THIEF
of the
ANCIENTS

An Abaddon Books™ Publication
www.abaddonbooks.com
abaddon@rebellion.co.uk

This omnibus published in 2014 by Abaddon Books™,
Rebellion Intellectual Property Limited,
Riverside House, Osney Mead, Oxford, OX2 0ES, UK.

10 9 8 7 6 5 4 3 2 1

Editor-in Chief: Jonathan Oliver
Commissioning Editor: David Moore
Cover Art & Maps: Pye Parr
Original Series Cover Art: Mark Harrison & Greg Staples
Design: Pye Parr & Sam Gretton
Marketing and PR: Michael Molcher
Publishing Manager: Ben Smith
Creative Director and CEO: Jason Kingsley
Chief Technical Officer: Chris Kingsley

ISBN: 978-1-78108-214-0

Printed in the US

TWILIGHT of KERBEROS

THIEF
of the
ANCIENTS

MIKE WILD

The Twilight of Kerberos Series

The Lucius Kane Adventures
by Matthew Sprange

Shadowmage
Night's Haunting
Legacy's Price

The Kali Hooper Adventures
by Mike Wild

The Clockwork King of Orl
Crucible of the Dragon God
Engines of the Apocalypse
The Trials of Trass Kathra

The Silus Morlader Adventures
by Jonathan Oliver

The Call of Kerberos
The Wrath of Kerberos

The Gabriella DeZantez Adventures
by David A. McIntee

The Light of Heaven

Twilight of Kerberos – The Final Adventure
by Mike Wild

Children of the Pantheon

INTRODUCTION

WHAT I REALLY wanted to do was put the fun back in fantasy. Okay, that sounds ridiculously flippant and not necessarily a good way to start an introduction, but bear with me on this as I have a serious point to make about the state of modern fantasy.

I'd never been one for huge epic fantasy sagas where each book weighs in around a 1000 pages and is usually one of a series of ten, or even thirteen! I struggled with *Lord of the Rings* at university, though I adored *The Two Towers*. The fantasy I was reading was the old stuff, and by old I don't mean creaky and redundant; I mean works by writers such as Fritz Leiber, Robert E. Howard, Clark Ashton Smith and others. Leiber's stories of Lankhmar were, in particular, a huge influence on myself and Matthew Sprange as we were putting together the world of *Twilight of Kerberos*. The other big influence on the series is the roleplaying game *Dungeons & Dragons*. Essentially what I envisioned for our sword and sorcery world was zesty, fun, stand alone novels that would still link together into a pleasing whole; books packed with incident, great characters, wild magics, vicious monsters and adventure. As I perceived it, there was certainly a niche for these in a market where every fantasy novel that came out competed with the last in terms of girth. Now don't get me wrong, I now do love a bit of epic fantasy and have since become a fan of such practitioners of the saga as Steven Erikson.

What we were trying to achieve with *Twilight of Kerberos*, however, was a new wave of pulp sword and sorcery, taking the classic model as our platform to present new exciting adventure-led fantasy.

Mike Wild got what I wanted to do straight away. When he pitched the first Kali Hooper adventure, *The Clockwork King of Orl*, he had fun and cool stuff happening from the start. And, what is more, he had a terrific character. Okay, there is perhaps a touch of Lara Croft about our tomb-exploring, kick-ass heroine but Kali quickly breaks that mould and becomes a living, breathing character that grows with each book. By the epic conclusion to the series, *Children of the Pantheon*, which will be available in the final omnibus edition, you'll come to think of Kali as a friend. A hard-drinking, sweary, belligerent mistress of the sword who is up there with Fafhrd, Conan and Solomon Kane as a great pulp hero; although, you know what, she's a little more sociable than any of those three.

So, turn the page and leap right on in. Fun is what I promised and fun is what you're going to get.

Jonathan Oliver (Editor)
December 2013

Sarcre Islands

Nurn

Drakengrat Mou

Vo:

Oweilau

Malmkrug

Scho

Turnitia

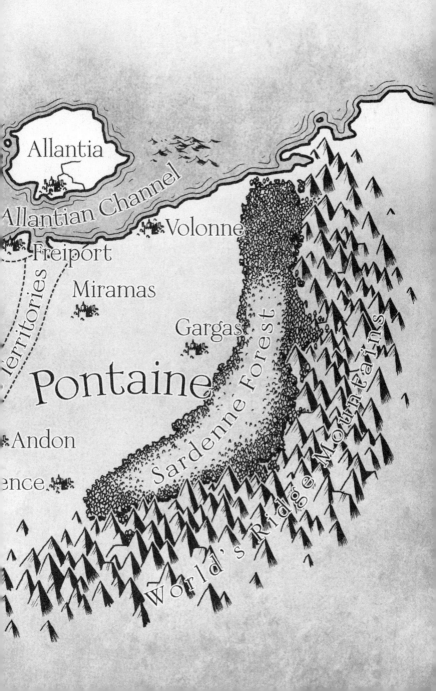

The CLOCKWORK KING of ORL

Original cover art by Mark Harrison

For Doreen – My Wife and Life

CHAPTER ONE

THE BEAST CRAVED flesh.

There, within the dark depths of the Sardenne Forest, that primal place curving like a great black bow beneath the frozen and fiery peaks of the World's Ridge Mountains, at the eastern edge of the peninsula, where civilisation stopped, the beast rolled insane and bulbous eyes, ground together huge and slavering jaws, and with a ravenous snort slowly advanced on the human it knew to be helpless before it.

The dark-maned young woman stood with her hands on the waist of her billowing squallcoat, head cocked to the side, weighing up the heavy creature as it came. She stood her ground, boots planted firmly against the foetid night winds of the forest, feeling her soles tremble as the ponderous beast thudded closer, unflinching despite the fact she was unarmed and facing it alone. There was no one nearby to help her. No one, in fact, anywhere within leagues of her, for this was a place humans rarely trod, and where the ones who had come before the humans had not trodden for countless aeons, since their civilisations had gone. She had long ago left behind what settlements dotted the edge of this dark expanse, long ago passed the silent stares and downed tools of their inhabitants as she moved between their homes and on into the darkness. Even those hardened woodcutters only ventured into the forest's outlying regions, and only then under the guard of their best fighting men, men who kept watchful eyes – and readied weapons – trained on the shadows that gathered about them. Beyond, the forest was considered impenetrable, and those who sought to prove otherwise – those who invariably never returned – to be foolhardy in the extreme. So it was the Sardenne had remained all but unexplored. The oldest of evils were said to lurk within its dark depths, and tales were told – in hushed tones, behind bolted doors – of creatures fantastic and terrifying that wandered there, waiting to corrupt or devour any intruder who entered their lair.

The young woman was not foolhardy but she was determined. By now, she had been travelling for three days, ever inwards, and so by all measures of the forest's dangers should be dead – or worse. With stealth, forestcraft and some alchemical guile, however, she had managed to evade the attentions of its darker denizens, though she had lost count of the times roars, rattles, whispers or blood-curdling screeches had alerted her to their presence, close by, in the darkness around her.

The darkness. What passed for night on the rest of Twilight – the haunting, azure halflight filtered through the gas giant Kerberos – was here more akin to Long Night, the greater darkness that only occurred when, four times a year, the world's distant sun passed behind Kerberos and the eclipses came. It was worse than Long Night, in truth, because while then the grey and silver-streaked surface of the looming giant could still be discerned above her, here the forest's canopy was almost total, as smothering and as dark as an oubliette.

Dark, that was, apart from the moist whiteness of the eyes of the beast, glittering, demanding saucers that had grown ever closer and loomed before her now. Yes, she might have made it this far but this was a confrontation she could not avoid. This particular beast would not allow her to progress until it had taken everything she had, its unnatural hunger sated.

She let it come, one hand slipping into a pocket of her squallcoat and wrapping itself in readiness around a small round object hidden within. Seeing her movement, and perhaps suspecting something, the beast reared its head and snorted steam from dark and expansive nostrils, and on the end of a thick, anvilled snout a pair of huge and fleshy lips curled back to reveal an array of tombstone teeth that, exposed in this way, appeared to grin as insanely as the bulbous eyes had rolled. The young woman steeled herself, her hand ready, but then without warning the beast lurched forwards and a slimy tongue the size of a rowing boat paddle slapped across her face. She batted it away, gagging and recoiling from a blast of foetid breath, took a step back and, with a groan of disgust, wiped a sliding patch of viscous slobber from her cheek and the lapel of her squallcoat. She flicked it to the ground with a grimace, shaking her hand until all of it was gone. *Gods, that was disgusting!*

Kali Hooper sighed.

"I taught you to wait," she said, exasperated. "All right, fine, okay. But this is the last, you hear me?"

The beast whinnied, nodding its head rapidly, and Kali produced the round object from her pocket, a lardon of bacon she tossed towards it. The meat hit the beast's snout, from where, its party trick, it was deliberately bounced back into the air before being caught in the huge mouth then manoeuvred beneath it. The beast rolled its insane eyes again and chomped down gratefully, drooling copiously as it ate.

"Those things will make you fat, Horse, you know that?" Kali said. "*Eff – ay – tee.*" She punctuated the letters with hearty slaps to the shire's thick neck, prompting a head-butting that almost pushed her over. "What use will you be then, you obese lump? Going to be you riding me to the Spiral, is it?"

The Spiral, Kali thought, and sighed again. The truth was, she'd be happy lugging Horse there if only she could find the damned thing. She slapped his neck a final time and slumped herself down at the base of a tree, once again unfolding the map she'd paid fifty full silver for from a contact in Turnitia some weeks before. Focusing on it in the dimness, she made a tired brubbing sound with her lips. Acquired from a collection whose legal ownership she wasn't privy to, the old and hand-drawn map purported to show the whereabouts of an Old Race site whose name she'd translated as the Spiral of Kos. She'd had her doubts about the map's provenance at the time but had handed over her money not because of what the Spiral of Kos was – frankly, she hadn't a clue – but rather its location here in the deeps of the Sardenne. Its very inaccessibility meant the site was likely untouched, and potentially that made it – and what it might contain – her most interesting find yet. Trouble was, authentic or not, the map was not to scale, and having found nothing so far she now had to decide whether to venture deeper into the forest, knowing that there lay Bellagon's Rip, reputed to be the stomping ground of the Pale Lord himself. While she didn't have any problem with that wayward necromancer – as long as he left her alone – she had to admit the vast army of undead under his command gave her pause for thought. If she wanted to spend the rest of her existence staggering around gibbering, she'd rather just be permanently betwattled, thank you very much.

Kali wished she could have a drink right there. Her chosen lifestyle – what she liked to think of as athletic archaeology – was one hells of a way to make a living.

She started. She had been so absorbed in her thoughts she had almost missed the fact that something had moved in the nearby undergrowth just then, something that alerted her with a crack of wood and a flash of something... *chitinous* at the edge of her vision. She instantly tensed, hunched to make herself small, and her eyes darted from left to right in her otherwise frozen form. *Dammit,* she thought – she'd broken her own golden rule, grown too complacent, stayed in one place too long. What was worse, she'd only just noticed that in wiping off some of Horse's drool she'd also smeared away some of the floprat render with which she'd been coating her squallcoat to deceive curious noses, and in doing so had released a whiff of her own human scent.

Humans were a delicacy here, and a whiff was enough. Whatever was in the bushes had found her because of it. And whatever it was, it wasn't friendly.

Kali didn't hang around, springing gymnastically onto Horse's back. Behind her, heralded by a sudden flight of panicked shrikes, she saw not one but maybe three predators – it was difficult to tell – glistening, angular carapaced things that reared out of the undergrowth on stickwood legs, and then in total silence, bar a sound like baby bones snapping, folded themselves around the trees towards her. Kali had no idea what the things were, and didn't want to know – and neither did Horse.

Her entreaty of "Go, go, go!" was entirely redundant as the great beast had also spotted the monstrosities and, with a panicked bray, was off, not at anything that could be described as a gallop but building his own hulking momentum, designed to get him and Kali the hells out of there, whether there were trees in the way or not. The pair ploughed ahead, gaining a few seconds as their predators sniffed at what Horse had involuntarily left behind, but then they could be heard behind them once more, folding and snapping themselves through the forest in a determined and slowly accelerating pursuit.

Accelerating some himself now, Horse thudded blindly on, neither he nor Kali caring where they headed. But then the pair of them broke through, suddenly, into an unexpectedly treeless area of the forest, a large glade where the canopy opened to the sky. Despite the openness the place was almost unnaturally still, thick with lazily hovering insects and bestrewn with strange vines that covered the ground and crawled in a tangle over a central, low but sweeping hill. Kali urged Horse on towards the rise, reasoning that if they could make it to the top she might be able to make a stand against their pursuers. But just before they began to climb, she threw a glance backwards and saw that though they had emerged into the glade they had ceased their chase, having come to a sudden stop at the edge of the trees. A nervous twisting and cracking of their chitinous forms suggested that for some reason they were wary of going on, and then they actually skulked away, back into the forest. Kali was so distracted by the development that it took her a moment to realise that Horse had stopped just as suddenly as they had.

Horse? she thought, but that was all, as the direct consequence of him halting so abruptly was that she was thrown out of her saddle and over his head. Kali's world turned upside down, and for a moment all she could see was the dizzyingly swooping sky, and then she landed hard on the slope of the hill, flat on her back, with an *ooff* and a crack that sounded like her spine had snapped in two. She lay where she was, stunned, while her brain tried to reorientate itself inside her skull. Rather ominously, she was dimly aware that Horse had begun to bray and snort and back away behind her.

Surprisingly, she found she could move – but when she did, stopped doing so immediately. There had been another crack beneath her, sounding this time not like her spine but the fracturing of ice on a frozen lake. It happened again – *kuuchruuck!* – and Kali hissed in a sharp breath as the slope shifted beneath her, a drop of perhaps only half an inch but one that felt so vertiginous it made her heart lurch. She didn't think twice, somersaulting from where she crouched, feeling the ground give again as she rolled to where Horse circled nervously below her.

What in all the pits of Kerberos – ?

Panting, Kali picked herself up and turned to look where she had fallen. The hill before her had looked solid enough but evidently wasn't, and had to be why both Horse and their chitinous friends had refused to go on. That, or they sensed something else. She had to admit the glade had a strange feel to it, a sense of something dormant and waiting, undisturbed for lifetimes. Something old.

Something old!

Kali felt a buzz of excitement – maybe, at last, she'd found something. Maybe. She calmed Horse then took off her squallcoat and tossed it over his saddle, revealing beneath the shnarl-hide working gear she'd had made in Freiport a couple of years earlier. The figure-hugging outfit, bespoke-tailored with artefact pockets on its arms and legs, was showing its age as well as some of her it shouldn't, but Kali didn't care, the kinds of places she wore it being well away from public gaze. She was rather fond of it, actually, as every tear or gash and every blood-stained hole brought its own memory. Around its waist she strapped a leather toolbelt she took from a saddlebag, and then to that a rope she took from another, securing the opposite end to the nub of the saddle itself. In the absence of trees in the glade, Horse would serve as an anchor for her safety rope. It wasn't the first time she had used his bulk in such a way.

Kali returned near to the spot where she'd been thrown, then knelt and swept her hand back and forth to brush away tiny plants and topsoil, creating an arc of investigation. The surface was thin and came away with surprising ease, and she realised this was because there was nowhere for roots to take hold. There was metal beneath. Riveted metal. By the look of it, some kind of supporting rib.

She sat back, surprised and confused. Not only because of the incongruous presence of the rib but the fact that metal would not have cracked beneath her the way she had felt the ground do. It was doubly odd. Checking the tightness of the rope, she inched her way up the rib until she overlooked the exact point where she had fallen, and again swept her hand back and forth. This time the topsoil offered absolutely no resistance at all, sliding away and trickling down to form a heap at the base of the hill. What lay beneath made her breath catch – a shiny, dark material as smooth as glass other than where hairline fractures marred it, fresh fractures that wouldn't be there except for her own ignominious crash-landing. She stroked the surface with her palm, realising two things. The material itself wasn't dark, it just had darkness beneath it. And it wasn't glass – it was crystal.

Kali stood, puzzling over what she'd found when she heard a shifting above her, and suddenly the trickle of soil about her feet became a small flood. She looked up and saw that where she'd wiped away the topsoil she had, in turn, disturbed the soil above it, and it, too, had begun to slip towards her. And with it gone, everything above had become unstable.

Horse brayed, hung his head and looked at her with chastising eyes. She'd caused a landslide. The entire bloody hill was coming down.

"Ohhh, bugger!" Kali said.

She staggered back along the metal, trying to get out of the way as the mass of soil and roots came crashing past her to the forest floor, almost dragging her off her feet and choking her in a dense, fibrous fog. She waded against the thick tide for what seemed like an eternity, and when, finally, it ceased, and its cloud had dispersed, found herself staring up at what remained.

Her mouth dropped open.

The hill hadn't collapsed, only the detritus with which nature had hidden what it really was over the course of long, long years. And now, rising away from her and sweeping off to her left and right, was a dome.

A vast, ornately ribbed, crystal dome.

Kali's heart thudded. Steaming pits of Kerberos, she had never seen anything like this!

There was no question about what to do next. She had to find out what was inside. Unlacing a pouch on her toolbelt, Kali dug through various odds and ends, took out a small hammer and clambered back up the rib to where she had knelt earlier, intending to tap the fractured crystal to create an exploratory hole. But as she raised the hammer to strike she felt tugs on the rope about her waist, minor at first but then hard enough to actually jerk her off balance. Unusually for Horse, it seemed he was getting skittish. But turning to see what the matter was, Kali realised Horse was more than skittish, he was clopping about in considerable agitation.

She looked past him and saw why. Something was coming at them out of the trees – *fast*. They must have worked up some courage because their friends were back with a vengeance.

There was no time to act, no time to hide, no time to dodge – Kali didn't even have time to brace herself. The chitinous things came swooping around Horse and straight at her, folding and flapping and then slamming into her with a speed that knocked the wind from her lungs. Their intent was presumably to pin her to the ground where they could rip her apart but, of course, there was no ground and, with a sound like a shocked and sibilant hiss, Kali and her three assailants crashed into and through the surface of the dome.

All four plummeted into blackness – Kali backwards with the things clinging on to her front – falling helplessly amidst countless shards of the partly shattered dome. Under different circumstances Kali might have found the susurrating crystal rain surrounding her mesmerising, but she was too busy bracing herself to hit the ground beneath the dome to pay much attention. No impact came, however, and she realised the dome must enclose something more than the forest floor itself – but what? For a moment she forgot the rope, imagined herself plunging ever downwards into some unknown abyss, but then the rope reached maximum length and she came to a halt with a whiplash jerk that made her internal organs collide and winded her worse than the folding bastards had moments before. Those same things, which until that moment still clung tenaciously to her front, triangular maws trying to snap at her face, were wrenched from her and tumbled away screeching, down and down into the dark. Seconds passed and then she heard the sound of three impacts from somewhere far below.

Kali groaned and hung where she'd halted, limp as a discarded doll, rotating slightly, the rope creaking above her in the silence that followed the fall. A dot in darkness, her head flopped backwards, she stared down into a vast and circular subterranean chamber lit vaguely by the half-light penetrating the broken dome. Whatever the place was, it seemed deserted and utterly still – the only movement motes agitated by her intrusion bouncing in the air – and the centre of it was dominated by a strange, shadowy mass that the whole structure seemed to have been built around. Also circular and broad at the base, but tapering gradually with greater and greater height, it rose towards her from the chamber floor like some huge ant hill – a hill within a hill – ever upwards, almost as far as the lip of the dome itself. It was a dizzying sight, especially when viewed upside down, and while Kali hadn't the faintest idea what it was, she did know she wanted a closer look.

The air in the chamber – *old air*, the kind she liked – acted on her like smelling salts and she snapped to, realising she had to find a way down from where she hung. But that was going to be easier said than done. Even if she whistled Horse to the edge of the dome, the rope on which she dangled was nowhere near long enough to reach the top of the mass, let alone the chamber floor, and unless she was going to be happy taking home memories of a bird's eye view of... wherever she was, she was going to have to find another way to descend. She pulled herself upright and turned on the rope, eyeing her surroundings, and had gone almost full circle before her gaze lit upon what looked like a platform, metal and ornately railed, running like a stretched-out horseshoe along the curving upper chamber wall. Some fifty feet away and below her, it would do as a start. It looked like one hells of a jump, however, and in taking it Kali knew she'd be committing herself to a descent with no return, because there was no way she'd be able to reach the rope again.

But she hadn't come all this way for nothing, and as Horse was probably getting a little disgruntled holding her dead weight, why not do him a favour and lighten his load? Besides, whoever had built this place must have built it with a front door, and in her experience of these old sites front doors were always easier to find from the inside than from the out.

Decided, Kali detached the rope from her belt and began to swing back and forth, building up an arc of momentum that would allow her to make the jump. She continued to swing until she had reached her desired speed and apex, and then with a determined cry let go of the rope. She flew, arcing through the air and then dropping, and landed hard on the platform, rolling to lessen her impact. Lessened or not, there was an eruption of dust and a loud metallic clang that echoed around the ancient chamber, quieting only after Kali thought she might go deaf. She very much doubted anyone was home but, if they were, they now sure as hells knew she'd come to visit.

All remained still and Kali stood, cautiously at first, but then, realising what she stood upon, throwing caution to the wind and instead grabbing the ornate railing to stare down, amazed. Still high above the chamber floor, the platform was clearly built for observation, and what it observed was the strange mass that dominated the place – the hill within a hill. Only it was no hill, she could see now, but a huge and vertiginous, winding metal stairway.

Kali swallowed because it really couldn't be anything else.

She was looking at the Spiral of Kos.

It was as incredible as it was mystifying. Overlooking its summit – still impossible to reach from where she stood – the dizzying structure was constructed in the same ornate fashion as the railing on which she leant, the steps of the stairway itself spiralling up inside a superstructure composed of flowing and curving ironwork the likes and artistry of which she had never seen. What drew her attention more than anything, however, was where the stairway led. Because there, at its top, completely isolated from the rest of the chamber, was another railed platform, and on it a large metal plinth.

And resting on the plinth was a giant key.

A key! Oh, she loved keys. Kali had no idea why it was there, where it had come from or what it unlocked, but she was certain of one thing – she wasn't leaving until she had it in her hands.

She turned, meaning to find a way off the platform and down to the first of those stairs, but as she did she caught a hint of movement from the Spiral itself. She turned back and squinted. Her eyes more adapted to the gloom, she noticed for the first time that the superstructure had apparently once housed some kind of hanging garden, for the dry and neglected remains of plants – thick tendrils and a number of presumably once-corpulent pods – still draped it now. That explained things. Perhaps one of those had shifted slightly in a draught from above – or then again, perhaps it had been nothing. A trick of the light.

Kali moved off the rail, searching for the way down that had to be there. Oddly, though, she found no connecting walkways, no ladders, no obvious way off the platform at all other than a small gate that led to... well, she wasn't sure what it led to. But as she walked closer, she felt a glimmer of recognition. The gate led to a cage, large enough that she could, if she so wished, step inside and which had a single entrance-cum-exit. Though it was different in many respects – more ornate, more complex, more *mechanical*-looking – it was clearly a version of the devices in use in the more industrialised areas of Vos – hoists and pulleys that had once lifted warehouse materials but now lifted men. Was that what this was, then? A... *lift* that could transport her off this platform? If so, where was the rope or chain suspending it? Curious, she leant around the edge of the cage, examining it more closely, and saw that though there was nothing to suspend it from above, the rear of the cage was secured to a thick metal arm that rested in the upper of two wide recesses in the chamber wall, recesses that swept away and down the wall in a reverse spiral to that of the Spiral itself, vanishing into the shadows below.

It had to be the way down. But after ages of disuse, could she trust it? Would the thing even *work*?

There was only one way to find out. Kali opened the gate and stepped warily into the cage, feeling for any kind of shift beneath her feet, all too aware that under the suspended floor there was nothing but a long, long drop. But she found it solid enough and so turned and closed the gate.

Kali waited. Nothing happened.

She waited more, and still nothing, and she frowned. Then she spotted a dust-shrouded lever on the wall of the cage next to where she had entered. Some kind of switch? Swallowing, she laid her hand on the lever and pulled it down. There was an empty clank.

Again, nothing happened – for a moment. Then, from somewhere inside the walls of the vast chamber, machinery that Kali knew to be older than her civilisation groaned as it stirred into life, filling the place with a bass cacophony as if it were haunted suddenly by its builders' ghosts. The noise resounded around the chamber, growing in volume until Kali felt the walls themselves rumble, and then silence descended abruptly and unexpectedly once more. *Dammit,* Kali thought.

And then the cage lurched.

Nothing could have prepared her for what happened next, and for a few exhilarating seconds she knew fully why she pursued the things she did. This was Old Race technology she was using, the first living being to have done so in perhaps a thousand years or more, and it was working.

Oh gods, was it working!

Kali laughed out loud.

The cage in which she stood released itself from the platform and swept majestically down along the chamber wall as if it floated freely in the air, the movements of the mechanisms that propelled it barely discernible at all. The passage down the spiralling recess afforded her a constantly rotating view of the Spiral of Kos, travelling so smoothly she could have been flying around it. Down and down and round and round she went, ducking involuntarily as, at what she guessed must have been the halfway point, a vast counterweight swept up the lower recess and beneath the cage with a heavy *whooooshh* that seemed to take the air away.

Kali watched the counterweight rise away and whooped, the magnitude of what was happening – what she'd found – hitting home. Her biggest find yet, *all* of this was hers to explore, and hers alone, the first person to tread within these walls since its Old Race occupants had gone. *All* of this – and that mysterious key.

Gods!

She looked down, almost clapping in anticipation of the cage berthing into a lower platform, and then she saw the light.

Her heart thudded.

It was hardly anything, a flare of whiteness perhaps two hundred feet below, but it was what the flare illuminated that was important.

People.

There were people below.

It couldn't be.

Kali stared at the shadowed figures, unable to distinguish who or what they were, only that a small group were crossing the chamber floor towards the base of the Spiral of Kos, their way lit by the raised hand of one of them. A glowing hand. Were they Old Race? Was it possible that some of them were still alive? Was it possible she was looking down at the builders? *It couldn't be. It just couldn't.*

One thing was clear. The cage in which she stood was going to deliver her right into their midst. And she couldn't chance that, having no idea if they were friend or foe.

Kali did the only thing she could. She rammed the lever back into its original position and, with a protesting groan, the cage lurched to a sudden halt, throwing her hard against its side. The groan caused the figures below to look up, and Kali threw herself to the cage floor, crawled to its edge and peered down, relieved as she saw them turn away. She'd been lucky – it seemed the figures had dismissed the noise as unexplained.

Nevertheless, she was too exposed where she was. All it would take to reveal her presence above them was another curious glance at the lift, a whim. She had to get out of there and down – and quickly. Keeping her eyes on the unknown group, she crouched and then swung herself quietly out of the front of the cage, twisting so that she could grab onto its side, and from there swung herself onto the metal arm on which it rode. Then she worked her way into the recess, wide and deep enough to accommodate her crouching form. Using it to get down would still leave her exposed but if she kept in its shadows, and her luck held, she would make it unseen.

She began to inch her way down towards the chamber floor. She had perhaps a hundred, a hundred and thirty feet to go.

And it was then that the vision hit her.

Searing agony cut through her mind, as if someone had embedded an axe in her forehead, and suddenly her world was yellow and red and white, everything the colour of raging fire. What had been a shadowy, abandoned chamber a moment before was now consumed by a blaze apocalyptic in intensity, the Spiral of Kos being destroyed in a conflagration beyond imagining. Things lashed and writhed within the flames – strange things that she had no time to identify before agonised screams swept them away. For a second she was outside the dome, staring as a pillar of fire rose high above the darkness of the Sardenne, and then she was back once more, in the fire's raging heart, in its midst. It couldn't be real but it was. She didn't just see it, she could *feel* it, the heat from the fire strong enough to sear and bubble her skin and to blind her with its bright, bright heat. *What the hells am I seeing?* she wondered. *What the hells am I feeling?*

Instinctively she flailed against it, and in that second realised where she was. Where she *really* was.

But it was too late. Her flailing had taken her too far towards the edge of the recess, beyond balance.

She tumbled out, and fell.

And when she landed, the fire faded to blackness.

And, as shadows loomed over her, so, too, did she.

CHAPTER TWO

KALI FELT SOMETHING thudding again and again into her side and, with slowly growing awareness and annoyance, realised that it was a boot. Her eyes snapped open just in time to see the offending article coming at her again, and she instinctively grabbed and twisted it, flipping its wearer heel-over-head to the accompaniment of a startled cry.

"Don't do that!" she growled, without even thinking who it was she might be talking to.

Great, she thought, reprimanding herself. Possible first contact with an Old Race and what does she do? Fling one of them on its arse.

She sat quickly up, bruised, throbbing and disorientated, and looked around. There was no more fire – no more vision – but neither any time to think about where it had come from or where it had gone as the wearer of the boot, a cloaked and hooded figure, had also risen and, snarling, loomed over her again, boot swinging back for another strike.

Kali was about to kick his legs from under him and punch his lights out when a hand moved across the figure's chest and pushed him back to where others stood silently looking down at her.

"Enough, brother," a gruff voice said. "Do you not see that our visitor from on high is awake?"

"My apologies... *brother*."

The speaker, becloaked and hooded like the rest, knelt by Kali, sighing as if somehow inconvenienced by her presence. The man was short, more accurately squat, and thickly muscled, his powerful bulk evident even beneath the loose folds of his cloak. Pulling back his hood he revealed a mane of grey hair flaring back from a face that was gnarled and scarred, inset with the coldest grey-tinted eyes she had ever seen. Whoever he was, Kali thought, if he didn't have some Old Race blood in him – and she knew *which* Old Race – then her name was Fundinblundin Hammerhead.

"Who are you?" the man asked slowly. His tone, civilised, patient and polite, was totally at odds with his appearance. "And what is it you are doing here?"

Old Race blood, but not Old Race, Kali decided, ignoring his question for a moment. The thought that had struck her before her fall – that some of the builders might still be alive – had never really been likely – next to impossible, actually – and now that she'd had chance to see these people close to, it only confirmed the fact. But though their origin was far more prosaic, who these people were came as only slightly less of a surprise than the alternative. Six of them in all, their garb, speech and, most of all, the crossed-circle talismans they wore pinned to their sleeves, left no doubt as to their identity. This bunch were Final Faith, members of the most pervasive, most consuming and most intolerant religion to blight the peninsula, zealots to every woman and every man.

They were not her favourite people.

That, however, was immaterial right now.

What *was* material was the obvious question. What the hells were the Final Faith doing in the Spiral of Kos?

The key. It seemed to be the only thing in the place so it had to be the key.

Well, if that was the case... Sorry, but she'd got here first.

"I asked you a question, girl," the apparent leader reminded her. His tone had already hardened somewhat.

Girl? Kali thought, and stared at him. "Oh, you know," she said innocently, "went for walk in the woods, got lost, fell down a sodding great hole..."

The man nodded then abruptly tugged her toolbelt from her waist, tipping out the contents of some of its pockets. Kali shrugged as he picked through a selection of pitons, hammers, clamps and other excavation gear, regarding her questioningly when he also came upon some marbles, a sock and a mouldy, half-eaten pie. Okay, so maybe she should have a clearout once in a while.

"Impressive tools for a walk in the woods," Mister Nosey nevertheless concluded. He glanced over at the broken, shard-covered bodies of the stickthings, which coincidentally she seemed to have landed on or nearby. "You managed to survive three brackan, too. Equally impressive."

Brackan, eh? Kali thought. *Have to remember that.* "Yeah, well, I –"

"You are intruding here!"

The statement came so suddenly and so forcefully that it threw her off guard.

"Excuse me?"

"Intruding. This... *reliquary* is under the jurisdiction of the Final Faith."

"Oh, really?" Kali said, bristling. "And since when did your little glee-club extend to the Sardenne?"

The man smiled coldly. "Since my arrival here."

Kali stared. She was only just getting over the shock that she had survived that fall – and its cause – let alone finding she had company, but one thing was already abundantly clear to her – this man was serious. And despite his superficial civility, he was dangerous. She could feel it exuding from his every pore.

The fact didn't stop her speaking up, though. That was her trouble, people kept telling her, though it never did any good.

"Well, then – you're a little off the beaten path, aren't you, *priest?*"

The man's hand – leather-gloved – shot out without warning and clenched itself about her neck. Kali gasped and fumbled to release its grip, but it was strong. Very strong.

The man stood, and, her throat constricting, she actually found herself being lifted from the floor.

"My name," he told her, "is Konstantin Munch, and despite your disdain I am not one of the Enlightened Ones." He used the phrase that described the Final Faith's priesthood with a degree of disdain of his own, which she found peculiar. "I am, however, an agent of that church, acting on its behalf and that of the Anointed Lord, and so I ask you again – *what are you doing here?*"

"Actually, I... bought the place," Kali rasped, choking. She hung a hand vaguely in the direction of the Spiral and its dead plants, twitched it. "Thought I'd open a herbalist's emporium but... was never very... green-fingered."

Munch's hand tightened, the leather squeaking. "Ah, I see."

"And you?" Kali ventured. "Mind... telling me what... you're... *kaa-hurr*... doing here?"

"Actually, yes. Why don't we just say that my friends and I were led here by the Lord of All?"

No surprise, there, Kali thought. These people did everything in his – *god's, her? Its?* – name, including all the sacking, raping and pillaging, by some accounts. But Lord of All or not, something had led Munch and his mates to the Spiral's front door, when even her map hadn't been specific about its location. And though she found it difficult to believe, she thought she knew what.

She flicked a pained gaze – already flaring and soon to blink out, if she wasn't careful – to the side, examining Munch's companions again. Sure enough, the clenched fists of one of them still pulsated ever so slightly with the aftermath of energy release – the same release, presumably, that had lit up the floor of the chamber earlier. She couldn't see much of his face beneath its hood, only that it seemed harsh, thin and sallow, but there was an overly intense penetration about the shadowed eyes that Kali had seen once before, and cared not to remember. They were the eyes of someone who would normally be denounced by the Final Faith. Eyes that stared out not only at this world but beyond, into another layer of being. Eyes that saw the threads of the universe, used them and followed them. The eyes of a –

"Shadowmage?" Munch said, sensing her recognition and puzzlement. He smiled, bobbing her dangling and struggling form almost playfully towards the mage in question. "The young lady wonders not only why we are here but why one such as I is in league with one such as you, Kallow," he said. "Are you offended?" Turning his attention back to Kali, he added, "Unusual, I grant you, but let's just say the Anointed Lord allows me some... latitude in my choice of companions, depending on the task she has set for me."

"*Tashk?*" Kali enquired, the one word all she could manage now. She could feel her eyes bulging painfully and her tongue thick between her lips.

Munch shrugged modestly, making her bob again. "Certain errands of import – troubleshooting, damage-control, the *elimination* of various problems." He smiled as he stressed the word before tossing Kali to the floor, where she scrambled back. "Whatever it is, in fact, the Anointed Lord wishes me do."

Kali hacked rawly, rubbing her throat, trying to ignore the pounding in her skull as blood rushed back into her brain. The man had almost killed her just then, and she had little doubt that was his ultimate intent, especially as he had just brushed back his cloak to reveal a particularly vicious-looking gutting knife.

"Last chance, girl, as I have no time for inconveniences. What is it that you are doing here?"

Kali thought fast. After that little ordeal, she was still too dizzy to run and too weak to defend herself, and so the only possible way out of this was to bluff. The question was, with what? It would have helped if Munch had given her a clue as to why he and his people were here, because without that juicy tidbit it would be so easy to say the wrong thing.

But then it struck her. Why was Munch so interested in what *she* was doing here? Surely that was obvious? Given that he hadn't just stumbled across the place, could it be that he'd come to the Spiral for the key without knowing what he'd find when he arrived? That he thought she knew something about the Spiral that might help? If that was the case, maybe he didn't know everything about the key itself.

It was something she could work with. A gamble, but worth the ante. If nothing else, it would buy her time.

"All right, all right!" she coughed. "The truth is, I came here for the... romfiffelypop."

Munch's eyes narrowed. "The romfiffelypop?"

Kali looked at him in a way that suggested everyone knew what the romfiffelypop was, then pointed towards the Spiral. "The *key*, dammit! I've been searching for it for years."

One of Munch's people – a woman by the sound of it – made a *pishing* sound, but Munch ignored her.

"The key?" he said, evenly. "Forgive me, I have never heard it called by that name."

Kali just knew she had him on the hook and shook her head wearily. "You wouldn't. It's an ancient Varondian dialect – a tribe in the Drakengrat Mountains – long extinct." *Oh, good one,* she thought.

"Is it, now? I see. And you are something of an expert in these matters?"

Kali nodded. "I've been around a bit, seen some things." She thought of others who did what she did, mainly blundering vandals – *tomb raiders* – in it solely for the money from the artefact trade. "The name's Orlana Dawn."

Munch pursed his lips, nodding. "Tell me, *Orlana* – have you experience of whirling blades, shooting spikes, rolling boulders, lava tiles and other lethal, death-dealing traps, triggers and devices?"

What? Kali thought. *Was that meant to be some kind of joke?* Sure, she'd come upon one or two 'protective measures' in her time but, for the most part, she'd had more problems with animals around the sites than anything inside them. Truth was, most contained nothing worth trapping at all.

"Why?" she asked, suspiciously. "Should I be?"

"We have encountered some such hazards recently. There is a possibility we may encounter some today."

Kali realised he was being serious, and couldn't help but be intrigued – where the hells had these people been? "Well, then," she said, "I'm your man."

Once again, the woman made a noise, but Munch silenced her with a slice of his hand. For the first time he looked Kali – openly and unashamedly – up and down. "Now," he said, "I know you are lying."

A lech as well as a psychopath, Kali concluded. But at least her gamble seemed to have paid off. For the moment, she would live – an extra member of Munch's team. The fact was, she resented that immensely – the Spiral should have been *hers* – but, on the other hand, she'd bought herself chance to examine it properly for the first time – and maybe when she knew more she could make it hers again. It had to be better than being sliced like a rack of shnarlmeat on the floor.

Munch, his people and Kali moved off across the vast chamber floor, their way lit by a fresh flare of light from the shadowmage. As her feet crunched on crystal shards, Kali looked up at the Spiral, noting the circular runics inscribed on massive plates that ran in a ring beneath the dome, wondering for what mysterious reason the builders had put them there. The sheer scale of what the Old Races had achieved never failed to leave her in awe, and now, with the advantage of this lower perspective, she found herself staring open-mouthed and more awed than ever before. Walking through the Spiral was like walking through a cathedral, a construction of staggering proportions, but however impressive it was, its actual purpose left her puzzled – and a little troubled. Her first thought – that it was some kind of museum – didn't really work, as what kind of museum contained only one exhibit? What, then? Some kind of memorial – but to a *key*? No, it had to be something else. A huge key perhaps suggested some accompanying huge vault, but then she had seen nothing here that a key such as the one atop the Spiral might open, and besides, what kind of vault, whatever its size, left the means to open it on public display?

Okay, so the place was hardly public. The point was, *it didn't make sense.*

The party reached the base of the Spiral and Munch and the others stared up the towering structure, assessing it. But left feeling uneasy by her inability to pin anything down, Kali's gaze was drawn instead to the grey remains of the plantlife that wrapped it, the nagging doubt about what she thought she'd seen earlier returning. As she watched, a tiny triangle of light – *natural light* – lit a patch of the lifeless tendrils and pods.

Kali looked up, blinked. The still-mottled but otherwise soil-free dome had begun to glow, the planet's distant sun rising and shining into that one patch of the Sardenne not obscured by its dark canopy – the clearing above.

Daylight was coming to Twilight.

And with it – in tenuous shafts that must have been intruding here for the first time in long and unknown ages – to the Spiral.

Kali looked down. She couldn't be absolutely sure but it seemed to her that the plants had stirred, as she thought they had earlier.

"*Uurrmm...?*" she said to the others.

Munch had apparently noticed something, too, as he had stepped back. He addressed her directly. "Did you see that, Miss Dawn?"

"I'm not sure," Kali responded. To her eyes, the plants seemed more... *fleshy*, too. "It could be –"

"It's nothing," the woman who'd protested earlier interrupted. "A trick of the light, that's all."

Munch looked again, but the plants – if they *had* moved – were now still once more.

"You are certain?"

"Of course I'm certain," the woman said, stripping off her hood and cloak, "or my name's not Orlana Dawn."

What? Kali thought. *What?* The woman had announced herself so casually that for a moment the name hadn't really registered. But nonetheless Orlana Dawn stood before her now, arms folded and smiling daggers, a buxom blonde putting all the right curves into a dark silk bodysuit. It was of a kind favoured by certain members of Vos and Pontaine's thieves guilds, which she had clearly adopted as her working gear. Kind of appropriate, really.

Still, it had a certain something. What Kali thought was: *I have to get me one of those.* What she said was: "Okay outfit, shame about the ass."

She looked at Munch. He had clearly been playing games from the start, probably even knew fully what the Spiral and the key were.

"If you knew – ?"

"Why didn't I kill you?" Munch answered. He inclined his head to the Spiral. "Frankly, because I do not know what hazards I face here, and I have lost too many people in recent months to waste an extra resource." He sighed lengthily. "The question, therefore, is which one of you goes first?"

"Konstantin!" Orlana Dawn objected.

Another sigh. "It's simple, Orlana. The two of you obviously share a passion for this kind of thing, but I have no idea which of you is the most competent at handling it. If I send you first, and you die, I send her in with the knowledge gained of what killed you. Or, I send her first and –"

"I get the picture," Orlana said. She looked suspicious of him, suddenly. "If she goes first – and succeeds – do I still get paid?"

Munch shrugged. "Sadly, the funds allocated to me are limited."

"Farking poxes from the pits! You're a bastard, Munch, you know that?"

"This I have been told before," Munch rumbled, unconcerned.

Their exchange faded in Kali's ears as her gaze flicked from the tower to the dome, the dome to the tower and back again, already ahead of them and working out what she needed to know. Then it struck her. The Spiral of Kos was no museum, no memorial and no vault, it was a greenhouse – a greenhouse specifically designed around its centrepiece, not the tower but the plants. In reaching that conclusion, however, she was still left puzzled. Because in the middle of the Sardenne Forest, what possible need could there be for *more plants?*

Unless...

"I'll go first," she said, suddenly, and what she hoped was decisively. She had no interest in the money but, as much as she disapproved of Orlana Dawn's motives for doing what she did, if her theory was right, she couldn't let her take the risk.

"Go to hells!" Orlana Dawn hissed at her. "She's a greenhorn, Munch."

"Hey, who are you calling a greenhorn?" Kali objected, despite herself. "The Maze of Moans," she cited, pointing proudly at her chest. "Me."

Orlana Dawn stared at her, momentarily nonplussed.

"Oh, really. How about the Lost Plateau of Thurst?" she retorted, with a snort.

Kali *piffed*. "Couldn't have been that lost. The Booming Room. The Booming Room, eh?"

"Quinking's Depths."

"Quinking's Depths."

"I already said that."

"Third level."

"Impossible. Look, this is my job, you interfering bitch. Konstantin, this is nothing I can't handle –"

"Miss Dawn goes first," Munch declared, putting an end to it. "The real one, that is." He gestured two of his people towards Kali. "In case she is tempted to help, hold the other one."

Kali was grabbed by both arms and struggled as Orlana Dawn sighed with satisfaction. "Munch, this is a mistake," she protested. "Orlana, don't –"

Munch hushed her. "Bring me that key, Miss Dawn," he ordered.

Orlana nodded, and Kali watched helplessly as her rival took one, two, then three tentative steps up the first turn of the Spiral. Even Dawn couldn't fail to notice that the plants *had* filled out somewhat now beneath the strengthening rays of the sun, but other than giving them a cautionary frown she continued slowly upwards, too inexperienced, too stubborn or simply too greedy to back down. As she did, one or two of the pods that Kali could now see formed the hearts of the various sets of tendrils belched something foul-smelling into the air, and Dawn stared down at them, curling her mouth in distaste. She was now past the fifth turn of the Spiral, and halfway round the sixth, and as she concentrated on putting her foot on the next step she failed to notice that some of the tendrils were, with a sound of sucking mud, slithering slowly onto those beneath her.

Kali pulled against her captors, but even if she had been able to break free, knew now that there was nothing she could do. What had become increasingly obvious to her – that the plants weren't dead but long dormant, untended since the demise of the Old Race and deprived of light as nature had reclaimed the dome – was, in truth, academic. What mattered was, reinvigorated, these things had a purpose, a purpose that answered the question of why the Old Race had needed more plants in the Sardenne. Because they weren't plants at all – not *just* plants. They had been grown here as guardians. Guardians of the key.

The Spiral of Kos hadn't been designed as a greenhouse – it had been designed to be a deathtrap.

"*Orlana!*" she shouted. "*Get down off there* – now!"

But it was too late – had been too late the moment Orlana Dawn had taken her first step onto the Spiral. Too late the moment the sun had begun to rise. And now, as it became fully bathed in light, the plants that covered it thrashed suddenly, shedding the accumulated dust of ages to reveal a horrible glistening green beneath – and the Spiral of Kos exploded into flailing, carnivorous life. Munch stepped back, raising an eyebrow, and motioned to one of his men, who pulled a crossbow from beneath his cloak and began to fire off bolts. Kallow the shadowmage, meanwhile, quickly rewove his threads to produce not light but thrumming balls of flame, pummelling the plants with a barrage of fire. Unfortunately, neither type of missile seemed to have any effect at all.

Orlana Dawn had no chance. Her way down the Spiral was now completely blocked, her way up – and it was still a *long* way up – filled with countless more of the plants that had manoeuvred themselves insidiously beneath her. While those above her snapped downwards like some deadly curtain, lashing themselves tightly about parts of the metalwork before whipping off in search of meatier prey, those below writhed graspingly upwards, slapping, probing and feeling their way around the Spiral like the tentacles of some inverted giant squid. There was nothing Dawn could do, and though she pulled a knife from her bodysuit to defend herself, spinning around and around in panicked circles, it was clearly going to be useless against the thick feelers that surrounded her, seeking out the intruder in their midst. Suddenly one of the tendrils darted at her neck, and though she dodged it, yelling, another darted from behind her to wrap itself quickly and tightly around her waist. Dawn doubled over, not only because she was struggling against its grip but because of the needles that even those below could see spring from it, puncturing both her bodysuit and her flesh. Dawn's mouth opened in surprise, some unknown toxin flooding her body, and as it did the second tendril struck at her neck once more, wrapping itself about her gulping throat as constrictingly as a slave's collar. Dawn jolted, her eyes widening in alarm as needles pierced again. Held in place by the two tendrils, others within reach sought her, found her and gripped by her ankles and wrists as well, and the struggling Dawn was lifted from the Spiral steps like a helpless marionette, tugged in every direction as each tendril sought to claim her for its own. She didn't scream, because she couldn't, whatever toxin had entered her system tainting her veins a pulsing shade of green, sending her into spasm as they poisoned every drop of her blood. It was, in a way, a mercy, because a second later other tendrils whipped in at her, their needles no longer piercing but tearing, ripping away first her bodysuit and, when that was gone, her flesh. Unable to move, unable to utter anything but the merest whimper, only Dawn's eyes reflected the agony of her paralysed and corrupted form as it was taken apart shred by shred. Her body jerked for a while longer but her eyes stared blindly now from a cadaverous skull, and soon after that she was nothing but a bloody skeleton, and then not even that. The pods opened, and, piece by piece, deposited inside by their tendrils, the skeleton, everything that had been Orlana Dawn, was gone.

The plants calmed, and then they were still once again.

A second passed, the remainder of the party staring up at the Spiral in shocked silence. Then Munch coughed and wiped a lump of cheek from his cheek, leaving a bright red smear.

"Well," he said, "that was a new one."

"Orlana was right, you are a bastard," Kali said without emotion. "You *knew* there was something, threw her life away –"

"There is always something," Munch said, wearily. "You just have to find out what. Which is why I am glad of your company today, because it enabled me to send the *stupid* one first. It seems that you are now in the employ of the Final Faith, Miss – ?"

"Kali Hooper. *Remember* it."

"Kali Hooper, good. So, Kali Hooper – explain to me how it is you mean to tackle the little problem that presents itself before us." Konstantin said, throwing her tool belt back to her.

"I don't mean to tackle it at all," Kali responded. "At least, not for you." The truth was, she had already worked out how she might beat this thing, not only for the key but now, also, for the memory of Orlana Dawn, but when she did, it would be on her terms, not those of a certain Konstantin Munch. She'd learned what she needed to know and – it was time to go.

Munch swept back his cloak, revealing the gutting knife once more. Almost friendly in his tone, he sighed and said: "Kali, if I have let you live for nothing, I *will* kill you."

"Stan," Kali replied, going with his familiar name, "you won't get the chance." Her adrenalin built during Dawn's death – the grips of her captors having weakened in shock, anyway – she knew this was her moment, and took it. Slamming her elbow into the stomach of the brother on her right, she doubled him over and flung him round so that his head rammed into the stomach of the one on the left, then booted the first up the backside so the two of them sprawled to the floor in a heap. That done, she ran like hells.

Munch growled, and Kali heard the unsheathing of his knife echo sharply. She also heard him bark orders to Kallow, and suspecting what might come began to weave to the left and right. Sure enough, a second later, fireballs impacted with the ground on either side of her, detonating bits of the floor and following her as she ran. Kali kept weaving and moving, heading for the shadows at the edge of the Spiral's chamber, where the light from the dome did not reach. Crouching and moving as quickly and silently as she could, she began to manoeuvre herself around the rim, searching for the way in that Munch and his cronies must have used. Not that she had any intention of abandoning the place – hells, no, the key was far too interesting for that – but she needed to reach the surface, and Horse, to get more equipment from the saddlebag before she could even attempt to go for it. The fact that the plants' sap made them impervious to flame did not necessarily mean that they were invulnerable to it, and she figured that if she could create a heat that was intense enough she might be able to burn away some of the plants at the summit of the Spiral and lower herself to the key from above. All she needed was the magnifying mirrors she used to illuminate corridors in the darker sites, then using the sun and the crystal of the dome itself...

Kali stopped dead, realising she had just scrambled by a door – not the exit she sought but another door – an arched door, made of crystal like the dome. She rose slowly, the hairs on her neck rising, thrilled not only by the door itself but what she could see through it, shrouded in gloom – workbenches, strange tools, shelves filled with belljars containing the dried remains of plants.

She spun around, flattening her back against the crystal, a thought striking her. And peering along the vast curve of the Spiral's edge she saw what she suspected she might. More doors like this one, that she supposed led to more rooms like the one she had already seen. Yes, it made sense. The plants that protected the Spiral were no natural species, that was certain, so they had to have been cultivated, engineered, maintained. And it was here that that had been done. These rooms were what made the Spiral tick.

It was incredible. She hadn't come across *anything* like this before. This vast place, these rooms, *all* of this effort to protect that key – *why*?

It was possible the room contained a clue. Kali turned back to examine the door, but there seemed no visible way of opening it. It was thicker than the crystal of the dome, too – too thick to smash. Then she noticed that the frame of the door was traced with a faint runic pattern – not a circle like beneath the dome but a squiggle that surrounded it like a vine – and she brushed her fingertips across it experimentally. There was a sound like a long intake of breath, and on the lower left the curls and strokes lit with a brilliant blue light that began to work its way around the frame as if it were somehow loading it with energy.

Kali staggered back, falling onto her rear, staring at the pattern, so stunned that for a second she didn't realise the light of it was illuminating her as if she were experiencing a visitation from the gods. She would have sat there still were it not for the sound of footsteps approaching. She scrambled up and away from the door but it was too late – drawn by the strange spotlight, Munch and his cronies had found her.

Munch stared at the glowing pattern and sighed.

"Miss Hooper, my job is hazardous enough, and I really cannot afford loose cannons," he said matter-of-factly. "Regrettably, then, I must find my own way to the key." He turned to the shadowmage. "Burn her!"

Kallow raised a hand that still flickered from the volley he'd launched earlier, flexing his fingers to combust it anew. Kali stared at the ball of flame that appeared hovering in his palm and backed away, swallowing. This time, there was nowhere to hide.

"No, wait," she said. "You're making a mistake."

"No," Munch said, already walking back towards the Spiral, "meeting me was *your* mistake."

Two things happened at once. Kallow punched his palm in Kali's direction, letting fly, and at the very same time the runic pattern completed, the door it surrounded sliding open with a hiss. Kali coughed and gagged as a noxious cloud – the product of the plants and gods knew what other strange materials that had rotted inside the room for years – erupted into the air outside.

Gas. And a lot of it.

The fireball never reached her. It ignited the cloud as soon as it left Kallow's hand and the space between them was engulfed in a sheet of flame that blew her pursuers off their feet, turning them into fireballs themselves. Only Munch escaped the worst of the blast, but even he was slammed across the chamber floor some fifty feet, bouncing and rolling, smoking and charred, even further beyond that.

"I told you you were making a mistake," Kali said.

She ran – because there was nothing else she could do. Behind her, the open room boomed as the gas remaining within ignited, and Kali felt the floor quake not once but thrice, the explosion starting a chain reaction that was beginning to work its way around each room on the rim of the chamber. As she ducked and weaved, the arched crystal doors blew out of their frames one after the other, shattering around her. Great plumes of flame erupted from where they'd been, carrying inside them vials and bottles that then also shattered, spreading who knew what upon the floor, but something flammable that added to and combined with the plumes to create a ring of fire in the heart of the Spiral – a ring of fire that was rapidly turning into an inferno. Kali looked for the exit, and with relief spotted it, but she did not run towards it yet, instead veering towards Munch, and aiming beyond him. The recovering psychopath loomed before her, and, without even thinking, Kali leapt upwards and somersaulted over his surprised form, twisting in mid-air and plucking his gutting knife from its sheath as she went. It was a move that rather surprised her, too. *Whoahh,* she thought, *you're getting good!*

But she was going to need to be. Because she wasn't leaving without the key.

Okay, it wasn't exactly the plan she'd had in mind, but the imminent destruction of the Spiral *had* forced a rethink. The sea of flame wasn't killing the plants at the base of the Spiral – not yet – but it wasn't sparing them, either. Already burning furiously beneath the lower steps – and refusing to go away – it had sent them into a sweating, writhing paroxysm that Kali hoped would keep them distracted while she did what she needed to do. Suicide, she knew, but since when had that ever stopped her? And unless she wanted the key to disappear forever in this conflagration, what choice did she have?

She sprinted straight for the Spiral and up, her footfalls clanging rapidly on its steps, gaining as much height as quickly as she could. All around her the lethal vegetation lashed and snapped as though it had a hundred victims in its malignant grip, tendrils twisting and twining with each other all about her, their needles locking and causing sudden, frantic struggles between them. Kali didn't wait around to see which won, the fire hot on her heels, spreading now not only with its own momentum but flicked ever higher by the panicked whiplashing of those plants it had already consumed. It was actually starting to damage them, the tendrils' outer flesh splitting in the intensifying heat, spurting their sap until they became slick with their own green juices. The resultant friction between them made them sound as if they were screaming – and perhaps they were.

Disgusting as it was, the sap was exactly what Kali needed. The acrid smoke that poured now from the plants she could just about cope with, but the heat was another thing, and the sap was as welcome as a mountain waterfall, enabling her to keep going. And keep going she did, using Munch's gutting knife to slice at any tendril that flopped in her path, not so much harming them as batting them out of the way to die. And the Spiral *was* dying, from the bottom up.

Still, it seemed neverending and Kali was starting to think that it would make one hells of a morning workout when, at last, she reached the top.

The key sat on its plinth before her, bigger than it had seemed from above, a peculiar thing – an oddly *disturbing* thing – carved in the style of gristle and bone. But far too unwieldy to carry, especially in current circumstances. Thinking quickly, Kali loosened her toolbelt, slung it over one shoulder, then hefted the key and stuffed it behind the strap.

Hells, it was heavy. But whatever it was, it was hers. She had done it. All she had to do now was get back down.

Kali took in two deep lungfuls of air and was about to begin her descent when the Spiral shifted beneath her. She stumbled and picked herself up. Then the thing shifted again, and she realised what she had been afraid would happen was happening. The heat of the fire was weakening – perhaps even melting – some of the Spiral's lower superstructure, and the whole thing was starting to collapse beneath her.

She looked down. The lower levels were folding in on themselves to create one mass of red-hot metal and superheated mulch. It was a giant furnace in the making.

There was no way down. Unless she got out of there now, the Spiral of Kos would become her funeral pyre.

Kali spun, searching for an alternative route. She could barely see anything, the explosions beneath her growing in their intensity and height. But then above the roar of the flames and the intensity of the heat haze she heard a peculiar clanking, looked down and saw the lift she had abandoned a seeming eternity ago bucking against its brake. But why? Another explosion drew her attention and, looking up, she saw it had reached almost as high as the observation platform – but obviously hadn't been the first explosion to do so, because the lift's counterweight was bucking against its own brake, the rail in which it sat mangled beneath it. And as she watched, the counterweight broke free.

It was coming down.

And as it did, the lift began coming up. *Fast*.

Once again, Kali didn't even think. Acting instinctively, surrounded by fire, the summit of the Spiral ringed by the thrashing tendrils of the last plants to die, she leapt into space, allowing one of the tendrils to smack her away through the air.

And she flew, in exactly the direction she wished. Her trajectory and timing must have been perfect because she slammed onto the lift's roof as it passed her by, falling heavily so as not to slide over the edge.

She stood, legs apart, riding it upwards, the wind of acceleration blowing back her hair.

The counterweight hurtled by like some heavenly hammer.

Kali looked down. In the light of the conflagration, the last thing she saw was the counterweight smashing through the buffers of the lower platform and screeing across the Spiral's floor towards a pursuing and furiously roaring Munch.

And then the lift impacted with the buffers of the upper platform, and she flew again.

Out, through the dome.

Out of the frying pan and into the fire.

CHAPTER THREE

KALI HAD TO give Horse his due – the old boy could move when he needed to. When he *really, really, really* needed to. And Hells, did he need to now!

Her explosive departure from the Spiral of Kos had not been quite the relief it should have been. Sure, she had escaped relatively unscathed and, sure, she had been glad to see Horse waiting faithfully where she had left him, but as she had flailed through the air, crash-landed and rolled to what she thought would be safety, what she had not been glad to see was the dome erupting with fire behind her. A great, roiling mass of it, the biggest fire she had ever seen, every second punching explosively higher and higher into the air.

It wasn't the explosions, or the fire, that was the problem – it was what they did. They shook that part of the Sardenne Forest to its core, and lit it up for leagues around. As a result, it seemed that every crawling, slithering, squelching, squawking, flying or ground-pounding denizen that lurked in that vast expanse was coming to see what was going on.

Coming towards *them*.

There was nowhere to hide, the billowing flames casting their light deep under the canopy and making it as clear as day. Kali and Horse were therefore not only able to see what horrors came, they could be seen by the horrors in return.

They were *exposed*. Which meant that if they didn't get out of the forest right away, they would be dead.

"*Hyyyah!*" Kali shouted, totally unnecessarily, to Horse, as he once again thundered through the trees. He was not so much a mount any more as a battering ram, his bulk crashing through wood and foliage, crushing small rocks and undergrowth, uprooting smaller trees. Kali squeezed her calves hard into his flanks and Horse responded without protest, but she could see the sweat breaking out on him and hear how heavily he breathed. She slapped his neck proudly. There'd be one of his favourite bacon stews in this for him – if they made it out alive. *"Hyyyah!"* she shouted again. *"Hyyyah!"*

Kali rode, covering in minutes a distance that, on their way in, had taken half a day. She considered it wise not to look at the creatures they passed, but those she glimpsed out of the corner of her eye were dark, rotting or slimy things, things of bone and things of glowing hide. Those of them that dared an assault, Horse barged through or she booted swiftly away, their tumbling, misshapen forms crashing into their counterparts and torn apart in an instant, for food or for fun. The two of them had to swerve in their flight once as what appeared to be a black puddle oozed up from the forest floor – and then again, narrowly avoiding instant death as a giant fist came swinging down at them from behind the trees.

At last the glow from the conflagration began to fade, and the horrors that surrounded them retreated once more into the dark. Instinctively, Horse slowed, but Kali rode him on for another ten minutes or so before she felt safe enough to rein him around and look back on what they had left behind.

In the distance, visible even through its canopy, a giant pillar of fire still rose above the Sardenne, identical to the one she had seen in the vision that had caused her fall. The moments she spent staring at it were the first chance she'd had time to think about what had happened to her, and she frowned. There was no doubt now that the conflagration she had witnessed was that of the Spiral itself, and that meant she had seen the future – how could that possibly be explained? *Gods*, she thought, *how could the whole bloody day be explained?* Death traps, the Final Faith, the giant key still slung across her back – *everything* about it posed a question.

Thankfully, she knew someone who could help her find the answers. She reined Horse around again, and together the two of them began the long trek back out of the forest. When they emerged from it, she knew, they would be taking the road to Gargas.

Their exit from the Sardenne – and subsequent trek across the eastern plains of Pontaine – took four days, and while it was a relief to be amongst such dramatically different scenery, the endless fields dotted by the occasional hamlet that comprised this far eastern part of the peninsula made for a wearisome journey. But at least Kali was able to make camp each night relieved that she did not have to watch the movements of every shadow, and by the final night's rest she had visibly relaxed.

"You ever wonder, Horse," she mused as she lay by her campfire nursing her sixth bottle of flummox, "if your ancestors are trotting around, looking down on you from up there?" She was gazing at the azure mass of Kerberos, where, common belief had it, souls went when the body died. There, they were meant to soar in endless majesty through the gas giant's clouds, but only if they'd been good, gods-fearing boys and girls – condemned to its pits, the hells, if they had not. Kali suspected she knew where *she* was going. She took a swig from her bottle and waved it around. "I'm asking only because then they'd have to have been *believers*, wouldn't they? You a believer, Horse? Is there some horsey church you go to when I'm not looking? Where you go clip-clopping up the *neeiigghhve?*" She giggled and yawned, stared at the distant sun. There was an eclipse coming. "No, I'm serious – wouldn't it be nice to just drift around as light as a feather?"

Horse chomped his bacon stew, ignoring her.

"Speaking of light as a feather. You're not listening, are you?"

Chomp, chomp, chomp.

"Thought not," Kali said, and promptly fell asleep.

The next morning they resumed their journey, the final leg, and reached the outskirts of Gargas by late afternoon. As they passed the sign to the market town, Horse perked up considerably, his trot breaking spontaneously into a canter without any prompting at all. Kali smiled and patted him on the neck. She was looking forward to seeing the old man too.

Kali had known Merrit Moon almost all her adult life, since the day he had introduced himself in the Warty Witch in Freiport. What had always stuck in her mind – become part of what drove her, in many ways – were the words he had imparted to her at the time. She had just returned from one of her first expeditions, only slightly less naïve than the day she'd been born, and had been sitting in the tavern bruised, battered and exhausted with a much-needed jug of ale and the artefact she had managed to extract from a ruined site some miles outside that town. As she sat there examining her prize, turning it in her hands, caressing it with a great deal of curiosity and no small sense of wonder, she'd been oblivious to the stares that the small, scintillating sphere was attracting from the Witch's other clientele. They, too, were curious about it, though their curiosity had little to do with the archaeology that motivated her and everything to do with lining their empty purses with gold. Two of what were presumably the more desperate among them, licking their lips, had begun to move over to her table when a hand had swept slowly across her own, pressing it down and hiding the object it held from view. At the same time, another hand waved the curious back towards the bar. The owner of both obviously possessed sufficient gravitas because the men left without question.

"What you are holding in your hand," a voice had said, "belongs to those who came before us, and is not a bauble to be toyed with. More importantly, it is not a bauble to be displayed in a place such as this."

A man had slipped then into the seat beside her, and she had looked over at a face of perhaps sixty years of age, weatherbeaten but at the same time gentle, with grey eyes that suggested a wealth of experience and a core of steel. Though a little portly, she'd suspected he hadn't always been so, much as she'd suspected that the shoulder-length silvery hair that now looked suspiciously like a bad wig, but wasn't, had once been more kempt. He was dressed, as she herself had favoured back then, in loose leathers but, rather startlingly, had slung about them a cloak of thick wool that looked and stank as if it belonged on a horse. And it was pink.

The stranger introduced himself as Merrit Moon. She had been sure she had seen him somewhere before, but he assured her she had not.

"Thanks for the advice, but I can look after myself," she had answered.

Merrit Moon had smiled. "Oh, of that, I have no doubt. But as much as that might be the case, don't you think it a little foolish to provoke the need to do so?"

He signalled for a drink and, as it came, continued, quietening only as the tankard was set down. "Ours is a rich world," he said, "but most of those who live upon it do not even begin to realise where its true richness lies. Nor do most of them wish to. They have closed minds, and to those minds all there is around them is Vos, Pontaine, the Anclas Territories, places busy with petty dealings and squabblings, trade agreements, embargoes and hostilities. They are, of course, aware, somewhere in their closed minds, that we all live with the legacy of older races who came before us, but they choose to ignore that legacy because their minds are too full of the mundane day-to-day struggles it takes to survive in this blighted land."

He'd gestured to the object she'd held. "Such objects might stir greed in some, as happened with those... gentlemen, but in others they stir fear – fear of the unknown, fear of instability, fear that their own lives and existences could as easily be snuffed as were the lives and existences of those who once crafted such things."

She had stared at him. Merrit Moon had the air of a man who had made his own way on Twilight, much as she had herself, and she instinctively trusted him.

"You sound as if you have knowledge of the Old Races."

"Enough to know when to keep that knowledge to myself, for fear of a knife in my back."

She had glanced up at the men and kept the sphere low, but had not been able to resist stroking it with her thumbs, wondering at its smoothness of manufacture. Smoothness, that was, apart from one intriguing dimple...

"This thing," she had asked. "What is it?"

Unexpectedly, Moon had laughed. "Do you know how many times I have asked myself that same question? Not, of course, with what you hold – I *know* that – but with many a hundred other objects – perhaps a thousand, I have found? And perhaps with one object in each hundred I have actually come up with answers." He'd smiled. "Though not necessarily the right ones."

"What kind of answers? I mean, what things have you found and what do they do?"

Moon had leaned in eagerly, almost conspiratorially, and his eyes had twinkled as he spoke. "Narrow cylinders of light that, unlike candles, never dim. A ring that when spun speaks with the voices of beings long gone, in a language long dead. A gauntlet that generates a field of force *nothing* to do with the threads of any mage, shadow or otherwise."

She had looked at him in wonder. In all her ventures up to that time, she'd found nothing so exciting. Except, perhaps, what she held then. Whatever it was. "And this one?"

"That one?" Moon had said, as if it were nothing. "That one's a bomb."

"Bomb," she'd repeated, thumbs frozen where they were.

"Icebomb, in actual fact. Quite ingenious but quite common, and I'd advise you not to touch the dimple." He'd sighed heavily. "I touched the dimple..."

"You did? What happened?"

"Froze my dog solid. Tried to fetch it when I threw it away."

She'd looked at him to see if he was joking but there was a definite tear in his eye. "*Pits!* Hey, wait, I wasn't going –"

"Don't lie. Yes, you were."

"Okay, I was." She'd quickly put the sphere down and changed the subject. "So what are you telling me – these objects you found, they harness magic?"

"Not magic, young lady. *Science.* Old Race science."

"They were that advanced?"

"That – and less, and more. The truth is, they dominated this land for a long time – through three ages – but tales from the Final Age tell of them actually preparing to send ships to the heavens. To explore Kerberos itself."

"Kerberos," she'd whispered. "But I don't understand. Other than this thing, I've never –"

"Found such things?" Moon had finished, chortling. "Perhaps

that's because you haven't been looking as long as I have. Or perhaps because you haven't been looking in the right places."

Without a word, he'd slid a map across the table in front of her.

"What's this?"

A shrug. "The location of an Old Race city. Only three streets remaining, but interesting nonetheless. I'm giving it to you because I'd like to help you in your pursuits, if I may."

She'd gawped at the map. "Why? Why would you help me?"

And he'd smiled. "Because of your very first question to me. 'What is this?' you asked. Not 'What is this worth?' but 'What is this?' because you are interested in its *history*."

"That doesn't mean I mightn't still want to sell it."

"But you won't, will you? Because you now know what it is. You have a great deal to learn before the things you see and find begin to make sense, but you have already learned the first lesson – that Twilight is not ready for its own past. Hide the sphere and keep it safe, because perhaps one day you will need it."

"Hey, old man – a girl's got to live."

"And you *will*. Oh, how you will! The true baubles you find? Sell them, as I have done over the years. Sell them so you can go to greater depths, in search of greater secrets. Sell them to finance the life you'll lead."

"The life I'll lead?"

"Finding out what happened to the elves and dwarves, of course!" Moon had declared with sudden passion. He'd squinted at her, a smile playing on his lips. "That is what you want to do, isn't it?"

"All I ever wanted," she'd breathed.

"Hah! Barkeep, two more drinks," he'd shouted, then, thumping the table in glee before turning to her. "Then join me, Kali Hooper. There's a whole world out there, and it *isn't* ours."

There's a whole world out there, and it isn't ours, Kali thought. The old man had spoken those words five years earlier, and in that time Merrit Moon and Kali had shared adventures and expeditions, the old man teaching her tricks and techniques that had proved invaluable since – but also in that time he'd become less physically capable and had eventually begun to act as advisor rather than active participant in their finds. And then, there had come a time when he had retired from the field altogether. He could not shed himself of his interest in the subject, of course, and on moving to Gargas had opened a shop whose income allowed him to maintain that interest, particularly when it came to acting as a sounding board for her more *intriguing* discoveries.

The smallest population centre in Pontaine, Gargas was a market town that sat alone amidst the eastern plains' northern farmlands. Merrit had chosen it as his home because, unlike Andon or Miramas or Volonne, it enjoyed a tolerably low level of interference from Pontaine's governing bodies and, latterly, from what he considered to be the scourge that was the Final Faith. For a large portion of the year its wide cobbled streets were empty, its inhabitants dots in a desolate community, but twice a year, when the harvests came in, it was transformed into a bustling centre of trade and commerce as farmers and merchants distributed their produce from all over Pontaine and beyond. Then, the city's population more than tripled in size, its streets thronged not only with legitimate salesmen but wheelers and dealers of every kind, the shops that lined them enjoying a week or so of frenetic prosperity that sustained them throughout the rest of the year.

It happened to be market time now, and as Horse trotted in through Gargas's southern gate Kali was almost overwhelmed by the riot of colour, noise and smell that greeted her. Garlanded and festooned stalls crowded every open space, their equally colourful owners selling cloths and spices, ales and trinkets, meats and fruits, and everything in between. Kali dismounted Horse and led him by his reins through the bustling throng, dodging hawkers who regaled her with tales of products that would change her life and worgles that rolled hopefully along the ground in search of scraps, and avoiding by as much of a margin as she could the foul breath of traders' mools, the black and white patched ruminants they used to ferry their goods. More than once she had to swerve swiftly off course, hurrying along as Horse nosebagged a sausage or a pie from its seller's stall, the baskets they sat in and all. With all this going on, it took her a good half-hour to wind her way through to her destination but there, at last, it was.

Merrit Moon's shop was hidden away down a side alley behind a flummox still run by brother and sister Hannah and Arthur Greenwood, and Kali winked to them as she passed. But though hidden, Wonders of the World was no less patronised for it – in fact, it was one of the most popular destinations for the punters filling Gargas's streets. The old man had certainly tapped a vein when he'd decided to market souvenirs of Twilight's more inaccessible areas, and it had become quite the thing in the cities to own a rock from the foothills of the Drakengrat Mountains or a walking stick carved from wood chopped on the edge of the Sardenne. It was all junk, of course, but it was profitable junk and it was genuine and it allowed Merrit to rid himself of some of the more useless items he had accumulated over the years. Not that he didn't still collect – in fact he paid good bonuses to the would-be adventurers he employed to gather his sticks and stones if they ever returned with something more interesting.

Few, of course, provided him with the kinds of finds she did. Spotting her as soon as the bell jangled above the door, Merrit tried to conceal his pleasure at seeing her by merely raising a finger to acknowledge her presence. Kali smiled – it was rare these days that her visits were for purely social reasons, and she could see the eagerness in his eyes to discover what she'd brought him this time. His interest in selling a throbsnake's shedded skin to some Vossian noble waned instantly, offering the man the supposed aphrodisiac at a significant discount just to get him out of the door. The rest, timewasters by the look of them, he shooed away with a Drakengrat death-rattle, flicking the sign on the door to 'closed' as soon as they had gone.

"Hello, old man," Kali said. She moved to embrace him but Merrit, as always, scuttled away, pretending some nonexistent business. Again, Kali smiled. She'd get him one day.

"You have the smell of the deep Sardenne about you," Moon said brusquely, sniffing the air in the room with distaste. "Have you been taking my faithful old friend somewhere less than healthy, young lady?"

My faithful old friend, Kali thought. The old man was referring to Horse. Sometimes she wondered whether Moon cared more about Horse than he did her – knowing that, if not, it would be one hells of a close-run thing. For the fact was, when he had stopped adventuring, she had stepped not only into Moon's metaphorical shoes but into his metaphorical stirrups as well, Horse having been his companion before hers, and for a good deal longer. They had been through a lot together, those two, but, when it had come time for Merrit's retirement, it was clear Horse would not be happy wandering in circles in some field all day, and had actually twice run away, lurking on the edge of town staring dolefully into the distance, where such adventures – and perhaps some exotic variant of bacon stew – lay. So Moon had offered him to her. She'd had her reservations at first, because Horse had seen a lot of miles in his time. But then in a sudden moment of insight it had occurred to her that time was precisely the point. All of the places she wished to go had already waited so many hundreds of years, so what difference would an extra couple of days – okay, in some cases a week – in getting there on a slower steed actually make? And, as it turned out, it even gave her time to prepare, to think. It was an arrangement that kept everyone happy.

Speaking of which, Moon was circling her, prodding and sniffing at the key she had bundled up on her back, eager to unwrap her latest find. Kali nodded to a trapdoor in the floor of the shop, indicating that what she had might be a little too important to reveal here. Even more intrigued now, Moon rubbed his hands together and lifted the trap.

A ladder led down to a cellar and Merrit and Kali descended, the old man waving his hand over light cylinders to illuminate the subterranean room where he kept his – and her – more unusual finds.

Kali stripped off her backpack and waited as eagerly as he had above as Moon unwrapped the key from the oiled cloth in which she'd wrapped it. She had lost count of the number of times she had brought artefacts here for him to examine, and had witnessed a gamut of reaction, ranging from vague disappointment to child-like excitement to awed reverence. But the way he reacted now she had not seen before, and it made her feel momentarily cold inside. The old man's face had darkened.

"Gods of the Great Pits," Merrit Moon said, slowly. His voice was filled with dread and he actually backed away from the key slightly, staring at it from the greater distance as if he could not believe what lay before him. When he spoke again, which was not for a few moments, his voice came out almost as a whisper. "Kali, where did you find this?"

Kali hesitated. *Merrit?* she wondered. *What the hells is the matter? Is there a problem here?*

"Tell me!" he barked, suddenly and totally uncharacteristically.

"All right, old man!" Kali shouted. She was surprised to feel her heart thudding. She had never seen him, never heard him like this. "In the Sardenne. A subterranean site called the Spiral of Kos."

"How old?"

"What?"

"This Spiral of Kos, girl – how *old* was it?"

Kali frowned, wondering where this was leading. "I don't know exactly, but from the architecture possibly Mid Age. The vegetation inside was of unknown genus, but I doubt that it was indigenous. I think it may even have been cultured. Oh, and by the way, it ate people."

"Yes, yes, yes," Moon hissed, impatiently. He was nodding vigorously, as if the information he had asked for was causing him pain and he was trying to shake it out of his head. "Oh, gods of the Great Pits," he said again.

"Merrit, what is it? What's wrong?"

The old man stared her in the eyes and said: "Kali, this... artefact has to be returned where it came from – right away – *right now!*"

"I don't understand."

"Returned *immediately*, Kali."

Kali could not hold his gaze. "Yes, well," she said, slowly. "That could prove to be a little difficult."

Merrit Moon paused. "Oh, gods, tell me you didn't –"

"I did."

"*Gods!*"

"Merrit, it wasn't my fault."

The old man flung his hands up in the air. "For Kerberos's sake, child, when will you learn to curb this... this *destructive* streak of yours? 'Thanks for the advice but I can look after myself'," he muttered.

Kali actually felt herself becoming annoyed with the old man. "I don't know, Merrit! Maybe when people or things stop trying to kill me." Her mind flashed back to the last time something like this had happened, and she felt a twinge of guilt remembering how in escaping the Temple of Rahoon she'd brought down its plinths like ninepins as she'd raced down the steps with the Rock of Ages rolling hot on her heels.

But at least Moon had *liked* that artefact.

The old man sighed. "Sorry. I'm sorry. Are you all right? What were you up against this time?"

"I'm fine. And it was Final Faith. But not normal God Squad. More like some special –"

"*Final Faith?*" Moon repeated, incredulous. He seemed more staggered by this revelation than by the appearance of the key itself. "It can't be," he said. "Tell me, Kali, did these people seem specifically interested in the key, or were they, do you think, there only by chance?"

Kali shrugged. "I can't really imagine any scenario where anyone would find themselves in the heart of the Sardenne Forest *by chance*. No, from what Munch said I'd say they were specifically interested in the key."

"Munch..." Moon said. He rewrapped the key in its shroud of oiled cloth and laid it carefully on the shelf behind him.

"This... *thing* needs to disappear, Kali. I need you to understand that. To be hidden again, this time once and for all. And its resting place needs to be far from prying eyes, scheming brains and grasping hands." Moon sighed again. "Which is why, the first thing in the morning, it and I will be heading for the World's Ridge Mountains."

Kali stared at him, speechless. It wasn't that he was taking the key from her, because in that decision she trusted him without question – it was just where he was talking about *going*.

"I'll be taking the southern road," Moon continued, aware of her reaction and expecting fireworks any time soon. "But even so I expect to be gone for some weeks."

"Then I'm coming with you."

Moon shook his head. "No, Kali. The fewer people who know the key's location, the safer the peninsula will be in the future. And you cannot get fewer than one."

"Are you saying you don't trust me? Tell me what the key is, Merrit!"

"No. And you know that I trust you. It is other forces out there that I do not. If the Final Faith are indeed aware of what this key is and knew that you were privy to its whereabouts, then their pursuit of your knowledge of its location would be... zealous indeed."

"But the World's Ridge Mountains – it's suicide, old man!"

Moon grabbed her suddenly by the shoulders. "I will be fine," he insisted, giving her a reassuring squeeze, "*Fine.*"

Kali told Moon about her vision, then, but the old man had no idea where it had come from, or what it meant, and she pursued it no further. Their business done, Moon prepared a hot supper of pot-roasted rufoon, redbread and dripping, which Kali devoured eagerly, sending the food on its way with a bottle of black wine that the old man swore was part of a batch he had found in an Old Race cellar years before, and which he reckoned was a still-palatable and particularly fine vintage. It was his theory that its owners had been saving the bottles for some celebration that ultimately had never come. Kali made the right appreciative noises, but the fact was the old man had never been very good on the booze front, and the reason it had remained in the Old Race cellar was more likely that it wasn't fit to be served to the rufoon they were eating – or perhaps was even what had killed it. She forced it down, though, trying her best to turn her grimaces into smiles, as Moon questioned her about what she was going to do next.

"Ar dunnof, really," Kali shrugged, her mouth filled with redbread. She spat sizzling crumbs and waved the half-torn loaf in the air, forming little spirals that burned into her retina. "Back to the Flagons for a few dayf reft and then one of the loft canals, mayfee. Had a tip there'f an entranfe to be found somfwhere near Turnifia."

"An entrance to one of the lost canals near Turnitia?" Moon repeated, intrigued. He stroked his chin. "Yes... yes, that would make a lot of sense."

Kali dunked her redbread in the dripping and took another bite, nodding. "Mmmmf, I'fe fought so, toof."

As they finished, the noises from the street outside diminished to the last clatters of carts leaving the market, a few scattered farewells and goodnights, and then to the kind of solid silence that could only descend on a remote and rural town such as this. Moon, of course, had an early start, and so wanting to retire, offered her a bed for the night, but Kali declined, ready for some fresh air after the heat from his fire and preferring, anyway, to travel by night. It was a preference that worried Moon – the isolated and winding country lanes that were the only way out of there had, because of their isolation, a reputation of being dangerous enough by day, let alone night – but Kali held to the logic that anyone who willingly travelled in the darkness would be perceived by whichever grabcoins lay in wait as probably too dangerous to be approached in the first place. So it was that she gathered together

her things and stepped out onto the cobbles, slinging and securing her saddlebags onto a snoring and slightly startled Horse as she readied him for the journey. She stared at Moon as he stood watching in the doorway, lit by the warm glow from inside, and then over his shoulder to the door to the shop, and the hatch to the hidden reliquary that lay beyond. An image of the key, wrapped in its protective shroud in readiness for its journey, flashed into her mind.

"Merrit," she said, "be careful, up there, please."

The old man smiled, reassuringly. "I am never anything else, young lady. Believe me, you do not get to my age in a world as surprising as ours without constantly being so." As Kali mounted Horse, Moon tossed his one-time steed a bacon lardon, and Horse bounced it off his nose into his mouth and munched down gratefully, eyeballs spinning. "Besides," the old man added, "it will not be the first time that the World's Ridge Mountains have welcomed these old bones into their cold embrace."

Kali raised her eyebrows and then nodded. She should have known.

"Another tale, Merrit?"

"For another time."

Kali smiled and squeezed her heels into Horse's flanks, then reined him in the direction of the road out of Gargas. "I'll be in touch, old man," she said, and urged Horse forwards. The old mount swung its head in the direction of Moon, whinnied a goodbye, and then began to clop slowly forwards.

"Safe journeys, Kali Hooper... and you, too, my faithful old friend," Merrit Moon said, smiling to himself. "Safe journeys."

The relic-monger watched Kali and Horse until they had fully crossed the market square and begun to descend the slope to the town gate, then turned inside to his parlour. The fire crackled, as welcoming as ever, but as he closed the solid wooden door behind him, the old man's smile faded. It was indeed not the first time that he had had cause to journey to the World's Ridge Mountains, but he did not regard the coming prospect quite as casually as he had led Kali to believe. The mountains were a wild and rugged place, as untamed as the Sardenne and as anywhere on the peninsula, and their dangers were not to be underestimated. To travel there alone, as Kali had reminded him, would be considered suicide by most.

Luckily, he was not most.

But he would need to prepare.

Merrit Moon bolted the outside door behind him, took a last swig of his remaining wine and then headed through to the shop and back down the ladder into the reliquary, this time bolting its hatch above him. As far as the reliquary went, he had never been wholly truthful with Kali about it – it was indeed where he stored his rarer items, but what Kali did not know was these items were neither the rarest, nor the sum total of them. Waving another light cylinder into life, Moon took a small key from his pocket and inserted it into the lock of a display cabinet against the far wall, turning the key not clockwise as might be normal but anti-clockwise, twice, until there was a dull click that did not come from the lock but from the wall behind it.

With the slightest touch of his hand the wooden cabinet swung away from the wall on iron hinges, revealing yet another room – a round chamber – beyond.

A small collection of objects glistened on stone shelves in the light of the cylinder outside.

Sighing, his heart heavy, Merrit Moon stepped towards them.

CHAPTER FOUR

KILLIAM SLOWHAND HAD become used to every kind of reaction to his performances, from laughter and tears to boos and hisses, showers of flowers and hails of rotten fruit. He'd had standing ovations and he'd had people who'd stood up and walked out. He'd been welcomed in towns, run out of towns, almost lynched in towns and had, in some, been called names which even he had not heard before. Most hurtful of all, he'd had women who'd cackled at his tights.

But before tonight he'd never felt the tip of a dagger pressed coldly and threateningly against his spine.

A tad overcritical, he thought.

The performance had gone well, and the sound of the audience's laughter and applause still ringing in his ears, Slowhand had exited backstage, it being divided from the front stage by a curtain slung over a rope – a method of construction which, in fact, made up his makeshift theatre, wherever he went. Once there, he had quickly begun to wipe off his greasepaint with a damp cloth, attempting at the same time to strip his torso and legs of his spotted tunic and stripy tights, the colourful costume he wore on stage. The ritual would normally have been a far more leisurely affair, done with a good stiff drink or three, but the night's show *had* been a good one, loud and raucous, and not only in terms of the numbers in the crowd but the number of them he had seen react to his little vignettes. Quite a few more seeds had been planted, this night, and if Slowhand didn't miss his guess there was a good chance he was going to be paid a visit because of it.

Sure enough, though a little too soon for his modesty, visitors had arrived, and he had heard the other curtain – the one behind him, the one leading to the outside world – suddenly ripping open, and in a flurry of activity had found himself cornered and grabbed by both arms while the cold, pointed metal was rammed into his flesh, almost but not quite piercing the skin.

Critics, he thought again.

He coughed and turned slowly, the dagger tracing a thin red line around his waist until it settled in his navel, and he found himself – wearing his tights around his ankles – facing three robed figures.

The three were strangers to him, but he knew exactly who they were. One was female – and cute. Or at least would have been had she not been the one sticking the dagger into him – or represented what she did.

Slowhand played it casual, ignoring the crossed circles on their sleeves. "Sorry but I never do autographs after a show. It's making the fluffy animals out of the balloons, you know... makes the wrists ache."

"We have no interest in your autograph, Mister Slowhand, or your fluffy animals. We are here regarding a different matter. That of your growing reputation."

"My, er, growing reputation?" Slowhand said. He couldn't help himself – he looked down then back up with a smile, winking at the girl. Rather disappointingly, her gaze remained impassively and steadfastly fixed on his face and didn't drop an inch. Not that an inch would have done the job, he reflected. Nope, not even close.

"It has come to our attention that certain... subject matter may not be serving the best interests of our church."

"Certain subject matter?" Killiam repeated. He adopted the same dramatic pause as the man who had spoken. "Are you talking about my... little play?"

"Your little play. The Final Faith does not take kindly to being portrayed as the Final Filth."

"Oh," Slowhand said, "dear."

"As a result, the Anointed Lord wishes to converse with you. Now."

"The Anointed Lord?" Slowhand said, feigning shock. Bingo, he thought. "Right... well. How can I resist? May I dress first?"

"We wish you would."

"Thank you."

Killiam turned to his wardrobe – a pile of clothes strewn on the floor – then turned back, indicating with a toss of his head that he'd like his visitors to turn their backs. In actual fact, despite what he was slipping on, he wasn't remotely concerned whether they turned or not – he just wanted to see if the girl had problems doing so. And yep, she was lingering, lingering...

Ha! Got 'em every time!

Satisfied and dressed, Slowhand found himself escorted from his makeshift theatre, noting as he was led outside that others in the robes of the Faith were already tearing it down, folding and packing the cloth into sacks for removal, probably to be taken away for burning. Some members of his audience who still remained milling about in

Ramblas Square made discomforted noises but, of course, none of them said anything to the demolition team. None of them dared.

Slowhand didn't mind. The Faith was doing itself no favours with this kind of behaviour, and it was something else that would hopefully lodge in his audience's minds.

It was a measure of the Faith's sensitivity that his little play had attracted such attention, but then by bringing it here to Scholten he had rather hoped that it would.

The Final Faith, he reflected. As churches went, Twilight had never known anything like it, or those that ran it. Appearing out of nowhere not so many years before, and rapidly growing to become the largest organised religion on the peninsula, the Faith preached belief in a single god named the Lord of All, said to be the creator of all things. Slowhand wasn't a religious man but he did know that before the Faith's arrival there had at least been a *choice* of gods, and to his mind this single deity must have made for much rubbing of hands in the church because its followers knew exactly who to give their money to. Oh, yes, the Faith had got quite a little business going on that front.

It wasn't, of course, the first church that had supported itself by means of its followers' donations, but what disturbed Slowhand was that with the Faith there was a price to be paid for everything. Its followers prayed to the Lord of All for little other than for what followers had always prayed – a good harvest, prosperity, or the simple wellbeing of their loved ones – but in each case there was a price – *a price for prayer* – that was all too eagerly levied by the Faith, more often than not on those who had little or nothing to spare in the first place. He had actually seen people reduced to ruin in their desperation to please the Lord of All, but the Final Faith's answer to these tragic turns of events? Prayer.

As he was led through the city, Slowhand scowled. Would that that was the all of it. He had travelled far and travelled wide, and in those travels had seen or heard examples of the Final Faith's influence in spheres where churches should really have no business – influence in spheres that made him feel at best uneasy and at worst actually fearful of their ultimate aim. The priesthood of the Faith – from the Enlightened Ones at the bottom of the hierarchy to the Eminences at the top – were taught that the Lord of All did not simply desire but demand unity for humankind, a distinction that made the heavenly helper seem less benevolent father figure and more malevolent dictator. Only through such unity, it was said, could humanity achieve ultimate and complete ascendance as a divine creation, but one only had to look at events in Turnitia and other cities in recent years to realise that *unity* sometimes came about by means of the rod, and was merely a euphemism for their true objective – nothing less than the complete and utter control of the peninsula, under the law of the Faith and the Faith alone.

And here, looming in front of him, was the heart of it. The base of Final Faith operations. The multi-spired monstrosity that was Scholten Cathedral.

Slowhand, dagger still held at his back, was ushered along Enlightenment Avenue towards it, the broad approach lined with red-tabarded cathedral guard and thronged with cathedral-goers and the officially sanctioned hawkers of religious tat who preyed upon them. The most blatant misuse of donated funds he could imagine, the structure towered over and dominated the city, serving not only as head office for the Faith but as a place of pilgrimage for those faithful who had clearly been sufficiently indoctrinated not to share his opinion of the place. They came from every region on the peninsula to bask in its magnificence, to worship in its endless banks of pews, or, if they arrived at the right time and were selected by the guard, to attend the weekly audience of the Anointed Lord – one of which, by the incessant clanging of the cathedral's bells, was happening now. Each of them would go home happy – if lighter in the pocket – because the pomp and the ceremony that was trowelled on to blind them to the truth made the experience seem like a little bit of Kerberos on Twilight.

Slowhand was spared the pomp and the ceremony. He had to settle for being shoved roughly along side corridors, any pretence of being a group of mates out for a stroll gone now that he was away from the public eye.

Again, he didn't mind. Being backstage, as it were, gave him chance to see with his own eyes the operation at work. All down the side of the corridor along which he was shoved, one after another until he was in danger of losing count, he could see into booths where the faithful were in consultation with priests. Alone or in groups, they passed over coin to the superficially sympathetic and nodding clergy, they in turn passing on benedictions in response to requests for divine favour ranging from fertility for their mool to a cure for a village's collective pox. And hells, they were good – so good they could have gone on stage themselves the way they made the money disappear, surreptitiously slipping it into tubes behind them and benedicting ever more loudly as it clattered down some central shaft into a communal coffer in the basement. It was a treasure trove that ever grew and never stopped, and one thing was certain – if for whatever reason the Final Faith didn't eventually subjugate the peninsula by rod, then they'd have no problem buying it outright. Even he hadn't realised just how massive a business it was.

Slowhand was shoved on, and his surroundings, other than for the sound of a distant choir, grew quieter. He was brought to a halt in a large chamber designed in such a way that anyone entering was channelled immediately and directly towards a raised dais in its centre, the path by which they entered unobstructed so that they might depart without turning, stepping backwards all the way. He knew the reason for this was that, as the Lord of All's supposed representative on Twilight, no one was allowed to turn their back on the Anointed Lord, the ruling no mere fancy of power but written – apparently – in the holy scriptures and enforced by its hard men – the Order of Dawn – as a crime punishable by death. Handy, that, he'd always thought, because if the Anointed Lord wished someone gone, then presumably all the Anointed Lord had to do was order them to turn around.

Speaking of which witch, here she was now. The head of the Final Faith swept into the chamber fresh from her audience with her flock, flinging off her holy vestments with a theatrical sigh of annoyance that suggested she was more than glad to see the back of them – in a manner of speaking.

Slowhand studied her, stimulated despite who she was. That the Anointed Lord was striking was undeniable, being tall and statuesque in build with a face that was handsome, if somewhat stern, this topped by a long, flowing mane of fiery red hair reaching down to her buttocks. Her eyes a bright green, they would have been attractive were it not for the way she used them, looking upon her underlings with some degree of disdain. They made him think that the term striking could also be applied to her in the way it was applied to a cobreel, fangs bared and about to lunge for your throat, and in that respect she certainly had the sinuous curves.

They had never met face-to-face, but Slowhand knew her.

Her name was Katherine Makennon. And the last time he had seen her, she had been a Five Flame General in the Army of Vos.

Makennon mounted her dais and flicked a glance at him, noting his presence, and he was about to step forwards, say 'Hi', when his escorts pulled him firmly back by his arms. It appeared that it wasn't yet his turn.

A man slammed through the main doorway and strode towards her, iron-capped boots thumping on the polished floor, though there was nothing polished about the man himself. A squat barrel of a thing, he struck Slowhand even from a distance as being distinctly ugly and unlikeable, and his dishevelled appearance hinted he had just this second returned from some assignment in the outside world. Wherever it was he had come from, it had to have been somewhere hot. The man was charred and blackened as if he had been caught up in some great fire, and Slowhand swore that parts of his clothing still seemed to smoke.

He was announced as Munch, and Makennon's expression darkened as he approached her – he had obviously not brought good news. There was an altercation. Words were exchanged. At one point, the Anointed Lord slapped him across the face. Slowhand wondered why he took it – statuesque or not, Anointed Lord or not, he could have snapped Makennon like a dry twig.

The exchange ended and she dismissed him, holding out the back of her hand in a clear sign that his audience with her was over. Munch kissed it, not once, twice, but three times, and Slowhand could almost hear the mantra that would have accompanied each contact of his lips – the very same mantra he heard almost everywhere he went.

The One Faith. The Only Faith. The Final Faith.

It should have been over, but the small brute of a man lingered still, his lips hovering over her flesh. He actually looked likely to go in again. *Ah, that was it,* Slowhand thought. *The little bastard has the hots for her.* Okay, that was understandable – he might, too, given a moment of flung-about-the-bedroom masochism. But really...

He sighed, loudly. "Look, I hate to interrupt, but have you done with the tonguing yet?"

The pair shot him a fiery glare, then Makennon ordered Munch to the sidelines with a flick of her finger. Another flick followed, this time commanding the lapdogs who held Slowhand to bring him closer.

He and Munch passed midway, and Slowhand bent to whisper in his ear. "Little tip, pal. If you wanna get your hands on the boss's bazooms, try to grow higher than her knees."

Munch roared and spun towards him with a balled fist, but Killiam caught it readily and solidly, stopping it dead and holding it, unwavering, six inches from his face. He held Munch's stare, veins pulsing in his temples, an unexpected steeliness in his eyes matching that in his grip.

"I wouldn't do that," he said.

Munch considered, a gamut of emotions crossing his face, not least surprise. Then a cough from Makennon reminded him that he had just turned his back on her. Growling, he snatched his hand from Slowhand's grip, turned, and continued to shuffle backwards.

"Quite a show of strength," Makennon observed, "for a common street player."

As the Anointed Lord spoke, Slowhand was jostled into position before her, where he bowed with theatrical exaggeration, sweeping his hand under his stomach and then up into the air.

"Actually, I prefer to think of myself more as an artiste. Troubadour, bard and all-round entertainer, in fact."

"Really."

"Absolutely." Killiam pulled a balloon from a pocket, blew into it and, with a series of tortuous squeaks, twisted it into the semblance of a fluffy animal. "I even do balloons."

Makennon slapped the shape from his hand, ignoring it as it bounced away across the floor.

"Why is it that you are doing what you are, Mister Killiam Slowhand?" she asked without preamble.

"Ah. So you know my name."

Makennon gestured with a flyer in her hand. "'Killiam Slowhand's Final Filth – Every Hour, On The Hour'," she read. "It wasn't hard."

Slowhand smiled. "No. Suppose not."

"And why is it that you have so little respect for our church?"

"I don't know," Killiam said, though, in truth, he had every reason in the world. "Why does your church have so little respect for the other ones out there? How does that little ditty go again? The One Faith, the – ?"

"Ours is the *true* faith."

"Right, of course. True as well. You consulted the Brotherhood of the Divine Path about that, lately? The Azure Dawn? Or the rest of them your mob have squeezed out or shut down or *disappeared* since you began annexing the whole damn peninsula?"

Makennon smiled grimly and stared him in the eyes. "Killiam Slowhand. That really is the most ridiculous name..."

"Hells. You should hear my real one."

"Those churches are irrelevant," Makennon declared, answering his question. "Misguided fancies, the beliefs of fools. They – and others like them – will come to understand the way of things."

"When you've knocked it into them, I suppose. If you really want to know why I have so little respect for your church, Anointed Lord, then I'll tell you." Slowhand remembered her as she had been. "This isn't Andon and the peninsula's no longer at war – but most importantly, you're not a general any more. Stop running your religion as if you're still trying to build an empire and maybe, just maybe, people will *voluntarily* listen to what you have to say."

Makennon laughed out loud, as if the whole idea were ludicrous, then stopped suddenly and leant forwards until she was staring Slowhand directly in the eyes. "I'm not the only one no longer serving my country as a soldier, am I, Mister Slowhand?" Her eyes grew curious and her tone deepened as she drew in almost seductively close to him and he could feel her hot breath on his cheek. "Oh yes, I know you just as you know me. So tell me, *Lieutenant* – what makes you do this? Just why is it that you are donning the garb of a fool and attempting to undermine us in this ridiculous, seditious way?"

Slowhand's eyes narrowed. "I have my reasons. And one of them is I just don't like people running other people's lives."

"Hmm. But surely someone has to do just that, don't you think? Otherwise the whole of society would simply degenerate into an unruly and unruled rabble."

"Rabble, eh? Why do I get the impression that as far as your opinion of your flock goes it rather neatly sums things up?"

"We provide them with guidance."

"They didn't *ask* for guidance."

Makennon sighed, then gestured around her audience chamber with her hand, sweeping it to indicate what lay beyond as well. "You think this all a sham, don't you?"

"A sham *and* a scam, actually."

"That we have no destiny? That our only concern is with our own material gain?"

"*Bang!* Nail on the head."

"That we do, in fact, lust solely after power?"

"Woohooh, you're good. No wonder they made you the boss."

Again, Makennon leaned in close. "What if I could prove to you that it was otherwise? That our future is plain? Would you then cease your public mockery of our church?"

"That would be something of a tall order."

"Then allow me to fulfil it."

Slowhand stared at her, unsure of where this was going. "What's this about, Katherine?" he asked with intended familiarity. "I'm far from the only seditionary out there, so why the special treatment – this personal touch? Why didn't your lackey's dagger go all the way in? After all, it's happened before, so I hear."

"Because I want you to join us."

"What?"

"The Final Faith needs people such as you. People possessing *certain skills*."

She turned and walked to the wall of the chamber, where she opened a compartment and Slowhand found himself staring at something he thought he'd never see again. "Where did you – ?"

"Does it matter? The point is, it's yours if you join us. Yours to use again, in our cause."

Again, Slowhand stared, but this time at Makennon – getting the woman's measure. It was clear her style of running the Final Faith was unorthodox, but it was also clear that she *believed* in what it did, at least to a degree. But despite the incentive she'd just offered, he had no interest in joining her, though, he had to admit, she'd got him curious.

"Okay, Katherine – what do you have to show me?"

Makennon led him out of her audience chamber and along another seemingly endless corridor, to the furthest reaches of the cathedral, the threesome who'd brought him to her trailing behind. There, she showed him into a library whose shelves were filled not with books but rolled-up scrolls. Other scrolls were unfurled on the walls, images daubed on them in red and black ink – images of hellsfire and damnation, praying and weeping souls, vast marching hordes. Before them knelt figures he didn't recognise – stylised, twisting forms that somehow didn't look quite human – and symbols splashed here and there, some of which reminded him of the crossed circles of the Faith, others vaguely of keys. He had no idea what any of them meant. But he knew who was responsible for them.

Hunched and twitching over long tables down the centre of the library, Final Faith brothers scratched away at scrolls with quills, creating more of the strange images. Hollow-faced and exhausted, the worst aspect of them was that they were not looking at what they were doing – their eyeballs, to a man, rolled up into the backs of their sockets, completely white.

"Hey, fella, are you all ri – ?" Slowhand asked, touching one, and then found himself somewhere else entirely, where other hands moved across another scroll, in another room he sensed was far away – *gods, was it the League, in Andon?* He spasmed suddenly, totally disorientated, and then felt his own eyes begin to roll upwards in his –

Makennon slapped his hand away and he gasped. He knew now who these people were – telescryers, remote-receivers, weavers of the threads whose particular use of magic wrecked their bodies and burned their brains away.

And Makennon had them working some kind of... production line.

"What *is* this?" he said.

Makennon smiled. "The future. The scattered pieces of a jigsaw held in a hundred sealed collections and forbidden libraries across Twilight, being brought together, here, for the first time, so that the path of the Final Faith might be fully divined. Prophecies, Mister Slowhand – prophecies as old as time. Prophecies that show the *destiny* of the Final Faith."

"Let me get this straight. You've got these poor bastards telepathically purloining a bunch of dangerous-looking old doodles because you think they are relevant to you?"

"Yes." She swept her hand across the walls. "Don't you see?"

Slowhand saw nothing – except maybe that Makennon had got a bump on the head on one battlefield too many. But he reminded himself it made her no less dangerous – if anything, more so.

"Join us," Makennon urged. "There are *many* things to be achieved."

"Erm, no thanks. I'll come back when your god's got his head screwed on."

Makennon's expression darkened. She summoned the escorts.

"Oh, let me guess," Slowhand said. "This is the part where you lock me up and throw away the key?"

"You are a nuisance to me, and I cannot afford to have a nuisance... *spoil* things at this time. I would have preferred to convert you to our cause because the removal of someone who has made himself so obvious on our streets is itself obvious, but then what choice do I have?" She directed her attention to the escorts and said: "He's a tricky one. Have him stripped and searched thoroughly. Take *everything* from his person."

"Everything? Katherine... not my balloons?"

"*Including* his balloons. When you're done, take Mister Slowhand to the Deep Cells. He'll be staying in our most prestigious quarters for a while."

The escorts grabbed Killiam by the armpits and began to shuffle him off, noticeably turning his back into which the knife dug once more towards the Anointed Lord. This breach of etiquette wasn't a privilege, he guessed, but a sign he was considered already dead. Nevertheless, he let them take him. Actually smiled. Because this was the other thing that the Final Faith excelled in – they made people *disappear*. And in forcing Makennon to make him disappear he'd got her exactly where she wanted him.

No, wait. Exactly where *he* wanted *her*.

At any rate, they had each other where...

"How long a while?" he called back.

"Until you come around to our way of thinking, or until you die."

"Right. In that case, about those balloons..."

Makennon watched him go and then returned to the audience chamber, summoning Munch back before her.

"I've considered your report," she said. "This Kali Hooper. I want her found."

Munch nodded. "Yes, Ma'am."

"Take whoever you need for the task and locate her. Quickly. Bring me that key."

"Just the key, Ma'am?"

Makennon stared at him, then laughed. "Has your pride been

injured, Konstantin? Is that it?" She waited a moment. "Very well, Munch, just the key. The girl is unimportant. Feel free to do with her what you will."

There was a pause, and Munch smiled in anticipation.

"The One Faith."

"The Only Faith."

"The Final Faith."

CHAPTER FIVE

You win some, you lose some, Kali mused. It was a week later and she was halfway down her third tankard of ale, draped at the table by the captain's chest in the upper nook of the tavern, the affair of the Spiral – despite a lingering nag about her vision – fading from her mind. Time to think about what to do and where to go next – there was, after all, enough choice out there. The Lost Canals, as she'd mentioned to Merrit? *Uummm,* maybe – she didn't yet know. But it was something that she intended to plan out, here, at this very table, over the next few days.

While at the same time getting some serious drinking done.

She quaffed the rest of her ale in one and signalled Aldrededor for another – no, make that two. The swarthy, grey-haired and ear-ringed Sarcrean winked and blew her a kiss as he set the golden brews down, pleased to have her back where she belonged. Behind him, down a small flight of bowed, skewing steps, business in the Here There Be Flagons was busy and lively, the air thick with laughter and banter, and a cloying mix of pipe, rolly smoke and sweat whose strength could still not mask the heady aroma of Dolorosa's Surprise Stew. The stew had been on the menu – was the menu, in fact – for as long as Aldrededor and his wife had been at the Flagons, and the surprise about it was the reaction anyone got if they were stupid enough to enquire what was in it. "*Why* you wanna know?" the tall, thin and equally swarthy woman would demand loudly. "You think Dolorosa trying to poison you, ah? You think maybe she cook witha the weebleworm anda the flopparatta poo? Well, Dolorosa tell you, iffa Dolorosa wanna you dead she would sticka the cutlass inna your belly and she woulda laugh! Like-a this – ha-ha-ha-ha-haaar! Now go! Getta outta theees taverno! Go away, go, shoo, go, go, go..."

Kali smiled. Dolorasa's more... unusual approach to business was, along with the captain's chest in a tavern landbound for leagues in every direction, a clue to the fact that before the elderly couple had fetched up here, they had pursued their own, long career on Twilight's roiling seas. Exactly what that career had been she had never felt the need to ask, because as far as she was concerned the ear-ring and the cutlass and the hearty laugh said it all.

It was what she loved – had *always* loved – about this place – the mixed bunch all of them were. Looking down towards the bar, she could see Fester Grimlock and Jurgen Pike engaged in a game of quagmire, the merchant and the thief staring daggers at each other as usual. There was Ronin Larson, the local ironweaver, and Hetty Scrubb, the herbalist. Between them weaved Peter Two-Ties, who had prepared the render for her expedition to the Sardenne. And then there, perched on his groaning and perpetually buckling stool, as he was perched every day – but only during the day – was Red Deadnettle, the flame-haired giant of a man who was the reason she was here in the first place.

All of them had made her welcome over the years, and all of them were friends, but to Red she owed it all. Kali knew nothing of her parents or her origin, only that she had been found, twenty-two years before, abandoned and naked as the babe she was, by an unknown adventurer exploring an Old Race site – a site she had never since been able to find. The becloaked adventurer had rescued her and walked the roads on a storm-lashed night, looking for somewhere or someone to take her in. That someone had been Red, who, seeing dawn coming, had brought her here. The rest, as they said, was history – and the adventurer had never been seen again.

A number of shadows darkened the outside of the small, whorled-glass windows of the tavern, before continuing on towards the door. Kali would not normally have given them a second thought – more customers – but their bulk and the way they had skulked for a second outside gave her cause to suspect something might be amiss. Sure enough, a second later, five half-uniformed thugs entered the tavern and headed straight for Red. They were heavies for hire, guards in the employ of local landowners to protect their interests on their estates, and while they had every right – at least in the eyes of the law as it had conveniently been written by their employers – to apprehend people on their land, they had no right to do so in a public place such as this.

"Mister Deadnettle?" their somewhat obese leader enquired. "Mister Red Deadnettle?"

Still hunched at the bar, his back to the man, Red did not move or respond to the question in any way. The thug swallowed and thumped him on the shoulder.

"Deadnettle, I know it's you. I insist you –"

There were sharp intakes of breath – warning hisses, really – from the others seated along the bar, and then a slow and universal shaking of their heads. The hubbub of the tavern quietened as Red rose from his seat, dwarfing the hulks before him as his fists balled.

Kali sighed. She was tempted to let Red continue but if she didn't want her relaxation – and indeed the Flagons itself – ruined by the earthquake that would suddenly and inevitably come, she knew she had better intervene. She leaned down and opened the captain's chest Aldrededor let her use, pulling a small blackjack from beneath a pile of maps, diagrams, schematics and other Old Race paraphernalia, just in case. Then she picked up her ale, descended the steps, and with a slow lowering of her hand bade Red sit down. That done, she tapped the guard on the shoulder.

"Is there a problem, officer?"

"No problem," the guard said tiredly, without even looking at her. "This gentleman and I needs a little chat, that's all. A matter of a small misdemeanour."

"He was taking a short cut across your boss's fields, unless I miss my guess," Kali said, though she knew full well that Red had been poaching again – it was in his blood. "Don't you think *misdemeanour* is a little strong?"

"It's the law of our lands, Miss. Or do you think that folk should just be allowed to wander wherever they want, eh?"

"I do, actually, yes. To wander... and explore." She gestured outside, beyond where the ramshackle tavern was slumped like a knackered cat beside Badlands Brook. "To see what's out there."

The guard turned and looked Kali up and down. She'd only got back to the place an hour before and, having spent a chunk of that time stabling Horse and reassuring him that Dolorosa's stew did have bacon in it, as yet hadn't changed, and the guard took in her sap-stained and torn clothing, the general dishevelment of her appearance. He sniffed as he saw the toolbelt at her waist.

"Oh, you're one of *those*. Take my advice and stay out of this, adventurer," he said with undisguised disdain. "Our business with Deadnettle is no flight of fancy – and no concern of yours."

Kali immediately railed at his attitude. She had never understood how people such as him could live on a world such as theirs and not be curious about it. As Merrit had said, their lives were mired in the mundane, obsessed with petty issues and their own selfish concerns. When all they had to do was look up at Kerberos and wonder –

Hells. She would have given him a lecture but he wasn't worth the bother. "Red is a friend of mine," she said.

"Yeah, he looks like he would be. Now off with you before I have the innkeeper eject you from the premises."

Red said something for the first time, then, leaning down to whisper quietly in the guard's ear. It was still a rumble. "That might be difficult, Mister Policeman. 'Cause Miss Hooper, she owns the place."

The guard guffawed and looked Kali up and down again. "Don't make me laugh. A strip of a girl like her owning a grub's den like this in the back of beyond. Why would she want to do that?"

Kali took a sip of her ale and stared at the guard measuredly. What Red said was true – the tavern had hit hard times a few years ago, and so, when she'd had the funds, she'd bought it, simple as that. But she hadn't changed anything. Except the name. You just didn't with this place. The year before one of the local gentry had objected to the fuggy atmosphere and had suggested it became a non-smoking tavern. After the laughter had died down – *a non-smoking tavern?* – Red had dragged the man to Bottomless Pit and thrown him in. *After* setting him on fire.

"It relaxes me."

Fatso guffawed again. "Bet that don't take much, either. Size of you, it'd only take a thimbleful before you was off your bloody head!"

"And ready for a good time, eh?" Kali said, calculatedly.

The guard's eyes narrowed, and he smacked his lips. "Tell you what – why don't we put that to the test?"

"I'm sure I don't know what you mean."

"A little competition. You, me, a few drinks. And if you're the one that remains standing, I let Deadnettle off the hook. Whaddya say?"

Kali slipped the blackjack back into a pocket, relieved she hadn't needed to use it. "You've got yourself a deal."

"Whoa, careful, little lady," another of the guards interjected. "At the Dead Duck in Miramas they call Sarge the Ale Whale."

Kali stared at the Ale Whale, hardly surprised. "*Phoo.* Well, it won't be a problem, then, will it?"

"'Ere, Sarge," another said. "You're supposed to be on duty."

Kali smiled her most girlish smile. "Surely he can hold his own against me? A thimbleful and I'm gone, remember?"

"Go orrrn, Sarge," one of the other guards snickered dirtily. "'Old your own against 'er, eh?"

"Why not, eh?" the sergeant cackled. "Why not indeed."

Kali looked at the bar but Dolorosa was ahead of her, having the first drinks lined up in readiness – four flummoxes with ale chasers. She dipped her head towards Kali as she swept them up.

"Poor bastardo," she whispered.

"Hush, woman."

Kali and the Sarge retired to the nook, and it began. One drink. Two drinks. Three drinks, four. An hour later, the Sarge's mates had lost count.

"'Ere, jush 'ang on a mo'," the Sarge said at last, slurring and straightening himself none too successfully in his chair. He made circles with his tankard, spilling great slops of ale over the side. "If thish is your hosteryl... your hotslery... your hoslerurry..." He hiccupped and frowned, determined to get something out. "If this is your pub, how am I to know your shour-faced wench ain't sherving you shome speshal watered-down muck?"

Kali looked down at her own ale, a thwack, triple the strength of his own. She'd tired of flummox and, besides, liked a challenge.

"Taste it for yourself," she said, smiling and proffering her tankard, which he took and quaffed greedily. All that was left, just to be sure.

"Okay?" she asked.

"Ish very nishe, yesh. *Blup. Orf.*"

Nodding, Kali motioned to Dolorosa to bring two more of the same. None too keen on being referred to as a sour-faced wench – or, indeed, any kind of wench at all – the concavity of the tall woman's cheeks clearly signalled she was sucking up to deposit a small present into the guard's beer, until Kali shook her head subtly. Dolorosa shrugged – *okay, maybe the man was suffering enough* – and instead slammed his tankard down hard, soaking his lap with beer. The guard looked down vaguely, his head bobbing, as the ale penetrated the cloth of his pants.

"Gawds, ah fink arve gone un me pished meself."

"No need to waste time going, then, is there?" Kali observed as he giggled. She raised her refreshed tankard to show she was still willing and able. "Come on, Sarge, drink up."

"Wha – ?" the guard said, startled. "Oh, yeah. *Cheershh!*"

The Sarge raised his tankard to his lips and stared hard at Kali. Or at least as hard as he could when he had finally managed to pull her into focus. Almost got her now, he thought to himself. *Ah mean, look at the state of the bloody woman... so betwattled she's blurred and swaying all over the place. Ey up, she was bringing on a reserve now, and all – another one who looked just like her. Nah, stood to reason that, as a gentleman, like, he was gonna have to say something for her own good, or she'd be off the bleedin' chair.*

"Wimmin," he bemoaned to himself. "They jush can't take their drinksh."

"Dolorosa!" Kali called. "Another!"

"Dolorosha," the sergeant repeated. "Godsh, sheesh uggle... uggloo..." He gave up and jabbed a finger across the table – jabbed it everywhere, really, including into his eye. "But you, Mish," he warned, "youse pretty an' oughts to givvup before youse lose your looksh... *ow, bloody 'ell.*" He looked stunned, suddenly, and then added, "Oh gawds... oh, *bluurrrfff!*"

Kali's tankard froze in mid-air as the sergeant's head hit the table with a thud. She sat back with a smile then motioned to his men to take him away, which they did, bundling him out of the door while their heads shook in disbelief.

Another triumph for the Tavern Tot, Kali thought.

She bounced down the steps and slapped the now reseated Red on his back. "Next time," she advised, "wait 'til Long Night, eh? Dolorosa, get this man another ale. Me, too, while you're at it. Please."

"You musta be hungry? You wanna some Surprise Stew?"

"Don't know. What's in it?"

"Oh, the beer hassa made the bossgirl funny, now! Hey, why not washa that outfit of yours because you steeeenk. Anda while you at it, sew uppa the pants because your bum it sticka out! Hoh, she smiles! Aldrededor, where issa my sharpeeest knife?"

Kali was halfway back up the steps when shadows darkened the windows again. Another group of men entered, clothed in common travellers' garb, but she recognised the leader of them immediately.

New recruits but same old story. The Munch Bunch.

But something was different. From the shapes that were barely concealed beneath his and his men's cloaks it was clear that they were more heavily armed this time. It wasn't the weapons themselves that worried Kali but the fact that their Final Faith talismans were absent from their sleeves, too. Munch and his cronies had obviously gone to lengths to distance themselves from looking like agents of the Final Faith, and that could mean only one thing. The gloves were off.

"Miss Hooper," Munch said. "You have been really quite difficult to track down."

"I like it that way. How's tricks, Stan?"

"They will be better when I have recovered what belongs to me. The key, Miss Hooper? Please?"

"The key? Oh, that key. Little difficult – I don't have it any more."

"You... don't... have it." Munch repeated, slowly.

"That's right. I threw it away."

Munch laughed out loud, spun to face the watching locals in the tavern. "Did you hear that?" he shouted. "She doesn't have it! She threw it away! Oh, well that's all right, then – we'll all just leave and go home to –"

Go on, Kali thought. *Say it. Say Scholten and give yourself away. Let all these people know who you thugs really represent.* But instead of continuing Munch slammed his fist down on the bar and with a roar swept away the drinks standing there. "Hey, watch out there," Red said, and made to move on him, but in under a second Munch had whipped a shiny new gutting knife from under his cloak and held it to the big man's throat. He pressed the point into Red's flesh until he was forced to sit back down.

Munch turned back to Kali. "Go home?" he said again, as if pondering. "No, I don't think so."

"I already told you, I don't have the key," Kali said. "Now, why don't you just leave before I tell everyone here who you are?"

"That would not be wise," Munch said. "Because then we would have to kill them all." As one, his cronies took crossbows from beneath their cloaks and trained them on the regulars.

"Miss Hooper, if you really do not have the key then I fear I have no choice but to change my plans again. This involves causing you great pain. Do you understand? Oh, and if you are thinking of fleeing from us as you did from the Sardenne Forest, I'm afraid that without the means that might prove a little problematic." Munch smiled coldly. "But if you doubt me, why don't you take a look outside?"

What the hells is he talking about? Kali wondered. Automatically her mind flicked back to her flight from the Spiral, the escape from its conflagration, the gallop away on Horse. *No,* she thought suddenly. *No! Surely even this bastard...*

Kali pushed past Munch and his cronies and burst out of the door of the tavern into the stable-lined courtyard beyond. There she stopped dead. Horse was being led towards her by another of Munch's men. But something was wrong. Very wrong. Horse stumbled as he came, sweating, whinnying sadly, his eyes rolling as they always did, but this time in pain. As Kali fought to take in what it was that was wrong with him her eyes were drawn to the reason for Horse's weak and unsteady gait. The fetlocks on both of his hind legs had been cut almost through. Sinew and cartilage dangled from raw and sliced wounds that bled freely and left a trail behind them, like red ribbons on the ground. The trails, Kali saw, led back to his stable, where this vicious deed had obviously been done, for there a puddle of blood the size of a small pond had already begun to soak into the straw. With that much blood gone and the wounds that he had, it was a wonder that Horse could walk at all. Kali already felt sick enough but then the true cruelty of what had been done to him – and to her – became clear. Horse's fetlocks had been sliced with an almost surgical precision, to the degree where they were held together only by the finest threads of gristle and tissue, and the fact that he was being forced to walk towards her now was providing the strain that would finish them off. As Kali watched in horror, the remaining threads of the fetlocks snapped away and, with a loud whinny of pain, Horse collapsed, dropping onto his rear, the blood beginning to run from him more freely than ever.

Kali roared and attempted to run to him, but Munch had stationed two more of his men on either side of the tavern door and they each grabbed one of her arms, holding her back. At the same time, more of Munch's men appeared on the roofs of the stables, aiming crossbows down. Munch stepped casually through the door behind her and said, "The nag was old. If the strain of fleeing once again hadn't killed it, the knacker's yard would have finished it soon enough." He stepped around to Kali's front, and smiled. "Trust me, Miss Hooper, I was doing you a favour."

Kali spat in his face, and struggled anew in the hands of her captors. Over Munch's shoulder she saw Horse fold down onto his front legs and then, with a winded and tremulous expulsion of breath, collapse heavily onto his side, his legs kicking spasmodically. Blood began to pool there, too, and he began to shake, soaked in his cold sweat. His dazed large eyes – as innocent as a child's eyes – rolled in confusion, for there was no way he could understand what was happening to him.

But Kali knew what was happening, and she couldn't believe it.

Horse was dying right in front of her.

"Let me go to him," Kali said. *"Please."*

Munch laughed. "The interfering adventurer shows her softer side. A compassion for all living things, all... *creatures* great and small. What a wonderfully pious attitude." He chuckled and, leaning in, whispered, "Perhaps you should consider joining our church?"

"Damn you!"

"The Lord of All knows my cause is righteous."

Behind her, the others were bundled out of the Flagons. Munch signalled his men on the rooftops to train their weapons on them.

Red and Aldrededor and Dolorosa stared grimly out at the scene before them, the woman raising her hand to her mouth. "Oh, no, no, no... oh, all the gods," Dolorosa said.

"'Ere, wosh goin' on out here?" another voice enquired, and the Sarge, his head looking as though it had been dunked in a bucket of water, strode from a stable, his men following behind. Munch scowled, and with a flick of his head ordered his men to lower their weapons. Idiots these men might be, but they still represented what passed for officialdom in these parts and, obviously, it was Munch's intention – perhaps *his* orders – to keep the situation as unofficial as he possibly could.

Unfortunately for him, it seemed to have already gone too far. The sergeant squinted at the dying Horse, then the restrained Kali, his brow furrowing. "'Ere..." he said again.

"There is nothing here to concern you," Munch said. "A tragic accident, that's all."

71

The sergeant pulled down his tunic, hiccupped and stared at him. "Looksh a bit more than that to me," he said. He gestured to his own men, who laid their hands on their weapons. "I'm afraid, sir, I'm going to have to ashk you for your provincial papers."

Munch scowled, considering the situation, and then actually smiled. But he made no move for papers of any kind. The poor fool confronting him had no idea how far he had just stepped out of his depth.

"Sarge, don't," Kali called to him. "Stay away."

But it was too late. Munch signalled his men and a rain of bolts took the sergeant's men down. Only the sergeant himself was left unscathed. For him, Munch had reserved something special.

It was over in seconds. Munch grunted as he forcefully levered his gutting knife from the chest of the sergeant fallen before him, and Kali could see him fighting the dull tugs on his bones as the roughened edge of his vicious blade grated and snagged between the dead man's ribs. Pulling it free of the corpse, he took a breath – a very satisfied breath – and then slowly turned and plunged the still-dripping blade into one of the gasping, weeping men who had survived his men's bolts. He did not go for a quick kill, instead impaling the man's guts and then twisting the hilt with both hands so that the end of the wide blade began to gouge a hole the size of an infant's head in the stomach of his screaming and helpless victim. The bucking man tried to grab the blade with his own hands, as if this would somehow ease his agony, but Munch pressed the sole of his boot onto them, slicing the grasping palms down the blade and, fingerless stumps now, into the gaping wound itself. As the man spasmed and uttered a final, guttural sob, Munch swiftly withdrew the blade, spewing a rain of intestinal matter onto his face and ending him.

Munch turned away from the corpses, wiping his knife on a patch of grass, but not replacing it in its sheath. It was clear to Kali that he hadn't murdered those men the way that he had just for fun. He had been *performing* for her – showing her how good he was.

How much of a challenge she was about to face.

Across the courtyard, Aldrededor knelt by the fallen Horse and trembled in helpless fury. Kali could see in his eyes how much he wanted to help her, to launch himself at Munch and his men for what they had done, and to kill them. But after his years of travelling the world Aldrededor was no fool – he knew the realities of life, of greater numbers, and of age. Instead, the old man stroked the neck of Kali's quickly fading companion, doing what he could to make the last minutes of Horse's life comfortable amidst the carnage. For his part, Horse's eyes were trained on Kali, perhaps wondering why it was she did not come. Wanting her badly to come.

"*Arrrrgh!*" Kali screamed, straining against the grips of her captors.

"She's mine," Munch shouted to his men. "Let her go."

Her captors released her, and Munch beckoned her to him, the courtyard having become his arena. Kali's first instinct was to charge at the bastard, to rip him limb from limb, empowered by the rage that had built – was still building – inside her like a volcano. But that would be foolish, she knew. She was no fighter, she just threw the punches she had to and, unless she was careful, Munch would likely skewer her before she could land a blow. Instead, she went halfway, starting to circle Munch in a half-crouch, ready, when her opening came, to spring. The trouble was, Munch was far too good a fighter to give her an opening, and as he too circled, expertly swinging his knife in a criss-cross defensive pattern, she knew that any such opening would likely be a feint, designed to draw her in. She had to play him at his own game, let him come to her.

"Something the matter, girl? Don't you hunger for my blood?"

"I'd prefer to just watch it leak away."

"Well, here's your chance," Munch said.

He raced at her, roaring loudly, swinging his knife diagonally right and left. The blackjack in her pocket useless to counter him, Kali knew she would have to rely on agility and speed to survive, and allowed herself to fall backwards to the ground. As his knife sliced above her, she rolled neatly out of his way and let his momentum crash him into a stack of barrels behind. Munch righted himself with another roar, and she quickly flipped back to her feet, beckoning to him, their positions reversed.

Munch came again, this time slicing his knife out in a wide arc before him, a manoeuvre that caused the air through which it passed to thrum.

Kali jumped back, jack-knifing herself at the waist so the tip of Munch's blade swept by her abdomen a few inches away and then, as it completed its arc, somersaulted forwards beneath Munch's plane of attack, slamming her soles into his gut. Munch buckled, winded, and, as he staggered back, Kali came upright again, grabbed him by the arm and, by sheer momentum alone, managed to spin him around. Once again Munch careered into barrels and, dizzied, collapsed to one knee. It was obvious he needed a second to recover but Kali had no intention of giving him the chance, and booted him in the face, knocking him onto his back.

Munch struggled to get back up. If his roar had been loud before, then now it was deafening, and purposefully not pressing her advantage – knowing Munch would use every dirty trick in the book and try impaling her from his prone position – Kali smiled. This was exactly what she wanted – to get the bastard angry, because if he was angry then he would start to make mistakes. Panting, she bounced on the balls of her feet like a pugilist, her fists clenched, waiting for him to come again.

Munch did, but quickly and with surprising agility, and Kali felt a surge of panic. She had known this was never going to be easy, but it was only at this moment she realised how hard her survival was going to be. Caught off guard, she flung herself desperately to the left as Munch's knife pierced the air in the spot she had stood a half-second earlier. That she had avoided, but unexpectedly Munch also rammed his elbow into the side of her head as he moved. Stunned, her head ringing, Kali felt herself weaving away and supporting herself on one of the beams holding up the stables, without a clue as to where her assailant would come from next.

The knife slammed into the beam hard, sending a chunk of wood and splinters flying into the air, and Kali felt the whole structure vibrate. Had the wood not been in the way, she would have been missing half her skull. With a gasp, she stumbled back into the stable proper, Munch wrenching his blade from the timber and following.

"Where's the key, girl? Tell me before I slice you in two!"

"Go to hells, you bastard!"

A distraction, she thought. She needed a distraction. Then, on the stable floor, she spotted the patch of straw into which Horse had first bled and, swallowing at its warmth, plunged her hand into it, flinging it in Munch's direction. Under normal circumstances it might have bought her a second before it was batted away, but with Horse's blood causing the straw to stick to Munch's face, it bought her two. Kali used the time to reorientate herself and ran back towards the yard.

"Come here, girl," Munch called from behind. No longer playing by his own rules, he signalled to two of his men to block her path. She spun to face two more, blocking the way she had come. And Munch came relentlessly on between them.

Kali spun where she stood, double-taking on any possible escape route, anywhere she could run to buy more time, but there was none. But then something clicked in her head. Whether it was her rage or the booze coursing inside her, she couldn't say, but she was seized suddenly by a rush of... well, she didn't know what it was, only what it made her do.

Surprising herself as she had at the Spiral, Kali ran straight for the nearest of Munch's men, and as he raised a sword to stop her she leapt upwards, using his sword arm as a platform to leap onto his shoulder, and from there onto the stable roof, the recoil from her heel sending the man staggering forwards onto his face. One of the men on the roof came at her and Kali spun, bringing her leg up and around, impacting with the side of his head and sending him flying from the roof, crashing into another of Munch's men on the ground. Another came and she ran straight at him, clutching his chest and flipping herself over and above him, maintaining her grip so that as a result he himself was flipped as she landed, slammed down, dazed. Working her way around the roof – kicking, throwing and punching any man who stood in her way, despatching them into the air until none were left above – she manoeuvred herself until Munch was directly below, staring up at her in some amazement amidst the chaos she'd caused. Kali panted and stared back, and she hoped her message was clear. *Get ready, you little bastard. Because I'm coming.*

She only wished she knew how, because she was making this up as she went along.

But so too now was Munch. Snarling, he flicked an arm at those men still standing, ordering them towards a stack of barrels that reached to the lip of the roof, and they began to clamber up towards her. Kali didn't give them a chance, booting the highest barrel down at them, scattering them aside. She booted another, and then another, and as they arced through the air, leapt out between them, landing and rolling in the midst of those who meant to do her harm. The first of the barrels had already crushed a man to the ground, and the second, come to a stop on its side, she booted again, rolling it into the legs of her nearest assailant, buckling the man over it, onto his back, where she leapt and knocked him cold. As another came at her, she dropped to her haunches, curled her fingers under the rim of the third, upright barrel and, with strength she hadn't known she possessed, spun it end over end, sending it smashing into his chest where he instinctively caught it, dropped it, and screamed. Kali didn't let it go to waste. Seeing another of the men coming straight at her from behind his broken-footed comrade, she ran forwards, heaved the barrel up and then kept going, using it as a battering ram to crush him up against the stable wall. The barrel shattered and, with a groan, the man slumped to the ground, unconscious.

Kali spun, panting and sweating, ready for the next.

But that was it – other than the men guarding Aldrededor and the others, she'd done it.

Now it was just her and Munch.

He stood there, his knife held in readiness by his side, smiling, waiting. Why the bastard hadn't attacked alongside his men, she didn't know. Maybe he wanted to use them to tire her out. Maybe he just wanted to see what she'd suddenly become capable of. It didn't matter, because all she could see, behind him, was a weeping Aldrededor and her now dead Horse.

Kali roared, and disregarding the caution she had felt when the fight had begun – knowing somehow that whatever move he made now she'd cope with – ran straight for Munch.

He raised his knife. But she didn't give him the chance to use it.

Kali used her speed to leap upwards, pirouetting in the air and sweeping her leg around to catch Munch with a sickening kick to his jaw that knocked him sideways. She landed, rolled and rose, spinning up from a crouch to bring her other leg around and deliver an equally numbing blow to his opposite side. *Turn the other cheek, you bastard,* she thought – *they teach you that in church?* Munch spat and grunted, as much with surprise as with pain, and, double-whammied, staggered about like the drunks he had slaughtered. Kali gave him no time to get his bearings, racing in at him and grabbing his knife hand by the wrist, at the same time bringing up her knee so that it impacted with his underarm, numbing his nerves and forcing him to release his grip. The gutting knife clattered to the ground and Munch stared at her, mumbling something incoherent. Kali didn't care what it was, using her leverage on his arm to twist him towards her and then ramming her elbow, hard and again and again and again, into his face. Munch grunted with each blow, blood spouting from his nose, and weaved backwards, totally stunned. As he did, Kali booted him first in the crotch and then the chest, and finally under his chin, sending him crashing backwards to the ground. She bent over him, panting, hot with rage, and pulled back her fist.

She was about to deliver the first of what she intended to be a volley of blows when it happened again. A vision. Only one much more painful than before. She suddenly couldn't punch anything, and all she could do was slam her hands to the sides of her head.

The last thing she saw of her home and her friends was Munch rising, snarling, and reaching for his knife.

And then agonising pain plunged her into blackness again.

CHAPTER SIX

Boots, again. Thudding this time not into her side but hard onto the ground. Many, many boots, thudding down one after the other, in militaristic rhythm.

The sound of marching.

But Kali saw nothing, saw no one. Only a sea the colour of blood. No, not just the colour of blood, for blood it seemed to be. Viscous and slow, it spread languidly across a flat and desolate landscape beneath a sky the colour of fog. A sea of blood that flowed ever outwards, seemingly without shore, until it covered all there was to see.

There was screaming, too. A distant and tortured screaming of many mouths that, though it seemed far away, was nevertheless all around her. But again, she saw no one – in the midst of the blood and the screaming, she stood all alone.

Kali stared down at the sea and wondered – was this the hells? Had she, despite everything she believed, been taken by Kerberos? Was she there? Would she see Horse?

There was movement on the horizon and she looked slowly up. Something was coming towards her. No, not something – *many* things whose bootfalls were in time with the marching she heard. Huge, looming figures that were somehow familiar in shape and somehow not, a dozen at first, and then a dozen behind, and then a dozen more still, marching towards her, advancing in rank after rank after rank.

Marching through the blood.

The ground trembled, and the blood flowed away in sluggish banks, revealing layer upon layer of bones – human bones – whose flesh had rotted where they lay. And the skulls and ribcages and femurs were crushed beneath the boots of the advancing horde as it came ever on. Kali could see now that the figures had looked familiar because they were human-shaped, but human they most definitely were not. There were no boots on those heavy, crunching feet. And it was not armour that clanked. And the sky of fog made their metal skins shine.

77

She turned slowly, struggled to run from the things, but her legs moved as if mired in sludge. The marching came closer and closer until it was right behind her, and her heart thudded. And then a great shadow loomed over her.

She turned again, looked up. Red and evil eyes stared at her and then a vast hammer came down hard.

"*AARRGH!*" KALI SAID, awakening bolt upright. That she awoke in such a position came as a bit of a surprise, but then awakening in any position would have been a surprise, considering she hadn't expected to wake at all.

Where? she thought. *What?* And then she remembered. She wasn't dead, then – she hadn't been finished by Munch. What she had seen had been another vision. But why the hells couldn't she move?

Ah. Kali realised she was restrained on a solid chair made of wood that could once have been butchers' blocks, on a raised platform in the middle of a cold, stone room. Thick iron collars integral to the chair circled her ankles, wrists and neck, holding her almost immovably in place. Her first instinct was to jerk against them, which she duly did, regretting the move when she found the insides of the collars had been inlaid with small sharp pins that stabbed immediately into her skin. Kali yelped, winced and stayed still. This chair had been designed by someone who liked inflicting pain, and she had a horrible suspicion who that might be.

All kinds of things went through her mind, not the least of them that she had been stripped of her working gear and was clothed only in her vest and pants. The goose pimples on her arms and legs were, however, the least of her discomforts, the greatest being the bloody great thumping headache she was not sure whether was the result of the second vision she had suffered or what must have been a knockout blow from Munch. Obviously the bastard had never intended to kill her – only make her think so – after all, he'd never find the key if she were dead.

The key. What was so important – and so *disturbing* to Merrit Moon – about that key that had driven Munch and his cronies first to the Spiral and then to the Flagons in its pursuit? Bloody images from the tavern that she did not want flashed into her mind, and she pushed them away.

Just what the hells was going on? And, more importantly, where the hells had she been brought?

Headache subsiding slightly, Kali looked around her place of captivity – as much as her iron collars would allow. There wasn't much to see – torches mounted on the walls illuminated a circular chamber accessed by a single heavy door, featureless other than the chair in which she sat, rather troublingly the obvious centre of attention. There were no windows, so it was likely a cellar, and by the absence of outside noise a cellar somewhere isolated and deep. But where exactly? She had no idea how long she had been unconscious and therefore no idea how far she had travelled. She could literally be anywhere on the peninsula.

Kali strained to listen, hoping perhaps to hear some noises from the outside world – perhaps a clatter of cartwheels on mud, cobbles or stone – an indicator of which town or city she was in, or snatched voices speaking in some regional accent. But there was only silence except for the vaguest hint of something in the distance.

It took her a few seconds to place what it was because it seemed so far out of context to the predicament she was in. But then she had it.

It was singing.

Somewhere above her, people were singing.

What sounded like a mix between a battle hymn and a song of praise. *The Final Faith,* she thought. Munch must have brought her to one of their churches, and she was sitting beneath one of their congregations. But which congregation, in which church, where? She strained to listen and, beyond the singing, caught the sound of bells.

Twelve bells to be precise, each of them pealing in turn. Kali felt her heart thump as recognition dawned. There was only one place she knew of that had such bell towers. Pits of Kerberos, the little bastard had brought her to Scholten – abducted her halfway across the peninsula, to the cathedral itself.

The realisation – and its implications – sinking in, Kali began to struggle anew against her bonds, but as she felt blood start to trickle, she let out a cry of frustration.

At the same time she heard footsteps approaching on the other side of the door.

A key turned in its lock and the door opened.

Three people walked into the room, studying her but staying silent. The first of them was Munch, the second a disturbingly tall, thin man she didn't recognise, and the third a woman she did – but only because she looked a bit like her statues.

It was Caroline MacDonald. The Anointed Lady.

No, hang on, that didn't sound right, Kali thought. *MacDonald, maybe but... Christine? Katarina? Katherine.* She was sure it was Katherine.

Yes, that was it. Katherine MacDonald, the Anointed Lady.

Hells, she really ought to get to church more often.

"We do seem to be plagued by pests of late," the woman sighed. She strode towards Kali and looked directly at her. "Kali Hooper," she intoned. "Age twenty-two, sex, sometimes, current occupation proprietor of the tavern formerly known as the Retching Weasel and now the Here There Be Flagons, situated in the hamlet of Stopford, in the western county of Tarn."

Kali smiled. "Thanks for reminding me. Now I'll be able to find my own way home. Whenever you're ready, that is."

"I'm not. Oh, and if you're thinking of shouting for help, don't bother." She pointed up. "The Eternal Choir never stops."

"That must get on your tits."

Makennon ignored her. "Not much to go on at all, Kali. And that is all the information in our records – tell me, don't you find that strange?"

Kali stared at her. "No, what I find strange is you have records about me at all. Tell me, Katherine, it is just a church you're running here, isn't it – not a dictatorship? And hey, I could have done without the crack about the sex."

"Proprietor of the aforementioned tavern and sometime tomb raider, I am led to believe."

Kali's eyes narrowed.

"Actually, I prefer to think of them more as repositories, or reliquaries – museums of the past. To be honest, I'd be pretty much gobsmacked if I found anyone dead in them, their owners having been gone for quite some time. But seriously, Katherine, you are really going to have to go to interrogation classes if you're going to ask me questions and then ignore everything I say." She smiled sweetly. "Kind of defeats the object, doesn't it?"

Makennon slapped her suddenly and unexpectedly on the cheek, hard.

"This isn't a damned game, tomb raider!"

Her head involuntarily snapped to the side, Kali worked her jaw and spat out a small glob of blood. Then she snapped her head back and glared at her captor, hair mussed over eyebrows that were deeply veed, her expression thunderous. But she spoke steadily.

"I'd kind of worked that out when your hired psychopath here slaughtered my horse."

Makennon smiled. "What can I say? Konstantin has a... passion for his work."

"Burn in the hells!"

Makennon cocked her head, almost curiously. "I hardly think that's likely, Kali, do you? I am Katherine Makennon, the Anointed Lord, head of the largest faith – the largest church – on Twilight. Hundreds of thousands of people see me as the Lord of All's representative on this world of His, and they revere me as much as they do Him. Each of these people pray for my well-being on a daily basis, and each of them will solicit my passage to the heavens when my time eventually comes. Think about it. With that kind of support, how could I possibly burn?"

"Oh, I'm sure there's a big enough match somewhere," Kali said. *Makennon, right.* "Why have you brought me here?"

"You know why, Kali. I want the key."

"I thought it was Munch who wanted the key?" Kali retorted. It was a weak retort but the best she could do in an attempt to halt the growing unease in her gut. "What are you going to do – fight amongst yourselves?"

"My desires are Munch's desires, and our desires are those of the Faith. The key belongs to no one individual but to the Church itself – it has been written."

"Oh, really? By whom?"

"The Old Races. The forefathers of we, the Divine Race."

"Oh right, them," Kali responded casually. Makennon was obviously referring to the elves and the dwarves, but other than that she didn't have a clue what she was on about. She just wished someone would tell her why the key was in so much demand or what it was that the damn thing actually *did*.

Makennon studied her, a smile playing on her lips. "You don't know what it is, do you? You haven't a clue. The key was just some... *bauble* you saw your chance to steal from us."

"Why don't you tell me what it is?"

"When you tell me *where* it is."

"You know, I am getting heartily sick of that question. As I told your flunky here – *I don't know.*"

"That we shall have to see, won't we?" Makennon said. She turned to Munch and the tall man. "Get on with it," she ordered. "Report to me below when you're done."

Below? Kali thought. *But weren't they already in the cellars?* She thought no more of it, though, as she realised Makennon was about to leave, and in her current circumstances being left with Munch and his mate as they got on with it made her feel more than a little concerned.

"Makennon, wait," she said. "You're the head of the Final Faith – a church – how can you countenance this?"

The Anointed Lord smiled. "I don't. I just ignore it."

With Makennon gone, Kali stared at Munch and he stared back, saying nothing but slowly rubbing his hand over large black bruises on his face, what looked like a broken nose, a stitched gash above his eye. He breathed shallowly and Kali noticed that bandages wrapped his ribs. She'd given him a good drubbing, all right, but right now it didn't make her feel much better. The bloody mouth Makennon had given her was nothing compared to the damage Munch could inflict while she was as helpless as she was.

But she was not going to let it matter what he did to her. She couldn't. Because if she told him about the key then she would have to tell him about Merrit Moon, and there was no way she was dragging the old man into this.

All she could hope for was that she blacked out quick.

Unfortunately, it seemed that oblivion was not going to be. As Kali swallowed in expectation of what was to come, it wasn't Munch who made the first move but the tall, thin man. With no expression showing on his sunken, sallow face he walked behind her, cupped her skull in his hands and then tipped it from side to side, fingers rubbing gently. The incongruity of what he was doing made her swallow harder still, her unease made all the worse by the fact that she couldn't see a thing. "What's with the massage, Munch?" she asked, sounding calmer than she felt. "You think maybe I need to relax?"

Munch spoke for the first time. He sounded calm and in control but Kali caught a flash of bloodlust in his eyes that belied his manner – the little bastard was looking forward to this. "This gentleman's name is Querilous Fitch," he said. "Mister Fitch is here to ensure our session lasts as long as is necessary. It is his job to ensure that you remain attentive and do not lapse into unconsciousness, a technique at which he is particularly adept."

"Then I'd better warn you I drop like a stone at the sight of blood," Kali said. "I don't think Fitch's massage is going to help very much."

Munch smiled. "His technique is a little more than a mere massage."

"Oh? What's he going to – " Kali began, and then stopped suddenly, gasping. It seemed to her that the fingers that a moment before had been caressing the back of her skull had somehow just slipped *inside* it, and while she was pretty sure the sensation couldn't actually be physical, it sure as hells felt like it. She felt cold and woozy and sick at the same time, and the really creepy thing was that she could feel different parts of her brain throb one after the other, as if the fingers were feeling their way around.

Thread magic, it had to be. Fitch was *weaving* inside her head.

Kali groaned loudly, and as she did Munch wheeled a small iron trolley into the room and locked it into place by the side of her chair. She flicked her eyes towards it. It looked innocuous enough but she somehow doubted it was there to provide her with a manicure to go with the massage. Too disorientated for a wisecrack, she found Munch speaking for her.

"I imagine you're expecting a selection of instruments crafted to cause you physical injury," he said slowly. "Branding irons? Pincers? Thumbscrews?" He lifted the lid. "Unfortunately, the Anointed Lord has decreed that such tools are only to be used should there be a failure in our more advanced techniques. I find these techniques rather *uninspiring* personally, but who am I to argue? The Anointed Lord has, after all, engaged some of our best alchemical minds to develop both these and their effects."

Kali looked numbly at what Munch had revealed. The trolley held a number of vials of coloured liquids, greens and oranges and reds, some of which looked more viscous than others, and each of which was marked with a strange symbol she did not recognise. They could have been reptile venoms or plant toxins or some other kind of poison and, though some bubbled of their own accord, what worried her most was that each sat next to a strip of needlereed, the hard, strawlike growth that, filled with a dart and the right ingredients, was a favourite tool of the assassins guilds.

But they were not going to poison her, surely.

So what?

Munch picked up a strip of needlereed and dipped it into one of the vials, the green, and then again, into the red. He tapped the end so that the viscous fluids mingled and slipped down inside, then raised and examined the reed, smiling in satisfaction.

"The dosage and combinations of these distillations have to be quite specific," he explained, "or can prove instantly lethal. But used correctly their effect is wondrously telling – though I'm told quite unpleasant – making your mind as pliant and as loose as I wish it to be. They do, however, cause some dizziness and lack of muscular control."

Kali swallowed. "Hey, then why don't you just give me a bottle of flummox? No, make that a case." She eyed the needlereed. "Is this going to hurt?"

Munch smiled. "This... no. But you may still feel some little pricks."

He flicked a lever on the side of the chair and the iron collars holding her clamped tighter, the pins piercing her ankles, wrists and neck. She bucked in her seat but found she could now barely move at all. Her limbs stung and blood flowed into the nape of her neck.

"Uuurngh!"

"As I said, they may cause some dizziness or delirium," Munch reiterated, "and it is essential for Mister Fitch's work that you remain absolutely still."

He dug the needlereed into the bend in her elbow, shoving it hard into her flesh, and Kali felt sick to the stomach as she saw the vein on her arm pulse and tinge green, the colour spreading up.

The noxious substance coursed quickly through her bloodstream, and there was nothing she could do to stop it, no way she could even try. Whatever it was Munch had given her, she felt instantly as if she had been on a week-long bender in the Flagons, the room about her tipping and swaying like a ship on the Sarcrean Sea. Sweat broke from every pore, her skin began to tingle, and as her stomach cramped agonisingly she vomited foam onto her chin. But however bad what was happening to her body was, it was nothing compared to what was happening to her mind. Her vision exploded suddenly with great bomb-blasts of orange and yellow and red that detonated and then spread like spilled paint, coating the inside of her eyes with a vibrant, cloying sea. Her head tipped back deliriously, and that part of her neck that thrust out as a result was pierced more deeply by the pins, making her blood run ever more freely. But she didn't care – the red of her blood was simply part of a rainbow that wrapped itself now around the inside of her skull, dizzying and disorientating, swooping and sick. As the colours swam, so too did her thoughts, and images of anything and everything began to flood her inner eye. Lost inside her own head, aware that she was dribbling and moaning, there was nothing she could do now but listen to the voice.

"The key, Miss Hooper – where is the key?"

"Told you... don't know..."

"Of course you know. The key, girl, where is the key?"

Kali tried to fight, to pull her thoughts into some kind of order, but the awareness of what the voice wanted produced precisely the opposite effect. An image of Merrit Moon flashed unbidden amongst a kaleidoscope of others and Kali railed against it, lest she blurt out his name. She tried desperately to make her mind go blank but it was a feat she had never been able to master – she wondered if anyone had – because there was always something in there, nagging away, even if it was only the panicked assertion to make her mind go blank, which perversely and inevitably conjured up the very images she wanted to forget. Kali consciously summoned other memories instead, the sights and sounds of previous adventures, but Merrit Moon hovered like a spectre in them all, smiling, advising, telling her when to run. She concentrated as hard as she could and shoved him away, back, into the darkness, and in his stead a cryptographic stone wheel loomed before her, set in a vine-strewn wall. *Three turns to the right and two to the left. No. Oops. Boulder, big boulder. Run!*

She could feel herself slipping, and all the time the question.

"The key, Kali. Where is the key?"

In the end, she fled to the only place she could – home. She surrounded herself with the laughter and the banter of the Flagons, the revelry and rivalry that was her tavern's soul. All her friends were there – Aldrededor, Dolorosa, Red – even Horse, alive once more. She swept away a sudden image of him dying and instead lost herself in memories of exploring the peninsula on his back, the discovery of Thunderlung's Cry, the Rainbow River, the mind-numbing Heights of Low...

"Such a *shame* about the beast," the voice said and, with a vertiginous panic, she realised that it was Munch, and that she must have unwillingly spoken Horse's name aloud. Her panic doubled, for she realised now that in thinking about Horse she was only one step away from thinking about Merrit Moon, and how easy it would be to speak *his* name out loud.

So she left even home behind, going back before the Flagons, before Horse and before Merrit Moon, back to her childhood and beyond – where lay no memory at all. But in doing so she found herself suddenly remembering what she had never fully remembered before, and she was there on a lonely road, during a storm-lashed night, crying like the babe she was, her tears indistinguishable from the rain. She felt herself being handed from one set of hands to another, caught a fleeting glimpse of a hooded man, and then, above her instead, was Red – a younger Red – smiling down.

Then even Red faded away, and she struggled to fill the gap he left behind. It was getting more and more difficult to concentrate now, she realised, and there was nowhere else to go.

But it seemed there was. Suddenly she felt something pull aside, like a curtain in her mind, and for the first time ever she saw, *actually saw*, the place where she'd been found.

Despite her escalating delirium, Kali gasped. It was there before her, clearer and more detailed than the memory of a babe had any right to make it. Clearly some kind of Old Race ruin, its interior was adorned with complex runes and trellised with ornate ironwork as artistic as that of the Spiral, or of anywhere she had ever been. But there was more, here – strange panels of light set into the walls, flights of iron steps leading to machine-filled platforms that *blinked* around the edge, corridors and doors leading away to who knew where. She could feel the whole place *tremble* with power. *Gods* – she wanted to get up, to explore, but she was, after all, only a babe and could not rise from where she lay swaddled and helpless, there, in the middle of it all.

Kali found it didn't matter. For the first time she was seeing what she had never seen or known before – her own origin. It was Munch's drugs, it had to be, and though she would never have believed it, she actually had something to thank the bastard for.

It was a revelation.

But nothing like the revelation that followed.

Because just as she thought it was over, the hooded man entered the room. The same stranger that on that storm-lashed night had taken her from this place and given her into the care of Red.

He bent over her, and she saw his face.

And it was the face of Merrit Moon.

Merrit Moon.

No! she screamed inside her head. The image – *the memory* – was so unexpected, so sudden, so startling, that she couldn't shed herself of it, and as a result couldn't trust herself not to speak his name. The only way – *the only way* – to beat Munch's drugs was to make herself forget the face, but how – *how* – could she possibly forget what she'd just seen?

She had to do something.

She cared too much about Merrit to reveal him.

She had to end Munch's flight of fancy. *Now!*

There was only one thing she could do. Kali rammed her ankles, wrists and neck into the collar's pins, hoping the pain would drop her into a state of oblivion from which even Fitch would be unable to bring her back. Through her agony, she felt him pulling at her, but that only made her the more intent, and instead of simply impaling herself on the pins she began to tug herself to the left and right as much as the collars would allow, letting the pins tear into her flesh, to rip it from her in jagged strips. The pain was excruciating and she felt as if her body was on fire, and her flesh was slick now with her own blood, but still she carried on, roaring not with pain but with unslacking determination. And, at last, she began to feel numb.

She heard distant, echoing curses. And then hands were pulling quickly and roughly at her restraints.

"Damn her," she heard someone say, and realised it had to be Munch. What followed made no sense. "Did you get it? *Did you get it?*"

"I believe so. But I will need time to absorb what I have."

"*Gah!* Make it quick."

Kali sighed, and someone took her, then. The collars released, she found herself being lifted from the chair, the room canting at strange angles around her. The figures of Munch and Querilous Fitch were merely blurs, as ghostly in their appearance as their disembodied voices were haunting. She heard the sound of doors opening, saw dark outlines looming, and realised she was being escorted through the underground of the cathedral. But that couldn't be right, surely, because as she moved she caught glimpses of bright lights, of lots of people, of activity that surely did not belong where she was. Had they taken her somewhere else, then, as she slipped between consciousness and delirium – somewhere where she could hear orders being barked, the sound of factory machines, the bustle of an army at work? Or perhaps she imagined it, because now those things were gone, and she was being led down a stairway that spiralled down before her, where it was quieter and darker and colder than even the chamber had been. Other faces swam before her now, peering at her through hatches in doors, faces that were bearded and straggly and desperate, and one that for a fleeting second she thought she recognised but couldn't possibly have. Some degree of awareness was returning now, and Kali realised she was in a corridor of cells, and even in the state she was in, one thing was clear – these faces she saw, leering out at her, these faces and their owners, they had been here a long time and, if she didn't do something *right now*, so would she be too.

She broke free of her captors and ran, lurching like a drunk, for the end of the cell corridor, to a ventilation shaft set into the wall. As deep and as doomed as they were, the prisoners here still had to breathe, and with a little luck the shaft would reach all the way to the surface. She leapt for a rung that was set just above the hole, and missed. She tried once more and this time found herself slumping down against the wall.

It was no good, the wounds on her ankles and wrists coupled with the loss of blood had left her too weak.

She could do nothing but capitulate as her captors loomed and roughly pulled her up.

Exhaustion overwhelmed her, then. All she remembered was being thrown into a cold, dark cell, and the door being slammed tightly shut behind her. Time passed, and then someone entered her cell and bandaged her wounds.

She slept, without any idea of for how long. And when she awoke, she heard singing.

But it was not the singing she had heard upstairs.

And of all the things that had happened to her in the last few weeks, it was by far the most disturbing.

CHAPTER SEVEN

THAT VOICE, KALI thought. *It couldn't be. Not him. Oh gods, please tell me it isn't him! Tell me it isn't.* But the seconds passed and, as had always been the case, the gods didn't tell her anything at all, and she thought: *It is, isn't it?* There couldn't be any doubt. That voice, that tune, those lyrics.

Gods preserve her, those lyrics.

She felt a dizzying swoon that was almost a panic. As the cell seemed to heat up and flex around her, she tried to shut her brain down but it was no good. And as the song concluded, she just couldn't help herself. It was like being some small, furry creature, its ears erect, transfixed by the sound of an oncoming cart, oblivious to the rumbling wheels of doom. She just had to listen.

> "...so ever since I've been in a stupor.
> Because of that lass named Kali Hooooooper."

A tin cup rattled on the bars of a cell door somewhere down the corridor. "For the sake of everything that's holy, will you *please stop!*" a desperate voice yelled.

"Wait – I think he has. Steaming pits, that was worse than the mangling room," said another.

"Something... I need something to stab my eardrums."

There was a very long, unappreciated sigh that echoed off the stone walls. "Fine," its owner said sulkily. "Just trying to cheer everyone up, that's all."

"We're cheerful, honestly!" someone cried, and then laughed manically, as if to prove it. "Really, really cheerful."

"Is it over? Oh, thank Kerberos... I feel I've been reborn."

Kali ignored the voices. Her heart thudding, she moved beneath the small grille that linked her cell to the next, from where the singing had come. She stretched and curled her fingers over its lip and then pulled herself up with a grunt, her soles skittering on the stonework below. It was something of a strain and her arms trembled with the effort, but as long as she held her grip she could see through the bars.

In the cell next door, there was a man wearing nothing but his undershorts. Just sitting there in the middle of the floor, with his legs folded, picking his teeth with a rockroach leg. Lean and muscular with an unkempt thatch of blond hair, many might have confused him with some debonair lord or playboy type, but she knew that nothing could actually be further from the truth.

Kali dropped back down, shook her head, took a breath, then heaved herself back up, unable to believe it.

The man looked up.

"Hello, Kali," he said.

Kali stared.

"'Liam," she said slowly and dubiously, in response.

"How are you doing?" he said, as casually as if they had bumped into each other on Freiport high street.

Kali's voice quavered with the strain of hanging on. "Ohhhh, you know..."

"Yeah."

"You?"

"Oh, fine, just fine."

There was a pause.

"So..."

"So..."

"Here we are."

"Yep. Here we are."

Kali dropped down again, and blinked. She knew full well what she had just seen but she couldn't shake herself of the conviction that it was impossible. The last time she had seen Killiam Slowhand – she slammed her eyes shut with a cringe, blanking out the details – had been on the Sarcre Islands, and that had been over two years earlier. After that night, he had seemingly vanished off the face of Twilight.

That night, she thought again.

Anger bubbled inside her, and she clambered back up, yelping as she saw Slowhand directly in front of her, working away at the grille to loosen it. "What the hells are you doing here, Slowhand? Come to *rescue* me again?"

"Nope."

"Stop grinning at me inanely."

"Can't help it. But it's still nope."

Kali gestured through the grille, indicating his cell, or rather his imprisonment therein. "Why are you here, then? It *is* me, I know it is – you heard I'd been taken by the Faith so got yourself taken to give me a helping hand!"

"You are unbelievable," Slowhand said, continuing to work at the metal. "Hooper, believe it or not some of the time I don't think about you at all."

"I'm hurt. Also vastly relieved." Kali's eyes narrowed. "So what the hells *are* you doing here? Don't tell me the great Killiam Slowhand was bettered by the Final Faith?"

"I have them where they want me. I mean, they have me where I... Oh hells, never mind."

"You were, weren't you! They caught you!"

"On purpose, all right?"

"What? Why in the gods' names would you want to do that?"

Slowhand sighed heavily. "Because I wanted to look around. See what really goes on behind the scenes with the Final Faith."

"From one of their cells?"

"Nooooo, not from one of their cells." He shrugged. "Well, not in the way you mean, anyway. Stand back."

Slowhand punched the grille out of its mounting and Kali instinctively caught it with an *oof* before it could clang to the floor. *Damn,* she thought, *we still make a great team whether I like it or not.*

But this was still going a little fast for her. She had no idea what was going on.

"Okaaay," she said. "So, what's that achieved? No, wait, don't tell me – you're going to escape from your cell into mine. Brilliant!"

"I see the wit hasn't deserted you," Slowhand said, wearily. "No, Hooper – it's the other way round. You're going to escape from your cell into mine."

"What?" Kali let the information sink in. "O-hoh, no, no, no," she replied forcefully, looking at herself still in the vest and pants in which she'd awoken upstairs. "If you think you're going to get me in a six foot square cell while we're both wearing nothing but our knickers you've another think coming. This isn't –"

"Because the way out is in my cell."

Kali stopped. She had to admit that had nonplussed her.

"You have a way out?"

Slowhand grinned broadly. "A-ha. Or, to be more accurate, have had a way out for the last week and a half I've been here. I've had to time it with the guard patrols, of course, but, an hour here, an hour there, it's allowed me to have a pretty good look around. Enough, in fact, to make tonight time to go. The escape route's a... little problematic but even in your state you should be able to manage it. So... excellent timing."

Her *state*, Kali thought. The odd thing was, she had already begun to wonder what her state was. She felt much better than she had when she'd first been dumped in the cell, better, in fact, than anyone who'd endured what she had had any right to feel. She had been here – what? – well, the truth was she didn't know – but surely not that long, and she already felt more than well on the road to recovery. She was tempted to look beneath her bandages but now wasn't really the time. Things had turned strange enough already.

"One tiny problem with your master plan," Kali said. "I'll never squeeze through that hole."

"Course you will. From what I've seen you've lost quite a bit of weight lately."

"Excuse me? Are you saying I was fat?"

"No! Great gods and pits of Kerberos, no. It's just that – well, you seem to have lost a bit of the puppy fat you had. You seem a lot more... *lithe*."

"Lithe?" Kali repeated. She thought again of her recovery. "Yes, well, I do seem to have developed something of a faster metabolism these days..."

"There you go, then," Slowhand said. He winked. "Besides, if nothing else it'll be fun to watch."

"Fun to watch," Kali repeated. "Wait a minute. Killiam Slowhand, have you been watching me in my cell? Lying here in a dungeon, in my underwear?"

Slowhand threw his hands in the air. "Of course I have, woman! Who wouldn't? No, I mean, how else was I to know you were there? And I – I wanted to know you were all ri –" He stopped suddenly, changed the subject. "Hey, if you're worried about getting through the grille, why don't you smear yourself with oil?"

"I don't have any oil."

"Damn! I'll just do my best to imagine it, then."

"Slowhand..."

"Fine, fine. Okay, look. The guards are going to change shift in fifteen minutes so if you're going to do this, Hooper, do it now. Or I leave you here."

Kali let out an exasperated growl and leapt for the opening, pulling herself up and then forwards on her stomach, her hands gripping the lip of the gap on Slowhand's side. It was a tight squeeze, but with a helping hand from Slowhand she made it through, flipping unsteadily into his cell and then, involuntarily, into his arms.

Slowhand grinned broadly. "Been a while."

"Don't even thi –" Kali began, and then stopped. "Whoa, hold on a second here," she said. "Killiam Slowhand, are you wearing make-up?"

Slowhand slid his fingers to that part of his neck which Kali stared at, and they came away smeared with greasepaint he had missed when cleaning himself up. It was amazing how long that stuff stuck around.

"Actually, yes," he admitted. "But it's not what you think."

"Really? And what do I think?"

"Knowing you, gods only know," Slowhand responded. He took an extravagant bow and added by way of explanation, "Killiam Slowhand's Final Filth – Every Hour On The Hour. *Ta daaaa.*"

"You've got to be kidding me," Kali said. "You've become a *troubadour?*" She couldn't help herself – she started to giggle.

"Hey, a guy's got to earn a crust somehow," Slowhand said, feigning hurt. "Besides, you'd be astounded the places being a travelling player gets you."

"Oh, that's it – it's all to do with getting in here, isn't it?" Kali said. Suddenly her smile faded and it was Slowhand's turn to study her up close. He whistled, looking concerned. "Pits, they really did a number on you, didn't they?" He stretched out a hand to stroke her cheek, but Kali pulled away, hesitated before speaking.

"'Liam... one of them... some bastard called Munch... he killed Horse."

"What? Oh, hells. Oh, hells, Kal, I'm so sorry." Slowhand's jaw tightened and pulsed, and for a second his eyes went distant, as though remembering – and noting – something. "I know how much the old nag meant to you."

"The old man, he doesn't know yet."

"The old man? Oh, you mean Merrit Moon. You haven't told him?" Kali shook her head. "He left for the mountains. To dispose of a key."

Slowhand pushed her to arm's length. "This key. It wouldn't be anything to do with the reason Makennon had you interrogated, would it?"

"The only reason. Whatever the thing is, it's important to her."

Slowhand sighed. "So I've been told. Look, it's going to be a few minutes before we're ready to move, and, in case you hadn't noticed, before then I'm a captive audience. So why don't you tell me all about it?"

Kali did, telling everything, including the find, the old man's reaction to it, everything, including the first and second vision, the one that had resulted in her being here. Slowhand took the news of a clanking army wading through a sea of blood in reasonable stride because, like her, he had seen some things. In turn, he told her about the scrolls Makennon had tried to woo him with – the images of the Old Races and the keys that were somehow meant to be the Faith's destiny – but after both of them were done, they were none the wiser.

Slowhand listened to the activity outside the cell. "Sounds like you have things to do," he said. "So how about we get you out of here?"

Kali looked around the cell, noting that its interior was exactly the same as her own had been, presenting the same obstructions to liberty she had faced. "About that," she enquired. "Just what is it you have in mind?"

Slowhand pointed to the lock in the door, and then, disturbingly, to his shorts, which shimmered slightly. "Krunt scale," he said, proudly. "The humble krunt's greatest weapon in the survival of the fittest." Kali looked blank and he sighed, explaining as he might to a five-year-old. "Krunts are native to the waters of the Stormwall, Hooper – their scales are polarised to repel stormbolts. That means they, themselves, are magnetised."

"They also make good butties, Slowhand. So?"

Slowhand pulled a face. "So," he declared, "they're pitsing uncomfortable to wear but very handy when it comes to manipulating tumblers." He pointed at the lock again, this time with some exaggeration.

Kali couldn't do anything but stare. "Let me get this straight. You've been opening this lock with your... underpants?"

"A-ha," Slowhand said, smiling.

Kali shook her head. "Oh gods," she said. Then the full implications of what he was saying struck her. "Oh gods, Slowhand, don't you dare!"

But it was too late. Slowhand was already pulling them down over his hips, and she spun quickly away.

"Pits – why does everything you do have to involve you somehow getting naked?"

"Don't know. Maybe it's *my* destiny."

"Just get on with it."

"Right," Slowhand said quickly. As he spoke, he stuffed his underwear into the keyhole, forcing it through with his finger, and then stretched an arm through the bars of the door to grab what came through on the other side. He then twisted his shorts into a tight roll and began to pull them back and forth, his face pained by the angle at which he stood, but humming as he worked.

Kali could hear tumblers rolling in their housing. She didn't even want to think about what Slowhand looked like. Definitely, definitely didn't want to loo –

"Are you done yet?" she asked, biting her lip.

"Almost there," Slowhand said, strained. There was a sudden sound of metal falling into place, and then she heard him step away from the door with a sigh of satisfaction.

"Done."

Kali didn't turn. "Put them back on."

"They're a little worn," Slowhand protested.

"Put them back on!"

Kali waited while there was another sigh, a slight shuffling and then a polite cough. These sounds were followed by a creak. She turned to see the door had been opened wide, and the corridor beckoned outside.

"Madam," Slowhand said, with an exaggerated flourish.

The two of them peeped out into the corridor, and saw for the moment that it was empty, the guards, as Slowhand had said, between shifts. But though they weren't there to sound an alarm, there was an immediate clamour from the other prisoners, who stared at them through their bars.

"Oh pits, it's 'im," one said. "No, no, what ah mean is nice bit o' singin', there, Mister. Voice of an angel, you 'ave. Come orrn, let us out."

"Don't say that – he might do an encore."

"It's a calculated risk. Look, do you wanna get yer arse out o' here or not?"

"Can I 'ave five minutes to fink about it?"

"Sorry, boys," Slowhand said. The truth was, he regretted having to leave them here but there was no other choice in the matter. Two might make it out of Scholten Cathedral alive but any more would leave them wide open to detection. He placed his hand on Kali's shoulder and ushered her along the corridor, following close behind. But as they reached its end, they heard footsteps on stone – the new shift descending the stairs.

Kali motioned for Slowhand to freeze and then flattened herself against the wall. As they passed her unnoticed form and saw Slowhand, they drew their swords, and she stepped out and tapped them both on the shoulder. She flattened the first with an open-palmed punch to the face, and Slowhand handled the second with a blow to the neck from behind.

Kali bent down to one of the crumpled guards and snatched his ring of keys. She tossed it to one of the prisoners they had left behind, who caught them in a hand projecting through the bars. "A half-hour before you make your move," she said, and pointed at Slowhand. "Or he starts to sing."

"Oh, funny," Slowhand said. He punched both guards in the face again to make sure they stayed out cold, then said, indicating the cells: "That's running a risk."

"Hopefully, they'll make it out. But if they don't, they'll provide us with a good diversion."

Slowhand looked at her, surprised. "A little cold and calculating, for you, Hooper."

"Last few days. I'm learning."

Slowhand nodded. As he did, Kali began to strip the tabards and unbuckle the armour from the guards. He placed a hand on hers. "What are you doing?"

"Getting us some clothing. You, in particular."

Slowhand shook his head. "Armour will do us no good where we're going, believe me. And you'd look a bit obvious in just a tabard. Cute, but obvious."

"If this is just a ploy to keep me nearly naked –"

"Trust me."

Kali sighed. "So what's the plan?"

"We head up."

"Up, eh? Here we are in what, some deep cells, and we head up? I'd never have thought of that one."

"Will you shut up and move?"

The two of them began to wind their way up the spiral stairway, staying cautious and keeping low, emerging eventually into the guard room that lay above. There, a guard was slumped in a chair, his feet on his desk, with his back to them, a faint snoring sound coming from the other side of his head. Slowhand seemed to know where he was going, and pointed. Without a sound, the two of them crouch-walked around the edge of the room, coming eventually to a door to a connecting corridor, which Slowhand peered through.

"The hard part," Slowhand whispered. "From here on in it gets a little crowded."

Crowded? Kali thought. And then she remembered being carried down from her interrogation – the sounds she'd heard, the sights she'd seen, or perhaps just imagined. *What was Slowhand saying,* she wondered, *that they had been real? Here, beneath the cathedral?*

"You've told me what you were doing here, Slowhand," she said as they moved into and along the corridor, "but you haven't told me why."

Slowhand hesitated. "The Faith and I have a bit of history. Or I should say they have a bit of history with someone close to me."

"Who are you talking about? Who did they have history with?"

Slowhand was uncharacteristically silent for a second. "That's a story for some other time. Point is, there's a lot more going on with the Final Faith than meets the eye. A *lot* more. And I needed to know what."

"And you found something?"

Slowhand nodded, pointing ahead of where they skulked. "Specifically, this."

Kali turned and, though used to some sights, actually gasped. The corridor ended a few feet ahead of them and, where it did, it opened out into a cavernous chamber carved into the rock and lit by the kind of light cylinders she had only ever seen in the possession of Merrit Moon. But it was *what* they lit that staggered her.

People milled about in what appeared to be some kind of warehouse and distribution centre, though from what Kali could make out very little of what they were storing and distributing consisted of either Final Faith tracts or any other religious baubles, bangles and beads. Instead, crates and packing cases piled high throughout the chamber were marked as containing supplies, both rations and medical, as well as various tools, implements, building materials and virtually anything else that would be needed in establishing Final Faith outposts throughout the land. There was a hint of how they would start to get there, too – iron rails in the floor of the cavern, with carriages upon them – some kind of rail *way*?

From what she had heard of their methodology there was something missing, though, and to satisfy her curiosity Kali crouch-walked into the cavern and forced open a crate that looked to her to be particularly suspect. Sure enough, she found what she had guessed they would contain.

Weapons. A lot of weapons.

She hadn't imagined *anything* when she'd been dragged from the interrogation chambers to the cells, it was all real. And the cavern she saw was not the only one – corridors led off everywhere. The sub-levels of Scholten Cathedral were not so much a religious base as a military complex.

Something else drew her attention.

"Slowhand, wait. What's that?"

Slowhand looked to where Kali pointed. On the other side of the cavern there were two openings in the rock wall, and in each a wooden construction that looked like some kind of lift, one of them rising and terminating at this level and the other, counterbalanced, going down.

Even *further* down.

Kali might not have noticed them at all were it not for the fact that they were heavily guarded, and that alone piqued her interest. What sent it into overdrive was that as she and Slowhand watched, Katherine Makennon emerged from the ascending shaft.

"Now, what do you suppose is down there?" Kali mused, slowly.

"Don't know. Ladies' toilets?"

"Witty. Why are the guards there, and nowhere else?"

"I don't know, but the question's academic. Wherever it is those shafts go, there's no way past those guards, not without alerting the whole of the Enlightened. We have to continue up."

"Slowhand, I thought you wanted the inside story on this place? Don't you want to know what's down there?"

"Of course I do. And I know you do. But not now, Hooper. There'll be another time."

Kali sighed. "Well, at least let's try to see if Makennon gives anything away. She seems to be going our way."

"Fine," Slowhand said, "we follow her. But don't get too close, and whatever you do, stay under cover."

"Stunning tactic. Never would have thought of that one."

"Just move."

"Yes sir."

Keeping behind crates, pillars and whatever else could provide cover, Kali and Slowhand pursued the Anointed Lord, gleaning little but nevertheless coming closer to what must have been an exit. Then, suddenly, Querilous Fitch appeared. Kali and Slowhand flattened themselves against a wall and listened in.

"I am here to report, Madam, as ordered," Fitch said.

"Sorry not to have been available earlier," Makennon responded, "but we had to seal below."

"More problems?" Fitch asked. "It has been... three days."

Makennon nodded. "We lost another two – including Salome. The defences in this dig are formidable."

Kali looked at Slowhand eagerly, about to speak, but he put his hand to her mouth and shushed her.

"That is unfortunate," Fitch said. "I'll arrange for disposal of the body."

"There *is* no body, Fitch."

"Ah, indeed." He hesitated for a second. "Madam, have you considered using –"

"The girl? No, Fitch, she is far too undisciplined, a loose cannon. Besides, following your recent treatment of her I very much doubt she would be sympathetic to our cause."

"She does not know what happened. And perhaps could be... persuaded?"

"No. I know her kind. You might beat her but you wouldn't break her. There'd come a time when she'd run into a trap rather than trip it for us. No, Fitch, I'll arrange for another. In the meantime, what did you learn from her?"

Again, Kali looked at Slowhand. What *did* Fitch learn? She'd been sure she'd said nothing.

Fitch paused. "The girl was extremely resilient, unexpectedly so for one so young. I suspect hidden depths with this one."

"Depths?"

"Great depths. I... needed to rest after the questioning. Some of the things she recalled were a strain and I needed to collate what I had gathered."

Makennon stared at him.

"Well?"

"The girl no longer possesses the key, nor is she aware of its exact location," Fitch said, his voice slow and tired. "However, there is a friend. An old friend. A relic-monger named Merrit Moon."

"And you believe that the key lies with him?"

"Yes," Fitch sighed. "But Moon travels."

"Where? Where does he travel?"

"Beyond Pontaine. To the ridge of the world."

Kali saw Makennon swallow. Even for one in such a powerful position as she, the World's Ridge Mountains instilled a sense of awe and unease. It was a place even the Final Faith did not tread lightly.

"Munch has arranged things?" Makennon asked.

"He and his men rode two days ago."

"Good," Makennon said. "Very good." And with that, she dismissed Fitch. Speaking to herself, unaware she was being overheard, she added: "This time, just bring me the key. I do not want an old man cluttering up my dungeons as well."

Kali watched Makennon follow Fitch up the corridor, stunned. She spun to face Slowhand, her expression pained. "How could he know that? I didn't say anything!"

Slowhand looked at her sympathetically. "Pits, you don't know, do you? That man's a psychomancer, Kali. Not so much a mind-reader as someone able to *realise* memories. I'm afraid he's been inside your head."

Kali seethed, knowing there'd been something wrong all along. "Munch told me he was there to stop me blacking out."

"It's a common trick. A dirty trick. While that little bastard was keeping your conscious mind distracted, his psychomancing friend was poking around in your subconscious and, in there, there's nowhere to hide. You couldn't help what they discovered, Kali, or stop them doing it. You literally weren't to know."

Kali snarled. Munch's abuse of her had gone far beyond the physical and, whatever it might have revealed to her by way of a side-effect, she didn't like that one little bit.

At the moment, though, that wasn't the issue.

"They know where Merrit went, and they know he has the key," she said to Slowhand. Her expression hardened. "As of this moment, the exploring's over. I have to get to the old man. You have to get me out of here now."

"Could prove a *little* difficult," Slowhand said, slowly.

"What?" Kali protested. "But I thought you – "

She stopped – because one of the two guards behind her had just discreetly coughed.

CHAPTER EIGHT

CLEARLY, THE TIME for stealth was over. Kali informed the guard of the fact by smiling sweetly and punching him hard on the nose. He staggered back against the wall, hands over nostrils pouring with blood, and with a satisfying metallic-cum-fleshy crunch Kali booted him up under his armour, bringing the knee of her other leg up under his chin at the moment he crumpled towards her, howling. The guard flipped onto his back, out cold.

Slowhand, for his part, performed a kind of spin that was half pirouette and half boxer's dodge that took him behind the guard so fast that the man barely had time to register the manoeuvre. As Slowhand came out of the spin, he wrapped his arm around the guard's neck, bent him double and rammed his head straight into the wall. Twice, to be sure he was out. And then, because he was Final Faith, just once more. The guard slumped and Slowhand dropped his unconscious body to the floor like a sack of wet wort.

The pair of them stared at each other, he smiling, she inwardly cursing – dammit, they'd always been good as a team.

Cries of alarm echoed down the corridor and urgent footsteps clattered towards them from all directions. Somewhere far above, they heard the peal of the cathedral's bells changing volume and pitch. The change would mean nothing to pilgrims going about their worshipful business, but to Kali and Slowhand it signalled one disturbing fact – the Final Faith knew they were on the loose.

They ran, not sure in which direction to head in the underground warren but moving with the surety that if they covered enough ground they must eventually come upon the exit. A number of avenues became blocked to them, however, barred gates sliding down from their niches in the rock to block off doorways to rooms and corridors, and to some degree the pair of them felt they were being herded. But herded or not, they were going to be no easy catch. Helpfully, the corridors here were stacked with equipment and supply boxes, and while they presented some impediment to their flight, forcing them to dodge and weave as they ran, they also provided cover and the means to discourage some of the guards from their pursuit. Three who tried to block off a corridor ahead were flattened as Kali forced over one stack, causing a mini avalanche, another two crushed against a wall as Slowhand hefted, without much difficulty, a crate of armour and tossed it towards them for them to catch. There was little room to manoeuvre in the tight confines of the corridors, however, and more confrontations were inevitable. The two of them refused to allow such inconsiderate encounters to slow them down, kicking, punching, leaping and dodging their way past them all, and as the numbers dwindled they started to believe that their escape might be successful. It simply never occurred to them that there would be nowhere to go.

The corridor ahead came to an impassable and totally unexpected end. The rock out of which this entire complex had been carved had, it seemed, provided a starting point in the way of natural caverns, and ahead of them now lay one such chamber. Dropping away from the corridor floor to a depth of about fifty feet, stretching away ahead of them perhaps three times that, the stalagmite-layered area was impossible to traverse around its edge, and even if they had been able to climb down to its floor, it would have been impossible to climb out the other side. The Final Faith had provided a solution to this natural hindrance – a slatted bridge that spanned the gap – but at that very moment, powered by the pumping arms of two of their people on the other side, it was moving away from Kali and Slowhand at a rate that made it impossible to reach.

They skidded to a halt, staring at the bridge as it retracted along guide cables in response to the turning of the large spoked wheel on the other side. An identical wheel on their side was of no help as it was impossible to operate while the other was in use. What was worse, the opposing wheel clearly had visible on it a clamp that could be swung down once the retraction operation was complete, effectively making the device on their side useless.

If they couldn't get across the bridge, they had no way out at all.

Slowhand summed up the predicament succinctly. "Hooper, we're stuffed."

Kali, however, wasn't listening. She stared at the retracting bridge, weighing up the widening gap, and then without a word to Slowhand ran back along the corridor down which they'd come. The troubadour looked at her dumbfounded, but then his expression turned to alarm as Kali turned and, taking deep breaths, began to pound back towards him. He looked at her, looked at the gap, and then back at her again.

She was going to try to make the jump.

"Hooper, don't be stu –" he began, but Kali had already drawn even with him, then was panting past him, and then she was in the air. Yelling with exertion as she took flight, legs pinwheeling beneath her, she flew forwards, describing a long arc that took her towards the ever-distancing bridge.

Her hands stretched out for a handhold before her – and missed.

But only just. Kali twisted, forcing an extra inch, and slammed into the lip of the retracting edge with an explosive grunt. She dangled there by her elbows as she took a second to recover before heaving herself up onto its walkway. One of the guards was already coming towards her but, as he approached, Kali slid aside, around him, then slapped him in the back with her arm, sending him careering over the lip to the unwelcoming rock floor below. The other guard, seeing what was happening, flung the lock onto the wheel and grabbed a pike from against the corridor wall, charging at Kali and intending to impale her. As he came, she grabbed both rails of the bridge and flipped herself upwards, the guard and his pike passing harmlessly beneath her. Spinning in mid-air, Kali landed behind his back, roared into him and, using his own momentum, rammed the wailing guard into the air to join his friend below.

She took a deep, satisfied breath, walked to the wheel and flipped off the lock, then began to swing it into reverse.

The bridge began to move towards Slowhand and she watched him fighting off those who caught up while it arrived, echoing her tactic of discarding them one by one into the rocky drop – so many of them, in fact, that with only a few more additions they'd be forming their own bridge across the gap. Kali smiled. He was enjoying himself, she could tell. At last the gap was narrow enough for him to make the jump, and as soon as he leapt for and landed on the walkway she began to retract it again, blocking the path of future waves of guards – perhaps mercifully – from their sweaty but grinning potential despatcher.

Slowhand joined her on the other side. They had escaped the complex but still had a way to go before they were out of danger. Forcing their way up the stairs was a running battle but finally they passed the dungeon level where Kali had been interrogated and reached ground level, bursting forth into the cathedral itself – right in the path of a group of advancing guards.

"This way, move!" Slowhand said urgently.

He raced down a corridor that branched off to the left, and then another to the right, heading towards the heart of the cathedral. Kali glimpsed more guards moving quickly along adjacent corridors, clearly manoeuvring to block off their route of escape.

"Where the hells are we going?" she shouted. She had to because of the bells and the singing.

"Up," Slowhand responded.

"Further up?"

"Further up."

"And how do we *get* further up?"

Slowhand snapped his head to the left and the right, then instead pointed ahead. "Through here. I think."

The troubadour burst through a large set of double doors into a transept, and Kali followed.

The pair of them stopped dead, stared.

Approximately two hundred people stared back. And as one they raised their eyebrows.

What else could the Eternal Choir do, faced with a heavily sweating man and a panting woman dressed only in their underwear in the heart of Scholten Cathedral?

Kali had to give them their due. They kept on singing.

"Slowhand?" she said, dubiously.

"Okay, that might not have been quite right," he admitted. He listened to the heavy footfalls approaching from behind and bundled Kali into the left rank of choristers before taking up a position on the right. "Sing," he mouthed across the aisle.

"What?" Kali mouthed back.

He gesticulated in front of his mouth. *"Sing!"*

Kali cursed but did as she was bidden, or at least moved her lips in time with the others. Across from her, though, Slowhand went at it with gusto. But though he was apparently oblivious to the guards who clamoured in through the door, Kali wasn't, and she had to remind herself to keep her gaze rigidly forwards as they moved up the aisle, heads turning to study the singers, eyes narrowing in suspicion.

It almost worked. *Would* have worked if the Eternal Choir hadn't chosen that moment to segue from one hymn to another. Because in the fleeting quiet between the two a broken baritone that had become utterly carried away – including from any key – was heard declaring, "...of that lass named Kali Hoooperrr..."

The game was clearly up.

"Idiot!" she hissed at Slowhand as the guards shoved their way through the choristers towards him. The guards snapped their gaze to her. "Idiot!" she hissed again, but this time to herself.

"Up there!" Slowhand yelled. He pointed to a balcony accessed by stairways sweeping up on either side of an organ positioned at the end of the transept, overlooking the cathedral nave. The curving archway the stairs formed there was lined with the organ's airpipes and draped with Final Faith pennants slung from the balcony's railings, and as Kali's gaze travelled up them she saw that another archway led off the balcony itself, stairs beyond leading upwards again.

"Oh, right," Kali said. "You mean where those *other* guards are?"

"What?"

Slowhand looked again. Four guards had appeared on the balcony, and each had a crossbow aimed directly at their hearts.

"Dammit!" Slowhand cursed. "Where did they –"

"Never mind," Kali sighed, peering at the organ. "You got us into this, I'll get us out."

"What?" Slowhand said. "Hooper, no, they'll –"

As with the bridge, he was too late to stop her. Kali burst from the choristers' ranks and sprinted along the aisle, leaping upwards, towards the organ. She used its keyboard as the first in a flight of makeshift steps – filling the transept with a discordant wail – and the organist's head as the second, eliciting a different kind of wail entirely. From there, she leapt onto the top of the organ, and then into the air, throwing herself forward and stretching to reach one of the pennants that hung from the balcony railing. It tore slightly as she grabbed it but the sudden downward jerk of the cloth granted Kali the extra manoeuvrability she wanted, allowing her to kick off from the balcony wall and use the pennant as a swing to run up and around the inside of the archway's curve. The soles of her feet danced across the organ's airpipes until her increasing speed took her out of the curve and she sailed into the open, first above the organ and then the choristers' heads, gaining height until she began to swing back towards the balcony itself. The guards positioned there tried to target her with their crossbows but the truth was they barely had time to register her coming before the pennant finally tore from its mooring and Kali slammed into them, booting them over the railing in a single yelling and flailing mass.

The organist scarpered as four heavy and heavily armoured bodies crashed like a ton of bricks onto the organ below, making it erupt with dust and buckling its wooden frame. Then one by one, each producing their own prolonged and discordant wail, the bodies slipped down over the keys and thudded to the floor. Their weight being the only thing that held the buckled instrument together, the organ creaked and groaned as each fell away, and as the last joined the pile it emitted a death rattle and gave up the ghost entirely. The organ fell apart.

There was a sharp intake of two hundred breaths, and for the first time in nobody knew how long the Eternal Choir fell silent.

"Er, sorry about that," Kali said in the pregnant pause that followed. "Slowhand, you coming?"

The troubadour ran, dodging the other guards whose mouths still hung open as widely as his had a moment before, and joined Kali on the balcony. They entered the archway and found themselves at the base of a spiral staircase that rose up into a tower, the purpose of which was unknown. But Slowhand again seemed to know where he was going and so Kali followed. And followed. And followed.

It was only as they burst at last through the door at the top of the stairs that she had cause to think her faith might – to say the least – have been a little misguided.

Kali looked down and couldn't believe it. *This was Slowhand's escape route? Bloody great steaming pits of Kerberos, there were birds below!*

Their flight from Makennon's guards had taken them up to the highest accessible point of the cathedral, a rope-and-plank walkway that at some point had been strung around the outside of its main steeple and hung there now as loosely as a whore's belt. Some fifty feet below where the steeple's tapering spire took over, the narrow, drunkenly undulating and half-rotten platform had perhaps once been used for repairs because as far as any other purpose went it was good for nothing, led nowhere.

Damn Slowhand! She should have known better than to trust him. *What the hells did the idiot expect them to do now – run round and round the thing until the guards following fell off, either through dizziness or exhaustion?*

She stared at Slowhand as he slammed the hatch behind them and barred it. No more than a second passed before there was an insistent hammering on its other side. If the hatch were as neglected as the walkway they balanced upon, it would not be long before they had company.

"So," Slowhand shouted casually above the winds that roared and buffeted here, taking a moment to sweep back his hair, "you're a tomb raider these days?"

Kali steadied herself on the swaying wood, positioning her feet with great care. Through a triangular gap between two planks she could see the toy-like rooftop of a Scholten steam factory belching a tiny plume of white fog in her direction. It was indeed a long way down. "A-ha."

"Like, erm..."

"No! Not like 'erm'."

Slowhand nodded vigorously, swallowed. "Fine. Fine."

Kali jammed her hands on her hips, regretting even that tiniest of movements when the walkway shifted beneath her and slapped against the side of the steeple, creaking loudly. "Look. Do you have a clue what you're doing up here, or not?"

Slowhand took a moment to reply. He was inching away from her along the precarious platform, his palms pressed against the side of the steeple, presumably for stability against the worst gusts of wind. "Hooper," he shouted back, "have I ever let you down?"

"Yes."

"I mean *apart* from the Sarcre Islands."

"Slowhand, those things almost had me *stuffed*. And yes, apart from the Sarcre Islands."

"Okay. Right. But let's get this straight. You have never, have you, actually come to any... *permanent* harm."

Rain suddenly began to hammer the walkway, soaking the two of them instantly. Standing there in her vest and pants, and from beneath dripping, slicked-down hair, Kali stared hard and ground her teeth. "*Nooooo...*"

"And that's because," Slowhand shouted slowly, "I always plan ahead."

He plucked a cloth-wrapped bundle seemingly by magic from the steeple's side, and Kali realised he hadn't been pressing his palms there for stability but searching for a hidey-hole. From the shape of the bundle, it contained one of the weapons that had once been Slowhand's tools of the trade.

"You hid a *longbow* up here? Why on Twilight would you do that?"

Slowhand stripped away the cloth, hefted the impressively sized crescent and pursed his lips. "The amount of anti-Makennon rhetoric I've been spouting of late, I knew it wasn't going to be long before she sent her goons to have a word. I just thought of every eventuality."

"Actually, I meant what *use* is a bow up *here*? What are you planning to do – spear a cloud for us to ride away on?"

"Oh, funny," Slowhand said. Acting quickly, he pulled a coil of thin rope from the same hidey-hole and attached one end to an arrow, the other to one of the more secure parts of the walkway. The coil certainly looked long enough to be able reach a cloud.

Slowhand squinted down at distant buildings, eyeing a trajectory, then aimed the bow high into the air.

"What the hells are you doing?"

Slowhand ignored a louder banging on the hatch. It sounded as if the guards were almost through. "Little idea I came up with. Call it a death slide."

"Nice," Kali said, and then put two and two together. "Hold on – you're going to fire that rope at a building down there and expect us to slide down it?"

"Nope. Building's no good – from this height you'd slam right through the wall. Need to hit somewhere open, target it through a ring."

"*A ring?*"

"Okay, a big, iron ring," Slowhand admitted. "One I tied between the Whine Rack and Ma Polly's, actually." He pulled back on the bow and winked. "There's a pack of supplies down there and a stables nearby so you should be able to find a horse to get you out of the city. Clever little bugger, eh?"

Kali said nothing. She couldn't even make out the places he talked about. She knew Slowhand was good – *very* good – but to make the shot he planned over such a distance, at such a target, and in *this* weather? Impossible.

Then Slowhand reminded her why he had gained the sobriquet *Slowhand*.

In the space of a second her ex-lover seemed to shut the world away. The wind and the rain and the hammering and the shouts seemed no longer to matter to the man at all, and an aura of great calm enveloped him, as if he lived now in a universe entirely his own. Gone was the happy-go-lucky troubadour he had styled himself as of late, and back was the famed archer who for what had seemed like an eternity had tested the hearts of the men he had fought beside at the Battle of Andon eight years before, during the Great War between Vos and Pontaine. Kali had heard the story told in a hundred of Andon's taverns, how their forces were in danger of being overwhelmed – were *being* overwhelmed – and Slowhand had stayed his hand as his comrades had clamoured at him to loose his arrow and take one more of the invading bastards down. But Slowhand had waited – even as enemy swords and axes had cut and sliced about him, he had waited – because he had chosen his target and would not fire until he knew his aim was true. Finally his arrow flew. Just one arrow across the length of a battlefield that was sheer chaos – through the flailing, bloodied forms of a thousand battling warriors and their dense sprays of blood – unerringly on until it found its home in the forehead of John Garrison, the commanding enemy general. One arrow into one man, but a man on whose survival the morale of the enemy depended. With his death, Slowhand bought Andon's forces the time they needed to gather strength, and the tide of that battle had been turned.

Slowhand let fly. His arrow sang into the sky then arched downwards. He must have calculated its flight perfectly because seconds later the rope it carried with it ran taut.

"After you," Kali said.

Slowhand stared at her, hesitated. "There's just one thing. I'm not going."

"*What?*"

"There's no time for two runs," he said, looking towards the hatch. "And in this weather it's too dangerous to risk the rope to two."

"I see. But you expect me –"

"*Listen* to me. I saw how you handled yourself during our escape, your reflexes, your speed – what you could *do*. There's something different about you, something changing... something *better*." He tested the tension in the rope that stretched out into the night sky, wiping the moisture from it on his tunic. "I knew it when I came up here. To be honest, in these conditions I don't know if I *can* make this slide, Hooper. But I know you can."

"I'm not just going to abandon you here."

"Call it payback for the Sarcre Islands."

Kali faltered. Was this Slowhand being serious?

"Use the bow," he said, quickly stripping it of its string then handing it to her, nodding in reassurance. "It'll hold. Go, Kali. Find your friend. Now."

Kali knew there was no other choice, not if she was going to save Merrit Moon. Even if that meant not only abandoning Slowhand, but abandoning him defenceless. She slung the stringless bow over the wire and pulled down until it became a horseshoe, gripping either end as tightly as she could. Then she felt Slowhand's hand in the small of her back, for a second almost tenderly.

"Enjoy the ride," he said. And as he spoke, Kali heard the door to the walkway crash open.

Kali looked down and let her body go loose. "Slowhand, I'll be seeing you again. I'll be –"

Slowhand slapped her off the walkway.

"Bye bye."

Kali gasped, the sky taking her as swiftly and as powerfully as if she had been snatched by a dragon's claw, and though those legendary creatures were now long extinct, she felt for a second what it would have been like to be taken thus. She appreciated also just how powerful they must have been to survive at the heights they had flown, for what she had stepped into was a maelstrom.

Every one of her senses was immediately and utterly overwhelmed as she dropped and the deathslide took her weight, her eyes and ears and flesh battered by the elements, blinding and deafening and, on her skin, as agonising as being slapped by open palms. No one before had been exposed to the heavens at this height – no one had seen Scholten from this unique perspective – but Kali had no opportunity or desire to appreciate the scenery, busy as she was shivering in her underwear and simply clinging on for dear life.

Slowhand's bow slid down the rope with a noise like some large insect, a deep *zuzzz* that made the muscles in Kali's arms flutter as if tickled but at the same pierced them through with pain, making even her teeth ache. The curve of the bow slick with the rain that pelted down, it was difficult enough to hang on without the added hazard of the wind that threatened to dislodge her with every passing second but, roaring with the effort of keeping her grip, she managed. At one point she even managed to twist her neck to look back towards the roof of the cathedral, but when she did wished she hadn't. The guards that had appeared on the rooftop had moved across and reached Slowhand, and as Kali watched the resultant scuffle she thought that she saw the troubadour go down at the point of a knife and tumble screaming from the steeple. And there was nothing she could do about it. *Nothing*.

She continued her inexorable descent, her momentum gaining, and with it the wind resistance against her. Her arms were now corded with the effort of gripping the bow but her increasing speed meant that the length of time before she reached safety was lessening dramatically with every yard she slid. The rooftops of Scholten were coming at her as blurs now, and above the roar of the wind and rain she could actually begin to hear the noises of the city and its people below. Soon she would be on the ground and be able to lose herself in their ranks. Soon she would be safe.

Suddenly, though, something felt different.

There was a lack of tension in the slide.

There could be only one explanation for that, and Kali felt a hard knot of fear in her gut.

Because she was still far from the ground. Far too far to survive the fall she was plummeting into now that the rope had been cut.

CHAPTER NINE

KALI ESTIMATED SHE was seventy or so feet from the rooftops, no longer hurtling towards Killiam's ring but dropping back and down, her forward momentum cancelled out by the sudden loss of tension in the slide. Letting go of the bow – a surprise present or a sore head for someone below – her hands flailed for the whipping rope, hoping to use it as a swing to at least get her closer to the ground, but her greater weight had already caused her to fall from its reach, and the lifeline was snatched away into the darkness, signalling its departure by momentarily blinding her with a few heavy drops of rain that had clung to the hemp. There was nothing now that would slow her descent – nothing, of course, but the impact that would inevitably come – and she plummeted towards Scholten like a rejected soul from Kerberos, spat back to Twilight on this dark and stormy night.

It was the Spiral of Kos all over again, only a hells of a lot worse. There, at least, the bones of the brackan had softened her landing, but here there was nothing between her and the hard stone streets except a packed and undulant layer of the city's jagged and sharply angular rooftops, all bedecked with a collection of chimneystacks, guttering and assorted pointy protrusions that from Kali's unique perspective seemed to have been cruelly designed to bounce her back and forth and shatter all of her bones *before* the ultimate pleasure she had to come.

She was, as Slowhand might have put it, stuffed. Actually going to die. The realisation brought with it a peculiar calm, and as time seemed to slow around her – prolonging her fall until it became almost dreamlike, *relaxing* even – Kali reflected that at least for *this* imminent demise no blame could be attached to the archer, for he had done all that he possibly could do to help her. Fine, she was still having problems getting her head around the fact that the bloody man could actually *be* so selfless, but the one thing she could not deny was that on the walkway he had bought her a little more time, by the look of things sacrificing his own life to give her a few more seconds on the slide. She wished – though very much doubted – that she was wrong about what she had seen, hoping for a second that even Katherine Makennon would not sanction cold-blooded murder on her holy premises, but then she remembered the way Makennon had left her to Munch, and immediately thought otherwise.

Munch. A memory of the courtyard outside the Flagons again flashed into her mind, the blood-soaked picture turning even redder with suddenly returned rage. Horse and now Slowhand, she thought – with Merrit Moon, a man who had never harmed and would never dream of harming anyone in his life, hunted down as well. Makennon and her murderous damned lackey seemed intent not only on ruining her life but of stripping it of everything she held dear.

Well, she wasn't going to let them do that.

No more, damn them both.

No pitsing more!

Kali's awareness of her immediate predicament returned to her, suddenly and vitally, but also differently than before, as if every one of her senses had burst into greater life. Though she still fell in the same slow and almost dreamlike way, every facet of what was around her and, more importantly, rapidly looming beneath her, seemed more distinct, the wind, rain and approaching rooftops separate parts of a jigsaw that she suddenly thought she could piece together in order to survive.

There was just one problem. There didn't seem to be time to open the box the jigsaw came in.

Time returned to normal and Kali dropped, the air above Scholten buffeting her as it whistled past at an ever-increasing rate. But then, instinctively, she turned in the updraught, angling and stiffening her body so that it sliced rather than fell through the firmament, causing her to nosedive towards – and at the same sloping angle as – the nearest and highest roof. The manoeuvre felt like suicide, and she herself figured that it very probably was, but some newly awakened part of her also figured that as reaching the ground was an inevitable given, why not do it in her own way, and in whatever style she could muster?

Hells. What did she have to lose?

The first roof came at her a split-second later, granted the honour of being the first to welcome her to town by the fact it appeared to cover the home of someone rich, building upwards rather than outwards in the cramped streets until the property was five storeys high. The tiles that coated it were a further sign of the owner's affluence, expensive redslate, and recently replaced or repaired. Sadly, whoever lived beneath them would have to give the slate quarry another visit.

Kali relaxed her body as she slammed into the roof, but the impact still sent jarring waves of agony through her and winded her severely, her loud explosion of breath drowning out the sound of shattering tiles as well as splintering timbers as the roof beneath them buckled to accommodate her form. From below came a screech of alarm and the sound of a shattering pot – perhaps some servant in the attic – but Kali could only apologise in passing as it soon became obvious she wasn't staying there for long. Loose tiles skittered down the roof before her, and she with them, sliding forwards on her front, hands clawing at gaps in an attempt to slow her descent towards the lip of the roof, but one that was to little avail. Her momentum uncontrollable, she skidded down, tiles snagging at her vest and pants and scraping her skin so that she felt as if she'd been thrown onto some giant cheese grater, the rough surface threatening to do her more damage than the impact itself. Grunting, she rolled onto her back as she slid but then realised she was heading towards the edge of the roof backwards and upside down, which was no good at all. She quickly flung her legs around at the hips, performing a kind of half-turn, half-roll manoeuvre that righted her so that she now slid feet first and on her behind, but with only a second to spare before she reached the roof's edge.

A hazardous rain of broken tiles and mortaring preceded her over the lip and tumbled towards the street below, soliciting another cry of alarm, and then Kali felt the soles of her feet slam into the iron guttering that lined the lip of the roof, the bolts holding it there loosening from the stonework with her impact. She didn't attempt to halt her descent as she was still sliding far too fast and the impact would have flipped her over and sent her flailing towards the street herself, so instead she used the disintegrating guttering to her advantage. She quickly scanned the buildings opposite, their roofs perhaps fifteen feet away and a storey or so below and, calculating the way the guttering was breaking, chose her target, the chimneystack-crowded roof of a seedy-looking boarding house called Dorweazle's. As the bolts on the guttering sheared Kali dug in her heels and – arms outstretched for balance – stood and rode it as it came away from the roof, using it and the drainpipe it served as a giant stilt to stride the gap between buildings.

It wasn't going to take her all the way, she knew.

The precarious assemblage of metal buckled beneath her when she was halfway across, and more evidence of her passage rained into the street below with a series of resounding clangs. Again, cries of alarm drifted up to her, but again she could only apologise in passing as she really had little choice but to keep moving, flailing and running through the air now as if she were some heavenly messenger who'd lost the power of flight but remained intent on delivering a missive to Dorweazle.

With a loud cry of exertion Kali made it – *just* – thudding down onto the roof of the boarding house in a crouch, though she knew her problems weren't yet over. The steep, badly maintained and rain-slicked roof offered little purchase and she found herself skidding backwards amongst streams of rainwater towards its lip, one still too far from the ground for her liking. She instinctively assessed her situation once more then quickly grabbed the edge of a passing chimneystack to brake her sliding form. The brickwork crumbled in her hands but she didn't stay around long enough for that to matter, instead throwing herself away from the chimneystack and increasing her downward momentum while at the same time skewing herself diagonally across the roof to where another stack jinked crookedly from the tiles. As bricks from the first clattered past her and down, Kali grabbed onto the second, used it as a pivot to spin around, and then flung herself away from it as she had done with the first. The second stack collapsed behind her completely, its bulk rumbling down the roof in her wake, but though Kali suspected Dorweazle might be less than pleased with her fleeting visit she was beyond apologising now – because for the first time she was starting to think that her suicidal manoeuvres just might work.

She was now sliding upright and face first towards the lip of the roof, in exactly the position she wanted to be. Only a couple of storeys separated her from the ground, the last leg as it were, and with luck she'd make it without breaking her own. For the final time she scanned the buildings ahead of her, decided on the way to go and then skied right off the roof of Dorweazle's.

She angled forwards, turning her ski-jump into a dive, and then curled into a ball. Tracing a perfect arc downwards, she fell for two seconds and then impacted with a shop's awning positioned between storeys, breaking her fall halfway. As she hit, and bounced, she uncurled herself from the ball and allowed herself to bounce again, flipping head over heels off the edge of the awning and laughing out loud as she saw her feet approach the ground. By all the gods, she'd made it. She was dow –

Something snagged and she jerked to a halt, toes a foot above the street. She dangled there for a second and then there was an ominous tearing sound. Suddenly, she dropped, the remains of her underwear remaining behind, fluttering from the awning like a flag.

Kali stared. She couldn't believe it. After all she'd just been through!

The second chimneystack, caught until now on guttering, smashed into the ground right behind her and exploded into a cloud of debris and dust. For a second she couldn't see a thing, and then the cloud cleared, and she could.

A small crowd of people stared, murmuring and pointing at her. The naked, ashen-white woman who'd just fallen from the sky. *Oh, this is just great,* she thought. *It was the Curse of Slowhand, come to get her from beyond the grave. Damn him.*

"What?" she yelled, holding her arms out. "They kicked me off Kerberos, all right?"

Bootfalls echoed suddenly, seemingly from everywhere, and Kali realised that the bells of Scholten Cathedral were still ringing, alerting everyone in the know to the fact there was a fugitive in their midst. Shadows loomed on the walls along the street, and she dashed for the nearest alleyway, double jinking and jinking again so that she emerged from another as the owners of the shadows passed it by. They could have been cathedral guard or they could have been city watch, she wasn't sure, because it was no small measure of the Final Faith's influence in the city that the livery they wore was almost exactly the same. But crossed circles or not, you never knew where you stood with the watch, because while some were indeed good men, others – sadly, an increasing number of others, along with a good percentage of the population – were in the expansive pocket of Makennon and her people, bribed to be their eyes and ears throughout Scholten by a regular pouch of full silvers or the promise of divine favour. It would be just her luck to run smack into the wrong ones.

The point was, she could trust no one, and that fact became all the more disturbing when she realised that she didn't have the faintest clue where in the city she was. She knew Scholten passably well but no one could possibly know all of its backstreets, and the rather unorthodox route she had taken to arrive here hadn't given her much chance to look for familiar landmarks, which had left her totally disorientated.

The only thing she did know was that she needed to find Slowhand's stash and the stables near to it. Where had he said it was – between the Whine Rack and Ma Polly's? Okay, the fetish house, as far as she knew, was near the eastern gate, so she'd make her way there.

Kali glanced at the stars to orientate herself and began to move, and it was then that it hit her. She ached like the hells. More, as the chimney's dust streaked off her in the rain so that she could see beneath, she was completely black and blue. Not to mention that she was limping like a trigon, her shoulder felt dislocated and a little finger throbbed like the pits, as if broken. One thing was clear, however. If she was somehow changing, then she was far from superhuman, and she'd been lucky that fall hadn't killed her. It was a handy lesson to bear in mind for the future.

Despite the night hour, the city streets still had traffic, and, regardless of the fact she was naked, Kali was forced to keep to the alleyways, take liberties sneaking through the occasional house and even return to the rooftops once or twice to avoid patrols or civilian spies. Even so, her route was not without danger, and she moved cautiously and stealthily through Gizzard Yards, Red Square and Thumper's Cross. Here and there she spotted the conical helmets, tower shields and red tabards of the watch engaged in less than official business but, in doing so, bided her time until they were done, and then moved slowly on. At last she came upon her destination, a muddy gap between the Whine Rack and Ma Polly's, confirmed where she was by looking up to see a rope dangling limply through a ring, and then searched in nearby bushes for the stash that Slowhand had told her would be there. She found it and, somewhat chilled by now and hoping for warm garb, pulled forth a filigree shirt and pair of stripy tights. She cursed. Slowhand might have been wishing to stay in his troubadour disguise but, sometimes, she worried about him.

There was, at least, a decent pair of boots and a considerable amount of coin also contained therein, and Kali took both. All she needed to do now was find the stables. That task – as it turned out – was relatively easy, because she would have been able to smell them a league away.

Kali followed her nose, slipping along more alleyways, keeping to the walls and in the shadows. The area through which she now moved was less than salubrious and she had to pick her way over collapsed drunks and weave through bins overflowing with rubbish, from which the head of an occasional scavenging polerat poked out. Cries and laughter and the louder sounds of disagreement and argument coupled with the odd smashing plate or bottle leaked from the houses all around her, echoing in the night air. At last, though, she came upon a fence, a slight whinnying and clopping of hooves from beyond leaving her in no doubt that she had found that which she sought. She scrambled up and peered over, and her heart sank. She had either found the wrong stables or Slowhand's requirement of what a horse was or could do was considerably less than hers.

There was some kind of junkyard jammed between the backs of four surrounding tenements, accessed through a covered passage between two of them. A tilting, half-chained sign declared it to be the business premises of one Poombar Blossom, Importer and Exporter of Exotica. And sure enough, the yard was piled high with exotica – if, that was, one considered rusted hunks of metal, old beds and broken cartwheels to be the mysterious produce of distant lands.

A ramshackle bank of three stables suggested that Poombar ran a little sideline in horse trading but, it seemed, his definition of what constituted a horse was about as accurate as his definition of the exotic. Only two of the stables were filled and then just barely, two emaciated nags who looked as if they'd snap in two if mounted chewing half-heartedly on carrots that were, themselves, thin and knackered. One of the horses – Flash, according to a sign on his stable – wheezed so badly that Kali suspected he'd drop dead at the merest mention of the word gallop. *Dammit,* she thought, *this has been a complete waste of time.*

She was about to drop back down from the fence when three things happened. Firstly, two men exited a shed that she presumed served as some kind of office and walked towards what looked like a tackroom near the stables themselves, apparently doing business. Secondly, something in the tackroom didn't like the sound of their approach, and suddenly the ramshackle structure all but exploded, every panel, including the roof, crashing outwards and upwards, shaken by violent impacts from within. Thirdly, Flash and his mate reared in panic, snorting so badly that they hyperventilated and, with two loud thuds, fainted to the stable floors.

Kali guessed that, whatever was being kept in the tackroom, it was not a fellow horse. And when a moment later its door was opened and she heard a rattling rumble from within, she knew it for sure. She smiled, because if she was right about what she'd heard then these stables might indeed provide her with a mount, as it appeared that Poombar Blossom dealt in exotica after all.

She leapt the fence and crept into the yard, hiding behind a pile of junk opposite where the men now stood. Through the open door of the tackroom she could now see its inhabitant as well as hear the exchange of the two men attempting to calm it.

"Easy, easy," the rotund thing that must have been Blossom said, and somewhat surprisingly the beast quietened. "There – ya see what I mean?"

"Bloody 'ells, you wasn't kiddin'. Where'dya find this fing?"

"Drakengrat Mountains. Came out o' nowhere an' got caught in the sweepnets o' the roob 'erders. Crippled five of 'em afore they managed to rope it. Me bro' didn't know what else to do so brought it to me."

"Bloody 'ell, Blossom. You know what it is?"

"Not a clue. You?"

"I've never seen anything like it in my life."

"You've never seen anything like it?"

"Never seen anything like it in my life."

"Make a nice addition to your menagerie, eh? Fifty full silver an' it's yours."

"You're 'aving a larf. Twenty."

"Forty."

The two men might never have seen anything like it, but Kali had. Seen and heard, once, and from a distance. And she would, in fact, be doing the man who was currently offering thirty full silver a very big favour by taking it off his hands. Slowhand, unfortunately, had left her nowhere near enough money to join in the bidding and that left her only one way of acquiring it. She debated some distraction to draw the two men away – even contemplated clobbering them both with a rusty horseshoe that lay on the muddy ground – but Blossom was clearly eager to sell the only sellable thing he had and the bartering was over before she knew it. Conveniently for her, part of the price was a tankard in the local tavern and, as the men departed wiping spit-slimed hands, she suddenly found that she had the now quiet junkyard to herself.

At least briefly. One second she could hear Flash's comatose wheezing and the next it seemed that she had somehow timeslipped back to the Great War and Scholten was again being blitzed by elemental bombs. The noise and the thudding made her pause for a moment, until she realised its cause. The tavern nearby – the one where Blossom had taken his punter to seal the deal – was the Knotted Noose, and the Knotted Noose was the home of the Hells' Bellies. Kali imagined the scene and cringed – the only tavern that sober people avoided bursting to life as *customers* entered its doors, its resident dance troupe dropping their pies and pounding gleefully to the stage to entertain the audience they never had. Great gods, she could hear the cannon-like snapping of their garters now...

The horror that was within the Knotted Noose would, however, work to her advantage, as Kali suspected that in the next few minutes she would be making rather a lot of noise of her own. Because breaking in a bamfcat was going to be far from easy.

A real live bamfcat, she thought. No one had ever got near one before, and whatever turn of events had led to this specimen being caught in the herders' nets was a fluke indeed. Bamfcats were found nowhere on the peninsula other than around the higher slopes of the Drakengrat Mountains, but the sheer incongruity of their presence there, together with their utter *difference* to the other indigenous species, had before now led her to wonder whether they were native to those mountains at all. Had someone or something brought them from elsewhere at some point in the past? Or had they, for some reason, migrated themselves? And if so, from where?

Wherever it was, they had evidently needed protection there. Approximately one and a half times the size of a normal horse, the bamfcat resembled such a beast in all but one very important respect – it was heavily armoured. It didn't *wear* armour, it was just the way it was built. Great plates of a glistening black shell-like material curved around its flanks, haunches, back and shoulders, and where the plates did not cover, on its legs and those parts of its body that needed flexibility, its hide was composed of a shiny, hard and knobbly substance that Kali could only equate to dried and bubbled tar. But as its defences went, that was not all. On the rear of its legs, all the way up the crest of its neck and down along its nose, the bamfcat grew sharp protrusions that were and were not quite horns, by the look of their slightly layered appearance retractable or extendable as a situation might demand. One thing was sure, it would win no beauty contests, despite its big green eyes.

"Easy, boy," Kali said as she eased into the shed to undo the beast's tethers. "Or should that be girl?"

There was a low, rattling rumble of indeterminate response. It would have to do as an answer because there was no way Kali was going to check. Slowly – very slowly – she eased it out of the tackroom into the yard, whispering in its ear, "Tell you what, why don't I call you boygirl? And boygirl, guess what? We're going for a little ride..."

Her statement was a little premature she knew because, before she could ride anywhere, she had two practicalities to overcome. The first was that there was no way any ordinary saddle was going to fit this thing, but she solved that by plucking two from the tackroom wall, slinging one above and below and using both sets of straps to circle the bamfcat's girth before cutting the main parts of the lower saddle away. The second was a matter of height – it would take a ladder to climb on the bamfcat's back – but that solved itself when she realised that she already had a ladder – the bamfcat itself.

Kali took a deep breath, muttered more soothing words to the beast and then ran up the horns on its legs. Throwing herself onto its back, she immediately grabbed another horn on its neck – the closest thing she had to reins.

As she'd suspected, it was the wisest thing she could do. All the accoutrements necessary for a ride might have been in place, but there was no telling that to the bamfcat. The sensation of being mounted obviously a novel one to the beast, for a second it stood there simply stunned, and then decided that it didn't like the development at all. And then all hells broke loose.

The bamfcat ceased its rattling rumble and instead roared a roar that drowned out the thudding of the Hells' Bellies, beginning to leap around the junkyard and spinning round and round in an attempt to throw its unwanted passenger from its back. Kali could do nothing but hang on for dear life, her hands clenched around the bamfcat's neck horn, thighs jammed against its flanks. At first she didn't find it too much of a challenge – the places she'd been, she was used to clinging to things – but what concerned her was how long she could maintain her grip – and how long, if at all, it would be before she succeeded in calming the beast. The bamfcat certainly didn't make things easy, deciding, when Kali refused to budge, that if it couldn't dislodge her with leaps and bounds, then it would do so with the aid of whatever lay around the junkyard, first impacting with and demolishing the tackroom and then having a go at the stables, where at that very moment Flash was just coming round. The emaciated nag sprang up, wheezing with terror, and began to run around the junkyard in hopeless circles, searching for an exit, before collapsing again. Kali, meanwhile, did the best impression of a circus performer she could, avoiding the bamfcat's protestations by dodging anything that threatened to crush her, throwing her legs over one side of the beast then another, at one point slipping under and over its girth, and at another lying flat on her back without a grip to pass beneath an overhanging beam that would otherwise have decapitated her. It seemed, for what felt like an eternity, that the bamfcat was never going to surrender its independence, but then, unexpectedly, it began to slow. A few more feeble bucks and leaps followed, together with a half-hearted brush against the collapsed ruins of the tackroom walls, but finally the beast was reduced to a few spasms that were little more than afterthought, and then to a begrudging standstill.

The thing stank overpoweringly of the sweat that oozed thickly from between its plates, but Kali knew that after what she'd just endured she was hardly in a state to win any floral competitions herself. This appeared to be no bad thing. The bamfcat turned its head towards her, eyes dolefully taking in the rider that had beaten it and, with a long and disgusting snort, sucked in the scent of its new owner.

"Good boygirl," Kali said, patting it heavily. She smiled as the bamfcat rattle-rumbled, because this time it sounded more like a purr. "Good, good boygirl."

It was time to go. Kali manoeuvred the bamfcat towards the passage out of the yard but then reined it back. On the other side of the gate she could hear the voices of two patrolling guards, who, despite the continuing thudding of the Bellies, were bemoaning the fact that it was too quiet in the backstreets, and how they'd each give coin for a little piece of the action. *Especially* if they could lay their eyes – and other parts of their anatomy – on the girl who was meant to have scarpered from the cathedral. She was a tasty little piece by all accounts. Running around in her drawers, too. A bit of all right. Worth a stuffing.

Really.

Be careful what you wish for, boys, Kali thought. She smiled and patted the bamfcat soothingly, prompting a rolling of its neck. If it was a piece of the action the guards wanted, then a piece of the action they would get.

"Yah!" she shouted, at the same time ramming her heels into its flanks and pushing its neckhorn forwards. With a snort, the bamfcat responded, galloping forwards and through the junkyard gate.

Through, because there was no need for Kali to bother opening it. Or rather, the bamfcat didn't need her to – because as it galloped forwards it demolished the entranceway in much the same way it had demolished the yard, ramming the gates with its armoured head and ripping them clean away from their hinges. As a result, twin sheets of wood arced through the air of the alleyway, flipping and spinning into the path of the patrolling guards.

"Wha – ? Oh, bloody *huuurk!*" one of them cried as half the gate smacked him in the face, flooring him, while the other, ducking to avoid the second half, swiftly drew his sword and advanced. But then he saw the bamfcat, and stopped. The bamfcat saw him, too, and roared into his face so strongly that his hair streamed back from his scalp. It was difficult to describe the colours the guard's face went, and the only change in colour about his person that could be pinpointed with any accuracy was that of his trousers. He slopped away.

Kali galloped the bamfcat down the alley and out, emerging onto Anclas Way, Scholten's main thoroughfare to its eastern gate. It, too, remained busy despite the night hour – was thronged, in fact, with revellers, tradesmen and, most of all, pilgrims returning from their visits to the cathedral. But as the bamfcat galloped forth, skidding into a turn on its wet cobbles, the area did its best to empty itself as fast as it could.

Kali ignored the screams and cries of alarm, the bodies falling through windows, the collapsed stalls and the rolling trinkets and fruit, and the bamfcat ignored the various objects thrown by some braver members of the crowd that bounced off its armour. Both of them ignored – completely – the cries of a number of startled guards that they should immediately halt.

A moment later, scattering those same guards in their path like ninepins, they exited the closing city gate.

Free at last of Scholten, Kali reined the bamfcat forwards. Towards a horizon that was tinged white and red from the glow of ice and volcanoes. Towards the mountains that formed the ridge of the world. Towards Merrit Moon.

CHAPTER TEN

IT TOOK KALI two days to reach the World's Ridge Mountains, but even without rest and at the sustained and full gallop to which she subjected her seemingly inexhaustible mount, the journey should have taken longer. The bamfcat, it seemed, was something more than just an armoured horse.

She couldn't put her finger on how it happened, where it happened or even precisely when it happened, but now and again in their journey, the world about them seemed suddenly to blur. This was not simple acceleration on the bamfcat's part – had it been she would have at least felt greater wind resistance – but a rather disorientating case of simply being in one place one second, another the next, as if unbeknownst to herself she had actually nodded off for part of the ride. The biggest hint that something unusual was happening was when they reached the town of Fayence, where, after such a blur, the startled faces of the locals were tantamount to what they might have been had mount and rider appeared right in front of their noses, out of thin air. Odd, that, because as far as Kali knew that was precisely what they'd just done.

Those faces were nothing, though, compared to the looks that followed when, during the brief hiatus, the bamfcat decided to feed. One moment the worgle was happily rolling along the main street in front of them, and the next the rodent was snapped up by a lizard-like tongue the length of two men, the furry ball hooting in panic as it was sucked in and devoured in a single swallow. A dozen of its startled brethren flared like toothbrushes and bounced away, trying to avoid its fate, but the bamfcat's lengthy tongue slipped into every nook and cranny and snapped them up in rapid succession, Fayence's worgle population suffering a devastating blow in seconds.

Kali didn't question how the bamfcat did what it did or how it fuelled itself, however, because it got her where she needed to be and faster than she would have dreamt possible. But with Munch having had such a head start, they still had a lot of ground to make up.

Thankfully, the journey so far had been the easy part, and the hard part was yet to come – and with some luck it would slow the bastard down. Kali looked up as they began to near the mountains, and felt the same sense of awe and insignificance that she always did when she came within riding distance of the range. Yes, if anything was going to slow Munch down, the mountains would.

Accessible only at the southern tip of the Sardenne Forest, the World's Ridge Mountains loomed massively ahead and above of her, a forbidding wall of rock that in places seemed to reach higher than the sky. Not just rock, either – the lower peaks of the range were dotted with live volcanic craters that belched lava onto their tortuous slopes, while the upper peaks were sheer faces of ice, glistening white in stark contrast to the orangey-reds of the fires below. Where the two met, and clashed, great steaming geysers blasted upwards, periodically disintegrating the ice and causing it and the rock behind to crumble and fall, the avalanches creating a roar that seemed to be that of the mountains themselves. No one knew what lay beyond the World's Ridge, and if anyone had ever attempted to traverse it, they had not returned. Like the Sardenne Forest, it was a barrier to the inhabitants of the peninsula, but in this case one that daunted even Kali, and she wondered, on occasion, whether there was anything to be made of the fact that the barrier was composed of earth, air, fire and water – the four elements themselves.

They reached the lower slopes, and the bamfcat slowed as it began to climb. It sniffed at her and then at the air, apparently picking up a human scent, and so Kali allowed the animal to lead her, negotiating gorges, precarious trails and natural rock bridges over bubbling streams and billowing pools, hot from the mountains' insides.

At least for part of the way. During the past few days, the bamfcat, apart from being inexhaustible, had manifested an absolute absence of reluctance to do anything it was asked, but after almost a day and a half climbing beyond the foothills there came a point at which even the bamfcat would not go further. As she watched the beast's nostrils flaring, Kali suspected why. Wafted down to them from the higher slopes on the occasional blast of bitter, whistling wind, came a stench that could only belong to whatever denizens called these mountains home. The stench was utterly feral, bestial, so strong it was almost sickening. Of all the sights, sounds and smells that they had encountered on their journey, Kali didn't know why this, of all things, should unnerve the bamfcat, but perhaps the inhabitants it sensed were its racial enemy, or perhaps even its natural predator in the place from where it had originally come. She wondered whether the beast that had become her new companion hailed originally not from the Drakengrats but from these mountains – or even beyond.

But that was a question for another time. For now it didn't really matter because the animal had served her well – had got her here when no other beast possibly could – and she had no right to push it any further against its will, even if such an act would be physically possible.

Kali found a suitable spot and dismounted, stripped the bamfcat of its saddle and then slapped the beast on its flanks.

It didn't go anywhere.

"What?" Kali said. "Don't tell me you're going to wait for me?"

The bamfcat flipped out its tongue, perhaps searching in vain for worgles, then hung its head, saying nothing.

"You're not going to be here when I get back, and we both know it. So go."

The bamfcat snorted and lifted its head to stare dolefully at her. There was a certain insanity its eyes that she found disturbingly familiar – and quite comforting.

"Okay, fine!" Kali relented. "Stay there – but something further up has obviously given you the spooks so don't try to follow me, okay?"

Kali left the saddle but flung the saddlebags over her shoulder. She started to climb, hesitated, then turned and patted the beast three times on its neck. "I'll... see you when I get back," she said.

She continued on alone, the foothills behind her, the true slopes of the World's Ridge rising precipitously before her. Snow covered the ground at her feet in increasingly larger and thicker patches, but here and there pools and rivulets of lava broke through the rocks and stained the whiteness, making it seem as if the jagged landscape was slowly haemorrhaging. She climbed higher and, despite the lava, the temperature dropped considerably, and while she had been too intent on getting here to feel the cold until now, Kali was forced to dig into Blossom's saddlebag for an extra layer of clothing, pulling out a ragged fur coat that looked as if it had seen too many trapping expeditions. That, or its donor had been trapped on a particularly bad hair day. She slung it on. The thing stank to the high heavens but did the job.

In the absence of the bamfcat, Kali had to rely on her own tracking skills to keep on Merrit Moon's trail, secure in the knowledge that as no one dared venture far up into these mountains the signs of passage indicated by dislodged rocks, broken branches and disturbed patches of scree – eliminating those caused by whichever wild animals lived on the mid-slopes – were most likely his. It was possible that as humans were such rare visitors to these heights, those same wild animals were wary of approaching for fear of their place in the food chain, and for the most part Kali managed to avoid encounters with local predators, driving off the odd pack of shnarls or curious bugbear with a wave of her knife and suitable warning noises. Only once did she pause warily, when from far above she heard the haunting echo of what sounded like prolonged screams. They could, though, equally have been the carrion calls of the strange birds that circled high above. In this place, it was difficult to tell.

Birds or not, Kali picked up her pace. Thankfully, tracking the old man became even easier when, after a further three hours' climb, she came across convergent tracks coming in by a different route, vaguely to the west. Seven people, six men and the smaller, slightly lighter tread of a woman – and horses – heavily equipped. It did not take her long to work out who they might be. Munch was probably using one or more shadowmages to track Merrit Moon, and, despite her fears for him, for once she was grateful for the presence of threadweavers as from there on in their talents resulted in the old man's trail being overlaid by the footprints of his pursuers, making it as obvious to follow as a flaming torch in the dark.

A flaming torch would have been something she'd have been very grateful for at that moment, because Kali was approaching the ice-slopes now, the snow that had become thick beneath her tread taking on the greater solidity of permafrost. A blizzard had begun to howl about her, too, and she huddled inside her furs as she tramped ever upwards, squinting to see past the needle-like flurries that threatened to white-out everything before her. Then, suddenly, she spotted something in a rockface ahead – the dark and variously shaped outlines of what could only be cave mouths. What was more, the trails of the old man and his pursuers – plain on the slight plateau that led to the caves – vanished right into one of them.

Kali's heart thudded and she hurried forwards, relief that she had at last caught up with the old man tempered by the worry that Munch's trail appeared to be only minutes behind his, and she hoped to the gods that she wasn't too late. But she had only taken a couple of paces when her foot crunched on something on the ground, and what she saw when she looked down made her momentarily pause.

The icescape about her was dotted with bones, human and animal, mainly old but some not so, seemingly torn from their respective bodies and stripped utterly clean, some lying in small piles, others resting alone where they had been dragged by... something. What was the most disturbing was that the something had precisely the same odour about it that had stopped the bamfcat in its tracks far below.

Here, the air was redolent with it, its strength almost overpowering. Kali trod cautiously in the direction of the cave, without doubt the source of the stench. She entered slowly, eyes alert for any movement or sound in the darkness. But she saw nothing, and the only sounds were those of her own feet crunching on the tinier deposits on the bone-strewn floor, along with a languid and incessant *drip-plop-drip* from the moisture-laden ceiling that echoed hollowly within the rock.

There should have been no light to see by, but as Kali inched her way inwards, her knife at the ready, she saw that the cave was illuminated by a dull green glow emanating from crystalline formations in the rock. It was hardly daylight but it was bright enough to stop her stumbling blindly over the body that lay mutilated on the cave floor a few yards in.

Merrit! she feared instantly, but quickly realised that it was not. Instead, she looked down at the body – the remains of a body – of what could only have been one of Munch's party, the corpse lying broken and missing an arm and both legs, eyes staring blankly and mouth frozen in a rictal, agonised scream. A black and glistening trail of blood led further back into the cave, and Kali guessed that the poor woman had tried to drag what remained of herself to safety.

Not Merrit. Merrit would not be capable of this.

There was nothing she could do for the woman, so Kali closed her eyelids and moved on. But it wasn't long before she came across another body, and then another, each in an equal or worse state of mutilation. Like the first, they appeared to have been trying to drag themselves to the exit but had never made it, the loss of blood from their amputations too great. Something in this cave had torn them apart like mools in a slaughterhouse, and it was beginning to look like it, not Munch's people, was the biggest danger here.

Kali could feel every fibre of her being warning her to get the hells out of there, but she knew she had no choice but to carry on, to find Merrit Moon, whether he was alive or dead. But as it happened, she did not have to look much further. No more than ten yards on, the cave opened out into a chamber where she found three more bodies heaped together in a small pile, almost indistinguishable from each other, they had been so badly torn. And next to them, covered in their entrails, lay Merrit Moon. The old man was face down on the floor, a staff and opened backpack scattered beside him, a dark pool of blood seeping from beneath his torso. But he was breathing shallowly. He was alive. Just.

"Oh gods," Kali said. She hurried to him and turned him gently over, cradling the back of his head in her palm. The old man sighed and his eyes fluttered open slowly, focusing on her with difficulty. From his complexion he had lost a lot of blood.

It was clear nothing could be done. Merrit Moon was dying.

Kali swallowed.

"Hey... old man," she whispered.

Moon coughed. "You have the smell of Vos about you," he said slowly, having to force the words out. "Have you ridden my faithful friend somewhere less than healthy once again, young lady?"

"No, Merrit, Horse... I mean, yes. But don't worry, Horse is fine... fine. He's waiting for me." She hesitated. "He's waiting for you."

Moon smiled. "You've been looking after him?"

Kali nodded briskly, trying not to let him see her tears. "Of course I have, you old fool. Bacon stew every day." She stared at her mentor, aware that they were both avoiding the issue, and what she really wanted to say erupted out of her. "Pits, old man, I told you not to come here alone!"

Moon shook his head, took her hand. As he spoke, his tongue clicked dryly in his mouth. "Here or elsewhere, it would not have mattered. It wasn't the mountain's cold embrace that finished me, Kali. It was the cold embrace of steel."

He slowly pulled up his tunic, wincing as the cloth tore from drying blood. Kali stared at three distinct puncture wounds in his torso – two in the gut and one near the heart – fury rising. The shape of the blade that had made them was unmistakable – a jagged-edged gutting knife. The worst thing about them was they could so easily have been killing blows but weren't – Moon's soon-to-be murderer had inflicted these mortal wounds and seemingly left him here to die.

"Munch," she hissed.

Moon nodded. "Kali, he took the key. Knew I had it..."

Kali sobbed. "I told Munch about you, old man. Gods help me, I didn't mean to but I told him."

Moon stroked her cheek. "Hush. Whatever you did, I know you couldn't help it. I told you, the Final Faith are zealou –"

"*Damn them!*" Kali shouted, interrupting him.

"Hush," Moon said, again. "Hushhhhh."

"Don't hush me! Damn you, Merrit Moon, stop treating me like a baby!"

Despite his dire state, Moon chuckled, coughed, his breath rattling. "Actually, I'm trying to save your life," he said. His eyes seemed to lose focus on her, stare beyond her. "More outbursts like that one and you'll... arouse them."

"Arouse them? Who?" She pointed at the bodies. "Are you talking about the things that did this? Merrit, for the gods' sake, what happened here? What killed these people?"

Moon sighed heavily, seemingly losing the thread. "The key. I meant to take it deeper... to where they live... but these old muscles are slow and Munch and his men weren't far behind... they found me here before I could..."

He took a shuddering breath, remembering. "Munch didn't even ask for the key. He just pulled me towards him, towards his knife, and then... my blood... the smell of my blood brought them up from below."

Kali's face darkened. "Where's Munch now?"

"I... don't know. I... think he ran from them..."

"Them, again," Kali said. For the first time she thought she could make out a low rumbling in the cave. "I guess we're not talking run-of-the-mill mountain cats here are we?"

Moon shook his head. "Creatures as old as the Old Races, probably much more so. They've lived in these mountains since the world was young, since before even the Sardenne grew – they, and their no-less-legendary cousins." His eyes flicked to the side, and he swallowed. "But I don't have to tell you about them, you can see for yourself."

"They're coming?"

Moon shook his head. "No, Kali. They're already here."

Kali felt the hairs on the back of her neck rise along with an overriding need to hunch down, to make herself small. Because even as the old man had spoken she had sensed the presences all around her, and she raised her eyes slowly and nervously from the old man to the shadows of the chamber. There were six of them, all but naked things, their flesh a green that had nothing to do with the crystalline light. Half as tall again as a human, their thickly muscled bodies and hunched shoulders made them seem shorter, especially while at that moment they squatted in what appeared to be their personal niches in the rock walls, regarding her. Not just regarding her – because as they looked on with their deep-set eyes, their hair lank about their bodies and their mouths protruding teeth, each gnawed droolingly on chunks of meat and bone identifiable as pieces of thigh, an arm, and even a head; meat recently ripped from the corpses around them.

These things. She'd heard tales of them as a child. Tales told in the Flagons meant to scare her but which instead intrigued her. Bogey men. She didn't know what their true name was but she knew what humans called them.

Ogur.

And as she realised she was kneeling in the middle of their dining room, they sure as hells scared her now.

Despite her fear, Kali moved to protect the old man but he held her where she was. "Don't," he told her. "They won't attack." He looked up as one of them took a tentative step towards Kali but then retreated when, much to her surprise, the old man barked at it in some unknown tongue. "At least," he finished wearily, "while I'm alive."

"You can control them?" Kali said, and remembered his words on his doorstep in Gargas, what seemed an age ago. "Don't tell me – this is your tale for another time."

Moon nodded, winced in pain. "I'd come here in search of Herrick's Passage – a tunnel said to pass under the mountains – but an avalanche meant I never found it. What I found was one of these ogur trapped beneath the ice, and I helped it."

"You're telling me one of these things was *grateful?*"

Moon half-laughed, half-choked. "Grateful? No. Had it not been so weak, it would have torn me apart. Which is why I shared with it the contents of my backpack."

"A quarrel of crossbow bolts, I hope."

"Eight bottles of flummox."

Kali stared at the old man dubiously. "Are you telling me you got an ogur pissed?"

Moon coughed. "Drank him under the table. But he wasn't used to the stuff. The point is, theirs is an alpha society and after that I was treated with a little more respect."

Kali laughed, but it was strained, redolent of a joke shared for the last time. Of all the tales the old man had told her over the years, she was never sure which he exaggerated, but clearly *something* had happened for the ogur to defer to him as they did. Something that had made him feel confident enough to lose the key in the lower depths of their cave, where it could never be reached.

In the odd way that these things did, it suddenly occurred to her to ask him why, now that he'd confessed to drinking flummox, he insisted on serving her that atrocious elven wine. She wanted to ask him many things, actually, but as the old man coughed again she realised there was no more time.

There had to be something she could do!

She dug in her saddlebag for something, *anything* to help, but as she did Moon placed his hand on hers, just as he had in the Warty Witch so long ago. The message now was as clear as it had been then – *put your hand down.*

"It's too late," Moon said, coughing. "What's important is the key. You have to get the key. But you also have to know what it is you're dealing with."

"Merrit, at least let me –" Kali began, but as she spoke thought: *At least let me what?*

"Listen to me, young lady." Moon insisted. "I don't know everything about the key, but I haven't told you everything I know. Snippets from across the years. The key you took is one of four, part of a set that unlocks something that should never see the light of day again. Something *evil* – so evil it is warned against time and time again in Old Race manuscripts written by a hundred different hands."

"What?"

Moon coughed again. "I never found out precisely. If I had I would have done everything in my power to find and destroy it – what the

127

manuscripts refer to repeatedly as an abomination." He paused. "What I do know is that it almost finished the Old Races, wreaked so much death and destruction amongst them that these bitter enemies forged their first alliance in order that they might end its threat."

"But you must have some idea what it is."

Moon nodded. "Oh, yes. Some tales describe it as a kind of giant construct – a supposed marvel of dwarven engineering that became instead a horror – a complex automaton called the Clockwork King of Orl."

"The Clockwork King of Orl?" Kali repeated. "What in the hells do you suppose it does – is meant to do?"

"The important question is what the Final Faith think it can do for them. If I know those zealots, their intent will be to use the king as a figurehead, a rallying icon for the spread of their church across Twilight. But if the old warnings are even half-truths, the people of Twilight will not be rallied, they will be destroyed."

Kali frowned. "I don't understand. This alliance. If they wanted the king stopped, if it was so dangerous, why not just destroy the thing, or at least destroy the keys?"

Moon sighed. "The king itself, I don't know – perhaps they kept it as a reminder of their folly. The keys, however... in the aftermath, when it came to it, neither side trusted the other in the matter of disposal. Even when both parties were present each suspected that magic might deceive the eye, that secretly one or other party would keep the keys for themselves. They decided instead that they should be sealed away, watched, protected by lethal countermeasures that would ensure no one could get their hands on them again."

"The Spiral of Kos," Kali breathed.

"And three similar containment areas. They each built two sites – two dwarven and two elven – and manned them with mixed representatives of their races." There was no blame in Moon's eyes when he added: "Kali, you have no idea what it is that you've unleashed."

"I'm beginning to get the picture." She bit her lip. "Merrit, please, what can I do?"

"If the Final Faith are going after the keys, you have to find them first, make them inaccessible, hide them, destroy them if you have to. If you cannot, then you must discover the location of Orl, destroy the Clockwork King before the Faith reach it."

"But I've no idea where to start!"

"Go to Andon, to the Three Towers, its Forbidden Archive. There are papers within that will tell you more than I know. They will be difficult to get to, Kali – they are protected – but you must reach them, find out what you can. And when you have, when you know what there is to do, you must do it. Make sure the Clockwork King is not reawoken, any way you can."

Kali felt somewhat daunted by her burgeoning responsibility. "Old man, I'm just a... tomb raider."

Moon slid his hand onto hers, visibly worsening. "No," he said, weakly, "you're not. There's something else you need to know. The night you were found as a baby, by the stranger –"

Kali stroked his hand. "It was you, old man. I know. I saw you when Fitch played with my mind. You and me in the Old Race site..."

Moon raised his eyes, surprised, then coughed, and this time there was blood. "Hells of a time for a reunion."

"Hells of a time," Kali nodded, sniffed. "Merrit, I –"

"Don't you dare hug me when I'm down, young lady," Moon warned, though after a second he, too, smiled. "Kali, please listen. You were my greatest ever discovery, believe that. You should know that I love you like a daughter. But that it was me who found you isn't what I was going to say. You have to know about the site itself."

"What? What about the site?"

Moon didn't answer directly. "There are things happening to you, aren't there? I can feel the changes, see it in the way you move, sense it in your aura. You are more than you were. It's what I always knew, right from the start – that you're somehow different."

"*Different?*"

"The site where I found you wasn't like the others, Kali. It was *uncompromised.*"

"What? What do you mean uncompromised?"

"You know what I mean. Nobody had been in or out in over a thousand years. It was completely sealed."

Kali stared at him for a moment, speechless.

"It couldn't have been," she said at last. "I mean, how did I get in there? What would that mean?"

"I don't know what it means. Only that it marks you out amongst the people on the peninsula – makes you different from them – and that is something you must remember at all times."

"But what –"

Merrit held up his hand, looked around at the gathered ogur. He was suddenly racked by a spasming cough, and sprayed more blood into his palm. "No more questions," he said. "You have to go – *now.*"

"Old man, I'm not just leaving you like thi –"

Moon grabbed her hand, squeezed it tenderly. "Kali, go. I am dying and there is nothing you can do, and as soon as the ogur sense I have passed they will tear you apart. You have to get out of here before I die."

"I can't do that!"

"You *must*, young lady." Moon was struck by another fit of coughing and then laid his head back with a sigh, his hand weak around hers. Kali choked back a sob. Dammit, she had to give him a hug whether he liked it or not.

She leaned in – gently, so as not to hurt him – and, as she did, her hand brushed an amulet resting on his chest. She could have sworn it was glowing slightly. She went to touch it but her hand was unexpectedly swatted away.

"*No!*" Moon shouted with surprising vehemence for a man on his deathbed. "It's too... near the time."

"Merrit, what – ?"

He actually glared at her. The old man actually *glared*.

"Go, Kali, *now*," Moon shouted. And then, more weakly: "Go now... and don't... look ba –"

Kali knelt there a second longer, stirring only as a series of grunts from the ogur signalled what she wouldn't, *couldn't* believe – that Merrit Moon was gone. Keeping her eyes fixed on the creatures she backed slowly away, settling the old man gently to the ground as she went. Then, with a final look at her mentor's body, she raced towards the cave mouth and safety.

She did not see the blue glow that suddenly suffused the cave behind her.

CHAPTER ELEVEN

KALI HAD SEEN more than enough death in recent days and had no desire to be reminded of it – but in approaching Andon she had little choice.

It was here that Killiam Slowhand had killed John Garrison, but he had been only one warrior amongst thousands, and the fields around the city still bore the scars of the pivotal battle they had fought. Andon had been besieged for almost two years while Pontaine's army had grown strong enough to repel the enemy, driving them back across the land that had become known as the Killing Ground. Such protracted and bloody engagements were not erased easily from a landscape, and the Killing Ground was littered still with half-buried skeletons uncovered by driving rain, the remains of defensive and offensive trench systems, and rotting and ruined engines of war. It was a ghastly and ghostly place, made all the more haunting by banks of slowly drifting fog that alternately concealed and revealed the horrors that remained.

It was before dawn, and Andon's gates were closed to traffic as Kali and the bamfcat appeared in the fog near its defensive walls, suddenly, in a blur. Even at this quiet hour guards patrolled vigilantly, on constant alert as many in the city believed it was only a matter of time before the forces of Vos attacked again, using as their base the forts they had constructed in the once-neutral Anclas Territories, only a few leagues away. Arriving seemingly out of nowhere as she had, some strange phantasm clad still in Slowhand's striped tights and Blossom's mangy furs, Kali had likely spooked the guards, and having no wish to feel the sudden thud of a crossbow bolt in her chest needed to make her business in the city known. She couldn't tell them the whole truth, of course, but a generalisation might do.

Kali got their attention by sticking her fingers in her mouth and whistling. Then she shouted: "Excuse me! I'm trying to save the world. Can I come in, please?"

It was an honest and bafflingly pre-emptive ploy that seemed to work. The guards studied her for a few seconds, shrugged and gave the order for the gates to be opened.

"'Yup, Horse," Kali said.

That she had referred to the bamfcat as Horse was no slip of the tongue. She wasn't sure when, or quite how, the beast had gained her affections but certainly it had started when she'd found it waiting for her on her descent from the ogur's cave – its welcoming and strangely familiar headbutts a display of companionship she'd needed badly when everything else seemed to have gone away. Their bond had grown during the journey to Andon and, after a while, she'd realised she really couldn't go on calling the beast good boygirl because it was just plain daft. Of course, she'd had some hesitation naming it Horse – Horse Too, to be precise – but the bamfcat was hardly a creature that would suit a name like Fluffy or Rex, and in an odd way it was a reminder of the old boy himself.

Horse, however, could not go everywhere, and inside the city it soon became clear that its narrow environs wouldn't take the bamfcat and he'd need to be stabled for the duration. Kali dismounted and walked him into one of a number of stableyards lining the outskirts, manoeuvring his oversized bulk into two stable enclosures, the beast straddling their low, dividing fence.

The stableman appeared and his jaw dropped open. But he did not let surprise interfere with business.

"Two silver tenths," he said.

"I thought the standard rate was one."

"That thing takes up two stables so it's two silver tenths."

Kali was in no mood. "Horse?" she said.

The bamfcat ate the fence and spat a mouthful of splinters at the stableman.

"One silver tenth," Kali said.

"Done," the stableman said, swallowing. "That's one hells of a mount, lady."

Kali patted the bamfcat, smiled. "He sure is. One word of advice – don't feed him anything that hasn't got a face."

"Face?"

"He likes worgles."

"Worgles?"

"Worgles." She pointed across the yard, where one of the furballs could be seen rolling into an overturned bucket. "Just shake 'em out and he'll handle the rest."

Horse's lizardine tongue whiplashed out and back again, as if to explain. The stableman did a little dance backwards.

"Yew, that's disgusting."

"Yep, that's what I thought, too."

Horse stabled, Kali made her way into Andon proper, working her way through the labyrinth of shadowed streets, alleyways and passages crammed inside its imposing walls. The walls were soon lost to view in the crowded conurbation, and it would have been easy to become disorientated, but as Kali made her way towards the centre of the city she could not have wished for a more obvious guiding beacon. Visible through gaps in the roofline, looming ever larger and more imposing, the beacon had actually been visible from *outside* the city walls – was visible, in fact, from some leagues away – but it was only now as she grew nearer that the sheer impossible scale of the largest building in Andon – indeed, anywhere on the peninsula – truly made its presence felt. The Three Towers made Scholten Cathedral look like a village church.

The twisting, semi-organic looking headquarters of the League of Prestidigitation and Prestige rose above the city fully forty storeys high, a structure that would have confounded the skills of the finest engineers in Pontaine – perhaps even the finest engineers of the Old Races – and its construction had only been made possible with the aid of the more powerful wizards who now studied within. Its rather incongruous presence in the otherwise somewhat seedy city was due to the fact that at one time, on a lesser scale, it had simply been the home of Andon's Magical Guild, housing parlour magicians and entertainers in the service of Pontaine's wealthiest families, but, since the Great War, it had gradually transformed itself into something much darker and now housed an organisation dedicated to the study of the effects of powerful sorceries on armies, and to the practice of war itself. Dark secrets were held within its half-built, half-grown heights – within the minds of those who moved there and within the manuscripts, tomes and artefacts that were said to fill its archives – and somewhere amongst those secrets was the information Kali needed to know.

The Three Towers was not a place, however, where one could walk up to the front door and knock. Even the Final Faith did not wield sufficient influence to enter there.

To get inside, Kali needed help. And she knew exactly where she was going to find it.

She continued on, breaking at last from the warren of small streets and out into the centre of Andon, a thronged circular marketplace filled with stalls, vendor carts and street performers surrounding the towers in a hub. Already gearing up for the day's trade, it was where the true hubbub of Andon was to be found and, as a consequence, where those who fed upon that hubbub could also be found. The largest and most successful thieves guild in Andon – the Grey Brigade

– were based somewhere here, and it was no small measure of their presence and influence in the area that their playful nickname for it had been adopted by the city's inhabitants, thereafter referring to the place as the Andon Heart.

Kali weaved her way through the milling crowds with no particular destination, at least none she yet knew. Her attention fixed seemingly on the endless array of gaudy stalls and goods, in actuality she had her senses trained on every subtle movement around her. She felt herself *accidentally* jostled or pushed once, twice, three times, and on each occasion felt hands slide gracefully into the pockets of her furs or vest, each of which she had filled with some coin. She had to admit that the dippers working this patch were very good, but when someone knew what to expect – in fact, hoped for it to happen – they had to be *very, very* good indeed if they wanted to go unnoticed.

Kali let the plunder continue until the fifth dipper made his move, and then she made hers. The boy's hand was sliding towards her side when her own lashed out and grabbed it tightly by the wrist.

"That's ten full silver your people have taken from me," she said, smiling. "Even accounting for your share, that's enough to buy me an audience with your boss, don't you think?"

"B-boss, Missus?" the boy said, struggling against her grip. "Don't know what you're talking about."

"Jengo," Kali said. "I'm here to see Jengo."

"Jengo?"

"Jengo Pim."

The boy smiled slyly. "So, you knows his name, eh? That counts for something, I suppose. But who's to say you ain't bringin' him some business old Jengo might not be inclined to undertake?"

"Who says I'm here on business? I'm his sister."

The boy guffawed. "Jengo ain't got no sister. Everyone knows he ain't got no kin and was dumped on the streets like the bastard he is."

Kali leaned closer, looming down on the boy, and tightened her grip. "Then I guess that makes me a bitch."

The boy swallowed. "A–all right, Missus – ah'll take you to him. But I tells you, it ain't no worry of mine if he slits you from ear to ear."

"From where to where?" Kali said, smiling.

"Eh? Oh, never mind. Just follow me."

Kali did, finding that the entrance to the Grey Brigade's den was hidden almost in plain sight, yards from where she stood. Nevertheless, it would have been impossible to take advantage of without her escort. She was led between two market stalls, the owners of which were obviously guild stationed as sentries, and then along a tight alleyway that jinked away behind them. Kali looked up as she walked, saw that she was being watched from a number of windows above. Clearly, no one who wasn't welcome could approach the guild unseen, and Kali suspected that for any *particularly* unwelcome visitor those who stared at her now, casually crunching fruit, might simply substitute the fruit for a loaded needlereed and the unwanted visitor would be incapacitated before they could take two steps. She guessed the resultant body – unconscious or otherwise – would be spirited away into one of the apparently sealed doorways she passed, there to be stripped, dumped in the river and never seen again.

She reached the end of the alleyway safely, however, and after the boy gave three irregular raps on the solid wooden door that terminated it, found herself inside the den of the Grey Brigade.

Impressive, she thought, as she was led through its busy interior, not only in the number of guild members she passed but also in the facilities provided for them. Everything the Andon thief could desire was provided here, from equipment and training areas to common lounges, dormitories and bar, all of them converted to their present use from the rooms of what looked to have been at one time a large hotel, an enterprise she imagined had been starved of business during the siege.

Grandly enough, Jengo Pim had chosen what had once been the hotel's ballroom for his court, and it was obvious which of those gathered within was he. The thieves guild leader was draped in an ornate, red upholstered chair in the middle of the room, swigging from a bulb of wine and gnawing meat he skewered on a dagger from a serving table beside him. As Kali was brought in, the appropriately roguish-looking man was conferring with two of his lieutenants, but as she approached he dismissed them and turned his attention to her. He jabbed the dagger into the table and wiped his mouth before speaking.

"So – I'm told I have a sister I never knew about," he said, blatantly looking her up and down. "Seems you got the genes I didn't. Nice. Very nice."

"Thanks. But I hear incest makes your bits shrivel and die, so I'd keep your hands off if I were you. The name's Kali Hooper. I'm here on business."

Pim sucked his teeth and spat a piece of gristle across the room. "Figured you might be. But as I have no shortage of business of my own, why should I have an interest in yours? What, in fact, stops me having you killed right here, right now?"

"Because you run a thieves guild, not an assassins guild. You'd need a good reason to bump me off and so far I haven't given you one."

"No," Pim said, lecherously, "more's the pity." He waved a hand at her striped tights and furs. "I could, of course, consider your current outfit a capital crime."

"Yes, well, that's a long story." Without being invited, Kali grabbed Pim's knife, stabbed a piece of meat and bit it off the blade. "Come on, Pim – aren't you just a little bit curious why I risked coming here?"

Pim took a swig of his wine, studied her, smiled. "Let's stick with mildly stimulated. Very well, you have a minute. How can the Grey Brigade be of service to you?"

"I need your help. To break in somewhere."

Pim pulled a face. "Oh, Miss Hooper, after so much promise you disappoint me. Pretty lass like you, what is it? Heard you can recruit some of my people to do an ex-lover's house? Perhaps empty his strongbox of compromising documents?"

"Actually, no, I need to do the job myself. And it's the League of Prestidigitation and Prestige."

Pim spluttered on the wine he'd just consumed, stared at her incredulously. "*The League?*" he repeated. He laughed out loud, and then with a bouncing of his palms invited the others in the room to join him in his jollity, which they duly did. "Bubbling pits of Kerberos, woman, that's impossible."

"Nonetheless –"

"Nonetheless, nothing. It's bloody suicide. Have you any idea what kind of traps are in there? Those sorcerous psychopaths have wired the place with every kind of thread threat you can imagine, and more. There are things that'll fry you, things that'll crush you, things that'll drown you, things that'll make your heart go boom." Pim slumped into his chair and swigged from his wine again. "Listen to me – only three men in the entire history of our guild have tried the towers. The first we found flapping around with his bones gone, the second was last seen ascending to Kerberos *before* he died, and the third came back in a bottle no bigger than this one." Pim shook the wine bulb he held. "No chance. Go home, girl. Go home."

Kali stayed where she was and folded her arms. "Actually, it isn't just the towers I need to gain access to, it's the Forbidden Archive itself."

This time Pim did not splutter. But he did stare and then quaff a mouthful of wine so hard that Kali heard him gulp and swallow it down.

"The Forbidden Archive," he repeated slowly. He turned to one of his lieutenants. "Kris Jayhinch, please give the lady a razor to slash her throat with – save herself some time."

"What's the matter, Pim? Too much of a challenge for you? Maybe I should take my request down to the Skeleton Quays, tell the guilds there you were too lily-livered to handle it."

The thieves guild leader's eyes flared darkly for a second. The mention of the Grey Brigade's rival guilds had the effect Kali desired,

Pim knowing full well that a loss of reputation was what no guild could afford.

"They would likely tell you the same as I," he said, contemplatively, "but then they are desperate enough to take your business." He rubbed his chin, considering. "I must be mad," he sighed before sucking in a deep breath. "Miss Hooper, do you have any experience of our noble art?"

"If by *noble art* you mean taking other people's property without their permission, I guess I do, but not in the way you mean."

Pim rose, handing Kali the bulb of wine. "I'll tell you what – there's a little test I have devised for new recruits, and I want you to take it. If you pass, you'll have my help. If you fail, well... I'll think of something *appropriate*."

Kali took a swig of the wine. "Mister Pim, you've got yourself a deal."

The mention of the test sparked the interest of everyone in the room and, as the thieves guild leader guided Kali through to another chamber, the pair acquired a small entourage of eager spectators. The room into which she was led was larger even than the ballroom – what looked to have been the hotel's reception area – but it had been converted from its original use to function as some kind of obstacle course-cum-training area for the guild. Various vaulthorses, gymnast rings, nets and other paraphernalia had been secured about its edges along with a number of racks containing exotic thieves' tools, but what drew Kali's attention was a small iron cage suspended from the centre of the ceiling, high above the floor. Hanging from a single chain, there was nothing near it and no obvious means to reach it – but Kali guessed that was exactly what Pim's test would require her to do.

"I see you're ahead of me," Pim said, staring up as she did. "The positioning of the cage is an approximation of the high-security containment for Bojangle's Baleful Bells, currently on display in the museum of Scholten. I have stolen them twice, returning them each time so that I might try again – what I like to consider a professional challenge. Said bells are not, of course, present here, merely a personal souvenir of sentimental value, but you should consider it a treasure of equal scarcity. Retrieve it for me and we will talk."

Kali nodded and walked forwards until she stood directly beneath the cage, craning her neck to look up.

"I have to inform you," Pim continued, "that to date not one of my would-be apprentices has managed this feat. Luckily for you, it is not success or failure that I will judge – only the originality of the methods employed in the attempt."

"A-ha," Kali said, not really listening.

"Please feel free to utilise any of the equipment in this room, and consider any of our tools to be at your disposal. There is a fine selection of gripgloves, pinshoes or spidersocks over here. Some even prefer the jumping jacks..."

"Okay," Kali said. Pim would have regretted turning his back to point out the selection because at that moment she was pulling off her tights.

"There is even a slight possibility of success with the..."

Tights off, Kali crammed the wine bubble she still carried into the toe of one leg, crouched, took in a few huffing breaths and then leapt, straight up. One arm outstretched above her, teeth gritted, she rose two and a half times her height, straight as an arrow, and then flicked the weighted end of the tights through the bars of the cage, grabbing it as it came out and dropped down the other side. Allowing the elasticity of the tights to drop her back down to the floor, she bounced with them, once, twice, three times, then sailed upwards to grab the base of the cage with a grunt. Swinging her legs up, she flipped herself over so that she was sitting on top of the cage, slid her arm in through the bars to retrieve the souvenir, then dropped it towards the floor. That done, she quickly wrapped the tights about herself, rolled down inside them like some carnival gymnast, flipping herself with a neat twist as she neared the floor, and then settled as lightly as a feather right in front of Pim.

The thieves guild leader stared at her through the dancer's tassel now draped over his head. Kali noticed it was labelled PROPERTY OF HELLS' BELLIES. Meanwhile, someone at the back of the room snickered.

"Original enough for you?" Kali said.

Pim coughed and, after a second, coughed again. "I don't know how you did that but you pass, Miss Hooper." He stared down at her now-bared legs. "By the gods," he breathed, "I could use someone like you on my team."

"Sorry, I work alone," Kali said, smiling. "Now, about your help. The Forbidden Archive. How the hells do I get in?"

Pim stared at her, knowing that, his agreement witnessed, he had no choice but to accede to her request. He nodded and led Kali back to the ballroom, but this time to a large table lain with maps and plans of all kinds. The pile reminded Kali of her captain's chest back home and, as was the case with her own papers regarding places that seemed too much of a challenge, Pim found what he was after buried right at the bottom of the pile. He swept away the less challenging plans to reveal a set of architectural drawings that looked to have been there for years, but that didn't matter because what they showed had not changed.

It was the inner workings of the League of Prestidigitation and Prestige.

Pim slammed a gloopy bottle on the corner of the document to keep it flat, and Kali wondered if it contained the remains of the Three Towers' last victim, perhaps kept as a reminder of the difficulty of the task at hand. He traced the confused patterns of lines on the paper – standard builders' marks and strange swirls that had to denote magical input – with his finger, frowning, remembering. "Big John Sinclair went in here... Hamish the Pumps here, and Nimble Neil Halliwell," his finger made a circle and stabbed down, "right here. As I said, none returned. At least, not in their original condition."

"So we can safely assume that whatever traps took them down are still in place in those areas," Kali said. "That could be an advantage – knowing what to expect."

Pim drew in a sharp breath, shook his head. "You might know the *what* of them, but not the *where* or *when*. Whatever did for them did for them quickly, and the trigger could be anything – weight, motion, sweat, breath, noise..."

"Difficult to counter all of those," Kali observed. She studied the plans, the bridges that connected the towers, what appeared to be the location of the Forbidden Archive in the third tower, then lowered her own finger. "What about this conduit here?"

Pim smiled. "You have a good eye for possibility. That was exactly what I was going to suggest to you. Its purpose isn't specified on the plans but from what we can tell it's some kind of alchemical dump shaft that empties into the sewers – dangerous but potentially difficult to trap as any waste potions might have, shall we say, *unforeseen* side effects on the thaumaturgical triggers. But there's a problem – the laboratories dump their waste regularly, every half an hour. The length of that conduit, you'd need to move fast. *Very* fast."

"All those wands, you'd think they'd just make the waste disappear," Kali sighed. "All right, fast I can do. Question is, will it get me safely inside?"

Pim traced the conduit's route. "See for yourself. Once through the conduit you'll be inside their perimeter defences. I don't know what you'll find after that but, with luck, you should be able to reach the stairs to the third tower."

"Any guards to worry about? Patrols?"

"Trust me, this place doesn't need them. It's *deadly*, how many times do I need to tell you that? So I ask you again – are you sure you want to do this?"

"Mister Pim," Kali said seriously, "I really don't have any choice."

For once, Jengo Pim stared nowhere but at her eyes, and, whatever the thieves guild leader saw there, a new note of respect crept into his voice. "Fine," he said, handing her the plans from the table. "Take these in case you need them – it's meant to be a maze in there. Also take whatever equipment and tools you think you'll need for the job. There's just one other thing. Kris Jayhinch goes with you."

Kali stared at Pim's lieutenant. "What? No chance."

"Every chance, Miss Hooper. If you succeed in this suicide mission – which I seriously doubt – then the Grey Brigade gets a share of the loot you find."

"I'm not after loot. I'm after information."

"Then there'll be all the more loot for us." He gestured to Jayhinch. "There is no discussion in this matter – take Kris with you or you do not leave."

Kali sighed heavily. "Fine. But I lead and he follows. And he looks after his own back."

Pim nodded. In truth it was Jayhinch looking after *her* back that for some inexplicable reason had become his greater concern. "Understood." He waved his arm to indicate the equipment racks. "Now, is there anything you need?"

Kali pursed her lips, remembering Orlana Dawn at the Spiral of Kos. "You wouldn't, by any chance, have one of those dark silk bodysuits?" she said.

KALI AND JAYHINCH left after dark, negotiating alleyways doubly shadowed by the night's azure gloom, until they came to a sewer entrance beneath the looming towers. Jayhinch pulled back a cover with a grating sound, then staggered back coughing as the area was suffused with a cloying and unnatural stench. What materials made up the stench Kali had no idea, but whatever they were they made the hole before them pulsate with an array of colours that looked considerably less than healthy.

There was a flushing sound that began high above them and, giving it a little time to clear, Pim's lieutenant gestured for Kali to drop inside the hole. "Twenty nine and a half minutes," he said. "You did say you wanted to go first?"

Kali did, manoeuvring her landing to avoid a rainbow sludge that was evidently the result of the purge from the towers, then a half-splash from behind her signalled that Jayhinch had joined her not so successfully in the mire. Wiping something that fizzed like acid from his boot, he then moved with her to a grate at the sewer's end – a grate smeared with the thicker contents of discarded experiments from above. Avoiding contact, the pair prised it away with disgust, and then began to climb a conduit that rose upwards, aware that they had just entered the Three Towers' outer wall. The knowledge made them move with increased caution but, however cautious they were, there was no way to prevent what happened next.

Kali wasn't sure what alerted her to the danger, whether it was some slight click or a subtle disturbance in the air, but something did – though unfortunately all she had time to do was shout a warning and then throw herself down. Kris Jayhinch was not as quick.

There was a whooshing crack and Kali kept her head low while whatever threat accompanied the noise passed. She heard an agonised cry and then an odd crackling sound that chilled her to the bone.

She turned to look back. Jayhinch was exactly where he had been a moment before but he would not be accompanying her any further. Arms outstretched towards her, eyes staring blankly and mouth wide in a silent scream, the now grey-coloured lieutenant blocked the conduit as still as a statue.

And with good reason. Pim had evidently been wrong about there being no traps here.

Kris Jayhinch had been turned to solid stone.

CHAPTER TWELVE

Kali blew out a long breath to calm herself, fully aware of how Jayhinch's fate could so easily have been her own. The unwanted thieves guild companion Jengo had thrust upon her had proved himself useful, yes, but in a way she would never have asked for, never have desired.

A gorgon trap was no way for anyone to go. The invidious magic could perhaps be thought merciful if it caused petrification in an instant, but Kali had heard that sometimes it took the internal organs – and most perversely the brain – as long as a day to fully turn to stone.

One minute in, one man dead – or as near as made no difference. That kind of put the Three Towers' quagmire cards on the table. No – it slammed them down with all the arrogant confidence of a winning bogflush, in fact. Suddenly the Three Towers seemed less of an entertaining, professional challenge and more the indiscriminating deathtrap that the thieves guild leader had threatened it would be. From here on in, if she didn't want to share Jayhinch's fate, she was really going to have to watch her step.

"I'm sorry," she said quietly to his immobile form, trying not to notice how a section of his skull – almost scalpless as a result of the lethally traumatic magic – remained as yet unpetrified and glistening, a bloody reminder of the man he'd been only moments before. She stared into his agonised, frozen eyes, wondering if Jayhinch heard her inadequate words, and then turned and continued on alone.

She didn't get far before the next of the defences hit. She experienced a sensation almost like a swoon, and then suddenly the conduit seemed to stretch away endlessly ahead of her, wavering slightly in her vision. Kali craned her neck and looked behind her, seeing that the conduit stretched into the distance that way, too, seemingly without end. But something was clearly wrong with the picture – apart from the fact she *knew* she hadn't crawled that far, the remains of Jayhinch were nowhere to be seen along its yawning length. It was also obvious to her that what she saw could not be real because the Three Towers, individually or as a whole, were simply not that expansive.

The sight that met her eyes, therefore, had to be some kind of illusion. An infinity illusion. But she couldn't see the point of such a trap. Any intruder who made it this far was unlikely to be dissuaded from progressing further as they'd know what they saw wasn't real, so why bother unless –

Unless it was a delaying tactic, meant to confuse while –

Kali's mind raced, wondering which way to go. Her natural inclination in such close confines would be to flatten against the floor as she had not long before, but the mages of the Three Towers clearly liked to play, to twist things, and dropping to the floor seemed wrong – *wrong!* Instead, she slammed her hands and feet against the conduit walls and with a grunt quickly heaved herself up above the floor, hoping to hells she'd made the right choice. At the exact moment she did a wave of ice hurtled towards her from along the conduit, turning the metal beneath her blue-white and sizzling and cracking it with cold. Limbs trembling with the effort it took to keep herself suspended, Kali hung above it, swallowing as she watched her breath condense into crystals over the super-chilled metal only a few inches below. The cold was spreading up the curve of the conduit, too – she could feel it in her palms, and, if she didn't let go soon, she'd be bonded to the metal so badly the only way to break the grip would be to rip the flesh off her palms.

Thankfully, the magically generated ice vanished as quickly as it had appeared, presumably because its job, for those with slower reactions, would have been done. Kali lowered herself back to the conduit floor with a groan, rubbing her palms to restore circulation to the throbbing skin, then did the same to her nose to alleviate a touch of frostbite.

She proceeded upwards, finding that the conduit levelled out some now, and as a result found her feet squelching in patches of alchemical waste that had not been fully flushed away. She avoided the muck as much as she could, stepped lightly and quickly through that which she could not, spurred to such action by the small skeletal remains of floprats who had chanced to crawl here. The remains of the rodents hadn't just been eaten away, their skeletons had been twisted and *changed*.

Her slightly increased pace made Kali no less aware of the danger around her, and she deftly avoided the triggers for another couple of traps – one apparently designed to release a cloud of living biomagical toxin into the conduit, another – which she purposefully triggered once she'd passed by – to make that section of the conduit momentarily discorporeal, meaning anyone unfortunate enough to be traversing it at the time would become part of the conduit on a permanent basis.

Pits of Kerberos! These guys really are bastards.

She continued on, relieved to find that at last the traps seemed to have stopped. Quite right, too, because anybody who had made it this far bloody well deserved to make it the rest. She couldn't relax until she was out of the conduit, however – the number of delays she'd suffered had eaten into the time she had for safe passage, and she reckoned she had less than a minute left before the alchemical laboratories were purged.

She hurried, the seconds ticking, and spied at last the access hatch marked on the map. The moment she reached it she heard dull, echoing rumblings from above, and grabbed quickly for the hatch wheel to swing it open.

Thread magic coursed through her, a crackling storm of blue energy that paralysed her momentarily before blowing her off her feet and slamming her into the conduit wall. Kali groaned and slipped to the floor, and lay there stunned, bucking and spasming involuntarily as small discharges continued to spark off her body.

Dammit, one last trap. They'd lulled her into a false sense of security and caught her unawares.

One thing she couldn't help but be aware of, though, were the noises. The echoing rumblings from above had become a series of metallic clangs, and as she lay there she realised with a dull knot of fear that the drop-hatches from the labs were opening.

Gods! She had to move now! Only she couldn't, not an inch. Not even to thump the conduit in frustration. Annoyingly, all she could do was dribble.

Dammit, Hooper, come on, come on. You've been an idiot, but do you want to die here? Do you want to die and prove Jengo Pim right?

The conduit filled with the sound of sloshing.

Hooper, she screamed inwardly, *do you want to fail the old man?*

Kali roared with exertion and, consciously forcing every movement of her body, lurched forwards, twisted the hatch wheel and heaved the cover open just in time. The last thing she saw before she dived head first through the hatch and it clanged shut behind her was a raging torrent of rainbow sludge.

She plummeted with a yell and thudded onto the floor below as if she had just been birthed by a pregnant mool, embryonic, twitching and covered in splashes of gunk. After a second she thrashed the gunk away, but stayed down while her spasms subsided, coughing and retching loudly. Only then did she perceive where she was – the middle of a corridor in the first tower – and lying there exposed and all but helpless, it occurred to her that her entrance had not exactly been the stealthy one she'd planned. She comforted herself, however, with the fact that the last trap would have killed – or at least hammered the final nail into the coffin of – anyone less bloody-minded than she.

She frowned, wondering. Was it just bloody-mindedness that had got her out of there? Or was it something to do again with the changes happening to her, the things that made her able to do the things she did? One thing was certain – now was not the time to think about it.

Kali groaned and picked herself up. The corridor in which she'd landed was a shimmering, smooth affair and, thankfully, empty, though it felt oddly not so. The corridor thrummed quietly to itself, as if the power of the Three Towers were contained within its walls, and Kali had the uneasy feeling that, while she saw no one, she was not alone. She felt as if she were being observed from all angles, almost as if she were being watched by the building itself, which, considering the nature of the place, it was just possible she was. Nothing happened as a result of her feeling, though, and she wondered if perhaps it was just a magical suggestion that hung in the air, designed to unnerve anyone who shouldn't be here. Even so, it was pitsing creepy.

Pulling out Jengo's map, she orientated herself and crept slowly forwards, thankful for the fact there'd been no alarms. She'd had more than enough alarms in Scholten. She began to weave her way through a maze of corridors towards the stairs that would lead her upwards and from there, across the bridge, to the third tower and her destination. The Forbidden Archive.

Despite Jengo's concerns, she moved with relative ease. Now that she was within the outer defences, there was little to be wary of in the way of traps, and as most League members were busy blowing up or dissolving things in the labs she passed, they presented little problem. Those mages that she did encounter in her path she simply avoided, a task made easier by the fact that in their flowing and colourful patterned robes it was easy to spot them before they chanced upon her.

Those robes. She found it perverse how these bastards still garbed themselves in the garish showbusiness style of parlour entertainers when their business was no longer entertainment but death. Still, she couldn't help but think that one or two of them were wasted here in the towers and should actually put themselves up for sale as a nice pair of curtains.

As she moved steadily on, only one thing hampered her – here and there certain corridors were blocked by shimmering curtains of different coloured energy and, while the mages moved through them with ease, presumably having protected themselves against whatever the energies did, a stray floprat that attempted to follow ended up as a small puddle of fur and blood. Kali did not want to chance her arm – or any other part of her body – by emulating it. Instead, she found the bottom of the stairs by a different route.

Following echoing, whispering corridors, they appeared before her at last, and Kali looked up their spiralling heights and cursed. According to the map, the connecting bridge to the Forbidden Archive could be found on the thirty-fifth floor. There was no lift. *The hells with a lift,* she thought. *These guys were mages so why hadn't they magicked some kind of... lifty-uppity zoomy tube?* But they hadn't, had they? No. Knowing her luck, they probably just spouted some kind of incantation that stopped them getting absolutely bloody knackered.

She began the long ascent, but it soon became clear that she would never make it all the way up without being detected – the stairs were simply too busy with mages crossing between floors. There was only one alternative. Much as she hated the idea of having to take one on, Kali secreted herself in an alcove near the base of the steps, reasoning that the best way to tackle a mage would be to surprise him from behind. This she did, waiting until she caught one alone then, as he passed cracking him on the head and catching him as he dropped. His robe came off in one.

The body concealed in the alcove, and suitably attired, Kali continued quickly on. She did not want to be anywhere near him when he woke up.

Thirty-five storeys later she emerged gasping through an exit into the open air, which led directly onto the bridge she wanted. Thirty-five storeys was a dizzying height and Kali expected a worse buffeting than she had received above Scholten, but to her surprise the bridge was totally calm and silent, protected, she assumed, by some invisible magical canopy. *Made sense,* she thought, smiling. After all, if they needed to visit the archive the last thing the League's mages needed was a nasty draught up their robes disturbing their forbidden musings.

Had Makennon got some of her own information from here? Kali wondered. After all, if ever a place needed to be infiltrated by a sender, this was it. The bridge leading to the Forbidden Archive looked harmless enough but Kali had by now seen enough of the things to recognise that the barely visible but variously coloured curtains of shimmering and sparkling energy that separated the bridge into sections promised something nasty the moment she tried to step through them. These were particularly powerful, no doubt about that – she could feel them buzzing in her brain.

She studied the bridge. It had no walls or railings and, naturally enough, no conduits, no side passages and no ledges. None, in other words, of her usual shortcuts. She tentatively touched where she imagined the magical canopy to be, and while her hand moved through it with ease, she guessed that if she passed through it completely there would be no way back in.

Handy enough for suicidal sorcerers but useless as far as she was concerned.

She had to admit, she felt stymied. There was no way across without indulging in some serious lateral thinking. She was beginning to think she was completely out of laterals when, fortunately, one arrived in the form of a mage coming through the door behind her. As soon as she heard the door open Kali twisted to the side and flattened herself against the wall, watching as a League member came through and began to amble across the bridge, seeming almost to float in his long robe. His relaxed attitude made her presume that he was not about to be frozen, incinerated or generally done to death by any of the traps so, like his brothers below, he had to have some kind of protection about him.

Normally, she would not have welcomed his presence at all, but this, she hoped, was her way through. She had to take the gamble, there was no other choice. She had to stick to him as close as a second skin. Used as she was to sneaking about places, she was about to find out just how stealthy she could be.

As the mage moved past her, Kali moved into step behind him, a living shadow, crouched but moving on tiptoe, matching his every move. As his left leg moved, so did hers, as his right, the same. Every pause, every hesitation and every subtle twist and turn of the mage's body was matched perfectly as he – and she – passed through the first of the defensive curtains and she felt nothing other than a slight fluttering in her muscles. But that she felt even that while she was protected proved her suspicion of how powerful these final traps were.

Two curtains, three curtains, four. Her plan was working – and then it wasn't. She was one curtain away from the end of the bridge when the mage stopped dead in his tracks, causing Kali to wobble and almost bump into him it was so unexpected.

There was what seemed to be an eternal pause. *What are you doing?* she thought. *Come on, come on, tell me what you're doing.*

The mage patted a pocket of his robe, shook his head in self reprimand and tutted loudly.

He's forgotten something, Kali thought. *The bloody idiot's forgotten –*

Oh, cra –

She moved as he did, a hundred and eighty degrees in perfect silence and synchronisation, staying in the same position behind him all the time. She couldn't believe she managed it, but she did, and the mage didn't even have a clue she was there. Though outwardly calm and in control, as Kali watched him walk back the way that he had come, she was surprised he didn't hear her heart threatening to burst out of her chest.

He disappeared through the door and she was left trapped between the last two curtains.

She threw her hands in the air and walked quickly around in a circle. There was no way forwards, no way back – and absolutely nowhere to hide when Mister Duh! Forgot My Head returned.

Idiot!

There had to be a way through – and she had to work out what it was fast. The first step was finding out what kind of trap she was looking at. Kali quickly tore a small patch from her dark silk bodysuit and tossed it at the curtain. There was a *zuzzz*, a puff of smoke and then nothing – the patch was gone. This was some kind of electrical trap and if she tried to step through she'd end up doing a dance that would put the Hells' Bellies to shame.

A very brief dance.

Dammit! She wasn't going to find out the location of the keys this way.

The keys, she thought, something nagging at the back of her brain. These differently coloured curtains with their different magics – surely the mages couldn't constantly invoke protection against each? What, then, if they instead carried with them some kind of key? She hadn't seen anything actually being used and so what could it – ?

She looked down. The pattern on her stolen robe scintillated slightly, more so when she moved closer to the curtain. *Gods,* she thought, *was that why the mages still wore them – because the robes themselves were the keys?*

Again, it was a gamble, but if she didn't take it she was stuffed anyway. Kali took a deep breath and walked slowly forwards, passing through the energy field with ease.

She cringed. All the effort she'd put into marking Mister Duh! Forgot My Head when she could have passed through any time.

Idiot!

She opened the door ahead of her and she was inside at last. The Forbidden Archive.

Her eyes narrowed.

Or... not.

What in the hells was this? Kali wondered, aghast. There was nothing here. After all her effort, the upper half of the third tower was an empty chamber, completely featureless apart from a solitary, podium-like structure at its centre and a red glow that suffused the place and seemed to emanate from the walls.

Okay – if this had been a guided tour, then she'd have demanded her money back.

She moved towards the podium, her footfalls clattering despite the fact she wore shnarl-hide soles. Of all the things she had encountered so far it was the clattering that made her shiver. This place was *weird*.

Kali mounted the podium and found it inscribed with a number of symbols, none of which she recognised, the symbols being magical not linguistic, and not her area of expertise. She pressed one, then another, and then each in turn, but nothing happened. She tried a different order and, again, nothing. On her fourth unsuccessful attempt she threw up her arms in frustration, then quickly stepped back as the air in front of her seemed suddenly to change. Then, spiralling down seemingly from thin air above came a number of tiny shapes that began to gather before her eyes, and as they did an object began to assemble itself from these tiny building blocks. Some kind of container – elven by the look of it – marked with the familiar circular symbol of their race.

Kali moved her hand forwards to touch the container but found nothing there.

An idea struck her, and she waved her hands again. As rapidly as it had appeared, the container disassembled itself and spiralled back towards the heights of the chamber, replaced by another object spiralling down and assembling itself in its place. This time it was a manuscript containing, by the look of it, some kind of outlawed spell.

Kali's gesticulations became more varied, and she dismissed and summoned more and more objects, each redolent to some degree of evil and possessed of an ominous aura. She had no idea what magics were involved, but it was becoming clear to her what was happening here – the League of Prestidigitation and Prestige obviously considered the collection of the Forbidden Archive too dangerous to keep physically in one location and so had devised this method of *virtually* retrieving each object for study from elsewhere – perhaps some plane that could not be physically reached at all.

It was an indication of their power and it was wondrous, but it did her very little good. How out of all the collection was she meant to find what she needed, because if she had managed to summon the items she had at random then the collection itself had to be immense, with infinite combinations of symbology. And hells – she didn't even really know what it was she was looking for.

There had to be a way of narrowing it down. Kali looked at the symbols on the podium again, reasoning that not even the League's mages could reasonably be expected to remember every combination, and that maybe they were subdivisions – some kind of cataloguing system. Instead of pressing it this time, she replicated the first symbol on the podium with arm movements, feeling what she had missed before, some kind of receptive magical field slightly thickening the air, and a second later a box not dissimilar to the first she had summoned assembled itself. Kali took a gamble and tried waving it on, and to her surprise the gesture worked – another curiosity assembling itself in its place. But she was clearly in the section for artefacts when what she wanted was manuscripts. She replicated the next symbol – spells – and the next – ancient relics. Only on the fourth and last did she find what she was looking for, or at least a place to begin.

Kali's gesticulations increased in pace and she began to summon, study and dismiss manuscript after manuscript, growing more and more adept with the practice until she looked as if she were conducting some complex symphony. She found she was able to pull writings towards her for closer study, turn them around or upside down to seek hidden illuminations and, in the case of actual tomes, flip from page to page with ease. The number of ancient documents stored astounded her, but her joy at discovering such a treasure trove was tempered by the knowledge that she had no time to truly study any but those she sought. Having still not found them and increasingly aware that the forgetful mage could return at any time, her efforts became more urgent, a degree of frustration creeping in as she hurled each document on with a snap of her hand.

Then suddenly, there. Images similar to those Slowhand had described from Makennon's archive in Scholten. There, on the first manuscript she saw, and on more following, diverse and variously decomposed references presumably collected here from different sources and different times.

Kali stopped cycling, hands moving slowly so that she could fold back and forth between the most telling documents, an illuminated manuscript, a map, and what appeared to be some ancient bard's tale of events. It was all there just as Slowhand had said. The hellsfire, the damnation, the vast horde marching under what appeared to be the crossed-circle banner of the Final Faith – not to mention the people kneeling before the horde in apparent worship. Also, looming over them in the background, a figurehead that could have been a representation of the Lord of All – what Makennon believed to be the horde's leader – but to less subjective eyes could equally have been anything else, including, troublingly, a gigantic and stylised version of your typical – how could she put this? – small, warlike person.

In fairness, Kali could see how Makennon had inferred what she had, but there were things here the woman must have been blind not to notice, that leapt off the pages and were simply wrong. For one thing, as had occurred to Slowhand, it seemed to her that the kneeling figures were not human, their physiognomy, though stylised again, more Old Race, elf *and* dwarf. For another, it struck her that they were not kneeling in worship but in supplication, praying to the marching horde and its leader, not for their help in divine ascension but for their mercy.

All of this, of course, was a matter of perception, but as Kali studied the text of the illuminated manuscript and then cycled to the bard's account, it became more a matter of interpretation. She was fluent in neither dwarvish or elvish – hells, who was? – but she had over her explorations picked up enough bits and pieces to recognise key words and put together the bones of a story.

The... middle times? A war between a clan of dwarves and a family of elves... dwarven defeat... no, near-annihilation. Survivors... and a sorcerer. Belatron? Belatron the Black? The Butcher? Anyway... a war machine... a *leader*... built to avenge... no, to *satisfy?*... the dwarven dead. But something wrong. Yes... something gone horribly wrong... a massacre. More death than in the war itself... genocide for both elf and dwarf... and a desperate alliance to stop it...

Kali blew out a breath. That, as far as she was concerned, clinched it – mostly. Everything here tallied with what Merrit Moon had told her, and was, in turn, totally at odds with what Katherine Makennon believed. The only thing she couldn't understand was why the symbol of the Final Faith and its prominence was on not one but two of the manuscripts she studied? Surely this was no representation of the Final Faith's future, it was a warning to everyone on the peninsula from the past.

So much for the history. Merrit Moon had wanted her to stop this thing and what she needed to do was find the information relevant to the here and now, to the threat they faced. She cycled to the map and studied it. The old man had said that between them the elves and the dwarves had built four containment areas for the keys, and there they seemed to be, marked in four widespread locations by two circles and two crosses, each with a representation of a key drawn in above. Why they were not marked by four circles or four crosses, instead of both, Kali wasn't sure, but she supposed the differing symbols were simply elven and dwarven equivalents of X marks the spot. Yes, she thought, remembering the runic circles at the Spiral of Kos, because as one of the circles here lay in the Sardenne Forest at the approximate location where the Spiral had been, that had to be what they were. Knowing that, even though the map was old and parts of the peninsula coastline looked different, she should be able to extrapolate the locations of the other keys from there. Only one thing confused her – the small amount of text on the map made passing reference to five keys not four. Had the old man been wrong and there was actually another, missing location? No, that didn't make sense – the map itself contradicted it. What, then, if there was a fifth key needed to access Orl itself? Yes, that could be it, even though there was no indication of a location for a fifth key on the map. *Dammit,* she thought, looking at the text again, she wasn't that good so maybe she'd just interpreted it wrong.

She had to concentrate on the matter at hand. She possessed the rough locations for the four keys but, for insurance, she needed the location of Orl itself. If this map, for whatever reason, had been meant to be some kind of overall guide, then it had to be here. Somewhere.

Kali took a deep breath and studied the map again, something nagging at her. Suddenly she pulled it towards her for a closer view of the key in the Sardenne. The whorls in the ornate head of the key looked familiar, and with good reason – the drawing was a stylised map of the topography of the area centred on the Spiral of Kos, a more detailed map of its location! But important as that was, there was something else – some of the whorls on the key seemed extraneous, nothing to do with the local topography and seeming to belong somewhere else entirely. Her heart thudded as she realised she was looking at part of a map within a map.

She waved her hand, flipping the document from side to side and slightly up and down, pulling it towards her to zoom in on each key in turn. For the moment she ignored the locations of the containment sites each gave, concentrating instead on the extraneous whorls, overlaying each set in her mind. Together, they formed a topography she recognised, part of the peninsula far to the west.

Kali zoomed to that part of the map. There did appear to be some kind of site marked, but the map was damaged around it, barely legible, and the marking could apply to anywhere within a number of leagues. But what she *could* make out appeared again to be the symbol of the Final Faith.

No, she thought, *that had to be wrong!* Because if it wasn't, what would that mean? That Makennon was right? That she was destined to find Orl?

There was something else that shook her, too – more dwarven text, but text that made no reference to the site being called Orl but... Mor... Mar... no, it was no good, she couldn't make it out.

Pits of Kerberos, she'd come in search of answers and all she'd found were more questions. But at least she had a rough location, and that would do as a start. She zoomed again, searching for landmarks that might help further, but then everything before her eyes suddenly faded. Kali blinked. The Forbidden Archive was a featureless red chamber once more.

"Find anything of interest?" a voice asked.

Kali spun and found herself facing a bearded figure who had to be Mister Duh! Forgot My Head. Only, seeing him from the front, his eyes and expression did not strike her as forgetful at all but instead rather threatening and intense.

Disliking tackling them head on or not, Kali didn't know what else she could do. She rushed the mage, intending to silence him before he could alert others of his kind, but with a sweep of his hand the man did something with the air in front of him and she found herself bouncing back off an invisible field of force that felt like rubbery water. She flung a fist at him instead, hoping that would penetrate, but another sweep of the hand wove a different thread and, this time, she was slammed back and away from him, without any physical contact at all.

Kali yelped as she crashed into the podium and flipped over it, then smashed jarringly and numbingly into the far wall. She picked herself up, wiping blood from her lip.

Again, she ran at the mage, and this time he simply raised an arm and she found herself rising with it, treading air before she could get anywhere near him. The mage smiled, slowly rolled her over in the air and then manoeuvred her helplessly floating body to the side of the chamber. Kali felt herself pressed against the wall and, as she struggled futilely against the invisible grip that held her there, the mage moved his arm again and she found herself being slowly dragged all the way around the circumference of the tower, as if she were dirt to be smeared from his hand.

It was, frankly, embarrassing. But embarrassing was all it seemed to be. Presumably the mage could have flung her around like a doll if he so wished, but he simply continued as he did, smiling, as if this were his way of proving a point.

He even let her down gently, positioning her back on her feet before him.

"Okay, that wasn't fair. You've got me, so what happens now?"

The mage smiled. "Absolutely nothing. I mean you no harm and will defend myself only as and when necessary. I have been employed to provide a client with the same information you now seek, and that employment is now done. It would be churlish of me to censure you for obtaining the same knowledge by your own means, would it not? And I *could* have turned you in the moment you fell through that hatch."

"It was *you* watching me."

"I... sensed you, yes."

"You're the sender," Kali realised. "The Final Faith's source."

The mage bowed. "Poul Sonpear at your service. Trusted archivist for the League of Prestidigitation and Prestige. But the Final Faith are quite generous when it comes to persuading people to bend the rules a little. Tell me," he added with genuine intrigue, "just why is it you and they find this material of such great interest?"

"You've seen it. What the hells do you think?"

"I have no opinion. I have seen many thousands of such manuscripts and these, as are they all, are open to subjective interpretation."

You can say that again, Kali thought. People saw what people wanted to see. Never more so than when they pursued their interest with religious zeal. And that remained exactly the problem here.

"What if I were to tell you these things warn against the end of civilisation as we know it? That unless I recover a key that the Final Faith took from a friend of mine, they're a quarter of the way to unleashing something –"

Kali paused, unsure how to go on.

"Something?" Sonpear urged.

"I don't know yet, okay?" Kali shouted at him, piqued. "But something very, very bad. A clockwork king."

Kali frowned, aware, after the intensity of her search, of how *unthreatening* that sounded.

Sonpear laughed. "Then I would suggest that you will not be able to stop them."

Kali balled her fists. "What are you saying? That this is, after all, where you call your friends to finish me off?"

"Not at all. I wish only to point out to you that the Final Faith's journey along their path of discovery has progressed somewhat further than you think."

"Say again?"

Sonpear sighed heavily. "My... exchanges with the Final Faith's receiver work two ways and, though I do not intend to, it is sometimes hard to avoid absorbing... *peripheral* information. This key that you refer to – the one taken from your friend and that I believe you originally acquired from the Spiral of Kos? – it is not the first to fall into their hands."

Kali swallowed. Suddenly what Munch had said in the Spiral about hazards he'd recently encountered made sense. "They have more?"

"There have been two previous expeditions – to forgotten sites called, I believe, the Shifting City and the Eye of the Storm."

Names that sounded suitably trap-like, Kali thought. And they must have been two of the sites the map referred to, but she – and, presumably, Merrit – had never heard of them. But then they didn't have the resources the Final Faith had – the bastards.

"And they were successful?"

"I gather so." Sonpear stared at her. "Young lady, the Final Faith are already in possession of three of your keys and are about to acquire possession of the fourth."

"What? Where?" Kali said, urgently.

"A site that has so far caused them considerable problems and loss, and by inference therefore the most dangerous of them all. And it is located beneath the most convenient and unexpected place you can imagine – the Final Faith's headquarters at Scholten Cathedral itself."

Kali's mind flashed back to her and Killiam's escape – the curious lift shaft, the place she had wanted to go.

"Slowhand, you fark," she said.

"Excuse me?"

"I have to go," Kali said, knowing she needed to reach the key first. "Listen, you're the spy – is there a back way out of here?"

CHAPTER THIRTEEN

MUCH AS KALI had negotiated her conduit above Andon, so the man without clothes negotiated his below Scholten – only here the conduit was constructed not of metal but of stone. Dank stone. The dank stone of a sewer, in fact, sheened and slimed by substances worse than those Kali had encountered at the Three Towers – vile, brown, smelly substances that a man as clean and fastidious as he should not even have to think about, let alone drag himself through.

Somewhere beneath the Scholten Cathedral kitchens Killiam Slowhand tried not to think about the sludge that coated him, especially as there was nothing at all between the sludge and him. *Every inch* of him.

The archer shuddered.

It could have been worse, he supposed. For one thing, he could be beneath the Final Faith's privies rather than their kitchens. For another, more importantly, he could be dead. The knife that had been lunged at him on the walkway had been intended to deliver a fatal wound but had instead only grazed his side, something to do with the fact that he had grabbed its wielder and thrown him off the towering building as soon as his arm had come towards him. As the guard's scream faded in Scholten's night sky, his friends would probably have avenged him, finished him off, were it not for the fact that the head guard, just caught up, had ordered him to be taken alive. The order came on the specific instruction of Katherine Makennon, but why she wanted him kept alive, he didn't know – perhaps so she could have her Mister Fitch turn him to her cause, or perhaps merely so that she could revel in his reincarceration. She had certainly seemed to revel as she had had him stripped of what little clothing he had, and he wondered whether something had been going on there, whether perhaps a little of his charm had rubbed off on her after all? Because surely she couldn't have rumbled the old abrasive underpants trick?

Whatever the reason, it had led him to his present unsavoury predicament. Makennon had returned him to a cell but this time somewhere she could keep an eye on him, a small oubliette she just happened to maintain in her private courtyard, which was obviously used only for very special guests. He had felt quite flattered by this and had returned the favour by singing romantic ballads night and day – his very own Eternal Choir. But all good things had to come to an end and, after two weeks, she had ordered his execution at the earliest opportunity.

This was fine by him, as he had never intended hanging around. He'd have been gone the first night had he not needed to lose a little weight first. Not that he was overweight, of course, just – well, a little *big*. A little big for the hole in the oubliette floor, that was.

It was a flaw in security but a necessary one, because with the amount of rain over Scholten, without it he or anyone else kept in the oubliette would have drowned. The hole had probably once been too small for anyone to pass through but it was also long unmaintained – its grate rusted – and, over time, the draining water had worn away its edges, providing a smooth-edged if extremely tight squeezeway through the floor. The fact was, if he had been fully clothed, he'd have had to strip anyway to get through.

Definitely. Yes, without a doubt.

Slowhand shook his head. Hooper would never have believed that he'd done it again. Once – *just once* – he'd like to catch her losing her clothes in the line of duty. Then she'd know that these things just had a way of *happening*. But no – there was no chance of that, was there? Not with little Miss Prissy Knickers.

Slowhand continued crawling forwards, estimating he'd pass beyond the cathedral walls in about ten more minutes. Ahead of him, he could actually see a dim circle of azure night sky that was the sewer's outlet.

Unfortunately, that same light was also partly obscured, silhouetting something coming straight towards him. And down here it could have been anything.

Slowhand cursed. Feeling somewhat vulnerable in his present state, he looked for somewhere to hide. His eyes darted ahead of him, behind him, down and up, but he was in a sewer and there was nowhere to go. He was actually so involved in doing what he did that he failed to notice how quickly the something was coming at him. And the something was so involved in getting where it wanted to be that it didn't notice him.

Heads collided.

"Ow, dammit!"

"Jeeeeshhh!"

A face popped up right in front of his.

"Slowhand?" Kali Hooper said.

He strained to see in the dark. "Hooper? Oh hells, don't tell me – you can see better in the dark, too?"

"Looks like it. *So...* how are you doing?"

"Oh, you know..."

"Mmm."

"Mmm."

The usual exchange went on for a while until Kali suggested they backtrack slightly in her direction, where an access shaft meant the roof of the sewer opened up. They moved to it, and Kali and Slowhand stood.

As he rose, the sewer's detritus slipped off his body, and Kali saw what was beneath. Or rather wasn't.

She turned quickly away. "Oh gods, you're naked again, Slowhand. How in the hells do you manage it?"

"Hey – don't blame me, blame Makennon," he defended himself. "Or maybe even yourself – in case you've forgotten *you're* the reason I got locked up again." He waved at himself. "Like this."

"You told me to go!"

"Of course I did – but I didn't expect you to come back! What the hells are you doing here, Hooper? Did you forget something?"

Kali's expression became serious. "I was too late to save the old man."

Slowhand faltered. "Gods, I'm sorry."

"I know you are. But before he died, he told me what's going on. Sent me to Andon. This whole mess is worse than we thought."

Slowhand bowed his head, sighed. "When is it ever anything else? Tell me."

Kali explained the gist of what she'd learned, omitting only those parts she was still working out in her own head, and, as she did, the expression in the archer's eyes changed from anticipation to resignation, and he rested his palms on the sewer wall, slowly banging his head against them. "I suppose this means I'm not escaping any more?"

"I... might be grateful for a little help."

Slowhand punched the sewer wall. "I knew it!" He pointed ahead, would have jumped up and down like a petulant brat if he could. "Do you realise I'm only a hundred yards from the exit! A hundred yards, Hooper. I see the light at the end of the tunnel!"

"I know. I came in that way. Slowhand, what can I say? The outside world's not all it's cracked up to be?"

"*Aaarrgh!*" Slowhand roared in frustration.

"Oh, will you stop it," Kali chided him. "Look, I hardly expected to find you crawling about down here, all right? In fact, I thought you were dead." She paused, quietened, and added softly, "I'm glad you're not, by the way."

Killiam stared at her in her new dark silk bodysuit, and his tone softened. "Yeah, me too. Like the new look, by the way. *Very* nice outfit. Clingy. It, er, shows off your good points."

Kali folded her arms. "It's damp and I'm cold, you pervert. Now, are you with me or not, because I want out of this sewer..."

"Oh, funnily enough, so did I!" Killiam offered, flinging up his arms, though by now it was obvious that he didn't mean it. Nevertheless, the action resulted in something flying off his hands and slapping Kali in the face. Slowhand looked down, apologised.

Kali wiped the article away, shaking her head. "There's an access shaft in the ceiling about two hundred yards back," she said. "Comes out near the Eternal Choir. We can work our way back down to the complex from there."

"Okay, I'll go first," Killiam said, bending back to enter the tunnel.

Kali grabbed him. "O-ho, no. If you think I'm going to crawl along looking at your rear end in all its glory, you've got another think coming." She got down on her hands and knees. "I go first."

"Fine, fine," Killiam said, tiredly. But as Kali moved forwards into the tunnel he smiled at the sight of her bottom, stuck his finger in his mouth to wet it, and drew a tick in the air. It was only a moment later he realised his mistake.

"Guh... uh... ahhhh... pits..."

"Hah!" Kali said. "What was that, by the way? On your – ?"

"Sewerkraut, I think."

"Don't you mean –"

"No, Hooper. I know what I mean."

The pair found the access shaft and up it a ladder that rose to cathedral level, which they climbed, shoving aside a grate. They emerged into a corridor filled with the singing of the Eternal Choir, and the first thing Killiam did was flatten a guard who stood in a doorway mouthing the words as he listened to it. He quickly stripped him of his armour, then donned it himself, bundling the body into a dark niche.

Kali looked him up and down. "Better," she said.

Slowhand shrugged, buckling up his collarpiece. "Yeah, well – this time we're not planning to go flying anywhere, are we?"

"The door's just down there – come on."

"Wait," Slowhand said. "There's something I need to get first. From Makennon's chambers."

"What? Are you nuts?"

"Trust me, Hooper. I've a feeling we're going to need this thing."

Slowhand led Kali to the Anointed Lord's audience chamber – deserted, Kali guessed because Makennon was down at the dig – and opened a compartment in the wall. Kali found herself staring at the most magnificent-looking longbow she had ever seen. She knew where it must have come from – the Battle of Andon, eight years earlier. This was the weapon that had killed John Garrison.

Slowhand weighed it in his hands, ran his palm along its sleek lines. "Suresight," he said. "Never thought I'd see her again."

"Careless of you to lose her."

Slowhand pulled a quiver from the compartment too, lined an arrow against the shaft, pursing his lips and nodding in approval. Then his expression darkened. "Yes, well... After Andon I'd had enough of killing. Everyone had." His tone lightened once more. "But times move on. Let's go."

"Hold on," Kali said, looking around. "If Makennon's in the habit of keeping souvenirs, maybe..."

She rifled through a nearby chest and with a cry of triumph pulled forth her toolbelt, removed from her prior to her interrogation. She also found her torn and tatty old outfit, and as she held it up to examine it, wasn't sure what disturbed her more – the fact that Makennon had seen fit to keep it, or the fact that Dolorosa had been right in her observation that it did indeed *steeenk*.

She left the remains of the garment where it was and they continued on to their original destination, moving down out of the cathedral and into its sub-levels once more. This time, they avoided all the guards they could, having no wish to announce their return to the lower depths.

There was only one problem. The bridge across the cavern had been retracted to the other side, the wheel there locked. What was more, two guards paced back and forth in front of it.

"Dammit," Kali said. "They've battened down the hatches."

"Not a problem," Slowhand said.

He unslung his bow.

Kali stared at the distant wheel and guards. So far they hadn't been spotted but...

"What the hells are you doing?" she whispered. "Take one of them down and the other will sound the alarm before you can hit the second. Oh, and even if you could get the second, then there'll be no one to activate the wheel. We need to think this through."

"No, we don't," Slowhand said. He primed an arrow and hefted the bow. A nerve in his jaw twitched as he waited, but then, at the exact moment the pacing guards crossed paths, he let fly. The single arrow pierced both of their necks, dropping them instantly, then carried on to impact with the wheel clamp with a solid thud, releasing the lock.

"Hells, you're good," Kali said.

Slowhand smiled, patting his bow. "It's good to have the old girl back."

Kali brought the bridge to their side and the two crossed, sneaking their way through the remainder of the complex until they neared the shafts that had so aroused Kali's curiosity what seemed now an age before. This time, they weren't guarded, but with the bridge supposedly retracted they didn't really need to be.

"Hooper, why here?" Slowhand asked. "I mean, an Old Race structure on this site, and then, centuries later, the cathedral built here too, presumably with the Final Faith not then knowing what was beneath it. Can that just be coincidence?"

"Maybe," Kali replied. "Or maybe this has always been a site of some significance, sociologically, historically or religiously. Maybe people, whoever they are – or were – are simply drawn here. Actually I've come across a few old manuscripts that suggest there may even be a number of nodes located across the peninsula, nodes that could be part of a network of –"

"Enough, Hooper," Slowhand said. "What do you expect we'll find down there?"

"Oh, that's easy. Something deadly."

"Something deadly," Slowhand repeated. "Right, fine, thanks for sharing that with me."

"My pleasure." Kali gestured towards the lift. "After you."

"No, no, I insist. After you."

"Slowhand, get on the bloody lift."

"You are getting quite domineering, you know that?"

"And you love every minute of it."

The lift was hardly the engineering marvel that Kali had ridden at the Spiral of Kos but it did the job, creaking on a rope as it descended a shaft that had been roughly cut from rock and felt strangely warm. The marks of modern tooling suggested to Kali that the shaft was the work of the Final Faith, which likely meant that the site to which they were heading had another – original – entrance elsewhere, but what or where that was she didn't know. She had never come across anything resembling an entrance in her explorations of the countryside surrounding Scholten, so maybe it had become blocked over the years by rockfalls or subsidence, or maybe had even been deliberately sealed. It didn't really matter because they were heading where they wanted to go.

The question was, where was that? The lower the lift descended, the less the creaking of its supporting rope could be heard, the sound overwhelmed by a growing hissing and pounding coming from below, as if machines were at work in the rock. As the sounds became so loud that the shaft itself began to vibrate, Slowhand looked to Kali for some kind of explanation, but she could only shrug. It was only when – at last – the lift reached bottom and they negotiated a small tunnel that their source became clear. Staggeringly so.

"My gods," Slowhand said. He, like Kali, was staring into a

natural cavern in the bedrock far beneath Scholten that was bigger than the Final Faith's distribution centre, looming above them into shadow and dropping away beneath them to a bubbling lava lake some hundred feet down. The lake surrounded an island of rock that rose out of it to their eye level, and on that island – connected to where they had entered by a narrow and recently suspended bridge – stood a structure that was far from natural and could only be the secure location of the fourth and final key. Looking something like a cross between a kiln and a furnace, its width that of seven men and its height of five, the stone dome sat solidly on the island perch, pistons positioned all around its circumference pumping out great bursts of black smoke while, in the centre of its roof, a round hole, some kind of chimney, belched out thick clouds of steam. If, Kali reflected, the Spiral of Kos had had a distinctly elven feel about it, then this site had dwarf written all over it in letters bigger than the dwarves themselves.

She wondered what kinds of traps dwarves favoured.

As if on cue, a piercing scream emanated from somewhere within the stone dome, and a few moments later Makennon and a bunch of cronies stormed out of the single entrance. Kali and Slowhand hid as the group passed, Makennon clearly cheesed off, and Kali presumed that she had just lost another of the tomb raiders she'd apparently been throwing at this thing.

This was her chance. The trouble was, she couldn't risk using the main entrance because Makennon had likely left guards behind and, as far as she could see, that left her with only one choice.

Slowhand saw her staring at the chimney, timing the gaps between its eruptions of steam.

"Oh, no. No, no, no. No, Hooper, no."

"Don't worry. You aren't coming with me."

"Of course I am. But not that way."

"There is no other way, Slowhand. But no, I need you to stay here. Watch my back in case Makennon returns."

"You think I'm letting you go in there alone?"

"Listen, you *just* said –"

"I *know* what I said –"

"Slowhand, listen. Think back to the night of my escape. Now look at those belches of steam. There's *no time* for us both to go."

Slowhand couldn't argue the point, and sighed. "Fine, I've got your back. But Hooper, this is still suicide."

"Since when did that ever stop me?"

Kali moved across the bridge, clinging to its cabling and staring down at the bubbling red lake below. *Lava,* she thought, *luvverly.* Reaching the dome, she worked her way around the outside rim of the structure until she had moved completely behind it, she wondering idly if this dwarven thing had remained active since the day it was built. That seemed unlikely. It was far more probable that Makennon had either accidentally triggered its mechanisms in her efforts to recover the key or one of the less than capable tomb raiders she'd hired hadn't been able to resist pulling some nice, shiny lever on the wall.

You just couldn't get the staff these days.

Kali wasted no time. She leapt for the side of the dome and scrambled onto its sloping surface, feet scrabbling behind her but maintaining enough purchase to enable her to grab a fingerhold on the rough stone. This done, she pulled herself slowly upwards until she reached the apex of the dome, ducking back as the chimney belched out a cloud of steam. Once it had done so, she peered inside the flue. A shaft dropped away before her, dark, dirty and utterly uninviting – just the way she liked it.

She sat back while another cloud erupted. Two minutes between belches. She was going to have to be very precise in the matter of timing. She would also have to be ready for anything as she would be going in blind, literally plunging into the unknown. But whatever was going on in this fiery hole, it seemed likely that the chimney would take her to the heart of the matter.

She stared across the cavern, found Slowhand and then jabbed her finger downwards, indicating she was going in. The archer's mouth opened, his head shook, and then he was holding it in his hands in disbelief.

Another cloud belched, and Kali scrambled inside.

She anchored herself against the sides of the chimney with her elbows and thighs, shuffling quickly down, estimating it would take her no more than a minute to descend the depth of the dome, more than enough of a safety margin between belches of steam. Quite how she'd exit the chimney near its base she hadn't yet worked out, but that she considered to be one of the challenges of her trade.

Something, though, was wrong – that was already becoming clear. All she could see beneath her was darkness, the perspective of the flue veeing below, and she suddenly realised that the shaft went deeper than she'd anticipated, the heart of the site not within the dome but the pitsing rock itself.

In other words, she'd never make it in time. Already she could hear booms coming out of the darkness below, what she presumed to be precursors of the next release of steam. There was only one thing for it – and that was to let herself freefall as far as she could.

Kali released her grip and immediately plummeted down the flue. She yelped as she slid down, down and down, her body thudding painfully into the sides of the shaft. More than once she crashed against unexpected ridges or bars, and the impacts bounced her sideways and around until she was in danger of becoming utterly disorientated in the dark. She couldn't allow that, however, or she'd be encountering the origin of the steam first-hand, something that just might spoil her day and the rest of her life.

She had to risk it. She jammed herself against the sides of the shaft once more, careering a further ten feet before she came to a jarring halt, and then looked down to see just where in the general scheme of things she'd ended up.

As it turned out, she'd made her move *just* in time. Not far below her the shaft widened and then branched off in a number of directions, splitting to envelop some central core. Had Kali continued down any one of them she would have been dead, because in each a lapping red glow was reflected from what could only have been the lava lake itself.

Kali didn't want to go there. But she did want to get inside the central core.

She eased herself down what remained of the shaft before it split, aware of the limited time she had but also that one slip would bring the same instant death as being consumed in a belch of steam. She dropped onto the roof of the central core and quickly heaved open a metal panel she found there. Dropping into a shaft of about her own height, she slammed the panel shut just as a final boom heralded a release of steam that made the metal above her rumble with the force of its release. Kali sighed with relief, but it was a short sigh, because as much of a challenge as getting this far had been, she suspected the hard part was yet to come. This was, after all, the site that Makennon had been trying to access since last she'd been in Scholten – and it was whatever lay below the *second* panel – the one she now found under her feet – that was going to be the true test of her mettle.

Kali pulled a rope from her toolbelt and secured it to the side of the shaft, dangling from it as she booted the panel open. Then she moved herself around until her head peeked through a hole on one side of a curving ceiling.

Well, she thought, *this is interesting*.

She was looking down into what appeared to be a dwarven forge, a circular chamber whose floor and walls were plated with metal panels decorated with the same repetitive runic shapes as had been at the Spiral of Kos, except here they were crosses instead of circles. The design of the walls made them look as if they might rotate, allowing access in and out, but for now they were tightly shut. Beyond this, the chamber was featureless apart from the forge itself, a raised and central metal mould carved with a complex coil design, in which lay the fourth of the keys. The parallel was obvious – other than for the fact this chamber was claustrophobic rather than vast, it was a dwarven version of the Spiral of Kos, right down to the presence of an observation area built into a curve of the wall behind a window of what appeared to be reinforced glass.

It was also, quite clearly, designed to be equally deadly. What Kali had ignored until now was the fact that the floor of the forge was blackened here and there by the twisted and charred remains of Makennon's unsuccessful tomb raiders, all of whom appeared to have been roasted alive, and one of whom still smoked where he or she had recently fallen.

It hadn't been too hard to work out that the trap here was going to be heat-based, but now it was time for her to find out exactly what she was up against. And if she was right...

Kali dug in her toolbelt and pulled out a small, polished stone she kept for such occasions, then dropped it towards the forge's floor. It struck one of the metal panels and bounced onto another, then another, and, with a moment's gap between them, the first and third panels sank slightly into the floor with a grating sound.

Kali smiled. She knew it. The panels were weight-sensitive, probably rotating at random to provide a false sense of security but in actuality trapping anyone who thought they'd found a safe path to the forge. All she had to do now was find out what they did.

On the subject of which...

She felt the heat before she saw it, the carved coils on the side of the mould turning first a dull red, then brighter, and then brighter still until they were almost white-hot. Kali knew now the reason for the dome's pistons and steam chimney – they had to be part of some elaborate mechanism that pumped lava into the dome from the lake surrounding the island, probably pressurising and concentrating its flow before delivering it here, to the forge itself. The carvings on the mould were not simple decorative patterns, they were sophisticated heating coils.

And what heat! Kali had to draw back into the shaft as the mould itself began to glow, gradually matching the intensity of the coils, and as it heated up, so too did the key inside. And after perhaps half a minute, watched through a heat haze, the key seemed to start receding away in her vision.

Only it wasn't receding, she realised, it was melting.

A few seconds later she stared down at a key that had become completely molten.

It wasn't what Kali had been expecting, but she had to admit it was ingenious. This place hadn't been built so much as a trap as a preventative, the mechanisms involved designed not to stop anyone stealing the key but to stop them *leaving* with it. The fact that that same anyone would die horribly, roasted alive by the heating coils, was simply a side effect.

The weight-sensitive panels reset themselves with a metallic chuk and the key started to cool again. Fitting exactly into the mould as it did, it started to regain its form in no time.

Kali knew now what she had to do. There was no way she could reach the key with her rope so instead she was going to have to play a game. And it was going to be exactly the same game she used to play as a girl, disturbing the regulars in the Flagons. Its aim was to get all the way around the bar using only furniture – okay, and the occasional head – and *without* touching the floor.

Exactly like that game. Only deadlier. So much so that every one of her movements had to be precise.

Kali took a steadying breath, and then slowly lowered and then removed her hands from the rope so that she was suspended only by the waist, then turning face downwards let her body find its own level as the rope took her weight. It was a delicate balancing act but, when stabilised, she was able to raise her arms and legs so that she hung horizontally spread-eagled, her limbs outstretched.

She gave a small kick, and turned, examining the chamber about her. There was a ledge there she could use, a ridge in the wall over there, and – *whoah, difficult one* – a slight rib between panels there. But then she'd be next to the key. *Okay,* she thought, running it through her head again – *One, ledge, two, ridge, three, rib... four, key.*

Oh, the hells with it, just go!

Kali swung forwards on the rope, building enough momentum to carry her over the first gap, then cut her rope cleanly with her knife. She sailed away, arcing forwards, hit the ledge and twisted, at the same time kicking herself away with her foot. Flipping forwards, somersaulting smoothly in mid-air, she felt her toes touch the ridge and lunged forwards, spinning this time slightly to her right, correcting her balance with a flap of her arms as her hip grazed the wall. There wasn't enough width in the ridge to keep that balance for long so she hopped quickly along it, only at the last second batting the wall with her hand so that she flew sideways out into the room. She let herself fall, inclining head first, then landed on the rib with the palms of her hands, immediately cartwheeling once, twice, then three times, and coming upright at the exact point the rib came to an end. Flexing her legs and bouncing as she returned to vertical, she leapt upwards and forwards, yelling with the exertion it took, and crossed the final gap between herself and the key. Landing on the edge of the mould on the balls of her feet, she windmilled her arms once more for balance, then stood upright, looking down at the object she sought.

Piece of pits, Kali thought. She only wished she could have done that sort of thing as a kid. It would have earned her a drink or two.

Kali bent and extracted the key from the mould – *oh, ooh, ow, ow, ow* – a little prematurely as it happened. She juggled it from hand to hand, her heart lurching as she almost dropped it on the third pass, then sighed with relief as it cooled. The key firmly in her grip, all she had to do now was get out of the place. She was about to start examining the walls for an escape route when a long rumbling signalled the rotation she'd suspected they were capable of. A number of doors were revealed, which then opened – a spiral stairway visible beyond them – and in each stood one of Makennon's people, aiming a crossbow directly at her. If that wasn't bad enough, framed in the last to open was Makennon herself – and beside her was Killiam Slowhand.

He didn't speak. But Makennon did.

"Miss Hooper, we meet again," she said. "Pray, tell me, what brings you here today?"

Kali smiled. "Oh, you know, out for a walk, fell down a hole..."

"And there was I thinking you'd taken up a career as a chimney sweep. You should, you know – as an occupation it's much less hazardous."

"But not as rewarding," Kali said, holding up the key.

"Give me that key, Miss Hooper."

"No." Kali looked down at the panelled floor. "Want to come get it, Anointed Lord?"

"I'd rather you just threw it to me."

"Not going to happen."

Slowhand spoke for the first time. "Hooper, just do it. The lady has you outgunned."

"Nice backwatching, Slowhand."

"They had us marked as soon as we entered the cavern. Took me as soon as you disappeared inside. I guess they wanted you to do the job for them. Give her the key, Kali."

"She's not getting the final key!" Kali shouted. She hovered on the edge of the mould, her intention clear. "It melts with me, if need be."

Makennon sighed loudly. "I gather that since our last talk you have been doing some research into the keys and what they are?"

"I've seen and heard a few things."

"And I imagine this *behaviour* is because you veer to the... darker interpretations of the facts to hand."

"That's right. End of the world, and all that. But hey, I'm not the one blinded by holy light."

Makennon smiled coldly. "I understand your concerns, I do. But

I have seen insufficient darkness to dim that light, and perhaps the opposite is true of you. So, as I once said to Mister Slowhand – what if I could prove to you that it were otherwise?"

Kali faltered momentarily, remembering what she had seen on the map. But she dismissed the concerns quickly. This was, after all, *still* the Final Faith.

"Makennon, you're not getting your hands on this key."

"Hooper..." Slowhand urged again.

"Slowhand, no! This thing is dangerou –"

Kali never even saw it happen. One second Slowhand had no bow in his hand, and then he did – and an arrow knocked the key from her grip, its trajectory perfectly aligned to bounce the key to Makennon's feet. The Anointed Lord bent to pick it up.

"Thank you... *Lieutenant*," she said.

Kali stared at the archer. She didn't know what to say.

"Hooper, they'd have –" Slowhand began, but broke off as a sudden push from Makennon sent him sprawling into the centre of the chamber. At the same time, Makennon and her guards retreated, and the walls began to rotate back to their closed position.

The last thing Kali heard from the Anointed Lord was, "Gentlemen, we have an appointment in Orl."

The wall sealed itself with a jarring thud. And the floor beneath Slowhand sank slightly with a grating sound.

The coils in the mould began to glow.

Slowhand took a look at the charred bodies and the reddening mould. "Oh, pits," he said.

"Pits?" Kali repeated. Now that the mechanism was activated there was no reason to stay perched where she was, and she jumped down, trying to find a way to reopen the wall. There was none. "That's all you can say after betraying me?"

"They would have killed you, Hooper, you know that. I was saving your life."

"Maybe," Kali said. Now she was pulling at the panelling, trying – desperately – to find some kind of off switch. Again, none, and sweat was already breaking out thickly on her body. "Dammit!"

She stared at the mould, at the window of the observation area and back again. That done, she moved with Slowhand to the rim of the chamber, but the heat was still intense – as intense as it would need to be to make the key molten in a matter of seconds.

And seconds was all they had, because her hair had begun to smoke. Her double take on the mould and the windows had given her an idea of how to get out of there, though, even if it would take split-second timing. But first she needed to deal with Slowhand. She needed him but his breathing was becoming increasingly laboured – he was having a much harder time of it than her.

Kali dug into her toolbelt and pulled out what appeared to be a small conch. The shape of it was something that could be bitten down on in the mouth, and Kali did this, testing the thing with a couple of inhalations before handing it to Slowhand.

"Use this," she said. "It'll be easier."

Slowhand took the conch, bemused. What, she thought he'd feel better if he could listen to the sea? He looked inside, and then recoiled. There were things inside – horrible, little, pulsing, slimy things.

"Don't ask me," Kali said. "But they produce oxygen. The supply's limited but it does gradually refill. Go ahead, chomp down, it'll make a difference."

Slowhand did so, reluctantly. And his eyes widened as the *things* did what they did, filling his lungs with cool air. "Fwer joo ged theef fings?"

Kali shrugged. "That one? That one I bought from a pirate in a little place called Crablogger Beach." She dug in her belt again. "*This* one, however, I found in an elven ruin – and I've had it for a long, long time."

Slowhand stared at her questioningly as Kali rolled the icebomb in her hand, remembering her encounter with Merrit Moon all those years ago. "Keep it because one day you might need it," he'd said. *Well, old man, guess what...*

"If this thing still works, things in this room are about to go from very, very hot to very, very cold very, very quickly. You know what happens when things do that?"

"They blow up in your face?"

"A-ha. So find somewhere to use as cover."

"Hooper, there *is* no cover."

Kali looked upwards. "Then Killiam Slowhand is going to have to be a little bit faster for once."

Slowhand followed her gaze. "Understood."

"Right, then," Kali said. She pressed the stud on the globe and threw it towards the forge. For a second nothing happened, and then everything before their eyes exploded and turned white.

The old man had not been exaggerating about the power of these things. It might have been tragically effective when he'd used one outside, but in these close confines it was almost elemental in its impact.

The forge frosted, and they waited. The floor cracked beneath their feet. The very air they breathed seemed to be crystals, and still the pair of them waited. The timing had to be perfect.

The two of them were covered in a thin sheen of ice now, and shivering violently. Their breath froze as it left their mouths.

There was a crackling sound from above, perversely sounding as though the forge were on fire.

The glass of the observation chamber frosted from left to right, as if something invisible had painted it white.

"Now, Slowhand!" Kali shouted.

The archer struggled to steady his grip. Kali could hardly blame him. She, too, was shaking like a leaf.

"Slowhand..."

Slowhand let fly three arrows in quick succession, the first spidering the frozen glass, the second cracking it and the third shattering it completely.

The glass blew out at the same time the forge exploded. Sharp slices of death – glass and metal – rained and hurtled at them from above and below.

They didn't hang around to feel their touch. As soon as his final arrow impacted with the wall of the observation chamber behind the glass, Slowhand grabbed Kali about the waist, circling her so his hand could still grab the rope, and then launched the pair of them up towards the broken window, frozen hand alternating with frozen hand as they climbed.

Behind and below them the forge didn't know what to do with itself, the chunks of the mould that had landed on its floor again triggering the heating coils at the same time as they crackled with intense cold. And as Kali and Slowhand reached window level, the stark contrast between temperatures caused a renewed series of explosions, and the whole chamber blew.

Kali and Slowhand were sent hurtling towards the observation area wall, thudded into it and landed on the floor, stunned. But as its floor subsided beneath them, they knew there was no time to waste.

The whole place was going up.

They ran, exiting first the observation area and then the dome itself, the whole place quaking beneath them. Makennon and her party had already left but some guards remained. They were not concerned with Kali and Slowhand, however, as they were too busy screaming and running for their lives.

The reason for this was that the lava lake surrounding the dome had ceased its gentle bubbling and become now a seething, broiling mass that lurched and spat at the rock that contained it. Thick, liquid fire had even begun to spit above its lip and, as Kali and Slowhand looked on one last, unfortunate woman was engulfed in a burning tongue that fried her screeching form to a skeleton in less than a second.

Those same lava spurts hitting them wasn't their main problem, however.

It was the lava spurts that had hit the suspension bridge.

Because as they watched, their only way off the central island warped and twisted in the intense heat, and then its cabling snapped away with a sound like a whiplash.

Almost instantly, the bridge was gone.

"Hooper?" Slowhand said, worriedly.

Kali looked down, her brow beetling. "We're stuffed," she said, succinctly.

What she neglected to mention was what Slowhand had not yet noticed. Because she didn't want to worry him more.

The lava lake was rising.

CHAPTER FOURTEEN

RESURRECTION WAS A second coming. Somewhat more than a second, actually, but in the circumstances Merrit Moon thought it would be churlish to complain about the delay.

The sharp intake of breath with which he returned to life echoed around the cave of the ogur, empty now apart from the ogur themselves, gathered in a tribal huddle where, by the look of the cleanly gnawed bones around them – *all* of the bones of Munch's people – they had been sitting for some time. They stared at him in silence, their expressions a mix of fascination and fear caused by what was likely the strangest occurrence they had ever seen.

The occurrence was no less strange to Moon himself, this being the first time he had died.

Or not – as the case seemed to be.

That the artefact had worked – albeit in a way and on a subject he would never have anticipated – renewed his faith in the Old Races and the wonders, rather than the horrors, they had once achieved. He doubted, however, that the ogur that had triggered the amulet had found its effects wondrous in any way, and he sighed. Perhaps it was a horror after all.

The poor creature knelt before him, hand outstretched and touching the amulet, but it was not what it had been. Where moments before it had been indistinguishable from the rest of its tribe – solid and formidable, awesome – it was now a shadow of its brothers, wasted and drained. The same ogur that had attempted to approach Kali – likely the alpha – it had obviously been the first to approach his body and it had paid the price.

The creature still breathed, haltingly and raspingly, and stared at him in utter helplessness and confusion, but there was nothing Moon could do to help it, and he felt deeply sorry. It had not, after all, been greed that had motivated the ogur to touch the amulet, just primitive curiosity. It had yet to learn – and he hoped it would have the chance to do so – that all that glistened was not gloob.

Therein lay the simple beauty – and horror – of what the amulet was. Moon thought back to his hidden room in his cellar in Gargas, and the mixed emotions the sight of it had engendered in him. Sitting there on the shelves amidst other acquisitions he had deemed too dangerous for even someone such as Kali to see, its physical beauty was undeniable – a scintillating, perfectly faceted gem inlaid in gloob that could have been used to pay the ransom of a king. It was for that reason that he kept the amulet locked away, because if the wrong eyes were ever to see the gem it would be impossible to resist, taken from his possession with no knowledge of what it truly was and what it truly did. Not that he didn't trust Kali implicitly on that level, of course. It was just that by the amulet's very nature – the fact that in the absence of the direst circumstances it could not be tested – it was unpredictable and therefore potentially very, very dangerous.

He had found the amulet in an elven site many years before, certain as soon as he had that it was more than it seemed, because if there was one thing he had learned in his long career it was that Old Race artefacts generally were. It had taken two years of research following the find to identify what it was, cross-referencing a dozen Old Race manuscripts, until he finally knew that what he had acquired was an example of a battlefield boobytrap that the elves called scythe-stones. Products of their science or their sorcery – or both, he still wasn't sure – they masqueraded as spoils of war, prime to be plucked from the fallen body of an elven victim, but in actuality what they did was transfer the life essence from a victorious warrior to the defeated at the moment of death, reversing their roles and effectively turning the tide of many a battle. The psychological effect on the surrounding enemy was not to be underestimated either, because the host body fleetingly absorbed some of the features of the victim, looking almost as if its soul were being stolen from the body. In a way it was, Moon supposed, and to the enemy – the superstitious dwarves – the supernatural aspect was often far more disturbing than the truth of what had actually happened.

Moon looked at the ogur again, and frowned. The efficacy of the amulet couldn't be denied – he was, after all, alive – but nevertheless something seemed to be wrong. For one thing, the process was meant to be almost instantaneous, and for another he... didn't feel quite right. Whatever was happening here wasn't happening the way it was meant to, and apart from his own discomfort it was evidently prolonging the agony of the poor creature before him. As Moon watched, the ogur's body and features seemed to shrink in on themselves even more than they already had, the blue wisps that were still being drawn from it by the amulet seemingly extracting its essence still. Moon was, as yet, still too weak to move, and so he had no choice but to witness the process continuing for another few minutes, at the end of which time he turned his eyes away. For the amulet had taken everything from the ogur, and now, in the end, the beast all but disintegrated before him, collapsing into a desiccated heap on the cave floor.

The amulet snatched what wisps of it remained in the air with a sigh.

Wrong, Moon thought. *That was wrong*. And the other ogur in the cave obviously thought so, too, because now they were stirring from their prone positions, grunting with what sounded like growing confusion and agitation. What was happening? Now that their alpha was dead, had their deferment to him ceased? Was he now as exposed to their primal hunger as Kali would have been had she remained in the cave?

No, Moon thought, *it wasn't that* – but it made his situation no less dangerous. Something had to have changed about him during the revitalisation process – perhaps something as simple as his scent – and the reason that the ogur were no longer deferring to him was because to their senses he was no longer the man they had deferred to before. The end result, however, was the same. He was no longer welcome here amongst the ogur – not as anything but food, that was – and he had to get out of their cave before their slowly revising opinion of him resulted in his being ripped apart.

Moon rose from the cave floor, slowly and cautiously, noting as he did that his resurrection seemed to have booned his old and tired limbs with a renewed resilience and strength that he had not felt for a good many years. This was hardly the time to celebrate the fact, however, because while the ogur's state of confusion seemed to have passed, their agitation had grown markedly. Their grunts were becoming more frequent now, their mannerisms more threatening – and their gaze more hungry.

Slowly, Moon bent to retrieve his staff and backpack, and then with equal slowness he eased towards the tunnel that led out of the cave. The ogur gathered about him as he moved, sniffing at him, clawing curiously at his clothes, and Moon realised that it was probably only a matter of seconds before one of them actually lunged. He was having to push his way between them now, and could feel their clawings becoming heavier, more insistent. And then one of them did what he'd been expecting and grabbed him roughly by the arm, attempting to rip the limb away.

Moon batted the ogur off and *roared*.

What? he thought. What had that just been? What had he just *done?* That he'd actually been able to physically repel the ogur? That he'd made that *noise?*

Oh, this wasn't good. This wasn't good at all.

It was not, however, the ideal circumstance to dwell on the matter, and for now all he could do – what he *needed* to do – was take advantage of it. The remaining ogur, it seemed, had been as disturbed by his unexpected actions as he had himself, and their clawings had become more hesitant, in some cases even ceased. And the ogur that had lunged for him was actually retreating submissively back into the cave.

What is happening? Moon wondered. Were the ogur, after all, deferring to him? Or were they perhaps sensing some of the alpha whose life essence he had stolen away? Whichever of the two it was, he knew that he needed to press the issue before they changed their minds again.

Instinctively, he roared for a second time. And this time, without even thinking about doing it, he repeatedly thumped the rock of the cave walls in warning.

By all the gods, what was happening?

The ogur – all of them, now – backed off into the cave, and, free from their threat, Moon turned towards the exit. A second later he emerged onto the ice plateau and, again before he knew what he was doing, began inhaling deeply of the air.

No, he realised, he wasn't inhaling it, he was *sniffing* it.

And on it, he could smell Kali Hooper.

Impossible. It was just impossible. He had no idea how long he had spent in the cave but it was not an inconsiderable amount of time, and yet Kali was *there* on the air, as if she had left him only a moment before, her scent traceable despite the stench of the ogur cave and the blizzard that still numbingly blew outside it. She was as clear as day to him, as vital as if she had remained nearby – but she hadn't, he knew, and he realised he was smelling a scent that should long ago have become undetectable to the human nose. A *human* nose, but not that of a creature that survived by...

Moon remembered the resilience and strength he had felt as he had risen from the cave floor, remembered the batting away of the ogur and his roar, remembered his hammering of the cave walls. Most of all, he remembered that he had not felt... *quite right*. Gods, he knew there was meant to be a fleeting transference from a victim but was it possible the amulet had somehow – ?

He lifted his palms to his face, feeling the features there. He half-expected to feel those of an ogur bulging beneath his fingers but, no, his face still felt like his own. He looked down at his body, and it too seemed to be the same. Only...

He gazed at one of his own footprints, frozen in the plateau ice. The footprint was from before he had entered the ogur cave and he turned to place his foot beside it. And the footprint was smaller.

Merrit Moon's heart sank. So, he had changed, then. Perhaps

was still changing. The only question was, to what degree and at what pace? The artefact that he had brought with him into these mountains in the hope that it – if it became necessary – would buy him more time to complete his mission had, instead, infused him with not only the ogur's life essence but part of the ogur itself. How and why that should happen, he didn't know – perhaps it was something to do with the ogur's body chemistry, or perhaps the fact that their species were so different that it was the only way the amulet could cope with the transference – but whatever the cause it left him with but a single thought: *Oh gods, Kali, what have I done?*

Thinking of his protégée made Moon's heart sink even further. He had taken no pleasure in not telling her about the amulet, in fact it had pained him greatly, but how could he have told her when even he was not sure whether the artefact would work? As she had knelt over his dying form, what right had he had to build up her hopes by telling her he might yet live if there was a danger those hopes would be shattered if the artefact failed to work? No, he couldn't have done that to her, any more than he could have let her touch the amulet at the moment of his passing. *Damn Munch*, he thought, because if that little thug had finished the job instead of leaving him to suffer then it would be him who would now be lying on the cave floor, as dried and as drained and as dead as he deserved to be.

Moon caught Kali's scent on the air once more, and he wondered where she now was. Had she succeeded in finding the information she needed, and was she on her way to protect the other keys? One thing he did know, he needed to find her, not only to help, if he could, but to let her know that he lived, even if it was not in quite the same fashion as he had lived before.

He began to trudge down the mountain, his legs feeling strangely powerful beneath him, and he drew a deep breath into his lungs so that they expanded as he had never known them to do before. There were obviously some advantages to his changing form, and if he could use his apothecarial skills to prevent any further changes – if they were to come – then he had to admit that he might not be too discomforted by his strange fate, after all. If he was going to find Kali, however, he would need to seek medicines or potions in Andon or Fayence, because there would be no time to sweep north to...

Merrit Moon faltered. He suddenly realised that he couldn't remember where he lived. Gar – ? Garg – ? *Oh, this was ridiculous. Damn the hells, where was it that Thrutt lived?*

Thrutt? he thought. *No, his name wasn't Thrutt, it was –*

Ah. So that was how it was going to be. Clearly, he was still changing, and the changes to him were not going to be merely physical, they were going to be mental as well. However much of this creature – this *Thrutt* – now resided within him, he was possibly faced with a battle for dominance that only one of them might win.

Far from fearing that possibility, the idea intrigued him. The ogur obviously had the advantage on the physical side, but on the mental he would equally obviously be the victor. This thing was a creature of instinct and sensation, a hunter and a cannibal, but nothing more. In other words, for such a big head, there was remarkably little going on upstairs. It had no rationality, no logic, no intelligence with which it would be able to hold its own, and so...

Again, Moon faltered. *Did that make sense?* he wondered. A situation such as this had no precedent after all. He wasn't talking about a possession here, and this was no mere battle of body and wills, this was something completely different, a process forged in the minds of beings who... of beings who...

Moon suddenly found himself confused by his own chain of thought, and then a wave of blackness washed through his brain that left him momentarily dizzy and blank. He tried to pull the thoughts back but suddenly realised that he no longer knew what they were. He'd been thinking about... thinking about...

The sound of Thrutt's roar echoed through the mountains.

No! Moon thought. He had to get a grip on this, on himself, at least until he could find those medicines or potions that might help. But if he was going to do that then he had to hurry, hurry, hurry, because Andon and Fayence were both so very far away and he had never been there before.

But wait – of course he had. So many, many times.

Hadn't he?

Moon began to pound down the slopes below him, passing a place where tracks intersected, forcing himself to think about anything and everything that made him what he was. He thought of his shop, he thought of Horse, he thought of his adventures and, inevitably, he thought of Kali. He was glad that he had been able to tell her how much she meant to him because he had never been able to do that before, as he had never been able to share with her the secret of how he had found –

There was a sudden stinging sensation in his right side, and he paused, rumbling curiously. Another such sensation stung him on his left, and this time he slapped at the part of his body where it had occurred. The sting transferred itself to his hand, and he lifted it – bigger than he remembered, and tinged slightly green – to see what had stuck there. It was a tiny dart that had caught in the soft flesh of the palm. And it looked like a piece of reed. *Needlereed.*

Moon's low rumble turned into a growl, and he sniffed the air around him, his nose jerking roughly as he did. There were men nearby. Men in hiding, at least four of them, and one of them smelled strangely familiar to him. Yes, he had the smell of one of the oomans who had invaded his cave...

No! Merrit Moon thought. Not his cave, the ogur's cave – but the smell of the man remained familiar all the same. And it made anger grow inside him – dark, uncontrollable, feral anger. He tried to stop it but he was losing his grip, could feel it, his thoughts running together, and the things that had stung him in his side, he saw that some substance dribbled from their ends, that it was on his skin and in it and...

Gods, no, what was happening, and why now – why?

As Merrit Moon roared more loudly, more primally, than ever before, the men with the needlereed darts came from behind the rocks and at him, but the toxins that had been fired into his system – the ones he had dimly thought had been meant to subdue him – had instead the opposite effect and stripped him of any fear of their coming. Primitive survival instincts taking over completely, Moon felt himself subsumed – drowned – by the primal reactions of a wounded beast and, dropping down into the depths of the dual consciousness he now seemed to possess, he found himself experiencing what happened next only as a kind of semi-aware observer. The observer was dully conscious of the fact, however, that it was not he who met the unexpected ambush but Thrutt the ogur.

Unfortunately, even he was not capable of defending himself against the ambush for long as the toxins were indeed working, albeit slightly more slowly than they might have done before, and as Thrutt batted away first one attacker and then another, the adrenaline – and strength – that had flooded his veins was slowly sapped by their effects until, by the time he had batted a man away for the seventh time, he was slowly sinking to his knees. As he did, three of the men picked themselves up from where they had fallen, examined the one who had been shattered against a rock and then cautiously moved forwards to loom above him.

Orders were given. And then he found himself being bundled into a wagon whose sides had been built as a makeshift cage. And as Thrutt stared out between the thick wooden bars, from somewhere within him Merrit Moon stared, too – right into the eyes of the man who had killed him.

"Make sure the wagon is secured and prepare to return to Scholten," Konstantin Munch ordered, slapping its sides. He stared at the ogur in captivity and himself growled. He did not like plans that did not go *according* to plan, especially when the plan was his own.

He thought back to the moment it had formed in his mind, the moment when, from his hiding place in a narrow crevice, he had observed the Hooper girl running from the ogur cave. That she had apparently somehow escaped Scholten's deep cells had come as little surprise – she was *extremely* resourceful, after all – but that she had seemingly recovered from her interrogation to such a degree *had* surprised him, though not as much as what had occurred after she had gone. The strange blue glow that had suffused the cave had drawn him from his hiding place with an overwhelming curiosity, and despite the danger he had eased himself painfully back down the cave, ignoring his own injuries from the ogur attack, to discover its source. What he had witnessed there, again from hiding, he knew of, but had never thought he would see. Perversely, though, the miracle of elven magetech was less important to him than the fact that the old man would live again – because now that he knew Kali Hooper was on the loose once more, it struck him that he might come in very useful as a hostage-cum-bargaining chip should the girl try to thwart his plans in the future. He would have taken the old man there and then, if he could, but the presence of the ogur and the fact that Moon seemed to have drawn a little more than life essence from his victim, stayed his hand. Instead, he had returned to his base camp and ordered his men there to construct the holding wagon in readiness for what would be the old man's inevitable descent from the hills. He knew he would be wanting to find his irritating pupil after all.

That, though, was when it had all gone wrong. Moon *had* descended from the hills, certainly, but the man he had caught in his ambush had borne scant resemblance to the man he had been when he had inserted his blade in his chest and guts and, in fact, had borne less resemblance as the ambush had progressed. Clearly, something had gone wrong with the scythe-stone process, which was tragic for the old man but even more so for him – for how was he meant to use Moon as a hostage when Hooper would be unable to recognise her mentor at all? No, unless this strange transformation reversed itself – which of course it *might*, which made it unwise to slaughter the beast – all he was stuck with was a sideshow freak, good only for the circus when it came to Ramblas Square.

Munch growled again and turned away from the holding wagon, wincing with pain. His injuries from the ogur attack were... troublesome and he ought to get them seen to. He turned to the mage he had left with the base party, intending to solicit some relief, but then saw that the woman was concentrating hard and staring into the distance in the way that those blessed – or cursed, he thought – with telescrying abilities did. Still, they did make life in the field somewhat easier.

Munch waited until she had finished, returning to reality hollow-faced, and with a shiver and a sigh.

"Well?" he asked.

"News from Scholten, sir. From the Anointed Lord. She wishes to inform you that she is in possession of the fourth and final key."

Munch drew in a deep breath. *At last.*

"There is something else, sir. A location where she wishes you to rendezvous with her party – the site known as Orl."

Munch laughed. *Yes, Orl,* he thought. *Orl indeed.*

He ordered his remaining people to break camp, and mounting the holding wagon instructed its driver to move out.

Towards the Final Faith's destiny.

Towards his own.

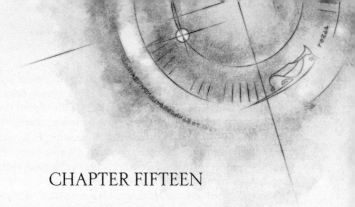

CHAPTER FIFTEEN

EVERYONE SEEMED INTENT on hot-footing it to Orl, and that included Kali Hooper. It was just that for the moment – oddly self-defeatingly – she was telling Slowhand not to move. Not an inch. In fact, she would have preferred it if he didn't even breathe.

It was nothing personal. Granted, it might have been *very* personal at one time but, since his recent reappearance, Slowhand had been somewhat helpful so the least that she could do was try to save his life.

The lava lake had calmed somewhat and was no longer belching out angry plumes of fire, but it was continuing to rise. It had almost reached them now and, any second, threatened to bubble over the lip of the rock on which they stood, at which time they would be hot-footing it whether they had escaped or not.

Thankfully, all was not lost – and, in a manner of speaking, Orl was not lost, either. The pair of them stood no longer on the island but on a small shelf of rock behind and across from the dome, on the opposite side to the incinerated bridge. They had managed to reach it through a combination of her gymnastics and Slowhand's ropes and arrows, an exercise in teamwork that had resulted in a couple of embarrassing tangles but had got them there in the end, she with a sprained thigh and he with a smile on his face.

The shelf, though, was a precarious perch, only a few inches wide and crumbling in an ever-increasing number of spots beneath their feet. But it did lead to a way out. Possibly.

Kali's reasoning that there had to have been an original entrance to the dome had, in their time of need, led her to seek it out as an escape route and, while successful in doing so, the tunnel she had found was blocked as she'd suspected it might be, manifesting itself now as a vague tracery of rocks beyond the remains of a long-collapsed stone bridge, some of the component parts of which had been visible as tiny islands in the lava before they had been consumed by the bubbling mire. Kali wasn't sure that the tunnel behind the tracery of rock was going to be passable and the only way she could find out was by removing the rocks from the tunnel mouth. The problem was, she had to do it very, very slowly and very, very carefully, otherwise the resultant rockslide would sweep them both into the hottest – and last – bath of their lives.

"You have to think of it like a jigsaw," she said slowly and quietly to Slowhand. She gently removed a rock with an archaeologist's hands, dropping it into the burgeoning lava with a plop. "Each piece dependent on the other to construct – or, in this case, deconstruct – the whole picture without forcing any one piece."

"Really?" Slowhand said, nodding, his arms folded tightly against his chest. He would have smiled at the way her tongue stuck out between her lips as she worked, other than for the fact the lava had reached the soles of his boots and they had begun to sizzle slightly. "Is this an easy jigsaw?"

"Urrm... somewhere between medium and challenging?"

"Right. Like a bowl of fruit with a binyano, an apple and a pear?"

"I guess so," Kali said. She removed another rock and dropped it away, freezing as the collapsed rocks left behind in the fall settled slightly. "If they've all been tipped on the floor and trampled by a betwattled cyclops."

"Fine. You are good at jigsaws aren't you?"

Kali's hand hovered over another rock before changing her mind and extracting the one next to it. Again, she dropped it away. "Nope. Never could stand the things."

"Oh, that's great. Hooper, look, how about that one there? No, that one. That one looks –"

"Will you stop waving your hands about and stand still?"

Slowhand hopped from foot to foot, his soles sticking and stringing whenever they made contact with the rock.

"Getting – a – little – difficult – to – do – that. Could you *please* get a move on?"

"*I'm trying, all right!*" Kali snapped. The sweat running off her now had as much to do with pressure as the heat of the lava. She bent and dropped a heavier rock, regretting snapping when Slowhand took the opportunity to wipe her brow.

"Just one more..." she said through clenched teeth. "Easy... easy..."

There was a sudden shift in the rockface, and then a low rumble, and Kali spun herself away from the front of the fall to flatten herself against the wall to its left. Slowhand needed no urging to do the same and, at the very second he spun to the right, the whole pile of rubble collapsed away from the tunnel mouth, avalanching down into the rising lake.

Behind the fall, the tunnel was clear.

"Go, go, go!" Kali shouted, and just in time. The sudden and dramatic fall of rocks into the lava had disturbed its recently calm rise and it began again to spurt and belch. Unnoticed by Slowhand as he darted into the shadowy tunnel mouth, a patch of the molten fire spattered onto his trouser leg, burning into the cloth, but before it could reach his skin Kali followed him in and tore the offending patch away.

"Don't get excited," she said. "That's all that's coming off."

"Hey, flesh happens," Slowhand retorted, and stared at her heavily perspiring form. "Hot stuff."

Kali shook her head – the man could never resist. She followed him into the dark, making out a winding tunnel that curved away into the rock. She hesitated to think when last it had been used, but for a second thought that she caught a stale whiff of whatever had been the last thing to tread the passage, something overtly male – the smell, perhaps, of dwarf? Her eyes adjusted further to the dark and all her instincts cried out for the time to examine her surroundings – especially as she could now see this was no mere cave but a constructed tunnel complete with those X-shaped dwarven runics – but that was simply not to be. The avalanche that had stirred the lava back into angry life had, it seemed, disturbed more than just the lake, perhaps ruptured another vent beneath the dome and, as she watched, the lava began to bubble into and then sweep with increasing acceleration up the tunnel behind them.

"Hooper," Slowhand said. "I strongly suggest that we run."

"Ohhh, running as we speak," Kali said, passing him.

Slowhand put on his own spurt and the two of them raced up the tunnel as fast as they could, but the collapsed rock at the dome entrance was not the only place where the integrity of their dark confines had been compromised, and every few feet or so they found their progress slowed by roof-falls which they had to clamber over. Thankfully, these same roof-falls acted also as makeshift dams – albeit briefly as it didn't take long for the lava to engulf them – and they managed to stay ahead of the flow. *Just.*

"Hooper, how far to the exit?" Slowhand asked, vaulting over another blockage in front of them.

Kali leapt in his wake, a spray of pebbles from her heel vanishing into the lava that was now immediately behind her. She slammed a palm onto the wall. "Not sure. But the temperature of the rock suggests we've still a way to go – maybe a tenth of a league?"

"Pits of Kerberos – *a tenth of a league?*"

"Excuse me! You *did* ask."

"I know but, hells, Hooper, sometimes I wish you didn't know as much as you do."

Kali stopped, slammed her hands on her hips and nodded back where they'd come from. "I got us out of there, didn't I?"

Slowhand sighed and grabbed her as the lava plopped over where they had vaulted, catching up with her heels. They ran on. "Maybe," he said, nodding ahead, though Kali was still so busied staring daggers at him that she hadn't noticed what he had.

"Fark."

"What?"

"The tunnel dips. Deeply. Some kind of U-bend."

"What?" Kali said again. "Why in the hells would it do that?"

Slowhand pointed towards the roof of the tunnel. "Maybe because of that."

Still moving, Kali looked up, then skidded to a halt. A few yards in front of them, the roof of the tunnel nosed downwards and changed in texture, no longer composed of rock but something else, some kind of fossilised remains, a dark and chitinous substance that reminded her of the brackan in the Sardenne. But these remains were not those of any brackan, because they were bigger – much, much bigger – and as well as nosing down they folded themselves through the walls on either side of the tunnel and into its floor, immortalised as an organic archway in the rock.

"The speed of this stuff, we'll never make it out the other side," Slowhand said.

Kali studied the dip, saw that the tunnel levelled out again beyond it and then turned her eyes on the fossil. These remains had to be hardy, considering it was clear to her that the dwarves had had no choice but to tunnel under them rather than through.

"Help me," she said, picking up a rock.

"Throwing stones at the lava won't make it go away."

"The fossil!" Kali shouted. "There, where it's been cracked by the tunnel subsidence! We can bring that part down!"

Slowhand looked exasperated. "Why?"

Kali leapt onto a slight rise of rocks at the tunnel's edge, avoiding the lava that had now caught up with them. Slowhand did the same on the opposite side, looking down warily as the red river overtook them and began to flow into the dip.

Kali smashed at the section of the fossilised remains with the rock. "'Liam, just help me!" she pleaded.

The urgency of her tone persuaded him and – though he still didn't have a clue what she hoped to achieve – Slowhand joined in. It took a fair number of strikes but finally the dark mass came loose from its resting place of ages and crashed down into the lava-filling dip, flipped over to become a bowl shape floating on the surface.

Some kind of carapace, it could just as easily have been a boat.

Kali began to hop from rock to rock at the side of the tunnel, towards it. "Move," she shouted.

Slowhand did as he was bidden, mirroring Kali, and it did not take him long to realise what she had in mind. And it was just a little bit frightening.

Kali reached the rim of the dip and hurled herself forwards, crashing into the bowl with an explosion of air and a grunt. Slowhand was half a second behind and almost didn't make it, but, as he threatened to shortfall into the roaring red river, Kali stood, balancing unsteadily, and grabbed his flying form by the scruff of the neck. She yanked him to safety and Slowhand crashed down next to her, winded.

The makeshift boat rose on the lava until it rode above the opposite side of the dip. And there, sailing the lava with its speed building slightly, it continued along the tunnel.

Slowhand stared at the passing rock walls, and down at the lava river, thinking it was a little like being on some carnival ride, only hotter. Like that new thing they'd had at Scholten Fair, the Tunnel of Luurrvv. The blupping of the lava even sounded quite romantic.

"Hooper..." he said, sweeping back his hair.

"Get your head down," Kali said.

Slowhand raised his eyebrows, looking surprised. "Don't you want to take things a little more slowly?"

"Down, you idiot!" Kali repeated and, as she spoke and Slowhand obeyed, the carapace slammed into a thick stalactite dropping from the tunnel roof. The impact sent the makeshift boat into a spin and it began to careen along the tunnel, crashing into its walls and generally out of control. As the pair of them clung to the carapace's sides, lava splashing all about them, it seemed to Slowhand that his Tunnel of Luurrvv had suddenly become a tunnel of soon to suffer very painful death.

Kali, though, didn't seem too perturbed.

"You get up to this kind of thing every day?" Slowhand asked, swallowing.

"Course not. Maybe once a week. Not enjoying the ride?"

Enjoying was not perhaps quite the word but Slowhand had to admit it was exhilarating, but only after the carapace had taken enough knocks without splitting open to reassure him that it might, after all, be safe enough to survive the trip. The flow of lava had sped up again beneath them, and now the carapace moved through the tunnel at dizzying speed, impacting and spinning with each new twist and turn as it made its inexorable way towards the tunnel's end. Then, suddenly, the tunnel began to slope downwards, its exit visible ahead. But the exit, too, was blocked.

"Hooper?" Slowhand said.

Kali smiled. "We'll be fine... fine."

Slowhand did not look convinced as they hurtled towards the pile of rocks blocking their only way out of the lava. He imagined the carapace shattering on impact, spilling them both into the lethal surge that would inevitably envelop them.

"You're saying you think this thing's strong enough?"

"Definitely," Kali said.

"How can you know?"

"Because," Kali began as the carapace slammed into the rock fall and broke through it. "This thing we're on," she continued as they sailed out into daylight, "has been down here a long, long time."

The carapace plummeted down some unknown hillside, the wind roaring past them, skimming the erupting lava flow as it went.

"Meaning?" Slowhand shouted.

"It belonged to something you don't see around any more!" Kali shouted back.

"What, for hells' sake –"

The carapace impacted with the hillside, bounced and flew. It bounced again, this time more violently, throwing them both into the air.

Kali flailed towards a landing and yelled, "*A drraaagggonn!*"

Slowhand stared at her and, while staring, thudded into the ground. He tumbled down the hillside, rolling, bouncing and cursing until, like Kali, he at last came to a bruised and aching stop. "A dragon?" he repeated.

"Oh, yeah," Kali said with exhilaration. She stood and stared at the carapace as it screed past them and then stopped further down the hill. Kali hadn't felt like it for quite some time but she whooped.

Slowhand stood and stared at the aftermath of their flight from the dome. The lava on which they had ridden was still gushing from the tunnel mouth above them, but the majority of it that had spilled forth was thickening in the outside air, turning grey and mottled on the slopes, smoke and steam rising from its curdling surface.

Kali stared into the distance. There, she could see that smoke also rose above the city of Scholten, and on the air she could just make out the distant ringing of the cathedral's alarm bells. She smiled. Makennon actually had something to be grateful to her for. If she hadn't opened the tunnel, giving the lava an escape route rather than letting it build as if in some huge pressure cooker, then there would be little left of the underground complex, and perhaps even her cathedral itself might now be reduced to rubble.

It was quite ironic. Kali Hooper – saviour of the Final Faith. Ah well, they could thank her later.

In the meantime, there was the small matter of a key to pursue. Four keys, actually.

"There's just one problem," Slowhand said. "We're stuck in the middle of nowhere and, in case you haven't noticed, we don't have any transport."

"Actually, we do," Kali said, and to Slowhand's surprise stuck two fingers in her mouth and whistled. "Little thing I've been teaching him," she said.

Slowhand looked baffled. "Teaching him. Teaching who?"

"Horse."

"Horse?"

"A-ha. Horse Too, to be precise."

"And where is this Horse Too?"

"Stabled in Scholten, where I left him."

"And you expect him to hear you whistle from here?"

"Horse is not your normal kind of horse."

"I see. Okay. Then just how is he going to get out of the stable, exactly?"

"Oh, he'll find a way."

Slowhand shook his head. Maybe the heat in the tunnel had got to Hooper after all. He was about to say something else when there was a sudden blur accompanied by the sound of heavy hoofbeats, and where there had been empty space between him and Kali a moment before he now found himself staring at something that resembled a Vossian siege machine. A large chunk of stable fencepost attached to a rope dangled from its neck.

"Slowhand, meet Horse. Horse, this is Slowhand."

The mysterious creature stared at him balefully, and snorted.

"What in the pits is that?" he heard himself asking.

"Bamfcat," Kali said simply.

Horse's tongue suddenly lashed out and wrapped itself around Slowhand's face.

Kali smiled. "I think he likes you."

"Mmmmrrrrumfff."

"Definitely."

"Grruuurrkk."

"Okay, Horse, that's enough. Let him go."

Seconds later, Slowhand found himself sitting behind Kali on the beast's back, Hooper leading him back to Scholten, a move he wasn't entirely sure was wise given the circumstances of their last visit. But Kali, as it turned out, only wanted to speak to the gate guard – and did so from a distance so she wouldn't be recognised.

"The Anointed Lord?" she shouted. "Has she left the city?"

"Three hours ago, Ma'am."

"Dammit," Kali said, looking to the west. Makennon now had the four keys – and therefore the location of the site – but she *still* only had a rough idea of where it was. "She could be taking any one of the three roads. If we lose her..."

Slowhand dismounted from Horse and examined the ground. It was thick with tracks heading into and out of the city, but he seemed confident as he pointed ahead and said, "Actually, she took that one."

"Slowhand, there's no way you could know."

"Take a look," the archer said.

Kali did, and laughed. "That woman's too full of herself for her own good," she said. She stared again at what could only be Makennon's tracks, because the horseshoes of her mount had been carved with the symbol of the Final Faith.

On her trail, they headed west, crossing Vos, and came within sight of Makennon's party as they travelled on towards the coast. Kali longed to pass the Anointed Lord, to reach Orl first, but she knew that without the exact location of the site, she and Slowhand could be seeking it out for weeks. The journey was long, Makennon and her party proceeding with the surety of something within their grasp that negated the need for haste, but their progress worked to Kali and Slowhand's advantage, allowing them to stop off in the coastal town of Malmkrug to acquire rations and essential supplies, including squallcoats for the worsening weather. Beyond Malmkrug, they passed along the southern rim of the Drakengrat Mountains, and there Horse sniffed the air, recognising the place where it had been found. The beast hung its head wistfully, though, because perhaps it did not recognise it as home.

The Drakengrats faded into the background as the party and their pursuers neared Oweilau, and here the coastline took a turn to the north-east, where eventually it would swing fully east once more, towards Dellendorf and, eventually, Freiport.

Kali did not think they would turn that far, however, as the location of the site had been towards the end of the peninsula, so they would likely stick to the western paths as far as they could go. This they did, and eventually came to point where they could be no more than an hour or two's travel from the Sarcrean Sea. Kali itched to continue ahead now that they were so close – was certain now that she would be able to find the site herself – but as Makennon's party made camp for the night it soon became clear that they could go no further for the time being. Camped bang in the middle of a gorge, there was no way they could get past them without being detected, and no way around without attracting the attentions of the shnarls who at night roamed the coastal rocks in vicious packs. No – all they could do was make camp for the night themselves, then get ahead of Makennon's party in the morning when they'd moved once more onto open ground.

The pair of them watched from a ridge as the Final Faith bedded down, their assorted wagons circled in protection. There was little to see, and Kali and Killiam were about to call it a night when, from the east behind them, more wagons made their way towards the camp. They had to have been behind them all the time and Kali and Slowhand hid as they passed, she snarling at the unexpected yet somehow inevitable arrival of the leader of the group.

"Munch," Kali said. "Pits, I should have known."

Slowhand frowned. "Munch, maybe. But what the hells is that?"

Kali looked at the caged wagon towards which Slowhand pointed, and immediately recognised the creature held therein.

"That," she said, "is one of the ogur from the World's Ridge Mountains."

"*They exist?*" Slowhand said.

"Oh yes."

"Care to tell me why Munch has brought it here?"

"Holiday by the sea?" Kali said. "No, seriously, I haven't a clue." She yawned.

"Time for bed, eh?" Slowhand said. "Just you and me and a seductively crackling fire?"

"You and me, maybe, but no fire, crackling or otherwise. This stage of the game, we can't risk them spotting us."

Slowhand sighed. There she went again, treating him like an idiot. "Actually, I already knew that. No matter," he added, winking, "instead we can get up close and personal, share some body heat."

Kali stared at him. "There's another possibility," she said. "In the Drakengrats, when bad weather hits and they can't get off the mountains, the high shepherds slice open the stomach of one of their flock and crawl inside for the night, using the intestines for warmth..."

Slowhand looked shocked. "You wouldn't – not Horse?"

"Who said anything about Horse?"

There was a moment's silence.

"I'll get some blankets from the saddlebags," Killiam said.

"Yes, you do that."

Minutes later, they had bedded down for the night, blankets a few feet apart. Lying in the azure darkness, each sipping on a bottle of flummox, Kali stared up at the night sky and its coming eclipse while Slowhand kept an uneasy eye on Horse, watching as the beast's tongue lashed out into the shadows surrounding the camp, snapping back every now and then with something dark, furry and squealing in its grip. The thing didn't *seem* to be interested in him any more, and so he turned his attention to Kali. The expression in her eyes as she stared at the stars troubled him.

"Hooper, how long have I known you?" he asked.

"Too pitsing long."

"I'm serious. I've known you long enough to know when something's bothering you. What is it?"

"What do you think, Slowhand? I lost two of my oldest friends."

"I know that. But I know there's something else." He paused. "The old man told you something in the World's Ridge Mountains, didn't he? Something about you, about the things you can do?"

Kali hesitated, and then told him about the old man's parting words, about how and in what circumstances he had found her, inside the sealed site.

Slowhand stared.

"How in the hells could it have been sealed?" he said. And after a delay, added, "Who are you, Hooper?"

"Slowhand, I wish I knew."

The archer saw Kali's expression grow reflective, and changed tack slightly in the hope he could cheer her up. "There's one thing I don't get. You came out of nowhere, an orphan with no family at all – so, why Kali Hooper? Where did you get the name?"

The question seemed to have the desired effect, and Kali smiled.

"Until I was about five, everybody just called me half-pint, but when I started to grow it didn't seem appropriate any more, so someone suggested I take Red's name instead. He wanted to call me after his mum, Dora. Dora Deadnettle, can you believe it? Needless to say, I vetoed that."

"Wise move."

"A-ha. So they suggested a number of other names but none of them worked, and I went back to being half-pint. Then, one night, Pete Two-Ties started staring at the beers and writing their names down, playing with the letters he got..."

"The letters?"

"The letters. And out of all of them, Pete found that one beer, in particular, worked."

"Which was?"

Kali took a swig of flummox. "Orki Hop Ale."

Slowhand couldn't help himself. He spat his flummox out.

"Wait a minute. Are you telling me that's all your name is – an anagram?"

"That's right. I'm named after a beer. Got a problem with that?"

Slowhand shook his head, swallowing hard. "No, no, no... no. Absolutely appropriate, really."

"I thought so."

Slowhand concentrated, mouthed letters. "Could have been worse, given what Two-Ties had to work with. Kira Pohole..."

"I don't think so."

"Erika Phool."

"No..."

"Karlie Pooh."

"All right, Slowhand, that's enough!"

They drank some more.

"Now it's my turn. You never told me – what is it between you and the Final Faith? Why the vendetta?"

Slowhand's expression darkened, and he stared off into the night. "That question's in a whole different league, Hooper."

Kali shifted onto her side, cradling her head in her palm. "I know. And if you don't want to tell me, that's fine. But I think you need to share with someone, Slowhand, and after what we've been through in the past few days..."

Slowhand sighed, and his eyes flickered as if viewing some distant memory. "I have a sister," he admitted, eventually. "A twin sister."

Kali had to admit she was gobsmacked. Somehow she had never thought of Slowhand as being, well, human. Not in the way of his having family, at least. She'd never really imagined him being a child, growing up – always seen him as he was now, having arrived in the world fully formed, grinning, winking and stroking back his hair. That there had been a sister that he had grown with was a double revelation to her.

"I never knew."

"There's no reason why you should have. Jenna was... taken before we met."

"Jenna," Kali said. "Hold on. What do you mean – taken?"

"The Final Faith," Slowhand said. "In their early days, and maybe still now – to build up their numbers – they had an indoctrination programme... actually, more like forced assimilation. Jenna was working in Freiport when the Faith's *recruiters* paid her a visit."

"She went willingly?"

Slowhand shook his head, took a long swig from his flummox. "Jenna didn't have a religious bone in her body. Before that day."

"What are you saying? That they brainwashed her?"

Slowhand stared at her. "You've experienced Querilous Fitch's manipulations first-hand. Yes, I believe they turned her, somehow – her and others."

Kali swallowed. "But why Jenna? And where is she now?"

"Jenna was a battlefield tactician for the Freiport Independents – I guess they had a use for her talents. As for where she is, I don't know – but not for want of looking. She could be garrisoned somewhere remote, maybe even a member of the Order of Dawn. But I'll find her, Hooper – if I have to tear the Final Faith apart, eventually I'll find her."

"I know," Kali said.

Slowhand lapsed into silence after that, and after a few minutes turned in his bedroll, settling himself down for sleep.

Kali lay there staring at him for a moment, deciding.

Maybe it was the flummox, but more likely it was the fact that Slowhand had just revealed a side of himself that she'd never suspected before.

She stroked his cheek.

"In the meantime..." she said.

And agony hit. Another vision. Only this time she was outside of herself, looking at her own body as it lay slung in the arms of an ogur. Her flesh was grey, her clothing thick with blood, and worst of all, she did not appear to be breathing.

The ogur pounded through the night, carrying her body and, as it went, it roared and roared and roared.

Kali heard herself scream.

"Hey, hey, hey!" Killiam Slowhand said urgently, soothingly, and as quickly as it had come, the vision was gone. Kali realised that she had screamed out loud and was wrapped in his arms and he was rocking her back and forth. "Bad dream, bad dream," he said. "Shush, shush."

The night had not turned out quite as she expected, but Kali did not move from Slowhand's arms. She continued to lie there and he continued to rock her back and forth, and she stared up at the stars.

So much had happened to her since this whole thing had begun – so much she didn't understand – but now at least she knew how it was all going to end.

She knew she was going to die.

Here. Soon.

And she knew what was going to kill her.

CHAPTER SIXTEEN

DAWN CAME – AND at the same time, didn't. The eclipse that had been on the cards for weeks was now finally coming to fruition, and instead of daylight replacing the azure twilight that had bathed them during a fitful sleep, a different kind of halflight made it seem as if the night simply continued on, imbuing the air with a languor that seemed to depress and slow the morning down. It was an atmosphere that failed to make Kali feel any better about her vision.

The languor did not last for long, however. The imminent cosmic conjunction also brought with it one of the worst storms Kali or Slowhand could remember, beginning with heavy and warm drops of rain that soon became splatters and then a downfall, this whipped by an increasingly tumultuous wind that Kali reckoned would be a full-blown hurricane within the hour.

The light and the weather worked to their advantage, though. Both of them donned squallcoats and, from the ridge that had sheltered their camp, watched and waited as Makennon and her expedition broke their own, ready to move out as soon as they did. Guiding Horse by a horn, they walked him through the gorge perhaps a hundred yards behind the Final Faith, their presence so close to the enemy group obscured and obfuscated by the driving storm. As soon as their party had passed through the gorge, Kali and Slowhand veered to the east, and when they were a sufficient distance away both of them mounted the bamfcat and rode him on. They could not spur Horse on to full gallop – the terrain near the edge of the peninsula was simply too treacherous, unpredictable and prone to landslip even in good weather – but that didn't really matter because, even at the rate they travelled, they had soon drawn ahead of Makennon and Munch.

They were going to find the site and they were going to beat the Final Faith to it. The only thing they had to do was work out what to do when they got there.

They continued on for another hour, checking occasionally that

Makennon's party remained behind them and that they hadn't missed something obvious – unlikely but still possible in the continuing storm. The sky darkened more and more as each minute passed, until it was a deep purple verging on black. It seemed logical that the worsening light would make finding Orl more difficult but, in fact, it was becoming an increasingly more simple task because they were running out of land. They could hear the Sarcrean Sea breaking violently on the far western edge of the peninsula now, and ahead of them Kali was just able to make out the looming and jutting stone of the coastal feature she had heard about but to this point never travelled this far west to see – the so-called Dragonwing Cliffs. The peculiar rock formations did sweep up on the horizon almost like wings, reminding them both of the fossilised remains in Scholten, but these were merely inanimate rock, carved over the years into their current shapes by the rather unique weather patterns of the nearby Stormwall. A meteorological anomaly that defied all natural explanation, the Stormwall wrapped the end of the peninsula about a league offshore, like a giant hand formed out of cloud, thunder, lightning and rain. No one had ever passed through it, only around it, and all shipping – what shipping dared this roughest part of Twilight's already tempestuous seas – avoided it by as much wheelage as they could. Why it was there – and why it maintained its roiling, booming and flashing presence in all weathers – no one knew, only that what lay beyond it – the Sarcre Islands – basked in a tropical weather system that was unknown anywhere else in the known world, and that, strictly speaking, should not exist.

The Stormwall and the Sarcre Islands, Kali thought. If she were to believe all normal accounts of this desolate part of the peninsula, there was nothing beyond them and nothing else here. But according to other accounts, there had to be.

Kali decided to tether Horse before they went any further, the terrain becoming too dangerous for his large and heavy form to negotiate. And, as it turned out, she did so just in time. Kali and Slowhand were making their way forwards, their long squallcoats flapping about them, when Twilight's distant sun moved fully behind Kerberos and its eclipse became full, plunging the Dragonwing Cliffs into almost total darkness. The pair could still see where they were going, by starlight, and just, but for the most part now the only guide they had to how close to the edge they were was the increasingly deafening roar of the waves crashing onto the rocks below. Even this, though, was only an intermittent guide, and they had to pause quite frequently when the sound of the sea was obliterated by the whistling and insanely howling wind.

Able to communicate only by gestures, they at last reached the edge, expecting to look down and see only the wild turmoil of the

Sarcrean Sea. For a moment their expectations were met but, then, glimpsed between squalls, they spotted what they might least expect to see in the presence of so much raging water – fire. Both faltered momentarily but, yes, fire it was – flickering and fluttering plumes floating on the surface of the water. No, Kali realised, after a second, not on the water but leading across the water, twin lines of wind-blasted and mounted torches, to be precise, forming a wide avenue that narrowed with perspective as it led out into the sea.

Kali followed the fiery avenue back with her eyes, able to distinguish more now that she knew what it was. The torches seemed to climb the cliff face, disappearing only the higher they came, where they were obscured by the very edge she overlooked. Swallowing slowly, she beckoned Slowhand to follow her, moving slightly along the cliff, and there the two of them found themselves standing at the top of a part of the Dragonwings that veered diagonally rather than vertically, an age-old projection down and beyond the cliff wall that was less precipitous than its bordering sides. The feature at first seemed natural but then revealed itself to be distinctly and unnaturally shaped. In fact, it appeared as if at some time long in its past the projection had been deliberately and laboriously carved into deep and broad increments that looked suspiciously like risers.

The hells with suspiciously, Kali thought. *They couldn't be anything else.* At the same time as Slowhand lowered his jaw in surprise, she realised she was looking down a mammoth flight of steps.

This was the site. Orl, it had to be, she'd found it. Her elation at the fact was, however, marred by the knowledge that, while the steps were clearly old, the torches were not. She might have beaten Makennon herself here but the Anointed Lord had obviously sent in advance troops, probably during the night, to prepare the place for her arrival. Gods, what was it with that woman – did she want everywhere she went freshly painted too? Would she only use a privy where people couldn't hear her tinkle?

Advance troops or not, she was still going in. The question was, into what? She hadn't until now known what to expect of Orl, but if she had pictured anything it wouldn't have been this. She stared at the avenue of torches again, leading into the sea. What exactly, she wondered, was Orl doing *out there?*

Kali patted Slowhand on the shoulder, pointing down, and the two of them moved onto the steps, but Slowhand halted her almost immediately, pointing out two sentries illuminated by the flare of the torches a good way below and away from where they stood. Both Final Faith thugs were positioned beyond what would have been the shoreline but on what, they could now see, was actually a rock jetty thrusting out between the waves. While their presence was a hindrance to Kali and Slowhand's immediate plan, what was more disturbing was what lay at the end of the jetty itself. For there, half-obscured by the lashing rain and battered by the thrashing waters, was an ominous-looking grey structure shaped something like a cowl. Enshrouding the end of the jetty, it sat solidly amidst the maelstrom, a great shadowed maw offering entry into whatever the cowl enclosed, what appeared to be gigantic black pipes arching from its roof and down into the sea – or from the sea into its roof – that from this distance appeared to thrust from it like an insect's legs. Whatever the hells it was, both Kali and Slowhand knew what it looked like. A giant, heavy spider, just sitting there, waiting.

Kali knew she had to get closer, find out what it was. But with the presence of the sentries, there were only two ways they were going to be able to do that.

Slowhand had already thought of one. He was already raising his bow and lining up twin arrows, but Kali stayed his hand, shook her head.

"Take them down and Makennon will know we're here!" she shouted. "We have to get around them!"

"There is no way around them!" the archer shouted back.

Kali nodded. "Yes, there is!" She pointed down the steps to the side of the stone jetty. "We swim around!"

"No chance, Hooper. If the cold doesn't get you, then the currents around the Dragonwings will. You'll be smashed and dead on some Sarcre Island beach before you know it!"

Kali stared at him. "No, I won't!"

Slowhand sighed. The trouble was, he knew Kali was right and that, really, they had no other choice. "Remind me again – why didn't I escape the sewers when I had the chance?"

Crouching and keeping low, using alternate torch supports for cover, the pair began to clamber down the weatherworn rock steps, each of which was half as high as themselves. As they did, they noticed that the tops of the risers were fractured and cracked in places, as if they had once been trodden by some immense and sustained weight, something *formidable* that had at some point in the past ascended these cliffs. They couldn't concern themselves with what, though, as their immediate priority was to reach the jetty unseen. Thankfully, the sentries appeared to be more concerned with what lay behind them than in front, and they managed the long descent without discovery. Once down, they crab-walked to the edge of the jetty and, other than a moaning hiss from Slowhand, slid silently into the water.

As Slowhand had no hesitation in pointing out, the water was farking freezing, and even right next to the shore Kali could feel strong, swirling undercurrents tug at her and try to pull her away into the darker depths, but she fought against them, keeping to the jetty's side and clinging to it with cold, wet hands. As Slowhand followed, she inched her way along the stone, and the further she went, the more uneasy she began to feel – a feeling that was difficult to explain, almost as if they were sharing the water with... something. But she saw nothing.

At last they drew even with the two sentries, waiting for a particularly strong gust of wind before continuing, lest the smallest ripple give them away. They pulled themselves perhaps another twenty yards along the jetty before deeming it sufficiently out of view to climb out, but just as they were about to do so, a series of clatters and rumbles from the shoreline made them plunge back into the water.

"Dammit, Makennon!" Kali hissed.

"Too late to make a run for it," Slowhand advised. "Stay down."

They did so, heads bobbing as if decapitated on the surface of the water, and watched as Makennon and her retinue rumbled slowly along the jetty towards their position. The woman had brought everything with her down the steps, including the wagons on strangely articulated wheels, and staring up from the water at the torchlit procession of horses, mages and soldiers – not to mention Munch and his cage containing the ogur – both Kali and Slowhand felt like small children watching the arrival in town of some bizarre carnival. The trouble was, it looked as if this particular carnival would be pitching tents just ahead of them, blocking the path to the cowl.

Or would they? As Kali and Slowhand watched, the procession reached the far end of the jetty and then continued on into the cowl-shaped structure, each of the wagons disappearing into the maw until the rear of the last seemed to tip and was gone. Slowhand stared at the front of the cowl, craned his neck to stare at its rear, and worked out that there was no way it was deep enough to take them all.

"Now there's a turn-up for the books," he said. "Like that magic trick where you pull worgle after worgle out of a hat." He paused. "Only in reverse." He paused again. "And with wagons instead of worgles."

"Make more sense if it just continued down, eh?" Kali said. She looked at Slowhand's bemused expression and found she had to explain by waggling her fingers. "More steps," she said. "It must be underwater. Orl must be underwater."

The concept was clearly difficult for Slowhand to grasp, and she couldn't blame him – she had never seen anything like it either. "Underwater? Hooper, you *are* sure this is Orl, aren't you? Not some forgotten tunnel under the Stormwall? Maybe they are taking the ogur on holiday, after all."

His question was half-rhetorical and, in truth, he expected an answer like: "Of course I'm sure," but what Kali actually said was: "No."

"No?" he repeated.

"No," Kali echoed. "The scrolls in Andon were... a little contradictory in places. Oh, don't get me wrong, this is Orl all right, I'm just not sure that it's called that. But now that we're actually here there may be a way to find out. Come on."

Kali heaved herself from the water and a confused Slowhand followed, shaking his leg to rid his pants of water. Kali had already reached the cowl and was examining it when he caught up.

"Old Race sites sometimes have identifying runics," she said, "particularly if they're of dwarven origin. I think it was a clan thing."

Slowhand smiled. "You mean they gave their houses names? Like Dunhammerin'?"

"Something like that. Should be one just about – *ah*."

Kali knelt by a rough inscription, brushed away seasalt and grime with her hand, concentrated and frowned. These carved runics were never completely decipherable – there were far too many cryptographic elements she simply didn't have knowledge of – but in general she was able to get the gist of what they were saying. And the gist of this one confirmed what she thought. This place wasn't called Orl, it was called Martak.

No, wait, she thought. The runic contained too many characters, there were gaps where they shouldn't be, and the emphasis was *wrong*...

Hells, Martak wasn't a word, it was a –

Kali's mind filled again with the images and accounts from the manuscripts in the Three Towers. Yes, what she read fitted with them, made sense. But if that was the case – if this place *wasn't* called Orl – then why the reference to the Clockwork King of Orl, a phrase that even the old man himself had used? Could it be he was mistaken – that Makennon and her people were *also* mistaken – and it was again a reflection of how difficult it was to decipher the Old Race language? That, or perhaps even some of the old manuscripts *themselves* were wrong, that somehow, over the long years, the phrase had become misinterpreted, corrupted? What she would need to do in that case was put the phrase in context, think about it in the overall terms of the accounts she'd read...

Unbidden, her second vision leapt once more into her mind, the desolate landscape, the pounding, the figures rising over the horizon.

My gods, she thought, *what had happened here at Martak? What had driven the dwarves here, to this lonely place at the edge of the world? What had become of them?*

Exactly what was the Clockwork King?

Questions, again. And only one way to find out the answers.

Kali peered into the cowl, making sure their way was clear. They were going in.

"Well, this is a new one," Slowhand said, gazing uneasily up at the shadows that enveloped them. He felt as if he were indeed entering some giant maw.

"What are you talking about?" Kali said, her voice echoing slightly in the dark.

"You – actually going in through a front door."

"Hey, there's a first time for everything."

They might have been going in through the front door but that didn't make them welcome guests – just the opposite, in fact. While there was little danger of their being confronted by the original inhabitants of Martak, there was no way to tell if Makennon had stationed any men on the steps down. They could also hear the clattering of her convoy further below – sound travelled easily inside the cowl – and they took care to move slowly, making no sudden moves whose echoes might alert the Faith to their presence behind them.

Thankfully, as they proceeded down more of the huge steps, the sea baffled most of the sound for them. While they could still make out the crashing of the waves outside, the sound was for the most part overlaid by the noise of the great black pipes that curved into the cowl from under the sea. Actually, they weren't strictly pipes any more, but tubes, each the thickness of two men, their casing after they entered the cowl changing from rough and barnacled metal to smooth, if age-grimed, glass. What could be seen inside was a murky detritus and seaweed-filled brine that glowed slightly and, agitated by the outside motion of the waves, slopped back and forth within. Bladed fans also stirred lazily along their length at regular intervals, their purpose, for the moment, unknown.

The steps that had led the way down the cliff continued down and down, and in the light from the betubed sea – caused by algae, Kali guessed – they could be seen in more detail than had been possible above. They were less weatherworn, too, and this extra factor drew Kali's gaze to their risers.

"Look at this," she said, kneeling and brushing away grime.

"Erm, what exactly?" Slowhand queried.

"There are more runics here. Carved into the fronts of the steps."

"So?"

"So..." Kali said. She frowned as she studied them. For once, the runics were easy enough to understand, common words in the dwarven language. "I don't like what they say."

"And what do they say?"

Kali pointed at each of the runics in turn. "Death. Kill. Destroy."

"Oh, that's nice. So I take it the people who lived here weren't very pleasant?"

Kali frowned. "I'm beginning to think no one lived here at all."

"What?"

"I don't think this was any kind of settlement, Slowhand. I think this was some kind of military outpost. An army barracks."

"An army?" Slowhand said in mock surprise. "Should have seen that coming the first time you mentioned the word 'dwarf'."

"Maybe, but –" She paused and stared at the steps again, at the same weight-induced cracks in them that she'd seen above. "I think this one was a very unique army."

"Oh?"

This time, Kali stared down the stairs. "What's more – I think it might still be down there."

Slowhand stared. "Okaaaay, now you're starting to worry me. Hooper, this place has got to be how old? A thousand years?"

Kali rose. "I know," she said in a tone which despite the circumstances was clearly excited. And with no further explanation she began to skip down the stairs. "You coming, or what?"

Slowhand stood where he was for a second. *Why does she never tell me anything?* he thought. *What am I? Lackey? Hired hand? Someone to just stand guard and shoot things? Hells – am I a sidekick?*

He sighed. *Yep, that's about the longbow and the shortbow of it. Gods, what was it about this bloody woman?*

He followed.

It was obvious now that the steps were continuing far under the sea – actually under the seabed, unless Kali missed her guess – and it was a feat of engineering that only dwarves could ever dream they could achieve. But the steps were only the half of it, and as they came to the bottom of their present flight, the true scale of what they had achieved here became awesomely clear. A long corridor stretched away before them, and one after another in rows against both walls, there were statues of dwarves. Each the height of five men, the bearded, behammered likenesses, posed in various battle-ready, grimacing positions, were clearly meant to be warriors, and despite being awed by the fact that she was for the first time looking upon faces from another age, Kali also shivered at the impression they gave. The runic messages on the stair risers, and now this – it seemed as if the entire exit from Martak had been designed to provoke bloodlust, to incite a hunger for violence and war.

Kali and Slowhand proceeded, coming eventually to another, shallower set of steps, and Kali sensed they were near now to the main area of the complex. The first sign of it was when they came upon the rear of Makennon's carnival, her people having reached the base of the steps but having had their progress halted there by the largest pair of doors Kali or Slowhand had ever seen. Sighting them, Kali flung out a blocking arm, slapping Slowhand in the face.

"Ow! Hey!"

"Shush!"

Both of them crouched on the steps, observing what was going on. The reason that Makennon and her people could not get the doors open was clear, and seeing what it was Slowhand stared at Kali, his expression questioning and concerned. But the expression on Kali's face told him that exactly the same concerns were running through her mind.

The huge doors had been sealed shut with a massive, glowing rune. A rune in the shape of a crossed circle.

"Hooper, isn't that – ?"

Kali swallowed. Pulsating slowly with a red fire, the giant rune was the symbol of the Final Faith, all right, but she could not believe that she was seeing it. There had to be another reason for its presence here, because otherwise all of Makennon's babblings about the Final Faith's destiny threatened to prove right. No, there had to another reason. *Had* to be!

One thing was clear. If it was the symbol of the Final Faith then Makennon was nevertheless having problems bending it to her will – and it was obviously not going to be wiped away with a wave of the Anointed Lord's hand. As they continued to watch, Makennon gestured to the mages in her party and the men and women congregated in front of the rune, beginning to weave their magical threads that would dispel it.

Makennon and company had clearly reached a temporary impasse and, as they worked out how to get the doors open, Kali realised it was her and Slowhand's chance to get ahead of their party. She looked around for a way to do so, certain with the knowledge of experience that there was always a way past these things, if you looked beyond the obvious. Her gaze fastened on one of the higher seawater tubes that ran along the corridor close to the ceiling. Where the tube met the wall in which the door was set, there was a small crawlspace around it. She nudged the archer, indicated it.

Slowhand knew what she had in mind. Quietly, he unslung his bow and took a roped arrow from his quiver, aiming upwards. The arrow flew and arced perfectly over the tube, taking the rope with it and wrapping it round and round until it was fixed firmly. Slowhand tested its grip and then indicated for Kali to climb.

She did, and he followed, and the two of them moved silently along the top of the tube in a crouched position, high above the oblivious Makennon and her people. There, they ducked into the crawlspace and through the wall. They passed through about twenty feet of darkness carved from the rock beneath the seabed and emerged finally into a space that was detectable only by their sudden freedom of movement as it was almost totally devoid of light.

Then their eyes adjusted slowly to the darkness, and they both gasped out loud.

Because the scale of the statues in the corridor outside was nothing compared to the scale of this room.

The first people to do so in over a thousand years, they had just entered what they, and Makennon, had journeyed to the edge of their world to find.

The throne room of the Clockwork King.

CHAPTER SEVENTEEN

THE THRONE ROOM was vast. That such an excavation could exist here, hewn from rock beneath the waves, was mind-boggling enough, but made even more so by the fact that as they stared around it in wonder the sea hung above them like a sky.

This – a bit to Kali's disappointment but to Slowhand's huge relief – turned out to be an illusion, the huge, stone buttresses of the throne room walls reflecting and magnifying the glowing seawater in the tubes, so that it seemed to ripple and shift in kind. But Kali's disappointment was mollified by the fact that the glow served a useful purpose, providing an effective, if haunting, illumination, bathing in a blue-green light this marvel of dwarven engineering that had been lost from sight and mind since before her own civilisation was born. What their eyes beheld as they further adjusted to the light was no illusion, however – but they could have been forgiven for thinking that it was.

The throne room stretched out ahead of them, bigger even than the inside of Scholten Cathedral, an immense rectangular chamber that could once have welcomed titans and giants as courtiers, and which, for all they knew, perhaps once had. A central aisle that was as wide as a road, inlaid with dwarven mosaics, led forwards, and at its end – distant but nonetheless still dominating the room – a huge and shadowed, seated figure loomed high in the dark. As compelling as it was, though, it was not the only figure in the room, and as Kali dropped from the pipe and began to wander slowly up the aisle, her head turned from left to right, staring up at three raised galleries, accessed by broad interconnecting stairways, that ran the entire length of the throne room on either side. As the corridor outside had been lined with dwarven statues, so were these, but in this case with many, many more, each and every one of them draped in cobwebs but otherwise identical and separated from the next only by their own width again. Kali swallowed as she studied one statue after another, the unease she had started to feel on the surface growing with each frozen visage she passed.

But uneasy as she was, Kali could barely control her other feelings. On the one hand, the sheer scale of this place and its contents made her feel like a starving mouse beneath a feast-laden table, and she longed to explore, to investigate, to catalogue the things she'd found – to *touch them*, the first person to do so for literally ages. On the other hand, however, she knew that was not why she was here, and the feeling of elation she felt at her greatest find to date was marred by the fact not only that – strictly speaking – *she* hadn't found it, but that, incidentally, she had to destroy it, too. Or, at the very least, stop it doing what it did.

Whatever it was that was.

Doubts resurfaced once more – that what the old man had told her was partly wrong, that perhaps Makennon's destiny did lie where she said – but the doubts were fleeting. She knew what she had seen and read in the Three Towers, knew what ideas of her own were forming, and most of all, she knew how this place felt – and it felt wrong. No, more than wrong. Troubled. Tainted. Bad. Something truly awful had happened within these walls, a long, long time ago, and its aura remained and resonated still.

She jumped as a hand touched her shoulder. "Nice place they've got here," Slowhand said. "Cosy."

Kali nodded, only half-listening, and walked further up the aisle until she came close enough to study the giant, seated figure at its end. No, not seated, *bethroned*. The idea that the Clockwork King might have been some kind of giant walking automaton had always verged on the edge of preposterous in her mind, but even so she'd been ready for anything. But looking at it now it was clear that the King was not designed as a giant that would arise from its throne, have a quick stretch, and pound across the peninsula sweeping all in its path aside. No, in actual fact, it seemed to be just a statue – a towering and staggering and very pitsing imposing statue, it had to be said, but a statue nonetheless.

Kali craned her neck, staring up to study it, and found herself being stared back at by a pair of giant stone eyes set in a gnarled, bearded and cruel dwarven face. Though the eyes were only stone, their stare was distinctly unsettling, made all the more so by the fact the face was draped in the same lengthy cobwebs as the statues against the walls, and Kali pulled her own gaze away, examining the rest of the statue instead. The giant figure wore – or had been *sculpted* wearing – the kind of studded leather armour she recognised as being from dwarven middle history, and in one hand held a like-period battle hammer, in the other a spiked dwarven shield. Again, cobwebs dangled from the shield's spikes, so long that Kali found she could walk through them like a curtain. It was only as she did that she noticed one of the less obvious features of the statue – one around the side.

Around the side and, then, to the rear, actually. For there the same kind of seawater tubes that ran into the cowl ran around and into the back of the Clockwork King. No, she realised, tracing the tubes back, they weren't the same kind of tubes – they *were* the same tubes, splitting and terminating here and in other places throughout the throne room as they ran around its walls like arteries.

Now that, Kali thought, *was odd.* And there was something else that was odd – now that she had seen that the statue was just a statue, why was it called the *Clockwork* King?

She sighed, moving to the part of the massive construction that she had purposefully saved for last. Directly in front of the throne was a large stone plinth inlaid with what looked like templates for the four keys, a complex-looking mechanism that seemed, in parts, to rotate and, presumably, lock into place.

There was a sound like a prolonged roll of thunder, and distracted as she was Kali had difficulty placing its source until Slowhand tapped her gently on the shoulder and, when he had her attention, pointed back the way they had come. It seemed that Makennon and her mages had managed to release the runelock, and the vast doors were opening. They were about to have company.

Makennon's soldiers came first, and then the Anointed Lord herself, sweeping into the throne room with a regal stride that suggested she had already claimed the place as her own. Nevertheless, for a few seconds she displayed the same reactions to the scale and content of the place as Kali and Killiam had, nodding to herself in approval. But then she spotted their distant figures standing before the king, and her brow furrowed in disbelief and annoyance. She gestured to the front members of her entourage, despatching them to various tasks around the chamber, and then strode up through the wide aisle towards the throne.

Kali's heart thudded, though not because the Anointed Lord approached. The reason for her sudden burst of adrenaline was the doors through which Makennon had passed – or rather what was now revealed upon them. Opened towards her and showing their outside face, Kali could see the remains of the fire runic that Makennon's mages had dismissed to gain entry, an embery half-circle that as she watched slowly extinguished and faded away into nothing. Suddenly everything became clear, and all the confused pieces fell into place. Gods – how could she have been so blind!

She turned to Slowhand, saw that he too stared and wondered if he had realised the same thing. But he hadn't. In actual fact, Slowhand was fighting a potentially embarrassing twitch of excitement. *Hells,*

Katherine looked good in her tight and shiny battle armour, he thought. *That walk, the way those hips swivelled when she moved...*

He swept back his hair, waiting.

And Makennon walked right past him without even a glance.

"Kali Hooper," she declared with a long sigh. "The Spiral of Kos, Scholten, the World's Ridge Mountains, Andon, Scholten again, and now, finally, here in Orl. Tell me – for the record – just how many of you are there?"

Kali remembered her first encounter with Makennon, and her *questioning*. "Oh, just the one – but enough to mess with your head."

"She does that a lot," Slowhand said, leaning in with a grin.

"And I'm about to do it again," Kali said, silencing him with a glance. "Makennon, listen to me, this place isn't what you think. It hasn't got anything to do with the Final Faith, and never has had, I know that now. Coming here was a big mistake."

"For you, perhaps, Miss Hooper," another voice said as its owner approached, boots thudding on stone. Kali scowled. "The girl does not know what she is talking about," Munch continued. "Like anyone young she adopts an overfamiliarity with things older than herself that is, at best, arrogant and, at worst, offensive in the extreme."

"Speaking of offensive..." Slowhand said.

"Makennon, listen to me," Kali went on, ignoring both. "This place isn't called Orl, it's called Martak. And Martak isn't a dwarven word, it's a dwarven phrase – M'Ar'Tak. You know what it means, Katherine? An eye for an eye."

"The girl spouts nonsense," Munch interrupted. "You have seen the evidence with your own eyes. Anointed Lord, we have worked hard for this moment – please, order the activation of the keys."

"Katherine, no –"

Makennon held her gaze for a few seconds. "The signs are clear," she said after some consideration. She turned and signalled for the remainder of her entourage to enter the throne room, prompting a smile from Munch. "Bring them forwards."

Kali spun in frustration. "Dammit, Makennon, you want to know about signs? Then let me tell you about the one on those doors, the one that was so difficult to break because it was so obviously there to keep you – to keep everyone – *out*. That runic wasn't the symbol of the Final Faith because it's actually *two* runics, one overlaid on the other. A circle and a cross, Katherine, different symbols but ones used by the elves and the dwarves to mean the same thing. *That's* why there were two of each on the map showing the sites of the four keys, because the elves and the dwarves built two sites each. They're *warning* symbols, woman! They mean stay away, danger. They mean *death*."

"Oh, now you tell me," Slowhand muttered.

"And the one on those doors?" Kali went on, pointing back along the throne room. "That was the elves and the dwarves combining their symbols to shout the meaning to the world. Because when together they'd finally managed to stop whatever evil came out of this place, they sealed it with the biggest warning sign of all."

For the first time Makennon seemed to waver, and Kali was about to press her advantage when the wagon containing the keys trundled into the throne room. What gave Kali pause, however, was what followed it – the wagon containing the ogur. The ogur spotted her, too, and began to pound against the bars of its cage, its roars clearly audible even across the distance that separated them.

Munch saw what was happening and frowned. The old man's... *changes* had not lessened and there was surely no way the girl could recognise him, so this reaction made him curious. But, he thought, what did it matter if it had thrown her off guard?

"Is there a problem, Miss Hooper?" he asked.

"No. No, I –"

"Then I suggest we do what we came here to do."

Munch turned to Makennon. The Anointed Lord took her gaze off Kali and looked at him and, after a second, nodded.

"Destiny awaits," Munch said, smiling.

He signalled to some of the soldiers and they unloaded four crates from the first wagon, then carried them forwards to the plinth, breaking the seals and revealing the keys packed safely in straw inside. Munch ran a hand over each with a reverence that made Kali frown. "With your permission, Madam?" he said to Makennon.

The Anointed Lord inhaled, drawing herself up to her full, imposing height. "Go ahead," she said.

Munch lifted the first key from its crate and placed it in its matching template, pressing it home with a sound like a shifting stone slab, then rotated the plinth until it locked into place with a grating thud. It struck Kali that he looked far too much like he knew what he was doing, and she frowned as he expertly did the same with the second, and then the third key, until only the last remained. As he lifted it from its crate she moved to stop him, but with a click of her fingers Makennon had her restrained by the soldiers, along with Slowhand.

"Please – you don't know what you're doing!" Kali hissed.

"On the contrary, Miss Hooper," Munch said, in a tone which made her feel suddenly very cold, "I do."

He inserted the fourth key, repeating the same procedure as before, and then stood back as the plinth took on a life of its own. Each of the keys now turned of its own accord, first clockwise or anti-clockwise, and then back again, and then in a seemingly random pattern that Kali realised had, in fact, to be some kind of combination. Her theory was proven correct when, after a further four or five turns – it varied with the keys – each again locked, but into a different position from which it had started, and then sank further into the plinth with more resounding thuds. A panel opened in its centre and from it rose a patch of what looked to be spikes arranged in the shape of a hand.

"Yes," Munch said. "At last, yes."

He placed his hand gently on the spikes.

Everyone in the chamber looked down as the floor trembled beneath their feet, then up and around as the seawater in the glowing tubes began to bubble and stir, the strange arterial system coming to life. The fans that punctuated their length began to slowly rotate and the detritus that had so long ago been sucked in with the seawater began to flop and toss in the glass tubes, and then began to circulate around the system with greater and greater speed. Bubbles began to bounce in the water now, a sign that more was being sucked in from the sea above, and the mounting speed of the fans increased its circulation and pressure, churning the murky water until it turned opaque and then a milky white. There was no sign of the seaweed or detritus any more, only a seething rush of pressurised liquid that raced through the tubes all around the throne room, heading towards what appeared to be each of the statues against the walls and, ultimately, the Clockwork King.

The roar of it was deafening. The whole of Martak shook.

But it was nothing compared to the shaking to come.

Kali swallowed as the water thundered into the pipes that fed the enormous statue, and as it did, the Clockwork King proved itself to be far more than a statue after all. As Kali and the others watched in amazement, great plates of stone detached themselves from various parts of its body, separating along hairline cracks for the first time in a thousand years. Dust poured from the edges of the rising plates and from the edges of the holes in the statue that remained, and as the dust fell away, the interior of the Clockwork King was revealed. There, powered by the inrushing seawater, great metal cogs and wheels turned and rotated, and pistons thumped, their movements extending the thick metal rams on which all could now see the plates were rising away from the component parts of the statue they had once been. As they did, the cogs and the wheels inside the king began to twist and turn, and then so did the rams, and as each plate followed suit, they slowly moved in different directions towards the walls and ceiling of the throne room. Kali looked up and around and saw that indentations in the stone matched each of the giant plates exactly.

It was at that moment that Kali realised there had been no confusion about the number of keys described in the scrolls in the Three Towers. The mention of a fifth key hadn't made any sense to her back then, but it sure as hells did now. And there was a fifth key, no doubt about it.

The fifth key was the Clockwork King.

And she suspected she knew what it opened.

She looked up again as a series of deep booms signalled that each of the stone plates had locked into their corresponding positions, and then she looked left and right towards the galleries, swallowing. Despite wanting to know all about the wonders of this place earlier, all she could think now was: *Let me be wrong. Please, let me be wrong.*

But she wasn't. That became clear as soon as the pipes that seemed to feed the statues in the galleries began to churn even more than before, and then a series of deep and prolonged rumblings drew everyone's glances towards the sides of the throne room. One after another, all along the walls, the dwarven statues were sliding upwards, the dust of ages pouring from them, their cobwebs tearing away. Moving slowly, each rose its own height and eventually came to rest with a thud, and revealed behind where each had stood was a space as dark as a tomb. And out of each space came a whiff of something foul.

Makennon's people had begun to scatter as soon as the statues had started to move, but now the Anointed Lord shouted for them to stand their ground. Kali glanced urgently at her and saw, despite the order, that she was looking increasingly uneasy, as if the soldier's part of her mind was weighing up the tactical advantages and disadvantages of what this place might offer, finding them at odds with that part of her that had been driven here by religious zeal. She might have brought a little too much of the warrior to her role of Anointed Lord, but it was highly unlikely she wished to further the Final Faith's cause by endangering all life on the peninsula, including her own.

"Makennon, stop this," Kali said. "I can see in your eyes you suspect what I said is true – or at least worth considering. Look at this place and think. How can anything in this graveyard fulfil the destiny of your church? I don't know what you expected to find but I'd guess this isn't it. This can't be anything good."

She grabbed Makennon by the shoulders, shook her and forced her to look at the tomb-like entrances. More cobwebs shifted slightly where they dangled in front of the darkness, disturbed, perhaps, by a breath of something from within.

"That monstrosity on the throne isn't the Clockwork King of Orl, Katherine," Kali persisted, shaking her once more, "it's the Clockwork King of *All*. Ask yourself, woman – *all what?*"

Makennon hesitated for what seemed to be an age, regarding Kali with unwavering eyes. Then finally she nodded, flicking her finger at Munch to stand him down. But he didn't move. Makennon instead flicked her finger at the soldiers to stand him down. They didn't move, either.

Munch laughed. "The problem with giving me autonomy to choose people for these missions, Anointed Lord, is that I chose carefully. And the people I chose on your behalf for this mission I did so because I knew you might have second thoughts." He sighed. "Second thoughts I cannot allow."

Makennon looked furious but knew better than to move. The soldiers already had their crossbows trained on her.

"What is this, Konstantin?"

"Destiny. But not, as I led you to believe, the destiny of the Final Faith. No, I simply needed its resources to find my way home."

"*Home?*"

"Home." Munch looked almost sad as he added, "It was my destiny to come here, Katherine – not yours. I am sorry."

"*Pff*, I'll bet," Kali said. "You know what, Stan – I had you pegged right from the start. Well, almost."

"Munch, what are you saying?" Makennon asked again.

"He's saying that he's a dwarf," Kali explained. "Or at least as much of a dwarf that the one million millionth drop of dwarvishness he'll have left in his blood after all this time qualifies him to be. And unless I miss my guess, that blood's from the clan responsible for what happened here."

"Quite correct, Miss Hooper. I am the last of Clan Trang – what became Clan M'Ar'Tak."

"Listen, pal," Slowhand interjected. "If I know my history, the dwarves were a noble, advanced race of miners, engineers and warriors, not homicidal bearded shortarses with faces like a mool's arse."

Munch glared at him, but his voice remained calm. "You wish proof of my claim, Mister Slowhand? Then I shall give you proof." He glanced up at the gallery tombs, which as yet remained as they had been. "The last part of the process to activate the Clockwork King of All."

Slowhand winced as, without flinching, Munch suddenly rammed his palm onto the patch of spikes in the centre of the plinth, smiling as his blood formed a pool beneath them.

"That had to hurt."

"Know this," Munch said. "The Clockwork King responds only to those whose veins still flow with the blood of Belatron the Butcher."

Slowhand shot a glance at Kali. "Who in the hells is Belatron the Butcher?"

"Bad guy," Kali answered. "I think."

"With a name like that I'd guess it's a pretty safe bet. Gods, you couldn't make this up," Slowhand added to himself in a whisper.

Neither could he have made up what happened next. Munch's blood seeped away into the plinth, and as it did the Clockwork King began to move again. Only this time, instead of sending out rams, its lower half reconstructed itself into the form of another throne on a circular platform. Except this throne was man-sized – more accurately, dwarf-sized. There was something else, too – it was surrounded by strange cylinder-shaped crystals.

"Oh, look," Slowhand said light-heartedly, though with tension in his voice. "He's built himself a chair."

Munch settled himself into it and the Clockwork King remade itself once more, smaller components from within assembling themselves into some kind of metal ring that moved forwards to encircle Munch's head. More spikes shot out of it and embedded themselves straight into his skull, and as they did the cylindrical crystals began to glow. Munch jolted and spasmed in the throne for a few seconds and then smiled. "Yes, Mister Slowhand, that hurt, too. But not, I am pleased to say, as much as my warriors are going to hurt you."

"Warriors?" Slowhand queried, dubiously.

"Not nice," Kali said. "I've seen them before..."

Munch closed his eyes and concentrated. A deep and rhythmic pounding suddenly reverberated throughout the throne room, and then from each of the spaces behind the statues figures marched before halting, more than one from each, and each of them thrice the size of a man. Standing there with their arms and heads slumped like those of ogur, they filled the galleries now and, like the interior of the Clockwork King itself, they were things of metal, of cogs and pulleys and gears, though they had been assembled in such a way that, like the king, they also superficially resembled dwarves, although grotesquely so. Each wielded a dwarven war hammer in one hand and a double-bladed axe in the other, but while the axe was of relatively normal size the hammer was as grotesquely enlarged as each warrior itself – a vicious-looking slab of iron-ribbed stone that was actually part of the ogur-like arm and would likely shatter walls, let alone bones, with a single blow. The only thing the warriors did not carry was a shield, but the giant hammer made such armour unnecessary, its bulk, used defensively, protection enough.

These were the things of which the manuscripts and all the tales had warned. Let slip once on Twilight, it had taken the combined technologies and sorceries of the elves and the dwarves to stop them. Let slip again, onto a Twilight where such abilities were as yet in their infancy, they would be formidable and unstoppable.

"By all the gods..." Katherine Makennon breathed.

"Don't you mean – ?"

"Slip of the tongue. What *are* these things?"

"They are M'Ar'Tak," Kali said. "Clan Trang's vengeance for the bloody carnage the elves reaped upon them. Isn't that right, Stan?"

Munch smiled on his throne. And then his face darkened. "History paints the dwarven races as the merciless ones, the warmongers, the roaring, blood-lusted, cold-blooded killers, but in our war with Family Ur'Raney it was they who proved to be merciless. Our war had raged for months, our forces driven back across the western territories we contested, the Ur'Raney seemingly able to summon endless reinforcements and our people falling before them – many to their blasted scythe-stones before they learned better. Before we knew it, our army was devastated, pushed back here, to the edge of the world. We thought they would stop, allow us to lick our wounds and leave, but they did not, instead driving us over the Dragonwing Cliffs, slaughtering us even as we fell, and forcing those who survived that slaughter into the sea. For the first time in the history of our race, dwarves were forced to hide, because there was nothing else they could do. They hid in the caves that permeate these cliffs like floprats because otherwise they – and Clan Trang – would have been exterminated."

"One of those who hid was Belatron, wasn't it?" Kali said. "He's what started all this?"

Munch nodded. "Belatron, our greatest wielder of magics. And within him a simmering hatred of the elves, a thirst for revenge that grew over the months – and then the years – into what you now see before you."

Slowhand spoke up. "You're saying that a small bunch of bloodied survivors burrowed into the sea and built an army of clockwork men to do their fighting for them. Apart from being a little unrealistic, that's not a very dwarven battle ethic, is it?"

"No, not to do their fighting for them," Munch said.

The archer gestured up at the warriors. "Then what do you call –"

"To do their *own* fighting," Kali said, cutting Slowhand off. "Because they're not clockwork men – at least, not wholly." She peered at the massed ranks and made out what the others had apparently yet not, that within the skeletal structure of each warrior were brains riveted into metal skulls, hearts suspended within metal ribs and, most grotesquely of all, eyeballs set deep within metal sockets. These things were not simply mechanical, they were vessels for the remains of warriors who had been slaughtered by the Ur'Raney.

And the most disturbing aspect about them was that, whatever mix of technology and dark magics had been used to create them, the organs remained fresh. Kali could tell that because each had a smaller version of the ring that encircled Munch's skull embedded in a still-pulsing brain.

"They called them the Thousand," Munch explained. "Dwarven warriors partly resurrected from where they had fallen to the elves and restored to fight again."

"Belatron harvested their bodies," Kali realised with disgust. "Returned to the battlefields and ripped their remains apart when they should have reached their final rest. That's why they called him Belatron the Butcher."

"They were *warriors!*" Munch exclaimed. "Each and every one of them would have given their right arm for the chance to fight for their clan once more!"

"Seems they did," Slowhand said. "Amongst other things."

Munch slammed his fist onto the side of his throne. "Clan Trang had to rise again! M'Ar'Tak had to march!"

"*Wo-hoah.* Steady, shorty."

"It all went wrong, though, didn't it, Stan?" Kali said. "This throne you're sitting in – this skullring you're wearing – is what Belatron used to control them. Only he couldn't, could he? Because by the time he'd done with them, by the time their brains had realised what they now were, and by the time he had forced them up those steps and indoctrinated them with his messages of death and killing and war, they had, all of them, become completely insane."

"They turned on their own," Makennon said. "And then they turned on everything else. A marching horde, but nothing to do with the Lord of All. How could I have been so blind, so stupid, so wrong?"

"You weren't wrong, Makennon," Slowhand said, looking at Kali. "Like Hooper, here, you just didn't have access to all the information. Something, in your case, I'm sure a certain short bastard had a lot to do with."

Makennon swung on Munch. "Why do you do this, Konstantin? Do you want to use your army to bring down the Final Faith?"

Munch laughed. "The *Faith?* The Faith is fleeting. My army is to be used to bring about a resurgence of the dwarven race, by giving them the freedom to emerge from their underground enclosures by annihilating anything that stands in their way."

"I've got some news for you," Slowhand said. "Your lot died out a long time ago. There *are* no more dwarven enclosures."

"Actually, there might be," Kali said, hesitantly.

"*What?*"

"Tale for another time."

"Oh."

Kali turned back to Munch. "Munch, listen to me. Belatron couldn't control these things, and neither will you. They won't wipe out *anything* that stands in your way, they'll wipe out *everything*, including yoursel –"

"Enough!" Munch barked. He inhaled deeply and his blood-stained brow furrowed with concentration. "It is time."

All along the galleries, the heads of the clockwork warriors rose from their slumped positions and stared ahead, ruptured vessels in their unnatural eyes making them appear to flare red. Then, in military step, they began to march forwards and pound down the steps from the three levels – an army on the move. Munch blinked and four separated from the horde, coming to stand around him as bodyguards, but the rest, assembling in ordered ranks of five abreast, stood ready to march towards the exit.

"No!" Kali shouted, pulling free of her captors. Determined to halt their progress, to prise Munch from his seat of power, she ran forwards, eliciting a warning cry from Slowhand. Munch looked at his clockwork bodyguards but then sniffed, as if using them was hardly worth the effort, and instead signalled to his people to turn their crossbows on Kali instead of Makennon – and fire. Their bolts slammed into her from every direction, the impacts forcing a series of grunts as she attempted to stagger on, and, though her reserves must have been considerable and she almost made it, she found herself faltering and staring at Munch with a look of pained surprise in her eyes. Munch sighed and drew his gutting knife from his belt, aiming it provocatively and directly at her.

"No further, Miss Hooper."

"Damn you, you bas –" Kali began. But she never finished her curse. The knife flew with as much force as Munch could muster and embedded itself solidly in her chest. It stopped Kali quite literally dead in her tracks and, her breath whistling strangely, she looked dully down at the protruding blade – what little of it she could see – then, stunned and confused, dropped to her knees and, slowly, onto her face. A small groan escaped her, and, as a pool of blood began to spread ever more largely beneath her, one thought overrode all others.

This wasn't how she was meant to die.

"Hooper?" Slowhand said.

"Should you be thinking of trying the same, *minstrel*," Munch advised, staring at the still and bloodied body, "there are plenty more bolts in my people's possession."

Slowhand stared. The throne room was utterly silent apart from the roaring of the ogur as it battered at the bars of its cage with as much fury as the archer had in his eyes. No words were necessary, though, as Slowhand's expression said it all. He was going to kill Munch – and very soon.

The standoff was broken by Makennon.

"Munch, this is insane! What if Hooper was right? If Belatron the Butcher – their creator – couldn't control these things, what chance do you have?"

Munch smiled, looked at his bodyguards and blinked. The four clockwork men stamped their feet as one, quaking the floor of the throne room.

"He's doing it," Makennon said quietly to Slowhand. "He's actually *controlling* them."

"Probably something to do with the fact that he's as insane as they are. The question is, how long will it last?"

Makennon tried to reason with Munch one last time.

"Konstantin, he's right. These things might obey you now but what about when you've razed Andon, Freiport, Scholten? Because that is what you want to do, isn't it? But how strong will you be, then? What's to stop your army going on to kill the very dwarves whose resurgence you desire? This is *fantasy!*"

Munch glared. "You call me a fantasist? You, a religious zealot who clutches at any straw and follows any carrot that is dangled before her eyes? You pathetic woman – your whole reason for existence is a fantasy!"

Makennon drew herself up to her full height. "I was a general, Konstantin Munch. It is my job to know when an army stands unfit to march."

"On the contrary," Munch said. "It is my job to tell them when to."

He closed his eyes and concentrated, and the massed ranks of clockwork warriors began to pound slowly towards the door. Their orders received, Munch opened his eyes, stared around at everyone in the throne room and then looked to his bodyguards. "Kill them all," he ordered.

All hells broke loose. Slowhand and Makennon staggered back as the four mechanical warriors began to systematically attack everyone who had been in the Anointed Lord's party, their axes and hammers slicing and crushing, chopping and pounding, beating and tearing their bodies apart. Those that were armed tried to defend themselves with their crossbows and blades, and those that were not – the mages – with their fireballs and storms, desperately weaving cones of protection as they fought to keep their attackers back. Screams of agony echoed around the stone chamber, and its walls were splattered and sprayed with blood, and there was nothing anyone could do to stop themselves dying. Nothing at all.

In his caged wagon, the ogur raged.

"You little bastard!" Slowhand shouted, and, without thinking, began to run towards Munch, but Makennon pulled him back.

"You'll never get near him," she said. "We have to get out of here."

Slowhand glared at her, knowing she was right. But still he shrugged her off, staring at Kali's body.

"I'm not leaving her down here."

"You won't get near her, either, you fool – those things will tear you apart."

"I'll find a way."

Again, Makennon grabbed him, but this time by both arms and more forcefully, spinning him to face her. Her gaze – her intense gaze – was for a second no longer that of the Anointed Lord, aloof and ruthless, but that of a professional warrior, the general she used to be. In it was the sadness of one who had lost one of their own together with the harsh pragmatism that acknowledged that in what they did someone had to fall in battle. It was inevitable.

"She's dead, Lieutenant. The battle is lost. Anything else is suicide. Retreat with me. *Now.*"

Slowhand was suddenly furious. "And where the hells do you suggest we retreat *to*, General? Have you any idea what your religious scheming has unleashed here? How many people on the peninsula are going to die?"

"I don't know! But there must be something that can be done to stop this. But first we need to *retreat*, regroup. You know that."

Slowhand swallowed. "There is something we can do," he said, suddenly. He unslung his bow, quickly strung an arrow and aimed it at Munch's head, squinting to get a bead through the clockwork warriors. "I might not be able to get near him but I can finish that bastard from right here."

But he didn't loose the arrow. Because what he had just noticed was that in all the confusion the ogur had escaped its cage.

And it, and Kali's body, were gone.

CHAPTER EIGHTEEN

THE STORM OUTSIDE Martak had worsened dramatically since Kali and the others had entered the sub-aquatic complex, and was now in stark contrast to its shelter, making it seem almost welcoming despite the nightmare the place had been. Forks of lightning split a night sky blackened by the eclipse, the flashes of light so severe it seemed the universe was, with homicidal slashes, slicing itself apart. A freezing wind caught and flung back to the cliffs by the Stormwall chilled and cut straight to the bone. The wind did not prevent the heavy rain from hammering straight down, however, and it was the wet, cold crashes of the raindrops on her flesh that kept Kali from fading into the oblivion she knew was very close.

She wasn't dead, that much was clear, but neither did she have long to live – she could feel it in every fibre of her fading being. Her body had been battered too much, pierced too many times, and she had lost too much blood to hope – even with her newly discovered powers of recovery – to survive. The fact made her feel immensely sad. She had hoped to live long enough to make a difference, but she hadn't. She had come so far, done so much, and yet she had failed.

Failed herself. Failed Slowhand. Failed Twilight.

Most of all, she had failed Merrit Moon.

Her regret and diminishing consciousness was so debilitating that for a while it did not occur to her to question where she was. But then even she couldn't ignore the violent shaking of her head any longer.

She groaned, eyes attempting to take in her situation, but her view bouncing everywhere. Then, what vestige of fear of death remained in her already dying form cut through her much more sharply than any bolt or knife, including Munch's, could ever have done. Because she saw that she was slung in the massive, green-tinted arms of a beast that was pounding up the cliff steps outside Martak, a beast that she dimly recognised – but mainly smelled – to be an ogur. What was more, the ogur was roaring, again and again and again.

This was it, then. The moment.

Her vision come true.

It was too much for her. Finally, too much. She hadn't asked for any of this, and she was no longer strong enough to fight the inevitable. With a great weariness and a long, drawn-out sigh that became hopelessly lost in the stormy night, Kali Hooper felt her body relax and then felt herself die.

I'm sorry, old man...

"There!" Killiam Slowhand shouted as he saw her slump in the ogur's grip. "She's there!"

"Slowhand, keep back!" Makennon warned.

Not a chance, Slowhand thought. The disappearance of Kali's body had been the catalyst he'd needed to flee Martak, his desire to rid Twilight of Konstantin Munch overwhelmed by his concern for his ex. He and Makennon had made for the exit just before Munch's army had begun their slow march through it and, frankly, he had all but forgotten about the dwarf and didn't much care. But if there was *anything* he could do to stop Kali suffering at the hands of this thing that, for whatever reason, had taken her, then he would do it.

He flung himself over riser after riser, pursuing the ogur all the way to the top of the cliffs, and there stood panting heavily, watching in disbelief as the ogur laid Kali's body gently down onto the rocky ground. Nevertheless, he ran forwards, attempting to shield her from whatever was the beast's intent, but the hulking creature batted him away like some buzzing insect, sending him smashing into nearby rocks. Slowhand picked himself up, wiped blood from his mouth and, roaring, went for the ogur a second time, but a loud roar from the beast that was much, much louder than his own – not to mention a steely grip on his arm from the now caught-up Makennon – held him back.

Panting even more heavily, Slowhand unslung his bow and aimed an arrow directly between the ogur's eyes, impossible to miss even though his grip wavered uncharacteristically with grief and fury. The pouring rain slicking down his hair, running in rivulets down his face and reminding him so much of the walkway on Scholten Cathedral. He addressed the beast through clenched teeth.

"*Leave – her – alone.*"

The ogur stared directly at him, an unexpectedly sad and thoughtful expression in its eyes making him falter in his intent. And then, while the still-wavering Slowhand shook his head to shake the water from his eyes, the ogur did something he hadn't expected at all. It pulled the crossbow bolts and the gutting knife from Kali's body, tossed them aside and then removed a strange blue amulet from around its neck and instead strung it about hers. It deliberately let go of the amulet – almost as if it were *giving* it to her – and then, after a few seconds, touched it again.

Again, the ogur stared at him, and somehow Slowhand knew it was asking him to *wait*.

Somewhere behind those primal eyes, Merrit Moon saw the desperate figure of Killiam Slowhand, continued to struggle for dominance of his transformed body and prayed the archer would give him time. He had no idea whether what he was about to try would work – as far as he knew scythe-stones had never been used twice, or in such a way – but if it did then Kali Hooper would live again.

His action would come at a price, though. The transference of his own life essence to Kali would likely kill him in turn, but even if it did not – if Thrutt had made him strong enough – then it would leave him so weak that he would no longer be able to fight the assertion of the ogur within, and he could be trapped within its form for the rest of his life. But it seemed a fair and just trade – after all, it was he who was responsible for her being here in the first place, was it not? Besides, she was his Kali – the closest thing to a daughter he had – so what choice was there, really?

He actually *willed* his life away.

A blue wisp appeared between ogur and corpse, and, feeling its hungry tug like a meathook through his heart, Merrit Moon had to struggle against his own instinct to survive, forcing himself to remain where he was as the process continued. The wisp became a snake, and then a cloud that filled the air between them, and then Kali's body took on a blue glow as it became suffused with the stuff of himself. Moon felt suddenly as if he had been folded inside out and pulled away, and then the cloud was snatched into Kali, and then it became a snake and a wisp once more, and then it was gone. The sound of the amulet doing what it did – a long sigh – was echoed by one of his own, and then his body slumped to the ground with a thud, breathing shallowly.

Kali Hooper's eyes snapped open. She coughed. And then she sat up, abruptly, ramrod straight.

"Great gods," Slowhand whispered.

"Lord of All," Makennon said.

"Slowhand?" Kali asked.

The archer scurried to her side. His voice trembled, partly in wonder at what he had just witnessed, partly in thanks that – somehow – he had Kali back. "H-hey, how you doing?"

"Ohhhh, you know..." Kali said weakly. "You?"

"Ohhhh, you know. Fled certain death, watched you come back from it, now starting to wonder once again whether we have a chance of stopping an invincible clockwork army intent on destroying the world – in other words, your usual." He hesitated, looked doubtful. "You up to speed with this?"

"*Unnh.* A-ha." Kali coughed again and held her chest, from where she found her fatal wound had gone. And as she did, she caught sight of the figure beside her, and scrambled back on the ground.

"It's all right... I think," Slowhand said. "I don't know how or why but... the ogur helped you."

"Helped?" Kali said, puzzled. She picked herself up, her own metabolism aiding the effects of the amulet, and studied the creature. It was weak but conscious, and its face seemed almost to ripple before her eyes, caught somewhere between the beast she thought it was and something heart-thuddingly familiar. She touched the amulet around her neck, remembered seeing it on the old man, then moved to touch the ogur's face. And as she did, the ogur's hand moved over hers and moved it gently down, much as another had in the Warty Witch a long, long time ago.

Kali swallowed. There was something familiar there – *and the eyes.*

"My gods," she said. "Merrit?"

"What?" Slowhand exclaimed.

"It's the old man," Kali said, excitedly. "I don't know how or why but he's here, inside this, this... *thing.* The cave in the World's Ridge, where I last saw him – he didn't die!"

"Oh, Hooper, come on –"

"Your friend is correct," Makennon said. "Munch told me how this happened, about an artefact. Its effects are meant to be temporary but..."

Kali looked at the ogur, concerned. What had, a moment before, seemed so familiar in its eyes was fading, as if Moon were going away, and as she watched the spark in them faded to something feral – the eyes that she remembered from the beasts in the cave. The ogur emitted a dull growl, then, and as if afraid something worse might follow, roughly shoved her away, rose and stomped along the cliff.

"We have to do something to help him," Kali said.

"Hooper, I'm not sure we can," Slowhand cautioned. "It seems to me that in doing what he did he's sacrificed something."

"Like what?" Kali said.

Slowhand looked grave. "Like himself."

"Then let us hope his sacrifice has not been in vain," Makennon said. Her attention had been drawn by a series of quaking thuds from far below. "Because they're coming."

The three of them turned to look down the steps leading to Martak, and at their base saw that the first units of mechanical warriors had completed their slow march from the throne room and emerged from the cowl. They marched in the same organised lines of five, in rank after rank after rank, filling the jetty with their broad bodies, metal feet pounding into the stone, and, as they gradually drew closer to the steps, rocks at the top of the cliffs began to tremble and shed scree that bounced and skittered below.

Their assault on the peninsula would soon begin.

"We have to stop them," Slowhand said.

"Oh brilliant. Just bloody brilliant."

"I see the old Hooper is indeed back."

"Well, honestly..."

"If you two are finished," Makennon said, "I think someone's already ahead of us on that one." She pointed a little way along the clifftop, where the ogur was pushing its shoulder into a boulder that balanced there, clearly trying to dislodge it and send it crashing below.

"I think it knows what it's doing," Makennon said.

"Damn right," Kali said, smiling. "The old man's still in there somewhere."

"Well, are we just going to stand here or are we going to help it?" Slowhand enquired.

"*Him*," Kali corrected.

"Fine, him. Come on!"

The three of them joined the ogur behind the boulder and leant their weight to pushing it, and with a dull rumble the giant piece of rock dislodged from its perch and went tumbling away, bouncing first off rocks and then onto the stone steps. With a series of crashes that were audible even over the storm, it continued down, bouncing two then three steps at a time, then more, gathering momentum as it went.

The mechanical warriors did not even react to its approach, their minds – Munch's mind – intent on their single imperative of reaching the surface and the humans who dwelled there. The boulder smashed into their front rank and sent five warriors staggering back, causing a knock-on effect behind them, and as the giant rock continued to roll through the second and third ranks their relentless march was momentarily thrown into confusion, the affected warriors trying to recover from the impact, those behind attempting to march on around them. Then, in unison, five of the giant dwarven battle hammers were swung at the boulder and it was shattered first to rubble and then, to dust. The warriors' march continued, the damage to them insignificant.

"We need more boulders," Slowhand declared. He repeated the statement more loudly to the ogur as if, somehow, being an ogur made it deaf. He then pointed at more boulders, just to make himself extra clear, but the ogur had already stomped towards them of his own volition. "Yes, more boulders!" Slowhand agreed needlessly.

Makennon assessed the ammunition available to them. Short of attempting to smash away the Dragonwings themselves, most of the rocks available to them were smaller than the first. "This isn't going to work," she said. "The last one barely scratched them."

"Maybe not," Slowhand responded, heaving. "But we can at least slow them down."

"And what will that achieve? There are no reinforcements coming."

"I don't know, okay? But I, for one, am not going to just stand here."

He and the ogur sent another boulder tumbling.

Kali, meanwhile, stared down the steps, and then inland, back along the peninsula. She bit her lip. "Slowhand, carry on with what you're doing because it just might help, but Makennon has a point. There's only one way to stop those warriors and that's to destroy what Munch used to animate them – destroy the Clockwork King. But that means first having to finish their general – finish Munch."

Slowhand and the ogur made another rock roll, and the archer nodded. "Finish Munch," he repeated, breathlessly. "Hooper, you have to be kidding. Even if you had a chance against his bodyguards, how in the hells would you get back down to him? Those things would mince you before you got halfway down the steps."

"There's one way," Kali said.

She swept up Munch's gutting knife from the ground and jammed it in her belt. Then, she stuck two fingers in her mouth and whistled. A second later, Horse stood next to her, braying, his broken tether dangling around his neck.

Kali mounted him and slapped his flank, welcoming his help.

Now it was Slowhand's turn to stare down the steps, Kali's intention dawning. "Oh, no," he said. "No, no, no. No..."

"*Hyyahh!*" Kali shouted.

She reined Horse around and galloped him towards the top of the steps, kicking his flanks to spur him on. Horse reached them and jumped, soaring in a determined arc over four of the risers before his hooves thudded back onto stone with an impact that made them spark and jarred Kali to the bones.

"*Hyyahh!*" she shouted again.

Horse thundered down the steps before them, Kali keeping her gaze straight ahead in the bouncing, rushing diagonal the world had become, and again kicked his flanks, spurring the bamfcat to greater speed.

"*Hyyahh!*"

They hit the jetty, and the world levelled, and still she kicked, bringing Horse to full gallop, the front ranks of the marching warriors now no more than ten yards ahead. As she'd hoped she would, she heard a distinctive shnak as the horns on Horse's body snapped fully from their housings, the bamfcat reacting instinctively to the danger to come.

Good boygirl, she thought, *good, good boygirl.*

And then they rammed straight into the army of the Clockwork King.

Kali was aware of little more than a sudden and rapid series of thuds and jarring impacts as Horse ploughed into and then through the advancing warriors, her world skewing this time into a seemingly endless number of fractured tableaux, flashes of hammers and axes and swinging arms, and of red, glaring eyes. There was nothing she could do but ride Horse as a helpless passenger, nothing she could do to affect their progress – all she could do was hope it continued, and that Horse's armour was strong enough to keep him from harm. The great beast ploughed onwards through the warriors, cutting a swathe through their middle, sending them staggering aside, and then, glimpsed through them at last, jarringly and shakingly, was the maw of the cowl. There were still far too many of the warriors between them and it, though, and within it, many, many more, still working their way up from the throne room, and the constant wall of metal and corrupted flesh was beginning to take its toll on Horse, not only in terms of slowing his momentum but in the amount of damage his armour was now taking. She couldn't – and wouldn't – push him any further, but that didn't really matter because it had never been her intention to reach the cowl, anyway. All she'd needed Horse to do was get her close to the water.

And now she needed to make sure Horse was safe.

Kali rose high in the saddle so that she touched only his stirrups, and then patted the bamfcat's neck. "It's time to do that thing you do," she said quickly, and hoped to the gods that he understood. "You know, the thing. Do it, Horse. Do it now!"

The bamfcat roared, and for a second Kali thought that perhaps he hadn't understood, but then she realised it wasn't that at all.

"Yes, you great lump, I'm fond of you, too, but you need to do the thing! Pits, Horse, do the thing and do it n – "

Horse reared, and the air cracked, and then the bamfcat vanished from under her, and suddenly Kali was flying over the heads of the marching warriors, all alone. She knew exactly what she was doing, however, and immediately turned what could have been a flailing tumble into an arched dive, taking her over the edge of the jetty. And then, like Horse, she, too, vanished – head first into the churning sea.

Kali hit smoothly, slicing beneath the surface like a knife. There, however, her smoothness came to an end, the churning maelstrom that was battering the side of the jetty flinging her around like a worgle in a whirlpool. It took her some time to orientate herself, arms and legs slapping and kicking against the currents, but finally she swam in the direction she wished. But she did not head for the surface, as might be expected. Instead, she swam towards the dark foundations of the entrance cowl to Martak. Slowhand had been right – there was no way to reach Munch through the warriors – but there *was* a way to reach him.

And there it was. Or, rather, they were.

The intakes for the water pipes loomed before her in the murky depths, the churning water around them exacerbated by the pumps somewhere inside Martak that drew it in. Kali had to fight against the pull so that she was not sucked against the grilles she saw protecting the pipes' mouths, and, thrashing and kicking again, manoeuvred herself so that she was able to grab both sides of one of the pipes, and there, amidst a cloud of bubbles as blinding as fog, tugged and wrenched at the grille until it came away. She let it fall to the seabed and then – her breath short – dug in her belt for her breathing conch before she thrust herself upwards and in.

It was almost peaceful inside the tube, the distant thudding of the pumps like a heartbeat, the rotation of the fans – slower now that their job in releasing the king and his army was done – a relaxing thrum. This was the first chance she'd had to appreciate the complex network of pipes that seemed to power the mechanics of the place, and, while she found it an achievement, she also found it rather odd because it was so distinctly *un-dwarven*. But then, she supposed, they hadn't had much lava to drive their engines here at the edge of the sea.

There was nothing peaceful about what was occurring beneath her, however, and as Kali wiped away the grime on the inner surface of the tube, and looked out, she saw the vaguely distorted forms of the advancing army of clockwork warriors marching in rank after rank along Martak's exit corridor. But she had no interest in them. They were the responsibility of Slowhand and the others now, and her concern was in reaching the man who controlled them and what he, in turn, controlled.

Kali swam along the tube, timing her strokes through the slowly rotating fanblades, heading horizontally and then downwards, rubbing the glass occasionally to determine how far into the complex she was. Eventually the light outside became shadowed and she realised she was passing through the section of tubing that ran through the surroundings of the first door, which meant there was only one short section of corridor remaining. There was, however, a problem. Her breathing was becoming laboured, and she realised the conch symbiotes had almost exhausted their current supply of oxygen. She would need to pick up her pace, get out of the tube quickly, or she'd become part of the flotsam floating around this hellhole for the rest of time.

She swam faster, ignoring her surroundings until a second batch of shadow told her she had at last returned to the throne room of the Clockwork King. But her breathing was becoming desperate now, and she could taste the toxic taint of her own used breath. She'd poison herself if she didn't get out of there right away.

Bubbles exploding from the sides of her mouth, Kali felt desperately around on the base of the tube, searching for some weakness in its length. She found a seal that linked sections and then pulled Munch's gutting knife from her belt, working at the strange, almost organic seal. It was more difficult than she expected, and her movements became increasingly jerky, imprecise, but at last a downwards spiral of bubbles indicated the seal was coming apart, water leaking into the throne room below.

She wondered if Munch would notice – notice that she was coming for him.

She stabbed his knife into the weakened seal, and a sudden lurch in the base of the tube warned her that it was about to give. Just in time she jammed herself inside the tube as the whole section dropped away from the rest of the network and hung down at an angle, water slamming into and over her back as it poured down into the throne room.

Kali released herself and went with the flow which, quite conveniently, washed her right in front of Munch, sitting there, on his throne.

"Miss Hooper," the dwarf resurgent said. "Even I have to confess this is something of a surprise."

"Hi, Stan," Kali said. "Have to say, you look a little rough."

He did, too. Munch was almost slumped in the throne he had so arrogantly adopted, looking drained and fevered. His eyes seemed unable to focus on her – or were, perhaps, focusing on a thousand things – and he involuntarily spasmed every few seconds. The blood that had leaked from where the spikes had stabbed into his skull had not dried, because the sweat that ran from his every pore wouldn't let it.

"Controlling the Thousand is proving to be something of a challenge," he said, wearily. "But one that I will master."

"Can't let you do that."

Munch paused. "Ah. You have returned to kill me."

"Not here to see if you've grown any higher."

"I am afraid," Munch said haltingly, almost as a gasp, "you are an inconvenience I cannot afford."

"Now, where have I heard that before? I suppose this is the part where you set your dogs on me?"

"Indeed." He blinked, and his four bodyguards snapped to face her, their feet thudding down as they adopted an attack stance.

Kali was ready for them. She'd been ready the moment she'd dropped from the tube to the floor. She only hoped that, in trying to do what she wanted to do, she was as capable as the events of recent days had suggested she could be.

Because if she wasn't, she was dead.

Again.

Four hammers slammed down from her left and from her right, impacting hard with the stone floor of the throne room and cracking it wide. They were clearly only warning blows but nevertheless Kali was already gone, backflipping away and feeling the heavy whoosh of the hammers' mass as she went. She straightened, turned and ran, inviting them to follow, which they duly did, their feet pounding on the damaged floor behind her.

Kali ran almost to the end of the throne room, seemingly intent on fleeing from their pursuit but planning nothing of the kind. For one thing, there was nowhere to go – the gallery steps and corridor were still filled with the mechanical warriors' slowly deploying ranks – but for another she knew exactly where in the throne room she wanted herself, and her would-be butchers, to be.

What she wanted to do, in fact, was let them drive her into a corner.

The mechanical warriors came on, hammers raised and axe blades swinging, while a somewhat weak cackling from Munch echoed in the distance. Kali stood her ground, waiting for her moment. As the four approached, she bounced on the balls of her feet, watching their axes, but, particularly, their hammers, not only for which of the warriors would swing the first blow but how they would swing it. She had, after all, learned a new trick in the Spiral of Kos.

The first two disappointed, and she dodged their downward swings by deftly rolling between them, but the third, swinging its hammer horizontally, was exactly what she'd been hoping for. As the hammer swung towards her, momentum guaranteed to carry it onwards and upwards, she ducked beneath and then instantly sprang onto its upper face from behind, letting it carry her into and then propel her through the air. She landed exactly where she wanted to be, on top of the very water tube she and Slowhand had first used to enter the throne room, but she did not use it to leave, instead simply standing there until her attackers swung at her again. This they did, and Kali glanced over at Munch as the hammers smashed towards her, watching to see if he'd realised his mistake. For at her current height, the deadly bludgeons of the bodyguards could not quite reach her, and instead they smashed into the tube itself. Glass shattered and water exploded, sending the bodyguards staggering back beneath its deluge.

Kali had leapt away at the moment of impact, and now ran further up the tube, in the direction of Munch, where she heard him roar in anger. Yes, he'd realised his mistake but, as was the way of these things, it did not stop him repeating it. The bodyguards pounded after her, hammers and axes swinging all the way, and as they swung they shattered more and more of the tube, so that entire sections of it fell away to the throne room floor. They didn't crash down, however, but splashed and sank, the increasing deluge of water from the ruptured system beginning to flood the throne room, the still rotating fans pulling more and more of it in from the sea. Kali continued her flight along the tubes and the warriors followed, almost berserk now, though their rage – Munch's rage – could do little to help them in what had become a forced wade through the rising waters. Again they swung, though more sluggishly now, their giant hammers slowed as they ploughed through the flood and, again, more sections of the tubes disintegrated before them. The water was deep enough for Kali's purpose now, and she stopped her flight, instead diving into the water herself, and there she clenched her gutting knife as she swam beneath the surface in the direction of her mechanical pursuers. There was always a way, she thought, not only to get into places but to defeat things, and swimming into the midst of the pack of bodyguards she slashed the wiry tendons on the ankles of all four, the water preventing them being able to manoeuvre fast enough to stop her. With a series of mechanical groans they collapsed beneath the ever-rising flood to the throne room floor.

Kali swam, and then waded from the water onto the base of the Clockwork King.

Munch, more feverish and manic-looking than ever now, seemed almost to shrink back before her.

"I knew that you were resourceful," he declared wearily. "I never realised quite how much."

As he spoke, an entire run of the water tubing collapsed from the throne room walls, weakened by the loss of the rest of its network, and beyond it, even more began to buckle. A crack appeared in the throne room wall.

"Yeah, well," Kali said, darkly. She was thinking back to the Flagons. "That slashing the ankle thing? Someone gave me the idea."

"Miss Hooper..."

"Stand up and face me, you bastard."

Blood ran slowly down Munch's forehead. "You know as well as

I that I cannot – I will not – leave this seat. I am helpless before you. So, go ahead – what are you waiting for?"

"*Aaargh!*" Kali roared, plunging the gutting knife downwards. But at the last moment she froze, the tip of the knife shuddering in her grip an inch from Munch's heart.

The dwarf chuckled deeply, and Kali regarded him with a hatred that could not manifest itself.

"You may have become some kind of fighting machine," Munch said, "but you will never be a true warrior. Not so long as you cannot finish your opponent. That is what differentiates the victor from the defeated on the battlefield."

"I can't let you continue this..."

"Then do what you came to do, girl. Stop me. Kill me. *Go on – do it!*"

Munch sounded almost as if he wanted her to. Kali pulled back her arm, ready to plunge the knife downwards once more, but again desire and conscience clashed, leaving the blade suspended and trembling, her whole body doing the same in furious frustration.

"Do it or all that you know will be gone, girl. Pontaine, Anclas, Vos, Gargas. Everything you know."

"You've already taken enough away from me."

"Soon there will be others who do what you do now – only they will be of the dwarven race. And it will be your bones they will pick over. *Your* bones, Kali Hooper. The bones of a fleeting and inconsequential speck in history."

"Not if I have anything to do with it."

Munch chuckled again. "Then do what must be done. Only you can't, can you? You have let down all those who trusted you, brought about the end of everyth –"

"No."

"The end of everything. You've lost, girl. You have los –"

There was a dull crunch and Munch's eyes widened suddenly in shock and disbelief, and for a moment Kali simply stared at him, wondering what had happened. Munch was staring back, directly into her eyes, but it took her a few seconds, during which a small tendril of blood ran from his left nostril, to realise that his eyes had already fogged and he was seeing nothing.

The arrow quivered slightly where it was embedded in the centre of his forehead.

Kali turned. How he had managed to get past the clockwork warriors she had no idea, but from the far end of the throne room a battered and bedraggled-looking Killiam Slowhand waded towards her through the rising and increasingly tumultuous water. He lowered Suresight to his side, its job done.

"In future, why don't you leave it to the sidekick to do the killing?" he said. He suddenly stretched his arms out and looked surprised. "What? You thought I'd let you do this alone?"

Kali inhaled a deep, trembling breath. There was no time for thanks or celebration, however, because there was still the problem of destroying the Clockwork King. But as Kali began to contemplate the problem, it was solved for her. The cracks that had begun to appear in the throne room walls widened suddenly, and as they did the ceiling itself began to crack and subside. Suddenly a wide gash appeared in what was effectively the sea bed and, along with chunks of rock, water began to pour down on the very spot where she and Slowhand stood.

Kali and the archer staggered back, watching the deluge pour onto the Clockwork King, and as the rocks crashed onto and shattered its cogs and pistons and gears, water poured thunderously onto the crystals that had brought its army to life. There was a series of sparks and then small explosions, and, at the opposite end of the throne room, the warriors that continued to march towards the exit suddenly stopped. Just like that.

Kali and Slowhand stared at them, watching to see if they moved again. But they didn't.

"Okaaaay..." Kali said.

Slowhand suddenly pulled her to the side as a chunk of rock hurtled down and smashed into the deluge next to where they stood.

"The whole place is coming down," he said. "Time to go."

"No argument there."

"After you."

"No, no, after you."

"Hooper, just –"

"Move. I know."

They swam towards the exit, manoeuvring themselves around the frozen forms of those clockwork warriors that had ground to a halt before it, and preparing to do the same with those in the corridor itself. Their red eyes stared as dully as those of Munch now, and they seemed strangely at peace.

The sea can have them, Kali thought.

Slowhand swam through the doors before her, and she was only an arm's length behind him when a sudden surge in the water caught her from behind and sucked her away in its backwash, returning her to the heart of the collapsing and flooding chamber. And, unbelievably, she saw that the doors to the throne room were closing.

"Slowhand!" she yelled.

The archer had already noticed her absence and had turned around, attempting to swim back to her aid. But it was almost as if the water was consciously trying to keep him back, one small surge after another catching him and holding him where he was so that he did little more than tread water. He stared up at the closing doors and roared with anger and frustration.

"Hooper!"

Dammit, Kali thought. *Dammit, dammit, dammit!* But as much as she tried to reach the closing gap, similar surges to those that frustrated Slowhand held her back. The rumbling of the doors could be heard even over the roaring of the inrushing sea, and the last thing she saw of Slowhand was his anguished face as they closed finally with a resounding boom.

Kali splashed around. The seawater continued to rush in with a roar and she rose slowly towards the throne room ceiling. Then, suddenly, the roaring stopped and she realised she was fully underwater, the throne room completely flooded.

As rocks fell about her in slow motion, an eerie silence descended. Kali fumbled in her equipment belt and withdrew her breathing conch, jamming it in her mouth, then floated there and stared into the murk. She might have been cut off from Slowhand but she was not alone, and below her the lifeless body of Munch drifted from its seat and rose up, ascending above the still forms of his warriors. Kali let the corpse float past her face without reaction, but then another shadowy shape in the water caught her eye and she almost spat out her conch in shock.

Because the seawater that had poured in from above had brought something with it.

Kali back-pedalled in a sea of bubbles. There, hovering before her in the water, was a humanoid figure – but humanoid was as close as it came to anything human-looking she had ever seen on Twilight.

Some kind of... fishman. She'd heard reports that similar creatures had been sighted in Turnitia but she'd dismissed them as the ramblings, perhaps even the ravings, of thieves too gone on flummox to be grounded in reality. But here one was, right in front of her – and it was staring at her.

Communicating with her.

Not talking, though. The thieves she had spoken with had described the fishmen as black-eyed, green-scaled, razor-toothed and bespined, but this one was different, its scales silver, face smooth and mouth toothless, with glowing nodules that hung from either side of its jaw. But neither mouth nor jaw moved as it spoke. Instead, Kali heard its words inside her head.

And, what was even more disturbing, it knew her name.

Kali Hooper. I am pleased that your path has brought you where you should be. That you have achieved what you must.

Kali found herself responding without even knowing how. And finding herself doing so without the need to speak, she found herself asking everything in her head at once.

Where I should be? What are you? Just what the hells is going on?

The creature floated where it was, regarding her, a paper-thin tail moving lazily behind it, and Kali felt a kind of smile – a very cold one.

Questions. Questions all the time, since when you were a child. Even then we could hear you – here, beneath the sea.

What? Are you saying you've been spying on me?

Spying? No. Watching. You, and the others. The Four.

The Four?

Four known to us. Four unknown to each other. Four who will be known to all.

Oh, gods help me, you're one of those who talks in riddles. I've come across your kind before. Statues, mainly, but –

Riddles? No. Only answers not yet formed.

Listen! You're doing it again! Hey, it's been a long day – how about some simple answers to some simple questions?

The creature floated before her, saying nothing. Kali took it as an invitation to continue.

Who are you?

Our name would mean nothing. We are the Before. The After. Those who have always been and will be again.

Will you stop it!

I... we... they... apologise.

Kali scowled, then frowned. *The Before?* she thought. *The After?*

My visions? she asked. *Were you responsible for them?*

Yes.

How? Why?

The first, to offer a solution. The second, to drive you. The third – the third to remind you of your own mortality... and, more importantly, that everything is not as it seems. The creature paused. *We know you but... we were uncertain of your resolve.*

What? You thought I'd give up? Back off because what I faced was too much? Then, Mister – you are a Mister? – however much you think you know me, you don't know me at all.

From this moment, no. Your path is what it has become. It was important to us only that you were here – at Martak.

Kali trod water. Martak. The way the creature spoke of it – spoke of her – it was almost as if they both had a place in some unknown scheme of things. It suddenly occurred to her once more how un-dwarven the water network had felt.

You were here when all this began, weren't you? You helped the dwarves to build this place – to build the Clockwork King?

They were dying. They had no resources. The balance had to be maintained.

The balance?

Too many of the elven ones, too few of the dwarves. The ferocity of the Ur'Raney was unanticipated, and their numbers after their victory had to be... curtailed.

Curtailed? You're saying you did what you did to give the dwarves an advantage? By all the gods, you wanted the Ur'Raney culled, didn't you? Only it all went wrong – the warriors you helped the dwarves create turned on their own as well – and then on everyone and everything else...

The creature remained silent for a second. *We chose our agent badly... everyone makes mistakes.*

But why would you do that?

The balance had to be –

Maintained? Kali shouted in her head. *What balance – why the hells are you talking abou –*

She suddenly choked and realised that, once more, her breathing conch was near to exhausted, something that her conversational partner had also spotted.

I would suggest that you have time for one more question.

One more question, Kali thought, and despite the fact she had a thousand in her head – about the balance, about this undersea creature, about the Old Races – she knew exactly what it had to be. Because, somehow, she knew it was relevant.

Do you know where I come from?

The creature laughed – not laughed in her mind but actually, physically laughed – and was suddenly obscured in a cloud of bubbles that came either from whatever orifice it used to breathe or simply from the stirring of the water created by its thrashing reaction. Wherever the bubbles had come from, when they went away the creature was gone.

Damn you, Kali thought. *Whoever or whatever you are, damn you.*

More rock fell about her from above, and with her last lungful of air she began to swim upwards, kicking and kicking until at last she passed through a fissure in the ceiling of the throne room and up, out into the sea. She broke its broiling surface and began to swim towards the shore. Slowly, wearily, she ascended the steps, glancing down at the jetty and the stilled warriors that would remain there now, until the weather of the area simply wore them away.

Slowhand, Horse and the ogur were assembled above. There was, however, one member of the party missing.

"Where's Makennon?"

"She skedaddled when the army stopped. Probably halfway back to Scholten Cathedral already, licking her wounds. Glad to see you made it, Hooper. But then, I should have known you would."

Kali waved him away, too knackered to speak. Her banter with Slowhand would, she knew, resume some time soon. There were, after all, things to do, among them find his sister and a cure for Merrit Moon.

Before that, however...

Kali patted Horse and took a bottle of flummox from his saddlebag. She drank deeply, and burped.

And then she stared down at Martak. At the sea. And she thought of what she had just encountered in it.

There were more questions to be answered than ever before. It was good, then, that she liked a challenge. In fact, she felt a renewed determination to discover the secrets of Twilight and the ultimate fate of the Old Races. And in doing so, she knew, she would leave nothing unexplored, nothing undiscovered, nothing untouched.

THE END

The CRUCIBLE of the DRAGON GOD

In memory of

JOE HALLIWELL
2001-2009

His game over far too soon

CHAPTER ONE

THIS IS HOW Kali Hooper would have escaped the things that had slaughtered four men before the first of them could scream. The same things that were coming to slaughter him.

That huge, seemingly unscalable rock, there, the one just ahead? That she would have scaled with ease. And that frozen vine beyond? The one ready to snap? On that she would have swung without thinking twice. The vine would have snapped at exactly the right moment, of course, and she would have soared with it over the abyss. This would not have worried her, though, because that ledge further on and down – yes really, *that one*, way over there – she would have flailed towards, rolling like some circus tumbler to soften her impact as she came in to land. And she would not have stopped there – oh no, though she might be grunting now – kicking up scree as she ran on and threw herself towards that crumbling ledge, and then the one beyond that, flipping, twisting and spinning, stretching all ways to grab the next small lump of salvation that would save her from a plummeting, broken death.

She would have made it, too, though rocks might have fallen in her wake – knowing her, perhaps there might even have been an accidental avalanche that would have destroyed half the mountainside – but, as usual, she would make it because she had to *succeed*. There, dangling from that last ledge, she would take a moment to catch her breath before her *piece de resistance*, a full body flip that would take her up and over until she could climb the rockface to safety. Her flight would have been done then and, from her refuge on the clifftop, she would have turned, bitten the cork from a bottle of flummox and downed the beer. And then, with a smile and a burp, she would have spat the cork at her pursuers. If she were feeling particularly mischievous, she might even have shown them her –

No. He did not want to think about that particular part of her anatomy. It seemed, now, somehow… disrespectful. Because this is how Kali Hooper *would* have escaped the things, had Kali Hooper not been dead.

That's right, he thought. Dead. Gone. Twelve hands under. The desperately running, blonde-maned archer had struggled to accept it but had come to realise that it had to be true – *had to be* given the facts. Hooper had been missing for weeks now and in that time there had been no sightings, news or contact other than that over which she'd likely had no control – the return to the Flagons, alone, of a half-starved and agitated Horse, and the discovery, washed-up as jetsam on a Nürnian beach, of her equipment belt attached to a blood-stained piece of her dark silk body suit. Where she had met her end he could not – *might never* – know, because she had left the tavern with a frown, telling no one what her destination was. But what he *did* know was that under no circumstances would she have missed the rendezvous she was meant to keep with him eight days before, at the base of the Drakengrat Mountains. He knew that because he knew *she* knew how important to him this expedition was. No, without doubt Hooper was gone, and whether she had met her end in the Razor Ruins of Rarg or the Blood Bogs of Bibblebobble or whatever other malignantly named hellshole had piqued her interest this time, it seemed the secret history of the peninsula she had worked so hard to unearth had, ultimately, buried her instead.

The painful truth was that he missed her like hells but it was what he, Killiam Slowhand, did that mattered now, and frankly, as far his imagined escape for Kali went... well, there wasn't a chance in the hells.

There'd be no impossible leaps up the rockface, no suicidal swings on snapping vines and no fairground acrobatics to leave his pursuers stymied. Because he wasn't Hooper. No, he was just her sometime lover, sometime sidekick and – oh, by the way, mere mortal. If he didn't spot a way out of this that was within his capabilities he wouldn't even be that. All he could do was run for his life. Oblivious to all but the pounding of his feet beneath him and the mountain winds that whistled around him, all he could do was keep moving and hope that something provided him with a means of escape.

The k'nid, he reflected as he ran, spinning occasionally to fire a volley of arrows in their direction, hoping to slow the blurry, crackling things down. Named by a Malmkrug baron after the local term for bogeyman, they had begun to appear near the town about the time of Slowhand's arrival there. Already a number of its inhabitants had fallen victim to them, lost to their sheer speed. They were not only fast, they were deadly and seemingly impervious to harm – and they seemed to be growing in number. People in Malmkrug had already shored up their homes in defence against them and their attacks on the town were as sudden and inexplicable as their origin was unknown.

Or, at least, had been until now.

For as he had ascended higher and higher into the mountains and seen the trails of more of the unnatural creatures – though most, thankfully, from afar – Slowhand knew something those below did not. That the k'nid, whatever the hells they were, seemed to be coming from somewhere around *here*.

It was typical. Pure Slowhand luck. To have fetched up in the apparent spawning ground of a plague of the deadliest things the peninsula had ever seen – and he had no one but himself to blame.

Over the past few months he'd put out a number of fresh feelers regarding his sister, and while the vast majority of them had returned nothing, the one that had led him here had shown promise. He had learned from a trader in Malmkrug that some two months before, a party of adventurers had purchased sufficient supplies for a prolonged ascent into the Drakengrat range. Despite the fact they seemed to have gone to considerable length to disguise themselves, their attitude, bearing and general demeanour very quickly gave them away as Final Faith. There was nothing, apart from the obvious, wrong with them being Faith, but the fact that they'd felt the need to disguise themselves meant they had to be up to something clandestine. That in itself was worthy of investigation. What was more worthy of investigation, however, was that the trader had said the party was led by a woman – a woman whose description he had found achingly familiar.

Jenna.

Slowhand still felt a burning rod of anger inside him every time he thought of what those bastards had done to his sister – recruiting and forcefully indoctrinating her into the Faith – and the thought that she was involved in something they found necessary to disguise their involvement with, made him as concerned for her safety as he was angered by her involvement in it. Unfortunately, that anger had had more than enough time to cool, the lead that had seemed so promising a week ago turning out to be as much of a wild frool chase as so many had before. Because if Jenna was up here, then she had discovered some chameleon spell that had transformed her into just one more of the endless snow covered rocks. No, there had been no Jenna, not even a *sign* of Jenna, and her presence had been supplanted by the k'nid, and all he could do now was cut his losses and run.

Slowhand's chest felt leaden now, and his breath was hot and rasping; symptoms not only of the altitude but of a speed and distance covered that he had not attempted since what his army passing out class, impressed and more than a little jealous, had dubbed the 'Night of a Hundred Wives.' And *that* had been quite some years ago. He was maintaining his lead on the k'nid, though, if only because one of his volleys of arrows had caused a rockfall on the narrow mountain path along which he fled. The rockfall hadn't harmed the k'nid, or even slowed them down, but it had forced them to take a detour, which was good enough for now. As he continued onward and upward, struggling more and more, he was even starting to think that he might lose them. But that was when he ran out of ground.

Slowhand came to a skidding, skittering stop, gasping with exhaustion and frustration, watching in disbelief as stones pushed by his sliding soles tumbled away only a few inches in front of him over a precipice. What made his predicament a hundred times worse was that not only had the terrain come to an end ahead of him but, unnoticed until now, to his left and right as well. In fact, there was little more than a half foot of rock on either side of him before –

Slowhand's focus zoomed in and out at the same time, and there was a vertiginous rush in his ears.

Oh boy.

Battered by wind, the archer turned slowly and carefully in a circle, taking in his precarious situation.

He was standing at the tip of a very long, very narrow outcrop of rock that, by all rights, should have collapsed under its own weight. Instead, it thrust itself defiantly and dizzyingly out into the night sky, seemingly ignoring gravity. In profile he guessed it would look like some part constructed bridge, stretching halfway across the deep chasm over which it jutted. But where a bridge might have had supports to stabilise itself, here there was nothing beneath it. Nothing at all. For a very, very, *very* long way down.

As Slowhand looked down at a river that height had reduced to the width of a hair, he realised his perch was impossible. A thing that *should* fall but didn't. And that realisation brought another – where exactly he was.

My gods, this is Thunderlungs' Cry.

He recalled Kali telling him how she had travelled here once with Horse – the original Horse, that was – to experience the legend that had been a favourite girlhood tale.

Two tribes, split by this vast chasm in the mountains, had met only once when freak weather had driven them both into the valley far below. That meeting had led to romance between two individuals but war between the tribes themselves. When each tribe had returned to their own side, the two lovers were prohibited from ever meeting again by their elders, and all paths to the valley were barred to them. The man, who became known as Thunderlungs, managed, however, to despatch a message to his lover, Mawnee, using a carrier bird, telling her that if their ancestors favoured their bonding, they would provide a bridge across which the two of them could be reunited.

He had come one Kerberos-lit night, and there she had stood, far across the chasm. He had cried out to the souls who scudded across Kerberos's surface, asking the aid of those who had gone before to unite the pair once more. This they had done, by growing a half bridge of rock from the side of his chasm, and another from that of Mawnee's side, and the two had begun to cross towards each other's outstretched arms. The ancestors had warned, however, that if their love faltered, even for a moment, then the bridge would be no more.

Thunderlungs' love was strong but *something* that night made Mawnee falter. To her lover's horror the bridge beneath her crumbled away, and she fell to her death.

It was said that Thunderlungs roared his heartbreak into the night – a roar that some said those who had lost loved ones could still hear – until he had frozen solid where he stood. Whereupon his ancestors had laid him down and made him part of the bridge itself, so that his shadow might touch, once a day, the place where his love had fallen.

It was a sad story, Slowhand reflected, and one that might have brought tears to his eyes if they hadn't already been streaming from this farking wind. And it was not as sad as his own would be if he didn't get off this rock right now. Because there had been that sudden, strange crackling behind him once more – as if he were listening to a tavern fire – and he had spun to see the k'nid had caught up with him, reaching the start of the Cry in a clammering rush but there coming to a dead stop, as if assessing what lay before them.

Now that they were at a stop, it was the first chance Slowhand had had to properly study the creatures.

A little over the length of a stretching man when they unfurled for the kill – a manoeuvre he had seen on four occasions and fervently wished that he had not – he saw now that they seemed to be neither animal, vegetable or mineral. They looked like a tangle of roots of glistening black wood that writhed about each other, as if suffering the death throes of the tree from which they had come. Except that they had come from no tree – the way his arrows had bounced from them proving that whatever it was they were made of, it was not wood. As tough as their bodies were, however, it did not prevent them being infinitely flexible. While they seemed to favour pursuit of their prey while in the form of a rough, gnarled, rolling sphere, chance glances had revealed that form shifting constantly between tumbleweed and what appeared to be a running shnarl and, on occasion when obstacles needed to be negotiated, even the briefly airborne form of some predatory bird. But of all their incarnations, it was the one that had slaughtered his companions that Slowhand could not shake from his mind.

He recalled his horror as he'd tried to fend off the k'nid who had closed rapidly on his guide and helpers, because while he'd expected them to be simply crushed beneath the rolling forms or smashed from the rocks to fall below, that wasn't what had happened at all. Instead the creatures had unfurled to reveal a red and fleshy interior and simply swallowed their victims before returning to a tangled sphere form. And no more than two or three seconds later each man had been deposited back outside the sphere, but all they were now were piles of stripped and steaming bones.

And now it was his turn. Unless some miracle occurred.

Slowhand looked around in desperation for a way out, but there was nothing. Thunderlungs' Cry simply projected too far from the rest of the rocks to provide any escape route. As the front rank of the k'nid began to crackle towards him, he was beginning to think the most merciful way out would be to jump, when he glimpsed something approaching from the north. Something in the sky.

What was that? A cloud? A bird? No, too small to be a cloud. Too big to be a bird. Unless it was a small cloud, of course. Or a big bird. Yes, a very big bird.

Then it slowly sank in what it actually was he *was* looking at.

It was a thing of inflated cloth like a giant balloon, with a thing of wood, like a gondola, slung beneath it. On the deck of that gondola he could just make out the tiny shapes of people. He realised then that he was looking at some kind of... *airship*.

A *flying* machine.

"Hey!" Slowhand shouted, desperately waving his hands above his head. "*Hey!*"

If the people on board heard him, however, they chose to ignore his cries, as the airship continued on its route without any reaction at all. He shouted again, but once more with no effect. The airship was closer now and he could see the people aboard, busied in the tasks he presumed were needed to keep the craft aloft.

If Slowhand couldn't bring the airship to him, then he would have to go to the airship.

Forcing his wonderment aside, the archer calculated its height and trajectory relative to the Cry, and while on the one hand the news was good – it would pass *beneath* the Cry – on the other it was bad. Too *far* beneath.

Slowhand double-taked on the k'nid and the airship. If he jumped from this height he would likely bounce right off the balloon and plummet to his death, so that height needed to be reduced. As far as he could see there was only one way to do that. He would need a rope. A rope he didn't have.

He sighed in resignation. It was as unbelievable as it was inevitable.

To make the ladder he needed, his clothes would have to come off. And to make the ladder long enough, that meant *all* of them. It was certainly the most unusual place he had had to resort to such action, and it was almost a pity he didn't have an audience but then, in the dire circumstances in which he found himself, there would be little if any time to show off his assets.

Okay, he thought as he pulled off and tore into strips his tunic, pants and shorts, and the mountain wind whistled around his lower regions, *his reduced assets.*

Standing there in just his boots, feeling disturbingly exposed considering the proximity of the k'nid, he quickly tied the clothing together and then, in turn, looped it around and secured it to the lip of the Cry. That done, he took a firm grip of the cloth and slipped slowly over the edge, where he dangled for a second before lowering himself down hand over hand as the flying machine drew closer.

A thought suddenly struck him.

I'm stark naked in a pair of thigh length leather boots, with a bow slung on my back, a thousand feet up in the air, and whoever's on that ship is in for a big surprise.

It was actually a bit kinky and he made a mental note to investigate the business possibilities of such goings on, on his return. Perhaps he could earn a few extra golds doing this for hen parties, birthdays and the like.

If he returned that was.

Because if he was going to do this it was now or never.

Slowhand hung there, his thighs clenched tightly around the stretched remains of his pants, revolving slightly as the flying machine nosed onward, manoeuvring itself at last beneath him. There was still a hundred and fifty feet or so between him and it, but for a second before it came directly under him and his view was obscured by the bag that seemed to keep it aloft, he could make out in more detail the deck of the gondola that was slung beneath it. There at least eight people continued to busy themselves with piloting the craft, a couple of them agitated, pointing and shouting roughly in his direction. But what they said was lost in the shrieking of the wind. Slowhand tried waving once more, one-handed, keeping a firm grip on his makeshift rope, but his potential saviours were clearly too involved with their duties to notice him.

Who the hells were these people?

Timing his drop to a split second, so that he would impact directly in the centre of the flying machine's airbag, he let go.

He manoeuvred himself as the wind whistled by him, turning so that he would impact on his back, glancing downward to ensure his target remained dead centre of his fall.

Slowhand suddenly found himself impacting so hard on the flying machine's airbag that the wind was knocked out of him. He lay there for a second, squirming and cringing in pain – not quite as soft as he'd expected considering this thing was light enough to fly.

The realisation came once more that he was lying on some unknown machine that flew like a bird or floated like a cloud but clearly wasn't either, and a sudden desire to feel something firmer than cloth beneath him possessed him.

The main centre of activity was towards the front of the airship, however, and until he knew who he was dealing with he thought it wise to descend from the airbag at the opposite end of the craft.

He turned onto his front and crawled towards the rear, using the thick ropes that reinforced the airbag to pull himself along. Slowhand was about to flip downwards when he pulled suddenly back with a "*Whoa!*"

The reason for this was what had so far been hidden from his view *behind* the vast balloon. A great, orange orb that pulsed there with an energy unknown to him, but which made his scalp itch, his eyes bulge and his skin throb. Whatever it was, it seemed to be powering the craft, but he wanted to be nowhere near it.

Instead, Slowhand manoeuvred himself to where he could drop to a quiet part of the deck and, using the ropes to restrain his descent, slipped downwards until he could grab the lowest rope and flip himself over to land feet first on the deck below. His impact was quiet enough but he still dropped into a gentle squat, as if his additional weight might prove too much for the airship and force it out of the sky. He stayed that way for a few moments, gazing left and right at the still level skyline, then experimented further by thumping the deck with his fist, harder and harder with each swing. Satisfied that the machine was still aloft, he rose to a standing position and jumped on the spot, once – tentatively – then again, and then, in a state of merry disbelief, over and over again. The deck remained solid beneath him.

There was only one thing left that he had to do to prove to himself that what was happening was happening. Slowhand ran to the side of the deck and peered over its railing, down towards the floor of the valley, far below. If he could have reached, he would have swung a hand below the hull, checking for invisible supports or struts. But he realised that was even more implausible than what he was seeing and, at last, came to accept that he was indeed up in the air with nothing underneath him.

No doubt about it. He was *flying*.

Well, okay, the machine beneath him was flying.

"I see your clothes still fall off at every opportunity. For the Lord of All's sake, throw him a cloak someone."

Slowhand turned around.

The crew had made their way from the nose to where he stood and were gathered in a semicircle, regarding him. Whatever individuals he had expected to be manning this strange craft, he had to admit he hadn't expected it to be *them*. He looked at the cloak emblazoned with a crossed circle without saying a word. It wasn't the fact that they were Final Faith that disconcerted him but rather who appeared to be leading them.

Tall, lithe and possessed of the same windswept mane of blonde hair as himself, she hadn't changed much in the six years since he had last seen her.

"Hello, sis."

"Brother."

Slowhand swallowed. It wasn't the unexpected encounter that made him do so, but the way Jenna had said that single word. For a moment he had forgotten that while his sister may not have altered physically, the Faith had long since indoctrinated her into their ways. She was not the person he had known, and that 'brother' had been delivered almost as if she were conversing not with her own flesh and blood but simply a fellow member of her damned religion.

"Jenna," he said. "*Jenna...*"

"As touching as this reunion is," a figure behind Jenna said, "we have a problem requiring your attention."

Jenna looked at him and the figure threw back his hood. Slowhand felt an involuntary snarl curl his upper lip. He was staring at a man he had not seen since his incarceration in the Final Faith's dungeons beneath Scholten Cathedral. Querilous Fitch. That he was here, with Jenna, made his blood boil – because this was the man who played with people's minds.

"Was it you?" Slowhand demanded. "Was it you who took my sister away?"

"I hardly think now is the time –"

"We're talking!" Slowhand growled.

"You will be *dying* if you do not heed my words," Fitch said matter-of-factly, and looked up.

Slowhand followed his gaze, as did Jenna.

The airship was now passing out from under the shadow of Thunderlungs' Cry, but the outcrop of rock was barely visible for the number of dark shapes that were dropping from it towards them. The archer felt his heart lurch. Seemingly with scant regard for their own survival, the k'nid were flinging themselves at the airship, many of them plummeting past into the abyss, but others falling on the balloon, whilst their brethren clawed for purchase on the hull of the gondola.

"Dammit!" Jenna declared. "Persistent little bastards, aren't they?" She spun to the crew. "All hands – prepare to repel boarders. Mister Ransom, Mister Leech, take us hard to port, full power. This'll be a rough ride, people, but trust me we'll shake our visitors off."

"Shake them off?" Slowhand said. "You must have weapons. Use them!"

"What good did *your* weapon do, brother?" Jenna snapped back at him, striking Suresight dismissively with the back of her hand. "Tell me that!"

Slowhand couldn't deny how useless his bow had proven, and looked desperately at the k'nid, biting his lip. "Is there something I can do?"

"Yes. Stay out of the way."

With that, Jenna moved off to position herself just behind the two men manning the airship's twin wheels, barking orders from where she stood, omitting only Querilous Fitch whose duty seemed to consist wholly of standing stock still and glowering at the archer. Slowhand ignored him, unable to help but be impressed with the way this crew handled their strange vessel.

Since the debacle of the Clockwork King, he had come to regard the Final Faith not only as dangerous but as dangerously irresponsible. Blundering buffoons whose interference in the peninsula's past could bring it close to doomsday. But here it was different and he was sure that was due in no small part to the tactical skills of his sister. She handled her crew with ease and they repaid her with utmost loyalty. Slowhand felt a momentary surge of pride, recognising that she had obviously come a long way since the last time he had seen her, even if her development had taken place under the auspices of the Faith.

The only thing that gave him cause for concern now was what the hells she was doing – especially as the airship was heading straight for the rock face.

"Urm, Jenna..."

"Steady as she goes," Jenna ordered, seemingly unphased. "Steady... steady... and... turn *now*!"

Both of the men manning the wheels reacted instantly, spinning hard to the left. Slowhand felt the deck tip beneath him as the gondola swung beneath the canopy. It swung so far, in fact, that as the dirigible went into its turn, the side of the hull and the airbag scraped against the face of the rock. The air was filled with a wrenching that sounded as if the gates of the hells themselves were opening.

Jenna's manoeuvre had been executed perfectly but there had to variables – the prevailing wind, air pockets – in an airship such as this, and what had been executed perfectly in theory did not necessarily turn out so in practice. It wasn't her fault, then, that the hull sounded to him like it was in danger of tearing itself apart. Despite being told to stay out of the way, Slowhand couldn't help but feel like the protective brother and raced to the guard rail, unslinging Suresight as he went and then using the bow to push off from the rockface. Slowhand staggered back, yelping, as he was punched in the face and then spun away from his position. He glared into the angered face of Jenna.

"What in the almighty hells do you think you're farking doing? You're tearing this ship apart!"

"Am I, brother?" Jenna shouted again. "Look! Look!"

Slowhand did, and suddenly realised his mistake.

The ship's impacting with the rocks hadn't, it seemed, been a miscalculation on his sister's part, but a carefully calculated strategy to remove their troublesome visitors. As he watched, those k'nid that were working their way towards them were scraped away from the dirigible's bag as they were caught between its surface and the rock. The screeching things tumbling away into oblivion. However, it only removed those k'nid that clung to that section of the hull. Slowhand was opening his mouth to point this out when he realised, once again, that Jenna was way ahead of him.

"Swing her round! One eighty degrees full rudder!"

The deck lurched beneath Slowhand as the order was instantly acted upon, and he was forced to cling to a handrail to prevent himself stumbling. Jenna, however, strode the tipping deck with ease, clearly practised with her 'airlegs' and still barking orders as she went. Slowhand watched as she executed a series of manoeuvres that made him swell with pride, making the airship do things it was clearly not designed for. Despite the fact that the airship collided with the rocks around it on a number of occasions – and the faces of its crew were clearly concerned about the battering it was taking – they nevertheless continued to obey without question, until the last of the k'nid had been ripped away. Only then did Jenna sigh with relief.

"Resume course. Steady as she goes."

Slowhand was about to move towards her and congratulate her on the flying display when Fitch strode towards her instead, whispering something in her ear.

"Dammit," Jenna said. "How bad?"

"The orb has purged energy," Fitch said. "We need to replenish it, enter Waystation One, or we will not reach Gransk."

"We can't afford to lose the time, but I suppose there's no choice. All right, prepare to take her in."

The orb, Slowhand thought.

Presumably the pulsating orb that seemed to drive the airship, but the waystation, what was that? And what and where the hells was Gransk?

"Problem?" he said, moving forward.

"Nothing that can't be rectified."

"Where, in this... Waystation One?"

"That's right, in Waystation One."

Slowhand was getting a little tired of being left out of the loop, even if, strictly speaking, he had no place in it. "What are you doing here above the clouds, sis? Where did this ship come from? What the hells is going on?"

"All hands," Jenna said. "Prepare to bring us around."

"Yes, Captain Freel."

Now Slowhand said nothing. Instead he simply stared at his sister instead.

That she had effectively ignored him – *was* ignoring him – after all this time spoke volumes for the depth of indoctrination the Faith had instilled in her, but that wasn't what disturbed him the most. What was with the Captain *Freel* bit? That wasn't her name. What was going on? He perhaps couldn't blame her for adopting another name but what he didn't understand was why Freel? It wasn't an assumed name like his own. So, unless she had become really boring in the intervening years, did that mean she had the name Freel for a reason? Had she been adopted? Gods, had she married? Whatever the reason it hinted at a history he knew nothing about, and considering that she was his twin sister, that simply wasn't right.

One thing was clear, however. The two of them were not going to be playing catch-up right now.

"Three degrees right rudder. Orb to half power. Ready a pulse on my mark."

"Aye, Ma'am."

"Half degree correction and... mark! Steady as she goes, Mister Ransom. Prepare to take us in."

The Final Faith crew obeyed Jenna's commands – with the exception of Fitch, who simply stood with his arms folded, staring at him, which Slowhand most definitely didn't like.

"This... *civilian* should not be seeing this," Querilous Fitch snapped.

"What would you have me do, threadweaver? Throw him overboard? He's my *brother*, dammit."

"No. *I* am your brother now."

That was it as far as Slowhand was concerned. He was about to go for Fitch when something took his mind entirely off his intent. Because Jenna's commands had turned the airship back towards Thunderlungs' Cry – or rather back and *beneath* it – and what he saw there he was immediately convinced was what had made Thunderlungs' lover falter and fall all of those many centuries ago.

Beneath the Cry was a huge cave mouth that was not a cave mouth at all – at least not a purely natural one. It appeared to have been bored out of the rock and led deep inside it. All along its sides – leading inward in two neat rows – were lines of great, glowing tubes set inside rune-inscribed arches. Tubes which pulsed in sequence as if designed to guide an airship in. And that, it seemed, was exactly what they did, because the airship passed between them and was swallowed by the huge cavern mouth.

My gods, Slowhand thought, gaping upward. *This is Old Race – the biggest Old Race thing I've ever seen. Pits of Kerberos, Hooper would have given everything to see this.*

He only hoped that whatever Old Race ruin – for it would have been nothing else – had claimed her life at last was as awe-inspiring as this one, because then at least his lover would have died happy.

If not, well, knowing Hooper, right now she'd be spinning in her grave.

CHAPTER TWO

"*AAAAAAAAAAAARRRRRRRRGGGGGGGGGHHHHHHHHH!*"

The cry of fury, of pain and of sheer frustration that boomed from beneath the ground was sudden and startling, shattering the desolate quiet of the dusty canyon and causing the strange black birds that nested there in twisted trees to take to the air with a chorus of haunting caws. The cry reverberated out of the canyon and across the landscape beyond. But there was no one out there to hear it – no one for leagues – and after a while, as its echo died down, the birds returned to their trees. There, they did not snatch up the dropped carrion on which they had been feasting but, instead, regarded each other with furled wings, cowed heads and darting, beady eyes. Troubled by this latest disturbance to their long abandoned, isolated piece of the world, their gaze turned along the canyon, past the rusted, age-warped rails of metal and the overturned, skeletal frames of the carts which once had rode them, and towards the dark and forbidding mouth at the canyon's end. And they wondered what it was they had done to offend the angry-spirit-who-had-come-to-live-beneath-them this time.

Ever since the spirit had arrived on its strange, armoured steed and gone into that dark mouth – there first announcing its displeasure with a deep rumble, an unknown curse and a great cloud of dust that had erupted from it by sunset that day – they had struggled to understand its subsequent outbursts, no doubt intended for them, but each time they had neared their answer another outburst had come and they had fled to the skies in panic once more. So it was now – as they felt the seed of an answer within them – the words of the angry-spirit-who-had-come-to-live-beneath-them came once more:

"Owww! Rollocks! Count to ten. One-two... no, soddit... You farking hoooor!"

Far below, through a labyrinthine series of tunnels and diggings, through galleries and chambers that had never seen the light of

250

day, and past tools and carts like those above, Kali Hooper grunted with pain as she pulled the lengths of cloth she held in each fist as taut as she could. The binding around the splints on her leg pulled tight, pressing the splintered bone in her shin tightly but agonisingly together, causing her to bite down hard on the gutting knife she had clenched between her teeth. Her groan echoed dully, joining the still audible reverberations of her earlier cry and reminding the solitary, bedraggled figure sitting pained, sweating and slumped in a small antechamber again and again of the mess she'd gotten herself into.

No, not exactly her, she reflected, but a certain completely mad little bastard whom Killiam Slowhand, in her stead, had long since despatched to the hells. Damn the man, she thought. Even dead Konstantin Munch continued to cause her pain.

The fact was, her current predicament *was* all the fault of Katherine Makennon's one-time right hand man. It might have been months since her final battle with him at the dwarven outpost of Martak, and the dwarf-blooded resurgent might even now be floating decomposed in the still and murky waters of its collapsed ruins, but that didn't stop his misconceived plan to resurrect dwarven glory from endangering her life yet again. Indirectly, at least. She should have known nothing good would come of it when one of Makennon's agents had contacted her with a set of papers which he explained the Anointed Lord wished to gift her in return for helping her with that affair. She should have said 'no thanks' there and then, but the fact was she hadn't been able to resist, had she? Oh no, because the papers turned out to be directions and maps to stores that Munch had established across the peninsula, and there was always a chance that there was going to be something more than a little interesting in there.

There hadn't been, as it turned out – the weapons and tools that Munch had collected to equip his fantasised army were as warped and useless as his masterplan – but in growing desperation to unearth at least *one* artefact, she had decided to give it one last stab, to follow one last set of directions. That stab and those directions had brought her here.

She really had no idea how long ago that had been, now, and she had all but forgotten that, ultimately, the trip had proven useless again, but that wasn't the problem. No, the problem this time was that it had turned out that it wasn't so much *what* Munch had stored away but *where* he had stored it away.

That this hellshole had been a mine at some point in its history – though mining what, she didn't know – was clear, but equally clearly the mine had become exhausted at some point and become... something else.

Maybe it was why Munch had chosen the place. Because, apart from its total remoteness, it was, as she had so painfully learned, a deathtrap. Not just neglected and unsafe and falling apart but a bloody *deathtrap*. The thought had even crossed her mind that Makennon had included the map to its location because she *knew* that and thought it a convenient way to be rid of her. Maybe she was being paranoid but she'd interfered once in the Final Faith's grandiose plans – even if in doing so she had saved the world – and with future plans likely in the offing maybe the Anointed Lord considered her too much of a loose cannon to be allowed to live. Not that she had any wish to get involved with that lot again.

Kali slumped against the rock wall and made a brubbing sound with her lips. The fact was, it had become increasingly unlikely that she'd be getting involved with *any* lot again if she didn't get out of here soon, not since she'd accidentally flicked that lever by stumbling over it in the dark.

One small mistake, that's all it was – an amateur's blunder – but that lever had been the key to this whole damned mess. It had transformed the mine's galleries in a loud and seemingly endless rattle of ancient chains and cranking of antique gears from the harmless tunnels they had been, into a deadly labyrinth constructed with one purpose in mind. To kill, as horribly and painfully as it could.

A testing ground was what it turned out to be. An ancient arena for dwarven rites of passage, designed to test their mettle to the full. She knew this because, whilst her own mettle was being tested by a selection of swinging blades and giant axes, she had come across a torn and blood-browned journal she could only presume had been written by a dwarf whose own rite of passage had come to a sudden end. As she had translated it, it told the whole sorry story of Be'Trak'tak, roughly translated as 'the beginning or end.'

Originating, she'd guessed, in the middle period of dwarven history – when their engineering skills were first beginning to evolve from the simple to the complex – it was to this place that the dwarven young were despatched at a certain age, sealed within the complex to face a series of elaborately designed traps and challenges whose survival would prove them to be warriors, or kill them in the process.

Gods, she'd wondered, *what the hells was it with those dwarves? Why couldn't they just go out on the twattle when they came of age like everyone else?*

Not that the dwarven traps would have proven *too* much of a challenge for her – not under any normal circumstances, anyway. The trouble was the unimaginable length of time since any of them had stirred into life, because in that intervening age most of the materials from which the traps had been constructed had become rotten, making them dangerously unpredictable and unstable. It was the very reason why she was slumped here binding her broken leg right now.

She had successfully negotiated her way through all but the last of a series of swinging hammer traps – itself just one more of an endless series of swinging, slicing or rolling *something* traps – when the beam that carried the final deadly bludgeon had splintered away as it swung, flinging the hammer where it was not meant to be *when* it was not meant to be. Kali remembered the agony as, halfway through a perfectly timed somersault manoeuvre, the hammer had sheared from its mounting and crushed her leg against the wall of the mine. Gods, that had hurt – and it had also proven to her that she was not quite as impervious to harm as events of the previous months had begun to lead her to believe. It was a salutary lesson and one she was not likely to forget so long as this farking splint remained on her leg.

Kali shivered, not so much from cold, but a combination of exhaustion, slight fever and a hunger that came from subsisting only on the edible, though thoroughly revolting, fungus that grew on the mine walls. Of course, the state of her dark silk bodysuit didn't help. Having improved on the original thieves guild design by having it retailored to incorporate pockets for artefacts, it now hung in virtual tatters about her, having fallen victim not only to her need for cloth to tie her splint but to the various traps she'd found lying in wait. That wasn't the worst of it, though. The gaping patch of flesh around her hip was a constant reminder that somewhere along the way she had also lost her equipment belt, torn from her body and flung into some deep, dark and, by the sound of it, watery pit by an intricate whirlwind of jagged blades of which someone, once upon a time, must have thought: *Whirling* and *jagged, eh? Oh, go for it, that's a good one.*"

She had lost Horse, too. She could certainly no longer sense him above, waiting patiently for her return as she expected he'd done for at least the first few days of her entrapment. No, Horse had become her faithful companion as much as the old Horse had been, but even he must have come to realise that Kali Hooper was not going to be returning to him anytime soon. She wondered where he had gone. Back to the Drakengrats where he had originally been captured? Or was he running free across the plains, the wind whistling through his horns? No, more likely he was galloping after some poor pack of worgles, terrorising them with his tongue.

Kali sniffed. Dammit, she missed him and she was getting maudlin. Hells, it really was time to get out of here, to beat these farking traps once and for all.

Kali heaved herself up against the chamber wall, thrusting a hand forward for balance as her bad leg took her weight, then hobbled out into the main tunnel, turning left and down rather than right and up. She knew that on the surface that seemed to make little sense but she also knew that there *was* no up – not since the landslide on the first day – and so she was going to gamble her survival on another possibility. Even the dwarves, with all their sadistic tendencies, surely couldn't expect any of their kind who had been 'warrior' enough to survive their traps to then *renegotiate* them on the way out. So it seemed logical that there had to be another way out, deeper into the mine.

There was only one problem with that. What was in the way.

Kali could hear it even from here. That rhythmic thumping, pounding and hissing that heralded the presence of the final trap. She had returned to it day after day for at least the last week, studying its timings and its intricacies and its foibles but making no attempt to pass. The reason for that was simple – this was the 'big one' and she was only going to get one chance at beating it.

There it was again, she thought, entering the cavern that opened out from the mine tunnel, a complex arrangement of giant hammers and blades, arranged vertically and horizontally, that completely lined the bridge crossing the chasm in the centre. It was no simple chasm, either. The rock walls flanking it had been carved into the shapes of giant dwarven faces whose roaring mouths randomly belched great fiery clouds of breath, hot enough to have singed the wood in the trap mechanisms over the years into hard, carbonised masses.

Kali couldn't help but admire the workmanship. The first time she'd had laid eyes on the construction she'd imagined it had once been named 'The Bridge of Doom,' 'Chasm of Chaos' or 'Gauntlet of the Gods.' But she hadn't liked the sound of any of those – so instead she'd called it 'Dave.'

Like the earlier traps, Dave would once have been negotiable with relative ease, but the rot of years had left some of its components askew, others working faster or slower than they should, still others partly broken loose from their matching components and set into motion by the movement of the mechanisms around them. As if that were not bad enough, the bridge itself looked as rotten as hells, likely to collapse under foot anywhere and anytime. The whole thing was as unpredictable as hells. One wrong move and she was over the side. One small miscalculation and she would be crushed to death or sliced to pieces. There was absolutely no room for error.

Kali narrowed her eyes and took a deep breath, studying for a final time the patterns of movement in the trap. She flexed her bad leg and pinwheeled her arms, loosening up her muscles. And then she swallowed. And then she ran.

Kali roared as her feet slammed onto the first few slats of the bridge, bouncing forward immediately as she felt the aged wood creak and give beneath her weight. As she bounced, the first of the trap's death-dealing devices came at her.

Kali eyed the trajectory of the whirling blade as it spun towards her and then actually ran towards it, flipping herself above and over the blade at the point metal and flesh would have met. The forward flip had to be timed slightly later than she would have liked – and she felt a sharp sting as the blade's edge sliced her thigh – but the delay was necessary for her to be able to meet the next of the bridge's dangers.

Righting herself, Kali landed on the upperside of a hammer that had just slammed down in her path and then balanced precariously on it as it began to rise. She did not let it take her all the way, instead she used its height to leap diagonally across the bridge so that she grabbed and clung onto a hammer rising on its other side. This, too, she rode until the very last second, allowing another blade to pass beneath her and then punching herself away from her perch as the hammer clicked in its mooring and slammed down.

She was between blades and hammers now but she didn't have a moment to rest. The instant she landed one of the dwarven heads belched fire towards where she was crouched. Kali didn't hesitate; snatching up a blade that had broken from its mechanism, she shored herself behind it, using it as a shield so that the fire was deflected past her on both sides. Then, the instant the fire died down, she used the now glowing blade as a wheel, rolling with it and behind it beneath the next hammer on the right side of the bridge.

The hammer came down hard, buckling the circular blade and straining the mechanism, but Kali had already dumped the metal and used the temporary jam to crawl swiftly beneath the area where the hammer would otherwise have impacted. This, in turn, enabled her to roll beneath the next circular blade before coming upright and flipping herself forward once more as its companion followed through a moment later.

Kali was moving fast and she was almost through to the end of the bridge now. She could barely contain the surge of elated adrenalin that accompanied that knowledge, because there she saw some kind of wooden elevator, as she knew she would, and all she had to do now was...

Wood splintered suddenly beneath Kali's feet and she fell forwards, cursing. The curse had barely left her lips before there was a sudden, heavy whoosh from her left hand side and the last of the mechanisms – a great hammer that swung across the bridge – came straight at her. She tried to throw herself out of its way, back into the space between hammer and blades, and would have made it safely, apart from the one small variable she had forgotten to factor into her equations. Making her leg thicker by as little as an inch, her splint made contact with one of the whirling blades she had already negotiated. Its teeth bit into the wood and cloth strip, ripping at it and tearing it away.

Kali felt her whole body vibrate bone-jarringly and then, as the teeth of the blade spat the splint out, found herself being flipped dizzyingly through the air back towards the hammer. There was no time to reorientate herself and, in the second she tried, the swinging bludgeon slammed directly into her front, knocking her, stunned and winded, cleanly off the bridge.

It could have been worse, she supposed, she could have lost the leg, but that was actually quite academic right now because she wasn't getting out of here. The place had become her tomb after all.

She looked down at the stalagmites and boulders that were now rushing towards her, estimated she had only a few seconds before she hit, and closed her eyes.

She slammed into the cavern floor. But it didn't hurt half as much as she'd imagined it might.

What? she thought.

Instead of the hard rock Kali thudded onto – and through – a layering of planks, that once upon a time must have been set there to prevent unwary miners stumbling into a dropshaft. They were so rotten she passed through without harm. Another layer was almost immediately beneath them, and then another, level after level of shoring. As Kali plummeted through, her momentum slowed slightly each time.

Kathuck, kathuck, kathuck.

It seemed to go on forever, and Kali was beginning to think she might die of suffocation as opposed to anything else when, at last, she slammed through the last of the layers and crashed, flat on her back, onto a small hillock of rotten wood on some deep, deep tunnel floor.

She lay there for a second.

"Ow," she said.

And then she flipped herself upright, ready for whatever trap was going to be thrown at her next.

But there was none. Kali knew instantly that this place was different to Be'Trak'tak. It looked different, felt different and even smelled different. And that could mean only one thing. The whole area she'd travelled through to reach Munch's mine had been riddled with other such excavations, and this had to be one of them. She'd broken through into another mine. And what was more, there was light ahead.

Wasting no time, Kali dusted herself down and began to move towards it, trying all the time to suppress the presumption that what was she looking at was an exit. After so long it was just too much to ask for, surely? And it was. Following the light to its source, Kali came up against a solid rock wall.

No, wait, not solid. There was *something* there.

Kali's disappointment upon discovering that the light source was not an exit was mitigated slightly by the fact that it seemed to be no kind of natural light, and she found herself intrigued. Also she saw that it was not one light source but two, only seeming to be a whole because they were embedded in the rock close together. No, not embedded, she realised as she examined them further. The lights seemed to be attached to something *else* embedded in the rock, something bigger that a roof collapse had buried at some time in the past and that had remained undisturbed since. The question was, how long had it remained undisturbed? Kali studied the collapse with a professional eye, noting the visible fossilisation, the settlement of the larger pieces of debris, and the compactness of the scree around them, which was absolutely solid. A very long time, then, she concluded. The only problem now being that, if that were true, how in all the hells could the lights – whatever they were – still be glowing?

She used her gutting knife to work away at the scree surrounding them, eventually revealing two small, orange orbs that seemed to throb beneath her touch, prompting a dull headache as they did. Suddenly, she realised what they had to be. Unless she'd missed her guess, they were some kind of power source for the thing to which they were attached.

Kali slapped the area she had revealed around the orbs tentatively, and then a little bit harder, and then harder still until her palms hurt. No doubt about it. Metal, and solid – apparently armoured or, at least, reinforced. But what on Twilight was it? She took a few steps back so that she could see the thing more fully and, with a pulse of excitement, realised that that the metal object was mounted on some kind of rotating tracks as if it might ride on them – *move* on them, in fact.

Kali continued her excavation anew, pulling now at larger stones and rocks that were embedded in the scree and then rolling each down over their predecessors until the pile was too big to accommodate more. But that didn't matter because she had managed to reveal enough of the machine for her purpose, and what she had revealed made her step back with a gasp.

She was standing in the space between the rock and what, it seemed, had been travelling *through* the rock, although what mechanism it employed to do this she could not see as she had not yet unearthed its front end. It was clearly a vehicle, however, as evidenced by the fact that there was a hatch in its side – and the hatch was covered in dwarven runics. Kali ran her palm over it in some wonderment, realising that while it was far from the first dwarven artefact she had discovered, it could very well be the first from the age that had produced it.

Through her own studies she had accredited three distinct periods of development to the Old Races – both elven and dwarven – during which they had progressed from opposing factions, utilising either magic or technology to build their individual civilisations, through periods of conflict where they had waged war using magic *against* technology, to the final age where, reconciled, both Old Races joined forces to expand each civilisation through *magical technology*. By this time both were so advanced that they would have been perceived almost as gods, and they could have been glorious and supreme if something hadn't happened. Whatever it was that had been powerful enough to wipe out these two great civilisations – to effectively *eradicate* them from the surface of Twilight – was perhaps the greatest of all mysteries but one that Kali intended one day to solve. The point was, that the vehicle she was studying appeared to come from the end of that last age, because what else could those orbs be but magical technology?

Becoming more excited by the second, Kali moved to the edge of the hatch, feeling around it until she had traced a round cornered, rectangular shape. It was sealed tightly but, being a hatch, there clearly had to be a way to open it. Perhaps that little niche there, marked with the rectangular symbol?

Kali felt inside and her hand wrapped around what felt like a small handle, which she gripped and pushed. Nothing happened, so she pulled instead. And then she staggered back as a giant, bronchial floprat with halitosis exhaled heavily in her face.

That, at least, was what it felt and smelled like. But there was no floprat, only the rank atmosphere coming from inside.

Kali watched the hatch release itself from its seal, punching away from the main body of the vehicle with a second exhalation and there waiting for a moment before, with a kind of wheeze, it slid slowly to the side. Kali understood now what she had just activated. The hatch was similar to the rune surrounded doors she had discovered in the Spiral of Kos, vacuum sealed by a method she did not understand to protect whatever lay behind them. But, where beyond those doors had lain ancient laboratories, behind this one lay only darkness.

No, she thought, not quite darkness. What appeared to be some kind of small, cramped cabin lay within, illuminated very dully by the same strange glow that had brought her to this part of the cave. As her eyes adjusted to the dark, she noticed that the glow seemed to be emanating from a number of places within, each of them small

– panels, perhaps, with levers. Some kind of control cabin then? But controlled by what?

Oh, she thought suddenly, *my gods*.

The panels were not so bright as they might have been, not because they were actually dim, but because something was blocking their glow. There was a *figure* within, just sitting there, staring straight ahead. Kali swallowed, knowing that if it moved she would very likely have a dicky fit.

But it didn't, of course. How could it? Who knew how long this machine had been stranded here, within the rock? Anything within it could not have hoped to survive. Hells, what a lonely, lonely death it must have been. But what nagged at Kali more than that morbid thought was, why had no one come to help? She wondered for a second whether it was possible that the inhabitant of the machine had died here because there *was* no one to come to help – that perhaps he had died here at the time the Old Races had gone away? And if that was the case then it begged the obvious question. *What* was she looking at?

Swallowing again, Kali leaned in and the figure emerged from the shadows before her eyes. Squat but, by the size of the ribbed uniform enclosing its now shrunken frame, once well-muscled and powerful. It remained utterly still. Dry, eyeless sockets stared straight ahead, gnarled hands gripping levers on the panel before it that had not moved since before the land was young. Though the body was completely mummified there was no doubt at all what it was she was looking at.

A dwarf.

Kali realised she had been holding her breath, and she let it out now in an exhalation that almost turned into a laugh. This was incredible! Something she had always hoped, but never thought, she would find!

The discovery was a momentous one and Kali took the appropriate length of time and appropriate reverence to appreciate it. After all, after gods knew how long stuck in this hellshole a few more minutes would make no difference at all. But then, with a deep sigh, she moved forward, grabbed the desiccated corpse by its shoulder and turfed it out of the cabin onto the mine floor. The dwarf's remains crumbled under her touch – clothing and all – and while the arms and torso hit the rock, they left the legs behind, half sitting on the seat. Kali heaved them off with a grimace and dropped them onto the collapsed torso – and only then realised she hadn't a clue where the head had gone. She scanned the cabin, peering into its shadowed recesses, and then spotted the missing appendage lying in the far corner, out of her reach. The head was looking right at her, its empty eye sockets baleful and reproachful, but Kali ignored them – what else could she do? – because her friend had been sitting in the driving seat of something that was still *working*. She slipped into the empty seat, thinking: *Sorry, my friend, but I have a lot more need of this thing than you do.*

Whatever this thing was.

Kali peered down at the panels and the levers and realised that she didn't have a clue how to use them even if she knew what it was they did. So what followed, she thought, was going to be interesting, to say the least. She did, though, have one starting point – a button marked with the same rectangular symbol she had seen on the outside of the machine. Humming softly to herself, she pressed it. With the same judder and sliding motion that it had opened with, the hatch closed and sealed itself.

Kali felt as if she were trapped inside a metal coffin.

But she just knew this thing was her way out of here. So, it was time to see what it could do.

CHAPTER THREE

DOLOROSA CONSIDERED SHE had better things to do than chase a herb up and down the hillside. The preparations for Kali Hooper's memorial evening – a drink-till-you-drop session which all the Flagons' regulars considered the most appropriate way to remember her – had taken the best part of two days. The last of them, a surprise stew for the evening – which was, of course, no surprise to the regulars, though none of them had told Dolorosa that – was all but done. But the hunt for one of its more vital ingredients was proving to be difficult. Said task had occupied her for the past half hour and, in that time, something of a murderous glint had appeared in her twitching right eye.

"I will 'avva you, you leetle red bastardo!" she threatened, her arm swooping down to grab the skittering bunch of macalorum.

But once again the leafy herb evaded her clutches, bouncing and flapping away down the hill towards the Flagons and causing the tall, thin woman to lose balance on the slope and flip heel over head, her skirt flapping after her and enveloping her like a tent.

"Bastardo!" she hissed again, from beneath the cloth.

A group of drinkers outside the tavern stared open-mouthed at an exposed pair of skull and crossbones bloomers and – possibly as a release of tension at the bad news they had all received – there was much pointing and loud and raucous bursts of laughter. Dolorosa's head popped out of the bundle of cloth and she flipped her skirt back over her dignity and squinted at them, *hard*. It was a squint that some said could kill – some even said it *had* killed – and the laughter stopped. Dead.

Dolorosa straightened, then squinted down at the tavern again. The drinkers had disappeared inside but she could still see their faces pressed up against the tavern's windows and she strained to listen for the merest titter from them. But there was none and they seemed only to be checking that she wasn't striding down the hill after them.

Lucky fora them, she thought, *because if they hadda tittered, I would havva to keel them horribly and withouta mercy.*

After *she had keeled the bastardo.*

Dolorosa spun as she saw that the macalorum had taken advantage of her unexpected halt to turn around and bounce back up the hill, chittering as it passed her. Once again she made a grab for it, and once again missed. What had made this essential ingredient of her surprise stew quite so skittish she wasn't sure – it was normally such a docile little herb – and she wondered whether it had anything to do with the reports of strange creature sightings to the west. These things nicknamed the k'nid. Certainly macalorum wasn't the only thing around here that was uneasy at the moment, as most of the smaller wildlife in Tarn seemed to be that, or worse. Whatever the cause, the macalorum's determination to avoid becoming an ingredient only made her all the more determined to catch it.

Dolorosa bent and slid her fingers into the rim of her right boot, then rolled up her sleeves and began to stomp after the herb.

The stiletto she had extracted from her footwear gleamed viciously and the woman grinned evilly and tossed it in her palm, weighing it up, before flipping it so that she held it by the end of the blade. All she had to do now was time her moment right. And there it was, she thought, where the herb was about to hop over that small ridge into the trees beyond. The macalorum tensed it roots and Dolorosa threw.

Victory issa mine! she thought, and began to scramble up the hill towards the impaled and struggling herb.

She was almost upon it when she found herself staggering backwards. The sky above her tipped dizzily, as if she were going into a swoon.

Greata Gods of the Seas, I havva overdone myself, she thought. *My 'usband, in moments of passion, hassa warned me ovva this.*

There was only one problem with that theory, she realised – she didn't feel remotely dizzy or weak. Why, then, did she continue to fall backwards, landing on her behind with a thud and a puff of dry soil?

Anda wotta wassa happening to the hill?

To her confused eyes it seemed to be getting bigger.

Pah! Eet ees impossible.

Impossib –

"Greata Grandma of the Gods!"

Above her, no more than a yard from her upturned feet, the grass that covered the hill was breaking apart, spilling roiling piles of soil onto the otherwise green landscape, like a pan that had begun to bubble over. Dolorosa scrambled back, thinking that perhaps she was being visited by a rarely seen undermuncher, but it soon became clear that it was bigger even than that. The roiling soil was spreading ever outward now, so much so that her feet and the bottom of her legs had begun to rise with it, tipping her further backwards so that she had to steady herself on the palms of her hands. The old woman watched, mesmerised, as the mound turned into a small hillock, and then one not so small, and her eyebrows raised as something suddenly poked its nose through the surface. Something big.

Dolorosa rapidly muttered a small number of hail glorias, and then far more curses, as she was once more tipped heels over head, her skirt enveloping her again, though this time perhaps mercifully as it shielded her gaze from whatever monster was emerging from the depths. She rolled down the hill in darkness, aware as she went that whatever was emerging from the ground was rumbling loudly and that it stank of the depths and something old. Totally unnecessarily, considering she was under her skirt, she closed her eyes and waited for whatever fate was going to befall her.

Suddenly the rumbling stopped.

The unknown beast hissed loudly.

And then... nothing happened.

A second passed. Two. Three. And then, with a gulp of apprehension, Dolorosa flung her skirt off her head, squinting ahead. There, silhouetted by the evening sun, something shadowed and bulky obscured the hillside. Something with a number of projections on its front, like cannon, that seemed to distort the air in front of them. As she stared the beast disgorged something from its side. No, not something, Dolorosa realised – a figure. A strangely familiar figure, as it turned out, with a what appeared to be a bum sticking out ovva its pants.

The figure looked around, taking in its surroundings.

"Pits of Kerberos," Kali Hooper said, "it worked."

She leapt down from the cabin of the machine she had nicknamed The Mole and limped past the prone and gaping old woman, pausing only to point back and declare with girlish enthusiasm: "Dolorosa, you have *GOT* to get yourself one of those."

"Bossa lady?" Dolorosa said. And then again: "Boss?"

She picked herself up and, with a backward glance at the strange machine, raced after Kali as she hobbled purposefully towards the Flagons, circling her as she walked and squinting with some concern, but mainly suspicion, at the bedraggled, dirt covered figure. Once she had truly established its identity, she poked it in the chest with a bony finger.

"You are notta dead?"

"Nope. But I am thirsty. *Very.*"

"Beer eet issa notta good when you arra dehydrated."

Kali snorted. "Yeah, right."

They reached the doors to the Flagons and Kali flung them open, frowning in puzzlement at the fact the bar was adorned with a great strip of bunting inscribed, in Dolorosa's strangled peninsulan, with the words: 'Kali Hooper – Resta Inna Peas.'

Rather unnecessarily, Dolorosa declared to all within that "the boss lady issa back", but before the expressions of joy had even had time to settle on the regulars' faces, Kali was already seated at the bar, pointing silently, but self-explanatorily, at the cask of *thwack*. Much to his wife's apparent disapproval Aldrededor was already pouring a tankard, and then another, and then – because he knew the occasion would demand it – another still. Kali downed them all in rapid succession, wiped her mouth with her forearm, sighed and burped long and hard.

"That," she gasped, "I needed. Hi, guys," she added, waving at the regulars and smiling as they welcomed her back.

"'Allo, Kaleeee!"

"Good to see yer, half-pint…"

"So – you are not dead," Aldrededor declared, taking the last empty tankard and placing another frothing one in her hand. "It is very good to see you home, Kali Hooper."

"Likewise, Aldrededor." Kali slapped the empty on the bar. "What made you think I was dead?"

Aldrededor shrugged. "The fact that you have been missing for six weeks. That there has been no news at all and, of course, this –" The one-time pirate pointed at Kali's battered and torn equipment belt, hung in pride of place behind the bar. "It washed up on a beach near Nürn. Luckily, Mister Larson was there on his holiday and managed to retrieve it. Thank you, Mister Larson."

"*Six weeks?*" Kali repeated. She nodded to Ronin as she reclaimed her belt. "That place really threw me out of whack. So have I missed anything?"

"Oh, the usual," Aldrededor said casually. "Red was arrested three or four times, Miss Scrubb has been nibbling the Dreamweed again and –" Rather surprisingly, Aldrededor stopped and suddenly busied himself wiping glasses.

"Aldrededor?" Kali prompted, but the swarthy Sarcrean only shrugged and devoted all his attention to erasing a tiny spot on one of the tankards, one that was seemingly *never* going to disappear no matter how hard he tried.

Suspicious now, Kali spun on her barstool to face the gathered regulars, but where a moment before it had been all "Here's to Kali!" and "We should have known you'd be fine!" there was now a totally uncharacteristic silence.

Kali stared at Pete Two-Ties on whom she could usually depend, but his head had descended into what was obviously a particularly challenging cryptosquare. She stared at Fester Grimlock and Jurgen

Pike, who in turn stared at their quagmire board despite the fact their game was clearly over. Then she stared at Ronin Larson, the ironweaver, and Hetty Scrubb, the herbalist, who were staring hard at their feet or out of the window, the former humming something tremulous and the latter giggling uncontrollably. Of Dolorosa herself, there was at first no sign, then Kali caught sight of her peering warily from behind the bravado barrel at the far end of the bar. The bravado barrel was a game of nerve with a single arm-hole in its front and there were a number of... interesting creatures provided by Red hidden inside it, but having someone hide *behind* it was a first.

Something was definitely up.

"Dolorosa?" Kali said, cautiously.

"What?" Dolorosa objected loudly, throwing her hands in the air. "You thinka that iffa there is something you will notta like it hassa to be Dolorosa's fault?"

That clinched it.

"*Dolorosa?*" she said again, emphasising her question. "What will I 'notta like'?"

Dolorosa squinted at her, saying nothing, but from the corner of her eye Kali saw Red Deadnettle pointing towards the rear of the tavern, mouthing something that looked like 'band.' Kali turned and stared up the few ramshackle steps that led up to her Captain's Table and saw that what had traditionally been her domain had been filled with a number of strange musical instruments, including a road-worn, sweeping, stringed affair that looked almost elven – what she thought was called a theralin. Frowning, she mounted the steps and saw that the Captain's Chest – storehouse of her papers and sanctum sanctorum of the peninsula's history – had also been buried beneath a spread of tattered music sheets for such appropriately forgotten classics as 'Boom Bang-a Thud', 'What A Wonderful Pie' and 'Yes, She's Heavy, She's My Mother.'

"What," she asked Dolorosa, "is this?"

The thin woman threw up her hands in protest but, nonetheless, looked guilty. "Wotta you theenk eet is? Eet is, eet is –"

Her words were lost as one of the thick timber beams, supporting the rooms above, suddenly curved downward with a stressed and prolonged groan that drowned out every other sound in the bar. Kali looked upward, blinking dust from her eyes. The next beam along bowed down, as did the floorboards in between, and then the next, and then the one after that. It was almost surreal, as if the whole infrastructure of the tavern had suddenly turned to rubber.

Then the top step of the stairs sounded as if it were splintering.

"Oh gods," Pete Two-Ties said. "They're waking up."

Kali double-taked. "What? Who? Pete – *who's* waking up?"

"Them," Pete pointed.

Kali spun. Whatever it was she expected to see, the last of it would have been a small mountain range, but that was exactly what appeared at the bottom of the stairs. A small mountain range squeezing itself into the bar and made up entirely of flesh. One of the mountains spoke. "Coo-ee, boys," it said, with a wink.

Oh gods, Kali thought. *No, it couldn't be. Not here.*

"The Hells' Bellies," she mouthed with dread. Her ordeals of the last few weeks notwithstanding she turned as white as a sheet.

The eyes in the peaks of the talking mountain lit up. "Our fame has spread! This young lady, she has heard of us!"

Kali was tempted to point out that the entire peninsula had 'heard' of them and that their fame wasn't the only thing that had spread. But she held her tongue and, instead, glowered at Dolorosa.

"Explain," she demanded, darkly.

"What issa there to explain?" Dolorosa said in a slightly high pitch, clearly going on the defensive. "We thoughta you dead and so we thoughta we woulda make a few changes..."

Kali caught Aldrededor waving from behind his wife, desperate to catch her attention. He was shaking his head vigorously and pointing at Dolorosa.

"Changes?" Kali asked, flatly.

"Entertainment!" Dolorosa declared. "Cabaret! Culture! And so I contracted the most popular dancing troupe in the two provinces!"

Kali felt her heart seize. "Contracted? For how long?"

"They havva performed for three nights," Dolorosa said, "and they havva forty one left."

Kali did a quick calculation. "You've contracted them for a *month*?"

Pete Two-Ties head thudded down onto his table in defeat and shook back and forth slowly.

"The whole of Cantar?" Kali said in disbelief. She signalled to Aldrededor to pour another thwack, which she grabbed and downed in one. "No, no, no, no, NO, NO, NO! Cancel it, Dolorosa, *now*."

A small moon suddenly orbited in front of Kali's face. Except that it wasn't a moon but another face. It took a second to fold itself into a jowly frown. "Cancel... contract?" it said, and Kali wished that Merrit Moon was there so that the Hells' Belly and the Thrutt side of his personality could communicate on equal terms.

She swallowed and used her words slowly. "Yes. Cancel. Contract."

"Pff," the moon said, throwing up its arms. Hairs the length of mools tails sprang forth from dim and horrible pits. "How can *you*, wisp of a thing, demand she cancel contract?"

"Because *I* own the place."

The Hells' Belly guffawed and Kali was blasted with the odours of stale and cheap wine, cigars, and the assorted yellow remains of potato crunchies still providing their money's worth where they were stuck between huge, horse-like teeth. "Missus Dolorosa, she owns the place. She told us this is so."

Kali turned to Dolorosa, but the door to the Flagons' courtyard was already slamming shut behind her.

"Look," she said, wearily. "I'll pay you twice your contracted fee to cancel the remaining performances."

The moon loomed again. A hand snapped a garter on a thigh the thickness of a tree trunk and Kali turned away before she was involuntarily mesmerised by what happened to the flesh around it as a result. "Our fee is nothing compared to the tips we receive from our... *gentlemen.*"

Across the room, Red Deadnettle and Ronin Larson coughed in embarrassment. Kali stared at them and sighed.

"Fine. I'll give you *three times* your fee. How's that?"

The offer was clearly tempting but a frown still crossed the Hells' Belly's face. It thrust itself at Kali interrogatively. "If we leave now, how will you guarantee our safety?"

"Your safety?"

"These are dangerous times, strip of a thing. What if we are attacked on the road?"

Kali pictured bruised and screaming grabcoins flying through the air. "Are you serious? Who in their right minds would take on you lo – ?"

She stopped as a hand suddenly rested on her shoulder and Aldrededor whispered in her ear.

"I do not think she is talking about grabcoins, Kali Hooper. I believe she refers to the k'nid."

"The k'nid?"

"Those things that have flooded our land and will soon be everywhere. The... *Wait, you do not know?*"

"There wasn't much news where I've been." Kali frowned. "Tell me."

Aldrededor told her of the reports of strange creatures coming from the west, of the deaths and invasions of towns, and Kali absorbed the information, worried but simply nodding. Again, she sighed. "All right... ladies. For now you can stay. But under one condition. While I'm around I do not, repeat *do not*, want any danc –"

Her words fell on deaf ears. The Hells' Bellies were already skipping, if that was the word, to the makeshift stage, clapping their hands in glee, and Red and Ronin turned their stools toward them appreciatively. As if from nowhere, a number of small, thin and sallow looking men

– their husbands? – appeared and took up the instruments that lay on the stage, stroking, blowing or strumming them respectively to produce a discordant wail that would have repelled a Vossian army. Then, without any tuning up, any rehearsal, it just... began.

Thudding.

Kali grabbed her tankard of thwack before it wobbled off the bar and looked around as others did the same. She stared up at the ceiling as streams of dust began to fall in columns. She gazed at the windows, expecting them to crack at any moment. She bit her lip. There was nothing she could do here. But there was something she could deal with outside. And her name was Dolorosa.

Kali slammed the main door to the Flagons behind her and stood with her back to it for a second, sighing in relief. Then she jumped away as the entire tavern shook. She moved across the relative silence of the courtyard and then frowned darkly as she spotted Dolorosa pottering about near the stables. Kali moved up behind her slowly and quietly, saw that the old woman was hastily wrapping what looked to be a new tavern sign in folds of cloth. It appeared that the Here There Be Flagons had been in the process of being renamed – as The Olde Crow's Nest.

Should be the Old Crone's Nest, Kali thought. *By the gods, I go away for a few weeks and when I get back my pub's been boarded by pirates.*

She was about to prod Dolorosa in the back, give her the fright she deserved, when her attention was distracted by a noise from the main stable. A low rumble, in fact. A strangely familiar sounding low rumble.

Horse? Kali thought.

Horse!

Kali slammed open the stable doors, making Dolorosa jump, and there he was, a living, breathing armoured tank desultorily poking his snout into a pile of hay. His big green eyes looked up as she entered and, as Kali said "Horse" once more, his head rose and a serpentine tongue curled out and slobbered itself with abandon all over her face. Kali moved forward and slapped his neck.

You came back, she thought. *You didn't return to the Drakengrats, after all. Hells, it's good to see you, boygirl.*

There was, however, something wrong. As pleased as Kali was to be reunited with her mount, Horse's whole demeanour seemed off kilter, eyes duller than usual, chitin plating less polished, and his general presence – usually quite comment worthy – less, well, *imposing*. Kali patted the bamfcat, murmuring a soothing *hey, he*y...

"Eet ees the worgles," Dolorosa explained from behind her. "They havva all gone away."

"Worgles?"

The small furballs were Horse's favourite snack – almost his staple diet, in fact – and were usually to be found in abundance all over the peninsula. It had taken Kali some time to get used to Horse's habit of scooping the poor little creatures up with his serpentine tongue, but used to it she had got, and the fact that they were apparently not around was even more unsettling than Horse's carnivorousness *before* their disappearance.

"Worgles, poongs, bladderrips, all of the small creatures they hide a fromma the k'nid. But the worgles, especially, seem to fear them greatly. It ees almost as eef –"

"These k'nid? Where do they come from? What do they look like?"

Dolorosa shrugged. "Where they come from, no one knows. Whatta they looka like is difficult to say. I have hearda many reports. All I know is thatta they are deadly. Butta you need notta worry, Dolorosa doubts they will find their way here to the Cro – erm, to the Flagons."

Kali frowned. "It doesn't strike you that the worgles and the rest have gone into hiding because the k'nid might be somewhere near?"

"*Fff.* No, the Flagons is special, isolated. Dolorosa feel it inna her plumbing – they will *notta* come here."

Kali grimaced and forced a certain image from her mind. But the grimace froze as, in the vitreous of Horse's eyes, she caught a glint of something low and dark behind her, moving into the Flagons' courtyard. "Think again," she said.

Working its way around a bush into the courtyard was an almost indescribable shape. It reminded Kali of the brackan she had encountered in the Sardenne Forest, but of many other things also. Somehow that made it seem many times worse. Moving slowly, and crackling strangely, like an open fire, it began to work its way around the edges of the courtyard, probing in a way that made Kali think it was some kind of scout. And where there was a scout, there would be the main party not far behind.

"I take it," Kali said with some distaste, "that's a k'nid."

She moved slowly out of the stable, shutting and bolting it behind her. Then she peered along Badlands Brook where, in the darkness, she could just make out what appeared to be a blanket of deeper darkness on the ground, extending back to the horizon. The blanket undulated and rippled slightly.

"Walk slowly back to the Flagons," she instructed Dolorosa. "Make no sudden moves."

The old woman nodded and did as bade, walking sideways so as not to lose sight of what lay outside the tavern's grounds.

They had only made it halfway across the courtyard before the scout k'nid reared and its friends tumbled forward, as if they were leaves swept into the courtyard on a breeze. Before either of them knew what was happening one leapt straight for Dolorosa, and the old woman screamed.

Kali stared, shocked and unable to believe what had just happened. One second beside her, the next not, Dolorosa was gone, as if she had never been.

That bloody *woman,* she thought, watching the door to the Flagons once more slamming behind her. *Hidden athletic depths or not, she and I are going to have to have serious words. But not now. Because, right now, there are more pressing things to deal with. Namely, thanks to a certain someone, that I'm now the only target.*

As the k'nid rushed at her in a sudden, swarming sea, Kali did the only thing she could to get out of their path. With a grunt of pain from her bad leg, she leapt upwards to grab the guttering of the stable roof, using this to flip herself up and over so that she ended up crouched on the lip of the roof itself, watching as the k'nid impacted with the stable wall.

As they recovered from the impact, it was a good position for her to study the creatures. She certainly couldn't disagree that they were ugly little bastards, flooding the courtyard like a colony of insects that had been disturbed from beneath some rock. But whatever rock that had been, she had certainly never come across one like it. These things struck every fibre of her being as *unnatural.*

They did not, however, seem to be quite the destructive force Aldrededor's reports had suggested. They were certainly making no moves to destroy the Flagons.

Now, why exactly was that? she wondered.

It took her a second to realise that the k'nid seemed to be reacting to the vibrations from inside the tavern – actually shying back each time a thud occurred. Was it possible, she thought, that these things had worked their way across the peninsula, attacking all in their path, only to be stopped here, by a dance troupe?

Kali chided herself, almost laughed. No, that was plain daft. In fact, it was the stupidest thing she'd ever –

The Flagons suddenly fell silent, doubtless in response to Dolorosa informing everyone that the k'nid had come to eat their face, and sure enough each lit window was suddenly eclipsed by a number of shapes peering into the night. What mattered more, though, was that as soon as the thudding stopped the k'nid had become more agitated and their attention had turned to the tavern – and consequently the people inside.

There was a sudden rush against the side of the tavern and Kali cringed as she heard masonry and wood splintering before the assault.

Dammit.

She had to warn those inside, but there was no way she could get back to the door. Instead, she raced along the stable roof, leaping from there onto the Flagons' outhouse, and from there onto the roof of the tavern proper. She clambered up its slates, slipping back twice as some broke from their fixings beneath her and then, at last, reached the apex. There, she found herself doing something and saying something – especially to its intended recipients – that she would never, ever, in a thousand lifetimes, have imagined she would.

"*Dance!*" she shouted into the Flagons' chimneypot. "*Dance, or die!*"

There was a few second's silence and then a puzzled and weak reply came back

"Wotta you say? Who issa speaking, please?"

Kali couldn't believe it. "Dolorosa, it's me."

"Who issa me?"

"Kali!"

"Kali? Why arra you uppa the chimaney?"

"I'm not *uppa the chimaney*, woman! Dammit, Dolorosa, just listen…"

Kali explained what was happening – what she *thought* was happening, at least – and how it was imperative not only that the regulars stay inside the tavern but also that the Hells' Bellies keep on dancing. She explained also that she wouldn't be joining them for her memorial evening or any evening in the foreseeable future. As she did she tried as best she could to hide the excitement in her voice. For her one glimpse of the k'nid had sparked in her a familiar and – considering the alternative – quite welcome feeling: the thrill of the hunt. No, these things weren't natural and to her that shouted Old Races from the veritable treetops. So, she was off on her travels again, and she knew already what her first port of call was going to be, a certain market town and a certain half-ogur who just might have some theories as to what they dealing with.

All she had to do was get there. But was Horse up to it? After all, he'd had better days.

She should have known better than to even question the fact as, at that moment, as if sensing her impending departure, Horse's growl was clearly audible from his stable. Then the door buckled slightly on its hinges as he gave it a gentle nudge with his snout.

Kali worked her way back down the rooftops until she was above his stable and then, keeping her eye on the k'nid, stretched down to unbolt the door.

As Horse trotted slowly out, his armour flaring slightly at the creatures, Kali reversed the manoeuvre that had got her on the rooftops in the first place, flipping herself down onto Horse's back. Then she eased Horse out of the courtyard, keeping him at a walk as they passed through the ranks of k'nid, which growled softly as they passed. Horse, in turn, growled at them and Kali could feel every inch of his body tense, ready to activate his armour fully at the merest sign of movement from the predators. The vibrations from the Flagons, however, still seemed to be rendering them passive. Passing without harm into the open countryside beyond, Kali spurred Horse first into a trot and then the beginnings of a gallop. There were likely more k'nid out here, she thought, and away from the Flagons their behaviour might be a different story, so she suspected it was going to be an interesting journey to Gargas.

As she and Horse traversed the first couple of leagues she turned back in the direction of the Flagons and the peninsula beyond, thinking of where she would be if she hadn't become trapped in Munch's mine. Because the thought of meeting Merrit Moon had made her think of another meeting she should have had, a certain rendezvous in Malmkrug.

Killiam Slowhand was out there, somewhere in the overrun west, searching for his sister, and wherever he was she hoped he was all right, and that he'd had the sense to keep his head – and the rest of him – down.

CHAPTER FOUR

DESPITE THE GLOWERING and threatening presence of Querilous Fitch lurking behind him, Killiam Slowhand could not take his eyes off what was in front of him. He leaned forward against the rails of the airship, like the excited child he had been on the deck of a far different kind of ship, a lifetime ago. Then, the *Merry B* had entered the bustling harbour of Freiport after his father had been posted from Allantia to the mainland, and to leave that island with the promise of a new life full of adventure on the much larger peninsula – even if then he'd had no idea just *how* much – had filled him with awe and a sense of wonder that he could barely contain. That wonder had returned now and Slowhand gazed upward, his mouth open, unable to believe what he saw.

The parallel with Freiport was more than the sense of wonder, however, because the sights he saw here were in many ways similar to those of that long distant shipping port. Moving slowly into a vast, and only partly natural cavern, hundreds of feet inside solid rock, the airship on which he was being carried aloft was entering its own harbour.

"Amazing, isn't it?" Jenna said, joining him at the rail.

She spent a few seconds leaning in silence by his side, watching as the airship passed gantries and loading cranes and other such devices that projected from rock walls and then, staring ahead, towards a strange cradle-looking dock towards which the airship was heading. "Before we came, no ship had docked here in thousands upon thousands of years. No one even knew it was here."

Hardly surprising, Slowhand thought. Human ignorance of such places was common – how many people had heard of Martak, for one? – but he had to admit there was something different about the place they were entering now. Its location, its position, its *isolation* suggested to him that it hadn't merely become lost like its contemporaries but had always been designed to be lost. In other words, hidden away from the world, even when that world was capable of constructing such a wonder. But, if that was the case, whatever clandestine purpose it had served was long past. Apart from one isolated area that he could see above him, the harbour was neglected, derelict, ill-maintained. Rusted and warped metal beams framed and criss-crossed the cavern like malformed ribs, twisted and time warped gears lay idle in unused machines, and crates sitting in loading bays rotted away along with their contents. Most telling of all, however, was that there were three more airships like this one – or, at least, once upon a time, there had been – and Slowhand simultaneously frowned and gaped as he stared up at the bedraggled remains of what had once been equally wondrous machines. Their canopies were rotted away now and hanging in strips from metal skeletons which would never take to the skies again. Identifying symbols that hung half obscured upon the rotted cloth left the archer in no doubt as to what he was looking at.

This was the remains of an elven skyfleet.

"You were thinking of Freiport, weren't you?" Jenna said. "The day we arrived?"

Slowhand stared at her, his surroundings momentarily forgotten. "You remember?"

"Of course I remember, Killiam. The Faith would have gained nothing destroying that part of me they valued in the first place."

"Your strategic skills?" Slowhand remembered the position she had held with the Freiport military. "They – or was it just Fitch – destroyed something, though, eh? Your free will? Your choice to leave?"

Jenna stared at him, strangely hesitant for the first time since their reunion. "Perhaps there were other reasons…"

"What?" Slowhand said, grabbing her arm and, as he did, part of her robe fell away to reveal a red choker around her neck inscribed with Final Faith runics. It was a wedding band.

"Outside, your man called you Captain Freel," Slowhand said. "Captain *Freel*. My gods, you married one of them didn't you?"

Jenna pulled her arm away, straightened her robe. "Sorry you weren't invited to the wedding, brother. The ceremony was in Scholten Cathedral. The Anointed Lord herself officiated."

"And how voluntary was *that*, Jenna? Who is he, your husband? Is he here?"

"Lord of All, you never change, do you? No, Killiam, he isn't here. He's on special assignment, just like me."

Just like you, Slowhand thought. And just like Konstantin Munch had been before the shit had hit the fan. "Do you ever think," he said, "that the Final Faith has its fingers in too many pies?"

Again, Jenna hesitated. "They… I…"

"What?" Slowhand demanded. But before Jenna could elaborate, the airship jarred suddenly and he realised that it had just entered the cradle they had been heading towards and that the cradle was, in fact, an elevator. Clamping them into position it then began to rise. Jenna pulled her arm away, suddenly all business once more.

"Mister Ransom, prepare to couple the orb feed. Mister Blane, disengage the canopy locks. Port and starboard rudders down and neutral, people. Let's get this done and get ourselves out of here!"

Despite the sudden burst of activity around him, Slowhand wasn't going to let Jenna's comment go, and he followed his sister as she went about her business, adjusting various dials and levers as the elevator reached its destination and began to turn on its own axis, positioning the airship's strange, pulsating orb before a huge panel. The crewman called Ransom began to link umbilical looking pipes up to it, and while he and the others were professionally adept at what they did – clearly familiar with the airship's workings – a number of things were now becoming clear to Slowhand.

"This isn't your ship, is it, sis? It's Old Race, scavenged from the remains of their technology and put together piecemeal. And this isn't your final destination, either, is it?" As Jenna helped crew position a gantry so that they could reach a rock platform filled with more modern machines and crates, which the crew then proceeded to load, he persisted. "All this equipment? What are you up to, Jenna? Where are you going?"

Jenna spun to face him. "Going, brother? We aren't *going* anywhere. In fact, we're running away from somewhere – as fast as we can."

"Somewhere or something?" Slowhand said with sudden realisation. "On the ship, what you said when those things came. You knew what the k'nid were, didn't you?"

"The k'nid?"

"Yes, the k'nid. The things that attacked your ship."

"Oh, so they've been given a name."

"Is it those things you're running from? What the hells are they? Where do they come from?"

Jenna stared at him defiantly, as if she were not going to answer, but then, as he held her eyes, she seemed to relent slightly. "There has been... a mistake," she said slowly, swallowing. "We need to rearm, reinforce, return to rectify what we have –"

"That is *enough*," Querilous Fitch interrupted, grabbing Jenna by the wrist and spinning her around. "This civilian cannot be allowed to know the business of the Final –"

"Hey!" Slowhand shouted, moving forward. "Get your hands off this civilian's sister or you're gonna find out just how *un*civil he can –"

Fitch's gaze snapped to him and, for a second, Slowhand swore he could see the blood vessels in his eyes dart and writhe like a nest of snakes.

"Or what?" he said disdainfully, and the archer suddenly found himself airborne, though this time with no dirigible beneath him.

The dismissive snap of the arm with which Fitch had accompanied his words had, seemingly without any effort on his part at all, flung him upwards and backwards with such force that he found himself hurtling through the harbour towards the energy panel from which the dirigible crystal fed. He impacted so hard that the wind was knocked completely out of him.

"My gods, Jenna," he gasped weakly. "What has the Faith done this time?"

Jenna stared but no answer came and suddenly, seemingly instinctively, his left hand shot out to grab a small node on the panel, gripping it tightly so that he dangled there. This, Slowhand found strange, because there was no way – instinctively or otherwise – that he would grab such a device having seen the kind of power it channelled. Sure enough, his whole arm buzzed with a strange energy that spread through his bones to his ribs, but however much he wanted to he found he couldn't let go. In fact, he suddenly realised, his *other* arm was reaching for the opposite node.

Slowhand felt a bolt of panic. He stared down at Fitch and saw the mage grinning coldly up at him. Damn it, it was the threadweaver who had made his arm lash out. And now he was forcing him to raise the other.

Querilous Fitch was in his head.

Below, Jenna snapped her gaze from Fitch to her brother and then back again, for a moment uncertain what was happening – but then it dawned on her. If his right hand connected with the other strut he would complete the circuit, and if that happened his whole body would be channelling the energy of the panel. Slowhand didn't want to know what would happen to him if it did. But the fact was, in his current position, there was nothing he could do to stop it.

His hand rising jerkily, face twisted and sweating profusely, fighting against Fitch's will, he looked desperately at Jenna. His sister was clearly uncomfortable with what was happening, but it seemed her conditioning was preventing her from doing anything about it.

Fight it, sis, Slowhand thought. *Help me.*

And as if she had heard his plea, her gaze snapped to him once more, her brow furrowing deeply.

Decide who and what's important to you, the archer urged. *Make your choice.*

Suddenly Jenna was struggling with Fitch, trying to turn him away from Slowhand, to break his hold. But despite his frame, the threadweaver seemed to be as strong in body as he was in mind, and would not be turned. As the struggle continued, so did Slowhand's, his grip no more than inches away from the second node now. Groaning, he tried to fight against Fitch, but whatever part of his mind the threadweaver was manipulating it was inaccessible to him. Slowhand craned his neck to watch as his right arm rose ever upward and then suddenly spasmed in shock as it made contact and completed the circuit. The effect was agonising and the archer screamed and bucked, held as the current locked all of his muscles, seemingly gluing him to the panel. But as his body danced, he nevertheless managed to form one word in a guttural tone.

"*Jennnnnaaaa...*"

Below, Jenna continued to struggle with Fitch but then, as if he had tired of a dog snapping at his ankles, he snapped his hand to the side and Jenna was thrown away from him to slam heavily into a pile of crates. Some of the crew turned, shocked that their Captain had been treated in such a way, but it was clear that none of them would do anything about it – dare challenge the threadweaver – and they continued to work. For her part, Jenna stared daggers at her so-called lieutenant, wiping a spot of blood from the side of her mouth. But for the moment she was evidently too weak to pick herself up and retaliate. *If* she even dared take Fitch on.

Slowhand realised that if he were going to live he had to get out of this himself. Thankfully, as Fitch had used some of his energy to throw Jenna aside he had felt a fleeting and slight reduction in the threadweaver's hold. Enough for him to be able to pull his right hand away from the contact panel. If he could work on that...

Slowhand moaned with effort, not only of trying to pull his hand away but also trying to make his intent as little obvious as possible. If Fitch spotted what he was doing, he had no doubt that his hand would be struck back to the panel in a second – and then he would be a dead man.

Slowly, though, it began to work and with a sudden jerk of his limb he realised it was free of the connection, though the panel behind him continued to throb with the charge it had built up. Slowhand took advantage of this, making his body buck as if it were still part of the circuit, but secretly concentrating on the effort involved in freeing his right leg. It, too, broke free, though for a second the archer held it in place, making Fitch think he was as much constrained as he had always been.

"Hey, Fitch," he gasped. "Shouldn't I be dead by now?"

The threadweaver's eyebrow rose in surprise that his victim was able to speak, let alone breathe. Suddenly Slowhand felt a resurgence of the power, Fitch forcing him further onto the panel and, teeth gritted, he fought against the push with all of his will.

"Threadweaver. I'm starting to think you couldn't weave your way out of a papyrus bag."

Below him Fitch growled.

"Querilous Fitch," Slowhand taunted further. "You think maybe that should be Querilous Oh-There's-A-Hitch?"

That did it. As Slowhand had hoped, Fitch was the kind of man who, despite his power, couldn't resist venting his anger in a more physical form. The threadweaver lurched towards him with a snarl.

As he did, his mental hold on Slowhand relaxed and, feeling his body untense against the panel, the archer made his move.

He dropped to the floor and, as he impacted, threw himself into a forward roll, hands snatching behind his back for Suresight and an arrow from his quarrel. He came upright, the bow readied. Slowhand could have killed Fitch there and then but, without knowing exactly why, he didn't. Instead he fired off, in quick succession, four arrows aimed at Fitch's arms and legs. Flitch tried to deflect them, but he had no chance. The threadweaver was suddenly picked up and carried off his feet by their speed and power, thudding into the packing crate behind him. Fitch roared with anger, trying to pull away from the arrows that held him, but they were so solidly embedded in the wood through the folds of his cloak that he was trapped.

Slowhand took a deep and satisfied breath and walked towards Fitch, pausing only to offer a hand to help the still prone Jenna up. She snatched it without thanks – without even a smile, of relief or otherwise – and rounded on the pinioned threadweaver, pointing at the control panel where Slowhand had been trapped. It buzzed now with a release of energy that, despite Slowhand not knowing what it should sound like, didn't seem quite right.

"You're action was irresponsible and stupid," she shouted. "Have you any idea of the amount of *power* contained in those things?" She pointed at Slowhand. "Inserting *him* into the circuit has destabilised the entire system and –"

Jenna broke off, ducking, as the upper left corner of the panel exploded.

"I think she's trying to say you broke it," Slowhand pointed out. He studied the panel as another section detonated, lighting up everyone's faces. "If you ask me, I reckon this whole place is going to go up."

"You fool!" Jenna yelled at the threadweaver.

Fitch actually looked chastised. "He shouldn't have done what he did. Shouldn't have been able –"

"He's my *brother*. He's a –"

She's going to say it, Slowhand thought. The name. And when she did, then the world would know the truth. But at the same time he considered this, the panel behind him detonated once more and the conversation abruptly ceased. Because, this time the explosion set off a chain reaction that spread to more panels next to it, and then more after that, and suddenly one entire side of the waystation was aflame.

"Yep, I was right," Slowhand said, smugly.

"Fark," Jenna shouted, and she began to move among her people, shouting orders. "Get everyone back on board, now! You, do as I say! And you! Leave everything not already loaded! Mister Ransom, loose the umbilicals and prepare for immediate departure!"

"Ma'am, we haven't finished refuel –"

"It will have to *do*, Mister Quinn! If we don't get out of here now, we're not leaving. By the Lord of All, I'll *glide* this thing into Gransk if I have to!"

Gransk, Slowhand thought. There was that name again. Where the hells was it? *What* was it? As troubling as the question was, though, something troubled him even more, and that was his sister's attitude to him since he had escaped from certain death. There had been no smiles, no hugs, no anything, and he was beginning to think that the only reason Jenna had fought with Fitch was because she knew how dangerous his unauthorised actions were – that the fact that her own brother had been the spanner in the works didn't really matter to her at all. The realisation left him with a heaviness in his heart that was worse than he'd felt at the loss of Kali Hooper, but it was a heaviness that he could not afford to indulge in right now.

He looked around him, ducking as the explosions from the Old Race mechanisms increased, sending plumes of fire into the paths of the airship crew. Most were on board now, only himself, Jenna and Ransom still uncoupling the ship not on the safety of the deck. And, of course, Fitch. The threadweaver was still struggling against the arrows holding him, and Slowhand was pleased to see an expression of panicked horror had overtaken the usual arrogance that filled that face. His temptation to leave the bastard exactly where he was almost overwhelming but –

Slowhand sighed, swiftly pulled the arrows from Fitch's robes and then bundled him towards the gantry. The last thing he expected – but *should* have expected – was that at the last minute Fitch would plant his palm on his chest and send him hurtling backwards into a pile of crates. Dazed, he watched as Jenna and the last crewmembers boarded, and the airship was already pulling away by the time he rose and ran after it. The archer tried to make the jump from dock to airship but stopped himself at the last moment by grabbing onto a rail. The gap between them was just too great.

"Jenna," he shouted as the airship receded further beyond his reach. "I have to know – *is there anything of you left?*"

His sister stared back, the wind whipping at her face, and Slowhand wasn't sure whether it was that or something else that made her eyes tear up.

Then she dug into a pocket, took out a small object and threw it across the widening gap towards him. Slowhand flung out a hand and then stared down at what he'd caught – a bracelet – before looking back up to question what it was. But, in the brief moment he had looked down, the airship had begun to turn away, as had his sister, perhaps not voluntarily, towards Querilous Fitch. Slowhand roared as the threadweaver approached her and then placed his palms on her skull and the hopes that he had harboured until that moment – that even now he might be able to turn Jenna away from the Final Faith – were finally dashed as his sister quivered beneath Fitch's touch.

Watching the airship descend to the harbour's entrance tunnel, Slowhand could not remember when he had last – if ever – felt so lonely. But there was no time to dwell upon the feeling as another fierce explosion from behind almost blew him off the gantry.

The archer looked around, searching for something – *anything* – that could help him get off this rock. But the only viable method of transport had already left and all that remained was the bones of its sister ships. Then it suddenly occurred to him that if Jenna and the Final Filth could build their flying machine piecemeal, then anything the Filth could do, he could do too.

Slowhand worked quickly but precisely, skewering bolts of cloth from the rotted dirigibles with arrows from Suresight, before pulling them down and framing them around struts of lightweight metal. He tied the pieces of cloth into place with catgut from his quiver, pulling each piece taut until, when he flicked them, they thrummed like drums above the two triangular sections he had created. Finally he linked the two sections together, creating a makeshift hinge by tying the metal struts to the flexible frame of Suresight itself, swung a strap beneath the two, and then stood back to admire his handiwork.

Looking like a pair of artificial wings, what he had created would not emulate a bird but he could *hang* beneath it and it would *glide*. He hoped that was all he would need. There was no time to test its airworthiness, however, as the explosions around him had now become so frequent that they were one solid, roiling mass of ever expanding combustion. The only thing that he could do now was fly.

Slowhand slung the device on his back, tightened the strap, and ran, the precipice that loomed before him doing nothing to discourage him – because if he stayed he was dead anyway. Suddenly, he was in the air and plummeting, and with desperate shifts of his weight from his left and to his right, he managed to manoeuvre the contraption between the numerous metal struts and beams that filled the cavern, dropping past and through them until the floor of the cavern was in sight.

Here, Slowhand arced his body upward, feeling the strain not only on his muscles but on the contraption itself. However, as it groaned in unison with him, his flight path gradually changed from the near vertical to the horizontal. He banked to the left, into the harbour's exit tunnel, its striplights blinking by him, and he could feel the wind from the outside on his face. But with a quite literal sinking feeling, he realised that the air currents within the tunnel were not enough to keep him aloft. Thankfully, the explosions in the harbour above obliged him at that very moment, blasting a wave of heated air and flame down into the tunnel and buffeting him forward as effectively as if he had been swatted away by some giant, invisible hand. Slowhand yelled with surprise and with exhilaration and, as the sky darkened around him, realised he had exited the tunnel and was above the Drakengrats once more.

He was just beginning to think he was safe when the entire underside of Thunderlungs' Cry began to blow apart in a series of thunderous and buffeting explosions. There was an ominous cracking from above, too, and as the air about him began, suddenly, to fill with falling stones, rocks and even boulders, he realised that Thunderlungs' Cry itself was coming down. Slowhand cursed and frantically began to manoeuvre the glider through the deadly rain, avoiding pieces of the collapsing bridge by inches and aware that even a single impact could slap him from the sky. Whether through some innate piloting skill or sheer luck, he emerged unscathed, and was about to whoop in triumph when a growing shadow on the distant ground made him instinctively look up.

Ohhh, fark! he thought.

Because Thunderlungs Cry had saved the best for last, it seemed, and – seemingly in slow motion – an entire middle section of the bridge was plummeting towards him.

Slowhand never thought he'd be grateful for more explosions, but for the final, momentous detonation from the rockface, he most assuredly was.

He suddenly found himself being punched across the sky. The shockwave from the final detonation had caught the glider and punched it into a spin away from the rock face and, to Slowhand's misfortune, higher rather than lower into the mountains. As he sailed dizzyingly above the immense chasm he realised that while he had been punched higher, this did not necessarily mean that he was going to *remain* high as the shockwave had severely damaged what little integrity his invention had possessed in the first place. Swallowing uneasily, the archer craned his neck to inspect how bad things were, and his worst fears were confirmed. His jerry-rigged frame was bent and warped, and where he had lashed catgut to hold it together, it was now either snapping away from the metal or uncoiling from it with a sound like multiple cracking whips. He estimated he had perhaps a minute before the whole thing came apart.

There was nothing, absolutely nothing, he could do to keep the glider aloft, and there was nowhere he could bring it in to a forced landing. He was going down.

Slowhand found his attitude becoming unexpectedly philosophical. Maybe Hooper and he were going to meet up again, after all, and he could imagine the conversation already.

"Hooper."

"Slowhand."

"How's things?"

"Ohhh, you know... dead. You?"

"Dead."

"Mmmm."

"Mmmm."

"*So...*"

"*So...*"

Killiam Slowhand smiled, but it was a smile that faded as it formed. Because one of the last things he saw from his aerial vantage point were the k'nid, spilling towards the peninsula.

Then, abruptly, there was no more time and the glider impacted with the ground.

There was a rapid and utterly disorientating series of cracks, thuds and crunches, accompanied by the sound of a whistling wind and breaking struts and bones. Then the world turned sideways, lengthways, diagonal, upside down and, ultimately, dark.

The body of the archer lay face down amongst the wreckage in the remote peaks, twisted and spasming, and he reflected that if there had been a small chance that he might ever be found, that chance was dashed as flurries of snow blew in around him, then over him, covering him in a thick, white shroud that, come night, would freeze about him completely.

His hand moved slowly, shakily towards a pocket, searching for the bracelet Jenna had given him, hoping for comfort in its company. But his fingers felt nothing, the piece of jewellery that had seemed so important to his sister had been lost in his frantic attempts to flee the harbour. The archer sighed lengthily, though knew the sound was only partly disappointment and that, in truth, the strength to care was deserting him.

His eyelids fluttered closed and, as white flakes began to settle on them, he did not blink them away. His face unmoving now, more flakes settled layer by layer until, at last, his features were indistinguishable from the snow.

High in the Drakengrats, nature had built Killiam Slowhand his grave.

CHAPTER FIVE

THE DRAKENGRAT MOUNTAINS flared for a moment with a light so intense that it whited out the eyepiece through which Merrit Moon watched the event occur. The old man turned quickly away, rubbed his eye, and then frowned deeply. The ancient elven telescope – a rune inscribed, hand-lathed and polished thing of great beauty – was infinitely more powerful than any such device humans could have made. However, even though, at full magnification, its lenses permitted him to gaze across what amounted to a third of the peninsula, it should not have made what he had just seen seem *quite* so intense or immediate. That could mean only one thing. The explosion in the Drakengrats had been incredibly powerful and, consequently, the catalysts or combustants involved, like the telescope itself, had to have been infinitely more powerful than anything his own race could have manufactured.

The conclusion was inescapable. Something Old Race was up there – *had been* up there – but what?

Moon bent back to the eyepiece but any details on the far distant mountains were now obscured by a strange, mushroom-shaped cloud and he'd see nothing for a while. Besides, the sun was coming up, and it was time to open the shop. He was about to turn away when a slight nudge to the telescope shifted its focus down to the plains of Pontaine and something there caught his eye.

What is that?

It looked like some strange black cloud moving over the landscape, or at least would have done had it not been at ground level. And it appeared to be heading towards Gargas. There was something else, too. Something familiar. In the middle of it. A bulky black thing with something on it, moving at speed, as if trying to outrace the cloud. Moon adjusted the magnification on the telescope but, by the time he had done, the object and the cloud had become obscured by what few hills existed in that part of the province.

This was surely a day for mysteries.

Moon sighed, covered the telescope with a cloth, and made his way over to the spiral staircase that wound down through two floors to ground level. The old man grunted as he began to negotiate the creaking risers, the wooden stairs having always been a tight squeeze but having become something of a tortuous ordeal since his unfortunate 'accident' in the World's Ridge Mountains. Though in the months since the events of the Clockwork King he had managed to concoct a number of potions and medicines that kept Thrutt's ogur form in relative check, his physical mass and bone structure remained twice what it had been. This left him with a physiognomy that had a tendency to make babies cry and small dogs bark. He had to force himself to be philosophical about this, however, as he had learned on a number of unfortunate occasions that what seemed to trigger the Thrutt transformation was a rise in his blood pressure. A condition flagged by a tendency for his nose and ears to turn a bright red, his eyes to bulge and his mood to become very, very angry. It was embarrassing, yes, but he supposed it could have been worse, even if he wasn't sure exactly how.

Calm, he told himself as he squeezed between the stairway's walls, dislodging pictures and ornaments as he went, cursing the resultant clattering. *Calm.*

The old man emerged into the shop, found it dark and, yawning, moved to the two windows and door to flip their blinds. Azure dawn light flooded Wonders of the World and, through a criss-cross of dusty motes, he took a quick inventory of stock, working out which lines he would need to replenish from the cellar. Goblin death rattles, for sure, always popular with the babies. Shnarl fur dice and the stick-on elf ears, too – the only non-authentic line he carried. And there had been quite the run on troll testicles of late, but then it *was* spring and they were always popular at this time of year.

The cellar, however, could wait. Despite the required restocking, things had been pretty quiet around Gargas of late, and there would likely be no customers for a while. It was a state of affairs Moon attributed to the rumours of new predators on the peninsula. He didn't know how much truth there was in the rumours – certainly there had been no sightings of the creatures this far east – but once these things got started, that was that, people simply weren't prepared for the unusual. Peering out through the glass of the door, however, everything looked normal to Moon. The market was gearing up and the flummox was starting to bubble on the Greenwoods' nearby stall. When it was ready he might even be tempted by a glass, maybe dunk some redbread to kick start the day, slurping the juices from his chin. Since he had become part ogur his appetites had changed, though thankfully not so far as getting the munchies for the heads of the babies who squawked interminably when they saw him. The temptation, though, had been there.

Moon flipped the open sign and suddenly a figure loomed in his face, leering in at him through the glass. A customer, already? And a fop from one of the cities or larger towns by the look of him, even if he seemed slightly on the down-at-heels side. City dwellers were the worst kind of customer, because even though everything in his store was genuine they never believed it so, for the simple reason that they had never encountered it – as closeted as they were in their own, small and so-called 'civilised' world. Moon sighed then opened the door, and even before he could say good morning, it started. Except this time it wasn't about the provenance of his stock.

"By the Lord of All! The butcher across the way was right."

"Excuse me?"

The fop jabbed him in the chest, and Moon got a whiff of a pungent underarm. "This ogur thing – great idea and I have to say you have it almost bang on. The perfect way to advertise your shop. Harmon Ding, by the way, consultant to the retail trade. Consultancy's quite the big thing in the cities, you know."

Oh, it would be, Moon thought.

The Old Races constructed unimaginable wonders but now that man was the dominant race, it concentrated its efforts trying to find a better way to sell sprabbage. But what was the man on about regarding 'this ogur thing'?

"Something I can help you with, Mister Ding?"

Ding gave a cursory glance around the shop, clearly uninterested in its wares. "Maybe, maybe. All in good time. The important thing is you. Like I said, *almost* bang on." He shook his head and sucked in a breath. "This ogur thing," he added slowly, "*not quite right.*"

Moon stared at him, nonplussed. "Not quite right?"

Ding stared back, in a way that suggested he was dealing with someone with the *brains* of an ogur. "The costume! The mask!" He narrowed his eyes, leaned in and then whispered conspiratorially. "Between you and me, looks a bit fake."

"Fake?"

Ding nodded. "Fake, yes. It's like you're half man, half ogur. Look, I know ogur – I've seen pictures of them in storybooks – and while we both know they're not real, if you're going for the effect, you've at least got to go all the way."

"Oh, ogur are quite real, Mister Ding. Trust me, I know."

"Yes, yes, of course, of course. What else could you say with this," he waved his hand dismissively, "*novelty* shop being your going concern?"

Novelty shop? Moon felt a rumble beginning in his throat and the lobes of his ears warmed slightly. "Let me rephrase my question, Mister Ding. Is there anything you would like to *BUY*?"

"Buy, Mister Moon?" Ding looked almost aggrieved. "No, no, not buy. I'm here to *sell*. My services. For a period of one month. For a one off fee of fifty full silver."

"Why on Twilight would I pay you fifty full silver?"

Ding stared at him, swallowed slightly, and then suddenly snapped an upright finger into the air, as if to demonstrate a point. Unbidden, he began to prance around the shop, pointing things out and occasionally gazing at the ceiling as if he were somehow receiving divine messages from the old man's bedroom.

"Because I'm seeing *special ogur days* to bring the punters in. I'm seeing spit-roasts and I'm seeing chase-the-child competitions. I'm seeing captive princesses, donkeys, face scribing and pig's bladders on strings. But most of all, I'm seeing you – yes you! – in a brand, spanking new costume designed by me. Huge, flappy ears. Big teeth. Green." He paused, finally, then pointed directly at him. "*You*, Mister Moon, will make a fortune!"

There was a moment's silence, then –

"I'm not paying you fifty full silver for anything."

"Forty, then!"

"No."

"Thirty?"

"*Nothing* at all."

Ding gazed at him, open-mouthed. "You're making a big mistake."

"I don't think so. For one thing, you're clearly not a full tenth. For another, I'm not *wearing* a costume or mask." His voice deepened. "*Of any kind*."

"And you're saying *I'm* not a full tenth?"

"Twilight is an unusual place, Mister Ding."

Ding laughed. "Oh, here we go! You mean the Old Races and their ancient technology? The Pale Lord? The Clockwork King? And these new things – the k'nid?" Ding curled his fingers at Moon and made nibbling sounds with his teeth. "Just *stories*, my friend – tales to be told around the fire during Long Night and that's all. *Not real*."

"Oh, you'd be surprised."

Ding smirked. "Trust *me*, Mister Moon. There is nothing in this world that could persuade me otherw..."

Ding trailed off, his mouth hanging open as, right in front of him, there was a crackle of energy, a whoosh of charged air and a yelling, half-naked woman appeared out of nowhere, right in the middle of the shop.

The woman was riding a roaring horse. Except it wasn't a horse, not really, but a huge, armoured, horned thing that looked like a Vossian siege machine. And *clinging* to the Horse – apparently trying to eat it and its rider – were a number of thrashing, clawing, slashing things that Ding found... indescribable. He would have blinked and rubbed his eyes, had he not been busy flinging himself out of the way, because the horse had arrived moving, and was *still* moving.

Taking in its surroundings with insane looking, rolling green eyes, it whinnied and tried to come to a halt but failed miserably, demolishing two of the shop's display stands and heading inexorably for the building's rear wall. Ding continued to watch transfixed as the beast's rider spotted where it was heading, shouted something like "oh, farking hells," and promptly threw herself from her saddle. The woman landed on her feet on a display counter, wincing slightly, and spun immediately to face three of the things that detached themselves from her mount to fling themselves after her. As they did, she unsheathed a vicious looking gutting knife and slashed it in an arc across the air before her, sending the creatures scrabbling back with yellow goo spurting from their flanks. The horse-thing, meanwhile, skidded itself into a half-turn as it approached the wall and hit it side on. The things still clinging to it were crushed with a sickening crunch, spraying yellow goo upwards in a fountain of gore.

Ding swallowed hard as dust streamed from stressed supporting beams and the shop began to creak ominously.

The woman threw herself into the air and across the room, taking the time to wave at the old man as she passed. He, in turn, waved back but Ding could see that he was clearly not as pleased to see her as she was he. As the old man regarded the wreck of a room before him, Ding could have sworn that his nose and ears throbbed a bright red, and that he appeared to *grow* slightly. This did not, however, stop him coming to the aid of the woman when she needed it. As she was now engaged in a losing hand-to-hand battle with the remaining creatures, the old man opened a cupboard beneath his sales counter and, with a yell, threw her a glove.

Oh, very useful, Harmon Ding thought.

But then his ears flapped as she slipped the glove on and blasted one of her assailants over each of his shoulders with an pulse of energy that drew crackling red circles in the air. Ding watched the two creatures crash screeching through the windows of the shop and then turned back, white-faced now, just in time to see the third creature lunge for the old man. The odd thing was, though, he didn't seem to be the old man anymore, and as the creature reached him something big and green and roaring that stood in his place simply tore it apart.

Nice costume, Ding thought, and fainted.

Or at least tried to. For as he began to collapse something shot from the horse-thing's mouth and wrapped itself about his neck, holding him up.

Oh, he thought, *it's a tongue. An impossibly long, slimy tongue.*

Instead of fainting, Ding decided, instead, to scream. As the girlish wail erupted from him, the tongue released him and Harmon Ding ran. Ran as fast as his legs could carry him, out of the shop and away. The last words he heard as he headed for the gates of Gargas were: "Fark, what a day. Who was that by the way?"

"That? Oh, don't worry about him. He wasn't real."

Far behind Ding, the old man sighed, not with relief but in an attempt to calm himself down and, as Kali and Horse looked on, his ogur physique began to dwindle until he had returned once more to his half-ogur form. Done, he looked around the remains of his shop and then stared at Horse and Kali. His eyebrow rose.

"You could have knocked, young lady."

"Mmm, sorry about that. These things attacked *en route*, tearing up Horse pretty badly, so we had no choice but to jump here. Should have been outside, of course, but obviously he's not quite himself and overshot." She looked guilty. "A tad."

"A *tad?*"

Merrit Moon walked slowly forward, feet crunching on broken vials and crushed souvenirs, shaking his head. Despite his obvious dismay about the state of his shop, however, his brow furrowed in concern as he approached Horse. Gently, he ran a palm over the wounds on his armoured flanks – wounds that bled slowly and made the huge beast wince beneath his touch.

"His armour should be stronger than this," Moon observed. "There's a discolouration in it that doesn't look right."

"I know. I think it's something to do with his diet – or lack of it."

"His diet?"

"Worgles. Won't eat anything else. But they've disappeared since these bastards came out of nowhere."

"Really?" Moon said, intrigued. He looked at the tumbleweed like bodies that littered the shop floor. "I take it, by the by, that these are the infamous k'nid?" Kali looked at him and he added: "Oh, yes, I've heard the rumours. I may even have *seen* them, earlier, out on the plains."

"Yep, that's where they hit us."

"Ah, that was you," Moon said absently. He turned back to Horse. "Well, let's see if we can get some of this fixed up." He collected some balms and a cloth from around the devastated shop and began to gently rub them into Horse's armour.

"Hey," Kali said. "I'm injured too."

"What? Oh, yes. Yes, yes, of course you are."

Kali threw up her hands but smiled. The fact was, since escaping the mine, which she now realised must have been inhibiting them somehow, her recuperative powers had worked wonders on her leg and, while not perfect, it would do. Horse was the patient now, and it was nice to see the old man tending to him so carefully. Because, despite her elation at finding he still lived on the Dragonwing Cliffs above Martak, there was one thing she'd dreaded, and that was informing the old man that his own beloved horse – the original Horse – had perished during the course of that adventure.

Constant companions, until the day she'd inherited him from the retiring artefact hunter, she'd never known a relationship between man and beast be so close and knew the news would be shattering to him – hells, it had been shattering enough to her. It was during the telling of it, however, that Horse Two had begun to gently nudge the old man's shoulder, and that not only seemed to alleviate the impact of the news but also create the same kind of burgeoning bond that she herself had felt with Horse's more.... unusual replacement. Over the intervening months, either with Merrit visiting Horse's grave above the Flagons, or they him, here in Gargas, that bond had grown until she had begun to think once more that the old man cared more about Horse than he did about her. Or maybe it was just because he was part of *her* that he cared. That theory made her feel a little better, anyway.

"Old man?" She kicked the remains of one of the k'nid, exposing its soft underbelly – red, turning now to grey. "What are these things?"

Moon regarded them as he continued to soothe Horse.

"First impressions? Hostile. Wrong."

"Hells, old man, I could have told you that."

"No, what I mean is, they don't belong. They're not a part of the order of things."

Kali kicked the k'nid again. "At least they don't seem as indestructible as the rumours make out."

"Ah," Moon sighed. "I wouldn't chance too many arms on that particular theory. These *specimens* were transported here with Horse, remember. Forcefully separated from their pack. I believe that together they might be far more formidable opponents. Certainly the number of reported deaths reflects that."

"What? So you're saying they're some kind of group entity?" Kali fought for a comparison. "Like fussball fans?"

"You never did like that game, did you?" Moon mumbled. He patted Horse, finished with his ministrations, and moved over to the k'nid, examining it. Suddenly he pulled his finger back with a hiss and flicked a clear liquid from it, which made a small patch of floor warp and burn.

"What is that? Acid?"

"No, some kind of *destabilising* agent," Moon mused.

He had used many, many substances in his alchemical experiments but this was a new one on him. He studied the k'nid more closely and frowned.

"This isn't right," he said. He took a small vial from his pocket and sprinkled its contents over the corpse. Nothing happened for a few seconds but then the dead creature began to wrinkle and twist, shrink in on itself, until it became utterly unrecognisable.

"Now that *was* acid, right?"

Moon shook his head. "It's the same potion I use to limit the influence of the ogur upon myself – to hold the change in check, as it were. Except, of course, that I just gave the k'nid far more than is safe to use on myself."

"So, what? You're saying this k'nid was *changed* like you were? That your potion reversed the changes, made it what it was before?"

"Exactly."

Kali pulled a face. "But look at it, old man – it's just a mess. It isn't *anything*."

"That's what worries me." Moon stood and sighed. "I saw something happen in the Drakengrats this morning. A great explosion."

"Well, don't look at me. I was nowhere near it."

"For once," Moon said, smiling. "The point is, Kali, the k'nid are swarming from the west, are they not?"

"Moving down in a fan shape from what I've seen. Freiport, Volonne, Miramas, now here. Merrit, do you think there's a link? That this explosion somehow *created* the k'nid?"

Moon shook his head. "Reports of their appearance precede that. But there may be still be a link. Something *else* up there."

"Any idea what?"

Moon hesitated. "There's a legend of an Old Race site I came across during research into my own condition. It spoke of a place in the clouds where the Old Races played at being gods. A fearful, unapproachable place. They called it the Crucible."

"A place in the clouds? You think that means the Drakengrats?"

"It seems a likely contender."

"And this 'crucible'? You think that's where the k'nid came from?"

Moon sighed. "Kali, if I'm right I think they might have been *born* there."

Kali took a deep breath. "Then, old man, I guess I'm going to the Drakengrats."

"And I'm coming with –"

The old man stopped as there was a distant sound of tolling. "That's the town's sentry alarm. The guards have spotted something on the plains."

"K'nid. They must be spreading faster than I thought."

"There's one way to find out. Come with me."

Kali trailed the old man up the spiral staircase, avoiding falling pictures and ornaments as she climbed, until the pair reached the attic. Moon uncovered the telescope, adjusted its warp lenses, and then tipped it down so that it was aimed towards the town's walls. He peered into the eyepiece.

"Not k'nid," he said. "Not yet."

"Then what?"

"Take a look."

The old man stood aside and Kali took a look, focusing on the main gate of the town through which a great many soldiers were marching. Their grey canvas and lace epauletted livery marked them out as Pontaine militia, forces financed by the local land barons as a kind of home guard, and guarding the home was clearly what they seemed to be doing – quite zealously.

Ranks of them were organising the civilians near the gate into small groups, keeping them in place with what seemed the unnecessary threat of their weapons. Unless the militia had suddenly decided to become a dictatorial force, there had to be a reason for their uncharacteristic behaviour. Kali tipped the telescope upward slightly, focusing first not far beyond the town walls, and then further out, at the almost featureless agricultural plains that surrounded Gargas. She could see them stretching away for leagues, or at least *would* have been able to were it not for the dark fog that covered them like a shroud.

Except it wasn't a fog, she knew. It was the same pack of k'nid she and Horse had become caught up in. If pack was the word to describe the hundreds and hundreds – if not thousands – of them she could see. It was almost as if, *en route*, the strange creatures had been *replicating* themselves. She muttered something with four letters under her breath.

"K'nid?" Moon said.

"Oh, yeah. They're here."

The old man urged her aside and peered into the scope. "By all the gods, they *are* fast."

"Here within the hour, I reckon."

"Then it's time that we were on the move."

He walked to a chest in the corner of the attic, opened it and extracted an equipment belt similar to her own, a few unidentifiable odds and ends which he stuffed into his pockets and then a pink, woollen cloak he slung about his shoulders. Kali couldn't help but smile. The old man had been wearing that cloak the day they'd first met and she hadn't seen it since the day he'd retired – and it *still* stank of Horse. This was beginning to feel a little like old times. As Moon began to descend the stairs she too dug into the chest, extracting a new bodysuit she'd asked him to keep there for emergencies, and quickly slipped it on.

"What about your shop?" she asked as she followed Moon down. "You know it'll be at the mercy of those bastards."

"I doubt a thousand k'nid could make much more of a mess of it than you did, young lady."

Kali reddened. "For all the gods' sakes, when will you stop treating me like a bloody chil –"

She quietened. There was a soldier at the bottom of the stairs. Another behind him. And another behind him.

"Come with us," the one at the front said.

"Excuse me?" Merrit Moon responded.

The soldier's face darkened. "You are ordered to come with us. *Now*."

"The shop," Moon said warningly, "is *closed*."

Kali looked at him, coughed gently and pointed out the front door of the shop which hung buckled and ajar, then a part of the wall which had started to collapse during their battle with the k'nid.

"Actually," she pointed out, "I think you could say you were still open."

"Funny. You know they aren't here to buy things, Kali. They're here to interfere, as their kind always do."

Kali patted Moon's arm. Much as she shared the old man's healthy disrespect for authority of any kind, there were things going on that they both had to take into consideration – not least the clearly scared and trigger-happy militia. Besides, Moon's temper had become noticeably more *fiery* since the Thrutt incident and, for obvious reasons, she needed to keep him calm.

She approached the soldier and, despite already knowing what was approaching, asked: "Why are you here?"

The soldier was blunt and to the point, although a slight bobbing in his throat revealed his nervousness. "Gargas is now under martial law. A curfew has been imposed and any transgressors will be summarily executed. The population is to be evacuated to Andon."

"Andon?" Moon said. "That's ridiculous... madness! The journey will take days!"

"We go with them, old man," Kali said, to his utmost surprise. "We go with them. No arguments."

"Young lady?"

Kali patted his arm again, this time squeezing it softly but reassuringly too. Because watching the militia enter through the town gate she had noticed something that he had not. But now was not the time to share it with him.

"Trust me," she said after a second. "We go with them, and we do everything these nice gentlemen say."

CHAPTER SIX

"Young lady," Merrit Moon said, with evident disappointment, "I am very, *very* surprised. It is most unlike you to capitulate so readily."

Kali smiled. "Oh, I'm not capitulating, old man. You know I never do. I'm just looking after our interests. Ours and everyone else's."

"And how is that exactly?" The old man stared ahead at the snaking line of people, hundreds of them, six abreast, being marched across the plains, then back at an equal number in similar formation behind them. He snarled at the soldiers who marched alongside, effectively herding the people of Gargas like cattle, as they had been doing for hours. "As I believe I pointed out, this is madness."

"Old man, I think they're genuinely trying to help," Kali said placatingly. "If only to guarantee the land barons next year's taxes. It's just that they've never experienced a situation like this before."

"As you say. But what the hells are we doing *with* them?"

"For one thing, there's no way we could have reached the Drakengrats directly – you saw the k'nid swarm yourself. For another, it *does* take us closer to the mountains, albeit with a slight detour to the south-west. But lastly," she added with a prod, "it's your best chance to get across the plains with your scowl intact."

Moon harumphed and stared into the distance. For the moment the horizon was clear but, having seen the speed of the k'nid with his own eyes, he knew that situation could change at any second.

"Horse could have had us to the mountains in three jumps," he said.

"Maybe, if Horse were up to par," Kali patted her mount as he plodded alongside, still weak but recovering from his injuries. Green eyes rolled. "Besides, whether Andon has the best defences in the region or not, I'm a little dubious about the logic of corralling all these people in one place. I want to make sure they're all right."

Merrit Moon sighed and shook his head, but Kali could tell she'd been forgiven. "You want to make sure they're all right. An admirable sentiment, but I don't really see what you can do to help and, I repeat, this is madness. Do you honestly think we can avoid the k'nid for the three or four days it will take us to reach Andon?"

"I don't think it's going to take three or four days. Look ahead."

Maybe a tenth of a league further on, a dust storm was beginning to brew on the plain, vast spirals of flotsam thickening moment by moment. "Oh, wonderful. We'll be blinded too."

"I don't mean the storm. I mean what's *causing* it. The people at the front. *Look*."

It was then that Moon noticed the gestures being made by a group of six individuals leading the march. Garbed in thick, plain cloaks but with hints of far more colourful robes beneath, they appeared hardly to move under their covering – except for a subtle but complex flexing of their hands.

"Are they what I think they are?"

"Yep. League of Prestidigitation and Prestige. Saw them with the soldiers at the gate. And they're *weaving*. In fact, they're brewing up the storm."

"But why on Twilight would they do that?"

"Perhaps to disguise what's inside it." She nodded forward, into the storm itself. There was a distinct glow visible inside, a swirl of energy that Moon recognised instantly.

"My gods, they're creating a warp portal. They're going to *teleport* these people to Andon."

"Without them even realising it," Kali said with a twinkle in her eye. "It wouldn't do to let the general public know just *how* much magic was around them, now, would it?"

"These people aren't stupid, they'll realise."

"They're scared, tired, hungry and facing the unknown. When they arrive in Andon, they won't even care enough to ask."

"You knew what you were doing all along, didn't you?"

"Oh, aye."

Kali, Moon and Horse continued forward and soon entered the storm. Cloaks or hands raised against their faces to protect themselves from the swirling dust, no one other than Kali and her companions realised what was happening. Even when the teleportation magic took hold of their bodies, causing a slight tingle of the flesh, a barely noticeable buzzing in the bones, as they suddenly left one place to arrive in another. Or at least they *thought* no one else had noticed. Because as the marching refugees emerged from the other side of the dust storm, finding themselves amidst the skeletons and ruined machines of war that littered the outskirts of Andon it was, ironically, Harmon Ding who noticed something amiss.

Towards the front of the line, the small twitchy man sniffed the air and bobbed his head from side to side, his brow furrowing in confusion and consternation and his fingers rising as if to question the soldiers and the mages at the forefront of the march. Thankfully, they ignored him for the most part, but then Ding's continuing and questioning gaze looked back down the line, spotted Kali, Moon and Horse in its ranks, and his face whitened. He grabbed one of the soldiers and pointed in their direction.

"This we can do without," Kali sighed. "Excuse me."

She began to work her way down the line, and the closer she came to Harmon Ding the clearer his entreaties to the soldier became.

"Don't let them into your city! They're not *normal*. This crazy woman has, well, a *thing*, and her friend, the old man, he isn't an old man at all, he's some kind of *monster*. A big, green monster. They're in league with those other things, I tell you. Armoured horses and big green monsters and crazy women and... and gloves that fire circles in the air."

"Excuse me officer," Kali said in an approximation of a backwoods accent. She could tell from his expression that the soldier had already decided he was dealing with someone less than a full tenth, so that made her task a lot easier. "Is cousin Ding botherin' you?"

"He seems to think your grandfather is a big, green monster, ma'am."

Grandfather, Kali thought with a smile. *Oh, the old man was going to love that.*

"Pssshh," she said, dismissively. Kali extracted a bottle of thwack she had palmed from the Greenwoods on her way down the line and shook it at the soldier, feigning clumsiness as the cap she had deliberately loosened came off and the noxious brew splashed all over Harmon Ding. "Sorry, cousin," she said. "But at least you can't stink of it any more than you already do."

"But – but I haven't touched a drop!" Ding protested. "Not a dro –"

Kali looked at the soldier and shook her head sadly. "Denial," she said, and rammed the neck into Ding's mouth, whacking him subtly in the stomach as she did so he couldn't help but gulp the thwack down. "There, there. You know it makes you feel better."

The bottle extracted, Ding sucked in a gulping breath. "Armoured horsh," he said, dribbling thwack while his eyes rolled. "Big, green monshter, gloves that – that..."

"I'm sure you have enough to deal with, so I'll take him off your hands," Kali said to the soldier. "I'll look after him, now."

"Thank you, Ma'am."

"No problem."

Kali took Ding by the arm and force-marched his protesting form back towards Moon. As they neared Horse she took a quick look around to make sure no one was watching and then suddenly elbowed Ding in the face, knocking him cold. She slung the body over Horse and then fell back into step with Merrit Moon.

"Nice work," the old man commented.

"Shucks, it were nothin'... *grandpa*."

The old man turned to protest, but then thought better of it as the exodus neared the walls of Andon itself.

They were formidable – and it was immediately clear why the barons had chosen to evacuate the populace here – because in addition to the normal ranks of catapults, trebuchets and giant crossbows that lined their tops, additional defensive weapons had been added to their number. Some, by the look of them, magical in their design. If – make that *when* – they came, the k'nid would certainly have a battle on their hands.

The soldiers at the front of the line called out and, with a massive rumble, the gates began to open. Gradually, the line filed beneath the stone arch, until it was the turn of Kali, Horse and the old man to enter.

It was then that the first of the problems Kali had envisaged hit them. Inside the city walls, refugees not only from the northern towns but, by their local dress, Fayence to the south-east, milled about in an ever thickening crowd, threatening to block the main thoroughfare. Nor did they just mill. Many were crying in fear of what they had been told might come; others beseeched the soldiers for help they could not give; still others protested volubly about the situation they had been forced into. It was, in short, chaos, and the soldiers looked as confused as they did.

Kali approached one of the city guards, asked what was to happen next.

"To be honest, Miss, it's kind of every man for himself. All accommodation is already taken, and the situation isn't helped by the fact that many have already barricaded themselves in their homes, threatening to put a quarrel through the heart of anybody who approaches. Frankly, the barons have made something of a mess of all this. All I can offer you is stabling for your, er, horse. We're stabling all the beasts in the bunkers in the city walls, should be safe enough there."

"Can't these people use those bunkers?"

"They could Miss, but try persuading them. If you knew things straight from the hells were heading for the city, would you hide in the first place that might be breached?"

The soldier had a point. For that very reason, she wasn't happy leaving Horse there either. But there was no other choice and he would, when it came down to it, be safer there than out in the open.

Kali slipped Harmon Ding's unconscious form from her mount and patted Horse on the neck, before handing the soldier his reins.

"Could you see to him for me? I need to find some shelter for our peop –"

Kali's words were drowned out by a sudden series of urgent cries from the city walls and a flurry of activity above as soldiers took up positions. There were mages amongst them too, standing tensed and slightly hunched, their faces dour, fists balling and beginning to flare or crackle with energy waiting to be unleashed. Within seconds there was barely an inch of space left on the walls as Andon's defenders readied themselves.

"They're coming! Seal the gates!"

My gods, so soon?

Kali raced up the steps to the walls, needing to know what the city was facing. Pushing her way between soldiers she stared out over the Killing Ground – or at least, what she could see of it.

The advancing swarm of k'nid completely obscured the abandoned battlefield as they tumbled, rolled and scuttled rapidly towards Andon's walls. As the k'nid came, Andon's defenders responded with devastating force, unleashing a rain of missiles and magical bolts that should have created an impassable wall of death but which, after the initial volleys ended, appeared to be having very little effect on the k'nid at all. It seemed, in fact, that for every k'nid that was pounded by the defensive assault, another two appeared. As prepared as it was, Andon looked as though it was about to be overwhelmed. Sure enough, only seconds later, the first wave of k'nid reached the walls, scaled them and rushed straight into the ranks of the now panicking mages and soldiers.

As men and women fell flailing and screaming, their cries muting as they were enveloped, spasming, within the k'nid, Kali knew that Andon's walls were already lost and the city itself would soon follow.

There was nothing she could to help these people now but she had to help her own – and quickly.

Kali raced back down the steps and quickly enlisted Moon and the Greenwoods to help marshal the people through the tortuous maze of twisting and jinking streets that led to the Andon Heart. For though the city guard had informed her that all accommodation was taken, she knew of one particular hotel that did not normally open for business that might be able to provide them with sanctuary. *If* they could get there in time. Because, with most of its residents barricaded behind their doors, the city was strangely quiet, making the sound of the continuing k'nid assault ever louder.

Screams were actually coming from the side streets around them now and, among them, they could hear officers barking desperate orders to their men and the crackle of magical discharges as mages made one last, desperate stand. The k'nid assault was, it seemed, relentless. As the walls around them turned rainbow-coloured with flashes of weapon fire and energy bolts, all Kali could say to her charges was: "Run!"

This they did without hesitation, and Kali led them to the Andon Heart, and there towards the alleyway that led behind two deserted market stalls to the entrance to the Underlook.

As Kali neared the mouth of the alley, a crossbow quarrel thudded into the wood right beside her, stopping her in her tracks. She stared at it, and then up at the window from which it had been fired, and then at the other windows which lined the alley. Like the first, they were occupied by the figures of a man or woman aiming a weapon in their direction.

What the hells? she thought. *This was hardly time for Pim and his guild to be playing their secret headquarters games.*

"These people need shelter!" she shouted. "Tell Jengo Pim they're with Kali Hooper!"

The only answer was another crossbow quarrel embedding itself firmly in a wall next to her head.

Dammit.

"Kali Hooper!" she shouted again, but her voice was lost in the clamour that was taking over the city.

"Forget it," Merrit Moon observed. "The place is a veritable fortress."

"Yeah?" Kali said. She studied the alley anew, weighing it up. The last time she had been here – immediately after the 'death' of the old man and before her trip to Martak – she had been escorted along its deadly length, but at that time she had still been learning of her new abilities and what had seemed impossible then now seemed less impossible.

"Stay here, old man," she said, and before Merrit Moon could respond, she was gone.

The first of the window sentries didn't even see her coming, Kali already having worked out her trajectory so that she could leap off some piles of rubbish to the alley's side and springboard herself off the wall above to its opposite number. There, her momentum allowing her for a second to actually run along the vertical surface, she flung herself forward, grabbed a drainpipe and slung herself around for a leap back across the alley. Somersaulting in mid air, she hit the first wall again with her feet, kicked off and propelled herself backwards towards the window that now lay opposite, jack-knifing herself as she went so that her legs wrapped themselves around the neck of the sentry positioned there in a scissor grip. Thus anchored, Kali allowed herself to flop loosely, hanging upside down from the window with her back to the wall. As she did, she jerked her legs so that the sentry was flipped forward and out. She opened her legs and he screamed as he plummeted to the ground, hitting with a dull thud.

Five or six crossbow quarrels slammed into the wall where Kali hung, but she was already gone, dropping down to the ground and pinwheeling on her hands across the alley's width.

Back on her feet once more she leapt straight upwards, directly beneath the second window, grabbed and twisted the front of the crossbow that was wielded there, then quickly pulled the trigger so that its quarrel impaled itself in the shoulder of its bearer.

Only seconds had passed since she had begun to run the gauntlet, but it was long enough for those sentries who remained to realise that she would now be coming for them. Shouts and cries of alarm bounced back and forth across the alleyway.

Kali went inside now, pulling herself through the window she had just vacated, knocking the groaning sentry cold then running through the room beyond, along the corridor, and into the adjacent room. She didn't slow her pace, however, indeed she accelerated, then launched herself straight through the room's window. Straight as an arrow, she flew across the width of the alley, waving a casual 'hi' to the stunned occupant of the window opposite, before slamming into him and winding him so severely that he sat down with an *oomf*.

The *oomf* became a groan as Kali wasted no time knocking him cold.

Here she changed her tactics, grabbed the sentry's crossbow and threw herself to the side of the window she had just entered. Then, with two perfectly calculated shots a second apart, fired a quarrel through the forearms of the next two sentries she could see from her position. Both cried out in agony and their weapons fell from their hands to clatter and break on the alley floor. Now, only one sentry remained, but she would be the most difficult to take out, and Kali quickly studied her surroundings, looking for a way to finish the job.

Old building, she thought. *Unused, neglected, probably riddled with woodworm and dry rot. Fine, that was the way to go.*

Without hesitation, she leapt upwards, straight into and through the ceiling of the room, spitting dust and splinters as she broke through plaster and slats. Heaving herself up into the roof space she ran a palm over the underside of the roof itself, found a weak spot and then punched through the tiles. Half a second later she was on the roof, racing along its sloping surface towards the end of the alley and the last sentry post in her way. Calculating when the window would be beneath her, she lay down on the roof surface and let herself slide down it headfirst, dropping off the edge of the roof and plummeting straight down. There was a gasp of surprise as she hit and grabbed the outstretched arms and crossbow of the last sentry, and then a cry of alarm as she realised Kali wasn't intending to let go. Weighed down by her mass, the woman was pulled from the window in to Kali's embrace. The two tumbled towards the ground, Kali wrapping herself around the Grey Brigade member to protect her, and then they hit the ground in a cloud of dust, the woman exhaling loudly as much from shock as the impact. Kali pulled her up. The two of them were standing directly in front of the main entrance to the Underlook.

The woman stared at Kali, gasping in disbelief.

"The door," Kali said. "Get it open. *Now*."

"It will do you no good."

"I got this far, didn't I?"

The woman shrugged and rapped on the door, a code that had changed from the one Kali remembered. As it opened, two men appeared on the threshold and Kali despatched them swiftly with punches to the nose. Moving inside, she worked her through the corridors of the old hotel until she came to its ballroom – the centre of operations and throne room of Jengo Pim.

As expected, Pim sat on his makeshift throne, and regarded her coldly as she entered.

"Pim, what is this?" Kali said.

"Kali Hooper," the thieves guild leader replied slowly. "So, which of my people dies horribly this time?"

Kali was somewhat thrown by the tone of her reception. Pim had understood the death of his man during her incursion into the Three Towers had been unavoidable and no fault of her own.

"I don't understand."

"Tom Daly!" Pim snapped. "You do remember how you got him turned to stone?"

Oh yes, Kali thought, *I remember. But I also remember that his name was Kris Jayhinch – and that was not something Pim himself was likely to forget.*

Something was wrong here. And now that she knew that, she was suddenly aware of the tension in the room – the beads of sweat on Jengo Pim's face and, more importantly, those on the faces of the men who surrounded him. She studied the man right behind Pim – a man she did not know – and saw how his arm was tensed, as if holding something to Pim's back. A knife, it had to be. It wasn't Pim who closed his doors to the refugees, it was these others. Pim had become the victim of a cowards' coup and, by the looks of things, quite recently.

"As you can see," Pim explained, "you are not welcome here. Leave now or... my men will fire."

Kali could see that well enough and, for a moment, she said nothing, biting her lip as she tried to work out a way out of this. The number of crossbows that were trained on them made it impossible to pull off any sudden manoeuvres. Deprived of that possibility she could only try to talk her way out. But that, in itself, seemed a likely unsuccessful path.

"Perhaps," a voice said, "I might be of some assistance?"

Kali turned and saw that Merrit Moon and the others had worked their way into the Underlook. But it was not Moon who had spoken. A figure pushed his way through the clamouring crowd and threw back his hood, and Kali found herself staring at a silver haired, bearded figure whose presence made him seem to loom tall over the others.

"You," she said.

The man inclined his head slightly. "Poul Sonpear at your service."

"Who's he?" Merrit Moon whispered in Kali's ear.

"Archivist for the League of Prestidigitation and Prestige, particularly the forbidden bit. Oh, and part time Final Faith spy." She glanced at Jengo Pim and then back to Sonpear. "Well, this is turning into quite the reunion."

"Odd, isn't it, how certain *pivotal* figures always seem to turn up in the right place at the right time." Sonpear smiled, but it was a smile that seemed aimed only at Kali. "One might almost say it was *preordained*."

Kali eyes narrowed. Was Sonpear alluding to something? Something, perhaps, to do with her own origins and place in the scheme of things, much as a certain fish thing had alluded in Martak some time back? If he was – in the presence of all these people – if he *knew* something, now was not the time to talk about it.

"What are you doing here, Sonpear? Shouldn't you be closeted with your buddies in the Three Towers?"

"I should, but clearly I am not." He shrugged. "A small distraction. A liaison in the Skeleton Quays, where I found myself detained. By the time I returned to the towers, they had already been sealed."

Kali smiled. Detained in the quays, eh? She knew just the place and wondered how business was down the Bound to Please. So, despite the fact Sonpear had already proven he was literally capable of wiping the wall with her, he was quite human after all. And now he was stuck here as much as they were. Or, then again, perhaps she was jumping to conclusions.

"I have made myself known to you because I believe I can help with our mutual predicament," Sonpear said.

"How's that, then?"

Sonpear said nothing and simply moved his right hand in a motion like he was turning some invisible dial, and the man with his knife in

Pim's back – as well as two others within stabbing distance – rose from the floor of the ballroom making choking sounds and clutching their necks, their feet kicking beneath them for a purchase they could not find. Kali had seen such magical 'persuasion' techniques before but not to the extent Sonpear seemed to be taking them. She swallowed as the eyes of the infiltrators began to bulge, then turned away as Sonpear suddenly flicked his wrist and their heads snapped around a hundred and eighty degrees. Three dead weights fell to the floor with a thud.

"You didn't have to do that."

"Didn't I?"

"He's right, Miss Hooper," Jengo Pim interjected, gesturing for the bodies to be removed. "We are nothing without our code. These men needed to be taught that there should be honour among our kind."

"I think it's a little late for them to learn anything."

"I wasn't referring to the dead," Pim responded. He nodded to the others in the room and, as Kali looked, she saw the change of attitude in them. The sense of insecurity that had pervaded the Underlook since she'd first arrived was gone now, replaced by a renewed and total allegiance to the true and proper leader of the Grey Brigade.

"I would suggest," Sonpear said to the other crossbow wielders around the room, "that you put those down. Now is a time to work together, not against one another."

Pim's men capitulated, and Pim himself rose from his throne with a relieved sigh.

"Right," he said. "Miss Hooper, get your people inside. Ferret, see to their wounded. Rathbone, once everyone's safely gathered in seal those bloody doors. I believe we have ourselves a siege situation."

The men went about their duties and it was only seconds later that the outside walls of the hotel reverberated with a series of impacts from outside, sifting dust from cracks in the ceiling of the ballroom. Many of the people from Gargas looked around in fear and hugged each other.

"They wasted no time," Kali said coolly. "Pim, are you sure this place is fully sealed?"

"Tight as an ogur's underpants," Pim said, glancing at Moon when his comment elicited a strange growl. "The question is, how long will the walls *themselves* hold."

Kali nodded. "The place is old but it's better than nothing. Still, we can't stay here for ever." She turned to Merrit Moon. "Old man, have you got any i –"

A sudden boom from outside, much louder than before, shook the hotel to its foundations, and Kali stopped speaking. Another such boom caused her to look around in alarm.

"What the hells?" she said.

"I believe that my people may be attempting to provide a solution," Poul Sonpear said.

"What the fark are they doing – bombing us?"

"In a manner of speaking."

Kali spun to face Jengo Pim. "Is there any way to see?"

Pim nodded. "Upstairs, on the top floor, in the old turret room. Follow me."

Kali and Sonpear raced after Pim up flight after flight until they came to a small, circular chamber which Kali noticed, with some amusement, Pim appeared to have turned into a shrine to the Hells' Bellies, the walls plastered with handbills and memorabilia. What was evidently his *sanctum sanctorum* was otherwise featureless apart from a panoramic circle of shuttered windows. Pim moved to open one but Sonpear redirected him to another. "No, there. The view will be... better."

Puzzled, Pim did as he was told and flung the shutters wide, then stepped back as the full scale of what was occurring struck him. Kali pushed in beside him.

"My gods!"

The eastern quarter of Andon spread out beneath her and there wasn't a street or an alleyway, a square or a cul-de-sac of it that wasn't overrun by the k'nid. Smoke, screams and chaos were the order of the day, and it seemed there was no escape from it anywhere. As Kali looked down in horror she saw at least ten people who had not managed to make cover stalked and taken by the k'nid, their skeletons left discarded on the scarred streets. It was not, however, the events that were occurring below her that made Kali gasp, but rather *above*. Because it seemed that, in reaction to the invasion of their city, the Three Towers were going on the offensive.

Kali had been inside that complex and had heard it thrum with its strange power, had known it to be magical, but it was not until this moment that she realised just *how* magical it actually was. The three towers, that were the headquarters of the League of Prestidigitation and Prestige, were *moving*, each of them twining like immense snakes, the bridges that connected them having seemingly retracted – or perhaps simply disappeared – to enable this new and unexpected freedom. But it wasn't just the fact that they were moving that stunned Kali, it was what they were doing as they moved – and what they were doing were blitzing Andon. From the top of each of the looming, swaying structures, huge, orange balls of energy were being fired down into the streets, each so powerful that, as it departed its tower with a *thwoom*, Kali felt the floorboards of the hotel beneath her vibrate. The vibration was nothing, though, compared to the shaking that followed as the spheres impacted, not only at ground level but occasionally on rooftops as they targeted the k'nid wherever they were. Explosion after explosion lit the battle torn streets. Not only k'nid but buildings and people were blasted apart, flailing and spinning through the air.

"What the hells are they *doing*?" Kali demanded of Sonpear.

"It's the League's self protection protocol. The towers are defending themselves as best they can."

"You arrogant – this isn't the way, you bastard! Your people are destroying their own to protect themselves. You have to stop this!"

"There is nothing I can do. The Towers are sealed."

"Well, think of something, dammit! They're tearing Andon apart!"

Sonpear hesitated, clearly torn between his League responsibility and the damage that it was causing. For a second he just listened to the sound of the fireballs and to the battering the exterior of the hotel was taking from the k'nid.

"There might be weapons," he said finally, "that may prove more effective in an offensive than those you currently possess. There will, however, be some hazards involved in obtaining them."

"Pal, they can't be any more hazardous than opening that front door or waiting here while it gets blown off," Jengo Pim interjected. "What do you have in mind?"

Sonpear sighed, as if what he were about to announce he should not even be considering. He was about to speak when there was a sudden warning cry from Kali and he stared toward the Three Towers. Or rather, at the space *between* themselves and the Three Towers. Because one of the towers had turned towards them and, thrumming deeply as it came, growing larger every second, one of the fireballs was on direct collision course with the Underlook.

There was no time to run, nowhere to hide and absolutely nothing they could do. Heart pounding, the last thing Kali saw was Sonpear rushing at her, pushing Pim into the fireball's path. And then the fireball struck and the top of the Underlook was gone in a blazing inferno, just like that.

CHAPTER SEVEN

ONE THING MADE Kali question whether she was in the afterlife and that was that Jengo Pim seemed to be sharing eternity with her. When their times came she granted they might be near neighbours in whatever level of the hells she was despatched to – close enough to pop round for a cup of sulphur, perhaps – but, hey, she hadn't led the life of crime he had. She guessed, she had one or two redeeming features he hadn't, hadn't she?

She stared at Pim, picking himself up off the ground. He was staring at her in the same way she was staring at him – which was to say completely bemused – and it looked very much like he was thinking the same thing as she was, too. There was no way on Twilight the two of them couldn't be dead.

Both of them then turned to take in their surroundings. Or rather lack of them.

Wherever they were, it certainly *looked* like the afterlife. At least if one subscribed to the idea of it being some almost featureless limbo; dark, unoccupied and silent. The kind of place where one might wander until the Gods had counted up your good beads and bad beads on their divine abacus, or whatever the hells it was they did. It certainly *felt* like the afterlife, at least in the sense that her arrival here had left her rather numb. The one thing it didn't do was *smell* like the afterlife. But, to be honest, that was more likely to be Jengo Pim.

No, wait, Kali thought, and sniffed her underarm. Okay, it had been something of an energetic twenty four hours.

"What," Pim said slowly, "just happened?"

Kali remembered the Underlook's turret room; a series of fleeting images that included the fireball, Sonpear shouting a warning cry, and then him staring her in the face, shoving her back into Pim, *hard.* The shock she had felt in that moment – that Sonpear was saving his own skin – didn't tally with the look she saw on his face. It no longer struck her as homicidal but somehow desperate, as if the mage were doing the only thing he could in the circumstances.

307

"I think he pushed us..." Kali said, vaguely.

"Oh, the bastard pushed us all right. Right into an early grave."

"Do you *feel* dead?"

Pim looked himself up and down, patted his arms and legs and chest, frowned slightly when he noticed one of his sleeves was smoking gently. He patted it down. "Well, no, but..."

"Like I said, I think he pushed us out of the way. *Magically*, I mean. I think we're somewhere else."

Pim took a moment to absorb what Kali said. "Somewhere else? This looks like nowhere."

"That's exactly where I think it is. Nowhere. I think this is Domdruggle's Expanse."

"Who's what?"

"Domdruggle. His expanse. It's *another place* – an echo of our own, existing on a different plane. At least that's how the story goes. It's very old, supposed to be something of a myth."

Pim shrugged. "Something of a boring myth, if you ask me."

"No, we're just becoming acclimatised to it." She stared out into the dark. "Look, Pim. *Look*."

The thieves guild leader followed Kali's gaze, where shapes were indeed forming out of the nothingness, but instead of displaying an expression of wonderment, he frowned.

"You said it was an echo of our plane of existence. But if we're still where we were, it looks nothing like it."

"No, it doesn't, does it?" Kali said, smiling. She continued to gaze into the darkness, making out rolling fields, and vast fortresses and soaring towers in the distance. Things other than clouds or birds scudded across the sky.

Great, winged things. "That's because we're looking at the distant past."

"Are you telling me we've travelled through time?"

Kali shook her head. "Nope, we're exactly *when* we were. This is what Andon looked like when Domdruggle conjured the echo. Of course there was no Andon then, only the cities of the elves and the dwarves..."

She trailed off, her wonderment at what she was seeing coupled with the promise of what she could explore out there leaving her speechless. She almost left Pim and walked off into the ghostly landscape.

"So this is the time of the Old Races?" Pim asked.

"The memory of it. I wonder what day it was, what season, what year? *When* in their calendar was this?" She gazed up at the stars to see how different from her own time they were, but instead of seeing the stars saw something else, and gasped.

Kerberos loomed above, twice, three times the size it should have been. So immense its sphere was almost enveloping the planet, creating an eerie fogginess to the light. And that light was not the azure light they were used to but a deep, blood red.

"My gods!"

"That doesn't look right," Pim observed, bleakly. "It's like it's *swallowing* Twilight."

Kali nodded. "I think this might be the End Time."

"End Time?"

"The time when the elves and the dwarves died. When the Old Races disappeared."

"What? You're saying that Kerberos *killed* them?"

Kali shook her head, not sure what to think. When she spoke, it was almost in a whisper. "I don't know. But by the looks of things I'd be willing to guess it had *something* to do with it."

"Perhaps one day soon, you should find out what, Kali Hooper," a voice said.

"What? *What*?"

"What?" Pim echoed. It seemed that he had heard nothing.

Kali rubbed the side of her skull, feeling a strange irritation, almost a scratching within.

"Awe inspiring, isn't it?" the voice said again, and this time it sounded more familiar. "Some say the whole expanse exists on the head of a pin."

"Sonpear?" Kali said.

"Sonpear?" Pim repeated.

"My apologies for your abrupt departure. In the circumstances, I am afraid I acted instinctively, my magic reflecting what was on my mind."

"Hey, don't worry about it," Kali said.

"You're talking to Sonpear?" Pim chipped in again.

"Yes!" Kali snapped. And then more slowly: "Although I'm not sure how."

"'Sending' and 'receiving' is my trade, Miss Hooper. Or had you forgotten?"

Kali hadn't. Sonpear's abilities as a telescrying spy had helped lead the Final Faith to the Clockwork King. She just hadn't realised his talents were quite so powerful.

"It isn't exactly telepathy," Sonpear went on, and Kali could almost *hear* a smile in his voice. "But I challenge any thaumaturgist to explain to me the difference."

"So you're a man of many talents. Does one of them include a way of getting us back from where you've sent us?"

"Do you not prefer to remain where it is safe? Do you not yearn to explore your new environment?"

Oh, Kali yearned to explore, all right – very much. But she also knew that now was not the time to do so. As it happened, Pim vocalised the question she was about to ask.

"How bad is the Underlook? How are our people?" he shouted into the air, turning as he did as if that might help Sonpear hear him better.

"There are no casualties. The fireball destroyed the hotel tower in quite dramatic fashion but the resulting damage was, thankfully, localised."

"I asked you a question! Answer me, dammit!"

"Um, I think only I can hear him," Kali pointed out.

Pim faltered. "Oh, right. Well, then, what did he say?"

"The fireball blew the roof off but, otherwise, everyone's all right."

"The turret's gone?" Pim said and, clearly thinking of his collection, his face darkened. "When this is over, I am going to sue the wands off those bastards in the League."

"*When* this is over. And somehow I don't think it will be unless we stop it."

"I'd welcome any suggestions as to what we can do," Pim said.

"Wait," Kali said, and then addressed Sonpear. "Earlier you said 'what was on your mind'? We were talking about weapons, Sonpear, so why should that make you think of this place? Are the weapons here?"

Sonpear sighed. "Among countless other artefacts. The Expanse was considered by the Guild to be a safe depository for such items, yes."

Kali remembered her visit to the Three Towers' forbidden archive, where she had summoned virtual projections of its treasures, mere *representations* of the real things. But this was where the real deal was. This was where the artefacts actually *were*.

"Tell me where. They could help."

Sonpear paused. "I remain reluctant to do that. Such weapons, were they to find their way into the wrong hands, could easily tip the balance of power on the peninsula."

Kali slammed her hands on her hips and shouted at the sky, without feeling even vaguely foolish. "Sonpear, listen to me. In case you hadn't noticed the balance of power has already been tipped. In favour of the k'nid. *They* don't belong on the peninsula any more than these weapons do. Give us the means to fight them!"

"Proceed west," Sonpear instructed. "But I warn you again, Miss Hooper – there may be hazards involved."

"What kind of hazards?"

Sonpear hesitated again. "I pray that you do not find out." He sighed. "I need to cease our communication for now. The effort is exhausting."

"Okay. But, Sonpear, don't go far."

"Fear not. I shall return to you as soon as I am able, Miss Hooper."

Kali and Pim moved cautiously through the ghostly darkness, in a direction that, if they were on their own plane, would be taking them towards the Andon Heart. It was somewhat disorientating, the knowledge of what they were passing through back home jarring with the sights around them, the towers and spires in the distance, the topology of this unknown time. Amidst it all, however, there soon became visible something that was strangely familiar – and strangely disturbing.

Ahead, soaring above them were three thick and writhing pillars of energy, powerful not only in appearance but in the discomforting buzz they produced in Kali and Pim's bones. As she and the thieves guild leader moved closer, Kali saw that they were more than just pillars and seemed to be filled with the ghost-like hints of a floor level here, a doorway there, a staircase between them.

"This looks like –" Pim began.

"It is."

The almost impossible structure that was the headquarters of the League of Prestidigitation and Prestige had always generated speculation among the people of Andon as to how *exactly* it had been built and remained standing – with sorceries, surely, but now Kali and Pim knew the truth. The Three Towers had its foundations here in Domdruggle's Expanse, magically rooted in another plane of existence. In other words, it was unique. The only thing on Twilight that spanned two worlds.

As revelatory as that was, what grabbed Kali's attention more was that this translucent echo of the Three Towers wasn't empty, filled not with the mages who thronged there in its physical reality but a variety of objects that glowed more brightly than the structure itself. Kali knew immediately what she was looking at. The Forbidden Archive. It was one hells of a warehouse.

"Come on," she said to Pim.

The pair of them approached the towers slowly, Kali's head craning upward, Pim's turning from side to side, still taking in the Expanse and clearly not at ease with it.

"It's lonely here," he said. "Eerie. Soulless. Why do you suppose whatsisname – Domdruggle? – did this, conjured the Expanse? I mean, what possible purpose could it have?"

"Before seeing it, I'd have said your guess was as good as mine. But now we know *when* it was created – the End Time – maybe it was meant to be some kind of bolthole. Somewhere to hide. And don't ask me from what, because I haven't a clue."

"Bolthole? What, for the entire population of the peninsula? *All* the elves and the dwarves?"

"Why not? It's as big as our world."

"Yes, but…" Pim trailed off. "There's *nobody* here."

"I know, and that's what worries me."

"I don't follow."

Kali thought about the body of the dwarf she'd found in the Mole, that lonely metal coffin buried far deeper than any grave or resting place should be, and wondered again how it was that no one had come to help him.

"*If* Domdruggle conjured the Expanse as some kind of sanctuary from whatever wiped out the Old Races, they obviously never had time to come here. That suggests to me that they were gone, just like that."

"Pits of Kerberos, that fast?"

"Maybe."

"Fark."

"A question for another time, though eh? Right now we have our own problems, the main one being what the hells we're looking for."

"Allow me to assist you with that, Miss Hooper," Poul Sonpear interjected. "I would suggest the artefacts you seek will be found on the third level."

"Suggest as much as you like, Sonpear, but I've a better idea. Why don't *I* choose what'll be most effective against the k'nid?"

"You are there and have that prerogative, of course. I would question, however, how you would endeavour to transport from this place a dwarven sonic cannon, say, or a –"

"Okay, fine, point taken. So what are we looking for?"

"Portable armaments, light but powerful. In this case, discharge weapons. The elves called them crackstaffs."

"Crackstaffs?"

"You will recognise them when you see them."

"Right, fine. Third level it is, then." Kali moved forward then hesitated. "Sonpear, the stairs in this place – they are negotiable?"

"This Three Towers possesses residual corporeal mass, yes. But the experience of negotiating it may be a little disorientating."

Sonpear wasn't kidding, Kali soon discovered. The disorientation hit her and Pim as soon as they entered the structure, mainly because all of their senses persisted in telling them that they hadn't entered anywhere at all, misled by the translucency – and, in some areas, almost complete transparency – of the sorcerous manifestation. Kali couldn't describe it any other way than as weird – like walking through a hall of mirrors where the mirrors cast no reflection at all. Nevertheless, she and Pim managed to navigate their way to the central staircase and, treading warily on its insubstantial risers, made their way up to the third level.

Kali's heart thudded, though not from the climb. Laid out before her were any number of objects that she had summoned in the Three Towers' virtual forbidden archive many months ago. Though here, of course, they were real. They could be touched. Examined. *Explored*. And she longed to do all three. For a moment she felt that it wasn't fair that she was stuck with having to risk her life exploring all manner of lethal ruins when the League of Prestidigitation and Prestige had such a collection – perhaps years' worth of adventuring! – here for the asking. But then she reminded herself of the lesson Merrit Moon had taught her long ago. Twilight simply wasn't ready for certain things, and to unleash these objects on the world might well bring about catastrophe. Even so, who were the League to make such judgements? And could they even be trusted to be the guardians of such potentially devastating might? To be honest, she was actually a little surprised that they hadn't rolled out these big guns during the last war, because they would have been pretty much guaranteed to put Vos in its place.

"Here," Pim said, interrupting her train of thought. "These look pretty staff-like to me."

Kali moved to where Pim stood examining four racks of what appeared, at first glance, to be simple lengths of metal. But closer inspection revealed them to be inscribed with complex runics and tiny studs that had to be part of a magetech device. The metal tubes seemed to be of different ages and all had been preserved in varying states of wear and tear. This suggested to Kali that they had been collected from various locations, rather than a single source. Perhaps some of them – the more dented and bashed ones – even from some long ago won or lost battlefield. But if they had been used in battle, she wondered who the combatants might have been, because from the look of them they came from the third age of dwarven and elven development, when the two races should have been at peace. She sighed at the fact that it was just one more puzzle to ponder over.

What mattered now was that they worked and, to that end, Kali hefted one of the tubes from a rack and was surprised to find herself thrown off balance because the object was so light. It was strange because the staff *felt* heavy – cold, hard, unyielding – and yet it was perfectly balanced and weighed so little that she could spin it in the palm of her hand. One possible reason for that, she discovered, was that it was hollow. Thinking that Sonpear had sold them a dud, she first shook it and then peered down its length, moving it around until she had Pim framed in a small circle. It took the thieves guild leader a second to spot what she was doing but, when he did, he waved and frowned.

"Do you mind?" he said, stepping out of the way. "That thing could go off."

"Don't see how. Unless there's a rack of blowdarts around here somewhere."

"Even so…"

"But," Kali mused to herself, "I suppose it has to be called a crackstaff for a reason."

It was, as Kali discovered that very second.

What *exactly* she had touched on the length of metal she had no idea but, whatever it was, it appeared to have been the 'on' switch. Kali suddenly found herself blown backwards as a bolt of blue energy fired from the crackstaff with a recoil like a kick from a giant mool. Winded and dazed, Kali slid to the floor and watched the powerful bolt of energy that had been discharged still fizzling away around the edges of a jagged hole in the far wall. Instead of a pained expression crossing her face Kali began, slowly, to grin.

"Wuhh-ow."

"Hells," Jengo Pim said softly, echoing the sentiment. "How the hells did it – ?"

Kali flipped herself up onto her feet.

"No idea," she said, moving over to the racks and sweeping up as many of the crackstaffs as she could carry, before thrusting them at Pim. "Maybe these tubes channel magical threads or maybe they somehow *concentrate* them but one thing's for sure – they work. Pim, we've got something with which we can even up the fight a little bit."

"I'm not so sure we have – *yet*." Pim said slowly.

"What are you talking about? Pim, we don't have much time so grab some more if you can!"

"Miss Hooper, I think we have company."

"What?" Kali said.

For the first time she noticed the thieves guild leader was staring past her, back towards the stairway they had used to get here, and followed his gaze. Several things were climbing – no, *sweeping* – up the stairs towards them. Spectral, ghostly shapes that Kali couldn't quite pin down enough to identify but knew immediately she didn't like.

"Oh, fark. I guess there is no such thing as a free lunch."

"I warned you this might prove hazardous," Poul Sonpear's voice commented. "I am afraid your careless use of the crackstaff has disturbed them."

"Them? Them, who? All right, Sonpear, so these are your hazards but what in all the hells *are* those things?"

"We call them residuals. They have become attracted to your vital energy."

"I'm flattered." The figures had reached the top of the stairs now and she could see them in a little more detail. "Wait a minute. Are they what I think they are?"

"They *were* what you think they are."

"How can that be?"

"It is believed that when Domdruggle created his Expanse there were sacrifices that had to be made. An area effect at the point of conjuration that ended the lives of Domdruggle and those who assisted with the ritual, condemning them to a half-life here in the Expanse. They volunteered for it, Miss Hooper, elves *and* dwarves, but now I doubt that they even remember who or what they were. They know only what it *felt* like to be and hunger for that feeling, still."

"Hunger. Okay, I'm not sure I like the sound of that. So, they're attracted to us *why* exactly?"

"To extract the life force from your bodies. Make your souls part of the Expanse."

"Gotcha. Sonpear, why didn't you tell me about these things before?"

"There was a chance you would not encounter them, and so I did not wish to worry you."

"Next time, Sonpear, give me *all* the facts." Kali grabbed another crackstaff from the rack, then shoved the thieves guild leader. "Out of the way, Pim."

Bracing herself this time, she aimed and pressed the same stud she thought she had previously used, gratified to find she'd made the right choice.

A crackling lance of blue energy shot impacted in the centre of the approaching residuals. But instead of blowing them apart, as she had hoped, the lance passed through them harmlessly, doing no more damage than a hand might wafting at some fog. It did something, though, because the spectral figures suddenly quickened their approach, coming right at her with a renewed determination.

"Shit."

Suddenly they were close enough for Kali to see them in full detail. She could make out wasted bodies and haunted faces with gaping mouths and what she thought might be weapons. With flowing beards or streak-like, angular heads, they looked as if someone had drawn them on the landscape and then had a hasty rethink, half rubbing them out with repeated swipes of an eraser.

Kali staggered backwards as one of them screeched like a banshee and slammed into her. Then, with a cry of alarm, she scissored back to avoid the wisps of a blade whooshing by where her stomach had been. The passing blade left behind tracers, like tiny furls of mist.

Somewhat aggrieved by the development, Kali threw a punch in retaliation but, as had the energy lance, her fist went straight through. Next to her, Pim suffered the same experience.

Now *that* was a little unfair. They could touch them but not the other way round? In the circumstances there was only one thing they could do. Dodging another rush, Kali pulled off her belt and made a makeshift strap for her back before grabbing an armful of crackstaffs and snapping her gaze at Pim, instructing him to do the same.

"Run," she then said to the thieves guild leader.

"Where? There are more of them on the stairs!"

Kali thought fast. "The hole I made. Out through there."

"This is the third level!"

"You got a problem with that?"

"Yes!"

"Pim, trust me – just do as I do."

Pim swallowed. "Go."

The residuals hot on their trail, the pair of them raced for the breach in the Three Towers wall and hurled themselves through. It was the first time that Kali had been grateful for what she considered the somewhat disturbing design of the Three Towers. Because, as she expected, the two plummeted out not into empty air but onto the tapering, semi-organic slope that, at their base, was a more gentle incline than further above. *More* gentle but they weren't out of the frying pan yet. The pair landed on the taper on their behinds, bouncing slightly and scrabbling for purchase to slow their descent before riding it down towards ground level, then tumbling into a heap at its base. Behind and above them, the residuals – probably about fifteen of them now – poured through the breach. Untroubled by such considerations as gravity, they began to sweep down towards them.

Kali quickly picked herself up. "Move!"

"I hate to repeat myself, but where exactly?"

"Away from here!" Kali shouted, already on the move. She tilted her head to the sky. "Sonpear!"

"You are doing the right thing, Miss Hooper. Avoid physical contact of any kind."

"I *know* that, dammit! Can you just get us the hells out of here?"

"I am endeavouring to prepare a return portal. Continue in your current direction and please be patient."

"Patient!" Kali repeated breathlessly as she glanced behind her.

The residuals had formed themselves into one amorphous mass that was pursuing them with even greater speed. What was worse, they seemed no longer content simply to chase. From within the mass they were hurling or firing the weapons they wielded and, disturbingly, they shot ahead of the mass in whip-like tendrils before snapping back to their owners to be launched at them again and again, narrowly missing each time.

"What the hells are those things?" Pim shouted. "Remember I'm only getting half this conversation."

"Er, can we go into that some other time?" Kali requested in a slightly higher pitch than normal.

She ducked as a hail of elven arrows pierced the air where her head had been a moment before, petering out into wisps ahead of her before, again, snapping back. Pim's question had raised one of her own. Namely why it was that Domdruggle's assistants – *if* she was right about the time he had conjured the Expanse – possessed such archaic weaponry. She could only put it down to some kind of race memory manifestation of their forms. It didn't really matter, though, did it? What *did* matter was that they were deadly and were not going to miss for much longer.

Kali muttered something as she continued to run, still seeing no escape route ahead of her.

"What?" Pim asked, breathlessly.

"Oh, just reflecting on something Sonpear said."

"What?"

"Just that this is a farking big pin."

"The portal is forming now, Miss Hooper," Sonpear advised. "Please try to stay alive a few moments longer."

"Oh, right," Kali responded. She could now see something materialising a couple of hundred yards ahead of her – like a small storm cloud. "Actually, I was going to stop, turn and blow them a kiss."

"There is no need for sarcasm."

"Well, for pits' sake!" Despite her words, Kali *did* turn, if only to glance over her shoulder to gauge the gain the residuals had made, and promptly wished that she hadn't. Because something *else* was materialising behind them, looming over them – something spectral and massive that, in the brief moment she saw it, she could have sworn was a giant face.

"Pim, I don't want to worry you but –"

"Now what?" the thieves guild leader said.

He, too, snatched a glance over his shoulder and promptly turned white. For what Kali had seen was indeed a giant face; gaunt, sunken and haunted. It regarded them hungrily with huge shadowed eye sockets and an oval of a mouth that was slowly widening into an all-encompassing maw.

It swooped down towards them, clearly intent on sweeping them into that maw. And it roared deafeningly as it came.

"What the hells!" Pim shouted.

"Domdruggle, I think."

"Ah. Run faster?"

"Run faster."

The pair of them put on a final, desperate burst of speed and closed the gap between themselves and the now partly formed portal. Kali thought that she could see the interior of the Underlook through it and, despite its current circumstances, nothing had ever seemed so welcoming. The only question now was, would they make it? Because behind them Domdruggle had accelerated beyond the amorphous mass of his assistants and the maw that had been his mouth seemed, like some dislocated jaw, to be stretching unnaturally forward, ready to scoop the pair of them inside. Kali could no longer hear Pim's shouts of alarm as the Expanse seemed now to consist only of a looming darkness and a deafening roar. For a second her own scream of protest at her faltering body was completely lost as the maw drew alongside, and then around, her running form.

Her last thoughts as the Expanse faded were: *Jump now, Pim, now! Sonpear, this had better farking work*.

Suddenly, she could hear herself screaming, and then she was crashing into something hard. The realisation that she was back in the Underlook was interrupted as she felt something collide with her equally hard. She and Pim found themselves in a tangle on the floor, being stared at by a number of the Grey Brigade and Gargassians whose mouths were agape. She was vaguely aware that, across the room, Sonpear was gesticulating madly, managing to just close the portal as a grey and fog-like snout burst through with the haunting echo of the roar that had been deafening her only moments before. Then, it was gone.

Kali coughed. "Okay, that was interesting."

"You have a knack for understatement," Pim said, dusting himself down. The thieves guild leader wasted no time in getting back to the business of their own reality, frowning as he listened to the k'nid battering still at the outside of the hotel.

"How's the situation?" he asked one of his lieutenants.

"The walls won't last very much longer. Reckon maybe ten minutes or so before they're breached."

Pim sighed. "Then it's time we took the fight to them." He dumped the bundle of crackstaffs on a table. "These are weapons. Anyone who feels they're up to it, take one. We'll show you how they work in a moment." Pim's men hesitated. "Well? What are you waiting for?"

"There's another problem," Sonpear announced, stepping forward. "The fireballs, the k'nid, they did something to your friend. He went crazy when the turret room exploded, *changed*. And he went outside, as if looking for revenge. The old man's out there in the middle of the bastards. He's missing."

CHAPTER EIGHT

KALI HAD NO idea how long she and Pim had been in the Expanse, but it had been long enough for Andon to turn into a full-fledged warzone.

The city was all but obscured by smoke and dust, filled with the sound of explosions and agonised screams. Her plan to take the fight to the k'nid began as soon as she, Pim and the other volunteers flung open the doors of the Underlook and began blasting their way out of the alleyway. Bolts of blue crackled into the narrow space, filling it with so much magical energy that it was at first difficult to tell whether the crackstaffs were effective against the k'nid. But the gratifying crunch of their blasted and twitching chitinous bodies beneath their feet, as they continued to advance towards the Andon Heart, soon told them what they wished to know. Their fight had just got a little more even.

Kali and the others burst into the marketplace and fanned out, beams lancing out to take down the k'nid who had made it their business to consume the market stalls. Their targeting was not random, each shot chosen quickly but carefully, and Kali found herself impressed by the marksmanship of Pim and his men. K'nid after k'nid were blasted, screeching, scuttling and dismembered. She supposed the dexterity of hands trained to slip a wallet from a pocket, without a hint it had ever been there, had other uses, too.

She wished only that the same were true of the Three Towers. The spires continued to blast away above them and this close to the structure, in its very shadow in fact, she could feel the raw power. A power that made her limbs feel weak and her brain tight. Such power did not, however, stop those k'nid who had chosen the towers as their target from flinging themselves at its sides. As she watched they joined an earlier assault wave, working away at the tallow-like walls to find a way to the mages inside. Kali debated giving the mages a helping hand by blasting the k'nid away, but only for a second. As far as she was concerned the League could stand or fall by its own devices, as they had so callously left the people outside to stand or fall by theirs.

The marketplace cleared, Kali and the others moved on into the streets where they split up to cover the warren of small streets and alleyways individually.

As she worked her way along one such street, Kali could hear the discharge of crackstaffs echoing all around her, and she smiled slightly at the damage that was obviously being meted out. Firing as she moved, her attention was nevertheless split between the next target and the location of Merrit Moon. She thought she caught sight of the old man – in his ogur form – once, but only as a possible presence amidst a small hill of swarming k'nid who were being batted and tossed aside. The chaos of the streets, however, prevented her from reaching him before he had moved on, leaving a path of destruction in his wake. Soon after, their paths almost crossed once more – but this time the old man's presence was announced only by a prolonged and savage roar of fury that was carried to her from beyond the rooftops, a street or maybe three away. By this time, however, Kali was beginning to realise that she had other, more relevant concerns.

The fact was, the sound of discharging crackstaffs that had been so prevalent not so long before was lessening somewhat. What was worse, she was beginning to hear cries of alarm and screams that she somehow knew came from Pim's people.

It did not take her long to work out why. The alarm bells from the city walls were ringing again and, glimpsed in streets all around her, Kali saw more k'nid were entering the fray, flocking to their unnatural brethren and bringing reinforcements into the battle that seemed inexhaustible. She and Pim and his people had made a difference in the defence of the city, but the fact was there were just too many of the creatures and more were coming all the time.

"We have to pull back!" Kali shouted to one of Pim's men as he stumbled out an alleyway nearby, his crackstaff firing into the shadows.

The thief looked at her, his face desperate, and Kali staggered back as she realised half of it was a bloody mess, all but gone.

"They just keep coming," he gasped. "There's no stoppi –"

As he spoke, two k'nid sprang from the alley and enveloped him. In the time it took his face to crumple in horror he was no more than a pile of steaming bones on the ground. Kali could do nothing but fire off a couple of bolts in retaliation and then, as more k'nid poured from alleyways and began to pursue her, she turned and ran. All she could do was try to carry the message to Pim and the others herself now.

Spinning occasionally to fire her crackstaff at the pursuing k'nid, Kali raced along the street, weaving from side to side as the fireballs from the Three Towers continued to pummel down, obliterating buildings all around her and forcing her to duck or roll as great chunks and shards of stone exploded across her path.

Damn the League, she thought.

They actually seemed – probably in increasing desperation – to be intensifying their bombardment and if their self preservation protocol continued like this, they'd be responsible for as many Andonian deaths as the k'nid themselves.

And she'd be one of them if she didn't get into some kind of cover soon.

Kali dodged into a side alley but there found herself tripping over her own feet, her route blocked by a man busied with another pack of k'nid streaming in from its other end. He was holding his ground well but, whoever he was, he wasn't one of Pim's men and he wasn't using a crackstaff to defend himself. In fact, he wasn't using any kind of weapon at all, except himself.

Bursts of fire, ice and magical energy roared and cracked from his fingertips, wielded against his attackers to devastating effect. She'd seen shadowmages at work before – mainly using their magics against *her* – but never one who handled the threads with such absolute confidence, dexterity and power. Tall and becloaked – with a handsome, if weather beaten, face visible beneath the hood – he wove complex patterns with his hands that seemed less the result of years of dedicated training than a natural, instinctive affinity with the craft.

"Nice handiwork," Kali said, running to his position. K'nid followed her in, thrashing at her heels. Too many of them.

"You, too," the man said. "Saw you earlier – some of the moves you pulled off. *Look out!*"

Kali spun, firing burst after burst at the k'nid, and found herself pressed back to back with the stranger. She could feel him lurch with each magical bolt that he unleashed and they balanced each other as she expended the power of her crackstaff.

"Yes, well, I seem to have a peculiar knack for what I do," she shouted over her shoulder.

"Me, too."

"The name's Kali Hooper."

"Lucius Kane."

"Pleased to meet you, Lucius. But unless we break this up and get the hells out of this pitsing bottleneck, we're stuffed."

"Not quite the language I'd use to describe our present predicament, but wholeheartedly agreed. Ideas, Miss Hooper?"

Kali glanced upward, at the walls tightly confining the alleyway. High and sheer, they seemed to be the only buildings in Andon that hadn't been buttressed with balconies, makeshift extensions or dropbogs of some kind. As such they would be near impossible to scale. She knew she could make it up with a few well-timed moves but the question was what good would that do her new comrade-in-arms?

"The only way out seems to be up. But..."

"Up it is, then. Shall we?"

"Shall we wha – ?"

Before Kali could finish, she felt Kane's back detach from her own, and then caught a glimpse of a flitting and dwindling shadow above. There might have been nothing for the man to cling on to but he apparently didn't *need* anything, rapidly flinging himself up some invisible ladder in the wall that only he could see. As far as Kali knew, there was no 'invisible ladder' spell in the grimoire or whatever it was these people used. So what the hells was he doing – using the *threads* themselves as rungs? Gods, yes, it seemed that was exactly what he was doing, using the threads as *physical* things, manipulating the world itself to his own ends. She had never seen any – *any* – shadowmage do that before.

He was looking back down at her and *grinning*.

Bastard!

Despite their predicament, he was clearly throwing down a challenge and, with a roar of determination, she kicked off after him, booting two k'nid out of the way. She used the subsequent scramble of the pack's bodies as a launching pad to throw herself up against one wall and then another, each time higher and higher, repeating the process until she had caught up with Kane.

Kali flipped herself over the edge of the roof.

"Not very gentlemanly," she gasped, "leaving a helpless girl alone like that."

"You're no helpless girl, and you know it."

"That's as maybe but –" Kali stopped suddenly, and it was her turn to shout a warning. "Kane!"

Somehow, one of the k'nid had managed to follow them to the roof, and was leaping for the shadowmage as she shouted. Spotting it, Kane's arm shot out and, for a moment, Kali thought he was about to unleash another elemental bolt, but that wasn't what he was doing at all. Instead, he punched the k'nid solidly as it came, but instead of knocking it back, his fist disappeared *inside* its chitinous shell so that the creature was caught, dangling, thrashing and impaled, on the end of his arm. Impossible enough that the man had somehow penetrated its natural armour, Kali thought, but what he did next actually made her stagger back. His mouth twisting into a grimace, his eyes widening and staring at the creature directly, Kane seemed somehow to suck the very life from it. The k'nid crumpled and decomposed in seconds, leaving behind a brittle and lifeless husk.

The shadowmage shrugged the remains off and crushed them beneath his boot. Clearly, what he had just done had been *nothing* to him.

Kali stared.

"Who *are* you?"

Silhouetted by the fiery oranges of the ongoing bombardment from the Three Towers, Kane stared back. And when the shadowmage spoke, somehow Kali knew his words were as much about her as they were about himself. What was more, she saw reflected in his eyes the same inner torment that she had felt ever since the day she had begun to realise that she was... different.

"That," he said, "remains to be seen."

With those words, Kane turned and manoeuvred himself over the other side of the roof. Their brief liaison had been, it appeared, just that.

"Wait!" Kali said. "What plans do you have now?"

Kane inclined his head towards the Three Towers. "I have business at the League of Prestidigitation and Prestige. Suggestions that might help the current crisis. And you?"

"Like you. Try to stop these bastards. But first I have to find the old man."

"Old man?"

"A friend. He went missing during the assault."

"And what is this friend's name?"

"Merrit Moon. Bad haircut, beard, pink horse blanket. Or, actually, he could still be big, green and roaring. It's, um, a long story. Have you seen him?"

"No. But I might be able to help you find him."

"Be glad of any help."

"Call it a professional courtesy."

"You're on. How about I take the west gate and you the – ?"

"Not *physically*. Have you anything that belongs to the old man?"

"No, I –" Kali began, then thought again. "Wait." She dug in her equipment belt, pulling something out from its very bottom and shoving it in Kane's hand. The shadowmage regarded the mouldy, half-eaten pie with an unfathomable expression.

"He baked it for me," Kali said. "About four years ago."

Kane smiled slightly and, without elaborating, moved his arm out above the rooftops in a gesture that looked half salute and half as if he were sowing seeds, and Kali swore that some kind of fine, shimmering dust took to the air. Kane waited for a few seconds while this dust settled and then pointed in the direction of the city walls, where a faint glow could now be seen rising from street level like a beacon. "There. Your friend is there."

"How in the hells did you –"

But Kane was gone.

"There one minute, gone the next," Kali shrugged, and smiled. "Lot like myself, really."

Wasting no time, Kali took a few steps back from the roof edge and then ran, leaping the gap between the building and its neighbour, reckoning that the safest and quickest way to reach Moon's beacon was by rooftop, avoiding the battleground below. Thankfully, her progress towards the city walls was taking her away from the epicentre of the k'nid invasion, the creatures – with the help of the towers' fireballs – having already devastated this part of Andon and moved on. Thus it was that when she finally dropped back down to street level, she found herself in an area of relative calm in the shadow of the city wall itself. There a few scattered guards and civilian survivors had set up a makeshift field hospital that, so far, had gone unnoticed by the k'nid. Still, they were close and while those who tended tried to help those they could, or comfort the maimed and dying where they couldn't, they were forced to stifle their moans or sobs with their hands as they worked.

The old man wasn't among them, but he was nearby. Kali found him in the doorway of the bunker where she had left Horse, talking to the beast. But her relief at the discovery that the two of them were still alive was lessened somewhat by the appearance of the old man.

Kali bit her lip as she approached, taking in the fact that he was all but slumped in position. The shallow breathing and raised and pulsing veins on his arms, coupled with his bloodshot eyes, were testimony to the fact that he had only recently recovered from a full Thrutt transformation.

But, by the look of things, Thrutt had sated himself before he had burned out. The bloodied and cracked remains of various k'nid covered the old man's clothes, along with a considerable amount of blood from the old man himself.

"We are losing this battle, young lady," Moon breathed, wearily.

"I know, old man." She only hoped that those she had despatched back to the Underlook were not facing their last stand. "I know."

"It is good to see, however, that you have not become one of its victims."

Kali smiled. "Not for the want of their trying. The k'nid *and* the pitsing League."

Moon sighed. "I don't think the latter will be a problem any longer. Observe, young lady."

Kali turned and, as she did, noticed two things – that all of those who were able in the makeshift hospital were turning to look the same way, and that the incessant thrumming and pounding of the fireballs from the League had ceased. And with good reason.

As the people around her stared, muttering curses, words of disbelief or even prayers to their gods, she saw that the Three Towers had given up on its offensive. Its soaring and majestic towers were doing something she had never seen them do before, or even *knew* they could do. They were *twining* around each other, apparently for protection, looking for all the world like the tails of whipped curs.

And, even from this distance, Kali could see swarms of k'nid skittering up their heights, scrabbling for a way in.

"If the Three Towers has fallen, Andon has fallen," Merrit Moon said, matter-of-factly. He eased himself up with a groan, to stand by his protégé. "It's up to us, now, young lady. We must reach the Drakengrats and stop these things at their source, find a means to destroy them. And we must *hurry*."

"You think more of the k'nid are coming?"

"Oh, that I don't doubt – but more coming is not the only problem. I saw it when I fought them, when *Thrutt* fought them. When the k'nid have consumed a certain amount, they *duplicate* themselves. Their numbers are doubling at a regular rate, Kali, and eventually there will be so many that their presence will be absolute."

"I saw it happening. When they first stormed the walls."

"That isn't all. They consume *everything* and their presence must already be changing the land, making it unsuitable for crops, for livestock, for *any* kind of habitation. Why they're doing this I don't know, but soon they will cover the peninsula like a living shroud and the damage will be irreversible."

"Gods, Merrit... how long?"

"A week."

"*Five days?*"

"Five days. No more."

Kali's face set with determination. "Then I'd better get a move on."

"*I?*"

"Old man, you're in no state to –"

"Pardon me, Miss," one of the guards interjected. He looked exhausted. "A moment ago, your grandfather mentioned travel to the Drakengrats?"

Despite the circumstances, Merrit Moon coughed and said something under his breath. Kali patted him.

"He did." Kali said, warily.

"Then I'm sorry, but our scouts report the Vos military have closed the border at the Anclas Territories. Apparently, their population centres have taken considerable damage and their people are crowding the old war shelters, and they refuse to compound their crisis by allowing anyone from Pontaine through. All refugees are being detained at the border."

"They're leaving us to our own fate," Moon said. "Sealing us in with the k'nid."

"The bastards. It isn't even *their* land." Kali said.

She considered their options. The fact was, she could probably make it through Vos's defensive lines but it would be a tricky business. One wrong move and, in the current state of trigger-happiness Vossian retribution might encompass execution of the refugees. She couldn't and wouldn't risk that. But, still, she had to reach the Drakengrats. There had to be a way.

She suddenly realised that there was. And that it might even expedite matters.

"Would you excuse us, please?" she said to the guard, and then turned to Moon. "Old man, I need you to take Horse and get to the Flagons, take a message to Aldrededor for me."

"I'm *coming* with you."

"*No*, you're not. You and Horse are both out of this fight but can still help by doing what I ask. I reckon Horse has one more jump in him so use it to get to the Flagons. It, er, might be a little noisy but, trust me, you'll be safe there."

Moon looked puzzled, and his eyes narrowed. "What are you planning, young lady?"

Kali told him.

"What? O-ho, no, young lady, no." The old man stared at her. "Impossible! It would take specialist equipment, mapping, planning, *weeks* of preparation. Your own research has shown what a potentially deadly maze they might be, unstable and likely collapsed at multiple points, to say nothing of the fact that you have no idea *what's down there*." He shook his head, adamant. "No, young lady, be realistic. You'll never make it through."

"Since when have I been realistic, old man?" She stared at him and smiled. "Besides, as far as specialist equipment goes, I think I have just the thing."

CHAPTER NINE

THE LOST CANALS of Turnitia.

Kali had been planning to explore them for as long as she could remember. They were, however, a massive undertaking. Some references she had unearthed about them suggested that they went on for hundreds of leagues and, until now, somewhere between the planning and the exploration of them, something had always managed to get in the way. Last year, there had been the matter of the Red Queen, for instance, and only a few months before she'd been considering their allure when she had been distracted by the small affair of the Clockwork King. Her current circumstances were perhaps not the ideal ones in which to finally fulfil her ambition, but Kali was quietly relieved that fate had pushed her in this direction and she had to admit that she was more than a little excited by the prospect ahead of her.

The journey from Andon had taken her a day and a half, moving slowly and cautiously through the stonewood forests of southern Pontaine, on a horse hired from the city wall stables, which she had dismounted and slapped back home when she had neared the Anclas Territories. She had used the cover of the forests not only to avoid the k'nid, but also to avoid the gaze of the surveillance scopes with which the Vossian army had equipped their forts.

Dividing the peninsula – and thus Vos and Pontaine – like a great thick belt, the Anclas Territories stretched from Freiport in the north to Turnitia in the south, and had once been neutral farmland. After the Great War between Vos and Pontaine, however, the former had wasted no time in establishing a number of forts on the land whose official reason for existence – the protection of the Vos Empire – had always struck Kali as somewhat ironic considering that it was they who had invaded Pontaine in the first place. Whatever the politics of it, Pontaine, battered by the war, had been in no position to dispute the placements. While they remained little more than observation posts, the number of additional forts, garrisons and service structures that had grown alongside and between them over the intervening years, had transformed Vos's presence in the area from a broken series of scattered bases to a virtual wall, over which they held complete autonomy and control. They hadn't exercised its strategic power until now, allowing relatively free trade and passage between the neighbouring states, like Pontaine, having no wish to precipitate another conflict, but in doing so it had become abundantly clear how insidious its growth had been to the area. Simply put, when they had closed the borders they had had the capability to do it literally. There was no way through.

Lucky, then, that Kali hadn't wanted to go through. All she'd had to do was make sure they didn't see what it was that was going *under* it. And the two bound and gagged and struggling guards at her feet were testimony to the fact that she had succeeded.

Kali stood, now, on one of the more remote guard towers towards the southern end of the Territories, staring through the surveillance scope with which the guards had unwillingly provided her. The looks on their faces as she had suddenly appeared before them, forty feet up in the air, had been priceless. While they weren't to know that she had, in fact, been dangling from a strip of shadow wire at the time, their surprise had lasted long enough for her to be able to slam their heads together, disabling them before they could sound the alarm. The action had been necessary because, out of all the towers in the Anclas line, it was this one that overlooked her destination. Or, to be more accurate, the *entrance* to her destination; one of the huge roundels to which she had given the name *dropshaft*.

That was the thing about the Lost Canals of Turnitia – they were not lost in the sense that no one had been able to find them. They were only lost in the sense that they had been long abandoned. *Long, long* abandoned by Kali's reckoning. Because, as far as she could make out, the inscriptions on the dropshafts were neither elven nor dwarven and seemed to her old enough to predate both. What exactly the implications of that were, she had no more clue than she had to what purpose the dropshafts served. In all the time she had been planning an expedition to the canals, she had located three of the dropshafts, one south east of Scholten, one west, near Malmkrug, and the third here, near the coastal city of Turnitia. That Turnitia had been honoured with giving its name to the canals was not, though, in reference to this particular dropshaft but rather that – unique among the canal network – this part of the coast had once had an entrance to the canals leading in from the *sea*.

Kali trained the surveillance scope to the north-east, and it was from that direction, from the Flagons, that she expected her companion to come. Anytime now.

Sure enough, as she watched a small, though bulky and unnatural, shape appeared on the horizon and began moving towards her, weaving erratically in a way that suggested its driver was not quite used to the controls. As she had instructed in her note, the headlights of the machine had been dimmed upon approaching the Anclas Territories.

It was time to go, to make her rendezvous. But first she had to make sure that two sets of eyes did not lay sight on something they shouldn't. It was Merrit Moon's old edict, told to her long ago in the Warty Witch. Certain discoveries from the world's past had to be kept to themselves, for *everyone*'s peace of mind. So, to ensure the guards neither saw nor heard the approaching dwarven artefact, Kali smiled sweetly and apologized. Then she bent down and punched both guards hard on the nose, knocking them cold before leaping onto the shadow wire and lowering herself to the ground.

Now came the hard part.

Kali had left the actual opening of the dropshaft until the last minute because she had not wanted any Vossian patrol stumbling across it in the dark, ruining not only her privilege of being the first person to access the network in an unimaginable time, but also any chance of a successful stealth operation into the bargain. She reckoned she had perhaps fifteen minutes before the Mole reached her and in that time, she would put into practice what she had been researching ever since she had first learned of the canals' existence.

One of the more unusual aspects of the dropshafts was that they were sealed with a metal door containing one of the most complex locking mechanisms Kali had ever seen. It was designed, if an attempt to open it was made incorrectly, to jam the chambers in place permanently, preventing anyone ever accessing it again. One thing was certain – whoever had built these things had gone to extreme measures to ensure no unauthorised person could access them, accidentally or otherwise.

Just what the hells were they going to such lengths to conceal?

Reaching the dropshaft, Kali worked slowly and carefully, following the diagram in her head that she had worked out over long nights at her table by the Captain's Chest. First, she disengaged the perimeter safeguards, then locked down the punchbolts in a predetermined order and, finally, released the chambers one by one, until the entire centre of the dropshaft door rotated counter-clockwise. She moved to the right of the metal plate, repeating the procedure – though, when it came to the punchbolts, in a different order – until, again, the centre of the door rotated, this time clockwise.

Kali sighed with relief. There was only one thing left to do.

Directly in the centre of the door, a circle of ten metal projections rose from the otherwise flat surface. These, she knew, had to be depressed in exactly the right order, otherwise the entire process would cancel itself out. There was only one problem – according to the ancient records she had found, the order was different for each of the dropshafts, and there was absolutely no indication of which order applied to which dropshaft. She had a one in three chance of success, so it was lucky, then, that she liked a gamble.

Tongue sticking out of her mouth, she crouched on her haunches and tried to put herself in the mind of whoever had last – if ever – operated the projections. Then, swallowing, she plumped for the third from the left, depressing it with a strenuous groan, until it was almost flush with the surface of the plate. There, with a metallic boom, it locked into place. Bingo – but that was the easy one, because two of the sequences started with that projection. The sixth from the left, then, or the eighth, the antepenultimate one? The eighth. She was sure it was going to be the eighth, and after that it would be plain sailing.

Be sure. Be very sure.

Kali depressed the eighth projection. There was another metallic boom. She cast a quick glance around all the perimeter chambers and they all seemed to be remaining in place. *Yes!* she thought.

Boom. Boom, boom, boom.

The locks were cancelling.

Shi –

All kinds of things went through Kali's mind, not least how stupid she had been. With her one-in-three chance of success, she had been presuming that the three sequences related to the three dropshafts she knew of, but if the sequence she was using was *wrong* that meant there was another one out there somewhere. This made the network potentially even bigger than she thought! The thrill she felt at the prospect was, however, rather comprehensively subsumed in the fierce rush of adrenaline produced by the realisation that she had only seconds to stop her work being in vain.

With a grunt of exertion she flung herself across the dropshaft plate, whipping a small metal bar from her equipment belt and jamming it between the chamber bolts before they could slam shut. The collision of metal on metal vibrated the whole plate and almost took Kali's hand off, but at least it had prevented the reverse sequence going any further. But it was not the only one. Kali back-flipped, grabbing another metal cylinder from her belt and jammed it into the second chamber feed before sighing in relief. That should have been that but Kali's interfering with the delicate balance of the locks and chambers had clearly knocked the whole mechanism out of kilter. She looked around in disbelief as chambers and punchbolts began to engage and disengage themselves in no particular order and with ever increasing speed.

Dammit. There had *to be an order to it somewhere.*

As she leapt around blocking or freeing those bolts that *looked* as if they should go this way or that, Kali tried to visualise the underworkings of the dropshaft plate. Rapid calculation after rapid calculation followed, Kali flinging herself here and there like something possessed, and she was beginning to think that she'd be doing this until she dropped dead of exhaustion when there was a sudden heavy clank from beneath her.

The plate had just released itself.

It began to rise.

There was only one problem. If Kali were to keep it open she had to remain in the position she was in, a kind of crooked spreadeagle with the sole of her left foot jamming one punchbolt, the calf of her right leg another, one hand pushing upward to block yet another, and a painfully positioned elbow blocking the last. She looked as if she were posing for some strange art class.

The plate had risen fully now, and Kali with it, and while she could not see what was beneath it, she *could* smell it. A dank, briny mouldiness that was redolent of the rot of ages. It made her want to gag. She didn't, though, because her mind was taken off the desire by a prolonged and bass rumble that originated somewhere from within wherever the opened plate led.

Or at least she thought that was where it came from. It was difficult to tell because he Mole was nearing her now, the sound of its engines drowning out everything around it. And all Kali could do was wait until it fully arrived. She was glad that she had incapacitated the guards in the watchtower because this, frankly, was embarrassing.

The Mole manoeuvred into position beside her and, after a second, there was the hiss of its opening hatch. A tall, wiry, moustachioed and ear-ringed figure eased itself out of the hatch, took in Kali's predicament with an amused glance, and then stroked his moustache.

"I see you are enjoying yourself," Aldrededor observed.

"Not... quite... the... words... I'd... have... chosen," Kali gasped as she strained to keep the punchbolts in place. "Do you think, maybe, you could give me a hand here?"

Aldrededor applauded softly.

"*Aldrededor!*"

The ex-pirate smiled again, sighed, and began to look around for suitable pieces of rock or detritus with which he could jam the spaces Kali's appendages currently occupied.

"Is it any wonder," he commented as he worked, "that we at the Flagons worry about you all the time? Why is it that you get yourself into these ridiculous situations?"

"I have a knack for it."

"Clearly. Tell me – just what would you have done had we not come along?"

"*I don't know,*" Kali said through clenched teeth. It took a second for what Aldrededor had said to penetrate. "Hang on. What do you mean, 'we'?"

"There," Aldrededor said, fitting the last block into place. "I believe you can climb down now."

"Thanks. *Ahhh. Ooohh.* Aldrededor, what do you mean, 'we'?" she repeated before becoming distracted as what appeared to be a thick cloud of brown fog roiled from the Mole's cabin.

A second later, it happened again, and Kali moved to the door, coughing as she was engulfed in a cloud of cloying reekingness.

Oh no, she thought, and stepped back as something tall and thin *articulated* itself, in the manner of a brackan, from the inside of the cabin and stood, cheroot in mouth, arms folded.

"Dolorosa?"

"Of coursa Dolorosa! Who you expecta, thatta red-headed tart, the Annoying Lord?"

"Anointed," Kali corrected, absently. "Dolorosa, what in the hells are you doing here?"

"Our land is plagued by man-eating *theengs* and you think I woulda let my 'usband make thisa journey alone?"

Kali stared at the aforementioned and Aldrededor shrugged, picking at a tooth.

"Who's looking after my pitsing pub?"

"Do notta worry. Horse issa behind the bar."

"*Horse!?*"

"Hah! I havva her! Eet ees a leetle joke. No, thatta reprobate Deadnettle, he looka after the place. Notta that there are any customers. Nothing, and I mean *nothing*, comes near while the fat women dance."

"The Bellies are still dancing?"

"They havva leetle choice."

"True," Kali reflected. She paused for a second, looked at the two of them, and shook her head fondly. "Look, I appreciate you bringing the Mole, but I have to go now."

"Offa to save the world."

"Again," Kali sighed.

She patted them both on the shoulder and moved to the dwarven machine. She settled into the pilot's position but found her legs bent up against the control panel, as they had been when she had first found the Mole. Again, she tried to push the seat back but this time it would not go, blocked by some object. Kali leant around and found that Dolorosa was not the only unexpected extra to arrive with the dwarven machine. Something was jammed behind the seat. A small, wicker basket. Kali flipped the lid and stared inside. There were a number of bottles of flummox and two small mountains of slices of bread, layered in pairs, with filling between them. Kali prodded the uppermost layer of bread tentatively then pulled back with a grimace as a thick, brown substance slowly oozed from beneath it.

"What," Kali asked cautiously, "is this?"

Dolorosa looked surprised. "It issa beer anda butties for our trippa into the mountains."

The beer Kali didn't have a problem with, but it was these 'butty' things, and what was still oozing insidiously from inside them, that had disturbed her. She picked one of the creations up and it flopped under its own weight, plopping a lump of brown stuff onto her lap.

"Surprise stew butties?"

"Ovva course!" Dolorosa looked affronted. "Wassa the matter, eh? You havva gone offa my signatura *dish* while you havva been away?"

"No, no," Kali said quickly, having no wish to incur the old woman's wrath, especially by mentioning you couldn't *have* a signature dish if it was the only dish you ever made. The fact was, while she had nothing against surprise stew as such, she'd rather have eaten her own knees than the mess that was being presented to her now. That wasn't really the point though, was it? "Dolorosa. This isn't a picnic."

The woman stared at her, squinting her eyes, then turned to her husband and threw her hands in the air. "Pah! Now she thinks I amma some kind offa buffoon! A madda olda lady whose marbles havva rolled away, eh?"

Aldrededor curled his moustache and smiled, saying nothing, and Dolorosa span back to face Kali.

"Ovva course I know this issa no piccaneek! Eet ees going to be *very dangerous*. Alla the more reason to keepa uppa our strength, yes?"

Dolorosa seemed to entering full flow, so it was going to be useless to argue. "Well, yes, I suppose so, but –" Kali began and then faltered. Dolorosa had just said what she'd thought she'd said, hadn't she? *Our* strength. Yep, she'd definitely said *our*, as in 'we.'

"*Ohhoohhhooooo no*. If you think you're coming with me, you've got another think coming. This isn't a day trip into the country, old woman, it's the *Drakengrat Mountains* we're talking about."

"I thought itta wassa the Lost Canalsa of Turnitia first?"

"Those, too! And you can guarantee that they became *lost* for a reason. There's *always* a reason with these places. Deathtraps, monsters, insatiable, grasping *hairy* things that lurk in the dark…"

"I havva shared my bedaroom with Aldrededor for forty-five years, this issa *nurthing*."

Aldrededor blew her a kiss.

"What?" Kali said, looking at him. "Oh no, uugh, I don't want to know. The point is, it's what I do – and I do it *alone*. You could die down there."

"Anda we coulda die uppa here. Or havva you forgotten the k'nid?" She leaned in towards Kali and added: "Havva you forgotten that when you take thissa *machine*, we woulda havva to *walk* home to the Flagons? Howwa long do you thinka we'd survive outta there, hah?"

"What?"

Dammit!

In all the chaos of the past few days she *had* forgotten that. Her own trip here from Andon had been perilous to say the least, and she couldn't reasonably expect Dolorosa and Aldrededor to make a journey ten times that length. And neither could she leave them here, where Vossian patrols might find and detain them, or worse. Maybe they could camp just inside the entrance to the Lost Canals, she pondered briefly. But then remembered the deep roar she thought she had heard when she had first breached its gates. It might have been nothing – an acoustic trick of the waiting labyrinth – but then again...

Dammit!

"All right, all right! But the two of you do *everything* I say, understand? You keep quiet when I tell you and you keep your heads down when I tell you and –"

Aldrededor interrupted her. "Young lady. My wife and I have survived the Mirror Maelstrom of Meenos and the Seven Sirens of the Sarcrean Sea, we have stood fast in the path of ripper gales and laughed in the face of the Chadassa themselves –"

"Like a this – *hahahahaaaar!*" Dolorosa interjected.

"– we have sailed the acid surf, we have swum the shadowed waters, and we have rode the boiling waves of the north."

"Enough!" Kali said. She had to admit she sometimes forgot that these two had... *history* and, being reminded of it by them, she felt vaguely chastised. She couldn't help but worry nonetheless. Neither of them were any longer in their prime and, when it came down to it, they were family. She made no apologies for trying to keep them safe.

But what choice did she have?

"Aldrededor... Dolorosa?"

"Yes, Kali Hooper?"

"What say we get this show on the road?"

The pair released a satisfied sigh. "Yes, Kali Hooper."

Kali gunned the engines of the Mole as Dolorosa and Aldrededor clambered into the seats behind her, checking they were settled before she flicked the lever that closed the hatch. The loud and sibilant hiss as it sealed made what they were about to do seem all the more immediate. But Kali wasn't sure what was worse – the unknown region they were about to negotiate or the sudden overwhelming odour of garlic and piratical aftershave that pervaded the Mole's cabin. *This* was going to be a long journey.

Having become quite used to the dwarven machine's controls by now, Kali pushed forward the lever that set it into gear, and then another that turned it on its tracks until its nose pointed towards the open hatch. Then, without further hesitation, she urged the machine forward, swallowing slightly as its front dipped onto the slope that lay beneath the opening. Outside the small observation portholes, the ambient light turned from the azureness of above to a strange and somewhat eerie rippling green.

"So theesa canals, they are what?" Dolorosa queried. "Some kind ovva sewer?"

"Not a sewer," Kali said. "But, to be honest, I haven't a clue what they actually are. All I know is where they go. At least, *part* of where they go."

"Whicha beggas the question. If you avva thees 'Mole', why is it you didda not drill into them somewhere else, inna stead of using thees hatch? Somewhere less dangerous?"

That, Kali could answer, and did. The fact was, she had made one exploratory dig at the location of one of the canal's branches over a year before, but had hit a layer of *something* that had been as impenetrable as the dropshaft plates she had later discovered. Whatever the material was, it defied damage from all the tools in her possession and then some. She seriously doubted that even the dwarven drill bits would make much inroads without taking damage. No, the dropshafts were the only realistic way in – and now that she was actually *using* one of them she hoped that she might find some answers as to what the material was. Because if she knew that, it might give her more of a clue as to who it was had built the bloody canals in the first place. Speaking of which, the Mole was coming to the end of the access tunnel.

"Lady and gentleman," Kali said as she flicked on the Mole's headlights. "The Lost Canals of Turnitia."

Both Aldrededor and Dolorosa leaned forward to peer through the portholes, and gasped. Kali almost did the same. Only the fact that her brain was working overtime to process what she was seeing preventing her from doing so.

Because with the affair of the dwarven testing ground and then the entrance passage to this network, she was beginning to think that she'd had enough of tunnels to last her half a lifetime, but the fact was tunnels were not what she had got. Instead, ahead of the Mole, she found herself staring at an arched thoroughfare that was as large and as grandiose as the inside of a cathedral. What was even more awe inspiring was that this passage was only one of the canals. Beyond further dark arches, to their left and right, as far as they could see, were many more of them, routing away to gods knew where beneath the surface of the peninsula.

"By all of the gods," Aldrededor breathed. "I never thought I would see this place."

"You know it?"

"From tales told on the high seas."

"Itta reminds me ovva the crystal caverns beyond Sarcre," Dolorosa whispered. "You remember, Dreddy? Where a we founda Davyjonz Locket?"

"I remember, darling," Aldrededor said, his eyes twinkling. "Ah – it is good to smell the sea again."

The sea? Kali thought, and then realised that what Aldrededor said was true.

That briny odour she had smelled above was stronger here, detectable even through the filters that were bringing air into the cabin. The fact that they were a good number of leagues from the sea, then, could mean only one thing. The canals down here were *seawater* canals, pumped throughout the network by who-knew-what kind of mechanisms.

"It's nice to be somewhere where there's a little peace and quiet," Kali commented.

Aldrededor's eyebrows rose.

"Wait – you do not know?"

"Know what?"

"These canals. The tales on the high seas tell of something that lives down here." He stroked his moustache. "As my beloved wife might say, something *beeeg*."

CHAPTER TEN

IF THERE WAS something *beeg* living in the Lost Canals of Turnitia there was, after half a day's travel through them, no sign of it. But then there was more than enough canal left for it to hide in. Or, if you were a glass-half-empty type, more than enough for it to leap *out of. If* it leapt, Kali mused. After all, it might crawl. Or slither. Or hop. Whatever it might do, Kali tended towards the glass half-empty principal, and so had been guiding the Mole through the canals cautiously and in low gear, its headlights dipped and sweeping slowly across broad banks and shadowed arches.

Despite Merrit Moon's warnings of tunnel collapse, they had come across few obstacles so far, and those they had, had been little more than piles of rubble which the Mole's sonic cannons made short work of. Having already made the decision not to stop until they were through the canals, Kali could only experience what they had to offer by peering through the Mole's forward viewing slat, and this she did, squinting, to occasionally purse her lips, occasionally raise her eyebrows and also, occasionally, frown. It was the way the canals made her feel. It was strange but, regardless of how many ancient sites she had visited, this place felt different. Though she couldn't quite put her finger on why. It was as if she had taken a step *too* far into the past and, for some reason, she felt like an *intruder* here. The feeling was not, though, one that would prevent her from intruding *again* – it actually quite intrigued her – and this she was determined to do, when she had the time.

Speaking of time, she had estimated that at their current rate of progress it would take the Mole about two days to navigate the canals beneath the Anclas Territories. Not as quick as other methods that might have gotten her to the Drakengrats but the only one she had.

When her unwanted passengers had joined her she'd imagined the journey was going to be interminable but Aldrededor had, in fact, turned out to be amusing company, sharing more of his tales from the high seas. As pleasant company as he was, however, the same had not turned out to be the case with Dolorosa.

Crammed behind them in the cabin, not only was her habit of smoking cragweed cheroots sending the air scrubbers into overdrive, but it had not taken long for her to start complaining that she was suffering badly from the bone-ache. This was only one of what turned out to be a series of complaints. Interruptions that included frequent prods in the back accompanied by suggestions of which way to turn, whether to slow down or speed up and, on occasion, louder cries of "stupid-woman-watcha-out-forra-that-bump ahead." There had also been repeated questions along the lines of "Are we there yet?" Last but not least, she had emitted an ear-piercing shriek when she had discovered there was a dried dwarf's head beneath her seat. This then promptly, and unexpectedly, ended up on Kali's lap, causing screeches from both she and Aldrededor and reducing everyone to a nervous wreck. Admittedly, Kali had forgotten about the head, and she might have given Dolorosa that one were it not for what happened next.

Dolorosa leaned forward and whispered something in Aldrededor's ear, but it was just loud enough for her to hear.

"You want *what*?"

"She wishes to answer the call of nature," Aldrededor whispered diplomatically. "To powder her wart. To enhance the realm of the gods of the sea..."

"I *know* what she means, Aldrededor! But hells, woman – can't it wait?"

"Eet issa the shock of this *theeng*, eet has sent my plumbing into spasm," Dolorosa objected, pointing at the dwarf's head and shaking her own. "No, I can notta hold it any longer. I warna you, Kali Hooper."

"Fark, haven't you got a *bottle* or something?" Kali said with exasperation.

"I cannotta – and willa notta – tinkle while you listen!"

It wasn't a thought that appealed much to Kali, either, and the fact was she doubted *she* could last two days. "All right, all right!" she said, sighing heavily. She squinted through the observation slat, looking for a suitable parking space and then, with a grinding of levers, brought the Mole to a stop. The hatch hissed open. "Go. But don't go far and make it quick."

"Actually, I too might..." Aldrededor said hesitantly, then smiled and shrugged.

"Pirates!" Kali cursed as the two squeezed by her. She sat there for a second, looking out of the hatch, and then thought *what the hells, let's have a look*. It was a good excuse for her to stretch her legs, anyway.

Trying to ignore the conspicuous head of Dolorosa behind a pile of debris and a whistling and flexing Aldrededor against the wall in the opposite direction, Kali stepped out onto the bank of the canal and took her first good look around since they had entered the network. She tried not to breathe in too deeply because, frankly, whether they were in an ancient wonder or not, the Lost Canals of Turnitia stank to the high clouds, worse even than a sludgestrider's socks. The reason for that was possibly as a result of its collapsed sections or simply because it had been long unmaintained. But whatever the cause, the whole system of canals had stagnated. Not only did thick moss – glistening and pungent – cover the walls of the tunnels like a thick skin, but the canals themselves seemed not to be filled with seawater but dark green vegetation. The entire surface looked thick enough to walk on. Despite all that, though – and something *beeg* or not – the arches that led off into tunnels in the distance pulled at Kali but, again, she knew that now was not the time. She looked towards Aldrededor and Dolorosa, willing them to hurry up, but while the former was already nearing her with a sigh and declaration of how much better for that he felt, the latter had not moved from behind her pile of debris. In fact, she seemed to be waving at her to join her with quite some desperation.

Gods, Kali thought. *What now?*

"I amma stuck," Dolorosa confessed as she neared. "My feet, they havva become caught in the weeds."

Kali took a step forward and then stopped. "Are you decent?" she said warily.

Dolorosa gave her one of her killer looks. "I amma stuck, notta the senile old bat, Kali Hooper."

"Sorry. Okay then, let's see what I can do."

Kali clambered over the debris and saw that the thin woman was indeed entangled in a mesh of aquatic weed, but nothing that couldn't be handled. She pulled her gutting knife from its sheath and began to cut at it with sawing strokes. The growth was larger than it looked, part of a mass that had climbed the wall of the tunnel itself. It took quite some effort and a number of tugs from both of them to free it. Unfortunately, when at last it did come free, it did so unexpectedly quickly. Kali found herself suddenly flying backwards towards the canal, plunging through the algae covered surface. She emerged safe, however, and gagging and choking, swam to the side and waded back out, her hand outstretched to Dolorosa for help.

"You arra the mess once more," Dolorosa declared as she heaved her up. "We cannota take-a you anywhere."

"Hey!" Kali objected, loudly. "It was *you* that –"

Kali stopped in mid-sentence and then, as Dolorosa started to protest, hushed her with a wave of the hand.

Without another word, Kali began to walk forward, gazing up, and Dolorosa gazed where she gazed, and gasped.

Because the mass of weed that they had pulled away had had a knock on effect on the weed that covered the tunnel wall, and part of that now lay exposed for the first time in no one knew how long.

And it was covered in symbols. Great, golden symbols from some iconography that Kali had never seen before. She pulled away more of the growth and the symbols seemed to go on for as far as the wall did.

"Gods of the Sea," Aldrededor breathed, joining them.

"What arra those? Do they belong to one of your olda races, like those, what issa it they arra called - dwelfs?"

"*Elfs*, Dolorosa. I mean *elves*. There were two races, elves and dwarves, tall and thin and short and bulky, not difficult to tell apart. But these don't belong to either of them."

"So, you arra saying there is a *third* race?"

"No... maybe... I don't know. It's just that..."

Kali trailed off, running her fingers over one of the symbols, generating a strange keening vibration as she touched the metal. This she ignored, more concerned that she was tracing a *familiar* pattern, even though she hadn't seen the symbols before now. One of the shapes was a dead ringer for the creature she had encountered in the murky waters beneath Martak – the strange, water-breathing life form that had known all about her.

"Boss lady?" Dolorosa said, prodding her.

"Hush, woman!" Kali snapped.

She wouldn't normally have been so short with her but her mind had suddenly gone into overdrive. *Fish symbols here?* she was thinking. But if that was the case that probably meant that fish people had built these canals. But why in the hells would fish people want a set of tunnels that stretched *everywhere* under the peninsula? What purpose would they have served? What did the fish people *want* here?

"Boss lady?"

"I thought I said –" Kali began, spinning on her, and then stopped.

Because she suddenly realised that Dolorosa hadn't been trying to interrupt her, she'd been trying to alert her. Something was coming. Something big.

Not that they could see anything, yet. It only manifested itself in the form of a distant roar. The surface of the canal had begun to undulate, like a tide coming in their direction, as if something massive had stirred it.

"Both of you get inside the Mole. *Now!*"

Dolorosa stood her ground. "I may have letta you down at the Flagons but do notta worry," she said, slipping her stiletto from her boot. "Whatever thees theeng is, I will – *heeeeeeeee!*"

The tall, thin woman made a sound like an expiring goose then promptly fainted, fortunately straight into her husband's waiting arms, who then swept her up and did as Kali had instructed. Kali herself remained where she stood for a second longer, just enough time to take in what had prompted Dolorosa's abrupt departure from consciousness.

What she saw was not the creature itself but the creature announcing its presence with its shadow as it emerged from a side channel far up the branch. A shadow that, despite the distance, filled the arched thoroughfare completely, looming like a fast approaching night.

Make that Long Night, Kali thought. Because the shadow went on and on and on.

There was another deafening roar and the tunnel began to pound and shake, as if the unseen creature were slamming itself against the sides of the canal in fury. And then, fleetingly, she *did* see it, emerging from the water, to flash at incredible speed up and *around* the roof of the tunnel, negotiating a full three hundred and sixty degrees before it reached the other side and slipped beneath the surface again. Not all of it disappeared at once, though and, briefly, its long shadow flitted here, there and everywhere, impossible to keep track of, before then it, too, disappeared. Kali suddenly found herself awash with the canal's sluggish water all the way up to her chest.

It was coming right at them under the water.

"Two-Faced Bob called it the *yhang-dor!*" Aldrededor shouted as Kali waded as quickly as she could towards the Mole. "He thought it was elvish for 'That which never ends.'"

"Actually, it just means *big bastard!*" Kali shouted back as she forced herself forward against the wash. She stared at the bobbing ridge of weed and algae moving disturbingly fast down the centre of the canal, realised she couldn't see its end, and swallowed. "Aldrededor, get the Mole moving, *now!*"

"Kali Hooper, you will not make i –"

"*I'll make it, Aldrededor! Do it!*"

Aldrededor sighed and the Mole began to move forward, slowly at first, fighting against the wash, but gradually picking up speed.

Kali stopped wading and threw herself into a crawl, head splashing left and right, spitting out small clumps of weed and algae as she swam. She was about a yard from the tail end of the Mole and she doubled her efforts to reach it with a grunt of exertion. She managed, with one stroke, to grab onto a rail on the vehicle's rear. Kali looked back and couldn't shake the feeling that the monster was going to swallow the lower half of her legs at any second.

Desperately, she twisted in the water and managed to grab a second handhold before heaving herself up onto the body of the Mole. The surface of the vehicle was slick beneath her feet and she slipped twice, each time looking back to see how much space they had – or hadn't – gained on the yhang-dor. The Mole seemed to be holding its own for the moment, but they really needed to get the vehicle out of the wash to escape its drag, because the thing seemed to become more determined with each second they eluded its clutches.

She looked up and saw that there was a rise in the bank up ahead, and hoped that Aldrededor had noticed the same thing. Thankfully, the ex-pirate proved to be as reliable as always and, a second later, the Mole veered up the bank, its tracks churning and sloughing liquid and weed as they went. Kali threw herself through the open hatch of the vehicle.

Aldrededor immediately swapped places with her, allowing Kali to take control of the levers, but not before activating the one to seal the door. Before it closed something long and serpent-like hove into view outside the hatch, overtaking the Mole. Suddenly, all that was visible through the observation slat was what appeared to be a large reptilian mouth filled with thousands of tiny, razor sharp teeth.

Oh no, Kali thought. *One bloody great gob trying to eat me is enough for one week, thanks very much.*

Kali quickly yanked and pushed levers, a combination of moves that threw the Mole into a skidding u-turn and shook the cabin, awakening Dolorosa just as the rear end of the Mole slammed into the body of their pursuer, before racing off in the opposite direction. Except that racing wasn't quite the right word. Because even though they were once more free of the drag effect of the canal water, The Mole was a machine built for tunnelling, not for speed. Only the fact that the lengthy creature seemed to need a few seconds to literally catch up with itself bought them distance. The trouble was, that distance would be eaten up in seconds. Kali decided to use the only advantage they had and steered the Mole towards where a number of branch junctions left the main canal. She hoped to use them and subsequent branches to stymie the creature's manoeuvrability, constantly shifting position to lose it in the maze of tunnels. But to do that she'd need to know the creature's location at all times.

"Dolorosa, open the rear slat. I need you to keep an eye on that thing."

"Whatta theeng?" Dolorosa said, shakily attempting to light a cheroot.

"The bloody great *theeng* outside!"

"Eeet was real?"

"Yes, Dolorosa."

"Eeet ees following us?"

"Yes, Dolorosa."

"*Heeeeeeeeeee...*"

"Oh, crap. Aldrededor?"

"I am doing it, Kali Hooper," Aldrededor said, climbing over his seat to stub out the cheroot and flip the observation slat. "My beloved," he said by way of apology, "she had the embarrassing experience with a large slithering thing many years ago."

"I'm betting I don't want to know the details, right?"

"You are correct, Kali Hooper."

"Hokay. Where is the bastard?"

"It has just finished turning towards us. Moving now."

"Then hang on – we're going right."

Kali spun the Mole, skewing it as she tried to eke as much speed as possible from the machine.

"Where is it now?"

"Turning into the junction. It does not look pleased."

"I don't care if it's suicidal. Aldrededor?"

"Still with us and gaining, Kali Hooper."

Kali spun the Mole into another u-turn.

"Turning left again, straight on, right," she warned her shaken passengers. "Sharp left, coming up... now!"

"Kali Hooper, what is this thing?" Aldrededor asked, clinging on. "Despite the tale of Two-Faced Bob, I do not recognise it as a serpent of the sea."

Neither did Kali. She'd seen a couple of such beasts in her time and this resembled neither of them, reminding her more of some *worm* than any subaquatic behemoth. From what detail she had managed to see, the thing was certainly the shape of one, though covered, along its considerable and most *unworm*-like length, with a thick coating of barbed bristles that appeared not only to give it traction on any surface to which it adhered but also propelled it along. From the amount of collisions it was shrugging off, it had to be quite hardy. She imagined that beneath the bristles there was a protective coating that was more shell than skin. Its bulk was another thing. No creature designed like this should be as big or as wide as it was. Kali was starting to suspect that the k'nid were not the only unnatural creatures she had encountered in the past few days. Its whole physical make-up and the fact that it had seemed to first be drawn to them when she had touched the symbols on the wall had actually begun to make her wonder whether the creature had not always been such as it was. Perhaps once upon a time it had been some *tool* of the tunnels' builders – a life form that kept their canals clean and navigable, perhaps – but, in the unimaginable length of time since they had become sealed and disused, it had nurtured itself on what it had once removed, mutating as it did into what they faced now. In that case, in a sense, it had every right to not look pleased, because it had lived here longer than humans had walked the peninsula. This was its home.

Kali was suddenly flung against the control panel as the Mole was impacted hard from the rear. Outside, there was a loud roar that sounded almost like one of triumph.

"*Aldrededor?*"

"Apologies, Kali Hooper. A sudden spurt of speed. It seems our friend is becoming more adept at the chase."

"Then let him chase this," Kali said, gritting her teeth. Suddenly she was pushing and pulling the levers as if she had used them all her life. The Mole started to buck wildly as she threw it through a number of accelerations, decelerations, sudden twists and skidding turns that the unwieldy creature could not possibly hope to keep up with, screeching at last to a halt in tunnel.

"Aldrededor?" Kali asked over the stressed rumbling of the engine.

"No sign, Kali Hooper."

"Then it looks like we're out of the... oh fark!"

Kali stared through the observation slat at a branch of the canal that was *branchless*, stretching ahead of the Mole for as far as its headlights could penetrate, which made it look like forever. And for all she knew, it might go on just that far. In other words, there would be no dodging left or right and no u-turns here. *If* the creature managed to catch up they would be totally exposed.

"Kali Hooper?" Aldrededor said again.

"What, Aldrededor? Can you see anythi –"

The creature slammed into the side of the Mole and sent it crashing from the bank into the canal, overturning it until its buoyancy righted it once more. In the cabin, Aldrededor clung on to Dolorosa, while Kali squeezed herself tight between seat and control panel. Outside the cabin, the creature roared while the rest of its lengthy form followed its head into the tunnel.

"Dammit!" Kali shouted, gunning the engine of the Mole, riding it up onto the canal bank. "Doesn't this thing ever stop?"

Aldrededor sighed. "It is as persistent as my wife's advances and there is no way we can elude it now."

"Wanna bet?" Kali said.

She was as fired up as the Mole itself. She rammed her foot to the floor and as the vehicle responded by accelerating to the speed it was designed for, even she realised that with their current limitations and circumstances they had no more chance of fleeing their now immediate pursuer than one of the Hells Bellies would have outrunning a shnarl.

"Kali!" Aldrededor said with uncharacteristic seriousness

"Aldrededor? You don't get out with me much, do you?"

"I do not."

"You don't really know how I work, do you?"

"I have a feeling I am going to find out."

"The fact is, Aldrededor," Kali said, making a slight course correction and ramming levers forward, making the Mole lurch, "I make things up as I go along."

"Kali Hooper, you are heading straight for the tunnel wall."

"Oh, yeah," Kali said, nodding determinedly.

Kali aimed the Mole at the wall and then, at the very last second, swerved. Instead of hitting the wall head on, the vehicle careened against it along its side, stripping away weed and algae until metal grated hard against the stone beneath. Rather than pulling away, Kali teased the Mole even further to the left, again and again, as if she were trying to smash through the wall. In fact, wasn't her intention at all.

Inside the cabin, a rather confused Aldrededor steadied his insensible wife while the Mole vibrated so much it seemed in danger of coming apart. Kali, however, seemed little concerned. She rammed the vehicle again and again against the wall and, as there was a series of judders and snapping and clanking sounds from its lower regions, it at last clicked with the ex-pirate what it was Kali was trying to do. She was not trying to destroy the whole vehicle, but only part of it.

Aldrededor turned to look out of the rear observation slat, directing his gaze right and groundward, and sure enough the tracks on the vehicle's left hand side were breaking apart, their connecting links buckling and separating as the bolts holding them together sheared and loosened. As he watched, the individual plates of the tracks folded, piling up against the hatch, and then the whole lot came loose, flapping away behind the Mole like a discarded belt.

The Mole dropped onto its metal wheels on its left hand side and was in danger of going into a spin. However, Kali handled it expertly and instead quickly plunged the vehicle through the canal to a rise onto the opposite bank, where she began the same process again. A minute later, the tracks on the Mole's right hand side joined their discarded opposites. Dropping fully onto both sets of wheels now, the vehicle accelerated along the canal bank, spurting a shower of sparks and leaving a rather confused looking yhang-dor in its wake.

Both Kali and Aldrededor were flung back into their seats.

"*Wahoooo!*" Kali shouted.

Behind her, Dolorosa stirred slightly. "My 'usband, what is 'appening?"

Aldrededor shrugged his arms helplessly and smiled. "Kali Hooper, she is making it up as she goes along."

The Mole continued its flight along the canal bank, three or four times its original speed now that its wheels had been freed of the constraining gears of the tracks. Kali smiled as the compass on the control panel informed her they were heading west, exactly the direction they needed to go. Her smile faded, however, as Aldrededor informed her that the yhang-dor was once more in pursuit. Now that it had a perfectly straight tunnel to traverse, it wasn't gaining on them as fast as it would had the tracks still been present, but it was still gaining.

"Okay, I've had enough of this overgrown toothbrush," Kali declared. "Aldrededor, take the levers."

The ex-pirate scrambled back over the seat. "Kali Hooper, what are you doing now?"

Kali flicked the hatch lever and grabbed the crackstaff she had stored beneath her seat, then climbed towards the opening, wind whipping at her hair.

"Just keep on in this direction, Reddy! Back in a mo..."

"You're the boss, Kali Hooper."

Kali heaved herself out of the now opened hatch and steadied herself against the side of the Mole, its passage far from smooth now that it was running only on metal wheels. Nevertheless, she managed to lock herself into a secure position so that she was staring back along the side of the Mole, and raised the crackstaff. Some two hundred yards behind the vehicle, seemingly untroubled by the shower of sparks the Mole still trailed, the yhang-dor roared, its maw opening, displaying its countless razor teeth.

Somewhat hampered by the fact that she had to cling on for dear life with one hand, Kali steadied the crackstaff as best she could and fired, loosing a bolt of energy that ricocheted off the canal bank and into the ether, while simultaneously almost blowing her off the Mole with its recoil. She anchored herself and fired again. This time the bolt impacted with the weeds on the wall, frying them before again ricocheting back down the long, dark tunnel. Trying not to look at the tunnel floor, as it raced blurringly by immediately below her, Kali fired once more. The bolt careened off the tunnel roof and back down at forty-five degrees into the stagnant water, where the canal erupted with a sudden geyser of steam.

Dammit! she thought, this was going to be next to impossible unless she found a better position.

She looked up and, deciding, flung the crackstaff onto the Mole's roof with a grunt, then climbed up after it until she was scrambling on top of the vehicle as it swayed under her. There, lying flat and facing straight back, she lodged the crackstaff beneath her, took aim and fired. An energy bolt slammed into the canal bank directly in front of the yhang-dor, blowing shrapnel in its face.

Adjusting her aim slightly, she fired again, and then again, and the bolts scythed along the creature's side, burning a path through its layer of bristle. The creature roared and reared, momentarily slowed, but then continued coming on. Kali fired again, again and again, the energy discharges reverberating in the confines of the tunnel. The length of the yhang-dor flared with multiple hits. It launched itself up and around the tunnel walls.

Keep still, you slippery fark! Kali thought as it spiralled towards her.

But it did not stop her firing and this time all but one of her multiple shots found their target. Almost pulsating with the blue of the energy bolts now, and shedding sections of skin from where its bristles had fried away, the creature's roar had become one less of anger and more of pain. But still it came on. It was a tough bastard, without a doubt. However, Kali was certain that all it would take to finish it was a few more shots. Particularly if she could get one straight down its throat.

She was lining up just such a shot when her world suddenly spun. The Mole was skidding, trying, for some reason, to come to an emergency stop. A moment later, it succeeded, and she found herself tumbling from the roof to land on the ground with an undignified *oof*.

Ahead of them, the roof of the tunnel had collapsed completely.

"I am sorry, Kali Hooper," Aldrededor said from inside the cabin. "There was nothing I could –"

Kali double-taked on the collapsed tunnel and then on the approaching yhang-dor, estimating they had perhaps thirty seconds before it caught up with them.

She leapt into the cabin, sealed the hatch behind her, and flicked the Mole's cannons on to full power. Through the forward observation slat she could see the sonic pulses staring to affect the fallen debris. A second later, she pulled back as a rain of pulverised stone and rock began to impact with the vehicle's front. But in her heart of hearts Kali knew that there was really no time, that the collapse looked far too thick to penetrate before the yhang-dor was on them. And sure enough, a second later, the Mole lurched horribly.

Suddenly all that Kali could see through the observation slat was a set of thousands of razor sharp teeth, then something horrible and squishy and, then, utter blackness.

In the darkness, Aldrededor swallowed so hard Kali could actually hear it. "Did what I think just happened happen?"

"A-ha."

On the back seat, no doubt disturbed by the impact, Dolorosa stirred. "All is quiet. Have we stopped being chased by the *theeng?*"

"In a manner of speaking, my dearest," Aldrededor said. "Why don't you go back to sleep?"

"Bossa lady? What issa wrong?"

"Oh, I think we're in the shit," Kali said, casually. And paused. "Or will be soon, anyway."

"Kali Hooper, I must ask you not to use such language in front of my delicate flower."

"Aldrededor, it was your 'delicate flower' and her desire to *flow* that got us into this mess in the –"

Suddenly the Mole lurched again, far more violently than the first time, and all three of its passengers clung onto their seats as it began to move forward. The relative quiet of the last few moments was replaced by the noise of a series of loud crashes that, together with the *thwooming* of the still active sonic cannons, was deafening. Kali realised that, with the combination of the yhang-dor's momentum and the cannons themselves, they were actually ploughing *through* the obstacle ahead of them. Not only that, if her senses weren't betraying her, but *up*.

What was more, the cannons were clearly damaging the yhang-dor from the *inside*, and by virtue of the fact that its resultant screeching was becoming louder than the cacophony caused by their passage through the roof-fall, it didn't like that at all. It began, in fact, to vibrate and spasm around them, and Kali was just beginning to wonder what would happen to the Mole when two things happened at once.

The yhang-dor smashed through the last of the blockages and promptly exploded, and the forward observation slat – after taking a moment to drain itself of clinging gore – exposed the interior of the cabin to a brilliant white light.

Either they had just ascended to Kerberos, Kali considered, or the Mole's two day journey through the Lost Canals of Turnitia had been considerably shortened by the fact that they had been forced to move a lot more quickly than anticipated. And if she was right, they were just where they wanted to be. There was only one way to find out.

Kali activated the Mole's hatch, then licked a fleck of snow from the end of her nose. Yup, that tasted right. She smiled and turned to a somewhat stunned Aldrededor and Dolorosa.

"Welcome to the Drakengrats. I think we walk from here."

CHAPTER ELEVEN

THREE DOTS MOVED across the pristine white landscape. Some leagues, and a day's climb, behind them, the landscape was stained by a great splotch of yellow gore that spread away from a jagged, irregular hole in the snow. Next to that sat the skewed, abandoned remains of a broken machine from which smoke curled lazily into the pure mountain air. Ahead of the dots lay a series of jagged peaks, rising ever higher until they seemed to touch the clouds themselves. But the majesty of these seemed, for the moment, lost on those who trudged wearily through the snow.

The crunching of their boots echoed through the ether, and then the echo of their voices – and then that of a slap.

"Do notta droppa the litter!"

"It is but a crust, my darling."

"Anda who willa pick up the crust in this gods-forsaken place, hah? No, 'usband, it issa the litter!"

"My wife, we are dreaded *pirates of the high seas* – we have done worse things."

"We *were* pirates, my 'usband! Nowwa we are the respectable proprietors of a tavern witha the great potential!"

A cough echoed alongside the voices, and a second passed.

"Nowwa we are the respectable *manageers* ovva taverno witha the great potential, and we –"

"Nice butties," the owner of the cough interjected. Its tone suggested the matter should be closed.

"I amma sorry, boss lady," the first voice said again.

Kali stared at Dolorosa and Aldrededor as the two of them ate and trudged wearily alongside her, chewing on her own surprise stew butty ruminatively. That she had finally decided to eat one of Dolorosa's mushy concoctions was a reflection that the current trek had, for all of them, turned out to be more gruelling than expected. Even her normal wariness about one disturbing aspect of the ex-pirate's signature dish –

that it never, *ever* cooled down – had been set aside in favour of getting something warm inside her. Because the one thing that could be said about the Drakengrats was that they were *farking cold*.

She hadn't expected to lose the Mole, of course. With the Mole this whole affair would have been one hells of a lot easier, but at least they had the furs and equipment she had instructed Aldrededor to bring with the vehicle. Trouble was, even with the Mole, they would have faced the same problem. That she didn't have the faintest idea where she, Aldrededor and Dolorosa were meant to be *going*. It was all right for the old man to send her to 'a place in the clouds' but there were a lot of clouds, and a lot of mountains beneath them – exactly which one of them had he meant?

Kali could only hope that she and the others stumbled across some kind of clue. A signpost 'To The Crucible', perhaps. Or another explosion that no one for leagues could miss. Or, best of all, another pack of k'nid swarming from the place they originated, so that they could follow their trail back whence they came.

Yes, just like those.

Exactly like those, in fact.

"Kali Hooper, something comes," Aldrededor pointed out, rather unnecessarily.

"It issa the theengs like-a leaves fromma the Flagons."

Kali stared up the narrow pass they had been negotiating. At its very top, the k'nid were swarming over the ridge like a dark avalanche, before tumbling down the white mountainside towards them. At the speed they were moving, she estimated they had about two minutes before the things were on them.

"Hide," Kali instructed, in a tone which left no doubt how important a manoeuvre that was going to be.

"Hide-a, she says," Dolorosa protested, throwing up her arms. "And-a how exactly are we meanta to do that?"

"My wife is correct, Kali Hooper. There is nowhere for us to go."

Her attention having been so fixed on the k'nid, Kali hadn't noticed they were in a part of the pass totally devoid of any cover and edged by sheer rock faces on either side. *She* might be able to make a leap up them to safety but the Sarcreans had no chance of doing so, and there was no way she was leaving them down here alone.

For the first time since they had started on their journey, she truly regretted allowing them to come along and, for a moment, felt a totally uncharacteristic bolt of panic. Her friends were going to die unless she did something quick.

Kali was about to unsling her crackstaff, ready to make a last stand when –

"Looka!" Dolorosa cried suddenly, and pointed up. "There!"

Kali snapped her gaze to where Dolorosa pointed and, at first, wasn't sure what she was looking at. Then she realised that *something* was caught, flapping in the wind, on a sharp piece of rock thirty feet above their heads. It looked to be, of all things, a large torn piece of white sailcloth. But that was impossible, surely. After all what kind of ship – wrecked or otherwise – would have been able to find its way here?

Impossible or not, it appeared to have galvanised Dolorosa. Eyes sparkling, she turned to Aldrededor and said: "I never though I would havva the chance to say this again, my 'usband, but we must *battena down the hatches!*"

Aldrededor's eyes also sparkled. "My wife, I love you!" He turned to Kali and pointed at the cloth. "Kali Hooper, if you would be so good as to…"

Kali didn't have a clue what they were on about. "Why?"

Dolorosa thrust her face in hers, her dark eyes narrowing. "Because, bossa lady, it ees oura turn to save youra life, forra once. *Nowwa do as I say!*"

That was good enough for Kali and she went for the cloth, reaching it in three acrobatic leaps, delivering it seconds later to the hands of Dolorosa. The ex-pirate and her husband pulled it taut and then held it about a foot above the snowy ground, whereupon Kali was ordered to lie underneath. This she did without argument and, a second later, Aldrededor and Dolorosa joined her, pulling the cloth down tightly over them all.

To an outside observer they would now look like nothing more than a small rise in the snow.

"We used to-a use the sails to secure our cargo inna the bad storm," Dolorosa whispered in what, Kali had to admit, were quite cosy confines. "Eet issa what gave-a me the idea."

"You are a genius, my wife."

"I havva my moments, yes."

"Hang on," Kali said. "All we've done is hide under a big piece of cloth. Do you really think that'll fool the k'nid?"

"Whya not? Itta fooled Short Jack Copper when thatta slimy bastardo boarded our ship. We-a waited for his men to come aboard and then sprang from beneath the sail like-a the… like-a the –"

"Springy things?" Kali offered.

"Like-a the springy things, yes! And thenna we *keelled* them all witha oura very sharpa knives! It wassa *horrible!*"

"A-ha. Dolorosa, why are you whispering?"

"So-a the k'nid do notta hear us, of course."

"Dolorosa, they're hurtling murderously down a mountainside

towards us, probably causing an avalanche as they come. I doubt they'll hear –"

"Be silent now, Kali Hooper," Aldrededor interrupted. "They are upon us."

Aldrededor was right. Distracted as she had been with her surreal exchange with Dolorosa, the approach of the k'nid swarm had somewhat taken a back seat but there was no mistaking it now.

The sound of their approach was audible even over the winds blowing through the pass, and it was building second by second to a level that would soon be deafening. The sound began to approach a crescendo and Kali, Aldrededor and Dolorosa remained utterly still, in readiness.

The sensation of the k'nid passing was difficult to describe – like being massaged by a horde of heavy insects, each and every insectoid leg discernable as a fleeting touch to the very bone – and for the few seconds it took for their numbers to progress over their hiding place, Kali felt every nerve in her body scream out with a desire to leap up and flee from her frozen position. She did not, of course, because that would have meant instant death, though resisting the desire was a struggle. Next to her she could see Aldrededor and Dolorosa suffering in the same way. The only way that they could communicate was with their eyes, but the message they sent to each other was nonetheless clear.

Do not move, do not cry out.

They remained that way for what seemed to be an interminable time but was likely only seconds and then, miraculously, it was over.

Even so, Kali waited a few seconds before moving the piece of cloth off their prone forms. It was heavier than she expected, laden with a layer of snow that the k'nid swarm had caused to avalanche over them, but Kali wasn't complaining as that snow had likely offered an extra layer of protection.

The three of them stood and stared down the mountain pass, catching view of the tail end of the swarm as it moved out across the peninsula.

Kali turned her gaze upward, biting her lip. "No doubt now where they're coming from. You two okay, ready to move on?"

"We are ready, Kali Hooper."

"Wait," Dolorosa said. "There ees something…"

The thin woman moved ahead of them, bending to pick up something glistening in the layer of fine, disturbed snow. It was some kind of band and Dolorosa bit it and turned it in her hands, shrugging, before handing it to Kali.

"What issa this theeng?"

Kali held the band up to the light. It was old, possibly of elven origin, and inscribed with a series of runics so small she couldn't make them out. It appeared to be, though, only decorative. "Some kind of bracelet, but how in the hells it ended up here is anybody's guess."

"May I see, Kali Hooper?" Aldrededor asked. "Hmm, yes. I have seen something such as this before."

"You have? Where?"

"The *Ramar'Est*. The wreck of an elven ship many believed haunted, for from within the sealed cabin of its captain, many, many centuries after he died, his voice could still be heard."

"I take it wasn't a ghost?"

"No, Kali Hooper. It was this."

The Sarcrean held out the bracelet and rubbed its side with his thumb. Kali and Dolorosa jumped back as the figure of a young woman materialised before them. Garbed in a cloak of the Final Faith, attractive and with a mane of long blonde hair, the figure was ghostly, flecked with the snow that penetrated its form, but Kali knew who it was.

"My name is Jennadayn Freel," she began. "Eleven years ago I was abducted by agents of the Final Faith under the command of Katherine Makennon's first lieutenant, Konstantin Munch. Since that day I have been stripped of my individuality, my liberty and free will, bent to the cause of the Faith through the machinations of the mindweaver Querilous Fitch. He is with me – he is *inside me* – always, and it is only in rare, stolen moments such as this that I am able to remember who and what I once was. This bracelet enables me to record my thoughts at these times. This I do under my own conditioning, so that when Fitch's influence reasserts itself I will remember nothing of the bracelet's capabilities or what I have said."

The figure flickered and faded for a second, and then reappeared in slightly different garb. It began to speak on another matter, one that seemed to have been recorded some time later, but the mountain pass in the middle of a snowstorm was no place to listen to what was said. Kali signalled Aldrededor to thumb the bracelet again, and the image disappeared. He handed the band to her.

"Who issa that woman?" Dolorosa asked.

"Slowhand's sister."

"*The* Slowhand? The one witha the snake-like hips and the cute-a ar..."

She trailed off, whistling and kicking her heels, looking sheepishly at her husband.

Kali coughed to hide a smile. "Yes, Dolorosa, *the* Slowhand. But the question is, if this bracelet belongs to Slowhand's sister, what in the hells was Jenna doing up here?"

"Perhaps," Aldrededor said, pointing, "something to do with that."

Kali and Dolorosa turned. What neither she or her companions had noticed until now – distracted as they had been by the k'nid swarm – was that further up the pass, high on its left hand side, smoke trailed from a gaping hole in the rockface, curling lazily and looking as if it were the dying tendrils of an explosion from some days before.

How about three days before? Kali thought. Because she had little doubt that was she was looking at was the aftermath of what Merrit Moon had seen through his elven telescope back in Gargas.

She had to find out what was up there, but she was not going to do so now, as the light of day was already fading into azure twilight, bringing with it a deeper cold that would make any route up to the mysterious gap in the rocks doubly treacherous. Instead, Kali yomped with Dolorosa and Aldrededor further up the pass, to a point perhaps a tenth of a league from where the hole loomed, and there found a small cave where they were able to make camp for the night. More surprise stew butties were consumed for supper and her two companions were soon wrapped up in their furs together, sound asleep and snoring. Kali took the opportunity to examine Jenna's bracelet once more, thumbing through her recorded entries and getting to know a little more about the woman who, until a few months before, she had never known existed.

It was a tragic and troubling tale, relating the abduction, years before, that Slowhand had told her about, and Jenna's subsequent indoctrination into the ranks of the Final Faith. But, more intriguingly, there were accounts of the various tasks she had thereafter been asked to perform on their behalf. Investigations into the strategical advantages of a considerable number of Old Race discoveries, some of which Kali knew about or, indeed, had beaten them to. There were other entries, too, but they were clearly meant for her brother alone and so Kali skipped through them quickly, until she came to the last entry of all.

Recorded only a week before, it detailed Jenna's last assignment and as Kali played it through she wandered, frowning, to the cave mouth and gazed up at the smoking remains of what she now knew was the first stage to finding the Crucible.

THE NEXT DAY Kali rose early and whispered to the still half-asleep ex-pirates that they should wait where they were for her return.

Moving out, she ascended the pass to the point where the hole loomed above, and there her heart sank. For the pass beneath had become blocked, recently by the look of it. While she scaled the massive pile of collapsed rocks with ease, using it to begin her ascent to the hole, she knew that Aldrededor and Dolorosa would never make the climb. Upon her return, they would need to find another way past the blockage, a delay she wasn't sure that they could afford. Her concerns on that matter were, however, soon replaced, by a growing sense of familiarity about the spot in which she climbed. She realised that the only reason she hadn't recognised it earlier was because the unmistakable landmark that was missing should not be missing at all. *My gods,* she thought; the rocks she was climbing were the remains of Thunderlungs' Cry. But that was impossible, surely? Because the Cry was a thing of magic and could never be destroyed.

No, that wasn't *quite* right, she corrected herself. Thunderlungs' Cry might be impervious to any *natural* threat but if the thing that had destroyed it was *itself* magical then it could tumble like anything else. Was that what had happened here? A *magical* explosion? If that was the case, it had to have been incredibly powerful, on a scale such as she had never heard of, and that told her one thing – that it was likely caused by something from the latter stages of the Old Races' evolution, from their third and final period of development, just before the End Time.

Another realisation hit her as she remembered the legend of Thunderlungs' Cry. What if it was no legend? What if what had distracted Mawnee was the hole in the rock she was climbing towards now?

Oh boy. Now *that* was exciting.

Kali climbed swiftly, moving beyond the collapsed rocks, flinging herself from outcrop to outcrop as she scaled the almost sheer face in a zig-zag fashion, then heaving herself into the lip of a tunnel. There she saw the burned and twisted remains of a metal superstructure that formed the tunnel walls and, further in, a massive gantry – some kind of elevator? – that could only have been produced by a more advanced technology. However advanced the technology that had constructed it, though, it was academic, because it was unusable now. As bent and twisted as every other piece of metal in the cavern.

But what pieces of metal they were! Even at this distance Kali could make out the burned metal skeletons of craft that were moored above her. Craft that, by their very situation, must have been capable of flight. Airships, then! She had suspected that the Old Races had been capable of as much but until now…

Kali's train of thought stopped and her nose wrinkled. As acrid as the air in the cavern entrance was, she had suddenly smelled something that had been caught upon it, as if in passing. But passing or not, it had made its mark and still lingered strongly. In a second, she had it.

It was Slowhand's aftershave.

Quiver.

Slowhand, here? How in all the hells had he gotten here?

And more to the point, where the hells was he now?

Kali moved along the cavern floor to the base of the ruined elevator and began to climb, picking her hand and footholds carefully, as the battered metal was in danger of collapse at any moment. Despite the creaks and the groans of the unstable structure, she made it without incident to the top and clambered onto the very same platform which, unbeknownst to her, Slowhand had leapt from three days before. She called the archer's name, but there was no response. Hardly surprising, she thought, for anything caught in the explosion that had taken this place out was unlikely to any longer have the capacity for speech. But if anyone had died here – and she tried not to picture Slowhand in such a conflagration – then there would surely be some remains. But there was nothing. Somehow, Slowhand must have made an escape.

For the moment Kali could only imagine what had happened here and she picked her way through the wreckage, searching for some clue to enlighten her, but anything that had been present before the explosion not made of metal had been reduced to ash. Still, what did remain offered hints to the place's original function. There were signs, for example, of great volumes of supplies, and the remains of a crane that must surely, at one time, have stowed such supplies aboard the airships. What these supplies had been for – and more importantly, where they had been *destined* – was, however, a question it appeared she would be unable to answer for the time being. Even the remains of what seemed to be some kind of refuelling device extending from the wall was so ruined that it was able to offer no clues. It did, though, help to explain one thing. For the remains glowed with the same amber energy she had seen glow in the Mole and her crackstaff. She realised that in some way it must *power* those devices and others. But what the hells was it? For future reference – and to keep things simple – she named it *amberglow*.

Kali continued her search without any other significant finds but then, bolted to the wall of what appeared to have once been some kind of office area, she found a metal panel that had been seared but left otherwise undamaged. A panel that seemed to be inscribed with some kind of map of the mountains. Amongst the diagrams depicting the mountains and their relative positions there were other symbols that showed, as far as she could work out, docking airships, which she could only assume were meant to represent places such as the one she was in now. Intrigued, Kali brushed away soot and studied the charred metal plate, tracing the symbols with her finger, jabbing the one whose relative position corresponded with her current location. Yes, it was the one lowest down in the mountains and, therefore, the first of four similar such locations inscribed on the plate. She *was* looking at a map whose purpose appeared to be as an aid to guide airships from one location to the next. The question was, what kind of destination required the amount of traffic that these waystations had clearly handled? What kind of destination needed this amount of raw materials and equipment on what had to have been a fairly constant basis? More – for what purpose?

Kali swallowed, looking at the one ideogram she had not yet studied in any detail. Because there, in a position that corresponded with the very heart of the Drakengrat Range, was a marker in the shape of... well, she wasn't sure what it was. But it *looked* like something half elven and half dwarven and it was big and it sure as hells wasn't natural.

Was this what Jenna had referred to in one of her log entries? Kali wondered. She took the bracelet from a pocket on the thigh of her bodysuit and thumbed it into life once more, finding and replaying some of the last entries. Jenna flickered into pseudo-life before her, and began to speak.

"Reports have reached us from the Drakengrat Mountains. An Order of the Swords of Dawn contingent has discovered something unusual that is believed to be an Old Race location worthy of further investigation. I have just received word that I am to leave for this location in the morning..."

Kali thumbed ahead.

"The location is of a scale hitherto unfound, though its purpose continues to elude even our finest investigators. I cannot shake the feeling that something *unnatural* happened here, though for the time being I can only guess at what."

Again.

"At last, a breakthrough! We cannot pretend to understand the science of it but it seems that the Old Race had developed a process of..."

And again.

"There has been a mistake. Something has gone horribly wrong with our equations and the capabilities of this place are out of control. Many of my people are already dead and, I fear, many will soon follow. We need to stop this but, to do so, we need help."

And finally.

"A number of us, including Fitch, have managed to flee the location on the airship we discovered. I intend to pilot the airship to Gransk, where our people are already aware of our problem. We shall, I hope, return to this place and end what we began. Even if it means we have to wipe this foul experiment off the face of Twilight. If we fail to do so, then the Lord of All save us."

Kali frowned, as she had the first time she had played these extracts, but now it was a frown exacerbated by what she had seen with her own eyes. The implications of it were worrying to say the least, but her greatest concern was for the fate of Slowhand himself. Dammit, if she hadn't gotten herself stuck in that *farking* deathtrap she would have been here to help him. She could only hope that the archer wasn't lying dead and frozen in some unmarked mountain grave.

Kali took a deep breath, realising that, while there was nothing she could do for Slowhand, she still had a responsibility to those who had accompanied her. If she, Aldrededor and Dolorosa were to follow the map she had found to its ultimate destination they were going to need more than Surprise Stew butties to keep them alive. There was a chance, perhaps, that, if they were packed in anything other than wood, some of the more modern supplies remaining here might be food.

Again, Kali searched. And came upon a number of charred metal boxes bearing the symbol of a crossed circle. Well, if there had been any doubt that Jenna and the Final Faith had been here, that was now dispelled. Kali broke the seal on one, stared, and laughed.

The supplies belonged to the Final Faith, all right. Who else would bring wafers and wine to the mountains?

But it was something. It didn't take Kali long to make her way back to the cave and she was actually quite looking forward to breakfasting on the alcohol, but then she stopped suddenly.

Something was wrong.

The place was too quiet.

And Aldrededor and Dolorosa were gone.

Kali entered the camp slowly, looking for any sign of her companions – or worse, what might have taken them. But there were no tracks. She moved over to the campfire, found it recently rekindled, then felt the cups the ex-pirates must have been drinking from. The liquid inside was still warm. In this temperature, that likely meant that whatever had happened here had happened in the past few minutes. But there was no sign of anything untoward.

There was, however, the slightest of sudden noises. It came from a previously unnoticed passage towards the rear of the cave and occurred at exactly the same time as Kali's sixth sense alerted her to the fact that something was wrong. She was about to unsling her crackstaff when the slight *pfft* she'd heard was followed immediately by a sting on the side of her neck.

Kali raised her hand, felt a tiny needle embedded there.

And then, her eyes glazed and, her body stiff as a board, she fell face down onto Dolorosa and Aldrededor's empty furs.

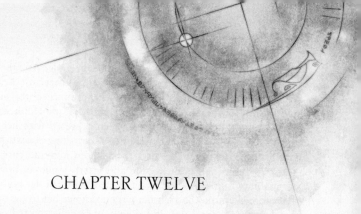

CHAPTER TWELVE

"UNKA-CHAKKA-UNKA-CHAKKA-OH-OH-OH!
"UNKA-CHAKKA-UNKA-CHAKKA-OH-OH-OH!

The chanting came from beyond the passage that led from the cave, loud and then soft, loud and then soft; never ceasing. The only visible signs of those responsible for the ominous mantra were the grotesquely misshapen shadows that loomed and rippled across the rough passage wall. Sometimes the shadows loomed so large that it seemed their owners were about to enter the cave, but then they dwindled once more, the only other activity the occasional burst of shadowboxing – perhaps jostling, perhaps some altercation – but, whatever their cause, they never lasted for long.

What did last was the gnawing and grunting that could be heard beneath the chanting.

And the smell of roasting flesh.

"UNKA-CHAKKA-UNKA-CHAKKA-OH-OH-OH!
"UNKA-CHAKKA-UNKA-CHAKKA-OH-OH-OH!"

Yes, yes, all right, enough already! Kali thought. *Will you please, for just one farking minute, shut up!*

She sighed heavily, and rattled the chains that bound her. She reckoned it had been about eight hours since the sting on her neck, and it was only now that the effects of whatever the tiny dart had been coated with were starting to wear off. Starting, mind, because although her paralysis had gone it had left her feeling distinctly betwattled. A condition she was not unfamiliar with but would have preferred to have enjoyed slumped in the Flagons rather than here, chained to a pillar and dressed in nothing but three strategically draped strips of animal hide. It was a development she had to admit had caught her a tad by surprise. Steaming pits of bloody Kerberos, it could only happen to her.

A sacrificial virgin!

Kali pouted.

Okay, then, sacrificial... offering.

Where the hells was she? Who were these people? And most of all, why was she dressed in this stupid, farking costume?

She frowned. The fact was, there were other, more serious questions. Specifically, what had happened to Aldrededor and Dolorosa? There was no doubt that the couple *had* been captured with her because she had caught glimpses of them, by her side, slung beneath the same kind of pole on which she herself had been tied and carried here. Those glimpses had been fleeting and utterly random, however, as her inability to move her eyes, let alone the rest of her body, during the enforced journey had left her with no choice but to see only what the twists, turns and ups and downs of her unexpected excursion had thrust before her frozen eyes. It hadn't helped that she had been lapsing in and out of consciousness, also.

What she *did* remember was that their captors seemed to have taken them higher into the mountains, and that the route had begun in the passage at the rear of the cave where they had sheltered. From there on in, it had become confusing – one minute exposed on the mountainside, the next travelling through rock, snatches of fur-hooded faces leering in both the light and the dark – leaving her with the impression that, far from being deserted as she had thought, the Drakengrats were riddled with a warren of caves and tunnels which were clearly inhabited. She remembered wondering whether she was in the hands of ogur, but then ogur would hardly dress her in a skimpy outfit as it would only stick in their teeth when they ate her. Besides, ogur would have downed her with club not dart, and she would have been in no position to wonder anything at all.

Also, her captors didn't smell anywhere near as bad – let's face it, nothing did. They just smelled... odd, actually.

Kali looked about the cave, gleaning what she could about her captors. Various skulls and other pieces of skeleton were hung on the walls. Animal skins were draped across the floor and littered across them were various implements and tools, bowls, cups and the like, all of which appeared to have been carved from bone. One thing was immediately clear. Everything here was designed or scaled for human use, though she had never come across a human settlement as primitive as this. What were they doing here in the Drakengrats, and why was their culture so stagnated? It was as if *nothing* had changed here since the days of Thunderlungs' Cry.

She needed answers – especially if these people knew anything about the Crucible – and she wasn't going to get them bound to this farking pillar. Again, Kali rattled her chains, pulling with wrists and ankles to test for signs of weakness, but all her struggles achieved was to dislodge the strips of hide from where they had been strategically placed and, cursing, she tried to jiggle them back. As she did, the chanting from the other cave suddenly stopped, and she snapped a look at the passage. Shadows loomed again, and this time they didn't go away.

"Shit" she said, and jiggled harder.

She succeeded just in time. Four figures dressed in skins entered the cave and stood in silence by the passage, just staring at her. She could barely make them out, silhouetted as they were, but they appeared to be human from what she could see. Human, if a little on the beefy side.

Kali swallowed, thinking: *One step and, I promise, you will regret it.*

The figures did not move towards her. Instead, a moment later, they stood aside to allow the entrance of a fifth figure – one who was more surreally dressed than they. It wore a loincloth, a plethora of dangling fetishes and, worst of all, a mask that covered its head and shoulders and made its upper half resemble that of an exploded chicken.

The figure approached then slapped both its palms onto its thighs. Then it suddenly squatted down, sticking its tongue out as far as it would go, which was quite some way, and waddled its head from side to side.

"*Wadaladalla!*" it shouted – or something like that. A curious sound that made even its companions look at him askance.

"Hey!" Kali shouted. "Unless w*adaladalla* means 'release the girl *right* now,' I am going to be very pitsed off!"

Everything went silent. The figure stared at her, and both hands suddenly produced ominous looking objects not unlike the goblin death rattles Merrit Moon dealt in and shook them violently in her general direction. Then it stomped gradually nearer, like some wrestler at the Scholten carnival, until it came face to face, whereupon it shook the rattles again and its tongue flicked at her nose.

There was just enough give in the chains for Kali to knee him in the groin.

"*Ohooooooo… huuuurrrr… Gods and farking pits!*" A man then.

As he staggered back cradling himself, Kali ignored the disturbed murmurs from his friends and stared at her victim hard. Something wasn't right here, she suddenly realised. For one thing, it had occurred to her that all that *unka-chaka* stuff reminded her very much of a song she'd once hated and, for another, it had only just clicked that this strange man wasn't anywhere near as hairy as his mates. Not at all, in fact. Above all else, though, there was the matter of a couple of familiar tattoos she could make out between the fetishes he wore – those and one she *wasn't* familiar with on his muscular left bicep. A declaration of love for someone called, of all things, *Endless Passion.*

Only one man would wear a tattoo like that, Kali knew.

"Slowhand?"

"*Guhhhhng…* h-hi, Hooper, how you doing?"

"How am I doing? Oh, you know, shot with a paralysing dart, kidnapped, stripped, chained to a sacrificial altar, *you*?"

The exploded chicken mask bobbed back and forth. "Oh, you know," he said, and paused to cup his lower regions once more. "*Hoooooo, hells...* fine, fine."

"Whatever you're doing wearing that farking thing, take it off! *What the hells are you doing here?*"

Slowhand slapped his palm over her mouth. "Trying to get you out of here. So will you please keep your voice *down*?"

Kali's eyes narrowed and, for a second, she debated kneeing him again. Instead, she spoke quietly. "*Whyfmychayndupwifnocloffson?*"

Slowhand withdrew his hand. "What?"

"Why am I chained up with no clothes on?"

"Oh, yes. Bit of a long story. Seems these people are having a problem with their god. Think it's angry because strangers invaded its – invaded *their* – holy ground."

"Strangers?"

"The Filth, from what I've pieced together." Slowhand said. He noticed the figures standing in the cave were regarding their lengthy and hushed conversation with some suspicion and, to appease them, did a little dance. Then, he frowned. "Led by my sister, as it happens."

Kali was already beginning to suspect that this 'holy ground' was the discovery Jenna had mentioned in her recordings – but that someone was *worshipping* it came as a surprise. Despite her current predicament, this was becoming more and more interesting.

"I know about Jenna. Aldrededor, Dolorosa and I found a bracelet."

Now it was Slowhand's turn to be surprised. "I *lost* that bracelet. She gave it to me before I fell out of the sky."

"You were on one of their airships?"

"Yes and no. Another long story." Slowhand glanced over at his companions, and shook one of his rattles for effect. "But now isn't the time."

"I'd go with that. So, exactly *how* are you getting me out of here?"

"I'm not."

"Excuse me?"

Slowhand hesitated. "Thing is, these people think a sign of their god's anger is the k'nid. That they're demons whose release into the world is a punishment which can only halted by the sacrifice of one of the strangers. They had their eyes on me when they found me but... I managed to persuade them otherwise."

"Don't tell me, you beguiled them by summoning balloon animals. Pits, Slowhand, you *still* carry balloons?"

He shrugged. "Well, they weren't *balloons* exactly, but..."

"I do not want to know!"

"Shush! Okay, forget the balloons. If you must know, I trained them in the making and use of bows, as well. They'd never seen such a weapon before and, with the scarcity of wildlife up here, believe me, they come in handy."

Kali sighed. "That explains the gnawing out there."

"Aha. Before, they sustained themselves mainly on mountain fungus and *vegetables*."

"Oh, gods."

"I know. Anyway, Hooper, the point is, I survived. But they still needed to sacrifice *someone*."

"Aldrededor!" Kali said, concerned. "Dolorosa!"

"No, no. They're *fine*. Because I suggested you."

"*What?*"

"I figured the only way to get us all out of this was to convince them we're *not* strangers, that we're like them. And our best chance of doing that was with you…"

"What are you talking about?"

"One of the first things I noticed about these people – they call themselves the yazan, by the way – is that they're different."

"Different?"

"Look, there's no time to explain," Slowhand said, and produced a vicious looking knife from beneath his fetishes. "Just be grateful I managed to persuade them to let me perform the sacrifice, my way."

Kali stared at Slowhand in disbelief as he placed the point of the knife on her sternum, then hissed in shock as she felt it penetrate the skin.

"Ow! 'Liam, what the hells do you think you're doi –"

"Don't move!"

"Don't move?! The hells I'm not going to move!"

Slowhand gripped her arm firmly and unexpectedly winked. "Trust me, Hooper, all right? The Death of A Thousand Cuts is the only way out of this."

"The Death of A Thousand Cuts!?"

"Will you please calm down."

"Slowhand, you're sticking a farking knife in my chest!"

The archer paused, leaning in and whispering in Kali's ear. "Hooper, I cannot tell you how good I felt when I saw you were still alive." He shrugged. "Do you really think I'd spoil that by slicing you open now?"

"It does seem a little odd, even for you."

"Fine, then trust me. *Please*."

Slowhand's grip on the gutting knife tightened. And Kali felt its tip being held against her measuredly.

"Do what you have to," Kali said, staring him in the eyes.

Slowhand nodded, and then drew the tip of the knife down her sternum, scoring a shallow red line about six inches in length, and she moaned softly as it began to ooze blood. As it did, Slowhand spun around to face the yazan, throwing his hands in the air to reveal the wound – what Kali fervently hoped was the first and last cut. But then the yazan stared at it and, to her discomfort, nodded. Their meaning was clear – *continue*.

"*Wadaladalla!*" the archer cried and spun dramatically toward her, knife raised. Then – rather too theatrically, Kali thought, he suddenly leapt back and pointed at her wound, uttering a shocked variation on his usual cry that sounded like: "*Wululadadalula?*"

The yazan stared where he pointed, and then moved forward to crowd around her.

What? Kali thought. *What?*

Had she suddenly grown a second head in her cleavage? Had the cloth come loose from her bits? Then she looked down to where Slowhand pointed, and gasped. She guessed that she'd never really thought too much about her recuperative abilities – just wondered at their presence – and, as a result, she'd never really studied them in action, but now she realised for the first time just how *dramatic* they were. Right in front of her eyes, the shallow wound that Slowhand had inflicted was sealing itself, healing in seconds.

Not for the first time, Kali thought, *what am I?*

But her concerns about her own abnormality were immediately replaced by a more pressing one. Namely, the implications of what had just happened for her current predicament. Slowhand had pulled a surprise card from up his sleeve, that was for sure, but the question was, how was he going to play it? Was he going to try to pass her off to these yazan as some kind of god? She sure as hells hoped not, because Twilight's mythology was littered with cautionary tales of why that kind of hubris was really, *really* not a good idea.

Slowly, she looked up at the faces of the yazan, and gasped again. For a second she wondered whether it was a trick of the light, but Slowhand's words seemed to suggest otherwise.

"That's why it had to be you, Hooper," he said. "Because you're *different*... like them."

Her mind reeling, Kali was only dimly aware that the yazan were backing off, gesturing to Slowhand in a way she guessed meant 'release her'. But, as momentous as what she had just seen had been, something else niggled at her as Slowhand freed her from her chains.

"Hold on just one farking minute," she said, and gestured at the pillar and chains and the hides that barely garbed her. "If you knew this was going to save me, why didn't you just slice me when I was paralyzed? Why all this pantomime?"

Slowhand coughed. "It was, erm, a tribal elder thing. Tradition. Yes, tradition."

"Really? And which ones are the tribal elders, then?"

"The elders... yes," Slowhand said, hesitantly. He moved his finger slowly round the cave and pointed at the yazan who stood near the entrance. "They would *beeeeeeeee*... that lot over there."

Kali folded her arms and tapped her foot. "I see. They don't look very *elderly* to me."

Slowhand paused. "Yes, well. They like their elders, er, young."

"It was you, wasn't it? The pillar, the chains, this *costume*. You said you wanted to do the sacrifice *your* way. Great Gods, you never miss a trick, do you? Hells, I'm surprised you didn't have me *oiled*."

"They only had yuk fat."

"You are a pervert, Killiam Slowhand."

"I know! I can't help it!"

"Well, I can't help this." Kali retorted. She booted him in the groin once more and, as the archer crumpled into a wheezing heap, turned and smiled at the yazan. "Sorry. Tradition."

The yazan accepting her as one of their own, now, Kali was permitted to leave the cave only to find herself in another, larger one. This appeared to be some gathering place for their people. Here, she found herself reunited with Aldrededor and Dolorosa who, despite their raised eyebrows at her garb, were, like the yazan themselves, comfortably seated around the fire whose glow she had seen from the pillar. She saw the reason for the shadowy altercations she had witnessed, too. The ex-pirates and the yazan were all gnawing heartily at chunks of roasted meat and, on occasion, some of the yazan tried to snatch Dolorosa's meat from her. The older woman was having none of it – as a rapidly unsheathed knife and a snarl proved – and, while Kali could appreciate her hunger after her ordeal, she found it quite *disturbing* how easily Dolorosa slipped into the tribal way of life. She smiled as the tall, thin woman winked at Slowhand as he hobbled in from the other cave, a greasy mass of dribble running down her chin.

Kali's smile faded, however, as she sat amongst the group, and it was replaced by a look of puzzlement. The yazan were different, all right. Human, yes, but sitting next to her was a man whose eyes were the colour of Long Night. Across from her, a woman whose skin was scaled as if her blood ran cold, and, next to her, another man whose skeleton, in places, grew outside his skin. She couldn't be sure but it looked as if one of them even had *gills*.

"Slowhand," she whispered as the archer, maskless now, settled beside her, "who are these people, what the hells is going on?"

"I don't know, but there are more like them, in caves all around here. Even some who are able to heal like you. Heal others, too. Believe me, I was in quite the mess when they brought me here."

Kali looked at him, concerned, but found herself staring instead at his *Endless Passion* tattoo. Was it, she wondered, anything to do with the younger female yazan who was blowing kisses at him from across the fire?

"Oh dear," she said, giving her a hard stare. "Still, you certainly seem to have *settled in*."

Slowhand harumphed, embarrassed. "Yes, that. Look, I told you, Hooper, they were thinking of offing *me*. I, er, had to *bond* with them."

"Bond with them? Right. And tell me, Killiam Slowhand, how many times, exactly, did you *bond*?"

"Hooper, it wasn't like that!" the archer protested, then reddened. "Besides, she's… different too."

"Pits, Slowhand, I leave you alone for a few weeks and suddenly you're setting up home with some tart with what, an extra orifi –? Oh, no, don't tell me, I don't want to know. I mean, it just occurred to me, even that chant of theirs – that *unka-chakka* – is the opening to that pitsing song I hate isn't it? *Isn't it!*"

"So ever since I've been in a stupor, because of that lass named Kali Hoooooper…" Slowhand sang, and smiled. "Truth is, Kal, I didn't feel much like coming down out of the mountains because what was the point? I thought you were dead."

There was something in Slowhand's tone that made Kali falter. "You're serious, aren't you?"

"Never more so."

"I thought you might be dead too."

"Well, I'm not," Slowhand grinned. "So… how you doing?"

"Oh, you know – *shit!*"

"Shit?"

"No, sorry, I…" Kali began and then trailed off.

Because, while Slowhand's *unka-chakka* had been nagging at her, something else had too. The name of the people they were with. The yazan, they called themselves. Despite her knowledge of ancient languages - elf, dwarf *and* human – she had never heard such a name before. There *was*, though, an elven word which was spelled differently but pronounced much the same. Only it wasn't a name, it was a description.

Yassan.

It meant *changed*.

She couldn't help but think of her own past, of how she had been found as a babe by Merrit Moon in that long lost and sealed Old Race site – and how different she had found herself to be in the time since. Just like the yassan. Neither she or the old man had ever found out where she had come from but could she have come from here? Was she really *like* them?

She shared her thoughts with Slowhand.

"Doubt it," Slowhand said. "There's a reason these people have never left the mountains, a reason their culture remains stagnated. Thing is, *if* they leave the mountains, they die."

"What? That's ridiculous."

"Tell the yassan that. They have funerals *before* they die – their old ones simply walking down the pass until they turn to dust. Dust, Hooper. Literally. As if abandoned by their god."

A place in the clouds where the Old Races played at being gods. "It has to be something to do with the Crucible."

"Crucible? You mean the Crucible of the Dragon God?"

"The Crucible of the *Dragon* God?"

"That's what they call it."

"They worship a dragon god? Why in the hells would they do that, when dragons have been extinct for thousands upon thousands of years, since before humans were around?"

"That is something I've been trying to work out."

"From what?"

"Their cave paintings."

"They have cave paintings?"

Slowhand smiled, as if he knew where he was going all along. He rose and offered her a hand up. "I know you love it when I talk dirty."

The archer took a flaming torch for each of them and escorted Kali through a series of caves heading upward, chatting as they walked as if simply out for a stroll.

"So, I guess the fact that you've turned up here means the world is ending again, right?"

"Pretty much."

"The k'nid?"

"The k'nid."

Slowhand nodded. "The yassan told me they've been pouring out of the mountains once every *seharn* – that's day to you. Met them myself. Lethal little bastards but I wouldn't quite have put them in the world-ending category."

Kali told him about Andon, and about the k'nid's ability to replicate.

"Hells. I shouldn't have been twiddling my thumbs up here. I could have done something to help."

"No, Slowhand, you couldn't. But you can now."

Slowhand stopped, smiled, swept back his hair. "Sidekick?"

"Sidekick."

"Gods, it's good to see you," the archer declared suddenly, and planted a smacker on her lips.

"*Iffgudderseyoodoo...*"

"What say that when we've saved the world we find a little cave somewhere, spread the furs and –"

Slowhand stopped as Kali froze in his arms then pushed him away, hard enough for him to collide with the wall. He raised his eyes as he realised where in the cave system they were, and what she must have seen behind him. The cave paintings.

The archer stood by her but Kali completely ignored him, already engrossed in what was depicted on the walls, running her fingers back and forth between the pictures as she concentrated on their meaning.

"Well?" he said. "They tell you anything?"

"Only the entire bloody history of the yassan. Gods, Slowhand, these people are descendants of Thunderlungs' and Mawnee's tribes, only they're not *true* descendants because the true bloodline was interrupted. It's possible even that the original tribes died out long ago." Kali paused, and took an excited breath. "No, this relates *another* legend about how their people were *taken* – taken to a place beyond the mountains – where they were changed by the god who lived there. A Dragon God, Slowhand! It goes on – *look* – saying that, in return for their service to the Dragon God, they would inherit the place beyond the mountains when the Dragon God ascended to... fark, that bit isn't clear. But the point, *the point is*, that this place beyond the mountains is described as a place in the clouds. A *place in the clouds*, Slowhand! It has to be what we're looking for. It has to be the Crucible!"

"So those jiggly lines are mountains?"

"The yassan – their Crucible – is it near?"

"Well, I don't know about the Crucible itself but the *way* to it certainly is."

"Where?"

Slowhand smiled in a way that suggested *he* now had the advantage, placed his hands on Kali shoulder's and turned her around.

"Oh!" was all that Kali could say.

Because, in her eagerness to examine the paintings, she hadn't even noticed that the part of the caves in which they stood was open on one side, a high snow-covered ledge looking out over a pass below. But it wasn't the pass that had left her lost for words. It was what lay across it.

Kali trudged onto the snowy ledge, exposed to a bitter night sky, hardly noticing the winds that buffeted her as she stared at a mountainside which, though some distance away, completely filled her field of vision. She was looking at one of the central peaks of the Drakengrats, heights almost as unscalable as those of the World's Ridge that should have had no way over them or through – except that this one did. Sort of.

The entire mountainside had been carved into the shape of an immense dragon's head, and beneath a pair of giant, brooding eyes and promontory sized snout, the dragon's roaring maw appeared to be some kind of tunnel. Appeared, that was, because the maw itself was exhaling a huge and constant, roiling mass of flame.

"They call it the Dragonfire," Slowhand said.

"Oh, we have *got* to find a way in there."

"Hooper, *finding* a way in might not be the problem. Chummy as we now are with them, I'm not sure how the yassan would react to us treading on their holy ground."

"Leave that to me," Kali said.

She turned swiftly away and retraced their steps through the caves, returning to the main gathering chamber and calling a meeting of the tribal elders – the *real* ones this time. Slowhand had to kick his heels as she conversed with them for an hour or more but, at last, she took up position on a raised part of the cave and addressed the yassan as a whole.

The archer wasn't to know how guilty she had felt manipulating the elders – telling them that she was obviously yassan but *special* yassan because she had lived beyond the mountains and survived – let alone breaking her own rules of hubris, because in the end the ploy seemed to work.

"Your elders have declared that I have been chosen!" Kali declared. "Chosen to calm the one you worship in this time of anger! Tomorrow myself and my followers depart for the Crucible of the Dragon God!"

For a moment the chamber was silent and then, increasing in volume as more and more voices joined in, echoed with a sound that despite the *followers* bit made the archer bow and preen.

"*UNKA-CHAKKA-UNKA-CHAKKA-OH-OH-OH!*

"*UNKA-CHAKKA-UNKA-CHAKKA-OH-OH-OH!*"

CHAPTER THIRTEEN

THEY STARTED OUT at dawn, taking most of the morning to reach the Dragonfire, the colossal scale of the cliff sculpture and its preternatural centrepiece deceptive, making the phenomenon appear much closer than it was and turning a seemingly short hike into a long, arduous trek. There were six in the party, Kali, Slowhand and four of the yassan. One to act as guide through a tortuous series of hidden mountain paths, caves and ravines, and three to tend and give offering before the enormous Godhead as other members of their tribe had done for countless years. Kali had decided she had already risked the lives of Aldrededor and Dolorosa too much to bring them along and so, to their frustration, had told them to remain behind with the tribe. They would rendezvous with them when they were done. The decision had, naturally, not gone down well, though the Sarcreans seemed somewhat mollified after she had taken them aside and suggested a way to make themselves useful.

Her overall plan was, she thought, a sound one, though with one pitsing great hole in it – the 'when they were done' bit. The truth of the matter was, she didn't have a clue what *was* to be done, because she didn't have a clue what to expect when they got where they were going.

The party arrived at last at the base of the Dragonfire and, standing beneath it, a somewhat breathless Kali found she could not crane her neck back far enough to take it all in. That the Godhead was awe inspiring was beyond question and their proximity to it had the effect on the four yassan that she had anticipated. Their heads bowed and eyes lowered, they diligently cleared its base of detritus and arranged their offerings of mountain flowers and intricately woven fetishes in rock bowls, their manner reverent and vaguely fearful. It was clear they dared not look upon the *Dragonfire* itself, let alone climb higher and actually approach it, which was handy for she and Slowhand because they could slip away without much attention being paid to them. Kali wasn't particularly happy that she had been less than truthful with the yassan, but if on the way up the rockface she suffered any *unchosen one* like falls, it was perhaps best they didn't see.

For a while as she and Slowhand clambered up the lower parts of the vast sculpture, she began to wonder whether that might indeed be their fate, because even though the wind whistled more harshly about them with each yard they climbed, it was as nothing compared to the roaring that reached them from above – from where the Dragonfire itself roiled into the world. It did indeed sound like the exhalation of some angry god, and only the fact that every bone in her body told her that it *couldn't be* stopped her turning back to rethink her plan. Slowhand reached the level of the fire before her and pulled himself up onto a ledge before it.

"Keep back!" she shouted up. "The heat could –"

To her surprise, Slowhand merely turned in a circle before it, his arms outstretched. "What heat? Hooper, it looks like fire, it roars like fire, but it isn't fire! It's just an illus –"

His words were cut short as his rotation brought him too close and the Dragonfire, rather than burning him, blew him back across the ledge. The archer thudded to the ground with an *oof!*

Kali flipped herself onto the ledge and made sure he was all right. "Serves you right. Idiot."

"Hey, how was I to know? You told me illusions are a favourite trick of the Old Races, right? Like the dancing beds at Cannista."

"Dancing *heads*," Kali corrected. *Gods, he really did have a one track mind.* "And I probably tell you far too much."

She offered a hand to help Slowhand up, and he grabbed it – the pair yelping as a spark of residual energy from his blow-back arced between them.

"Fark," Kali said, shaking her hand

"The power of the Dragon God?" Slowhand mused as he rubbed his own tingling fingers.

"More like the power of ancient technology. Some kind of force barrier. Very old and much weaker than it probably once would have been. Otherwise, you wouldn't be standing here now."

She stared up at the Dragonfire. The area over which it roiled was massive. Large enough, she realised with growing excitement, to permit an airship to pass through it.

"You're not telling me the yassan built this thing?"

"No, only the Godhead around it. The fire thing goes part of the way to explain their choice of deity, though, don't you think?"

"I think a better question is, is there any way through?"

Kali examined the area. "Doesn't seem to be any way to shut it down so I guess anything *meant* to pass through it, like an airship, must be recognised somehow – perhaps some kind of onboard, runic key."

"Doesn't do us a lot of good, then. All out of airships *and* runic keys."

"True, but maybe we can fight the magic with magic, *force* it to recognise us."

Slowhand spread his hands, looking around. "Except we seem to be lacking a mage."

"But we do have this," Kali said, unslinging her crackstaff. "It made a hole in the Expanse's echo of the Three Towers so maybe it can do the same here."

Remembering the force with which Slowhand had been blown back, she eased the tip of the staff into the Dragonfire, intending to build its charge slowly. "Better hide," she advised, feeling the tingle of the force barrier running through her body. "Don't want this blowing all your clothes off, do we?"

"Oh, funny," Slowhand said. Kali sensed him disappear from her side, then heard, "This do?"

Kali looked at him looking at her, his face wavering on the other side of the barrier. "Yes, that's fi –" she began, then stopped when she realised what she was seeing.

"Not so much of a know all, then," Slowhand said, with a grin.

"How in the hells did you – ?"

"Think about it, Hooper. If the ancestors of the yassan – who obviously didn't inherit the place because they're *out here* – and the k'nid escaped the Crucible, then they had to have a way out, right?" Slowhand looked insufferably smug and then cocked his thumb left. "Spotted it a moment ago. A small fissure just over there."

Kali looked where he indicated. "Dammit."

"Nice hairstyle," the archer commented as she retrieved the crackstaff and made her way to his side. "Vertical."

Kali patted down the stiffened stack. "Shut it."

Slowhand pretended to stagger back. "Are you *sulking*?" he asked, and glanced at the fissure. "Just because I found – ?"

Kali slammed her hands on her hips. "I am *not* sulking."

"You *are*. You're *sulking*."

"Look, can we just get on with this, please?"

"Fine, fine," Slowhand capitulated, then winked. "But you'd best let me go first, eh? Just in case you miss anything."

Kali growled and elbowed him out of the way, taking the lead into the tunnel. Her initial stomp soon turned into a slower and more awed tread, however, her neck craning again as she gazed upwards, realising just what a tunnel it was. Absolutely circular and clearly cutting right the way through the mountain, it was easily the size of one of the Lost Canals of Turnitia. The perfect smoothness of it indicated it had been bored using technology similar to the dwarven Mole, except on a much more ambitious scale. Hers was not the only mouth to hang open as she and Slowhand walked its length, their way lit by the same massive glowing tubes as had lit the waystation. Their passage through the mountain took some considerable time but, as they neared its end, they began to glimpse slivers of sky ahead, obfuscated by what appeared to be a mass of thick vegetation, possibly the tops of trees. That there was such growth here was surprise enough, but exactly *where* it grew was what took the proverbial redbread.

"Hooper," Slowhand said as they finally reached the tunnel's end. "Are you seeing what I'm seeing?"

"Oh, yeah," Kali responded, breathlessly.

They had emerged half way up another cliff-face and spread out before them, here in the highest heart of the Drakengrat Mountains, was a lush jungle valley. Completely surrounded by impassable and overlooming peaks – between which appeared to roil another barrier like the one they had passed through – it was a strange and fully verdant lost world that sat amongst the clouds. And there were structures in it. Structures that were not part of the jungle but had been overgrown by it. It was difficult to make out the details of them from where they stood because much of what they saw was obscured by the jungle itself, but both Kali and Slowhand got the impression they were looking at a number of *worlds*.

"The Crucible of the Dragon God?" Slowhand hazarded.

"Why don't we go ask him?"

"That looks as if it might be easier said than done."

Slowhand was right. The structures loomed high in the jungle and so they were going to have a problem accessing them. There was another problem, too, though one that was more theoretical than practical. It was now clear to Kali that this valley – *these worlds* – were meant to be reached only by air, and as a consequence of that only by those with the *technology* for air travel, and that troubled her. That they were here, so remote, so hidden, and that the force barrier at their only entrance was designed to stop unwanted intruders, made one previously unrealised question nag at her mind. If this place *was* Old Race – and in her mind there was little doubt of that – who exactly was it that its inhabitants had been protecting themselves against? There would have been no one else around at the time who *had* the technology to reach here except more Old Race. So were the people who had built here defending against their *own*? Why? What the hells was the Crucible of the Dragon God for?

There was only one way to find out. They had to negotiate the jungle.

Kali and Slowhand began to carefully descend the rockface into the thick and overgrown mass. She had the impression that the valley – if, indeed, it was a natural valley at all – had been razed some time in its distant past. Razed to allow the construction of these worlds, but in the endless years since these structures had last been inhabited nature had reasserted herself, entwining, enwrapping and growing between the artificial interlopers to their present state. That fact was reinforced as they moved across the jungle floor where, progressing towards the centre, they began to come across various constructions attached to them – support struts and the like – which *had* to have been built in the absence of the rampant vegetation. Both of them were on constant alert for any creatures that might call this place home, but none came, and the feeling that Kali hadn't been able to shake – that they were the first to tread here in an unimaginable age – became all the more pervasive. There was, she felt, a *reason* nothing was here. There was something horribly lonely about the place, almost unbearably still and sad, as if once upon a time something momentous had happened but that its effect upon the world had, in the end, been ultimately insignificant.

She and Slowhand continued to work their way through the jungle – he pulling branches out of the way, she slashing through the tendrils with her gutting knife – and eventually reached the centre of the valley. Here they were beneath the largest of the worlds they had seen, whose size completely obscured what little sky they had previously been able to see. It was a vast sphere, supported high into the trees by a framework of girders that made it look like a giant bulbous spider suspended in a metal web. It was impressive and inviting but Kali's appreciation of it was somewhat dulled by the fact that, from her and Slowhand's position, there seemed to be no way in. None designed, anyway. But the fact that the valley had returned to the wild offered an alternative.

"We can use the vegetation to get part of the way up," Kali said. "After that, we'll have to make it up as we go along."

Slowhand craned his neck and saw the branches of trees twisting and spiralling heavenward until they were lost from sight. "One hells of a climb, Hooper."

"I'll go first."

"Oh, be my guest."

Kali gestured for Slowhand to give her a boost up and, kicking off from his entwined hands, she leapt for a branch, grabbing onto it with a grunt. She pulled herself up and walked its length, before leaping for another branch above. The thickness of the foliage was stifling and she was already beginning to lose sight of Slowhand. For a moment she wondered why he hadn't yet started following. He was probably waiting for her to get out of the way, she reasoned, so the smaller branches didn't slap him in the face. Continuing on, she worked her way higher and higher, through branch after branch, until the trunk's appendages became more pliant beneath her hands and feet. Kali used this, however, to her advantage, bouncing and springing from the lower ones to their higher counterparts, speeding her ascent to double what it had been before. At that speed, it took her no longer than five minutes to reach the uppermost part of the tree, and suddenly she found herself able to peer out across the canopy.

Unfortunately, the canopy was still not as high as the metal structure, and from here on in her makeshift ladder would no longer be natural but Old Race made.

As Kali worked her way to the outer tip of one of the highest branches, coming closer to the upper side of the sphere, she saw that it was definitely of Old Race construction. The smooth, runic covered and organic quality of its material was a dead giveaway. The only problem was that said material, though close to the end of the branch, was just beyond a distance that she could leap, even though her leaps could be considerable. But the tree came to the rescue once again as Kali realised she could use two of the branches to slingshot herself across the gap.

Tricky, but possible.

Kali positioned herself back near the trunk, pulling the branches with her until they were tense, then, releasing one, used it to fling herself into the second, releasing the tension in that as she did so. The double spring effect catapulted her from the foliage of the tree and into open air, and then she slammed onto the curve of the sphere itself.

From here it became trickier. Although the sphere's incline was not acute, it was slippery, and Kali found herself scrabbling for purchase as soon as she landed, then having to flatten herself on its surface to prevent herself sliding off. Thus positioned, she began to inch her way forward and upward. But though vegetation had so far aided her ascent, now it stymied it.

Unmaintained and exposed to the elements for countless years, the upper curve of the sphere was covered in a slippery lichen and each time Kali tried to pull herself across it, she slipped back. There was no way around it and the only other access to the top of the sphere was via some kind of walkway that curved above it, but that was at least a hundred yards higher than her current position.

There was nothing else for it. She had to negotiate the lichen.

Pulling herself upward, even more slowly than before, Kali began to inch her way over the grassy coating, digging her fingertips and toes into the material for purchase. But the purchase was slight and, again and again, Kali found herself taking one step forward and two steps back. Increasingly frustrated, she found herself flinging any attempt at a negotiated passage to the wind, and instead simply clawed her way forward whichever way she could.

She had gained perhaps fifteen feet when a whole swathe of lichen became detached from the sphere, its tiny roots ripped away beneath the weight of her body. Kali tried to throw herself over it but felt one foot skid under her, and the other, and then thought, *oh-oh*.

Suddenly, she was accelerating back down the sphere, the carpet of lichen on which she lay now acting as a sled.

"*Whooooooaaaaaahhhhh!*"

She was too distracted by the likelihood of imminent death to hear the *ziiiip* of something thin and fast shooting past her. She was too distracted to notice had it been an inch to the left the shaft of wood that had made the sound might have gone right through her. But she was not too distracted to feel herself jar to a sudden stop, in the arms of something that smelled strangely familiar.

"Slowhand?"

"Hi, Hooper, falling for me?" the archer said, with a broad grin.

Even as she watched his long mane of blond hair being buffeted by the wind, and as she felt the two of them begin to rise, she couldn't believe he'd said it.

Kali looked down. There was nothing beneath them, nothing at all. She looked up, and saw a thin wire stretching up to where it was fastened by an arrow in the underside of the walkway. And she looked at Slowhand's free hand, clutching a small and complex looking device, which seemed to be, thanks to some mechanical workings, carrying them up the wire.

"Little something I worked on during my time with the yassan."

"Really?"

"Yup. Call it a whizzline."

"A *whizzline?*"

"Yup."

Slowhand's smile of satisfaction was rapidly erased as Kali suddenly shouted in his face.

"Are you telling me that I just went through all that for nothing!"

"Hooper, now hang on –"

"Hang on, he says! Do I have a lot of farking choice!"

"Well, no, but –"

"Slowhand, you are a –"

"Hey, I saved you from a horrible death, didn't I?"

"You wanna know about horrible deaths? I'll show you..."

The exchange might have continued were it not for the fact that, at that moment, Slowhand's whizzline device reached its apex and the two of them found themselves dangling beneath the walkway, having come to a dead stop. They stared at each other as, beneath their combined weight, the line creaked above them, and then in unison yelped as the arrow holding it loosened slightly from where it was embedded.

"I think we'd better – *yaaaarrgh!*" Slowhand said.

They fell.

Kali didn't hesitate, swinging her legs up so that they wrapped Slowhand about the middle, and then flipping backwards in mid air so that her feet hooked over a small rail on the underside of the walkway. Then, with a grunt, she jacknifed herself upwards and grabbed onto the same rail, lowering her legs until Slowhand dangled between them, beneath her. The archer stared up from between her thighs.

"This," he said, "is like a dream."

"You want me to open them?"

"Er, not right now, no."

There was a moment's pause.

"Right."

A few seconds later, Kali had manoeuvred the pair of them onto the walkway and they stared at what lay in front of and beneath them.

"Slowhand," Kali said, bending to place her palms on her thighs and taking a deep breath. "I think we're here."

"*Hoooo, boy.*"

As the highest point amongst the whole, strange series of structures, the walkway afforded the two of them their first proper view of the complex. Kali realised then that she hadn't been far wrong with her first impression that the valley was full of worlds.

A number of spheres of various sizes – though all massive – dotted the hidden place, some projecting ornate walkways to their neighbours, others on, or attached to, huge metal tracks or arms – one of which bore cradles and the rotted remains of more airships like those at the waystation – all sitting there amidst the overgrown trees. *Literally* complex and wondrous, Kali could see no reason why such should be its purpose but she couldn't help being reminded of something she had once seen used by the Sisters of Long Night. A mechanical contraption they told her was meant to emulate the movement of the celestial bodies on and around which they lived – something they called an orrery. That was what the Crucible reminded her of – a giant orrery, constructed for reasons she couldn't yet begin to imagine.

There, roughly speaking, was Kerberos, the largest sphere and the one beneath them, there, in its shadow, Twilight, and there, further out, its size perhaps representative of its actual distance, Twilight's sun. The only sphere Kali could not reconcile with what she knew of the heavens was one that was positioned somehow jarringly amongst the others – a sphere constructed of a darker material than its companions that looked as if had once drawn ever closer to them on a perfectly straight track through the trees. Kali frowned – in all her explorations she had never come across anything like this, and the only way she was going to discover the purpose of the spheres was to get inside them. Fortunately, there appeared to be a gap in *Kerberos* – as if once upon a time the upper half of the sphere had, for some reason, opened to the skies. Its edges now browned with great patches of rust, it seemed jammed in that position, but it was wide enough for their purposes. The only problem would be in reaching it without a repeat of her recent, almost fatal mishap.

"Remember Scholten?" Slowhand asked, winking.

He unslung Suresight and strung an arrow with a wire attached. Kali nodded. She wouldn't easily forget that stormy night and the suicide slide from the heights of the Cathedral. A slide that had come to a rude end when Katherine Makennon's guards had cut the line.

"You joining me this time?" she queried.

"Wouldn't miss it for the, er, world," Slowhand told her, nodding at the sphere.

He raised Suresight, aiming the arrow on a shallow trajectory, and then fired it through the gap. A second later he tested its tension and then attached the zipline. "Grab hold."

Kali did as instructed, wrapping her arms around Slowhand's torso and her legs around his, ignoring some ribald comment as the archer shuffled himself against her. Then he lurched and the two of them began to speed down the wire towards the shadowy gap.

As they slid through it into a dark and still interior, the metallic *zuzz* of the zipline sounded suddenly sharp, though not as sharp as would have been their cries of pain had they struck any of the odd, unidentifiable shapes that whizzed by them in the gloom. Thankfully, the interior of the sphere was vast, and none were in their way. Exactly what they were sliding into remained a mystery but, as was her habit on entering any Old Race site, Kali sniffed as she descended, trying to take in the odour of the place. There was metal and oil and the rough, sour tang of machinery. An odour she had smelled before in a site called Kachanka, one of her finds that had been some kind of dwarven factory. She never had discovered what it made. For all she knew it could have been dwarven razorblades, in which case, no wonder it had gone out of –

"End of the line!" Slowhand warned suddenly, and the two of them released their grips, dropping with a clang onto metal where they rolled to soften their impact.

Unexpectedly, they continued to roll, and – after mutual yelps of surprise – they realised they had landed on a sloping surface and were apparently sliding now towards the base of some huge bowl. When at last they came to a stop, they were up and ready to defend themselves,

Slowhand panning a primed Suresight around him, Kali the same with her crackstaff. They saw nothing coming at them out of the dark, however, and reslung the weapons. Now, they listened, but the only sounds they heard were those of their own, heavy breathing and of the sphere itself – loud, eerie creaks and groans of metal shifting and settling. One such shift was so pronounced that the sphere actually shook, and the pair rocked on the soles of their feet.

"Whatever this place is," Slowhand commented, "it feels as if it's coming apart at the seams."

"It's *ancient*, Slowhand. What do you expect?"

"I've a feeling it's more than just age that's caused this."

Their eyes began slowly adjusting to the gloom and, as they did, they gasped.

Because they seemed to have landed on a walkway that curved along the base of the sphere, and off to their left and their right. The trouble was, as their slide had testified, it didn't *stop* to their left and their right. Instead it curved up the sides of the sphere and then, disorientatingly, not least because of the dizzying height involved, curved across its top, crossing the gap through which they had entered, and down again in a complete loop, coming full circle back to the spot where they stood. Nor was it the only walkway to do so. The interior of the sphere was criss-crossed with them, weaving a web-like pattern over its cathedral sized interior, as if the terms up, down, above and below had no meaning here. To be certain what she was seeing was true, Kali attempted to renegotiate the curve of the walkway but made it only so far before its incline slid her back. Craning her neck and turning on the spot, she gazed open mouthed, tracing all the walkways and wondering whether some sorcery that had enabled people to traverse these impossible ways had, once upon a time, been at play here. This remained a possibility until Slowhand noticed that the walkways were suspended a little way above the shell of the sphere, and that between the two a series of tracks, gears and gimbals hinted that they had been designed to move around its inside. A latticework sphere *within* a sphere, apparently rotatable through three hundred and sixty degrees in every direction so that any point of any walkway could rapidly shift into any position it needed to be in. It was a more prosaic explanation than sorcery, for sure, but was no less staggering for it. An incredible achievement of Old Race engineering unlike any they had ever seen. One question nagged at Kali, though. What exactly was it *for*?

Maybe part of the answer lay in what slowly became visible *between* the walkways. The vague shapes that had had whizzed by them during their descent were revealing themselves now to be tools and machines of various shapes, unknown purposes and sizes, all of which were aligned towards or – on their *own* independent tracks – capable of being aligned towards the centre of the sphere. Strange instruments like giant thrusting lances and claws, huge lenses and multiple-jointed things that looked like nothing less than upturned metallic spiders. The central focus of these tools made Kali rethink her initial impression of the place, feeling now that this was no razorblade factory but designed to build something big, and she suddenly desired to see the ancient machinery in action. The huge inner sphere whirling and swirling about its task – whatever it was – and all of those various machines and tools at play, perhaps flashing and sparking with unknown energies, would have been of such complexity that it would have made the mechanics of the Clockwork King seem like those of a child's toy.

It *would* have been wondrous but, sadly, Kali doubted that it would ever work again. The interior of the sphere was almost as decayed as its exterior and, in parts, as overgrown as the jungle beyond. Swathes of lichen draped the walkways and machines, choking them, while great curtains of the stuff hung from the sides of the opening itself. Here and there plants had actually taken root amidst the machines. The sphere had gone almost to ruin, the vast mechanism that seemed the reason for its existence appearing, for all intents and purposes, dead.

Almost.

It was Slowhand who noticed it first, squinting at the heart of the sphere.

What had previously appeared to be empty space shimmered and rippled slightly, as if he were looking at some great globe of transparent liquid suspended in the air, extending out as far as the machinery around it and big enough that, if he so wished, he could almost reach out to touch it. The liquid reflected its surroundings in such a way – refracted them, in fact – that it seemed almost not to be there at all. It hung undisturbed, as if it were somehow part of an entirely different reality.

"Erm, Hooper?" the archer said. "What the hells is this?"

Kali turned her attention to where Slowhand pointed. Her heart missed a beat. What she was looking at was something she knew existed from her researches but which, before now, she hadn't encountered. It was one of the older sorceries of the elves, a thing that toyed with existence and was designed to mislead, to obfuscate – to *hide* those things that they wished kept secret from the world. The elves had a name for it. They called it a glamour field.

"You know what it is?"

"A-ha. But the question is, what's inside?"

"Some magical portal? To the realm of the k'nid?"

Kali frowned, bit her lip. Here in this place of technology that didn't feel *right*. "Somehow... I don't think so."

"So what do we do, shut it down?"

Kali shook her head. "Even if we knew how, that wouldn't be wise until we know what we're dealing with. We need to take a good look around."

Slowhand raised his eyebrows. "That's a tad cautious for you, Hooper. What happened to 'ooh, ooh, ooh, what does this big red button do?'"

"Funny. But usually the sites I explore don't have the bloody k'nid pouring out of them."

"Point taken. Well, there's no sign of the little bastards here so... the other spheres?"

"The other spheres," Kali agreed.

The pair began to look for a way through to the next sphere but, while they found it, accessing it was easier said than done. The non-manoeuvrability of the internal walkways meant that the entrance to one of the connecting bridges – a passage near to the construction's equator – could only be reached either by Slowhand's zipline or a long and complicated climb. Rather than risk an arrow coming loose at the wrong time if the sphere shook again, they decided on the latter. The archer took the lead, deftly negotiating the various projections, and Kali followed noting, as she did, that despite their condition some of the machines still seemed to thrum slightly beneath her feet, a sign that their surroundings were not quite as dead as they had first appeared.

Something else, however, was.

Slowhand had just reached the lip of the passage and grabbed onto it, ready to heave himself up, when his hand skidded away from the surface and he fell back with a cry, only escaping a rather swift and bumpy return to his starting point when Kali grabbed him by the wrist. She held on tightly as he dangled beneath her, giving him a chance to regain his footing, helping him roll himself over the lip. Unexpectedly, he cried out again, but only because he had discovered what it was that had made his hand slip in the first place.

"*Ohhhh, hells!*"

"What is it?"

"Trust me, Hooper, you don't want to know."

"I do. It might be important."

"Oh, I've no doubt that it is. But –"

Kali quickly leapt up next to him then, with a squeal, leapt just as quickly aside.

"Warned you."

Kali grimaced. She had been standing on – more accurately, *in* – the rotting corpse of one of the Final Faith. The slimy and bubbling remains were clearly victim of a k'nid attack, brought down on this spot as it – its gender was hard to determine – had apparently tried to run. What made it so repulsive and different to other victims they had seen was that it clearly hadn't been fully absorbed. As if, for some reason, the k'nid involved had abandoned the process part way through. But, as Slowhand rather irreverently pointed out, it wasn't like them not to finish a snack.

"So what happened?" he asked.

"I don't know. Maybe it was interrupted by something."

"Interrupted?" Slowhand repeated, panning Suresight about him once more. "By what? The place is abandoned. Isn't it?"

"That's the theory."

"*Right.*"

"I know one thing, though," Kali added, nodding ahead, "and that's that we're on the right track."

Slowhand looked. "Ohhhh, hells."

"Exactly."

Kali and Slowhand moved into the passage they had found and, at its end, onto a bridge between spheres – half overgrown with trees – picking their way carefully past more of the Final Faith; ten or so, all similarly and horribly dead. As they crossed, the *Kerberos* sphere shook once more behind them, more violently than ever.

"I guess these are the ones that didn't make the airship," Slowhand commented.

Kali swallowed. "Do you think your sister abandoned them?"

Slowhand took a second to answer, the face he pictured in his mind not Jenna, then said through gritted teeth, "I'd like to think she didn't have a choice."

The pair reached the far end of the bridge and entered the sphere Kali had designated *Twilight*.

The first thing they noticed was that the difference between it and 'Kerberos' couldn't have been more marked. For one thing, this sphere was not hollow like the other, possessing a floor at the level they entered which was divided into corridors and chambers. For another, its style of interior construction was distinctly opposed to the sphere they had left. Where *Kerberos* and all its heavy machinery had struck her as being predominantly dwarven, the almost organic and membranous make-up of *Twilight* was unmistakably elven. The fact that both spheres co-existed in the same complex – together with the presence of the elven glamour field in the dwarven *Kerberos* – led Kali to only one possible conclusion: this was a joint venture of both of the Old Races. That in itself wasn't unknown in the latter years of their civilisations' existence – where their magics and technologies had combined for the good of both – but in a place such as this, in such a way and on such a scale? What had brought them together to do this?

Kali and Slowhand began, slowly and cautiously, to explore the corridors and chambers about them. Some of these, however, were not immediately accessible as their doors were either sealed with thick membranes or they appeared to have been barricaded by the Final Faith in some desperate attempt to stave off the k'nid. The latter tactic had not been overly successful, judging by the number of bodies they found littering the place. Kali found it astounding that the Faith had sent so many of their people here – top-ranking academics judging by their robes – and realised that they had obviously attached great importance to the complex's capabilities, whatever they were.

Some clues started to present themselves as they explored further, not only *in situ* but also in a number of containers the Faith academics had packed with carefully preserved anatomical and biological diagrams of ancient origin as well as information crystals of a type Kali recognised from previous sites. That these containers were found in laboratories filled with vials, test tubes, examination slabs and other kinds of scientific trappings, including complex and delicate machines beyond understanding, suggested that they were records of experiments the Old Races had conducted – perhaps that the Faith wished to replicate – but experiments into what, with what, and for what purpose? A further clue came when Slowhand somehow triggered the opening of a number of small and strange, crystalline drawers in an adjacent chamber. Kali looked and saw that inside, indexed with elven pictograms, were what appeared to be organic tissue samples of every animal that she knew existed – and many, many that she didn't. There was the grank at the top of the food chain, to the bassoom in the middle, all the way to the humble worgle at the bottom. There were samples of insect life, too, of avian, reptilian and aquatic lifeforms, and there, in a section of their own, those of elves, dwarves and – Kali swallowed slightly – humans.

What disturbed her the most was that, in almost every case, the indexing attached to the specimens was cross-referenced to others – sometimes two or three, sometimes seven or eight, or sometimes as many as twenty other specimens in the collection.

"What *is* this?" Slowhand said.

"Disturbing," was all Kali could say in reply.

Again, she and Slowhand moved on, working their way towards the hub of *Twilight* now, passing chambers even more mystifying than those they had already investigated.

Here was a chamber whose circumference was lined with membranous booths, most of which stirred with what looked like variously coloured gases; here one whose laboratory equipment was, bafflingly, positioned on the ceiling; and here a considerably larger and perfectly circular chamber whose only content was a strangely shaped chair suspended on the end of a metal arm looking like the hour hand of some giant clock. The purpose of these devices was, for now, beyond their ken and, shrugging to each other, they ignored them, coming at last to a point where the corridor joined – *became* – a circular affair surrounding the hub itself. This was clearly a centre of activity as other corridors joined it at regular points but, like some of the earlier doors, they had all been barricaded by the Faith. Neither Slowhand or Kali were very much interested in what lay along them, however, because their attention had instead become fixed on what actually lay at the heart of *Twilight*.

"Slowhand?"

"Don't look at me. I haven't a clue."

They were staring at another sphere within the sphere, or at least half of one. For a broad hemisphere lay in front of them – one that perhaps would take a hundred men to surround with arms outstretched – but this one was transparent, made of a substance that felt like soft glass, and its interior slowly roiled with a thick green fog. From what Kali and Slowhand could see through the fog, the interior of the hemisphere did not end at floor level but went much deeper, and they realised that they were looking through some kind of observation dome into the lower half of *Twilight*. There was some kind of chamber down there, a completely organic space whose uneven floor was punctured by perhaps fifty circular holes, each the size of a farmstead's well. They appeared to contain liquid, too, but it was not water. Instead, there was a slowly bubbling, lava-like gloop the colour of the mist it produced that was slightly overflowing their edges.

"Looks like pea soup," Slowhand commented.

"Oh, I think it's *some* kind of soup, all right. Just not the kind you'd serve at dinner."

Kali studied the chamber further, noting three demi arches that arced over the wells, their tips almost meeting above their centre. An odd looking runed prism was suspended between the tips, though it looked damaged and skewed. But even so, every few seconds, it discharged spidery, slowly dancing bolts of energy into the wells themselves, as if it were in some way *vitalising* them. Kali's attention turned to the hemisphere itself, and here she noted that it was not completely transparent but instead etched all around its circumference with the same pictograms that had indexed the specimen drawers.

Thousands of them, one after the other. The fact that these etchings glowed slightly suggested they were more than simple decoration. They reminded her of the 'orchestral' selection controls she had once used in the Forbidden Archive and she knew instinctively that if she danced her palms over them she would be combining one species with another in whatever combination she wished. Merrit Moon had been right when, back in Gargas, he'd said that the Old Races had been playing gods. The wells beneath them were not wells, they were *birthing pools* for whatever was created within them.

"The Crucible of the Dragon God," Kali said. "We've found it."

"So we know where the k'nid come from. Unfortunately, I don't think we've come at the best time."

"What?"

"Time's up, Hooper. They're spawning again."

Kali snapped her gaze back into the fog and thought, *dammit*.

Their exploration of the spheres had obviously taken longer than they had reckoned because something was indeed happening down there. Something they had come to prevent but were now forced to be witness to. From each of the birthing pools a small platform was rising and atop each platform, gloop dripping from its irregular, angular flanks, was a k'nid. The dark, unnatural creatures did not move until they had fully risen from their pools but then they burst into frantic activity. Some sped up what appeared to be a circular pathway just discernable around the wall of the chamber and a second later could be heard battering at one of the Faith-erected barricades, others headed out of view of the observation dome and did not return, perhaps finding some other exit from the chamber. Still others, sensing Kali and Slowhand above, launched themselves the not inconsiderable height towards the dome itself. One actually made it, thudding upside down against the transparent substance, and was followed in quick succession by another, and then another.

"Whoa!" Slowhand said, backing up. He unslung Suresight and aimed at the dome.

"I wouldn't worry too much. This stuff is probably tougher than it loo –"

The soft glass tore before her eyes, rent by the scrabbling of the k'nid. Fog billowed through – noxious and foul.

"Yeah?" Slowhand said, loosing three rapid arrows while coughing. "You wanna think that one through again?"

"Shit!" For a moment Kali considered blasting the k'nid with her crackstaff, but she had no idea how volatile the fog that accompanied them might be. There was only one alternative. "Run!"

"Where?"

"Anywhere!"

The sound of the dome tearing accompanied Kali and Slowhand's footfalls. These were soon drowned out as more of the k'nid trailed the others through the newly created exit. Kali didn't look back to count, but from the noise she reckoned at least another five of the things were in pursuit. It didn't take an arithmetical genius to work out that eight k'nid was eight too many. Nor did it take a genius to work out that if they didn't get the hells out of their way, they were dead. But where to run to? All of the laboratories they had explored so far were open and offered no protection, and the sealed doors were out, but there had to be somewhere. Finally, she noticed one of the chambers they had passed earlier – the one with the gas filled booths – and ran towards it. One of the booths appeared clear of gas and, hammering on it to test its strength, Kali punched a panel on its outside which she hoped would open it. The front of the booth slid aside.

She grabbed Slowhand and threw him into the chamber, before following him. As she squeezed up to the archer the door slid shut. A second later, the k'nid slammed into their makeshift refuge, shaking it but otherwise unable to gain entry.

Slowhand stared out at the scrabbling things, the sound of their assault muted, his face pressed up against the side of Kali's head. "Cosy."

"Cramped is the word I'd use."

Kali shuffled round so that they were face to face, trying to avoid as much body contact with Slowhand as she could. But it wasn't easy – thigh pressed against thigh and breasts against torso – she could barely raise her arms before they were touching the smooth walls of their circular confinement.

"Closet?" Slowhand hazarded.

"There's nothing in it."

"We're in it."

"I'd noticed."

"Okay. One of those elevators then?"

"Not going anywhere."

"True." Slowhand smiled as the tips of their noses touched, and he puckered up. "Maybe it's a private *lurrrvv* chamber."

"Then maybe Endless Passion would like to join you in here." Kali said through gritted teeth.

"Hey, I already said, nothing happe –" The archer stopped, looking taken aback. "Hooper, are you *hissing* at me?"

"I *do not* hiss." But she had heard the sound herself. "I thought it was, you know... your problem."

"What problem? Hooper, I do not have a prob –"

If Kali had been able, she would have put her fingers to his lips, shushing him, but all she could do was body-bump him to keep him quiet. "I think you do now."

There was indeed a hissing but neither of them were responsible for it. For a second, Kali worried that the chamber was flooding with gas like the others, but if it was it had no colour or odour. Then, both isolated the source at the same time and looked up. There was some kind of fan above, rotating ever more swiftly, and as Kali watched it was time for Slowhand's hair to progress in an upward direction. Amusing as that was, it clearly wasn't right. Neither was the fact that she was having difficulty breathing.

"Slowhand, do you feel hot, breathless, as if you're expanding?"

"Every time I'm near you," the archer said. The fact that he wheezed and his eyes bulged, took some of the humour out of it.

"I think something's sucking the air out."

"Oh, come on! Why would someone build a room that sucked the air out? Hooper, are you making eyes at me?"

"No. The pressure's dropping, fast, and if we don't get out of here right now, we're dead."

Despite the fact the k'nid still scrabbled no more than an inch away, she was willing to take her chances outside rather than in, and thumped the booth. But the door did not reopen. She tried again. Nothing.

"Must be on some kind of timer," she said.

"What? *Ow!*"

"Ow?"

"My ears just popped!"

"Ow! Mine too. Hey, Slowhand, you know you're getting fat?"

"Hey, *you* can talk!"

Kali stared at the archer, who was indeed fatter, his face, particularly, bloating to perhaps twice its normal size. She was aware of her own doing so, too. But it wasn't just their faces – their whole bodies were starting to expand now, pressing them even more tightly together. Kali could see Slowhand's blood vessels bulging on his temples and neck even as she felt her own blood beginning to pulse painfully in her veins. *The air's gone!* she tried to say, but nothing came out – no sound at all – and across from her Slowhand's mouth moved uselessly. Kali tried to reach her equipment belt for her breathing conch, but it was too late, their expanded forms too crushed, and instead all she could do was look at Slowhand in panic, noticing how his tongue had begun to swell from his mouth, as she felt her own doing from hers.

Hooper, Slowhand mouthed, though it was difficult to make out the forming of even that one word. She didn't really need to, though, because the expression on her lover's face said everything that he wanted to say. He was confused and knew they were going to die, but he was also glad he was by her side and wanted to say goodbye.

She mouthed his name in return, so very, very sorry that she had gotten him into this mess. Furious, too. But only with herself. Gods, how could this have happened so quickly? How could she have come so far only to let it end like this? By stupidly stumbling – stupidly dragging them *both* – into something she didn't understand?

Her vision began to flare and darken until she could barely see Slowhand. Then, in that darkness, she felt her brain began to thud in time with her heartbeat, each beat clutching and agonising.

The beats got heavier and slower.

Heavier and slower.

Then her heart seemed to explode, and she no longer felt anything at all.

CHAPTER FOURTEEN

"Hooper, can you hear me? Hooper?"

The voice filled her mind, resonant and familiar. All there was in an otherwise deep and dark world. She floated there until the voice spoke again, and this time shook at the sound of it. No, something shook *her*. *Was* shaking her, again and again. The darkness began to swoop about her, blooming and flaring with light, and then her mind seemed to surge upwards, bringing a dizzying confusion, a lurching imbalance and a desperate need to steady the world. But all it did was shake some more.

"Hooper? Hooper, dammit, wake up!"

She sat upright, her eyes snapping open. There was a man in front of her, holding her tightly by the arms. Instinctively, she nutted him.

"*Ow! Dammit!* Steaming pits of... easy, Hooper, it's me."

"Slowhand? Shit, sorry."

"You okay?"

"Think so," Kali said, though from the lump on the side of *her* head she'd taken one hells of a bump. She looked around, saw she was sitting on the floor of the booth. "What the hells happened?"

Slowhand pulled her to her feet. "Dunno. A noise. Don't know how to describe it – wailing, spooky, like the sound of some old elven instrument. Whatever it was, it spooked the k'nid. They left the booth alone, disappeared, and the next thing I knew, the door opened and we were falling out. That's where you got the bump."

"Someone chased away the k'nid and let us out?"

"Looks that way. And that's not all. One of the doors in the corridor – one that was sealed before – that opened, too."

Kali raised an eyebrow. "Then why are we waiting? Let's go meet our saviour."

"Hold on. Our *saviour* could be the one who built that bloody deathtrap in the first place."

"I don't think it *is* a deathtrap."

"Pitsing well feels like one to me. I mean, come on, Hooper, what else could it be?"

"Don't know. But if the other door's open, maybe it's an invitation to find out?"

She moved out and, shaking his head, Slowhand followed. The pair passed through the unsealed door and neared another that was still sealed, seemingly a dead end until, somewhat unnervingly, it opened of its own accord. The same thing happened further on, and then again, their route clearly being manipulated through areas of the complex which, judging by the undisturbed layers of dust and cobwebs, the Final Faith had not been allowed to tread. In fact, these new chambers had a lonely feel to them that suggested to Kali that no one had entered them since the time of the Old Races themselves.

At last they came to a spiral staircase winding up the wall of an otherwise featureless chamber and both paused at its base, peering through thick and foreboding strings of cobweb to darkness above. The fact that the sphere shook at that moment seemed somehow appropriate.

"I think we're there," Kali said. She brushed the web aside and placed a tentative foot on the first riser. "Lair of the Dragon God, anyone?"

"Hooper, are you sure you – ?"

Kali gave him a look and Slowhand shut up. Because he knew that look – *the* look – the one of girlish excitement she couldn't contain when she knew she was near some significant find. Sometimes he wondered why she just didn't jump up and down, clapping her hands...

"There's something here, 'Liam. I feel it. There's *intelligence* here."

Slowhand nodded, and the pair of them took the steps slowly, one at a time, until they emerged into a spacious, yet almost featureless chamber. The one feature it *did* contain, however, was another sphere. In this case a large, membranous one filled with a liquid clearer though not dissimilar to that in the birthing wells. Stirring within it was what appeared to be some kind of plant. A fragile, multi-stranded, frond-like affair that made Kali think of some wavering growth on the ocean floor.

"It's a fish tank," Slowhand said flatly, pulling a face. "Gotta say, bit anticlimactic."

"Probably not a fish tank, Slowhand..." Kali said, patiently. She hoped not, anyway.

"Oh, *come on*. Can't you just see some little gogglefish darting in and out of that water feature ther –"

The archer quietened as Kali touched the sphere and, in response, another voice overrode his own, booming around them.

"Welcome, Kali Hooper. I have awaited your arrival for a very long time."

Kali and Slowhand stared at each other as the greeting resonated through the chamber, but while both waited in expectation of what might follow, no more words came. Kali stared around the chamber, hoping to discern the origin of the voice but, failing, fixed her attention back on the sphere. She guessed some reply to the greeting might be in order but, in the circumstances, she wasn't quite sure what she should say.

"Really?" she hazarded, after a second. "That's nice."

"That's nice?" Slowhand repeated, incredulous. The more cautious archer was already readying Suresight to loose an arrow at anything that came at them. "You may have been around a bit but don't you find the fact that something in this graveyard knows your name just a little disturbing?"

Kali couldn't deny that she did find it disturbing. But not because she had been referred to by name – as far as she knew her name could simply have been overheard sometime during their explorations. No, what disturbed her was the fact that the voice had said she had been *awaited*. Because this reminded her once again of her conversation with the fish-thing in the ruins of Martak, and its comment then that she was *where she should be*. Ever since that encounter, she had railed against what that meant, and to be faced with a similar comment now brought back all the worries that somehow, without her knowledge or consent, her life was following a preordained path.

"Who are you?" she asked. "Where are you?"

"My being, all around you. My physical form, before you."

"You? You're – ?"

"Hooper," Slowhand said worriedly, "maybe that bump did more harm than we thought. You do know you're talking to a plant?"

Kali ignored him and studied the sphere again. What she saw could easily be mistaken for a plant, that was for sure, but there was something more to it. A complexity about the hairy fronds and an energy *inside* them that suggested something more advanced, more *alive*.

"I don't think it's a plant. I mean it *looks* organic, yes it *is* organic, only not in that way."

"Not in what way?"

Kali stroked the sphere, tracing the outline of the shape within. "Strip away our flesh and our bone," she said, "our veins, organs, muscle, sinew, tendons, and what do you think you get?"

"A bloody mess?"

"I mean what's *left*, Slowhand. The very core of our being."

"Your companion shows a knowledge beyond that of her world,

archer," the voice said, startling them both. "You see before you the nervous mesh central to the body of everything that lives. The threads, if you will, within us all."

"*Right.* So, your sphere, it's some kind of grow bag?"

"Slowhand!"

"*Joke*, Hooper. Breaking the ice with the plant is all."

"It *isn't* a plant."

"*I know that*, for fark's sake. Of all the steaming pits – you really do think I'm thick, don't you?"

"No, no, of course I don't. Not at all."

Slowhand stared challengingly and found Kali couldn't hold his gaze. He shook his head in resignation and ran his own palm over the sphere. "What I don't get is, are you saying it was once one of us? Human?"

Kali looked around at the decay of ages, and smiled. "Oh, I wouldn't think human, no."

She was only just beginning to appreciate the possible nature of the being whose presence they were in, and despite the gravity of the situation that had brought them here she couldn't help but almost giggle with the thrill of it. The mummified corpse in Be'Trak'tak was the closest she ever thought she would come to meeting a member of the Old Races, but now?

"Why don't you ask him?"

"Him? How do you know it's a him?"

Kali was getting a little tired of questions when so many of her own were clamouring to be asked. "Maybe because if it was a her – maybe someone called Endless Passion – you'd already be working on some unlikely contrivance to make your pants disintegrate."

"Hey. That is below the belt."

"No, we know what's below the belt. And where it's been."

"*Hey!*"

"*Hey!*"

They stopped, remembering where they were. Kali turned towards the sphere to apologise but then stood back, gasping.

"What the hells...?" Slowhand said.

Inside the sphere, the liquid had begun to flood with clouds of grey. They were clearly more than clouds, however, as not only did their mass seem to be made up of tiny organisms but they moved with purpose, variously wrapping, obscuring and agitating the fronds of the 'plant' until they began to change, thicken and grow. What their unexpected host had described as 'the threads within us all' were beginning to take on a fuller form, one gradually becoming more recognisable as a living being.

First came a skeleton, one bit of bone at a time, the bones lengthening to join others, creating joints, limbs, ribs, a skull. Next came sinews, organs, tendons and muscle, these growths in turn becoming interlaced and overgrown with capillaries, blood vessels and arteries, which, when whole and connected, began to flow with blood the colour of sky. Over these vessels grew tissue and then flesh, a body forming before their eyes. And, lastly, came eyes, hair, features, until both Kali and Slowhand found themselves staring at a fully formed being, floating before them in the sphere.

But it was like no being either of them had seen before.

At least, not quite.

The thing was, Kali recognised elements of the creature she saw before her – the musculature of the limbs, the shape of the torso, the physiognomy of the face – but what confused her was that they seemed to come from two different anatomies. She was familiar with this creature and yet wasn't at the same time. Because while it had always been her dream to meet a living, breathing member of one of the Old Races, she had never, ever dreamt she would meet a living, breathing member of both Old Races *simultaneously*. It was hardly what she'd expected the Dragon God to be.

"You?" she said breathlessly. "You're –"

"The first of the dwelf. The last of the dwelf."

"My gods!"

"Dwelf?" the archer said, confused.

"Work it out, Slowhand."

"Are you telling me this thing is half dwarf, half elf? A hybrid?"

"Yup."

"Glad I wasn't hiding in the wardrobe in *that* boudoir."

Kali raised her eyes. "I doubt it happened like that."

"No? You wanna tell me another way you know of making," Slowhand paused and shuddered, "little dwelfs?"

"I am not the result of physical procreation," the dwelf explained, "but of other processes."

Slowhand wasn't sure what that meant. "Are they as much fun?"

"*Slowhand!*"

"Sorry, sorry."

"You said 'other processes.'" Kali said to the dwelf. "You mean those birthing pools? Is that what this sphere is - your own birthing pool? Were you *created* here?"

"Created when your race was young."

"Looking good on it, pal," Slowhand said, then pulled a face as he visualised the frond thing the dwelf had first been. "Now, anyway."

"Actually, I doubt he's as old as we are," Kali corrected the archer.

"That's right, isn't it? When we saw you grow, you were being created all over again, just like the first time, weren't you? The liquid in this sphere is the same as that in the pools but... more complex, somehow. It enables you to form and reform at will?"

"Nutrients, proteins. The essential building blocks of life. I would not have survived this long had I not been able to revert to a state of stasis among them."

"You're thousands upon thousands of years old," Kali breathed. "But at the same time, *so young*."

"Oh, come on," Slowhand objected. "He can pop in and out of existence, just the same as he was, every time, with all his memories intact? I may be just an old soldier boy, Hooper, but –"

"Perhaps you simply do not have all of the facts, Killiam Slowhand," the dwelf said.

As he spoke, his body *faded* into a state of translucency for a second and something that looked like a length of stretched and shimmering gold could clearly be seen coiled throughout his body.

Slowhand stared. "What the hells?"

Kali could hardly believe it herself. She thought back to her meeting with Kane in Andon, the way he used the threads as *physical* things. It seemed the Old Races had too, but in a way that even Kane would likely find hard to believe. The Old Races, particularly in their last age, had been outstanding engineers, but she had never imagined – never could have imagined – that they had begun to engineer *themselves*.

"I think that's a line of thread magic," she said. "An actual magical thread interwoven with his very being."

"Yeah?" Slowhand responded, perhaps not quite grasping the enormity of what she said, or perhaps, being Slowhand, simply asking the sensible question. "Why?"

"It is a necessary part of the process," the dwelf said.

"Necessary for what? To churn out those *things* from the pools? Or maybe just try and *suffocate* anyone who pops by?"

"The atmosphere chamber," the dwelf said. "That was not I."

"Oh? Then who?"

"No one. Your entrapment was accidental, the process automatic. However, I regret the facility was left unsealed."

"Atmosphere chamber?" Slowhand asked but Kali placed a hand on his shoulder, preferring the conversation walked before it ran.

"If you were the one that freed us, thank you," she said. "And for chasing away the k'nid, however you did."

"That is what you call the spawn? Interesting. But yes. The *k'nid*, like most organisms, are susceptible to certain harmonics and vibrations which cause them discomfort, in this case forcing them to flee."

"Harmonics and vibrations you've used before. To interrupt the absorption of those bodies out there."

The dwelf was silent for a second.

"I had no interest in saving the intruders," he said. "Only in protecting this place." As he spoke, the structure shook once more, rumbled deeply. "The birthing *k'nid* have inflicted considerable damage on the complex."

"The Faith, too, by the look of what we've seen out there," Slowhand chipped in. "Why the hells didn't you use these harmonics to get rid of them, too?"

"Because I have observed your world and know their motives, the singular, dark mission of their Church. Had my presence been revealed to them it would have served no good and perhaps have led to other discoveries. Also, my influence over the complex is no longer absolute. The damage it has sustained even without the k'nid – *naturally* over the long, long years – has left areas of it dead to me."

"Like the birthing pools - the Crucible," Kali said, and the sphere rumbled again as she spoke. "The Final Faith turned it on, didn't they?" she said, remembering Jenna's recordings. "That was what she meant by their *mistake*."

"And now you can't turn it off," Slowhand said.

"The Faith disturbed the precise calibrations of minds long since dust, spawning the k'nid in numbers not intended. Worse, the prism central to the birthing process – the same prism that could *abort* the process – became misaligned beneath their meddling hands." The dwelf sighed. "You are correct, archer. I cannot stop it."

"Stop it?" Slowhand repeated. "Why in the hells did you *start* it? For gods sakes, why on Twilight would you want to create such creatures in the first place?"

The dwelf's answer sounded regretful and – considering what it seemed he, or at least his people, were responsible for – also somewhat unlikely. "To save the world."

"News for you, pal, that's her job," Slowhand said, nodding at Kali. "So what's the real story?"

Kali wasn't as hasty in responding. The dwelf's regret had sounded genuine enough for her.

"Do you have a name?" she asked.

"I was created to be a guardian," he said. "The elven word for such a role would be Tharnak."

"Tharnak it is, then. Tharnak, please, I don't understand. How would creating these *things* save the world?"

"Our world faced a threat foretold in tomes of as great an age as divides our civilisations now. A threat both from the unknown and unknown in essence. Though both elven and dwarven races knew of its coming, we knew also that it was *alien* to us. We did not know what could stop it because we could not know what its weaknesses were. And so we constructed the Crucible. Its purpose was the creation of a singular life form specific in its purpose – to combat *any* threat."

"Must have been a pretty unique threat."

"It was. As unique as the solution we devised. The creatures you call k'nid were the result of complex manipulations of Twilight's life forms – extracting from them those elements which brought them victory in the survival of the fittest. In the process we gave birth to *other* creatures, and these, too, became part of the process. Our survival was at stake and so we had to create the ultimate defence. A life form capable of surviving any environment, of winning and *transforming* that environment and becoming its dominant life form. The *only* life form."

"So overwhelming it would spread like some disease," Kali said, "consuming the enemy. Tharnak, we're not the enemy and your creations aren't saving our world, they're *destroying* it."

"Because," the dwelf said, "they were never meant to be unleashed here."

"Unleashed *here*? I don't understand."

"On this world."

"*What?*"

"The k'nid were destined for the heavens."

"Okay, pal, that's it," Slowhand cut in. "Hooper, don't waste breath on this guy. He's a short wick in a long candle."

"Slowhand, let him fin –"

"No, Hooper. Think about it. What isn't ringing true here? Apart from this *heavens* rubbish? If this project of theirs was so damned important – so vital to the future of both their races – why is it stashed away up here at the top of *our* world, hidden in a secret valley behind the Dragonfire? I'll tell you why. Because it's a farking loony bin, is why."

"My friend has a point," Kali said, biting her lip. "If elves and dwarfs were working together, in a time when there were only elves, dwarves and a handful of primitive humans who would have posed no threat, who exactly were you hiding yourselves from?"

"Many of our peoples were against what we would achieve."

"Hardly surprising," Slowhand said.

"Do you imagine that because we were races who had attained greatness, that we did not have as many fundamental divisions among us as divide the peninsula today? There were those who ignored the threat to us, those who courted, even welcomed it, and those who actively sought to prevent us stopping it, for their own reasons, insane as they may have been. We were called blasphemous, sacrilegious, and even within our own ranks there was doubt. Doubt that could only be assuaged by my creation. A living compromise between elf and dwarf factions, a believer of *both* sides."

"So the Crucible was built in secret?" Kali said. "Your rulers, governments, churches, knowing nothing about it?"

"For three years our people – those who *believed* – worked with and within them, utilising their resources and hoping, also, to recruit some to our cause. But – as is the case with your own Final Faith – the ideals and aims and beliefs of most were too intractable, entrenched to change. Had we been discovered we would have been banished, or worse. Still, our people managed to establish a chain of contacts, supplies and the means to transport them, the cooperation of sympathisers to our cause and, eventually, began to establish their presence, here, in the Drakengrat Mountains."

"The waystations," Kali said.

"Constructed, again, in secret, and as defended in their time as the Crucible itself. Not only a means to ferry our materials but designed to intercept any who might wish to stop what the Crucible hoped to achieve. Some of the airships therein were fighters."

"Fighters? It sounds like a war."

"More than just a war. A holy war. We had no wish to spill the blood of our own but we *had* to protect the complex whilst its purpose was achieved."

"A holy war?"

"As I said, the k'nid were designed with a specific purpose and that purpose was to destroy the *deity* in our heavens."

"Destroy the deity?" Slowhand echoed. He almost laughed. "Are you saying their purpose was to *kill God*?"

"Some called it God."

Kali found herself almost physically staggering. "Deity," she said. The dwelf had spoken in the singular so presumably he was not referring to the various gods whom most on Twilight had worshipped before the coming of the Final Faith. Was he, therefore, speaking of *their* God, the one God? If that was the case, did that mean the Old Races acknowledged its existence literal ages before the Faith came into being – as an actual entity? That it might be real was something she struggled to accept. "Tharnak, are you talking about the *Lord of All*?"

The dwelf almost spat his response, so vehement was it. "I am talking about the Lord of Destruction, the Lord of Nothing!"

Kali frowned. Lord of Destruction? Lord of Nothing? What the hells did those phrases mean? Were these just other terms for the Lord of All, or for something else entirely? She was about to ask when another tremor ran through the Crucible, more violent than any that had come previously, and she was forced to steady herself against the sphere as growth fluids sloshed about inside. Even Tharnak himself seemed concerned.

"Would that I could show you," the dwelf said with a sigh. "Make you understand. But there is so little time."

Tharnak's weary resignation made Kali realise that she was unlikely to get any further with this line of questioning for the moment and, while she still didn't understand the meaning of the threat, there was something becoming increasingly obvious to her – something made inherently clear by the fact that the Old Races were no more.

The threat, she thought. *Is this what happened to the Old Races? My gods. Is this how they died?*

"Your attempt to eradicate this deity," she said, "it failed, didn't it? *Why?*"

"Hubris, arrogance, *foolishness*. At that stage in our civilisation, though we possessed the technology to do what we did, it was not enough. We needed the magic, too. But the magic, by then, had become weak, for we had destroyed those who made it whole."

"Destroyed? Destroyed who?"

"The Dra'gohn."

"The Dra'gohn? You mean *the dragons*?"

"If that is what you call them, yes."

Kali didn't have a clue why the absence of dragons should affect the magic – make it whole – but that hardly seemed the point. The Old Races were the reason they had gone away?

"How?" she asked. "Why? What happened?"

The sphere shook again and the dwelf's weariness returned, almost as if he were dying with the Crucible. "Cowardice... greed... does it really matter? They were gone – and with them, our only chance to survive."

"But this place," Kali protested, aware as she spoke of how naive the question seemed. "All of its potential – couldn't you have somehow *remade* them, brought them back?"

The dwelf actually laughed, although the sound was guttural and bitter. "How many times over these countless, lonely years do you think I have been tempted to try? To rectify *our* mistake, and to *apologise* to them, even though it would have been too late? No, it would have been an empty exercise, for that is why we failed. The magical threads that bind our creations are weak. Nothing *made* here can survive for long if it leaves the Crucible." The dwelf paused. "How could I bring the dra'gohn back knowing that when they took to the skies I would once more be responsible for their end – that they would *die?*"

"You mean like the yassan, you bastard?" Slowhand said. "How do you think they feel – out there, *changed*, unable to leave that frozen wilderness they call home? Tell me, *Tharnak*, did you really need to make them part of your *soup* or were you just playing games?"

"We took no pleasure in our experiments on them. It was our wish that, when we left, we gifted this valley to them in return. But, of course, we did not leave."

"And that's meant to make things all right?"

"'Liam, don't," Kali said. She stared at the dwelf. "If that's the case, why are the k'nid able to survive?"

"They are not. Their capability for self-replication grants them a longer life span than others but eventually they, too, will revert to nothing. They would not have reached the heavens. Beyond this valley they have, perhaps, a matter of days."

Which we don't, Kali thought. "Then, please, is there a way to stop them?"

"The prism above the birthing pools. It holds upon it the runics capable of reversing their creation, *removing* them. Combined with the magic of your Three Towers – if your men of magic channel their threads of destruction through them – the plague upon the peninsula will be ended."

"It's that simple?" Slowhand said, beginning to revise his opinion of the plant.

Easy for you to say, Kali thought. She calculated she had some hours before the next wave of k'nid were spawned but, from what she'd seen of them, that didn't necessarily make the birthing pools any less dangerous. "So this is the bit where I risk life and limb in some potentially lethal hellshole to save the world once more, right? Fine. I'll go get it."

"Then you must do so with all speed. There is little time."

"There should be hours yet."

"Until the next birthing cycle, yes. But that is not the threat you face." The dwelf's eyes closed, as if he were sensing something far away. "The Final Faith have returned. They have their own airships. And sorcerers who, even now, are attempting to break through our force barrier."

"Airships?" Slowhand said. "There was only *one* airship."

"Gransk," Kali said. "I think Jenna had a telescryer in her party, sent them the information how to build them."

"'I'll glide this thing into Gransk', Jenna said," Slowhand remembered. "Hooper, what the hells is Gransk?"

"Final Faith shipyards, on the coast between Turnitia and Malmkrug. Top secret."

"Right."

Kali turned to the dwelf. "How long do we have?"

"The force barrier weakens. They will gain access by dawn."

"When they'll blow this place to bits," Kali said.

"Sounds good to me," Slowhand said. "So why don't we get the hells out of here right now?"

"The prism," Kali said.

"Fine. Then we get the prism and *then* get out of here."

"I cannot allow you to leave this place, Killiam Slowhand," the dwelf said, unexpectedly. "Not yet."

Slowhand raised Suresight without hesitation, an arrow pointed unwaveringly at the hybrid.

"Yeah? Difficult to see how you'd stop us with this sticking out of your forehead."

"Please. I do not intend my words to be a threat."

"Sounding pretty pitsing much like one to me."

Kali raised an arm and lowered Suresight, much to Slowhand's consternation. "'Liam, wait. Let's hear what he has to say."

"Hooper, I do *not* see the problem. Whether this guy's on our side or not, it was his people who caused this mess in the first place. You tell me – what exactly is wrong with having the Crucible destroyed right now? Isn't it what we came here for?"

"Because there's something else, isn't there, Tharnak? There has to be." She thought back to Slowhand's comment about the yassan, and about the atmosphere chambers and other strange rooms the two of them had seen. The dwelf had said that they were creating the life form but he had also said 'that and those who could deliver it to its goal.'

The dwelf nodded and, across the chamber, on a shimmering patch of air, a view of the *Kerberos* sphere appeared – in its centre the glamour field.

"We learned early in our experiments that we, the elves and the dwarves, would not survive the journey to the heavens but that humans – *changed humans* – would. We were creating four such travellers when the end came."

"What happened to them?"

"I do not know. It was necessary that I reverted to my hybernartion state to survive the end and when, finally, I awoke they, like the races which sired me, were gone and I was alone."

Slowhand saw the disappointment cloud Kali's face. He knew she needed to know *exactly* how the Old Races had died.

"In other words, you were here when it happened but you missed it because you were *asleep*?"

"In essence, yes. But perhaps you will be able to glean some knowledge from this..."

In the *Kerberos* sphere, the glamour field began to dissolve.

"In my solitude I became guardian not only of this place but what remained within it, hidden from view for countless years. But now my time is over, and another guardian is needed."

Kali and Slowhand stared.

"Is that what I think it is?" Slowhand gasped. "I mean, I'm not sure what I think it is... *but is it?*"

"*Oh, my gods!*"

CHAPTER FIFTEEN

KALI KNEW RIGHT at that moment that everything was going to change – *fundamentally* change – and life would never be the same again. She didn't know how it would change, she didn't know when it would change, but this was the *beginning*. She knew it.

The resulting numbness she felt had barely wavered even when, in the image the dwelf had called forth, Kali could see two familiar piratical figures clambering into the *Kerberos* sphere; having presumably come to warn them of the Faith only to end up gawping at what had been revealed, as she was. Because in that same moment she had been back in the Warty Witch in Freiport, having her first conversation with Merrit Moon, he the twinkly eyed exponent of the world's lost past, she the wide-eyed girl. The topic had, of course, been the Old Races and the wonders they had produced. In his cataloguing of such wonders the old man had cited one whose seemingly sheer implausibility had haunted her ever since.

"Tales from the Final Age," he had said, "tell of them actually preparing to send ships to the heavens. To explore Kerberos itself."

Ships to the heavens.

In truth, she had never really believed they could exist.

But now she was looking at one.

SHE AND SLOWHAND worked their way in a daze down to the *Kerberos* sphere – there reuniting with Aldrededor and Dolorosa – and now the four of them were gazing up at what was clearly the ultimate achievement of the Old Races.

Sitting on some kind of fluid, semi-organic cradle, the ship was a great flowing, sweeping creation that was unlike any mode of transport Kali had ever seen, human *or* Old Race. The main part of its hull the length of ten cattle carts and the breadth of four, it widened further where its wings curved majestically and seemingly without join from port and starboard down to the hangar floor. As Kali and the others drew closer, they saw that the wings, like the hull, were seemingly made up of, but in fact overlaid with, hundreds of small and overlapping sets of fluted funnels, like flattened panpipes. Combined, these gave the impression the ship was covered from bow to stern in rippling scale. The impression that it was some kind of living organism was further enhanced by the fact that every one of the funnels was inscribed with delicate runics resembling the porous flaws of skin. They, in turn, rested on a membranous, flexible underlayer that was soft like flesh. Kali stroked one of the wings almost reverently, realising that here was another reason why the yassan had chosen what they had as the basis for their religion. They were not misguided, their ancestors had simply been mistaken in what they had seen. Because by accident or design, the Kerberos ship looked for all the world like some stylised dragon ready to take flight.

"A thing of beauty, is she not?" Aldrededor observed with a heavy sigh.

"As beautiful as I, my 'usband?"

"Ohhhh, definitely not."

"But, er, what is it?"

Kali smiled. "I guess you could call it a… spaceship."

"A *space* ship?" Dolorosa repeated. "What kind ovva space?"

Kali pointed upwards – straight upwards – and the tall, thin woman inhaled sharply. Then her eyes narrowed and she stared with great suspicion. "You take-a the peees, yes? You havva the laugh atta Dolorosa!"

"Nope," Kali said, shaking her head. In truth, she only had half a mind on the conversation with the Sarcrean woman, still absorbing the words of the dwelf when he had revealed the ship to them.

The Final Faith will destroy our creation along with the Crucible. You must take it from this place, to a place of safety, where it, and its cargo, must remain in your care.

Its cargo, Kali had thought. Tharnak meant k'nid. This beautiful thing was laden with their ultimate weapon, he had said, sealed in a magical stasis inside its shell, lying dormant, awaiting the day when they would travel to the heavens. Only they couldn't travel to the heavens now, could they? Because without the dragons the magic that would keep them alive was not *whole*, whatever the hells that meant.

Maybe one day, Tharnak had said, the magic would return.

Kali exhaled. The fact was, she had no idea why they should save these k'nid. That, though, wasn't really the point, because what had *really* been given into their care was the ultimate artefact of the Old Races, the ship itself. As such it was invaluable – a source of information about those who had gone before that was absolutely unparalleled in its importance. Gods, even if she hadn't been asked, she would have *had* to save it herself!

The only problem now was how to get it out of here.

The ship will accept you, Tharnak had said. *The ship will choose its saviour.*

But what did that mean?

There was only one way to find out.

Kali took a step up the sloping cradle, towards the stern of the ship, pausing warily as the spine of the semi-organic hull parted before her, as if someone were slipping the covers from a wagon. Where it parted, a long, narrow, railed deck was revealed, running from stern to bow, and at the far end an organic-looking control panel glowed a dull green. Kali took a breath and stepped onto the deck, noticing now that it was translucent, another organic membrane, and beneath could be made out the still forms of dormant k'nid. It was something of an uncomfortable feeling treading over the lethal predators but, when it became obvious that they were not going to stir, Kali's confidence grew and she began to marvel at her unique surroundings. The combination of structured hull and semi-organic interior clearly marked the ship as a co-endeavour of both the Old Races and, born in crisis or not, it was a magnificent achievement.

She beckoned the others aboard and Slowhand, Aldrededor and Dolorosa stepped tentatively onto the deck, joined her at what seemed to be the controls; a collection of fleshy nodes forming a sweeping curve. But though they glowed that dull green Kali had noticed as she'd come aboard, nodes were all they appeared to be – lifeless.

"Now what?" Slowhand said.

"The ship will choose its saviour." Kali whispered, and stepped closer to the panel. The nodes made a squishing noise and pulsed at her approach, like pods about to open.

"Easy, girl," Slowhand said, pulling her back. "We have no idea what the things *are*, let alone what they'd do to you."

"Slowhand, someone has to *do this!*"

"I don't deny it. Only it isn't going to be you." As Kali opened her mouth to protest more, he placed a finger on her lips. "It's more than concern. Don't you have a prism to find?"

"Mister Slowhand is correct, Kali Hooper," Aldrededor said. He examined the still pulsing nodes and pulled his moustache, intrigued. "This, I think, is a task for Aldrededor."

"Husband?" Dolorosa queried.

"With you at my side, wife, I captained a ship of the outer seas for over forty years," the ex-pirate pointed out. "I should be the one to captain her now."

"No, Aldrededor," Kali said. "This is *my* responsibility."

"No, Kali Hooper. *Your* responsibility is finishing the job *you* have to do."

Dolorosa stuck her face into Kali's. "Or do you thinka you canna do everytheeng, heh?"

"Aldrededor –" Kali began again, but it was already too late.

The ex-pirate placed his hands onto the two central nodes and, with the same squishing sounds as earlier, his hands were absorbed *into* them. The Sarcean's eyes widened in surprise and, for a few moments, he suffered a series of small spasms that made Dolorosa slap her palm over her mouth. Her husband seemed, though, to be unharmed, managing, a few moments later, a small and slightly stoned looking smile.

"Aldrededor?" Kali enquired. "What's happening?"

The Sarcrean did not reply immediately, but only because he did not know how to answer Kali's question. Because he was seeing things which no one had seen before, the world on which they lived in a new light, and not through his own eyes but those of the ship. And what the ship *saw* were the very threads on which Twilight's various magics depended, filling the air around the craft with ribbons of colour, thick and thin, long and short, like the component parts of some as yet unmade, planet sized tapestry. But the ribbons were not still. Instead, they wove in an out and around each other like snakes, in places touching and releasing bursts of more vivid colour, in others drifting apart and fading, but all in constant motion. If the waves of the seas were coloured silk, Aldrededor thought, this is what they would look like.

One thing marred the beauty, however. Here and there amongst the ever moving patterns were black threads that hung heavily, disturbed occasionally by the other, coloured threads but themselves unmoving, apparently lifeless. And when they touched their vibrant counterparts, they seemed momentarily to leech them of colour. It was as if these threads had once been a part of the flowing sea but were no longer, remaining within it now with no purpose other than to fill the space they had left behind, yet at the same time weakening the sea as a whole.

"Dra'gohn," the pirate whispered sadly to himself.

"What?" Kali said. "What did you say?"

"I amma worried," Dolorosa said. "Aldy has notta been like this since last he smoked the weeds of the sea."

"Wait," Kali instructed. "Give him a little longer."

Still amongst the threads, Aldrededor heard Kali's words and nodded. A little longer, yes. Because the threads were starting to make sense now – at least in the way they related to the ship. Or rather, the way the ship related to them. *Used* them, in fact. Because it was the way that it *flew*.

Eddies and tides and currents of threads. The ship navigated them not with wheel and rudder but with the funnels that coated the ship, drawing in and then channelling and manipulating the threads a thousand different ways to propel it through the sky.

Aldrededor pulled his hands from the nodes with a long sigh.

"My 'usband?" Dolorosa said.

"My wife," he replied. "The ship has shown me what I need to know. It has shown me the invisible ocean of Twilight."

"Aldrededor," Kali said. "Are you telling me you can fly this thing?"

"I believe I may even be able to *sail* it." His chest puffed. "It has chosen me, Kali Hooper."

"Then what are we waiting for?" Slowhand asked. "Hooper, let's get that prism and get the hells out of here."

"Unfortunately, Killiam Slowhand, we are not yet able," Aldrededor advised. "The ship's energy has leaked away over the long years and is all but depleted. It needs to feed."

"Feed?" Slowhand repeated, with a note of distaste.

Amberglow, Kali thought.

After all, if the other Old Race magical technology – the Mole, the crackstaff, the airships – relied on it, why shouldn't this? The only question was, what would it feed *from*?

"We must depart the sphere, that is all I know." Aldrededor said. "But first we will need to free these holding mechanisms or we will go nowhere."

"Free the mechanisms, feed the ship," Slowhand recited. "Will we get that done before the Filth arrive?"

Aldrededor paused. "I do not know, archer. But the question, in any case, is academic. We cannot travel through the Dragonfire while the Faith wait on the other side."

"Am I missing something here? This is a *spaceship*, right? So why the hells don't we just fly it *over* the mountains and bypass the Faith entirely?"

"Because the ship's depletion of energy is not the only damage it has accrued over time. There is some damage to the integrity of the ship itself and it will be unable to withstand the stress of high-altitude flight. Air turbulence above the mountains, or higher, would tear us apart."

"Oh, luvverly."

"Sounds like we need to get a move on," Kali said. "Sorry I can't stay to help but try not to leave without me, eh?"

"Try not to leave without *us*," Slowhand added, and turned to Kali. "I'm going with you."

"No. You're not."

"The bossa lady is correct, bow bender, I need you here," Dolorosa said.

"*You* need me here? I thought Aldrededor was Captain? And don't call me bow bender, it sounds vaguely dirty."

"I need you here," Dolorosa said, "because while my 'usband was Capitano for forty years, I was sheep's engineer, and now the sheep's engineer needa your help freeing the mechaneesms."

Both Kali and Slowhand stared at Dolorosa. The idea that she had been 'sheep's' engineer had tempted a smile onto both of their faces, but it faded quickly when the old woman took to the job at hand with surprising skill.

"Okay, okay," Slowhand agreed, begrudgingly. "But, Hooper, you watch your back down there."

"Always," she said, and was gone.

Wasting no time, Kali retraced her route through the complex to the gallery overlooking the birthing pools, and there took a rope from her belt and tied it to the frame of the membrane the k'nid had penetrated. She eased herself through the rent, coughing as the noxious gases from the pools thickened about her and sucked at her lungs, though this time she *could* reach her breathing conch and slipped it on. She dropped to the floor with a squelch in the coloured fog. If the k'nid spawning cycle remained true to form, she had plenty of time to do what she needed, but still felt a distinct sense of unease now that she was in their midst. Thankfully, she would not need to stay for long, intending only to retrieve the prism and leave the k'nid to the ministrations of the Final Faith.

It was then that she noticed something that had been blocked from her and Slowhand's view from above earlier. A ring of spheres encircling the edge of the birthing pool area. They were not unlike that which held Tharnak, though smaller, and they appeared to have objects *crammed* within. She frowned and began to make her way slowly across the organic floor. The birthing pools bubbled and popped, as sluggish as pits of lava, the occasional overzealous discharge spattering the bottom of her dark silk bodysuit and boots. The pools discharges were not hot, however – the processes occurring in the soup beneath here were things of biology and chemistry, not heat. It did not stop her hopping away from them *as if* she had been burnt, however, almost falling once or twice as the floor ruptured slightly beneath her.

Kali reached the spheres and rubbed the surface of one, then leapt back. Curled within, like a foetus in a womb, was a seven headed beast. The beast would never be born, however, as the sphere had long since leaked the life-giving liquids it had contained and the poor creature was mummified, having, from the look of it, died in some considerable pain.

Kali turned away, feeling sick, and examined the other spheres. Some were empty, torn apart, as if their occupants had escaped, but most were occupied by the long dead remains of other beasts she did not recognise, confirming her suspicions. She was looking at a menagerie of creatures that must have been produced in the Crucible's program of intermixing and artificial breeding. Creatures whose reason for existing had been but a means to an end and that could not – *should not* – exist in the normal scheme of things.

Again, she felt sick. *This* was what they had to do to save the world? *This* was the price for their salvation?

Kali froze suddenly, slapping a hand over her mouth and, for a second, almost *was* sick. Because right in front of her, in an adjacent sphere, was Horse. Or at least *a* Horse. Because the huge, slumped, armoured, horned corpse couldn't be anything but a relative of her own steed. *Now* she knew why Horse had been found in the Drakengrats, and now she knew why the so-called bamfcat was unique, because he had to be descended from creatures who had escaped this strange laboratory, creatures which must have bred the weakness inherent in all the Crucible's creations out of them before they died.

The discovery of Horse's origin should have been a welcome revelation but it only made Kali feel worse. How many versions of Horse had there been, she wondered? That they had probably been in pain as a result of their mutation made her think of what might have happened to *her* Horse had he been alive at the time. That such a fate could have befallen the intelligent, loyal animal she knew made her succumb to a sudden, uncontrollable fury. Without thinking, Kali raised her crackstaff and then raked its energy across the sphere, staggering back as it exploded towards her in a rain of membranous casing. Despite that, she did not dull the beam, holding the crackstaff with steadfast determination and, roaring, moving it from the bamfcat's sphere to the others, reducing their occupants to the dust they should, long ago, have been. Finally, she stopped, breathing hard.

All Kali wanted now was to find the prism and get the hells out of the Crucible. But as she made her way to the tri-arch, she suddenly found herself thrown off her feet as *Twilight* shook with one of its most violent tremors yet. And when she stood, she saw that the birthing pools had started to bubble rapidly.

What the hells? There should be hours yet!

Clearly, though, the last tremor had disturbed the processes, and the spawning cycle had begun early.

Things were rising from the floor.

Things was the only way to describe them because they were not k'nid. Not yet. Whatever processes occurred in that unnatural soup, they had clearly been interrupted part way through because what emerged before her eyes were more than monstrosities, they were true horrors. Demented things that thrashed and bashed themselves against the sides of the pools and up onto the floor like landed fish, all the while screaming in the manner of things possessed. Some of the part-formed k'nid headed directly for a rent in the side of the Crucible but a good number began throwing themselves around the chamber in a lethal hail that threatened to tear her to pieces.

Kali didn't hesitate, running straight for the tri-arch and throwing herself onto it, scrambling up its length towards the suspended prism. The deformed k'nid leapt for her as she climbed, but thankfully, in their current state, seemed to lack the agility of their fully formed counterparts. Kali, her legs wrapped around the arch, thumped the prism repeatedly to loosen it, finally freeing it as the beleaguered structure quaked violently beneath her. She had just managed to secure the prism in her equipment belt when the whole tri-arch collapsed. Kali was already in the air, though, launching herself towards the rope on which she'd entered and grabbing onto it with a grunt. The last thing she saw of the Crucible were the screeching k'nid being crushed beneath the tri-arch as it smashed into the birthing pools.

Kali's problems were only just beginning, however, because now that she had returned to the sphere proper, the extent of the damage from the last, dramatic tremor was clear. The whole of the sphere was skewed and groaning loudly, in danger of collapse. Worse, fires had broken out, fires that were triggering explosions in some of the laboratories – and each of those explosions were triggering others in turn. As the sphere shook once more about her, Kali realised that this was the end for *Twilight*, and she had to get back to *Kerberos* fast.

There was one thing, though, that she *had* to do first. And that was find out what Tharnak had meant when he had said she had been awaited. Because if the dwelf could answer that, maybe he could answer other questions too. Namely, why was she *different* and what, if any, connection was there between herself and the yassan?

Her hopes were dashed as soon as she entered Tharnak's chamber, however. His sphere was collapsed and leaking and the dwelf was sprawled half out of it, dying. It was a tragic and inappropriate end for such a creature and Kali knelt by him, trying to offer some comfort as she listened to his last, almost incoherent words. Then the dwelf slumped in her arms, and she realised there was nothing more she could do.

Twilight continuing to detonate around her, Kali raced for the bridge between spheres, hoping to the gods that Dolorosa and the others had managed to free the holding mechanisms on the ship. As explosions followed her out of the doomed sphere, blowing the bridge apart yard by yard right on her heels, she burst into *Kerberos* and yelled: "*Get her up! Don't wait for me! Do it now!*"

Below, Slowhand and the others looked up quizzically. A sudden explosion that blew Kali yelling and flailing off the ledge, and into the air between them, quickly spurred them on. Within seconds Aldrededor leapt to the controls and the ship sat began to shudder upwards. Kali, meanwhile, slammed onto one of the sphere's walkways with a loud *oof* and, after a moment's disorientation, realised that the explosion had blown her within running distance of the cradle. As it rose a yard above the sphere's base, she was starting to think she might actually make it when a series of explosions from beneath the walkways blew flooring plates into her path and made a direct route to the ship impossible. Instead, she began to weave around the explosions, trying her best to estimate where the next might occur. But while she got a number of them right it *was* guesswork and, inevitably, she also got some wrong. It was during one such mistake, as she found herself being blown left, right and centre, surviving the blasts only through a series of dexterous somersaults, that she noticed Slowhand throwing the levers that had raised the cradle back to their original positions, and the ship juddered to a halt.

"We're not leaving without you!"

"Like hells you're not! Slowhand, you have to get that thing out of here!"

"We'll *do* it, Hooper, but not without you!"

A detonation blew Kali forward and she cursed. "Go!"

Dolorosa joined the archer at the rail. "We cannot, because the sheep it has notta been named. Eet is very bad luck to launch a sheep withouta the name."

"It isn't launching yet, you stupid woman!"

"Eeta still musta be named!"

Kali knew full well that this was just Dolorosa using a delaying tactic, and she loved her for it, but time was fast running out.

"All right, all right!" she cried as she picked herself up and ran. "I name this ship –"

"That issa no good, Kali Hooper."

"*What?*"

"Eet is traditional to shatter the bottle of feezzy wine against the hull."

"Where am I going to get a bottle of *feezzy wine*, you daft old bat!" Kali shouted in exasperation, but it was already becoming clear that she was not going to win this exchange.

Even Aldrededor got in on the act, crowding in between them at the rail. "The alcohol is necessary, Kali Hooper. The... er... *feezziness*, it drives away the evil spirit."

"Oh, and what evil spirit would that be, Aldrededor? Your wife?"

"Hoh!" Dolorosa cried. "She thinka she issa the funny woman again!"

"Put the knife away, my angel. We are trying to save the boss, not kill her."

"Yes, yes, that ees right. I willa keel you later ..."

"Is the message clear yet, Hooper? We're *not* going without you."

"Dammit!" Kali shouted as she continued to dodge, digging into her equipment belt as she did. "Fine, you want booze, here's booze!" She plucked a bottle of thwack from the belt and hurled it towards the ship. "Now bugger off!"

"That was notta feezzy wine."

"No, but it *was* my last bottle. *That do?*"

There was a collective intake of breath.

"Her..."

"...last..."

"...bottle?"

Slowhand worked the levers, winking broadly at Kali as he did so. "Then I guess it's time to go."

Damn the three of you, Kali thought, still moving. Because even though the cradle was rising again – her friends knew what was at stake, after all – they had delayed its rise just long enough.

"Aaargh!" Kali yelled with determination, and began to pound forward, forcing everything she had into the attempt.

But the explosions beneath the sphere's floor were almost constant now, making it buck and chop like a stormy sea. Kali found herself leaping from walkway to machine and back again as if the world itself were coming apart beneath her. The situation worked somewhat to her advantage, though, as the more plates that blew, the more she could see the fiery, roiling mass below, and she was able to time and locate the next explosion with greater accuracy than she had before. With Slowhand and the others urging her on, Kali began to use the plates as stepping stones. Dancing, sometimes nimbly and sometimes not so, between them as they rose, fell or flipped across the hangar. Finally, she reached an almost leapable distance to the rising cradle and, in a last ditch attempt to reach it, she quickly calculated where the next explosion was going to come from. Slowhand, Aldrededor and Dolorosa all realised her intent at the same time, and there was a simultaneous and rapid shaking of heads. But Kali knew that really, she had little choice. She leapt forwards just as a further heavy boom from beneath the floor sent a panel shooting upwards and, calculating her trajectory perfectly, landed on its just as the force of the detonation flipped it over in mid air. Kali, however, didn't wait for the flip to complete, instead letting it throw her into the air, into a position where she was able – just – to make a grab for the cradle with one hand. This she did, and then another hand slapped onto her own. A strong hand. Slowhand's.

"Welcome aboard," he said, heaving her up.

"It isn't over yet," Kali said. "Hold on!"

Her advice was well timed because, at that very moment, what remained of the sphere floor exploded upwards, rocking the cradle as a fist of fire and debris punched it from beneath with such force that the conflagration mushroomed momentarily about its edges, bathing them in searing heat. Thankfully, though, the launchpad had moved high enough to avoid serious damage. It wasn't just moving higher any longer, either, whatever dwelven mechanisms had come into play to raise it seemingly only the first stage in an orchestrated series of manoeuvres. As they drew closer to the top of the sphere, the cradle began to revolve slowly and, amidst much groaning of metal, the two halves of the upper part of the sphere began to open. At first Kali thought that they were not going to make it, the hemispheres so rusted that they would fail to part far enough before the ship was crushed against them. But then, with some shearing of ancient and massive bolts, they juddered free and began to open. The sky was visible now, at first as an ellipse and then a much broader swathe, and then in all its azure glory as the inside of the sphere and its massive workings became fully exposed to the evening sky. Kali and the others were no longer *inside* the sphere, however, but watching, staggered, as the sky panned before them, the cradle having begun to swing out on a massive arm the moment the hemispheres had become low enough to permit it to do so, and Kali's attention moved from what they were leaving behind to what they were heading towards. Now she knew the purpose of the walkway from which she and Slowhand had gained access to *Kerberos*. Because as the giant arm continued to move it also turned slowly, the cradle rotating to fit neatly into position next to it, embraced within its stretched horseshoe shape. As the cradle docked at last inside the walkway with a vibrating *thunk*, Kali could barely hold back a giggle of admiration. She had thought the Clockwork King of Orl was a staggering achievement of Old Race engineering but *this*, this was a true marvel.

But it wasn't over yet.

"Hooper, look." Slowhand said, equally awed.

Kali watched as one of the other spheres – the one she had nicknamed *Sunsphere* – began to move on a giant arm through the trees, swinging towards them – *under* them – while at the same time opening to reveal what could only have been the power source that kept the Crucible's creations intact. This was the fire painted on the cave walls of the yassan – the fire they could not leave. Glowing bright against the azure night sky, like some vast brazier, she was looking at the biggest concentration of amberglow she had yet seen.

It came to a stop beneath the cradle and crackling fingers of energy began to dance between it and the underside of the ship. Kali stared at the hull and saw that the runes over its surface had begun to glow.

"The ship feeds," Aldrededor said from the controls. He drew a deep breath as though he himself were being vitalised. "All we can do now is wait."

"Good job, Aldrededor. Good job, everyo –" Kali began, but then stopped as a sudden massive explosion from *Kerberos* blew its interior and half of the sphere into the sky, the arm on which the cradle rested buckling partly as a result. She and the others clung onto whatever they could as the cradle dropped and skewed, coming to rest, creaking and groaning, at a thirty degree angle above the amberglow. All waited a few seconds, listening to the protesting metal beneath them, and then exhaled in relief when nothing else happened. It had been close, but they were safe.

"I guess that saves Jenna a job," Slowhand said, staring at the burning shells of the spheres.

"I guess it does," Kali replied, trying not to think of Tharnak. "So now we wait for them to come through."

"Family reunion," Slowhand said, biting his lip.

"Do you suppose that when Jenna sees what we've rescued, she might have second thoughts about blowing us out of the sky?"

Slowhand stared ahead, shook his head.

"Jenna's Final Faith now, Hooper. The Faith haven't seen this ship and they won't know what it is, but they won't care. If they *did* know, they wouldn't care. Think about it, Hooper. This thing can reach the *heavens*, and do you think they'd allow that? Gods forbid anyone knew the *truth* about what is up there, whatever it is. Because one thing's for sure – it won't be what *they* say it is."

Kali nodded. She turned away, staring beyond the platform over the valley, towards the Dragonfire. They were safe for now, but only for a matter of hours. There was no going back to the sphere now, and nowhere else to hide. They were alone out here. Alone on a precarious arm of metal, in a long lost valley, somewhere at the top of the world.

Outlined by the glow of the fires – natural and magical – she couldn't help but feel like a target.

CHAPTER SIXTEEN

THE FINAL FAITH breached the Dragonfire at dawn, just as the dwelf had predicted. Four airships as black as Long Night nosed into the lost valley, each of them emblazoned with the crossed circle of the church Kali knew all too well. But much as she hated everything that symbol stood for, she could not fault the machines behind it. Because while their airships differed from those of elven design – being uglier, ribbed things with more primitive gondolas and with rotors turned by steam rather than amberglow – they were nonetheless similarly and equally functional to the Old Race vessels that had inspired them.

The lead ship was larger and more ornate than its companions – the *Kesar*, *Voivode* and *Rhodon* respectively – and sported a huge gondola lifted by a double gasbag with two huge, thrumming rotors driving it from behind. This was obviously the flagship and its status was reflected in the name Kali could make out on its side: *Makennon*.

It wasn't the ship that drew her attention, though, but the figure she could just make out standing at its prow before a contingent of shadowmages. Even at this distance, a familiar blonde mane of hair could clearly be seen billowing behind the figure as it stared ahead.

"It's your sister," Kali said. "Back to mop up the mess she started."

"Then it's time we were on the move," the archer said. "You got a name for this thing yet?"

"Thought we might call it the *Tharnak*."

"Nice."

Kali followed Slowhand onto the *Tharnak* and, with a nod to everyone, decoupled the clamps securing it to the gantry.

"Aldrededor?"

"I am ready, Kali Hooper. All we need is a destination."

Actually, there are two, Kali thought.

The first had been obvious – Andon because she had to get the prism to the League – but the second had proven difficult. In fairness, it wasn't every day she had to work out where on the peninsula she could hide a *spaceship*. The problem lay in the fact that their civilisation was growing all the time, and there was no guarantee that any choice made today might not be encroached upon in a month's time, six months or a year, as both Vos and Pontaine continued to vie for dominance across their limited land. But at last she had decided. There was one place where they were unlikely to ever go. An inhospitable and downright pitsing dangerous place that defied any attempt at settlement and with which she'd had passing acquaintance. And there, in its vast sprawl, one specific location. An Old Race site that had once had a deadlier purpose but, since its destruction, would provide them with an underground harbour that should keep the ship safe for as long as needed.

"Andon and then east. We're taking this thing into the Sardenne – to the Spiral of Kos."

Aldrededor nodded in approval. Then his eyes closed. A second later, the *Tharnak* stirred, the thin traceries of hull visible between its thread funnels glowing brightly with their restored amberglow charge. There was a barely perceptible vibration in the ship and then the thread funnels themselves began to slowly move until the hull rippled like the reptilian hide it resembled. Dolorosa gasped as the *Tharnak*'s wings shifted slightly and Kali could hardly blame her – because the ship seemed *alive* beneath them.

"Take her up, Captain," Kali ordered.

Aldrededor concentrated and the *Tharnak* rose unsteadily from its cradle, tipping left and right as the ex-pirate became used to the feel of it. The sensation of leaving the ground – becoming airborne – was, Kali had to admit, a little unnerving. Even Slowhand, who had already flown, clung to the deck rails, his knuckles white. Though that, Kali suspected, might have had more to do with the fact that he and Jenna were about to become mortal enemies in a confrontation only one of them might survive.

Aldrededor steadied the ship, the ex-pirate growing more confident in its handling, before turning it towards the approaching airships. It was a manoeuvre that shifted perspective in a way that Kali had never experienced before and that first she found discomforting and dizzying, but then exhilarating.

Watching the walkway skew away beneath the ship, and then the horizon tip diagonally, Kali felt an overwhelming sense of how impossible her current situation seemed. She'd come across many artefacts that were beyond her ken but she couldn't help but wonder how the people of the peninsula might react if they knew that a battle for their future was about to be fought between airships and a flying machine here at the top of the world.

The Final Faith airships were clear now and, sure enough, their decks swarmed with figures, all gathering at their rails to stare at the Crucible's remains. The fact that she and the k'nid had done their job for them would not, Kali suspected, garner a grateful slap on the back and, equally sure enough, once the situation sank in, all eyes – including the coldly narrowing ones of Jenna – turned in the direction of the *Tharnak*. Kali wondered what she made of the strangely shaped craft, and whether, for a moment, she might reconsider her intent and call a truce to examine this remarkable find.

As the ships began to move towards them Kali stared at the *Tharnak*'s controls. "I wonder if any of these farking things are weapons?"

Aldrededor spoke from the piloting panel. "Have no fear, Kali Hooper – we have other means to defend ourselves."

"We do?"

"We have the ship itself. Or rather, how it flies."

"You mean use the threads?"

"Indeed. The *Tharnak* stimulates them, and if we can fly close enough to the enemy ships we should be able to disrupt their stability, bring them down."

"Sounds good. But you've only just learned how to pilot this thing. Are you sure you – ?"

Kali and the others wrapped themselves around rails as the *Tharnak* executed a perfect roll, three hundred and sixty degrees, leaving a reddened Dolorosa clutching her skirt about her knees when it righted itself.

"Convincing," Kali said, swallowing. "Do it."

Aldrededor winked and concentrated once more. The gap between the *Tharnak* and the airships closed rapidly. On the decks of the airships crewmen and shadowmages yelled in shock and surprise and, for a fleeting second as they hove in on the *Makennon*, Kali caught sight of Jenna frowning before racing along the deck, barking orders to her people.

All hells broke loose.

As the *Tharnak* drew level with the flotilla, the shadowmages aboard the *Makennon* and its sister ships began to weave their powerful magic. Suddenly the sky was filled with bolts of lightning, fire and ice. It was a devastating barrage and had Aldrededor not deftly manoeuvred their ship out of the way, the battle would have been over before it had begun. Having avoided the first barrage, the Sarcrean quickly brought the ship in close to the *Rhodon*, before veering suddenly away to starboard. The resultant play of the threads rippled along the sides of the *Rhodon*'s gasbag like a squall wind and the moorings of the cloth tore away in places, leaving flapping rents in the envelope. The *Rhodon* lurched suddenly, narrowly avoided collision with the *Voivode*.

Aldrededor wasted no time. As the *Voivode* pulled up to avoid its sister ship, the Sarcrean brought the *Tharnak* about, climbed, and then headed bow to bow with the second craft, intending to climb once more at the last second, generating a thread *wave* to slap the enemy ship down. The *Voivode* was more prepared than her sister ship, however, and even as the *Tharnak* headed towards her, the shadowmages had already discharged a volley of defensive magic, expanding circles of fire that would have been difficult to avoid even without the fireballs that accompanied them. Rather than take their impact on the most vulnerable area of the ship, the prow, Aldrededor did the only thing he could and swung the *Tharnak* around hard, flinging Kali and the others against the rails. The sky steadied itself after a second and Kali realised that while they had been forced to turn and run, they had still managed to inflict damage on the *Voivode*, which was bucking violently in their thread wake. She had no doubt that the same thought had already occurred to the Sarcrean, but she voiced it anyway.

"Aldrededor. Accelerate, *now*."

The air behind them rippled with distortions as their slipstream kicked into overdrive. The *Voivode* flew into the disturbance and was instantly kicked back, spiralling out of control towards the valley walls. Kali had to give its pilot their due, because they managed to regain some control before the ship impacted. Even so, the *Voivode* found itself colliding with, and badly snarling on, some of the sharper, projecting rocks.

It was their second victory but any element of surprise their manoeuvrability had granted them was gone, now, and even before Dolorosa had finished yelling and punching the air, the *Kesar* was heading in on their bow, moving hull to hull and tight against them on an opposed heading. It was a manoeuvre clearly meant to give the shadowmages already clustering at its rails chance to rake their energies along the *Tharnak*'s side and Kali knew there was no way they would be able to avoid damage.

It was time to give Aldrededor a helping hand.

Unslinging the crackstaff, Kali lodged herself against the rails and let loose a burst of energy towards the nearing shadowmages. However she found she had underestimated them as, one by one, they deflected the incoming charges with hastily erected shields, ricocheting it back in her direction.

"Hooper, go for the envelope," Slowhand urged, suddenly beside her. "I'll cover you."

Kali didn't question the archer, immediately bracing the crackstaff and angling it upwards just as the *Kesar* nosed into range.

The shadowmages spotted what she was trying to do as she aimed and prepared to launch another volley at her. But before they could loose their magical assault, they fell to the deck bucking and screaming as Slowhand unleashed rapid volleys from Suresight. His arrows provided Kali with the cover she needed, and she used the time to unleash a raking assault from the crackstaff, moving it slowly and determinedly across the enemy airship and tearing a gash in its envelope Suddenly venting gas, the *Kesar* tipped violently and, amidst much scrabbling and screaming, the shadowmages tumbled from the gondola to fall through the trees to the valley floor below.

"Hah!" Dolorosa shouted after them. "Thatta is whatta you get fora working with the *Final Feelth!*"

Aldrededor banked the *Tharnak* to starboard, pulling away from the battlegroup and the *Makennon*, taking advantage of the chaos to head for the Dragonfire rather than challenge the superior ship of the Faith flotilla.

Unfortunately, the *Makennon* had not been idle while he had outmanoeuvred her smaller sisterships, bringing its heavier bulk about in a manoeuvre that was perfectly timed. Even as the *Tharnak*'s bow turned to the Dragonfire, Jenna's flagship came seemingly out of nowhere to loom massively and directly in front of them, nose to nose, blocking their way to the exit from the valley, their artillery trained on the Old Race craft.

The message was clear

You want a fight? I'll give you a fight.

Kali moved to the front of the deck and found herself in direct eye contact with Jenna. Seeing Kali, Slowhand's sister smiled coldly. Slowhand came to stand by Kali's side, but if the archer had any hope at all of his sister's resolve weakening in his presence, it was dashed as her smile failed to falter.

"I see Fitch hasn't returned with her," Kali said through clenched teeth. "You still think there's no chance we can talk her round?"

"Hooper, the *fact* Fitch hasn't returned with her answers that one. Look at her – that cadaverous bastard's job is done."

Kali swallowed. She could tell that Jenna was actually enjoying this moment.

"Back us up," Kali said to Aldrededor. "Gently."

The *Tharnak* began to slowly reverse. Slowhand looked at Kali questioningly and, on the *Makennon*, Jenna frowned. But then with a wave of her hand she ordered the *Makennon* to follow them. Keeping the ships nose to nose.

"Keep going," Kali said.

"Hooper, what the hells are you doing?"

"*Keep going.*"

The *Tharnak* continued to reverse and the *Makennon* followed her. Had they continued the game that way, they could have played all day, nudging through the valley, but then Slowhand spotted something that would soon put paid to their backward flight.

"Er, Hooper..." he said.

Kali turned and saw that, behind them, the *Rhodon*, *Voivode* and *Kesar*, scarred and damaged though they were, had taken up positions in their path, enclosing them in an arrowhead formation. And those shadowmages that had survived the first clash lined their rails ready to unleash a fresh assault.

Jenna seemed to have them exactly where she wanted them.

"Bring us to a stop," Kali said.

"So what now?" Slowhand asked. When Kali didn't answer, he added, "Hooper, she's an expert tactician. There's no shame in being outmanoeuvred."

Kali looked at the archer, but couldn't hold his gaze. Had she been facing anyone but his sister her next move would have been delivered with some degree of satisfaction but –

"I'm sorry, 'Liam."

"For what?"

"Finishing what you started."

"I don't understand."

"For once," Dolorosa elaborated, "the bossa lady did not make it up as she went along."

Slowhand stared at the two women as they moved to the ship's rails. He looked down. Below them, a great number of small, wavering flames were visible in the treetops, covering the canopy like stars. Slowhand knew instantly what he was seeing and snapped a look at Dolorosa and Kali – just as they raised their arms and dropped them down.

From the cover of the jungle more than a hundred burning arrows were unleashed by yassan archers and arced upward towards the three smaller airships, puncturing their envelopes and firing their rigging and gondolas. A second volley came, firing those parts of the ships untouched by the first wave and doubling the damage. There was no escape and nowhere to hide from the devastating rain and, as the third volley filled the sky, it was intermingled with a renewed chorus of panicked and agonised screams. Their was nothing the shadowmages could do to prevent the surprise attack, though some of them tried, sweeping the jungle canopy with energy bolts that cut a swathe through the vegetation. But for every Yassan that was caught, three more still wielded their bows and the shadowmages themselves became targets, falling to their arrows. It took only seconds before the *Rhodon*, *Voivode* and *Kesar* were little more than flying funeral pyres and then they were only pyres, not flying at all.

Kali watched the remains of the airships spiral down into the jungle. Only the *Makennon* remained. As the flagship hung there, the yassan archers emerged fully from their cover, and once more Dolorosa and Kali raised their arms. All across the jungle canopy the Yassan waited poised. Kali and Dolorosa swallowed and turned to Slowhand, their arms stayed, awaiting the archer's word. Aldrededor, too, turned. The decision – *the word* – had to be his.

For his part, Slowhand simply moved up to stare across the gap between ships, his mane of blond hair blowing in the wind. Across that gap, her own hair blowing and eyes defiant and unblinking, Jenna stared back.

A second – an eternity – passed.

The archer's jaw tensed.

"Fire!"

Their eyes tearing, aware of the enormity of the decision Slowhand had just made, Dolorosa and Kali dropped their arms, and the volley of arrows turned the flagship into a flying inferno within a matter of moments. While Dolorosa had not had much time to train the yassan, train them well enough she obviously had, because amidst the volley, certain arrows did not randomly target the ship itself but instead those members of the crew manning the cannon, dropping them as they prepared to return fire.

Finally, the bow of the *Makennon* began to dip.

As Dolorosa pointed out, to a chorus of curses, the flagship of the Final Faith, while indeed beginning a slow dive, did not seem to be diving fast enough. Its angle and rate of descent was sluggish and lumbering, perhaps fitting of a ship its size. This was not a problem in itself but a problem *did* lie in the fact that that same angle and rate of descent was forcing her stern upward. If it continued as it did it would soon flip completely over toward the *Tharnak*. If it hit, it would swat the ancient spaceship out of the sky.

Aldrededor was visibly struggling to pull the *Tharnak* out of its path. As the Final Faith flagship continued to nose heavily downwards, the ex-pirate finally managed to force the *Tharnak* into the beginnings of a climb. It seemed they might make it – but it was going to be close. Close enough, in fact, that they found themselves able to watch the last moments of the *Makennon* and her crew in intimate detail.

Pulling up even as the *Makennon* angled down, the *Tharnak* flew along the *Makennon*'s deck, finely manoeuvring through the metal ribcage that had supported its all but burned out envelope. As they accelerated past they could see just how much damage the yassan archers' arrows had done.

Kali watched Slowhand watching the deck of the *Makennon*, following the actions of his sister amid the chaos rapidly developing there. It was testimony to Jenna's command skills that the ordinary crewmen still followed her orders – though the contingent of shadowmages aboard had already succumbed to panic – trying to beat back the flames despite the fire's inevitable triumph. Jenna strode the deck as if she could restore the *Makennon*'s flightworthiness though, even at a distance, Kali and Slowhand could see the strain thinning and greying her face. But, in the end, Jenna had little choice other than to accept the ship's doom. The sheer amount of collapsing rigging, support struts and explosions defeated any effort that could be made to stay what had to come. And at last it happened. A combination of spreading fire and detonations that conspired to separate the ribbing and remains of the envelope from the gondola completely.

The *Makennon* began to fall to the jungle below.

Jenna faced her demise with dignity, anchoring herself at the airship's wheel and standing steadfast The last thing Slowhand saw before she was obscured by the overturning hull was his sister staring directly into his eyes.

Goodbye, brother. I wish I knew what might have been.

"She's going to clip us!" Kali shouted over the roar of the dying ship as its tail swung towards the *Tharnak*. Even as Aldrededor struggled to gain more height there was a bone-shaking vibration that juddered the ancient craft right to its core, throwing Kali, Slowhand and Dolorosa to the deck.

As the Sarcrean struggled at the control panel there was a dull boom from the underside of the ship and the amberglow layer beneath the thread funnels crackled and darkened.

"We have lost the use of half of the funnels on our port side and a third on our starboard, Kali Hooper. The retro funnels are gone completely. Though we have some limited manoeuvrability remaining, I fear it is not enough to enable us to negotiate the Dragonfire."

"We're going to crash?"

"We are going to crash."

Behind her, Slowhand slammed his palms onto the rail and walked to the *Tharnak*'s stern, staring down at the smouldering remains of the three smaller airships and the *Makennon*, reflecting with a certain calm that perhaps it had indeed been fated that he and his sister should die together.

They were going down and what they needed was a miracle.

What neither he, or anyone else aboard expected, was that they got one.

From the still burning remains of the Crucible, something was rising. Something that, at first, looked like a plume of smoke but, on second glance, turned out to be something else entirely.

It moved more slowly than smoke, for one thing, and seemed to be made up of countless tiny shimmering particles. As all aboard the ship watched, the particles began to coalesce.

For Kali and Slowhand, it reminded them of the dwelf slowly taking shape within its sphere. But this was something quite different. A long, undulating worm-like was body was forming, kept aloft by majestic wings that stretched far and wide.

The red eyes of the creature regarded them. Then the dragon flew towards them.

"Oh, shit," Killiam Slowhand said.

"Great Grandma of the Gods," Aldrededor and Dolorosa breathed together.

Only Kali said nothing and smiled to herself, knowing what was actually happening. This was what the dwelf had meant when he'd said that there had been one last thing he had to do. Whatever technology and magics he had left – and she suspected this was more magic than technology – the doomed ancient one had somehow reconnected them to the dying Crucible and produced at last the one creature of peninsulan legend they had never recreated. Why he was doing this now, she didn't know, and nor did she know how much of the dwelf's consciousness existed in his creation but, in the end, it didn't matter. As its people watched in awe from the jungle canopy, the Dragon God rose over them.

"It's coming right at us!" Slowhand warned.

"There is nothing I can do," Aldrededor confessed.

"I don't think it means us harm," Kali said. "It might even be coming to help..."

"Help?" Slowhand repeated.

"A-ha. Look."

Slowhand and the others did, but not for long, as they were too busy ducking. Because despite Kali's assurance, they could not help but instinctively drop as the massive creature flew directly at the ship and then swooped overhead, so close that the downdraught from its wings beat the air around them. As they watched in amazement, the claws attached themselves to the *Tharnak* and pulled the entire craft up beneath it, towards its belly, as if for protection. As soon as the ship was secure the creature proceeded to fold its vast wings about the craft, pulling it in tight.

The very last thing they saw, before the creature entirely enfolded the craft, was the Dragonfire before them.

"Hold tight!" Kali shouted. "It's taking us through!"

"What the hells do you mean, taking us through?" Slowhand screeched.

"Slowhand, sometimes you've just got to have a little faith!"

Faith and a pretty good sense of balance, Kali thought to herself. Because for the next few seconds – but what seemed like an eternity – she and the others found themselves being flung from one side of the deck to the other as the creature manoeuvred through the cave system. And then, suddenly, they were through.

The dragon's wings opened and the *Tharnak* was lowered by its claws, and they found themselves being flown high along the pass.

"My gods!" Slowhand said.

"No," Kali corrected. "*Their* God."

The archer, like the others, looked to the rails, and saw the yassan emerging from a hundred cave mouths along the pass. As the Dragon passed over them they fell to their knees and emitted a great roar of worship that resounded deafeningly through the mountains. And as it did, the dragon's long neck waved slowly from side to side, as if in acknowledgement.

"This is the moment that they – that their ancestors – have waited countless years for," Kali said. "In a strange way, in believing what they did, they were right all along."

"I hate to spoil the moment," Slowhand pointed out, looking somewhat less elated than Kali, "but while they may have been right, something here is wrong."

"What are you talking about?"

"Well, for one thing, our friend here isn't letting go."

Kali looked up, and frowned. "I'm sure it will soon."

"No, bossa lady, it is more than that," Dolorosa said. The ex-piratess had climbed up on a rail to examine the creature more closely and she, too, frowned. "Look atta this," she added, nodding at a scabrous wound that seemed to be spreading by the second all along its underside. "Eet is injured."

"Hardly surprising," Aldrededor said. "Our passage through the Dragonfire was a rough one."

"Except only its outside hit the walls," Kali pointed out.

Slowhand bit his lip. "Hooper, are you saying – ?"

Kali nodded. "Nothing except the k'nid can survive outside the valley."

"Then we are in trouble, Kali Hooper," Aldrededor piped in. "Because as my wife would say, we 'havva another problem'."

"What, Aldrededor?"

"Perhaps you and Mister Slowhand would care to take a look over the side."

"Ohhhh, fark," the archer said.

"You can say that again," Kali answered.

"*Ohhhh, fark.*"

The curse was wholly appropriate. Whilst they had all been speaking, not only had the dragon flown them out of the pass and beyond the Drakengrat Mountains but it had also, for its own reasons, climbed. Features on the landscape below were now little more than dots, the dragon having gained at least a thousand metres in height.

A thousand metres.

And it was still climbing.

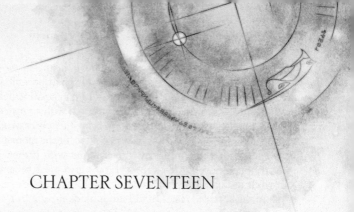

CHAPTER SEVENTEEN

THE DRAGON CONTINUED to climb, so high now that daylight began to give way to the azureness of night as the air around it and the ship thinned, and that azure glow in turn began to give way to an inky blackness that was neither night or day. Kali and the others had been unable to do anything to prevent their continued ascent and they could do nothing now except experience, in stunned silence, that which no one of their world had ever experienced before.

It was an hour after dawn.

And the stars were coming out.

"Hooper?" Slowhand said, his voice tinged with wonder.

"Oh gods," was all Kali could say in reply, as she stared out into the void.

That either of them could speak at all was a surprise. And not only because of what lay revealed before them. All four on board the ship had suffered near unconsciousness as they had been carried further and further from the now impossibly distant and patchwork ground, breathlessness giving way to burning lungs and then an inability to breathe at all. Thankfully, though, the effects of their rising altitude had not lasted, the ship forming a membrane around the deck that sealed them in while also generating fresh air for them to breathe. This was alongside another, far more peculiar and unexpected effect which was that, a few seconds later, she and the others seemed to be able to fly!

It was as if they weighed nothing at all, victims of some mischievous sorcery wielded by an invisible hand. The expressions on her companions' faces reflected the same emotions Kali felt – that it was unbelievable and strange and incredible. And liberating. *Too* liberating in one case.

Slowhand's clothes were beginning to float off.

Fortunately they didn't get chance to float all the way.

The ship dropped suddenly, Kali and the others' weightless forms thrown into turmoil within, and as Kali scrambled to see through the membrane, paddling upside down across its surface, it was clear that the dragon had begun to struggle above them. The wound on its underside that Dolorosa had noticed earlier had become livid now, and the flesh around it was falling away, first in small flakes and then larger chunks, as if the creature were infected with a virulent leprosy. Whatever had possessed the dragon to bring them here, whatever had driven it on this suicidal climb, didn't matter for the moment, because it was clear that its journey was over – and with it their own. The ship dropped once more as the dragon's grip on it became weaker, but while it didn't let go, the creature itself began to turn, as if to dive back to the surface. The turn did not look deliberate to Kali, though – as if the creature were simply too weak now to remain aloft, listing rather than manoeuvring, merely suspended momentarily in this alien space. A second later, that proved to be the case.

Both the dragon and the ship began to plummet, and Kali and the others were propelled into the membrane. As it stretched Kali began to pray that it wouldn't break. She did not have to pray for long, though, as the dragon's rate of descent was so great that the weightlessness they had experienced soon dissipated. This resulted in all four of them being thrown about the craft like peas in a pod.

"Hooper, what in all the farking hells is going on!?" Slowhand shouted.

"Gravity, I think."

"That isn't what I mean and you know it!"

Kali stared up at the dragon and her brow furrowed. The wound on its underside had spread, encompassing now its sides and the beginnings of its wings. Cartilage and muscle and even bone were becoming visible beneath the flesh now and it was obvious to Kali what she was seeing. A reversal of the process that had formed the creature in the first place. This, then, was the fate of all those creations, bar the k'nid, who left the influence of the Crucible. The dragon was coming apart before her eyes.

And if it came apart at this height, then the ship would too.

Their dizzying fall continued and, as they dropped below a certain altitude, the membrane that had held them from the void disappeared, exposing all on the deck to the raw maelstrom of the wind. It was impossible to communicate with the others, words and even screams whipped away in the deafening roar, and it was almost as impossible to maintain their hold on the ship, winds ripping at them and making the flesh on their faces flap and ripple. Aldrededor, though, was fighting his way back to the controls, presumably in a desperate attempt to try and level them out. Even if he made it, the Sarcrean certainly had his work cut out for him, the decaying dragon having fallen now into a spiralling descent that spun the world around them.

Kali willed the dragon to quite literally keep itself together for just a little longer, until they were at an altitude where Aldrededor might be able to safely regain some control. She had no doubt now that the same benign intelligence – perhaps all that was left of the dwelf – that had guided them through the Dragonfire was still at play here, because the dragon was clearly trying to raise and flex its wings and pull them out of their terminal dive. Even as great scaled and fleshy chunks of it were torn away by the tumultuous descent, the dragon, for whatever reason it had brought them here, was now trying to bring them safely home.

Kali pulled herself down the deck to Aldrededor's side, where the ex-pirate was linked to the ship once more but clearly straining to impose his will upon it. As he did, she stared at the dragon again, heart sinking as she saw its flesh had now all but been stripped away.

It was surely only a matter of minutes before there was nothing left of the creature at all. Still, as it fought, its wings, slowly, began to lift.

And as they did, the ship began to level out.

Kali looked down. Their angle of descent was still way too steep, way too fast. But it was a start. The dragon was trying, and they had to try too.

"Aldrededor, you have to pull us up!" Kali shouted. "You have to pull us up when I tell you!"

The ex-pirate's flowing moustache was plastered against his cheeks by the wind now. "I... will try... Kali Hooper."

Kali slapped him on the back. "I know you will!"

"Hooper, our friend is a goner," Slowhand shouted.

"Just a few moments more," Kali willed.

Again, she looked at the dragon and was staggered and awed as, quite deliberately, its head – actually more a cadaverous skull now – turned on its long neck and looked at her, as if acknowledging its complicitness in her plan. The creature knew what it was doing, all right, and it could *only* know if it did indeed carry the consciousness of the dwelf. Kali looked up as a beating that could be heard even above the roaring wind began and saw that at last the dragon had managed to fully flex what remained of its wings. As they slowly, majestically, swept at the air it began to pull the ship onto a more level keel.

But it would not be enough unless they did their bit.

Kali stared one last time at the dragon, swallowing as its saddened eyes began to dull, then turn grey, and then, like the rest of its form, began to discorporealise. The air around her filled with a dry, golden rain that coated her face and tasted bitter on her lips.

"Aldrededor, now," she said, a tear in her eye.

"Everybody hold on."

The Sarcrean's eyes shut, his jaw clenched and his temples throbbed with concentration. Above him, the dragon was now nothing but a skeletal afterthought and, even as he pulled back on the ship's controls, that too began to stream away into the wind.

Thank you and goodbye, Kali thought sadly, wishing she had more time to mourn the passing of the ancient creature.

As the dragon vanished on the wind, the Kerberos ship soared from its ashes, punching through its discorporealising remains into clear sky, pulling up from what had become a forty-five degree dive into a much gentler descent. Only the angle of the descent was gentle, however, the ship still hurtling through the air at previously unimaginable speed.

As Twilight rolled beneath it, Kali could not work out how high they still were because she could see no landmarks below. But then as the ship drew lower, penetrating a thin layer of cloud, she understood why – they were coming down over the sea.

Storm tossed waves roiled beneath them and lightning flashed. How far out they were, Kali didn't know, but she understood instantly why the Twilight Seas were considered so dangerous by those who sailed them. Here, beyond the Storm Wall, she could see that vast areas of the deeps were whorled by giant whirlpools. Waves clashed like opposing armies, the fallout of battle spreading for leagues and, in one place in particular, Kali saw a wall of water so high it was moving dizzying slowly, but seemingly with purpose, across the turbulent expanse. *What the hells was that?* Kali thought. It even seemed to have things riding the side of it, *something* on top of it.

Whatever it was, their passage was such that it was soon gone and at last, ahead of them, Kali began to make out the jagged edges of what looked like a large island. From its shape she recognised Allantia, and beyond that a much larger landmass that, by extension, had to be the northern coast of the peninsula. As the ship passed over Allantia, a dark mass flecked with both red and white rose ominously on the eastern horizon, bending southward for leagues after leagues – a mass that was without doubt the World's Ridge Mountains.

Kali felt a momentary stab of disappointment, that of missed opportunity, because if only they had come in the other way she might have been able to see what lay *beyond*. She shrugged the feeling aside in favour of a much more positive one, however, because Aldrededor had brought them almost exactly where they needed to be.

The ex-pirate brought the ship onto an almost level keel and Kali turned to congratulate him but, as she did, the ship shuddered violently beneath her. It sounded and felt as if it had taken far more of a battering than it could stand.

Kali looked to the east where the thick bow of the Sardenne Forest could now just be made out, wrapping the base of the World's Ridge Mountains. The problem was, she could feel the ship moving ever so slightly away from it, on a south-easterly course.

"Aldrededor, can you turn us towards the Spiral?"

The Sarcrean shook his head. "I fear not, Kali Hooper. Our manoeuvrability remains all but non-existent and many thread funnels are damaged. We are locked on this course unable to climb and, what is worse, unable to attempt a controlled descent."

"You mean we arra going to crash?" Dolorosa asked.

"Not so much crash as fly into the ground... eventually," Kali corrected. "Aldrededor, where will we come down?"

The ex-pirate closed his eyes, calculated. "With our rate of descent and crew complement we will impact several leagues outside Andon, to the east of the Anclas Territorial border."

The Anclas Territories, Kali thought. *Dammit!*

Because in other words, that meant right under the hawklike noses of the Vos military. She had never been partisan in her life, and she wasn't about to start being so now, but if that happened, even if the ship took damage, the dwelfen technology on board could unfairly tip the balance of power in Vos's favour for years to come. They *had* to get past them, bring the ship down elsewhere somehow.

But where? As Kali studied the ground flashing below, she asked herself not for the first time just where on the peninsula it would be safe from its burgeoning civilisation.

And the answer was nowhere.

Kali paused, a plan forming. A plan she was amazed she hadn't thought of before now.

"Aldrededor," she said suddenly. "You said with our 'current crew complement.' So if our crew complement were fewer, namely one, would the ship avoid coming down near the territories, even overfly Andon?"

"By a narrow margin, Kali Hooper. But I do not understand – you are thinking of hiding the ship beyond Andon?"

Kali smiled. "Something like that, Mister Pirate."

Aldrededor frowned, not understanding but willing to comply nonetheless.

"Very well, Kali Hooper. But how do my wife, Mister Slowhand and yourself plan to leave the ship exactly?"

"*I* don't. It's you lot I need to walk the plank."

The ex-pirate's eyebrows rose. "This ship needs a pilot, Kali Hooper."

"No, Aldrededor, not any more. The ship's locked on course, right?

429

So even if you detach yourself from the threads, it'll get me where I need to go, yes?"

"Yes, but –"

"Then it's settled," Kali looked at the ground. "Get yourself ready, there isn't much time."

"Whoa, whoa, whoa," Slowhand protested. "There isn't much time for *what*? How exactly are we going to abandon ship, Hooper?"

"Once, whenna our sheep was swept into the sky by the Great Gusts of Groom," Dolorosa interjected, "Aldrededor and I escape using the sheep's flag anda feathers from its mascot. We called itta the parrot-chute!"

"You have to be kidding, right?" Slowhand sighed. "Well, unfortunately, we're all out of parrots, too."

"You havva the better idea, preety boy?"

"Pretty boy?"

"Yessa, preety boy!"

"Hey!"

"*I* have the better idea," Kali interrupted. "We use the Roaring."

"*The Roaring?*"

Kali nodded, picturing the giant, coolwater geyser that erupted north of Miramas and Gargas, the strange wall of water she had seen at sea having given her the idea. No one really knew what the source of the Roaring was, though some said it was an outlet for water surging underground from the other side of the World's Ridge Mountains. What she did know was that it thundered into the air for an hour each day at about this time, and the phenomenon was right in their flightpath. What was more, when the geyser crashed back to ground, its overflow became the Rainbow River which, flowing south-easterly, eventually fed Badlands Brook near which sat the Flagons. If Slowhand and the others gave themselves to the geyser and the current of the river they should not only be home in no time but – assuming they stayed in the moving water – relatively safe from any k'nid infestation between here and their destination.

"Let me get this straight," Slowhand said. "You want us to *jump* into the Roaring?"

"Only if it's spouting."

"What ees the matter, preety boy – afraid of a leetle water?" Dolorosa taunted. She joined Aldrededor at the ship's rails, her husband having already detached himself from the controls, trusting Kali implicitly.

"I'm not going anywhere," Slowhand said to Kali. "I'm staying with you."

"Slowhand, you *can't*. One person on board, this ship gets where I need it to go. Two, it crashes and burns."

"Then you jump, too!" the archer retorted. And then, more softly: "Dammit, Hooper, I've already lost one person I love today."

Kali stared at him, momentarily speechless. The fact was, she didn't exactly relish what she planned to do as it was as potentially dangerous as Slowhand feared, but if her plan was to work she *had* to stay with the ship. "There's no choice."

"What are you going to do, Hooper, hit me again? Well, try it. You just try –"

Kali's fist landed hard. The archer staggered back and then collapsed to the deck.

Kali took a deep breath, then leaned over the rail and looked down and ahead. The Roaring was already looming, spray from it spattering her face.

"Time to go."

Both Aldrededor and Dolorosa climbed onto the rail, ready to jump, the latter hesitating slightly.

"Bossa lady? Arra you sure you know whatta you are doing?"

Kali smiled. "I thought I told you, I make this up as I go along." She looked at the prone archer. "Look after him, okay?"

"Pretty boy, he willa notta be pleased."

"I hope you survive to find out, Kali Hooper," Aldrededor said.

"Both of you," Kali said, "thank you. For everything."

The ex-pirates nodded, he with a twirl of his moustache and a twinkle of his eye, she with a smile that cracked parts of her face Kali hadn't ever seen move. And then the two of them waited until the wide geyser was beneath them and leapt.

Kali watched the two Sarcreans plunge into the seething plateau and then quickly heaved Slowhand's unconscious form onto the rail. The archer was groaning, beginning to stir, when she grabbed his legs and tipped him forward. Slowhand's semiconscious form tumbled from the ship, his clothes snagging awkwardly on some protrusion from the hull and, before Kali's disbelieving eyes, they were ripped from him, leaving him completely naked, bar his bow and quiver, to fall after the pirates.

Pits of bloody Kerberos! Just how in the hells did he do it?

Shaking her head, Kali moved to the rear of the deck and watched as Aldrededor and Dolorosa caught the spluttering archer, and then the three of them began to recede from her view as the giant geyser reached its zenith and began to drop from whence it had come.

Kali moved to the bow of the ship and stared down to study the landscape as it continued to roll beneath her. The ship was following the course of the Rainbow River. There was the Rainbow Delta and one of its various offshoots, Badlands Brook, there Ponderfoot's Copse, there Bottomless Pit, and there – suddenly – the Flagons itself.

The sight of home – surrounded, though thankfully still untouched, by the k'nid – tugged at her, and the desire to be down there, downing her eighth glass of thwack was almost so overwhelming that she was tempted, for a second, to leap overboard herself. The desire became all the more tempting when unexpectedly – no doubt drawn by the sound of the ship, the kind of *off key* sound that only he would recognise – Merrit Moon emerged from the doors of the tavern and stared upwards. It was odd but Kali had become somehow so used to the concept of the Kerberos ship over these last hours that she had forgotten how staggering it might be to another's eyes. She watched the old man's face gurn through a number of indefinable expressions before he mouthed the words: "My gods."

He actually *did* stagger back when she waved to him from the deck, and for a moment she thought he might spontaneously turn into Thrutt.

Interested in Old Race artefacts, old man? Well, I got you a doozy.

She wished she could explain what was happening, have the reassuring presence of the old man with her somehow, but that task would have to be left to Aldrededor, Dolorosa and Slowhand.

The ship moved on and, after a while, Kali wondered whether she were close enough yet to put the next stage of her plan into action, studying the ground once more to sight landmarks to indicate her proximity to Andon. The effective range at which her plan might work was a complete unknown, however, and she would really lose nothing by trying to instigate it now. Decided, she steadied herself on the bow of the ship and focused all her mental energy and concentration into the formation of a single word. A name.

Sonpear.

It was a gamble, of course – a gamble that the telepathic link that the League sorcerer had established with her while she was in Domdruggle's Expanse remained effective.

Sonpear, she attempted again, trying to amplify her thoughts. *Can you hear me?*

No reply.

Sonpear.

SONPEAR!

Kali's eyes squeezed shut and her brow furrowed in concentration. She was oblivious to the wind that buffeted her as the ship continued its long descent, oblivious to everything but the image of a man on whom she would never have dreamt the lives of so many would depend.

SONPEAR, YOU BASTARD, HEAR ME!

Miss Hooper? There is really no need to shout. Or, I might add, to get personal.

Kali's eyes snapped back open and, for a second, she felt the link that had just been established slip away. But she fought against it until she could once again feel the sorcerer in her grasp.

Miss Hooper, it is pleasing to hear from you. Tell me – was your mission successful?

There'll be no more k'nid from the Crucible. But the danger isn't over yet.

Indeed? And I gather that this communication is occurring because you once more need my help?

Not only yours, Sonpear. The League.

The League? Miss Hooper, I thought you already understood that the League has sealed its doors. That they are offering their help to no one.

And doing so because they know nothing works. Tell me, Sonpear – how are things in Andon?

The k'nid are ubiquitous. There is little more that can be done to prevent the city falling to them completely. Thankfully, we have managed to evacuate many of our people to the sewer network. Not the most salubrious place of refuge, as I can testify, but one that has become a necessity.

Keep them there, Sonpear. But I need you to bring a message to the League, however you can.

And that message is?

That I have the means to eradicate the k'nid. But I need you, and them, to do something for me in return.

Which is?

Open another portal to Domdruggle's Expanse.

The Expanse? But surely I alone could attempt –

I doubt it, Sonpear. This one needs to be a little bigger.

Bigger?

And in the sky.

Sky?

It's a long story. Trust me.

Sonpear went silent, and whether it was the telepathic link or not, Kali could almost feel him cogitating.

Very well, Miss Hooper, I shall do as you ask. How long do we have to prepare the portal?

Ohhh… about ten minutes.

Hmph. I see.

Not yet, you don't. But you will. Later, Sonpear.

The sorcerer's voice sounded vaguely puzzled. *Very well, Miss Hooper. Later, as you say.*

Kali broke the link and returned her attention to the physical rather than the mental, staring ahead of the ship to determine its current location. Its trajectory had not wavered while she had been otherwise occupied and, while it was inevitably now slightly lower in the sky, it was also closer to Andon, whose tallest structure – the Three Towers – had now become visible. She guessed that she would know if Sonpear had been successful in his task if she saw the structure unfurl from its defensive position. For now there was nothing that she could do.

She gazed down at the passing landscape once more. Soon she would pass over the desolation surrounding Andon that was known as the Killing Ground. But, before she reached that, she was already encountering a number of smaller settlements that had established themselves between the Anclas Territories and the city. They were mining towns, mainly, what their inhabitants liked to think of as frontier towns, and they provided Kali with her first chance to see the effects of the k'nid on populated areas. Having slaughtered, absorbed or driven into hiding everyone in the area, the k'nid were now the only living presence – and they were everywhere. It was as if someone had lain a grey blanket over the countryside. She realised that if the k'nid were not stopped, then the peninsula would be lost forever.

Kali looked to the horizon, filling now with the diverse shapes that made up the skyline of Andon, from besieged battlements to ramshackle merchants' houses, from the warehouses at the Skeleton Quay to Archimandrate Thomas Marek's solitary, Final Faith church; each and every structure quiet and abandoned and obscured beneath a layer of feasting k'nid. The only structure that seemed – perhaps through some magical means – to have escaped absorption was the Three Towers, but even so the headquarters of the League looked battered after enduring days of what must have been continuous assault. It did not, though, matter a jot what the Three Towers *looked* like, so long as its offences were still functional.

Dammit, Sonpear. This is cutting things fine.

But at that very moment the towers began to unfurl.

Standing at the prow of the ship, Kali watched as the three separate spires of the headquarters of the League of Prestidigitation and Prestige began to return to their normal state, shedding those k'nid that determinedly clung to the sides. It was an awesome sight but, as she watched, Kali was uncomfortably aware that she was the only spectator. The city below was deserted. But the restoration of the Three Towers to their normal state was a sight that instilled confidence, and not a little pride, in her. And her confidence was further bolstered when she began to make out a considerable number of figures exiting the spires and lining the bridges that were beginning to snap back into place.

Sonpear had done it. He had managed to persuade the mages to come out of their hidey-hole and join the final battle.

Still, what she was asking them to do was, as Sonpear himself had admitted, going to be far from easy. She wasn't exactly convinced that it was even possible – there was certainly no sign of any portal that she could see. Kali reckoned that she had approximately two or three minutes before the ship intercepted the Three Towers and she was knocked out of the sky. They all had only one chance at this, and if they failed the rune-covered crystal she carried with her would be lost, possibly for ever.

Suddenly, however, something began to happen. The mages lining the bridges turned as one to face the approaching ship and though she could not hear them, the gesticulations they made with their arms made Kali realise that they had begun to chant. Led by Poul Sonpear – and Kali was convinced she spotted Lucius Kane in there too – every man and woman present was mouthing the same invocation over and over again, the volume growing as she neared them. And as the volume grew, so did something else.

Kali's previous experience of a magical portal had been pressured and fleeting to say the least, but there was no mistaking what was forming before her and the ship now. Smack in the middle of the triangle formed by the three towers, above the bridges, the sky was opening. The portal began to spread across the sky like a bleeding wound, as if the heavens themselves had been knifed, and through it Kali could see the shadowy netherworld that was Domdruggle's Expanse. The perfect hiding place, she thought, where the ship could remain in limbo until, if ever, it was needed. And the ship was heading straight for it. Which, of course, meant that it was time to go.

Kali had had her escape route mapped out from the moment Andon had appeared on the horizon, a sequence of buildings she intended to use as stepping stones to get her safely down to ground level, starting with the steeple of the Final Faith church. She was sure the Archimandrite in charge of the place wouldn't mind the sacrilege, after all it was his lot that had started this mess in the first place. Of course, she would have to contend with the k'nid on her way down, but she still had her crackstaff and that should keep her safe enough until she could reach the Three Towers and hand over the crystal whereupon – hopefully – *that* particular problem would become academic. All she had to do was time her drop right so that she didn't break her legs.

She was beginning to unfurl a rope from her equipment belt, intending to tie it off and lower herself part of the way, when the ship shook violently and unexpectedly beneath her. She glanced worriedly ahead, saw that the ship was veering off course slightly. And if it continued the way it was going, it would veer away from the portal and into one of the towers themselves.

Dammit! Kali thought, dropping the rope and returning to the controls.

She had little, if any, idea of their internal workings and so did the only thing she could – thump them. *Hard.* She thumped them again but there was no response. And then, for the sake of variety, she kicked them. There was a slight response then and the course of the ship corrected slightly. But only for a second. Clearly the ship had leaked too much charge to continue without some persuasion and the implications of that couldn't have been worse.

She couldn't abandon the ship. She had to ride with it into the portal. And this time she doubted she would be coming back.

Kali looked up. The portal was directly in front of her now, fully formed, filling her world. The junction between realities seemed to slow the world around it, so that the ship edged rather than raced forward, but Kali wasn't sure whether that was a good thing or not, because it gave her more time to see what was waiting for her *inside.* Looming large, directly on the other side of the portal – *filling it* – was Domdruggle's face. That angry, wizened, no longer human face. And it was roaring at her.

"Hooper!" it shouted.

Or did it? The voice seemed to come from behind and below her, faint on the wind, and somehow not possessing the rumbling, vocal *gravitas* one might expect from an ages old, spectral wizard.

"Hooper!"

No, she thought. *It couldn't be.*

Kali raced to the rear of the deck and looked down. *Oh Gods, no, it really, really couldn't be...*

But it was.

There was a naked man on a horse following the ship.

Correction. There was a naked man on *Horse* following the ship.

Riding him across the rooftops.

Kali stared, and despite her predicament couldn't help but smile. The fact was, Slowhand wasn't so much riding Horse as Horse was allowing him to stay mounted as he galloped in pursuit, the great beast taking the gaps between buildings with powerful leaps, flinging the archer about in the saddle. Quite how he had gotten here so quickly she could only guess at, but presumably filled with indignant anger at being unceremoniously – and literally – dumped, Slowhand had survived the Rainbow River and hot-footed it to the Flagons and coaxed Horse from his sickbed with warnings about how she was in mortal danger. The bamfcat's unusual abilities took care of the rest. Kali's heart lifted to see how well the beast had recovered under Merrit Moon's tender ministrations, and having him nearby made her feel less alone against what she faced. The archer, too, she supposed begrudgingly.

"Hooper, jump!" Slowhand shouted, his voice faint across the distance between them.

"I can't!" she shouted back, hoping that he not only heard but realised there was a reason for her refusal beyond the dizzying height. Fortunately, the ship juddered once more to illustrate her point.

A second passed, Slowhand sizing the situation up. As Kali corrected the ship's course once more, she heard: "Hooper, just time it!"

Time what? Kali thought.

Because despite their mutual effort, Slowhand and Horse remained too far away. But at that second the nose of the ship impacted with the portal, squelching as it entered, and the effect the portal had on seeming to slow time was magnified tenfold as it slowly began to suck the ship through the bridge between worlds. Two things became immediately apparent to Kali – one, that this would give Slowhand and Horse time to draw closer and, two, that the ship no longer needed to be steered. It was entering the portal now no matter what and that made the difference between heroism and suicide. The jump itself might be suicide but at least she could *try*.

Again, she raced to the back of the ship, saw Slowhand and Horse had drawn closer, galloping now across some of the higher rooftops surrounding the Andon Heart. But they were still some way away and one hells of a long way down. She'd never make it.

Still, Slowhand had to have some kind of plan. She knew he thought she thought he was an idiot but he was an idiot she had learned to trust. Even Slowhand wouldn't suggest she leap to her death. She *had* to trust him, whatever his plan.

As he had said, she had to time it, wait until the last possible moment before she leapt. Decided, Kali returned to the bow of the ship and stood directly before the portal, drawing a deep breath to steady herself against Domdruggle's immense, looming visage. And as the ship penetrated ever further into the portal she began to back up, keeping the threshold at a safe distance all the time. As she did, she mentally envisaged the deck shortening behind her, waiting for the *exact* moment when it had become just short *and* long enough to make her leap a viable one. And then, with a roar of determination, she turned and ran.

Kali pounded along the remaining deck, legs thumping, arms pumping, her panting drowning out every other sound as she watched the Andon skyline bob before her. And then she was in the air.

She soared from the end of the ship, legs still pumping, arms windmilling as, behind her, the ship continued to be absorbed by the portal, but she was no longer interested in what was behind her, only what was in front and below. As the air whistled about her she tried to orientate herself enough to spot Slowhand and there he was, spurring Horse up the sixty degree slope of the roof of an inn. And then, at full gallop, he spurred Horse off it so that the great beast seemed, momentarily, to be making a jump towards the heavens.

Then the pair of them disappeared.

Suddenly they were gone. Completely.

Oh crap.

She had recognised the disturbance in the air about Horse enough to know that he had just made one of his 'leaps' but she had no idea if the leap had been made by accident or design. Maybe Horse had simply panicked at what the archer had made him do, or maybe it had been a deliberate, if mistimed, attempt to somehow reach her.

Alone now, Kali watched the rooftops grow beneath her and tried not to anticipate the impact she would soon feel. It wasn't the first time she had been in a situation such as this but it *was* different. Falling from a suicide slide above the rooftops of Scholten was one thing but here she was, having leapt from somewhere almost forty stories high, and that was something else entirely.

Suddenly Horse appeared directly in front and a little below her, a roaring Slowhand on his back. The shock was so great that Kali almost dropped right past them thinking: *Hey, that was neat.* Then her survival instincts kicked in and she grabbed for the beast – and missed. Luckily, in the second she'd made her attempt, Horse's momentum had carried him slightly further forward and, with the aid of a horn that he suddenly thrust forward, she was able to flail and grab again, flinging herself up onto his back behind Slowhand. At the exact moment she did, all three of them succumbed to gravity and they fell.

The world disappeared around her.

Reappeared.

Horse impacted with the ground so hard that his hooves shattered the stone flagging.

But they were down.

Safe.

Almost.

"Thanks, Slowhand," Kali said, and leaving a stunned and naked archer behind, began to run off along the street.

"Where the hells are you going?"

Kali produced the prism from her equipment belt, waved it in the air.

"Have to see a man about a god!"

CHAPTER EIGHTEEN

THE SKY ABOVE the Here There Be Flagons raged with a storm unlike any heard or seen before – a storm of turbulent, clashing clouds and roaring thunder, green forked lightning and a strange syrupy rain. The same storm as raged over Tarn raged over the rest of Pontaine and over the Anclas Territories and Vos too. Coast to coast as far as the Storm Wall, reaching every edge and every corner of the land to cleanse it of those who would have destroyed it. There was nowhere for these things – for the k'nid – to escape, because this was a storm visited on the land not by nature but supernature. A phenomenon born somewhere between the ancient magics and the final, doomed technological achievements of the Old Races.

The storm had raged for three days now, and would rage for three more. It was not a time to go out.

Watching the tumult at the windows of the Flagons, its violence muted by the thick glass and offset by the warm glow of the fire, Kali sipped from a tankard of thwack and reflected that the contrast between where she stood now and what she had seen and done in recent days couldn't have been more dramatic.

The crackling of the fire, the whinnying of horses from the stables and the simple talk around the bar – of work needed to repair the fields, of blacksmithing new tools and of the coming harvest – only served to heighten the difference between her world and that of the Old Races. There were no damned airships here, no damned mad scientist laboratories and, most importantly of all, no damned race against time. The pace was slower, gentler, and she realised how much she appreciated that right now. How much she *needed* it. That wasn't to say that she might not be off on her travels once again when the storm died down, but for the moment she needed time to think.

And, of course, to drink.

Kali downed the remainder of the thwack in one and went for another, squeezing in at the bar. She found one waiting for her, already poured by Red, who had volunteered to play host for the festivities; giving Dolorosa and Aldrededor a break from their usual duties, a break which Kali felt they had wholeheartedly earned. Red's displacement from barstool to his position behind the bar seemed to suit him, and despite the fact that the Flagons was jam-packed, he was doing sterling work.

Kali wandered through the crowd, nodding to those she knew and those whose acquaintance she had made in the past few days, pleased that she had invited them all here. The fact that the storm effectively stymied any normal outside activity had, to some, presented a problem. Namely, how to occupy themselves while it lasted, but the solution had seemed obvious to her.

Let's get betwattled.

At the Flagons.

On me.

Kali smiled. Her unusual tolerance for alcohol had, of course, given her the advantage in this prolonged session. Looking around now, it was clear that some of her guests were becoming somewhat the worse for wear. Sitting by the temporary stage, Jengo Pim and his lieutenants were waiting patiently for the appearance of the night's cabaret – if the slumped and, in some cases, face down on the table positions they had gradually adopted could be called waiting patiently. Still, they weren't completely out of it yet, stirring with a groan every time there was a creak on the stairs, only to collapse again despondently when the objects of their affections – Pim's, in particular – failed to appear. She could hardly blame the Hells' Bellies for taking their time in getting on stage. After all, they had been nowhere else for a week and they had only agreed to one final performance when, on his behalf, she had told them that Jengo Pim was their greatest admirer and fan. It hadn't hurt that the Grey Brigade's leader had personally agreed to treble their fee too.

Kali looked towards the crowded bar and smiled again. At first she had thought Poul Sonpear and his friends from the League were holding up – somewhat surprisingly – better than the streetwise, heavy drinking thieves, but now she saw that the mages were hardly playing fair. Sonpear himself appeared to be handling his drink naturally, standing tall amongst them, downing shot after shot, but his companions were clearly using a couple of old tricks to maintain the illusion that they were still one of the boys. Kali noticed the giveaway pink puff of smoke following a belch that denoted a sobriety spell and, further along the bar, two mages who were taller than when they had arrived, due only to the fact that they were hovering a few inches above the floor so as not to betray any unsteadiness on their feet. Kali moved past them, gave them both a nudge and they rose like balloons, crashing back to the floor when their heads hit the ceiling. She noticed as she did that Sonpear appeared to be muttering to himself between slugs. Ah, so that was it, she thought. He wasn't handling his drink naturally at all, it was the old Hollow Legs invocation.

Kali turned and crashed right into Dolorosa, who was weaving her way back from the bar with two more 'stalkers' for herself and Hetty Scrubb. The two women had been hitting the lethal cocktails – so named because they lurked before hitting you from behind – since the morning, and even the fact that both umbrellas flew out of the drinks in the collision didn't stop the Sarcrean making a narrow-eyed and dedicated beeline back to her seat, where she and Hetty continued cackling as if Kali had never been there. Kali shook her head, hoping that Aldrededor served up some food soon, not only because it might help to sober the old bat up but also slow her down so that she and the herbalist didn't bankrupt the Flagons with their drinking.

Kali nodded to Merrit Moon at a table further along the bar and then popped her head into the kitchen to see how Aldrededor was getting on. The Sarcrean had volunteered to cook, as everyone was heartily sick of Dolorosa's Surprise Stew after the batch she had prepared for Kali's memorial drinking session the week before.

"How goes it, Mister Pirate?"

Aldrededor looked up at her from the stove as he stirred, then bent, inhaling deeply from the cooking pot. "Ahhh, sproing, crackfish and limpods, everything the stomach of a true mariner could desire."

Kali smiled, and dipped a spoon for a sample. "At least you're willing to admit what's in it."

"Indeed. And in honour of these ingredients, I name it Seaman Stew."

Kali's smile froze, as did the spoon at her lips. "You know, Aldrededor. I might be tempted to have another think about that..."

"Oh?"

"You know. *Think* about it."

"Why should I think about it, Kali Hooper?"

Kali stared at him as he stared at her, wondering whether he was going to crack a smile. "Well, *because*..." She shrugged when there was no response. Maybe pirates had a different sense of humour, she thought. Or maybe, more worryingly, it was just her.

"I'll get Slowhand to explain it. See you later."

She returned to the bar, noticed that Pim and his men were once more staring in expectant hope at the stairs, and looked up herself to see what had caused the creak this time. Still no Hells Bellies but, as the thieves slumped once more, she smiled, seeing the one person who had so far been missing from the festivities. Though she had given Slowhand Jenna's bracelet in the yassan caves the night before they had left for the Crucible, the archer – perhaps so as not to be distracted from the task at hand – had decided not to activate it until now, and had spent the best part of the day watching his sister's recordings over and over. She had, every now and then, gone up to check on him, but had never made it through the door, Jenna's voice speaking so gently to Slowhand – of their childhood together – that she had felt it improper to intrude.

"Hey," she said, "fancy a drink?"

Slowhand nodded and smiled.

"Except there doesn't seem to be anywhere to sit."

"Not a problem," Kali said. She moved over to the bar and nudged two of Sonpear's hovering companions, so that they floated off across the tavern, clearing two stools. There was a belch and a pink puff from the mage next to them.

"Want to talk about?" Kali said.

Slowhand took a sip of thwack. "If you're asking if I'm all right, Hooper, yes, I am. It's funny but, despite her conditioning, Jenna remembered more of our early years than I did myself. Maybe that's the reason she was able to resist as she did, by holding those memories close."

"I wish there could have been more," Kali said softly. She hesitated. "'Liam, I'm sorry about what had to be done."

"Don't be. I'd have done the same myself. Besides, it was me who gave the order, wasn't it?" Slowhand downed more beer. "I found her too late, Hooper, but in a funny way I also found her in time. She would not have wanted to be what she had become and at least I helped her... not be."

Kali studied Slowhand. He wasn't quite as calm as he seemed to be, that she could tell, but she didn't think the reason was Jenna herself. No, there was a tension in his face that was more anger than grief, and it didn't take much to realise who that anger was directed towards. She wouldn't like to be in Querilous Fitch's shoes when her lover found him.

"Can we talk about something else?" Slowhand asked.

"Sure," Kali said, signalling for two more drinks from Red. "For one thing, I never got a chance to thank you for coming after me at Andon. That was quite a stunt with Horse."

"Don't mention it."

"There's one thing I don't get, though. Horse. How'd you manage to get him out of his sick bed – sick stable, I suppose?"

Slowhand produced a small vial from his pocket. "Essence of worgle. Swiped it from one of the laboratories in the Crucible. Here, have it."

Kali took the vial. "I'll save it for emergencies."

"Don't give him any more than a drop, though. It makes him frisky."

Kali laughed but the sound was drowned out by a sudden clamouring from Jengo Pim and his men, the thumping of hands on table. She and Slowhand looked over and saw that they were staring at the stairs and, this time, with good reason. The Hells Bellies' musicians were descending the creaking risers, and where musicians came the Hells Bellies themselves could not be far behind. Jengo Pim was on his feet now, his tongue hanging out, applauding loudly as a female leg appeared at the top of the stairs. The leg was followed by its owner and then the rest of the dancing troupe. And then Jengo Pim's applause stopped and the thief collapsed back into his chair, his arms hanging limp by his side. Seeing this, Kali almost choked on her thwack, because she had never seen a man look so crestfallen.

The reason for Pim's dramatic disappointment was the equally dramatic difference in the Hells' Bellies since he had last seen them. Because each of his beloved dancers must have shed at least twenty stone, the obvious result of a week's hoofing to stay the advance of the k'nid. They were now, Kali had to admit, really quite elfin, and their new stage costumes – made, it seemed, from the pockets of their old – while not making much of an impression on Pim, had certainly got the attention of the rest of the men in the Flagons.

The music started, the dancers began to dance, and the tavern *didn't* shake.

"At least the k'nid caused something good to happen," Kali said to Slowhand's back.

"What?"

"I said, at least the k'nid caused something good to happen," Kali repeated, cursing as Red poured beer over her hand. "Oh pits, Slowhand are you *listening* to me?"

The archer stared at the stage as the Hells' Bellies slithered provocatively through their old garters. "Of... course... I... am."

"Well, then – all that dancing," Kali persisted. "The dancing that stopped the k'nid?"

"Actually," Slowhand said slowly, "I don't think it was the dancing."

"What are you talking about? What else could it have been?"

"Remember that eerie wailing in the Crucible? The one that sounded like an old elven instrument...?"

It took Kali a second to register what he meant, but then she stared at the Hells' Bellies, or rather the stage behind them where the musicians were beamingly strumming and fiddling away. One on his old elven instrument.

The theralin?

Kali swallowed. "You think that I made them dance all week for *nothing*?"

"Yup."

"My Gods, they'll *kill* me."

"Ah well, never mind."

"What the hells do you mean, 'ah well, never mind'?" Kali protested. She looked towards the stage again, where the dancers were now slithering *two at a time* through their garters, a manoeuvre that evidently required them to slither rather slowly over each other as well. "Oh, fark it, you're not listening again, are you? ARE YOU?"

Kali shook her head and gave up. She grabbed her thwack and left the bar, debating whether to chance her arm in the bragging barrel while everyone else seemed occupied. But then she caught sight of Merrit Moon, the old man sitting exactly where she'd seen him last, alone at a table at the far end of the bar, and looking as if he wasn't enjoying the festivities at all.

No, she realised. It wasn't that he wasn't enjoying himself. He was concentrating on what was in his hand.

Ah. So that was it.

The fact was, the essence of worgle hadn't been the only essence that had been taken from the Crucible, she herself having removed a sample from that part of the laboratory that dealt with human specimens. And she had taken it to give to the old man. She didn't know whether it would be of any help to him, but she figured there had to be some link between the body-changing experiments at the Crucible and the scythe-stone that had originally transformed Moon into the half-ogur he now was. The point was, she thought it might help him in his own experiments to find a full cure for himself – or thought it worth a chance anyway. But by the look of things it hadn't been.

"No good?" she asked, slipping into a seat opposite him and nodding at the vial he was rolling between his hands.

Merrit Moon looked up from it slowly.

"On the contrary, young lady. This essence is really quite potent, far more powerful in its capabilities than that responsible for my original condition. I imagine, in fact, that were I to imbibe it, it would effectively eradicate all ogur tendencies within my body."

Whatever answer Kali had been expecting, it wasn't that and she sat back, stunned.

"What? You're joking, right?"

"I wish I were. Because then I wouldn't be facing this dilemma."

"*What* dilemma? For pits' sake, it's what you've been looking for, old man. Knock it back! Hells, I'll even get you a brolly for it!"

"No. The time is not yet right."

"What the hells do you mean, not right? *Why?*"

The old man stared her straight in the eyes.

"Perhaps because there is something you're not telling me."

Kali tried her best to hold his gaze, swallowing slightly. "What's to tell? We won and the k'nid are gone or, at any rate, will be soon. Slowhand and I saw them starting to dissolve on the way here from Andon. And the *Tharnak*'s safe in the Expanse. Hells, Sonpear even told me that when the portal closed the Expanse reverted to a state of stasis, so the ship didn't even crash!" She smiled in a way she hoped would bring the conversation to an end. "Let's hope we never need it, eh, old man?"

"But we will, won't we young lady?"

"What do you mean?"

"What are you not telling me?"

Kali stood up. "Look, will you *stop* it. It's a day for celebration, so why don't we *celebrate* okay? Enough talk about the end of the farking world."

Moon raised his eyebrows. "Did I mention the end of the world?"

"No, but... oh, look, I don't want to hear any more – really I don't!" Kali shouted, much to Moon's surprise. "I mean, why me, why Kali Hooper, or whatever the hells my true name is? All I ever wanted to do was get drunk, find places and poke around in the dark. Instead, what do I find? That I'm some kind of demi-human, that you died and became some half-ogur *thing*, that Horse isn't a horse, that Slowhand's sister died, and now – now..."

Moon's surprise at the unexpected outburst turned into a look of concern. "Kali, what is it?

"Steaming pits of Kerberos, old man, I'm twenty-three years old. *Twenty farking three!* I don't want the weight of the whole world on my shoulders!"

"Young lady..."

"It just isn't fair!"

"Kali..."

"*It isn't farking fair!*"

"Hey, hey, hey, what's going on?" Killiam Slowhand said, suddenly behind Kali and taking her by the shoulders. He turned her towards him, surprised to see the tears in her eyes. "Hooper?"

Kali thumped him on the chest, repeatedly, as he drew her close. "Godsdammit, Slowhand, this never ends!"

"Hey, whoa, whoa, whoa, what's the matter, what do you mean. We won didn't we? Didn't we?"

The old man nodded, but his face remained troubled. "This is about something else."

"What?" Slowhand asked Kali, softly. "What is it?"

Kali tensed in his arms but said nothing. And then, after a second, she broke away, grabbed some bottles from the bar and, without a word to he or Moon, headed outside, slamming the door behind her. Slowhand started to follow but Moon stopped him, spinning him around with a hand on his shoulder which, being half ogur, Slowhand could hardly resist.

"Leave her be," he said and then, after a few more moments, led him over to the bar, signalling drinks from Red. "So, young man. Why don't you tell me *exactly* what your intentions towards my protégé are..."

Outside, Kali leaned for a few seconds with her back against the door, catching her breath. The fact was, her reaction had surprised her as much it had the old man and Slowhand, but she guessed that a bellyful of thwack and the fact that what was on her mind had to come out somehow was pretty much responsible for her uncharacteristic display. But what could she tell her friends? She knew full well that she couldn't have done what she'd done over the last few days without their help. So how could she tell them that it might all have been for nothing?

That's right, she thought, *nothing.*

Gods, she had to talk to someone about this, didn't she? Or she would likely go insane.

Kali drew a deep breath and made her way to the top of the hill beyond the tavern, ignoring the syrupy rain. There, she pushed her way through a gap in the bushes into a small glade, wherein a solitary grave was illuminated by a flash of green lightning. The grave's headstone was carved with one simple word – Horse – and Kali touched it and smiled. It had become her habit to escape up here on the occasional night to tell Horse of the adventures she'd had since he'd been taken. And these chats were usually relaxed, meandering affairs, but the events of these last few days had left her hardly knowing where to start.

Kali slumped with her back to the headstone, cracked a bottle of flummox and began. She told him how the world – *her* world – had changed so much this past week that he would barely recognise it, and then she told him that what troubled her the most was that she had seen what the Old Races had ultimately been capable of, but that for all their greatness and the levels of technology, they had still been unable to stop whatever it had been that had wiped them out. And if *they* had been unable to prevent their extinction, then what hope did she and the others have of preventing theirs? Because the threat was as real to them as it had been to the Old Races, she knew that now.

She knew that because she had finally realised why the dragon had taken them to the edge of the heavens – it had wanted to show them something. And that something had been a smudge on the side of the sun. With that realisation she had also worked out the purpose of the strange black sphere at the Crucible, the one that had once moved slowly forward on its straight tracks. It had done so because it wasn't a sphere, it was a *countdown*. A countdown the dwelf had obliquely referred to in the fading moments of his life.

She never had found out why she had been *awaited*. And she never had found out why she was like she was. And, now, she knew, there was a possibility that she never would.

Kali took a slug of her flummox as she remembered the dwelf's last words once more.

"This world is called Twilight for a reason," he had told her. "Once in an age, to every civilisation, a great darkness comes."

THE END

ENGINES *of the* APOCALYPSE

Original cover art by Mark Harrison

CHAPTER ONE

THE END OF the world began with a scream. A very high-pitched, girly scream.

Not Kali, then. She wasn't a girly scream kind of girl.

No, the scream in question came from her guide, one Maladorus Slack, hired only hours before in the Spider's Eyes when he'd claimed to know the location of a lost passage leading directly to the fourth level of Quinking's Depths. It was an audacious claim and it wasn't every day Kali trusted the word of some ratty little chancer in a seedy tavern, but there had been something in the way he made it – with wariness as well as greed in his eyes – that had made her take a gamble and hand over fifty full silver for the privilege of having him share what he knew.

As it turned out, it was money well spent, Slack guiding her at twilight into a cave in the hills above Solnos and, deep within, tearing creepers off an ancient cryptoblock he swore, once unlocked, would enable her to bypass the Depths' upper levels and find treasure of such value that she might, as he put it, come over all tremblous in the underknicks. Kali had been forced to have words with him about this, pointing out that it was *her* business what went on in her underknicks and also, while she had him pinned against the wall, that she wasn't your common or garden tomb raider doing what she did for the money. Unless her taxes were due, of course.

Later, she would feel a bit bad that Slack had spent some of his final moments being throttled, especially when she recalled the hungry roar that followed the poor sod's scream. Not that what happened to him was her fault. Nor Slack's. In fact, there was no way either of them could have guessed what was going to happen after she picked up the Claws.

Okay, okay, okay, she'd been at this game long enough so perhaps she *should* have known better. Perhaps, given the way things had been going until then, she should have sensed the whole thing was going to go tits up.

"This cryptoblock..." Slack had queried as she worked on the numerous etched blocks that formed the seal. The conditions in the cave were cramped, and he was balanced awkwardly between the skeletal remains of earlier treasure seekers who had found their way to the threshold, trying to ignore the fact that all their bones were utterly and inexplicably shattered. "It is some kind of puzzle, yes?"

"Not some kind of puzzle," she replied. "A very specific kind."

"You have seen such puzzles before?"

"Once or twice. Cryptoblock seals are typical of an ancient race called the dwarves."

"The Old Race?" Slack said. "Tall with pointy ears and bows?"

Kali sighed, but took time to set the man straight because he had at least heard of the Old Races, which was more than could be said of most people on the peninsula, especially out here in the sticks. "No, the other lot. Short-arsed with attitude and axes."

"But surely both are stories for the children, yes? These Old Races did not exist?"

"Oh, you'd be surprised..."

Slack sniffed. It was the kind of rattling snort where you could hear the contents of his nostrils slap wetly against his brain and Kali grimaced in distaste. But the man seemed to accept the truth of what she was saying.

"The dwarves. They were supposed to have been masters of deadly traps, were they not?"

"Not supposed."

"Then this door is a trap?"

Kali glanced at the skeletons on the floor of the cave. "Either that or these guys had a very bad case of the jitters."

Slack glanced fearfully around the cave, looking for hidden devices.

"You won't see a thing," Kali advised. "They were master engineers, too."

"You *do* know what you are doing?"

"Wish I did," Kali said. She ran a finger down the join between two blocks, concentrating hard, tongue protruding between teeth. "Trouble is, no two cryptoblocks are the same... springs, balances, counterbalances... you just have to feel your way around." She gasped as something suddenly sprang inside the cryptoblock and slammed together where she delved. "Farker!" She cursed, whipping out her fingers and sucking their tips. Then she almost casually grabbed Slack's sleeve and pulled him aside as a solid stone fist the size of an outhouse punched down from the cave roof onto the spot where he'd stood, reducing what remained of the skeletons to dust. With a grinding of hidden gears, the fist retracted, and Kali returned to her work, smiling slightly as Slack had, himself, come over all something in the underknicks, a small stain forming on the front of his pants.

"Sorry about that," she said, wrinkling her nose. "Might be a while."

She'd worked diligently on the puzzle well into the night, Slack staring warily about him all the time, flinching or whimpering each time there was a click, clunk or clack from the door. At last, though, there was a sound that was different to the others – somehow *final* – and, as he watched, Kali stood back with a sigh of satisfaction, brushing the dust off her hands.

Slack regarded her and the cryptoblock with some puzzlement, because, at first, nothing happened. Then, with a soft rumbling and puffs of ancient dust, the blocks making up the door began to punch in and out. Some then slid behind those next to them, which in turn slid in front of others next to themselves. Yet more ground up or down, obscuring or obscured by their neighbours, or simply retracted backwards into darkness, never to be seen again. The movements became faster and more complex, the cryptoblock shrinking all the time, until at last all that remained was a single block, floating in the air, which Kali grabbed and casually tossed aside. Slack found himself staring at the discarded stone.

"I do not understand," he said. "It is gone. How can it be gone?"

Kali frowned. Questions, always questions. "Translocation mechanics," she said, adding in response to his puzzled stare, "It's a dimension thing." It might well have been, for all she knew; the truth was, despite having cracked a few of these bastards, she really hadn't a clue where they went.

Luckily, Slack hadn't been interested in analysing her statement too deeply. His attention had been side-tracked by the passage that lay beyond the cryptoblock, and the ore that glittered in its walls. It was only triviam, all but worthless, but its shine held the promise of greater things, and as Slack wiped sweat from his lips with his arm, she frowned. The man might have saved her the trouble of negotiating the first three levels of the Depths, but there was a growing air about him suggesting that, while he'd been happy to guide her to the cryptoblock, he'd never really expected her to *open it*, and now that she had was having second thoughts about who deserved the treasure beyond. Her suspicions were confirmed as Slack raced ahead of her into the opening.

Kali cursed and threw herself forward, grabbing his tunic from behind – just in time, as it turned out. Slack was already skidding helplessly down a sharp incline and, now a dead weight on the end of her arm, wrenched Kali onto her stomach and pulled her down after him. The stone floor of the passage was rough beneath her, tearing her dark silk bodysuit, and grazing her exposed torso with sharp scree. She ignored the pain, concentrating instead on jamming her legs against the sides of the narrow incline in an effort to slow their progress. The walls tore at her ankles, stripping them of skin, but she ignored this, too, groaning as she stretched out her other hand to get a firmer grip on Slack. He suddenly yelped and lurched, and Kali willed all her weight onto the floor of the incline, praying for enough traction. She was yanked forward and her arms were almost pulled from their sockets, but the two of them came, at last, to a tentative stop – again, not a moment too soon. Kali sighed. Below her, Slack dangled over a seemingly bottomless abyss, too terrified to struggle or even object to the rain of stones that bounced off him, clattering down into the dark.

Kali twisted herself into a stable position and heaved him up. "Looks like I need to keep an eye on you in more ways than one," she growled.

"I was only... making sure it was safe," Slack said, breathlessly.

"Of course you were." Kali winced and rubbed her bare stomach, ignoring Slack's hungry stare. "But there are rules to this game," she added. "Rule one is watch *every* step."

A flash of resentment crossed Slack's face as he dusted himself down, but he turned to stare into the dark, swallowing deeply. It was not in reaction to the end he had almost met, however, but a stare of undisguised greed.

Kali joined him at the edge of the abyss, wondering fleetingly whether it might have been less bothersome if she'd just let him fall, but considering what it was they faced, it was obvious Slack could make no move without her.

As always, her research had given her some idea of what to expect when coming here, but the expectation never quite did the reality justice. The two of them were staring into a vast cavern that must have extended beneath the whole of one of the hills above Solnos, an underground expanse hung with immense stalactites and dimly lit by a strange, golden glow in front of them. The glow was the only illumination and emanated from the top of an isolated pillar of rock, maybe six feet across, which thrust thinly and dizzyingly up from the abyss. It appeared unreachable from their position. Kali bit her lip and studied her goal. She could not yet make out the source of the glow, but was sure she knew what it was. The light was pulsing, dreamlike. The glow of something magical.

Kali had no doubt that she'd found what she'd come for. All she had to do was reach it.

"There?" Slack observed incredulously. "But there is no way across!"

"Rule two," Kali said, pulling a small object from a pocket in her bodysuit. "Plan ahead."

Slack stared at a small, ornate piece of stone – some kind of key – that Kali held in her hand, then watched her move along a narrow ledge to a carved niche. She brushed lichen away from an indentation in the stone, inserted the key and, with a grunt, turned it solidly to the right, the left, and then twice more to the right. Something grated behind the niche as, below in the darkness, something rumbled. Slack watched in amazement as another rock pillar rose judderingly from the abyss, shedding thick cobwebs, dust and the detritus of ages as it came. The top of the pillar stopped level with the ledge on which they stood, some hundred feet out into the void.

Kali withdrew the key from the niche and smiled. Slack, meanwhile, stared at the pillar and then Kali, regarding her quizzically.

"I do not understand," he said. "That is still too far away to reach."

Kali nodded. The fact was, it was too far away for a running jump, even for her. But even had she been able, she wouldn't have tried. Revealing her abilities to a man who would, for the price of a shot of boff, tell all and sundry about it was not a wise move in a backwoods such as this. It could easily reach the ear of some overzealous Final Faith missionary, and she had no wish to be dragged to a gibbet and burned as a witch. Besides, jumping would take the fun out of it all.

"Rule three," Kali said. "Be patient."

She smiled again as, from under the lip of the ledge where they stood, a scintillating plane of blue energy snaked out towards the newly risen pillar, zigzagging around the stalactites in its path to form a translucent bridge wide enough to take them both. Slack squinted, frowned, and Kali realised he hadn't a clue what he was looking at. It was easy to forget that while she'd come to live with such wonders on an almost day-to-day basis, the average peninsulan hadn't much experience of magic.

"It isn't witchcraft," she explained. "The bridge is made of something called threads."

"Threads?"

"An elven thing but the dwarves weren't averse to their use when needs suited. They –" Kali paused and contemplated. How exactly *did* you explain the threads of magic to a man such as Slack? "They allow you to use the world around you... to do things with invisible tools."

Slack looked enlightened. "So, I could use these tools to dig a new dump-pit?"

Kali pulled a face. "Uh, yeah, I suppose," she conceded, thinking that she was the only one digging a hole around here. "Let's move on, shall we?"

A wary Slack dibbed a toe onto the bridge, clearly not trusting its solidity, while Kali strode casually by him into the void, slapping the stalactites she passed and humming a happy tune. She reached the pillar and waited for Slack to catch up before inserting the key into a second indentation carved in its centre. This time she turned it left three times, right and then left again. There was another grating sound, and another rumbling from below.

"Six pillars," Kali explained as another rose ahead of them, "six combinations. If all are entered correctly, they form a bridge all the way to where we want to go..."

Slack sniffed. "This is really quite easy, then."

"Easy?" Kali chided as she waited for the bridge to form before skipping onto it. "You think I got this key from some adventurer's junk sale? Oh, no. This key is a complex construct of separate components, each of which was hidden in a site rigged to the rafters with every kind of trap you could imagine. These past few weeks I've been shot at, scalded, suffocated, stifled, stung, squeezed, squished and squashed, so maybe, Mister Slack, you should rethink your 'easy.'"

"And you say you're *not* doing this for the money?"

"Nope," Kali said. "Holiday."

"*Holiday?*"

"Holiday."

The fact was, she was still reeling from recent revelations about 'the darkness' coming to Twilight – so much so she'd had to get away, from friends, the Flagons, all of it. Not that there were actually that many friends around right now. Slowhand was off avenging the death of his sister, and she'd barely seen hide or hair of Moon or Aldrededor since she'd rescued the *Tharnak* from the Crucible – the old man, whose shop was being rebuilt after the k'nid attacks, and the pirate were spending all their time tinkering with the ship in Domdruggle's Expanse. Dolorosa had dismissed it as boys and their toys but there was a serious side to their tinkering, readying the ship for when – and for *what* – it might be needed. Not that she missed any of them – her holiday had been chosen specifically to keep her busy. She had, in fact, lost count of the times she'd barely avoided it becoming a funeral. In short, she'd had one hells of a time, and the acquisition of what lay ahead was the last challenge she had to face. Because what she had so far not told Slack was that forming the bridges was only half of it.

"One wrong move," she said, "and the entire mechanism resets itself. Bridges gone, pillars back where they came, carrying us with them into the depths."

Slack peered down and glimpsed something huge, white and serpentine slither through the darkness. "But there is something down there! Something horrible!"

Kali looked over her shoulder, smiled. "Of course. There's always something horrible."

With the more restrained Slack in tow, Kali negotiated more bridges, coming eventually to the last one – the one to the resting place of the artefact.

This time she wielded the key but hesitated as she held it before the lock, drawing a worried glance from her companion.

"There is a problem?" Slack asked.

"No, no, no problem," Kali responded.

Well, not much of one. It was only that at this point she might most likely get them both killed. The fact was that while her studies of the dwarven key had revealed a pattern to her, she'd been sure of all the combinations except this last. The combinations represented a really quite simple series of nods to the inclinations of the dwarves' multifarious minor gods – lightning equalling from above, or up; sunrise, east, so right; sea, which at this point on the peninsula was to the west and therefore left. The problem with the last combination was that it contained a glyph for the god of wind and, frankly, that one had left her stymied. Wind, after all, could come from any direction, so how in the hells was she meant to know which was correct? In the end, she'd whittled the possibilities down to two answers – up, because the wind in this valley was predominantly northern, and down, or south, because... well, because.

Hesitantly, she inserted the key in the final niche, turned most of the combination and stopped before the final twist.

North now, or south? If she guessed wrong, the last thing she'd see would be Slack wetting himself again, and she could think of better images with which to depart the world. She stared at the odorous little man and, in doing so, made up her mind. It had to be, didn't it?

Kali turned the key south, locked it in place and, after a few seconds, the bridge appeared.

She sighed heavily; she'd gambled correctly. On a dwarven joke. A crude but effective joke, much like the dwarves themselves, and she could imagine them roaring with laughter when they had thought of it.

Hey, Hammerhead, how about this? There's more than one kind of wind!

Kali was not about to tell Slack that she'd just gambled both of their lives on the strength of a fart gag, so instead she sauntered nonchalantly across the bridge, finally setting foot on the reassuring solidity of the central pillar. And right in front of her was what she had come for.

The Deathclaws.

Legend had it they had been forged by the renegade blacksmith Dumar, who had pledged his allegiance to an elven rather than dwarven court. Commissioned by that court's Lord, the mysterious metal from which they were made was said to have washed up as jetsam near Oweilau millennia before. That the metal *could* wash up – that it could float – was just one of its unusual qualities and had led many to speculate its origin lay with those said to live deep under the sea. True or not, the metal was unlike any worked before. It was pliable yet all but indestructible. When fashioned into the claws, they were sharp enough to slice through anything, natural or man-made, most importantly the unbreachable brodin armour in which the dwarves of that time garbed their warriors. It was even said that, wielded with skill, they could bypass the armour completely and slice away a dwarf's soul.

Unsurprisingly, the Lord who wielded the Deathclaws became unstoppable on the battlefield, and thousands of dwarven warriors had fallen before him, until, one night, the claws had simply vanished from the Lord's chambers.

The fact that, thereafter, Dumar returned to live among his own people in such circumstances that ten lifetimes' smithing could never have paid for may or may not have had something to do with the disappearance. But, by whatever means the dwarves acquired the claws, they had thereafter sealed them here, on the lowest level of Quinking's Depths, so that they might never be wielded again. They were, in short, a priceless treasure, a one of a kind artefact that Kali had had on her 'to find' list for as long as she could remember.

She sighed and lifted them from the podium on which they rested, then slipped them onto her hands. As light as silk, each of the metal handpieces was attached to five curved rune-etched blades by intricately crafted hinges and studs that allowed for perfect freedom of movement. It was hard to believe that something so delicately and lovingly constructed could have been intended for such deadly use. It wasn't simply the workmanship that belied their purpose, however. The legend also said that the elven Lord had imbued the runes with additional sorcery that ensured the blood of the fallen never tainted their beauty, and it was this that gave them their golden glow. Kali couldn't resist wielding them for a short time – slashing at the air like a cat, grinning as they cut the air with a hiss – and then she moved to return them to the podium.

"What are you doing?" Slack asked, aghast.

"Putting them back," Kali said.

"Are you *insane*?"

"Nope. I made a promise to a friend a long time ago that certain things should stay where they are, for the good of Twilight."

Behind her back, Slack hopped up and down, gesturing at the key, the bridges. "Then why all *this*?"

"Because I could."

"Because you could?"

Kali nodded. "It's about the thrill of the chase."

For a moment, Slack stared at her open-mouthed, then moved with hitherto unsuspected speed, putting a knife to Kali's throat. It was as dull as a twig compared with the treasure she had found but could still cause a nasty gouge. More uncomfortable by far was the fact that Slack was pressing himself tightly up against her rear, rubbing her exposed midriff slowly and panting in her ear. Kali sighed, but only with bored resignation.

"I will be taking the claws, Miss Hooper," Slack said.

"You sure about that?" Kali responded.

"What? Of course I am sure!"

"Only it's just that if I drop them to the ground you'll have to pick them up, and while you're doing that I'll kick your nuts so hard people'll be calling you 'four eyes.'"

There was a pause.

"I told you, Slack, plan ahead..."

"Then pass the claws to me slowly, between your legs."

Kali drew in a sharp breath in mock sympathy. "Or 'no nuts.'"

"Over your shoulder, then!"

"'Twilight's silliest hatpins'?"

Slack tightened his grip. "You are toying with me, woman."

"Actually, I'd prefer to get this over with. Have you any idea how much you *stink*?"

"*Give me the claws.*"

"Won't."

"Will."

"Won't."

Slack sighed in exasperation and Kali smiled. All you ever had to do was wait for the sigh that said your opponent was off guard.

She elbowed Slack in the ribs and flung him around in front of her, kicking his legs out from under him as he came. It should have pinned him to the ground with the Claws at his throat, and that was exactly where they would have been had the entire cavern not begun to quake violently, almost spilling the pair of them into the depths. As it was, Kali stumbled to her knees, the Deathclaws skittering from her grip, and Slack took advantage of the moment to grab them and run. Kali growled and made after him, then suddenly stopped dead in her tracks.

What the hells?

That some kind of quake was occurring was beyond doubt, the cavern shaking and thick falls of rock dust pouring from the roof. The rumbling was almost deafening. The quake, though, was not what had caused Kali to stop in surprise. Something seemed to be interfering with the thread bridges throughout the cavern. As Kali watched, they faded and flickered. The magic seemed to be destabilising for some reason and, if it disappeared completely, she and Slack were going to be trapped down here.

Slack himself had a more immediate problem, however. Oblivious in his flight, the rat was already running across the fifth bridge and, from her vantage point, Kali could see it was the most unstable of them all.

"Slack, come back!" Kali shouted, but the only response she got was a backward flip of a finger. "Fine, you moron, run, then! Just get off the farking bridge!"

She'd meant the warning to galvanise him but it actually had the opposite effect. Slack paused in his tracks, turning to face her. That he was listening was good, but it was also the worst thing he could have done.

Kali stabbed a finger downwards, trying to make the man aware of his situation, and comprehension slowly dawned as Slack looked down. His mood turned from triumphant glee to undisguised panic as he saw the bridge flickering in and out of existence. The sudden realisation that, at any moment, there might be nothing between himself and an abyss filled with *something horrible* spurred the thief into running for his life but, unfortunately, time had run out for Slack.

"*Aaaaaaaaaaaiiiiiiiiiiiiieeeeeeeeeee!*"

"Bollocks," was Kali's honest response. But she couldn't help raising her eyebrows when she saw the Deathclaws remained where Slack had been, still held in his bloody, severed hands, amputated by the flickering bridge the moment he'd fallen through. For the bridge, like the others, had not yet gone for good. She had time – though not, necessarily, any to waste.

Kali ran. As the six bridges continued to blink on and off, she knew that crossing each successfully was going to be a matter of a timing, using the pillars that connected them as staging posts.

The first bridge was, at that moment, in an either/or state of flux, and she ran on the spot until she felt it safe enough to traverse, then put on a sudden burst to reach its other end. She did the same with the second, and then the third. The fourth presented a problem, almost as unpredictably erratic as the one on which Slack had met his doom. The effects of the quake on the cavern were worsening. What the dwarves had intended to be a protective sanctum for as long as the hill above existed was now starting to come down about her ears. While she ran on the spot waiting for safe passage a rain of dust and stones left her coated in a grey shroud, and she had to dive out of the path of several large chunks of debris.

Then, when the bridge finally seemed stable enough for passage and Kali began to race across, all of the pillars began to move up and down.

Kali felt her stomach lurch as the pillar ahead rose and the one behind sank, taking the bridge with them so that she suddenly faced an uphill flight.

Oh, you have got to be kidding.

Kali pumped her legs until she neared the rising pillar ahead, and, with a bellow, threw herself onto it, rolling into a ready position for the next, crouched to leap.

There were only two bridges left now, but she was painfully aware that the next was the one that had so abruptly ended Slack's time on Twilight. It was once more flickering every half second or so but, interestingly, the claws had still not fallen through, which suggested it was stable enough to take her. The problem lay in timing it right, because if she moved at the wrong moment the pillar ahead would have risen too far and she'd once again face a steep incline to reach the end.

Kali ducked as the cavern shook violently and further falls of rock poured from the roof all about her, and then scowled at the bridge ahead. It looked as right as it was ever going to be.

Kali moved, faster than even she thought possible, but once again the quake scuppered her plans. As she began to race for the final pillar a massive boulder detached itself from the cavern roof and plummeted straight down. The boulder seemed to hit the pillar in slow motion, splitting asunder before bouncing off into the abyss, and in its wake the pillar started to crack and break apart. What was worse, it severed the link with the last two bridges. Kali staggered and yelped in protest as the threads there began to sputter and die, and now it was her mind rather than her body that raced. She took in all of the possibilities presented by the changing circumstances and moved again, heading not for the pillar but for the Deathclaws. It had never been her intention to remove them from the cavern but now they were coming with her whether she liked it or not. In fact, they might even save her life.

Kali didn't even slow to pick the ancient weapons up, executing a rolling somersault as she ran, one hand slipping into each of the claws and shaking to lose Slack's disembodied grip. His appendages spun down into the abyss, arcing trails of blood, until something white snatched them out of the air to join the rest of him, but Kali was already gone.

Her sole interest now was in reaching the collapsing pillar before the bridge died or it broke apart completely. The pillar was more or less level as she reached it, though far from intact, and as Kali landed on its buckling and crumbling surface it finally relinquished its hold on the bridge ahead, which blinked out of existence before her eyes.

She didn't need to turn around to know that the bridge behind her was also gone, but neither did she let the fact that she was seemingly now trapped on a disintegrating finger of rock hinder her pace. Kali ran full pelt across its surface and then, even as she felt the pillar tipping and tumbling away beneath her feet, she let out a loud "gaaaaaah!" and launched herself into the air.

Arms and legs flailing to stretch as much distance out of the leap as possible, she seemed to hurtle though the air for ever. But then she thudded into the stalactite ahead of her, the claws embedding themselves effortlessly into the spine of rock.

Kali simply hung there for a second.

"Oh, yes," she breathed to herself.

From the stalactite to the ledge and the exit was now only a minor jump, and Kali made it with ease. She would have taken a moment to pay her respects to Slack but the cave was rapidly filling with rubble. But as Kali moved into it she did cast a backward glance into the cavern that had almost claimed her life. The last of the bridges were flickering out now, leaving the ages old resting place in darkness but even as the roof caved in, she sensed that it hadn't been the quake that had caused the bridges to go away. No, something else had killed the magic.

Maybe when she reached the surface she'd find out what the hells was going on.

CHAPTER TWO

HELLS WAS THE right word. As in all of them breaking loose. Kali dragged herself spluttering and squinting up into the dawn light, disorientated and wrong-footed. Not only because the landscape she remembered from before her descent was now obscured by a dust cloud so thick she could *bite* it; she also immediately found herself dodging rivers of scree flowing rapidly down the hillside. As the treacherous stones threatened to sweep her off her feet, Kali hopped left and right.

There was no escaping it. The whole range rumbled as if the world itself were coming to an end. The boulders she dodged smashed into others below, cleaving apart with cracks like thunder, the guttural, groaning, thrashing sounds of uprooted trees and vegetation and the strange, hollow clattering of falling rock everywhere. There was another sound, too, not particularly loud in comparison, but one to which demanded Kali's attention. It was the agitated snorting and roaring of Horse, whom she had left tethered nearby – safely, she'd thought at the time.

Kali scanned the hillside, trying to locate the bamfcat in the chaos. As she did she caught sight of a dark, spherical object, the size of a fussball, darting here and there through the dust-filled air. As she saw it, it stopped dead, hovering right in front of her eyes. Kali recoiled instinctively, thinking *what the hells?* But by the time she'd recovered enough to try to work out what the sphere was it had already gone, darting away into the fog as quickly as it had come.

Weaving to dodge the tumbling descent of yet more stones, Kali began to work her way across the hillside once more, at last spotting Horse rearing against his tether, horns and armour plating deployed to deflect falling rubble. She moved to him quickly, slapped his side solidly and whispered calming words in his ears, and, though his nostrils still flared and he bucked slightly beneath her, the bamfcat no longer fought her. One thing was for sure, though – she had to get him out of there. Kali quickly untied his tether and led him away from the quake. At least that was her intent. The problem was, there didn't seem to be any *away* to get to. What Kali had thought to be a phenomenon specific to the hills was actually affecting an area much wider.

Exactly how much became clear as soon as she and Horse topped the next ridge.

When she had ridden up into the hills with Slack the previous evening, she had left below her a town lying peacefully in the savannah and forest lands east of Andon. Solnos was positioned beyond a sun-bleached but solid wooden bridge, the river meandering gently around its northern outskirts, and at the other end of town a grassy escarpment rose to the south before sloping away in the direction of Fayence. The town itself was a little smaller than Kalten, without defensive walls because none had ever been needed, and its buildings were one or two-storey affairs, constructed of blindingly white plastered bricks over a wooden framework. The buildings were centred around two squares, each strung with bunting and paper lanterns, one lined with shops selling everything from food to farming implements to bolts of silk, the other home to the town's well and church, a twin-turreted and bell-towered affair that was rurally typical of the Final Faith. The Faith's 'missionary' presence in such an otherwise idyllic spot had been the only thing that had stopped Kali musing on the possibility of opening a second Here There Be Flagons in the town, but it had been something she'd remained willing to consider should the Faith ever be kicked out on their arses, as they thoroughly deserved.

Now, it was likely she never could. Solnos was turning rapidly to ruin.

Where only the previous afternoon children had been laughing and playing in the streets, their parents sampling the exotic fare of the town's communal dining plaza, all had degenerated into chaos.

The white buildings were now criss-crossed with a growing number of cracks, each widening by the second as the buildings were shaken to their foundations. Many of the inhabitants of the town were racing in and out of the buildings, desperately gathering valuables or loved ones, or rushing in panic about the streets, trying to understand what was happening to them. The destruction wasn't limited to the buildings, either – even those who had safely evacuated their homes could not escape the effects of the quake, as they found themselves fleeing dark, jagged rents in the streets themselves, bunting and lanterns falling and fluttering about them like dying birds.

It was utter calamity and confusion. The people of Solnos hadn't the slightest clue what was hitting them. But Kali did. From her vantage point on the hillside, she could see it, even if she couldn't quite yet take it in.

"Okay," she said with a levity she didn't feel, "that's a new one."

To the west of the town, in the midst of its farmlands, massive machines were drilling out of the valley floor. There were three of them in all, emerging one after the other, the first already risen to the height of the ridge on which Kali stood, filling the sky and dwarfing her with its mass. The machines resembled, of all things, giant fir cones. The comparison was hardly apt, however, because these were not the products of some unbelievably huge, nightmare tree, but things of metal which spouted steam as they rose. Things which crackled with electrical energy. Things which Kali had no doubt had been *manufactured*, which only served to make them all the more staggering.

She could only stand stunned beside Horse as the second and third machines rose to join the first, churning slowly out of the ground with a deafening crunching of substrata and roots, carrying with them great scoops of soil, shrub, and even whole trees, sloughing from their sides in lethal downpours. Rising ever higher, they inevitably became visible to the town beyond the ridge, and Kali's gaze flicked to the people of Solnos, who as one had momentarily forgotten their immediate concerns to stop and point, or scream.

As one, the massive machines had begun to turn slowly on their vertical as well as horizontal axis so their pointed peaks would eventually face towards the ground. As they did this they emitted a siren sound that reminded Kali of the last, desperate calls of some dying leviathan, or of some impossibly loud and haunting foghorn, blaring endlessly into the night. The sound drowned out everything, even the clatter of the crumbling hills.

What in the pits of Kerberos were these things? The style of their construction and the runes Kali could make out carved into their eaves were dwarven, and the devastation they'd caused upon emerging suggested they had lain underground for millennia. Their history and reasons for construction were only two of the questions that intrigued her, though. What had brought them to the surface? Who or what controlled them? And why?

No, Kali mentally kicked herself. *Honestly, sometimes...* The question she should be asking was, what could she do to help the people below?

Kali turned her attention back to the west of town, to the farmlands. There, a number of Solnossians, little more than dots from her vantage point, were scurrying across the fields, their tools abandoned. Kali had no doubt that when these most unexpected of crops had emerged from the ground, the farmers had been as staggered and transfixed as their neighbours in town and now that they had collected themselves to flee, reaching safety appeared to be almost impossible.

The fields were nothing less than a disaster zone, subsiding not only into the three gaping pits that the machines had created but into rents in the ground like those that had split the streets of Solnos. Even as she watched, Kali saw two of the fleeing figures sucked into oblivion, clawing desperately for purchase as they went, and she knew that things were only going to get worse. Beneath all of them was the subterranean expanse that she had only just escaped, and if Quinking's Depths collapsed further, Solnos might as well say goodbye to anything or anyone this side of the ridge.

Kali mounted Horse and spurred him down the hillside towards the fleeing figures. She frowned, the fleeing men and women were some distance apart, and to aid them all she and Horse would have to perform some pretty fancy manoeuvring.

With a "hyahh!" she drove the bamfcat toward the nearest group, shouting at them to raise their arms as she leaned sideways to scoop the first of them up. The man arced up onto Horse's back, landing with a thud in the saddle, and Kali repeated the rescue with a second farmer and a third. She could carry no more behind her for the time being and reined Horse away from the landslips and to the safety of a patch of stable ground.

Kali had no choice but to ignore their pleas about rescuing husbands, wives or brothers and wasted no time, turning Horse again and scanning the fields for those in the most immediate danger.

One group of five or six – in the chaos it was difficult to tell – were struggling, their escape route cut off by a fresh fissure. Attempting to backtrack, they were once more caught in the middle of the subsidence.

Another "hyaah!" sent Horse hammering towards them and, almost as if he had read her mind, the bamfcat deployed more of his natural armaments. The extra horns which had just sprang from Horse's body were, for once, meant neither as defensive or offensive appendages but provided hand and footholds for the group of farmers it would otherwise have been impossible to carry. Quite what the farmers made of the great armoured beast as it pounded towards them she'd never know, but as they staggered back before his fearsome sight, Kali had to indicate as best she could what they should do. Thankfully, in their desperation, the men and women seemed quick learners, and as Horse galloped into their midst, they leapt for and clung to the armoured protrusions.

"Hang on!" Kali shouted and, wondering vaguely if there was some kind of obscure world record for the number of farmers dangling from a bamfcat, she quickly reined Horse around once more, riding him into a jump across the fissure that had earlier stymied the farmers' flight.

The bamfcat roared triumphantly as they arced over the collapse, and, as they thudded down on the other side Kali, too, let out a whoop. But it wasn't over yet.

"My girl!" One of the women pleaded as Kali dropped them off with the others. "Please, she was frightened, she ran, I couldn't reach her..."

"Where?" Kali said, already turning Horse.

"She ran *beneath* one of those things. Lord of All, please, you have to help her!"

Kali stared back into the chaos, seeing no sign of the girl but spotting instead another group of stranded victims, whose escape route was blocked by fallen trees. They were attempting to hack through the barrier of vegetation but their going was slow and all the while, behind them, the ground broken by the machines was growing ever larger.

Kali swallowed. She had no choice but to ride to help these people, and all she could do was hope she'd spot the youngster on route – the problem being, if she did, what the hells was she going to do then?

A second later, the dilemma became stark reality, a scream managing to make itself heard over the strange wailing of the machines. Kali stared hard and spotted a small figure struggling on the edge of the pit in the shadow of the first of them, and cursed. There was no way she could reach both the girl and the others in time, and for a moment she reined Horse's nose left and right, left and right, tortured by the decision to save the lives of a whole group or of one, however young. Thankfully, it was a decision she didn't have to make, the sound of further heavy hoofbeats signalling the arrival of a second horse by her side.

"You take the girl!" Its flame-haired rider shouted from her solid white mount. "I'll fetch Treave and the others!"

There was no time to think about who the woman was or where she had appeared from. Once more Kali booted Horse's flanks and steered him towards the girl. But if her chances of success had been precarious so far, they had just gotten a lot worse.

Kali found herself weaving Horse through the masses of soil that poured from the machine hanging above the girl in a deadly rain, at one point even having to turn him abruptly as a tree crashed back to the ground directly in their path. It was a close run thing with far too many near misses and, the further in she rode, the thicker the falls became, leaving Kali with no choice but to ignore the painful hammering of falling detritus on Horse's hide and on her own, far less protected flesh. At last, though, she reached the girl and scooped the dishevelled, but miraculously unhurt, child up behind her, turning Horse for the return trip.

But again, she cursed. What seemed like a whole field by itself was falling in a solid curtain that would be impossible to pass without being crushed. Nevertheless, Kali spurred Horse on, leaning forward as she did to whisper in his ear, "If ever there was a time for you to do your thing, my friend, it's right now."

Horse was of the same mind, galloping straight ahead. One moment the bamfcat, Kali and the girl were heading into the roaring soilfall and the next they were heading away from it, on the other side.

Kali kept Horse at a gallop until they had reached the waiting farmers, slowed him to a trot, and stopped beside the anxious mother to swing her daughter down into her arms. She dismissed the woman's thanks, but not ungraciously, being more concerned with the fate of the one who had come to aid her in the rescue attempt. She stared back into the disaster area, a hopeless mass of uncontrollable landslides now, and bit her lip. Long, long seconds went by but then, bursting through a cloud of debris, a white, if somewhat soil-stained, horse appeared at full gallop. The farmers she had rescued clung to her saddle in much the same way Kali's had clung to Horse's horns, and a moment later they were with their own.

Kali watched the woman dismount, nodding modestly as the farmers thanked her for what she had done, but seemingly more interested in tending to the welfare of the animal she had ridden. Kali dismounted Horse and walked to the white horse, casually palming between its gravestone teeth one of the bacon lardons she kept for sentimental reasons, and then, without a word, the two women stood side by side to stare up at the strange, rotating machines which had come to dominate the whole sky.

All three of them now fully inverted – or perhaps the right way up, who was to tell? – their rotation appeared to be speeding up. The sound of their sirens faded to be replaced by a strange and very deep thrumming that seemed to be produced by the rotating eaves. The faster the machine turned, the more intrusive and painful the thrumming became, and all in the fields were forced to press their hands to their ears to block it out. The painful effects seemed to last no more than a minute, however, although both bamfcat and horse snorted in protest a little longer. As the animals calmed, Kali guessed the thrumming had passed beneath the range of anything's hearing, leaving the machines to rotate in apparent silence.

Kali glanced at the woman beside her. She still stared up at the machines with narrowed eyes and a steely set to her jaw, as if these things were an affront to her. There was also the same determination on her face that she felt herself – to find out just what these bastards were and what they would do next.

"Hells of a morning," Kali said.

"Not exactly what I expected when I got out of bed," the woman said.

"Kali Hooper."

"Gabriella DeZantez."

Kali studied her more closely. With her bone structure and fiery red hair she looked like a younger version of the Anointed Lord, Katherine Makennon. Kali didn't usually notice such things but it was also clear to her that the hair had been cut by her own hand rather than the prissy fingers of the primpers and preeners who'd begun to appear in the cities. She could tell immediately that Gabriella was different, like herself having little time for people's expectations or normal conventions. Her attitude was reflected in her clothing, too, the woman dressed for practicality rather than fashion, in a dusty surplice and working trews. Unfortunately it was the surplice of the Order of the Swords of Dawn, the Final Faith's warrior elite, bearing the faded crossed circle of the church. Kali had no idea what had caused Gabriella to end up as she was in a backwater such as this but she knew instinctively that she liked her. Which made it all that more of a shock when, with no preamble at all, the woman's next words were, "As the Enlightened One of the town of Solnos, I am placing you under arrest."

"What?" Kali protested. "Why?"

Gabriella DeZantez turned to face her directly for the first time, and Kali started slightly. Gabriella's eyes were unlike any she had ever seen, one a clear sapphire blue, the other a striking almond flecked with gold.

"I should have thought that was obvious," she said.

Kali surveyed the devastation. "You mean this? I had nothing to do with this."

"There is evidence to the contrary."

"Evidence? What evidence? Now wait one farking minute!"

But before she could argue her case further Gabriella DeZantez quickly unsheathed her twin blades, whirled them full circle and slammed their hilts into her temples.

Kali dropped to the ground like a stone.

"Treave, Maltus, bring her," the Enlightened One said as she strode by two of the farmers in the direction of what was left of the town. "As the Overseer has decreed, this 'Kali Hooper' must answer for her crimes."

CHAPTER THREE

FOR THE LAST hour the archer's aim had been unwavering, the tip of the arrow pointing precisely where it had pointed when his wait had begun. It had not moved a hair's breadth in any direction. In the hands of any normal bowman, the strain of holding it so would have long ago become too intense. The bow would have begun to shake and skew, the shaft unstable and tremulous between two crooked fingers of the right. The nock of the arrow would, by now, have begun to buck spastically on the bowstring, and the strain would have transformed the tendons of the arms into agonising webs of red hot wire. Under such circumstances the bow would have to have been relaxed, lowered, and the trembling, cramped limbs exercised and massaged. The intended target of the bow might, as a result, have been lost.

In the hands of *this* archer, there was no such concern. The bow remained steadfast and its aim true. Everything was perfectly still, the only sounds in the flue where he hid the subtle creaking of wood and his soft, measured breathing. His concentration was sublime. Where others' gaze would have long ago started to wander, their vision to blur and lose focus, his blue eyes remained focused and alert, waiting for the moment – *the one, fleeting moment* – that he knew would eventually come.

Man and weapon were the best there were.

It was why the bow was called Suresight.

And why the archer went by the name of Slowhand.

The moment arrived. A small flicker of shadows betrayed motion some twenty yards outside the flue, framed in the one inch square formed by four bars of the iron grille through which his arrow was aimed. Despite the imminent arrival of his target, Slowhand's breathing remained calm. All that changed was that he smiled.

Smiled because this was not the first time in the last few days he'd waited for the perfect shot, and depending on how things went it might not be the last. For the last thing Slowhand intended was to kill the man whose shadow approached – that would be far too easy. He did not want Querilous Fitch to die *quite yet*.

Oh, Querilous Fitch. Slowhand so much wanted the psychic manipulator to suffer. He wanted him to suffer in the same way the corpse-like bastard had made Jenna suffer, stripping from his sister everything that had made her who and what she was. It might have been Slowhand himself who had given the order to fire upon her airship, and consequently end her life in a flaming crash, but in truth it had been Fitch who'd ended it long before. Independence, spirit, freedom of will: Fitch had taken them all until Jenna was nothing more than a puppet of the Final Filth. Slowhand did not have the abilities that Fitch possessed, of course – to literally stick his filthy little fingers in unspeakable pies – but he had his own, and so far they were working just fine.

During the past days, wherever in Scholten or beyond Fitch had been, he had been also – unseen, undetected, undetained. And on each occasion he had sent Fitch a message to let him *know* he was there, an arrow despatched from whichever hiding place he had used which could almost, but *not quite*, have dropped him dead where he stood. By these means he had gradually robbed Fitch of the very same things the bastard had taken from Jenna, reducing him to his current state – a furtive, quivering hostage to mortality, unable to do anything or go anywhere without the presence of the living shield of bodyguards he had so desperately employed.

There the bodyguards were now, Fitch huddled in their midst. The passage along which he walked was one that rose from the cells and torture chambers beneath Scholten Cathedral to the central level of the Final Faith's sprawling underground complex. It was a route Fitch followed daily at roughly the same time, depending on how thoroughly he had attended to his 'guests.' The fact that he had not varied his routine was probably reflective of the fact that he considered himself safe in the bowels of the secret stronghold, but the time had come to prove him wrong.

Slowhand waited until Fitch was outlined in the dead centre of the one inch square and let his arrow fly. It cut perfectly through the grille, flew through the narrow gap between supply crates that blocked the flue from view and then embedded itself solidly into the wall next to Fitch's face. The psychic manipulator and his guards fell into immediate, blind panic; Fitch, clearly torn between gathering them more closely about him or sending them in search of the origin of the arrow, settled for half and half. Some guards pounded towards the flue, while others bundled Fitch away, swords raised defensively as they attempted to get their charge out of sight.

As the first batch of guards kicked open the flue and examined its interior, Slowhand was already gone, having slipped out and replaced the grille the moment he'd released the arrow. Now he circled the crates, keeping out of sight but, as the opportunities presented themselves, unleashing more arrows in Fitch's wake, until a line of them dotted the wall of the passage along which he fled.

Turning with a look of horror each time one hit, Fitch made the decision that might make these his final moments after all. He ordered his protectors to guard his flank.

No problem, as far as Slowhand was concerned – he simply clambered up onto a stack of crates, leapt for a support beam and passed over the guards' heads.

Fitch, he thought, *you really should have invested full gold and bought in decent mercenaries from Allantia. The kind with brains, because you only get what you pay for.*

It was just him and the psychic manipulator now. As Fitch fled into the warehouse and distribution area, Slowhand followed, passing the Faith workers there unopposed, creating confusion as they hurried through. Once or twice Fitch looked to his rear, trying to defend himself by unleashing fireballs, but, born of haste and panic, they ricocheted wildly off the walls.

Querilous Fitch reached the other side of the central area and entered one of the railway tunnels that fanned off it, dodging between the couplings of stationary wagons. The expansive network of tunnels that spread far across the peninsula – beneath both Vos *and* Pontaine – were thought to be the remains of dwarven mines which the Faith had extended into a transport network, and the cable-driven, funicular trains which rode their rails simply developments of the ore-collectors once used. It was what the Faith did – purloined technology and then adapted it for their own insidious purposes – but it gave Querilous Fitch no advantage here.

Just the opposite, in fact. In his panic, Fitch had clearly neglected to take into account what lay some distance into the tunnels – and Slowhand knew what lay there because he'd had to bypass one to enter the Cathedral.

Since last Slowhand had been here with Hooper, security had been upped dramatically on the surface, and without offing every guard between himself and Fitch he would have had the pits' own job of reaching him undetected. But, as was so often the way, when security was increased on one front, it was often left vulnerable on another. Instead of heading for Scholten Slowhand had made his way to a tiny and purposefully underwhelming Faith mission some leagues east. The Church of Divine Intervention was more than it seemed, the fact that it had never been open for worship a clue that it had another purpose more fitting to its title. The mission was but a hollow shell concealing an access shaft to one of the Faith tunnels that led from Scholten to Volonne.

The mission also had only one guard, and he was swiftly despatched with an iron-tipped arrow to the helmet that concussed rather than killed. After that it had been easy to gain entry to the shaft and drop onto the first train heading back west. The train had been carrying naphtha for the cathedral gibbets, and he had used some of the oil mixed with grime to apply facial camouflage before he reached the complex.

But before the complex, of course, had been the shields.

Fitch had forgotten about the shields.

Slowhand smiled. The tunnel along which the psychic manipulator now fled was not the one through which he had rode the train – appeared, in fact, to be long unused – but that didn't matter, for its defences would be the same. He allowed Fitch his rein, letting him increase the distance between them, exhaust himself as he fled into the darkness. Slowhand followed at his own pace, knowing he had all the time in the world.

Fitch now gasping and staggering had negotiated most of a broad bend in the tunnel, and the blue glow that he could see illuminating the walls seemed to him to be some kind of salvation, a heavenly exit, perhaps, which would end this dark pursuit. It was nothing of the kind, of course, and as Slowhand appeared along the tunnel behind him, the stark reality of what he faced hit home.

The magical force barrier that sealed all of the tunnels against intruders into the sub-levels of Scholten Cathedral closed off the tunnel, its surface rippling gently. The only things capable of passage through its lethal charge were the trains, their front carriages embedded with crystals that momentarily nullified its destructive effects. Given time, Fitch might have been able to use his own sorcerous powers to break the barrier down, but time was something he no longer had. The psychic manipulator weaved left and right, as if trying to find some alternative escape route, but unless the first train in who-knew-how-long came through the shield in the next few seconds, there was no way out.

Fitch turned to stand against Slowhand, his brow darkening and hands dancing in an attempt to weave threads. Slowhand gave him no chance, rapidly loosing two arrows that nicked the tops of Fitch's hands and drew blood, breaking his concentration. Fitch tried again and Slowhand loosed more arrows, deepening the same wounds. The archer's message was clear: he was in absolute control. Any of his arrows could be solidly embedded in Fitch's forehead in an instant, if he so wished.

That, though, would be far too quick.

Slowhand didn't want it to be quick.

The archer sighed and closed on the man responsible for Jenna's death, Suresight now slung casually by his side. As he came, Fitch fell to his knees, tearing away parts of his robe to wrap around his bloodied hands. He stared up at his nemesis, trying and failing to disguise the fearful bobbing of his adam's apple, and was wise enough not to raise his hands again. He studied Slowhand intently, working out his identity through the smears of camouflage the archer still wore.

"The brother," he said, with disdain. "So it *was* you all this time."

"The brother," Slowhand confirmed. "But isn't that a redundant term?"

Fitch smiled coldly. "From what I've heard, she died at your order, not mine."

Slowhand paused. For Fitch to know that meant there had to have been a survivor of the *Makennon* and he'd thought all hands had gone down in the battle with the airship above the Crucible. Not that a survivor was necessarily a bad thing. News of the Faith's comprehensive defeat might very well serve to deter them from taking to the skies again anytime soon. In any case, it didn't alter the facts – Jenna would not have even been aboard the *Makennon* when it crashed in flames, were it not for Querilous Fitch meddling with her very being.

Speaking of which, the bastard was trying it with him, right now.

Slowhand recognised the slight dip of the head and pulsing of the temples that signified Fitch was trying to *influence* his actions as they spoke, but he wasn't going to be turning his bow on himself today, thank you very much. He tutted and raised Suresight, aiming an arrow directly at the manipulator's head.

"Don't try it, stick-insect. If I feel the slightest scratching in my mind..."

Fitch capitulated but, Slowhand got the impression, not wholly because of the warning he had just received. The man seemed confused, troubled somehow, as if he had been trying to gather the mental reserves to pull off his insidious little trick but had, for some reason, failed.

"Maybe you should try to *talk* me round, instead," Slowhand suggested. "Though I can't really guarantee that will work."

Fitch glared up at him, but there was an element of desperation in his gaze.

"There's something..." he began, then shook his head, unable to grasp what. His mind was, in any case, on other matters. "So what happens now, *brother*? Do you plan to execute me in cold blood?"

"Actually it's running a little hot at the moment. But yes, that's the plan."

Fitch began to laugh, softly at first, but then with a volume Slowhand knew was designed to unnerve him. It was exactly the type of tactic he'd have expected – mind games of a more prosaic nature than Fitch usually played, but mind-games nonetheless. And he knew what they were about. Fitch didn't believe that Slowhand had it in him. He saw him as one of the good guys who, when it came to it, wouldn't actually *murder* someone in revenge.

Fitch didn't know Slowhand at all. Didn't know what had made him not really care.

Slowhand drew the bow tauter still, pressing Fitch's head down with the tip of his arrow. The creaking of the weapon was the only sound in the silent tunnel.

"Say goodbye, Querilous Fitch."

The psychic manipulator began to tremble beneath him, waiting for the arrow that, in all likelihood, he would never feel. And in the eternity that he seemed to wait he became aware that Slowhand could play mind games, too.

"What are you waiting for?" He hissed. "*Do it!*"

"Get up," Slowhand said.

"What?"

"On your feet, you bastard. Move away from the shield."

Fitch sneered. "What is this, some kind of trick?"

"No trick. Do it."

Dazed and pained, Fitch regarded him with confusion. But Slowhand's attention was fixed above him. Because what had stayed his delivery of the fatal arrow hadn't been sadism on his part. As he'd been about to loose his killing shot something had drawn his gaze. Something beyond the energy barrier.

A horde of people – hundreds of them – were approaching. And each and every one of them appeared to the archer to be dead.

He plucked Fitch up and span him around. "You wanna tell me who *they* are?"

Fitch gasped, actually staggered back. The apparently dead things, meanwhile, walked into the barrier in a single mass, recoiling from its charge in waves, but otherwise unharmed.

"I think they want to come in," Slowhand said. "Fitch, are these things your doing?"

"No," Fitch said quietly.

From his expression, though, he clearly recognised what he was seeing, and his face was as white as those beyond the barrier. Even when he'd been facing death Slowhand wasn't sure he had looked so afraid.

"So," Fitch continued, "the First Enemy moves at last."

"The First Enemy?"

"We have to get out of here," Fitch declared, pushing past him. "Now."

"Whoa, whoa, whoa, tiger," Slowhand persisted, grabbing him by the arm. "Whatever these things are, we're safe behind the barrier, right?"

"It was designed to be impenetrable."

"Then why are you so afraid?"

It was Fitch's turn to rail on Slowhand. "*Because the barrier is shutting down.*"

"What?" Slowhand said, and saw that what Fitch said was true.

The Final Faith's shield was flickering on and off, as if something was interfering with the magic that made it whole. He stared at the figures pushing against it.

"Are they doing this?" He asked. "The First Enemy?"

Despite his evident fear, Fitch began to chuckle. "*They* are not the First Enemy, archer. They are only his representatives here."

"Fitch, what in the pits of Kerberos is go –"

Slowhand didn't finish his question. The barrier had vanished completely. His nose wrinkled as it was flooded with the stale air of the long unused tunnel, but it was nothing compared to the stench of those who approached them now.

Slowhand could see that his first impression of their health hadn't been entirely accurate, but neither had it been wide of the mark. Grey of flesh and white of eye, with chests that barely rose with breath, they were alive, but not in any usual sense of the term. They seemed suspended, somehow, between life and death, and had an odour about them that reminded him of an outbreak of the tic. An odour that came when bodies ceased to function properly, when things were fundamentally wrong inside. The odd thing was, none of the people seemed wounded or showed any obvious illness. It seemed to Slowhand to be more of a spiritual thing.

That was it, he thought. The clothing these people – men, women, and even a few children – wore was blackened or torn but still recognisable, and it betrayed them as being from the woodcutting villages that bordered the Sardenne. He knew these people, had spent time with their kind, and they were hard-working, rugged individuals. But now, from their empty eyes, to their emotionless expressions and the way they moved as one, they may as well have been the walking corpses he had first taken them for.

They began to move towards himself and Fitch. Each shambling figure brandished an axe, cleaver or scythe.

"What the hells?" Slowhand breathed.

The archer raised Suresight and unleashed an arrow which thudded into the chest of a man at their front. He faltered slightly but continued walking. He hadn't made a sound. Slowhand swallowed and unleashed another into a different target, with the same effect. As the group continued to advance towards them, he backed Fitch along the tunnel and loosed Suresight again and again, into hearts, necks, right between the eyes. The shambling group just kept coming.

"That will do little good, archer," Fitch said. "As you've seen for yourself, these things are no longer normal flesh and blood."

"What *happened* to them?"

"They have become puppets. As such, even an arrow into the brain will barely slow them."

"Whose puppets? No, forget it. You wanna tell me what *can* stop them?"

"I can," Fitch said after a second.

Slowhand shot him a look. The psychic manipulator was displaying his bandaged hands, clearly seeking permission to use his powers without penalty.

"Magic is the only thing that can stop them," Fitch insisted.

"Do it." Slowhand said.

Fitch raised his arms towards the group, his temples pulsing. But moments passed and there was no sign of lightning bolts or fireballs or any offensive magic at all. Not a fizzle.

"Fitch," Slowhand said, "this is no time for projectile dysfunction."

"I – I don't understand," Fitch said.

"What's to understand?" Slowhand countered. "This, Fitch, is the day the magic died."

The stick insect gave him a horrified glance. "What do we do?"

Slowhand glanced towards the approaching figures. The walking pace which they had so far adopted was turning into more of a trot.

"Run maybe?"

"For once, archer, we are in agreement."

The two of them began to pound back along the tunnel, but at the same time the pace of their pursuers increased even more, until it was almost a charge. The eerie thing was that, other than for the sound of their footfalls, they proceeded in absolute silence. There was no need for them to utter a battle cry to chill the blood because the *thud, thud, thud* of their relentless and accelerating progress was chilling enough. Within seconds, Slowhand and Fitch were near to being overwhelmed, and the archer pushed the manipulator to the side of the tunnel, deciding the only thing to do was to make a last stand.

He wasn't sure whether to be relieved or offended by the fact that, other than an instinctive swing of weapons from those on the group's edge, their supposed attackers passed them by. It made him sure of something else though. These things weren't interested in the two of them, they were merely in the way. The horde's purpose was to reach the cathedral.

"We have to warn them," Slowhand said, and pushed Fitch on.

Paralleling the horde's advance now, he could see the light of the warehouse sublevel and, silhouetted before it, the wagons Fitch had dodged between on his way in. There were now also a number of workers who, guided by some Eminence, were delicately loading boxes onto them, oblivious to the deadly wave heading towards their way.

Slowhand had no love for anyone of the Faith but they *were* people. "Get out of there!" He shouted. "Get out of there now!"

The workers looked toward the sound of his cry, and tools were instantly dropped. They stared in incomprehension, something for which Slowhand could hardly blame them, but that reaction and their position – right in the path of the horde – cost them their lives. The horde met them and they were reduced to a pile of twitching, dismembered body parts by axe and cleaver and scythe.

The carnage did not last long but it gave Slowhand and Fitch enough time to overtake the horde and burst from the tunnel, the archer shouting warnings. But the distribution centre had already been alerted by the workers' screams, and the cathedral's cloister bells were sounding a security breach.

Guards were pouring from the sublevel's barracks to take up position before the tunnel. Slowhand bundled Fitch behind their lines, amazed that he had started the day intending to kill the man and was now getting him to safety.

"Arrest this man," Fitch ordered, intercepting two of the guards. "He tried to kill me."

The guards stared at Fitch questioningly.

"The First Enemy moves. For all we know he is in league with him."

The guards faces paled at the mention of the name, but they nodded and seized Slowhand by the arms. The archer glared – that was what you got for being the good guy.

"Fitch, don't be a fool," he pleaded. "I don't know what's going on here but let me help."

"Take him," Fitch ordered, and headed for safety.

"Dammit, Fitch! Can't you see this is about more than just saving your skin!"

Slowhand's protests fell on deaf ears as the horde continued to pour from the mouth of the tunnel. The guard commander hesitated for a moment before barking orders to his men. Crossbows were loosed and fifty or more quarrels slammed into the front ranks of the horde, the archers reloading instantly to despatch a second volley. By their sheer weight of numbers the quarrels slowed the horde more than

Slowhand's arrows had, but they were as ultimately ineffective at stopping them and, despite a third volley, the horde gained ground into the sublevel itself.

Ordering his crossbow men to continue firing at will, the guard commander turned to a number of robed figures who had hastily shuffled into position at the rear of the line, and with a downward sweep of his arm instructed them to deploy their defences.

Nothing happened, for the figures were shadowmages, and the magic here, too, was gone. A wave of desperation crossed the guard commander's face and, despite his evident fear, he changed tactics, breaking forward from the line and unsheathing his sword, ordering his men to follow and do the same.

It was a mistake and a massacre. Only Slowhand and Fitch had so far witnessed how the horde behaved in close combat, and it hadn't just been the utter lack of mercy with which they had mutilated the tunnel workers, it had been the way they had done so with no regard to mutilation to *themselves*. They didn't care, didn't feel anything, and the only way to stop them was utter dismemberment.

The cathedral guards didn't get the chance. As they ploughed on, swords raised, into the front of the horde, the grey-fleshed intruders responded in kind, their makeshift weapons all the more deadly because of the suicidal way in which they were wielded. The guard commander and first wave of his men were bloodily felled without claiming a single foe, and even those who miraculously survived the sweeping attacks died horribly moments later, torn apart. More guards joined the fray and the horde began to slaughter these, too, fighting in eerie, absolute silence. The only noise was the wet sound of butchery, and the desperate cries and screams of the dying.

"Stop!" A voice commanded suddenly.

Slowhand glanced towards its source and saw that reinforcements had arrived, summoned from the upper levels by the tolling of the cloister bells. The Anointed Lord herself – Katherine Makennon – stood at their fore.

The archer drew a sharp intake of breath. He hadn't forgotten how striking Katherine Makennon could be, but as the Anointed Lord strode towards the tunnel, shoulder to shoulder with her men, his thoughts were not on the way her shining armour accentuated rather than hid her statuesque form, nor on the feral mane of long red hair that swept behind her like a fiery comet's tail. All he could think was that, for once, she might be biting off more than she could chew.

"Makennon, don't," he implored her as she passed. His words were barely heard above the clanking of her armour. "I don't know what these things are but I'm not sure they can be stopped."

The Anointed Lord halted briefly, her face a mix of recognition and curiosity at the archer's presence, swiftly replaced with cast-iron determination. "I will stop them. This is *my* cathedral."

Slowhand struggled against the guards as Makennon strode on, but their grip was firm. All he could do was watch as the Anointed Lord marched at the horde, her battleaxe swinging down before her with an audible *swoosh*. Scholten might well have been her cathedral but for the moment at least she was no longer its Anointed Lord, reincarnated instead as the battle-hardened Vossian general she had once been.

Makennon directed her men to the peripheries of the horde and then, roaring, waded into the heart of them, battleaxe carving a path as the invaders' weapons sparked and clanged on her armour. While it looked as though she was wielding the heavy weapon with as much carelessness as the enemy were wielding theirs, it was in fact with great precision. Its twin blades bypassed, by hairsbreadths, her own people fighting beside her, cleaving only into the things that flailed about them. The horde might have been unaffected by damage from lesser weapons but the sheer mass of Makennon's axe, to say nothing of the expertise with which it was used, was something they could not withstand. Within seconds she had reduced their numbers by twenty or more. As damaging as Makennon's incursion was, though, the numbers involved were great, and as more guards fell beside her it was clear she faced a war of attrition with an inevitable conclusion. This did not deter Makennon from continuing her impassioned defence of her domain, however, and while she shouted for what few men remained to pull back to a safer position, she herself continued to wade forward until she had carved a sea of body parts that reached almost to the tunnel entrance. There, fatigue at last started to get the better of her, and she was forced to stand her ground. Breathing heavily and slightly bowed, her blood-slicked hands nevertheless levelled her axe before her, ready to swing it in a circle and cut down any or all of the horde who closed in about her.

But the horde did not close in. Instead, as one, they collapsed to the ground.

Slowhand's surprise was as great as the Anointed Lord's, but their interpretations of the unexpected development differed. Obviously concluding her efforts had somehow won the day, Makennon's heavy breaths turned into shuddering gasps of relief, and slowly she raised her gaze to him, displaying flaring and victorious eyes. The archer was considerably more wary. Puppets, Fitch had called these things, and if that was the case their strings had just been cut. But he seriously doubted that, with such an advantage, this First Enemy – whoever he was – would have cut them in defeat.

Something was wrong.

Every one of the horde that remained intact began, slowly, to laugh. They didn't stir from where they had collapsed, and their faces showed no more emotion than they had before, but from each of their upturned, gaping, black mouths came the sound of laughter. It was a cold and calculating laugh that echoed throughout the now otherwise still battlefield, and it seemed to come from very far away.

Makennon turned in a circle, her eyes on the collapsed forms, her axe ready to be wielded once more. And as she turned, she faced the tunnel.

She stared into the darkness. Something darker still seemed to grow there.

And then that darkness exploded in her face.

CHAPTER FOUR

KALI STIRRED, BLINKED in confusion. After the clout she'd taken from DeZantez she guessed it was normal to see stars, but the Enlightened One's clout had clearly been an Almighty Clout because she was seeing balloons, bunting and flags as well. There was also a worgle right in front of her nose, staring at her in what seemed to be a very accusing way. Worgles had no eyes but it *still stared*, conjuring up flashes of Horse's darting tongue and a pang of guilt she'd never realised she'd felt.

Kali shook her head to free it of weirdness, then groaned. She was surrounded by the stuff of festivals and fun, but the way DeZantez had turned on her she wasn't feeling much like either. Wincing at the pain in her bruised temples she gently picked herself up off the floor to see she'd been confined in a small storeroom with a tiny window and solid wooden door. She tried to open the door but, naturally, it wouldn't budge, no doubt barred on the outside as there was no lock within. She pulled a crate under the window and climbed up. The window was too small for even her lithe frame to squeeze through but at least the view enabled her to glean where she was and how long she'd been out.

By the look of the sun, it was just after midday, and she was in Solnos – what was left of Solnos anyway. The storeroom had clearly been sturdy enough to survive the quake – which explained why it was serving as a makeshift jail – but outside was devastation. She was looking out onto the town plaza, which was now deserted, many of the tables and chairs upturned, plates shattered, the remains of meals scattered across the mosaic floor. There was smoke everywhere, a pall of it pouring from a jagged rent that split the plaza in two. Beside the rent was the body of a small dog.

Kali craned her neck so that she could see beyond the plaza. The destruction that the machines and the quake had wrought had flattened almost half the town, spreading as far as the second square, where, though the well and church had survived, the adjoining graveyard had disgorged its dead, many of the coffins lying broken in the sun, others half sunk in the river along its edge.

A few people were gathered around the well, cleaning and caring for the wounded as best they could. More simply cradled those who were beyond care, slowly rocking them back and forth. The only sounds were those of distant coughing and gentle weeping.

Kali sighed. If there was one small mercy, it was that it all seemed to be over. The quake had ceased completely. The strange machines, still dominated the horizon, and as she narrowed her eyes to discern the spinning objects against the brightness of the sun, she thought she could make out pulsing waves radiating from them, as if the inaudible sound they made was almost physical.

What the hells are *these things?* she found herself wondering once more. She had to find out. But that wasn't going to be easy in her current circumstances.

Kali considered her options. Horse had to be somewhere nearby, likely constrained like herself, and for a moment she considered whistling for him. Little would hold the bamfcat for long and, at full gallop, his armour would make short work of even these walls. She quickly rejected the idea, however, knowing that if she used the steed to instigate a jailbreak it would only confirm her guilt in the minds of her captors, however the hells they had concluded she was responsible in the first place. No, she had no desire to have her face on bounty posters all across Pontaine. It was better to get things cleared up.

Speaking of which, figures were moving towards her from the church right now: DeZantez and some fat, shaven-headed, jowly guy in fancy Final Faith robes. With him were a pair of meatheads, Faith again, who appeared to be his bodyguards. What a Faith dignitary was doing in Solnos she had no idea, but while she was never pleased to see one of Makennon's lackeys, if he was coming to sort this mess out, fine.

Kali heard the sound of a bolt being drawn back and the door opened, light momentarily flooding the room. Then fatso filled the gap, plunging it into shadow.

"I'm sorry about what's happened," Kali began. "but –"

"My name is Randus McCain," the fat man said, speaking over her. "It is my honour to be the Overseer for this region."

Kali's eyes narrowed – she didn't like to be interrupted. What she liked less, however, was the detail she could now see on her visitor's fancy robe. The usual crossed circle of the Final Faith was present but at its centre the pattern had been interwoven with the symbol of a wide open eye. Kali felt a tug of concern. She knew the Faith hierarchy fairly well but the eye and this 'Overseer' role were new ones to her.

"Nice eye, Randus," she said. "What's that about, then?"

"Bring her," the Overseer ordered the two bruisers. He moved back into the sun and the two men grabbed Kali roughly by the arms.

"Hey, now, wait," Kali protested, struggling in their grip. Her instinct was to nut one and knee the other but the sound of sharp metals being unsheathed halted her action before it began.

Gabriella DeZantez stood in the doorway, head slightly bowed but gaze fixed on her, twin blades ready for use in her hands. Kali paused, she could see how perfectly posed for combat the woman was, how honed her muscles were, and, quick as she knew herself to be, realised that to challenge her would be folly. What affected her more than anything, though, was again the appearance of her cat-like eyes. They had an arresting presence about them – a *genuine* presence, that was, not the kind affected by fatso – that made her feel that, if she could appeal to anyone here, it would be her.

"What's happening?" She asked her, swallowing slightly.

DeZantez didn't answer, merely continued to stare, jaw muscle twitching. Randus McCain loomed behind her.

"You are charged with the manipulation of forbidden artefacts," he said. "You are to answer for your crimes."

Forbidden artefacts? Kali thought. McCain could only be referring to the machines. So the Faith were taking it upon themselves to police Old Race finds now? They really were arrogant bastards.

"Look, I keep trying to tell you –" she tried once more, but the Overseer merely nodded to his guards and she found herself being dragged from the storeroom.

Gabriella DeZantez stood aside as she passed but Kali sensed her immediately swing back into position behind her. Herded as she now was there was little chance of escape. Just one of DeZantez's blades could sever her spine before she managed a step.

It wasn't just the presence of the woman she sensed, though. There was more than a whiff of resentment coming from her, too. Resentment directed not at her but McCain. That was interesting and something she might be able to use when she found out what was going on. For the time being Kali allowed herself to be marched towards the church, noticing two things. The first was the fact that DeZantez faltered slightly as they came within view of the graveyard, as if someone close to her had suffered the upheavals there. The second was that Horse was chained beyond the well, guarded by more goons who had presumably escorted McCain into town. The bamfcat registered her predicament as she drew closer and began to snort and pull against his chains. Kali knew he could snap them in an instant but stared into his flaring green eyes and shook her head. Horse calmed.

Prisoner and escorts reached the church and paused. McCain turned to DeZantez.

"Wait outside," the Overseer ordered. "Ensure we are not interrupted."

DeZantez protested. "I am the Enlightened One of Solnos. My place is inside the church, where I should witness these proceedings."

"I have given you an Overseer command, Sister of the Swords of Dawn. Need I remind you that yours is a temporary position and that our office holds jurisdiction over your own."

DeZantez's face darkened, her hands tightening on the hilts of her blades. "Need I remind *you* that your office did not, until recently, even exist. This town has been my responsibility for months and I have lost many of my people today."

Kali noticed McCain's goons go for their own weapons but the Overseer shook his head. "Very well. But you are to take no part in these proceedings, do you understand?"

DeZantez glared but nodded briskly. Kali could hardly blame her for her attitude. If she'd just had her authority stamped on like that, she'd be pitsed off too. The irony was, DeZantez could have whittled both goons down to a knucklebone in a second but, as a Sword of Dawn, the Faith's chains of command were sacred to her, whoever rattled them.

The interior of the church was pleasantly cool as Kali was ushered in. The wooden door was shut firmly behind her, DeZantez taking up position before it, and Kali looked around. Where she had expected some one-to-one questioning from McCain she found herself instead confronted by a number of townsfolk filing into pews as if to act as a jury. And when the Overseer stood in a shaft of light at a podium before which she, in turn, was forced to stand, she knew exactly that a jury was what they were going to be.

Hang on, she thought. Things were getting a little out of hand here. Moving a little too fast for her liking.

This was no questioning.

This was a trial.

"Kali Hooper, you stand accused –"

"What the hells is this?" Kali shouted over him. "I've done nothing to be tried for."

"Nothing?" McCain retorted. He pointed at the jury, raising his voice. "The loss of this community's loved ones at your hands is 'nothing'?"

Kali faltered. She was being charged with these people's deaths? Oh no, this was wrong. Wrong, wrong, wrong. She stared helplessly at the jury and then steadily at McCain.

"You're talking about the appearance of those machines. I had nothing to do with that. What happened was as much of a surprise to me as to you."

"A surprise?" McCain repeated. "A *surprise*? You make it sound like those *machines* were nothing more than some cheap trick gone wrong!"

There was a mumbling in the jury, shaking of heads, and Kali swallowed. Scant few hours had passed since the disaster, and these people's horror and anger were still raw. Even though she knew she shouldn't have to, she sought another choice of words.

"A shock, then."

McCain let her response hang in the air a second. "A shock," he said, nodding to himself. "A shock. What are you girl, an adventurer? One of those tomb raiders who make their living scrabbling for shiny things in the dirt?" He paused and gripped the sides of the podium, rattling it until his jowls shook. "In doing what you do," he thundered, "how many other shocks have you caused by sticking your nose where it doesn't belong?"

The jury stirred angrily, and glared at Kali. She, in turn, glared at McCain. And he had the gall to accuse *her* of cheap tricks, the fat bastard. McCain didn't care about these people's feelings, wasn't interested in meting out justice for them. All he wanted to do was manipulate them, and her. The shaft of light, the shouting, the flair for the dramatic – McCain, wherever in the hells he'd sprung from, seemed to have his own little travelling roadshow, and the trouble with roadshows was that they always ran to a script. Just as well, then, that this hadn't been a 'one-to-one' discussion because she would have been wasting her time. If she was to avoid being rail-roaded into whatever outcome McCain had in mind, she'd need to appeal to the jury directly. And to DeZantez.

"You were *there* this morning," she said to the Enlightened One, and then turned to the jury, "some of you people too. You saw how I tried to help. Ask yourselves – would I have done that if I had caused the quake in the first place? Why would I have *wanted* to cause the quake? To hurt you? Again, why? It makes no sense."

Faces remained impassive.

"These... machines," Kali continued, "I want to know why they've destroyed your town as much as you do, but to find that out the first question you should be asking isn't who's responsible, but what in the hells *are* they?"

"Exactly that, tomb raider," McCain said from behind her. "Instruments from the very Pits of Kerberos. From the hells themselves. Instruments which *you* made rise from where you plotted beneath the ground."

Kali whirled to face the Overseer. Though his office might, as DeZantez had suggested, be new to the Faith, McCain himself clearly wasn't. His jowls and girth evidence of a number of comfortable years in its hierarchy. As such, he'd know very well that he was talking bollocks, that his so-called 'instruments from the pits' were Old Race technology, whatever their purpose might be. This wasn't something he'd necessarily care to share with the people of Solnos. After all, the Lord of All Himself might struggle to create such wonders and He couldn't be seen to be inferior in their eyes. But that didn't explain why McCain was pursuing her with such zeal. He might still think her guilty, yes, but why not deal with her quietly rather than persist with this whole charade?

There was only one reason she could think of. McCain enjoyed it. The fat bastard had been tempted to stir from behind his dinner table by the chance to play god.

"How did you know?" She asked McCain. She and Slack, had, after all, headed to the cave when no one was around and had told no one their destination. "How did you know I was underground?"

McCain smiled. "Because, Kali Hooper, the Eyes of the Lord are everywhere."

"Of course they are." But what she'd meant as a flippant response took a darker tone when McCain addressed the jury.

"Would you like to see, my children?" He asked. "Would you like to see what this woman has done?"

In response there was a murmuring. Kali, meanwhile, looked about in confusion.

McCain thrust both hands towards Kerberos. "Then let me show you what the Eyes of the Lord beheld!"

Oh, for fark's sake, Kali thought, *enough!*

But then she froze. Because, between herself and the jury, an image had flickered into view and before their eyes they saw Slack leading her towards the cave and out of sight.

The view segued to show the machines burrowing from the ground, starting the quake, and then fleeing and terrified townsfolk, trying desperately to escape the effects of the catastrophic machines. Again the image segued, and this time showed Kali alone, emerging from the cave, moving across the crumbling hillside towards Horse, and then mounting him and riding away. There was a collective gasp from the jury as she did, both at what the recording implied and because Horse, with his armour fully deployed as it had been, was something of a disturbing sight.

The images began to loop, showing themselves again and again, and with every loop the jury shifted more uneasily in their pews. McCain certainly knew how to charge an audience, allowing the images to play a couple more times before raising his hands to stop them.

"With your own eyes, people of Solnos, you have witnessed

how this *careless adventurer* and her pits-born beast activated the machines that destroyed your town. With your own eyes you have seen her guilt!"

"Hey, fatso!" Kali shouted. "Horse is no pits-born beast, he's a bamfcat, okay! And your little performance here proves nothing! The destruction of your town began while I was underground, yes, but that doesn't mean I started it!"

"Really?" Randus McCain said slowly, and once more an image appeared.

This time the image zoomed into Kali's face in a sudden close-up, dusty and bloodied after her ascent from the cavern, and recoiling, wide-eyed, in shock. "Do you see the blood?" McCain went on. "Proof she murdered your own kinsman lest he interfere with her plans! Do you see the startled look upon her face? Proof she believed she could deliver this act of evil upon us without realising that the Eyes of the Lord see all!" He paused again. "Ask yourself, people of Solnos, why would the Lord of All reveal such things to you unless he wished this evil act to be punished!"

"But that isn't what happened!" Kali shouted.

She was about to launch into an attack on McCain that would reveal him to be the charlatan he was but then realised she was taking the things she had seen in her stride. It had been immediately obvious to her that the images McCain had presented to the jury had come from the dark sphere she had fleetingly encountered on the hillside, but how was she to explain that to the people who, thanks to McCain's manipulation, held her fate in their hands? Explaining the presence of such technology to them was like explaining magic to Slack. Here, in this once idyllic town, they simply had no knowledge of it, and the Old Races were stories for children.

Kali looked around. True enough, it was reflected in their faces. Even the face of Gabriella DeZantez. The woman was clearly intelligent, but she was also a dedicated Sword of Dawn, and the Faith carefully chose what they exposed the Swords to. Without something tangible to contradict it, why shouldn't she accept what she had just seen?

Only Kali knew otherwise. She stared up into the shadows of the church, following the flickering light that created the imagery, and saw it. The sphere. It had to contain one of the memory crystals she had encountered in the Crucible of the Dragon God, the same kind of crystal that had recorded Jenna's messages to Slowhand, and was perhaps held aloft by some miniature version of the rotors that had driven the Faith's ill-fated airships. Makennon's mob might have lost their battle for the skies in the Drakengrats but they had adapted both technologies for another far more insidious purpose. The Eyes of the

Lord were no messengers of the Lord of All, they were surveillance devices.

Overseers.

Gods, no wonder McCain was enjoying himself. The Filth had a new toy for its voyeurs to play with.

Despite how difficult it might be to explain, Kali knew she had to tell the people of Solnos what was going on. It wasn't just for her or their sakes, but for those of everyone where these things might already have been deployed.

"This isn't divine proof!" She shouted to them. "This is a *recording* of only part of what occurred. The Lord of All didn't see what happened underground because 'He' couldn't follow us there!" Kali paused, looking up. "There is a device," she went on, "a device constructed with the aid of Old Race science – a science developed long ago by the elves and the dwarves." She stared at the blank faces before her and then turned on the Overseer. "Why don't you tell them, McCain? Tell them about memory crystals and airships and your sphere, and how those machines out there in the sky aren't from the hells but from civilisations far older and more advanced than our own? Why don't you tell them that it was *they* who left the shiny things in the dirt? Or are you afraid? Afraid that if these people learn the truth, know how you use their tools, that you'll no longer be able to bend them to your beliefs?"

McCain gave Kali time to take a breath and then turned to stare at the jury as if he had no idea what she was talking about. Only she caught the knowing flare of his eyes as his gaze passed hers. "'Memory crystals'? 'Airships'? 'Sphere'?" he said with a chuckle that became a laugh. "These terms are unknown to me. The only truth I know is that which is shown to me by the Eyes of the Lord."

The Overseer raised his hands once more and the images returned, playing over and over again.

Keep going, Kali thought, seeing Gabriella DeZantez edging forward from the door, peering up into the shadows.

Unfortunately, just as the Enlightened One was about to become more enlightened, McCain sensed her movement and the sphere, controlled by some unknown mechanism, zipped out of sight.

"It was a trick!" Kali shouted to the jury, but received only unsympathetic glances. She turned to DeZantez. If she was going to bring her onto her side, now was the time. "You have to believe me," she said. "It was there. The images showed only part of the truth, not the whole truth, and certainly not *divine* truth. It's circumstantial. Give me time and I'll show you the sphere. Give me time and I'll prove to you what happened."

DeZantez hesitated. Her gaze alternated between Kali and McCain.

"May I remind you," McCain interrupted, "that the Enlightened One plays no part other than that of an observer in these proceedings. Her opinion carries no weight."

"Hey!" Kali shouted at McCain. "You want an opinion that carries weight, you bastard, I'll show you one!"

She leapt the podium, intending to land a fist in his smug, fat face, but found her neck scissored between DeZantez's twin blades before she could swing. Barely able to speak because of the blades pressing on her throat, barely able to move her head, she strained to look into DeZantez's eyes.

"*Please*," Kali implored.

"Not until I *know*."

So, that's it, Kali thought. With four words DeZantez had declared her independence, but shattered her hopes that she would act on the injustice that was happening here. The fact of the matter was there was no evidence of injustice, and until there was, the Sword of Dawn was bound by her oath to the Faith.

"Ladies and gentlemen of the jury," McCain said. "What is your verdict?"

Kali swallowed, waiting for the word that she knew was going to come.

"Guilty."

"Guilty."

"Guilty."

One after the other, the jury members stood and delivered the same verdict, and Kali was powerless to do anything about it. DeZantez remained stony-faced during the delivery, even when McCain delivered his sentence.

"The Eyes of the Lord have witnessed your crime. The sentence is death."

"No," Kali said quietly.

McCain nodded to DeZantez. "Prepare the gibbet."

Kali struggled against the grip of the guards that now surrounded her. She had been fully aware that the gibbet was the Final Faith's preferred method of punishment – had been fleetingly aware of it hanging outside as she had been led into the church – but had refused to acknowledge its presence until now. Things all of a sudden became very unreal and she felt a dreamlike coldness ripple through her body. As she watched DeZantez exit the church and found herself being hauled after her into the sunlight, Kali realised that her holiday had finally come to an end here, far out in the backwoods, among strangers who intended to burn her. She felt suddenly, desperately lonely and yearned for Slowhand, Merrit Moon, anyone who could say *no, don't do this, this is wrong*. But all of her friends were far, far away, thinking other thoughts, and all they would know of her death would be that she never returned home. She was alone and, worse, about to die for a crime she would never dream of committing.

Well, hells, she wasn't going without a fight.

Kali drove her elbows into the stomachs of the goons holding her and slammed her fists into their faces as they doubled over. The pair staggered backwards and she dropped to a crouch, swinging herself around her hands and kicking out, knocking their legs from under them. The guards fell on their backs in a clatter of armour and, as they struggled to pick themselves up, Kali punched both in the face, knocking them cold. She sprang upright, twisting to face Randus McCain. The Overseer swallowed and backed up against the church wall before her less than happy gaze.

Then, Gabriella DeZantez casually walked in front of her, between them.

The Enlightened One had both blades unsheathed and assumed a low, defensive stance. One blade was thrust forward, wavering slightly as if tempting Kali to make a move, the other held back and unwavering, ready to follow through. DeZantez was, in short, prepared for a swift and deadly double strike.

DeZantez spoke one word, but it was enough.

"Don't."

Kali slumped, her battle tension reluctantly leaving her body, and the guards once more took her. DeZantez sheathed her blades and returned to the duty McCain had given her. Kali stared at the Overseer as he watched DeZantez manipulate the chains that lowered the gibbet from its hanging position on the side of the church, then open the front of the cage. The look of abject terror he had exhibited moments before had been replaced by a twisted smile, and he wiped a small amount of drool from his mouth as he turned to his guards.

"Strip her," he said.

Strip me? Kali thought.

"Get your farking hands off!" She shouted as the bodyguards began to tear at her bodysuit. Thankfully, she saw DeZantez move forward, at last seeming willing to intervene. Instead of halting their actions, however, she regarded Kali steadily.

"It's better this way," she said. "Trust me, when the naphtha comes, you will not wish it to first burn your clothes."

Naphtha. Perversely, the word made Kali feel even colder than she had before, and she stared at the pipes that ran from the side of the church into the top of the gibbet cage, at the spark ready to ready ignite the substance as it poured onto the victim within. Well, nightmare as this was, she sure as hells wasn't going to entertain McCain more than he already would be.

"He isn't concerned about how easily I die," she said, with disgust. "Let me remain as I am."

DeZantez hesitated, then nodded to the bodyguards. They bundled her into the gibbet, slamming and locking the cage behind her.

"It's your choice," DeZantez said, turning away.

Kali stared after her and, as she did, became aware of McCain laughing.

"What did you expect?" He said. "That the Enlightened One would balk at the horror of what is about to happen to you, force me to release you from my custody?" He shook his head. "The gibbet is an *everyday* occurrence, girl, don't you understand? Your enlightened friend here has burned countless sinners in her career. Have you not, Miss DeZantez?"

DeZantez stared at Kali, still emotionless, and nodded.

"This might seem like the ultimate horror to you," McCain continued. "But it is her *job*."

Kali grabbed the bars of the gibbet. They were rough beneath her grip, coated with a substance that once had been the flesh of 'sinners' but was now only a permanently caked layer, as hard as coral.

"McCain," she said. "You do this and I promise you *I* will regret it."

McCain smiled. "I like a sense of humour. But I equally dislike modesty. Raise the gibbet, Sister DeZantez."

Gabriella DeZantez paused for a second but then turned a wheel on the wall of the church.

Kali felt the cage floor shift beneath her and sway and creak as it was lifted well off the ground. The climb brought her within the full glare of the sun and she blinked and prickled in the brightness and heat. It was nothing, though, compared with what was to come, and she stared down at McCain, DeZantez and the goons, swallowing dryly as they were joined by the jury, filing slowly out of the church to witness what was to come. Any hope she might have had for a last minute reprieve or hint of compassion was instantly dashed as she saw their upturned faces; vengeful and convinced of her guilt. Suddenly she appreciated the awful reality of the situation she was in. To her this was a waking nightmare, but such was the iron rule of the Faith here in the sticks that to these people, as McCain had said, it was just an everyday occurrence. A *normal* way to die.

"The taps, Miss DeZantez," McCain ordered.

"No…" Kali said softly to herself, clenching her fists around the rough bars.

She began to struggle as she watched DeZantez turn the taps on the wall of the church and they vented steam. Drops of moisture fell to the ground. The pipes above her hissed, shook and gurgled as the naphtha entered them and began to build up pressure inside. It would take seconds for the lethal substance to travel their length and Kali was suddenly overwhelmed by how close to death she was. She had never been afraid of dying – had faced it many times – but to have it occur like this was somehow tainted and wrong, and filled her with despair and fury.

She renewed her struggle against the bars, rocking the cage violently on its chains. The pipes groaned under the strain of the protest she unleashed and, for a moment, Kali thought that was the way out. If she could only dislodge the pipes, she would escape this after all. But then she saw that the pipes were flexing with her, joined at various points along their length by some rubbery substance that could presumably withstand the heat of the naphtha.

"Really, Miss Hooper," McCain said, "do you not think that all who have died before you have not tried the same..."

Kali looked up at the pipes and then quickly down again, for the gurgling was louder now and *closer*. Before she jammed her eyes shut in a futile attempt to block out the pain she glanced over at Horse, her loyal mount bucking in agitation beneath the restraining hands of a dozen of the townspeople, and wondered what would happen to him now. Then she felt the first tiny hot spits of naphtha searing the back of her neck.

Something cracked like thunder, and there was the sound of wrending metal. No further naphtha came and Kali opened her eyes.

She saw that the pipes had been torn apart at their mid section and were dancing about in mid air, vomiting their lethal content to the ground. Below, McCain and his goons were stepping back awkwardly, trying to avoid the oil, while DeZantez threw herself at the taps to stop any further release before lowering the gibbet to the ground.

The flow stopped. Kali's gaze turned to McCain, whose face was red with fury. The subject of his fury seemed to be behind her, out of sight, and so she had no idea to whom McCain addressed his next words.

"What," the Overseer rumbled angrily, "is the meaning of this?"

A figure strode into view and Kali frowned. She wasn't sure who she had expected miraculously to have appeared – Slowhand, perhaps, Aldrededor, Dolorosa or Moon – but the man she saw was a complete stranger to her. Tall, muscular, and garbed like a huntsman in leather britches and squallcoat sewn from irregularly cut pieces of hide, his stubbled face with its piercing brown eyes regarded McCain with some degree of contempt.

"The meaning of this," he replied in a voice clearly used to having the last word, "is that your execution is over."

As he spoke, he wound back into a coil a whip made of nine lengths of chain, clearly the weapon which had ruptured the pipes, and moved around to the front of the cage and released its door. He offered Kali a hand down and she took it silently, still assessing what the hells was going on here.

"On whose authority?" McCain demanded.

"The highest authority. That of the Anointed Lord."

I wonder what the Lord of All would make of that? Kali thought.

It was clear what McCain's opinion was. The Overseer narrowed his eyes and beckoned his bodyguards to the fore, where they placed hands on their weapons.

"Forgive me," he said, "but you hardly have the appearance of an agent of the Anointed Lord, and I know, or know of, most of them. What is your name?"

"My name is Jakub Freel."

"Freel?" McCain repeated, dismissively. "I have never heard of you."

McCain may not have heard of him but Kali had, and she stood back slightly in some shock. She stared at her rescuer, her own eyes narrowed. Jakub Freel. This was the man whom Jenna, Slowhand's sister, had married. Other than that, however, she knew little about him. As to his role here, she was as much in the dark as McCain himself.

"How is it that you carry the authority of the Anointed Lord?" asked the Overseer. "What office do you serve?"

"Let's just to say that the office I occupy was once occupied by another, now deceased."

McCain sneered. "And this other was?"

"Konstantin Munch."

Freel's answer gave the Overseer pause. His sneer disappeared and, somewhere beneath his jowls, Kali saw the man swallow, hard. That was hardly surprising. Munch's remit in the Final Faith had been to tackle those jobs that might prove *embarrassing* in others' hands, the head of a shady group whose powers, as a result, transcended the otherwise rigid structure of the Faith, allowing them to go everywhere and exist nowhere at the same time.

Kali found it interesting to note, however, that while Munch had surrounded himself with lackeys, Freel appeared to be working alone, and she got the impression that this was his preference. Whether that was because he was capable of single-handedly dealing with what the Faith threw at him or not, she didn't yet know, but she did know that it was time to start getting her own handle on things.

"So, you're Stan's replacement," she said casually, and nodded at the cage. "I like the new approach to the job. Getting me out of there was not something he'd have done."

"Oh, he might. In these circumstances."

"Which are?"

"I tracked you here because the Anointed Lord has need of your help. We need to leave for Scholten right away."

Kali was stunned.

"You're kidding, right? You're here because Makennon needs *my* help? *Again*? This is the same Makennon whose arse I saved at Orl but who then sent me a map to a dwarven deathtrap as thanks? The same Makennon whose people nicked the plans for the *Llothriall* from my own tavern? The same Makennon whose skewed religion nearly got me fried alive just now? The same Makennon who... fark it, never mind."

Kali turned and began to stomp towards Horse. "Tell her to go to the hells..."

"I wish I could," Freel said, striding after her.

"Wish you could what?"

"Tell her to go to the hells."

Kali span. "Look, at least Munch was an *obvious* nutter. Do you want to tell me what you're talking about?"

"The hells," Freel said. "We fear they have already taken her."

CHAPTER FIVE

THERE WAS NO way that Kali could resist a hook like that, was there? She agreed there and then to accompany Freel, at least until she knew more about what was going on.

There remained, however, the small matter of Randus McCain, who refused to recognise Freel's authority and thus to release her to him. Kali knew full well that it was little to do with authority and more with the bastard's desire – stripping her whether she liked it or not this time – to get his fat hands on her again, and her immediate inclination was to stuff the Overseer in his own gibbet with a naphtha pipe up his arse. She sensed Freel felt the same – seeing through the pretence of procedure to recognise the tin god pervert for what he was – but while McCain himself would prove no obstacle if Freel chose to remove her by force, his goons about the town might. Not than any of them looked as if they'd stand a chance again him – it was just that, new to the job as he was, he might not wish the paperwork that would result from mopping up a town of his own people.

Freel suggested a compromise.

Kali would be returned to McCain if she failed to deliver the help the Faith was asking of her. To ensure her return, Gabriella DeZantez would accompany them where they needed to go.

"What?" Kali said.

Once again she began to stomp towards Horse.

And once again Gabriella DeZantez stepped in front of her, blades drawn.

Kali whirled on Freel. "*Are you serious?*"

Freel folded his arms. "It appears Sister DeZantez is serious."

"But I already agreed to come!"

"Ah. But not necessarily to help."

"I'm innocent, dammit!"

"That remains to be seen."

Kali's gaze snapped between the two of them, exasperated. What the hells was going on here? One minute this... *enforcer* was asking for help, the next taking her into his farking custody! Then a small wink from Freel mollified her. He had no intention of returning her to the Overseer, just getting her away from him without the need for bloodshed.

"It is better all round, do you not think?" Freel said.

Kali did think. Once again the enforcer had demonstrated an approach to the job that was different from Konstantin Munch's and shown himself to be something of a manipulator in the process. It made a refreshing change from a punch in the face, but she realised she'd have to keep an eye on this Jakub Freel.

"Maybe it is," she agreed.

Kali again moved to Horse, and this time actually reached him. She debated manually unshackling the various chains that had been wrapped about his body and legs but, having had more than enough of this town, snapped her fingers instead. Horse bucked, the chains exploded and links flew like rain.

"Good boygirl," Kali said.

She began to check her saddlebags ready for the journey. As she did she noticed DeZantez emerge from rooms behind the church with a single, if fairly hefty, saddlebag of her own. She slung it over a dusty, chestnut horse, and the clank it made suggested it contained her armour.

Kali frowned. Gabriella was something of an enigma and she couldn't quite work out how serious she was taking her assigned role as her custodian. Whether, indeed, she was aware that Freel himself had not been serious about it. Certainly, she had to keep up appearances for now, but the question was, were they more than appearances? Would she, if it came to it, return her to McCain if she failed to help Freel? Would she, even, cut her down if she tried to flee? Kali decided she might have to have a word with Freel once they'd left town, request that he make his little deception clear to DeZantez, because she appeared to be a soldier who followed orders to the letter.

Or... maybe not.

Kali watched as DeZantez returned to the church and emerged with its collection coffers. The gold inside was destined, like them, for Scholten, and it was a cardinal sin to remove it, but DeZantez had no hesitation in distributing it instead to the people of the town. She clearly thought it better used for the repairs Solnos would need.

Kali was about to move forward, tell her that was a kind gesture, but hesitated as DeZantez moved to the edge of the ruined graveyard and stood, staring in. Kali didn't know why, but she sensed that had the graveyard still been intact the Enlightened One might have been a little more reluctant to leave. With its destruction, she had found an excuse for a decision that she had struggled with for a while; that it was time to leave Solnos, and whatever memories it held, behind.

After a while DeZantez turned and mounted her horse. Kali and Freel mounted up too. The three of them rode to the edge of town and then up onto the ridge where, for Kali, this whole affair had begun. They stared at the rotating machines. A rumble of thunder in the sky behind made them seem all the more ominous.

"I was going to find out what these bastards are," Kali said to Freel. "Before you came."

"Actually, Miss Hooper, you were going to die, screaming horribly."

"You know what I mean."

"I know what you mean. And believe me when I say you are still going to get the chance."

Kali snapped him a look, but before she could question him further, Freel spurred his horse on, and she and DeZantez had to gallop their mounts to catch up.

The enforcer kept them to a strenuous pace for most of the journey to Scholten, slowing to rest the horses – the bamfcat needing none – only infrequently. Kali could, of course, have had Horse make a few 'shortcuts' but there seemed little point in reaching Scholten before Freel. Still, she would have liked to see DeZantez's face if Horse jumped right in front of her eyes. What would she do about returning her to McCain then, eh?

It was during one cooling off period – she and Jakub Freel riding side by side in silence, DeZantez lagging a little way behind, lost in thought – that she decided to tackle what had so far been unsaid.

"I know who you are."

Freel simply nodded. "And I, you. In fact, I understand you were something of a thorn in my predecessor's side."

"More like an arrow in his head," Kali said. "But, strictly speaking, I wasn't the one responsible."

"No?"

"No," Kali repeated. "It was my lover. Slowhand. Killiam Slowhand."

The mention of the archer, and her relationship to him, was careful and deliberate. She let both facts hang in the air. She hadn't known how much Freel knew of her and Slowhand's involvement with Jenna's death in the Drakengrats, but got a notion now – a flicker in Freel's eyes that went beyond recognising his wife's brother's name. It was obvious he knew full well that Slowhand had given the order that had killed Jenna.

"Killiam Slowhand," Freel repeated. "A joke of a name. Not even his own."

"He has his reasons."

"That, then, is his role in your relationship? He is your assassin?"

"Assassin? No, of course not. He's a soldier and..." Kali hesitated and decided that she may as well take the bamfcat by the horns. "Freel, you have to understand, what happened... it was Jenna or us."

Freel pursed his lips, nodded slowly, but said nothing. Kali did not press him.

"Was it worth it?" He asked eventually.

"What? Was what worth it?"

"What you fought so hard to save? The reason so many died that day? The ship?"

The question threw Kali and she frowned. The fact was, other than generalities, she had no idea what role the *Tharnak* had yet to play. "Honestly? I don't know."

"Are you saying that it remains to be seen?"

"I guess I am, yes."

Freel turned to her for the first time. "Then, Miss Hooper, if you are trying to discover what my opinions of your lover are, my answer is they, too, remain to be seen."

With that, the conversation ended and Freel spurred his horse on. They didn't slow again until they had reached their destination.

Scholten Cathedral. The last time two times Kali had trodden its supposedly hallowed halls she had been with Slowhand, and on both occasions she and the archer were intruders, either running for their lives or sneaking about in the dark. In either case they had been able to pay little attention to the details of their surroundings, other than to the whereabouts of Faith patrols. She wished she could say it made a nice change to be able to take a good look around but the opposite was true. Everything about the place – the grandiose architecture, the ceremony and particularly the smug faces of the cathedral's Enlightened Ones, tending to their flock in exchange for donations – made Kali sick to the stomach. She wondered why she hadn't, in fact, jumped away with Horse on the way here, as had crossed her mind.

The One Faith, The Only Faith, The Final Faith, she thought. *Gods!*

They were a blight selling the false dream of ascension to their followers, and she wished she could tell every one of those followers what she had witnessed done in the church's name, just what it was that went on behind the gold-thread tapestries and hand-carved wooden doors – show them the real face of the Final Faith.

She, of course, bore scars both old and new to remind her of exactly what that was. The old scars on her ankles, wrists and neck had been acquired deep beneath these very halls, where Konstantin Munch had submitted her to the comforts of his 'nail chair' and the tender ministrations of Querilous Fitch. Though the scars had faded, her disdain for the Faith would never go away. The new scars were the red blotches that she now bore on her shoulders and neck: evidence, if any were needed, of these bastards' propensity to burn first and not ask questions later, to immolate any who spoke out against their cause, as they had done in the thousands over the years.

It gave Kali no small pleasure, then, as, with the sound of the Eternal Choir fading in their ears, Freel led her and DeZantez down into the sublevels', where it seemed the Faith had undergone some suffering themselves. The transition from the ornate cathedral to its gritty underbelly was always dramatic, but the signs of recent battle in the distribution and rail centre made it more so. Bodies had clearly been removed from within it, but cleaved or broken pieces of armour and torn surplice cloth were scattered here and there, some pieces of which still contained the odd chunk of severed flesh. And there was blood. A great deal of blood that had to have come from a great many people.

Something had hit the Faith and hit them hard.

The question was what?

"Come with me," Freel said, wasting no time.

He led the two women to some kind of bunker that, judging by the crates of belongings waiting outside the door to be removed, had recently changed hands. Kali recognised some of the belongings, particularly a small trolley containing a number of needlereeds and vials of viscous liquids and a duplicate of her own gutting knife. This must have been Konstantin Munch's hidey-hole when he wasn't torturing poor unfortunates in the holding chambers below. But as they passed through the door, no further evidence of the dwarf-blooded psychopath could be seen. Freel had put his own stamp on the office.

Kali's eyebrows rose. The bunker could have been an Old Race site, so much of their technology had been installed. Except that where most of the devices she encountered in such sites had been decayed and broken down, rotten after countless years of neglect, this stuff looked as if it had come straight out of the box. Amberglow light-panels illuminated an array of exotic machines of unknown purpose, security cages were sealed with runic arches and, most disturbingly, a raised platform in the centre offered views from a dozen Eyes of the Lord spheres, projecting goings-on in different parts of the Faith's empire. These images were being monitored by a handful of grey-robed men.

Gabriella DeZantez seemed discomforted in the presence of so much technology, as if it had no place in her vision of the church. Freel immediately dropped a few notches in Kali's estimation, too.

"Seems like there's a difference between my manipulating forbidden artefacts and your doing the same," Kali observed, nodding at the spheres.

"Oh, those things," Freel responded, "those weren't my idea." He signed a chit handed to him by one of his men. "The rest, though... well, the Faith has to move with the times. Even if, ironically, those times are the ancient past."

"Still meddling with things you don't understand," Kali said.

Freel paid her little attention, his face darkening as another man entered and read out the latest confirmed casualties – supply workers Bogle, Krang, Rutter and Flank, and an Eminence named Kesar.

The latter name seemed to shake Gabriella DeZantez.

"Rodrigo Kesar is dead?" She said.

The guard looked regretful. "The Eminence was supervising a... volatile incense shipment when the assault began, Sister. Was the Eminence a friend of yours?"

"No," Gabriella DeZantez said quietly to herself, and shook her head.

Kali looked at her, puzzled. The man had obviously been important in some way, but she had already said not as a friend. It seemed almost as if she had had some door slammed in her face. Maybe she'd ask her about it when she had the chance. For now, though, there were more important questions to be addressed.

"You want to tell me what the hells has been going on here?"

Freel guided her and DeZantez to the viewing area and, as he did, three other men joined them from across the room. "General McIntee of the Order of the Swords of Dawn, Cardinal Kratos," he said by way of introduction. "And this is the developer of the Eyes of the –"

"I know who this bastard is," Kali interrupted. "And I should have known. Hello, Fitch."

The psychic manipulator bowed slightly, his hands steepled. They were bandaged, Kali noticed. "Kali Hooper. What a pleasant surprise."

"What the hells are you doing here?" Kali demanded.

"Helping, Kali, just like you. All hands on deck, and all that."

"What – you run out of heads today?"

Fitch smiled and suddenly noticed the burns on Kali's neck. He tutted sympathetically.

Kali snarled.

"I suggest," Freel said hastily, "that we get down to business."

"No argument here," Kali agreed. "You said Makennon needed my help? That you feared she'd gone to the hells?"

Freel nodded. "The Anointed Lord has been taken."

"Taken? By which I presume you *don't* mean she's currently prancing through the clouds annoying the rest of the poor souls with Kerberos?"

"He means abducted," General McIntee said. "Here from the very heart of the Faith."

Kali pursed her lips, nodded. "Neat trick. So who's got her?"

Freel nodded to Fitch who promptly shut down all of the images being projected from the Eyes of the Lord. He then picked up an inactive Eye of the Lord from a nearby table and readied it for viewing.

With DeZantez, Kali found herself watching the horde's assault on the tunnels. She saw an overview of the grey figures pouring from the tunnel, zooming images of agonised or dying Final Faith soldiers and the flashes of the intruders' makeshift but lethal weapons. She had to disguise her shock as she saw Slowhand struggling in the grip of Faith guards. She had already met with indisputable proof that his mission to kill Fitch had failed, and now she knew why. Just like herself, events had overtaken him. Not for the first time, she reflected that she and the archer had a knack for being in the right place at the wrong time. It was almost as if, as Poul Sonpear had pointed out some months before, their presence in these places was somehow predestined. Now was not the time to worry about that, however, or Slowhand's current fate. If she were to make sense of what was happening before her, she had to give it her full attention.

Katherine Makennon was visible in the fray now, the armoured form of the Anointed Lord striding into the sublevel at the head of her men. Again, Kali caught a glimpse of Slowhand, trying to stop Makennon wading in. Wade in, of course, was what she did, and Kali had to give the woman her due – she could certainly bollock the bad guys. What happened next, however, was so unexpected and shocking that she wasn't at all surprised to see Slowhand and his captors reel from it.

Something hurtled out of the dark, darker than the tunnel from which it came. A thing of indeterminate shape, a storm cloud streak that moved at breakneck speed, whose outlines writhed before the eye. A shifting, octopus-like morass and an insane blur at the same time, as seemingly insubstantial as shadow as it shot straight at Makennon and whipped back towards the tunnel, wrapping about her as it did, absorbing her in its mass and carrying her away. In that instant – and only that instant – it was almost identifiable, as a black carriage drawn by wild-eyed, snorting horses from the pits. A moment later the shape and Katherine Makennon with it were gone.

"Farking hell," Kali said, as the image from the sphere flickered and died.

Gabriella DeZantez was a little more controlled. "What in the name of the Lord was that?"

"Interesting, isn't it?" Freel said. "All I can say is that it – and the preceding events – were repeated at twelve other locations across the peninsula. And in each case the leader of that community was taken by that... thing."

"By previous events, I presume you mean the attack from the soul-stripped?" Kali said.

Fitch looked surprised. "You know of the First Enemy?"

The First Enemy, Kali thought. Only the more senior of the Final Faith called him that, those who *remembered*. DeZantez seemed not to be one of them, and so for her sake –

"Why don't you remind me, Fitch?"

Fitch shrugged. "The result of a conceit of the first Anointed Lord, Jeremiah Nectus Dunn. He mistakenly believed the teachings of the Faith could be taken to the farthest reaches of our empi... of the land."

"The Sardenne Forest you mean."

Fitch nodded. "But Dunn was wrong. The people who live in that forsaken hinterland have greater things to fear than the Lord of All, as our people discovered to their cost."

"My, my, Querilous Fitch, that's almost blasphemous," Kali chided.

Fitch could have been talking about any of the multifarious creatures that called the Sardenne home, and it would have served Dunn's missionaries right if they had encountered them and not come home as a result. But he wasn't talking about them, she knew. It wasn't the bogarts and beasties of the great forest coming out of there that they had to worry about – the assault on Scholten Cathedral was far too coordinated for them. This was without doubt the work of the one ruling intelligence that called the Sardenne home. In an area called Bellagon's Rip.

Most people called him the Pale Lord.

"He was the first serious resistance our Church encountered," Fitch continued. "A sorcerer of power unprecedented, then and now. He found the presence of our people in the forest – in *his* forest – distasteful, and made that distaste abundantly clear. Those who 'survived' the encounter remain with him, I imagine, to this day. In the end the Faith and he made a truce. The Sardenne would be left alone and, unless we attempted to return, so would we."

Kali nodded. It was pleasing to see that some things made Fitch sweat as profusely as his victims. But with good reason. In Pontaine, at least, the Pale Lord had become something of a bogeyman. A necromancer by the name of Bastian Redigor, he had been banished from civilisation long ago and had retreated into exile in the depths of the Sardenne Forest, whereafter occasional sightings of his almost albino features and tall, thin, cloaked figure – who never seemed to age – had earned him the nickname of 'the Pale Lord.' It was what the Pale Lord *did* during these sightings, however, that had earned him his fearful reputation over the years. People near to the forest began to disappear, first in ones and twos and then in ever increasing numbers.

If these people were ever seen again it was as a fleeting form glimpsed among the trees, empty and grey and engaged in mysterious business. These people had become slaves of the Pale Lord – he had taken their souls for purposes unknown – and they became known as the 'soul-stripped.' As the years had passed, more and more had been taken – the soul-stripped themselves taking people on their Lord's behalf – so much so that unruly children were sent to bed with a promise that, if they did not behave, the Lord or his growing army of minions would come to 'kiss them' and take them away into the night.

Oh yes, Kali knew that, because she'd been one of those children who'd lain awake night after night, peeking out fearfully from under the sheets. Thankfully, rather than turn her into a gibbering wreck, it had eventually instilled in her a curiosity for the unexplained that had defined the rest of her life.

But why, after all these years, and as the Faith hadn't returned to the Sardenne, was the Pale Lord attacking them?

And how the hells had he been able to do what he did?

"I thought your tunnels were shielded," she said. "Weaved so powerfully nothing, not even the Pale Lord, could get through."

"They are. Or rather, were. The shields collapsed before the assault began. Just vanished. As, incidentally, did the abilities of every mage or shadowmage in the complex."

Kali's eyes narrowed suspiciously. "Vanished how?"

"We don't know. They just –"

"Fizzled out," Kali finished, and sighed. "Just like Quinking's Depths."

"Quinking's Depths?"

"Below Solnos," Kali said absently. "The same thing happened there."

"Then I imagine you're thinking that the reason the shields collapsed is related to the appearance of the machines near Solnos. And you would be right. But only partly so."

"Oh?"

"Those machines are not the only ones of their kind. There are three groups of them."

"*What?*"

Fitch moved to a map of the peninsula, pointing out three locations. "Three groups of three machines rising from beneath the ground at precisely the same time. Their appearance was reported to us by our senders, just before their abilities... left them."

Kali hesitated. "Wait one minute. Are you trying to tell me this phenomena is peninsula-wide? That magic has been cancelled out *everywhere*?"

"Yes. Our theory is that these machines have been activated from some central location by forces of the Pale Lord for just that purpose. It is with this that we need your help."

Kali folded her arms. "I thought that's where I might come in. You want me to find out where this location is and shut these things down right?"

Fitch nodded. "Only then would we have an effective defence against the First Enemy. Only then would we be able to effect a rescue of the Anointed Lord."

"And the others who were taken, of course..."

"Of course."

"Okaaay," Kali said. "And just what do you lot do in the meantime?"

"Try and find out more about what the Pale Lord is planning," Freel said. "To that end I ordered an Eye of the Lord despatched to the Sardenne."

Kali was impressed. She doubted very much that such a course of action would even have occurred to Fitch, who could think of nothing to do with his new toys other than spy on his flock.

Sometimes you just needed to think, as it were, outside the collection box.

"Show me," Kali said.

"I will," Freel reassured her. "But the journey to and from the Sardenne takes time. We expect the Eye's return in the next couple of hours." The enforcer shrugged, half-smiled and spread his arms. "In the meantime, I suggest you make yourself at home."

CHAPTER SIX

MAKE YOURSELF AT *home,* Freel had said. How exactly did you do that in the bosom of the most intolerant religion the peninsula had ever seen? Kali had contemplated popping upstairs to do a few numbers with the Eternal Choir – maybe something with a bit of a *beat* – or perhaps sneaking into Makennon's quarters to grab herself a nice, hot bath, but she didn't want to give Fitch a chance to play with his balls. She had even thought of getting the hells out of the cathedral for a while to down a flummox or three in the Ramblas, but the information she was waiting on was too important to miss.

She tried to get to see Slowhand, But the archer was under heavy guard – access to no one but Fitch – and instead she found herself wandering the sublevels. She came at last to the naphtha chamber where the soul-stripped, who had been left behind after the Pale Lord's assault were meeting, without objection, their ultimate end. The creatures' fate was indicative of how Redigor had used them as nothing more than cannon fodder to draw Makennon out, and now their purpose was done, they were discarded.

Kali was surprised to see DeZantez in the chamber, watching the mindless victims with sorrow rather than disgust in her eyes. As one soul-stripped after the other was placed within a naphtha cage, mindlessly compliant, she seemed even to sag before the weight of them, as if each victim took with it a little part of her. Maybe it did, Kali reflected. After all, as a Sister of the Order of the Swords of Dawn, these were the people whom DeZantez had sworn to protect, and they had been taken from her by the Pale Lord in obscene numbers.

Watching them burn, Kali cringed, recalling her own close encounter with the gibbet and trying not to think how agonising her death could so easily have been. She was aided in this by what was perhaps an even greater horror. As the naphtha consumed them, the Pale Lord's soldiers remained perfectly still, making no attempt to escape their gibbets and absolutely no sound other than the crackling and spitting of their own burning flesh. By all that was natural, they should have filled the underground with the sound of their screams but, whitened eyes staring unfeelingly ahead, their mortal forms departed the world uncomplaining, supplicant until the last to their dark master's will.

When it was done, Gabriella DeZantez touched all four points of the crossed-circle on her tunic and then placed her right palm on its centre, her head bowed in prayer. When her gaze rose once more Kali was surprised to see teardrops beading the corners of her eyes.

"Maybe now," DeZantez said, "their souls can somehow reach Kerberos."

Kali regarded her, and nodded non-commitedly. Considering the treatment she had received at this woman's hands, she hadn't expected such a human response from her but, then, she had already sensed that there was more to her than the average Filth drone. She shared their devoutness, yes, but she was clearly not part of the pack. There was an air of independence and a sense of humanity and, more importantly, *justice* about her. For a moment she wished she could share her hopes for the victims.

"You don't believe in ascension to Kerberos." Gabriella observed, seeing her expression.

Kali shrugged, bit her lip. "Let's just say I've seen and heard a few things that make me question the received wisdom, particularly the teachings of the Filth."

DeZantez actually smiled at the slur. "That it is our destiny to ascend – to become something greater than our whole?"

"Yes."

DeZantez pondered for a moment. "We have time. What if I could prove to you that when a deserving soul departs its body it does indeed travel to the place to which we all aspire – to the clouds of Kerberos?"

"And just how would you do that? With some Faith parlour trick? No, I don't think so."

"No trick. And nothing to do with the Faith. Except, of course as a reinforcement *of* our faith. No, this is something that was here before our Church. Something much, much older."

Gabriella snapped instructions to a nearby brother, an initiate by his cowl, to fetch something from her saddlebag, and he departed, returning a little while later with a small cloth-wrapped object. Gabriella unfolded the material almost reverently, revealing what appeared to be a shard of glass or crystal.

"This is a piece of Freedom Mountain," she explained. "It was loosened during a recent... let's say *visitation* and removed from the site by a man named Crowe, as a souvenir of what happened there. Travis... he neglected to take it with him when we parted company."

"I don't see what geology has to do with anything here."

"Take it," DeZantez urged. Kali did, and found the shard unexpectedly light. "Now come with me."

Kali frowned, but did as asked, finding herself led along a number of corridors to a small chamber which had been converted into a makeshift field hospital to treat the few survivors of the recent attack. One of the cots held the badly injured body of a Faith brother for whom nothing more could be done. The dying man stared up at DeZantez with dimming eyes as she stood over him, a rattle of recognition at her Swords of Dawn surplice escaping his dry throat. Gabriella smiled with genuine warmth and sat gently down on the side of the cot, taking the man's hand.

"This is Brother Marcus," she explained, squeezing his hand. "Brother Marcus is a good man, with simple beliefs. Chief among those beliefs has always been that when his time comes he will ascend to Kerberos and there find the greater glory that awaits us all, just as the Final Faith teaches." She leaned forward to Brother Marcus's face and spoke softly. "You understand, don't you, Marcus, that your time is coming soon?"

Brother Marcus nodded almost imperceptibly and swallowed, as did Kali. DeZantez had clearly spent time here while she'd been wandering around.

"I am with you," Gabriella said.

Kali shifted uneasily on her feet, but said nothing as DeZantez continued to comfort Marcus and wait for the man to die. There was, she presumed, some point to this. After a few more minutes, Marcus's hand suddenly tightened in Gabriella's, he bucked once and gave a long sigh. This particular member of the Final Faith had breathed his last.

DeZantez sighed. "What do you see?" She asked Kali.

"A man gone to meet his maker," Kali responded. "But who, or what, that maker is I wouldn't want to say."

"Look again," Gabriella instructed. "Through the shard."

"What?"

"The shard. Freedom Mountain had a direct physical connection to Kerberos, and that has given it some unique properties. Look again," she added. *"Hurry, girl, or it will be too late."*

Girl? Kali thought. There wasn't that much difference in their ages and, in fact, she was pretty sure she was the elder here. Nevertheless, she shrugged, warily raised the shard before her eyes, and caught her breath. Because what the shard revealed was that Brother Marcus hadn't yet gone anywhere. His soul, his essence – Kali wasn't sure what to call it – separated itself from the physical form like pollen shaken from a flower by a spring breeze. It was made up of sparkling, scintillating beads of light as vibrant as anything Kali had ever seen.

As they emerged from his lifeless body, they formed themselves into a recognisable semblance of Brother Marcus – albeit distorted, as if viewed through a carnival mirror – forming and stretching upwards, towards the ceiling of the chamber. And then, with an actual, noticeable glance down at his corporeal remains, *through* the ceiling.

Kali continued to stare upwards, working out where beneath Scholten this particular chamber was located, trying to rationalise what she had just seem. But she couldn't. Because unless Brother Marcus was heading for a final tankard in the Bloody Merry – which, considering the Faith's abstinence laws, seemed unlikely – there was only one thing up there. Quite some way up there.

"The clouds of Kerberos." Kali said softly.

"The clouds of Kerberos." Gabriella confirmed.

"I... I don't know what to say."

"Then say nothing. But understand that this is why I have given myself to the Faith. That, despite what you think, some of us truly believe."

Kali stared at her. DeZantez turned as the messenger who had delivered the shard returned, in a hurry and bringing news. "Sister DeZantez, Miss Hooper, Enforcer Freel requests your presence," he said breathlessly. "The Eye of the Lord has returned."

The pair looked at each other and began to make their way to the bunker.

"There's something that I need to ask you," Gabriella said en route. "Something I don't understand."

Kali was grateful to return to more familiar footing. "Shoot." "That *thing* that took the Anointed Lord. It was borne of sorcery, it had to be. Of magic. But I thought the magic had died."

The same seeming contradiction had occurred to Kali, and while she had no answer, she did have suspicions. The threads might have been cancelled by the machines, but what if this wasn't the threads at work? Something close to them, yes, something similar, but not the threads everyone knew? She recalled Aldrededor telling her that while he had been piloting the *Tharnak* he had seen strange *black threads* lying dormant amongst the others, no longer a part of their tapestry but still there. They'd appeared lifeless, he'd told her, but nevertheless occasionally leeched colour from other threads.

"It has," Kali said to DeZantez. "That's what worries me."

They reached Freel's bunker where he and the others were gathered once more about the central platform, where a new sphere had been positioned for viewing. The returned Eye was blackened and damaged, still smoking slightly, as if it had been caught up in some incredibly vicious firestorm. Kali wondered how it had managed to limp home. But limp home it had and, by the looks on the faces of Freel, Fitch and the others, they had already viewed what it had brought back with it.

"I have a feeling this isn't good news," Kali said.

"It isn't." Freel replied.

He nodded to Fitch and the manipulator activated the sphere. The flickering image showed the rolling plains of east Pontaine for a moment, before the target of the Eye of the Lord's flight came into view.

The sphere approached the perimeter of the Sardenne at a height of about a thousand feet, so that the demarcation between the ancient forest and the plains was clearly visible. It was darker than Kali had expected it to look, however, although she had experience of just *how* dark the Sardenne could be. The reason wasn't immediately obvious, the distance still too great, but from Jakub Freel's expression it was going to come as quite the revelation. She studied the image intently as the small recording blimp drew closer, and gradually began to make out exactly what it was that constituted that greater darkness.

Gabriella DeZantez crossed herself once more, praying under her breath.

Soul-stripped, thousands of them, standing shoulder to shoulder in the border of the forest, absolutely motionless and as grey as the shadows in which they stood. Distinguishable as individuals mainly by the whites of their lifeless, staring eyes, they were crowded together in an almost crushing mass but none reacted to the others, none complained, none jostled. Kali had no idea how far back into the forest these witless creatures lurked but, as she watched, more, presumably recent victims, shambled to join them and take up positions by their sides. As if those already assembled weren't enough.

This was a gathering of the Pale Lord's servants on a massive and hitherto unprecedented scale. The necromancer was, it seemed, building an army.

"Their eyes," Fitch said. "It's said that the First Enemy can, if he wishes, see through them all at once, and that when he does his gaze is powerful enough to see people's thoughts."

"What the hells is going on?" Kali asked.

Freel placed a hand on her shoulder. "There's more."

Kali glanced at Gabriella, who looked as confused as she did, and turned back to the projection. The Eye of the Lord was heading beyond the edge of the forest, now, and the vista it displayed was an unending, rolling landscape of ancient and massive trees, a thick canopy that hid the presence of the multifarious creatures and horrors that lived beneath. As the sphere progressed, Kali mentally traced her own journey through the forest almost a year before, the only way that she could map the progression of the Eye of the Lord over the otherwise unchanging topography. She guessed it was nearing Bellagon's Rip, now, which was generally accepted to be the stomping ground – or hiding place, depending on which way you looked at it – of the Pale Lord. Her guess turned out to be accurate as, after a minor alteration of its flight path, the view of the Eye of the Lord changed slightly and *something* hove into view.

"Oh, my gods," Kali said.

The Eye of the Lord had turned to look over the Sardenne's canopy, Kerberos's azure curve clearly visible above the forest. It was neither the canopy nor the gas giant that drew the eye, though, but the space between the two, where a massive pillar of energy, the width of a small village, punched up from the forest *towards* Kerberos. The pillar pulsed regularly and, each time it did, seemed to rise a little higher.

"What are those things you can see in it?" Gabriella DeZantez asked.

"I wish we knew," Freel responded. "Miss Hooper, have you ever come across anything like this in your travels?"

Kali shook her head. She was gaining a better view of the pillar now as the Eye of the Lord moved closer. The 'clouds' were revealed to be an agitation of the entire insides of the pillar, the shapes thick within it, slapping and battering against each other like leaves in a storm. Kali squinted, peering at them to make out more of their exact form when a thought struck her. She nudged DeZantez, indicated the shard and then raised it to her eye to view the projection.

Kali swallowed before speaking.

"They're souls," she announced.

Freel, Fitch and the others snapped their gazes towards her but, before Kali could elaborate, the projection suddenly juddered and flickered and, with the sphere perhaps thirty feet from the surface of the pillar, blackened and disappeared.

"The Eye of the Lord closed at this point," Fitch pointed out. "And returned to me."

"Did you say *souls*?" DeZantez asked Kali, clearly disturbed by what she had seen.

"But the ascension is meant to be a *personal* calling," Cardinal Kratos said, seemingly of the same mind, though Kali wasn't sure she believed him. "An individual journey. Not this... this –"

Kali offered him the shard. "Watch again and see for yourself. I'm sorry but they're souls. One for each of those soul-stripped."

Freel blew out a breath, looked at Kali. "I have to ask again – have you ever come across anything like this?"

She shook her head. "Believe me, it's only recently that I've got aboard this whole 'soul' thing."

Kratos sighed. "I think the enforcer had hoped to benefit more from your experience."

"Hey," Kali protested, "do I look like a farking encyclopedia?"

"No," Fitch joined in. "What you look like is the owner of a disreputable tavern in the middle of nowhere."

"That's it, I'm off..."

Gabriella DeZantez blocked Kali's way.

"I *thought* we'd gotten past that," Kali snarled.

"Gentlemen, ladies, please," Jakub Freel said. "The pressure of this current situation has obviously affected us all. May I just ask you all for your conclusions on what you've seen?"

"What other conclusion can there be?" General McIntee answered. "You saw the number of those things. The First Enemy is planning a full-scale invasion of the peninsula."

Beside him, Cardinal Kratos accepted and read a scroll handed to him by a messenger. His expression turned grim. "Faith riders report that more of the Pale Lord's forces have launched assaults on most of the settlements within twenty leagues of the Sardenne, and are moving farther afield. We believe we are looking at the total loss of Verity, Rasoon, Prayer's End, and countless communities, including Gargas."

"What about the rest of it?" Kali interrupted. There was something very wrong going on here. "That... phantasm that came for Makennon and the other twelve? This... pillar of souls? Where do they fit in? It doesn't make sense."

Freel sighed. "Are you suggesting an alternative theory?"

"No, but you asked for my help, so give me time and I'll have one."

"How much time?"

Kali faltered. "I think it has something to do with the speed at which the pillar of souls is rising. I think its meant to touch Kerberos. And I think whatever is going to happen will happen then." She paused, calculating. "Three days. Give me three days and I'll shut down your machines *and* find out what you need to know."

Freel was silent for a few moments, considering. "Agreed. But in the meantime, I have no choice but to convene a council of war."

"You do that," Kali said. "But there's one other thing."

"Oh?"

"I want Killiam Slowhand to be in on this too. Fitch has him and I want him released."

Freel's expression was unreadable. But he nodded briskly.

"Under no circumstances!" Querilous Fitch objected. "The man is insane, a killer!"

Kali smiled. "That he is. And a very good one. But he only kills those who deserve it."

"No," Fitch insisted. "I refuse."

Cardinal Kratos and General McIntee regarded the psychic manipulator with distaste. McIntee was the one who voiced their thoughts. "The decision is not yours to make, manipulator. In the absence of the Anointed Lord we are responsible for decisions for the good of the Faith." He turned to Kali. "Very well. I'll have him brought up from the cells."

A few minutes later, Slowhand appeared in the doorway, and immediately tried to lunge for Fitch, but Kali, standing unnoticed beside the door, grabbed his arm and pulled him back. The archer turned on her, ready to lash out, but froze as he saw who he was facing.

"Hooper?"

"Slowhand."

"How you doing?"

"Just for a change, working for the Final Faith. And so are you."

"Nice company," Slowhand said. He paused, then his eyes narrowed. "This is something to do with what happened to Makennon, isn't it?"

"Uh-huh. The Faith think their First Enemy is planning some kind of invasion."

"Him again? Who *is* this First Enemy guy?"

"The Pale Lord."

"Ah," Slowhand said. "Oooooh." He looked in Kali's eyes, then leaned forward to whisper in her ear. "Is he?"

"He's planning something," Kali whispered back, "but nothing about this feels right to me. Keep smiling, anyway."

Slowhand did. "So we need to sort this out, right? So where are we off? The Prison of Pain? Ranson's Remains? The Mound of Thunder?"

"Actually," Kali responded, "to the library."

"The library?" Slowhand repeated, not sure that he had heard right.

"We need to do some research."

"The library," Slowhand said again, deflated. "You know, one thing about working with this woman is there's never a dull moment."

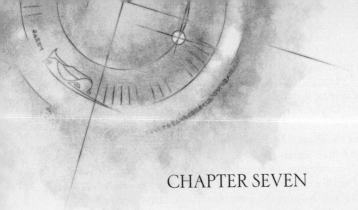

CHAPTER SEVEN

THE HALL OF Proscribed Knowledge, the largest of the collections in the Final Faith library, was situated in a wing of the cathedral all of its own. The vast depository was packed with shelves towering as high as the ornate architraves and each shelf, in turn, was crammed to bursting with tomes of all shapes, sizes and provenance, the evident age and titles of many of which almost made Kali drool. The ones set in elven or dwarven script, particularly.

The books on the lower shelves were reached through a claustrophobic and labyrinthine network of narrow passageways which jinked left and right unexpectedly and along which two people could not walk abreast. These, however, were the more common tomes, and the loftier ones – literally and metaphorically – were accessed by a precarious and dizzying network of crooked and seemingly unlinked metal stairways that reminded Kali of a structure she'd struggled for weeks to scale in a recurring dream. As she had in the dream, she wondered quite how it was they managed to stay up. She doubted magic, because from the moment she and Slowhand had entered she'd sensed the library was somehow isolated from the rest of the cathedral, and whatever sorceries or technologies were in use elsewhere in the complex had no place here, lest they damage the tomes. There was probably even – under normal circumstances – a dampening field in place. The contents of at least some of these books also explained why so few people were present: a cardinal here, an eminence there, and white-gowned curators whom she presumed had been thoroughly vetted before being trusted with the information in their charge. This was a domain accessible only to the Faith elite, though Kali struggled to reconcile them with the term as over the sounds of scribbling and dry parchment pages being turned, there was the occasional consumptive cough, belch and blatantly delivered fart.

"As I said," Killiam Slowhand muttered, "never a dull moment."

"*Shhh!*" A voice admonished.

Slowhand stared at the white-gowned curator, a wizened little man about half the height of Suresight, who was as dusty as the shelves.

"Hey, I can mutter, can't I?"

"*Shhh!*"

Slowhand shook his head and pulled Kali aside. "I don't get it," he whispered. "Why here? Surely whatever we can find here, the Filth already know?"

"Maybe, maybe not," Kali whispered back. "I'm willing to bet there are thousands of books here that have been confiscated simply because they *could* be confiscated, and haven't been touched since. Hopefully we'll find something they haven't."

The archer looked dubious.

"Come on, Slowhand, how many people do you know who've read the entire contents of their *own* library?"

"You, for one."

"Yes, well..."

"And Merrit Moon," Slowhand said. "Well, all apart from –"

"The Flesh Rituals of Elven Slither Maidens? With pictures by P'Tang?"

"Oh, yeeeah." Slowhand looked at her suspiciously. "How did you know?"

"Because I was reading in the corner when you crept down and nicked it from his shelf."

"*Borrowed.*"

"A year ago. Frankly, I'd be amazed if you can still open the thing."

Slowhand coughed and abruptly paled. He hissed, "Wait a minute. You're not seriously suggesting we work our way through this entire place!"

"*Shhh!*"

"Will you fark off!"

"There is no need for –"

"Hey!" Slowhand shouted. He unslung Suresight from his back and mimed using the little man as an arrow and shooting him out a window. The curator scuttled off.

"Not if you know what you're looking for," Kali went on. She hopped up steps and plucked a pile of tomes, dropping them on Slowhand for him to read. "But it is going to be a long night."

Kali browsed more shelves for tomes for herself, and then she and Slowhand made their way to a reading table. Kali rolled her eyes as she flung her backpack onto the table. The bag clattered and there was a long sigh from beyond the wall of books.

They hadn't been working long when a shadow loomed over them.

"Need any help?" A voice asked and Slowhand looked up. Then

he looked down, then up again, before stretching back in his chair, hands linked behind his head, beaming.

"Be our guest," he said, showing all his teeth.

Kali, too, looked Gabriella DeZantez up and down. The woman had washed off the dust of the trail and changed into a clean white surplice, its brilliance accentuating the subtle but powerful musculature beneath her bronzed skin. Kali pouted inwardly – she spent far too much time underground to get a tan like that. "You don't strike me as someone who has spent a lot of time with her head in a book," she responded, after a moment.

Gabriella smiled coldly. "You disappoint me, Kali. I'd have expected you of all people not to judge a book by its cover."

"Oh?"

"A girl from a backwater tavern with an over fondness for drink, an absolute disregard for authority and a tendency to repeatedly cross swords with the Final Faith? Hardly the kind of person you'd expect *them* to turn to for help."

"What can I say? We go back a ways."

Gabriella nodded. "I know, I've done some research of my own. The Clockwork King. The Crucible. Greenfinger's Wood. The Faith holds quite a file on you."

"You surprise me. That crack about 'sex occasionally' still in there?"

"The Anointed Lord's small attempt at a joke. She's human, too, you know, despite her calling from the Lord of All."

"Yeah, right," Kali spat. Then she apologized. What DeZantez had shown her earlier had proven that there was at least some basis to the Faith's beliefs, even if she remained convinced that their interpretation of it was deeply suspect.

"For the record," DeZantez went on, "I spent a good deal of my childhood in a place such as this. Not on the same scale, of course. My mother ran – still runs – the Faith archive in Andon."

Kali raised her eyebrows. "Marta DeZantez is your mother?"

"You know her?"

"Not well, but I've had... occasion to consult her records. She's a good woman – non-partisan."

For the first time DeZantez's smile warmed, and she nodded her acknowledgement, still a little uneasy.

"Listen," Killiam Slowhand said loudly, in an attempt to defuse the situation. "Seeing as we are all in the employ of the Fil – the Faith for the foreseeable future, what say we all be friends here?" The archer patted an adjacent chair. "Sit by me."

DeZantez stared at the proffered chair and then the archer,

regarding him as she might a mollusc. "So you can pretend to read a book while you ogle my thighs? I don't think so."

"I guess she's read your file, too," Kali said.

"Uh-huh," DeZantez confirmed.

Slowhand did his best to look innocent, then attempted to change the subject. "Gabriella DeZantez," he said, with his best grin. "Quite the mouthful. How about I call you Dez?"

The swordswoman's eyes darkened. "Sure. How about I call you Slow?"

The archer's smile faded and it was Kali's turn to smile. She indicated a seat beside herself instead. "There's a lot to get through. We'd welcome your help."

Gabriella slid into the proffered seat. "Okay. What are we looking for?"

"Two things. Anything about the machines, their origin and history, but particularly any mention of how they are activated and controlled. Secondly, dates and details relating to the legend of the Pale Lord, known experiments and movements, anything that might cross-reference with the Engines or this 'pillar of souls.'"

DeZantez nodded. "Fine. Who's doing what?"

"I'll tackle the machines, with Dez," Slowhand volunteered.

"Nice, but how about you tackle the Pale Lord and Gabriella and I take the machines," Kali corrected. It had been a while since she had seen the archer go into a sulk, but he did as he was told, and a few minutes later three heads were buried deep inside books.

The hours began ticking by. Kali hadn't been wrong when she'd said it was going to be a long night, and the reading table was soon stacked high with tomes from all sections of the library. Most offered nothing, and a few gave snippets of information useless by themselves. Gradually, however, and after Slowhand had been kicked twice for snoring, some snippets began to correspond and a sketchy picture emerged.

It seemed that during one of the bloodiest times of their later history, having been routed by the increasingly powerful magic of their elven enemies, the dwarves had constructed a number of weapons or deterrents – the meaning wasn't exactly clear – said to be capable of nullifying the magic of the elves, effectively interfering with the threads manipulated by their song-magic. That interference, Kali guessed, had to be caused by the sound the machines emitted; it was possible that the sound could also interfere with other types of magic, including the barriers to the cathedral's railway tunnels, whose magical origins lay with the elves in the first place. One thing puzzled Kali, however. Although there were several references to the machines there was no subsequent mention of them having been used successfully against the elves. History, in fact, recorded that there was no such change of fortunes in the elf/dwarf wars and that they had soon after declared a truce that was to be the starting point of their third age of existence, where the Old Races had advanced their civilisations in peace. But if that was the case, one obvious question needed to be answered – *why* hadn't the dwarves used the machines it had clearly taken them a great deal of time and effort to develop?

It was Gabriella who found the answer. Or at least something that pointed to an answer. Records from around the time of the machines' development spoke of severe upheaval across the peninsula, of unnatural storms and quakes, and of coastal settlements being consumed by the sea. It didn't take much of a leap to imagine that perhaps the cause of these phenomena lay with the machines themselves – that perhaps they affected more than just the threads and the dwarves had inadvertently, created some kind of doomsday weapon.

The theory gathered credence when Gabriella came upon one further reference. It needed to be translated from the dwarven by Kali but this one gave the machines a name.

The Engines of the Apocalypse.

Kali sat back with a sigh. They had discovered what they were dealing with, but it was now all the more imperative they find out how these engines were controlled, and from where.

A further number of hours research produced little on the former, but eventually Kali lit upon, of all things, a number of dwarven engineers' requisition forms buried amongst other preserved papers. Sometimes it *was* the small things, Kali reflected. The requisitions were for heavy construction materials, all of which were to be delivered to a particular location. The materials by themselves were no proof of any connection but the fact that the location was smack bang in the centre of the three groups of machines and had, from somewhere, acquired the name 'the Plain of Storms' sounded somewhat more promising.

They were, however, not yet done. The more she learned, the more Kali became convinced that the Pale Lord had to be planning something other than a simple invasion of the soul-stripped. After all, what could he possibly hope to gain from a devastated peninsula inhabited solely by the near-dead? No, Redigor's use of the engines to take Makennon and the others as well as render their mages powerless against his army was part of a greater plan, she was sure, and anything they could find out about the man himself might have a bearing on it.

"Anything, Slowhand?" Kali asked.

The archer shook his head. "I've been through a hundred books and other than the usual guff about the Pale Lord being banished from Fayence for meddling with necromancy, then buggering off into the Sardenne to form his army of the soul-stripped, there's very little. But there is this one phrase that keeps recurring..."

"Oh?"

"Here they lie, still," the archer quoted.

"Here they lie, still?" Gabriella repeated. "Any idea what that means?"

"Reputedly, they were the last words spoken by Redigor before he entered Bellagon's Rip," Slowhand said, consulting a passage. "But who 'they' were and where they 'lie still,' nobody records."

"Could he have been referring to the engines?" Gabriella mused. "Maybe the dwarves moved them to the Sardenne? Their equivalent of decommissioning them?"

"Maybe," Kali said, biting her lip. "Anything else?"

Slowhand shook his head and thumped another large, dusty tome down in front of him. He had no sooner opened it, however, than he stopped with a start, his gaze flicking to Gabriella sitting opposite him. The archer coughed, squirmed slightly, then smiled and gave her a sly wink.

"Are you all right?" Gabriella asked suspiciously.

"Fine," Slowhand answered, squeaking and clearing his throat. He jerked his head towards Kali, occupied with a new book, conspiratorially.

"You sure?"

"Oh, I'm sure," Slowhand said, leaning forward and whispering in Gabriella's ear. "Only I thought you weren't interested."

"Interested?"

"Your foot," Slowhand breathed, "on my thigh."

Gabriella's eyes narrowed. "Mister, believe me, the only place you'll ever find my foot is *between* your thighs, but you'll be too busy peeling your gonads from the ceiling to enjoy it."

"Funny," Slowhand purred, "that sounds just like something Hooper would say."

"What sounds like something Hooper would say?" Kali joined in.

"Oh, nothing," Slowhand said. He turned to give Gabriella another knowing glance but she'd already stood to replace some of the books on the shelves. He glanced quickly under the table, where 'her foot' was still at work.

"Er, ladies..."

Kali glanced up, stood and pushed back her chair with a curse. Beside her, Gabriella unsheathed her twin swords with a metallic ring that echoed throughout the vast library.

"*Shhh!*" came an admonition from beyond the shelves.

Kali ignored it. "What the hells?"

The book which lay open in front of Slowhand, who was leaning well back and staring at it warily, was *exuding* something from its spine. A number of thin, black tapers were curling from the top and bottom of the book, growing by the second, one of them now fully curled around Slowhand's thigh. Multiplying and thickening, accompanied by a dry, sinister hiss, they were redoubling their interest in the archer.

"Hooper, one of 'ems heading for my –"

"Slowhand, get up slowly," Kali said.

"That might be a good idea," he responded. It took him a second to react, however, the tapers having a strangely mesmeric effect on those who watched them, and it was only when the taper made a sudden dart for his crotch that he stood and kicked his chair back with a "Whoa!"

It was, unfortunately, a little too late, and before Slowhand knew what was happening twenty or more of the things had wrapped themselves around different parts of his body and were holding him in their grip. The archer struggled against them but, with as echoing thud, they tipped him off his feet and slapped him to the floor.

"Mmf... ooper?" Slowhand said, his eyes wide, as one of the tapers wrapped around his jaw. "Youf wanna helf me ouf here?"

"Hold on," Kali said, and attempted to tear the tapers away. "Shit," she shouted. "*Shit!*"

Not only were the tapers binding Slowhand as tightly as barrel hoops, but Kali's attempt to sever them prompted a backlash against herself. Suddenly they were far from mesmeric, a wild, thrashing mass that struck at her. She had no choice but to back off from Slowhand, and as the archer writhed helplessly on the floor, increasingly constricted, she adopted a defensive stance, gutting knife drawn in front of her.

"What are they?" Gabriella asked. She stared at the book's spine, which had thickened to accommodate the roots of perhaps a hundred of the tapers. "They look like some kind of..."

"Bookworm?" Kali suggested.

"I'm glad you said that."

"Hells, I call 'em as I see 'em."

Gabriella threw herself on top of Slowhand and, gripping him between her thighs, slashed at the tapers with her own twin blades, again to no effect. She, too, was forced back, Slowhand groaning in pain.

"There has to be something we can do." Gabriella said.

"Yeah, and fast. Before these things pop him out of his clothes." Gabriella looked at her strangely. "Trust me. It happens."

The Deathclaws, Kali realised. They might free Slowhand *and* prove to be a better defence. She leapt for the table where her backpack lay, snatched the blades from within and returned to slash at the tapers about the thrashing archer. They did the job, but the tapers had now multiplied to a degree where they were beginning to fill the entire reading area and, as Gabriella pulled Slowhand up and staggered with him down an aisle, Kali was forced to leap out of the path of the evil-looking mass and cling to the side of a bookshelf. At the same time she shouted to the curator who was approaching to see what all the commotion was about. "You! This book – where did it come from?"

"W-which book, Madam?"

Hanging there, Kali gave him her best, bemused look. "The one with the things growing out of it?"

"I d-don't know," he said, staring and stammering. "I'll need to ch-check the catalogue."

"*The catalogue?*"

The little man actually looked affronted. "M-Madam, there are over ten thousand tomes gathered in this library, subdivided into –"

"Just do it!" Kali shouted, slashing at the tapers with the claws. Severed sections spiralled away but more tapers darted in from her left and she threw herself from the shelf on which she clung to one on the opposite side of the aisle. "Because if you haven't noticed, things are getting a little out of hand here!"

The little man scuttled off and Kali found herself leaping from shelf to shelf as more and more tapers emerged from the book and snapped at her. The Deathclaws hummed in the air and the amputated tapers began to pile up below her, but there were always more, growing from the severed ends. Their tenacity was unrelenting and Kali wasn't sure how long she could keep up her defence. She saw one of the Eminences appear in the aisle, no doubt come to see what all the fuss was about, and the man stared in horror as a single taper shot out and punched into his chest. Kali actually saw it punch out of his back and then snap back, clutching his heart, leaving the dead man to slowly collapse to the floor.

"Keep back!" Kali warned as the curator returned, and it only took one look from the man to the still body of the Eminence for him to immediately obey. "Well?"

"This book and a number like it originated in the town of Fayence, Madam. They were acquired by the Hall of Proscribed Knowledge quite some years ago."

That sounded about right, Kali thought. "And their original owner?"

"A gentleman by the name of Bastian Redigor."

The name hung in the air for a second.

"The Pale Lord," Kali said.

The curator looked almost sheepish. "The Pale Lord," he repeated. "They were confiscated from his estate."

"Where the bastard must have trapped them before he was banished."

"Trapped?"

Kali sighed in exasperation. "Just what did you think we were dealing with here, Mister Curator? One of his collection of pop-up books?"

"No... I... oh, Lord of All, what do we do?"

Kali leapt from shelf to shelf again, veering mid-course so as not to bring the tapers that targeted her closer to the curator. He'd doubtless ask them to keep the noise down just before they ripped out his heart too. "*We* find a way to stop these things," she advised. "*You* get yourself and everyone else the hells out of here."

The curator looked non-plussed. "But my readers do not like their studies disturbed!"

Kali couldn't quite believe what she heard. Staring at the ever thickening spine of the book, she was about to explain that unless they all departed right now there was every chance they wouldn't be going anywhere, ever again. All of a sudden the spine of the book exploded and the entire section of the library in which they stood or clung was filled with a tree-sized growth of the things, thrashing toward the ceiling. The curator needed no more convincing and turned and ran, screaming to Kali to please, please, please not damage his books.

Kali flung a glance towards Gabriella, who stood with Slowhand, staring in horror at what had manifested itself, here, in the very heart of her faith. Kali understood, this was the same magic that had taken Makennon – something dark and very, very old that the Engines had not subdued like normal thread magic, that might even be related to the *black* threads that Aldrededor had seen while piloting the *Tharnak*. A magic that had no place in the Faith's or anyone's doctrine, and that was *unknown* to them all. The realisation only served to reinforce what she'd thought about the Pale Lord, that there was something much more to him, much more to this whole affair, than met the eye. It was also clear that Bastian Redigor would not have seeded the tome with such a trap if he didn't have something really interesting to hide. The only problem lay in living long enough to find out what that was.

Kali dropped from her perch and raced towards Gabriella and Slowhand, the roiling mass of blackness pursuing her, batting aside bookshelves as it came. They skidded into another passage as one, the tapers lashing at their heels.

"I'm beginning to think they've got something against us!" Slowhand shouted, ducking as more woodwork exploded all around.

"What the hells makes you think that?" Kali shouted back.

"So what do we do now?"

"I don't know!"

"There's something that might stop them," Gabriella gasped. She was staring up into the highest reaches of the library as she ran, above the precarious stairways, where a caged platform was visible. "The Dellendorf Scrolls."

"The Dellendorf Scrolls?"

"An archive of Old Race, perhaps *older*, scrolls – assorted incantations, enchantments, destruction spells and so on. They were found by an excavation team twenty years ago."

"What's the point?" Kali said. "Only Redigor's magic is working!"

Gabriella shook her head. "My guess is that the Engines interfere with the stability of current spells or the casting of new ones, but the magic of the scrolls is sealed into their parchment, *already cast*. All one of us needs to do is release it!"

And I wonder which one of us that's going to be? Kali considered.

She stopped and stared up at the scrolls' store. It certainly wasn't going to be easy; and between her and them, a veritable forest of tapers now thrashed, expanding into other passages, attempting to catch them in a pincer movement.

"We're trapped!" Slowhand shouted. The archer loosed a number of arrows at the nearest tapers but they were batted away. Gabriella slashed at the encroaching mass with her blades, but this time the tapers snatched her weapons from her hands, flinging them away over the shelves.

"Yeah?" Kali said, as her companions backed up. She leapt onto one of the walls of books enclosing them and slashed the Deathclaws from top to bottom, landing back on the floor with a grunt. Slowhand stared at her, puzzled, until Kali booted the wall and the entire section tipped away before her, crashing into another shelf beyond it, starting a domino effect across the library towards the stairway.

"Neat," Slowhand observed.

"Take these and try to slice yourselves a way out!" Kali shouted. She stripped off the claws and flung them towards Gabriella. The Enlightened One plucked them neatly from their flight. She nodded to Kali and donned them.

"Hooper – ?" Slowhand began, but Kali was already gone, leaping along the downed bookshelves, the tapers snapping at her from beneath and around their sides. Her alternative route seemed to have confused the dark magic strands, and Kali made it over several of the fallen shelves, but she saw that the tapers had extended ahead of her and were now punching in through a gap. She rolled, dodged and weaved, the stairs drawing ever nearer, until a taper managed to whip itself around one of her ankles and she found herself flipped high into the air.

After a moment of dizzying disorientation, Kali thudded to the floor beyond the final row of shelves and lay on her stomach, winded. To her right lay the base of the stairway she needed to reach, but to her left, hurtling towards her at a speed that in her state she couldn't hope to outrun, was a solid, seething mass of the black strands.

Kali struggled to her feet, looked for a way out, found none. She spun in a circle and punched shelves of books in frustration, furious with herself. A peculiar rumbling sound came from the direction of the stairs and she turned to face it, wondering what new threat she faced.

Her eyebrows rose. Gabriella DeZantez was racing towards her in mid-air, straddling two of the sliding ladders the curators used to access books on higher shelves. Between her legs, pushing the ladders as hard as he could, was a red-faced Slowhand.

"What, you think we'd let you do this alone?" He shouted as Kali ducked to let the ladders pass.

Kali watched their progress. Gabriella's hands blurred, the Deathclaws slicing constantly, the Enlightened One spinning and leaping between the two ladders in a dance that ensured not a single one of the tapers got near her or Slowhand. She and the archer cut a swathe through the mass, the black strands falling in their hundreds. The whole thing lasted no more than thirty seconds and, the tapers briefly repulsed, Gabriella leapt from the ladders and Slowhand released them.

"What are you waiting for?" She shouted to Kali. "Move!"

Kali didn't need telling twice. She ran for the stairway but, even as she did, more tapers lashed in from beyond the shelves, wrapping themselves around the lower risers, preventing her mounting them. This time Slowhand came to the fore.

"Hooper!" He shouted, and two of his arrows whizzed over Kali's head to embed themselves solidly in the wall. She leapt onto the first Slowhand had fired as another arrow struck the wall above her, feeling it snap under her but giving her enough upward momentum to carry her to the second, and then the third. Kali climbed Slowhand's makeshift staircase above the level of the tapers as he continued shooting, and threw herself onto the stairway beyond their reach. Her feet clattered on metal as she ascended, and the tapers raced after her, but Kali tumbled and leaped, leaving them behind as she negotiated the complicated structure. At last she reached the cage containing the scrolls, booted off the padlock and threw herself inside, slamming the cage closed behind her. The tapers swarmed about and rattled the metal enclosure but the mesh was too fine for them to penetrate. Kali let out a relieved breath.

Her relief was short-lived.

It was all right for DeZantez to say she could use one of the Dellendorf scrolls to blitz the tapers but, dammit, which one? There were hundreds stacked before her and, as far as she knew, the one she chose might make things worse, not better. It seemed, though, that whichever curators had been assigned to investigate these mysterious scrolls were possessed of frustrated egos and somewhat fanciful imaginations, and Kali found a clue to what she wanted in their attached notations. Quite clearly named after the curators themselves, the scrolls glorified in such names as Hamish's Wandering Eye, Charles's Dream of Domination and Gleeson's Worrisome Whiff, and one which sounded as if it might be up to the job – Strombolt's Devastator. Yes, that sounded pretty unequivocal. Now, how was it Gabriella had demonstrated it should be used?

Kali took a breath and stood in the centre of the cage, sweeping her palm across the scroll she held. As she did, the script upon it – a strange collection of symbols unknown even to her – parted company with the parchment and flew out through the mesh of the cage. Nothing happened for a second, and then the floating symbols raced together and collided, forming a dense, pulsating cloud above the centre of the vast library. The air grew immensely heavy, the light dulled, and a charge in the atmosphere made Kali's hair stand on end. The last thing she thought as she wrapped her arms about her head was how the curator had pleaded with her not to damage his books.

The Hall of Proscribed Knowledge, all of it, detonated with an explosion so powerful that its walls buckled momentarily outwards, prompting screams and cries of alarm from outside. The stained glass windows lining its upper storey disintegrated, shards falling as a rainbow rain. The chandeliers were propelled upwards, bouncing off the ceiling and dropping broken metal and molten wax before crashing to the floor below. The explosion finished the job the tapers and Kali had started, smashing each and every piece of furniture – tables, chairs and bookshelves – against the walls, leaving them as a shattered tide washed against the hall's perimeter. For quite some time afterwards countless cream and white leaves – all that remained of the books that had crammed the shelves – fluttered to the floor. If there was any saving grace to what Kali had just unleashed, it was that the tapers had flopped to the floor, dormant or dead.

"Oops," Kali said as she picked herself up from the floor of the cage. She coughed and picked splinters from her hair. From far below she heard other coughs and looked down to see Slowhand and

Gabriella emerging, battered and bruised but otherwise unharmed, from behind a heavy shelf that had miraculously landed at an angle over them. Gabriella backed cautiously away from Slowhand, looking puzzled and disturbed as to how the explosion, which left her relatively unscathed, could have blown him so neatly out of his clothes. Kali worked her way slowly down towards the pair.

"Well, that seemed to work," Gabriella DeZantez said.

"You know something?" Slowhand added, seemingly uncaring that he was naked, "I'm beginning to think we might make a pretty good team."

CHAPTER EIGHT

SLOWHAND HAD TO hand it to the Final Filth – for a bunch of God-Botherers, they did military mobilisation rather well. Preparations for their response to the Pale Lord's threat were already well under way at dawn the next day, the sublevel a hive of activity as engineers and support workers prepared and supplied funicular trains while the men and women who would ride them gathered in ranks, waiting to board. The sides of the railway tunnels were packed with swordsmen, axemen, archers and lancers, many of them young and, considering what it was they were being sent to face, understandably nervous. Steadfast, if no less grim, were the hardened warriors draped in the livery of the Order of the Swords of Dawn, and mages – lots and lots of mages. Quartermasters and Enlightened Ones walked among them all, the former inspecting weapons while the latter blessed their bearers for the trials ahead.

Impressive as it all was, Slowhand frowned. The war council had convened while he, Hooper and DeZantez had been occupied in the library and had informed them of their decision when they had emerged. Despite Hooper's doubts about the Pale Lord's intentions – reinforced during their researches – the Faith remained committed to their belief that he planned a soul-stripped invasion. The plan was to establish a cordon along the length of the Sardenne after the last of the Pale Lord's strange army had filed in. The cordon was to be a defensive one – they at least had the sense to realise *offensive* strategies would be suicide while the Engines were active – and would only engage in combat if the Pale Lord made a move. Once the Engines were shut down and magic restored, however, they planned to advance on the soul-stripped – to go in, as it were, with all hands blazing. Of course, the Faith alone did not have the numbers for such a massive endeavour, which was why some of the trains were to remain empty for now. The Faith had arranged not only to second thousands of troops from the Vossian army, who would board at

Faith 'missions' en route, but to enlist aid from the Pontaine militia too. Considering the attacks that had been occurring in their half of the world, Slowhand had no doubt they would agree.

Hence the frown. The Faith was, tactically, putting all the peninsula's eggs in one basket, an approach he had never been particularly fond of, and he could only hope the basket wasn't dropped somewhere along the way.

Slowhand moved through the frantic activity towards what would be his train. The fate of the Anointed Lord not forgotten in all of this, it had been decided that he, Freel, DeZantez and, of all people, Fitch – along with Hooper, when she returned from what she had to do – would not be part of the cordon but instead form a 'strike team' to infiltrate the Sardenne to try to find and rescue Makennon. As such, they were not to travel to the edges of the cordon, but to the main base camp – what had once been 'the pulpit.' To reach the pulpit meant they'd have to travel along the disused tunnel, where this nightmare had started and the thing that had taken Makennon had emerged.

Slowhand yawned. For what he'd expected to be, thanks to Fitch, a quiet night in the Faith's deep cells, things had turned out markedly different. Hooper's announcement that they were both temporarily seconded to the Filth had initially made him feel quite uncomfortable, and he had even felt slightly resentful that she had taken it upon herself to forge such an alliance on his behalf. Now, though, even though he'd slept little, spending what had been left of the night 'conferring' with Hooper and then fletching some special arrows for the rigours ahead, his discomfort had faded. As he moved towards his train he was actually beginning to find that the Filth's resemblance to an army on the move had instilled in him some of the feeling of his old, military days. It wasn't nostalgia exactly – he had seen and done too much for that, some still regretted – but there was a fondness for the sense of directed mass purpose that part of him still missed. Filth or not, it felt reassuring to be part of such a large force working together to a common aim, even if there were one or two tarnishes on the force's collective armour.

He could see tarnish number one ahead of him right now. The archer had hardly believed it when he'd finally been introduced to the man he'd be working with and, pulling the belt holding his special arrows taut across his chest, he nodded now to Jakub Freel. The enforcer nodded back noncommittally, the barest of acknowledgements and hardly the greeting of a comrade-in-arms. The atmosphere between the two of them had been neutral while Hooper had been around but distinctly cooler in her absence, each tolerating the other's presence only because they had little choice in the matter. Considering the loss they had both endured, and the circumstances of it, they were hardly going to become bosom buddies were they? He would have to keep an eye on him.

Tarnish number two was another matter. Standoffish in a different way and for reasons he was still struggling to understand, Gabriella DeZantez was perched on an upturned railway sleeper as he neared her, sharpening her twin blades on a stone and examining the results with a practiced, expert eye. A fresh surplice was bulked out with armour, gleaming beneath the cloth. She wore it utterly naturally, as comfortably as a second skin. Slowhand had come across a number of the Swords of Dawn in his travels – had even, on occasion, had cause to avoid them – but he could remember few, if any, who had looked so born for the role. What had caused her to relinquish that role until now, he didn't really know, but her reaction to him the previous night suggested that, one way or another, she had been badly hurt at some point in her past – the kind of hurt that could only have been caused by a man. Who that man had been, and where he was now, he couldn't begin to guess.

DeZantez glanced up at him as he approached, and Slowhand smiled rather than nodded. *What the hells,* he thought, it might be a fault of his but the woman had helped to save his life and he couldn't help still wanting to break the ice.

"I didn't get chance to thank you," he said. "For last night."

"You make it sound as if we lay together," DeZantez said, her attention having returned to her blades.

And he'd thought they'd worked together so well. "No, I didn't mean –"

"I know what you meant, Slowhand. It's just a little irksome when you couch everything in innuendo."

He found himself staring at the top of her head, and swallowed. "That wasn't what I –"

"As for the fact I saw you naked last night, don't make the mistake of thinking it has planted a latent seed of desire in me. It hasn't."

Slowhand tried a grin. "Most girls remember the sight, at least."

"I'm not most girls. And most men I've seen naked were wetting themselves or worse as they pleaded for their lives within the gibbet, which tends to temper any erotic aspect, believe me." She looked up. "Let's get this clear. We work together, that's all."

Slowhand's grin faded. "Look, is there a problem here? I mean, more than just me?"

"Your girlfriend is gone."

Ah, yes. That had been the other part of the plan. When it had been arranged for Hooper to leave to stop the Engines that morning, she was meant to have taken DeZantez along.

"I know. She gave me a goodbye kiss."

"She was meant to be in my custody. That was the deal I made with the Overseer."

Slowhand shrugged. "Yeah, she told me. Thing is, it's nothing personal. Hooper has a problem with authority. And she likes to work alone."

DeZantez made a particularly violent sweep along her blades with the sharpening stone, making Slowhand wince. "She isn't coming back."

"What? Of course she's coming back!"

"Then why did she sneak out of here before daybreak?"

"Because she could."

"Not funny."

"Not meant to be. But she left you these."

DeZantez looked up. The weapons she had returned to Kali after the library were being proffered to her once again.

"The Deathclaws?"

"The Deathclaws. She thought you might make better use of them than she could."

"But they must be priceless."

"Oh, they are. She asked me to ask you to consider them as bail. If she doesn't come back. To fix a church roof or something..."

DeZantez hesitated, then said in a resigned tone, "The City Watch reported her heading south-east, not due east towards the Plain of Storms. What's she up to?"

"Said something about having to make a house-call first. Don't ask me why because I'm always the last to know. It's what she does."

"Slowhand," DeZantez said after a second. "Do you trust her to get the job done?"

"With my life."

"That might come to be the case."

"I can handle myself."

"I don't doubt it. But I mean will she succeed, before the Pale Lord mobilises?"

"She said she'll rendezvous with us the day after tomorrow, at 'the pulpit.'"

"That doesn't give her much time."

"She'll make it. You might have noticed she has a rather unusual Horse."

DeZantez nodded then slid off the railway sleeper and sheathed her blades. She accepted the Deathclaws from Slowhand, attaching them to her belt.

"Then I guess it's time we got this show on the road," she said, and pointed.

Slowhand turned to see Jakub Freel striding along the tunnel past them, climbing onto the front carriage and waving back along the train's length. It was a signal to the gathered soldiers, and all along the tunnel they picked up their gear and boarded the carriages.

Slowhand stared at Jakub Freel. The enforcer was in command of this particular train and, as such, could have waved Slowhand aboard too. But he just stared as if he didn't care whether Slowhand boarded at all. The archer shrugged and grabbed a rail on the side of the last car, using it to swing up onto the train's roof where he had already decided he could serve the expedition best by riding shotbow. DeZantez mirrored his move, opting for the first car, as far away from him as she could get. It wasn't – he hoped – personal. Whatever the darkness that had come for Katherine Makennon was, for all they knew, it could still lurk somewhere in the tunnel ahead, and they would all need to be on the alert.

The train lurched beneath him and was off. There was a long journey ahead and Slowhand settled himself down into a cross-legged position, watching the curved, moss-covered ceiling of the tunnel roll by. It grew monotonous over the hours, the train seemingly limited by its funicular cable to trundle along at only a few leagues an hour.

Despite the danger of their situation, Slowhand found the rhythmic clacking of the train soporific and, tired from his almost sleepless night and lulled by the soft, warm breeze created by the train's passage, he began to nod off. Dimly aware that they were passing beneath the Anclas Territories right now and would, in an hour or so, be under the Pontaine plains, he found himself traversing them overland rather than underground.

He was flying above flowery, rolling fields, and in each field beneath him naked women danced from behind giant blooms to frolic and wave at him as he passed. Slowhand smiled, his clothes vanishing like thinning clouds, and saw he was over Miramas and Gargas, now. Their streets were devoid of naked women, but every bedroom window was flung wide, a happy, expectant trilling coming from within. Slowhand swooped down, but before he could pass through any of the colourful curtains that fluttered invitingly in the breeze, he became aware of something else – something beyond the towns – a great, dark mass on the distant horizon that swept to the east and to the west as far as the eye could see. It seemed that whatever worries were playing at the back of his mind wanted in – there was no escaping the Sardenne Forest and its appearance halted his reverie like a slap in the face. Literally.

Ow.

"Wake up." Gabriella DeZantez said. "We've got trouble."

"What kind of trouble?"

"The tunnel roof," the Enlightened One said. "Looks like the Pale Lord left a few of his friends behind."

Slowhand followed her gaze forward and upward and swallowed. *A few?* He thought.

Where the front of the train was nosing into darkness, the gently curving rock that they had been passing beneath seemed rougher somehow, and the reason could be made out as they drew close. Perhaps a hundred or more of the Pale Lord's soul-stripped were clinging to the roof of the tunnel like insects – blackened by tunnel grime, their whitened eyes their only distinguishable feature.

"Oh, crap," he said.

"My thoughts exactly." DeZantez responded.

Both she and Slowhand raced along the carriage roofs, shouting warnings to those within. There was little the occupants could do to escape the impending threat, however, and little room to use any of their weapons effectively. Their only real recourse was to steel themselves as best they could and raise shields at each car's entrance. Consequently, of course, any proactive defence of the train was left to those who rode on its roof, and Slowhand was actually quite pleased to see Jakub Freel climbing up from the driver's cab as the first of the soul-stripped dropped from the dark.

"Here we go," DeZantez said. Her jaw was set and her weapons drawn – the claws rather than her blades, Slowhand noted, if only because they were the only effective weapon against their current foes.

All he had was Suresight, but despite his trusted bow's failure – through no fault of her own – to halt the soul-stripped previously, he raised her anyway. The arrows would do little damage, he knew, but damage wasn't his intention. He let fly again and again, targeting the dropping soul-stripped half way between tunnel roof and train, aiming not for the vitals but for peripheries – shoulders, hips and thighs. Because the archer's intention wasn't to drop the soul-stripped as they landed, but to hit them before they did.

One soul-stripped, two, four and then ten were hit in mid air by his arrows, solid impacts knocking them sideways in their descent, away from the train. The soul-stripped spun helplessly, silently down to the tunnel floor on either side, hitting the sides of the tracks with a crunch of muscle and bone, twitching rapidly where they lay.

Slowhand couldn't get them all, of course, and inevitably many landed on the roof. Thankfully, most of those the archer missed were immediately intercepted by DeZantez and Freel in a blur of claws and chain. The Deathclaws were, as expected, singularly effective in despatching the cadaverous forms, slicing and amputating them at every joint, but Freel suffered the same handicap as he. But his whip lashed out to wrap around ankles and wrists, flipping the soul-stripped from the train.

But even all three of them couldn't handle everything, and those of the soul-stripped who escaped their triple defence began swinging themselves down into the cars below.

Orders were barked and what weapons could be used came into play, but the relentless and uncaring manner in which the Pale Lord's puppets threw themselves at their targets, scrabbling ferally, took its toll. Slowhand stared over the edge of the train at the warriors, young and old, being tossed to the tunnel floor, where he witnessed the true horror of the soul-stripped, the means by which the Pale Lord was building his pillar of souls. Each soldier who fell was instantly seized upon, drawn up into a lover's embrace as a cold mouth was pressed to theirs. They quickly surrendered to the Pale Lord's puppets, their eyes rolling back in their heads, their skin paling to a waxy sheen. For a few moments they lay still, before rising up to join their new brethren.

"They just keep coming," DeZantez said, suddenly next to him. The claws she wielded were ribboned with flesh. "How many more *are* there?"

"Let's find out," Slowhand said.

It had been his intention to save the special arrows he had adapted for use in the Sardenne but, of course, things rarely turned out as intended. He plucked one of his naphtha dipped creations from his belt and struck it against the flashpad he wore as a ring, igniting the arrow as it launched. The billowing projectile arced through the tunnel and illuminated the way ahead.

Freel was silhouetted in the heart of the fire, his squall-coated figure striding up the train, whip lashing left and right like something out of the hells. But beyond him were the hells themselves.

It hadn't been a one-off gauntlet they'd been passing through. Some few hundred yards ahead, there was another mass of them. Only this time the dark shapes didn't just cover the tunnel roof but the tunnel's sides, and thickly blocked the tracks themselves. The soul-stripped were everywhere and they went on for ever.

"Lord of All," Gabriella breathed, "the tunnel may as well end here. We'll never get through alive."

"We'll get through," Slowhand said.

Setting his jaw manfully, he smiled at Gabriella and raced for the train driver's cab, jumping in next to the man's sweating, but so far untouched, form.

"We need to use the train as a battering ram!" Slowhand shouted. "Can you crank it up to top speed?"

The driver nodded and thrust a lever forward. Slowhand was hardly rocked off his feet. They had gained maybe a third more speed. At a push. If this was the train's top speed, the only thing it was going to be capable of battering was a fish.

"What? That's *it*?"

The driver nodded again. He flinched as a number of soul-stripped crashed onto the front of the train and ripped at the metal cage that protected the cab. Though two of them tore their arms away in the attempt, the cage thankfully remained intact. "It runs on cables," he said through clenched teeth. "And the cables' speed is regulated by controls at either end of the line."

Slowhand shot an arrow into the eye of a soul-stripped who had worked out the cab had a side door, and booted it away. "Then what the hells does it need a driver for?"

"To flip the lever that moves the grip from the slow to fast cable!"

"The grip?"

"Under the train!" He stared at Slowhand as if the last thing he needed was an idiot. "The grip grips the cable and the cable pulls the train!"

Slowhand just stood there, desperately considering his options. Going back to DeZantez and telling her he'd set his jaw for nothing wasn't one of them.

Grip, cable, cable, grip, he thought – *come on, Slowhand, you're an archer, and cables are just like thick bow strings, right? Is there anything you can do with them?*

"What happens if the grip slips off?" He asked.

"The train stops."

"I mean, how do you put it *back on*?"

"There's an access panel under your feet."

Slowhand looked down, tore open the panel. The track below was hardly racing by but, this close up, it was a little unnerving. He fixed his attention on the cables instead – three of them, not two as he'd expected. "There's a middle cable here that isn't moving," he shouted to the driver. "What does that do?"

"It's the torque cable," the driver shouted back. "It regulates the tension in the other two."

"And if it severs?"

"What?"

"If it *severs*, what would happen then?"

"I don't know. I guess the other cables would snap and whiplash away."

"Like the one we're attached to now?"

"Yes but –" The driver paused. "Oh, no. No, no, no..."

"Bingo," Slowhand scrambled back up out of the cab. More soul-stripped had landed on the train's roof in his absence and he simply didn't have time for them. As Slowhand raced back towards the train's rear he aimed Suresight as he moved, loosing naphtha arrows with such force that their flaming shafts simply punched any attacking soul-stripped into the air, off the train, and out of his way.

He paused only once, grabbing one of the Deathclaws from a surprised DeZantez's hand, before reaching the end of the train and launching himself into the air.

Slowhand landed on the tracks behind, rolled, and swung the claw through the torque cable. It severed immediately and began to unravel, as did the one pulling the train. The archer grabbed onto its end, allowing the whiplashing cable to carry him into the air and back towards the train. It arced above the last carriage and he let go, crashing onto the roof, and immediately shouted a warning to DeZantez, Freel and all of those in the cars below.

"Hold on tight!"

Beneath him, the train, still gripped to the cable which was no longer restrained at one end, began to pick up speed, and Slowhand threw himself flat.

The front of the train ploughed into the wall of soul-stripped, bucking slightly on its tracks as it did. As always, there were no screams of cries of protest from those it hit, but a series of sickening fleshy crunches and a rain of dismembered body parts. The rattling and clattering of the train's wheels faded as the vehicle travelled not on bare metal but a thick layer of gore and blood. Slowhand cautiously raised his head and found himself staring into the blood-spattered face of Gabriella DeZantez. He offered her a hand up.

"You okay?"

"You know the personal motto of every Sword of Dawn. 'I always rise again.'"

Slowhand smirked. "I thought that was my motto."

DeZantez shook her head. "Quick thinking with the cable."

"I'm sure you would have thought of it yourself," Slowhand replied.

"Oh, I did. I just wanted to see how quick Slow was."

Slowhand nodded with a small smile, an acknowledgement that the prospect of their working together might not be as bad as it had seemed. He found himself staring up at Jakub Freel too, but the leather-clad man merely wiped a patch of gore from his cheek and slapped it to the train's roof with some disgust.

"It might not be over yet," he said, with no hint of gratitude. "We need to check for stragglers, any of them that might still be on or near the train. I'll check the front, DeZantez you get the sides, and Slowhand, you get the tracks to the rear."

Slowhand picked himself up, nodding as he wiped away gore. He made his way back down the cars and looked down. But other than the occasional piece of limb or bloody chunk of flesh being dragged along in their wake, there was nothing – the soul-stripped were gone.

Slowhand bowed slightly, placing his palms on his thighs and breathing a sigh of relief, when a hard shove in the small of his back sent him flying into the air.

He cried out in shock, twisting in mid air, and saw Freel standing on the lip of the last car. Slowhand fully expected to hit the tracks once more, but Freel's whip lashed towards him, coiling about him and slamming him against the rear of the train. Slowhand hung, dazed, and saw Freel glaring down at him, his teeth bared.

What the hells is this? Slowhand thought. *First the bastard shoves me off the back of the train, and then he catches me, and now he leaves me dangling here?*

This was about Jenna, it had to be. Freel was playing mind games, for sure.

The Faith enforcer stared down at him for what seemed an age, his face red, his eyes wide and wild, and then suddenly jerked the chain upward, bringing Slowhand with it. The archer clutched the lip of the car's roof and pulled himself up, and Freel snapped the chain off him, turned and walked away.

Slowhand stood, breathing hard and rubbing his wrists, staring after the man. His every instinct was to follow, to grab him and to sort the problems between them out right now, but somehow he didn't have it in him.

Instead, as the train sped inexorably towards the Sardenne he returned wearily to the cross-legged position he had adopted at the start of their journey, and once more his mind began to wander.

This time, however, his imaginings were not of naked women, of the rolling plains of Pontaine, or even of the Sardenne. Instead, they were of his sister's face, staring at him from the burning gondola of the *Makennon*. One word kept repeating itself, over and over in his mind. An order, delivered in his own, sure voice.

"Fire!"

CHAPTER NINE

IT WAS SAID that a fistful of full golds could buy you anything in Fayence, but the bigger the fist the better the anything it bought. Not that any of the personal services of this town were in any way unsatisfactory. The local Lord, who maintained a fiscal and hands-on interest in them all, made sure of that. It was merely a matter of how long it would take to recover from the relaxations on offer, whether they were mental, physical, or both. Stimulation-wise, Fayence boasted it catered for all six senses, sometimes all at once, and it wasn't for nothing that the many hotels in the town were known as convalesalons.

Kali moved through a noisy crowd of the coming night's – or possibly week's – guests-to-be, many of whom, by the look of them, should have checked in some hours before. She was making her way along Fayence's main thoroughfare – known to one and all as Sin Street – and the air was a fug of exotic perfumes, stimulating massage balms and dreamweed clouds, the odours brushing off on Kali in the jostling melee. Though she knew exactly where she was heading, she found it impossible to get there in a straight line, the sea of revellers carrying her first towards Maloof's Erotivarium, thence the Palace of Pleasure and Pain and its patented 'Sinulator' by way of the Slither Baths and the Womb Chambers, the barkers in front of which deafeningly promised a sensory experience such that "you'll wish you'd never been born!" Kali knew that the so called 'Womb Chambers' were, in fact, the extracted bladders of globe toads from the Turnitian marshes but if the owners weren't going to tell the punters that little trade secret who was she to spoil their fun? You sure as hells had to admire the inventiveness of this place.

Not that Kali was *that* familiar with Fayence's attractions, she would be at pains to point out to anyone who asked – no, no, no, not at all. Slowhand, of course, had been badgering her to come here since they'd first become an item, but as that prospect was the equivalent of letting a very greedy little boy loose in a very large sweet factory, she had consistently denied him her company – and knowing she knew, he hadn't dared come alone. She smiled, thinking how galled he'd be if he knew she were here now. Even if she currently had only a passing curiosity in the establishments of Sin Street and was actually heading towards one of the town's more unusual attractions, a little more off the beaten track.

That was the thing about Fayence. It hadn't always been like this. For hundreds of years, in fact, the town had been the favoured home of those who studied the old Wheel of Power, and had once even been considered as a potential site for the Three Towers, the headquarters of the League of Prestidigitation and Prestige. That it had lost out to Andon in this respect had been an early blow for Fayence but one which had ultimately served it well. When their more conformist brethren had decamped to the north-west, the mages who subsequently came here – followed, in turn, by such complementary professionals as apothecaries, herbalists and suppliers of various arcane needs –shared a certain streak of independence, an *individual* approach to their studies that would have made it difficult for them to gain acceptance amongst their peers elsewhere.

They had their limits, however, and while many of their experiments might have stretched these to breaking point there were areas of their craft that, by general agreement, were considered too dangerous for exploration and, therefore, forbidden. Creation magic was one. Necromancy another. Thus it was that when Bastian Redigor was discovered to be waving his wand around in such murky waters – the specifics of which had not survived the passage of time – the man was banished forthwith from Fayence, never to return. It was at this point that the town's fortunes had begun to wane, not least because it was rumoured that with a wave of his hand upon his departure Redigor had left behind a legacy in the form of an incurable and agonising *taint* that quite literally consumed mages' brains, reducing the skull to an empty shell within a day.

Whether the rumour were true or not, one by one the mages died, and with them gone the livelihood of the apothecaries, herbalists and suppliers went too, and while a few remained to this day – albeit providing services for a clientele with more *intimate* requirements – Fayence was reduced to a little more than a ghost town.

So it remained for a number of years until the present Lord of Fayence, Aristide, inherited his position, whereupon he reinvented the town to reflect his own predilections, a change of emphasis he knew would be lucrative bearing in mind the amount of coin he himself had spent elsewhere over the years.

There was one area of the town Aristide did not change, however. Whether for fear of a return of the taint, or whether because the aura of the outcast who had become known as the Pale Lord still, after all this time, lingered there, it was left to rot, untouched, abandoned.

It was where the mages had died. They called it the Ghost Quarter.

Kali approached this forgotten part of town between the ignominious landmarks of a derelict comfort parlour called Whoopee Kushen's, outside of which an out-of-date courtesan swatted flies, and a grimy street stand trading in spit-roasted mool and bottles of thwack that gloried in the name Abra-Kebab-Bar. It was doubtful if either enterprise was licenced by Lord Fayence, but they had attached themselves to the outer periphery of his salacious empire to engage in its spirit nonetheless. As Kali neared the latter, its proprietor – a huge, fat, greasy-bearded man three times the size of his stand who presumably was Abra – almost fell off his stool at the prospect of an actual customer. But his ear-to-ear grin faded as Kali nodded, smiled and passed on by.

"Girly, lady, madam, missus-woman," he protested as she passed, "I assure you, there is nothing for you beyond my small but perfectly formed establishment." He stroked his beard. "A little like yourself, if I may say..."

Kali smiled. "You can forget the flattery, Abra. I'm not looking for food or drink."

Abra coughed, and actually looked embarrassed. "Ah, I see."

The man's redness made Kali flush too. "No, no, not that either – not *anything*." She resorted to her failsafe tactic when she found herself in an impasse situation. "Actually, I'm trying to save the world."

"The world?"

"Umm. Think so, anyway. Not quite so sure about what's going on this time."

"The world," Abra said again and then, aghast, "My advice to you is forget the world, save *yourself*."

"Why do you say that?"

"Because if you are heading within, you must be heading for the Pale Lord's house yes? There can be no other reason to go there. I say do not do so, because those who do, they do not come back."

"*Other* people have gone there?"

Abra made a dismissive sound. "Oh, not often. The occasional mage or relic hunter, eager for a memento of our infamous son. Young, drunken couples with their underknicks already about their ankles, clearly acting upon a dare." He sighed and shook his head. "I do not see any of them again, other than as a stain upon a wall, a smear across a window, a splatter beneath my feet." Abra emphasised his point by suddenly squeezing a large dollop of kebab sauce onto the ground with a loud and flatulent plop, making Kali jump.

"I see," Kali said. Redigor had obviously trapped his old home the same way he'd trapped his books, which made her destination all the more interesting. "Thanks for the warning, Abra. I'll watch my step."

Abra sucked in an amazed breath. "You *still* go?"

Kali placed her hands on her hips in what she hoped was a heroic stance. "It's what I do."

"Then you are the loopo," Abra exclaimed, rotating a finger at his temple.

"That's what people keep telling me."

Kali moved on into the Ghost Quarter, shaking her head as Abra produced another sigh and flatulent plop. But she had soon left the Abra-Kebab-Bar behind her, Sin Street far behind her. The difference between the two locations could not have been more marked. Kali was now the only living thing in a warren of utterly silent streets, shattered glass cracking underfoot, the odd piece of rubble skittering away from her. There were no birds in the azure night sky, not even any vermin peering from the empty houses on either side – rich nesting grounds though they'd be. Lifeless and dark, the houses themselves were remarkably well-preserved, some even retaining the black 'T' daubed there long ago to warn others that their owners had succumbed to the taint. Kali was pretty certain that the 'T's would have served no useful purpose. The Pale Lord was powerful and, if his taint had your name on it, sooner or later it would have got you, no matter what.

The Pale Lord's home was the eeriest in the eerie warren of properties – a foreboding, rambling structure at the end of the street which, despite being long-abandoned, seemed to glow faintly of candlelight from within. Kali approached slowly, looking around to make sure she was alone, and climbed the step to the entrance. The door was half-obscured by thick cobwebs and half-hanging off its hinges and, when pushed, fell to the floor in a cloud of dust. Shadows danced slowly within. Kali eased into the hallway, and could have sworn she heard the sound of footsteps from the upper floor. She swallowed.

Disappointingly, though, as Kali cautiously began to explore, there were no ghosts – and very little of anything else – to be found. Apart from a couple of fairly obvious traps which she carefully defused, the house seemed exactly what it appeared to be: empty and derelict. For an hour, she worked her way minutely through all its rooms, finding nothing and ending up in the building's main parlour where, from the looks of what remained, Redigor had once kept his library and laboratory. But as elsewhere, there was little to see. What the passage of time had not rotted had been removed, most noticeably in the bookshelves lining the room. Even the laboratory was a disappointment. A dust-covered and vaguely horseshoe-shaped workbench occupied the heart of the room. Kali could imagine Redigor standing there conducting his 'unique' experiments, but the only evidence which now remained of them was the odd upturned belljar or shattered pipette. Kali pursed her lips. Not quite what she'd expected of an infamous necromancer's laboratory, it had to be said.

Still, though the dwelling seemed to offer her nothing, Kali couldn't shake the feeling that she was missing something. She had the feeling there was something *wrong* with the room that she couldn't quite put her finger on, something to do with space. For some reason, it felt bigger than it was, more open. Kali backed up to the door and studied it anew – nothing. Maybe she'd been wrong to come here after all, she thought, frustration flooding her.

It was in that moment, her mind returning to the bigger picture, filling with images of the Sardenne and what lay within it, that she stopped looking – and that was when she *saw*.

It wasn't much, like something in the corner of her eye *right in front of her*, but it was there. Something odd about the way the workbench curved, as if its relations with the rest of the room were oddly misaligned. She noticed then how it wasn't just the bench that appeared odd but the other trappings, too – bookcases, furniture, even the tiling on the floor. Where their lines should have been straight, they curved ever so slightly, and where surfaces should have been flat, they were very gently concave. The only comparison Kali could draw was that it was like looking through a very weak fish-eye lens, but what she saw was there – something bending the reality of the heart of the room.

Kali moved into the 'u' of the bench and waved her hand slowly back and forth where light seemed to bend the most. She felt a slight thickening of the air and, for a moment, her fingers brushed against something almost, but not quite, insubstantial. Dammit, she knew what this was now. It was a glamour field like the one she'd encountered at the Crucible, only in this case highly localised, highly concentrated. So concentrated it was able to confound every sense. To manipulate reality with such finesse would have taken great skill indeed, and such a degree of skill would surely only have been used if, as she suspected, Redigor had something very significant to hide.

Kali's elation was fleeting. The problem that remained was finding out what. Even though she *knew* there was something there, her perception remained too wrong-footed to tease it out into the open. Frustrated, she flopped down against a wall, clucking her tongue as she stared at the field.

Come on, Hooper! There has to be a way to work this, a way to skew my senses so that I'm not looking at what the field wants me to look at.

For a while no solution presented itself and then, slowly, she smiled. What was that old adage about mixing business with pleasure?

A moment later, Kali was out in the street, racing back through the Ghost Quarter to Abra's stand.

"Your thwack," she said. "I want it."

Shock at her sudden appearance mingled with surprise at actually making a sale. "H-how many bottles?"

"All of them."

"*All* of them?"

"And flummox. You got any flummox?"

"I – I think I may have a few bottles, yes..."

"Those, too. What about twattle?"

"*Twattle?*" Abra gasped. He glanced about himself guiltily. "I have one bottle. But it is deadly. And illegal. It is also very, very expensive."

Kali pulled a coinpurse from her pocket and emptied its golden contents into Abra's hands. "I'll take it. I'll take everything. The lot. But I'll need you to wheel it to Redigor's house."

The suggestion brought even more sweat to Abra's face than was already running down it but, as he watched Kali bite the cork from the bottle of twattle and down it in one, he realised she was not to be messed with. He had, after all, once seen a bottle of twattle make someone's ears drop off. Quickly, he began to unlock his stand's complex arrangement of brakes and supports. Kali, meanwhile, grabbed two armfuls of bottles and was gone.

Back at the house, she ploughed into the various ales with industrial zeal, popping out to Abra when necessary for more, and the wall where she slumped was soon stacked with a small mountain of empties. The booze hadn't yet achieved its desired result, however, her preternatural capacity for the stuff preventing her from getting drunk enough to loosen her hold on reality. Not that it wasn't having *some* effect.

As she once more sought out Abra for supplies she felt an overwhelming desire to tell him what a very nice fat man he was – no, no, *really*, Abra – and, on returning to the laboratory, she accidentally booted half the bottle mountain across the room. Kali hopped up and down flapping her arms, trying to shush them as they rolled and rattled everywhere, but the little farkers wouldn't listen, so she called them names instead.

She dropped to her knees, snorting, eyes moving in circles over her fresh supply. *Which to pick? Which to pick? Which to pick?*

Having decided that the fourth of the identical bottles was by far the prettiest, she stood precariously and raised it in a toast to the glamour field. There was still no change in its appearance but the small manoeuvre threw her off kilter and her feet momentarily forgot which of them was which. Kali staggered into one of the bookcases, bowed and apologised profusely, then soothed its hurt feelings by drawing shapes in the dust of one of its shelves. It was as she was doing this that she realised she could murder a kebab.

Kali staggered to a window and shouted to Abra at the top of her voice. As she turned back, it suddenly occurred to her that she had stumbled upon actually quite a cool concept, having food delivered to your door. Maybe she ought to jack in all the world saving stuff, go into partnership with Abra and open a home delivery shop. Hells, with Horse she could have the food anywhere in a five league radius in no time, still warm and at no extra charge. Now, what would she call it? Kebakali? Kalibabi? Kebabkalbulbu –

Pitsh!

There was something wrong with her lips.

The realisation suddenly struck Kali that for the last few seconds she'd been staring at a spiral staircase in the centre of the room. Mouth gaping, bottle dropping to the ground, she half walked, half stretched towards it, as if any sudden move might make it vanish once more. It didn't. It was there, all right, as real as everything else in the room, solid beneath her touch. Kali burped and pulled herself in, turning sinuously around its metal core like a dancer, head angled to peer up the spiralling steps into shadow.

"Boo!" She said suddenly, and giggled, blowing a hole in a thin blanket of cobweb, which dropped down onto her face like a flap of skin.

Kali puffed it away, peered through the hole and frowned. Even sobered up slightly. From what she could see through further cobwebs, the staircase went up high. Higher than the house itself. Maybe it was something to do with her pickled brain, or maybe it was because she had become used to such things, but Kali didn't find anything odd about that at all. Nor did she find its shadowed heights unnerving or daunting. Far from it, because she knew she was staring at a threshold that hadn't been crossed since Redigor had abandoned the house. This staircase was what he had been hiding, his little secret, and at its top she might very well find out just what the Pale Lord was *really* all about.

Did she go up or didn't she? Kali placed a finger on her lips. Difficult one.

Under normal circumstances, she'd have taken the spiral steps slowly, but, fuelled by booze, she raced up them as fast as she could - which was just as well, as they seemed to go on for ever. It was only after she had passed through the house's attic and found herself still going up that she began to slow, but this was more to do with the ever thickening cobwebs – almost like netting now – than any dwindling enthusiasm.

Becoming swathed in so much of the stuff that she began to resemble something bored of its sarcophagus, even Kali's boundless energy was taxed as she went round and round, but she found strength in the realisation that she had to be ascending some kind of magically constructed tower hidden from the outside world by the same kind of glamour that concealed its base. She found it slightly disconcerting that, in a sense, this meant she was climbing up into thin air, but the tower felt solid enough about her. Solid and *very old*. Old enough, in fact, to explain the preternatural thickness of the cobwebs: this, for some reason, was the growth of thousands and thousands of years.

The tower's top was becoming visible, now, and the shadows above lightened. Not much, the kind of illumination one might expect if daylight were projecting through a number of narrow windows, but enough to suggest the presence of a chamber above.

Kali didn't know what to expect up there. But it wasn't this.

Bastian Redigor waited for her at the top of the stairs.

"Shit!" Kali shouted, and almost fell back the way she had come. Saved only by a patch of the thick, sticky cobweb, she clung to the tower for a moment, fully expecting the clang of footsteps from above, but Redigor did not appear. Very slowly, she peered back around the last turn of the stairs. "Girl," she chastised herself.

Kali climbed into a chamber dominated by a portrait of the Pale Lord. It, too, was almost entirely obscured by cobweb, as indeed was the rest of the room, but the part she could see – *had seen* – showed the piercing black eyes, flowing raven hair and handsome, aquiline features she was familiar with from illustrations in books. Even represented in oils, Redigor had presence, and he wore expensive robes of a fashion not seen on the peninsula for a very, very long time.

Kali drew her gaze away from the portrait, turning her attention to the chamber, and tore away blankets of cobweb. If she had been looking for information, she guessed she could pretty much say she had found it.

A desk in front of her overflowed with books, journals, scrolls, notes and charts, most of which pertained to necromancy in one way or another. The assorted papers were not limited to the desk, either. The floor was littered with more of the same, the walls covered in diagrams and maps of every size and description, including, interestingly, one of the sprawling expanse of the Sardenne. Across this Redigor had marked in sweeping scrawl the location of Bellagon's Rip.

Kali sighed. What she needed was new information. It was here, she was sure of it, but she didn't have a clue where to start digging. She decided after a second to thrust her hands into a stack of papers to see what came out.

For the next few hours Kali ploughed through notes on anatomy, alchemy, conjuration, revivification, holding and other kinds of magical constraint. She flicked through sketches of Twilight and of Kerberos, and through diagrams of what appeared to be the pillar of souls she'd seen at Scholten. There were starcharts, too – in the kind of detail she'd heard only the Final Faith's astronomer had compiled – but she had no idea why. She had no idea, either, of the meaning of endless reams of calculus, columns of figures in their thousands, that Redigor seemed to have constantly annotated in his strange, sprawling script. One document did, for a moment, seem to bear out the Faith's theory that Redigor planned an invasion – a map of the peninsula overlaid with countless thin, sweeping lines – but unless the Pale Lord planned to despatch his soul-stripped on a thousand or more fronts, it made little tactical sense.

That was the problem. All this effort and the only conclusion she had drawn was that nothing here made sense.

Gahh! She needed a break.

Dumping a batch of papers, Kali strode to one of the windows that lit the tower, stretching, and froze.

Instead of staring out high over Fayence, she was gazing on a sprawling panorama of glistening towers whose architecture she had never seen but which, after her time in Domdruggle's Expanse, was cloyingly familiar – architecture out of the distant past. Except that it *couldn't* be out of the distant past. It was new and thriving, figures moving along the streets below, sleek objects darting through the sky between towers, and between them a crystal clear river meandering into the distance.

It was a vast, Old Race city. An elven city. The warm breeze from it was fresh.

It was *real*.

The conclusion was inescapable. Somehow she and the tower in which she stood were in the past. It was incredible, not only the wonders she could see but the sorceries that must have brought it about. Maybe that was what Redigor had done with the tower, she thought. Maybe it wasn't concealed from Fayence with a glamour field because it didn't need to be. Maybe it projected itself further into the past the higher it rose.

My gods, I'm there, she realised. The time of the Old Races. The temptation to climb out of the window, regardless of the insane height, was almost irresistible. But why would Bastian Redigor have done this? Why would he have expended the vast amounts of energy needed to stare out over a vista long gone? Maybe he just had a thing for elven architecture, she thought. Or maybe he couldn't stand looking out over the depravity in which Fayence excelled. Or maybe –

Maybe it simply made him feel at home.

Kali's heart thudded, and she spun back to face the inside of the chamber. *That* was what had been missing from all this, why she hadn't been able to make any sense out of what she'd studied, because all along she'd been trying to work out the plans of your average human, world-dominating necromancer. But there was much more to him than that, wasn't there?

Kali raced to the portrait, tearing away cobweb to reveal more of its detail. Of course. In pictures of himself elsewhere, Redigor had appeared as he wanted to appear, but here, in a portrait that would be seen by no eyes other than his own, he seemed almost to have taken pride in sweeping back his hair.

It was an ear thing.

Bastian Redigor was an elf.

Kali swallowed. It wasn't just the revelation that somehow this bastard had survived down the long years but what she saw in the rest of the exposed portrait.

The woman next to him bore a striking resemblance to Katherine Makennon. It wasn't her, of course, because even had she been alive when the picture was painted, there was no way Makennon would allow herself to be pictured garbed as this woman was – which was to say, in very little at all. That Redigor, smiling slightly, also held a fine chain attached to a collar about her neck, put paid to the possibility fully.

Kali's mind reeled. The woman was clearly *mu'sah'rin* – in human terms, somewhere between forced consort and slave – and that could mean only one thing. Redigor wasn't only an elf, he was Ur'Raney. The most misogynistic, cold-hearted, sadistic so-called 'family' of the elves there had ever been. The Ur'Raney were the same family who had relentlessly pursued and slaughtered the dwarves at Martak, who had brought both Old Races to the brink of war, and who, because of their gleeful, unremitting cruelty, were reviled even by their own kind.

Most contemporaneous texts had been of the opinion that Twilight would be better off without them.

Kali calmed herself. So, Redigor was an elf. The fact was, she couldn't say she felt *that* surprised, because something had occurred to her in Scholten that seemed to have been missed by everyone else. The Engines of the Apocalypse being what they were, lost to and forgotten by countless generations, should have been exactly that – lost and forgotten. Unless the Pale Lord had stumbled upon their control centre while out for a walk one day – an unlikely turn of events, to say the least – they had to have been activated by someone *old enough* to know it was there. Well, that was Redigor, all right. He had revealed his true heritage at last. But the question remained, what the hells was he up to?

Here They Lie Still.

Kali replayed the phrase Slowhand had quoted in the library through her mind, analysing it in a different light now she knew Redigor's true identity. As she did, she studied the assorted papers again, trying to piece together the jigsaw that was the Pale Lord's experimentation. Why should an ancient elf wish to unleash an army of soul-stripped onto the peninsula? What the hells was he going to get out of that? Unless, as she had suspected, that wasn't what he was planning at all. Her gaze rose back to the portrait of Redigor and the woman and once more she asked herself – what the hells did the Pale Lord want with Makennon or the other 'dignitaries' his soul-stripped had snatched from all over the peninsula? What was special about those thirteen people?

Another question. With so much power at his disposal, why had Bastian Redigor allowed himself to be banished? From what she had seen here, he could have wiped the floor with any mage on Twilight, and certainly the berobed fops and jesters who made up Lord Fayence's court wouldn't have stood a chance in the hells against him, and he could have taken the town any time he wanted. So why? Why move from what was clearly his home, as well as a well-equipped base, to the unforgiving wilds of the Sardenne? And just why did he already have a map showing the Sardenne and Bellagon's Rip?

Kali studied the map again. If she expected to see any previously unseen feature she was soon disappointed, but her eyes were drawn once more to Redigor's flowing script. Bellagon's Rip. It was written there as plain as day and yet there was something not quite right about it. She suddenly realised that her mind had been filling in the gaps and she was reading what she expected to read, because that was the name by which that area of the forest had always been known. But what if it was misnamed? What if some more modern cartographer had chanced upon some previously scrawled notation of Redigor's on some other map, and had misinterpreted it as she was doing now? Maybe this was a matter of perception rather than interpretation, because although Redigor had used human script on everything she had so far read there was still an elvish flourish to his hand that potentially gave a whole new meaning to what was written. Bearing that in mind, Kali reread the name, seeing each letter on its own rather than as a component part of a word, and gradually they began to flow together. That was *it*. It wasn't a name at all but an elven phrase. Not Bellagon's Rip but Bel'A'Gon'Shri. She concentrated hard, eyes closed, trying to pull together all the elvish she knew to make sense of the phrase, and her eyes snapped open in alarm.

Bel'A'Gon'Shri.

Here They Lie, Still.

Gabriella DeZantez hadn't been far wrong in her theory about its meaning. But the phrase wasn't referring to the Engines and it wasn't suggesting that anything was lying idle. It was suggesting that 'they' were lying where they'd lain for a long time and were *waiting*. And Kali suspected she knew who.

The charts, the maps, the diagrams, the calculations, they suddenly all made sense. Rather in the manner of an Eye of the Lord, she imagined herself descending from the sky into the map, the image no longer two-dimensional but a living canopy of trees through which she swept down, down, down. And waiting for her beneath was a structure of gothic horror overgrown with the vegetation of thousands of years, a structure that she knew was sitting deep in the Sardenne.

An elven necropolis.

An Ur'Raney necropolis.

Oh gods.

The Faith, as she'd suspected, and as farking usual, had got it all wrong. There was going to be an invasion, all right, but not in the way they thought. She had to shut down the Engines of the Apocalypse and then get to the Faith, let them know what was *really* going on.

She ran for the stairwell, trying to ignore the staring eyes of Bastian Redigor, and heard a click beneath her feet. She looked down.

Trap, she thought. *Dammit.*

In her eagerness to leave she'd triggered something she'd missed, and as a result could already sense that something was coming. Something from outside.

Kali raced to a window, seeing the same wonderland as earlier. Now, thin, grey shapes were hurtling towards the tower through the sky. Whatever they were, they had the same aura about them as the death coach that had taken Makennon, as the tapers in the library, and had again to be born of the black threads. As Kali looked on in horror, the shapes resolved themselves into the figures of hags, skeletal things clad in translucent shrouds. Their talons were grotesquely overgrown, blurred streaks of things that seemed to stretch from this world into another.

Kali swallowed, knowing now what had caused Abra to see stains upon the walls, smears across windows and splatters beneath his feet, and she stumbled back from the window as the hags shrieked into the tower. They seemed, though, to have no interest in her, tearing around the circular chamber like a dark whirlpool. They moved faster and faster, Kali ducking under Redigor's desk, trying to work out what the hells was going on as a loud tearing sound rose over the creatures' shrieking. Kali looked out and saw flashes of sky. The hags' talons were slicing through the tower, not as the Deathclaws might slice through stone but seemingly through its very *existence*. Redigor had conjured the tower for his secret researches but must have booby-trapped it so that, if discovered, it would be obliterated.

The whole place was coming apart around her. Being erased.

Kali lurched from under desk, the flight of the hags – nothing more than blurs, now – whipping at her bodysuit and hair. She stared in horror as she saw great streaks of sky visible where, moments before, there had been a roof. Her heart began to pound as, around and beneath her, the walls and floor began to disappear slice by slice.

Kali dashed for the stairwell, hoping she would be able to outrun Redigor's trap, but then staggered back as the hags' talons eradicated the entrance to the stairs.

Oh, fark, that was not good. Not good at all.

Kali looked around the room in desperation, searching for an alternative means of escape, but the only one that presented itself was to jump. Despite the fact that was ancient sky out there – thousands of years before her time – it was better than the alternative of staying where she was and being sliced from reality. Hells, if by some miracle she survived the jump, she could leave the Faith a note and experience the wonders of the Old Races first hand.

She wasn't completely suicidal, though, and needed something to slow her fall. The rope in her backpack would be nowhere near long enough. There was only one other thing that she could see might work, even if it was one hells of a gamble. Moving almost in a blur herself, Kali spun around the remains of the chamber, gathering its thick and sticky coating of cobwebs about her body in layer after layer, then, when she felt she had gathered enough, turned to face the remains of one of the windows, took one deep breath and ran and leapt. The coating of cobweb wrapped about her body pulled masses of the stuff after her, almost stripping the tower clean.

Kali plummeted. And marvelled. As she fell, she travelled not only downward, but forward through the ages. In a flash, the elven city crumbled and disappeared, and clouds scudded across wasteland. The course of the river changed, twisting like a striking snake. Another city arose, then fell, and one after that, though none were yet Fayence. Faster and faster the images came until Kali could no longer keep up, each year, maybe even each century, a flash in the mind, gone before she could register anything she saw. The feeling was incredible, marred only by her sadness at falling through all she had ever wanted to know. Then, building by small building, Fayence appeared below.

Kali was keenly aware that the next thing that might flash through her mind could be the pavement. Though still distant, the ground was coming up fast and the cobweb wasn't yet slowing her fall. Just as she started to worry that her plan wasn't going to work, the thick layers wrapped about her jerked subtly and began to tear themselves away in ever increasing strips. That was it, cobweb's end, and all she could hope for now was that her descent would be slowed enough to negotiate some kind of safe landing.

What she hadn't counted on was that, as the strips tore away, they twined about and adhered to each other until they had formed a kind of elasticated rope. The only thought that went through her mind as she reached the end of her drop and continued on was that jumping from great heights attached to something that, if it didn't smash you into the ground, was going to snap you back into the air like a pea from a catapult, wasn't a pastime she could ever see anyone choosing to do for fun.

Unless she wanted to be on nodding terms with Kerberos, she needed an anchor.

And there was one, still distant but coming up fast.

"Abra!" She shouted.

"Yes?" A puzzled voice responded from below.

The fat man was waiting patiently at Redigor's front door, clutching an immense and, by now, stone-cold kebab. The vendor slowly rose before her, and, catching a glimpse of a pair of Hells Bellies' socks while thanking the gods that the cobweb seemed to have stretched its furthest, Kali grabbed onto his belt. Momentarily they were face to face – albeit with her upside down – and Kali stared Abra in the eyes and smiled. "Never mind," she said.

The pair of them shot into the air where, to his credit, Abra remained stoically silent, as if this kind of thing happened every day. He managed a weak smile.

The return flight reached its apex and they dropped again. Then rose. Then dropped. At last the cobweb seemed to recognise that enough was enough, and they ended up dangling a foot above the ground.

As the remains of the cobweb began to tear themselves slowly apart, dropping them towards the pavement, Abra coughed.

"Did you," he asked slowly, and with a crack in his voice, "discover what you needed to know?"

Kali stared back up at where the tower had been.

"Oh, yeah," she said after a second. "The Ur'Raney. He's planning to bring them back."

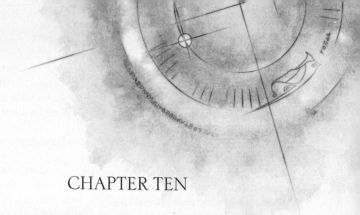

CHAPTER TEN

HEAD DOWN, KALI rode hard and fast, pushing Horse to his absolute limit. The bamfcat was, as usual, loyal and uncomplaining, though he did seem somewhat confused at being unable to do what he normally would and shorten the journey. But he could not jump; for the last few leagues they had been riding across the Plain of Storms.

It was one of the peculiar features of the area. Surrounded by the temperate farmlands of mid Pontaine, the almost perfectly circular valley was a meteorological anomaly, prone to a stultifying heaviness of air and battered by constant electrical storms. Those who lived on the periphery of the area said that sometimes the catastrophic conditions on the plain affected other weather it had no business affecting, *pulling* at the northern lights and bending them toward the ground, or even snatching a maelstrom from the Storm Wall, far away on the coast, for a few hours. If this were true – and Kali had seen enough of the raw potential of Old Races creations to believe it could be – it was likely that the energies of the control centre for the machines, what she had nicknamed 'the hub,' were responsible.

In other words, she guessed she was in the right place.

Nearing the centre of the plain, Kali slowed Horse to a stop and stared into the rain-lashed, thundering vista before her. She dismounted, took her squallcoat from her saddlebag and slipped it on, fastening it securely. From there on in, she led Horse by the reins.

It was hard going, fighting the unnaturally heavy atmosphere and taking deep, grasping breaths as she went. Here and there, tornadoes whirled across the barren ground, threatening to pluck her up if she strayed too close. Not that it was much safer out of their path – where the whirlwinds didn't manifest themselves, Kali found herself having to dodge sudden bolts of lightning that struck the ground about her, leaving small, smoking craters where they hit. One or two almost got her, but she soon learned to anticipate their arrival, the dense air further thickening a few seconds before each strike, as if someone were pressing down hard on her head. No pitsing wonder the area was so desolate, she thought. Other than a few scattered hardy plants, tanglevine and redweed among them, it was like walking through a bad dream. No one had ever tried to fully explore, let alone colonise the region, but why in the hells would they?

Once again, she thought, to find the hub you'd have to know it was *there*.

And suddenly, unexpectedly, it was there. A dark cave mouth loomed before her out of a dust storm. Not just a cave mouth, though: the eroded rock still retained the faint remains of carvings chiselled into it millennia earlier, shapes Kali recognised as dwarven. The most obvious clue to its provenance, though, was that the cave mouth itself was the shape of one of the Engines.

Kali tethered Horse, moved to the mouth and paused. If this was indeed the entrance to the hub then surely it was once a prime target for the dwarves' elven enemies, and as such she'd have expected it to be protected by the usual array of dwarven defences and traps. There was no evidence of anything, however, and Kali wondered if perhaps the traps, like the mouth itself, had been obliterated by the ravages of the plain. She bit her lip, deciding all she could do was proceed with caution.

Kali entered the cave mouth, briefly disappointed. To be frank she had been expecting to find more than just a cave. But that was all she'd got. A plain tunnel sloped gently downwards, ending in a chamber devoid of features but for a large hole in the ground. Kali eased her way to its edge and peered down. While deep, it appeared, for all intents and purposes, to be simply that. A hole in the ground. Then Kali noticed that the floor of the cave leading towards it was scarred and grooved. Once upon a time heavy objects, and a good number of them, had been dragged towards that hole. She pictured teams of dwarves pulling their burdens on ropes and then –

And then what? She wondered.

Because unless she had been completely wrong about this being the hub and she had, in fact, stumbled across some dwarven landfill site, surely they hadn't simply been dumped down there? She looked around. There was no sign of any haulage mechanisms with which they might have been lowered. As far as she could tell there was also no sign of any mechanism which might raise an elevator from far below. Frowning, Kali conducted a thorough search of the surrounding rock, but nothing. It did indeed appear as if she had come all this way to be stymied by a hole.

Kali sat herself against the wall and made a flubbing sound. If she were going to make the rendezvous with DeZantez and the others, she did not have the advantage she normally might in such circumstances –

to take as much time as she wished to ponder the problem. Frustrated, she plucked stones from the cave floor around her and began to lob them towards the hole. If she listened carefully, she might at least be able to determine how deep the farking thing was. It was then that she noticed two things – one, a thrumming from below that was barely audible over the lightning strikes outside and, two, the fact that the stones she had lobbed at the hole hadn't fallen in.

What the hells? Kali picked herself up and moved to its edge, leaning forward to grab one of the hovering stones from mid air. It seemed to contain metallic ore. As she leaned forward, she felt a resistance, placing her hand in a soft pillow, and stood back, her heart thumping. Did that mean what she thought it meant? That if she –?

Kali stripped off her backpack and threw it out over the seemingly bottomless drop, raising her eyebrows as it, too, bounced about as if tossed by currents of air. But this was not air she was dealing with – she felt nothing on her flesh, on her face, in her hair – it seemed instead to be something that *warped* the air.

Perhaps, even, the same force that kept the Engines of the Apocalypse aloft?

Okay, what's the worst that can happen? Kali thought. *If I step over the breach I end up hovering there and have to claw my way back.*

But what if the only reason that the rocks and backpack were hovering was because they were lighter than she was? What if this resistance, whatever it was, allowed the gradual descent of something with more mass – the objects that had scored the floor of the cave, perhaps? What if the strange force warping the air acted as some kind of invisible elevator?

Kali stepped forward, her foot wobbling slightly on the air, and then drew herself over the hole. She stuck her arms out straight like a wire walker and giggled as she floated. Then, very slowly she began to descend. Instinctively, Kali took a deep breath, but then smiled to herself. This wasn't water she was dealing with, this was something else entirely, and it had so far proved to be harmless, so she saw no reason why she shouldn't enjoy the ride.

Down she went, slowly down. At long last, Kali felt solid rock beneath her feet once more.

She stared at a solid rock wall. Disappointment threatened to overwhelm her once again. But then she turned around.

Kali smiled. *Hello, hub,* she thought.

Stretching away ahead of her, cut to the same dimensions as the vertical shaft, was a tunnel running horizontally through the rock, disappearing into the distance. Kali took a step forward, shrugged away a moment of giddiness, and waited while her eyes adjusted to the dim light of the underground.

The smooth, curving walls here were not bare rock, but lined with a softly-glowing metal, as was the floor, both inscribed over every inch of their surface with thousands upon thousands of delicate etchings. There were far too many of these etchings for Kali to be able to make sense of them as a whole, but they were undoubtedly dwarven in style and, what was more, of a kind that she had never come across before. The archetypal dwarven symbology was, of course, usually to do with war but Kali didn't see a single battleaxe, anvil or roaring dwarven visage. Instead, the fine etchings were flowing, swirling patterns – millions of them, perhaps – that reminded her of mathematical or algebraic symbols, all interlocking and sweeping in every direction and along the curving walls, combining as a whole into a thing of beauty. But were they just decorative or did they serve another purpose? Kali placed her palm on one small area of the etchings and immediately snatched it away, her flesh jolted, tingling and numb. Well, that answered that. Whatever they were, they were more than just decorative.

The answers lay ahead, they had to, and Kali began to walk the tunnel's length. She moved with caution, her concerns about the lack of traps playing on her mind. Again, though, there was no sign at all of anything threatening. The one thing that made her slow in her tracks turned out not to be any kind of hazard at all.

Lying on the floor of the tunnel, apparently torn apart, was the remains of some kind of machine. Multi-limbed, with appendages that resembled tools, it reminded her of some kind of giant spider.

Kali took a wide berth around it, just in case, and proceeded along the tunnel.

With all of her concentration focused on detecting traps she felt sure should be there, she found herself suddenly caught off guard, her progress impeded not by any trap but an unexpected wave of dizziness and disorientation that threw her off balance and sent her staggering.

"Whoa," Kali muttered.

Her head thumped, the passage seemed to spin about her, and she felt suddenly very hot with a wash of tingling saliva in her mouth, and a wave of nausea. Palms pressed against the passage wall, Kali swallowed and shook her head, feeling it buzz as she did and bringing a sudden stabbing pain behind the eyes. What the pits was going on? She suddenly felt as if she had the hangover from the hells. The previous evening had been a little heavy, even for her, but it felt all wrong. There was a throbbing heaviness of the head there, for sure, and an acid biliousness in her gut, but she knew what a hangover felt like and this wasn't it.

There was only one other conclusion. Something about – something *in* – this place was messing with her insides.

The sensation passed as she moved a few feet further on, and returned once more as she drew nearer to the end of the passage, before inexplicably disappearing again. Thrown, Kali continued, experiencing a few minutes of normality, before, abruptly, the debilitating sensation hit her once more. And if anything, it was worse than before. The resurgent feeling slapped her like a wave and, never mind her stomach, she felt as if her brain itself was sloshing about in her head. This time Kali buckled and actually did throw up and for a few seconds remained on her hands and knees, trailing spittle and groaning. She didn't want to get up but she knew she had to, that the sensations were connected to particular spots in the passageway and, perhaps by extension, in the whole place. Unless she wanted to suffer an ignominious death by a thousand heaves, she had to find a safe spot, and quickly.

Kali picked herself up, her vision wavering and blurring, and, her brain feeling like one of Slowhand's balloon animals, weaved like a drunk towards the end of the passageway. The current section seemed to have no safe spot whatsoever. She was dimly aware of passing another couple of the wrecked, spidery machines – in fact, almost tripping over one of them in her reduced state – and tried to think more about what function they might serve but found her concentration slipping away from her, unable to focus on anything but placing one foot in front of the other.

As bad as she felt, however, she could not help but react to what she saw as she reached the end of the passageway – even if for a second she thought it might be some vision induced by her delirium. Once more, Kali fell to her knees, not due to the disorientating effects of the place but because she was so staggered by the chamber she found herself in.

No, chamber was not a word that did this place justice. Spectacular as it had been, chamber was a word that described the lower level of Quinking's Depths, but this was...

Kali was kneeling on a platform overlooking a vast dwarven machine room, its metal-ribbed heights soaring as high above her as they plunged into the depths below. It was a vertiginous, spherical *world* of a place that made her feel as if she had stepped into the very core of Twilight itself. Great, irregularly-shaped metal objects rose and fell in the centre of the massive sphere, other smaller devices hovering around them like the satellites of metal moons. Other masses simply hung in the air, rotating slowly, while around the edge of the sphere, along its equator, a massive band of metal spun constantly, alternately clockwise and anti-clockwise, blurred by its speed – some kind of accelerator. And working on and around all of it – skittering on, about and around the devices – were spidery machines like the ones she had seen wrecked in the tunnel.

Kali couldn't take it all in, let alone make any sense of it, especially in the state she was in, and she crouch-walked along the platform until she found the blessed relief of a safe spot. Here, she felt able to crawl forward and peer down over the lip of the platform.

The machine room went far deeper than she had envisaged, burrowing down into the natural, rocky depths, so that the whole place was the shape of an upturned teardrop. Rising from that rocky depth was the reason 'the hub' had been built here, a narrow and tapering pinnacle of rock that disappeared into the confusion above, forming the centre around which they turned. The rock seemed, somehow, to be exerting an influence on the objects, keeping them afloat and in motion, and even from where she studied it Kali could feel the force it was emanating, as if she were leaning into a strong wind. She realised suddenly what it was she was dealing with here. The pinnacle of rock was an unimaginably massive lodestone – a giant, natural magnet – and its satellites had to be magnets, too, repelling and attracting each other in a geological dance choreographed by unbelievably complex forces. By the gods, they said the dwarves were masters of the very rocks themselves but this... this was incredible. It was magnetism on a massive scale, a peninsula-wide field controlling the Engines of Apocalypse.

Kali shook her head, another wave of dizziness hitting her, and, as she did, she caught a glimpse between the gaps in the revolving magnets of something else – something perched *on top* of the lodestone secured by bent struts. Some kind of platform, with what appeared to be a control panel on it. There was something else on the platform, too, and Kali felt a knot of dread in her chest as, through increasingly wavering vision, she made out four of Bastian Redigor's soul-stripped, at their feet another wrecked spider. They had clearly been despatched to activate the Engines, and as far as she could see it would be impossible to access the controls without them detecting her presence.

But wait. There was something not right about them. The soul-stripped were less than animate when not under the direct control of the Pale Lord but these four seemed to be not so much standing at the panel as slumped there. But that didn't make sense. Wouldn't Redigor would have kept them alive to ensure the continued operation of the Engines, or at the very least to stop anyone coming along to turn them off? What, then, was going on?

Kali swallowed as the brief glimpses of the soul-stripped the revolving magnets permitted her revealed more about their state. The soul-stripped were not moving because they could not move. Each of them was quite, quite dead, rivulets of blood congealed beneath their mouths, ears and nostrils. Where their eyes had been were simply empty sockets still slowly oozing gore. It was as if some external influence had taken hold of their heads and squeezed until they popped.

Kali raised her fingertips to her own nostrils, and they came away red and wet. The dwarves had established no defences here because no defences were needed. The spider machines had been built to maintain the hub once it was running because the dwarves knew the overwhelming magnetic forces at play would prove deadly to any living thing, including themselves. While Redigor's puppets were no longer strictly alive, their bodies were still flesh and blood, subject to the same physical vulnerabilities as anyone.

Kali wondered if Bastian Redigor had felt the agonising pain that must have accompanied the soul-stripped's deaths. And she wondered, more resilient than most or not, how long it would be before she started to feel her own.

She had to reach the control panel.

Get the job done and get out of there fast.

Kali stood and found herself staggering, forced to steady herself on a nearby strut. Oh, that was just great. Under normal circumstances getting the job done might have involved a couple of daring leaps across the magnets and then onto the control platform, but in her current condition there was no chance of that. She had to find an alternative route.

Kali studied the chamber and its central platform. Once upon a time it had to have had some kind of access walkway but that had clearly been removed once the structure was finished, meaning there was no direct way to it. The pattern in which the magnets orbited it, however, did present one or two moments when protrusions of the rotating stones almost touched the platform. If she could get onto one she should be able to make the jump across. There was no way onto them from this side of the chamber, but on the other side one of the objects that passed near the platform also passed near the edge of the chamber, and that distance, too, looked jumpable. It sounded easy enough – A to B to C – but the only problem was that getting to B would involve having to hitch a ride on the accelerator. The very, very, very fast accelerator.

Kali looked down. There was some kind of access hatch beneath her feet and she bent and flipped it open, staggering back as a wave of velocity seemed to slam through the gap. The accelerator lay directly under the hatch, as she'd hoped, but there was no way she could drop onto it while it was in motion. Kali swallowed, watching it ram first one way and then the other, each transition marked with an almighty clang. Gods, it was fast – the moment in which it paused to change directions fleeting – and her timing would have to be perfect. She waited while it stopped once, twice, and on the third time dropped without hesitation, flattening herself and grabbing hold as tightly as she could before it started again.

Thankfully, the accelerator was layered with tiny ridges and these afforded Kali a better grip than she would otherwise have had. Even so when, a heartbeat later, the accelerator punched back into life, she was almost ripped from its surface like a leaf. Kali skidded backwards, grabbing at the ridges to slow herself, and heard herself screaming, partly in exhilaration, partly in shock. She felt her teeth bared, her cheeks flapping and the flesh of her face rippling against her skull as she was carried around the perimeter of the chamber at unimaginable speed, the room blurring. The ride was over almost in an instant, however, and Kali screamed again as she found herself flipped heels over head, her grip snatched away, skidding helplessly forward on her back. She had only a second to react and she clamped her fingers onto the ridges and, with a grunt, flipped herself over, grabbing them once again.

The accelerator punched itself in the opposite direction once more, and now Kali found herself travelling backwards, her bodysuit almost torn from her body. She suddenly hadn't a clue where in the chamber she was and, for a moment, nearly panicked. Then her eyes fixed on the central control platform, the only constant in an ever changing blur, and she kept her gaze trained on it, marking its position and the magnets around it each time the accelerator stopped. At least she was no longer being thrown, having splayed herself over the accelerator like a human limpet.

Kali had to endure another five of the sudden punches while she waited for the floating magnet to rotate into a position where she would be able to reach it. It was hellishly slow and, by the time it finally did come round, she felt as if she'd been locked in a stable with a rampaging bamfcat. She simply wanted to lie down and die. This was hardly the spot to do so, however. If she relaxed, even for a second, her only memorial would be a Kali Hooper shaped hole in the chamber wall which no living thing would ever see.

Kali rode the accelerator for what was hopefully the last time, slowly and very, very carefully lifting herself into a crouching position. With even her hair whipping at her, she was almost torn free before the accelerator even stopped – and in that position certainly would be when it did stop – but her plan was to make the leap between accelerator and magnet in the split second *before* it did, using the speed and angle to propel herself to the target. Despite her calculations, this was going to be a leap of faith and the last thing she needed was the sudden, dizzying pounding in her head. Kali didn't even have the strength to curse, and certainly not the strength to hold on any longer, so she simply allowed herself to be thrown into the air.

Impact with the magnet was, of course, potentially as lethal as impacting with the chamber wall, but somewhere within her throbbing world of pain Kali calculated just how much she needed to adjust her trajectory to lift herself above the magnet. It seemed to have worked because she wasn't staring at her own backside splattering the surface of her destination. She quickly scrabbled beneath her for the surface – all she was capable of doing, really – almost broke her fingers as they touched, and then grabbed. She was once again thrown head over heels, slamming hard onto her back, but roared with determination and clung on despite her arms being wrenched so hard she thought for a moment they'd been ripped off. Kali lay stunned for a second as the magnet rotated beneath her, her eyes beginning to bulge slightly, and groaned loudly.

Something tickled her feet. She looked up to see one of the spider machines poised over her legs, ready to sweep down with a blade that would have amputated them. She was so thoroughly pitsed off that she just booted the maintenance machine off the magnet, sending it clattering into the abyss below.

More weary than she had ever felt, Kali picked herself up, waited for the slow rotation of the magnet to bring it into alignment with her destination and leaped.

She landed, at last, on the control platform and found herself among the collapsed remains of the soul-stripped who had been deployed there. She tried not to pay too much attention to them, to wonder who they might have *been*. She tipped their stiffened forms over the edge of the platform to tumble silently after the insect machine. Then she turned her attention to the control panel itself.

Oh hells.

Kali had lost count of the number of Old Race cryptograms, riddles, puzzles and traps she had been forced to decipher or solve in her time, but this one took the biscuit.

The panel was etched with a fine and impossibly intricate pattern of lines that glowed slightly and seemed to move, an optical illusion that didn't help her dizziness at all. The pattern was made up of circles, ellipses, ovals, plumes, radial spreads and whorls, all in various sizes and all overlapping. There were no other kinds of control mechanisms, buttons, levers or otherwise, and Kali felt her heart sink, wondering why for once, just farking once, the Old Races couldn't have designed something with a simple on/off switch.

Kali gazed at the panel woozily, and for a second thought she was about to make the task of deciphering the panel even more problematic by splattering thwack and kebab all over it. She swallowed the impulse down, however, and tried to ignore the pounding in her head. Each of the curving lines had to represent the line of a magnetic field, surely, so was it possible that somewhere in the pattern were also representations of what they affected? Working on that theory, she gradually began to discern three shapes that seemed static within the shifting of the etching, and guessed that these could be what she was looking for – the Engines themselves. The problem was that while the Faith had pinpointed the real locations of the Engines, their positions here, forming the three points of a triangle, seemed only symbolic, not relative to the sites they physically occupied. She was missing something, clearly – some term of reference that could relate how the magnetic fields interacted with the Engines in the real world – and without it she had no idea how they could be manipulated.

Suddenly, however, a thought struck her. Or rather, an image. She once again saw the map she had discovered in Redigor's tower – the one she had at first thought represented battle manoeuvres and had subsequently dismissed – and realised that it could be, after all, a vital piece of the jigsaw. If it *wasn't* battle manoeuvres it was illustrating, what if it were magnetic fields?

Kali once again shoved aside the pain in her head to concentrate hard, struggling to summon what she remembered of the map, its lines, and where they were positioned in relation to the coastline of the peninsula. She kept the image in her head and stared down at the control panel, trying to match up the slashes and curves. It seemed next to impossible, but she realised that all she really had to do was find the *first*. And there it was, a great sweeping line that ran from Scholten and across the Anclas Territories to grasp Miramas in its encompassing curve. Another ran across it, roughly paralleling the Territories themselves and was bisected by a third in the region of Andon. More of Redigor's smaller scrawls then became discernible, but they weren't really necessary. With their main counterparts identified, Kali was able to work out where on the control panel the coastlines of the peninsula lay, and with that knowledge the overall pattern laid out before her began to make a lot more sense. It really was quite ingenious the way every field of magnetic force affected every other across the whole landscape. What the dwarves might have accomplished had they survived could have been staggering. Now all Kali had to work out was how to ruin their achievement of a lifetime. To throw, as it were, a spanner in the works.

The problem was that there were still no visible controls and yet, clearly, the lines on the panel had to have been set somehow.

Experimentally, Kali moved her hand across the surface and nothing happened. She tried once more and still nothing. Then she looked up and realised that by looking at the control panel for changes to its settings she had been looking in the wrong place. Her gaze fixed ahead of her, she moved her hand experimentally once more, this time in a circle, and smiled as one of the magnets across the chamber rotated as it did, at exactly the same speed and for the same duration. She was onto something. Now all she had to do was work out how to get that magnet to interact with the others, from there determine how exactly they influenced the magnetic forces on the surface, and from there to determine a way to use them to disable the Engines.

For the first time in her life Kali began to regret dropping the moroddin lessons that Pete Two-Ties had once tried to thrust upon her, because the more she experimented with the controls the more she realised it was like playing some complex musical instrument. Still, she had to try.

Kali began to move her hands in a more relaxed manner, remembering Pete's words before she had aborted his teachings to *feel* the instrument in her hands, to let it be the guide, and as she did she found that she was gradually moving all of the magnets in the chamber at once, and not only that but managing to slow and speed up the accelerator as well. The whole process gave her an overwhelming feeling of power. If she weren't feeling so much like death, she might even have begun to enjoy herself.

The feel of the control panel much more familiar now, the magnets moving at her whim, Kali began to concentrate instead on the panel, which seemed to have warmed beneath her hands, so much so that she could feel the flesh of her palms beginning to tingle. Then she realised that it wasn't heat that was causing the sensation but the softest of magnetic pressures being emitted by the metal. As she moved her palms across its entire surface once more it was like moving them over a series of small, invisible hills and valleys – a miniature topography made of magnetism.

That was it!

Eager now, Kali placed her palms above the three spots that represented the positions of the Engines and there felt peaks of magnetic push far sharper than elsewhere on the etched map. As she began to gently manipulate them they actually began to soften in their resistance and began to *move*.

I have you now.

It would take a good deal of concentration and dexterity but, in theory, she should be able to move the Engines anywhere she wanted.

Kali set to work.

CHAPTER ELEVEN

KALI MADE THE rendezvous that evening, helped along by three jumps from Horse, the last of which brought them atop an escarpment overlooking the dark border of the Sardenne. The forest stretched to the west and east as far as the eye could see, as did, about half a league back, the Final Faith cordon. Dotted by campfires along its vast length, it was as yet impossible to make out the individual figures waiting around them, but the numbers involved were staggering. Bolstered now by legions from both the Vossian and Pontaine militaries, the force represented the first time the two armies had come together since the Great War, and the first time ever that they had done so in peace. It was a reflection of the seriousness of the threat they faced. As Kali watched them from on high she felt almost like a party pooper knowing she had to tell them they had no choice but to stay their arms.

Her gaze rose into the azure twilight. As massive as the cordon was, the escarpment afforded a ringside view of something even more daunting – something now utterly unavoidable. The thick pillar of souls rising from deep within the Sardenne was now twice the height it had been when Kali had last seen it. A vertical maelstrom that swirled endlessly and chaotically and, whether it was her imagination or not, seemed to scream out at the darkening sky. Maybe the poor souls trapped within sensed their time was coming, Kali thought, because the pillar appeared, from her perspective, to be already piercing the outer layers of Kerberos, actually making contact with the gas giant itself. It wasn't – yet – but at the rate the pillar was growing she reckoned she'd been more or less bang on with the deadline she'd estimated.

Tomorrow was when it would happen.

Kali bit her lip and spurred Horse gently on, walking him down the hillside and to the perimeter of the central camp. Two Faith guards nodded in acknowledgement and parted to let her pass. She tethered Horse near a gathering of tents, clustered around a crackling campfire. A few acolytes were clustered around the fire, where Slowhand was fleecing them in a game of quagmire. By the look of his upturned cards, the archer had just stymied his opponents with a five-card plop and was raking in a handful of silver tenths.

"Hooper, how you doing?" He said casually as she approached. He nodded to the acolytes, a request for privacy, and they left shaking their heads and pulling less than pious faces.

"Oh, you know. Been introducing the pure of heart to the evils of gambling?"

Slowhand inclined his head to the east. "Didn't fancy a walk in the woods."

"Understandable." Kali sat herself down beside him and cracked open a bottle of thwack from her backpack, downing two thirds of it and heaving sigh.

"Introducing the pure of heart to the evils of drink?" Slowhand countered.

"Nope. It's all mine."

Slowhand smiled.

"Besides, there's no such thing as evil drink, only evil empty bottles." She took another swig and then upturned the one in her hand, scowling. "See."

"Rough couple of days?"

Kali shrugged. "No more than usual. Discovered Bastian Redigor is an elf, travelled a few thousand years into the past, give or take a teatime, almost got sliced apart by spectral hags, and then nearly turned into a doily by magnets the size of farking mountains."

"Right."

"Oh, and I had a kebab."

"Ooooh. There's that death wish again. But I take it the elf thing is what I should be paying attention to?"

Kali nodded. "I need to talk to the others."

"Well, Freel's patrolling the camp. Fitch is off somewhere, avoiding me. And Dez – sorry, *Gabriella* – is in her tent. I think she's... you know, the thing with the hands."

"Praying?"

"That's the one."

"For once, it might not do any harm. Which tent is she in?"

"The one behind you," DeZantez said. She was folding up a shnarlskin prayer mat as she exited, appearing casual, but by the look of her Kali had risen in her estimation for having returned. "Did I hear you say something about an *elf*?"

Kali stood. "I think you'd better get your people together."

Gabriella studied her, then nodded.

A few minutes later she, Freel, General McIntee, Fitch and assorted other senior officers were gathered in war council, listening to what Kali had to say. The relief of the magic users following their realisation that magic was, as it were, back on line, dissipated when Kali told them what she had discovered. There was almost universal silence, the only person to speak Gabriella DeZantez. And perhaps because what she heard conflicted so much with her own faith – everything she believed about the sanctity of souls and Kerberos – the only word she was able to utter was an incredulous, "What?"

"The return of the Ur'Raney," Kali said. "It's what the Pillar of Souls is for. To act as a conduit between Twilight and Kerberos, allowing the exchange of the human souls Redigor has taken with those of his dead elves. One for one, every one of his subjects reincarnated, right here, as an army, in the bodies of the soul-stripped."

"The bodies of farmers and their wives, their children?" General McIntee said doubtfully. "I do not see how they could pose much of a threat."

"I seem to remember them being pretty threatening under your cathedral," Slowhand countered. "To say nothing of the shit that's been hitting the fan everywhere else."

"Actually, the general's partly right, 'Liam. When the Ur'Raney inhabit the soul-stripped they will be alive again, and physically vulnerable as a result. But it's my guess that during whatever ritual Redigor is going to conduct he'll also transfer some of the *physical* essence of the Ur'Raney to alter the hosts." She turned to McIntee. "If I'm right, General, they'll be transformed, and you won't be facing farmers, their wives and their children, you'll be facing thousands of elven biomorphs."

"That's the bit I don't get," Slowhand said. "This necropolis you mentioned. It's got to be just bursting with pointy-eared stiffs, yes? So why doesn't Redigor just 'ritualise' the Ur'Raney back into their old bodies?"

"That, I don't know," Kali admitted. "Maybe it's just been too long."

Freel took a pensive breath. "You called them Redigor's 'subjects,'" he said. "Are you saying Redigor was some kind of elven king?"

"King, no. Lord, yes. The elves had no monarchy as such. What they did have were elven 'families' or courts – the Ur'Raney, Pras'Tir, Var'Karish and others – each autonomous but led by their Lord and twelve lieutenants who made up a kind of high council called the rannaat."

"Coincidence?" Gabriella pointed out. "The Anointed Lord and the other dignitaries who were taken by the soul-stripped?"

Kali nodded. "I think Redigor has them marked as hosts for his lieutenants."

"Except thirteen were taken," Freel pointed out. "Thirteen, not twelve."

"Yes, well," Kali said slowly.

She had her own theory on that particular discrepancy and her mind flashed back to the portrait in Redigor's tower. Makennon's resemblance to his one time *mu'sah'rin* must have seemed to him to be a gift from the gods or, at least, *his* gods.

Because, at one and the same time, the 'First Enemy' had the opportunity to behead the Final Faith of its leader *and* humiliate them in a way only the Ur'Raney knew how. The effort of reactivating the Engines of the Apocalypse might have been worth it to him for that alone.

"I think I can explain that," Kali continued carefully, considering the loyalties and sensitivities of the company she was in. "The Ur'Raney had little respect for the females of their court and I don't think Makennon has been taken to be one of his lieutenants."

"Then what?" Fitch queried.

"It's... difficult to explain. *Mu'sah'rin*. A kind of... submissive partner."

Slowhand almost coughed up his tonsils.

"Sorry," he said, after a moment.

The reactions from the others varied slightly. Freel took a second, then nodded. Fitch turned away to stare into the trees. Gabriella flared with anger and embarrassment. The only vocal reaction came from General McIntee.

"We order the advance immediately," he growled. "End this now."

"You can't," Kali said.

McIntee looked to the west and east, nodding to the ranks of soldiers and Swords of Dawn, and the mages amongst them. In an ever extending line in both directions, weapons were drawn and determined fists flared with fire, lightning and ice. "Oh, young lady, I assure you, we can."

"No!" Kali persisted, slapping a palm solidly on his chest as he moved to lead them. "That isn't what I mean."

The general halted, glaring. Freel stepped in to draw Kali's hand from his heaving chest, defusing the confrontation. "What *do* you mean, Miss Hooper?" He asked.

"Think about it, Freel," Kali said. "All along we've been assuming the soul-stripped are lost to us, dead, but if Redigor plans to use them as hosts for the souls of the Ur'Raney, there may be a way we can return the souls of our *own* people to their bodies."

Gabriella stared at the pillar of souls, thrusting into the night sky. "She's right, Enforcer. They haven't reached Kerberos yet."

Freel looked helplessly between the two women.

"Bring them back? Is such a thing possible?"

"Obviously Redigor thinks so," Kali said. "Right at this moment those soul-stripped are as much hostages as they are threat. Could you live with yourself if you at least didn't *try* to save them?"

"Madness," McIntee growled. "This might be our only chance!"

"You know what?" Kali shouted. "He's right. If Redigor manages to get his people into those bodies, they are going to march from the Sardenne and they are going to absolutely kick your arse. They drove an entire dwarven subrace to the point of extinction, for fark's sake. Clan Martak was helpless, utterly defeated, yet still they routed them, massacred them, drove those they couldn't kill into the sea to drown. Freel, your predecessor Munch himself told me – and believe me, that little bastard wasn't averse to a bit of carnage himself – they just never stop."

"We will hold them," McIntee insisted.

Kali slapped his chest again. "Are you *listening* to me? These elves were an Old Race who enjoyed rape, torture, pillage – even amongst their own kind. They sacrificed every tenth newborn to Yartresnika, their god of destruction. They added blood to their wine to make it *tastier*. Are you forgetting what happened when your lot first encountered The First Enemy? All you faced then was just one man. What happens when Redigor brings his friends to the party, eh? Thousands of them?"

"You seem to have defeated your own argument," Freel pointed out.

Kali shook her head. "Only if they're not stopped. Freel, let me ask you again – do you really want to slaughter thousands of your own, innocent people if it isn't necessary? Give me a chance."

"The girl was enlisted to shut down the Engines," McIntee said. "She's done that. Send her home."

"I was also 'enlisted' to save Makennon," Kali reminded him. "Let me try to do that. And the soul-stripped, too."

One at a time, Freel stared them in the eyes. His gaze, however settled on Kali.

"What if you fail?"

Kali faltered, swallowed. "Then you'd better hope your general here is as good as he thinks he is..."

"At least," Gabriella added after a moment, "you won't have the blood of your own on your hands."

Freel let out an exasperated sigh. The lives of thousands hung in the balance.

"What do you propose we do?"

"We go in as a strike team to find Makennon as planned. But with fifty mages and some Swords of Dawn, the best you have, as support. And while we're there, we do as much damage as possible to Redigor's ritual. Hopefully enough."

"Any ideas how?"

"One, but it's a long shot. I tend to work on the hoof."

Freel turned to Slowhand, the beginnings of an actual smile playing on his lips. "I heard a good way to deal with resurrectionists is to put an arrow in their head."

"Damn right," Kali and Slowhand said at the same time.

"There is one problem we still haven't resolved," Gabriella said. "If Fitch is right about the Pale Lord's eyes being everywhere, how do we bypass the soul-stripped?"

"With eyes of our own," Freel said. "I've already adapted an Eye of the Lord to make a low level reconnaissance and determine a safe, or at least safer, route through them."

"But wouldn't the Pale Lord still detect its presence?"

"I'm gambling his eyes can't be everywhere at once. There has to be some kind of trigger that opens them. Something *alive*, for example."

Kali nodded at Gabriella. "Makes sense. When can you send it in?"

"Right now. But before I do..."

Freel turned back to General McIntee, who seemed to have taken the reality of the situation facing his forces a little more on board. "Keep your people here," he instructed. "If this doesn't work, if we don't come back... just... do what you can do."

McIntee swallowed, and nodded. "Good luck, Sir." He turned to Kali, Slowhand, DeZantez – even Fitch. "Good luck to all of you."

The war council disbanded. Freel moved off to despatch the Eye of the Lord and, knowing once more that it would take some time to report its findings, to personally assign the mages and Swords Kali had requested. Slowhand decided to use the hiatus to fletch more of his special arrows and settled himself back before the campfire. Kali and Gabriella took up positions on the other side of the flames, giving him the room he needed to work. They sat in silence for a while, the Enlightened One regarding Kali carefully before she spoke.

"Why do you do it? What you do?"

Kali prodded the fire with her gutting knife, a fresh flare of flame illuminating her face. "What? You mean rub people up the wrong way?"

Gabriella smiled. "You know what I mean. Spend your life digging around in the dirt, trying to learn what's gone?"

"You admit finally that I was just looking for the Deathclaws? That I had nothing to do with the Engines?"

"Oh, I think you're pretty much off the hook. So why?"

Not so long ago Kali would have said to find out what happened to the Old Races. She hadn't yet even shared it with her friends, and she certainly wasn't ready to share it with DeZantez, but her goals had changed – to find out what had *killed* them, yes, but now also to find out what 'the Darkness' was.

"Urm, because they were there?" She said.

"And now they're not?"

"That's right. It's important I find out why."

Gabriella nodded, poked the fire again. "Did they leave much behind?"

Kali shrugged. "It varies from site to site. Most are empty shells, stripped by tomb raiders down the years, or by your mob, if they manage to beat me somewhere. But you're one of them, you should know that."

"I tend to avoid that side of the Faith's affairs. They... don't sit well with me."

Kali raised her eyebrows. She remembered their meeting outside Solnos, how she had felt that DeZantez was a lot like herself – following a calling, doing good, trying to help – but that somehow the world had changed beyond her control.

"The more inaccessible sites offer the occasional trinket," she continued. "And, every now and then, there's a special site that delivers something like the Deathclaws. Also those that promise much but usually – when you've worked your arse off for days trying to get into the thing – deliver bugger all. The Lost City of Fff, for one."

"The Lost City of Fff? You're making that up."

"I promise you, I'm not. Learned about it from the Followers of Fff at their annual Faff. Should have known better than to listen to people who Faff." Kali shook her head. "Treasures undreamed of, they told me..."

"And what did you find?"

"A chest full to the brim with crap."

Gabriella laughed, an actually quite embarrassing bass, guttural bellow, but the first genuine humour Kali had seen the Enlightened One display. Clearly, she needed the release that a little laughter brought but it soon faded, her smile dwindling until she wore her impenetrable mask of introspection once more. Her guard seemed to have lowered somewhat, though, and Kali couldn't resist asking the question that had been bothering her almost since they had met.

"The graveyard in Solnos," she said. "It's obvious you're not from the town but I got the impression there was –"

"His name was Erak Brand," Gabriella interrupted her. "He was the Enlightened One of Solnos before me. A kind, faithful man."

"You were close?"

"Erak and I were lovers. We were to marry."

"Gods, I'm sorry. What happened?"

Gabriella tensed and the stick she'd been about to throw onto the fire she snapped in half. "He was murdered. By a man named Dai Batsen."

"Why?"

"Batsen was a rogue shadowmage. A hireling of someone who didn't want us to discover an unsavoury truth."

"What truth?"

Gabriella let out an exasperated sigh that turned into a cracked, humourless laugh. "The truth is, I don't know. And now I doubt I'm ever going to find out..."

Kali frowned. "Rodrigo Kesar had something to do with this, didn't he? I saw your face back at Scholten when you learned he was dead."

Gabriella nodded. "And with him my chance to avenge Erak. May that bastard Kesar be burning in the hells."

Gabriella's cold ferocity took Kali aback, but more than that, it struck her that her companion meant exactly what she said. She wasn't speaking of the hells in any metaphorical sense, she was speaking of them as real places. It was clear she believed they existed as much as the Clouds of Kerberos floated above their heads. After what she had seen through the shard at the cathedral, it sent a shiver down her spine.

"Is there no other way you can find out what was behind Erak's death?"

Gabriella shook her head. "My position as Enlightened One of Solnos was only ever meant to be temporary. But I waited and waited and, as the months passed, no one came to replace me. Eventually I found out, from friends, that the Anointed Lord had arranged to have me watched – and then, simply, forgotten."

"You think Makennon was responsible?"

"I don't know. I don't think so. But I do know I seem to have little place in a changing Faith. I believed in their mission – *still believe* – to bring Ascension to the people, even if we have to purify some with fire. But after what happened to you with the Eyes of the Lord – seeing how they accused you and how they were *wrong* – I realised just how out of control they have become. The Faith threatens to become a dictatorship, ruling with an iron glove and I think something is rotten at its core."

"Can I take that as an apology for trying to burn me alive?"

"Kali –"

"Joke," Kali said. "But if you realise all of this, why are you still here?"

Gabriella stared at her as if the answer were obvious. "As a Sister of the Order of the Swords of Dawn, I remain sworn to protect the Anointed Lord."

"Now that's a joke, ri –" Kali began, but halted as Gabriella suddenly placed her palm on her forearm, beckoning silence.

At first she thought the Enlightened One had simply had enough of the subject but then saw that she was staring into the dark boundary of the forest, where Slowhand had wandered minutes before to collect wood to whittle into shafts. The archer seemed alone in the shadows but then she sensed another presence in the darkness, watching Slowhand from hiding. Kali stared at the spot, gradually discerning a shape, but she had difficulty making out what it was until there were two simultaneous flares about a foot and half apart at waist height. For a fleeting moment the flares illuminated curled palms, a dark-robed torso, and a white, cadaverous face, steadily regarding Slowhand with malignant intent.

"Fitch!" Kali said, starting to run. "One bastard who should never have got the magic back!"

Gabriella was up and by her side in an instant, the two of them pounding towards Slowhand, but the archer was hacking at vegetation, unable to hear their shouts. The fire in Fitch's palms, meanwhile, had transformed into crackling spheres of energy. As Kali and Gabriella watched helplessly, Fitch drew his palms back and threw the fireballs at the preoccupied archer. Luckily, Fitch's aim was slightly askew, and the fireballs impacted with a tree trunk next to Slowhand, knocking the archer off his feet. He scrabbled back in shock and raced towards his assailant, roaring as he recognised Fitch.

He suddenly stopped dead in his tracks and Kali saw the psychic manipulator smiling and weaving some distraction thread with one hand while nurturing a third fireball with the other. There was no question that this one would hit Slowhand full on and she and Gabriella were still too far away to do anything.

"You tackle Fitch!" Gabriella yelled, and then pounded toward Slowhand. Kali ran at the psychic manipulator along with Jakub Freel, who had been alerted by the noise. As she watched the fireball grow all Kali could feel was the pounding of her heart, and the certain knowledge that the fireball was going to leave Fitch's hand before she or the enforcer reached him. She snatched a glance towards Gabriella and, like herself, the Enlightened One still had too much ground to cover.

Fitch launched the fireball and everything became dream-like and slow. Kali came to a faltering stop and tracked the crackling sphere of fire helplessly, her mouth falling open. As it passed the halfway mark between Fitch and Slowhand, she turned slightly, yelling to Gabriella to drive her onward. Ripping away her armour as she went, driven as much by momentum as muscle, Gabriella left the ground, throwing herself forward through the air, but it wasn't Slowhand she was throwing herself at, it was the fireball.

Enlightened One and fireball collided in mid-air and Gabriella DeZantez was consumed by the magic, disappearing inside an explosion of super-heated fire. The infernal heat it contained would, had she still been wearing it, have turned her armour red hot in an instant, roasting her inside, but with only her surplice she would likely suffer a quicker death than that. She had no chance of surviving, none at all, and so it came as something of a surprise to Kali when, as the fire blasted about Gabriella and then dissipated, the Enlightened One fell to the ground with her surplice burnt away, smoking and stunned, but otherwise apparently unharmed.

Slowhand looked about him in confusion. Fitch, meanwhile, stared at the recovering form of Gabriella DeZantez in disbelief. For his part, Jakub Freel covered the remaining ground between Fitch and himself where he flattened the psychic manipulator with a single punch to the face.

Kali turned her attention back to Slowhand. The archer had stripped off his shirt and was wrapping it about Gabriella as he lifted her slowly from the ground. The woman was clearly stunned, but there wasn't a mark on her, not a single blemish or burn. It was no time for questions, however, and Kali and Slowhand took Gabriella between them and slowly led her back to her tent. Slowhand paused mid-route and nodded to Freel.

"Thanks," he said.

"Don't mention it."

The Final Faith enforcer watched them depart with their charge. Neither of them noticed as, behind them, he hauled Fitch to his feet with one hand and roused him. Neither did they hear the words that passed between the enforcer and the cadaverous manipulator.

"I told you not to make a move," Freel said. "I told you that when the time comes, Killiam Slowhand is *mine*."

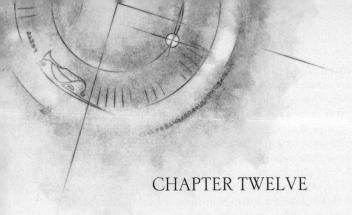

CHAPTER TWELVE

THEY ENTERED THE Sardenne at dawn, not that Twilight's distant sun ever made much difference in the heavily canopied forest. The first few yards of their ingress plunged them into shadow, the next few beyond that to a darkness equivalent to longnight, and with every step thereafter the ambient light lessened until, in parts, their surroundings were as black as a windowless room. To aid their progress, the mages in the party wove soft and subtle light threads that played about them like fireflies, not bright enough to attract unwanted attention but enough to make the individual members of the party aware of where they stepped and distinguishable from each other. Their beacon, albeit an ominous one, was the pillar of souls. The column of spiritual energy continued to grow, and offered a continuous reminder of why they were treading such dangerous ground.

They were amidst the soul-stripped now and followed the route that the Eye of the Lord had suggested was safest, though watching the images the device had returned to them had still been a discomfiting experience. The small sphere had woven a meandering course through the soul-stripped, manoeuvring up to and around them, between them, but never drawing too near and – in case Kali was wrong about what would alert the Pale Lord – never lingering too long. The Eye's passage nevertheless allowed it to see a level of detail that no human would have survived long enough to absorb, snatches of facial features of the soul-stripped – an ear, a nose, a mouth, a dangling lock of hair. That close, they almost became individuals again, might have been husbands, wives, sons, daughters or friends, but it only took one glimpse of their rigid forms or whitened eyes to remind all who watched that they were nothing to each other or their loved ones now.

However uncomfortable watching the images had been, the party's progression along the route mapped by the Eye was worse.

They moved in silence and almost in single file. Every breath, every footfall brought with it a palpable sense of fear. It seemed that each piece of tinder that snapped beneath a boot, each branch disturbed, would alert the soul-stripped, and that it was only a matter of time before one of them turned its gaze toward them. As a result, Kali moved everyone forward with great caution.

It had fallen to her – as one of the few, and certainly the only member of the current party to have ventured deep into the Sardenne and survived – to take point and in that role she had advised them of a few of the realities of the sprawling, ancient domain. The most important was that the soul-stripped were not the only things to be afraid of. The further they progressed into the forest the stranger and more dangerous the threats they might face. She had allocated everyone some floprat render, the olfactory camouflage she found worked best within the Sardenne, but some, the Swords particularly, wore the foul smelling substance awkwardly, as if they thought she was playing some practical joke at their expense. Kali's sincere hope was that they didn't have to find out otherwise. Familiar with the Sardenne's unnatural menagerie first hand, she doubted that any of the men or women present would believe her if she tried to describe some of the things she'd seen, so she didn't bother.

Oddly enough, though, there were none of the hisses, caws, growls, rumbles, rattles or shrieks from the surrounding undergrowth that she would normally expect to hear. She wondered whether the presence of the soul-stripped, or the aura of Redigor, had actually done their party a favour, driving the wildlife deeper into the forest and leaving the path ahead of them clear. They would only know the truth as they forged deeper.

Though their passage through the soul-stripped was tortuous and took some hours they miraculously avoided detection, reaching a point at last where the Pale Lord's puppets thinned. Soon after, they had passed beyond them completely.

It was at this stage that Kali instigated the second part of her plan to negotiate the Sardenne successfully. Her main reason for including the mages in the party was not for them to help tackle Redigor – five *hundred*, not fifty, would have been nearer the mark for that – but because she knew they did not have time on their side. Travelling in a normal fashion, it would take days to reach Bel'A'Gon'Shri, and the pillar of souls would have touched Kerberos long before that. But by using the mages to generate portals – effectively *teleporting* their way through the forest – they could reduce a journey of days to one of hours.

The ploy was not without its logistical problems, however. For one thing, the effort and energies involved meant that the mages would have to work in turns, and would only be able to move them a league or two at a time. For another, they would be teleporting blind. It was the reason they could not use the same technique to bypass the soul-stripped – the last thing Kali wanted was to materialise in the middle of a mass of them – and they could only hope that more of them, or other hidden hazards, did not lie ahead.

Slowhand looked uneasy as the first wave of mages began to weave the threads. They were helpless to sudden attack from the forest while the weaving took place, so the Swords stood vigilant around them.

"You've done this before?" The archer said to Kali.

"Sure. The old man and I travelled from Gargas to Andon during the k'nid invasion. It's what gave me the idea."

"And you arrived okay? I mean with... all your bits?"

"My bits? Gods and hells, 'Liam, is that all you ever think about?"

"*Did* you?"

"Of course I did! Stinking pits, I would have thought you'd have noticed by now!"

Slowhand faltered. "Oh. Right. Yes. They seemed okay."

"*Okay?*"

"Dammit, Hooper, you know what I mean!"

Before them, the mages had completed their weaving and the portal had formed, a shimmering circle that flared outward briefly before just hanging in the air a few inches off the ground. Slowhand swallowed as, with a distinct squelching sound, Jakub Freel stepped into it and vanished. DeZantez, Fitch and the ranks of the mages and Swords followed.

"Our turn," Kali said. "Want me to hold your hand?"

"I don't think so," Slowhand answered through gritted teeth. "Much as I love you, Hooper, I don't want us spending the rest of eternity as some three-handed, twenty-fingered *thing*."

"Be a bit more optimistic. We might end up joined at the groin."

"Yeah?"

"Dammit, we are *not* going to end up either way, okay?" Kali said, but Slowhand still seemed unconvinced. "Fine then. Go by yourself."

"If we end up on a different planet..."

Kali had had enough, and pushed him through the portal. She materialised beside the archer a second later, turning away quickly when she saw him looking down and squeezing himself unashamedly. She looked up; the pillar of souls was closer. The portal had worked.

Spurred by their success, another portal followed, and another, and another after that, by which time the party had progressed so far into the Sardenne that Kali was certain she could smell the faint tang of the long burnt-out shell of the Spiral of Kos. The forest felt different from when she'd fled the explosions that had destroyed the Old Race site, however, wildlife still conspicuously absent. What had been a vital, if life-threatening, region of the forest back then now felt abandoned, as if every participant of its predatorial food chain had deferred to a far greater appetite and retreated into caves and broad burrows, or beneath large stones. Even those creatures who hunted not for food but fun had disappeared. The worst thing was, Kali sensed it was neither the soul-stripped or Redigor that had caused this, but something else.

She had to admit to being quite relieved when Gabriella DeZantez joined her at the front of the ranks. The Enlightened One was fully armoured once more and recovered from Fitch's attack. They walked together in silence for a while, but then Kali found herself broaching a subject that just had to be broached.

"That fireball thing last night. You feel like telling me what *that* was about?"

"I wondered how long it would take you to ask."

"Well, hey, a fireball brushed off as easily as a nibble from a worgle? People tend to notice such things."

"Does anyone ever interrogate you about the things you can do?"

"Things?"

I saw you in action in the library, remember? And some of the eye witness accounts of your exploits in your file – well, let's just say they raised eyebrows."

Kali faltered. "Generally I try not to show off."

"Show off what?"

"I wish I knew."

Gabriella seemed genuinely surprised. "You don't know?"

"Hells, no."

"And yet you always seem to show up where your abilities are most useful. Almost as if it were –"

"Don't say it," Kali interrupted. "Predestined? Well, if it is, I wish to gods someone would tell me, because believe me, all I do is make it up as I go along."

The two of them lapsed into silence again. But only briefly.

"It's happened before," Gabriella admitted. "In Solnos. A fireball full in the face and... and nothing. There was another time, too, when I was a child, in some ruins south of Andon. We... that is, my friends and I, used to play there."

Kali's eyebrows rose. "The Seventeen Steps? Every level is an inaccessible deathtrap."

Gabriella nodded. "Because of the Dust Curtains."

"So named because they strip to the bones anyone who comes within fifty feet. I've been trying to crack them for two years."

"Not me."

"I'm sorry?"

"The Dust Curtains. I walked right through them." Gabriella took a slow breath. "My friends didn't react well to that and it wasn't long after I signed up for the Swords of Dawn."

Kali felt her heart thud. After all her efforts, all she *should* have wanted to ask was what lay beyond the Dust Curtains but what DeZantez had just admitted to her was a revelation that made the secrets of the Seventeen Steps utterly insignificant. She turned to face Gabriella, and grabbed her by the shoulders.

"Are you trying to tell me you're immune to magic?"

Gabriella swallowed. "I guess I am."

"Hells."

"*Hells?* That's all you have to say?"

"What do you expect me to say or do?" Kali hissed. "Abandon you like your friends – turn you into some kind of freak, outcast, pariah? We're more alike than that, remember?"

Gabriella stared at her, then nodded. "And I'm not sure we're the only ones."

"What?"

Gabriella sighed, but it seemed a relieved sigh because she could finally talk to someone about what she knew. "I told you I sneaked a look at your file in the Faith record but what I didn't tell you was that next to it I found one on me too. And two others."

"What the hells are you talking about?"

"Two other files, each relating in some detail the strange abilities of their owners. A thief based in Turnitia, by the name of Lucius Kane. And another, a mariner called Silus Morlader."

"Kane?" Kali said. "I met him. He was something more than your average thief."

"Exactly. And from what I read, this Silus isn't your average fisherman, either. You heard anything about him?"

Kali shook her head.

"Apparently, he now commands a ship by the name of the *Llothriall*. A ship stolen from the Final Faith. What's more, the *Llothriall* is an –"

"Elven ship," Kali finished.

Gabriella shrugged. "I suppose the clue's in the name."

"Not really. I found the plans for it." Kali sighed. "This world gets smaller every day."

"I don't understand."

Kali paused. "What if I told you that a year or so ago I had an encounter with something beneath the waves? Some form of water dweller, who spoke to me in my head. Mind to mind."

"Water dweller?" Gabriella said.

"Water dweller," Kali repeated. "Most of what it said was couched in riddles, about it being part of the Before, the After. But it also spoke about a group of people known as 'the four'."

"The Four?"

"'Four known to us. Four unknown to each other. Four who will be known to all.' That was what it said."

"And you know what that means?"

"Haven't the remotest idea. But it's one pretty big coincidence, don't you think?" Kali paused, frowned. Despite her reservations about discussing the subject with Gabriella, the situation had clearly changed and she deserved to know something more. "In fact, it's two."

"Two?"

"Tharnak, the dwelf creature I encountered in the Crucible, also spoke of 'four.' In his case, of four humans who were being prepared to travel to Kerberos – alive, that is."

"In that ship you found? But why?"

"To save the world, I think. The point is, these four had been changed, altered, somehow physically manipulated so they could survive the journey. Their abilities had been *enhanced*."

"Surely you're not suggesting..."

"Gabriella, I'm not sure what I'm suggesting – but what I *know* is the Faith is keeping files on you, me, and two others. Four. The question is, why?"

The Enlightened One was silent for a second, then said, "Maybe the person who holds the halo versions of the files has the answer."

"Halo versions?"

"Faith security classification. Halo files contain additional information. More *sensitive* information. The locations, for example, of supporting physical evidence on their subjects."

"Who has these files, do you know?"

Gabriella nodded. "But you're not going to like it when I tell you."

"*Who?*"

"Querilous Fitch."

Kali stopped dead. Without a word, she turned and began to push her way back through the ranks to where Fitch, avoiding Slowhand, trailed at their end. Gabriella followed, ignoring the confusion on the faces of the archer, Freel and others who had been pushed aside, catching up to Kali as she neared the psychic manipulator.

"Lord of All, we're in the middle of the *Sardenne*. Are you always this impulsive?"

"Yes."

Kali was almost in Fitch's face now, his features all the more gaunt in the wan light. He started slightly but smiled coldly, as if knowing what Kali had just learned and knowing, too, that he held all the cards.

"You –" Kali was about to say, "have got some farking explaining to do!"

But she had barely formed the first word when a massive shape swung into view between them, brushing by her and Gabriella and dashing them to the ground. Fitch was not so fortunate. Struck full on, his cadaverous form was sent hurtling away through the trees with a shrill scream – gone, just like that.

Kali and Gabriella scrambled to their feet, trying to adopt a defensive position, although they had no clue what they were defending against. As they did, the shape swung again, and they ducked. Whatever the hells was coming at them, it was huge; the Swords charging, weapons drawn, into its path had no chance against it. Kali heard the crunch of metal and bone and dimly registered their broken forms flying into the undergrowth. She and Gabriella stared at each other, horrified, and rushed for cover. Others nearby were not so well practiced and, as the massive shape swung back for a third pass, another four Swords shrieked as they were knocked away by the impact.

"What in the name of the Lord of All?" Gabriella breathed, and a great, primal roar erupted from the darkness above them, sending those below into a panic, colliding with each other or freezing on the spot.

Kali wanted to shout to them to *move, move, move*, but she was desperately trying to process what it was they were dealing with. She remembered many things about her last visit to the Sardenne, but none were stamped quite so indelibly on her mind as the one she was remembering now.

It had occurred during her desperate flight from the Spiral of Kos when, with vast swathes of the forest lit by the detonations behind her, the creatures who dwelled within had flocked to her. As she and Horse, bless his bacon-lardon-loving heart, had galloped towards safety, they had been assailed by the full spectrum of nightmares that called the forest home, wooden things and armoured things, things of bone and of things of blood, things of moss and mud and stone. But there had been one creature, felt more than seen – a giant fist, registered fleetingly as Horse pounded along, swinging down at them from behind the trees. It had impacted with the forest floor with such force that Horse had momentarily lost his footing and she'd almost been thrown from his back. Naturally, they hadn't lingered to meet its owner, and Kali had no idea of what kind of creature it was, but it had to be the same creature that was attacking their party now.

"Move, move, move!" Kali shouted, but the command would do their ranks little good.

She stared up into the trees, trying to make out the creature that was attacking, but could see little. In truth, she didn't really *need* to see it. It was obvious that for every hundred yards their people could run, a single stride would bring their attacker back into reach. Gabriella DeZantez made the same assessment and unsheathed the Deathclaws in a determined, if futile, attempt to defend herself.

Nor was she the only one. Amongst the group – most of whom were torn between running or standing their ground and fighting – she saw Slowhand flip Suresight from his back and unleash a volley of arrows into the trees above, and Freel snap his whip from his side, eyes narrowed, scanning for a target. Some of the Swords, who had at last pulled themselves together, unsheathed their weapons as the mages unleashed bolts of fire or ice or lightning. Many still panicked or blundered around. The attack had come so suddenly, so unexpectedly, that with the first swing their battle readiness had been reduced to a complete and utter shambles.

The fist returned, and while the soldiers were ready for it, throwing themselves out of its path in a clattering of weapons and armour, a second fist slammed down on the spot where they moved. There was an explosion of weaponry, bone and gore and the unfortunates were crushed like bugs. Now the creature's feet pummelled the ground too, stomping onto a growing carpet of crushed bodies. The survivors were not idle, however, Slowhand having fired at least twenty arrows into one of the feet as soon as it appeared, and Freel having lashed out at the wrist of one of the hands with his whip. Neither seemed particularly effective, though. Freel found himself being swung through the trees as the creature tried to rid itself of his weapon. Gabriella, too, was moving, racing at the behemoth to slash at its exposed flesh with the claws, using the corpse of a soldier as a springboard to launch herself into the air, twisting her body as she flew to slash through a briefly exposed forearm and bring forth a rain of blood.

Green blood, Kali noted with horror.

Few creatures that had ever stalked the peninsula had green blood, and there was only one that she knew of that was this size, and it had been extinct as long as the Old Races, primarily because it had been *created* by one of the Old Races and used as their pet. *Gods*, she thought, could that be what they were dealing with here – an elven juggennath? Had it somehow survived here in the Sardenne for all of those countless years? The juggennath was a relentless, all-but-indestructable killing machine without emotion or mercy, and it absolutely would not stop in its efforts to crush them beneath it. They had to get out of here and right now.

It was easier said than done and Kali had difficulty reaching those she needed to warn.

The wound inflicted by Gabriella seemed to have opened an artery in the giant's arm – serious but not serious enough, apparently, to slow the bastard down – and as it swept back and forth once more, its blood soaked the vegetation and defending ranks, obfuscating and adding to the chaos and carnage unfolding before her eyes. DeZantez wasn't to have known but one of the more unpleasant aspects of juggennath blood was its corrosive nature, burning and mutilating those it struck. Kali could do little to help those caught in the heat of battle, but grabbed those she could and flung them towards cover. She shrank back from a soldier who wheeled on her, clutching his face, smoke pouring from his helmet as he collapsed to his knees.

"'Liam!" Kali cried, "DeZantez, Freel!"

No response came and, having rescued all those she could, Kali leapt into the fray herself, aware of how pitiful her gutting knife was. All she could hear was the shattering of limbs, the clatter of blades and arrows. But despite all these efforts, there was no respite in the assault at all.

A cry of frustration drew her attention. Gabriella was attempting to pull an injured Sword out of harm's way, and was too preoccupied to notice the giant hand swinging towards her. In the instant before it struck, however, she saw Kali racing to help her, and for the briefest of moments their eyes locked.

Thanks for trying, DeZantez's expression seemed to say.

Kali felt each impact of her feet as they thudded onto the forest floor, her legs dragging beneath her, bringing her to a skittering halt, and as a cloud of leaves thrust up in her path she could only cry out and look on in horror at what unfolded.

Gabriella had turned slightly, attempting to throw herself away, but it simply wasn't enough, and the juggernnath's swipe caught her on the side. The cracking of bones echoed in Kali's ears like the shattering of wood. As Gabriella was hurled into the air, Kali heard her armour crumple beneath her surplice. She sailed towards the edge of the glade and slammed into the base of a tree. The Enlightened One's body crumpled, folding into a grotesque distortion of the human form.

At that point, at last, things seemed to quieten. The ground shook as their attacker retreated into the forest, and the frantic sounds of battle were replaced by the wails and pleas of the injured or dying.

Kali looked slowly around. Though there was no sign of Slowhand or Freel. Gabriella remained where she had fallen and Kali moved to try to help her. The last thing she remembered before rough hands bundled her away was Gabriella's face, blood trailing from her mouth, staring at her once more.

But this time the Enlightened One's head lolled to the side and her eyes grew dim.

CHAPTER THIRTEEN

GODSDAMMIT, GODSDAMMIT, GODSDAMMIT!

Kali hunched in the roots of the bajijal tree, hugging her knees, sucking in deep breaths. She ignored the look from Jakub Freel, the only other survivor of the assault and the one who'd pulled her from the melee. Now here they were beneath this overgrown pot plant – hiding, dammit, *hiding* – and while Freel's look was concerned rather than accusing, as far as Kali was concerned it didn't matter an ogur's turd. The Faith enforcer had enlisted her to help him sort out this whole mess and instead she'd managed to turn it into even more of a mess, and people were dead as a result. There was no two ways about it. Freel had put his trust in her and she'd farked up badly.

Pits, she had been *stupid*. Fitch, Gabriella and, gods knew, even Slowhand. How many had died in the last hour? How many more lay maimed in the undergrowth, never to be found again or, worse, found by something they couldn't imagine in their darkest nightmares? Gods, she had become embroiled in this whole affair because, for just a while, she had wanted to forget about how she'd endangered the lives of Dolorosa, Aldrededor and the rest, and now she hadn't just endangered lives but *ended* them. Oh yeah, 'stupid' was the word. Stupid to expose the uninitiated to the Sardenne. Stupid to have become self-obsessed and let her guard down. Stupid to have thought she could even start to second guess an elven psychopath who had been preparing for these moments since the towering trees about her were striplings.

"Your friend the archer said there is usually a moment like this." Jakub Freel said.

"What?" Kali asked, without much interest.

"Crisis. Doubt. A stage in every one of your adventures when you feel you have failed and let down all who placed trust in you. A moment when you freeze, impotent, scared, feeling like a lost little girl..."

Kali flinched, Freel's words hitting close to home, but looked up indignantly.

"Slowhand's been *talking* about me?"

"I asked him whether he thought you were truly capable of doing this. He answered."

Kali bridled. "You sought me out. I guess you must think so."

"Oh, I do. But it isn't what I think – it's what your *friends* think."

"Slowhand might be dead, for all I know. Does it matter anymore what he thinks?"

"I think so. Especially when he says that *after* moments like these you invariably pick yourself up, dust yourself down and... make it up as you go along."

"Make it up as I go along," Kali repeated, looking to the skies. "Not a phrase that inspires much confidence today, is it?"

"Maybe not. But doing so, I am told you almost always succeed." Freel sighed. "Tell me, Miss Hooper, are you going to make a liar out of your friend?"

Kali stared at him. *What is it about this man?* She wondered. She'd seen from the start how different he was to Konstantin Munch, but it was more than just the way in which he approached the job he'd inherited. There was a confidence about him, a way with words, a bearing that made him difficult to dismiss. In a way she wasn't surprised that Slowhand had opened up the way he had.

"Are you playing mind games with me?"

"Is it working?"

Kali bit her lip. Things so far had gone badly against plan, but there were always other possibilities that might yet succeed, and didn't she owe it to the dead to see if they did?

"Freel, do you truly understand what we're up against? Things could get ugly."

"Miss Hooper, 'ugly' is my middle name."

Kali laughed, despite herself. "That sounds just like something Slowhand would say."

"Maybe he and I are more alike than you think."

"Opposite sides of the same coin?"

"Precisely."

Kali raised her eyes to Freel's, half expecting to see a smile. But if there had been one, it had already faded. Her gaze returned to the enforcer's hand, and she drew in a deep, shuddering breath, and then slapped her palm solidly into his, allowing herself to be hauled to her feet.

"For Slowhand," she said.

Kali and Freel were no sooner upright than they froze again. While they had been talking, a number of shapes had detached from the roots around them, Kali didn't need to hear the dry cracking of their joints to recognise some of the forest's nastier progeny. Her heart lurched as the stick-like predators unfolded, drawing themselves up to their full height, and the cracking came, like the breaking of baby's bones, from six of them in all.

"What in the name of the Lord...?" Freel breathed.

"They're called brackan," Kali said. "They're tough, fast and –"

Kali didn't finish. Three of the brackan hurled themselves at her and three at Freel, though one was instantly decapitated by his chain whip. As its body flailed blindly in the confines of the bajijal roots, the enforcer yelled at Kali to duck and spun in a full circle, scything over Kali's head and slicing two more of the brackan in half. The remaining brackan slammed into the pair of them, flattening them to the ground. Kali and Freel struggled beneath the creatures, rolling from side to side to dodge their sharp, pointed, jabbing limbs, and trying to ignore the fact that the brackan Freel had already incapacitated were even now splintering and regrowing.

"You were trying to say?" Freel growled.

"A pain in the arse," Kali growled back. She stabbed at her attacker with her gutting knife.

"Not much help," Freel went on. He gasped in pain as the brackan broke through his defence, gouging a thick red runnel down his cheek. "They must have a weakness!"

"Oh, they do, they do," Kali gasped. "Unfortunately, we're a little out of –"

"Fire?" A voice said.

Two flaming arrows thudded into the backs of the brackan and suddenly the things rolled over, desperately defending. Not that it did much good, their panicked flailing setting fire to the others in turn, transforming all of them into thrashing torches. Kali and Freel booted the brackan off them and backed out of the bajijal roots, soot-streaked but otherwise unharmed. Their weapons remained cautiously trained but the brackan began to break apart, collapsing into a pile of burning wood. Kali and Freel watched as a dishevelled, tall, blond figure walked to the fire's side, sat, and casually began to roast a chunk of meat skewered on the end of a dagger.

"Hells of a morning," Killiam Slowhand said.

"Nice shots," Kali responded. "Is that *breakfast*?"

"Mmm. How you doing, Hooper?" As an afterthought, he added, "Freel."

Jakub Freel waved away the offer of a piece of meat which Kali then took and devoured.

"You two don't seem particularly shocked to see each other," he commented.

"Oh, you'd be surprised how we keep popping up together."

Freel's expression became more serious. "Other survivors?"

Slowhand looked up, swallowed, and shook his head slowly. The gesture might have seemed casual but there was pain in the archer's expression.

"Guess it's time for Plan B, huh?" Slowhand said.

"Plan B," Kali said. "The three of us finish the job ourselves."

She stared up through the dense forest canopy, which, while it defeated most attempts by daylight to brighten the murk, could not fully obscure the brilliance of the pillar of souls as it lanced into the sky.

"We're close enough to the necropolis to make it without portals now," Freel observed. "But we still have a journey ahead of us."

Slowhand stood and snuffed the remains of the brackan with his boot. "Then the sooner we get started..."

They moved on into the forest, trying not to think of the dead they were leaving behind. For some hours they worked their way through the treacherous terrain, which grew still denser as they neared the necropolis. The vegetation was changing, from the vines and sub-tropical plants Kali associated with the Sardenne to thick patches of dry scrub and coarse, thorny bushes. They felt wrong somehow, tainted, and the further they moved, the more hostile the plants became, until at last there was little doubt that they formed a defensive barrier around Bel'A'Gon'Shri, likely conjured by Redigor himself. As Kali and the others hacked their way through she reflected that the Pale Lord had missed at least one trick by not infusing the vicious barbs with poison. Still, knowing that bastard, she supposed there was time yet.

Kali approached Slowhand and spoke quietly.

"What were you doing, talking about me to Freel?"

Slowhand looked surprised. In truth – considering what had happened on the train and all – he wasn't really sure.

"What? Hey, it was a trek, Hooper, and you and Dez were busy with girly talk."

"*Girly talk?*"

Slowhand nodded. "Nothing wrong with that. Nice to see you making a friend." He paused, smile fading. "Kal, I'm sorry she didn't make it."

"Me, too. Don't change the subject."

"What is the problem? I'm willing to bet you talk about me, don't you? Don't you?"

"Actually, no. What would I tell people? About the collection of underknicks pinned to your bedroom ceiling? Or how a girl would be lucky to get through a first date without your clothes falling off?"

"Hey, I took the underknicks down, didn't I?"

"*Pshyeah*. And then kept them labelled in a drawer. How *was* Luci Lastic, by the way? Or Nikola Start? Those *were* their names, ri –"

Slowhand suddenly slapped his palm over Kali's mouth, and her eyes widened in shock and rage. She was about to pull free, demand to know why it was she couldn't get a *full farking sentence* out today, when the archer nodded between thorn bushes, at a feral shape moving towards them fast.

Breaking apart, he and Kali readied bow and knife while Freel dashed into cover, his whip to hand.

A second passed and something wild-eyed, torn and filthy burst into view. But rather than some slavering denizen of the Sardenne, it was human. Garbed in the shredded remnants of a green robe and considerably older than any of their party, however, he wasn't one of their own.

The man collapsed at Kali's feet. "Help me. Lord of All, help me, please."

"Where the hells did you come from?" Freel breathed.

"The Lord... the Pale Lord," the man gasped, pointing back through the thorns.

"Easy," Kali said, kneeling. "You've come from the Pale Lord?"

The man nodded, taking slugs of water from a skin Kali handed him. As he drank, Freel studied him warily. The man was terrified, but beneath the dirt and sweat he was well-groomed. He did not belong in the Sardenne.

"Be careful," Freel suggested. "This could be Redigor's doing."

"No, wait a minute, I know this guy," Slowhand said. "We've met before."

"Before?" Freel queried.

"It doesn't matter where."

"*Yes, it does.*"

"Fine. In court, if you must know. He gaoled me for a longnight for... well, let's just say I know what colour sheets cover a lot of beds in Kroog-Martra." He stared at Kali. "And before you say a word, Hooper, it was a bet and I had no *time* to collect their underknicks, okay?"

Kali gave Slowhand a weary shake of the head. "This is the magistrate of Kroog-Martra?"

"Yeah. A magistrate in the middle of the Sardenne. A fat lot of use he's going to be."

"'Liam, hang on. If you're right, this guy is one of the twelve taken for Redigor's High Council. He might know something about what we can expect at Bel'A'Gon'Shri." Kali took the magistrate by his shoulders, forcing him to look at her. "How and why are you here? Did you escape? Did you escape the necropolis?"

"Kroog-Martra was attacked. By things hardly alive. Something came. A coach as black as night. Brought me to that place. Oh, Lord of All, that *place*..."

"Hey, *m'lud!*" Slowhand pressed. "The lady knows that, okay? You maybe wanna cut the pie and get to the meat?"

"In the depths," the magistrate went on. "Tombs. Vast, cold tombs. There they lie, still. The elves." He struggled in Kali's grip, remembering, suddenly desperate to get away. "But they're coming back. Lord of All, they're coming back!"

Freel strode to the magistrate and gripped him by the head. "*How did you escape?*"

"The Anointed Lord," the magistrate said, flinching. "She was taken with myself, the others. The Pale Lord took something from us, everything seemed like a dream, a nightmare. But the Anointed Lord she fought him... she was defiant... she was *strong*."

"Makennon escaped with you?" Kali asked.

"Makennon?" The magistrate repeated, and shook his head. "No, no. But while the Pale Lord fought to bring her under his control, I felt his magic weaken. Not much... not much at all... but enough for me to run, to flee the Chapel of Screams."

"The Chapel of *Screams*?" Slowhand repeated "Oh, the day just keeps getting better and better."

Kali sighed, looked up at Freel. "I think he's telling the truth."

Freel nodded. "The Chapel of Screams sounds like where the ritual is going to take place."

"The ritual," the magistrate said. "Yes, yes, the ritu –"

He stopped abruptly, eyes widening with fear. The forest had begun to resonate with a slow, bass tolling.

"The ritual begins," the magistrate said. "The Time of the Bell."

"Time of the Bell?"

"The *summoning*."

Freel snapped Kali a look. "Does that mean we're too late?"

Kali bit her lip. "I doubt it," she said, although in truth she wasn't really sure.

The magistrate had said *it begins*, and if her calculations were correct they had some hours yet, so likely the Bell was only the start of a ritual they should yet be able to stop. She was about to question the magistrate further when he at last managed to break from their grip and run. Slowhand leapt after him, but halted as he saw countless soul-stripped heading towards him. Slowhand, Kali and Freel stared at the approaching horde open-mouthed, as they passed through the thorns – and through *them*, too – insubstantial and translucent, leaving them with a feeling that somebody had walked over their graves.

"What's happening to them?" Freel asked. "They're like ghosts."

Kali had wondered how Redigor intended to bring the soul-stripped to Bel'A'Gon'Shri across the sprawl of the Sardenne. And now that she knew, she didn't like it one bit.

"He's using a different plane of existence to phase them to the necropolis," she said.

"But if he has the power to do that, with such numbers?" Freel calculated. He did not need to voice the next question for Kali to answer.

"Once he brings his people back, he can send them anywhere, right across the peninsula."

Freel kicked a tree-root. "The bastard's one step ahead of us all the time! Tricked us into forming a line at the Sardenne. And for nothing. Miramas, Volonne, Andon, Fayence, and Vos beyond – they're all but defenceless. We'll never make it back in time."

"Then we'd better make sure we get to Redigor in time," Kali said.

Slowhand and Freel stared as she stepped into the stream of spectral figures and, absorbed by the mist-like cloud wreathing the figures, began to walk amongst them.

"Hooper, what the hells are you doing?"

"Going along for the ride. Can you think of a better way of getting where we want to go?"

Freel smiled and joined her. "This, I take it, is the 'making things up as you go along'?"

"Aha. But be careful. We'll be in direct contact with the Pale Lord and he could sense us, so try to empty your mind."

The pair concentrated while Slowhand, too, stepped into the stream.

"Empty your mind, 'Liam."

"Done."

"What?"

"Mind. Empty. Done it."

"Are you taking the pits?"

"Hooper, I'm *ready*, okay. Now are we doing this thing or not?"

They did the thing, now reduced to phantasms, staring at each other in wonder as they moved. Whole swathes of the Sardenne, including the thorn barrier, passed in instant blur as they, along with all the soul-stripped who had no choice in the matter, were drawn ever closer to Bel'A'Gon'Shri.

Redigor's enchantment did not take them right to the necropolis's door, however, but to a deep, creeper-lined gorge on the approach to it, and there the soul-stripped began to return to corporeality. As they did, some turned to stare curiously at Kali, Slowhand and Freel.

"Redigor's getting his eyes back," Kali warned.

"Then it's time to break ranks," Freel said.

Kali and Slowhand trailed the Faith enforcer as he walked to the side of the gorge and took cover behind a dense wall of creeper. From there, the three of them watched the soul-stripped file in, emerging only when all of them had finally passed by. Then, after waiting a few more seconds, they followed some distance behind.

"Oh, crap," Slowhand said.

Freel stared. "Lord of All."

Carved out of the gorge's end, soaring above them, was the entrance to Bel'A'Gon'Shri. A threshold of utter blackness punctuated only by the occasional circling, cawing shrike. It wasn't the entrance itself that was disturbing but what surrounded it. Angled away from her, rising up on either side of the blackness to the twin horns tolling the Time of the Bell, great rock ramparts had been sculpted into a grotesque statuary which, decrepit and strewn with creepers, loomed malevolently over everything below. Great, winged creatures – the hags Kali had seen in Fayence – thrust stone claws at the world, while sweeping carvings of the black coaches that had come for Makennon and the others raced around and between their malformed limbs. Most unnerving were the screaming faces that covered every remaining space on the ramparts, which whispered as the wind blew past them, murmuring half-heard warnings not to approach, to leave this place while they still could.

"Bloody hells," Kali said at last.

"Not exactly welcoming, is it?" Freel added.

"It's going to be less welcoming in a second, if we don't move it." Slowhand nodded towards the top of the threshold.

While the three of them had been examining the necropolis, the ranks of soul-stripped had continued to file towards it, *into it*, and now the very last of them were being absorbed by the blackness within. The entrance began to seal, a mountainous stone slab rumbling slowly down. The three of them were still some two hundred yards away from it.

"Shit!" Kali cried, and began to run, Slowhand and Freel hot on her heels.

Negotiating the tangled floor of the gorge at speed was not easy, however, and the entrance was half closed before they had covered a third of the distance.

Kali continued to pound along the gorge, shouting to Slowhand and Freel to *move, move, move!* The two men were already slowing behind her. Kali struggled for a few more steps before she, too, was forced to accept that the attempt was hopeless, and she roared in frustration. As the last of the soul-stripped vanished, the slab closed with a rumble of ground-shaking, deafening finality. She pounded on the door as the others caught up.

"Hooper, it's useless..." Slowhand said.

Kali continued to pound, staring up at and around the slab as she did. "Dammit, I will not be stopped now!"

"Miss Hooper, I fear the archer is correct."

"No! There's a way. There has to be a way."

Slowhand slumped with his back to the slab. "Well, we're open to suggestions..."

Kali stared at him, hot, angry, and breathing hard. She was about to bite his head off when she suddenly turned away from the slab, staring back down the gorge, toward the forest.

She began to stomp off, Slowhand giving her a curious glance.

"Hooper, where the hells are you going?"

"Redigor's not going to stop me now," Kali reiterated. "You two stay here, do what you can."

"And you?" Slowhand shouted after her.

"Plan C!"

"Which is?"

"We have a locked door, right?" Kali yelled. "Then what we need is a key!"

CHAPTER FOURTEEN

SLOWHAND AND FREEL watched Kali work her way back down the gorge and into the undergrowth with a mixture of puzzlement and concern. The archer thought he caught sight of her a few minutes later – of all things, *climbing trees* – but he couldn't be certain and his attention was caught by Freel, anyway. The Faith enforcer had been studying the huge, statue-covered frame of the slab, apparently working out a way to climb the incline. Now he seemed to have decided where to start and lashed his whip upwards so that it wrapped around one of the lower statues, then, with a grunt, began to pull himself up towards it.

"Where the hells are you going?" Slowhand said.

"Doing what I can. Looking for another way in."

"Hooper will get us in there, Freel. Trust me."

"I believe she will *try*. But in all truth this whole operation has been a disaster so far, though through no fault of your Miss Hooper. And now she's out in the Sardenne, alone. Face it, archer, there's no guarantee she'll be back."

"*She'll be back*. She always comes back."

"And if she doesn't come back this time? Like Jenna didn't?"

The question completely threw Slowhand. "I –"

"I knew Jenna had been assigned to the Drakengrats," Freel said. "And I didn't know why, or for how long. But you sense, somehow, when it's been long enough, and then you start to wonder. I wondered, in fact, until Makennon summoned me, with news. The news came from the one survivor..."

"Freel..."

"You love her, don't you?"

Slowhand hesitated, momentarily unsure whether Freel meant Jenna or Kali, until he realised that he'd spoken in the present tense.

What had brought about these sudden revelations, he wasn't sure, nor why he was about to again be so candid with the man.

Was it because of what had happened to Jenna at *his* hands? Did he feel the need to justify himself, giving Freel the full picture of the circumstances, and his place in them, that had brought about his sister's – and Freel's wife's – death?

"Sometimes I love her. And sometimes she annoys the fark out of me. And sometimes I wonder whether I'm in way out of my depth. I'd follow her anywhere and do anything for her but one thing's for sure – she isn't the innocent tavern owner and sometime adventurer she was when we first met. Something's *happening*, Freel, but whatever it is, she won't let me anywhere near it."

Freel nodded. He lashed his whip around a second statue now, and began to haul himself up. "You coming?"

Slowhand looked back down the gorge, but if he had indeed seen Kali she was now gone. He nodded and, without hesitation, unslung Suresight, attached one of his whizzlines, and fired it towards a statue above Freel. A second later he had hoisted himself to a position where he waited for the enforcer to catch up.

"Useful toy," Freel commented. "But this isn't some kind of competition..."

"I know. I'm just trying to get the job done."

Now that they had bypassed the initial lip of the slab's frame, where the statuary was sparser, there was no need to continue using the whip or Suresight, and the pair were able to pull themselves manually from one statue to the other. The going was slow. Some of the grotesque figures were unstable in their settings, and needed to be negotiated with the utmost care. When, finally, they reached the halfway point of the incline, the men paused, breathless and sweating.

"How did you meet?" Freel asked. "You and Miss Hooper."

Despite himself, Slowhand smiled. "On the Sarcre Islands. I'd bought passage with a pilot named Silus. He, in turn, had been hired to pick up a female passenger from one of the outlying islets – but I don't think he knew what he was going to get. Hooper came running at us out of the jungle, down the beach, dropping ancient artefacts as she ran, she was trying to carry so many. She yelled at us to rig for top knots, and a mob of angry natives poured out of the jungle after her. All of a sudden about a thousand fire arrows came arcing through the sky and Silus had no choice but to get the boat out of there. I was pitched overboard and ended up on the beach, with Hooper, surrounded by the natives. Turned out what she'd thought was an Old Race site was actually a temple to their fertility god... Rumpo-Pumpo, or something." Slowhand paused and shrugged in the manner of someone convinced the name couldn't be quite right. "Hooper was new to the game, then."

"You obviously lived to tell the tale."

"Just. The two of us ended up stripped and dumped in a pot to be blanched for the native's supper, jammed together thigh to thigh. Only got out when I told them we had the hic."

"That would do it. You actually sound as if you enjoyed yourself."

"Ohhhh, yes. Took Hooper back a year or two later when the natives had started dabbling in tourism. Room with a hot tub. Wasn't my fault the native eldress recognised us. Hooper almost got stuffed and I... well, I was cursed."

"Cursed how?"

"Something about me always being dressed for dinner. Never could work it out myself."

Freel looked at him sceptically. He'd read the report of the number of times Slowhand had been arrested for losing his clothes, so it was either an astounding set of coincidences or the man was in complete and utter denial.

"Let's move on," Freel said.

He grabbed the base of the next statue and heaved himself upward. Slowhand was about to follow when, with a crack, the statue broke away from its base. Freel tried to throw himself free but was snagged in the statue's hands and found himself tipping over the edge of the buttress. The statue dropped another foot with a sharp jerk and the remainder of its base began to crumble. Slowhand steadied himself and thrust out a hand but couldn't reach.

"If you're thinking of making a rope out of your clothes, don't," Freel growled through gritted teeth. "I'd rather take the fall."

Slowhand studied the crumbling statue. "Fall, then."

Freel snapped a look upward, glaring at him. And the statue jerked again.

Slowhand's jaw pulsed. "*Fall.*"

A strange expression crossed the enforcer's face – disappointment, perhaps? – but there was no time to work it out as the statue came free of its base and began to fall, Freel still trapped in its grip.

The moment it did, Slowhand snatched Suresight from his back, primed an arrow and aimed it at his falling companion. But he didn't fire. Not yet. Instead he waited while the falling statue impacted with the incline of the entrance slab, breaking apart. His eyes narrowed, picking out Freel's flailing form amid the cloud of debris. Suresight moved infinitesimally but, again, Slowhand did not release his arrow until his aim was true.

The arrow flew through the coils of chain whip at Freel's waist, and ricocheted off the entrance slab beneath to wrap around the neck of one of the statues further below. Freel came to a sudden stop, bouncing on Slowhand's rope, and looked up at the archer calmly securing its other end. He blew out a relieved breath.

"I thought you were..."

"I know what you thought," Slowhand said. The archer climbed back down a number of statues and thrust out a hand, which Freel grabbed.

The remainder of the climb was laborious but uneventful, and at last Slowhand and Freel pulled themselves up onto the necropolis roof. A slight mist curled on its lip. They walked forward between the towers of the Time of the Bell, mouths agape at the pandemonium beyond.

Both men swallowed. On reaching the roof, they had, of course, expected to see the pillar of souls, for it was now originating from beneath them, but neither had given much thought as to how it might be rising from Bel'A'Gon'Shri. Through some kind of dome, maybe, or perhaps even just a channel in the rooftop. But ahead of them there *was* no rooftop. They faced a surreal, broken landscape that seemed half part of reality and half not. It looked as if the entire top of that part of the necropolis had exploded upward and, moments after detonation, frozen, component parts suspended in a slow-motion limbo. A gently rotating jumble of bricks, lintels and stones dangling the moss and detritus of ages, starkly illuminated by the blazing pillar.

The pillar itself was a screaming, roaring, constantly whirling maelstrom of ghostly forms and presences, these once human manifestations, thousands of them, writhed and churned about each other, even tore at each other, as they sought release. Stripped from their bodies as they had been, drawn inexorably into this insane captivity, it must have seemed to them that they had been condemned to the hells themselves. As Slowhand and Freel moved closer, they found themselves recoiling as the desperate souls tried to punch through the surface of the maelstrom – a horrifically distended eye here, a screaming mouth there, half a face or a spasming, clutching hand on the end of an arm made of spectral bone. Nor were these horrors occurring only before them. The pillar of souls was so vast that the victims passed out of sight in all directions. They craned their necks to try and see the distant top of the pillar stretching out to Kerberos.

"Not something you come across every day," Slowhand shouted.

"True," Jakub Freel agreed. His jawline throbbed as he regarded the morass with a steely gaze. "The Pale Lord will answer for this."

"Come on. There might be some way we can get down into the necropolis."

The two men picked their way onto the floating masonry at the pillar's periphery, taking care to avoid stones whose orbit took them too close, lest the grasping maelstrom pull them in. Hopping slowly from stone to stone, they caught glimpses of the necropolis' interior between the jumble of tumbling rubble. Hair and clothes whipping about them, they found themselves a relatively stable platform and stared down onto a floor they guessed was a few hundred yards in from the necropolis' main entrance. At the base of the pillar of souls, the chamber could only be one thing.

The Chapel of Screams.

Their position, in truth, did them little good. Despite Slowhand's best attempts to find an anchor for a whizzline, there was no way down. All the pair could do for now was reconnoitre from here and then look for another route.

The Chapel of Screams was blood-red. Arranged around a central aisle were tombs, six to the left, six to the right, and before each but one stood a rigid figure, but who these figures were was impossible to tell. At the end of the aisle, the Chapel widened into a huge circular chamber, and a raised stone platform overlaid with a complex magical circle. This was the base of the pillar of souls, and its screaming captives, for the most part, obscured it. All that could be made out with certainty was that the patterns were not carved, because they pulsed and shifted occasionally, darting about the circle like angry snakes.

Or perhaps threads. Black threads.

Standing before the platform, dwarfed by the pillar of souls, were two more figures, one as rigid as those by the tombs, the other, much taller and with a mane of flowing hair, thrusting his hands high into the air, as if summoning the gods themselves.

Bastian Redigor. The Pale Lord.

Slowhand shifted towards the edge of the platform they stood on, and Freel held him back.

"What are you doing? We already decided there's no way down."

"I'm not going down," Slowhand said, pulling Suresight from his back. "I'm going to end this thing right now."

Freel stared at the distant figure of the Pale Lord. "In these conditions? Impossible."

"Yeah?"

Slowhand notched an arrow and aimed directly at Redigor's forehead, right between the eyes. The shot wasn't impossible, but it was challenging, even for him. There were a number of factors he had to compensate for – the height, the movement of the platform beneath him, the disturbance from the pillar of souls – but doing so was just a matter of patience. Unfortunately, patience wasn't only a virtue, it was time-consuming, and by the time Slowhand had locked his aim, the platform beneath him had begun to move again, rotating about the pillar of souls.

It became suddenly like finding a target through a kaleidoscope.

Slowhand narrowed his eyes, unfazed, and loosed his arrow. The tip raced unerringly towards the Pale Lord and would, a second later, have punched directly into his brain – but the arrow stopped dead in the air, an inch from his face, and dropped to the floor. The Pale Lord looked up, directly at Slowhand, smiled, his mouth widening into a razor-toothed maw.

"We're out of here, now," Freel said, and pulled Slowhand up by the shoulder. He bundled him across the floating stepping stones.

"Dammit, Freel. I can take another shot."

"To what end, Slowhand? You saw what happened."

"I'm quicker than he is – I'll get an arrow through!"

"Really? How exactly? By making it up as you go along?"

"What the hells is that supposed to mean?"

Freel span to face him. "That sometimes you have to think about things. Maybe if you'd thought about things a bit more at the Crucible you could have avoided a confrontation. And maybe my wife might still be alive."

Slowhand stared at him. *Is this it?* He wondered. *Is this when it all finally boils over?*

"Jenna intended to blow us out of the sky," he said, more calmly than he felt. "And without that ship, the k'nid would have obliterated the peninsula."

"The Faith would have found a way to combat them. *I* would have found a way."

"Are you *sure* about that, Jakub? It was, after all, your wife – my *sister* – who could have avoided a confrontation. But that doesn't seem to have occurred to you, does it – it never does in the Final Filth."

Freel's grip tightened about the stock of his whip but he made no move.

"Face it, Jakub. Jenna became a puppet. The Faith's puppet. *Your* puppet."

Freel roared, raced at him, and the archer was winded as the enforcer piled into his stomach and threw the two of them back over the floating stones.

Slowhand found himself with his head only yards from the pillar of souls, but his greater concern was Freel's hands, slowly tightening about his throat. For a second the two men stared at each other, faces red and taut with strain, before Slowhand found enough strength to growl, "Is this it, then? Where you kill me?"

"Kill you?"

"Like on the train? What stopped you, Freel? That DeZantez would be a witness? Or was it just what it felt like – some kind of warning, a game?"

"What the hells are you talking about?"

"The shove in the back? The almost but not quite death on the tracks? The whip?"

Freel's eyes flickered over him, as if suddenly shocked to find someone in such a helpless position beneath him and he snatched his hands away. He rolled onto his back and snorted. "I guess working together finally got to us both. I wasn't trying to kill you, you fool! That cable you cut came lashing back, almost cut you in half. I was pushing you out of the way."

"Bullshit."

"Why on Twilight would I want to kill you? I helped save you from Fitch, remember? Even went so far as to steer him away, told him you were mine."

"And just why would you do that?"

Fitch laughed, rough and guttural.

"Has it ever occurred to you that we are, in fact, brothers-in-law, you and I? That out of all the people on this godsforsaken world we are the only ones with something unique in common? Someone we loved?"

"Jenna," Slowhand said. "No... no, it hadn't." He shifted uneasily. "Even so, I find it hard to believe that an agent of the Final Faith would let family get in the way of removing a thorn in their side."

Freel paused. "Let me ask you something. Were you to work in a tavern, would that make you a drunk? If you yanked teeth for a living, would you necessarily like causing pain?"

"I've known a few in both cases. What's your point?"

"Simply put? That the job doesn't always make the man."

"You work for the Filth. You're their chief enforcer, for fark's sake. I'd say that was more vocation than job, Jakub."

"So much so that I almost never pray."

"Come on. I'd have thought that was mandatory."

Freel shrugged. "Abstinence is a privilege of the position."

"Wait a minute," Slowhand said. "Are you telling me that while you're an agent of the Faith, you're not *of* the Faith?"

"What can I say? I prefer a choice of gods myself."

Slowhand blew out a breath. "Oh, this day is just full of surprises. Then *why*, Freel? Why do what you do?"

"Let's just say that certain... factions in Allantia have growing concerns about the Faith's ultimate mission here on the mainland, because Allantia is not so very far away. And that the demise of Konstantin Munch provided them with an opportunity to place one of their own in a position of some seniority – and perhaps influence, if and when needed. Thank you for creating the vacancy, by the way."

"You're a spy."

"More of an observer."

Slowhand said nothing for a second.

"Jenna. Did she know?" He asked at last.

Freel shook his head. "I couldn't take the chance that she'd reveal what she knew under Fitch's influence. But I like to think that the man she fell in love with was the real me."

"I always thought..."

"What? That our marriage was a forced one? Decreed by Makennon and orchestrated by Fitch? No, Slowhand, we loved each other. And she, in turn, loved you and me both."

"Then why in the hells didn't you get her out of there?"

Freel smiled, though it was tinged with sadness. "I had been making plans for her removal after the Drakengrats. A disappearance – a convenient death – during a mission arranged by me. She would have been free."

Slowhand looked up at the enforcer.

"Gods, I'm sorry."

"Don't be. You did what you had to."

Finally, Slowhand heaved himself to his feet. "The tension of these last few days. From you. It struck me as pretty genuine."

"Oh, it was. I didn't know you, archer – as you didn't know me – but I knew your reputation. Since then I've learned more about the man you are. I needed to be sure that this, all of it, including Jenna's death, was more than a *game* to you."

"Oh, it's no game," Slowhand said. "Not any more."

Freel regarded him steadily. "So... what say we get on with it?"

"What say we do."

Slowhand held out a hand, and the enforcer took it.

"Tell me one thing," Slowhand said. "Why since your first question to me have I been unable to keep my mouth shut?"

"Ah, that," Freel said. He ran his hand down his squallcoat. "This whole thing is stitched together with mumbleweed."

"Mumbleweed?"

Freel leaned in almost conspiratorially. "I'd have thought you'd have come across it in your travels. It relaxes people's inhibitions. Very handy when you're a spy."

The two men turned, distracted by a noise from the forest. They leapt from the stones and returned to the roof's edge. Something big was approaching through the trees, and approaching fast, and it made even the temple roof pound like a drum skin beneath their feet.

Freel looked at Slowhand.

Slowhand looked at Freel.

The two men turned and ran, almost falling over themselves in their efforts to shield the other and push him away, and they cried out in unison.

"*Ohhhhhh, shiiiiiiiiiiiiiit...*"

CHAPTER FIFTEEN

KALI GRUNTED, PUSHING her boot against the tree trunk as she pulled the vine taut and knotted it in place. It was the fourth time she had carried out such an operation, and the fourth time she wondered just what it was she was getting herself into. As usual, she decided her plan didn't bear too much thinking about.

She slapped the vine to test its tension, and dropped from the tree and moved on. More coils of the stuff were slung over her shoulders, and they would all be used. For once in her life she didn't resent the number of times she had needed to bail Red, her adoptive father, out of trouble – both financial and physical – now that the time she had spent with the old poacher was at last coming in useful. He had a way with traps, did old Red.

Kali ducked as a flock of shrikes burst from the thick branches above, but ignored them. The wildlife had returned to the forest since she, Slowhand and Freel had reached the necropolis, which was an added complication, but she frankly didn't have the time to be bothered with it. It had taken some effort to renegotiate the thorn barrier. If she had to hide every time she had a close encounter with the forest's denizens the Pale Lord's plan would be done and dusted before she got anywhere. Even so, she wasn't stupid, and had taken added precautions to conceal herself from the creatures around her. Having decided that floprat render alone might not be enough to confuse predators' senses, she had trapped and butchered a yazuk, stripping the flesh from the creature and draping it about her like a cloak.

It stank to the pits but, once more, thank you Red.

Amidst the noises and movement of the forest were the sudden, horrified screams of soldiers and mages who had survived the juggennath assault. She had no time for them either, but each time she heard them she closed her eyes and bit her lip. They may have been why she had made it so far without being attacked but she could not be grateful for them. There was nothing she could for them other than to will them not to run, to panic, to stay still, to *pray*, but she knew, ultimately, it would do no good. If she were in their place in this godsforsaken hellshole wouldn't she do the same?

A young, sweating Sword suddenly crashed through the undergrowth before her, falling to his knees on the forest floor. He spotted Kali and stared at her imploringly, shouting "Help me! Help me!" but it was already too late. The tendrils coiled about his ankles snapped him back in an instant. The sounds of his thrashing struggle – and screams – continued for several seconds before they were abruptly silenced by a gelatinous *gloop*.

Kali kept moving, not even looking back, and chose another tree.

Once more she lashed vines about its trunk, stretching their length in a tense line to another opposite, where she climbed and lashed them tightly again. She repeated the procedure two more times, with trees further ahead and hundreds of yards apart, and at last seemed satisfied that all she could do with the vines had been done.

Girl, she thought, *you've taken risks before but this time you've got to be mad.*

Kali negotiated her way further into the forest, fighting a growing sense of isolation and wishing she had Horse by her side. The area she was entering was where she and the first Horse had almost given up on their search for the Spiral. Yes, there was the acrid stench of the Spiral's ruins and there was the mix of odours – metallic, biological, faecal – that meant the juggennath was still nearby. She had successfully made her way back to its stomping ground.

Stomping ground. Never was a phrase more appropriate, because Kali felt her prey before she saw it, vibrations in the forest floor that resonated in her bones.

Kali moved forward cautiously, weaving her way through the undergrowth. The trees thrashed and snapped back and forth, as if caught in the throes of a violent storm, but the sky above was clear of clouds. Abruptly, the air was split by a series of angry, deafening roars.

She eased her way to a clearing ahead.

Kali had been presuming that the creature that had attacked their party had been a juggennath, she had been calling it a juggennath, and it certainly smelt like she imagined a juggennath should smell, but it was only now, setting eyes fully upon on it that she really appreciated what a juggennath was.

Legend had it that the elves had grown six of these creatures in huge vats. They were unnatural, undying behemoths nurtured of thousands of gallons of offal, sinew, hide and bone, the mashings of huge creatures, individually terrifying, who roamed the peninsula long ago. Elven alchemists had grown them with one purpose – to empty the battlefields of the dwarves they had fought in the oldest of the wars. It was said that the six could reduce a line of ten thousand men to a bloody smear. Armoured in spiked metal plates, shaped over vast anvils, and armed with stone hammers hewn in blocks higher than a man, they were said to be unstoppable, and only by choosing their battlefield cleverly – in a place known as the Hollow Fields – had the dwarves eventually rid the world of their destructive blight. The abyssal caverns of the Fields, lying beneath thin layers of topsoil and roots, had swallowed even the juggennaths whole, and the dwarves had given those caverns a name, too – in dwarven, Yan'Tuk – which in human speak meant something roughly along the lines of 'Up Yours'.

Okay, Kali had never been sure about that last bit. But she liked it.

Clearly, though, one juggennath had survived. The thick, heavy mass that blocked her view was its *legs*. She craned her neck as far back as it would go, past legs the width of redwood trunks and a torso the size of a small hill, to a head and shoulders as high as the treeline, if not above.

The only thing that Kali could think was, *no wonder the dwarves wanted rid of them.*

Well, that was precisely why she was here, wasn't it? But before she made a move she needed to work out a route.

Kali studied the juggennath further. On a colossal scale, the creature resembled the primates of the higher World's Ridge Mountains – the ogur, for example – and was covered almost entirely in hair, muscular arms and legs concealed by the thick and straggly coat. In places jagged sections of rusted and tarnished metal clung to its body, some pieces still bearing the remains of the spikes that had once covered it. They would come in handy. The remains of some of her party were strung and slung about its massive frame, at least thirty men and women bounced lifelessly against the juggennath as it shifted, and whether they were worn for decoration or for food, Kali almost turned away seeing the state they were in.

She had seen what she needed, and was ready. All she had to wait for now was for the juggennath to move again.

It did so, the trees and branches about it thrashing and breaking as a wave of shrikes and razorbeaks circled its head, at least twenty of them taking it in turns to dart at the giant figure as it flailed against their attacks. The giant batted them out of the air but there was no way it could stop them all, and they dived for its flesh, returning with chunks of bloody flesh and matted hair held in their beaks. The juggennath roared in irritation and frustration, the wounds insignificant, but the attacks had clearly been going on for some time – and the reason that they had commenced them was, she believed, the same reason that the rest of the wildlife had emerged from its cover in the forest. For the first time in its impossibly long life, the juggennath had been injured – slashed by Gabriella DeZantez and the Deathclaws – and the great beast that had so far held dominion over them had seemed weak, as they had smelled its blood.

Kali almost felt sorry for the ancient creature, the bemused beast once king of its domain, but there was little she could do to help it. Wouldn't have helped if she could, in fact. She was banking on the distraction to make the next part of her plan easier.

She had to act quickly.

If the juggennath decided to flee its tormentors, went pounding off deeper into the Sardenne, she might never catch it again.

It was time to hitch a ride.

Kali burst from the treeline and raced across the glade. She made it with only a couple of minor scratches into the shadow of the juggennath itself. Only one, particularly persistent brackan tried to take a slice out of her, but with a running twist she managed to manoeuvre it into the path of a hackfire toad and, with a cheery wave, it was goodnight stickface. This done, she threw herself upwards with a grunt, grabbing two fistfuls of the matted hair on the giant's legs. She hauled herself up onto the limb proper and took as firm a purchase as she could, the giant pounding about the glade in its efforts to defend itself, and was flung to the left and the right like a small doll, but she gradually scaled the phenomenal creature. Kali doubted that the giant even recognised her presence.

Kali rose higher and higher, aiding her climb with a couple of somersaults from spike to spike, and at last she found herself on its shoulder, headed for the neck and clung onto the nape as she might cling to an exposed rockface. There, she took a breath.

Before she could move further, Kali found herself snatched from the juggennath's neck by one of its giant hands, swung around to the front of the creature and held before its face. If, that was, it could be called a face. She had never actually considered what a juggennath saw if it shaved in a morning. There was no nose or mouth as such, only a twitching orifice where both should be, and above that a single, bar-shaped eye that stretched almost across its forehead from left to right, giving it a perpetual frown.

"Gods, you're ugly."

Kali struggled in the giant's grip as she stared into its looming eye, and wondered why everything had gone suddenly quiet, the attacking shrikes and razorbeaks gone. Then she realised that the eye, previously a feral brown, had become as white and dull as those of the soul-stripped, so that she felt as if she were held before a cold, snow-filled sky. Whatever intelligence the juggennath possessed – and Kali suspected it wasn't much – seemed to have been replaced by another.

The fist of the juggennath tightened ever so slightly around her.

"Who are you, girl?" A voice boomed. "What are you doing in my forest?"

The voice was arrogant, cold and cruel. Bastian Redigor, it seemed, was introducing himself.

"Hello, Baz," Kali said. "You don't mind being called Baz, I hope?"

"I asked you a question. What do you want?"

"Er, world peace? A cure for the hic? No – how about an all-over tan?"

The fist tightened.

"Okay, okay, just breaking the ice." Kali leaned forward and peered into vast orifice. "Dark and smelly in there, huh?"

"I am not here, stupid child. This beast is but a means of communication."

Kali rolled her eyes and tutted. "Farking hell, I know that, elf. I should have known the Ur'Raney would have no sense of humour."

Redigor laughed. "So you know who I am. Would it surprise you to know that I, in turn, know who you are... Kali Hooper?"

Actually it did, but Kali didn't let it show. Maybe there was something in what Fitch had said about Redigor's gaze being so penetrating it could read minds. She concentrated on keeping her true thoughts – and plans – to herself.

"I see the little girl, wide-eyed with stories that I would come for you," Redigor went on. "I sense the fear, the desire to run and curl beneath the bed..."

"Forget it, Redigor. I wasn't afraid then, I'm not afraid now."

"I would not say that. I can feel your sweat leaking onto this creature's pores."

"You sure it's my sweat?" Redigor's laughter was a rumble this time.

"Listen, Puce Lord or whatever your name is, I've been in tighter spots."

"Really?"

The juggennath's grip tightened suddenly, not enough to crush her but enough to squeeze all of the breath from her lungs. She had no doubt that Redigor *could* have crushed her had he wished, but was enjoying playing with her. Knowing his predilections she wouldn't be surprised if the immense fingers of the giant he controlled soon started to peel away her clothes.

"I ask you again," Redigor's disembodied voice said. "What are you doing in my forest?"

"I've come to stop a dirty old man returning his perverted rule to my world."

"Bel'A'Gon'Shri is sealed and the exchange will soon begin. And I hardly think you are in any position to stop it."

"No? You don't know me very well, do you?"

Kali suddenly rammed her gutting knife into the tender flesh of the juggennath's palm and, with a roar of pain, the creature opened its hand. She had gambled on the fact that, even though Redigor was ostensibly in control of the mammoth creature, its reaction to pain would remain instinctive. Of course, she'd hoped that the giant's grip would simply loosen enough to allow her escape from it, and hadn't expected to be dropped.

Time to improvise.

As the juggennath's other hand swept around to swat her from existence, Kali twisted in mid-air, booting herself away from it, and once more found herself heading towards the hairy hide of the beast, somewhere about its midriff. She struck, clung, and began another slow climb.

She didn't want to know what it was she was climbing up and as she ascended the thick, matted hair she instead concentrated on what mattered – that it was getting her where she needed to go. One way or another she had Bastian Redigor by the short and curlies, and when she had finally returned herself to the juggennath's neck she told him so, whispering into the beast's ear, "Redigor, I'm coming."

Kali heaved herself up on top of the living mountain, avoiding its hands. She leaned forward, holding her gutting knife in both hands, and plunged it viciously into the creature's eye. Vitreous humour spurted forth and the creature reacted once more as she had hoped.

Roaring and slapping at the eye, the juggennath staggered forward in the direction from which the pain had come, seeking out the cause and attempting to crush it. There was, of course, nothing there, and Kali had already flipped herself away. She dangled, now, on a length of hair by the left side of the beast's head, and after a few seconds kicked herself around and delivered another blow with her knife, this time to the juggennath's cheek. Again, it roared, turning to identify its new attacker, but once more there was nothing there. As the beast lurched forward, she did a quick calculation, working out that only one more application of the knife would be needed to get the creature to go where she wished it to go, and then she could effectively sit back and enjoy the ride.

Kali returned to its head and this time used the fringe of the beast to drop herself down until she dangled directly in front of its eye. The blinded eye had reverted to a natural state, a sign that Redigor had departed his host, most likely in response to the pain. That suited her needs perfectly. Glancing behind her to double check that she, and more importantly the creature itself, were on the course she wanted, Kali rammed her gutting knife into the eyeball once more.

The creature roared louder than ever, scaring away those of its predators that still remained in the nearby undergrowth, and charged through the forest, swatting its great hands before it as it did, trying to locate and remove its tormentor. Kali, however, was once again, gone, perched now just above the beast's forehead like a driver. From that position she occasionally jabbed her knife into the wrinkled flesh of its brow, reminding it, when needed, of where she wanted it to go. Then the first of the traps she had laid became visible just before its stomping feet, and just before the rampaging beast triggered it, Kali wished herself luck and hung on tight.

The trap caused the beast no pain, of course, but it roared anyway, this time in confusion, as Kali's meticulously arranged vines wrapped themselves around its feet, throwing it off balance. The trap was not enough to bring it down, of course, but it *was* enough to send the giant stumbling blindly and out of control further through the forest and towards the second trap she had laid. This one was strung at a different height to the first, and this time the tension in the vines turned it as well, sending it careening to her goal. Kali tightened her grip on the giant's matted hair as it slammed through the trees surrounding it. She could make out the remaining traps ahead of them and, beyond those, the gorge that led towards the necropolis.

She couldn't help but yell out loud – "go, boy, go!" – as the juggennath impacted with her next trap, this one designed to catch the giant at the waist, throwing off its centre of gravity.

Kali suddenly found herself atop a rampaging mountain that could not stop itself from flailing forward, a victim of its own momentum. The last two traps she had lain came into their own now. As the giant stumbled into the complex arrangement of crossed vines, breaking each with a sound like a musket shot, the branches and, in one case, log that Kali had secured in place sprang from their lairs and struck the juggennath full on, slapping it forward. The giant roared in protest and confusion, brain unable to register what was happening in such swift succession, flailing all the more.

Perfect, Kali thought from her position at the creature's summit. All she needed to wait for now was the final trap and she could be off, leaving nature – and gravity specifically – to take its course.

The Juggennath broke through the thorn barrier surrounding Bel'A'Gon'Shri, and was in the gorge leading to the necropolis's front door. From her height Kali could actually see the stone slab ahead of them. She encouraged the Juggennath once more, ramming her knife into what remained of its eyeball. As the giant beast roared in pain she saw two tiny figures on top of the necropolis – Freel and Slowhand – turn at the sound.

The Juggennath staggered forward and Kali counted down the seconds until it triggered the trap.

If she did say so herself, there was no doubt that she had saved the best for last.

As the two tensioned vines stretched across the gorge floor were snapped by the Juggennath's staggering feet, a complex series of weights and counterweights were set rapidly in motion, and the two overhanging trees that Kali had tied back using ropes and pulleys sprang out from the gorge wall and slapped it hard in the back, somewhere in the region of each shoulderblade. Flung forward, the Juggennath roared and swung its mighty arms, trying to regain its balance, but its enforced momentum had already tipped its centre of gravity, and its mass was far too great to recover from such a complication in time to save it from its inevitable fall. It careened forward head-first, the heavy and uncontrolled pounding of its feet travelling up its body and shaking Kali to the bone, and she knew it was time to leave. She turned away from the eye and began to scramble down the back of the beast's neck, then unexpectedly flipped forward with a yelp, suddenly halted in her flight.

What the hells? She thought, and twisted her body, struggling to look above and behind her.

She saw that her foot had become entangled in a knot of the Juggennath's hair and she was now dangling from it like some kind of decoration.

Oh, that was great. Just great. Just farking great. How many seconds did she have before her plan came to fruition? Three? Two? One?

Roaring herself now, Kali flipped herself upward, tugged at the constraining mass of hair and then, realising she could not get free, instead heaved herself around the side of the Juggennath's neck as far as she could go.

One, in fact.

The last thing she saw with any clarity were the figures of Slowhand and Freel on the upper lip of the sealed entrance to Bel'A'Gon'Shri, their mouths agape. Then she saw the two of them throw themselves out the way.

By an odd coincidence, her cry echoed their own.

"*Ohhhhhh, shiiiiiiiiiiiiit...*"

The Juggennath struck the sealed entrance to the necropolis like a battering ram, cracking the thick stone. For a moment it seemed that that might be it, that the slab would give no further, but the Juggennath's vicious spikes had embedded themselves in it. Clinging still to its neck, having at last managed to kick loose from its hair, Kali felt the Juggennath strain and lurch as the spider-web cracks widened and the slab crumbled before it. The Juggennath let out a last great roar of pain and protest and fell through the gap, hitting the floor with a force that rocked the very foundations of the necropolis. The Juggennath tried to pick itself up, but the remnants of the broken slab broke free and crashed onto its helpless form. It seemed unlikely that it would rise again.

A dusty, coughing figure picked itself up from next to the crushed, bloodied mass and stared into the darkness ahead. It wasn't exactly how she'd planned to make her entrance admittedly but, what the hells, the end result was the same. She'd promised Redigor she was coming and here she was.

"Knock, knock," Kali growled.

CHAPTER SIXTEEN

THE FIRST THING Kali noticed as she moved into Bel'A'Gon'Shri was how *old* the necropolis felt. It wasn't the usual sense of age she experienced when finding Old Race sites, but a feeling that she had somehow stepped backwards in time – not into the past exactly, but certainly out of the present. It was as if, when the place had been built, it had somehow clung onto its time and never been willing to let go.

Her world seemed suddenly far away and she was therefore grateful to see Slowhand and Jakub Freel silhouetted in the entrance, descending together on one of the archer's whizzlines. The pair climbed over the debris to join her.

"Quite the entrance," Freel commented.

"That?" Slowhand countered. "You should have seen how she got into the Hoard of the Har'An'Di."

"The lost artefacts of the forgotten tribe? I'm sorry I missed that."

"Don't be," Kali said. "They collected thimbles."

They fell silent as the dust settled. A vaulted corridor stretched away into the distance, as high and as broad as the massive door itself, and lined with carved representations of those in whose honour it had been built – statues as high as a house.

"The Ur'Raney, I take it," Freel said.

"The Ur'Raney," Kali repeated.

Freel nodded. "Nice."

In every case, the statues depicted the Ur'Raney inflicting some kind of torture or pain on helpless victims, ranging from dwarves to ogur, humans to fish-like creatures. The carved victims were shown as far smaller than their torturers. Freel slowly unwound his chain whip, keeping it at the ready, as they moved on through the avenue of horrors. He had a point, Kali and Slowhand realised, and unsheathed their own weapons, gutting knife and Suresight alike.

The silence that had met them at the entrance gave way to an unsettling chanting in the distance, that sounded as if it were coming from human mouths yet did not chant human words, and a chorus of agonised and desperate cries that could only be coming from the Chapel of Screams – the same tormented sounds that Slowhand and Freel had heard on the necropolis's roof, here amplified by its stone corridors until the whole place seemed to be suffering.

As they moved along the corridor no horde of soul-stripped came to meet them. Bastian Redigor did not stand threateningly in their way. The business now occupying him, it seemed, was being conducted deeper within. Their only company the leering statues, they came at last to an ornate double door and Kali halted them.

"Trapped?" Slowhand wondered.

"Can't see anything," Kali said, scanning the door and its frame.

"Maybe Redigor put all his faith in the slab back there," Freel guessed.

Kali nodded. Tentatively, she pushed the massive golden door with her fingers and it opened with ease.

The path became a bridge beyond the door, crossing a vertiginous chamber carved wholly out of some substance that looked disturbingly like bone. From the floor of the chamber to the ceiling on either side – and it was a long way up and a long, long way down – the frontages of countless tombs could be seen, each of them inscribed, in elven script, with the name of its occupant. Kali tried to count them but gave up after the third ledge of tombs, but there were thousands here. These were Bastian Redigor's people. This was the final resting place of the Ur'Raney.

But there was something wrong with the whole picture. Kali couldn't immediately put her finger on it but something was very wrong. Straining to read the script on the tombs, for the most part ignoring the names, her eyes flicked from one to the other until what was nagging at her clicked into place.

It was the dates accompanying the names. They were all the same.

"Yantissa 367, Interlude Third," she whispered to herself.

"Something wrong, Miss Hooper?" Freel queried.

"Yantissa 367, Interlude Third," Kali repeated more forcefully. "It's elven chronology. According to these tombs, all of these elves, thousands of them, died on the same day."

"So?" Slowhand said. "I thought it was generally accepted that the Old Races were wiped out in one go. Maybe that's when it happened?"

Kali pondered. "If it was, I'd be ecstatic, believe me, because we'd be able to pinpoint the end day exactly. But I don't think this date has anything to do with that."

"Why?"

"Think, 'Liam. If that was the day the Old Races were wiped out..."

"Who buried them?" Jakub Freel finished.

Slowhand looked from one to the other. "Redigor?"

"One man, all this?" Kali mused. "Even with an eternity to play with, I don't think so."

"Okaaay," Slowhand said. "So maybe Yantissa 367, Interlude Third isn't a day. I mean, I know your elven history is better than mine but as you admit yourself, you've still a lot to learn. Maybe Yantissa 367, Interlude Third refers to a *period* of time, and maybe it took the Ur'Raney a while to die out?"

Kali stared at the archer. "You know, Slowhand, that's not bad. Not bad at all."

"Hey, I'm not just a pretty face..."

"Completely wrong, mind. Because it still doesn't make sense." She indicated the tombs and structure around them. "Think about it. If the world was falling apart around you, would you take the time to build *this*?"

"I wouldn't," Freel said. "But if it wasn't the end day that killed them all, what did?"

The question was momentarily forgotten as Slowhand pointed. "Hooper, Freel, look."

Above and below the bridge they were standing on, obscured in the shadows of the huge chamber, other, smaller bridges crossed the bone chasm. Each of these bridges led to one of the ledges of tombs, and each was filled with slowly filing figures. The soul-stripped who had been phased through the Sardenne, all chanting that strange, elven chant, were making their way to the fronts of the tombs and, one after the other, taking up positions before each of them, simply standing there, staring blankly ahead.

"It's as if they know which tomb to go to," Freel whispered, for fear that his words might alert the soul-stripped to their presence.

"Redigor knows," Kali said.

"And it strikes me," Slowhand offered, "that he's the only one who can tell us what happened on Yantissa 367, Interlude Third."

The party crossed the bridge, casting wary glances about them as they did, and the wailing, haunting, tortured cries that had been audible since they first entered the necropolis grew louder with every step, reaching a deafening pitch as they reached the door at the far end. A door which could only lead to the Chapel of Screams.

Again, Kali scanned it for traps and pushed it open. Before them was the tableau Slowhand and Freel had caught glimpses of from the roof, only the Chapel seemed much bigger, stretching away before them, the figures barely discernible at the far end. Behind them – silhouetting and warping their outlines with its churning, chaotic energy – was the base of the pillar of souls. It was, of course, from here that the screams were emanating and, again, as Slowhand and Freel had seen on the roof, souls captured within struck and writhed at the surface, giving the occasional close-up glimpse of a struggling form or tortured face, even the odd hand outstretched in pleading to be pulled from the turmoil. The proximity of the pillar of souls – its sheer size and power – seemed to be of no concern to the two figures, however, presumably because one was the Pale Lord himself, the master of all he had conjured, and the other, under his control, was Katherine Makennon.

They walked down the central aisle of the Chapel of Screams, Makennon's fellow abductees lining the Chapel on either side of them like a guard of honour. The tombs were far more ornate than the masses they had passed on the bridge. The eleven men and women had been stripped of their own clothing and garbed in uniform, flowing robes, making them look like sacrificial victims – which for all intents and purposes, of course, they were. There was little doubt that those who lay in the tombs behind them were the individuals for whom they had been hand-picked to become hosts – Bastian Redigor's Ur'Raney High Council. As they passed between them Kali recognised the faces of Kantris Mallah, the mayor of Gargas, Thilna Pope, Volonne's Ambassador to Vos, and Belf Utcher, Thane of Miramas, among others – though, of course, none of them recognised her in return. Redigor, it seemed, had not soul-stripped the hosts for his most important returnees as he had the masses outside, but it was clear from their haunted, staring eyes that neither had he left them entirely intact. The expression in their eyes begged her for release from bodies that had become prisons.

There was nothing Kali and the others could do for them. Yet.

The three of them, Slowhand and Freel walking either side of Kali moved on up the aisle, coming at last to stand before Bastian Redigor and Katherine Makennon. Despite herself, Kali faltered slightly. The portrait she had seen of the Pale Lord in Fayence did not, in reality, do him anywhere near justice. He soared above both Freel and Slowhand, a tall, gaunt, angular figure with flowing black hair who should have seemed cadaverous but who radiated an aura that Kali had to admit made her go weak at the knees. The man – the *elf*, she corrected herself – was sheer presence, more magnetic even than the hub, and she could see how he had become lord of his people. Bastian Redigor stared down at her, smiling coldly, and for a few seconds she found she could not draw her eyes away.

She kept telling herself how much of a bastard he was and, with this mantra, dragged her gaze to Makennon, and the sight of what he had done to the Anointed Lord quashed the elf's glamour.

Redigor had wasted no time in preparing Makennon for her role, stripping her armour and clothing and dressing her in a diaphanous shift that fell loosely from her shoulders to her ankles and did little to conceal her nakedness beneath. A high, stiff collar had been placed around Makennon's neck, thrusting her jaw upwards; a *zatra*, a collar of obedience whose prime purpose was to denote the status of a woman as a pet. Kali's eyes travelled down her body, noting the recent bruises, and then back up until her gaze met Makennon's. Though Kali had little time for the woman, her eyes teared at what she saw – fury and frustration at what had been done to her, yes, and shame and utter humiliation that she should be paraded in this way, knowing that all *knew* the indignities she must have suffered. Kali tried to offer her some look of reassurance but wondered whether anything could offer solace for what had happened, and after a second she was forced to turn her gaze away. She looked at Slowhand, but even the normally libidinous archer was staring at the floor, unable to look up.

"Proud of yourself, Baz?" Kali queried, snapping her gaze back to the Pale Lord. "Is this what we're to expect when the Ur'Raney return?"

"This, and more," Redigor replied, his smile widening. He turned to look at Makennon and then back at Kali, his eyes widening in anticipation. "Perhaps when I tire of her I shall take you as *mu'sah'rin* in her place. I sense in you a stamina that I think will be able to satisfy even my demands."

"You keep your slimy elven hands off her," Slowhand threatened, making a move forward, but Kali placed her hand on his arm, stopping him. Redigor might be dripping sleaze but she could feel his raw, unadulterated power. The reason there had been no traps on the way in was that Redigor didn't need any. Slowhand would have no chance against him.

"In your filthy, farking dreams, pal," Kali said to Redigor. She motioned to Makennon and the others. "At least give her the dignity of oblivion. Why must Makennon know what's happening to her? Why must any of them?"

Redigor smiled. "It is necessary that I retain some of their knowledge of the leaders of your civilisation, such as it is. Their familiarity to their people, superficial as it might be when the ritual is done, will be of some advantage. It will make our transition to power... less bloody. It also makes things so much more *fun*."

"Since when did the Ur'Raney care about spilling a little blood?"

"We don't. In fact, we intend to spill a lot of blood. But that," he added with a sigh, "will come later."

"I hate to point out the obvious," Slowhand said, "but this High Council of yours, you're one missing."

"The magistrate of Kroog-Martra," Redigor said. "Convenient, then, that you saw fit to include a replacement in your party."

"What the hells are you talking about?"

The Pale Lord waved a hand and the whip at Jakub Freel's waist suddenly took on a life of its own, uncoiling from his side and wrapping itself around his neck. As it lifted him from the floor, Freel had the presence of mind to react quickly, to jam his fingers between chain and flesh to prevent himself being hanged. Even so he gagged and choked as, with another wave of his hand, Redigor manoeuvred his floating body into position before what had been the magistrate's allocated tomb. Freel dangled there, his legs kicking, his eyes bulging as he stared down at Kali and Slowhand.

"Hey," Slowhand said. "It was me speaking. Let him down, take me instead."

"*You?*" Redigor boomed. "Why should I wish a bedraggled commoner when I have Prince Tremayne of the Allantian First Family?"

Both Slowhand and Kali turned to look at their helpless comrade.

"You didn't *know*?" Redigor said.

"Prince Tremayne?" Slowhand said. "My sister married royalty?"

"Indeed. So you see why I have absolutely no need of riff-raff such as yourself."

"Yeah?" Slowhand challenged. "Well, let me show you what riff-raff can do."

The archer released a clutch of arrows at the Pale Lord in blinding succession. Redigor managed to deflect four of them but two breached his defences, embedding themselves solidly in his right thigh. Redigor gasped and stared down at the protruding shafts in incredulous fury and waved his hand again. Slowhand was propelled violently backwards along the length of the Chapel, impacting with the wall above the entrance with a bone-cracking, sickening thud. The archer slumped there, held by an unseen force, one arm dangling at an unnatural angle through Suresight's string.

Kali stared at her helpless lover and swallowed, then turned back to Redigor.

"Nice party tricks. But when do we get to the main event?"

Redigor raised an eyebrow. "You seem strangely eager."

Kali shook her head. "Nope. But if we've a few minutes, I wouldn't mind the answers to a few questions."

Redigor steepled the fingers of both hands, intrigued. He nodded for Kali to continue.

Kali again looked at Slowhand and Freel. The questions she had in mind, she would not normally have raised in anyone else's presence for fear of burdening them with what she had learned at the Crucible, but both men had lapsed into semiconsciousness. Still, she wanted to take no chances, and spoke to Redigor in elvish.

"Now that we're alone," she said. "What's this all about, Baz?"

"What? You are trying to buy time, child. You know this already."

"Of course I know you're bringing your people back. What I'm asking is, why now?"

"Now?"

"I saw the charts in your tower in Fayence, and I know the intellect you possess. You know as much as I do that a darkness is coming – the same darkness that obliterated the Old Races – so why would you want to resurrect your people when the world's about to come to an end?"

Redigor stared at her and burst into laughter, as if she were a child who had said something profoundly foolish. Kali frowned and pouted.

"Forgive me," Redigor said at last, though his tone still quaked slightly. "Forgive me, but I believe I have overestimated you. All you know is that the darkness is coming, isn't it? But you don't know what the darkness is, or why it comes. You don't know *anything* about it."

Kali felt her heart skip a beat.

"I'm willing to learn."

"An exercise in redundancy, believe me. There is nothing you can do."

"No? Then what did your people do, Baz? They all died at the same time, I know that, but no other member of the Old Races – elf or dwarf – had the luxury of his or her own tomb. They were just... gone."

Redigor's lip curled in amusement yet again. "Your point being?"

"That somehow your people survived the darkness. That somehow they –"

Kali stopped, something in Redigor's expression and something in her own head making the truth click into place.

"My gods, they didn't survive, did they?" She said. "They died *before* the darkness came."

"All of them on the same day," Redigor confirmed. "Thousands of Ur'Raney ascending to Kerberos to wait for this moment, the moment of their return. It was glorious."

Kali felt suddenly, intensely cold. "You killed them?"

"They died at my behest. A subtle, mostly painless poison."

"A suicide pact?"

"A *survival* pact, child!" Redigor's eyes flared as he spoke. "Though even in their tombs I knew they would not be safe. Still, I knew the darkness would find them, ravage their physical remains, reduce them to husks. Only I remained whole. I, their guardian, their leader, their lord, curled like a babe, cocooned deep beneath the surface, swaddled in the thick, protective wraps of magic older than time. Only in this manner could I conceal myself from what came."

The thought of even someone as powerful as Redigor having to *hide* chilled Kali to the bone. But a question nagged at her.

"Why kill your people? Why didn't you just let the darkness take them and then restore them from Kerberos?"

Another laugh bubbled up from the Pale Lord.

"Because, child, when the darkness takes you, your soul does not *go* to Kerberos."

"What?" Kali said. "What is it, Redigor? What is the darkness?"

"The Hel'ss."

"The Hells?" Kali said.

"The antithesis of Kerberos. The Other."

Kali staggered with the sheer weight of the revelation. But whether what Redigor seemed to be telling her – that the fundamental beliefs of Twilight's religions were correct and there *were* two places to which souls went, Kerberos and the Pits, or in other words, the Hells – was true or not, another question nagged for an answer.

"But if it's coming again, how do you intend to survive it this time?"

Redigor shook his head almost sadly.

"We do not *have* to survive it this time, child, because this time it does not come for us."

"What? What are you saying?"

"That the last time it came for the elves and the dwarves. And this time it comes for you."

"Humans?" Kali gasped. "Are you saying it *chooses* what it wipes out?"

"I am saying that there is an order to these things."

"So that's your plan, you bastard? To get your jollies from enslaving us humans before inheriting what we leave behind? You disgust me. You're vultures."

Redigor smiled. "No. Vultures are creatures of instinct, their pickings what they find. We, on the other hand, are creatures of refinement, and the pain we shall inflict upon you will be exquisite. Think of it, child – as the darkness comes and the screams of your race echo across the land, we shall *thrive*."

"Not if I can help it..."

Kali roared and leaped for Redigor, unsheathing her gutting knife as she did, but her hand was caught in a vice-like grip and Redigor's eyes stared down at her, wide and wild.

"What is it you are trying to do?" He said, almost compassionately.

"You said it yourself, Redigor," Kali gasped as she twisted in his grip. "There's an order to these things and you've had your turn. The Ur'Raney don't belong here any more."

"And you intend to stop me how? By scratching me with your knife?"

"I'll stop you, you bastard."

Redigor released his grip, but Kali found herself frozen before him. The Pale Lord gazed at the pillar of souls and took a deep, satisfied breath. "This isn't a time for weapons, child, this is a time for celebration. Dance for me."

"What?"

"*Dance for me!*"

Kali didn't do dance, she didn't like dance, she didn't understand dance, but she danced. Danced for the Pale Lord. Spasming and twitching at first, trying to resist, her feet began to tap the floor, and then she began to spin, moving away from the Pale Lord, down the aisle, her body whipping around again, and as much as she wanted to, she couldn't stop – couldn't stop, didn't stop, until she reached the far end of the Chapel of Screams. She slammed into the wall beneath Slowhand with numbing force and, her dance done, slumped to the floor.

"Did you really think you would be able to make a difference?" Redigor asked.

Kali shook her head and wiped a slick of blood from her face. She realised it was dripping on her from the archer suspended helplessly above her. *Oh gods, Slowhand,* she thought as her head spun. What was it she had gotten her lover into? What had she gotten them *all* into?

Kali struggled to rise, staggered, retched, intending to go for the Pale Lord again. It was only as she began to weave between the tombs that a whisper from the helpless Slowhand halted her in her tracks.

"No, Hooper... no, it's too late..."

Kali turned to look up at him, but focused again on the pillar of souls spearing the Chapel roof. It was impossible from where she stood to see the top, but she didn't need to see Kerberos to know that it had at last been reached. The pillar of souls suddenly pulsed brightly, its helpless captives rushing up, and a second later pulsed again, this time downwards. The pillar of souls darkened as if flooded by a rush of arterial blood. Not so dark that Kali couldn't see what was within, though, and she drew back as the base of the pillar struggled to contain a miasmic wave of grasping, clutching, spectral forms, tearing at their own and screaming so loudly it seemed to pierce the very fabric of her ears.

One triumphant cry could be heard above the screaming; Redigor, his hands held high.

"They come!" He declared, laughing. "*They come!*"

CHAPTER SEVENTEEN

KALI HAD WONDERED how exactly the final exchange might take place – how Redigor's *delivery* of the Ur'Raney back to Twilight would occur – and as she staggered back she got her answer.

The expansive, seething, screaming base of the pillar of souls filled and bloated, and exploded, dazzling those present. As Kali watched it through her fingers it blasted harmlessly through her and the wall of the Chapel behind her, towards the tombs. It *wasn't* harmless, though, was it? It was deadly, conjured across the millennia to be as insidious as anything could be. At least to those who had been chosen to be the recipients of what it contained. Kali could not help be awed by the sight, but knew full well that, within the next few seconds, it was going to end the existence of countless innocents who, through no fault of their own, had become caught up in the schemes of a madman who had plotted against them almost since before the human race had been born.

How would they end, though?

Despite herself, Kali couldn't help but ask the question. She pictured the soul wave expanding rapidly through the tombs, individual tendrils of it darting into each of the thousands of ancient resting places like snakes before snapping back out, carrying within each of them the physical essence that had been preserved in the remains of the Ur'Raney. Then, perhaps with a violent spasm from each of the soul-stripped assembled before the tombs, these snakes would strike, darting into necks, eyes, mouths, preparing to infuse themselves into the horrible emptiness from which the true inhabitants of these bodies had been so cruelly torn.

It sickened Kali – the awareness that somehow these things had to *know* which tomb to seek out, which body to violate, and they would move to them as unerringly as salmon returning to their spawning ground.

This, though, was all her imagining, and by the time she could see the Chapel once more, she realised she might never know.

Those souls belonging to Redigor's Ur'Raney Court had already found their homes, slipping into the bodies of Katherine Makennon and the other dignitaries as easily as worms into soft soil, and the effects on their hosts was immediate. Soft groans escaped each of them. Their eyes widened in response to the intrusion, then took on a peculiar blankness. This faded away, to be replaced by *new* eyes that took in their surroundings first with an almost childlike innocence, then a growing curiosity, and then a hunger unlike any Kali had ever seen.

They began to metamorphosise – ever so slightly but enough – taking on the slightest sharpening of their physiognomy, a subtle elongation of the ears, and the lightest of green tints to their skin. Kali could also have sworn – but this may only have been because of the manner in which they carried themselves – that they grew taller.

With almost reptilian twitches of their necks, each of the Ur'Raney *rannaat* sighed and, as one, turned to face Bastian Redigor. Their Lord stood smiling at them, a welcoming smile, his *mu'sah'rin* already draping herself languorously about his neck.

"Hooper..." Slowhand's voice said weakly from above Kali. "This might be the time for that 'long shot' you mentioned to Freel."

Kali said nothing.

"Hooper, the long shot?"

This time, Kali bit her lip.

"Hooper, you do *have* a long shot, right?"

Don't ask me that, 'Liam, don't ask, Kali thought.

What was it she had said to Freel, back in the Sardenne – I tend to work on the hoof? Well, she wasn't on the hoof now, was she, she was on her backside, collapsed helpless against a wall, and it didn't look like her long shot was going to be materialising at all.

"Sure, 'Liam. I'll ask Baz to stop, shall I? Get him to send his people home to Kerberos?"

A drop of blood fell from the archer, and he spoke slowly, quietly. "They have no home other than the hells, you know that. They don't belong on Kerberos and they don't belong here. Hooper, *come on*, you always have something up your sleeve..."

"Not this time. I'm sorry."

"Kali..."

"*Not this time!*"

Shocked, Slowhand stared down at her. But Kali was not looking up and all he saw was the top of her head.

"Kal," he said. "We've all lost people close to us, and we know how much that hurt. Now that's about to happen again, only on a massive scale. As I see it, as soon as that pillar disappears, they've lost their loved ones for ever, but so long as it's *there* we have a chance to bring them back... somehow."

Kali's eyes slowly rose to the base of the pillar of souls, still emptying itself of the last dregs of Ur'Raney souls. What the archer said was true – while that pillar still existed, there might still be time to save them somehow, to bring them back, for *something* to happen – no matter how much of a long shot it might be.

"Hooper," Slowhand said. "You're the only one who can do this..."

"I know," Kali whispered to herself.

"What?"

"I said, I know!" Kali shouted, picking herself from the floor. Between her and Redigor, the *rannaat*, who were just about to move away from their tombs, turned at her defiant cry. She uttered a primal roar as she ran along the aisle to launch herself at the Pale Lord. The *rannaat* looked almost amused, and looked to their Lord for guidance. Redigor, looking less amused, shook his head.

Kali pounded towards him, beads of sweat falling from her.

"Enough," Redigor said. "You are a meddlesome pain, child. I could easily strip your soul and take your body for my collection, but I do not believe I wish to keep either."

Redigor's arm shot out and he curled his fingers. Kali found herself halting in her tracks and collapsing to her knees with a cry of agony as something seemed to close around her heart and pull. She looked down, her mouth falling open in shock and pain. Whisps of light were being drawn from within her. As he had with so many before her, Bastian Redigor was extracting her soul – and doing so, it seemed, in as slow and as agonising fashion as he could.

"Hey," Kali uttered between clenched teeth, "that just isn't fair..."

"And since I do not wish to keep your soul, child," Redigor continued, ignoring her. "Why don't I simply tear it out?"

The elven sorcerer jerked his outstretched hand again and Kali wailed with pain. Though she remained on her knees, she was bent backwards, her spine and neck arched like a bow, throat taut, mouth stretched open as far as it would go. The light poured from her and across the Chapel to Redigor's fingertips. There the Pale Lord breathed in deeply and with satisfaction, as if he were drinking her.

Kali groaned. The more her soul was drawn from her, the more agonising it became. She was struggling desperately now to hang onto the last of her being, but she was fighting a losing battle. Her vision darkening, her thoughts dimming, feeling as though she were adrift in some dark expanse, she was only peripherally aware of a shape that staggered into her distorted vision, and then of two blurry flashes that sliced through the air before her. Through the air and through her departing soul. Kali screamed in agony as the whole of her self suddenly snapped back in like an elastic band, and she bucked on the floor taking deep, gulping breaths.

In that instant she realised that Redigor's grip was gone, and that she was whole again.

Whole, and not alone.

"Stay behind me," Gabriella DeZantez said, wielding the Deathclaws. "I guess what they say about these things slicing souls is true."

What? Kali thought. *What they say about the claws is true? But Gabriella has the claws and Gabriella is dead... she died.*

Gabriella was dead... she had *seen* her die in the Sardenne, at the hands of the juggennath. But at the same time here she was.

Kali shook her head and saw Gabriella, pulling her to her feet. The Enlightened One was scarred and battered, her armour crushed and misshapen beneath her torn surplice, and a dark rivulet of blood leaked from the side of her mouth, but she was there. And behind her, staring with a strange mixture of curiosity and rage, was the Pale Lord.

"No, no," Kali said to Gabriella, trying to push her away, "he's too powerful. Get out of here, get out of here now."

Gabriella grabbed her by the shoulders. "It's *all right*, remember."

"All right?"

"Yes, all right! Now, stay behind me."

Kali nodded, not really understanding. And then she began to remember. Remember because Redigor was attempting the same trick on Gabriella that he had tried on her, but with absolutely no effect at all. Gabriella, in fact, still had her back turned to him, and she hadn't even *noticed* what he was attempting to do. Then – Redigor still trying without success to rip out her soul – she turned and began to limp slowly up the aisle towards him, drawing Kali in behind her.

From over Gabriella's shoulder Kali saw the Pale Lord hesitate.

"What is this?" He said. "Some kind of resistance? Who are you, girl?"

"My name Gabriella DeZantez. I am a Sister of the Order of the Swords of Dawn."

The Pale Lord's eyes narrowed. "And pray, Sister, what brings you here?"

"I come to smite thee."

The Pale Lord looked, for a second, amazed, and – as Gabriella and Kali continued their approach. But then his face reverted to its usual arrogant mask and he raised his arms towards Gabriella. Kali knew what was coming and it was clear that so, too, did Gabriella.

The Enlightened One's fingers curled into the top of her breastplate, ripping it away, and she drew in a deep, preparatory breath.

"Bring it on, you unholy bastard!"

Bastian Redigor's lip curled.

"Very well. We shall see how strong you are."

Lightning burst forth from his fingertips, smacking Gabriella directly in the chest. It had no physical effect other than to slow her slightly, discharging in bright arcs and cracks about her shoulders as she pushed against it. Redigor loosed another bolt, equally ineffective, and his eyes widened. He thrust his arms forward once more and this time a plume of fire lanced towards Kali's protector, bursting about her body. Kali ducked, but still Gabriella moved forward.

Now Redigor tried ice, and the crackling, steaming bolts of magical energy slammed into Gabriella with a serpentine hiss but, again, only slowed her in her tracks. It was like struggling forward against a strong wind, and this was exactly what Redigor tried next, summoning a gale to pummel Gabriella that, while it set every loose object in the Chapel flying, she strode through as if it were an inconvenient breeze.

The pair of them were halfway up the Chapel's aisle now, nothing stopping them reaching Redigor.

The Chapel was filled with shrieking hags as phantom horrors materialised out of every corner and swept at Gabriella, threatening to tear her apart. As they came, so too did great, writhing snakes whose wide, fanged maws bit down on her. Nor were they the last of what Redigor had to offer. Spectral daggers hurled themselves at her in wave after wave, fist-sized explosions detonated about her body, and stone barriers assembled themselves out of the floor, only to crumble before Gabriella's determined march. The Pale Lord actually looked visibly shaken now – was perhaps even becoming drained – but rather than feel a sense of impending victory Kali felt increasing concern for Gabriella. It was true that the Enlightened One seemed unstoppable in her progress, but Gabriella seemed at last to be weakening before it.

She moved more slowly now and, above the noise of the assault, Kali thought that she even heard Gabriella wheeze with strain. She wanted to say *stop now, that's enough, you've done what you can,* but she knew she couldn't. If Gabriella gave up now the two of them would be dead, and any chance of stopping Redigor gone for good. Suddenly all of Kali's attention was focused not on Redigor's continuing barrage but on Gabriella herself.

A great, unremitting river of destruction poured from Redigor's fingertips, slamming relentlessly into Gabriella. No one, however gifted, could withstand such destruction for much longer, and Kali's heart sank as Gabriella at last began to falter. She felt the sheer impotence of her own position, the fact that she couldn't help the woman at all. Knowing that she would be inviting instant obliteration if she stepped from behind Gabriella's protective guard, all she could do was will the Enlightened One onwards despite her mounting pain.

And more than pain.

At first Kali wasn't quite sure what she was seeing, but Gabriella's muscles were now less pronounced than before, and somehow deteriorated. Her skin had lost its golden sheen, becoming less vibrant. With horror Kali realised that this wasn't simply a reaction to the suffering Gabriella was enduring; she wasn't just weakening before Redigor's onslaught, she was *aging* before it. Kali placed a hand on her shoulder, felt bone rather than muscle beneath her fingers.

Oh gods, what's happening to her?

The answer seemed clear. As immune to magic as Gabriella had announced herself to be, she might have had the ability to spend her entire life shrugging off any one of the Pale Lord's individual attacks – of anyone's attacks – and somehow recovered. But what she had suffered from Redigor collectively in the space of minutes was *already* a lifetime's worth. She had been drained of everything she had in attempting to save her, in attempting to save *everyone*, and Gabriella DeZantez's life was ending right before her eyes.

Redigor's barrage continued and Gabriella, having almost reached him, faltered, staggered, and crumpled to the floor, more bone than flesh.

Redigor lowered his arms and looked down. His eyes widened and he bent and plucked the Deathclaws from Gabriella's twitching hands.

"Ah," he said, "I've been looking for these for a long, long time."

Kali's rage was incandescent as she stood before him, but she could do nothing. If she made a single move, the elf would reduce her to dust.

"Now," Redigor said, "wouldn't you agree that was just a waste of time?"

Kali's eyes rose to him, but the Pale Lord was calmly looking at her, awaiting an answer to his question. He *wanted* an answer, Kali realised, so that he could bask in his supremacy, and, in all honesty, she wasn't sure that she wouldn't have to give the one he desired. But not yet. Not yet. She looked slowly around the Chapel of Screams, at Slowhand, at Freel, down at Gabriella DeZantez, and then up at Makennon, from whose eyes a stranger stared haughtily down. She hoped that they understood she'd tried her best, and that this time her long shot hadn't paid off.

Her eyes returned to the Pale Lord. As they did, she heard something that the Pale Lord hadn't yet picked up on. It was a sound that she had been hoping to hear almost since she'd arrived at the Sardenne, a sound that when she had first heard it had filled her with dread, but which, now, buoyed her heart.

That was the thing about long shots, she guessed. Sometimes they took a while to arrive.

"Actually, no," she said to Redigor, "I wouldn't agree at all. What Gabriella did wasn't a waste of time, it *bought* us time."

Redigor looked up, now recognising the disturbance in the air above.

"That's right, Baz," Kali said, springing up and hissing in his ear. "Remember those?"

Redigor stared through the shattered roof of the Chapel of Screams, his face twisted with anger. Three massive machines hove into view, and whether Redigor had personally set eyes on the Engines of the Apocalypse before or not, there was no mistaking the immense cones for anything other than what they were. But if any more proof were needed, the sudden blare of their positioning sirens as they began to spin above the necropolis was more than adequate. Redigor snapped his gaze from them down to Kali and then to his *rannaat*. The twelve-pseudo elves looked at him with pleading, but already their features were reverting to human, his hold over them disappearing.

His hold over other things was disappearing, too. At the far end of the Chapel, Slowhand fell from where he was pinned against the wall, crashing to the floor with a thud. He picked himself up, his expression dark, and, clutching his broken arm, began to weave his way down the aisle towards Kali.

"No," Redigor whispered.

"Yes," Kali corrected. "That's right, Baz. That old black magic is going away. Quite ironic, don't you think, since that's how this whole thing began?"

"Impossible!" Redigor protested. "The Engines are designed to negate only elven threads, and my magic is... is –"

"The dead bits in between?" Kali said. "What remains of dragon magic, perhaps?" Kali shrugged. "Under normal circumstances, yeah. But, hey, you know, if you twiddle the dials, turn everything up to eleven..."

"*No!*" Redigor cried.

His voice echoed throughout the Chapel of Screams and he raised his arms, trying to propel Kali and Slowhand back along the aisle. Only Kali staggered back, and only because he physically shoved her. Redigor threw his arms wide, somehow finding the reserves for one last outburst of energy, trying to infuse his people with his own essence, to slow their reversion, but the energy fizzled even as it began to spread, dissipating into a cloud of nothing, and Redigor collapsed to his knees, spent. He stared in disbelief and could do little but watch as the whole sequence of soul exchange reversed itself before his eyes, the souls of the Ur'Raney pulled from the bodies of their hosts and back towards the pillar, and the pillar, in turn, brightening with the return of the human souls from Kerberos. Kali doubted that Redigor felt the same but the whole process was quite magical to watch, the whisps of humanity slowly twisting and twining throughout the

Chapel, finding their rightful homes first in those who had been doomed to be the High Council and then travelling further afield, to the general tombs, to reinhabit those who waited there.

The exchange complete, both Kali and Slowhand stared up at the pillar of souls. The essences of things still writhed within it, still sought somehow to escape, and perhaps even to snatch at those whose flesh they were now denied, but there was one important difference – these souls were Ur'Raney, and they were going back where they belonged.

The pillar of souls disappeared and Kali and Slowhand found themselves staring at the looming masses of the Engines, still rotating above.

"Hooper, I thought you said..." Slowhand interjected.

"Sorry, 'Liam. For one thing I didn't know if I had programmed them correctly but, more importantly, I couldn't even think about them in Redigor's presence. He'd have sensed it, stopped them somehow..."

"You worked out a way to bring them all the way here?"

"Made it up as I went along," Kali said, smiling.

Their smiles faded as they heard Katherine Makennon groan and were reminded of the ordeal she'd been through. Slowhand was about to offer aid, but Kali placed a hand on his arm, holding him back, allowing the Anointed Lord to emerge from her nightmare by herself.

Her gait stiff, her head erect and proud, Katherine Makennon moved slowly from the altar by the kneeling Redigor to a slab where her clothing, armour and weapon lay neatly folded and stacked. For the moment, she ignored the garments, regarding them curiously, fingering them, but nothing more. Instead, she took the shaft of the battleaxe in two hands and wearily dragged it towards her. Seemingly lacking the strength to lift it again, Makennon paused a second, drawing in a deep and contemplative breath, and then turned to face the Pale Lord, her expression devoid of emotion. Then, equally slowly, she began to walk towards Redigor, dragging the battleaxe with her. When she stood in front of him, she stopped and, in a dry croak, demanded he rise.

Showing no fear, no remorse, only the arrogance that had marked the man for all his long and depraved life, Bastian Redigor stood. For a second his eyes seemed to flick beyond her but then he leaned forward, and whispered in her ear.

"Your church will crumble at my hands. I will destroy it."

Makennon's gaze rose until it met his. Her eyes were unblinking, her face blank. Almost imperceptibly at first, the muscles about her mouth began to spasm, her face contorted into a mask of rage and fury, and then she swung the battleaxe up from between her legs with a guttural roar that shook the Chapel.

Bastian Redigor had no time even to cry out. With a sound more at home on a butcher's block than a chapel's altar, the blade sliced into the Pale Lord at the groin and continued up through him until it swung out over Makennon's head. Arcs of blood and entrails spattered the faces of those watching but no one moved. The Anointed Lord held the battleaxe over her head, dripping blood and gore, and then gradually set it down. Before her, the halves of Bastian Redigor parted and crumpled to the floor, landing with wet thuds.

Makennon's words were whispered.

"I'd like to see you try."

Kali looked around her at those assembled, seeing in their eyes the same return to humanity that she had witnessed in Makennon's. Then her eyes moved to the prone, shrivelled form of Gabriella DeZantez and she knelt by her side. The Enlightened One was still alive, just, but the life was already fading from her eyes.

Kali cradled DeZantez's head, wanting desperately to offer some comfort but not knowing what to say. In the end, it was Gabriella who spoke first, though her voice was not what Kali remembered – a cracked, aged thing, little more than a sibilant whisper.

"Do you see the light? Gabriella DeZantez sees the light."

"The light?"

"Kerberos," Gabriella said slowly, and smiled. Her eyes were focused upward, not on Kali at all. "My time is close."

"You saved my life. Bought the time to save all our lives. Is there anything I can do... to make things easier?"

Gabriella emitted a low chuckle. "Are you offering to pray for me?"

"Yes. Yes, yes, I am, if that's what you want."

Gabriella shook her head, laughed again. "Maybe it would be... more appropriate if... you had a drink for me instead..."

Kali smiled. "I'll do that. More than one. The whole of the Flagons will."

A cough. "Such a request from a Sister of the Faith is, of course, prohibited."

"What the hells, eh?"

Gabriella suddenly tensed beneath her. "Looks like we were wrong."

Kali frowned. "About what?"

"My being one of the Four."

"Hey, I don't think so," Kali said. "You did more than your bit to save the world today."

Gabriella shook her head again, but this time didn't laugh. "No. This wasn't the time, I sense that. Not the threat that is meant to bring the Four together..."

Kali turned away, biting her lip. When she looked at Gabriella again, the Enlightened One was staring directly at her.

"There's more you haven't told me, isn't there?" Gabriella asked. "You *know* something, don't you?"

Kali took a second before she spoke. "Not much. Something's coming. Darkness."

Gabriella absorbed the information, swallowed, and her body spasmed once more. But she retained enough control to study Kali intently. She clutched at Kali's hand, squeezed it. "*Tell someone.* Tell Slowhand. Don't go through this alone."

Kali nodded, while beneath her, Gabriella groaned.

"Do something else for me," she said. Slowly, her skeletal hand slipped into her charred surplice and withdrew the shard of Freedom Mountain, which she pressed into Kali's hand. She swallowed again, dryly, and her next words emerged almost as a wheeze. "Please. Watch me go."

Kali looked at the shard and at Gabriella and nodded. The Enlightened One squeezed her hand in thanks and held her gaze. Only after a few moments had passed did Kali realise that she was never going to look away again.

Kali took a shuddering breath and slowly raised the shard. She gasped, eyes widening, and smiled.

Gabriella's soul rose from her body in much the same way as Brother Marcus's had done, but there was something that distinguished it, not only from the Faith soldier's soul but from every other soul she had now seen.

Gabriella's essence shone brightly, blindingly. As it slowly wove its way upwards, towards Kerberos, it flared with all the colours of the threads, a rainbow burst filled far more with life than it ever could be with death.

Kali thought about everything she'd learned about Kerberos in the past few days. About how it might, despite her previous disbelief, be a part of everything.

And maybe, she thought, Gabriella had been wrong about not being one of the Four. Maybe, just maybe, she might yet still be.

A hand fell heavily on her shoulder.

"Hooper, I'm sorry," Slowhand said. "The Engines – there's something wrong."

CHAPTER EIGHTEEN

THERE WAS SOMETHING wrong, all right. Great shadows loomed over Kali even as she stood to take in what Slowhand had said. As she looked through the collapsed roof of the Chapel of Screams she saw that the Engines were lower in the sky than on their arrival. Their sirens were blaring in a deafening, urgent tone.

"Oh gods," she said. "They're coming down."

"Down?" Slowhand repeated. "Hooper, I thought you had control of these things?"

"I do... I did! They just weren't meant to come down *so soon*."

"So *soon*?"

"What, you thought I'd leave them up there? Slowhand, there's a reason they're called the Engines of the Apocalypse!"

"Right, right, fine," Slowhand said.

He looked around at the former members of Redigor's High Council, all of whom were shuffling slowly about the Chapel, disorientated "But I suggest we get these people out of here now."

Above them, one Engine tipped suddenly to the left, its siren blaring louder still, and grazed one of its companions. The sound of the immense machines grinding together drowned out even the increasingly distressed wail of the siren, and the explosion that followed drowned out even that. The first Engine shuddered on its axis and sheered off. The second came to a stop, hanging above them like a steel storm cloud.

And then, though strangely slowly for something of its size, it began to drop.

"Move, move, move!" The archer commanded, slapping Kali on the shoulder with his good arm and herding Makennon, Freel and the rest towards the Chapel's exit.

The Anointed Lord glared at him furiously for a moment, snarling over Redigor's remains, but she capitulated, turning to help Freel and Slowhand with steering their groggier counterparts from the Chapel.

As they ushered the nobles, lords and ladies onto the tomb bridge, the first Engine fell, burrowing into the hole left by the exploded chapel roof. As it came, slowly and inexorably, the edges of the hole began to crumble and collapse, bringing a rain of falling masonry. From near the exit, having just manhandled the last of Redigor's victims through, Kali stared back into the Chapel, picking out Gabriella's corpse through the resultant cloud of dust and debris. She started towards it, intending to carry it out with her, but two slabs of the roof collapsed in her path. Coughing and spluttering, Kali staggered back, looking for another way around. The Engine had begun to burrow itself into the base of the Chapel, and great jagged rents were splitting the floor, spidering out in all directions. Kali finally had to concede that there was no way through. Reluctantly, she turned and stepped onto the bridge.

As Kali began to race after the others, making their way slowly across the bridge, the second of the Engines slammed into the chapel roof and through it and the Chapel of Screams was no more. Kali looked back and swallowed as cracks began to pursue them across the bridge. Many of the former soul-stripped still milled by the tombs lining the chamber, free of their possession but lost on the crumbling walkways.

"Get a farking move on!" Kali shouted to those on the bridge, and to those above and below, "Hey, do you *really* want to die?"

Miraculously they all made it, bursting from the entrance of Bel'A'Gon'Shri and racing to safety along the gorge just as the entire necropolis collapsed. Kali and Slowhand ushered them on along the gorge, at last reaching a safe distance where the dust and debris from Bel'A'Gon'Shri choked and coated them but otherwise passed them harmlessly by.

The rest of the party out of harm's way, Kali told them to carry on while she and Slowhand paused for a while. She wanted to make sure that the third and last of the Engines followed its companions, not only to confirm that the peninsula was rid of the things but also because, in a sense, it would be like watching the final nail being hammered into Bastian Redigor's coffin.

Unfortunately, things didn't go quite according to plan. Explosions rocked the third Engine, and it began to spin faster and faster, before it fell.

Kali and Slowhand looked at the crooked remains of its companions beneath it, and did some quick mental calculations.

"Please tell me it's not going to do what I think it's going to do," Slowhand said.

Kali stared. "It's going to do what you think it's going to do."

"Oh. Hells."

"Shall we run?"

"I think we'd better."

Despite their words, they remained where they were for another couple of seconds, staring up.

The third engine was coming down on the other two and still spinning at full tilt. Exactly how the engine would react to that Kali and Slowhand couldn't be sure, but it wasn't likely to be gentle or quiet.

The third engine, its sirens blaring, listed badly to the side as it continued its fall, presenting itself side on to the remains of the engines below. The strangely shaped mass slewed into its companions with a grinding and clashing of metals louder even than the noise of the sirens, jamming itself between them and, with an almighty explosion, hurled itself out from between its grounded companions, tumbling end over end towards the necropolis's entrance. The Engine shattered and scattered statues as it came and, when its nose hit the ground, flipped itself end over end once more, bounced along the gorge for perhaps three or four rotations, and slapped down onto its belly with ground-quaking force, skewing along the gorge towards them.

"Now?" Slowhand asked.

"Now." Kali said.

The two of them turned and began to run like the hells, the engine demolishing trees, boulders, *everything* behind them, and still coming. The pair snatched glances over their shoulders and wished they hadn't, as it was beginning to look as if they had turned to run just a little too late.

The engine, seemingly unstoppable, continued to tear up the ground as it advanced, creating a solid tsunami of soil, rock and shredded vegetation. It would not, both of them reflected, be a very nice way to go.

The first ripples of soil and debris nudged at their ankles.

They looked at each other, and gulped.

Then Katherine Makennon was standing before them and the Anointed Lord was not alone. A group of ten mages, who had presumably teleported in to be by her side when they had witnessed the arrival and demise of the Engines, stood to either side of her. Makennon gestured to them and, as one, they raised their arms, releasing visible pulses of energy over Kali and Slowhand's heads, designed to slow the rampaging Engine down.

The strain was written on their faces. Veins pulsed beneath their flesh. From the noses of one or two blood began to trickle, and then pour.

The Engine began to slow. Gradually, the sounds of destruction from behind Kali and Slowhand quietened. And then it was over, the two of them rather embarrassingly pushed right in front of Makennon on the crest of a final, slow wave of soil.

"Thanks," Kali said, after a moment.

The Anointed Lord regarded her. The cloak she wore to restore her dignity had, it seemed, been 'donated' by the mayor of Gargas, who stood shivering in his britches behind her.

"I think that makes us even," Katherine Makennon said. Her tone made it clear that there would be no discussion as to what had happened. *Ever*.

Kali nodded. As she did, Freel emerged from the undergrowth and stood by Makennon's side. He snapped his fingers at those mages who weren't holding handkerchiefs to their noses, and they began to weave the threads. After a few seconds, the air before Makennon and Freel parted into a rift through which Kali glimpsed a view of Makennon's inner sanctum back at Scholten Cathedral. The rift hovered a couple of feet off the ground but, in an ostentatious touch presumably designed to ease Makennon's passage, a small flight of steps formed so that she could reach it.

As if they were departing after a simple day in the countryside, Makennon's retinue filed through one by one, until only the Anointed Lord and Freel were left. Then it was Freel's turn. At first it seemed that Jenna's husband was going to leave without a goodbye but he paused, one foot on the steps, and turned to Slowhand.

"I'll remember this," he said.

Slowhand nodded and, with a bow to Kali, Freel was gone.

Makennon stepped up to the threshold of the portal. Like Freel it seemed that she, too, was going to depart without another word but then she turned to Kali and beckoned her to her side.

"That girl in the Chapel. Who was she?"

"Her name," Kali said, "was Gabriella DeZantez."

"DeZantez... DeZantez," Makennon repeated as if she were dredging the name up from some dark and forgotten depth. "Ah, yes."

Then Makennon – and the portal – were gone.

"Well, they could have offered us a lift," Slowhand said. But the only response he got from Kali was a crashing of the undergrowth. "Hooper? Hooper?"

Kali was storming away from the necropolis as fast as she could go. Slowhand hurried to catch up.

"Farking woman!" Kali cursed.

"Hooper, I'm not sure you should be storming through the forest like this."

"No? You know any better way to get the hells out of the pitsing place?"

"Hooper, what I mean is *slow down*, or you'll bring every freak and monstrosity within a league's radius down on us!"

"Bring 'em on."

"Don't be stupid."

"I said, fark 'em, Slowhand!"

The archer pulled a face, grabbed her by the shoulders with his good arm, and turned her around. "Hey," he shouted. "Hey!"

Kali wrenched herself out of his grip, turned in a frustrated circle, not knowing what to do with herself, and finally kicked a nearby tree trunk. Something with wings that flapped like wet cloth took to the sky but Kali didn't care, her breathing fast and hard.

"Hooper," Slowhand gasped, "if you don't stop crashing around you're going to get us *both* killed."

Kali bent and ran the back of her hand across her mouth, speaking breathlessly. "Leave it alone, 'Liam."

"I can't do that. Because this isn't about Makennon, is it?" Slowhand challenged. "It's about Gabriella."

Kali shot him a look, found his firm but concerned blue eyes holding her gaze, and gradually brought her breathing under control. The archer was only partly right, but right enough. It was about Gabriella, yes, but about Makennon, too – the way the woman had swanned off just now. Pits of Kerberos, she didn't want any gratitude herself – gods knew, she hoped she wasn't *that* petty – but she *did* want some kind of acknowledgement for the people who had died to win her the freedom to go home. Not only Gabriella DeZantez but those many who had died at the hands of the juggennath or in their subsequent flight from it. Still, it was Gabriella that stuck in her mind, and what stuck more than anything were Makennon's words about her.

Who was she?

Who was she?

Kali pulled away from Slowhand and continued, with him trailing behind. The pair managed to negotiate a couple of leagues without incident, but found themselves freezing at a sudden thrashing from the bush beside them. Kali drew her gutting knife, ready to wield against whatever warped denizen of the forest had them in its sights. Nothing came at them though, and, after a few seconds, Kali pulled the undergrowth aside.

The source of the thrashing was a warped denizen all right, but not the kind that she or Slowhand had expected.

Querilous Fitch lay in a ditch beneath them, having presumably landed here after he had been struck by the juggennath. The extent of his injuries were plain to see.

Fitch saw Slowhand and the broken body of the psychic manipulator spasmed in the ditch, hands desperately trying to rise and wield some kind of magic, offensive or defensive, but his arms simply flapped by his sides ineffectually.

"That old problem again, Fitch?" Slowhand growled. "You really ought to see a doctor about that."

The archer moved in and took Fitch by the neck, staring him in the eyes as he tightened his grip.

"'Liam, don't kill him," Kali said.

"What?"

"I'm asking you not to kill him. He has information that I need."

"What the hells do you mean, he has information that you need?"

Kali hesitated. "Something... well, I don't know if it's important, but it might be."

"Oh, really," Slowhand hissed without loosening his grip. Fitch was struggling, turning blue, his tongue bloating between twisted lips. "Hooper, this guy was responsible for the death of my sister and in case you hadn't noticed has tried to kill me twice, both times without compunction or hesitation, and frankly I don't want him running around anymore. You tell me – what could be more important than that?"

"I –" Kali began, and stopped.

She rocked back and forth on her heels, torn. *Share this with someone*, Gabriella had said. *Don't bear it alone.* But how could she burden her sometime lover with the knowledge that the world he knew – and all of the beds and women in it – might soon be coming to an end? The answer was, she couldn't – at least until Slowhand, with a sigh, suddenly released his grip on Fitch, dropping his choking victim back into the bottom of the ditch, and turned to face her, more concerned than she had ever seen him.

"Dammit, Hooper, this is about that night at the Flagons, isn't it? The night you stormed out of the party? Because you learned something in the Crucible, didn't you? Something you haven't told anyone?" He took her by the shoulder again, and this time Kali didn't pull away.

She did just the opposite, in fact.

"Kal, what is it?" Slowhand asked, as she sobbed in his arms.

She told him everything. About what the dwelf had said about the coming darkness and about what she had learned about 'the Four' and how she had come to believe they might have a role in preventing it. When she had finished, Slowhand said nothing, his eyes like those of a drowning man. In the end, it was Fitch who broke the silence.

"Everything your girlfriend says is true," the manipulator admitted, "and I have the information she needs to make sense of it."

"Then spill it," Slowhand said.

Fitch smiled. "Not here. Hidden. I can tell her how to find it, how to retrieve it, but first you have to get me out of here."

"No deal."

Kali looked at Slowhand, hesitant. She knew the decision she was about to make was not going to be popular. "Deal," she said. "Can you help me get him up? We should be near enough to the perimeter now for me to whistle Horse."

"No," Slowhand said.

Kali shook her head and clambered into the ditch. "Fine. I'll do it myself."

Slowhand held her arm. "I mean no, he's not coming, Hooper. The bastard stays here, takes his chances."

"Slowhand, *please*."

"No."

"No?" It was the first time Slowhand had ever openly disagreed with her.

"No, Kal," Slowhand said more softly. "Because it strikes me that if it's your *destiny* to do these things, your destiny to find these things out, then you're going to find them out whichever way things happen. *If* it's Fitch who's destined to tell you what you need to know then he'll find his way out of this and he'll tell you, but I'll be damned if I'm going to help him do so."

"What if that's *your* destiny? To help him?"

Slowhand slapped his forehead in frustration. "No, Kali. No, I'm not having that. I'll not accept that my every move is predestined." The archer felt the need to explain further, sought an analogy. "Look, I believed it was Pontaine's destiny to win the Great War – every one of us did, which is why we fought so hard and for so long – and in the end we *did* win, spilling the blood of thousands on the Killing Ground. *Thousands*, Kal – but you know that. The point is the battle was won as a result of thousands of decisions that I and those fighters made each and every second we fought – split second choices to cut or to thrust, parry or raise shield, shoot or hold that made the difference between our lives and our deaths. And all of those decisions were based on what our *enemies* chose, out of thousands of choices of their own. Just how many choices is that in all, Kal? It was chaos on the Killing Ground, *chaos*, so can you really tell me that every one of those decisions was predestined?"

"Of course not!" Kali said defensively, aware of the strength of Slowhand's argument. "But I'm talking about the bigger picture." She struggled. "The way it needs all the pieces to fit together... like a jigsaw."

"Didn't you once tell me that you were crap at jigsaws?" Slowhand said.

Kali stared up at him, tearful, then down at Fitch, torn.

"Hooper," Slowhand said, "wars are won as they're meant to be won, through dedication to a cause and a determination to see it through. I know you – you might hate every minute of this, but I also know you *will* see it through whether you're one of these fabled 'four' or not. And you know why? Because that's *who you are*, and not because it's your destiny. But if you let Fitch manipulate you like this, you'll be just as much one of his puppets as Jenna was."

"Will you... see it through with me?"

"I don't know, Kal. I just don't know."

Kali bit her lip, then nodded. She whistled for Horse and, a few minutes later, the bamfcat appeared. Kali mounted, slapping the thick of his neck hard in thanks for coming to collect her. "Sorry, Querilous," she said to the protesting, groaning figure in the ditch, and then, to Slowhand, "You coming?"

"Give me a second," Slowhand said, "I'll catch up." He watched as Kali nodded once more then walked Horse forward through the forest, and then he turned back to Querilous Fitch.

"Are you going to kill me now, archer?" The manipulator said. He nodded at Suresight. "I should imagine that would prove difficult, with only one arm."

Slowhand whipped an arrow from his quiver and held its tip shaking above Querilous Fitch's chest. "I only need one arm."

"You really should listen to your girlfriend, you know. It's your *destiny*."

Slowhand almost plunged the arrow down right then, but he held it, his unblinking blue eyes looking into Fitch's, *through* him. *Thousands of choices a second*, he thought, *and through those wars are won.* He stood and began to walk away. Whether it was the low, sick cackling from behind him or the sibilant, murmuring, protesting voices in his own head he didn't know, but a moment later he turned, returned to Fitch and, with a shout, rammed the arrow into the manipulator's chest with such force that it pinned him to the ground. Wide eyed, Fitch was so stunned that he couldn't even wail.

"I make my *own* destiny," Slowhand said, and followed Kali's trail.

BOTH KALI AND Slowhand wanted to take the journey slowly, and, camping at their leisure, took three days to return to the Flagons. The last thing they expected when they arrived was an invitation to attend a memorial service in Scholten for those who hadn't made it out of the Sardenne. Kali thought for a second that she had, after all, misjudged Makennon – but on closer inspection it turned out that their invitation had been signed by Jakub Freel. At any rate, the service was scheduled for the next day at Midchime and, after both she and Slowhand had been thoroughly polished and preened by Dolorosa – "you notta go in anything from which your bum sticka out, young lady!" – the two of them set out on Horse, reaching the Vossian seat of power overnight, in four jumps.

They spent the morning in the Gay Goblin, the Kegs O'Kerberos and the Bloody Merry, marking time in the way of those aware that, on a fundamental level, things were moving on. Gradually, eventually, they worked their way towards the cathedral, the front of which, by the time they arrived, was filled with people considerably more sober than they. The two of them were content with a place in the jostling crowd, but one look from a guard at their invitation had them elevated to the front platform where they were positioned instead alongside Freel, the Anointed Lord and a number of dignitaries including Cardinal Kratos and General McIntee.

Freel nodded as they took their places. Makennon, however, did not even acknowledge their presence, remaining aloof. Whether that was because she was maintaining her public face or, as Kali suspected, this whole thing and their part in it had been Freel's idea and Makennon resented it, she didn't know – but it was interesting to note that the Faith's new enforcer seemed far more willing to adopt a prominent public role than Konstantin Munch had ever done.

Quite what he intended to *do* with it was a matter for another day.

Bells rang, silencing the crowd, and Makennon's address began. Kali was hardly surprised that in the Anointed Lord's account of the events in the Sardenne, neither she nor Slowhand got a mention, and in fact she had difficulty recognising any of it. All the crowd seemed to want to hear, however, was that – aided by the Lord of All – the forces of the Final Faith had defeated their First Enemy and that once again its flock could look forward to the glory of the day of ascension. The very mention of the word brought a rousing cheer from the crowd, and both Kali and Slowhand shuffled uneasily as the all too familiar mantra began to sound from the crowd, growing in volume with each repetition.

"The One Faith!"

"The Only Faith!"

"*The Final Faith!*"

Eventually, the Anointed Lord raised a hand, and the crowd lapsed into silence. Bells rang once more, but this time more slowly, a dirge rather than a call to attention. Makennon nodded to Cardinal Kratos and the robed figure moved solemnly forward. He began, as was way of these things, to intone platitudes about the dead.

The names were read out, the accompanying comments saying nothing at all about the people who had died, or what had led them to make the sacrifices they had made. As banality followed banality, Slowhand saw the growing tension in Kali's face. The thing about Hooper was that she never got drunk unless she wanted to or she was upset. It was almost as if she could open a sluice gate somewhere halfway down her throat, and all the alcohol she consumed simply went somewhere else. Today, however, that sluice gate had remained firmly closed, and while he'd *thought* she was handling herself well, considering the amount of thwack they'd poured down their necks, he now saw that slightly unfocused look in her eyes.

Trouble was brewing, he knew it.

Sure enough, as the roll call of the dead reached Gabriella DeZantez and the platitudes began to spout, Kali suddenly lurched forward and shoved the cardinal out of the way. The noise Kratos made as he tumbled down the platform's wooden steps were amplified by the complex arrangement of shells positioned around the podium to amplify speech, and three quarters of Scholten gasped.

Behind Kali the Swords of Dawn honour guard reached for their weapons, but a subtle shake of the head from Makennon halted them.

"You want to know about Gabriella DeZantez?" Kali began. "I'll tell you about Gabriella DeZantez..."

As Kali began to speak about the woman she had known, her loyalty, her dedication, her embarrassing laugh and even her *eyes*, Slowhand stared at the back of Kali's head and mouthed, *goodbye*. He had decided that morning that it was time to go, that he had to spend time away from Hooper and work out what was to happen in the future on his own, and now was as good a time as any. Maybe he'd be back, maybe not, but whatever happened he knew that at least Kali had another friend she could rely on, one within the Faith itself.

Slowhand nodded to Jakub Freel as he made his way off the platform and down into the crowd. Kali was in full swing now and didn't notice him go.

"...if it wasn't for Gabriella DeZantez," Kali shouted, pointing at the Anointed Lord, "this woman would be spending the rest of her life with tassels on her tits!"

Slowhand smiled, working his way through the crowd. A few days ago he'd have stopped to help with the commotion that comment would cause, but Hooper would be all right.

Look after her, Prince Jakub Tremayne Freel, he thought.

What Slowhand did not know was that as he had left the platform and stared into the eyes of the Faith enforcer, it had been Bastian Redigor staring back.

THE END

The TRIALS of TRASS KATHRA

Original cover art by Greg Staples

CHAPTER ONE

ONE YEAR AFTER Kali Hooper last laid eyes on Killiam Slowhand she came face to face with her lover once more. The reunion, if such it could be called, was brief; he a sketch on a stray handbill plastered to a storm-lashed steeple high above Scholten Cathedral, she a flailing, cursing figure sliding hopelessly down its slates in the direction of thin air and certain death.

Despite this, Kali couldn't help but snatch up the sodden parchment and gaze on it curiously. The bill advertised a travelling carney and its main attraction, Slowhand. Except Slowhand was now 'Thongar the Golden Archer!' with the emphasis very much on the 'thong'. The tiny posing pouch in which he was pictured hid little – which, okay, was quite a lot, she'd grant – but she'd seen those bits before. It was the burgeoning beer belly, sparkling body paint and peaked feathered cap that were new to her.

So it was that when she plunged off the steeple, her cry was a mix of bemusement, hilarity and desperation.

"Waha? Wahahaha! Wahaaarrrggghhh…"

The wind snatched away the handbill and Kali shut up. It wouldn't do to alert the Faith with her noise – especially if that noise was a splat. She concentrated instead on finding a way to halt her fall, perhaps to make the violent night that had caused her to lose her footing in the first place work *for* rather than against her.

She was high enough, fortunately, to allow herself to simply drop and look for a second, and this she did, though unfortunately there seemed to be nothing more substantial nearby than the curtain of water pouring from the steeple, acting as a backdrop to her descent.

Then, lit by a sudden and powerful sheet of lightning, she made out a ramshackle trellis-work of iron behind the filthy liquid curtain, guttering meant to carry the ocean unleashed by the heavens which, like herself, had been overwhelmed by volume and unremitting strength. What rain the guttering did carry filled it beyond capacity and bubbled, foamed and spurted from every joint, threatening to break the protesting labyrinth of pipes and send a tangle of iron crashing into the courtyard far below.

Kali spotted one pipe ready to go and, twisting with a grunt in mid-air, snatched through the waterfall at the column of over-stressed iron. Already loose in its mooring, pulled further by her weight, its top half broke from the wall, a jet of filthy grey water erupting in her face. Another jet came from its disjoined gutter above, plastering her hair flat, and Kali flubbed her lips, spitting away the clinging strands. Dammit, she'd just had her hair done, too.

Jerking to manoeuvre the pipe, Kali clung to the roughly wrought metal as, with a groan, it bent further away from the steeple until it projected at the diagonal, then swung her weight around, forcing the metal to the side and rotating it back in against the wall. The stress on its lower half was now so much that it was starting to snap but that didn't matter – if it did crash to the ground the Faith would think it a victim of the storm, and it had served its purpose anyway. Even as she had manoeuvred the pipe, Kali had already spotted where to leap next, and she threw herself through the air to grab a horizontal section some feet away.

Water splashing and beading coldly on her already chilled hands, Kali dangled there for a second, gasping, and watched the piping she had abandoned break away to tumble down the vertiginous side of the steeple tower. It turned end over end until it almost disappeared from sight and then bounced across the courtyard below with a series of barely audible clangs. It gone, she looked around her, regaining the orientation she had lost in her fall. Her sudden departure from her well-planned route across the rooftops had caused her to lose sight of her destination – the reason she had come to Scholten tonight – and it was a few seconds before she found it again. Then there, between annexes of the sprawling cathedral complex, she once more pinpointed her goal.

Perched high above her, atop a sheer wall dotted with maybe a hundred or more yellowed, candlelit windows beyond which berobed shadows roamed, the dark dome that was the domain of Brother Incera sat.

It remained a long climb away, but Kali knew she had to reach it during the azure night hours. Not only was this the only time she could guarantee Brother Incera would be present, but she would simply never make it through the complex during full daylight. There were too many Faith around for that. Far more than there had ever been before.

Kali was about to move again when, far below, she heard the solid slamming of a heavy door and looked down to see a small group of Faith scurrying across the courtyard cobbles to investigate the noise of the fallen pipe. For a second they paused in the rain, staring up at the cascade of water and shaking their heads in dismay, and as another flash of sheet lightning lit the wall Kali pulled her legs up towards her middle, making herself as small as she could to avoid detection. Luckily the downpour left the Faith in no mood to tarry, and they returned whence they came. The door, caught by the wind, slammed shut behind them.

Kali breathed a sigh of relief and lowered her legs. Her feet found purchase on another piece of guttering running parallel and below that to which she clung, and she used the two in tandem to inch her way to the corner of the steeple tower and onto its east facing. There, sheltered some from the storm, she transferred to another vertical stretch of pipe and, testing its solidity, began to ascend to a position where she could again work her way to the dome.

She climbed haltingly, moving from shadow to shadow, because the wall of windows was right behind her now, and she was acutely aware that all it would take was one casual glance out into the darkness for her game to be up.

It was an unusual feeling, being so wary of the Faith. But then, as with her own life, things with Makennon's church were not what they had been. The Anointed Lord's self-proclaimed 'Only Faith' had begun to change not long after the encounter with Bastian Redigor in the Sardenne, transforming over the year from the despotic though superficially benign church it had been, to the simply despotic. Many of its flock now lived as much in fear of its torch-wielding priests as they had once lived in awe of them, and as if the Eyes of the Lord, the Overseers and the Order of the Swords of Dawn hadn't been enough of a handful, there were some new kids on the block. Recruited from mercenary factions, the Red Chapter had swollen the Faith's paramilitary forces until they had begun to rival the Vossian army itself and, working alongside their more pious comrades, their presence across the peninsula was total. So total that most people had become afraid to even think.

What was more disturbing, those brave souls who did dare speak out against the apparent hardening in attitude of Katherine Makennon had started vanishing. It wasn't, of course, unusual for dissenters of the Faith to vanish but, where previously they might have expected to meet their end in the naphtha chambers beneath Scholten, there had been no sign of the smoke that meant the burners were in use. No, these people were simply gone, and the words on the lips of those who had lost loved ones was that it was to 'a fate worse than death.'

She herself had narrowly avoided being one of them. The day of the memorial service to the victims of the Sardenne a year ago had, of course, ended with her verbal attack on Makennon and, while she was willing to concede that her comment about the tassels on her tits might have been a little inappropriate, she *had* been unusually shit-faced and so would have expected little more than a prompt ejection from the speakers' platform. That, though, hadn't been what happened. In the absence of Slowhand, the one other person she'd have thought she could rely on had instead ordered her arrest. Jakub Freel. Dammit, how could she have been so wrong about him? How could she *and* Slowhand have been so wrong? The bonds of friendship they both thought they had forged with the undercover Allantian prince were clearly not as strong to him, and the fact that Freel had subsequently ordered her to be incarcerated in the Deep Cells pending what he called 'relocation' severed them completely. It was only the fact that after a month her cell had been unlocked by some unknown ally – to this day she didn't know who, though from the peculiarly misshapen handprint on the lock she was certain it wasn't Freel – that she hadn't found out first-hand what it meant to become one of the 'disappeared'.

Ironically, thereafter, she'd been forced to make herself disappear. Declared an outlaw by Freel, she'd been hunted wherever she went by Overseers and Eyes of the Lord, by every priest in every town, and by the mercenary-bolstered Order of the Swords of Dawn, some of whose ranks had scant regard for the vows taken by their brothers. They were, in short, a bunch of psychopaths fit to rival Konstantin Munch or even the Ur'Raney, and their constant snapping at her heels made an already difficult task even more so. This past year she'd been forced to skulk in the shadows and rely on the shelter of friends during her investigations, and there had been a few close shaves during it. One particular group who'd had the temerity to get *too* close were now entombed for all eternity inside Black Johnson's Crypts, and if they had any hopes she was going to return and release the seals, they had another think coming.

Fark 'em. She had a world to save.

But the question remained, from what? Or, more accurately, from what *exactly*? Kali heaved herself onto the roof and took a breather, crouching at its edge like a gargoyle, silhouetted by the body that dominated the azure night sky. The gas giant hung there like a giant, malevolent eye and was the reason she had come here in search of Brother Incera.

The gas giant was not Kerberos, however.

It was the Hel'ss.

Kali bit her lip as she stared at the object she had first seen from the deck of the *Tharnak*, when it had been nothing more than a smudge on the side of Twilight's distant sun. It was a smudge no longer, but a fully fledged part of the heavens in its own right. And while it shared many characteristics with Kerberos, though was of a more violent, redder colour, it differed from its counterpart in one very important respect.

It was drawing closer to Twilight every day.

Kali recalled what she had managed to piece together about this cosmic entity since she had first learned of its existence, and whichever way the facts were interpreted, things did not look good. From the vastly expanded and darkened sphere of Kerberos that she and Pim had experienced during their visit to the past in Domdruggle's Expanse, to the countdown that marked its approach at the Crucible of the Dragon God, to Bastian Redigor's revelation that the last time the Hel'ss appeared his race died, and that this time it was the turn of the humans, there was only one inescapable conclusion.

It wasn't just the Hel'ss that was drawing near, it was the End Time.

"This world is called Twilight for a reason," the dwelf at the Crucible had told her. "Once in an age, to every civilisation, a great darkness comes."

And it seemed to have fallen to her to help stop it.

Whatever 'it' was.

Her destiny as one of 'the Four'.

The Four. Gods, she was coming to hate the phrase. Because despite having learned what she had about the Hel'ss, her knowledge of who and what the Four were was almost as scant as it had been the day she'd first heard the phrase beneath the floodwaters of Martak. The strange undersea creature she'd encountered there had spoken cryptically of 'Four Known To Us, Four Unknown To Each Other, Four Who Will Be Known To All', but the fact was its comments remained as annoying a riddle now as they had then – more so considering she had met two of the Four and they were as much in the dark about things as she was.

Oh sure, she knew who her brothers-in-arms were: Lucius Kane, Shadowmage; Silus Morlader, Mariner; and Gabriella DeZantez, Sister of the Order of the Swords of Dawn, now deceased and ascended to Kerberos, but what was the connection between them other than the physical and mental gifts they each possessed? What the hells were they, was *she*, meant to do? To make matters worse, the only one to whom she had not spoken, who just might know something, Silus Morlader, hadn't been seen for months, and the rumour was that both he and his ship had been lost at sea.

That was the problem. It seemed she was being stymied at every turn. Even what had been such a promising lead – the so-called 'Halo Files' that Querilous Fitch was meant to possess – had, after months of effort, ultimately proved fruitless. A seemingly endless amount of cajoling, bribery and tracking of Querilous Fitch's past movements had led her eventually to a priest to whom Fitch had given the files for safekeeping, but on going there she had found the priest's house razed to the ground by forces unknown. The only lead she'd gained was from a remnant of parchment that mentioned the island of Trass Kathra, but that wasn't much of a lead at all, because Trass Kathra – the Island of the Lost – was exactly that: lost. The place was a myth, a rock in the middle of nowhere that had vanished long, long ago, pummelled under the waves supposedly by the gods themselves.

Banging her farking head against the wall. That was what she had been doing. Then it had occurred to her – if doors were slamming in her face every time she tried to find out more about 'the Four' then maybe, instead, it was time to find out more about the threat they faced.

To take a closer look at the Hel'ss.

Literally.

And with Merrit Moon's elven telescope having been destroyed in the k'nid invasion, there was only one other place on the peninsula she could do that.

Kali moved on, working her way across the storm struck rooftops towards her destination. The route was complex and treacherous, and for anyone with normal abilities it would have been suicidal, an impossible challenge. But Kali's preternatural prowess got her where she needed to go in a little over an hour. Not that her passage was without incident – at one point she was forced to negotiate a precipitous wall of old but barely rooted ivy, flinging herself from one section to the next as each ripped away, at another to shimmy above a rumbling portcullis as the crunching boots of a Faith battalion marched through it into the night, and at yet another – somehow the most nerve-racking of all – having to inch her way past the apartment windows of her old sparring partner, Katherine Makennon herself. The Anointed Lord was home and awake, silhouetted with her back to her before a large, roaring fire, staring motionlessly into it, but her presence made Kali feel strangely uneasy and she felt it best not to disturb her reverie by knocking and saying 'hi'.

The most dangerous section saved itself for last. The 'bridge' between the wing she was on and the wing she needed to reach was a stretch of flat rooftop filled with lightning rods that caught the raw power of the heavens and transmitted it to the sub-levels of the complex and the Old Race technology in use there. The violent night meant that bolts of lightning were striking one or more of the rods every few seconds and, threatening to overload, the rods were subsequently discharging the strikes to other rods, causing arcs of bright blue energy to flit between them randomly. There was no way Kali could predict a safe route and a single touch would burn her to a crisp, and so the only thing she could do was trust in her reactions, pray to the gods, and run like the hells.

Her brain buzzed heavily, feeling like lead, as she rolled, somersaulted and flung herself through the deadly and ever moving web but she made it, the only sign of her running the gauntlet a scorched and smoking bodysuit with a few slashes across the arms and one particularly revealing one on her arse that was going to give Dolorosa a dicky-fit the next time she snook home.

Gasping, she came at last to the dome within which she hoped to find Brother Incera. The structure was much larger close to than it had appeared during her approach, as one might expect considering it housed the Faith's so-called cosmoscope. The immense arrangement of lenses and mirrors that magnified the skies above Twilight had been considered by many within the Church to be a blasphemous, sacrilegious object but somehow it had survived the Faith's puritanical purges over the years, as had its keeper, Incera himself. The aging Brother probably knew more about the vagaries and mechanisms of the heavens than anyone else on Twilight, and for that reason Kali hoped that he, amongst a Faith who, troublingly, seemed to have accepted the Hel'ss as a part of their religion, might be able to enlighten her as to what the entity was and what the hells was going on.

A sheet of lightning illuminated Kali as she paused at the base of the dome, frowning. She might have reached it but getting inside was another matter. The actual entrance to the dome was one floor down, inside the cathedral, and other than risking further close encounters with the Faith the only other way in was the gap in its curved surface out of which the cosmoscope viewed the heavens. And that was currently positioned almost at the apex of the dome, trained, it seemed, on Kerberos.

Kali jumped back at a sudden grating in the rooftop beneath her feet, and realised that the dome was turning. She looked down at its base, where thick greased wheels revolved along a circular track, and then upwards, where she could just make out the nose of the cosmoscope being realigned to a different viewpoint. The angle and degree of rotation left little doubt in Kali's mind that it was turning to face the Hel'ss, and Kali guessed – hoped – that Incera was doing what she'd hoped he would be doing – comparing the two celestial bodies like the man of science he was. Because if Incera's curiosity was piqued sufficiently for him to do that, then she just might not have to force the information she needed out of him.

Kali dug into a pocket of her slashed silk bodysuit and withdrew a small tube, the base of which she rotated. The tube was one of a number of Old Race devices she'd scrounged from Merrit Moon some months before, reasoning that if she'd become Public Enemy Number One she needed all the assistance she could get. From the top of the tube a magnetic wire shot upwards to wrap itself around the cosmoscope, and Kali pulled the wire taut and climbed, grabbing onto the broad cylinder of metal. She heaved herself upwards with a grunt, her chest pressing against the cosmoscope's outer lens, and then she flipped herself onto its top from where she was able to work her way inside the dome.

It was a tight squeeze but at last she made it through. She dropped to the floor of Brother Incera's observatory; a wet, smouldering and bedraggled figure looking like something that had dragged itself from the depths of the Strannian Sulphur Swamps.

Three acolytes stopped what they were doing and stared. One of them made a move for a bell suspended in a niche in the wall, but as the young woman was about to raise its accompanying hammer to sound the alarm a voice from the operative end of the cosmoscope said, "No."

Kali turned, water sloughing from her to form a puddle at her feet. The man who had spoken continued to stare into the eyepiece of the cosmoscope but waved a hand behind him, shooing the acolyte away from the alarm. Though she couldn't see his face, Kali guessed that the older, more hunched looking form beneath the Faith robes was who she had struggled here to see.

Brother Incera turned a moment later, a look of curiosity on his face. There was also an intrigued twinkle in his eyes and superficial resemblance to the old man that reminded Kali very much of Merrit Moon.

"Leave us," Incera said to the acolytes. "And say nothing to the guards."

The acolytes did, though casting vaguely suspicious glances behind them.

"Thank you," Kali said after they'd gone. "For not raising the alarm."

Incera shrugged. "It isn't every day an old man has the chance to gaze upon two new and, may I say, impressive celestial bodies."

"I'm sorry?"

The astronomer coughed, glancing with some embarrassment at her chest, then up at the cosmoscope itself.

Kali blushed. What she had wasn't much but she guessed if they were magnified a few hundred times...

"Oh. Right. Look, I'm sorry about that but it was the only way I could get to see you. Brother Incera, my name is Kali Hoo –"

"I know who you are, Miss Hooper. Among the Faith, your exploits have become a matter of some... consternation over time. I know also why you are here."

"You do?"

"Take a look," Incera said without preamble. He gestured at the cosmoscope's eyepiece and Kali moved hesitantly towards it.

"Kerberos and its new companion," Incera said as she did so. "To the naked eye, so very similar, aren't they? On closer inspection, not so at all."

Kali placed her eye against the eyepiece and pulled back slightly, blinking. For a second she was puzzled as to why a device so advanced should produce such blurred results, but then she realised that the lenses would have been set to Brother Incera's eyesight, which was likely not so acute as her own.

Her hand moved to the side of the cosmoscope and her fingers found and manipulated dials there, adjusting the instrument's focus until the Hel'ss was outlined clearly and starkly against the background of the cosmos.

She gasped.

Brother Incera had been correct in his observations that while the Hel'ss superficially resembled Kerberos, in close up the difference between the two was marked.

Where the azure surface of Kerberos was scudded with the layer of clouds Kali now knew to be the souls of Twilight's dead that were drawn there, the surface of the Hel'ss was, in comparison, almost bare, resembling less a gas giant as some impossibly large, translucent brain. The more Kali studied it, the more she began to discern gaseous filaments reaching out from its surface across space and almost stroking the atmosphere of Kerberos, and the more uncomfortably aware of some sentient presence up there she became.

It could just have been her imagination, of course, but it wasn't, as what happened a moment later proved beyond doubt.

For a second, just a second as Kali watched, the entire surface of the Hel'ss suddenly and unexpectedly reorganised itself into a reasonable semblance of a face. Her face.

Kali pulled back with a gasp.

"Are you all right, Miss Hooper?"

What the hells *was* that? Kali thought. Was it even *possible*? But she had seen it with her own eyes – whether the Hel'ss was trying to scare her off or else imprinting itself with a knowledge of who she was, it had just demonstrated that it was a living thing.

It was telling her it *knew* her.

"Miss Hooper?"

Kali shook her head to clear it of the image. "Yes... yes, I'm all right. Sorry."

"My brethren have come to believe," Incera continued, "that the entity is some form of herald of Kerberos itself. That it is the first sign of the beginning of the cycle of their becoming one with their God."

That would explain a lot, and not for the first time in her dealings with organised religions Kali wondered where they got this shit. "You, I take it, are not of the same mind?"

"I am a man of science, Miss Hooper, not so easily persuaded."

"You also said *their* God. Hardly the kind of scepticism I'd expect from such a long-standing member of the Faith."

Again, Incera shrugged. "When we began, the Faith were not quite so fanatical as they are now. There was room within their ranks for people with open minds. Free thinking souls. Our acceptance was tolerated for the tactical advantages our pursuit of knowledge might bring to them. But, one by one over the years, our numbers became depleted, until only I remained." Incera smiled. "Somehow up here, in my little nest, I managed to evade the fundamentalist brooms that swept away the unworthy."

Kali realised at last that, in coming to see Brother Incera, she had made the right choice.

"The Hel'ss," she said. "What do you think it is?"

Incera sighed, moving to the walls of the observatory where a number of large parchments were strung one atop the other. The astronomer flipped them, revealing his sketched impressions of objects the cosmoscope had revealed to him over the years.

"There are many strange things in the heavens, Miss Hooper. I have seen worlds of flame and worlds of ice, worlds verdant and worlds long dead, and worlds that seem nought but smoke or shifting shadow. I have seen the stars by which they are lit and, on occasion, I have seen the children of worlds flit between them in tiny ships. I have seen great coloured clouds seemingly of no substance that take the shapes of everything imaginable by man. I have seen flares and streaks of fire that would incinerate Twilight would we be unlucky enough to feel their touch. But nowhere, Miss Hooper – *nowhere* – have I seen anything like the body that grows nearer to our world every day."

"You're saying that it isn't just some kind of... wandering star?"

"I would stake my reputation on it."

Kali thought about the filaments. "It seems, somehow, to be connected to Kerberos."

"Indeed it does. But what form, what purpose, that connection takes, I cannot say."

Kali decided it was time to let Incera in on everything, and the astronomer listened with growing horror as he learned about the fate of the Old races and its cause, and how the same threat was now returning to Twilight.

"It has to be stopped," Kali concluded. "But I have no idea how to do that."

Incera swallowed. "Miss Hooper, I'm sorry – neither do I."

He hesitated for a second, as if remembering something, but whatever it was remained unspoken as there was a hammering at the door to the observatory.

"One of my acolytes must have reported you to the guards," he said. "You have to go."

"In a minute," Kali said. She was used to the hammering of guards on doors and had become quite adept at calculating exactly how long it would take them to break through. She had time yet. "I want one more look at this thing before I go," she said, moving back to the eyepiece of the cosmoscope.

Incera glanced nervously between her and the door. "You must hurry."

"Don't worry," Kali muttered, and then, "Oh gods."

"Miss Hooper, is something wrong?"

"I've a feeling the guards are the least of our problems," Kali said. "It's the Hel'ss. Something's happening on the surface."

"Let me see."

Incera shoved Kali aside and stared into the eyepiece for a second. Kali knew he was looking at the same sudden and strange disturbance on the surface of the body that she had – a kind of broiling – and then the eyepiece flared with a light so bright it left a burned circle on Kali's retina. She didn't want to know what it had done to Incera's eyes.

"Oh," the astronomer said, staggering back from the cosmoscope. "Oh, Lord of All."

Whatever had caused the light, for it to be so intense through that tiny an aperture could only mean it had been blindingly so on the surface of the Hel'ss. And, what was more, the reason for it no longer needed to be viewed through the cosmoscope.

Through the break in the dome, Kali could see the entire night sky above Scholten filling with scintillating drops of light, intermingled with the rain and falling towards them.

"I think we should leave."

"Is something happening?" the astronomer said, blinking to restore vision. "What is it. Tell me!"

"I don't know. But trust me, it doesn't look good."

"What do you see?" Incera demanded.

But before Kali was able to give him an answer two things happened.

The first was that the guards at the door managed to break through and moved towards them, and the second was the first of the drops falling from the Hel'ss arrived, punching right through the metal of the dome.

Most hit the floor in short, sizzling spurts but one hit the palm of Incera's right hand.

"What is that – rain?" he said, dumbfounded. "How can it be raining inside the dome?"

Kali looked up, biting her lip at the impossibility of it. If there was any advantage to this unexpected development, it was that the guards had stopped at the sight of the strange downpour.

"It *hurts*," Incera said.

He groaned as the flesh of his palm seemed almost to liquefy, spiralling slowly about itself as if a corkscrew had been stuck into the flesh and turned. Kali grabbed his hand and stared as the skin and the bone beneath it melded together in a moving circle of white and red scar tissue, forcing out blood, that then slowly progressed through his flesh until it had burrowed a hole right through to the back of his hand. Incera groaned again, more loudly, as the ends of lost sections of cartilage and sinew snapped or contracted, twisting his hand into a grotesque parody of itself, like the misshapen claw of some old crone.

What the hells was this stuff? Kali thought. Some kind of acid? It was certainly acting like acid on the dome and the apparatus beneath it but she had never seen acid act the way this was doing on flesh. The liquefaction, the strange warping of Incera's hand, the lack of actual burning, it was as if the flesh were somehow being undone and *remade*.

Gods, if the stuff should hit something vital...

Kali wanted to shout *get out, get out now!*, not just to Incera but to the guards as well, but knew it was already too late.

The first tentative drops of the glowing rain were but a vanguard of what the Hel'ss had released on them, and the true downpour hit the dome with a vengeance.

Hundreds of drops punched through the dome and impacted with the observatory floor, creating a sea of sizzling holes. They were followed in rapid succession by more, many splashing and burning into the wall of the round chamber, incinerating Incera's charts, others punching into the cosmoscope itself, shattering the lenses mounted at both ends.

His eyes only now focusing, Incera stared at the ruined device and its cracked, smoking glass half quizzically, half in horror, but then found himself being bundled away from where he stood, thrust to safety by Kali. Her sudden manoeuvre sent the two of them crashing to floor where Kali rolled them over and over, their bodies narrowly avoiding the impacts of more of the potentially deadly projectiles.

The guards possessed much slower reactions and were not so lucky, and the first of them were felled instantly; one clutching at his heart through a widening hole as he collapsed with a gasp to the floor, the other simply toppling forward with a stunned expression in his eyes and a hole the size of a gold tenth in his head that was spiralling into his brain. This sent their brothers in arms into panic, stumbling over their fallen comrades in a dash for the door, but the rain was heavier still now and they had barely made a move before each of them was struck multiple times.

Kali caught fleeting glimpses of the same strange spiralling of flesh as the rain did its work, and within seconds they were writhing in agony on the dome's floor, their limbs and joints twisting and bending until they were grossly malformed, in some cases reduced to vestigial flaps of skin, until the guards resembled a twitching, spasming collection of involuntary circus freaks. Even the two who had been killed instantly were not spared the horror, their bodies shrinking and morphing before her eyes, spreading patches of flesh now just exposed veins and arteries seeping dark puddles of blood onto the floor.

Kali wanted very much to close her eyes – wished she could do the same with her ears, too, against the agonised screams – but she couldn't. She had managed to roll Incera under the cosmoscope but he was struggling against her, unable to cope with what he was seeing, trying to get away. That wasn't her only problem.

Above them the cosmoscope was buckling beneath the rain, its own integrity compromised, and it was only a matter of seconds before it fell onto them, crushing them beneath its riddled mass. Then, suddenly, a chunk of it did drop a foot, and as Kali struggled to hold it off them, Incera fled her grip, making a dash for the door.

Kali had no choice but to leave Incera and the guards to whatever fates might befall them and just do her best to stay alive. There was nowhere to run, nowhere to hide, and survival would be purely a matter of luck.

Dodging beneath chunks of metal she hoped were thick enough to absorb the lethal impacts, she darted from one to the other until, in turn, they began to collapse above her. Increasingly desperate screams sounded from all about her but all she caught were fleeting glimpses of bodies between metal – legs stumbling, torsos falling, heads slamming fatally to the floor – as she kept moving and the rain continued to fall.

Trembling, Kali moved and huddled, moved and huddled, and thought that the downpour was never going to end. When, suddenly, it did, she was left with a slight ringing in her ears and an inability to accept, for a second, that she had, in fact, survived. Then the groans of the deformed and dying, audible now that the rains were gone, coupled with an ever growing pool of blood that was seeping almost languidly into her last hiding place told her that she was, indeed, experiencing the aftermath.

Slowly, cautiously, Kali emerged from beneath the buckled metal, and gasped at what she saw.

The observatory dome was all but gone and most of the guards dead but, miraculously, Incera lay propped against the remains of the far wall of the observatory still, though barely, alive. Kali quickly moved to him, noting he was in a very bad way, his legs all but useless, part of his torso appearing to have been turned inside out, revealing glistening organs, head slumped to the side, blood trickling slowly from a mouth that gaped now almost to his ear.

"I'll get you some help," Kali said.

Incera held her back.

Through his deformed mouth, he spoke in a kind of half gurgle, half drawl. "Nohh. Theh'el khill yooo."

"I can't leave you here like this!"

Incera gave a weak laugh. "Mhaybee is worshe than it lhooks. Yooo harve to gho. Shtop... whatever ish happenink."

"I wish it were that easy. Without the Halo files, I don't have the faintest idea where to start."

Incera's eyes widened. "Haylo Fihles? Thart what I wash goin to tehll yoo. The enforsher, Freel, has the Haylo Fihles."

"Freel has them? How do you know that?"

Incera pointed weakly at the shredded remains of his research. "Brought me something to anahlyze frohm them – a stahrchahrt."

"He wanted to know about the stars?"

"Yesh. Nho. Nhot the stahrs themselves but what they would lhook lhike from a location here ohn Twilight. Whanted me to calchulate where iht wars."

"And did you?"

Incera nodded. "Aht sea. Fhar beyond the Storhmwall. Ttharn any ship has ehver sailed."

"At sea? But that doesn't make sense."

"If there were an ihsland there. Freel mentioned ah name. Trahss Kathra."

Kali felt as if she had been hit with a sledgehammer.

"Freel's found Trass Kathra? It exists?"

"Having ship built right now. At Gransk."

Gransk, Kali thought. The Faith shipyards. She couldn't believe that she had a lead after all this time, and it had to be her next destination.

Beneath her, Incera convulsed suddenly with pain, and she moved to lift him, to find him help, despite the danger. But then the sound of bootfalls on the stone stairs leading to the observatory signalled the approach of more guards, and Incera once more shoved her away.

"The uhniverse should be constant," he said, staring up at the exposed sky and the Hel'ss in particular. "Bhalance, counterbalance, everything in plhace." His face darkened. "But that... *thing* doesn't belong. You are the only one who can shtop it. Gho..."

Kali stared at Incera for a second, then nodded. She moved to the edge of the observatory and then, with a last, concerned glance back, disappeared beyond the remains of the dome.

Incera stiffened as the sound of bootfalls reached the broken door and a fresh group of guards flooded in, recoiling from what lay before their eyes. Then the guards parted and Jakub Freel himself strode into the remains of the dome. Ignoring the gasps for help from Brother Incera, the studded leather clad man ran the links of his chain whip through his hands as he slowly and thoughtfully gazed at the carnage before him.

"Sir!"

Freel turned in response to the cry from one of the guards, who had moved to the edge of the newly created parapet and was pointing out across the rooftops of the cathedral. In the distance, a small, body-suited figure leapt from one building to another, gradually working its way towards the edge of the complex.

"It's the Hooper woman, sir!"

Freel sighed heavily. "Why does that *child* always leave such destruction in her wake?"

"Sir?"

"Never mind."

"Do we go after her, sir?"

"Don't be a fool. You would not have a chance of catching her."

"But, sir –"

Freel glared at the man, who staggered back as if physically struck.

"Th-then your orders, sir?"

"Have this mess cleared away," Freel said, his gaze deliberately taking in Incera along with the other bodies. Then he paused, deep in thought, his jaw twitching. A whole year and the combined efforts of the Final Faith had not delivered Kali Hooper into his grasp, and now the little minx had reappeared at what he considered to be a pivotal moment. Maybe it was time to adopt a different tactic – to, as it were, take out some insurance against any further interference. Even if it did not prove necessary, it would at least bolster the numbers for his plans for the near future.

"Alert the Red Chapter," he said, "Have them mobilise the Eyes of the Lord and the best men they have, and find everyone Kali Hooper has contacted in the last year. If I can't lay my hands on Miss Hooper herself, then I think it's time that her little network of helpers started to disappear..."

CHAPTER TWO

THE PALE LORD pushed the problem of Kali Hooper to the back of his mind and strode the shadowed halls of Scholten Cathedral as if born to them. The delicious irony in the fact that he, the Final Faith's First Enemy, was now as accepted a part of these rarefied environs as the Anointed Lord herself was not lost on him, and frequent flashes of lightning so strong as to wash away all colour from the hall's stained glass windows – mirroring his own, true pallor – illuminated a self satisfied smile. Neophytes, Enlightened Ones and Cardinals alike mistook the smile for a sign of his blessing and nodded reverently, bowed in supplication or scurried aside, dependent on rank, as he proceeded with single-minded determination to his apartments.

These humans' attitude amused Bastian Redigor. But why shouldn't they treat him so? Since he had taken possession of Jakub Freel's form in the Chapel of Screams, they had come to owe him much. The changes he'd instigated in the Faith had both strengthened and buoyed their Church, hardened it in its resolve and redefined it in the face of its flock, all of these things ostensibly preparing it for what both its ministers and ever-growing number of worshippers believed was soon to come.

The Ascension.

Yes, the Ascension. The central tenet of their Church. The long-awaited and much sought moment of rapture when they would, each and every one of them, become one with their God.

What utter nonsense.

The poor, deluded fools really did have as little idea of what was happening as the Hooper girl had when she'd faced him at Bel'A'Gon'Shri. Less so. At least the bloody and battered little tomb thief had known some kind of threat was nearing her world, if not its actual nature; whereas these zealots, blinkered by their own teachings, believed it harmless, even benign.

It was not wholly their fault, this ignorance. The fact was, he could control many things, but the one thing he could not control was the appearance in the skies of the Hel'ss. Visible in Twilight's azure haze for months now, its presence lessened little even during the day. There was no avoiding it, no escaping it, and, if only to prevent the inconvenience to his plans that a mass panic might cause, it had needed to be explained. In such a way that suited his purposes. The glamour he had therefore insinuated into the minds of key members of the Faith's elite had ensured they interpreted the approach of 'the other' as part of the process that would, as they wished, deliver them from their mortal coil into the embrace of their Lord of All.

He had given much thought as to what form this glamour should take, considered many scenarios, but in the end it was a corruption of the actual truth that served him best.

The 'other', he said, was a herald of the coming Ascension, which appeared in the heavens to facilitate the rapture itself. While it was true that the Hel'ss *was* linked to Kerberos, it was, of course, nothing of the kind, but he saw no reason to share this part of the entity's sordid history with the humans. They would, after all, all be gone before they found this out.

Oh, how simple it had been. While initially worried about the degree of will it would take to weave such a deception in the minds of so many, it had not taken long for the part truth to take on a life of its own. Such was the pliability of true believers that they were willing to accept anything that bolstered their own beliefs, and while it was true that he had been forced to 'tweak' the minds of a few who began to express doubts, the slavering vegetables they had become were no longer a problem. Otherwise the elite of the Final Faith had delivered his wondrous news to their underlings who had, in turn and through means subtle and otherwise, dutifully instilled that belief in the minds of the masses.

So it was that the thing that was about to annihilate them all was perceived to be an object not of death but of life. Glorious, everlasting afterlife.

Yes, they were fools. But they were happy fools.

Even Makennon – although it was true to say she was less happy than most.

Ah, Katherine, Redigor thought. He missed the feel of her, her *inner fire*, as it were, but in his new guise it would not have been appropriate for him to take advantage of the Anointed Lord in that way. If he had been capable of feeling sorry for anyone, he would have felt sorry for Katherine. The woman – strong, proud, but fallibly human – had barely been released from servitude to him when her mind had once more become no longer her own. She, of all of them, had required the most delicate manipulation because she had felt his touch before, and with one slip he could have revealed his true self to her. He could not remove her faculties in the way he had with the others, she was too prominent for that, so instead it had been necessary for him to... *deaden* certain parts of her mind. On the surface, she continued to perform her role as Anointed Lord as she always had but, when her official duties ended for the day, Makennon could now be found locked in her apartments, staring into her fire, in whose flames she sought but failed to find that part of her mind she sensed was awry.

It was almost a pity. He had promised Makennon at the moment of his 'death' that he would crush her church, but now, through his own manipulations, she was likely to miss it.

Bastian Redigor sighed and reflected on events of the past year. A year – it was nothing to an elf, not even the blink of an eye and, yet, saddled as he was with this human form, it had seemed eternal. Probably no less so for Jakub Freel who, in unguarded moments, he could hear screaming in fury from somewhere deep within. Redigor admired the Allantian for his strength – even after all this time, when he should have become nothing more than a whimpering echo of his former self, Freel protested with the same strength as he had when first been lost. He was not, however, quite strong enough, and it took only a few moment's concentration on his part to quell the internal rebellion. Yet still, when his energies could have been engaged in other matters, it was bothersome.

But not for much longer, he hoped. Because in doing what he was going to do for the Hel'ss, he very much hoped that the Hel'ss would do something for him in return.

Guards stiffened to attention and then moved aside as he reached his apartments. The Pale Lord barely acknowledged their presence as he swept inside. As the door was closed behind him, he allowed himself a moment of weariness, and leant against the wall with a sigh.

As always, when he entered this so-called sanctuary, the first thing that struck him was how painfully *human* it was, and he rued the pretence that made it necessary to keep his private space in the style of Jakub Freel. Long as he might for things elven, he instead had to surround himself with the trappings of the sometime prince of Allantia, and these *creature comforts* sickened him. No less so, in fact, than the sound of that damnable Eternal Choir, whose caterwauling voices and specious songs penetrated even these thick walls. It had been beyond his – or rather Freel's authority – to have them silenced, and so, instead, he had ensured that they suffered for their art by living up to their name. A small conjuration had bound each and every one of the singers to their positions, where they had been forced to remain since he had taken up office that seeming eternity ago. A secondary, smaller conjuration ensured that observers saw and heard nothing beyond the norm, and only he knew how they stood there now, their emaciated, undying forms with their desperate eyes struggling for release but finding all they could do was continue to sing.

It wasn't much but it was poetic. And it would have to do.

Thankfully, there was one part of his apartments where he could escape both Freel's trappings and the Eternal Choir. The inner sanctum – or prayer room – that was common to the quarters of all the Faith elite was sound-proofed and sacrosanct, and no one bar the occupant would dare set foot inside its walls. Safe in this knowledge, Redigor had removed the small altar and kneeling stone that had sat in the centre of the round, windowless chamber and replaced it with a circle of power drawn upon the stone flags of the floor. It was inert as he entered the chamber but, with a small wave of the hand, the runes that made up its pattern pulsed with a bright blue light and, a second later, an equally bright blue and slightly sparkling fog swirled dreamily in the centre of the sanctum.

Not even slowing his pace, Redigor walked into it. Through it.

And was somewhere else.

The cramped, circular confines of the prayer room gave way to a much larger space, one that not only looked different but felt and smelled different, too. Here there was a chillier aspect to the air, and a tang of brine about it, and if you listened very, very carefully, the sound of waves and gulls could be heard from somewhere in the distance.

Away from the cathedral, in this quiet place, Redigor succumbed to a greater tedium than mere weariness, and for a second actually staggered then steadied himself against a wall, his lips pulling back in pain. Only here, far from the stage on which his act needed to be maintained every day, could he acknowledge that it was far more than weariness affecting him.

The fact was, his possession of Jakub Freel required little effort on his part, but what *did* require effort, and sometimes a great deal of it, was ensuring the body did not succumb to the rigours of the dark magic he would have it employ. The channelling of such forces through an elven form exacted some small price on the physiology, but channelled through a human it was the cause of a biological rot that had to be monitored and addressed almost constantly.

Redigor pulled up the sleeves of his tunic and examined the black weals that writhed on the skin of his forearms like living tattoos, leaving necrotised patches of flesh, and knew this pattern was reflected on other parts of his body as well. He knew this because he could feel the burning the writhing brought with it.

A year in human form was, indeed, a long time, and he was unsure for how much longer he could stem the tide of the rot. Already he could feel it manifesting itself in his internal organs, feel them throb and twinge as they threatened to collapse. If that happened there was every chance he would not survive to see the arrival of the Hel'ss. What he needed was a way to rid himself of it. The problem was that though he possessed the capability to take another host, that act would be self-defeating, not only because it would remove him from this position of power but also because he was running out of time. There was no chance he would be able to reestablish himself before the Hel'ss arrived. The only solution, therefore, was not to run from the rot but to eliminate it completely, and it was with this, that if the legends were right, he believed the Hel'ss could help.

Redigor took a deep breath. In the centre of the chamber was a large tank-like structure, wrought of iron and studded with thick rivets strong enough to contain the weight of water that one or two portholes on its side revealed to be contained within. The water was the colour of algae and had clearly come from the sea. There was a dark shape barely discernible at its heart, the size of a tall and stocky man.

Redigor waved a hand and wheels on the side of the tank began to turn. From within, the sound of sloshing and draining water was heard. It was not the first time Redigor had drained the tank but, each time, it had been refilled in order to preserve the items he'd contained within. Different items. This time as the water drained away, foot by foot, what was revealed was not the figure of a man but a woman – a woman carved of wood.

The water gone, Redigor proceeded to a hatch between the two wheels and heaved it open with a metallic groan. Water continued to stream down its inside and pooled at his feet, but Redigor paid it no attention, his eyes fixed on the ship's figurehead.

Half rotten, encrusted with barnacles and with its joints accentuated by embedded layers of seaweed, the figure was twice his height. It thrust forward, staring over and beyond him, and looked almost desperate, as if seeking a wave it knew it would never ride again. Its features were smoothed by the erosion of years at sea, yet still distinguishable: the half-gown that had once connected it to its ships prow, the curve of its torso and breasts, its arms pressed to its sides, and its head, once crowned with flowing locks of hair, reduced now to a layering of rotten, jagged and jutting wood. What stood out the most, though, were its eyes, larger than those of a real human; blank orbs veined not with blood vessels but the grain exposed by their carving, that stared straight ahead and yet saw nothing at all.

But he would make them see.

It was time to awaken this lady.

Redigor closed his own eyes, falling into a deep concentration in the silence of the chamber. After a second, a sibilant whisper could be heard drifting from him, although his lips appeared not to move at all. The words he spoke were strange, short and clipped at first, though became longer and louder, and each began to overlap the other until eventually it sounded as if a crowd of people were whispering in unison with Redigor. Still, though, his lips did not move.

But as the volume increased yet more, others did.

With a sudden, almost horrified inhalation of air, the mouth of the figurehead opened, and at the same time, its eyes. What had previously been dead wood was suddenly transformed into the semblance of human eyes, though they were grotesquely distorted, bulging, matching the size and shape of the carved orbs themselves. Cartoon eyes, fishmen's eyes – or perhaps the eyes of a suffocating and drowning man.

Which was exactly what they were.

The eyes' grotesque appearance was made even more so by the fact that their gaze flicked about the chamber in panic, settling on Redigor, their surroundings, even trying to look down, presumably in search of the form that should hold them. They saw nothing, of course, for the body they had once inhabited wasn't there, and the eyes widened in terror.

Water vomited from the figurehead's mouth.

"Who were you?" Redigor asked.

The eyes shot to him, though still flickered wildly, trying but unable to tear themselves away, to make sense of what was happening.

"*I don't know.*"

Redigor sighed, wearily. The human race's hold on their existence was stupefyingly weak, hardly worth the effort of their drawing their first pathetic breaths at all.

"Answer me," he demanded.

"*My... my name was William... William West, sir.*"

"And *what* were you, William?"

"*I... I was second mate on the Fulsome Wench, sir.*"

Redigor nodded. This at least confirmed he had summoned what he wished – necromancy was so prone to strays and intruders, chancers from the fringes of the planes. It confirmed also that West was on the crew manifest of one of the ships he had despatched beyond the Stormwall. The translocation rituals that Makennon's people had perfected recently had come in very handy in that regard: one moment these ships had been sailing safe waters, the next unknown and lethal seas thousands of leagues away. The magical cost of such translocations – and of retrieving their almost universally doomed remains – had left him exhausted physically, but, as the Eyes of the

Lord he had earlier attempted to send beyond the Stormwall had been brought down by its preternatural energies, he'd had little choice.

"You know, do you not, William, that you are quite dead?"

"Yes, Sir. I'm sorry, Sir."

"There is no need to apologise, William."

"I… I wasn't, Sir. What I mean is, I'm sorry for my Meg, my wife, and Rob, my boy. They're all alone now."

The smallest of smiles curled Redigor's lip. West could not know that it was he who had sent him to his death. "Do not worry yourself, William… the three of you will be together again soon enough."

"Can you promise me that, Sir?"

Redigor's smile widened. "Oh, yes. I can."

William was silent for a moment and his eyes stared beyond Redigor, as if picturing that time. Then he spoke again.

"Is there something you wish of me, Sir?"

"Yes, William," Redigor said. "I want you to show me what you saw."

"Sir?"

"Before you died."

The dead sailor's eyes started to flicker. "I… I'm not sure I want to do that."

"And why is that? Because it would cause you pain?"

"Yes. The memory."

Redigor's eyes, and his tone, darkened. "Is this the kind of pain you would like instead, William?"

Something carried with Redigor's words and suddenly the mouth of the figurehead began to wheeze and gurgle. Its eyes, in turn, became even more grotesquely deformed than before, flecked with veins that bulged with blood, threatening to burst despite the fact their owner was already dead. William's voice became a series of strangled, bubbling gasps, the sound of a man desperate to breathe but finding only water where air should have been. Where a few seconds of these gasps would normally have ended with the silence of liquid filled lungs, and of dimming eyes, however, here they simply continued, a frantic and agonising and wild-eyed struggle for relief that the Pale Lord let continue for two minutes or more. When at last Redigor released his hold on his summoning, William West's eyes stared forward glazed.

"That's better," Redigor said. "Now… show me."

Before him, the vitreous of West's eyes began to cloud over, as if beset by cataracts, and then began to swirl. At first it was like looking at a reflection of something indistinguishable in a mottled and tarnished mirror, but then the swirls began to coalesce into the view of a storm-tossed seascape at night. Redigor leaned forward and allowed himself to be drawn into the scene – in, and very far away.

He found himself travelling out from the peninsula, through the Stormwall and over an endless expanse of ocean. Land disappeared far behind him until there was nothing but water. After what seemed like an eternity an object became discernible on the horizon, and after a few seconds it resolved itself into the shape of a vessel. Then he was sweeping up to the hull of the ship, and then aboard, where at last he came to rest, or at least as at rest as the vision of a man who was trapped on a sinking ship could be.

This was what West had seen moments before he died, and as his gaze shifted across the panorama before him, his fellow, doomed crewmen could be seen, too, frantically working the sails and ropes on the deck of their ship. The *Fulsome Wench* was already breaking apart, and there was nothing they could do to save themselves, but that didn't matter to Redigor. He didn't care about their deaths and it was not their deaths that he had summoned West to see.

Redigor waited patiently, disappointed too many times. The seascape of the other side of the world was by now a familiar vista to him – as familiar, that was, as an endless expanse of maelstrom could be – but he needed to see more. And to see more, the location had to be right, the conditions had to be right, the *stars* had to be right. The chances of a translocation bringing him close enough for these conditions to be met were, of course, infinitesimal, and he was already prepared to be disappointed once more. Then, suddenly, his eyes widened.

Something…

Redigor's eyes narrowed as he studied the last moments of William West's mortal existence for the finest detail, and at last drew in a sharp breath. There, a glimpse between masts and rigging, of a star pattern that seemed similar to that on the chart from the Halo files. Then as Redigor watched – or rather as West's perspective shifted – a clearer view, the heavens revealed in all their glory.

Not just similar to the star chart. A perfect match.

This was the place. He had found his destination at last.

All he needed to do now was confirm what he believed.

Redigor's attention shifted from the night sky to West's immediate surroundings. The *Fulsome Wench* was sinking, its hull already half beneath the waves, and as a result what the second mate saw was wildly skewed, disorientating, obscured at times by the flailing bodies and screaming faces of his shipmates. Redigor was annoyed that they were stopping him seeing what he wanted to see in the few moments of their lives that remained.

West sank beneath the surface and suddenly all was a maelstrom of air bubbles and darkness, but then, for the briefest of times, he came up and Redigor smiled.

There. No more than snatches and glimpses, but enough. Outlined against the night sky, in the distance, a darkened island of sharp and jagged rocks whose desolation was palpable even through this vision. And before it – washing the island again and again from view – a swirling, unnatural body of water that was responsible for the sinking of the *Fulsome Wench*.

It was fitting that William West should choose that moment to breathe his last and drown. Fitting that the eyes of the figurehead dimmed and reverted to wood once more.

Because their job was done.

He had seen something *in* the water. *Part* of the water.

The legends, it seemed, were true. There was hope for him yet.

The Hel'ss wasn't just approaching Twilight.

It was already here.

CHAPTER THREE

"EXCUSE ME," A voice said, loud and demanding enough to be heard above the general hubbub in the tavern, "but I think there's something wrong with this stew."

Everything in the Here There Be Flagons stopped. Red Deadnettle half way down a jug of thwack; Fester Grimlock and Jurgen Pike about to slam down winning hands of Quagmire; Pete Two-Ties and Ronin Larson arguing, as they always did at this time of day, about the true depth of Bottomless Pit and how many times one of them would have to throw the other idiot in to fill it up. Even Hetty Scrubb, gigglingly high on one of her many 'combustible herbs' lapsed into silence with an uncharacteristic look of horror on her face.

Behind the bar, Aldrededor stopped towelling down the bowls of those regulars who had seen nothing fit to complain about and mouthed, "Oh, gods, no…"

All eyes turned towards the kitchen door.

It was a delayed reaction, but the sound came soon enough from within. Hoarse yet high pitched, and, to those who didn't know otherwise, somehow strangely… reptilian.

"*Heeeeeeeeeeeeeeeee…*"

The man who had complained, some kind of city fop by the look of him, couldn't help but look at the door, too. And though he couldn't say why, he started to swallow rapidly and involuntarily.

"Did I say something wrong?" he said, glancing around in exasperation.

A hand slapped down on his right shoulder. "If I were you, friend, I'd get out of here now. Get out while you can still father a child."

Another slapped down on his left. "But run fast, for her knives, not to mention her tongue, can sever your manhood half a league away."

"Knives? Tongue? What? the man gasped. "You're joking, right?"

Both regulars burst into raucous laughter, and the man looked relieved. But the laughter stopped abruptly, leaving only shaking heads and deadly serious expressions.

"No."

A dagger thudded into the wooden beam right next to the man's head, quivering so fast that a few seconds passed before it ceased to be a blur. The fact that bits of moist, sliced onion slithered down and then dropped off its blade did not make it appear any more homely or less lethal.

The frame of the kitchen door outlined something long and thin and oddly disturbing that appeared there and began to make its way towards the table where the man sat. He tried to run, as advised, but suddenly, almost preternaturally, the something was there, looming over him, and despite all his survival instincts he couldn't help but sit and stare in mesmerised astonishment at its long, hawk-like nose.

"*Oh, please, don't stare at the nose,*" someone whispered urgently from nearby.

Dolorosa shot them a look, and then, with an intake of breath, drew herself up to her full height, folded her arms and smiled. With the lipstick she was wearing, the smile looked something like a spray of blood at a murder scene.

"You havva the complaint?" she said.

"No, n-no. L-lord of All, no," the man stuttered quickly, but then realised there was no denying what he'd said. "Well, all right, yes, it's your Surprise Stew…"

"And wotta seems to be the problem?"

"Urm, for one thing, look," the man said, pointing, "there's something moving in it."

"Yes?"

"Well, something moving in it wasn't quite the 'surprise' I was expecting."

Dolorosa's eyebrow rose. "The leetle redda thing? It issa macalorum. It infussa your dish with flavour. Itta loves to do so."

"Macalorum?"

"It issa local 'erb. It ees a bastardo to catch."

"Catch? Excuse me but herbs don't run away."

"Nor do they 'ave bladders." Dolorosa watched as the small red herb squirted something into the stew, and shrugged. "Whatta can I say?"

The man swallowed. "Are you saying that this macalorum is *peeing* in my stew?"

"It issa full of vitamins."

"Okay, right," the man said doubtfully, poking in the stew with his fork. What looked like a couple of white eyeballs bobbed to the surface. "But what about these?"

Dolorosa peered intently into the bowl. "Ah. You avva me there."

"What? You don't know what they are?"

The question prompted a slap about the head. "Of coursa I know whatta they are. Eet wassa the joke, you stupeed man."

Dolorosa emitted what for her passed as a laugh – *hahahahaharrrr!* All of the regulars in the Flagons echoed it. *Hahahahaharrrr.*

"Then," the man asked hesitantly, "what are they?"

"They are, owwa you say, the love spheres ovva the purple skoonk."

The man paled. "You mean its –"

"Delicioso, yes?" Dolorosa interrupted proudly. "A rare delicacy and," she cast a glance at Red Deadnettle, the ruddy-faced poacher raising his tankard and nodding back, "locally sourced."

The man picked up his napkin and wiped the edges of his mouth slowly and solidly, as if trying to erase even the memory of what he had so far consumed.

"Let me get this straight. Am I to understand I've been eating vermin's gonads and the waste products of an over-excitable, incontinent weed?"

"You havva the problem with that?"

The man stood abruptly, his chair making a loud scraping sound on the wooden floor. He tossed his napkin angrily down onto the table.

"Madam, do you know who I am?" he declared.

"You'd be wiser asking who *she* is," Aldrededor muttered behind the bar. He shook his head. "Be merciful, my wife."

"Have you ever heard," the man continued, "of the *Miramas Times*?"

Dolorosa had, of course. It was the oldest news-sheet on the peninsula and, back in the day, had often reported her and Aldy's maritime exploits. Out of the many headlines the two of them had engendered, her favourite remained *Perilous Pirates Pillage Pontaine – Again!*

"I see that you have," the man said, smiling. "Have you heard, then, of its respected food critic, H. Borton Jeckle?"

"Yes!" Dolorosa blurted. "Wait, no."

"*I*, Madam, am H. Borton Jeckle."

"You *never* are."

"Indeed I am. And I came to your establishment today to consider bestowing it one of my coveted Jeckle Moons."

Dolorosa's lips curled back. "You feelthy purravert…"

"Madam?"

"No one flashes their bottom inna my taverno!"

"It is an *award*, Madam. A mark of distinction that is highly regarded by anyone of taste. A Jeckle Moon means that the food in an establishment is of an exceptional quality."

Dolorosa's smile suddenly reappeared, twitching, and this time on the other side of her mouth. She swept her hand back through her hair.

"Anda you say I am to be considered for one of these Moons?"

Jeckle considered his stew one more. "I regret, Madam, only if it is indeed provided by my arse. And only then while it is leaving your establishment. The fare you have served me today was the most disgusting and repellant concoction it has ever been my displeasure to con – "

The last syllable disappeared down Jeckle's throat along with two of his teeth, and with surprising sprightliness for a man of his age Aldrededor leapt the bar to support the critic as he staggered against a wall.

"You must forgive my wife," he said, glancing towards the far end of the tavern where, up a small flight of skewed steps, sat an empty Captain's Table. He grabbed Dolorosa's arm as it tried to go for the knife still embedded in the wooden beam. "She is... missing a friend."

"She is missing her marbles," Jeckle protested through bloodied lips. "I demand an apology, Sir!"

Aldrededor sighed as he and his wife struggled. "Dolorosa, apologise to the nice man."

"I willa not."

"Perhaps," Aldrededor gasped, "it might be better if you leave. Your meal is, of course, on the house."

"Correction, sir. The meal belongs in a horse."

"*Heeeeeeee...*"

"Oh, now you have reminded her of her friend again. Please, for your own safety, leave now."

"Sir," H. Borton Jeckle said, "you do not have to ask me twice."

The much respected food critic of the Miramas Times exited the Flagons with an harumph and the swish of a tailor-made cloak. Outside, his carriage awaited, his driver slumped in a doze at the reins. As H. Borton Jeckle mounted the rig and deposited himself into his upholstered seat, he reflected that while the county of Tarn was indeed a delightful place, and the Flagons itself ideally situated for the sort of weekend sojourn his readers might appreciate, there was no way on Twilight he could recommend it to them. Just the opposite, in fact. On reflection, he supposed he should have expected little more from a tavern that was reputedly owned by a female outlaw.

He prodded his driver in the back, demanding they begin the long journey home.

The driver tipped forward onto the reins, causing a disquieted stirring from the horses. It seemed he was not dozing but dead.

"Broggle, Lord of All, man," Jeckle said, slithering back out of the carriage. Maybe the sun had got to the poor fellow, or maybe his heart had seized, but whatever the cause it was damned inconvenient. If he couldn't find another driver he might have to spend the night in this hellshole while he sent a runner for a replacement.

"Broggle, you're fired," Jeckle declared.

The body of his driver twisted as he prodded it, falling onto its back on the seat. He stared, glassy-eyed, up at Jeckle and the critic's mouth opened and closed like a fish as he saw the blood red slash across the driver's throat. The man's livery was sodden and stained through.

Grabcoins, he thought, with a thudding heart. Probably in league with that Hooper woman. Well, that settled it. Another reason to warn his readers to stay away. Actively discourage them from coming anywhere near here, in fact.

A hand clamped tightly over his mouth while the point of a blade pressed into his spine.

"Who are you?" a voice breathed into his ear. The hand was released briefly so that he could provide an answer.

"Jeckle. H. Borton Jeckle," he answered quickly. He swallowed as some kind of flying sphere hovered in front of his face, as if examining him.

There was a moment's hesitation from his assailant. "The food critic for the *Times*?"

Jeckle's eyebrows rose but, his mouth covered once more, he could only nod. A half sob escaped him, muffled by the hand.

"Then this is unfortunate, Mister Jeckle, for I find your column edifying. But you are not who we hunt and we cannot alert those inside to our presence. Do you understand this?"

Of all things, H. Borton Jeckle thought, what, don't be ridiculous, man! What could a grabcoin know of my column? He never vocalised the thought, though, as a moment later he felt something so sharp it didn't even hurt slash across his throat, and the only sound he could make was a gurgle.

His wide-eyed, spasming body was lowered quietly to the ground, where it subsequently produced a large red puddle, and died. His assailant stared down, thinking how Jeckle's job would have benefited had he lived. In his profession it would be a distinct advantage to have two mouths.

He signalled his men, who emerged from the bushes in which he himself had hidden, and in absolute silence they moved towards the Flagons. The shadows that they, and at least six Eyes of the Lord flitting about the tavern like angry flies, cast fleetingly at the windows went unnoticed as, inside, there was a communal burst of laughter.

"LOVE SPHERES!" PETE Two-Ties bawled, his voice cracking into a hoarse wheeze as he used a dirty handkerchief to wipe tears from his eyes. "The man was a buffoon!"

"Flashing his arse!" Fester Grimlock cried.

"He didn't realise you knew who he was!" Red Deadnettle joined in. He took a deep slug from his jug. "The bit about the macalorum!"

"No, Red, that bit was true," Aldrededor said, eyeing him steadily across the bar.

"It was?" Red said, shrugging. "Well, it's never done me any harm."

"Whatta makes a man like heem think we would like to be in his stupeed guide," Dolorosa said. "'Madam, do you know who I am?'" she mimicked. "Pah!"

"Perhaps you should have keeled him," Jurgen Pike mimed, "lika thees." His hand stabbed down repeatedly, as if holding a knife.

Dolorosa suddenly loomed over him as she had over Jeckle, arms folded tightly across her chest, fingers drumming. "What issa thees stupeed accent in whicha you speak?"

Hetty Scrubb splurted out the cocktail from which she had been attempting a quivering sip, and once more giggled uncontrollably. But the giggle faded a moment later as the surface of her drink was unexpectedly covered by a fall of dust from between the skewed wooden beams of the ceiling. The Flagons being so old it was normal practice to cover drinks against the possibility of such falls, but only on the occasions there was someone upstairs.

Hetty's eyes moved suspiciously upwards, one slightly slower than the other, and just as the two levelled out the fall of dust was followed by a low creak of the timbers. From behind the bar, Aldrededor looked over at Dolorosa and shook his head at the slight look of hope in her eyes. They were all aware of the circumstances that dogged Kali and neither of them had seen her for over two months, and when she did return to say hello and dump her washing, their adopted offspring always used a different means of entering the Flagons, in case she had been compromised.

The last time she had come, she had come from upstairs.

"My 'usband," Dolorosa hissed. "I theenk we havva the uninvited guests."

"Then, my darling wife," Aldrededor responded, with a twinkle. "I suggest we prepare to repel boarders..."

Aldrededor moved to the chest by the Captain's Table, heaved it open and drew out a crackstaff – one of the few still working that had been left behind by one of Jengo Pim's men – and flicked it on. It crackled softly, like hand-held lightning. Dolorosa, meanwhile, plucked her kitchen knife from where it remained embedded in the wooden beam, and from her garter produced another, far more deadly looking blade, which she proceeded to toss full circle in her palm. The two of them looked towards the base of the stairs.

"Stay where you are," Dolorosa whispered to Hetty Scrubb and Pete Two-Ties. "Red and Ronin will look after you."

"Give 'em one for me," the diminutive herbalist requested. She rose and hopped from leg to leg, punching the air before her. "In the nuts. Yes, yes, in the nuts."

"The only place she can reach," Pete Two-Ties sighed.

As Dolorosa and Aldrededor approached the first two risers, Red Deadnettle slid from his stool, far more gently and quietly than might be expected from such a giant of a man, and, from beneath, withdrew a large wooden club. Ronin Larson, the blacksmith, joined him in standing guard, his weapon a molding hammer he kept perpetually slung on his broad leather toolbelt and which he now pounded into his open palm. From his grin, it seemed he was looking forward to molding a few Final Faith faces rather than metal for a change.

Unfortunately, neither he nor the others were prepared for the type of attack that was to come. The ground floor of the Flagons was thrown into chaos as three of the whorled glass windows were smashed in a series of determined blows from sword hilts, and through them came three canisters that spewed a green fog across the bar area.

"Swamp gas!" Dolorosa hissed, and began to cough uncontrollably. As did the others. A few seconds later they were all on their knees, weapons dropped. The gas began to dissipate and, as it did, the door to the tavern was kicked open. Swords of Dawn flooded the room, each placing a weapon at the throats of those who were incapacitated.

But other than stand guard, they made no further move.

They were waiting for something.

And that something was the creaking of the tavern's stairs as they signalled the arrival of a figure descending them. Their uninvited guest, it seemed, knew how to make an entrance.

"My name," he said, "is Gregory Morg."

Dolorosa squinted at him through stinging eyes, a man dressed in robes and armour that identified him as neither Swords of Dawn or Faith, but somewhere in between. He was likely one of those damned mercenaries Jakub Freel had conscripted. "This tavern is now commandeered, and you are in the custody of the Final Faith."

From their prone positions on the floor, Dolorosa and Aldrededor cast worried glances at each other, knowing full well what this was about. The bastards were finally coming after those near and dear to Kali, presumably in an attempt to flush her out. It wasn't for themselves they looked worried, however, but for the innocents in the bar – Peter, Hetty and the rest – whose only connection to Kali was to provide her with a cheery welcome home after one of her adventures. They didn't deserve to be treated this way.

"The old man and woman, these others," Aldrededor pointed out, "know nothing. Let them go."

Morg smiled coldly and stepped off the stairs so that he towered over the Sarcrean.

"If I let one old man go, then I would have to let another go, too," he said, clearly referring to Aldrededor. He sneered. "Along with his ancient crone of a wife."

Dolorosa spat on his feet.

"Calm, my darling," Aldrededor soothed. He stared up at their captor, touching the sword held at his throat. "Do you intend to execute us, is that it? Send a message to Kali Hooper?"

"Then you do not deny your association with the outlaw?"

"Would there be much point?"

"Not really."

Two other Swords of Dawn entered the tavern. "The perimeter of the property is secure, sir. No sign of further insurgents."

"You have checked all of the outbuildings?"

"All apart from the stables, sir. They seem to be locked."

"Then *unlock* them, man!"

"We tried, sir, but the lock is strange. Inscribed with patterns."

Morg's eyes narrowed and he grabbed Aldrededor's chin and forced it up. "Runes. What do you keep in the stables?"

"What do you normally keep in stables, Gregory Morg?"

"Behind a rune-inscribed lock?"

Aldrededor grinned widely. "We stable some rare breeds."

"The bamfcat. If it's here, the girl may be close by. Shatter that lock and slay anything within."

"Horse isn't here," Aldrededor said. "Neither is Kali Hooper."

"We shall see. As for our captives," Morg said, "bring the wagons."

"Wagons?" Aldrededor repeated.

Morg smiled. "You'll all be taking a little trip. Relocated, as it were."

"Interesting," Aldrededor commented. "I hope somewhere sunny."

"My 'usband," Dolorosa whispered urgently in his ear, "we cannot allow ourselves to be taken, and we cannot allow them into the stables."

"I know this, my lovepeach," Aldrededor responded through still grinning teeth. "Be patient."

Dolorosa looked about herself, confused. What was her husband on about, patient? They all of them had swords at their throats and as far as she could see there was no immediate way out of this predicament. Then her eyes caught sight of what Aldrededor had obviously been referring to. While the rest of them had simply dropped their weapons her husband had managed to conceal his. The crackstaff was perched at an angle between the flaps of the bar and, what was more, remained charged, crackling softly to itself, out of sight. Dolorosa did not fully understand these strange devices but one thing she did know was that, if left idle like this, the crackstaff would eventually purge itself of pent-up energy.

There was going to be a bang.

"Everybody," she said, meaning her own people, "I suggest you sticka your heads between your knees."

Regulars and Swords alike looked at Dolorosa questioningly, but it was already too late.

From the tip of the crackstaff erupted a bolt of darting, twisting blue energy that blew the flaps off the bar and struck a Sword who had the bad luck to be standing in its way. The energy bolt tore through his body armour into his chest, exposing the white bone of his sternum. He was punched into the air, slamming into and smashing another of the tavern's windows. The flaps, meanwhile, both solid chunks of wood the size of sewer grates, blew to the left and the right in an explosion of splinters, hitting two more of the Swords, decapitating one and shattering the sword arm of another. These men, or what remained of them, flailed into their own, and in the chaos that ensued Aldrededor and the others made their moves.

The swarthy Sarcrean pushed his captor from him, leapt and rolled back over the bar, then snatched the crackstaff from where it now lay on the floor. He discharged it into the face of a Sword who tried to follow. Dolorosa used far more primitive but no less effective weapons, snatching her twin blades from beneath her and simultaneously thrusting them back and up, hissing in satisfaction as she felt them puncture flesh. As she rolled from beneath the Sword's collapsing body, she booted Red's club over to where the giant poacher could grab it. As he bent to do so, a Sword who tried to stop him found himself with a new and unique perspective on life as Red's club swung round solidly, knocking his head permanently sideways.

Dolorosa snatched a glance at Morg, whom she noticed had retreated a few risers back up the stairs from where he watched the battle with narrowed eyes, and then at her husband, who was sweating and grinning as much as she.

"Justa like the old days on the sheep!" she declared and, though it showed her skull and crossbone bloomers for all to see, couldn't resist bounding onto and from a table, using a curtain as she might a sail to swing out across the room and boot two more of their captors in the face and off their feet. She landed on the bar and from there urged on Red and Ronin. The giant first swung his nailed club up between the legs of another Sword, and then grabbed the poor unfortunate by the neck, racing him across the tavern to ram his head into the bragging box, where he collapsed twitching and screaming, stung by whatever was inside. Ronin, for his part, moved through the Swords with his hammer swinging in a blur, forcing all before him to dodge or duck the momentum of the heavy blacksmithing tool. Even Hetty Scrubb and Pete Two-Ties helped out, the former reducing one Sword to a spasming heap by blowing him a faceful of her latest herbal concoction, while Pete confounded another by more intellectual means.

"Stop!" he shouted, as the Sword was about to bring the hilt of his weapon down on him. The Sword was surprised enough to do so. "I half faint, sorting out these idiots!"

"What?" the Sword said, bemused.

"Anagram!" Pete emphasised, punching a finger at the cryptosquare in the newssheet he held. "Five, five…"

"What the fark are you talking about, old man?"

Pete rammed the rolled up newssheet into the Sword's eye, causing a cry of pain. "The answer's 'Final Faith' you moron," he announced.

It wasn't the deadliest of attacks but it served its purpose. Pete slipped by him while the Sword stumbled against the wall clutching his face.

Slowly, he and the others fought their way to the exit, Aldrededor providing covering fire with the crackstaff as they moved. Furniture, glassware and ornaments were shattered or sent flying from the blasts, and Aldrededor comforted Dolorosa as she watched the inside of her beloved tavern blown apart. Both knew there was no choice in the matter, however, as their first priority was to protect what was within the stables, to say nothing of their friends. But as they, the last to back out, emerged from the door of the Flagons, they noticed an unexpected quiet in the courtyard behind them.

Both ex-pirates turned slowly. Their friends were lined up before more Swords, weapons once more at their throats. Behind the line of prisoners two barred prison carriages stood waiting.

The regulars of the Flagons stared at them apologetically.

"Sheet," Dolorosa said.

A slow crunching from the doorway of the tavern heralded the reappearance of Gregory Morg as he walked slowly out to them. He took the knives and crackstaff from their hands.

"What do you think this is?" he said. "*A game?*"

For the first time, Morg hefted his own weapon, a cruel looking battleaxe that had been slung on his back. He walked to the line of prisoners, considering each but then choosing one seemingly at random. He nodded to the Sword holding Fester Grimlock and, as he moved away, span with a roar and sliced the battleaxe up through Fester's torso. The merchant was thrown off his feet, twisting in the air with the force of the impact, and when his already dead body landed with a thud, his innards were forcefully spewed from his body in a glistening, steaming heap.

Hetty gagged, while the rest of the regulars railed ineffectually against their captors.

"Bastardo," Dolorosa said slowly.

"Any further resistance and I kill another of you," Morg said, reslinging his weapon. The murder of Fester Grimlock had meant nothing to him.

Dolorosa studied the mercenary, and Aldrededor smiled as she spoke. His beloved had always possessed a keen tactical mind. "It is my guess that we are being taken as some kind offa insurance, yes?" she said, nodding at the wagons. "A deterrent against our Kali acting against Jakuba Freel. If that issa the case, I doubt he woulda be very pleased if he discovered you had keeled *any* of us, hmm? Or arra you going to prove me wrong?"

Morg's eyes narrowed and he sighed.

"Put them in the wagons," he said to his men. "I'm going to take a look at this mysterious locked stable of theirs."

Again, Aldrededor and Dolorosa shot each other a glance, trying, and failing, to work out a way of stopping him. It was obvious that what they needed was some kind of diversion but what was not so obvious was who provided it.

Hetty Scrubb nodded at them, then mouthed for them to be ready to get the hells out of there. The ex-pirates' eyebrows rose – neither had been aware that the perpetually high herbalist even knew they had something to protect.

Puzzled, they watched as Ronin, Red, Jurgen, Pete and finally Hetty were bundled into one of the wagons, its barred door slammed shut behind them. They shot a glance at Morg, who was fiddling with the rune lock on the stable door, and then were themselves ushered to a wagon. Whatever it was Hetty had in mind, they hoped she would do it quickly.

She did.

Just as Aldrededor and Dolorosa were about to be bundled into darkness, the rear of Hetty's wagon began to pour smoke, a cloud so thick and cloying it immediately threw the Swords surrounding it into confusion.

"Fire!" one yelled, but Dolorosa knew better than that. This was Hetty's *special* pipe in action, the one she'd been forced to ban from the Flagons, and if anything was going to take the Swords' minds off things, this was it.

Aldrededor and Dolorosa took their cue, racing through the black hallucinogenic cloud of while the Swords battled to re-open the wagon and extinguish the pipe. They met Morg half way. The mercenary made an immediate angry dash for the two of them and, while Aldrededor steeled himself for a confrontation, Dolorosa shoved him on, rolling up her own sleeves instead.

"I will 'andle thees. You do what you 'ave to do."

"My wife," Aldrededor protested, "this is not some errant customer you are dealing with, Morg is a dangerous man."

"And it is a long time since I have had the pleasure of keeling one. Now, do as I say, 'usband!"

The Sarcrean was about to protest further but it was too late, battle joined.

Before Morg could make a move on him, Dolorosa pivoted on her right leg, skirt flying, and delivered a roundhouse kick that sent the mercenary staggering back, snarling at a bloodied lip. It took Morg only a moment to recover and come at her, but Dolorosa was ready once more, meeting him with a flying kick that again sent the man staggering, this time flat on his back. As his wife roared and raced in with the intention of keeping Morg down, Aldrededor made the sign of the gods and left her to it, heading for the locked stable door. Where it had proven problematic for Morg and his men, however, it was nothing for the ex-pirate. As the sounds of confrontation continued behind him the lock fell away before a series of rapid and deft gestures. The stable door creaked open and Aldrededor span back to face Dolorosa.

"Hurry, my darling. We have –"

The Sarcrean's words dwindled into silence as he saw Morg had proven himself the better after all. He held Dolorosa in a neck lock, her back pressed against his front. The love of his life no longer looked furious or determined, only ashamed and defeated – and somehow old. Older than she had ever looked to him before.

Time, he reflected, was indeed catching up with them.

"Dolorosa..." he breathed, and then, to Morg, hoping that his wife had been right. "You will not kill her."

Morg smiled coldy. "Perhaps not, Sarcrean. But if you do not surrender, I can and I will do almost as much..."

"Aldrededor," Dolorosa hissed. "You must go."

"Not without you, my wife."

"My 'usband," Dolorosa insisted, eyeing the shadows beyond the stable door. "You know what is at stake – *go*."

Morg's eyes narrowed suspiciously.

"What exactly is at stake, old man? I warn you, don't make a move."

Aldrededor's eyes flicked from Morg to Dolorosa, lingering long and hard over his wife's distressed face. But as their eyes met and he held her gaze he knew she was right. What he *should* have known, after Fester's death, what that Morg would not hesitate to act.

Morg made good on his threat. Without any further warning, he shoved Dolorosa out in front of him and, as she stood there looking confused, two sharp blades – her own sharp blades – were thrust suddenly through her. Dolorosa stiffened, her eyes widened and, as the projecting lengths of the blades glistened with blood in the light of the sun, she made a sound that was not unfamiliar to Aldrededor but was nevertheless horribly strange.

"*Heeeeeeeeeee...*"

"DOLOROSA!"

"A crone as scrawny as this," Morg said, "she's lucky I missed the vital organs. She will, though, bleed to death unless I grant her medical attention. Now, old man, why don't you show me exactly what's in that stable?"

Aldrededor was about to do exactly that, caring about nothing other than getting help for his wife, when Dolorosa vigorously shook her head. The act clearly caused her great pain.

"Aldy," she said, in a guttural voice, "do what I said. 'E will not let me die."

Aldrededor swallowed rapidly. "*I cannot take that chance.*"

"You *must*. They cannot get their 'ands on the sheep."

It would have been funny, had it not been so true, and Aldrededor knew it.

"If my wife dies," he growled at Morg, "there will be no place you will be safe, no sanctuary you can hide in or shield you can cower behind. I will hunt you down, I will find you, and then and I will kill you."

"Lika thees," Dolorosa muttered weakly.

Aldrededor stared at her wavering smile, swallowed again, and immediately turned. He was inside the stables and slamming the door shut behind him before Morg could make another move. The rune-inscribed lock re-configured itself.

"You and you, get this woman in the wagon," Morg snarled to his men, who had just relieved Hetty of her pipe and were working their way through what remained of the smoke. "The rest of you," he added, releasing Dolorosa's body and slamming his fist on the doors of the stables, "raze this thing to the ground."

Morg's men responded, and within a minute they had gathered torches and surrounded the stable. The soft thrumming of the flames of their torches was, however, drowned out from a growing sound from within the stable's walls – a thrumming again, but this time one which made their heads ache and was quite clearly caused by something other than fire.

"What in the name of the Lord of All?" one of the Swords muttered.

The roof of the stables suddenly began to rise upwards, not from any mechanism designed to make it do so but from the sheer force and pressure of something rising inside. As the roof broke apart in broad splinters, the walls, too, began to press outward as if the something inside were turning slowly as it rose. The walls began to fall away like discarded cards.

Bowing to these pressures, the entire stable exploded outward and something rose from its ruin, a sleek flying shape the length of three carts, that then hovered in the sky. An uncountable number of black vents flapped on its side, shiny and looking like the shifting of reptilian skin, and on the underside of its hull, orange orbs pulsed.

The Swords, even Morg, staggered back. But Dolorosa, being dragged to captivity, caught a glimpse of her husband at the flying thing's helm and smiled. Seeing the repaired *Tharnak* airborne once more, she watched as it hung there for a second, acknowledging her, before banking gracefully and disappearing above the rooftop of the Flagons.

Morg stared after it, his lip curling in anger. He stared at the Flagons and then at his men.

"Burn it. Burn it all."

CHAPTER FOUR

THE RED CHAPTER'S cull of Kali's friends was swift and simultaneous. Their targets tracked by Eyes of the Lord, squads of Freel's mercenaries struck across the peninsula at the same time Gregory Morg raided the Here There Be Flagons.

Exiting the Three Towers in Andon, on his way to a certain club in the Skeleton Quays for an engagement he hoped he couldn't get out of, Poul Sonpear spotted a number of spherical shadows scudding about his own as he progressed down the alley he used as a short cut. He immediately dropped into phase, thinking himself safe in the half realm accessible only to members of the League of Prestidigitation and Prestige, and was somewhat surprised to be joined there by four black-clad figures – shadowmages, by the look of them. Sonpear began to muster defensive spells – skull shield, ball of immunity, flash – but his assailants were ready for him. One countercasted with slow, another with silence, while the final two physically wrestled him against a wall, restraining him while a scrambling collar was clamped around his neck.

Sonpear recognised the collar as proscribed technology, Old Race, and as he felt its effects numbing his faculties, his mind raced. Why was he being targeted? Who were these men? What did they want? There was only one possible answer, and he tried, but failed, to send a telepathic warning to the one person with whom he maintained a permanent link. The message that would never be sent was, *Kali, they're coming for us...*

ELSEWHERE IN ANDON, Jengo Pim lay on his bed in the Underlook Hotel, clutching his greasy knife as he imagined the Hells Bellies writhing before him. The hideaway of the Grey Brigade was unusually quiet, most of his boys out on jobs for the night, leaving only twelve or so snoring in nearby rooms. As Pim gnawed on the leg of meat his knife skewered, swilling it down with a chunky Allantian red, there was an unexpected creak from the floor below. The thief frowned, then shrugged – the Underlook was an old building, prone to shifting. He rejoined his fantasy, wiping juice from his mouth with a satisfied sigh, when a second creak – this time the drawn out, pressured creak of foot on floorboard – impelled him to extract his knife and slip off the bed, eyes narrowing suspiciously.

He moved onto the landing and stared down the main staircase. As he did, a candle was snuffed below, then another and another, until all was black. A shape – possibly more than one – flitted through the darkness. Visitors, Pim thought, but no problem – the old hotel didn't take kindly to *unexpected* guests.

Pim tapped gently on bedroom doors, rousing sleepers, and then flipped a lever on the wall. A dull clank and ratchet sound signified that all of the traps on the ground floor were now active, and as his men slipped silently down the stairs with garrots tensing and daggers gleaming, he was confident that caught between a rock and a hard place, whoever had checked into the Underlook this night had no chance.

A series of screams met him from below, and protesting cries as traps were tripped, but a chill went through Pim as he realised the voices in both cases were those of his own men.

He called out – no reply. How could a dozen of the best thieves in the business be taken out so easily? His mind raced, trying to identify who might possess a strong enough grudge against the Grey Brigade to launch such an offensive. It was only at the last moment, after he had slowly taken the stairs himself and swift, shadowed figures came at him, driving him to the floor with a yell, did he realise what this was all about. Her name, as blackness descended, was the last thing that passed his lips.

"Hooper!"

As Pim's ROAR echoed through the Underlook, Martha DeZantez knelt by her daughter's graveside in Solnos. There was no body in the grave, but that didn't matter, because it was here that Gabriella was remembered in spirit, next to the grave of the man she had loved, and it had become a place of peace and remembrance. She would find no peace today, however, as for a second her heart seized as she heard Gabriella's voice, as clear as day, warning her against something, and then shadows loomed suddenly over her. A second later all that remained of her presence was a flower with a broken petal lying on the ground.

* * *

IN FAYENCE, ABRA Sarkesian had just wheeled his Abra-Kebab-Bar into its lock-up for the night, woeing the takings of the day, when a shadow at the rear of the storage area caught his eye. The lock-up had provided an emergency bolt-hole for Kali Hooper on more than one occasion, he dropping awnings to hide its existence the moment she rode into it, and his heart lifted to see she had sought his shelter once more. But the face that emerged from the shadows was not Kali's – not even close.

SO IT WENT. Peninsula wide from Oweilau to Malmkrug to Turnitia, Vosburg to Freiport to Volonne, anyone with recent contact with Kali Hooper, however minor, simply disappeared. But not everything went according to plan. At that moment in Gargas...

A GLOVED HAND prevented the bell on the door of Wonders of The World from tinkling as it opened. Yan DeFrys motioned his heavily armed men into the shop in silence. He'd been told his target was a strange one, rumoured to possess a faculty for bodily transformation, and had decided his best tactic for capture would be to simply overwhelm him. He'd hoped to have all of his men inside before he was alerted but it seemed that was not to be. Though the shop had appeared empty through its windows, the old man was suddenly there, appearing as if by magic.

Yan DeFrys sneered. With a shock of white hair and beard, and what looked like a pink horse blanket over his shoulders, the old man shuffled about the shop waving a feather duster over piles of stock. *This* was his target?

"I'm closed," Merrit Moon said.

"Then you should lock your door, Mister Moon."

"Why? Others respect the sign hanging there. You see what it says, hmm? 'Go Away' is what it says, and I'd be obliged if you did so."

"We're not here to shop, old man."

"No? Some pongbegon for you, I think. Wooh-hoo, yes. And you, sir – in you I sense a man with a frustrated wife. Knickerknocker Glory's what you need. Direct from the Sardenne and very good for the old early *oooh*, if you know what I mean."

The mercenary to whom Moon had spoken moved forward, but DeFrys held him back.

"We have no interest in your trinkets, trivia or fetishes, old man. We're here for you."

Moon continued to shuffle about, apparently not listening. It was odd but for a second DeFrys got the impression he seemed to blur between locations rather than physically move. DeFrys nodded to two of his men, who moved to apprehend him. Moon looked up as they began to weave their way through piles of stock, and manoeuvred himself behind others when they drew close. This happened twice more and the mercenaries cursed in exasperation finding direct pursuit impossible. The stock had been arranged in such a way that it formed a miniature maze seemingly designed to frustrate their every attempt to reach their quarry.

"That's right, that's right," Moon said. "Have a good look around."

"I already told you, old man," DeFrys barked. "We have no interest in your goods."

"Today's special is a boozelhorn made by the Yassan of the Drakengrats. It's said if you blow a boozelhorn your enemies comprehensively fill their trousers. Would you like a demonstration?"

DeFrys growled; game over. He bashed away a pile of stock, hurling pots and jars to the floor. Some clattered through an open trapdoor which Moon moved towards.

"I expect there'll be quite a mess," he said. "Now where did I put that shovel?"

"Stay where you are, old man!" DeFrys ordered as Moon began to descend. His men crashed after him, reaching the opening just as the old man's head vanished below. It was odd but just for a second he thought he saw the old man disappear *before* he disappeared – that was, before passing out of view beneath the floorboards. It had to have been a trick of the light. It was difficult to tell with his men crowding around.

"What are you waiting for?" he shouted. "Follow him!"

DeFrys expected to hear the sounds of a scuffle before the old man was dragged back to the ground floor. But there was only a puzzled cry from one of his men.

"Sir, he's gone, sir!"

"What?"

"The old man, he just seemed to disapp... no, no, wait, he's here. I think."

"Make up your mind, man!"

"I could have sworn..."

DeFrys bit his lip. This whole thing was damned peculiar.

"Don't let him out of your sight," he said. "I'm coming down."

DeFrys descended the ladder. Half way down he paused, running his hand over a light tube that illuminated the lower level – the kind of light tube, Old Race technology, that he had only ever seen in archaeological sites or the sublevels of Scholten Cathedral. What were they doing in a primitive market town in Pontaine?

What, for that matter, were all the other objects down here?

The old man stood on the other side of the cellar, smiling. In the artificial light he looked somehow strange, almost flat and two dimensional.

"An impressive collection, isn't it?" he said. "Reserve stock which I normally only make available to special customers. Those I trust to use it properly." His expression darkened. "Some of it I don't make available at all."

DeFrys looked to where the old man was pointing. Beside him was another small chamber beyond the cellar, one that appeared to normally be hidden behind a display cabinet that was, for the time being, swung open on concealed hinges. His eyebrows rose at what he saw in there – even if he didn't necessarily know what it was he was seeing.

"Do you realise how many years it has taken me to collect these items?" Merrit Moon said. "How many sites I have risked my life to explore to bring them here, to safety?"

"Proscribed technology," DeFrys said.

"What has come to be known as proscribed technology," Moon said. A needless repetition that brought a momentary frown to DeFrys' face. "Proscribed by a Church which has neither the wit or wisdom to use it properly." He turned towards the chamber, staring wistfully at each object in turn. "Here there are devices that can change the nature of a man or his surroundings. Devices which can control the weather, bringing rain or sunshine depending on which is your desire. Devices which can turn the tide of a war…"

DeFrys stepped off the bottom rung of the ladder and took a step towards the old man.

"Why are you telling us these things, old man?"

"I once told a protégé of mine – perhaps you've heard of her – Kali Hooper?" Moon went on. Again it struck DeFrys as a non-sequitur, "that she had to take great care in what she released into the world. I have to tell you the same now."

"These objects will be confiscated, old man," DeFrys said. "Examined by experts within our ranks…"

"I doubt, however," Merrit Moon continued, "that you will pay much notice to what I say."

"What?"

"I couldn't take them with me, you see. Had to leave them behind. But I cannot let them fall into your hands. Simply cannot. It would not be right."

"What?" DeFrys said again.

He stared hard at the old man, his face questioning, but Moon simply stared impassively back. A sudden tug of fear gripped the mercenary, for now that the old man was so close the sense of unreality about him that had been so nagging seemed more pronounced. He took a step forward so he was standing nose to nose with the man he was to arrest. His target had no body heat, no body odour, no substance at all.

"For that, I am genuinely sorry," Merrit Moon said.

DeFrys swallowed and put out his hand. It passed right through Merrit Moon.

"Genuinely sorry…" Merrit Moon repeated.

Suddenly everything made sense to DeFrys. Moon's seeming to blur as he moved. His momentary disappearance at the trapdoor. But most of all his inability to answer a direct question. The old man wasn't being obstructive or evasive – he simply wasn't answering questions because he hadn't heard them!

These last few minutes this… projection had been delivering a pre-recorded lecture.

And class had just been dismissed.

"It's a trap, get out, get out!" he shouted to his men, but too late.

As the walls around DeFrys began to throb and glow with strange green veins, he found himself scrabbling for the rungs of the ladder alongside his men. Forcing them off it, in fact.

His breach in officerial responsibility was academic, for his men would never report him. The cellar of Wonders of the World exploded with a force no human bomb could have achieved, and a second later the rest of the shop – ground and upper floors – followed suit. DeFrys was running for his life from the building when it was wiped from the map, and the concussion hit him like a giant sledgehammer in the back. He was thrown forward to land crookedly and heavily on his front, the impact forcing out an explosive grunt.

As Gargassians began to run towards the site, pointing and gasping, it took a few seconds for the mercenary to cease moving forward, his twisted body ploughing a furrow in the ground where he'd landed, his jaw carving a rut.

HUNDREDS OF LEAGUES away, Merrit Moon was eating a sandwich when he felt his old life vanish forever, the event transmitted to him by the elven sensory sphere he had left behind with the holographers in the shop. The One Faith, the Only Faith, the Fewer Faith, he thought philosophically. And continued to chew.

The knowledge that he no longer had a home did not come as the wrench he thought it might, surprisingly. The old place had never been the same since being all but demolished by the k'nid, and even as he had been packing the cracks they had left with the elven compound he had named detonite, in readiness for the Faith forces he knew would inevitably come for him, he hadn't felt particularly sad. There were some things the k'nid attack had destroyed that could never be replaced – his elven telescope, ironically the first thing that had seen them coming, among them – and he was far too old to seek out and gather such treasures again. To surround himself with such seemed folly in these changing times, in fact.

There was, of course, also his health. He wasn't ailing – in fact, for a man of his age he was in quite superior shape – but that was wholly due to the ogur corruption that continued to taint his body. The solutions and elixirs he had perfected to keep his transformative affliction in check continued to do their job, and while he still possessed the thread-engineered antidote that Kali had brought from the Crucible, he resolutely refused to use it. It wasn't that he didn't trust it – because of its provenance its efficacy was beyond question – but that, as he'd told Kali that night in the Flagons, to use it just didn't feel right. If he were honest, he had never been able to shake a conviction that what had happened to him had happened for a reason, and in the light of recent developments he was becoming more convinced still.

He had not told Kali this but the fact was, since the Hel'ss appeared, he was changing more than he had been. Not changing more frequently – although the bouts did seem to have their own accelerating timetable – but more dramatically. He sighed and raised a trembling hand, watching as the sinew and tendons beneath his skin pulsed and throbbed. These painful phenomena were not just linked to his hands, either, the same effect manifested itself at different times throughout his body, and he could not stare at himself in a mirror for more than a few minutes before one such tic or another materialised. All of these felt different to the Thrutt transformations – for one thing they occurred spontaneously, without the raised adrenalin that normally acted as a trigger – and the only conclusion he could draw was that his body was responding in some way to the presence of the Hel'ss. The question was, why?

This, he had no answer to – yet. What he did know was that these occasions were something to which he could not risk exposing his friends. The feeling of unfettered power that accompanied them both terrified and awed him, and if it were to be unleashed, beyond his control, when anyone was nearby... he didn't like to think what would happen.

So, in the end, he'd decided to leave. What choice did he have? The interesting thing was that it hadn't been at all difficult to choose where to go. And for one simple reason.

He could not stop dreaming of the World's Ridge Mountains.

They were calling to him.

And he had answered – or at least relocated to their vicinity in the hope he would there find out what the dreams meant. The lower to middle heights of the World's Ridge still hid Old Race sites he had been too inexperienced to challenge as a young man, and too incapable of challenging when old, but now he had, if needed, the physical means to survive, what better time to explore them? He had not, after all, lost his interest in *learning* of the past, far from it – the ever growing presence of the Hel'ss in the skies was surely an indication that the fate of the Old Races was more relevant than ever.

Moon picked himself up, biting into an apple to finish the lunch he'd eaten, and strolled to the mouth of the cave he was using as a bivouac. It actually wasn't so much a cave as a recess halfway up the side of a sheer and precipitous wall of a much, much larger cavern, and what Moon's dwarfed figure saw as he looked out made him crunch deeply and appreciatively on his fruit. The bite and subsequent self-satisfied sigh seemed unnaturally loud in the vast expanse. Every archaeologist on Twilight – what few true ones there were – dreamed of the ultimate find, but most had to content themselves with second best. But not he. Not any more. The sense of wonder and magnificence he had felt when he had first set eyes upon this site was not misplaced, and he once more revelled in the name he had given it.

The Gallery.

Most caverns had galleries somewhere within them, of course, but few in an artistic sense, and none on the scale of what he'd found here.

As soon as Moon stepped into the bosun's cradle he had strung beneath his makeshift living area, he came face to face with a small section of ancient cave painting, covering the entirety of the vast wall in which his bivouac was set. So close to, it was impossible to discern what the painting depicted and, even from the other side of the cavern, it was difficult, the primitive art obscured by growths of vines, creepers and other vegetation. Moon had spent the last few weeks negotiating the wall in the cradle, laboriously clearing the growths away, but had even now completed only perhaps a quarter of the work needed to fully reveal the painting. Further clearance was not on his agenda today, however, and had not been for the past two days, ever since he had discovered what appeared to be the entrance to a chamber hidden *within* the complexity of the painting itself.

It was all really rather exciting, and Moon hummed to himself as he used the complex system of rope pulleys and fulcrums it had taken him a week to assemble to pull himself along the wall. Stone projections at certain points required that he moved down and then across again, and then down, up and across once more, but the old man was patient, in no hurry to get where he wanted to go. The cradle at last ended up suspended before a small ledge.

Moon stepped from the cradle onto the ledge to face a cryptoblock. What lay before him was not quite so daunting as it seemed, however, he having worked on it full-time since its discovery. Though cryptoblocks had become something of Kali's speciality, he'd retired the previous evening having only one last element to arrange, and though its proper positioning had confounded him through the night, the solution had at last popped into his head over lunch.

It was all very simple, really.

Moon pushed a block of the puzzle inwards and then immediately pulled it out again. A second later the ratchet that had been triggered by the pressure sprang into place. The cryptoblock collapsed before him.

"Well, well, old man," Moon whispered to himself, "I guess you haven't lost it, after all."

He took a breath and stepped into the unsealed chamber. He cracked an elven lightstick that he took from a satchel and moved it slowly about. A flare of light bounced back from something reflective in the centre of the room.

Just one object in the whole of the chamber.

My, my. That *had* to be important.

The old man cracked more lightsticks and scattered them about the floor of the chamber. He found himself staring at an object perched on a podium that appeared to be some kind of metal dodecahedron. It was difficult to tell because its material was so polished that it shone like a tiny sun.

Moon circled it slowly, his hands almost but not quite touching, as if the object were his partner in a slow waltz. Then he dropped to his haunches, licked his lips, examining it only with his eyes.

"What have we here?"

Tentatively, he reached out a hand, intending no more than the gentlest caress of the object's side, but a sudden spasm – the kind of spasm he was by now all too familiar with – made his arm jerk violently, and instead of caressing the object his hand knocked it fully from the podium to bounce across the opposite side of the chamber.

Not *now*, Merrit Moon demanded of himself.

But it was too late.

There was a grinding noise from the surrounding walls.

Protective failsafes. Preventative measures. Proof that the mysterious object was as important as he'd suspected it to be.

Or, to put it another way, a trap. And very likely a deadly one.

Moon wasted no time. Despite the pain and the throbbing in his arms and legs, not to mention the agonised flaring at the back of his head that made him feel as though someone was scooping out his brainstem with a spoon, he loped around the edge of the podium and grabbed the object, jamming it into his satchel. Then he turned towards the entrance, noting that a thick stone slab was already descending where the cryptoblock had been. His days of rolling beneath such things were beyond him and he knew he didn't have much time, and so the last thing he needed as he made a dash for the shrinking exit was for another spasm to hit him, this time harder than ever before.

He belly-flopped onto the floor, lay there gasping and groaning. The same hand that had triggered the podium's weight sensors stretched out quaveringly towards the closing gap but the slab was already two thirds of the way down. He knew there was no way he could make it.

Too slow. Too old. Despite thinking that his… *condition* could help him be young again.

Merrit Moon's head slumped to the floor of the chamber, and he sighed. But despite the fact that he was clearly doomed to die, he smiled to himself. Perhaps better this way – doing what he loved – than facing the unknown future that his physical instability offered him. It was, he reflected, the way Kali would have preferred him to die.

Kali. He swore he could almost hear her now. Though, admittedly, sounding less articulate than imagined.

"*Gahh! Uuung. Get in there, you farking…* "

He looked up and saw the silhouette of a figure outlined in what remained of the exit. A figure which rammed something into the dwindling space between slab and floor. The length of wood, if that's what it was, was already splintering and cracking beneath the weight of the stone.

"Kali?" Moon queried.

"That's me," the figure said. A head appeared in the gap. "Look, old man, I'm sorry to be a pain and I know this is all a bit last minute but I need someone to look after my bamfcat."

"What?"

"Well, y'know, putting him in kennels is just *so* expensive…"

"What? What are you talking ab –"

He broke off, just as something else did the same. "Look out!"

"Shit!" Kali yelled, seeing the wooden support give way. She at least proved herself capable of rolling out of danger, even if it was in the wrong direction. As she bumped into Moon, the stone slab slammed shut behind her.

Kali stared at the old man, saw how the entire surface of his body seemed to be… rippling.

"Hi," Kali said breathlessly. And then, "Old man… are you all right?"

Moon felt his spasms start to subside, struggled into a sitting position and dusted himself down.

"Am I all right? Do you realise what you have just done?"

Kali gave a cursory glance around. "So we're trapped. Not the first time for either of us, right? And for once we have two minds to figure a way out."

The walls surrounding them rumbled again. And with an expulsion of dust juddered an inch closer to them.

"Quickly?" Kali added, with a sheepish grin.

"Oh, there's no rush," the old man said wearily, all too aware that their predicament was his fault. "You're inside a Bevvel's Conundrum."

"I am?"

"Otherwise known as Bevvel's Chamber of Unending Torment. Think yourself lucky you've never come across one. In the time it takes to contract – about a week, I believe – they say that in your mind you die a thousand times. Each time imagining the final, slow constriction of the walls, the pressure as your internal organs are squeezed, and the cracking and splintering of your bones as they're crushed beyond recog –"

"Do you *mind*? Fark me, have you always been this blunt or is it an age thing?"

"There is no need for foul language, young lady."

"Well, I'm sorry, old man but... don't you think we'd be better employed trying to determine a way out?"

"There is none, believe me. Bevvel's construction is based on cryptoblock dimensional dynamics."

"No trap is foolproof, old man."

"You are welcome to try to prove that."

Kali did. During the time it took her to exhaust possibilities, the trap contracted once more.

"Shit," she said softly. "Shit, shit, shit."

"I told you..."

"I had to try."

"...about the language."

Kali glared, and slumped in a corner, hitting the stone petulantly as it rudely juddered forward once more. Then it occurred to her.

"Hang on," she said. "Wasn't that a bit... quick?"

Moon's eyes widened and he stuck his ear to the floor. "There is something wrong," he said. "The gears sound misaligned."

"Cryptoblock dimensional dynamics have *gears*?"

"It's... complicated. It took me a lifetime to work out how much so."

"Well, I'm not going to have a lifetime to catch up unless we do something."

At Kali's feet the elven lightstick that Moon had activated fizzled out. In the resultant darkness there was another crunch of gears.

"Don't suppose you have any more of those?" Kali asked.

Moon held up one more, lit it and laid it at their feet.

"Dark soon, then."

"Quite so."

The two of them sat there in silence for a while – or at least silence punctuated by the juddering of stone. Kali reckoned she'd got about two hundred and forty seventh into imagining her thousand deaths when it proved too much. She started to hum.

"What are you *doing* here, Kali," Moon asked.

"I came to say goodbye. Found your note at the shop. Just before they came and... you know."

"Goodbye?" Merrit Moon repeated, ignoring the reference to the fate of his shop. "Kali, I wouldn't have stayed out here without seeing you once more. I would have found a way."

Kali shook her head. "I'm not talking about you, old man. I'm talking about me."

Moon hesitated. "You're imagining you're going somewhere you might not come back from? That isn't like you."

"No. Yes. I don't know. I... just have a feeling about this one."

The old man placed his hand on hers. "Where?"

"The Island of the Lost."

"Trass Kathra?"

"Trass Kathra," Kali repeated. "It exists."

Moon turned away. His mind raced, weaving and reweaving a thousand separate strands of knowledge he had accumulated over the years with an equal number of theories. He shared none of them with Kali because she was involved in every permutation and every permutation ended the same way – he would lose her from his life in the same mysterious fashion she had arrived. It had been so convenient to forget this child had been found as a newborn in some kind of Old Race 'pod' that hadn't been seen since. He had pretended to himself that she had been normal but, of course, she wasn't – with such an origin how could she be? – and, now, maybe, if Trass Kathra was involved, was the time her past came home to roost. The fact was, all the old legends associated Trass Kathra with the End Time, so maybe Kali had found her ultimate destination at last.

One thing seemed undeniable. If that was the case, he had to be certain she got there. And to do that, he had to get her out of the deathtrap that his own curse had stuck her in.

Moon broke suddenly from his introspection, and began to slam his fist on the stone floor of the chamber, making Kali start at the unexpected violence of it. As he continued and the skin of his fists split, leaking blood, she tried to stop him, but he shrugged her off, intent on achieving what could be their only salvation.

"What the hells are you doing?" Kali asked.

"Leaving," the old man said, simply.

His blows became more powerful because he became more powerful, his head snapping back and the irises of his eyes changing as he purposefully unleashed his inner ogur – and what he had found lay *beyond* the inner ogur. Sitting in the corner of the shrinking chamber, Kali swallowed, because although she had witnessed his transformation into Thrutt a number of times, what was happening now went far beyond anything she had ever seen.

Every muscle in the old man's body was expanding, he himself becoming taller, broader, bigger, and with the extra strength this granted him he was able to shatter the stone of the floor and expose the gears beneath. These, too, he pounded, though not mindlessly, and suddenly the contractions of the Bevvel's Conundrum became more pronounced and more frequent, reducing the area of their confinement by half in a matter of seconds.

"Old man...?" Kali said.

The chamber jerked inward once more, and Merrit Moon stood.

"Get beneath me," he said. There was a timbre in his voice deeper than any previously heard. Kali looked at him, saw his expression, and obeyed, huddling in the old man's shadow, though the truth was he appeared hardly old, in fact hardly a man, any more.

The chamber shuddered again, and Kali felt the cold touch of stone nudging at her heels.

It was at that moment that the light went out. The old man's explosion of anger had subsided but, instead, she heard a low growl. An inhuman and even un ogur-like growl. The growl of something *incredibly* powerful. And then the growl turned into a roar and she heard the sound of massive fists punching outward, fists which shattered the stone around them, reducing the walls of the Bevvel's Conundrum to dust.

As the dust settled, she looked up. Something massive and incapable of speech loomed over her. But its message, as it offered her a hand, was clear.

Time to go.

Kali followed the beast like creature to the exit from the cavern, watching its form dwindle as they progressed upward. By the time they reached the surface, Merrit Moon was almost himself again, though Kali couldn't shake the image of the old man's transformation from her mind, far more violent, far more dramatic than it had ever been. She waited until his breathing steadied before asking the question that had to be asked.

"Merrit, what happened to you down there?"

Moon raised his eyes to meet hers. "I'm sorry if I frightened you."

Kali smiled, touched the old man's arm with its enlarged cartilage, tendons and muscle that even now throbbed and pulsed beneath the skin.

"You could never frighten me, old man. I'm just concerned. I don't understand what's going on..."

"Then that makes two of us."

"It's unlike you not to have some kind of theory."

"Oh, I have a theory, all right. But you're not going to like it."

"*Tell me.*"

"I'm staring to believe..." Merrit began, then paused.

"What, old man?"

"I'm starting to believe that I was never meant to leave the World's Ridge Mountains. I mean after what happened, after I died. That it happened, how and where it did, for a reason."

"The ogur cave?"

"The ogur cave," Moon repeated. "I think it's.... calling to me."

"What?"

"Don't ask me to explain it – I can't. But I think there was far more to my transformation than corruption by the soul scythe. A purpose."

"Some kind of destiny? Gods, old man, you know how I feel about destinies."

Moon sighed.

"We may not be talking about destinies, young lady, but a single destiny. That somehow you, me, Slowhand, Aldrededor and Dolorosa, *everyone*... we're all caught up in something beyond our control. Something that, in different ways and perhaps with different participants, has happened before."

"There's a hole blown in your theory, right there," Kali said. "Slowhand's gone, right?" Her voice changed in a way Moon couldn't quite fathom. "Doing his own thing."

Moon sighed again, more heavily.

"I wouldn't be too sure of that."

Kali span on the spot, trying to take in a hundred different possibilities at once. But the only thing that made sense saddened her deeply. It was that there was something she had to do, and there was something Merrit had to do, and that their paths were going to take them to opposite ends of their known world, perhaps never to return.

"Merrit," she said, "is this goodbye?"

"I don't know."

Kali pulled in a breath, huffed. The sun was rising over the peaks of the World's Ridge, far above. "Well, I know one thing," she said perhaps a little too quickly, moving towards Horse, "and that's if you're going, you're taking Horse with you. If anyone can look after you, he can."

"Kali, I don't even know what my ultimate destination will be."

"Then," Kali said, stroking Horse's snout and refusing to turn around and face the old man, "when you no longer need him, let him go. It may not be the Drakengrats but it is the mountains, and he'll feel at home there." She stroked the bamfcat's snout again. "One thing's for certain – he can't come with me."

Moon didn't move for a second but simply stared at Kali's back, understanding that she didn't want to prolong this any more than he did. The bamfcat snorted softly, plaintively, and it was clear that he, too, knew what was going on.

The old man rose, kicked out the remains of the campfire, and slung his bags across Horse's back. But he kept one small bag back, handing it to Kali.

"A few toys I salvaged from the shop's cellar that might help to keep you safe," he said. "Also something I found in that trap. And my notebook, incomplete but –" Moon shrugged.

Kali nodded, took the saddlebag. Again, she did not look at Moon as the old man heaved himself up into the saddle, seemingly trying to close off the world. She did, however, start involuntarily as the bamfcat began to move off.

"Old man," she said after a second, staring after him. The physically altered Moon looked so *natural* on Horse's back, and Horse beneath him, as if somehow they had always belonged together. "Take care of yourself."

Moon smiled and then aimed his gaze at the rising slopes ahead.

"You, too, my daughter. You, too."

But what he thought was, *Please let there be someone out there, so you don't have to go through this alone.*

CHAPTER FIVE

THE ROAR OF the crowd, the smell of greasepaint and everything covered in shit. All the fun of the fair. While the towering, brightly-lit wine-glass that was Miramas's famous Theatre of Heaven dominated the stormy horizon, the Big Top drooping in a sodden field a couple of leagues outside the city was another class of venue entirely. Rain hammered down here as it had for hours, battering the already unstable looking canvas and threatening a blow-down, while the muddy footprints of those who had risked life and limb by venturing inside the tent for the night's performance splashed and popped incessantly, flooded to overfilling.

Among the sideshow stalls, freak cages and calliope music machines of the abandoned midway, pigrats – the usual inhabitants of the field – snuffled up half-eaten mool kebabs and sugarfloss, which they chewed greedily before adding to the mire. Attending to their toilet, they had no interest in the occasional cheers from inside the tent but looked up briefly when, from the other side of a candle-lit stretch of canvas, came the sharp snap of a thong followed by a pained hiss and a word that sounded like "*nyyyyyynnnhg.*" A moment later they scattered, farting and honking, as a shadowy mass stumbled into the canvas, making it bulge out like an oversized balloon animal gone wrong.

The strange shape emitted a rumbling burp and attempted to right itself, stumbling again not once but twice. The pigrats were not to know it but the player in this unusual piece of shadow theatre went by the name of Killiam Slowhand.

And Killiam Slowhand was shit-faced.

The archer was taking another slug from his bottle of twattle when it was snatched from his hand, pouring beer down his bare torso and washing away the glitter he had half-heartedly rubbed on only minutes before. He blinked, and then the sound of the bottle being slammed onto his dressing table made him start.

"Started early again, I see?" Shay Redwood said. The petite, dark-haired Oweilaun woman kept her voice low but it was no less cutting for it. "Or is it that you just haven't stopped?"

The archer regarded his interrogator with half-focused eyes, wobbling backward slightly. Hands planted firmly on her hips, Shay stared solidly back up at him, though her expression was not so much accusing as concerned.

"The second one," Slowhand burped after a second. In all their time together he still hadn't worked out why he couldn't help but be honest with the woman. "The 'not having stopped' bit, I guess."

"Fark, Slowhand. You know this can't go on."

"Can't see any reason why not."

"No?" Shay said. She plucked the archer's quiver from the dressing table and extracted one of the arrows. She used the tip of one to prick the soft flesh of her thumb, which took no pressure at all. "These things aren't toys."

Something flared in Slowhand's head, an old memory, but he kept control of it. "I know that," he said steadily.

"I'm no toy, either," Shay responded, unphased. "Slowhand, it's me out there, in front of your arrows, and the only thing that stops me dying at the hands of a drunk is that what you do comes naturally to you, like breathing. You're just too good an archer to ever miss."

"So what's the problem?"

"*You*. You're the problem, can't you see that? Look at you! You're stagnating here. You jump through the same old hoops every day, not because you enjoy it but because it stops you thinking of anything else."

"The only thing I'm thinking of is paying my keep."

"Yeah? That's not what I hear when you talk in your sleep. Talk of traps and treasure, of long lost secrets. And night after night, without fail... Kali Hooper."

Slowhand hesitated. "Sorry. It... she... doesn't mean anything. It was a long time ago."

"It was a *year* ago, 'Liam. Only a year. And I think you have unfinished business."

"Shay, I promise you, I'm not –"

Shay placed a hand on his cheek. "I know you're not, lover. But clearly you were involved in *something* back then that just isn't letting you go. Think about it, eh? Maybe it's time for you – for both of us, if you'd like the company – to find out what."

"I'd have no idea where to go."

"Maybe you'll know when you get there." She cocked an ear as there was an announcement from the ring. "But for now, Mister Thongar, what say we get this show on the road?"

She went on before him, disappearing through the vorgang with a smile and a flourish that was greeted with rapturous applause. A few moments later, the chanting began. And then the drums. And then the screaming.

The screaming was his cue and – glancing at the bottle but forsaking it – Slowhand pulled in his stomach, put on his best heroic grin and followed his partner into the ring.

There, Shay was already in the grip of the orcs. They weren't real orcs, of course, but Griffin, Mosk, Thane and the rest of the crew in moth-eaten and less than convincing orc costumes, but that didn't matter as neither he nor, he was willing to bet, anyone in the audience had ever encountered a real orc in their lives. It was a matter of debate whether the creatures existed on Twilight at all.

The whole act was the grand finale to the show and presented as a set piece in which he, Thongar, had to rescue Shay from a sacrificial ritual orc-estrated, as it were, by the supposed beasts of the mountains. To his surprise, it had become a runaway success. Maybe with that thing – the Hel'ss – hanging in the sky people, despite what the Filth told them, needed to believe they could still cope with the unknown and, in however small a way, he was satisfying that need. Despite the scenario's pure fiction, it had, ironically, been only a few performances in when he'd realised he'd gladly sacrifice himself in order to rescue Shay for real. Ever since they'd met in that tavern in Scholten – she persuading him to run away to the circus, just for fun and just like kids, that very night – the pair had grown closer and closer, their relationship blossoming until he had begun to think of them as soulmates. He would have been more than happy to forget that he had even *had* a previous life, if it hadn't been for the dreams.

The dreams.

As he'd had to night after night for months, Slowhand quashed the lingering images of the dreams by throwing himself into his act with gusto. As the crowd cheered him on, he leapt from papier-mâché rock to papier-mâché rock, despatching the monsters who threatened Shay with a dazzling display of bowmanship. As Shay struggled against the bonds on the sacrificial frame built on the highest rock, his arrows thudded into the orcs from all directions, and Griffin and the others made their pratfalls on cue, roaring as they clutched the shafts embedded in the thick padding of their costumes, tumbling to their deaths. That they, as much as Shay, trusted him to deliver his arrows with unwavering accuracy said a lot about the bond he had developed with them all and, as usual as the climax of the act approached, Slowhand was concentrating so much as to not let them down that he had forgotten his dreams completely.

The last of the marauding orcs fell and the climax of the performance arrived. It was the most difficult shot of the evening, one that required him to be static, and he struck a suitably heroic but steadied pose on a rock halfway up the fake mountainside.

In his sights was an orc shaman dancing directly behind Shay, and the arrow he was about to fire was firstly to sever the chain holding Shay's arms aloft, and then continue to strike the taller shaman in the chest, punching him off the rocks and 'killing' him triumphantly.

Slowhand tensed. Despite the gap of only inches between Shay, chain and shaman, it wasn't the aiming of the arrow that presented problems but the power with which it was delivered. Too little and the chain would not shatter; too much and it would puncture the padding of Thane, his friend. Slowhand's grip on his bowstring tightened. His eyes narrowed. On the summit of the fake mountainside, Shay winked and smiled.

Her eyes were filled with the same absolute trust when they jerked wide in shock, and then almost instantly glazed over. As Shay slumped on her chains, she did not react at all to the pulse of dark blood that ran down from the centre of her forehead and over the bridge of her nose to drip onto the papier mache rock.

A rumble of unease ran through the audience, and then came deafening silence. All eyes stared at the projectile embedded firmly in the centre of Shay's forehead, registering part disbelief and part expectation, benumbed by the fact that the shot had been so perfect, so unwavering, so exact, that it couldn't be a mistake. In other words, it had to be part of the act, and the great Thongar had amazed them again, if only they could work out how.

Slowhand himself simply stood there, Suresight hanging at his legs. The sights and sounds of the ring – that place of smoke and mirrors, of unreality – seemed suddenly painfully loud and vivid. He saw crew and fellow performers move to him from backstage and through the crowd, their movements slowed as if in a dream, cries of shock coming as drawn out drawls. Bent Dez Fagin, Little Jack The Giant, Five Ropes Lucy, none of them could believe what had happened.

Slowhand didn't know what to think. All he knew was that Shay had trusted him, and had died at his hand. He raised that same appendage, his arrow hand, palm up, before his eyes, and stared at its shaking form as if it were nothing to do with him at all. It took him a second to realise that in his other hand, hanging as limply as Suresight, the arrow remained.

Did it matter? Shay wasn't to know that, was she? She would have had no time to realise that the projectile that had instantly snuffed her life and thoughts had not been unleashed by him, for there was no reason why she would think there should be another. In one stunned moment his love would have gone to her grave believing, however infinitesimally fleetingly, that he'd failed her and the drink within him had let them both down.

But it hadn't. *He* hadn't. The arrow was still in his hand.

Slowly, with a rush of pressure in the ears, the world about him returned to normal. The first thing he heard were the screams from the audience – screaming not because of what had just happened but because they, like his friends, were being manhandled out of their seats and propelled towards the exits. The people doing the manhandling were strangers, but there were a lot of them, and all dressed in black. It wasn't difficult to guess who they were but, if further proof were needed, the black spheres that moved through the air between them provided it.

Filth, Slowhand thought. Then, feeling the slightest disturbance in the air, he instinctively span as a projectile identical to the one that had killed Shay – a crossbow bolt, not an arrow – sheared by him to thud into the fake rock on which Shay slumped. His archer's expertise immediately calculated the arrow had not been fired to take him out, too, but only to incapacitate by hitting him in his drawing arm.

Slowhand's eyes narrowed as he stared at a figure clad in black standing on the opposite side of the circus ring to him. Unlike the others – males – the black she wore hugged a lithe and supple figure with flowing red hair, and her crossbow was raised and primed once more, and she smiled as she fired.

The smile faded as Slowhand instantly brought up Suresight, re-notching his arrow as he did, and released it without a moment's hesitation or calculation. It split its opposite number in two as it came.

As the broken halves of the bolt and Slowhand's arrow dropped to the sawdust of the ring, Suresight was already primed to fire again. But across the ring his attacker had jettisoned her crossbow in favour of twin swords that she drew from sheaths on her back, and even as Slowhand's arrow sped through the air towards her, the swords moved, reducing the arrow to slivers.

A trick reciprocated, the smile returned.

"Who are you?" Slowhand hissed.

"Someone employed to do a job. A *real* job, that is, not this posturing and preening that passes for your excuse of a life."

That sounded *personal*, Slowhand thought, but now was not the time to explore why. "What kind of job?"

"Shepherding. If you weren't so out of the loop, you'd know that most of your heretic friends are now guests of the Final Faith. You took a while to track down. I volunteered for the job."

"Is that so? So what happens now?"

"I deliver you. I get paid."

"Confident. But you just killed my girlfriend, so I think I'll have to spoil your plans."

"I don't think so."

"You really don't have a lot of choice."

The girl nodded and, out of the corners of his eyes, Slowhand was aware of Faith moving down the aisles between the now empty seats, closing on the circus ring. A second later, he was surrounded by a solid wall of crossbow wielding robes. The message to him was clear – you're outnumbered, archer. You might take down some of us but you'll never stop us all.

No? Slowhand thought. And in that instant heard Shay's voice in his head.

It comes naturally to you. Like breathing.

Maybe Slowhand didn't need telling, but he might have needed reminding, and he moved in a blur, plucking arrow after arrow from his quiver and unleashing them before his newly found circle of friends had chance to react. Six of them went down with arrows embedded in their throats or through their hearts, three more with tips positioned as exactly as had been the bolt that had killed Shay. Slowhand moved as he fired, allowing none of the figures to draw a bead on him while at the same time circling the ring so that the girl and her swords could not draw close. Despite this, his accuracy was undiminished, and the eyes of those who were not felled by arrows widened as much in shock as those who were.

But Slowhand was not quite as invincible as he appeared. Though his archery prowess was indeed undiminished, the physical effort it took to maintain was already starting to take its toll, and Slowhand found himself uncharacteristically breathless. There wasn't really the problem, though, because while he could nevertheless maintain the pace needed to eventually finish off every single one of his attackers, he carried a quiver stocked not for battle but entertainment.

In short, he didn't have enough arrows to go around.

Slowhand felt the contents of the quiver as he plucked the next arrow from it, confirming, as he'd calculated, there were only four arrows left. Three of these he used to drop twice as many Filth, each arrow shot with such force that it passed through two men at a time. The last arrow he withheld. The smile returned to the girl's lips and was echoed on the faces of the survivors as they saw the archer's predicament, and as one they began to move in.

Slowhand turned in a slow circle, bowstring creaking, the arrow pointing at each Faith in turn but not released, until it was aiming directly at the girl's heart. Still, he did not release it, holding her gaze as she sensed victory and her smile grew. Then, as she raised her swords, he swung Suresight directly upward and released the tension that had kept the arrow from play.

The arrow shot high above the ring, tearing through canvas and anchoring itself, and Slowhand rose on the whizzline attached to it. He leapt from it into the web of rope rigging that filled the hemisphere, that part of the Big Top where the aerialists performed, and sat like a spider in its nest. His attackers now far beneath him, Slowhand saw there were nine of them left, ten with the girl. She was already angrily despatching her men towards various ladders and poles that accessed the upper tent, but Slowhand was ready for them, clambering swiftly along the ropes to the centre of the hemisphere, where lay the riser ring through which most of the Big Top's rigging was tied off. The band that encircled the king pole – the central support of the whole tent – was a confusing snake's nest of thick and intertwining guy lines but, as everyone mucked in together on the road, he was no stranger to them and knew precisely which to loosen or untie to create the utmost havoc beneath him.

His new friends were about to discover just how dangerous a place a Big Top could be.

Two ropes brought down the gantry from which handlers controlled the trapeze lunge ropes, and another one of the wheels from which hung the cloud swings, the ropes on which support performers swung out over the audience to hold their attention while the next aerialist 'trick' was readied. Both structures first collapsed sideways, dropping to forty five degree angles as their guy lines whizzed through their pullies, then, as they whipped free, both fell to the big top's floor, those Filth who were using them as a means to reach him falling with them, screaming. Slowhand's satisfaction on hearing the crunching impacts of his attackers' bodies was, however, short-lived, as three crossbow bolts thudded into the king pole next to his head, and he immediately dropped down through the rope spiderweb, grabbing onto one of its strands and swinging rapidly, hand-to-hand, down it towards its connecting quarter pole.

The quarter pole – and the seven others that ringed the arena – were the medium supports of the Big Top, positioned where they were to prevent sagging, and each rose to a point where the Big Top's triangular roof flaps were lashed together, separable in case of an emergency. This, Slowhand reckoned, qualified as an emergency and, dangling by one hand, he quickly undid the lashings on one side, then rapidly shimmied, crossbow bolts thudding about him, along the skirt of the tent to the other. He undid the lashings there, too, and the entire section of canvas roofing flopped inwards, dropping down like an exhausted dog's tongue. From the expressions on the faces of the Filth it headed towards, climbing the tower to the high-wire, it was clear they thought it an inconsequential threat, but they had seriously underestimated the weight of such a section of canvassing – wet or not – and were slapped from their positions with another bone-crunching thud and appropriate screams as the flap hit them, almost overbalancing the tower itself.

Slowhand needed to gain height once more, and he flipped himself from the guy rope into the air, grabbing onto the lip of the flap adjacent to the one he had dropped, then heaving himself onto the roof of the Big Top. Dressed as he was, he hissed against the cold and hammering rain, and his bare soles slithered frustratingly on the buoyant canvas as he pounded determinedly up, but eventually he reached the Big Top's cupola, and, through the gap in the roofing, out of which projected the king pole, flipped himself back inside once more.

The last of the Filth – the girl aside – had now managed to reach the spiderweb of guy lines some twenty feet below him and, spotting his return, were aiming crossbows, but Slowhand had already worked out what he needed to do. He dropped from the cupola onto one of the guy ropes that made up the spiderweb, the impact of his landing sending a tremor throughout the lines, and the Filth staggered, one of them involuntarily loosing a bolt he'd primed into the chest of a comrade-in-arms on the line next to him. The skewered Filth fell, clutching the line desperately for a moment before dropping away, and the resultant second tremor gave Slowhand all the time he needed to work his way across the web and boot his unsteady opponents from their perch.

Far below, the girl side-stepped the falling bodies as they exploded beside her, and raised her gaze slowly upwards. Eyes locking with Slowhand's, she smiled and then made her way to the ladders that would eventually bring her to him. Slowhand's jaw tensed, knowing his final opponent was in a different class entirely to the rest, and his eyes darted around the hemisphere, working out the moves he would need to counter those she would doubtless bring. Unarmed, dressed in nothing but his thong, the possibilities seemed limited, but then, almost unwillingly, he remembered a phrase that had many times been used by Kali Hooper.

Make it up as you go along.

Slowhand calculated the girl's route and made his way to one of the surviving lunge gantries, drawing in a trapeze on a guide rope. As he'd guessed, she was already doing the same, stepping onto the horizontal swing, intending to use it to reach him. She didn't get the chance, Slowhand bringing the fight to her by kicking off at the same time she did.

The two of them clashed in the heart of the hemisphere but, neither practiced on the acrobatics tool, did so clumsily, and the wind knocked from the pair of them, they were sent spinning wildly in opposite directions. Slowhand struggled to bring the trapeze under control, the Big Top and, more threateningly, the girl looming in his vision in a series of skewed, disorientating and vertiginous flashes, and then the two of them impacted again with a thud and an explosion of air and spittle. The collision was slower this time, accidental, but that didn't stop the girl taking a swing at him with one of her swords, and Slowhand only just escaped decapitation by dropping from his standing position to grab the trapeze bar with his hands.

He swung away from the girl, knifing his legs to gain momentum to cross the hemisphere, and gained a moment of precarious rest on the edge of the trapeze platform from which his opponent had kicked off. Twisting, he saw that she was doing the same on his, using the time to position herself with her lower legs wrapped about the trapeze ropes, freeing both hands for her swords, and then he was swinging once more, as she was swinging towards him.

Heading inexorably towards her, Slowhand had nothing with which to block the coming blades but the trapeze itself, and with a grunt he flipped himself back into a standing position. As the girl rushed towards him, he violently jerked his body sideways and downwards so that the hand rail of the trapeze rose up to parry the blows. Swords met wood, one deflected harmlessly but the other cleaving the trapeze in two, and the archer immediately grabbed the guy line of its left half, swinging out with it as it broke from the right.

The manoeuvre caught the girl by surprise, and Slowhand already had another one coming as, with a further twist of his body, he swung his now singular support around in a sweeping circle, heading directly back towards her. The girl gasped as Slowhand's feet smashed into her side and her trapeze was again sent spinning, this time so violently that its guy lines wrapped themselves about each other like plaiting hair. As she struggled to bring it under control, Slowhand swung in again, wrapping his legs about her entangled form and twisting an arm so that she released one of her swords into his grip. The girl roared in fury and swung at him with her other weapon, but Slowhand had already released his legs and was swinging away. It was only after a second that he realised she had nevertheless cut cleanly through his thong, and he was now completely naked. Once upon a time he might have reflected that the combination of nakedness, girl in black leather and lots of ropes would have held much promise but what had happened since – who was he kidding? What had happened *today* – quashed any such thoughts. Make no mistake, this girl might have been hired to capture him but this was rapidly turning into a battle of life and death.

But here was not the place to fight it. If he was going to take the girl on on even terms, now that he had one of her swords, he needed space, and needed it quickly. The girl already freeing herself from her entrapment, Slowhand swung away, flinging himself from the trapeze rope onto one of the surviving cloud swings, and from there shimmying up the rope to the wheel that suspended it. From there, another couple of leaps took him back to the section of roofing he had released, and then back onto the exposed upper surface of the Big Top.

The girl was right behind him, and Slowhand backed up as she pulled herself up onto the outer canvas. For a second the two of them stood there bent and gasping in the hammering rain, weapons poised, and then the girl came at him, yelling like something possessed. Slowhand did his best to defend himself under her furious barrage of blows, blocking and feinting, but he was being constantly forced back and barely managed one thrust himself, and it didn't take him long to realise that, despite the weapon, they were not on even terms at all. The girl was good. Very good.

She swung again, and Slowhand jack-knifed at the waist, avoiding her blade. The move threw his balance and he fell onto his back, slithering into one of the valleys of the undulating canvas, and cold water rushed to pool about him in the depression he had made. The girl launched herself at him, blade destined for his throat, but a moment before she struck Slowhand raised his legs, caught her, and sent her tumbling over him. He scrabbled around as she scrambled up, and the two of them circled each other, struggling to regain their footing.

"Who are you?" Slowhand gasped.

"You asked me that."

"No. I mean who are you, *really*?"

"I'd have thought you'd have known that. After all, we don't look that different, he and I. And after what you did, I'd have thought his face would have been etched in your mind forever."

"Who?" Slowhand asked, confused, but then her brow, her nose, her mouth started to transform into another face, one that, as she'd said, didn't look that different at all. He was suddenly back on the battlefield outside Andon during the Great War – *the Killing Ground* – lining up his shot to take out the general of the enemy forces as his brothers-in-arms breathed expectantly, desperately about him.

"My gods," he said, "you're John Garrison's daughter."

"John Garrison's daughter," she replied, her face hardening. "And Ben Garrison's *sister*."

The boy, Slowhand thought. He had never told anyone, not Shay, not Hooper, about the boy. The reason why he had laid down Suresight and left the military after the events of that battle. Pits of Kerberos, what the hells had he been doing there, on that worst of days? A *child*, no more than eight years of age. No one had ever quite been able to work it out but later, when casualties had been identified and someone had told him who it was that had died, speculation was that he had been running to help his father in the face of defeat, help him in the way only an eight year old boy would have thought he could.

And he, Slowhand, had killed him. Because the fact was there had *never* been a perfect shot that day. But there had been *a* shot. A shot through the heart of a figure who had looked bigger than he was, clad in the battered helmet and chain of a dead soldier. A shot that had punctured his body and continued on to impact with Garrison's forehead. A shot that, in a spray of arterial blood, had killed the child instantly.

"What's your name?" he asked.

"Beth."

"Beth, I'm sorry. I didn't know."

"You took the shot."

"*I didn't know.*"

"You murdered my family that day. All I had."

"Yeah? Well, you just murdered mine."

Garrison's daughter laughed. "You think that makes us even?"

Slowhand studied her eyes. It was clear the girl had only used the Final Faith's resources to help track him down, and it was equally clear that there was going to be no reasoning with her. As much as he'd like otherwise, there was no way Beth was ever going to understand or accept his remorse, and there was no way that, because of what she'd done to Shay, he was just going to lie down and die. The Killing Ground, it seemed, was never going to let him rest.

"No. But it means one of us has to die here."

"Yes, it does."

Both paused as, through the opening in the canvas from which they had emerged, three Eyes of the Lord appeared, hovering.

"So what about your contract?" Slowhand said, indicating them.

"Fark it."

Beth roared and flung herself at him again, sword cleaving the air. Slowhand blocked and his blade locked with hers, and for a second they strained against each other, but then, with a deft flick from her wrist, the archer found himself disarmed, his weapon flipping away to land, tip down and quivering, piercing the canvas some feet away. He leapt for it but Beth was there before him, throwing herself forward to skid on her stomach along the wet surface, snatching it back into her grip as she went. She stood, possessing both swords once more, and, grinning manically, sliced the air in a complex pattern before her. All Slowhand could do as she came again was retreat, sometimes tumbling, sometimes skidding and sometimes somersaulting, until the two of them had completed a full circuit of the roof of the Big Top.

Momentarily, he found himself teetering on its edge, wondering if he would survive a slide down its outer surface, but the cages and calliopes were far below, and without clothing or padding of any sort – unless, he reflected bitterly, you counted his slight beer gut – it was unlikely he'd emerge unbroken. He finally had to admit to himself that, despite his challenge, he'd been bested, and his best chance of survival was to return from whence he'd come.

Slowhand began to scramble back up the sloping canvas, to the cupola, intending to flip himself back inside the Big Top. He was aware with every step that Beth was right behind him, swords slashing, but while he half expected to feel one or the other or both of them slicing into his flesh, he didn't at all expect to hear the tearing of canvas beneath him. He span, saw that the girl had clearly changed tactics, and the multiple rents in the canvas that she had sliced with her swords were lengthening towards him, their pace exacerbated by his own weight.

A gap appeared beneath him and he plummeted. Desperate grabs at the rigging in the hemisphere failed, and there was nothing between him and the floor of the circus ring far below.

Slowhand hit hard and at an awkward angle, having twisted himself to avoid being impaled on rigging beams, the wreckage of his own making, which projected up on his either side. Landing on these might have been more merciful. He roared as his bad arm snapped under him, emitting cracks as loud as gunfire he heard again and again, reverberating in his other bones. His leg, almost rigid as it impacted, thrust its bone up into his pelvis, creating further waves of agony as the pelvis shattered and the sheared bones of his leg punched out through the flesh of his upper thigh. He felt his ribs snap, puncturing his insides so that he felt as if he'd been flooded with hot soup, and as the shockwaves from the impact travelled up his spine, he felt vertebrae mash together until something sharp and pointed rammed up into the base of his skull, filling him with a dizzying disorientation that made his consciousness swoop in and out of a black pit.

He barely heard his own loud, long groan as his body at last settled into a shattered heap.

From somewhere, however, he retained enough awareness to realise that though the fall hadn't killed him, he had far from escaped death. He forced himself to turn over, tears flowing involuntarily with the effort and pain it brought, and through pulsing waves of shadow stared upwards and saw the wavering shape of Beth descending on a guy rope. She would take a few seconds to reach him and he knew he had to get away. All he could do, however, was roll sideways, the pain causing him, despite himself, to mewl like a baby, and find a hiding place under the crumpled sheets of canvas he had earlier released and which had now fallen completely to the ground. It offered little to no protection – would only prolong the inevitable by a matter of moments – but still he was possessed by the urge to swathe himself in the darkness, like a wounded animal returning to the depths of a cave.

His breath was loud beneath it, but in the darkness he shuffled himself further and further in. But then, when he could move no further, he simply lay there, his heart pounding.

An eternity seemed to pass but he could *sense* his opponent drawing closer. Then, as the canvas tightened about him, he knew Beth was standing right over him, trapping him.

What would it be? Slowhand thought. A swift blade thrust through the cloth. Or would she simply wait there as he suffocated beneath a shroud of his own making?

All Slowhand could see in the darkness was Shay's face. For a second it transformed itself into that of Kali Hooper, but then, as quickly as she had appeared, Hooper was gone and Shay was back again, smiling her unjudgemental, caring smile. He chuckled softly. Too late, it seemed, he'd found where he belonged. With *whom* he belonged. Too damned late for both of them.

Slowhand blinked as the canvas was torn from him and Beth loomed over his broken body. Surrounded by the hovering spheres of the Eyes of the Lord, she seemed like the centre of some dark universe. But then something else appeared in the universe, a hazy, blurred shape that trundled into existence behind her, and he was dimly aware of her turning in shock, gasping a name that he surely misheard. He hadn't imagined that Beth would be afraid of anything, but she was afraid of the owner of that name.

"You are disobeying orders child," a voice said. It was a strange voice, breathless and high. "The Faith want him alive."

"I… I'm sorry, sir," Beth responded. "But this man is a murderer."

"No. He's a soldier. A mindless, regimented drone."

No, Slowhand wanted to respond. *That's not right.* But the sudden sound of a larynx being crushed silenced him. It wasn't his own. He tried to focus, work out what was going on, then saw. Beth was a foot above the ground, legs kicking, hands struggling to free herself of an invisible grip.

"You can't do this," she gasped.

"Why is that?"

"Because we're on the same side!"

"I think not."

Beth Garrison stared imploringly at the hovering Eyes of the Lord.

"But they'll see! At the cathedral, they'll see!"

"I don't think so," the shape said. Slowhand saw the outline of a hand being raised and, simultaneously, the Eyes of the Lord detonated, the resultant shrapnel tearing holes into Beth's shocked face. But she didn't suffer. Instead, her head snapped abruptly to the right, neck broken by the same invisible force that had held her aloft, and she dropped to the floor like a stone. Slowhand could feel her body heat already fading beside him.

The shape trundled closer, revealing itself to be some kind of wheelchair. But a wheelchair built by a madman. Looking like a mobile torture device, tubes with needles wove slowly about its surface, occasionally injecting its occupant with coloured fluids, while bladder like things inflated and deflated, hissing and gurgling with air and water that seemed somehow to sustain him. It was an impossible, nightmare thing, but nowhere near as impossible or nightmarish as the shrivelled figure that was the centre of its attentions. Despite the state of its occupant Slowhand recognised him immediately.

He hadn't misheard the name, after all

It was Fitch.

Querilous Fitch.

The psychic manipulator stared down at him, smiled.

Not long after, Slowhand felt what was left of his bones begin to crack, and he began to scream.

CHAPTER SIX

KALI REACHED GRANSK lying on her stomach sandwiched between slices of creev. The thick, blubbery material used to line the hulls of ships for buoyancy did not feel very buoyant, pressing down on her and holding her immobile like the blankets of a tightly made bed. It was damp, hot and stifling between them, and the creev stank so badly she was constantly on the verge of throwing up. It was an urge she'd quelled by snatching swift lungfuls of air through a raised flap of the stuff whenever it had been safe to do so.

She was denied that luxury now. Her last glimpse of the outside world had been of the cart which carried the creev itself becoming sandwiched between Final Faith wagons, part of a convoy which was forming to snake down the cliff road into Gransk. Just before she'd closed the flap, she'd studied the wagons pulling into line behind her, wondering what the large, cigar-shaped, canvas covered objects they carried were. The only thing she did know was that they were not the only wagons out there. Far from it. Whatever kind of ship Jakub Freel was building here, he seemed to be throwing at it every resource the Final Faith had.

Kali felt the cart dip beneath her, beginning its descent into the town, and she pictured the scene outside her hiding place.

Once a small and tranquil fishing community, Gransk had grown into something quite different since the Filth had adopted it as the location for their shipyards. Adding both docks and dry docks for the construction of their coastal clippers and patrol boats, most of the original fisherfolk had over the years been driven away, replaced by a coarser breed of peninsulan labourer who'd stamped their own identity on the town. She'd visited the place on a couple of occasions before now, and while the Filth had found it necessary to garrison a few Swords of Dawn to ensure that the work they commissioned was actually carried out, they had for the most part left the inhabitants to run the town for themselves. Now, though, it seemed to be a different story. From the number of delays, shouts and barked orders Kali heard from beyond the slices of creev, security had been upped considerably. It didn't take much to figure out by whom, or why.

The cart came to a stop and Kali was aware of the presence of soldiers gathering about it. She felt a slight lurch as the cart's driver climbed down, presumably in response to a signal from one of them.

"Your goods?" a deep but muffled voice enquired.

"Creev, sir," the driver responded. Kali was relieved to hear his voice remained calm. He was aware of her presence but there was not a hint of betrayal in his weary tones.

"Creev? That's all?"

"Yes, sir."

There was the sharp scrape of a weapon being withdrawn from a scabbard, and then another, and Kali sucked in breath, knowing what was coming. What kind of lunatic they imagined would secrete themselves in this pile of shite she couldn't imagine, but the guards had clearly been ordered to be thorough.

She froze as swords thrust into the slices of creev. The blubbery substance deflated and released puffs of noxious gas. She was grateful that the odour was so rank that they were reluctant to make the inspection *too* thorough. Nonetheless, one or two of the thrusts came too close for comfort and Kali quietly contorted herself each time, like a magician's assistant inside a sword trap.

"You're clear. Papers?"

A shuffling, and a cough.

"These seem to be in order. Pondeen's Maritime is on the western harbourside. Proceed directly there, unload your shipment and then turn your cart around."

"Around?" the driver said. "But I intended to stay at the tavern. It's been a long haul."

"Turn it *around*, old man. Trust me, you don't want to be in town tonight."

Kali frowned, wondering why. The old man questioned the soldiers no further, however, and the cart sank once more as he resumed his position. A clicking of his mouth spurred the horses on.

Kali remained still, listening to more muffled voices and sounds, not of soldiers this time but the activity of Gransk. The cries of men at work, the shifting of cargo, the screeching of razorgulls as they circled overhead hoping for pickings from the goods being loaded. She did not listen without reason – if she were to slip from her hiding place unnoticed, she'd have to time her move carefully. After a few more minutes of the cart negotiating the narrow streets of the town, the sounds became more mooted and Kali knew that the cart's driver had steered her to a place of relative inactivity, as requested. Listening again to be certain no one was around, she slithered from between the slices of creev, placed a bag of full gold in his hand, and then vanished into a side alley, from where she intended to get her bearings.

The other end of the alley opened onto a main thoroughfare. Kali took her squallcoat from her backpack and slipped it on. A sailor's cap she had procured elsewhere she jammed on her head, the peak lowered to obscure her features. Then she took a breath and, with hands in her pockets and head down, slipped from the alley and joined the throng of people heading towards the dockside.

The port came alive around her, voices amplified among the packed and overhanging buildings of the streets.

"Ragfish and jumpo, guv'nor? Two tenths a bag."

"Ropes, hawsings, nets!"

"Hey, sailor, fancy yer chances with Mair behind the crates, do yer? Goworn, you'll never get the chance out there now, will yer?"

"Hand over yer purse, lad or... ow! Fark! Pits o' Kerberos, what d'ya do *that* for?"

Kali smiled and lowered her elbow as the grabcoin raced off into the crowd nursing a bloody nose. She ignored all further solicitations, weaving slowly through the crowd. It had been her intention to spend some time listening to gossip, trying to glean information, but where she'd expected the locals to be quite forthcoming considering the amount of work Freel had brought to town, there were surprisingly few mentions of the ship, and these only in hushed tones. Instead, she began to work her way directly to the dockside where she had at least gleaned Freel's ship was berthed.

And then stopped.

The ship had come into view far before she expected it to, a consequence of its size. She could see little detail of it from where she stood but that made it none the less awesome. Made of materials that were almost entirely black, including its sails, it appeared in view like some gigantic wall, towering over the dockside, blotting out the horizon completely, casting a shadow over the lower half of the town. It left no doubt in her mind that this was the place where she would find all the answers she needed.

"Don't you go near that ship, young lad," a voice said suddenly from beside her. "Arsk me, she's cursed."

Kali turned to see a grizzled old seadog. "Cursed?"

"Aye, cursed. I've seen men carried out o' the bowels o' that thing with their flesh rottin' off 'em, as if they got the worst case o' the hic there ever was. An' before I did I heard their screams from inside its hull."

"Screams?"

"Agonised screams. As if their souls had been touched by the devils themselves. An' that ain't all…"

"It isn't?"

"Oh, no. I swear to ye, the very instant they rolled that monster outta dry dock an' into the waters, the ocean *boiled*. Stay away from 'er, I tell ya. Stay away!"

Boiled, eh? Kali thought. That was certainly enough to get a girl's attention.

She nodded, flipped the seadog a coin, and began to move with renewed determination towards her destination. But she had not got far before her progress was rudely interrupted.

Her gaze fixed on the looming wall of the ship, she did not notice the sudden kerfuffle in the crowd about her, and the first thing she knew of its cause – something moving at speed out of a side alley – was when that same something barrelled into her so hard she was winded and knocked off her feet. As she thudded unceremoniously onto her backside, Kali cursed her assailant for not even having the good grace to apologise for the collision. Then she realised there was good reason for the omission.

Three Eyes of the Lord darted out of the alley, spinning about while they re-orientated, and then tore through the air after the figure, which was now half way across the street.

Kali double-taked on the spheres and the fleeing figure. The first thing she noticed was the Eyes of the Lord's prey wasn't so much running as rolling along, the reason for this being that he appeared to have no legs. Instead, he was perched on a small, wheeled platform which he was thrusting along with sweeps of thick and powerfully muscled arms. Kali wondered if he was perhaps a veteran of the Vos-Pontaine war and, like so many, had lost his limbs in one of its horrifying battles. He didn't look like one, though, when, for a fleeting second, she caught a glimpse of a solid, gnarled face almost wholly obscured by a thick beard which had, of all things, a number of small, tin bells woven into it.

Her first instinct was to spring upward and help him, but before she could she realised she had problems of her own. Unnoticed until now, her tumble had dislodged her cap from her head and, with it lying a few feet away, her true appearance was revealed to all.

One of the three spheres stopped dead in its pursuit of its prey, backtracked a few feet, and then darted towards her until it hovered directly in front of her face, staring her, as it were, in the eyes. Kali realised she had only a few seconds before the information it was gathering was processed by the Overseers back at Scholten Cathedral, and then she would have been tracked by the Faith. She leapt up and rid herself of the problem with the only thing that came to hand. Plucking a large fish from where it lay, dull-eyed, on an adjacent stall, Kali held it tightly by the tail, swung it round in an arc and batted the Eye of the Lord hard enough to send it careering through the air. As bits of fish splattered the crowd, the sphere ricocheted off one wall and then another and yet a third before it plummeted, smoking and sparking, through the cloth awning of a stall further up the street, bringing the whole lot down around it.

"Fore!" Kali shouted.

Her unique solution to the problem couldn't help but attract the attention of the other two spheres, and also, for a second, the figure on the wheeled platform, who paused and regarded her curiously. There was no time for introductions, however, as one of the two remaining spheres veered off towards Kali while its partner resumed its pursuit of its original prey.

Kali cursed – an ancient Drakengrattian powerword that made even the hardened inhabitants of Gransk gasp and step back in shock – reflecting how her plan to clandestinely go about her business had so rapidly turned to shit.

The Eye of the Lord now in hot pursuit, Kali fled into a side alley running parallel to that taken by the bearded stranger, and as the alley jinked to the right, his must have jinked to the left, because the pair found themselves meeting again, though heading swiftly in opposite directions. A few seconds later, when Kali jinked once more, they were again heading directly towards each other. They nodded as they passed. By the time they encountered each other for a third time, Kali had had enough, but thankfully another plan had popped into mind.

While she considered it a little unnecessary to shout "duck!" to her fellow escapee, she did so anyway, and then ran right at him, seemingly playing chicken. At the very last instant before their two forms collided, she flung herself to the side, bouncing off the alley wall with an *oof!* before continuing her flight. As she'd hoped, the pursuing Eyes of the Lord were not so nimble in their reactions and the two spheres impacted with each other directly above the bearded stranger's platform, knocking each other askew, taking a few seconds to regain their equilibrium. It was enough time for both parties to lose them in the backstreet maze. The last thing Kali saw of the maybe veteran was his platform throwing up dust as it disappeared into yet another alley, and then she, too, veered left, right, right, left and left again in what she hoped was a dizzying enough series of manoeuvres to ride herself of her sphere for good.

Breathless now, Kali turned at last into a long, featureless alley – and stopped dead in her tracks.

One of the Eyes of the Lord hovered at the other end, blocking her escape route. Kali turned and found the second hovering where she had come in. She span on the spot, studying the alley for an alternative means of escape but seeing none, and even if she took to the rooftops – a favourite ploy guaranteed to confound any normal pursuer – it would do little to help her against the omnipresent spheres.

Both Eyes of the Lord began to move towards her, closing the gap between them, but just as they drew near a staggering, singing figure suddenly emerged from a plain and hard to spot doorway just a few feet away. Though she would clearly be observed going in, it would have to do for now, and Kali grabbed at the door before it closed, spinning herself inside.

Fug and the smell of her favourite thing greeted her, because on the other side of the door was a bar. The fact that it had been unsigned hinted that it was likely frequented only by those who knew it was there, clearly the kind of back street watering hole visited by sailors who traded in exotic and illicit goods. Consequently, the face of every customer within snapped towards Kali with expressions ranging from curiosity to startled guilt to snarling, outright belligerence, and more than one hand dropped to a blade sheath concealed under clothing. Even a game of arrows taking place in the far corner stopped – literally, with the tiny projectile frozen in mid air – the ship's first mage whose throw it had been pausing time to weigh up the unexpected arrival.

Kali had no time to weigh up anything, knowing the spheres were only one or two seconds behind her, and she darted for a booth in the most shadowed area of the bar, vanishing into the dark. This action alone seemed to mollify the regulars – if the girl was hiding, and in this town she could only be hiding from the law, then she was all right by them – and they turned back to their business.

"This booth is occupied," a voice growled in the darkness beside her. "Fark off."

Kali jumped. The ill-mannered request had come from right next to her. But, dark as it was, the booth was clearly empty. Kali shook her head. Must have been a trick of the acoustics in the place.

Something prodded her sharply in her ribs, near her breast, prompting an indignant "Ow!"

"Go on, ar said. Fark off."

"What the hells?"

Another prod.

"Are ya deaf, smoothskin? Or is yer just plain stupid?"

"Now wait one pitsing min – " Kali began. She turned with the intention of snapping off whatever it was doing the prodding but at that moment the door to the bar was booted wide open and sunlight flooded in. The regulars, who were used to the door never being open for longer than it took someone to duck quickly and furtively inside, squinted and shielded their eyes against the brightness.

Silhouetted shapes appeared in the light. Two spherical shapes that floated slowly inside, followed by two armoured human shapes, Swords by the look of them. The Eyes of the Lord had brought reinforcements.

"Aw, me mother's bollocks, now ya've gone and done it," the voice next to Kali cursed. "Come on, then, smoothskin, ya'd better get under here."

Kali felt something thrown over her, the weight and texture of one of Merrit Moon's horse blankets. She became immediately aware of two things: that the blanket stank worse than possibly anything else she'd smelled in her life, and that its stink originated with the hunched figure she was sharing it with. He was so bad he seemed to have to transfer his excess stink through some form of osmosis. What Kali didn't expect, therefore, was his next comment.

"Great gods, smoothskin, ya stink like a mool's arse after a bad case o' the trots."

"*I* stink?" Kali gasped. But then realised the creev had likely left her with a body odour problem of her own.

"Keep ya bloody voice down, or ya might bring more attention than me cloak can stand."

"Cloak?" Kali blurted. "You plan to hide from the patrol under a pitsing *cloak*?"

"It fooled you, didn't it?"

"It was dark, then!"

"Trust me, smoothskin."

"Oh, sure. Better idea. I'll go stand in that corner with a lampshade on my head!"

The figure sighed. "For a small 'un ya've got quite the gob on ya. Do me a favour and shut it for a second, eh?"

"*You* are asking for –" Kali began, but stopped as the spheres and Swords, so far having concentrated their activity on the patrons near the bar, turned their attention to the booths. Kali froze as the Eyes of the Lord floated before her, and could almost feel the Overseers in Scholten peering at her intently.

"You, Allantian," one of the Swords barked. "We're looking for two fugitives – a girl and a short, thick-set man." He hesitated. "On a trolley."

Allantian? Kali thought. Not only did she – and, as far as she could tell, the Great Pongo – not look remotely Allantian, but the numbers were wrong. The Sword also paid no heed to the fact that the two of them were hiding under a blanket, which if she'd been him she might have found just a tad suspicious. She supposed you got what you paid for.

"Seen no one," the figure next to her said. "Just enjoyin' a drink."

The soldier's eyes narrowed, as if suspecting something but unable to put a finger on what.

"Your trade?" he demanded. "What business have you in Gransk?"

"I grease knobs. Luggleknobs."

"What?"

"They assign ya to a docks an' ya don't know what luggleknobs are?"

"Well, no…"

"Then ar suggest ya watch your footing around town, greenhorn. Now why don't ya leave an old lag to his drink, eh?"

The soldier hesitated, but the bluff – if that's what it was – seemed to work, and he turned away from them with a grunt.

Kali gave it a moment before she spoke.

"What are luggleknobs?"

"Haven't a clue."

"Thought so. What just happened? Why did he think *we* were an Allantian?"

"Ah, that. Cloak o' Many Contours. Handy bit o' kit."

Kali felt a stirring of excitement, despite the stench. "This is an artefact?"

"Artefact?" the stranger repeated. "No, just me old cloak."

"And what does this cloak do?"

"Fools the eyes, mainly. You thought this booth was empty when you sat here, right?"

"Right. But the Sword clearly didn't."

"That's why it's called a cloak o' *many* contours. It adapts to what it's covering. You were a bit too bulky ta simply hide."

"*Bulky?*"

"Don't get your knickers in a twist, smoothskin. Yer can't help yer size."

"Are you talking about glamour?"

"Aye. Portable glamour."

"Then it *is* an artefact!"

"I told yer –"

"It's just your cloak," Kali finished. She sighed, getting nowhere. She looked at the bar, saw the Swords and the spheres were leaving, and then pulled the cloak off their heads, sucking in fresh air. She, too, made to leave.

"An' where is it yer think you're goin'?"

"They've gone so I'm going. I wish I could say it's been a pleasure."

A hand clamped about her forearm, solid as iron, and Kali turned to look at her companion for the first time. Wreathed once more in shadow, his face was gnarled and grizzled, hairy and a little pug-like, and comprehensively covered in scars. Even the scars had scars. None of these features were how Kali recognised him. It was the bells in the beard that were the giveaway.

"*You*."

"Aye, me."

"Okay, that's it. I'm definitely off."

"Ar wouldn't. The Swords'll be on full alert after our little runaround. Probably take 'em til nightfall to calm down. Whatever business ya have in Gransk'll have to wait."

Kali slumped back in her seat, supposing he was right.

"Okay," she acceded. "So what do you suggest we do for the next few hours?"

A guffaw. "What else do ya do in a bar, smoothskin? We DRINK!"

He shouted to the bartender and, a second later, two pitchers of frothing ale were slammed down on the table. They were followed in rapid succession by two more. And two more. And two more. Kali matched her companion drink for drink, wetting her whistle with the local brew – clanger – then suggesting they moved on to something stronger. She ordered the guest beer – wobblehead – and not pitchers this time but the full barrel. The bartender eyed her suspiciously as he rolled it over, but Kali simply wiped her mouth, burped and tossed him a pouch of full bronze. The weight of it erased all worries from his face.

Kali drank and thought about her companion's odd appearance, the artefact that was 'just' an old cloak, the way he had of speaking. "You're not from around here, are you?"

"Depends on what ya mean by 'here'. I haven't fallen from that thing that's appeared in the sky, if that's what yer suggestin'."

"I'm not. I've a lot of theories about what's up there but one of them isn't that it's filled with rude little men."

"Bugger off."

Kali thought carefully about what she said next, but was pretty certain of her suspicions before she spoke. "What happened to your legs?"

"That's somethin' of a personal question, don't ya think? Why don't you tell me why yer tits are so small?"

"Hey! I know they're small, all right? So, come on, answer the question – were they blown off? Amputated? Eaten by a ravenous shnarl? Or did they just rot away holding all that beer?"

"Mind yer own business."

Without warning, Kali pulled away the remainder of the cloak covering her companion. As she'd suspected, the trolley on which he'd ridden had been discarded under the table and he was sitting there with a pair of legs that were fully formed – small, but fully formed.

Her companion sighed and struck a match, lighting a huge pipe he had produced from a pocket. He blew smoke from his nose. Three distinct plumes of smoke at the same time.

Kali nodded. There was only one kind of nose that could do that, and the last one like it she'd seen had been on a desiccated and mummified face sealed inside the Old Race machine she had purloined to reach the Crucible, the machine she'd named 'the mole'.

Three nostrils.

"Fark me," Kali said. "You're a dwarf."

The figure snapped his gaze further towards her, so much so that the tin bells woven into his beard jangled. Then he took a deep, thoughtful draught of his ale and a pull on his pipe, inhaling hard before replying.

"Ya seem to be quite unphased about that fact. Most people might find it surprising that they were sitting having a beer with one o' the Old Races. Particularly as most of 'em think we're a myth."

"I'm not most people. I've met some of your kind before. Sort of."

"Pah! Bollocks."

"It's true. Okay, one of them had only a bit of dwarf blood running through his veins and the other, well, he was half dwarf, half elf – a dwelf called Tharnak."

The dwarf's eyes widened and without so much as a by-your-leave he planted both his palms on Kali's chest.

"Hey! What the hells do you think you're doing?!"

"Just checkin' summat," the dwarf said, apparently satisfied.

"Yeah, there are two, all right!" Kali snapped. "Pits of farking Kerberos, are you some kind of pervert?"

"What do you know about the dwelf?" the dwarf asked, ignoring her protest.

Kali, despite her indignation, was intrigued.

"Long story. The question is, what do *you* know?"

The dwarf stroked his beard, regarding her with great care.

"You haven't told me. What brings you to Gransk, smoothskin?"

"I intend to take passage on the Black Ship."

"Is that so? Well, now, that might present a bit of a problem."

"How so?"

"Because I intend to sink it."

"What the hells are you talking about?"

The dwarf began to chuckle heavily into his beer, as if she had asked the question of all questions. "That, smoothskin, is also a long story. A long, long, long story. Longer than you can imagine. And it begins where that ship is goin'."

"You're talking about Trass Kathra."

"That I be."

Kali's eyes narrowed. "Is that where you're from?"

The dwarf didn't answer for a second. And when he did, it wasn't an answer at all.

"Jerragrim Brundle," he said, sticking out his hand.

"Kali Hooper."

"Well, now, Miss Hooper. You and I have a lot to talk about."

"We do?"

"Not least that I think I've been expecting you."

"What?"

"As I said, it's a long, long story. But here is not the place for it's tellin' –"

"Where, then?"

Brundle studied her. "That rather depends on what happens later."

She got little more out of him, there and then, other than small talk over their continuing drinks. So many continuing drinks that even she began to feel their effects. But no more so than Brundle. After a few hours she was rocked back in her seat as the dwarf slammed his tankard into hers, sending ale flying everywhere.

"Ya know, for a smoothskin, you can down yer drink as well as a dwarf!"

Kali flushed. Despite the circumstances, she suddenly felt immensely proud, as if holding her own with one of the Old Races was vindication of everything she had tried to discover over the years. Maybe, she thought, that all she'd ever wanted – all she'd ever *really* wanted – was to get shit-faced with the people she admired the most.

"Yer not so bad yerself!" she responded, slamming her tankard into his.

Ale foaming and dripping off their heads, she turned to one of the bar's tiny windows.

"It's dark. Time to go?"

"Time to go," Brundle agreed.

As Kali and Brundle exited the tavern, a figure sitting hunched at the bar turned slightly to watch them go, the light from the doorway illuminating a hard face framed with greasy black hair, and a strange 'x' shaped scar on his upper left cheek. He didn't know who the shortarse was or why he was here – didn't, in fact, even recall him coming in – but the presence of Kali Hooper came as no surprise at all. He expected he'd be seeing her again quite soon.

First, of course, he, too, had to get aboard the boat. The security he'd checked out earlier that day was comprehensive, and while he could have got aboard by taking down a couple of guards where they stood, they would eventually be missed, and that would spoil everything. No, if he wanted to get aboard he'd have them *take* him aboard, and for that the fact that even some veteran sailors in town refused to sail on the vessel worked in his favour. It was already short of crewmembers and he had significantly increased the odds that they would need to find more by arranging a little accident by the dockside some hours before. The cargo crates that had inexplicably sheared from their crane had crushed at least six of the pre-assigned crew and injured a good few more. Enough for Freel to have to resort to emergency measures to find replacements.

Gransk was not that big a port and so it was only a matter of time.

The stranger stared into his drink and waited for the crack on the head that signalled the arrival of the press-gang.

CHAPTER SEVEN

THE FAITH HAD indeed stepped down from alert as Kali and Brundle emerged into the darkness, and though patrols were still present in the streets, their regular circuits of the shadowy alleyways were easy to predict and avoid. The pair of them made their way down to the waterfront, but from the shouts and hammering and clanging of tools it was clear before they got there that the coming of night had not quietened their destination as it had the rest of Gransk.

The dockside remained a hubbub of activity, all of it centered around the Black Ship Kali had until now seen only from a distance. She and the dwarf hid behind crates – Kali the only one needing to duck to do so – and watched as Faith came and went on the gangplank, labourers carried supplies aboard, and workmen dangled on ropes at various points along the hull, securing rivets and otherwise effecting preparations for the ship's seaworthiness. One of the strange, cigar shaped objects she had seen in the convoy was being loaded by crane, joining seven others which had already been secured to the deck near the ship's stern.

All in all, It looked to Kali as if the ship was going to sail that very night.

And what a ship. Kali couldn't take her eyes off it. As huge as it had seemed from the street, it seemed huger still here. Constructed of rune-inscribed metal plating rather than timber, its prow curved threateningly downwards like some great insectoid proboscis, and sweeping back from it, overshadowing its decks, were a series of static sails made not of cloth but metal again. The shape of half shells, eight of them, they appeared to be currently at rest, receding one atop the other, as squat almost as the ship itself, like some armoured carapace. The effect was so streamlined and organic, the vessel looked less ship than predatorial beast.

What struck Kali more than anything was that it also had two hulls. Each resting in the water some twenty yards apart, the vessel straddled them as a bridge might straddle pontoons in a river, and this made the ship seem even more solid, seemingly unstoppable in all of her dimensions.

Kali whistled softly.

"Never seen a cat before, eh?" Brundle said.

"Cat?"

"Catamaran. Two hulls make the vessel much more stable in the water. Standard design for a dwarven warship."

"This is a *dwarven* warship?"

"Based on one, anyway. Though ya can tell not built with *passion*."

"Why in hells would they build a dwarven warship?"

"Seein' as there's no one to go to war with anymore, survival'd be my guess. They have to get through the Stormwall first, don't forget. And then there's uppards o' two months' sailin' ahead o' them, in some o' the wildest seas there is. Then there's the things that live out there. Chadassa Raiders, untershraks, the Great Weed. And, o' course, there's the weather – the sunderstorms can rip an ill-clad ship apart wi' one strike."

"I'm beginning to get the picture," Kali said.

"Oh, that's not all, smoothskin," Brundle cautioned. "'Cos if they survive that lot, they're gonna need somethin' as immovable as me tenth wife's arse when they face the swirlies..."

"Swirlies?"

"The swirlpools, smoothskin," Brundle said, as if it were obvious.

"What are swirlpools?"

"They're the barrier between the island an' the rest o' the world." Brundle tilted his head upwards, at the looming shape of the Hel'ss. "A little legacy of our friend up there. Quite the *lasting* legacy, I might add."

"Hold on again. There's a relationship between the Hel'ss and Trass Kathra?"

Brundle laughed. "I wouldn't call it a relationship as such. Unless o' course yer thinkin' o' me and me thirteenth wife, may the bulbous bitch rot in Zlathoon. Nah, smoothskin, last time around that thing up there did its best to obliterate the island, an' what it left behind makes what's left o' the Stormwall look like a squirt o' piss from a babby's knob."

Kali shook her head, struggling with the surfeit of information. "Wait a minute? Last time around? Are you trying to tell me that the Hel'ss has been here *before*? And what do you mean – what's *left* of the Stormwall?

"Like I said, it's a long –"

"Enough! Who the hells are you, Brundle? Where do you come from?"

The dwarf shot her a glance, raised an eyebrow. "Didn't ah tell ya, smoothskin? Trass Kathra's me home. I'm what yer might call its caretaker."

"What?" Kali said. "*What*?"

But her befuddlement fell on deaf ears. Brundle was already moving, taking advantage of a quiet moment on that part of the dock to shift position. With a growl of exasperation, Kali followed him to another hiding place nearer to the ship, behind a stack of barrels.

"Will you *please* tell me what's going on?"

"Right now ah think we'd be better concentrating on what's going on with the ship." The dwarf pointed. "Take a look."

Kali turned her gaze in the direction Brundle indicated. There was fresh activity on the gangplank – or for the moment, to be more accurate, before it. A number of wagons were arriving on the dock, and from the first of them Jakub Freel alighted, followed by a number of mercenaries. Kali was hardly surprised to see Freel here, but what did surprise her was what was forcefully disembarked from the wagons that lined up behind his.

Civilian prisoners. Hundreds of them.

"Well, now," Brundle muttered. "This is interestin'."

Kali ignored him and looked on as Freel and his men took up position at the head of the gangplank, inspecting the prisoners as they were ushered aboard the ship. Led by them in wrist and ankle chains, like slaves, Kali saw men, women and children who, by their varying modes of dress, seemed to have been taken from all across the peninsula. She knew instantly that she was looking at the 'vanished', those who had spoken out against the Faith and been imprisoned for their beliefs, and she gasped as she began to recognise some familiar faces amongst them. *Too many* familiar faces.

There were some of Jengo Pim's men – among them, Pim himself – and there... oh, gods. Red. Hetty. Pete Two-Ties and others from the Flagons. There, too, were people who had become friends after helping her with supplies and information in the last year: Martha DeZantez, Gabriella's mother; Abra, and Poul Sonpear, the mage from the Three Towers, his powers clearly constrained by what appeared to be a scrambling collar about his neck.

And there...

Dolorosa.

Dolorosa but not Aldrededor.

Alone.

The woman was injured – badly. Being carried aboard the ship on a stretcher. But despite her condition, still scowling. Spitting in the faces of the Faith gathered around her. Had she been able to wield a knife, she would have been slitting their throats.

Good girl, Kali thought. Yet still cringed as the woman was taken below decks with those who had preceded her.

Kali wasn't having this. She made to move from behind the barrels but Brundle's iron grip held her back.

"Easy, easy," he said.

"Those people are *friends* of mine. Family.".

"All the more reason we get aboard that tub secretly," Brundle countered. "You'll not be able to help with one o' the Sword's namesakes stickin' in yer belly, now, will ye?"

"Oh, so now *we're* going aboard, are we? I thought you were going to sink her?"

"Ah may still have to. But for the time bein', things have changed."

"You're right, there," Kali responded angrily. She tried to struggle from his grip but Brundle reasserted his strength, pulling her back.

"Listen to me, smoothskin," he growled, more serious than she had ever seen him. "It is imperative that you stay alive. *Imperative*, do you understand me?"

Kali swallowed, shocked by the outburst. "Why?"

Brundle smiled. "Ah think yer know that, lass. Ah think you know that."

Kali pulled her arm away, and Brundle let her, knowing she was going nowhere. At least for the moment. Because then events took an unexpected turn.

Prisoners continuing to be ushered aboard, Jakub Freel took up position at the head of the gangplank and shouted across the harbour.

"Miss Hooper, I know you are out there And I would suggest you surrender yourself to me now!"

Dammit, Kali thought. The Eyes of the Lord must have got a good enough look at her after all. Or maybe Freel just *expected* her to be there – let's face it, if she were in his shoes, she would. The question was, what was he up to? What happened if she didn't surrender herself?

"Kali," Freel went on. "We know each other well enough for me to call you Kali, don't we? As you can see I am amassing a good number of your friends aboard this ship. A sufficient number that I am able to spare a few. Therefore if you do not reveal yourself within one hour, I shall kill one of them. If you do not reveal yourself thereafter, I shall kill another every ten minutes. Do I make myself clear?"

As crystal, you bastard, Kali thought. In fact the message was so clear that Freel didn't dwell on it. His ultimatum delivered, he stepped down once more, going about his business as if a threat to commit mass murder was nothing to him. Nothing at all.

Beside Kali, Brundle blew out a breath.

"Ah don't think ah like this man," he said.

721

"I thought he was a friend, once," Kali replied. She made to rise again and Brundle once more held her down.

"I thought we'd been through this?" he said.

"What choice do I have?"

Freel had her in a stalemate and the only way to break it was to take the initiative. But if she was going to give herself to Freel, she was going to do it her way. The *only* way she could.

And as the ship showed every sign of sailing soon, the time to act was now.

"You'll get yourself killed," Brundle warned.

Kali winked. "That's never stopped me before. You sticking around?"

"Oh, aye, I'll be sticking around," Brundle replied. He seemed to find his answer amusing somehow.

Kali sighed. "And let me guess – you'll tell me about it some other time?"

"That's about the long and the short of it, smoothskin."

Kali narrowed her eyes. "Was that a joke?"

"No," Brundle said warily. "Why?"

"Well, you know..." Kali said. She flattened her palm and moved it up and down, comparing their heights. But all she received in response was a blank expression. "Oh, never mind."

Kali continued on, darting from crate to crate along the dockside, until she reached a spot behind where the prisoners' wagons had arrived. Most of them had been embarked now and, as she'd hoped, those remaining were being manhandled by only a couple of Faith, confident their charges in chains would present them with little resistance. They were also just out of sight of the main part of the dockside, which served her purposes perfectly.

Kali waited while one of the two was occupied dragging a particularly recalcitrant prisoner from the wagon's rear and then stepped up behind the other and tapped him on the shoulder. Clamping one hand over his mouth, she swiftly delivered four nerve-numbing blows to spectacles, testicles, wallet and watch, – and then caught his boggle-eyed, paralysed form as it fell, dragging it out of sight. There she delivered a knockout punch to the man's face, just because she felt like it, and no more than a couple of seconds later, dressed in the Faith robes she stripped from her victim, stood beside his brother, who had only now managed to extract his charge.

Kali apologised mentally and jabbed the prisoner in his side, forcing him into line with his fellows. Their passage to the ship coincided with that of more Faith who, between them, dragged the semi-conscious forms of men who appeared to have been press-ganged, and, for the sake of camaraderie, she jabbed one of them in the side, too, quite harshly. The man, with a mane of long, black hair and a strange, 'x' shaped scar on his left cheekbone, bucked and, clearly not as out of it as he seemed to be, raised his head and glowered at her. The glower turned into an unfathomable expression as he caught sight of her face under her hood.

Kali frowned, though had no time to ponder the look as she and her companion, the last of the prisoners shuffling in their midst, reached the gangplank. A few yards above Jakub Freel stood momentarily studying each prisoner and, though this was the first time Kali had managed to get this close to him since the Sardenne – longed to find out what had *happened* to him – she knew she dared do nothing. If what she had planned was going to work convincingly, she had to walk a fine line between success and failure.

She kept her head low as she and the prisoners passed beneath Freel's gaze but, despite herself, couldn't help but pause as they almost touched. Though she and Freel hadn't known each other long, the experiences they'd shared had been intense, and such experiences tended to stamp the aura of a person indelibly in one's mind. And the thing was, the aura felt wrong. Everything about the man beside her rang alarm bells – his stance, his attitude, even his body odour, and Kali felt a shiver run through her, as if someone had walked over her grave.

Or as if someone had crawled out of a grave.

Kali shook herself, and began to push the prisoners forward once more. But it took all the willpower she had not to freeze when a voice behind her spoke two words.

"Kali Hooper."

Though Freel had apparently recognised her, there was still a chance he'd think himself mistaken – that her stance, attitude or perfume had triggered some erroneous mental connection. What she had to do was continue bluffing her way through by giving no sign of recognition at all.

It was a reasonable plan, spoiled only by the fact that two Swords of Dawn immediately blocked her path. As they did, she felt Freel move up close behind her, and then her hood was pulled quickly back.

Okay, Kali thought. It was a fair cop.

She turned. A face she had not seen in a year filled her vision, staring down at her. The sight was strangely disconcerting. The same rugged, unshaven features were there, the same intelligent, piercing and curious eyes, even the slight smile which, though rarely seen, had betrayed the humanity of the man she thought she had come to know. This *was* Prince Jakub Tremayne Freel of the Allantian Royal Family. And yet. And yet his humanity seemed missing, somehow, as if some unknown events since she had last seen him had erased that aspect of him. Now, despite the smile, a cold cruelty seemed to seep from every pore.

"Jakub Freel," Kali said.

The strange, cold smile curled slightly at one side, and Freel bent almost melodramatically to whisper in Kali's ear. He was making it clear that this was just between the two of them.

"Sorry. No."

Kali's heart missed a beat. Her gaze snapped back to Freel's eyes and what she saw there made all of her confusion of the last year make sense. Though she had struggled to reconcile the actions of the man she had come to know in the Sardenne with those of the man who had returned with Makennon to Scholten Cathedral, changing the nature of the Church completely, it had simply never occurred to her that the two men were not necessarily one and the same. And if this wasn't Freel she was confronting, there was only one other man – though, of course, man was not the word – who had the power to take his place. Someone who had considerable experience in the exchanging of souls...

"Redigor," Kali said. "You farking piece of –"

Freel motioned to the Swords who'd blocked Kali's path and they each grabbed her by an arm, holding her firmly. Then Freel cocked his head to one side, his smile broadening, and when he spoke once more, it was to all.

"I have no idea what you're talking about."

"Listen to me!" Kali struggled in the grip of her captors. "This man is not who he seems to be!"

There was a murmuring from the ranks.

"This woman," Freel countered, "is Kali Hooper, the outlaw."

The murmuring intensified. Kali would have been flattered were this not all so *wrong*.

"I'm no outlaw!" Kali shouted, piecing together why it was that the Faith had such a price on her head. "This man, this *imposter*, made me so – the same as he has done with all these prisoners – so that I, they, couldn't interfere with his plans!"

"My *plans*?" Freel roared. He regarded the massed ranks and then pointed up at the evening sky, where the strangely nebulous shape of the Hel'ss loomed on the opposite side of the horizon from Kerberos. "All of the Faithful here know my plans, and they are to do all we can to welcome the Herald of the Lord of All. The Herald of our Ascension!"

"The Hel'ss is no herald!" Kali argued. "And the man standing before you knows this! He knows because he is the Pale Lord. Your First Enemy!"

Kali's revelation didn't quite have the effect she desired. While some townspeople did draw in a breath and make the sign of the crossed circle of the Faith, the ranks of Swords and brethren began, disturbingly, to laugh.

"The Pale Lord is dead!" one shouted. "The Anointed Lord did smite him."

"He wasn't smited... smoted... pits, he wasn't smitten!" Kali protested, cursing herself for her lack of religious vocabulary. "He's here! Before you! Now!"

"No! His plans crumbled before the might of the Final Faith!"

"Heretic!"

"Outlaw!"

"I was there!" Kali shouted. "I was there, saw what happened. I understand your believing what you do but he still lives and –" Kali indicated the ship " – this, *this* is his plan..."

The ranks roared. Jakub Freel raised his hands to quieten them.

"If this outlaw is correct," he told them, "then perhaps she can explain this plan." He turned to Kali questioningly, the smile still playing on his face.

Kali looked as though she was about to speak, but growled in frustration. "You know I can't do that. I don't know what the fark you're up to."

Redigor leaned in. Another little confidence. "Maybe it's something to do with the fact that as you denied me the return of my race, I intend to deny you yours."

"Bullshit. There's something more to it than that. With you, there always is."

"Do you hear?" Freel shouted to his people. "She doesn't know!"

"But I'll find out," Kali added with determination. "I promise you that."

Freel sighed and ordered all men, but those who held her, back to their duties. It was clear that Kali had lost any advantage, even if she had one to begin with. Their attention away from the pair, Freel leaned into her once more.

"I doubt it," he said. "Only one of us can come back from the dead."

Freel withdrew a glinting dagger from his tunic and raised it. Kali's eyes widened and in that moment she knew that if there were any vestige of Jakub Freel left inside his own form, Redigor must have snuffed it like a candle flame.

"You'll regret doing this to my friend, elf," she said.

"No," Freel answered. "But you will regret coming here."

Kali stiffened as he ordered his men to hold her more firmly, and then grasped the back of her neck with one hand. She gasped in shock and pain as, slowly and deliberately, he carved two intersecting lines into the skin of her forehead, following these with a carefully drawn circle, enclosing them. Kali didn't need to see the pattern being cut into her flesh to know that she had just been branded with the mark of the Final Faith.

Blood began to seep into her eyes.

"The best place on the human body to guarantee a healthy blood flow," Freel said. "And one of the longest to heal. Even with your powers of recuperation these cuts will take time to recover... more than enough time for our purposes."

Kali shook her head and blinked to try to rid her vision of blood, but it was flowing too freely and she stared at Freel through a veil of red.

"Lash her to the figurehead," Freel ordered. "Once we pass beyond the Stormwall, the untershraks can have her..."

Kali struggled in the Swords' grips as they attempted to turn her away from the gangplank, but their gauntlets were clasped tightly about her, impossible to shift. This coupled with the fact that she was all but blinded made it difficult to gain any advantage against them and she knew it was only a matter of moments before her plan – of which being lashed to the figurehead was not part – was ruined. The one thing she couldn't have anticipated was that it wasn't Freel she'd be dealing with but Redigor, and his method of despatching people was far too final for her liking.

Thankfully, though, a sudden commotion from the gangplank provided her with just the distraction she needed.

At first, Kali wasn't sure what was going on, but soon saw that one of the Faith's press-ganged sailors had fully regained consciousness and wasn't at all keen on what was happening or where he was being led. Kali saw it was the same man who had glowered at her earlier. Not emerging from unconsciousness, then, but merely choosing this moment to make a pain of himself. Whether he was doing it deliberately to help her, she didn't know.

Unexpected ally or not, the sudden flurry of activity surrounding his protestations gave her the chance she needed, and she threw her weight forward, making her captors stagger onto the gangplank with her. She immediately felt a lessening of their grip as their minds were filled with more overriding concerns, namely that on either side of them was now a drop into the waters of the harbour, and heavily armoured as they were, this was a place they'd prefer not to be. Armour and water did not mix. Their potential fate was illustrated quite graphically as, in the midst of the chaos her lurch had caused, one of the Swords near to the base of the gangplank suddenly found himself colliding with the protesting prisoner and his centre of gravity was thrown. With a cry of alarm the Sword tipped over the rope that edged the gangplank and plunged into the dark waters of the harbourside, sinking instantly beneath the surface.

Kali reminded her captors of the precariousness of their situation by swinging herself around as much as she could, and as their own momentum threatened to tip them after their friend, both released their grips. Freel, caught in the middle of the turmoil, spotted Kali's sudden freedom and his hand dropped to the chain whip at his belt, but by then it was too late. Kali blundered back up the gangplank and fled along the deck.

Freel ordered his men to follow, and they did so eagerly, welcoming the renewed solidity of the deck beneath their feet. Kali, meanwhile, ran, tearing away part of her bodysuit to wrap as a makeshift bandana around her forehead. The cloth did not stop all of the blood, but helped some.

As she heard the thudding of the Sword's boots after her, she made her way to the rear of the deck, finding herself amidst the cigar-shaped cargo she'd seen earlier. This close to them, she realised just how big each canvas shrouded object was – much taller than herself, and broad, too – and she dodged between them, hiding. A second later the Swords arrived and Kali waited until they had passed her hiding place to burst forth and head down the other side of the ship's superstructure. Between her and the bow, however, more Swords appeared, and Kali had no alternative but to go either into the superstructure, or up. She tried one door and another but all were locked, and so, with a grunt of exertion, grabbed onto a rail and heaving herself upwards and upwards again. She was standing now on the forward sloping, ridged carapace formed by the ship's folded sails.

Kali looked down. The Swords climbed after her but she'd bought the time she needed.

"Just where is it that you expect to go, Miss Hooper?" a voice asked.

Kali span. Jakub Freel stood at the opposite side of the carapace. He held his chain whip coiled before him.

"I was looking for the bar," Kali answered calmly. "The ship doesn't do room service."

"No. Only doom service."

Kali paused. "Did you just say that? Did you just say 'doom service'? Gods, man, did you really used to speak like that? No wonder the elves died out..."

Freel – Redigor – didn't answer. Only moved towards her over the rise of the carapace, allowing his whip to uncoil and trail full length behind him.

Kali readied herself for what was to come, knowing full well how proficient Jakub Freel had been with his singular weapon. She saw no reason why Bastian Redigor wouldn't have inherited this particular prowess, too. This was quickly confirmed as, with a flick of his forearm, Freel brought the whip to life and the single strand of chain separated into nine tails, each cracking down and sparking on the metal sail beneath them.

As sparks shot towards her face, Kali flipped backwards, increasing the distance between herself and Freel's deadly lashing. Freel was just as fast, however, and even as Kali landed on her feet, the multiple strands were sweeping out, each trying to trip her before she fully regained her balance. Kali's instincts were quick enough that she was able to dodge the majority of the sweeping chains, leaping above or cartwheeling over each as it passed beneath her, but a subtle flick of Freel's wrist brought the last one in faster than it was appearing to come, and with a bone-cracking impact she felt her ankle struck and then give beneath her.

Kali rolled with the blow, turning a tumble into a shoulder roll, but the slight miscalculation had given Freel momentary advantage. Her ankle didn't feel broken but it did throb like the hells and couldn't take much weight, and as Freel's whip came at her once more, Kali was forced to throw herself backwards rather than hobble out of the way.

She landed awkwardly on her behind, winded, near the edge of the sails, and cried in pain as a second dart of the metallic snake caught her on the forehead, tearing away her bandana, lashing the wound there and allowing the blood it was producing to flow freely once more.

Kali shook her dizzied head in an attempt to clear it, and stared down over the sails' lip, towards the waters of the harbour. As she did, those Swords climbing after her pulled themselves over the lip. They didn't approach her, but spread themselves around the periphery of the sails with crossbows aimed.

Deferring to their master. Kali rolled as Freel's whip sliced the air, this time at a level which would have cleanly decapitated her had she remained where she was. He'd clearly given up on the idea of simply incapacitating her and lashing her to the figurehead, and that suited her just fine because, in truth, she wanted him to bring it on.

Kali allowed the roll to bring her back to her feet, wiped blood from her face, and then charged at Freel before he had chance to retract the chains for another lash.

She somersaulted again as she neared him, timing the roll so that she came out of it feet first, and with those feet slamming directly into his chest.

Freel staggered back with an involuntary exhalation as Kali impacted with him, and she took advantage of his imbalance to come upright and strike him with almost simultaneous left and right jabs to the jaw. Freel reeled before her and Kali immediately raised herself onto one leg, spinning as she did to bring the other about in a roundhouse kick that sent Freel's already battered face snapping to the side, throwing an arc of spittle to the wind. As he staggered, attempting to recover from the assault, Kali circled him, her breathing slow and heavy, almost *challenging*. Freel wiped blood from his face, smiled coldly and reined in the chain whips, reducing their length so that they might function better at close range.

This was exactly what Kali wanted, and as Freel began to lash her anew, she backed away, dodging each of his strikes as they came. The manoeuvres kept her convincingly endangered but, in reality, safe from any injury that might lessen her chances of success. There were quite a few close calls – too many, in fact – but eventually she managed to lead Freel all the way to the rear of the sails, which was exactly where she wanted him to be.

It went against everything she believed to bring the fight to a close. Her deepest desire was to finish the bastard now. But that wasn't the solution to the problem Freel had presented her.

Kali began to run, surprising Freel, angering herself, but knowing she was doing the right thing, the *only* thing she could.

She headed with grim determination down the carapace, jumping the small ridges that delineated the folded sails, following the curve in the direction of the ship's prow. Behind her, having expected a confrontation, Freel was caught off guard, and by the time he had released the coils of his whip to take in the extra distance between them, Kali was already out of the deadly chains' reach.

Freel smiled grimly, however, because this didn't matter. It was clear to him that the girl was making for the water, but it was equally clear that she was not going to make it.

The gauntlet presented by those Swords who had followed her from the deck was inescapable, their crossbows covering her from port and starboard. Freel watched as Kali began to run, but there were limits to what even Kali Hooper could do.

Before she had even made it half way to her destination a dozen quarrels had been unleashed, and while Kali did her best to dodge them, twisting and spinning gymnastically so that their deadly barbs whizzed by a hairsbreadth from her skin, at least a third of them found their target; two piercing her right thigh, one her shoulder, and another her side.

Kali staggered slightly and continued on, though the multiple impacts had slowed her, and the second wave of quarrels found their target more easily and with a greater degree of success. She cried out in pain as two quarrels slammed into her back just beneath her shoulderblades, and then another into the soft flesh at the back of the knee, bringing her down. Kali slammed down onto the carapace and began to crawl forwards, roaring with the effort and with her own frustration.

"Surrender, Miss Hooper," Jakub Freel said as the Swords' wound the tension on their crossbows for another assault. "There is no escape."

Kali stiffened momentarily and then managed to get a grip on the ridge of the last of the sails and pulled herself forward. The lip of the carapace was just ahead, below that the ship's prow and the sea. But then the sound of the crossbow's quarrels being slipped into place and locked for firing made her freeze once more. Slowly she tried to pick herself up, and though the Swords were ready to fire, Freel raised a hand to them, momentarily staying the release of their deadly projectiles.

Kali Hooper drew herself up to her full height and turned to face him. Malignant eyes stared from beneath a brow thick with blood. She was slick with it and its loss made her waver slightly where she stood, but she had enough strength to bare her teeth.

Jakub Freel stared up at Kerberos and the ever looming presence of its new companion, then down to Kali.

"It's time for a new dawn, Miss Hooper. A new era where you have no place."

"Go to the hells," Kali growled.

"No. Not I."

He dropped his hand and the Swords fired. Multiple quarrels struck Kali in the legs, arms, torso and head, their impact so powerful she was propelled from the carapace, arcing backwards over the prow and then out into the dark waters below.

Freel moved to the edge of the carapace just in time to see her crash into the sea.

Kali's body floated for a second, and then sank beneath the waves.

CHAPTER EIGHT

THE BLACK SHIP sailed at midchime that night. The torches that had been lit all along the harbourside were presumably present only to keep the crowd that had gathered there warmed against the chill sea winds, for they made little difference beneath the azure glow of Kerberos.

It was tradition that all who worked on the construction of a vessel should watch it depart on its inaugural voyage, though in truth none of them were there by choice that night, roused from their beds by the Swords and forced to attend. Why the Church should insist they assemble for the occasion none could guess, for it knew how they felt about the ship's presence in their town. To them, it was an abomination, unnatural, and, because of the many deaths that had occurred in the months it had taken to build, clearly cursed. None of the town's doctors or apothecaries could explain why the cause of death in most of those cases had been severe burning of the flesh, though some speculated it had something to do with the strange devices with whose assembly they had assisted, or even with the mysterious mineral the Faith had imported into the town and loaded aboard by the ton under conditions of utmost secrecy.

As a result, there was none of the usual cheer and acts of celebration that would normally accompany such a launch, and as the ship's ropes were cast off the people of Gransk regarded the dark hulk silently and with relieved expressions, glad that they would soon see its back. Maybe then, at last, their town might return to normal.

Kali trod water some thirty feet under the surface, her limbs moving slowly and lazily. The constant stream of bubbles from her breathing conch as she pulled quarrels from her flesh went unnoticed by those on the harbourside, though their shadows, backlit by torches and distorted by the surging of waves, appeared to be looming over her. Dammit, Kali thought. That had hurt. But the subtle gymnastics necessary to make sure the quarrels hadn't hit anything vital had achieved her aim. As far as Redigor was concerned, she was dead, and the Black Ship would sail with its hostages safe.

Down here, the sounds of the Black Ship's imminent departure were muted – a dull rumbling of engines and sporadic, almost ghostly clangs as its hull plating shifted – and the only sure way to tell the behemoth was about to sail was from the churning froth of its propellers and the slowly pulsing glow from the amberglow generators concealed beneath the ship's plimsoll line. These orange blisters, two to port and two to starboard, looking from Kali's distorted perspective like wavering suns in some alien sky, had presumably been what had made the waters boil when the ship had been launched, and with them acting as a boost to the ship's sails, she reckoned that Brundle's quoted sailing time of two months would be more like two weeks.

Kali wondered what the people of Gransk would make of the Old Race technology at play here. Doubtless they had been involved in its installation – as the ship's builders how could they not? – but none of them could have truly realised with what it was they were dealing. The Faith had doubtlessly come up with some explanation for the strange sights they had seen, perhaps each would receive a visit from one of Querilous Fitch's alumni and, following a brief but effective mind probe, simply forget everything that had happened.

Kali shifted her attention from the surface to the darker depths below her. She was pleased to note that she had positioned herself correctly as, from the shadows beneath her feet, a large and heavy shape hove into view. It trailed bubbles and silt from the harbour floor as it rose, and Kali kicked herself into position next to the thick chain to which it was attached. Brundle had remained secretive about how he was going to gain access to the Black Ship, and so had she, mainly because she hadn't worked it out at the time, but the simple expedient of hopping a lift had come to mind not long after.

The Black Ship's giant anchor, one of four that held its bulk steady, took shape as it neared the surface, and Kali grabbed at it through swirling silt as it passed. She was feeling quite pleased with herself for choosing this method, but the slight smile on her face was replaced by a look of shock as instead of touching the hard metal she expected, her hands brushed against something organic. She back-pedalled, involuntarily spitting out her breathing conch and gagging on water. The shock made her almost miss her only chance to reach the ship before it departed. Disregarding whatever it was she had touched, Kali lunged forward once more and this time felt the unyielding curves of the anchor's hooks beneath her grip. Flustered – had she imagined what had just happened? – Kali allowed herself to be carried upwards by them for a second while she stared down into the wake of the anchor's ascent and for a moment, just a moment, caught a glimpse of a silvery figure receding into the depths. She was just able to pick out its smooth features, its toothless mouth and the glowing nodules that hung from either side of its jaw – not to mention the fact that it was staring right up at her with eyes that seemed to penetrate her very soul.

Kali's heart thudded. Her unexpected companion looked just like the creature – or at least the same *kind* of creature – she had encountered beneath the collapsing ruins of Martak more than two years before.

The End Comes, came the alien voice in her head. *The Truth Awaits*.

What? Kali thought. What? But she knew she was not going to get an answer, for her strange visitor was already being absorbed into the darkness below, and a second later it was gone. The words resonated in her mind but she quickly shook them away, knowing she had only seconds before the anchor on which she rode broke the surface. Trying her best to ignore what had just happened, Kali began to scramble up the body of the anchor, getting herself into a readied position.

SOME TWENTY FEET above, on the starboard stern deck of the Black Ship, Brother Kelleher stared grimly at the press-ganged men who had been ordered straight into service to struggle with the vessel's anchor chains. He did not attempt to help as, sweating and straining, they heaved it from the water and the anchor began to rise up the sheer wall of the ship's hull. On the port side of the stern, he knew, a similar operation was underway, and similarly two more at the bow. What Brother Kelleher did not know was that, unlike his compatriots elsewhere, his men were being forced to strain just that little bit more.

Brother Kelleher nodded to the men as the anchor rose into its housing and was locked off, and a moment later they were dismissed. The initiate remained behind for a second, watching the anchor spill water and turn slowly where it rested in its housing. He contemplated the voyage ahead – how he would be venturing where no one else had been, into strange and unknown waters, and all for the glory of the Final Faith. He reflected that it was an honour to be chosen to do this, and for a second bowed his head and prayed aloud, thanking both the Anointed Lord and the Lord of All for the privilege that had been granted him.

"I'm pretty much sure that neither gives a toss," a voice said.

Brother Kelleher looked up. The anchor had turned fully turned round in its housing and, spread-eagled so that she matched its cruciform shape, a young woman hung upon it. It was difficult to make out her features through the plastered down fringe that obscured her forehead, but then she flicked the hair aside, slowly spat out a spout of water, smiled and winked. A fist swiftly followed these actions, but this Brother Kelleher didn't really see coming, and he had no chance to reflect on the fact that he had been remiss.

KALI HOPPED STEALTHILY down off the anchor, landing in a crouch over the prone body of the Faith initiative. She delivered another swift punch to his groaning form, making sure he was out cold, stripped him and then quickly dumped him overboard. Far below, Brother Kelleher crashed into the harbour waters and, his underknicks inflating like a balloon, began to bob away on his own, unexpected voyage.

Kali turned back to the deck, lit by the ship's running lights. The fact that she was still sloughing water like a naiad was a pain, but at least her dip had rid her of the stench of the creel, something for which Brundle, if they were eventually reunited, would doubtless be eternally grateful.

She slipped the brother's robe over her own bodysuit and stared about, noting that in the distance the men dismissed by the initiate were entering the bulkhead, leaving that part of the deck clear. There was no one to notice, now, that she had replaced the brother, and as far as anyone seeing her from a distance was concerned, she would be taken for him. She walked to the ship's rail to look back at the departing Gransk.

Oh gods, no, she thought.

Because from her perspective she could see what the crowd gathered there could not, namely that the guards positioned behind them were lifting the tall-staffed torches from where they had been positioned and wielding them like lances. She had her answer, now, to how the Faith intended to deal with the problems of the builders' exposure to their secretive Old Race technology, and, unless she wanted to give away her presence, she couldn't even shout out a warning.

The bastards were making it look as if this were an attack from those sea-dwellers who had raided more than a few coastal towns of late. Kali closed her eyes as the first of the people of Gransk were impaled on the flaming skewers and unceremoniously thrust into the dark waters below. She kept her eyes closed as those who turned at the cries of their friends were cut down by rapidly unsheathed swords.

Damn the Faith, she thought. Damn Makennon, damn Freel, damn them all. If this was the future of their Church, it had no place on her peninsula.

This ends. If not tonight, then one night soon. This ends.

The End Comes, she heard again. *The Truth Awaits.*

Kali took a deep breath and turned away from the scene of carnage, and it mercifully grew more distant as the ship's amberglow generators began to pick up its momentum. Soon the sounds of screams from the shore were replaced by the rush of sea winds and the constant thrum of the vessel beneath her. Kali shivered. She had to get inside, not only to rid herself of the cold but because it was there that she might begin to find some answers as to what exactly was going on on this ship. On the latter, she didn't act immediately, first finding herself a hiding place in the ship's ballast bulkheads and venturing forth occasionally to work out the pattern of the ship's watches and patrols so that when she did emerge, she could do so clandestinely.

It was two days, during which the Black Ship passed through the crackling maelstrom that was the Stormwall and she was forced to insulate herself from the electricity that danced through the ballast bulkheads, before she ventured on decks. There, she had two destinations. As it was likely that the ship's crew knew little – if anything – of Redigor's plans, one of these destinations was the elf's cabin, which she had located towards the stern of the ship. Before that, however, she had a higher priority. This involved her travelling the length of the ship to where she had previously located a set of steps leading down to the cargo hold, where she suspected the prisoners were being held.

Having donned her Faith robe once more, she made her way as far as she could along the open decks, swapping from starboard to port to avoid patrols, and then ducked through a hatch back inside. Here she stowed the robe, the heavy cloth counterproductive to stealth and because it would do little to conceal her identity in the close confines of the interior anyway, and began to negotiate the corridors.

It was like beating a maze where no other wanderers were allowed to see you, but thankfully Kali had always liked mazes. She dodged left and right, right and left, pausing at corners and then moving on, sometimes only a second behind crewmembers in whose steps she silently walked. It took half an hour during which time she hardly dared breathe, but at last she came to the steps she wanted.

She headed down into the hold, three decks below, gratified to find that her suspicions had been proven right. The entire area below decks had been converted into a makeshift prison for the many brought forcefully aboard, kept in groups in cages laid out in a chequerboard style. Guards wandered the shadowy criss-cross of spaces among them and Kali was once again forced to 'dodge the Filth' as she worked her way towards the people she wanted to see. Others – people she didn't know, just innocents who had spoken out against the Faith – rose hopefully as she slipped passed their cages, but for now there was nothing she could do to help or comfort them. Kali continued to move between the cages, inspecting their occupants, and coming at last to two adjacent cages which held her friends from the Flagons and Jengo

Pim and his men. The fact that these were positioned the farthest back and together suggested that Redigor wanted those closest to her well incarcerated, but it also worked to Kali's advantage as it was an area the guards only glanced towards occasionally.

Inside the first cage, Red Deadnettle caught a glimpse of her face and was about to holler out when Kali put her finger to her lips, silencing him. The huge poacher nevertheless moved eagerly to the bars, Hetty Scrubb and Pete Two-Ties squeezing in beside him. At their rear, Kali could just make out Martha DeZantez tending to the stretchered Dolorosa.

"How are you?" Kali whispered, glancing sideways to keep an eye on the guards.

"Could do with a drink," Red shrugged.

"Me, too," Kali agreed.

"They could have given me a cryptosquare, to pass the time," Pete Two-Ties moaned.

Kali smiled; the man lived to complete his cryptosquares.

"Nihc," she said.

"Pardon?"

"Chin up."

"Oh, ha," Pete responded, dryly.

"Personally, I would like to rip off their balls," Hetty Scrubb hissed. The tiny herbalist was never at her best when unable to sample what she sold, and every sinew and tendon thrust prominently through her parchment skin. "Rip off their balls and ram them in their eyes."

"You'll both have what you need soon," Kali said. "I promise."

Red stared at her. Giant that he was, it was amazing how much like a child he looked. "Then you are not here to get us out?"

"Soon."

Swallowing, she checked the positions of the guards once more, ducked momentarily into shadow, and then moved across the aisle to the opposite cage.

"About time you showed up," Jengo Pim said. "We need out."

"There are what?" Kali said. "Twelve of you? Twelve thieves locked in a cage and you can't *escape*?"

"You can see that this is a rune-inscribed lock," Pim hissed.

"Even so. I really should report you to your union."

"Funny. Now are you going to find a way to get us out of here or not?"

It was only at that moment that Kali realised the reality that she had so far been denying to herself. Had denied to all of them. It was a reality she didn't particularly like.

"I... I can't."

"Can't?" Pim repeated.

"Think about it, Jengo. We're outnumbered two, maybe three, to one on a ship we don't know how to control, heading for a destination only Redigor knows the location of."

"We can handle odds like that. And unless I'm mistaken, didn't you and your people once take control of a spaceship? How hard can the Black Ship be?"

"If we take them out, we might not have enough people to run the ship."

"Then we *force* some of them to run it for us. And Redigor must have charts."

"We can't take that risk."

Pim thumped the bars, then eyed Kali carefully. "Just between you and me, these are just excuses, aren't they?" he said quietly. "You *want* Redigor to get where he's going."

Kali swallowed. She should have known it wouldn't take someone as astute as Pim long to work out the truth. "I didn't know you were all going to be here, okay? I honestly didn't. But I have to reach Trass Kathra."

"Why?"

"I don't know."

"Pits of Kerberos."

"Trust me, Pim. I think this ship needs to get where it's going, for all of our sakes."

"Even the old lady? What's her name? Dolorosa?"

Kali took in a sharp breath. "Even Dolorosa."

Pim took a second and then nodded reluctantly. "Promise me one thing. That you get us out of here before the shit hits whatever fan it's going to hit."

"Nothing's going to happen until this ship reaches Trass Kathra, I'm sure of it. And when it does, I'll have you out of there, okay?"

"Okay."

Kali hesitated, bit her lip. "See you later, Pim."

"I hope so."

Reluctantly, Kali left the prison deck and made her way back the way she had come, all the way to the stern. Her second destination, Bastian Redigor's cabin, awaited. The only problem was that Redigor didn't leave his cabin. Not then and, when Kali returned, not for the whole of that day. Nor the next. Nor the one after that. Eventually Kali concluded that, for whatever reason, the elf was going to spend the entire voyage in isolation, and resigned herself to the fact that the information she wanted would have to be sought later.

Kali didn't go back above decks for the remainder of the voyage, returning to her nest in the ballast bulkheads and spending her time foraging for discarded food, sleeping – as best she could on the violent seas – and befriending and feeding two sodden and sorry looking floprats she named Makennon and Munch. She also read through the journal Merrit Moon had given her in the World's Ridge Mountains. Kali flipping the pages eagerly, as intrigued as much by the old man's journey of discovery as the one she herself was on. The chamber from which she had rescued Moon was, according to his notes, the first of three which together formed the passage through the World's Ridge Mountains he had speculated existed. The Hall of Tales was the first, the Hall of Howling Faces the second, and the third the Hall of the Mountain... thing.

Obviously he hadn't managed to translate that last bit.

A few events distracted her during this time. The first was the ramming of an untershrak herd against the hull, sometimes so powerful she expected their triple-jawed snouts to punch through the watertight plating beside her head. The second an attack by the Great Blob itself. No one knew the exact nature or intent of this much feared aquatic denizen, though it struck Kali as being fundamentally benign – an observation based on its plaintive and almost befriending cries as it circled the Black Ship, occasionally rubbing itself up against it. Kali didn't interfere as the Faith fought the creature off – how could she? – and felt monumentally saddened when the blob's cries turned pained and then faded away into the distance.

One night – on what she calculated was the twelfth night of the voyage and in relatively calm seas – music drifted down from somewhere above, a familiar melody that reminded her of Slowhand, and for the few hours until daylight came again she felt agonisingly homesick.

At last, a burst of activity on the upper decks signalled what had to be the end of the voyage. Kali stole from her hiding place, figuring that if it was all hands on deck she should be able to go unnoticed in the crowd. Sure enough, as she emerged into natural, albeit a stormy grey, light for the first time in two weeks, the decks were awash with so much activity that no one had time to give her a second glance.

Kali made her way to the prow, and immediately saw why. Couldn't miss why, in fact.

The Black Ship was heading towards a stretch of ocean that could only be the swirlpools that Brundle had described, and while the dwarf had intimated these obstacles were dangerous, the word dangerous hardly seemed to do them justice.

Kali gasped. For what seemed like leagues ahead of them, and leagues to port and starboard, sweeping away in a broad band, the ocean was in upheaval. Great, circular eddies, hundreds of them whirling away, crammed together and crashing together, forming other, new manifestations of themselves, making the waters they were about to sail into seethe and boil and explode upward into the sky. Far higher than the Black Ship itself, these violent eruptions of ocean seemed almost alive, made of stuff more viscous than the seas that birthed them, somehow almost sentient in the way they hung there before plummeting whence they came, worsening the chaos beneath. It was like the ocean was at war with itself, and Kali knew instantly that to enter this battlefield would be deadly.

A shadow darkened her view. Redigor stood calmly by her side, hands holding the rails, as if they were two friends on holiday, enjoying the view.

"Spectacular, are they not?" the elf said.

"Personally, I prefer the banks of the Rainbow River, or the Shifting Sands of Oweilau."

"Both beautiful, especially seen as I have seen them, awash with the blood of battle."

"Thanks for reminding me what a fruitcake you are, Baz. You don't seem surprised to find me alive."

"Not surprised at all. I could *feel* you infesting the bulkheads like a filthy floprat. What is it you call such vermin these days? Pests?"

"Then why didn't you subject me to pest control?"

"I had... other concerns."

"I can tell."

Kali studied the elf's profile as he stared impassively beyond the prow of the Black Ship. His – that was Freel's – condition had deteriorated dramatically even since they had met on the ship's gangplank, and was presumably the reason he had locked himself away inside his quarters. His long black hair was thinning and billowing about his body like a shroud, his skin flaking away, peeled from him by the sea wind and trailing behind him to be slowly scattered amidst the grey, cloudy skies like ashes from a burnt-out fire.

The man was a ghost even though he wasn't dead yet.

Not yet.

"It's over, Redigor. Give this up."

"I am touched by your concern for my health."

"I don't give a flying fark about your health, elf. It's Freel's health I'm concerned about."

Redigor's jaw tensed. "Forget your friend. He's gone."

"Not while I'm drawing breath, Mister."

"Then I shall once more have to address myself to making sure that you don't."

Kali glanced casually down over the edge of the deck, saw the white of the angry ocean rushing by the plimsoll line. There was no way she'd survive that. And even if she did, where would she go, in the middle of nowhere, here, on the other side of the world?

"Shouldn't you be ordering a full stop?"

"On the contrary. The island is my destination. I intend to reach it."

"But the ship will be torn apart."

"Yes."

Kali gasped as a particularly violent surge caused her to lose her grip and she was slammed around, her back impacting painfully with the prow. It was in that moment that she realised something that she – and Brundle, wherever the dwarf was – had missed. The only thing that mattered to Redigor was that he made landfall, and to that extent the ship was nothing more than a means to an end. It had been built the way it had to be used as an ocean-going battering ram, to get them as close to the island as it could, and if it was wrecked in the process, he didn't care.

He wasn't going home. No one on the ship was going home.

This was a voyage of the damned.

"My god, Redigor, what have you got planned?"

"Salvation," the elf said.

And with that he raised his hand, signalling those on the bridge behind him not to slow but to speed their knottage. The Black Ship ploughed ahead.

Heading straight for the swirlpools at ramming speed.

CHAPTER NINE

THE ELF TURNED suddenly away from the prow. "You must forgive me, Miss Hooper, but it is time for your friends to be released from their confines. You may help if you wish."

Kali felt the Black Ship groan beneath her. Heard the bang of exploding rivets and creak of plating from its hull as it encountered the first of the stresses that the swirlpools presented. They had only just reached their edge.

"I don't know what you've got planned but damn right I'll help," she said, following.

"Then be quick. There is no time to waste."

The two of them made their way back below decks and down to the prisoner's hold, Redigor enlisting men to help as he moved. Watching the elf dance his hand over the rune-inscribed locks of the cages, opening them, wasn't exactly what Kali had imagined when she'd promised Pim she'd get him and the others out of there, but considering the unexpected development it would have to do. Pim gave her a glance as, along with his men, he was pulled from his cage, still in chains, to join the other prisoners being ushered onto the upper decks. All Kali could do was give a shrug that said, wait and see.

Redigor opened the cage holding Red and the others from the Flagons, and Kali quickly moved inside to help Martha DeZantez with Dolorosa. The sour stink of infection assailed her nostrils as she bent to wrap the old woman in her blankets, and Kali had to quash a flare of fury that Redigor had provided no medication for her wounds.

Dolorosa groaned and shifted as her stretcher was lifted, and a hand slipped free. A small object trailed from loose fingers onto the floor of the cage. The old woman's prayer beads.

"Red, take her," Kali said to the poacher, and turned to retrieve the beads. When she turned back the cage was empty and Redigor was standing by its door. He closed it with a clang, his hand dancing once more over the rune-inscribed lock.

"Should have seen that one coming," Kali said.

"I believe you should have," Redigor agreed.

Kali glanced between the cages to the steps where the last of the prisoners were being taken to the upper decks. At their rear, Red Deadnettle turned and looked at her hopelessly. As he did, the entire ship rocked, almost turned onto its side despite the stability of its twin hulls, and, rather disorientatingly, began to rotate.

They were entering the swirlpools proper, and, if the sounds of the tortured hull around her were anything to go by, the swirlpools would soon be entering the ship. A second later, a bulkhead beside the steps burst and a torrent of seawater began to flood the prison deck.

"Goodbye, Miss Hooper," Redigor said.

And with that, he and the others were gone, the hatch to the upper decks shut behind them.

Kali thumped the cage bars, cursing her own stupidity, and as the floodwaters began to swirl about her ankles and then her waist, her hand searched instinctively for her breathing conch in the side pocket of her bodysuit. Feeling empty space, her mind flashed with the image of the conch dwindling into the depths of Gransk harbour, and she cursed again.

Then Kali remembered the small bag Merrit Moon had given her in the World's Ridge Mountains. A few things that might help to keep you safe, he had said, so let's see.

She dug inside, extracting first an elven memory crystal, second a small sphere that looked like one of the old man's ice-bombs and which she wasn't willing to risk finding out, and third an object that rattled and hummed in her hand but of whose purpose she had no idea at all. Fine. If she wanted to record herself being frozen in a solid block of ice while some kind of weird clockwork toy got on her tits, then Moon had provided her with the perfect tools. But if she wanted to use them to get out of here, she was bollocksed.

There was one more item. A small bag within the bag that had gone almost unnoticed in her search. She pulled it out, undid its drawstring, and then yelped in pain as a length of thin vine covered in tiny leaves wrapped itself tightly around her index finger, extracting more of itself from the bag as it did. Kali knew what this was. Tourniqueed. Back when, the elves had used it as dressing to staunch the flow of blood from wounds in battle, and it still grew to this day in the marshes of Rammora. Kali could only imagine that Moon hadn't realised it was in the bag, a forgotten piece of a first aid kit he had perhaps used in his earlier adventuring days, but ironically it was of more use than any of the other objects he had given her.

The water having risen to her neck, Kali pinched the leaves of the tourniqueed, releasing it from her finger, and wrapped it instead around one of the bars of the cage. She pinched the leaves again and the vine contracted. Many an elf had lost a limb before he or she had come to realise how to stop the vine's contractions, and left to its own devices it was strong enough to cut through anything, even metal.

It took time, though, and time was one thing Kali didn't have. The seawater was splashing about her mouth and nose now, making her gag, and when at last the tourniqueed severed the bar she had already been submerged for almost a minute. Kali quickly snatched the vine from the water and reapplied it two feet further down the bar, and as it began to cut its way through once more she hammered the bar repeatedly, knowing she'd never survive until the tourniqueed had completed its job. She lost count of the number of desperate strikes she made, but she did know that her blows were becoming weaker each time, and finally she resorted to holding onto the surrounding bars, twisting her body and booting the face of the cage. Her vision was darkening and for a second she was only vaguely aware that the bar had become weak enough and was slowly spiralling away from her. She twisted and pulled herself through the opening it had made.

Kali swam directly for the steps and the hatch above, but as she turned the wheel to open it, it stuck fast. Redigor, or one of his men, must have jammed it. Kali's eyes widened and she turned desperately, seeking another way out.

But there was none.

She pounded on the hatch, bubbles of air exploding from her, but who was she kidding? Who did she expect to come to rescue her?

Maybe the person who was now turning the wheel from the other side, opening the hatch to the equally flooded deck beyond.

Kali's mind was so starved of oxygen now that it all seemed like a dream. Maybe it *was* a dream because the person who had opened the hatch – her rescuer – wasn't a person at all. In the grey, murky waters, Kali found herself looking at the same creature she had encountered in Gransk harbour, possibly the same creature she had long ago encountered in the floodwaters of Martak. Whether it was the same or not, she didn't know, for this time the creature did not speak in her mind, but merely took hold of her floating form and pulled her after it. Familiar ship's corridors, their angles warped by the waters that filled them, segued by, and in what remained of her conscious thoughts Kali recognised that she was being taken to safety.

Thank you, she wanted to say. *Please tell me, who are you?*

But she couldn't. Finding herself lying face down on the deck above, her sodden form gasping, the creature was gone.

Kali picked herself up, but her problems were only just beginning.

The stresses she'd witnessed tearing the ship apart below were far more evident above, and the ship pitched suddenly and dramatically, flinging her across the deck and almost hurling her into the sea. Except there was no sea. Clinging onto the rail, Kali looked down the precipitous drop of the hull to the part of the maelstrom in which it was caught. A section of one of the swirlpools churned right below her – or maybe above, in the constant skewing of the world it was difficult to tell – battering and lashing the ship while all the time staring back like some unblinking, giant, malevolent eye.

But the swirlpool was no eye, she knew that now. It was a mouth to the hells. A mouth that was fully capable of swallowing the ship whole. And the only reason it hadn't yet done so was that it vied with maybe a hundred others that made up the barrier around Trass Kathra.

A hundred.

And the ship was caught in the heart of them all.

As it was pulled from one to another, increasingly battered and twisted, the sound of the swirlpools' roaring hunger almost, but not quite, drowned out the sound of dull, periodic explosions and screams from along the deck.

Redigor and his people. And the hostages. It had to be. Despite her enforced delay, they must not yet have made it off the ship.

Kali began to move towards the screams. Reaching their source was not easy, however. Even as she forced herself off the rail against which she'd been thrown, the ship pitched again, and she found herself staggering back towards the hatch from which she'd emerged, slapping into it and then onto the deck as a crash of water soaked herself and the deck about her. This time, for good measure, the ship turned, too, its bow being forced around by the edge of an adjacent swirpool, and the creaks and groans of its protesting bulkheads began anew. There wasn't much time. The ship was coming apart.

The sky revolved giddily, and Kali found the only way to negotiate the wall in which the hatch sat was to allow herself to slide along it, carried by the water that flooded towards the stern. This, too, turned into a treacherous exercise as the ship dipped violently, transforming what had been a level, if unstable, deck into an acutely angled slide. Again, Kali let herself go with it, gaining speed as she skidded down, then, at the last minute, grabbed onto another passing rail before she impacted with what would have been bone-crunching finality against one of the deck stanchions.

"Woo!" she cried, feet dangling and kicking in mid-air.

She jerked herself aside as two Final Faith brothers, presumably having been engaged in some last minute business at the bow, sailed past her, robes flapping as they plummeted to their inevitable end.

Their sudden departure from the ship reduced the numbers she had to deal with and she didn't feel the slightest guilt in taking pleasure from their demise. It was the silly bastards' own bloody fault for coming here in the first place.

This handy method of reducing the opposition was only momentary, however, and the ship's bow crashed back onto the water with an almighty belly-flop that jarred every rivet in the hull and loosened yet more of its plating. A sheet of seawater splashed down onto the deck and Kali was punched off the rail and found herself spiralling along, caught in a series of crashing waves and rolling banks of water. This time she could not avoid being slammed into one of the stanchions, and the wind was knocked out of her, leaving her briefly dazed. But when she recovered her orientation, she found the waters had carried her to the part of the deck from which the explosions and screams had been coming.

Kali hid behind the stanchion and stared at what she saw there.

The explosions came not, as she'd expected, from disintegrating parts of the ship, but from explosive bolts that secured the mysterious, cigar-shaped objects to the deck. As these detonated, Redigor's men were tugging the canvas sheeting from them, revealing large, dark metal objects the purpose of which Kali couldn't make out for the throng gathered about them. One thing was likely, though. From the desperation with which they worked, these things were a way off the sinking ship.

Kali's attention turned to the throng. Something was wrong here. Counting Redigor's people and the hostages – who were being forcefully jostled amongst them, still in chains – there seemed far too many potential survivors, especially as it seemed one of the cigar-shapes had been damaged during the voyage. Redigor himself was already scowling at this and, among his men, shouts of recrimination and accusations of negligence were being bandied around. This got them nowhere, of course, because it was clear that there could be only one conclusion to this realisation.

Some people would have to be left behind.

Oh gods, Kali thought. The hostages. If it was a choice between his own men and the hostages, Redigor would surely dispose of them here.

She was about to break cover, simply take a chance and go all out to save them, when she faltered. A bright blue flash in the middle of the throng was followed by a scream, and the body of one of the Faith thudded to the deck, as a smoking and charred heap of meat. Others around him backed off, muttering fearfully, and this revealed the cause of the first flash as it happened again.

It was Redigor. Fists burning, the Pale Lord was frying his own people, any and all of them who tried to clamber onto the objects out of turn or objected to the fact that they seemed not to have a place there. For these, their desperation to escape the doomed ship overrode their fear of their leader, but it was a bad choice, a fatal choice.

What disturbed Kali the most about it was that Redigor smiled as he so casually doled out their deaths.

No, that wasn't quite true – what disturbed her most was why Redigor was favouring the hostages over his own people. If he was so intent on saving them and taking them with him, surely that suggested they had a purpose that went beyond their being hostages or simple prisoners. But what?

The ship twisted again and groaned beneath her, louder than ever before, and Kali knew it could not take the stress it was suffering for much longer. As waves crashed about her and parts of the ship's superstructure broke away to crash onto the deck, she moved closer to the desperate gathering, keeping to cover, trying to see if there was any way that she herself could find her way onto one of the mysterious objects of salvation.

There was none, however, and she could only look on as the objects revealed themselves fully. Groups of Redigor's people – the hostages scattered amongst them – were positioned beside each of the 'cigars' and, now that Kali could see more clearly, she watched as each in turn began to unfold, transforming from their original shapes into something quite different.

Kali knew immediately what she looking at – flutterbys. The deceptively charming name for elven troop carriers. Triangular shaped wings extended from the objects' sides, retractable blades from their tops, and, from the main bodies of the objects, riding platforms in the form of interlacing metal struts on which passengers were clearly meant to stand. The flutterbys fully deployed, they sat on the deck of the ship like a swarm of giant insects.

Impressive, Kali thought. They looked original, too, and she reflected that while she had never physically come across one, Bastian Redigor clearly knew where to look.

The flutterbys were filling up now, but there remained far too many people to be accommodated by them. But, as before, Redigor was ensuring that the numbers became more manageable in his own, inimitable fashion. The whole group fell into chaos as more of his own men died thrashing and screaming, and Kali thought it the ideal moment to make a dash for one of the machines to guarantee her own passage off the sinking ship.

But she paused. The balance of numbers between Redigor's people and his hostages was favouring the latter now, and for her to take a place in one of the pods meant one of the hostages would not make it, and she couldn't condemn them that way. Of everyone on board, with the possible exception of Redigor himself, she was the one most physically capable of surviving the ship going down, even if she didn't yet know how she was going to manage it.

She was sure something would pop up. It always did. But it was going to be one hells of a rough ride.

The last flutterby being boarded, now, Kali bit her lip as she watched Redigor and his personal retinue, accompanying the last of the hostages, step into position. Just as the last, a man whom she'd swear she'd last seen as one of the press-ganged, stepped onto his foothold, he turned and spotted her hiding behind her cover. For a second their eyes met and Kali wondered if he would reveal her presence to Redigor. He did nothing, however, apart from nod as if wishing her luck.

She was going to need it. As the flutterby rose from the deck, turning in a sweeping circle to head towards the island, the ship groaned beneath her as if poisoned to its core.

Suddenly the whole of the stern, where the flutterbys had been, began to break away from the hull, a rift opening from below decks that spread upwards until it began to tear the deck itself asunder. As decking warped, popped and tore under her, revealing the equally torn lower decks spilling their contents into the sea, Kali joined those few of the Faith whom Redigor had left behind alive in running towards the bow and relative safety. That they had such commonality of purpose made it all the more irksome when one of them – clearly acting above and beyond the call of duty – grabbed her and demanded to know what she was doing there. She flattened the idiot and threw him over the side.

The deck buckled as she and the others continued to run, sending a wave of wood and metal nipping at their heels, but while it caught up to and brought down a number of the Faith, Kali herself leapt for the safety of a handrail to one of the upper decks. It provided only a brief respite from the surging destruction below, however, and a few seconds after grabbing onto it, it, too, buckled and fell.

Kali cursed. The first time in her life she had been on a sinking ship and it didn't even have the decency to sink properly, which was to say slowly and languorously beneath the waves. At least then she might have had a chance to formulate some kind of plan, perhaps even grab a drink and sing a rousing song or two as the sea proceeded inexorably towards her feet. But no – the increasing stresses from the swirlpools all around were tearing the ship apart, and the screams, rather than songs, that came from all around her reflected that fact.

A scream from one Faith as the deck suddenly opened and then closed again beneath him, cutting him in two at the waist. A scream from another as a stanchion broke from its mooring and decapitated him instantly if not cleanly. A scream from a third as the deck rail against which he hoped to gain respite broke away, plunging him into the maelstrom below.

Screams. Screams everywhere.

And then, just like that, the ship broke cleanly in two. The hull finally gave way to its stresses and parted right in front of her, bringing Kali to a skidding halt. She was suddenly surrounded, overtaken, by screaming, flailing forms as the Faith who had been following in her wake flung themselves desperately across the widening gap. One or two reached the opposite section of deck cleanly, somersaulting and continuing to run, some didn't quite make it, gaining precarious handholds and dangling desperately from struts exposed by the rent, while still others missed their mark completely and plunged into the churning mass of hull and water that waited beneath.

Kali didn't know what had made her halt in her tracks but the decision had proven to be the right one. The irony was that what they all – herself included – had thought to be the safer half of the sinking ship was not that at all. The final battering that had broken the ship's back had been caused by the confluence of two massive swirlpools challenging each other for their prize, and as Kali watched the bow of the ship was immediately taken by one, while the stern was swept away by the other. As the distance between the two halves of the ship grew, the stern section a quarter of the way around the periphery now and receding all the while, the bow was already being pulled directly into the heart of the furthest maelstrom. She could see the figures of the Faith who had made it across realising their situation and flinging themselves off the sinking ship into the water, but this was the worst thing they could have done, serving only to accelerate their deaths as their tiny forms were sucked beneath the surface in advance of the much larger wreck. Not that they would have survived that much longer, because the bow of the ship was already tipping forwards as it succumbed to the terrible forces in which it was snared, and only a few seconds later it sank beneath the waves.

Kali turned to look about her, and realised she on her own now. As the stern half of the ship listed beneath her, she was sent tumbling across the deck to its far rail, so that once again she was staring directly into the hungry sea. The list was only the result of the ship finding its natural position, however, and as it began to circle the sloping rim of the swirlpool she would, had it not been for the deafening roar of the chaotic sea, have found it almost relaxing, like being the sole passenger on some weird carousel.

But there was only one way this ride was going to end, and as the stern section spiralled gradually but inexorably ever deeper into the giant, watery crater, Kali bit her lip, deep in thought. One by one she assessed the circumstances of her situation – sinking ship, swirlpool, middle of the ocean a long, long way from home – and it didn't take her long to reach a summation of her predicament.

Farked. She was farked. All she could do was ensure that as the stern section began to sink she stayed as far from the all consuming water as she could, and when she could do that no longer... well, she was just going to have to make it up as she went along.

Round and round the wreckage went. And down and down. Its descent into oblivion more gradual but no less inevitable than that of the bow. Kali was backing up in what remaining space she had, the churning surface of the swirlpool literally lapping at her feet, when something burst through the surface of the water some hundred yards away.

It was some kind of machine that sped towards her, pumping the discoloured sea through membranes that seemed to drive its solid and barnacle covered frame forward. She didn't have the remotest idea of what it was but she did know who was sitting in what could only be the driver's seat.

Jerragrim Brundle grunted as, with the whine of some unknown engine, the strange machine slewed up onto the deck and skidded halt beside her. It still pumped out the water it had used for propulsion. Its streamlined shape was etched with dwarven runes and, though simple, its controls were far more complex than anything anyone on the peninsula could produce. Kali grinned. This was the aquatic equivalent of the mole machine she had found many months before, and she wanted one. Hells, did she want one.

"Are you gonna continue grinning like a loon or are yer gonna jump aboard?" Brundle demanded. He flicked his head toward the water. "Cos if yer haven't noticed, we don't have a lot of time."

Kali slammed her hands on her hips. "Oh, so now it's all rush. Just where the hells have you been for the past two weeks?"

"Close by, smoothskin. Close by."

The dwarf looked down.

And Kali looked at the machine. She noticed that some kind of breathing tube protruded from its control panel. There appeared to be one for a passenger, too. "Are you telling me that this thing's been attached to the hull all this time?"

"As tight as the piles up me arse."

Kali pulled a face. "How did I know you were going to say something like that? Couldn't you have just said 'limpet'?"

"Why?"

"Because... oh, never mind."

The waters began to slosh and slap over them, threatening to wash the machine off the deck. The last remains of the ship tipped dangerously as it began to be pulled down to the heart of the swirlpool.

"Are you coming, or what?" Brundle asked with some urgency.

"What do you call this thing, anyway?" Kali asked as she settled herself into the space for a second rider.

"Scuttlebarge. Now hang on."

Whatever response Kali might have had emerged only as a startled yelp as Brundle slung the scuttle barge around and, with a roar of its engine, it shot nose first into the churning sea. Kali scrabbled for the breathing tube, convinced that it was simply going to slip right beneath the waves but, as soon as it was waterborne, the membranes that pumped the water rotated in their housings so that they pointed straight down, and the machine gained its buoyancy on the surface with the force of their thrust. They didn't remain there once their job was done, however, rotating once more into a position half way between the two, and with a kick that threw Kali back in her seat the scuttlebarge began to skip across the sea.

To say that it was a bumpy ride would be an understatement. But Brundle appeared to be an expert pilot. Despite being continuously slapped and drenched by waves, more than one of which threatened to knock her overboard, forcing her to hold on tighter, Kali couldn't help but be impressed by the way the dwarf handled the scuttlebarge, playing the tumultuous surface of the sea with practiced ease, going with the flow here, using it to gain momentum there, never once hesitant as he threw the machine into each new manoeuvre.

The one thing that did come as a surprise – and caused a small lurch of shock – to Kali was that rather than piloting the strange craft to avoid any swirlpools in their path, Brundle aimed it straight for them. What appeared to be a suicidal ploy was nothing of the kind, however, as at the very last second on approaching the first of the maws, Brundle veered the scuttlebarge to starboard so that rather than heading right into the swirling water it skirted its rim, using the power of the swirlpool to carry them around the maw. Once on its other side, Brundle gunned the pumps of the craft so that they flipped over the crest of the maelstrom and then immediately flung her around so that they were carried along in the rim of another, this one swirling in the opposite direction. After successfully achieving this a couple more times, it became clear to Kali what it was he was doing – using the coriolis effect of the swirlpools to catapult the scuttlebarge between them. It could not have been the first time he had attempted such a task.

But what lay ahead of them might not prove such an easy task.

Roaring with a sound that drowned out of all its compatriots, out of all the swirlpools that surrounded Trass Kathra, this was the daddy of them all.

"You might want to use that tube now!" Brundle warned, and even as Kali fitted it tightly into her mouth, the pumps to the rear of the scuttlebarge rotated so that they were pointing upwards, forcing the machine beneath the waves. Everything was replaced by the turmoil of grey water, and all that Kali could make out was Brundle's beard, previously in danger of slapping, with all its bells, into her face, floating about her.

The reason Brundle had submerged had already become clear to Kali. Even with his expertise there was no way he could have negotiated the sheer power and violence of this swirlpool on the surface, but here, under the water, things were just that little bit calmer, even if it did still appear as a maelstrom from the hells. Brundle used the same technique he had above, riding the scuttlebarge into the outer edge of the underwater spiral and then allowing it to carry them around, to what would hopefully be calm on its other side. There was, however, something different about the swirlpool down here – caught up in the churning waters were patches of a whiter substance, still liquid but slightly more viscous than the surrounding element, which moved within it and yet not *with* it. Whatever the stuff was, it was clearly not simple seawater, and Kali noticed that Brundle put all of his effort into grimly and steadfastly avoiding it.

Dark shapes bounced around the scuttlebarge, and as the currents brought one of them smack bang into Kali's face, fleetingly revealing a horrified though quite dead visage whose lips had pulled back from its teeth, she realised they had hit a pocket of drowned men from the ship. A couple of the bodies bumped against the side of the scuttlebarge, forcing Brundle to correct his course slightly, but then, thankfully, they were through the cluster of dead. Kali couldn't help but turn to look behind her as they passed, however, and for the briefest of moments thought she saw one of the bodies caught up in the whiter substance whose nature she still knew nothing about. All she knew was that she was glad Brundle had managed to avoid it, because, as it touched the drowned Final Faith, his whole body seemed simply to drift apart.

What the hells? Kali thought.

The scuttlebarge began to rise, and Kali realised Brundle was returning it to the surface, using the last of the power of the swirlpool to throw them beyond its influence into calmer waters. They should, now, be nearing the island, she calculated, and, sure enough, as the machine lurched above the surface, slewing water from its barnacled frame, the coastline of Trass Kathra was right ahead of her.

Oh gods.

The island was not so much an island as a mountain in the middle of the sea, and built into its shadow and into its sides were structures so ancient and overgrown they'd come to resemble the rocks themselves. Accessed by a precipitous network of carved steps that led up from a small cove on the shoreline – what, perhaps, had once been a landing point – Kali saw strange bunkers and metal towers, many of these collapsed and bent at unnatural angles, a couple of carapaced structures that looked as if they might be some kind of warehouse, and numerous other, oddly shaped buildings whose purpose she couldn't even begin to guess at. Dominating them all, though, was the most impressive looking structure of them all. Almost at the island's highest point, on the slope of a great, thrusting clifftop, was what appeared to be a huge observatory dome.

Kali's mouth dropped open. Out here, far beyond the known world, where nothing at all should be, was the work of those whose secrets she'd spent a lifetime exploring.

An Old Race outpost.

She couldn't wait to set foot on those steps.

Disappointingly, however, Brundle wasn't piloting the scuttlebarge towards the cove but keeping an equidistant course along its coast. If they continued the way they were, they would leave the steps far behind and round the island's farthest point.

She tapped the dwarf on the shoulder, shouting above the noise of breakers on rocks.

"What the hells are you doing?"

"We're not landing here, smoothskin," Brundle responded. "Too dangerous."

Kali frowned. She looked back towards the cove and saw what her enthusiasm had denied her seeing before. The cove was filled with the grounded flutterbys from the Black Ship. And though she saw many of the guards and their prisoners snaking their way up the steps to whatever destination Redigor had in mind, others of his landing party – prisoners and guards – remained behind. A number of the guards having positioned themselves as sentries on the steps, there was no way they would get past them.

"Oh, and one more thing," Brundle shouted over his shoulder. "Yer got the name o' the place wrong. People always get it wrong. It ain't Trass Kathra, the Island of the Lost. It's Trass *Kattra*... the Island of the Four."

Kali almost fell off the scuttlebarge.

"*What?*"

Brundle smiled and turned his attention back to ploughing through the waves.

"Child of Trass Kattra," he roared, "welcome home!"

CHAPTER TEN

CHILD OF TRASS Kattra, Welcome Home! The words reverberated in Kali's mind, begging a hundred different questions, but her attempts to gain an answer to any of them were thwarted by the choppy coastal waters they had entered. Brundle couldn't hear a thing – or chose not to hear a thing – as he gunned the scuttlebarge's engines, expertly playing the breakers, slapping and lurching the old and battered machine ever closer to land.

They rounded the end of the island, and there approached a patch of darkness at the base of a cliff. A cave. It seemed this was their destination and, considering Brundle's other words – about this being the Island of the Four, whatever *that* meant – Kali couldn't help but start to imagine what wonders it might hold.

Nothing, was the answer. Bugger all. Because as the cliff face swallowed the scuttlebarge, plunging it into shadow, there were no wondrous Old Race machines, no looming statues of ancient heroes, nothing, in fact, that suggested the island would live up to the promise of its name. Instead, as Brundle cut the engine and they drifted in, she saw a primitive jetty and walkway that was all but falling apart, lit by the few torches that hadn't been broken. Those that weren't picked out nets and seafood pots dangling from railings, spears, tridents and harpoons. There was even a pair of wellies stacked amongst them. The only signs of technology were the remains of three other scuttlebarges, in various states of disrepair, one of which bobbed by the jetty, the others lying skewed where they had been driven up against the sides of the cave for makeshift berthing.

Something splashed near her right leg as it dangled in the water and Kali looked down. She spotted a huge keep net in which scores of fish the likes of which she'd never seen swam. One, the size of a floprat, bared sharp teeth and darted at her, and she snatched her leg from the water with a yelp.

"Thrap," Brundle stated. "Vicious little sods but good wi' a shake o' sea salt."

Kali nodded, not really listening. It was still here. Too still. The acoustics of the cave were such that they blocked out the sound of the raging seas beyond, and as she continued to look about in the flickering torchlight, listening to the slow lap of waves and almost soporific drips of water from the roof, she sensed that her surroundings had been like this for literally ages; a backwater at the end of the world, never, ever changing.

"What is this place?"

"Home."

"You live here?"

"Aye. It ain't much, but it satisfies our needs..."

"*Our* needs?"

Brundle pointed down at the keepnet. "I like a piece o' thrap, lass, but not that much."

"How many of you are there, then?"

"Two."

"Two?" Kali echoed. She stared at the keepnet. "Maybe still a little greedy."

"Aye, well... yer haven't met the wife."

"Wife?"

"Brogma," Brundle said. "Wife number... blast it, ah forget what number she is, now." He sighed, but Kali couldn't tell whether tiredly or regretfully. "Believe me, there've bin a few."

"And Brogma – she's a dwarf, too?"

"O' course she's a bloody dwarf! Are yer thinkin' ah'd marry an elf?!"

"That isn't what I meant. Don't forget from my perspective dwarves are, er... a little short on the ground. I thought maybe that in the absence of anything else she might be human?"

"Human? Pah to bloody human! There's mendin' to be done! Cleanin'! Cookin'! Forgin'! A human could no more satisfy me needs than one o' them posin' ponces, the elves!"

Equality was clearly not big with dwarves, but Kali couldn't help smiling. Of all the ways the ancient tales referred to the elves it was the first time she'd heard them called 'posin' ponces'. It almost made her feel better about Redigor's presence on the island.

The thought of the elf returned her mind to business – and the many questions she had. As the scuttlebarge bumped against the jetty and Brundle disembarked, hooking the machine's nose with a thick hemp rope he then tied off, Kali ignored his offer of a hand and hopped up under her own steam, turning to block his path with hands on her hips.

"Explanations," she demanded. "*Now*."

"What explanation did yer have in mind?"

"Oh, let's see," Kali said. "How about that little fondling act back in Gransk? Or why you wanted to blow up the ship to stop it coming here? And hey, while we're at it, what was that thing out there in the swirlies, what the hells is this place and why's it called the Island of the Four, and – oh, oh, last but not least – *what the fark did you mean by welcome home?*"

The dwarf waited while his hair settled and the bells in his beard stopped jangling.

"Have ye done?"

"Yes!"

Brundle sighed. "I can answer some o' yer questions, lass, but not all. That tale's a long one, and it ain't mine for the tellin'."

"Then whose? Brogma?"

"No, not Brogma."

"There's someone else on the island?"

"In a manner of speaking."

"In a manner of speaking," Kali repeated, increasingly frustrated. "What is it with you, dwarf? Were you born awkward or did you take special classes?"

"Special classes. I've had a lot of time to kill."

"Funny. Take me to them, then. Whoever can tell me the *whole* story."

"You'll have yer little chat soon."

"Soon?"

Brundle smiled. "Why don't we have a little bit o' tea first?"

Kali growled in exasperation as the dwarf weaved his way past her, and, having no choice, followed. Brundle neared a rockface and, purposefully this time, jangled the bells in his beard. The sound they made was loud and distinctive. After a second, a chunk of the rock face before him, what Kali had thought was the end of the cave, rumbled aside, revealing a torch-lit passage. A waft of something cooking – powerfully fishy – came from within.

"This way, smoothskin," Brundle directed. And then shouted, "Hi, honey, I'm home!"

Kali took one last look behind her and followed Brundle, possibly more bemused than she'd ever been. She wasn't sure what she'd expected when she reached Trass Kathra – Trass Kattra, she corrected – but this certainly wasn't it. And what she expected least of all, just before they exited the passage into what lay beyond, was a set of flowery curtains that Brundle, with some embarrassment, pulled aside.

"Don't blame me," he growled. "We live with what we find."

"Live with what you fi –?" Kali half repeated, then stopped. The passage had led them into an inner cave which opened out before her, and though it was much the size of the one they had just left, there was barely an inch within it to move. The whole place was crammed with enough junk to fill a city of scrapyards, piled up against the walls, across the floor, in great piles in the corners of the chamber. At least Kali presumed they were the corners of the chamber, because as far as she could tell this rubbish might go on for ever. It was like looking at the World's Ridge Mountains made out of crap.

Despite being overwhelmed by the sheer volume of the stuff, however, she couldn't help but be drawn to specific items contained in the mounds. Because most of this stuff was old – very old – and despite it being bruised and battered she still felt a little like a child let loose in a confectionarium.

"Where the hells did you get all this?"

The dwarf shrugged. "Plenty is washed up by the storms or makes its way on the tides. Or was salvaged from the wrecks o' those daft enough to try to take on the Stormwall. When that bastard *really* packed a punch, that was."

"That's the second time you've suggested the Stormwall is less than it was."

"All ah can say, smoothskin, is that one upon a time she were magnificent. Stretched around the peninsula like a necklace o' heavenly fire, she did, from both ends o' the World's Ridge to the Sarcre Islands. Nothin' could get through it. Nothin' at all."

"You mean it was some kind of *wall*?"

"Just something that was where the mountains weren't."

"What the hells is that supposed to mean?"

"That, smoothskin, isn't me place to tell."

"How did I know you were going to say that?"

"Now, where was I? Oh, aye. That which doesn't find its way here otherwise is foraged around the coast of the mainland. Ah make trips five or six times a year with the scuttlebarge an' a sled. Generally tie 'er up in Ten Bones Bay. It was the trip before last ah learned about the buildin' o' that bloody Black Ship, an' scuttled back here as fast as ah could for me bombs..."

Kali nodded, only half listening. She was working her way through the twisting avenues created by his collection, hands caressing shapes and objects of all sizes as she went, most of them unscathed by what might have been millennia in the sea. Even though she didn't have a clue what the pieces were – especially as they were only bits of pieces, as it were – she lingered over one or two of them as she might over works of art, trying to find meaning in the precisely turned metal objects, perfectly curved and rune-inscribed plating, the sheer craftsmanship involved in their smallest parts and in every other aspect of their making. They sure as hells didn't make 'em like that anymore. Yet.

One piece she came across *was* a work of art. It was a painting of what she at first thought was herself and Brundle on the scuttlebarge, but on closer inspection realised that couldn't be the case at all. For one thing, how could it be here, now, and for another the figure she'd thought was her own was sitting in the pilot's seat, not the dwarf. The fact that the woman was also considerably older than she – more, what was the word they used, handsome? – seemed to confirm the fact. It was intriguing, though. At least until Brundle punched her on the shoulder.

"Take a left just up ahead," he instructed. "Six paces and a right, twenty left and straight on. I'll be right behind ye."

Despite the dwarf's words, he wasn't – lagging behind grumbling, tutting and occasionally striking a piece of junk with his fist, as if he'd noticed a flaw somewhere. Kali was therefore alone when, having followed his directions she emerged cautiously into what appeared to be a living area in the heart of the tunnels. It was as packed with junk as the rest of the place but one small area had been set out with chairs, a table made, it seemed, from the panelling of an elven dirigible, and a kitchen with a ferocious looking stove on which three cauldrons bubbled.

A short, squat – that was, shorter and squatter than usual – dwarf, a female of the species, stirred them one by one. Her back was to Kali and she was dressed in a pinny and flowery skirt which looked to have been cut from the same cloth as the curtain that Brundle had pulled aside.

"Hello, dear," she said, without turning. "Did you have fun blowing up your boat?"

"Er, hi..." Kali said.

The dwarf span, ladles in hands, and some fishy gloop splattered Kali's face. It was hot but she didn't move, letting it drip from her chin. The best course of action here, it seemed, was to simply stand there and smile.

"Hammers of Ovilar," the dwarf gasped. "You almost made me rust me pantaloons."

"Sorry," Kali said, cringing.

Brogma, for this was presumably she, waddled forward and prodded her in the chest. It had to be, Kali was beginning to think, a family trait.

"By the gods, who are ye, girl?"

"This," Jerragrim Brundle announced, slapping Kali in the back and almost sending her face first into a cauldron, "is Kali Hooper. You've heard of Kali Hooper, haven't yer, wife?"

"No."

"No, neither had I. But she's –" Brundle moved forward and whispered something in the female dwarf's ear. Her eyebrows rose. Very high.

"*Is she?*" she said.

Brundle nodded conspiratorially. "But where are me manners?" he declared. "Smoothskin, this is me wife, Brogma. Brogma, this is... well, bugger it, yer know the rest."

"Sit yourself down, dear," Brogma said. "You're just in time for tea."

"Look, that's very kind but I don't have time for tea. I have to help my friends and –" Kali paused, staring daggers at Brundle "– find out what's going on."

"Yes, of course, dear. As one of the Four, you must."

Kali couldn't hide her surprise. "You know about the Four?"

"Of course!" Brogma declared, ladelling up food. "Keep an *eye* on things, I do. Now, let me see – there's the shadowmage, Lucius Kane; the Sister of the Order of the Swords of Dawn, Gabriella DeZantez; the mariner, Silus Morlader; and the explorer, Marryme Moo –"

Brundle coughed. "That'll be enough now, Brogma."

"I'm sorry," Kali said. "What?"

"Keep an eye on things, I do."

"That isn't what I meant," Kali said. "*What* was that name you said? Who in the hells is Marryme Moo?"

Brundle coughed again and motioned for Kali to bend, so that he might whisper in her ear. "Brogma's gettin' on a bit," he explained. "This Marryme Moo is someone she once knew – someone much like yourself – and she's a little confused."

"She's not the only one," Kali said. She wasn't at all sure that Brundle was being truthful with her, but how could she argue? Looking at Brogma, just standing there smiling, she couldn't deny that she seemed a little, well, challenged. What to do? The obvious answer was to ask the question she hadn't yet asked, but was becoming the most important of all.

"Jerry – can I trust you?"

The dwarf looked affronted.

"It has been the Caretaker's job to wait for you since the day the Old Races died," he replied, as if that were an answer. "Now do as the lady wife asks, and sit."

Kali hesitated for a second. Two weeks of living off scraps on the Black Ship had left her starving, and she'd be of little use to anyone if she didn't eat soon. Reluctantly, she did as asked, and Brundle plopped a bowl of grey sludge in her lap. The act was the first of many which would lead to her regretting her decision.

"What is this?" Kali asked.

"Starter."

"No, I mean, *what* is this?"

"Thrap."

"Oh. I thought – I mean, from the smell – that the main course was thrap."

"It is."

"Ah. The pudding wouldn't by any chance be thrap?"

"No, smartarse. A big, juicy steak."

"Steak for pudding?"

"Okay, I lied. It's thrap."

It got worse from there. Despite the monotony of the menu, Kali devoured her food, trying to fire off questions between mouthfuls, but getting nowhere. Brundle ate like a pigrat, a series of slurps, chomps, sucks and grunts drowning out her words. His table manners were nowhere near as disturbing as Brogma's, however, who simply tipped her head back and dropped fish after fish into her gullet, like a seal. Kali almost expected her to oink and clap.

"Essential oils," Brundle said, smiling.

The meal ended at last, and Kali was about to fire off her questions once more when Brundle let out an almighty belch and excused himself for the bathroom, farting loudly as he went. Brogma, seemed to have no such need, and instead waddled to a cupboard and extracted a great tangle of what looked like wire. She slumped into an armchair and, from its side, took two large needles and began to play the wire with them, teasing, turning and pulling it up towards her. As she caught two strands, the needles began to clack, and soon the wires were being knitted together with such disturbing dexterity the act was almost a blur.

The strange thing was, Brogma didn't even look at the wires – not once. Stared straight ahead all the time. Kali frowned and eased herself from her chair, noticing for the first time a strange, silvery tint to the old woman's eyes. She waved her palm up and down in front of them and there was no reaction. Brogma, it appeared, was blind.

"Is there something I can do for you, dear?"

Kali started. "What are you, erm, knitting?"

"Brains, dear,"

"Brains?"

"Yes, dear."

"*Right*," Kali said, and backed off.

She decided that any other queries, knitting-related or not, could and should wait until Brundle returned. To pass the time – and take her mind off the noises emanating from that part of the cave into which Brundle had departed – she examined some of the odder objects she'd spotted earlier. The first was a piece of thin metal which, whichever way it was bent, returned to its original shape, which was always that of a parrot. The second, something that looked like a tuning fork but which shattered a rock when she tried it, she put quickly away. A third object appeared at first glance to be some kind of jack-in-the-box, but when Kali opened the lid it wasn't a grinning head that popped out but some strange spherical device that flew straight up and began diligently to drill a hole in the cave's roof. Kali coughed, whistled and walked away.

Her path brought her to an object that was perhaps the oddest of all. The base of a large tree trunk secured to the wall by its splayed, gnarled roots, looking like a wooden sun. The trunk had been cleanly sawn through to reveal its rings, the number of which attested to its great age. It did not seem to have been treated with the respect it was due, however, having been used as a dartboard at some point, and what was even more disturbing was the 'darts' were the feathery, desiccated remains of three small skewerbills, their tiny eyes still frozen wide with alarm from the moment of impact.

Kali turned her attention to a number of inscriptions carved into the wood. They were in a very ancient dwarven script she struggled to translate and, when she had, wondered whether she should have bothered. *Brogma 32 Gone Today, Miss Her. One Thousand Years, Candles Broke the Cake. Fish For Tea Today, Tomorrow an' the Day After. By Bollocks, I'm Bored...*

Kali was, by now, quite convinced that instead of learning something of world-shattering importance from Brundle and his missus, they were in fact inmates of some offshore institution – that this particular part of the island wasn't Trass Kathra or Trass Kattra, the island of the lost or the Four, but Trass Kuckoo, the island of the insane. She was out of there, she decided. Right now.

Kali wandered the aisles looking for an exit, and at last found a ladder leading up a shaft to, she presumed, open air. But when she reached the top, her way was blocked by a circular metal hatch. The wheel at its centre suggested that it, like everything else here, had been salvaged from some ship, but when Kali tried to turn it, it wouldn't budge. She tried again, straining, hoping to break whatever was blocking the rotation, but then noticed the entire hatch, and the rock surrounding it, was coated in some substance set as hard as nails. Nothing was blocking the hatch as such – it had been completely sealed over.

Kali slid down the ladder and negotiated more of the maze, coming upon another exit and finding it exactly the same. Then another. She felt a small stab of apprehension, wondering what exactly it was she *had* stumbled into, but then reason took over, along with no little anger, and she stormed her way back to the heart of the maze.

There, Brundle was at last returned from his toilet. Pulling up his pants unselfconsciously, he patted Brogma on the shoulder and asked, "How are the brains comin', wife?"

"Fine, dear. Just the way you like them."

"You want to tell me why all the hatches to the surface are sealed?" Kali demanded.

"I –"

"Time to spill the beans, Jerry. What the hells is going on here?"

Brundle stared at her, then nodded.

"Ah suppose ah can't avoid it for ever. This island you're standing on – or under – is, or rather was, the generation station for the Thunderflux."

"Generation station? Thunderflux? That sounds like tech speak to me. If I didn't know better, I'd say I was back at the Crucible of the Dragon God."

"In a way, you are. Trass Kattra was its sister facility. O' course, it wasn't called Trass Kattra then."

"Then what?"

"Nothin' at all. Strictly speakin', it didn't even exist."

"I think," Kali said slowly, "that you'd better start at the beginning."

"You've already been to the Crucible, so I'll spare you its history. Suffice to say it had one purpose, and this island another. Both part of the same plan."

"The Crucible was meant to launch the *Tharnak* and its k'nid payload, to destroy the deity in the heavens," Kali said, remembering what the dwelf had told her. "But it never happened. He said nothing about this place."

"He wouldn't. It was need to know. Tell me, smoothskin – have your travels ever brought you into contact with Domdruggle's Expanse?"

"Big, roaring, bearded face? Gob the size of a planet?"

Brundle laughed. "Roldofo Domdruggle. His bark always was worse than his bite."

"And you're saying he was part of this plan?"

"Not just part, smoothskin. Its architect."

Kali took a moment to collect her thoughts, particularly those involving Poul Sonpear and what he'd told her about the Expanse.

"You're losing me, shorty. The way I heard it the Expanse came about as a result of some great magical ritual. Lives were lost. Sacrifices made."

"Aye, they were. But not in the way you think."

"Then Domdruggle wasn't a wizard?"

"Oh, Roldolfo was a wizard, all right. A wizard of temporal mechanics. Of the threads. He conceived the Expanse as a plane separate from normal time. A kind of –"

"Bolt hole?" Kali finished. "Meant to be used to escape the End Time?"

Brundle smiled. "Catchin' on, smoothskin. The Expanse was meant to be a hidin' place for the entire population o' the planet while the k'nid did their work. But ah don't need to tell ya that both parts o' the plan failed…"

"But the Expanse exists," Kali said. "So what went wrong?"

"Nothin' went wrong," Brundle said, and sighed. "The Crucible project failed for its own reasons and we –"

"Something about the dragons dying, right? The lack of their magic?"

"Aye. We just ran out time."

"What do you mean?"

"We had the heavens themselves thrown at us."

"I'm sorry?"

Kali hadn't imagined that a dwarf's face could become any more gnarled, that its angry furrows could become any deeper or darker, but in this case they did.

"A rain o' fire. A rain that changed, twisted an' warped everythin'. Got inside things an' people an' turned 'em ta sludge."

Kali swallowed.

"I encountered something similar at Scholten Cathedral."

"It wouldn't be somethin' similar, lass, it would be the same thing. The Hel'ss. And that beasty out there in the swirlies is what remains of its attack. The Hel'ss Spawn."

"What?"

"They lasted as long as they could, but that bastard was determined to stop them," the dwarf said. "Roldofo and his aides stayed at their machines and atop their towers until they were reduced to ruin. The generation field started to break down, closing the expanse, until finally Domdruggle and his people had no choice but to sacrifice themselves to the void in the hope that somehow, from inside, they could keep it open long enough to allow the exodus they'd planned."

"But it collapsed completely and they became trapped," Kali said. "Alone and desperate for a way out. Ghosts of themselves."

"Aye. The Thunderflux lost focus. Dartin' an' hoppin' about it was, until it were startin' timestorms all over the planet. Those that remained were forced to cap it, workin' up there at the top o' the island while that rain continued to pour." Brundle sighed, as if lost in a distant memory. "A lot o' good people were lost that day, to the void and to the spawn."

"Jerry, I'm sorry –"

"When it was over, the Expanse was severed for ever. But in the chaos, the Thunderflux severed the Hel'ss Spawn from its parent, too. The bastard's remained here ever since, like a great blanket o' deadly snot."

"That's why your hatches are sealed," Kali realised. "The Hel'ss Spawn comes on the island, doesn't it?"

"Every now and then. As if, after all these years, it's still tryin' to sniff out those the Hel'ss itself missed. Too stupid to realise they all died a long time ago."

Kali had stopped listening a second ago. "Brundle," she asked coldly, "is this one of those times?"

The dwarf sighed. "Aye."

"Oh gods," Kali said. "The people up there."

She burst away from the dwarf and climbed back to one of the hatches, starting to hack at its seal with her gutting knife. A second later the knife was pulled from her hand and tossed back down the shaft.

"Are you some kind o' bloody loony?" Brundle demanded.

"Nope. But you've finally confirmed to me that you are."

"*Do you want to die?*"

"I'd rather die saving my friends than hiding away down here, like you!"

Brundle roared and grabbed at her, and the two of them fell from the ladder and went the way of the knife, landing in a crumpled heap. Kali was the first up, fired by incandescent rage, and grabbed the dwarf by the throat, heaved him off the floor and pinned him against the wall. His legs dangled, unkicking and unresisting.

"That's quite some strength yer have there, smoothskin," Brundle gasped. "Quite the *legacy*, eh?"

"You bastard!" Kali shouted. "That's why you've been feeding me all this crap, the fish and the potted history of this arsehole of the world! You just wanted to save your own skin!"

"No, lass, not mine," Brundle croaked, shaking his head. "Because ah'm not just the caretaker o' this island, ah'm the caretaker o' you, too."

That took some of the wind out of Kali's sails. "What do you mean?"

"That strength o' yours – or any o' yer other abilities – they aren't yer only legacy. Ah told yer there's someone here yer need ta speak to. Who's left a message for yer, if you like. An' it's vital that yer live ta hear it."

"*Why?*"

"The reason this place is called the Island o' the Four an' why ah said welcome home. So yer can save the world, o' course."

Save the world, Kali thought. How many times had she heard that phrase? How many times had she tried? She was tired of jumping onto what she thought was the last stepping stone only to find another one in front of her.

"What's this little chat going to teach me, dwarf? Where to go next?"

"No, lass. This is the end of the line."

Kali felt an icy cold envelop her, and slowly released her grip. Brundle let out a sigh of relief and slid to the floor.

"I'm not having this 'chat' until I save my friends," Kali said.

"Smoothskin," Brundle said, "that's what I've been tryin' ta tell yer. There's nothin' yer could have done ta help, either the Faith or yer friends. The moment they set foot on this island, they were already dead."

CHAPTER ELEVEN

"Dead?" Kali repeated. "No, I refuse to believe they're dead."

"I'm sorry," Brundle replied. "By Ovilar, I should a' sunk that bloody boat in Gransk. At least then they'd have had a fighting chance."

"No, it's my fault."

"Yer mean for bringin' them here?" Brundle questioned. "Look, if it's any comfort, it wasn't your fault they were on the Black Ship. And if yer hadn't finished yer journey there'd soon be millions more souls followin' yer friends into the clouds. Trust me on *that* one."

Kali forced images of the Hel'ss Spawn consuming her friends from her mind, but, as she did, a thought nagged. She recalled her conversation with Redigor, when he'd *been* Redigor, a year before, in the Chapel of Screams. He'd known then what the Hel'ss was – how it had been responsible, however indirectly, for the death of his people, the last time it had come to Twilight. Though he hadn't been very forthcoming about the nature of the spaceborne entity, he'd clearly recognised the dangers it presented, and she was pretty sure he wouldn't expose himself to such danger – even if it was via its spawn – without some kind of plan. No, Redigor hadn't brought all these people all this way just to die. At least, not yet.

"Jerry, you said the Hel'ss Spawn invaded the island every now and then. Does that mean there's a way for you to know when?"

"Aye, me vertispys. Why?"

"Because I think you're wrong about what's gone on up there. I think they're alive. Take me to these vertispys."

Brundle sighed, but a glimmer of hope sparked in his eyes. He nodded and indicated Kali follow him. The pair moved towards a set of stone steps carved in the corner of the cave.

"Shall I carry on with my knitting, dear?" Brogma asked after them.

Brundle stared at her, and then at Kali, rubbing his beard thoughtfully. If there was the smallest chance that she was right…

"Aye, wife," he said. "An' it mightn't do any harm to get a bit of a move on."

Brogma nodded. And her needles clacked faster than ever before.

Kali and Brundle ascended the steps, which rose and wound through a small passage, one of many that Kali could see veering off in all directions, and she guessed that Brundle must have carved out a network of the things over the long years, granting him access to all parts of the subterrain. The passage they followed brought them to a small, round chamber in the centre of which was a device that looked, like everything else in the place, to have been built from the cannibalised parts of Brundle's wreckage. A pipe affair that dropped down out of the rock, it had a projecting, hooded eyepiece at its base and two handles made of sawn-off broomsticks jutting left and right, a means, it seemed, of rotating the pipe. The dwarf gripped the handles, leant into the eyepiece and began to turn in a slow circle. What he saw above made him mutter to himself.

"What do you see?" Kali asked.

"Boots."

"Do they still have feet in them?"

"Aye. Seems you were right, after all. I just don't understand why."

"Maybe a different vertispy'll give us a clue?"

Brundle nodded. "Come on."

The dwarf led her through passages again, to another pipe in another chamber. The angle of this vertispy offered him a view of the steps through the ancient ruins, and was much more revealing than the first. This time boots *and* their owners could be seen, enough of them to have been posted as sentries on almost every other step. Between them what Brundle estimated to be about a hundred of the prisoners from the ship were being force marched upwards. He turned the vertispy, backtracking along their route, and saw the remainder of the prisoners corralled and guarded on the small beach where the flutterbys had landed.

"They're bloody everywhere," Brundle growled. "But I'd have bet me left bollock they wouldn't have survived."

"Then that's a bollock you owe me," Kali said, then pulled a face. "On second thoughts, never mind."

Brundle frowned and was off again, this time bypassing a number of vertispys, heading for one high in his labyrinth. As he rotated the spy he muttered softly to himself before jolting to a halt, clearly having spotted something.

"Impossible," he growled. "They made it to Horizon Point."

"Horizon Point?"

"Strictly speaking, *Event* Horizon Point. But that's another story."

"It would be."

Kali determined the only way she was going to find out what was going on was to see for herself, and she shoved the dwarf out of the way. She saw the surface through a scratched and smudged lens half overgrown by vegetation. The view it offered was of the summit of the island, where, as seen from the scuttlebarge, the massive, observatory like dome was perched. She could see now that it wasn't an observatory at all, or at least had no opening to allow the projection of a cosmoscope, nor any sign of one even closed. The only detail she could make out on the convex structure was a deeply etched layer of flowing and complex runes that pulsed with raw power, and the mere sight of them made the hairs of her neck stand on end *and* sent a shiver down her spine. She guessed this was the 'cap' for the Thunderflux that Brundle had told her about.

Her attention was drawn by a flicker of activity to the right. Turning the vertispy, she saw what she guessed was Horizon Point itself, the great, thrusting clifftop she'd first seen from the scuttlebarge. Flanked by six shadowmages whose arms moved in a complex dance, presumably manipulating threads, a figure stood at the very edge of the clifftop, facing out to sea. The figure's arms were thrust out, as if trying to embrace the sky, and the flowing mane and black robes immediately identified it as Bastian Redigor.

"Do yer mind?" Jerragrim Brundle protested. "This is my bloody vertispy."

"Shush!" Kali chided him. "What the hells is he doing?"

"*I don't know.* Let me see."

"No."

"*You* are beginnin' to get on me tits."

"I get on most people's tits. Deal with it."

Brundle grumbled as the reason for Kali's dismissive response kept her glued to the spy. It was true that the dwarf obviously knew a great deal more about the Hel'ss Spawn than she did, but having heard what he'd told her about it she doubted even he'd seen it act this way. Rising from the sea far below were great patches of the viscous, milk-white substance they'd barely avoided in the swirlpools. Here, though, they had formed themselves into one semi-liquid mass that, if it resembled anything at all, looked like a jellyfish standing to attention. Any comic effect this might have engendered was, however, dispelled by the size of the thing. Towering far higher than the clifftop, and just as wide, it could have been some vast, organic cloud, and it made the silhouette of Redigor seem like that of an ant.

The Hel'ss Spawn swayed curiously, almost languorously, above him, blotting out the sky.

Its presence didn't seem to phase Redigor one bit.

The elf appeared to be trying to bargain with it.

"What's happenin'?" Brundle prompted.

Kali told him.

"Impossible. That thing's a lump o' sludge, driven by instinct alone. It doesn't bargain."

"Maybe that's how it's been all these years," Kali said. "But maybe now the Hel'ss itself is back, things are different."

"You mean he's using the spawn as some kind o' conduit ta talk wi' our friend up there? But why? What could he possibly want from it?"

"I think the more worrying question is what could he possibly *offer* it," Kali said. "Wait – something's happening."

Kali returned her full attention to the view of Horizon Point and saw that the prisoners Brundle had earlier observed on the steps had now reached the summit. They were being assembled by their guards on a patch of open ground that sloped up to the clifftop, each and every one of them staring about them in helpless confusion. Kali didn't like what she was seeing one bit, even less so when roughly a quarter of the group – Ronin Larson and Jurgen Pike among them – were separated from the others and force marched up the slope to stand behind Redigor. By the slight movements of his body, Kali could tell that the elf was once more speaking with the Hel'ss Spawn, but with his back turned she didn't have a clue what he was saying.

"Dammit," Kali snapped. "Brundle, can you get any sound on this thing?"

"Aye," Brundle said, reluctantly. "But if that is the Hel'ss Spawn up there, ah wouldn't like ta say what yer might hear."

He popped down a couple of earpieces, and Kali listened. Unfortunately, at the distance the vertispy sat, whatever there was to be heard was swept away by the wind that buffeted the promontory.

"No good," Kali said. "Can you turn it up?"

"Up? No. But ah can get closer."

"Closer?"

Kali heard the dwarf fiddling with more controls behind her back, and a second later something moved into view before the vertispy. It looked very much like an ear trumpet, and, trailing what appeared to be a hosepipe behind it, skittered towards Redigor on tiny, mechanical legs. Kali shook her head in the manner of someone who was seeing things, because as much as she applauded Brundle's inventiveness, there were some things that were just *too* weird.

The peculiar device did, though, do the trick.

"...and I bring these people before you as a foretaste of what is to come!" she heard Redigor announce. "The first of many I can bring to you in advance of your arrival. Think of it. Of the strength you'll gain. Of how much easier it will be to challenge the other!"

The other? Kali thought. Hadn't Redigor once called the Hel'ss 'the other'? If that was the case, did he now mean Kerberos? But what was he talking about – challenge?

"A whole Church – no, a whole religion!" Redigor went on. "The largest religion on this planet – the Final Faith! Hundreds of thousands of followers, all of whom once followed their Anointed Lord, but, through her, now follow me. Hundreds of thousands who have but a single mind – mine!"

Redigor's ego clearly hadn't diminished since he'd been chopped in half, Kali mused. But it wasn't the ego that was important here, was it? It was the position he was in. Now that he was, apparently, the power behind the throne of the Final Faith, it was just possible that he *could* influence the majority of the population of the peninsula, whether directly or indirectly, and through belief or through fear. The question was, why would he want to?

"They can follow you, too!" Redigor's rant continued. "Follow you, who, because of me, they believe to be the herald of your enemy! *Give* themselves to you, willingly, in the ritual they mistakenly call Ascension!"

Oh gods, Kali thought. Was that was this was about? Redigor up to his old tricks – some kind of exchange that would once again resurrect his psychopathic elven 'family', the Ur'Raney? But, no, that couldn't be, could it, because the souls of his people were with Kerberos. She'd seen them dragged back into its azure clouds kicking and screaming herself.

"And all I ask," Redigor requested, "is that I be remade as what I once was. That I walk this world in my own form once more. That I live!"

What? Kali thought. That's it? All this was about was Baz getting himself a makeover? One lousy, should-have-been-long-dead Ur'Raney pleading for the chance of a few more years of torture, incest and bloodletting? Why would an entity like the Hel'ss be interested in a bargain like that? And how – come to that – could it achieve it for him, even if it were?

Redigor's address to the Hel'ss Spawn seemed to be over for the moment, and Kali watched as the viscous behemoth swayed slightly before him, offering no sign of reaction at all. That's right, blobbo, she encouraged it, send him home with a flea in his would-be pointy ear. Of all the stupid, ridiculous...

The Hel'ss Spawn folded itself over Redigor and his shadowmages and – Kali could think of no other word for it – *licked* the group of prisoners assembled directly behind them. The lick stripped the flesh cleanly from their bones and twenty five or more skeletons stood there for a second before collapsing to the ground with a clattering sound that Kali thought she might remember forever. The last thing she saw was Redigor's shadowmage retinue gesticulating at the sky beyond the Hel'ss Spawn – where loomed the red sphere of the Hel'ss itself – and firing what she recognised as souls in its direction. Then she staggered back from the vertispy, collapsed against the cave wall and vomited.

"Oh, shite," Brundle said. "I thought it might come to this."

"It isn't what you think," Kali said, taking deep breaths. "This wasn't just the Hel'ss Spawn, it was the Hel'ss itself. It murdered them – murdered two of my friends. It's actually made a bargain with Redigor. Something about being strengthened, about a challenge, and about being able to *remake* him. Does than make sense to you?"

Brundle moved to the vertispy to see for himself. "Aye, it makes sense. All apart from *why* Redigor should want to be remade. Inta what?"

Kali laughed, a little bitterly. "Oh, I'm sorry, didn't I tell you? Redigor isn't what he seems. You might think you're looking at Prince Jakub Tremayne Freel of the Allantian Royal Family but one year ago he was possessed by Bastian Redigor, otherwise known as the Faith's First Enemy, the Pale Lord."

Brundle started. So violently that his head thudded into the hood above the eyepiece. He pretended it hadn't happened, though, and kept his grip firmly fixed to the vertispy's handles, his eyes steadfastly on the lens.

"Ah thought that name sounded familiar," he growled. "That elf's meddlin' in things he has no business being near."

"Brundle, we have to get the rest of my people out of there, before more of them die. What can we do?"

The dwarf disengaged himself from the vertispy, flipped up its handles and thrust the pipe back up into the ceiling.

"What we can do is get that bastard off me bloody island."

"Aren't you forgetting something? Redigor has a small army up there."

"Don't you worry, lass," Brundle replied. "The Missus'll take care of everything."

"The Missus?" Kali said in disbelief as Brundle led her at some speed back through the underground warren. "The Missus? What the hells is Brogma going to do? Stab them with knitting needles? Beat them with wet thrap? Or is it more than coincidence that thrap rhymes with crap?"

"Just wait and see, lass."

"No, Jerry, no. No, no, no," Kali persisted. "I finally find myself in the place that's meant to provide me with all the answers and what have I had since I've arrived? Riddles, half-truths, hints of mysterious chats with someone who as far as I know might be a figment of your imagination. So tell me now – how exactly is Brogma going to *take care of everything*?"

At that moment they re-entered the main cave. Brogma gave them a cheery wave with her needles. Brundle waved back but continued on through the cave, leading Kali into yet another series of tunnels on its other side.

"Brundle, answer me!"

The dwarf span to face her, beard jangling, all three nostrils flaring, face redder than any face she'd seen before. She took an involuntary step back.

"Have ye no respect for yer elders? By the farting denizens of Tapoon, what's happened to patience these days?"

"Patience? I've been waiting a year to find out what the pits is going on."

Brundle snorted. "A year? A whole year? Bah! Try waiting a few millennia."

"What are you talking about?"

"Let's just say that caretakin's a full time job, eh?"

"Wait a minute, wait a minute. When you told me the caretaker had been waiting for me since the day the Old Races died, I thought you were talking generally. I mean about the *role*."

"Well, in a way ah suppose ah was…"

"But now you're telling me you're the only one who's occupied that role?"

"Aye, that's what ah'm tellin' yer. An' yer know what's the worst about it? No farkin' bastard's ever presented me wi' so much as a carriage clock."

"I –"

"Now," Brundle barked, making her jump. "Will yer let me do me farking job?"

Brundle continued his march through the tunnels, Kali dogging him every inch of the way.

"I don't believe you," she said.

"What's not to believe? Yer met Tharnak at the Crucible didn't ye? He survived. And that pointy-eared bastard upstairs. Him as well."

"That's different."

"How is it different?" Brundle growled.

Kali shrugged as she moved. "Well, Tharnak was the result of experimentation by some of the greatest minds of the Old Races, and the Pale Lord is an ancient and powerful sorcerer with all of the dark threads at his command. You – well, you're just an obnoxious, little arsehole who moans and farts a lot."

"Hmph. Why don't yer tell me what yer *really* think of me?"

"Okay," Kali said, warming to the subject, "why don't –"

She stopped as Brundle entered a large chamber carved, as far as she could tell, at the far end of the subterranean labyrinth. The reason for her sudden cessation of hostilities was that in the few seconds in which Brundle had preceded her, he'd wasted no time in tugging another embarrassingly flowery dust-shrouded curtain from before a long recess carved into the chamber wall. The way he slapped the curtain to the ground and glared at her left Kali in no doubt that he was hoping – *really* hoping – that this would shut her up.

It did the trick. Kali stared open-mouthed at the number of dark shapes, ten of them, that were standing immobile in the shadows of the recess. Squat, humanoid shapes, though forged of metal, some of them missing parts of an arm or a leg, they were all similar in one startling respect. They all wore the face of Brogma.

"Hello, my beauties," Brundle said.

The figures were so old, so neglected, that Kali was sure Brundle didn't expect a response. But then she staggered back as a slight glow lit their eyes and, as one, the figures stamped a foot onto the ground in recognition of the dwarf's greeting. A heavy and metallic crunch brought a fall of dust from the ceiling.

"What the hells is this?" Kali said, stepping back some more.

"Don't you worry," Brundle said. "There's nothing to be afraid of."

"Nothing to be afraid of?" Kali repeated.

It was all right Brundle saying that, but what she had just witnessed had brought a pang of recognition and fear she thought she would never feel again. The shape of these things, the way they were constructed, their very *aura*. The last time she had seen monsters like these they were being left to rot in the floodwaters of Martak after she had put paid to their would-be resurrectionist, Konstantin Munch.

Smaller and squatter they might be, but in every other respect it was like looking at the army of the Clockwork King.

"The Brogmas won't hurt you, lass," Brundle insisted. "Come on, come closer."

Kali hesitated, then did as bade. She studied the Brogmas' faces – their identical faces – noting they seemed made of some flexible rubbery material. They were in varying states of decay, and if she had to hazard a guess she'd have said each of them had been stored here after being active at different times in the past.

They weren't the only Brogmas stored here either. Brundle whipped away coverings from further recesses all around. There were more

Brogmas in each; in some Brogmas who had all but rotted away. Kali wasn't sure whether to be shocked, disturbed or, when she saw how tenderly Brundle looked at them, deeply saddened.

"Smoothskin, ah'd like ta present wife thirty-three," he said, gesturing at one. And then, at others in no particular order or without any favouritism, "Wife nineteen, fifty one, three…"

"Jerry," Kali interrupted. "What have you done here?"

The dwarf wiped his beard, snagging his bells so that they were pulled up silently and then flopped back with a dull tinkle.

"Made meself some company, lass, what else."

"Company?" Kali said. She hated to refer in such a manner to the constructs which the dwarf regarded with obvious affection but she could see no other way. "But these things. They remind me of a place. A place I wished I never had to go."

"M'Ar'Tak," Brundle said. "It's where ah learned mah trade."

Kali stared at him, everything falling into place even as she struggled to accept it. The sheer number of Brogmas before her, like the deceased members of a family entombed for generation after generation, back to the start of their lineage. The tree trunk whose annotations, now she came to think about it, had all been written in the same hand. But most of all, Brundle's tale about the attack of the Hel'ss Spawn on the Thunderflux. It wasn't *as if* he'd been lost in memory, he *had* been lost in memory.

"My gods, you really have been here all the time. Jerry, how can you be so old?"

Brundle pulled back his shirt and rapped a fist on his chest. There was a metallic clang. "Mechanical ticker. Doesn't last for ever but every few hundred years Brogma gives it a service."

"You worked with Belatron," Kali said, still struggling with the implications. "Belatron the Butcher, the architect of the Clockwork King."

"Aye. But don't you worry. It didn't take me long to work out what a psycho he was. Upped and left wi' me tools, wandered the world and eventually ended up here."

"But you were there when – ?"

"The Ur'Raney drove the dwarves into the sea? Aye, ah was. Which is why you'll forgive me for me temper. This has become a wee bit personal."

"Jerry," Kali asked cautiously, "was there ever a wife number one? Was Brogma ever… real?"

The dwarf's eyes lowered, and when he spoke it was softly, fondly. "Aye, she was real. So many thousands o' years ago that I've lost count, she was real." The dwarf sniffed; a strange sound through three nostrils. "The old girl lasted almost seven hundred years, not a bad age fer one o' our kind, not a bad age at all. Didn't want to leave me on me own, ya see?"

"I'm sorry."

"Smoothskin, it were so long ago they could 'ave named a geological age after it. Besides, she went in her sleep. Never knew a thing. No chance ta worry about me wakin' up alone."

"That's good. Is she... buried on the island?"

"What? And let the Hel'ss Spawn have her bones? No chance. No, lass, ah took Brogma to the mainland and our clan's burial grounds 'neath what yer now call Freiport. She lies there still."

"I've never found that site," Kali said. "I'll make sure I never do."

"I thank ye."

Kali let Brundle's response hang in the air, unsure of what more, if anything, there was to say, but as it happened she was spared the problem. The mention of the Hel'ss Spawn seemed to have galvanised the dwarf back into his old self, and his mind seemed focused on his task once more.

At least she thought so.

"Wife!" he shouted. "Have yer finished that knitting yet?"

"Yes, dearest!" came the echoing reply.

"Then what are ye waitin' for? Bring it through."

"Coming, dear."

Kali said nothing, merely waited while Brogma waddled into the cave with the armful of wiring she had been working on all the while. Kali wasn't sure what to expect – an overly baggy jumper, a scarf, some baby bootees? – but it certainly wasn't the tangle of wiring that looked to her exactly the same as it had when she'd first begun. She frowned as Brundle took it and then shooed his wife away. Brogma returned to the main cave without protest. Of course she did.

"Brundle?" Kali said.

"Ah had the wife start knittin' before ah left for the mainland," he said. "Just in case ah was compromised and that bloody Black Ship got here after all. Should o' been ready but me old darlin' isn't as fast as she was."

"She isn't?" Kali asked, remembering the blur.

"Nah. Which is why ah told her to hurry up, on the slim chance that you were right. About yer know, up top."

"Jerry, what the hells are you talking about?"

"Oh, this is beautiful work," the dwarf said, ignoring her. He picked at and examined the wiring as he might fine filigree. Then he started to pull chunks of it away, opening the chest plates of each of the Brogmas as he did, and stuffing the handfuls inside. That done, he started to finger each bit of wiring individually, delicately, and, in turn, each Brogma started to exhibit further signs of life, the rotation of an arm here, the bend of a leg there, the sudden turn of a head followed by a wink in the dwarf's direction.

Kali watched as he worked.

"Jerry, I don't understand. Belatron's clockwork warriors were part organic but these aren't. They look like his army but they're not. I've never come across this kind of technology before, even at the Crucible, where they were building spaceships, for fark's sake."

"Interestin', isn't it?" Brundle said as he continued to tinker. "Scraps that washed up a long, long time ago. The remains of... well, to be honest wi' ye, ah don't know what, but ah know they had silver eyes and must 'ave walked this world long before I did. Took me centuries ta work out their ins an' outs an' what went where's but, when ah did, ah was able to build the Brogmas without the need for any poor sod's brains bein' scraped off some battlefield. Brogma – the latest Brogma, that is – is a mistress of knittin' some o' the more advanced functions together."

"More advanced functions?"

"See, when ah first built the Brogmas, they weren't just for company but designed for defence, too. Defence o' the island. Trouble was, they sat here for thousands o years wi' nothin' to defend against, an' started gettin' trigger happy. The day one o' them almost blew me brains out when all ah'd asked for was a light for me pipe was the day ah decided to strip them o' their sentry circuits." The dwarf sighed and stepped back from the Brogmas, closing their chest plates. "Well, now, here they are, restored to what they should be."

Kali stared at the Brogmas. They looked exactly the same.

"Nothing's happening."

"Battle stations, girls," Brundle said. "We've got an elven arse ta kick."

"Yes, dear," said ten Brogmas in unison.

The Brogmas stood to attention and Kali watched in amazement as their forms expanded, arms thickened and legs extended, so that each Brogma was now as tall as she was. They didn't just grow either, they sprouted – small hatches and panels sliding or flipping open on their forearms and their thighs, on their chests and in their torsos, each cavity whirring and clicking as it unleashed a weapon of some description or another, designed to operate independently or in the construct's hands. Blades, hammers, axes, small, star-like discs designed to be fired, morning stars and flails, each of Brundle's wives became in an instant a one woman arsenal. Simultaneously, they all span full circle at the waist, and as the weapons sliced the air or were beaten on their open palms with the rhythm of a war drum, their eyes flared with power.

"Oh," Kali said, numbly. "Oh, that is so cool."

"Aye," Brundle said proudly. "Now, are we goin' to take back Trass Kattra, or what?"

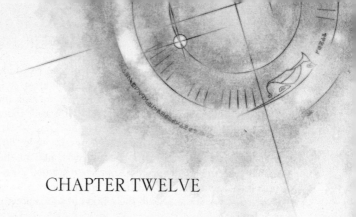

CHAPTER TWELVE

BRUNDLE HAD INFORMED Kali of all the exits onto the surface, and she chose the lowest, the one closest to the beach where the flutterbys had landed, from which to begin the assault on Redigor. The dwarf had left the planning to her, and the first thing she had decided was to send him in alone.

What might have seemed counter-productive folly – a lone figure emerging at the furthest point from their target – was, she'd decided, the best route to success. Because as she'd seen through the vertispys, Redigor had proven himself quite the tactician, doubtless a throwback to his days of being Lord of the Ur'Raney, where he would have led his forces into many a bloody battle. Deploying his sentries in positions perfectly calculated to offer uninterrupted and mutually supported surveillance across the island, he had the place sewn up tight. Each sentry kept an eye on not only his territory but two or more sentries, depending on their position on the rocks, at the same time. The result of this was that there was no way through them and no way other than this one to emerge onto the surface without being observed. To try to take out any one sentry elsewhere would instantly alert the others.

She could, of course, have had Brundle deploy the Brogmas to take out *more* than one sentry, but as impressive as the mobile arsenals were, they were hardly built for stealth. The last thing she wanted was for Redigor's major force – the one on Horizon Point – to be prematurely alerted to their presence as that would likely result in the execution of the prisoners, either through the sword or being fed to the Hel'ss Spawn before their time. No, they had to make it up there while Redigor was still involved in his negotiations with the parasite. Negotiations that she suspected would end not only with the sacrifice of the prisoners but those guarding them as well. It was a pity she couldn't just tell them what a bastard Redigor could be.

No, the Brogmas would have their moment, but it wasn't yet. For the time being, it was Brundle's play.

The dwarf emerged from an unsealed hatch concealed in a tangled mess of scrub grass and washed up kelp, grumbling not only because of the effort it took to shrug the detritus from the long unused exit but that Kali had chosen him for the task. It wasn't that he didn't trust her damn fool plan – in fact, it was rather good – but, all things considered, he'd rather be where she was, preparing to do what she was going to do. Now *that* was the fun part, not this floprat like scrambling up out of the ground. But she'd wanted – *really, really wanted* – to do it, and who was he to argue? He was, after all, only the caretaker, while she... well, she'd find out soon enough what she was, wouldn't she?

Apart from being a bloody annoying little girl.

Brundle sighed and quietly lowered the hatch behind him, then pulled his Cloak of Many Contours fully about his body, shoulders and head. Had any eyes been watching at that moment the cloth might have transformed from its rank and basic dingy state into the semblance of wind-blown seaweed or perhaps a chunk of driftwood that rolled in the tide. But a second later, when Brundle actually stepped out from the small lee in the seashore and into the view of actual eyes, it, and he, resembled a berobed member of the Final Faith.

The sentry standing on the shore above started slightly but Brundle simply nodded and strolled on by as if about his business, which seemed to put the man at ease. Beneath the hood of his cloak, the dwarf smiled. The first chink in Redigor's armour had just been exploited, and he suspected the sentry was more disturbed that he'd allowed what he perceived to be one of his comrades patrolling the beach to get so close without noticing, than anything else.

Brundle continued along the beach, passing the base of the path that led up into the ruins and towards the hostages that had been left behind under guard there. Nodding to the men who stood in a group watching over them – four, a number deemed sufficient not to have to be overlooked by other guards – he casually continued to their rear and then, producing the twin-bladed battleaxe he'd held under his cloak, swept the weapon around in a silent arc. Its sharpened edge cut cleanly through the necks of all four men and their heads bounced away into the tide.

"Now then," Brundle said. "Which one of you sorry looking bastards is Jengo Pim?"

Most of the prisoners watched their guards' bodies collapse onto the sand and up at the dwarf, shifting uneasily in their bonds. One, however, regarded him with steady, dark eyes and thrust himself unsteadily to his feet.

"I'm Pim."

"Well now, Mister Pim," Brundle explained as he released his chains, "your friend Miss Hooper has a message for ye..."

"She's alive?"

"Do I look like a clairvoyant?" Brundle snarled, and then realised he was still shrouded in his cloak. "Oh, sorry, maybe ah do." He shrugged the garment off and some of the prisoners gasped as for the first time in their lives they set eyes on a dwarf. A dwarf with what appeared to be a large trident stuck to his back. "Yes, she's alive, and very soon she's going to be kicking. That's where you come in..."

Brundle asked Pim's men to identify themselves and then moved to release their chains. The other prisoners he left as they were. The last thing he and Kali wanted was for a number of panicked civilians to be running around while there was a job to be done.

Brundle explained Kali's plan as he worked, and by the time the last of Pim's men was freed of his bonds, they and Pim himself knew their part in it. The leader of the Grey Brigade knelt in front of his people and gestured to each, then at the rocks above. Each man nodded, his instructions clear.

"Good luck," Brundle said, patting Pim on the back.

The group was about to move out when a figure appeared from behind the mass of one of the flutterbys. A tall, dark-haired, swarthy looking man with a peculiar x-shaped scar on his cheek, he had to be one of Redigor's men. But as Pim and his men froze, the stranger simply nodded to them. *Carry on.*

Nodding back, Pim and his men slid into the lee of the rocks, as silent as the shadows that swallowed them. Brundle, meanwhile, regarded the stranger.

"Whoever ye are," he said. "Jerragrim Brundle thanks yer. I've already enough blood ta clean from me blade."

He began to move off into the rocks himself but a question from his rear stopped him.

"Wait," the stranger said, pointing at the trident slung on the dwarf's back. "What *is* that?"

Brundle looked quite pleased to be asked.

"This, my friend is a transmitting aerial. A little something I call 'faraway control'."

"Faraway control?"

"A-ha."

The stranger frowned, none the wiser. In the rocks above, so did Pim. Why was it, he reflected that any encounter with Kali Hooper seemed to bring out the weirdest in people – or, to be honest, just the weirdest *of* people. He quickly returned his mind to the task at hand, however, for in the few seconds he and his men had been moving, they had already come close to the first of the guards on the steps. Hooper wanted he and his friends removed from their positions silently and, more importantly, simultaneously, and Pim watched as one of his men peeled off from the group, melting into the shadows behind him. More men peeled off the higher they climbed, concealing themselves directly behind the guard that Pim had allocated to them, and Pim, having reserved the highest of the guards for himself, continued on alone. The Grey Brigade's leader seemed not to exist at all as he used the patches of darkness on the rugged landscape to his advantage, darting from one to the other with the silent surety of a man who had spent a lifetime being where he was not meant to be. Without generating the merest amount of suspicion from the guards he passed between, he took his own place and waited for the rest of Kali's plan to unfold.

You'll know when to make your move, the dwarf had told him. This presumably meant that Hooper was going to give some kind of signal, but what form the signal would take he hadn't a clue.

Pim therefore waited, as still as a statue, watching the guard above him shifting slightly as he tried to make himself comfortable on his watch. All was silent other than for the crashing of the waves on the shores of the island. There was nothing to hear that was out of the ordinary, nothing to see but rocks. Then, suddenly, Pim's keen hearing picked out a slight drone coming from the sea, like the buzzing of an insect, and when he looked in its direction he made out a small dark speck, heading towards the island. The guard heard the drone, too, and began scanning the water for the source of the sound. Pim found it, his gaze suddenly locking onto the dark speck, much closer now, its droning louder, and he tensed, ready to call out a warning to his comrades in arms.

That was it.

Pim unfolded himself from his crouched position so that he was standing directly behind his victim. His preferred method of despatching him would have been a clean blade across the throat, but as his weapons – along with those of his men – had been removed on the mainland he was forced to use an unarmed though no less effective technique.

Pim slid one hand onto the side of the guard's neck and another onto the side of his forehead, locking his head in place. At various positions below him, he knew, his men would have done exactly the same. And in the same moment that Pim snapped the guard's head sharply to the right, so too were snapped the heads of all of the guards lining the steps. As one they fell to the rocks below them, their necks broken.

Pim grinned and scooped up his victim's weapons.

Miss Hooper, he thought. *You're on.*

* * *

SOME QUARTER OF a league out to sea, having swung in on an accelerating course that had skirted the swirlpools and brought her into a trajectory heading directly for the island, Kali watched the distant shapes drop and gunned the scuttlebarge on which she rode. The machine kicked beneath her, far more violently than the last time she had ridden it thanks to the extra two engines that Brundle had installed. The controls of the device fought against her grip and her knuckles whitened as she struggled to keep the scuttlebarge on course, because she knew that the slightest deviation from her target would end in disaster.

That target loomed ever closer ahead of her; a section of hull that had been sheared away from the Black Ship to be slammed into the rocks of Trass Kattra, where it now rested, thrust up against the cliffs. What Kali knew she needed to do in order not to endanger the hostages was generate as much of an element of surprise as possible, and to that end the section of hull suited her needs perfectly.

She gunned the engines of the scuttlebarge until they began to smoke and whine in protest, and the dwarven machine slapped and bounced across the waves towards its destination.

Kali felt the scuttlebarge jerk violently and then tip sideways as it parted company with the sea and crashed down on the shattered section of Black Ship. Kali leaned hard in the opposite direction to maintain equilibrium, and while the engines no longer had anything to work against, the sheer momentum of the scuttlebarge propelled it up the hull, aided in its passage by the slithery accumulation of seaweed it gathered as it went. Sparks flying where it stripped away the growth, its own metal shearing away in chunks, the scuttlebarge reached the top of the hull and, looking like some airborne sea monster, took off. For the briefest of moments Kali caught sight of Brundle below her, the dwarf looking up and shaking his head in some envy, and then of Pim and his men, giving her the thumbs up, and the sense that her plan was coming together was reflected in her own long and drawn out cry.

"*Ohhhhhhh yeeeeaaaaahhhhh…*"

The fact that Kali cried out so loudly was no longer a matter of concern to her, for the fact was that the 'stealth' part of her plan was over. Considering the method of her arrival onto the island, it really couldn't be anything *but* over.

Rising higher and higher into the air, above the rocks that had formed Redigor's first line of defence, the airborne scuttlebarge and its trailing fronds of seaweed came into view of the soldiers the elf had left in charge of the prisoners. As it did, they gaped upwards to a man. It was exactly the reaction that Kali had wanted, for as long as they were gaping they would not be harming those she had come to liberate, who were doing a considerable amount of gaping themselves. Kali winked as, down below, she spotted the cheering forms of Red Deadnettle and Hetty Scrubb, the latter having become so excited that she was attempting to punch the air despite her chains, the action making her repeatedly fall to the ground.

Speaking of which, as memorable as Kali's arrival had been, what went up had to come down, and in that respect she had little control over what happened next.

The scuttlebarge's nose began to dip a second after it passed over the main group of soldiers and prisoners, and Kali saw she was heading directly for a ridge from which four more soldiers overlooked the rest of the group. Two of these ceased to be a problem the moment the nose of the dwarven machine slammed into them, and they departed their duties in an explosion of blood, while the third was sent fleeing in a desperate attempt to escape the spinning chunk of metal that broke away from the hull on impact. The last of the guards was the only one to offer a challenge, standing his ground with sword drawn, ready to knock Kali from her seat, but sadly he had failed to take the scuttlebarge's continuing momentum into account. Kali yanked the controls around so that the rear end of the scuttlebarge span in a half circle, and as the soldier yelled in protest, holding his sword uselessly to block its approach, the hull slammed him off the ridge to fall screaming onto the sharp rocks below.

That particular manoeuvre brought the nose of the scuttlebarge pointing down the slope of the ridge and, taking a deep breath, Kali bucked her body to send it on its way. The machine began to slide down the slope, picking up momentum again. The juddering, bucking mass of metal with its engines whining more than ever was clearly not an object to be in the path of, and soldiers threw themselves left and right as it came, some of them not quite in time. A trail of severed, twitching limbs and screaming victims left in her wake, Kali rode the scuttlebarge across the level of the plain until it finally slewed to a halt, where she leapt out to face the remainder of the soldiers in charge of the prisoners.

They stood before her in a line, twenty or so of them with weapons drawn, sneering at what they thought was a foregone conclusion. None of them seemed eager to make the first move, however, the woman in their midst quite clearly insane. Kali played to that belief, regarding them with determined upturned eyes and a smile of invitation to come try it on. And when at last they did begin to move in on her, it was already too late, because a solid mass of metal had risen between them.

Kali smiled as the Brogmas rose on the freight elevator that Brundle, visible on a nearby rock, had activated with his faraway control. The old mechanism, he had told her, had once serviced the Thunderflux, but, since its capping, had fallen into many centuries of disuse, a situation reflected in the fact that until now it had been totally invisible, buried beneath an overgrowth of grass.

The elevator was not the only thing the faraway control activated, however, and as Brundle fiddled with it once more, the Brogmas repeated the foot stomping, weapon twirling ritual which had so impressed Kali below. 'Impressed' was not a word that could be used to describe the reactions of the soldiers for whom they now performed on the other hand, because clearly there was one thing more off-putting than a solid mass of metal between they and their target, and that was a *moving* mass of metal between they and their target. Especially one moving in their direction.

One or two of the men ran away. A few more, who might have heard barrack room tales of the rout at Martak, which only the Anointed Lord herself had survived, froze in their tracks in much the way Kali had when she'd first seen the machines. The majority, however – if only because they were perhaps more fearful of what Redigor might do to them if they did not – raised their weapons to defend themselves.

Kali admired their guts.

No, really.

The soldiers which the Brogmas proceeded to go through like a hot knife through butter were not the only ones that had to be contended with, of course, and as soon as that battle had been joined a further phalanx of Redigor's troops poured down the slope. As if that were not enough, those soldiers who had been positioned on the ridges around the slopes roared to spur themselves on and then raced at Kali and the Brogmas from two directions, closing on them in a pincer movement.

Thankfully, Kali and the Brogmas no longer had to fight alone. Having activated his machines, Brundle himself waded in with his battleaxe, and one by one, up the top of the steps, brandishing the weapons they had acquired from the sentries, came Pim and the rest of the Grey Brigade. Pim directed a couple of his people to start releasing the prisoners from their chains, and then, with his other men behind him, raced into the furore.

The battle, as all battles do, soon degenerated from an initial, full on clash to a series of smaller skirmishes fought across the slope of Horizon Point. With the aid of the Brogmas especially, the tide soon began to turn their way, though Kali herself had a couple of close calls. The first came when she was bashed on the back of the head by the hilt of a sword and went down, stunned. The soldier responsible stood above her and was about to swing down the weapon's more lethal component when help arrived from an unexpected source.

Burrowing up through the ground, having made its way to the surface at last, the small sphere that Kali had released from the jack-in-the-box, shot straight up into the air before him and, taking advantage of his momentary distraction, Kali leapt up, grabbed and twisted the soldier's swordarm, and thrust the blade into his stomach. The soldier doubled over and fell, impaling himself further, and Kali rammed the point home by booting him up the behind.

The second close call came immediately afterwards. Kali was about to salute the small sphere as it sailed away into the sky, but with her hand half in the air noticed she'd been targeted by three bowmen who had come out of nowhere. Their weapons primed, their arrows aimed directly at her heart, there was no way even she could avoid them. Then, suddenly, all three flew backwards into the air, as if they themselves had been hit in the chest by arrows, and crashed away behind a ridge into oblivion. At first Kali thought Poul Sonpear had been released from his scrambling collar and had despatched her assailants with projectiles of his own summoning, but then she saw that one of Pim's people was still trying to free him from the restraint and there was no way he could have done what she had thought.

Strange.

Kali turned, wading back into battle, and found herself joining what was effectively an advancing line consisting of Pim and his men, Brundle, the Brogmas and herself. All of the separate skirmishes were over and all that was left was a retreating line of the survivors of Redigor's forces. Those that put up any resistance were swiftly taken care of by the whirring blades or swinging flails of the Brogmas, and those that didn't – or decided there and then that they really *shouldn't* – began to stumble away in shock. Brundle raised his axe to behead one in front of him but Kali stayed his hand. They'd surrendered; let them live.

Unfortunately, Redigor had other ideas. Whether as a demonstration of his dissatisfaction with these men or of his last line of defence, each of them transformed before Kali's eyes into a cloud of dust, the result of the crackling strands of energy fired from the clifftop by the Pale Lord's shadowmages. Redigor himself stood, as he had throughout the battle, with his back to them, still engaged in whatever business he was conducting through the Hel'ss Spawn, but it was clear that a part of him was still controlling the proceedings.

Proceedings that, one way or another, were about to come to an end.

The six shadowmages stood steadfast before Kali and the advancing party. Their balled fists crackled with an energy more powerful than she had ever seen. It arced between them, across their line, forming an ever intensifying curtain of blue. It made her brain hurt.

"This could be a problem," Brundle said.

The shadowmages flipped backwards, as if hit by arrows, disappearing over the cliff.

"Or not."

"What the hells?" Kali said. She looked behind her for the source of the attack. Nothing.

"Does it matter?" Brundle growled. "We have the bastard now."

"Not we," Kali said. "He's mine."

Brundle was about to protest when he saw Kali's expression. He turned and looked at the Brogmas, who were juddering on the spot, ready to advance.

"Stand down, girls," the dwarf sighed. "Everybody stand down."

Kali nodded and began to stride up the slope to Horizon Point where Redigor remained with his back to her. The higher she rose, the worse the wind became, and as her clothing slapped against her, she was forced to shout to get his attention.

"Hey, Big Ears!"

At last, Redigor did turn, and Kali saw that her description, although facetious, hadn't been far off the mark. For what had been occupying the Pale Lord all this time was clearly the Hel'ss Spawn's – or, more accurately, the Hel'ss – response to the sacrifices it had been offered earlier. Redigor had given it a little, and it, in turn, had given a little back. Jakub Freel didn't resemble Jakub Freel as much any more. The Pale Lord Kali knew and loved was on his way back.

The process, however, was far from complete. No doubt pending genocide. But if her plan worked, it would be nipped in the bud right now.

"Is there a problem, Miss Hooper?" Redigor asked.

"Yes, there's a problem, shithead. This island's my destiny, not yours. And I'll not have you destroying my world just because you don't have the sense to know when to die."

"Brave words, Miss Hooper. But can you back them up? All by yourself?"

"Ah, well," Kali said. "There's the thing. Because I'm not all by myself, am I?"

Kali hoped that Redigor would interpret that as meaning Brundle and the others who waited impotently down the slope, but in actual fact that wasn't what she meant at all. She'd gone up against Redigor before and had only survived the encounter because of Gabriella and the Engines, and in a straight confrontation she knew she had little chance now. No, what she was gambling on was what she had learned *during* that encounter in the Chapel of Screams, when Redigor had revealed a little of the nature of the Hel'ss. If she was right, it could not only be used to her advantage but might even, however fleetingly, bring the Hel'ss onto her side.

"Look at you, Redigor – you're struggling to survive every second, rotting, being eaten from within. Face it. You're coming apart at the seams."

"I will survive long enough."

"Really? Because you know what it is that's eating you alive? It isn't the fact you don't belong in a human body, it's the fact that the body is that of a good, brave and honest man. A strong man. One who's been fighting you every step of the way."

"It's been over a year, girl. Jakub Freel is gone."

"You want to place a bet on that?"

Kali raised her gaze, addressing Redigor no longer but the Hel'ss Spawn that loomed beyond them both like a giant cowl.

"I'm willing to bet," she went on, "that there's *too much* of Jakub Freel left in this form for your bargain with this elf to ever work. I'm willing to bet that contact with it will leave you tainted, corrupted, as rotten to the core as he is. Because that's *your* destiny this time around, isn't it? Not to eradicate the Old Races but humans? And how can you do that if you help one spark of humanity to remain alive, even in a different form?"

The Hel'ss Spawn hung there, silent.

"This hybrid… this *freak* isn't part of your natural order. The elves' time has passed and we, the humans, walk this world. Humans you have returned to destroy. Isn't there, then, no other choice but to destroy this man?"

Redigor laughed softly. "That is very clever but aren't you forgetting something, Miss Hooper? If the Hel'ss takes it upon itself to destroy me, then your friend dies too. And I'm sure you wouldn't want that to happen."

Kali's brow creased. "You're right. I wouldn't. If I could help it. But I can't help it. And neither can Jakub Freel."

She paused. This was the only part of her plan that was utterly out of her hands, and it depended very much on how good a judge of character she was.

"Isn't that right, Freel?"

Redigor laughed louder. "What are you trying to do? *Talk* to him? Do you have any idea how deeply he is suppressed? How far away I have sent him?"

"I *said*," Kali reiterated. "Isn't that right, Freel?"

"Really, Miss Hooper, this is just –"

Redigor stopped. His eyes lost focus and he staggered. He snapped a look at Kali – venomous, hateful – and then as his face twisted in an attempt to prevent it, a single word was forced out from between his lips.

"Yyyyyyeeeeeesssssss."

"Hello, Jakub," Kali said, smiling.

"No!" Redigor protested. Despite his vast age his voice sounded like that of a petulant child. "You will remain where you are!"

"What's the matter, elf? Is it that you just can't understand why someone might be willing to sacrifice themselves for a greater cause? You wouldn't, would you, seeing as how you buried yourself the last time this bastard came around. Buried yourself while the rest of your people died. You called yourself a Lord? Well, let me tell you something – a Lord is as much responsible for the welfare of his people as their rule."

"O-ho no, girl," Redigor spat, barely able to stand. The wind whipped at his clothing, making cracking sounds. "I know what you're doing. Trying to distract me while your friend reasserts himself. But it won't work. I've come too far, done so much, to be halted now."

"Yeah? Well then, why don't we ask Jakub once more. Freel, tell the man. Tell him that if it stops what's happening here, you're more than willing to die."

Redigor's gaze snapped around him, as if seeking some defence from what threatened him. But there was no defence from that which came from within. He doubled over, clutching himself,,and from his mouth came words once more unbidden by himself. This time they came through gritted teeth, even more forced, and all the more determined.

"Damn. Right."

"This... will... not... happen!" Redigor screamed. He span to face the still looming cowl of the Hel'ss Spawn. "This... human has been purged. He is nothing but an echo. You cannot touch me. I am *clean*."

The Hel'ss Spawn, though, had clearly decided otherwise, and as Redigor turned, it pulled back from the clifftop as if from something horribly disfigured and diseased. Redigor opened his arms to it, pleading, and over the watery roaring of the entity Kali even heard him beg. Words she never thought she would hear from the First Enemy of the Final Faith.

Please. God.

It was too late. Severed from the process, the alterations the Hel'ss Spawn had made to Freel's body were already starting to reverse, the exotic, aquiline cut of his face, the thinning out and elongation of his limbs, the shape of his ears. And as all of these features became more human looking once more, the dark shapes that had roved his body like living tattoos returned to again consume him. Weakened, Redigor collapsed to his knees, and then onto his hands, on all fours, like a dog.

His gaze moved slowly up to meet the looming Hel'ss Spawn, his body trembling with a mix of fear and rage.

Before him, the Hel'ss Spawn rose to its full height, and both Kali and Redigor knew what was coming next.

Redigor's whole body quaked.

"No!" he screamed. "I am Bastian Redigor of the Ur'Raney!"

Redigor's head drooped, and his back heaved in great, wracking breaths. When, a second later, he looked up again, he spoke with a different voice.

"NO! I AM JAKUB TREMAYNE FREEL, PRINCE OF ALLANTIA. I AM HUMAN!"

Kali swallowed as the Hel'ss Spawn darted down, as quick as a snake, enveloping him and lifting him from the ground in an unbreakable embrace. As Redigor/Freel thrashed helplessly in its grip, Kali saw some discolouration as it started to leech his soul, and Redigor/Freel began to scream.

It was a scream of the damned and Kali wanted so much to turn away, but couldn't. Freel had made the decision to sacrifice himself for the greater good and the least she could do was stay with him until the end. She steeled herself, therefore, as the Hel'ss Spawn continued to suck at its victim, contenting herself with the knowledge it would all be over very soon.

It was, though, taking *too long*. Longer to consume Redigor/Freel, and in a seemingly far more agonising way, than she had witnessed with any of the Hel'ss Spawn's earlier victims.

Something was wrong.

Kali's first instinct was to rush in, unable to allow herself to condemn Freel to this, but then she forced herself to stop.

What, she thought, if something wasn't wrong?

What if something was *right*?

That had to be it, she realised. What was causing this was exactly what she'd said. She'd called Redigor a hybrid, a freak who belonged in neither the old world or the new, and when it came down to it, that was exactly what the Hel'ss Spawn was, too. The Hel'ss had left this spawn behind during its *last* assault on Twilight, when it had come for the elves and the dwarves, and that imperative had somehow remained with it. In other words, it was following the natural order of things, taking Redigor's *elven* soul before it started to consume that of Freel the human.

Gods, if that were true, Kali thought, she could save Freel. But she didn't have much time. She had to time this exactly right.

There was only one question. Time *what* exactly right?

Kali realised that she hadn't a clue how she was going to get Freel out of this but, as usual, that didn't stop her. As Freel/Redigor continued to scream, the elf's essence continuing to be absorbed, she tensed, running every kind of scenario through her mind and coming up with nothing. But again, as usual, that didn't stop her. There was a moment – a fleeting moment – where the Hel'ss Spawn seemed to pause, perhaps sated by elf and ready to begin consuming the human, and in that moment Kali roared and ran right at it.

She grabbed Freel about the waist, tore his body from the Hel'ss Spawn and, with legs pumping, took the two of them over the edge of the cliff, into the vertiginous drop towards the sea.

With the wind slapping at Kali like wet sheets of cloth, a more than little confused Freel struggled in her grip as his elven features began to fade. This was good. What was bad was that they were both plummeting towards the tempestuous sea crashing onto the rocks below. It was not an ideal situation to be in, but got instantly worse. Even as the two fell, another raging sea – the liquid form of the Hel'ss Spawn – came at them from the top of the cliff, plunging downward with the hunger and determination of a predator that had momentarily mislaid its prey. The entity roared as it came, and with both it and the sea closing on them at an ever increasing rate, it was like being trapped between two deadly, vertical jaws.

Kali wasn't sure whether to be pleased or cheesed that Jakub Freel chose this particularly troubling moment to regain some awareness, staring at her in confusion.

"Kali Hooper?"

"All right, mate?"

The Allantian craned his neck, looking down, and then up, at the pursuing Hel'ss Spawn.

"Erm, we seem to be falling to our deaths while being chased by a... well, by a –"

"Yep," Kali said. "Trying to deal with it."

"I'm presuming that, as usual, you're making this up as you go along?"

"Yep. Sorry."

"Oh, please," Freel managed, attempting to be polite but unable to disguise a slight break in his voice, "don't be, don't be..."

Kali narrowed her eyes. "I'm thinking," she said, "that we could maybe separate and dive into those rock pools down there."

"Yes," Freel answered, totally unconvinced.

"Or perhaps angle our fall so that we glide – you know."

"Perhaps."

"Or –"

"We could pray?" Freel offered.

"That's the one."

There were mere moments before the two of them impacted with the water – and rocks – at the base of Horizon Point, and they spent a couple of them staring at the Hel'ss Spawn as it accelerated beyond their own rate of descent, threatening to catch up an instant before the impact came. As a choice between horrible ways to die, it was no choice at all, and both Kali and Freel closed their eyes. With the roaring of the Hel'ss Spawn and the crashing of the waves, neither of them heard the sharp, almost insect-like *zzzzzz* that played about them for a second before being replaced by a sound something like the lashing of twine.

They did, however, feel something wrap itself tightly about both of their bodies, and then snatch them up into the air. For a few seconds neither of them had a clue what was happening but then they were swinging across the cliff face, out of the way of the Hel'ss Spawn.

They watched as, like some great waterfall that had been severed from the river that fed it, the viscous mass plunged by them with a scream that sounded distinctly elven to impact with and dissipate into the sea.

CHAPTER THIRTEEN

KALI AND FREEL hung suspended for what seemed like an age, the line that bound them tightly together creaking loudly as it swung back and forth across the cliff face like a pendulum on an overwound clock. They might have been rescued from the Hel'ss but they were not out of danger yet. Twisting and turning on the end of the line, waves crashing beneath them, both Kali and Freel had to take it in turns to kick out to avoid being smashed into projecting parts of the rock, or to prevent the line becoming dangerously snared around them. On occasion their kicks sent them into an uncontrolled spin, one or the other of them colliding with or being dragged painfully across the rough rock face, and after a few such impacts both of them were beginning to wish that they hadn't been rescued at all.

Gradually, however, the creaking softened, the swinging became less pronounced, and they came to a stop. The two of them stared at each other – in the position they were in, having little choice – and after a second the line jerked, and they felt themselves being hauled up.

They rose in fits and starts, their combined weight clearly causing whomever or whatever was doing the hauling problems. The sheer height of Horizon Point meant that they had to wait a good half hour before they found out who or what that was, and in the end they heard it before they saw it.

A deep grumbling, lots of cursing, and a slight jangling of bells.

Kali grunted as they finally reached the clifftop and she grabbed onto solid ground, being helped up by Jerragrim Brundle. He did the same for Freel and then unwound the line from about both of them. The dwarf was breathing heavily, eyes bulging and his face inflamed.

"Thanks," Kali said.

"Ye can thank me by going on a diet," Brundle countered. "Startin' with that unfeasibly well-rounded arse of yours."

"I'm sorry?"

"The one sticking out of yer troozers."

"Hey!" Kali shouted, then looked behind her. Dammit, she must have caught her bodysuit on one of the rocks. Double dammit, why was it always her arse? She *had* to get that part of the suit reinforced.

Normally she would have flattened Brundle but what he had just achieved took the wind out of her sails. "I meant it," she said, "thanks."

"Aye, well, I only did the pullin'. The man yer've got ta thank for firin' ya yer lifeline is over there."

Kali looked to where Brundle's head inclined, and noticed another figure on the clifftop for the first time, reeling the wire that had saved them into a coil. The black-garbed figure with the scar on his face was familiar to her – and yet at the same time wasn't.

"Him again?" she whispered. "I saw him in Gransk, and on the ship..."

"If yer expectin' me to know who he is, ah haven't a clue," Brundle said. "All I know is he turned a blind-eye down by the flutterbys at the moment we needed it."

Kali nodded and, bidding Freel to stay where he was, walked over. Something about the stranger suggested that she should approach him alone. The dark-maned figure continued to patiently wind his wire but he eyed her warily from under lowered eyelids as she approached.

"I wanted to thank you," Kali said. "For what you –"

She stopped mid-phrase. The line fully wound now, the stranger was twisting himself around to place it in a quiver on his back, and as he did she caught the outline of a bow slung beside it. Partly hidden by his body before now, it was of design uniquely familiar to her. This wasn't just any longbow. There was only one longbow like it on the whole of the peninsula.

"Where did you get that?" Kali asked suspiciously.

"This?" the stranger queried. "Why do you ask?"

"Because it's called Suresight and it belongs to a friend of mine. A good friend."

"Really? Even one who deserted you?"

Kali felt surprise and a slight pull of anger, her mind flitting back to Scholten a year before. But Kali quashed the feeling, more concerned with how the stranger knew what he knew.

"I don't know what they were but I'm sure he had his reasons," she replied, tight-lipped. "What I *do* know is he wouldn't voluntarily relinquish ownership of that bow."

"He wouldn't. And he didn't."

Kali's hand lowered to her gutting knife, interpreting the words as a threat. "So I repeat – where did you get it?"

The stranger looked at her fully for the first time. A slight smile pulled at his lips and, though it was colder than she remembered,

Kali recognised it instantly. But more than that it was the eyes. She *knew* those eyes.

"Slowhand?" she breathed, in disbelief.

The archer regarded her steadily, as if reluctant to admit what she evidently knew, and his smile remained as cold as when it had formed.

"Hi, Hooper," he said. "How you doin'?"

"Ohhhhh, you know," Kali said tremulously.

Her mind was spinning, not just with the impossible reappearance of her ex but his look, attitude, the fact that after vanishing from her life without so much as a by-your-leave he could be here, standing in front of her at all.

"It was you – you who killed the archers and the shadowmages. I should have guessed. Killiam, what the hells are you *doing* here?"

"Long story," the archer said, and, the line stashed, began to move away across the cliff. As he did, he nodded to Freel who, having overhead the exchange, nodded numbly back.

Kali wasn't going to have Slowhand abandon her in the same way he had in Scholten, and she trod heavily after him, grabbing him by the shoulder.

"Where do you think you're going?"

The archer span. "Why don't you tell me where I'm going?" he barked. "After all, I can't seem to make a move without you. A *successful* move, that is."

"What the hells are you talking about?"

"Like I said, long story."

"I'm listening."

"Nothing to hear."

Kali's grip tightened. Her eyes narrowed as she spoke.

"You've changed," she said. "And I don't just mean physically. Something's happened."

"*It's personal.*"

"What, and the fact that I've spent a third of my life with you, sleeping with you, saving your life and you saving mine, going through all kinds of shit together, means you don't know me well enough to tell me something personal?"

"There was a girl, okay!" Slowhand barked. "More than a girl."

"So what else is new? *And*?"

"She died."

Kali felt herself reel, but said nothing.

"She died, Kal," Slowhand repeated, after a moment. The way he spoke suggested a return to their old familiarity and the break in his voice suggested he did want to talk about it, after all. "Her name was Shay and she died because of me."

Kali stared at her ex-lover, gaze flickering, and then slowly, hesitantly, put her arms about him and pulled him to her. "Tell me," she whispered in his ear.

Slowhand did. About the carnival, about Shay, about the attack and about Fitch.

"FITCH," HE GASPED, lying there.

"Fitch," the psychic manipulator had repeated in that strange, high-pitched voice. It was as if he'd had his voicebox transplanted by that of a child's, or perhaps a bird's. "Querilous Fitch. Abandoned Fitch. Dead Fitch." He'd cocked his head to the side. "Or would have been had that master of destiny, Killiam Slowhand, had his way."

He – Slowhand – had thought back to their last meeting, a year before, in the Sardenne, when their roles had been reversed. The psychic manipulator, smashed and broken by the juggenath, had lain helpless beneath him, more so when he had rammed one of his arrows cleanly through the bastard, impaling him to the ground.

"Looking good," he'd said, trying to disguise the fact his throat was so dry.

"Flatterer." Fitch took a breath and the bladders deflated like tiny lungs. Briny liquid bubbled and popped from the tops of tubes. "Not a pretty sight, am I? Unfit for the eyes of women or children. It's really quite remarkable how much damage the body can take and yet not die. In my case, as in your's, the damage was extensive – bones shattered, internal organs crushed – and were it not for the sheer power of my will I would be one more pile of crumbling bones whose flesh had succumbed to the many dangers of the Sardenne." The psychic manipulator almost giggled. "I thank you, by the way, for the arrow you... left with me. It gave me the means to defend myself while my mind effected sufficient repairs to drag myself to safety."

"Willpower can achieve remarkable things, I'm told," Slowhand answered through gritted teeth. "You know, I once stopped – well, *dating* for a week."

"I'm not talking about willpower, you fool. If it were simple willpower, stand up!"

"*You know I can't.*"

"I can help you do so."

"How and why in the hells would you do that?"

"The abilities I began to hone in the Sardenne were, sadly, not enough to repair myself. But have since become as precise as a surgeon's tools. I can restore you to what you were."

He swallowed. "That's the how. What about the why?"

"Because I need your help. Against the Final Faith."

"Excuse me?"

"I realise how that must surprise you, but much has changed within its ranks. When at last I returned from the Sardenne, I found – how do you say – a cuckoo in the nest?"

"The biggest thing that's cuckoo in that nest is you, you sadistic bastard."

"I enjoyed my work, I do not deny it. But ceased to enjoy it when I found the whole reason for it was being subverted at the highest level."

"Subverted? By Makennon?"

"Not Makennon. The Anointed Lord no longer holds primacy over our Church. Instead, it is in the hands of one who would make a dark covenant with the Hel'ss."

Fitch told him, then, what Kali and he had, by now, learned of Redigor's duplicity, and his mind whirled as he worked out the identity of the only member of the Faith in a position to do what had been done.

"Freel?" he'd said disbelievingly.

"Your friend is no more. The wheel of destiny has turned."

"Oh, there's a wheel, now," he said with some exasperation. "Newsflash, Fitch. I turned my back on that life for this one because that whole 'destiny' thing left me with no choice."

"Look around you, archer," Fitch said matter-of-factly. "This life is ended."

His gaze moved across the Big Top, settled on the pathetically slumped body of Shay. Her eyes were staring right at him, but instead of the support and comfort they once offered, they were not seeing him at all.

"And do you know why this life has ended?" Fitch continued. "Because of the choice you made. Because of that choice, your little sweetheart over there died. The simple truth is all our destinies are linked. Because of you she was *destined* to die…"

Whether Fitch's was deliberately provoking him or not, he'd roared. But it was the roar of a declawed beast, and all he was able to do was writhe impotently on the ground.

"… and because of you *I* was destined to live."

For a moment, he didn't realise what Fitch had meant. And then –

"The arrow," he breathed, and laughed with the sick realisation.

"The arrow."

He lay there in silence, his breathing becoming shallower, until Fitch spoke again.

"Kali Hooper is once more in pursuit of the Pale Lord," he said. "Will you help her?"

"Hooper doesn't need my help. She'll survive. She always does."

"Perhaps not this time. And if she falls, someone will need to take her place."

He laughed again. "What are you trying to put over on me, Fitch? That I could step into her shoes? That in all this talk of 'the Four' someone got their sums wrong and I am, in fact, 'the fifth'? Moolshit."

Fitch smiled. "I admire your pretensions, but sadly you will always be a supporting player – one of many, whether they know it or not. No, what I attempt to suggest is that if Miss Hooper falls, *I* will need you as my eyes and ears if *I* am to defeat the Pale Lord."

"Why this sudden interest in everyone's welfare? I thought the whole point of the Filth was to coerce them into surrendering their existence to Kerberos in some kind of... rupture."

"The word is *rapture*, archer. And so it is. Not to be taken by the Hel'ss."

"The way I see it one big blob in the sky is much the same as another."

"Then you couldn't be more wrong. Kerberos is our God, our Lord of All, not the Hel'ss. It is with *his* power that the future of this world lies."

"Like I said, moolshit. Fundamentalist moolshit."

"Do you want to stay here and die? Or do you want to find out? Make a *choice*, archer. Choose your *destiny*."

He stared up at Fitch with vision that was already beginning to fade. He was dying, there was no doubt about that, so there was nothing to lose. For Shay, he might even be able to find out what wasn't letting him go. Sometimes, he guessed, being in league with the devils was better than being in league with nothing at all.

"This is all some kind of game to you, isn't it? But I'll play. What do you want me to do?"

"Stay close to Kali Hooper, for wherever she is, Bastian Redigor will be close by."

He swallowed. "Do what you have to do."

And so Fitch began. To restore him. But also to change him. It made sense when, later, he saw in a mirror a different body, a different face looking back. After all, if he was to be Fitch's eyes and ears, it wouldn't have done to be recognised by the Pale Lord.

Yes, it had made sense. But it hadn't stopped the screaming.

"It had to hurt," Kali agreed. "But not as much as... oh, gods, 'Liam, I'm sorry. So very, very sorry."

"I know. But, hey, at least the bad guy is dead."

Kali nodded. "That's what bothers me. What are you supposed to do now? Report to Fitch? How? Where? What exactly is it that he wants out of all this?"

"Your guess is as good as mine, better, probably," Slowhand said. "But in the meantime, I guess there are other things to think about." He pointed down the slope of Horizon Point, to where Redigor had corralled his hostages. There, among the stilled forms of the Brogmas, Jengo Pim and his men were liberating them all from their chains and, as Kali walked down, three figures emerged from the crowd. Hetty Scrubb and Pete Two-Ties were overjoyed to see her but it was Red Deadnettle who physically demonstrated how much, scooping Kali into his arms and giving her a bearhug that almost made her projectile vomit her thrap. As it was, as she felt herself being squeezed tighter and tighter, she couldn't help letting out a prolonged fishy burp.

"Oops," she said. "Sorry."

"No me," Red said. "Me sorry."

"How you doing, Red?" Kali said as she was plonked back on the ground. "You all right? Hetty? Pete? You?"

"We have been prisoners of *kunto*, but have survived, Kalee," Hetty declared, somewhat fierily. "We are all fine."

"Apart from," Pete Two-Ties said, "'door also a woman', eight letters."

Kali nodded. Much as she loved the others, Dolorosa had been the one foremost in her mind, and she moved through the crowd to her. The old woman was on her stretcher at the heart of the group, being tended by Martha DeZantez. Gabriella's mother mopped her brow with a torn piece of skirt while Dolorosa herself stared at the sky, wincing as she did.

"How is she?" Kali asked quietly, squatting down.

"Her infection has spread," the archivist said. "In a wound this serious, she should be dead. Tough old girl."

"Eet issa nothing," Dolorosa mumbled unexpectedly. "Randy Cromwell Quaid once hadda me impaled witha his throbbing sabre."

Martha reddened and coughed embarrassedly.

"No-a, wait," Dolorosa said, only half there, "it wassa the *Robbing Sabre*."

"I'm sorry," Martha said. "She's delirious."

"No, she's not," Kali smiled, stroking Dolorosa's hair. "She used to be a pirate."

"*Did she*?" Martha said, impressed. In an effort to keep Dolorosa with them, she asked, "What was the name of your ship?"

Dolorosa sighed happily. "Eet wassa the *Fluffy Bunny*."

"That doesn't sound very... piratey."

"It was the *Run For Your Money*," Kali corrected.

"Better," Martha agreed.

Kali paused. "Has she mentioned her husband at all – Aldrededor?"

"Something about running away with a space sheep?"

"Right. That's not what it sounds like, either."

It was good to hear Aldrededor had evaded the Faith's clutches, but, wherever he and the *Tharnak* now were, she couldn't begin to guess how he must be feeling having left Dolorosa behind. Kali bit her lip. "Martha, is there anything you can do for her?"

The woman shook her head. "Keep her comfortable is all. I'm sorry, Kali."

Kali nodded, and stood. Mercifully, she had no time to reflect on her friend's mortal state, as Brundle barrelled up to her and dragged her towards the cliff.

"You should see this," he said. "Somethin's happenin'."

Kali joined the dwarf at the cliff edge, as did a number of others who'd spotted the same thing he had. Directly below was the spot where a portion of the Hel'ss Spawn with which Redigor had communicated had plummeted into the sea. It was still there, and still agitated, though not as agitated as the rest of its mass, farther out to sea. As they watched, it moved to reabsorb itself, but when it did its agitation seemed to be exacerbated, not calmed. A ripple effect headed inland and water began to crash against the cliffs in great spumes, some of it almost as high as the spot on which they all stood, catching them in its spray.

"Aw, shit," Brundle said. "Ah think there's a storm comin'."

"I'm guessing you don't mean a normal storm, right?" Slowhand queried.

The dwarf ground his teeth. "Nay, mah friend. Ah don't mean a normal storm."

"He's right," Kali said, pointing. "Take a look out there."

Everyone's gaze shifted offshore, towards the main body of the swirlpools, where the maws had begun to spin even more violently than before. Spumes had become plumes, and exploded into the air where the swirlpools clashed, and where they crashed back down again they rolled from the lips of the maelstroms in the form of huge, destructive waves. These, in turn, disrupted the swirlpools further, carrying them with them on their crest, raising them and tipping them so their normal rotation was stretched and skewed, and as a result they began to move through the waves erratically, unpredictably, more liquid tornados than the swirlpools they had been.

The deadly band that surrounded the island seemed to be going absolutely insane.

What was worse, it was heading directly for shore. Directly for them.

"You think we've pitsed it off?" Slowhand asked.

"No," Kali said, frowning. "I think something's wrong."

"Maybe Redigor stuck in its throat."

"Something more. There, where the Black Ship went down..."

There was no exact spot where the ship had sunk, of course, merely great swathes of water filled with its shattered wreckage. But wherever wreckage could be seen, so could something else. A glowing orange tint that was spreading through the swirlpools like a powerful dye.

"What is that?" Slowhand mused.

"The ship's amberglow reactors," Kali said. "They're disintegrating."

"Why would that affect the Hel'ss Spawn?"

"Gods know."

"Aye, well, we can play twenty questions later," Brundle growled. "Right now, we need to get these people underground."

Brundle was right. The deadly ring of the Hel'ss Spawn was already closing on the island and great splashes of it were pummelling its shores and cliffs, rising higher and encroaching more inland every second. A heavy and viscous orange rain started to splatter the steps and the ruins, and then the edges of Horizon Point itself, and wherever the rain fell chaos was the result. Ground fleetingly became fog-like or gaseous, or as solid as stone, flickering through all the colours of the spectrum and more before liquefying before their eyes. The shapes of boulders changed, spherical one second, square and spear-like the next, taking on the textures of glass or wood or sponge and ultimately nothing at all. Some of the upper buildings of the ruins folded and bent on their foundations, as if viewed through a funhouse mirror, as flexible as rubber one moment, fragile as paper another, before the stresses they suffered made them, too, lose their solid state and drain slowly away.

It was a mind-boggling vista, a nightmare landscape, as if the Hel'ss Spawn was trying, but failing, to find a form that it could maintain, as if this might rid it of whatever poison it seemed to have absorbed. No one wanted to imagine what would happen if it touched a human, and it galvanised them all into action.

"You two," Pim ordered two of his men, "take charge of the old woman's stretcher."

"Be gentle," Kali said. "Slowhand?"

"Already on it," the archer said.

He was moving through the crowd, ushering those too stunned to act for themselves towards the hatches to Brundle's underground warren. The dwarf himself was darting around, using his axe to unseal others, ensuring there were as many routes to safety as possible. Sonpear, Red and even Abra helped but, even so, it was a slow process, each hatch able to take only one refugee at a time, the age or health of some making it a frustratingly arduous descent.

Inevitably, there were casualties, first the stilled Brogmas – whose armour to some degree resisted the rain but smoked and sparked nonetheless, shifting out of shape until they slumped – and then the humans. The orange downpour, soaked a group of three and for a second they became one; a horrible, flailing blur of misshapen limbs, and then all that was left was the fading echo of their agonised cries. Another man stumbled as he tried to take a short cut across some rocks, and the rain caught him mid-fall, and when he hit the ground he burst like a water balloon. Yet another, a woman, stood frozen to the spot, staring at the heavens and screaming with mouth open wide, but the scream soon turned to a gurgle as her mouth erupted with her liquefied insides, coating and disintegrating her from the outside in.

Kali spotted two people towards the edge of Horizon Point, cut off from safety by a river of orange ooze. She moved to help them but found herself forcibly held back by Brundle. The two of them struggled at arm's length, the wind whipping at their hair.

"No," the dwarf shouted. "Let someone else help."

"They're going to die!"

"*Everyone*'s going to die unless you do what this island's waited for you to do."

"Which is?"

"Find out the truth. It's time for yer little chat."

"Fark it, dwarf, this *isn't* the time. Not for more of your riddles. The truth about what?"

Brundle's free arm pointed at the Hel'ss Spawn, at the Hel'ss itself, at Kerberos. "About that, and that, and that." He pulled her towards him, as if they were engaged in some strange dance, then growled in her face. "The truth about *everything*, of course."

Kali stared at him hopelessly, unable to break free, sensing somehow she *shouldn't* break free, that what Brundle insisted upon was indeed what she needed to do. Her dilemma was alleviated somewhat as Slowhand half ran, half hopped by, slapping her reassuringly on the shoulder as he headed towards the stranded pair.

"Look around ye, lass," Brundle growled. It wasn't just Horizon Point that was taking a battering from the Hel'ss Spawn but all of the island, and everywhere the disruption caused by the spawn's instability was manifesting secondary, natural effects. The island trembled, scrub and rock tumbled from its edges into the sea, and here and there sudden cracks of varying widths sundered the ground, generating clouds of dust that were starting to stifle the surface in a smoking fug. "This is lookin' to be the worst batterin' Trass Kattra's ever taken," the dwarf said. "Maybe even worse than the day the Hel'ss arrived."

"So? You said we could survive it."

"Not the problem. In case yer hadn't noticed, this entire island is riddled wi' caves, many o' me own makin' but not all. Some are safe enough but others are ancient and ain't seen shorin' for a god's age. If they go, there's a good chance the Thunderflux'll go wi' them."

Kali stared up at the huge dome, which was trembling like the rest of the island. Brundle's fears seemed justified as the glow that was emanating from its covering of runes seemed slightly diffused, as if their integrity were breaking down. One particular patch of its convex surface was already spewing a thin beam of brilliant blue light into the sky.

"What does the Thunderflux have to do with this?"

"It's where yer have to go. For yer little chat."

"It is?"

"Aye. And *now*, lass."

Kali swallowed and gazed across Horizon Point, saw the last few of the refugees vanishing through the hatches, and that Slowhand had managed to rescue those she'd intended to herself. She caught the archer's eye as he passed, supporting one in each arm, and pointed up towards the dome. Kali smiled as Slowhand – bless him – nodded in acceptance, without even knowing what was going on. Neither did she, really, but she'd missed him because of that. He didn't need to know. He was just always there.

"Fine," she said to Brundle, starting to march up the hill. "Let's go."

"Wrong way, smoothskin," the dwarf said. "The way we're headin' is down."

"Down?"

"There's no way into the Thunderflux through the cap, that's why it's a cap," Brundle said. He turned and strode urgently down the steps through the ruins, dodging the rain that continued to fall. Kali followed, instinctively but rather redundantly shielding her head with her hand, knowing all the time that if one splatter – or worse – hit it, the hand might as well not be there at all. There were a couple of close calls – Brundle cursing and ripping off a piece of his leather armour that dissolved even as it was thrown; Kali gasping as a stray spot blistered her cheek, but which her regenerative abilities seemed to keep under control – but at last they made it to cover. It was there, in the interior of a ruin whose floor had remained intact and which had steps leading down, that Brundle continued the conversation of some minutes before.

"And o' course," he said, with some hesitation, "first yer have ta go through yer trial."

Kali stopped dead. "Come again? Trial? What kind of trial?"

"Och, nothin' legal. Nothin' borin' like that. Just a trial of life and, er... death."

"Life and, er... death? Now I really am confused. You said that I was meant to be here on this island? That I have to have this chat? But you're going to try to *kill* me before I do?"

"Smoothskin, understand," Brundle said, unusually flustered. "What yer'll hear in the Thunderflux is not for anybody's ears. Addressed to the wrong person, it could cause mass panic, and ta a person wi' the sense to understand it, grant power they shouldna have. That elf of yours is a case in point."

"Redigor's dead, Brundle. All I see is that Trass Kattra – the world – is about to fall apart, and before I can stop it you want me to jump through *hoops*."

The dwarf scratched his beard. "Ah don't recall any hoops."

"You know what I mean, dammit!"

"Ah'm sorry, smoothskin. The secrets of Trass Kattra are just too valuable. Your trial – and the trials o' the other three, had one of 'em made it here before ye – are designed so only that member of the kattra has a chance o' gettin' through."

A *chance!* Kali was about to yell, but then bit her tongue. What Brundle was saying was only, after all, what Merrit Moon had said years before in the Warty Witch. A truism she'd taken on board and used as a code throughout her life. That Twilight just wasn't ready for some things. If the Thunderflux really did contain what Brundle said – the truth about everything – could she really blame him, or blame whoever was ultimately responsible for this trial, for protecting it this way?

"I'm the one who should be sorry," Kali said. "What do I need to do?"

"Just follow me," Brundle instructed.

Kali did. Down the steps in the floor of the ruin and into a new cave system. Down into shadow. The rumbles from above quietened as they descended, becoming almost inaudible by the time they came to a cobweb shrouded arch. Beyond it she sensed a larger chamber. She swallowed. The darkness within was total.

"Tell me one thing," she said to Brundle as he ripped the thick cobweb away. "If I make it through this trial, what can I expect on the other side – in the Thunderflux?"

For once the dwarf's response was simple and to the point.

"The past, smoothskin. The past."

CHAPTER FOURTEEN

BRUNDLE MOVED INTO the chamber, taking a flint from his pocket and striking it four times. A matching number of torches flared into life with a rush of sound like a sudden squall.

As their strange, greenish light revealed their surroundings, Kali saw that each torch lit an archway carved through the chamber wall ahead. Each archway, in turn, possessed a curving lintel of gold inscribed with a large, ornate, ancient looking symbol – a different one for each arch. From left to right, Kali saw what she first took to be a snake but then realised might represent a magical thread; then a pair of hands, palms pressed tightly together as if in prayer; then a rolling crest of a wave; and finally, a clenched fist. Clenched, Kali felt, not in anger but determination, rather in the way she'd been known to clench her own.

Hanging from the lintels was the accumulation of ages, great sheets of cobweb stirring in response to sighing breezes from beyond.

"Spooky," Kali said over the flutter of the torches. "So this is the start of the Trials, huh?"

"Aye, this is the start. Each o' these arches leads to a path built to challenge the abilities of one the Four, and be traversable only by them. The first is the Path of Magic, the path of Lucius Kane. The second, the Path of Faith, the path of Gabriella DeZantez. The third, the Path of Water, the path of Silus Morlader. And the fourth, the Path –"

"The Path of Confusion, right? The Path of Kali Hooper."

Brundle gave another of his strange looks.

"The Path of Endurance," he corrected.

The chamber shook slightly, the conditions on the surface clearly worsening. A skitter of dust fell from the roof.

"There isn't much time," Brundle said.

"Okay. But if there are four paths, shouldn't all four of us be here? I mean, if this 'truth' the paths lead to is so world-shattering, shouldn't we all be here to listen?"

"The Truth awaits all four, but not all four need to hear it. The first will pass the Truth to the others... to the world."

"Four known to us, Four unknown to each other," Kali countered. "Four who will be known to all."

"Is that meant to be some kind o' weird cod philosophy?"

Well, at least Brundle was in the dark about one thing, Kali thought.

"No. You just reminded me of something a fish once told me," she said mischievously. "But if I told you, I'd have to brill you."

"Hah!" Brundle laughed, appreciating, if not the bad pun, having the tables turned. But he wasn't going to let her get away with it. "I'm glad to hear you still have your sense of humour," he said, his face looming up at hers and darkening. "You'll need it."

Kali's face, too, darkened, but not in response to his comment.

"There are only three of us, now – you know that? Gabriella... she died."

"Did she?" Brundle said.

Without another word, the dwarf moved towards the entrance to the Path of Endurance, seemingly ready to usher Kali in.

"Wasting no time, I see?" Kali said, swallowing. "Is there anything I need to do?"

"There's an antechamber beyond the arch where you can pray if you wish, or bless yourself with holy water after removing your kit and clothes. 'Course, I don't expect you –"

"O-ho-ho, back up there, shorty," Kali broke in. "Naked? You want me to do this naked?"

"The Path tests you and your abilities, not the tools at your disposal," Brundle said. "But don't worry, smoothskin, ah promise ah won't peek."

"And how am I to know you haven't got more strategically placed vertispys in there?"

Brundle sighed. "Because ah'd be letchin' over summat so thin ah could use it to clean me ruddy pipe, is why. Ah'm a dwarf, and you ain't. Yer might as well accuse me of fancyin' a worgle."

"There are some who do."

"There are?"

"Sure," Kali said. "They meet in secret. In, er, furry costumes. And they, um, have this secret handshake. Well, not a handshake exactly as worgles don't have hands but they do this kind of wobbling thing with their..."

Jerragrim Brundle's eyes narrowed suspiciously. "Yer wouldn't by any chance be tryin' to delay goin' in there, would ye?"

Kali swallowed, caught out. "Why would I do that?"

"Ah don't know, but here's a stab in the dark. *Because yer might die*?"

Kali turned to face the arch. The fact was, she *was* trying to delay the start of the Trial, but not because of the danger. No, if she were honest with herself, after all her years of trying to solve the mystery of what happened to the Old Races, it was *that* she was afraid of. Finally learning the truth. Would it place more responsibility on her shoulders? Or take that responsibility away? What was she to do in either case, being at the centre of things or being out of it completely, her job done? It wasn't death but *survival* that she feared, the knowledge that whatever happened from here on in was going to change things – *change her* – for ever.

Right then, as she stared at the billowing curtain of cobweb draped from the symbol of the clenched fist, she would have given anything for Lucius Kane to be standing before his arch in her place. Let the shadowmage burden the responsibility, when she'd encountered him in Andon he'd seemed capable enough, after all. Or Silus Morlader. She didn't know the man but was aware of his supposed legacy and somehow this place – far out to sea and battered by the swirlies – seemed more appropriate to his skills. Even poor Gabriella, had she lived. Despite the doubts the Sword of Dawn had started to feel about the Church she had served all her life, surely her own admirably unshakable faith would have carried her through?

But none of them were standing here, were they? It was just her. Alone. And she could either stand here all day talking pits with the dwarf or get on with it.

"I'm ready," she said.

Brundle nodded and moved to the arch, slowly pulling away the thick cobweb. Taking a deep breath, Kali moved towards the shadows beyond.

"Smoothskin," Brundle said, placing a hand on her side as she passed, "if it's worth anythin' ah know yer can do this."

"Thanks, shorty."

"See you on the other side, eh?"

"'k."

Kali moved through the arch, and the world behind her was gone. Not gone physically but in her mind, subsumed by the feel of the chamber she found herself in.

It felt indescribably old and, despite the rumbles from above, indescribably lonely. The knowledge that this place had been created for her and her alone – that no one else had ever, *ever* set foot here and likely never would – weighed heavily on her mind. Kali examined its meagre contents; a stone trough of water and a stone bench, illuminated by what appeared to be glowing crystals in the walls, and then another cobwebbed arch which led out from the chamber opposite to the one by which she'd entered. Through there lay the Trial and whatever it had in store for her, and where in any other circumstances she would have ignored Brundle's instructions, tackled it under her own terms, here that somehow felt wrong. Here she suspected she should follow the rules to the letter.

Even if it was so farking cold.

She sighed and stripped off her bodysuit, folding it neatly and laying it on the bench. She stood over it for a second, shivering in the breeze that came from further within, allowing her naked body to acclimatise to the environment. She looked at the trough and wished that instead of blessed water it held a few gallons of thwack. That was the only spiritual aid she needed, right now, thank you very much.

Despite the temperature, she scooped up a handful of water and splashed her face and neck. She hissed but the cold liquid invigorated her and reinforced the reality of her situation. She took three deep breaths, then turned to the second arch.

She was ready.

She stepped through into the darkness.

Found the floor ceased to exist under her feet.

And fell.

Kali's yelp of surprise segued into a longer wail of alarm as she tumbled down a steep slope. Whatever she'd expected beyond the arch it wasn't to be wrong-footed from the word go, and in the seconds it took her to come to terms with her situation she repeatedly impacted hard with the walls of the passage as its curving descent bounced her down and down, left and right, deep into the bedrock of the island. Then her survival instincts kicked in and she flung out her arms in an attempt to halt her progress. For a few seconds her flesh grated against rushing rock but then the walls of the drop were no longer within her reach. Feeling only air on her palms, and then suddenly also beneath her, it didn't take much to work out the passage had ended and she was now in freefall in some kind of vertical shaft. Knowing the nature of this place, it wasn't likely there was going to be a cushion beneath her.

She flailed in the darkness, seeking a means to prevent her ending the Trial almost before it had started as a mass of shattered bones. Her hands closed on some kind of rope – ancient hemp but tarred, it felt, to preserve it – and with an organ jarring *oof* she halted her fall, bringing a shower of clattering stones and dust from far above. The respite was only momentary, however, as, while she swung there, she heard the metallic *klik-klak* of some kind of ratchet releasing itself as a result of her weight, and suddenly the rope was snaking heavily down about her and she was dropping once more. She flailed again, made contact with another rope, and the sound of another *klik-klak* made her heart thud.

Shit!

But part of her had already worked out what was going on. She leapt into dark space again, found another rope – *klik-klak* – and then another – *klik-klak* – each time falling further towards the base of the shaft, and with increasing speed. To her left and her right, throwing herself upwards and downwards amidst what she now knew to be a veritable forest of dangling deathtraps of different lengths, she moved from rope to rope all the time sensing the ever accelerating approach of whatever lay beneath her. Still shrouded in total darkness, she at last clutched a rope that seemed not to produce a response from a ratchet, and she hung there gasping, the ancient hemp creaking as she moved slowly on its end.

Klik-Klak.

Bastard!

Kali lunged, desperately, instinctively, and so violently that the next rope she grabbed onto swung wildly back and forth, crashing her against the walls of the shaft and sending her spinning in the opposite direction. This didn't exactly improve her mood but, after a few seconds one thing did.

It held. As it stilled, the rope held.

Her weight on it also seemed to activate some kind of mechanism, and to her right part of the blackness rumbled. A square of light – a doorway to another passage – appeared in the shaft's walls. As it did, it illuminated the area where she dangled. Directly beneath her Kali could now see the entire base of the shaft was rooted with spikes taller than she was, and though they were clearly as ancient as the ropes she was willing to bet they had lost none of their keenness. Kali flexed a foot, dipping the flesh off her big toe onto the tip of one of them, then snatched it away with a hiss as a bead of blood appeared.

Cliché, she thought, but couldn't help but admire the design of the trap that could so easily have left her impaled upon the spikes. Right from the second she'd stepped through the arch, the whole thing had been a test of reaction – the kind of reaction only she, as one of the Four, would possess. That this was, she suspected, only the start of what her Trial had in store for her, brought a summation of its designer's ingenuity that consisted of just one word.

"Twat."

Despite that, Kali did now feel advantaged. She had some measure of the Trial. And if the rest of it consisted of the same perverse, impossibly difficult challenges she had just faced, it might even be fun. With a grunt of determination she began to inch her way up the rope to draw level with the doorway, then swung, let go, and landed.

The passage she was in was lit by the same growths as in the preparation chamber, but the fact that she could now see where she was going did not make Kali any less cautious. Just as well, too, as a sudden grinding of ancient gears gave her a moment's notice of the crescent shaped blades that began to scythe rapidly across the passage before her, all along its length. The *vwoop, vwoop, vwoop* of the blades was constant, and though Kali had encountered similar deathtraps in other locations, this one differed in one vital respect. The gaps between the blades were unforgiving, no wider than she was, making the old run and stop, run and stop strategy impossible, and unless she wanted to lose the bits that Brundle had fondled in the bar in Gransk, or the arse he'd commented on at Horizon Point, she'd have to use a different technique.

The sudden rumbling of a wall behind her, closing the exit from the passage and moving forward to shunt her towards the blades, forced Kali to act without thought, and she crossed her arms tightly against her chest, sucked her stomach in, and began to pirouette through the blades.

She span and span and span again, with ever increasing acceleration, feeling stupidly dizzied but forcing herself to remain upright and straight as a dye while the blades scythed within a hair's breadth of her flesh, carrying away with them long streaks of her sweat. Every spin, every quarter second, brought with it the conviction she was about to be cleaved in two but amazingly, miraculously, she sensed suddenly that she was through. There was no relief, though, for the same acute senses that had served her so well over the years warned her this wasn't quite done yet, and Kali flung herself onto her back as a final blade swept *along* the passage, between those that had stopped after her passing, and sliced a thin red line from her groin to her sternum.

Like she'd said. Twat.

So it went. Kali fought her way on, besting such classics of the athletic archaeologist's trade as the punching walls, the stomping hammers and the bubbling lava pits of doom, each challenge perversely tweaked to deliver that extra pound of her flesh. She even half expected to come up against the revolving razor rabbit, though didn't, but that was probably because she'd only encountered that once, in the dark, and in truth had been very drunk at the time.

She at last emerged onto a narrow rock bridge spanning a vertiginous void and, before she proceeded, collapsed to her knees to take a breather. But the breather didn't last for long. Her first thought as the bridge beneath her began to rumble was that they were rolling out that old chestnut, the giant boulder, but then the ceiling began to rain debris and she realised she must be somewhere near the surface, where the death throes of the Hel'ss Spawn were continuing. Cracks started to appear in the bridge before her, and Kali picked herself up and ran, heading for the safety of another cave mouth with the symbol of her Path at its end. But before she could reach it a fall of rocks blocked her way through. Her Path of Endurance, it seemed, was at an end.

Or was it? As dust settled after the tremor, leaving the bridge intact if skewed, Kali looked into the void the bridge crossed and found it not to be a void at all.

The design of the Trials was cleverer than she'd thought, not in terms of the challenges they offered but the fact they also seemed to intersect each other, for below and, indeed, above her, she could make out cave entrances with the symbols of the Paths of Magic, Faith and Water – the latter a pool in the floor rather than an entrance – inscribed in their frames. Staging points, like this one of her own.

The solution was obvious. She could no longer continue on her own Path so would have to choose another. But which?

No choice, really. It seemed fitting that she took the one she felt closest to.

Gabriella's Path.

Not that it was easy jumping tracks. With a series of grunts, Kali threw herself from the bridge and managed, precariously, to gain a hand and foothold on the cavern wall. From there she began to inch her way upward, almost losing her grip more than once, but at last found herself in a position just below the lip of the entrance inscribed with the symbol of the praying hands. She flipped herself upwards, ready to journey in, when it occurred to her that the direction she was facing was back the way she had come.

She turned and found that the way ahead lay through a similarly inscribed portal – but one that was at least two hundred yards away on the other side of the cavern. There was no bridge that connected them like her own.

How in the hells was she meant to get across? How in the hells had Gabriella been meant to get across? Was there in fact a bridge there like one of those she'd heard about, built in such a way it disguised itself against its background? Or was it one made of perfectly carved crystal, refraction free, that would only reveal itself when sprinkled with dust?

Kali almost kicked herself. It could be neither of those, of course, because if it were, how could she have flipped herself upwards? All she would have ended up doing was flattening her arse on rock.

What, then? A bridge that revealed itself stage by stage with every footstep you took? A bridge controlled by some mechanism handily concealed in a nearby room full of monsters? Dammit, there were just too many kinds of bridge.

Including one she'd forgotten.

This was the Path of Faith, right?

What if this was a bridge of Faith? Had Gabriella been here, would all that would have been required of her be a *belief* that the bridge was there? A bridge that was provided by her God?

There is a bridge, there is a bridge, there is a bridge, Kali thought as she closed her eyes tight and took a tentative step forward. She must have been doing something right because she didn't tip into the cavern below. Another step. *There is a bridge, there is a bridge, there is a bridge*. Another, then another, then another. Oh, this was a piece of pits, she thought, and began to run. *Bridge, bridge, bridge, bridge, bridge*. All right! It was really quite astounding how you got religion when you needed it.

Oops. Impious thought.

Kali suddenly felt air beneath her feet. Well, not beneath so much as rushing by. Her eyes snapped open and saw that, luckily, she had almost made it to the other side. She roared and flailed forward, grabbing onto a vine that dangled from the opposite entrance, and pulled herself up. She rested for a second. Close call, smartarse.

Kali strode through the entrance into the next stage of Gabriella's Trial – and straight into an inferno. The passage ahead was blocked by fire burning with a heat so searing she wondered if it was meant to represent the Hells. The religious hells, that was, not the bastard in the skies – the place where Gabriella and her fellow devotees preached you went when you'd been a naughty boy or girl. Another test of her faith, then? A demonstration that as a Sister of the Order of the Swords of Dawn she could walk through the hells unscathed? Maybe. But the Trials were tests of the person *and* their abilities, so what if this was meant to challenge Gabriella's magical resistance? What if this was a magical fire that Gabriella might be able to saunter through but would roast anyone else alive?

Kali reached out a hand and pulled it back with a hiss, her palm reddened and blistered. Okay, it felt like real fire but that didn't prove anything. Maybe all she needed to do was concentrate like she had on the bridge – or, considering her surroundings, maybe a little bit more. Kali closed her eyes and put out her hand once more. The heat of the fire began to lessen. And when it had lessened enough, she began to walk forward. Flames enveloped her but she continued on unharmed.

She'd been right the first time. She had to admit that Gabriella's Trial was a bit of a breeze compared to her own.

Kali was halfway along the passage when she began to smoke.

Began to hurt. And however much she concentrated the pain wouldn't go away.

Oh gods, she realised. This wasn't a test of Gabriella's faith *or* her magic resistance. It was a test of both.

Kali ran. Ran faster than she ever had in her life, the flames licking at her, blistering her, turning patches of her skin an agonisingly raw red. She burst forth onto another bridge but it too was lined with fire. There was nowhere to go but down.

Kali threw herself off the bridge without a clue what was below, and landed hard, on rock. She patted herself down, wincing, and saw that once again she was in some kind of juncture between Paths. Looking around, guided once more by the symbols carved into the rock, she saw that the only other Path accessible from this point, and again only with difficulty, was Lucius Kane's.

Kali picked herself up and made her way across the rocky hinterland. The entrance to whatever stage of Kane's trial she would face lay some eight metres away, on the other side of a precipitous and apparently bottomless ravine. She backed up, taking deep, preparatory breaths, then raced forward with arms and legs pumping and leapt over the unwelcoming depths.

Her roar of determination echoing throughout the subterrain, she made the leap with a foot to spare, but landed hard, and the pain of the sharp rock on her bare soles made her somersault forward not once but three times. The last of these gymnastics took her onto Kane's symbol-inscribed path, and even before she could right herself she spotted three coruscating, variously coloured orbs in a triangular formation heading directly for her, and fast, along the narrow passage beyond. Kali squealed, rose and span, intending to retreat while the orbs shot by, but an invisible wall now blocked her in, and she span back, mind racing. The orbs had resolved themselves into balls of blue crackling energy, hissing ice and – oh great – more fire. Kane's trial was wasting no time and she guessed this was a test of his reactions, his ability to swap between threads at speed, finding the right ones to counter the different elemental threats, diffusing, destroying or repelling them before they hit.

Yep, that made sense. For him. But what the flying fark was *she* supposed to do?

Fly. It was all she could do. Fly through the lethal looking orbs as they came, launching herself through the small gap in the heart of their formation. This she did, feeling like some kind of circus act, turning almost three hundred and sixty degrees as she kept her body streamlined. But she was a human thread passing through a needle's eye, and some contact was unavoidable. Kali took the pain from grazing the fire orb almost as a matter of course – how could it be any worse than Gabriella's inferno? – but she gasped in pain as the ice orb grazed a hip and ribs, the temperature contrast on her reddened skin agonising enough, but not quite as agonising as then having that same skin instantly frozen and stripped away. A streak of raw flesh now running half the length of her right hand side, the last thing she needed was contact with the last of the orbs, but this was unavoidable, too. The blue, crackling energy sent her entire body into spasm in what remained of her flight, and Kali hit the ground clumsily, twitching and coated in sweat, small darts of lightning dancing over her before discharging into the air.

She watched the orbs hit the invisible wall and disappear. Her eyes narrowed.

She hated this farking place. It had actually made her pee.

Kali forced herself up on trembling arms and wearily began to limp further down the passage. She remained on guard for more lightning, thunder, acid rain or whatever was going to be thrown at her next, but in actual fact she reached a chamber that was in stark contrast to any she had encountered before. That wasn't to say it wasn't equally dangerous, of course, even though all it seemed to contain was a door.

That was it. A door. A door standing all by itself in the centre of the chamber. A door that you could walk all the way around. And in the centre of the door, a lock. But what was the point of a lock if all you had to do to get through the door was move to its other side?

Kali frowned. The sheer fact that she was looking at a locked door seemed to indicate this was a test of Kane's thieving skills rather than his magical legacy, but that wasn't necessarily so. If this path had the same duality of purpose as Gabriella's it could be either.

No, she realised suddenly, it couldn't. Or at least she didn't think so. Because if it were a test of thieving skills and it was Kane who was attempting this trial, if he'd reached the island before her, then he, too, would be doing it naked, and what was he supposed to pick the lock with, his – well, she didn't need to picture it, did she? She wasn't denying the shadowmage might have hidden talents but she doubted that was one of them, so this had to be a kind of a hybrid test – a thief's challenge that needed to be solved by magic. If that *was* the case, then she could...

No, again. Who was she kidding? Either way she was bollocksed.

Frustrated, Kali kicked the door.

And then found out what would have happened if Kane had failed this test.

The rapid *shnik! shnik! shnik!* was a dead giveaway, and she would have been dead had she not encountered similar traps on more than one occasion. She berated herself for not having noticed the myriad circular holes that punctured the walls of the chamber, even though they had become filled and disguised by the dust of ages, and once more leapt into the air.

What was it to be, she wondered? The tree, the stag or the teapot? In the end, she found herself in an unidentifiable and vaguely sillier position than any of them, suspended where she'd leapt between the hundred or so pointed bars that had erupted from the walls, roof and floor horizontally, vertically and diagonally, ramming themselves into the opposing areas of the chamber in a series of thuds and explosions of dust. Kali hung there immobile, her neck trapped between an intersection of bars so tightly she felt it had been removed and mounted, her left arm bent back and behind her at the elbow, her right thrust straight down under her, toes almost but not quite touching the ground. Her torso and right leg, meanwhile, were twisted at such an angle she could easily see all the way down the livid scar on her right hand side. She reflected she hadn't done badly considering what the chamber had thrown at her, but the bar that had skewered her left thigh, punching all the way through by the bone and impaling her on the latticework, elicited a long and weary groan. Kali waited, watching the drips of blood from her leg puddle on the chamber floor, then, as she'd hoped, the trap reset itself. With the dull rumble of some hidden mechanism, the bars slowly retreated to their housings, and, bit by bit, Kali was released from her confinement, slithering downwards from bar to bar.

The one that had punctured her thigh, the dust it had gathered grating on her inner flesh, hurt like the hells as it came out, and she gritted her teeth, finally thudding to the floor with a gasp.

That was it. Sod the world. She wanted to go home. Now.

There was no going back, though, was there? Only forward. And in that respect, the trial was offering Kali the first break she'd had. This trap, like all the others, was multilayered, and though she had failed the door test – as Kane conceivably *could* have – the trap itself was as much of a test of skills as the door had been. Whatever magical wheeze the shadowmage might have used to avoid a change of career to a pin cushion – some spell like skin of steel, spongeflesh or size of a worgle, whatever he called the bloody things – survival satisfied the test's conditions as much as success.

The locked door was gone. Transformed into a shimmering portal.

Kali sighed, picked herself up and, leg slick with blood, limped through.

Another bridge.

That'll do, Kali thought. She'd had more than enough of the Trial of Lucius Kane.

She dropped down into what she thought was going to be another hinterland, hoping to find a cave inscribed with the symbol of Endurance. But all there was was a dark and uninviting pool of water in the rock floor.

Guess who? she thought.

The memory of what had happened on the sinking Black Ship still fresh in her mind, it was the very last thing she wanted to do, but Kali inhaled one slow, very deep breath and then dived beneath the surface into the Trial of Silus Morlader.

CHAPTER FIFTEEN

IT WAS LIKE swimming through soup. Cold, leftover and half-rotten soup filled with every unwanted ingredient that could ever be imagined. As Kali propelled herself down with determined strokes, still moving painfully slowly against the swell – the murk around her offered up great patches of silt from the cave floor, wooden flotsam that bobbed and bumped against her, detritus that had accumulated over the ages, and finally, but by no means the least, lengthy, cloying strands of seaweed and other marine vegetation that slithered over and clung to her body and, on occasion, her face, making her want to release her air and gag.

These were not the only obstacles she faced. The crystalline formations that lit the rest of the Trials were far less abundant here, worn away for the most part by the roiling water and eroding effects of its contents, and the further Kali swam from the entrance the darker the waters became. The darkness itself was not the danger, of course – with no idea of what form these submarine caves took, or even of which direction she was meant to be heading, she was blind in more ways than one, and her hands scraped repeatedly and painfully against boulders, sharp growths of coral, and rock walls. Kali began to trail blood, and at one point another length of the seaweed wrapped itself around one of her legs, sliding down to entangle her ankle. Repulsed, Kali kicked herself away so violently that she span in the water, her head cracking an unseen boulder so hard she saw stars.

Disorientated, having involuntarily released a quantity of her air, Kali scrabbled back to what she thought was an upright position. But the disturbed water had become thick with silt, and there wasn't even the faintest patch of light, and for all she knew she could have been attempting to swim downwards or sideways.

The first stirrings of panic set in as all Kali could feel, whichever way she stroked her hands, was rock, and she turned again and again, this way and that, but finding no hope for her predicament. She twisted herself around once more. This time her hands dug into the base of the cave, scooping up fistfuls of sand and shells and, as she cast them away as if they were contaminated, another flare of panic came. She found the rock wall – *a* rock wall – once more, and groped her way along it, hoping that this time she had chosen the right direction in which to kick off.

She had, finding a bend with her fingertips which she pulled herself around, but as she began to thrust herself forward once more the stark reality of her situation was already starting to hit home. It had been all right telling herself that she could negotiate the path designed for Silus, that her abilities would get her through, but the fact was if this path was meant to be as much of a challenge for him as her own had proven to her, then, despite the fact she was already faltering, she would only have, as it were, dipped her toes in the water.

The realisation brought with it a desperate burst of energy, and Kali propelled herself through the water as fast as she felt it safe to do so, ignoring the bumps and scrapes to her arms and hips that had earlier given her cause to tackle the liquid path more cautiously. One pain that she couldn't ignore, however, was the one growing in her breast, a searing heat of constrained, exhausted breath that was beginning to feel more and more as if someone were scraping the blade of a knife up and down her trachea. The pain made her want to cough and, more dangerously, swallow reflexively, and, as she did, her mouth opened slightly, expelling some of what was left of her air in a cloud of bubbles and allowing the taste of the mire through which she swam inside her. Kali swallowed it, for there was nothing else she could do, and knew it was only a matter of time before her lungs would involuntarily start to fill with more of the tainted liquid. There was nothing else for it. She swam on, determined but ultimately not built for that which she had been forced to endure, and then felt her stomach, her chest, her entire torso begin to spasm, fighting against her to draw in the great, gulping breath that she didn't want to take.

More bubbles exploded from her mouth and struggling, slowing to a stop, Kali hung there and then gradually began to incline vertically upwards, her limbs floating. She flailed in the water, bucking, resisting, knowing her fate was inevitable. She could hear her own resistant moans inside her head, magnified because she was unable to release them, whimpering and animalistic. Her eyes widened in desperation, even now seeking a way out of this deathtrap, but seeing nothing but the mire that was sure to become her watery grave.

Then suddenly, waveringly, *there*. Kali wasn't sure whether she was actually seeing it or whether it was the result of the increasing, spotted flaring of her vision, but above her seemed to be light. She began swimming upwards, brushing gleefully welcome, upwardly sloping rock as she did, and then unexpectedly burst the surface with a single, long gulping inhalation of breath. The breath caught on the muck that had settled within her and immediately she vomited up the dire water she had swallowed.

Taking another gulping breath, hacking and spitting, Kali looked around. There wasn't much to see. Illuminated by a small collection of crystals, a small, hollow niche surrounded her, not quite big enough for her to fully stretch out her arms. At first she thought it might have been some kind of rest area for Silus – a staging post on his trial, maybe – but she then realised he would have no need of such respite. Studying the rock, she realised it was a natural formation, the result of erosion into which the swirling waters below must periodically rise, trying to find an alternate exit from the labyrinth through which they flowed.

Kali forgot what such a feature was called but, in actual fact, didn't give a toss. She was just grateful it was there. Had she been able to reach it, she would have kissed the rock above. Shagged it, if the rock had been in the mood. This tiny pocket of air could prove to be her salvation. It could even prove the means by which she might survive Silus's trial after all. Using it as a base, a central point, she could reconnoitre the labyrinth that lay ahead, gauge distances, directions, each time returning here for vital oxygen. And each time, hopefully, having managed to map the trial a little further. This was nowhere near a guarantee, of course – who but its builders knew how far the trial extended – but it was a *start*.

Kali wasted no time, filling her lungs, dipping her head back beneath the water and power-stroking down. Less panicked now, with a brain filled with thoughts rather than adrenalin, she twisted, eel-like, around a bend in the cave she could now discern. The bend led to a narrow flue that dropped vertically and she twisted again, doggy-paddling herself into position to descend it. The flue dropped about a hundred yards and, at its base, she found a number of passages radiating off a small chamber. Kali decided to explore them clockwise, and swam into the first, finding, after about ten yards, a dead end. She retraced her path and was about to tackle the second passage when she started to feel the familiar burning sensation in her midriff. Time to return and refuel, as it were.

Done, Kali tried the second passage, and then the third – dead ends again – though the second proceeded so far in that she thought it was leading somewhere, and only just made it back to the airhole. On her return trip, the fourth passage proved to be the one she wanted and, after a winding route, she shot with surprising speed into another chamber, one much larger than the last. Again, though, she had reached the limit of her explorations, and twisted herself around in the water to return from whence she came. But there was a problem. Her accelerated arrival into the chamber had been the result of the strong current generated in the passage she'd used, and returning to the passage, swimming against the current, wasn't possible. Kali struggled, her arms pumping and legs kicking, but she made no headway at all, and, ever weakening, found herself spat back into the heart of the chamber, where she was tossed and rolled helplessly.

Panic flared within her once more as she felt more currents tugging at her and, using what little strength she had left simply to remain stable, realised she was in the middle of a maelstrom. The chamber, like the one above, offered a variety of exits, but in this case many, many more, riddling it like Gargassian cheese, and from each and into each water poured under such pressure that attempting to fight or resist its flow was a lost cause. Not that she had time to fight or to resist as her breath was almost gone now, the searing pain in her chest urging her to take one breath, just one breath...

An involuntary burst of bubbles escaping her mouth, Kali's mind raced as fast as the currents clashed with each other around her. Like the rest of the aquatic labyrinth this chamber had clearly been designed as a challenge for Silus, but surely not simply to confuse and to trap him here, because for a man with no need of breath, what would be the point? He could take all the time in the world to negotiate his way through. If not a trap, then, what? Some kind of gauntlet? A test of his endurance and skills? If that was the case, what skills, other than the ability to breathe under water, did Silus Morlader possess?

Think, woman, think! He was a mariner, right? He had lived all his life with the sea. The fact that his legacy had endowed him with the preternatural ability to survive in a submarine environment could, in a way, almost be considered a bonus. But there was little doubt that his abilities, even when latent, must have drawn him to the sea, because that, after all, was his destiny, as much as it had been her destiny to spend her life burrowing beneath the ground. Silus Morlader and the seas of Twilight were complementary forces. They were one with him, and he was one with them.

One.

That was the answer. You didn't fight that which made you whole. You didn't struggle. And the purpose of running a gauntlet was to prove it presented no danger to you, that you accepted its dangers and were comfortable with them. Yes, that had to be it.

Unless she wanted to die here, decomposing until her flesh became one with these waters, her bones battered on the chamber's rock walls until they, too, were silt, it was her only chance.

Kali relaxed her body, closed her eyes, and allowed herself to drift into the strongest of the currents. She forced herself to remain relaxed as it snatched her away, ignoring the presence of the rocks that projected all around her, trusting, as Silus would have done, the tumultuous ebb and flow of the chamber's currents, allowing them, with only the slightest instinctive changes in her posture, to deliver her where she was meant to be.

Her body was carried through the waters of the chamber, bending and twisting, supple and slithery as a snake, and, while occasionally she felt looming masses of rock flashing at her or within inches of her side, or her whole body buffeted as one current crossed another, she did not resist and simply went with the flow. Even the now agonising tightness of her chest seemed to dull as she proceeded, accepting the inevitability of her underwater journey, which could now only end one of two ways, neither of which she had any say in at all.

On through the waters she continued, until at last the current transported her into one of the many passages that led off the gauntlet, which Kali was only aware of because of an increased darkness about her. Down, then sideways, then up she travelled, the slight shifts in her posture occasionally misjudged, her body scraping the passage walls but unharmed, the rock worn to an organic smoothness by the force of the water that travelled through it. But the darkness around her wasn't the only darkness, now, her body finally succumbing to lack of oxygen, and heavy shadows began to close in on her mind. As unconsciousness loomed, insidiously, like slipping into a dream, any attempt at manoeuvring was forgotten and, less Kali Hooper now than piece of living flotsam, her body began to drift in the current, bouncing and then slamming with increasing force off the passage walls as it was carried seemingly forever onward.

And as it did, her mouth yawned opened, and water began to enter her lungs.

Kali's eyes snapped open. The cold shock of the liquid inside her brought her back from the brink of oblivion, extinguishing the fire within her breast but not welcome for doing so, and with a loud blub she expelled it back from whence it came. The urge to inhale again was immediate, and she almost did, but, angry now – angry that she had almost allowed herself to die, angry that these Trials conspired to kill her when she was so close to the truth – she decided that she wasn't dead yet.

No way. No farking way.

Kali forgot everything except reaching the end of the Trial. Her body already black and blue from the battering it had taken against the walls, she cared little what further damage it took, because this was do or die. Instead of allowing the current to simply carry her along, she began to kick, punch and throw herself off the walls, rolling, flexing and punching herself ever forward, like a sentient bullet trying to find the end of the barrel of a gun. Her progress was lost in a welter of bubbles, thrashed water and flailing limbs as on and on she went, but, so long as she felt the current still pushing her from behind, she was going to be all right.

She had to be...

...she was going to be all right...

...going to be...

...going to...

...going...

A sudden, deafening roaring filled Kali's ears, she felt air on her face, and she heaved in a gasping breath so deep that for a moment she felt that her upper half was going to implode.

The roaring resolved itself into the sound of thunderously rushing water through which, feeling it smash into her back from above, she was falling. Kali looked down and saw that far below her, almost obscured by a billowing cloud of white spray, the water was pouring into the base of another cylindrical flue, but this one much broader – and, of course, unsubmerged – as those earlier. The fact that it *was* unsubmerged gave her a sense that she was at last close to the end of Silus's Trial, but it wasn't quite yet time to rejoice, for if she didn't do something about her uncontrolled plummet the impact into the waters below would snap her into pieces.

Kali twisted and flexed until she was pointing headfirst at the water, her body straight and her arms outstretched beside her. As she cut through the waterfall, wind that had never been more welcome whipped at her. Then, a few seconds before she disappeared into the cloud of spray, she inclined her arms beneath her, as straight as the rest of her, waiting for her fingertips to slice neatly into the waiting water.

Kali plunged into the foaming mass that filled the base of the flue, feeling its swirling, roiling presence strangely warm and all over her skin like a reaffirmation of life, and then she burst the surface with the cry that she had been wanting to vent the moment she had been able to breathe again.

"*Yeeeeeeeee-haaaaaaaaahhh!*"

She'd done it, she'd survived the Trial, and not her Trial but Silus's Trial. The cry she'd emitted, even though it was inaudible above the sound of the waterfall, segued into laughter as Kali looked up and splashed her face. Gods, she was good. Yes, Kali Hooper was *good*. She'd *proven* herself to be one of the Four.

Kali's laughter faded as she began to turn involuntarily in the waters that surrounded her, and then she frowned as, amidst great disturbance on its surface, the water began to rise, taking her with it. Within a second of the phenomenon occurring she had risen twenty feet within the vertical flue, spinning dizzyingly all the time, and all that she could see above her were its revolving walls becoming submerged ever and ever faster. What the hells was this? What was happening now?

But if Kali had learned anything during this Trial it was to let things simply take their course – not that she really had any choice – and as she rose she studied the flue's sides, trying to gauge, to prepare for what was to come. There seemed to be some kind of opening on what was momentarily the left, and another opposite, slightly higher, on the right. The purpose of both were unknown. Pits of Kerberos, she thought, if she was going to be dumped into either of these, this whole process beginning again, she'd save the Trial the trouble and quaff the waters down like thwack. Enough was enough.

As it turned out, however, the whole process was not going to begin again, because as Kali rose to the level of the first opening she saw that the rising water was already beginning to spill into it, flowing down a short, sloped channel then cascading away as a waterfall like the one through which she'd been dumped here. She turned in the water and saw that the opposite opening had a set of ancient stone steps leading down, bridging the gap between the two. So that was it, she thought, the flue wasn't a flue but a means to bring whoever had survived the earlier journey into it to this point, the whole thing acting as a kind of giant cistern and the water that cascaded away recycled, no doubt, through another labyrinthine series of passages so that the process would repeat over and over again.

She felt the tug of the new waterfall drawing her towards the first opening but kicked against it, and a second later drew herself onto the steps that the second proffered. Water dripping from her, hair plastered to her head, she ascended them slowly, to an arch that awaited her at their top.

Kali stepped through the arch and gasped.

She had entered the most massive cavern of the underground labyrinth yet, what had to be *the* most massive cavern, as it seemed to fill the entire centre of the island, a hollow core beneath a rock roof whose inverted topography matched what she knew to be the landscape above. It wasn't the above that drew Kali's gaze, however, but what was ahead of her, and below. She was standing at the beginning of a narrow rock bridge, one of four that entered the cavern from each point of the compass, the other three what could only be the ends of the Paths of Magic, Faith and Survival. She might have reached this place by the wrong route but it didn't matter, because they converged here.

Each bridge spanned the cavern across a raging body of water, and as she looked down Kali could make out various caves that she presumed opened into the sea. This was doubtless the same water which supplied Silus' Path, the one she had just negotiated, and now she would have to negotiate it again, this time from above. This wasn't a path she was looking forward to any more than Silus's, because the water, thrust by violent tides and slapped by the walls of the cavern – and doubtless made all the more tumultuous by what she had seen happening to the Hel'ss Spawn – frequently crashed above the height of the bridges, momentarily drowning them with such force that if she timed her crossing badly she'd be instantly washed away.

But cross the bridge she must. Because at its far end, in the exact centre of the cavern and towards which the other three bridges also led, was what she presumed was her ultimate destination. A huge column of intertwined, multicoloured lightning that shot powerful whips of energy throughout the cavern and towards its roof, dancing and dissipating where they struck its walls with a force Kali could hear and feel even this far below. This had to be the phenomenon that Brundle had mentioned to her.

The Thunderflux.

Whatever the Thunderflux was.

Kali swallowed. It wasn't so much because the phenomenon looked as though it might be capable of incinerating her at the merest touch, but because, if what Brundle said was true, that inside it the truth lay. *The* truth. The truth she had been searching for for years. The fate of the Old Races. The secret of who she was. The destiny of mankind.

All she had to do was reach it, and the answers would be hers.

Kali's heart thudded as she stepped onto the bridge, immediately backtracking as a wave crashed down directly in front of her, swamping the narrow thoroughfare and leaving behind a detritus of seaweed that dangled from the stone like vines. Kali took another step forward, feeling some of the aquatic matter crunch beneath her bare feet and some, its surface suckered, adhere to her soles like glue. She kicked it away and continued on, watching the ebb and flow of the waters beneath her every step of the way. A wave crashed directly under the bridge and a heavy spray buffeted her on both sides, and then she ducked, clinging onto the rock, as the bridge was swamped in a backwash. Kali was knocked onto her side, almost slithering off the bridge on the slime that coated it, but managed to hook a foot in some of the seaweed on its opposite edge, preventing her fall. She heaved herself onto her hands and knees again, most of her body coated now in a green marine goo, and uttered a small curse as she stared ahead and saw there was perhaps still two thirds of the bridge to go. She would not be stopped now, though, and decided to use the bridge to her advantage rather than treat it as an obstacle.

Kali waited where she was, hanging on for dear life, as three more waves crashed about her, and then, having worked out a rough pattern to the water's movements, raised herself into a sprint position and flung herself forward. The slime caused her to lose her footing almost immediately, of course, and she managed only three pounding steps, but that was exactly what she wanted, and she allowed herself to fall forward, crashing back onto the slime and allowing it to do what slime did best. Grimacing as her body became coated in an ever accumulating layer of green sludge, pulling a wrapping of seaweed with her, Kali slid along the bridge until she came within yards of the Thunderflux.

And didn't stop.

Shit. *Shit, shit, shit.*

Kali felt the surface of the Thunderflux prickling her bare flesh, *warming* it, as she neared, and having no desire to enter it until she had a far better idea of what she was dealing with she fought madly to bring herself to a halt. Her desperate scrabbling and slapping at anything and everything that might halt her progress turned her in a slow circle as she slithered closer and closer, as if she were coming to the end of some carnival ride, but she came to a stop at last, mere inches away from the crackling column.

The waves were not striking this close to the Thunderflux, but Kali still rose hesitantly, unsure whether one of the whips of energy might catch her and fry her where she stood. Other than the prickling, warming effect of the column itself, however, they seemed harmless enough, one even passing directly through her, leaving her with little more than a slight sense of disorientation.

Slowly, Kali stretched out her arm, her palm touching the column's surface, and she felt a thrill she'd struggle to describe. The closest she came brought a smile, as she remembered a phrase from a year before, the speaker of which was no longer with us.

All tremblous in the underknicks.

The phrase – and the feeling – reassured her. There was nothing to be afraid of here, surely? After all, what would be the point of having her – of having any of the kattra – go through the Trial only to have them zapped into oblivion when they completed it?

This thing had waited a long, long, long, long time. It wasn't going to hurt her.

Kali took a breath and was about to step into the Thunderflux when she stopped dead. There was something she'd forgotten. The bridge on which she was standing was not her bridge. And if the truth was protected from those who were not meant to hear it by the

Trials, who was to say she wouldn't be committing some grave error by entering the way Silus was meant to enter? Should she somehow try to make her way to her own bridge?

Kali didn't know whether her hesitation was valid or not, and as she weighed up its pros and cons – not least the seeming impossibility of reaching her own bridge from where she now stood – she failed to notice what was happening below the bridge, in the still tumultuous waters behind her.

Through one of the sea caves that fed the cavern, a slick of orange goo had mingled with the waters within, and as Kali continued to stare at the surface of the Thunderflux, the slick moved closer to her. Thicker and more soup-like than the liquid through which it flowed with a clear intent, the first thing that Kali knew of its presence was when it exploded from the waters to loom above her.

Kali span, but it was too late. In much the same way as it had earlier on Horizon Point, the Hel'ss Spawn darted at her and slapped her off her feet and the bridge. With a yelp, Kali found herself falling into the waters below, her heart almost seizing when the cold struck her. Momentarily numbed, she struggled to come to terms with what had just happened, and when she did, despite being underwater, roared in fury. Thanks to the Hel'ss Spawn she was going to have to do this whole damned thing again!

Fury, however, was not nearly a powerful enough word to describe the emotion that overtook her a few seconds later. For as Kali kicked her way to the surface the orange slick enveloped her like the caress of a rough lover, and as it did she felt a fundamental difference between what had attacked her earlier and what was attacking her now.

The Hel'ss Spawn had meant to do her harm, of course it had, but in a sense it had been impersonal, the attack of an entity which cared not at all for the individuality of its victim. This, though, was different, and she sensed something – a presence – almost immediately. There was, as far as she was aware, only one dirty old bastard who'd try to cop a feel in this way.

"Redigor," she growled. "You just don't know when to farking give up, do you?"

There was no answer, of course. How could there be? Redigor's body had gone and all that was left of him now was the same non-corporeal parasite that had been hitching a lift inside Jakub Freel. It seemed he'd gone up in the world – literally – having presumably infested the Hel'ss Spawn as it had plunged with his soul off Horizon Point, and she reflected that only the Pale Lord could be arrogant enough to try and possess a god. Or at least the agent of a god.

Kali had to admit, though, that he was making a pretty good job of it.

The Hel'ss Spawn, under Redigor's control, seemed determined that she was not going to win, dragging her back under the water and flinging her about until her breath, hastily snatched as she went under, was forcefully expelled by the battering she was taking. Thankfully, Redigor provided her with an opportunity to replenish her lungs as she was hauled from beneath the waves and flung violently towards the distant walls of the cavern. Here Kali's lungs exploded again, this time as the impact winded and dazed her, and she tumbled from the wall onto a rock below, where she rolled weakly back into the raging sea. Undulating, constantly shifting shape, the Hel'ss Spawn came at her again, enveloping her and then plunging to the bottom of the submerged cavern, dragging her along the rough sand there until her flesh was rubbed raw and bleeding. Then, lifted through a cloud of her own diffusing blood, Redigor returned her to the surface and high up into the air.

Kali dangled in the entity's strange grip like a marionette whose strings had been severed, glowering, despite her pummelled state, at the viscous form before her. For one fleeting second she was transported back to the observatory at Scholten because the Hel'ss Spawn rearranged itself into a semblance of Redigor's features and returned her gaze, smiling coldly.

She knew then that she was only suffering the first act of Redigor's perverse game. The battering he was giving her was not meant to kill her, only soften her up. Redigor wanted her utterly helpless, broken not just physically but mentally, so that she could do nothing when he eventually rammed the Hel'ss Spawn's hungry tendrils inside her, ripping away her very soul.

Well, she'd felt Redigor's touch before, when he'd tried to drain her of her essence in the Chapel of Screams, and she'd be damned if she was going to let it happen again. If Redigor wanted to knock the fight out of her, she'd show him just how much fight she had left.

Kali began to kick and pummel in the Hel'ss Spawn's grip, only for it to fling her through the air towards the cavern's unforgiving rock walls again. The undulating form followed immediately, ready to snatch her up again, but this time she was ready.

As she flew through the air, Kali grabbed onto one of the lengthy strands of seaweed that dangled from each of the bridges, and swiftly swung herself around so that she smashed back into – and through – the viscous entity that Redigor controlled. As she'd guessed, the manoeuvre was so unexpected that even the Hel'ss Spawn had difficulty adjusting, and part of the shape-shifting entity collapsed, unable to reform itself in time to stop her. Redigor's avatar did so a second later, of course, but by then it was too late, Kali having used the seaweed in the manner of a vine and swung herself to a point where she let go, flailing through the air towards the hanging detritus of the cavern's adjacent bridge.

Swinging from marine vine to marine vine, Kali built up a momentum that enabled her to use them all as ropes to evade Redigor, and changing her course frequently and unexpectedly the entity found itself being stretched to the limits of its shape-shifting abilities, breaking apart, as it pursued her about the cavern. Exactly where this was leading, Kali wasn't sure, but she suspected that the orange taint from the amberglow that had caused so much disturbance to the Hel'ss on the surface – the same glow that infused it here – was damaging it somehow, and hopefully it was a chink in its armour that she could exploit.

All she had to do was keep moving. Survive long enough to find out.

What Kali hadn't taken into account was that in some way Redigor himself seemed aware that his alien host was damaged, and rather than be cowed by the fact that the Hel'ss Spawn was breaking apart in its crazed pursuit of her, he pushed the entity to double its efforts to succeed. Kali was guessing but it seemed to her that Redigor *didn't care* that the Hel'ss Spawn might be destroyed, that this was no longer about his survival, or his insane plan being resurrected, but just between he and her. It was revenge Redigor craved. Petty revenge.

This was personal.

There would be no stopping a madman, Kali realised. This coupled with the fact that even she couldn't keep this up for ever, that she was rapidly tiring from the exertion involved, led, inevitably to a moment where Redigor's avatar gained the upper hand.

It was an appropriate phrase, for as Kali made a minor error that caused her to miss a leap between seaweed strands, forcing her to swing for it a second time, what remained of the mass of the Hel'ss Spawn exploded from the water and clenched her in what resembled a giant fist. Kali struggled and slithered within it but the fist held her fast, and she roared in frustration as Redigor's features appeared fleetingly in the viscous matter once more.

The bastard was smiling. He had everything that he wanted.

All that remained was for him to deliver the finishing blow.

Kali swallowed repeatedly, tensed in anticipation, remembering how Redigor had invaded her in the Chapel of Screams, tried to strip away her soul, and would have succeeded had it not been for the intervention of Gabriella DeZantez. It had been the worst pain she had ever felt, agonising beyond words. But this, this was going to be different.

It was going to be one hells of a lot worse.

Kali flung back her head and roared in pain as the Hel'ss Spawn coated her body and began to insinuate itself into her flesh through every orifice, every pore. She watched horrified as it travelled beneath her skin, seeking out muscle, tendon, sinew and bone, every vital organ, and she began to buck and groan as each part of her began slowly to be reworked from the inside. It couldn't be happening but it was, it was, and as her vision pulsed with blood pumped wrongly through her body, in great, warm washes where it should not have been, she saw that her flesh had already begun to dissolve, her arms and legs shrinking, deforming into shapeless, liquid things, her stomach collapsing and her flesh running from her in streams, like candlewax.

She would be nothing soon, and her universe consisted of one endless, deafening scream.

Then, suddenly, as one small part of her recognised the Hel'ss Spawn had worked its way up, was spreading now over her thumping heart, ready to take that, too, she felt another kind of pain. No, not pain, but the kind of red-hot, nagging insistence in her chest she had felt when almost drowned. This feeling was different, though, not the result of a desperate need to draw air from without, but the need of something to be released from *within*.

Images flashed unbidden into her mind. The moment at the Crucible when Tharnak had told her she shared a legacy with him. Brundle, placing his hand on her in the tavern in Gransk, the gasp he had uttered thereon. Herself, standing in front of a mirror in the Flagons that one dark night she had told no one about.

The night that she had become aware of the thing she believed made her what she was.

The night that she had seen the thread within her *glow*.

Oh gods, Kali thought, as it began to glow again, brighter than ever before. What was this? What the hells was this? And then the pain of what the Hel'ss Spawn was doing to her was forgotten as her spine arched so acutely it seemed to snap in two, and she screamed with an agony she thought could get no worse as something broke from within her and the cavern exploded with light.

Kali felt herself falling, released from the grip of the Hel'ss Spawn, remade miraculously whole. Instinctively, unthinking, she grabbed onto a strand of seaweed and swung there breathlessly as before her the Hel'ss Spawn roared. She had no idea what she had done but suddenly the entity – Redigor's screaming face within it – was retreating from her and flinging itself about the cavern as though infected with some deadly toxin. Against rock after rock and wall after wall it crashed, each time breaking itself apart into smaller and smaller segments, and then, when there was little of it left, what remained of it collapsed into the waters and, bobbing on the waves, began to drift lifelessly away.

Kali hung where she was, gasping, unable to believe what had happened, waiting for the Hel'ss Spawn, for Redigor, to rear up once more. But after five full minutes had passed, it, and he, did not.

The Hel'ss Spawn was gone.

Bastian Redigor was gone.

Slowly, Kali lifted herself hand over hand up the seaweed strand and then collapsed onto the bridge above. She lay there on her back for a few seconds, her palm caressing her chest, feeling the place the light had come from. It was back within her now, that she could feel, but, despite what it appeared to have done, it was of no comfort.

Gods, what was it? What was *she*?

Was this a part of the Truth?

Kali stood and stared ahead of her. The lightning column that was the Thunderflux waited no more than ten yards along the bridge on which she stood, and somehow she knew that this was the right bridge, *her* bridge, and that whether by accident or design of fate she'd been delivered to the right place. Whatever lay within was the end of the Path of Endurance, the end of the path of Kali Hooper.

Her destiny.

Kali took a breath and strode inside the Thunderflux. She found herself rising and then stopping inside a domed chamber, and she guessed she was inside the Thunderflux cap. The same energies that had danced in the column danced here, too, all around her, beating at the walls, but they did her no harm.

The only shock she felt was when a face appeared before her.

A woman.

An elf.

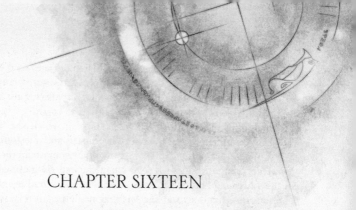

CHAPTER SIXTEEN

"HELLO, KALI," THE elf said. She spoke slowly and her words trembled in the air, as if they were the most delicate things in the world. "As I speak, I am separated from you by many thousands of years, and the civilisations I represent are about to end. They shall be gone from this world soon – taken by the entity you will already have encountered. The elves and the dwarfs and all of their grand achievements will be no more. But we leave behind us the seeds of a new race – the human race – whose origins lie in the depths of the oceans of this world, and not, like us, in the skies above… or on other worlds, far beyond your skies." The elf paused. "I expect you have many questions. Please feel free to ask anything you wish."

"I, er, don't suppose you have a towel?"

The elf smiled. "No, I don't have a towel."

"Right. Sorry about that. I guess I'm a little nervous. How about who are you? And how can we be speaking like this?"

"My name is Zharn. And I am able to speak to you because I am trapped in a moment of time. A moment created when the Thunderflux was capped, that links the Trass Kattra that is now with the Trass Kattra that was then."

"You're here on Trass Kattra. In the past?"

"Not just the past, Kali. The End Time. Even as I speak, the darkness is upon us, and were it not for this moment, I would already be dead."

Kali swallowed. "Who are you, Zharn?"

"One who tried to help save our world. One of four."

"Four?" Kali repeated. "You mean like the *Four* four?"

"Yes, that is what I mean. I was of the kattra of this time. And it was I who was chosen to come to the Thunderflux to relate the tale you need to hear."

"Okay," Kali said cautiously. "I don't seem to have anything else on at the moment."

"We share a singular heritage, Kali – and a singular foe. One that will be difficult to explain because its history is ages in the making. But it must be explained if you are to succeed in what you must do. It is a tale of growing knowledge, of constant adversity, and, until now, of failure. Steady yourself, for we are about to begin."

What? Kali thought. But then the dome in which she stood was suddenly a dome no more. Its walls vanished and she found herself adrift in a void, floating, and somehow knew she was in the centre of the strange expanse she had seen when she had risen above Twilight in the *Tharnak*. This 'space' was as immense as it had been then, her confines utterly gone, and she felt that if she began to travel in any direction, she might never reach its limits.

There was only one difference: where within this void she had then been able to see Kerberos and Twilight's distant sun, marred slightly by the body she now knew to be the Hel'ss, here there was nothing. Nothing in the void. Nothing at all.

"My gods," Kali breathed.

"In the beginning," said Zharn, "there was night. Worlds without light. Rocks without life."

Kali found herself stunned, backpaddling as she might in water to keep afloat, as a number of blindingly bright spheres appeared out of nowhere in the space all around her.

"And then, the gods came."

The spheres hung about Kali at various distances – unimaginable distances – illuminating the void and the lifeless worlds she could now see scattered throughout it. Each was also far more than a sphere, Kali sensed, because from them all she could feel the same strange and powerful sentience emanating.

"They came to this desolate corner of the universe," Zharn continued. "To this dead space. They were the Pantheon."

Kali swallowed. "The Pantheon?"

"Twelve entities – creatures, powers, gods – call them what you will. Kerberos, the Hel'ss, Faranoon, Chazra-Nay, Rehastt, along with eight others whose names we might never know, for they are long gone."

"Wait. Are you telling me one of these spheres is Kerberos?"

"As Kerberos was, when it was young. Like the Hel'ss, it shone brightly, then. It had feasted well before it came – as had the Hel'ss, as had the others."

"Feasted?"

She gasped and began to drift through the expanse before her – or was it that the expanse drifted about her? – she wasn't sure. She found herself directly above the surface of one of the spheres as it rotated beneath her, massive and filling her vision completely. But it was what filled the sphere that drew Kali's attention – a swirling sea

– no, ocean, entire *world* – of writhing forms that resembled Bastian Redigor's Pillar of Souls. But there was a difference – where then she had seen only human forms, the dead of Twilight, here she was looking at what could only be the dead of other worlds, a multitude of strange forms that both awed and disturbed her at the same time. Octopoid things and serpents that were leagues long, pyramidal creatures and creatures of jagged contours, gaseous entities, distinct from that in which they were trapped, and dark, flowing shapes, like liquid shadow. There was nothing familiar about them, and Kali realised she was looking at the souls of another universe.

"Gorged is perhaps a better word," Zharn said. "Gorged until there was nothing left in their old domain. And so they came, came in search of new life, so that they might feast again."

Kali looked at the planets around her. "But these are dead worlds."

"All worlds are dead," Zharn said. "Until their gods come."

Kali watched as each of the spheres – each of the Pantheon – began to move to one of the worlds and take up position above it, hanging there as Kerberos hung above Twilight. Though she could somehow see them all, she knew that billions upon billions of miles must separate them.

For as she continued to watch, the spheres that were the Pantheon infused their individual dead worlds with life, life that from her heavenly vantage point she could see begin to spread across the worlds as their respective civilisations grew. What kind of lifeforms thrived beneath her she didn't know, but thousands upon thousands of years of their history must have passed before her eyes, and when it had, the process that each of the Pantheon had begun was, it seemed, done.

Each sphere had lost its brilliance now, each of the Pantheon became a different hue, and as Kali observed a barely distinguishable thread connecting each sphere to its planet below, a thread which pulsed upwards constantly, she knew from what that hue had grown.

The fact that she was witnessing each member of the Pantheon feeding on its planet's souls was somehow forgotten as her eyes were drawn to the sphere with a familiar azure hue.

To the planet from which it fed.

"Oh gods. Is that Twilight?"

"No, Kali. It is not. For there begins the next part of this tale.

"I don't understand."

Zharn paused. "This is what the Pantheon were, and had they remained so, these worlds, these civilisations, would have enjoyed millennia of existence before their gods moved on. With this there was nothing wrong, for that was the nature of things."

"Something changed?"

"The Pantheon changed. They were ancient beings when they came here, and now they were more ancient still, and some of them chose their worlds unwisely and fed less well than others. Across the vastness of space some began to sense their more successful brethren, became jealous of their conquests, and instead of moving onto neutral worlds the weaker among them began to follow in the wake of the stronger. For a while they were allowed to bask in the essence of those they followed but the worlds available to the Pantheon were becoming fewer, too, their resources scarcer, so that, gradually, the Pantheon were drawn into conflict with each other. They began to draw souls not only from the planets they had created but from each other. They began to consume themselves..."

Kali watched as one of the Pantheon – she didn't know which – hung above a world whose surface glittered with the light of campfires, signifying life, if a primitive form. Then she became aware of another of its kind encroaching on its space from afar. The second of the Pantheon gradually began to move towards the first.

"What am I seeing?" Kali said. "Is this the Hel'ss and Kerberos?"

"No, Kali. You are seeing the merging of Faranoon and Chazra-Nay. Witness, Kali. Witness the end."

It might not have been the Hel'ss and Kerberos that Kali was observing, but the similarity to what was happening above Twilight right at that moment was clear. As the Hel'ss was nearing Kerberos, so too was Faranoon nearing Chazra-Nay. But in this case drawing close enough to touch. As Kali watched wide eyed, the edges of the massive, gaseous spheres came into contact and then, slowly, Faranoon began to eclipse Chazra-Nay. Chazra-Nay did not disappear, however, remaining visible inside the other, like a nucleus within a cell. At least for a while. Then, at first in pockets and then in great spreading clouds, the atmospheres of both bodies became increasingly disturbed, as if each raged with unimaginably large storms – but if they were storms, they were storms of souls, the meeting and conflict of the life force of each of the so-called deities. Seething and roiling ever more tumultuously, the surfaces of the spheres changed hue and composition again and again, sometimes so rapidly that they appeared to pulsate in anger, and it was apparent that a great battle was being raged. Kali had no idea of the length of time that passed during this struggle but in the end Faranoon emerged the victor.

The way that victory came would have made Kali stagger, had she something solid on which to do so. Because though Chazra-Nay vanished inside Faranoon, the size of Faranoon suddenly doubled, and as it did its hue changed and it enveloped the atmosphere of the world below.

"This," Kali gasped, "I've seen this. With Pim in Domdruggle's Expanse. Kerberos was bigger, darker, more threatening. This is the End Time, isn't it! This is the darkness!"

"Wait, Kali," Zharn countered.

Faranoon was now enveloping the alien world like some giant membrane. Hanging there in space for what seemed an eternity, it seemed to be passing on a message to the cosmos. This world is mine. And then, from the surface of the alien world to the surface of Faranoon, countless strands of light began flow. Kali knew instantly what they were – souls – the souls of every living creature on the world being consumed all at once by the deity. She knew now why the elves and the dwarves had vanished so quickly from Twilight, seemingly unable to prevent their fate, because it took only a matter of minutes before the strands of light were fully absorbed into its biosphere and the world below was emptied of life. All across the surface of the world, the campfires went out.

"That is the darkness," Zharn said.

Kali was momentarily speechless.

"How many worlds have the Pantheon destroyed like this?"

"Those it took to reduce their ranks. Faranoon was consumed by another as little as five thousand years later. Rehastt took two worlds before it was itself consumed by the Hel'ss. Ten worlds in all lost to their conflict until only two of the Pantheon – Kerberos and the Hel'ss – remained."

Kali hated to sound flippant about what she'd witnessed but it seemed relevant.

"Kerberos didn't seem to get the munchies."

Once more she was on the move, zooming through space towards the azure sphere and the world she had mistaken for Twilight. It was her longest journey yet.

"No. Kerberos was the most distant of the Pantheon, here, on the very edge of this space. It had found a world whose own god it had subsumed and which satisfied its needs. Because of this and of the great distance between itself and its brethren, it took no further part in the affairs of the Pantheon."

"But Kerberos is above Twilight now, right? So something must have happened."

"The third part of our tale. Of the many races the Pantheon created, this was one of the few that developed the capacity for travel in space, and with it the means to escape Kerberos' domination of their world. A band of refugees managed to leave the planet in search of a new home. What they did not know was that Kerberos, angered by their audacity, would decide to follow them. But what Kerberos, in turn, did not know, was that its passage across the vast void would bring it close to the realm of the Hel'ss."

Kali watched as the great azure orb that was Kerberos moved across space. There, perhaps billions of miles distant but close enough, it briefly eclipsed another orb, purple in colour, which also began to move. Very, very slowly, it began to close the gap between them.

"The hunter," said Zharn, "became the hunted."

The distance between the spheres was so great, Kali realised, that thousands of years could conceivably pass before the Hel'ss caught up with its prey, but this was nothing to the two deities, and she knew from experience that the end of the pursuit was inevitable.

She found herself following Kerberos through space, then floating around its axis, where she gasped. Below her hung Twilight. At least she thought it was Twilight. Because there was something about it that was *wrong*.

"The refugees from the dead world eventually led Kerberos to this world, your world," Zharn explained, "where they mysteriously vanished. Despite this, Kerberos had no choice but to remain, for the journey here had left it weak."

"Twilight looks different," Kali said. "But I can't work out why."

"Yes, Twilight is different. Because there was a fundamental difference between this world and any other that Kerberos had seeded."

Kali began to swoop down into Twilight's atmosphere, at first soaring high above the clouds and then punching through them. She flew above an unfamiliar landscape, across which figures raced. No, not raced – pursued each other. She stared as the predatory creatures – strange, green-skinned hulks and short, vicious, rat-like things – then engaged in battle.

"Oh gods," she said. "Twilight was already populated."

"Indeed it was. But Kerberos was angry that the fugitives he had pursued across space had once more escaped him, and he was also desperate. For the first time since arriving in this universe, Kerberos chose to transform an inhabited world."

"Transform?"

"First it sent its dragons, creatures who appeared to magically create life but who, in fact, were assessing the make-up of the world, ready for disassembly. And when they had done their job, it sent the Great Flood to cleanse the world. The creatures who called it home – those your myths call orcs and goblins – were swept from their lands in the flood and became assimilated in the endless waters. A few survived – somehow – but they no longer belonged on this world."

"This 'assimilation' – it was what was happening in the swirlies? I mean the swirlpools off the island?"

"Yes. The creation – or uncreation – of life."

Kali cringed. "I never thought I'd feel sorry for an orc or goblin."

"Their fate was perhaps merciful considering what happened next. Others eventually would come to live in the great ocean – the Chadassa, the Calma – but the landmasses which the orcs and goblins called home were about to be changed for ever."

"By what?"

"By the more powerful form of the dragons. By the dra'gohn."

Kali sailed back into the skies until she was facing Kerberos. Shadows seemed to be building within its gaseous mass and, then, after a second, burst from the entity's depths. Kali recoiled as these cloud-like things resolved themselves into creatures that were all too familiar. Somehow translucent and more ghostly here, perhaps, but the last time she had seen one of the same it had carried her to the edge of a space before disintegrating before her eyes.

One single dra'gohn that was no more.

But this time, there were hundreds of them.

"The dra'gohn were sent to your world, as they are to every one of the Pantheon's worlds, when the time is right. Spawned in the core of Kerberos, these creatures would make the land on which its people would grow, and on which they would live. The dra'gohn were beings that channelled the very stuff of the universe, of creation, and they were magnificent."

Kali swallowed as her perspective changed once more and she found herself back on the flooded world, standing on the summit of a mountain that appeared to be the only piece of land anywhere. Except it wasn't land, because the mountain was made of glass. Then one of the dra'gohn flew directly at her. The massive creature filled her vision, its wings blotting out the sky, and then she was somehow scooped up and found herself riding on its back. The glass mountain was left far behind her and they flew above an endless expanse of water that spread from horizon to horizon. The sky darkened about her as other dra'gohn joined the one on which she rode, until they were once more present about her in their hundreds, and as one they began to angle down towards the sea.

And then, they made the land.

Kali found herself gasping for breath, so overwhelmed was she by what she saw. The mouth of each dra'gohn opened wide and each *breathed*, massive jets of red and yellow that intertwined and together looked like roaring fire. But this was not fire – this, as Zharn had said, was the stuff of creation itself. The dra'gohn were breathing threads.

Below her, where the ocean had been, a strip of land began to form, the water evaporating, transforming, solidifying gradually into a desert landscape, as the dra'gohn flew above. Kali twisted on her mount's back and gasped again, for behind her a great ridge of rock rolled in the dra'gohn's wake, a crease in that which was being made, nothing less than a mountain range separating the land that was fully formed from that still being breathed.

The dra'gohn ceased breathing and turned, swooping back over the mountain range. Here, they peeled away from each other, some heading to the east, others to the west, and began to breathe again. The somewhat featureless land that they had created on their first pass began to be shaped more now, the weaving patterns of the dra'gohn in the sky creating the shape of a coastline, of river inlets, lakes and valleys and gorges and hills, and when at last they stopped breathing once more, Kali found herself looking not at a strip of land anymore but a landmass that was whole and complete.

A landmass that was as familiar to her as the back of her hand.

The peninsula.

The location of all her adventures.

Home.

"My gods," Kali said. "It's all there. The World's Ridge Mountains, the Sardenne, Vos, Pontaine. All there."

"Except of course," Zharn pointed out, "they were not yet known by these names. For as yet there was no one to name them."

"The Old Races," Kali said. "But that means that Kerberos *was* their god, because it created them!"

"In a way, I suppose. But Kerberos's motives were not those of a god, they were those of survival. Knowing how little time it had – relatively speaking, of course – before the Hel'ss reached Twilight, it made the decision that the battle for survival between itself and the Hel'ss could no longer continue as it had. They were the last of their kind and one of them needed to gain the advantage. To this end, it determined to create not one but two races to inhabit its new domain, gifting each with the potential to be more than just mere fodder but to actively assist it in the fight against its old enemy."

"The elves and the dwarves," Kali said.

"The elves and the dwarves."

"But that doesn't make sense. If Kerberos wanted their help, why create two races that were at each other's throats for millennia? It was only in their third age that they found any kind of peace at all."

"You are wrong," Zharn went on. "Of course the two races fought, but that was exactly why they had been created so. To be diametrically opposed. The el'v, meaning, in the ancient language of the Pantheon 'of the mind', and the dwarves, a corruption of dou'arv, hammer and anvil, 'of the body'. It was only by throwing mind and body into conflict that Kerberos believed they would, eventually, reach their full potential. I suspect it is the same story on a thousand worlds, far beyond the Pantheon. That many of the indigenous races' greatest achievements come about – can *only* come about – as a result of war."

Kali stared at a peninsula overrun with soaring towers and factories, fortifications and battlefields.

"The whole of the peninsula was a forge," she realised.

"A forge for the dwarves, perhaps, a laboratory for the elves. The distinction is immaterial. Each managed, in their own way, to create horrifying weapons of destruction. And the souls of the hundreds of thousands of each race who fell before them across the long years served only to strengthen Kerberos."

"So wouldn't it have served Kerberos better if it had created lifeforms with potential for nothing other than destruction? Some kind of a… warworld to supply it with victims for evermore?"

"Even millions of souls would have been insufficient for Kerberos' needs, so weakened was it. What it needed to recover was the constant ebb and flow of *billions* of souls. The population, in other words, of a full and thriving planet."

"But," Kali said, "all there is is the peninsula. It would never support that many people. Are you telling me that there are lands beyond the World's Ridge Mountains – beyond the Stormwall – beyond the seas?"

"On the contrary. I am telling you there are not."

"I'm sorry. I don't understand."

"Each time one of the Pantheon grants life to a world, it begins, as you have seen, with the creation of a small section of land – in your case, what you call the peninsula, what is to you, in effect, Twilight. This land serves its purpose until the demands upon it begin to exceed its capability, at which time it must expand."

"The deity having drawn strength from what it's already created," Kali gathered.

"You are perceptive."

"So," Kali asked, "the dra'gohn return?"

"Yes, the dra'gohn return," Zharn said. As she spoke Kali's viewpoint changed yet again, and she found herself so far above her world that she looked down on the peninsula as she might a representation of it on a map. Its coastline was fully visible from end to end, all but featureless at this height, looking almost unreal. Then she became aware of massive shapes that momentarily blocked her vision – the dra'gohn swooping once more from the heart of Kerberos – and when she looked again, these shapes were clearly delineated above the peninsula, heading as one to where a small ripple in the map indicated the presence of the World's Ridge Mountains. Kali gasped as the heavenly forms flew majestically above the towering range and once more began to breathe their red and yellow threads, and, as they did, land began to form *beyond* that which she knew to be the edge of the world.

And as it formed, as she'd seen in her earlier flight, the World's Ridge moved with it.

"Wait," Kali said. "There's something wron –"

For the first time since their conversation had begun, however, Zharn did not pause in what she was showing to her, as it if were something she *had* to witness. It didn't matter because, anyway, Kali's question trailed off into silence. How could it not? She was, after all, seeing something she would likely never see again.

Far below her, as the land grew, the flights of the dra'gohn diverged once more, banking gracefully out to all points of the compass, and where they went, they continued to breathe. Kali's heart thumped until it felt fit to burst as she watched a vast continent begin to take shape, spreading for thousands and thousands of leagues in every direction, rich with forest and lakes, prairie and desert, rolling hills and mountain ranges that, this time, remained where they were created. A coastline that would take her lifetimes to explore weaved, darted and thrust itself out into the surrounding sea, but even as a multitude of small and large islands began to dot its waters offshore, the growth of the land did not stop, continuing on out of view, far, far beyond the curve of the world.

It *was* a world. A whole, new world.

Kali could hardly breathe. Her eyes ran with tears.

And then the world was gone.

"You had a question," Zharn prompted gently.

Kali swallowed, gathering her wits before she spoke.

"It's what I meant when I said something's wrong. I understand now what the World's Ridge Mountains are. They're a *barrier*, aren't they? A barrier meant to prevent exploration. To prevent people leaving their world before they – before the rest of the world – was ready. Before Kerberos *wanted* them to leave."

"As, along the coast, was the great elemental barrier – the phenomenon that you call the Stormwall – designed to prevent exploration of the seas. Such exploration would have been, after all, a voyage that would never end..."

Kali suddenly felt very heavy, the weight of 'the truth' beginning to hit her.

"But something happened to the Stormwall, didn't it?" she said. "Just like something happened to the World's Ridge Mountains."

Zharn smiled. It was the smile of someone who knew she had chosen her audience well.

"Why do you say that, Kali?"

"Because the World's Ridge Mountains never *moved*."

Zharn drew in a trembling breath, and the void in which Kali hung seemed to tremble too.

"It is true," the elf said, after a second. "What you have just seen was what *would* have been, were it not for the unimaginable tragedy that occurred. Something that broke the cycle of Kerberos, damaging the deity so badly that it might never be restored."

"What?" Kali said.

"The death of the dra'gohn."

CHAPTER SEVENTEEN

"Oh gods," Kali said. She did, of course, know that the dra'gohn were gone, but she had never learned the circumstances of their demise – or realised they had such an important link to Kerberos or Twilight itself. "How did it happen?"

"The time came when the civilisations of the elves and the dwarves were at their peak, thriving in every sense," Zharn said. As she spoke, the chamber flared to life again and this time Kali found herself with a far more intimate perspective of the peninsula, swooping down across the land, passing over – and sometimes between – the buildings of towering cities of both elven and dwarven origin, witnessing the wonders that filled them. From the technology on view – steam-powered but nonetheless impressive dwarven engineering; the more organic path that the elves favoured – she guessed that in time she was somewhere very near the end of the second or at the start of the third age of the Old Races, the time where, at last, the two had begun to work together. But it seemed Zharn had been almost understating the facts when she'd said they'd thrived in every sense of the word. Their populations growing with the prosperity that peace between them had brought, both races had spread across the peninsula until there was little of it left, taking with them their phantasmagorical devices, their clockwork chariots and their flying machines, the remains of many of which she had come across in her travels. Kali even recognised the genesis of many of the sites she had explored as ancient ruins: Robor's Skyway, the Avenue of the Fallen, and on the coast the bay-encompassing Amphibitheatre of Rossox, where now lay Vosburg but where once the Calmamandra had come to play.

It was clearly time for the Old Races to expand, for the land to grow. But as Zharn had already intimated, there was nowhere for them to go.

"Tell me," Kali said.

Zharn nodded. "Whether it was by accident or design there was an... encounter between the Old Races and one of the dra'gohn," she said. "The encounter ended with the death of the dra'gohn, its form torn asunder by the weapons and powers that its opponents wielded."

"The death of one dra'gohn caused the collapse of Kerberos's plan?"

"Not one, no. It is what happened *after* its death that was to lead to the collapse. Many flocked to the site of the encounter, wishing for whatever reason to observe the remains of the heavenly form, and it was one of these visitors who eventually noticed something very strange. Where the essence – blood or threads, think of it as you will – of the dra'gohn had seeped into the ground, the rock below changed, infused with some kind of energy that made it pulse as if alive."

"This rock," Kali asked hesitantly. "It wouldn't by any chance have been orange?"

"I see you are once more ahead of me, Kali."

"Amberglow," Kali said, swallowing.

"Amberglow. What was to become the power source for most of the elven and dwarven machines that followed. The element that sparked the Old Races final era of magical technology."

"Are you trying to tell me –"

"Its discovery," Zharn spoke over her, "led to the wholesale slaughter of the dra'gohn. The extinction of the very creatures that were needed to save them. Even as the dra'gohn returned to breathe the land, the elves and the dwarves were waiting for them with their airships, with their mages, their ballistas and their cannon emplacements atop the highest peaks."

"I can't believe it. How could they be capable of such greatness and yet so stupid?"

"They were not to know how integral to their future the dra'gohn were. How could they? Besides, if you were handed the power of the Pantheon – the threads, the power of the gods – are you sure you would be able to resist?"

"Of course I –"

Kali stopped. Would she? Would she really? How much had she enjoyed being at the controls of the scuttlebarge? The dwarven mole? Carried into the skies and beyond by the *Tharnak*? Even wielding something as simple as a crackstaff? None of these things would have been possible without amberglow.

It was a question she might never answer, and certainly not now, for the images resumed. This time she witnessed the effects on the land the end of the dra'gohn had wrought. Their slaughter, Zharn explained, sent ripples through the threads that became tsunamis of change, and Kali saw the peninsula they had created reforming once again, this time in turmoil. Great cracks appeared in the land, into which many of the Old Races' achievements tumbled, to be lost forever. Earthquakes felled building after building and shattered roads and trade routes. A huge rolling ridge of land – similar to the World's Ridge but here rolling free and uncontrolled – came to rest in the heart of what would become Vos, the upheaval leaving behind it what were now the Drakengrat Mountains. Most dramatically of all, the coast of the peninsula to the west and to the north began to break apart as a result of the stresses elsewhere, and Kali gasped as she witnessed huge chunks of land shearing away into the sea. She was awed by the sight for what she was watching was the formation of the Sarcre Islands and of the home of Jakub Freel, Allantia itself.

"The Stormwall," she said. "This is what destroyed the Stormwall."

"Yes," Zharn confirmed. "Following the Great Upheaval all that remained of the barrier was that which now separates the Sarcre Islands from the mainland, and a much weakened zone of meteorological disturbance along other parts of the coast."

"Much weakened?" Kali reflected. "Pits of Kerberos."

"This, then, was the last time the dra'gohn had any influence on the future of our lands. What remained was to become the stage on which would be played out the final act of the Old Races."

"The darkness," Kali said.

Zharn nodded. "It was three thousand years, measured in the Old Race's calendar, before the Hel'ss reached this world, and in that time the elves and the dwarves became masters of the magical technology their wholesale slaughter had brought them. But in mastering it, they forgot the roots from which the amberglow had come. The threads that the dra'gohn had breathed were but one segment of the Circle of Magic – sometimes called the Circle of Power – with which Kerberos had imbued this world and on which its survival depended. Had the dra'gohn threads – the dragon magic – remained in the Circle, Kerberos might just have had the strength to fight the Hel'ss, but without them the entity was the weakest it had ever been."

"Kerberos's experiment to defend itself against the Hel'ss had succeeded," Kali said. "But because of the folly of its creations, one vital component was missing."

"Yes. The ship and its k'nid were ready to be launched at the Hel'ss, while here, on Twilight, Domdruggle's Expanse was ready to be used as a sanctuary by our people during the chaos that might ensue. But the ship was found lacking. Without the armour of the Circle of Power it would have carried with it, it could not penetrate the Hel'ss defences, and was never launched. And without the Circle of Power defending Twilight, the Hel'ss was able to launch its attack on Trass Kattra."

"By the ship, I take it you mean the *Tharnak*," Kali queried. "Strange, flying thing?"

"The guardian's name," Zharn said, and smiled.

"If only they'd waited. They'd have developed another means of power."

"That is the tragedy of it. Soon afterwards, the darkness came."

"Now, that's what I don't understand," Kali queried. "If the darkness *did* come, if the Hel'ss merged with Kerberos and fought that battle you showed me, why didn't Kerberos die like Chazra-Nay, Faranoon or the others? Why wasn't it consumed?"

"You might equally ask why Kerberos did not consume the Hel'ss. Both entities had travelled so far that they were equally weakened – starved of souls – and what should have been the final, decisive confrontation between them ended in stalemate. The struggle for supremacy lasted a thousand years and more but neither the Hel'ss nor Kerberos emerged victorious, in fact they emerged as far from victorious as they could possibly be, wounded, scarred and almost dead. Kerberos became the shadow of itself that looms above your world to this day while the Hel'ss retreated to deep space, regaining, through the long ages, what strength it could. The strength it knew it would need to one day return."

"And now, here it is," Kali said ominously.

"Yes. Returned for an unprecedented second confrontation – the first time in the history of the Pantheon that this has occurred. And because of it, the Four have the best chance to end their war that we have ever had."

"Okay, here's the other thing. Who the hells are 'the Four'?"

"The last survivors of a world Kerberos drained long ago. A world before this universe but with a race not dissimilar to your own. Four individuals who came to perceive the true nature of their god and who voluntarily surrendered their souls to it. Souls which, through their mental discipline, were able to insinuate themselves into Kerberos's Cycle, to be reincarnated once on each planet it seeded. Souls that might eventually find a means to rebel against the Pantheon and end their devouring of worlds."

"Which is why you're where you are now? Or why you involved yourself in what was going on? To help the Old Races destroy the Hel'ss."

"The Hel'ss, and then Kerberos."

"Hold it right there," Kali said. "You said the Four were reincarnated *once* on each planet Kerberos seeded. And you also said you were one of *your* Four. But this is the same planet, so where did we – Morlader, Kane, DeZantez and me – come from?"

"The past. Now. My now, that is."

"Whoa, whoa, whoa. Are you saying that your souls are *our* souls?"

"I am."

"How is that possible? I mean, how is… oh, fark."

"It must be difficult for you to understand, but I will try to explain. When the End Time came, or at least when it was near, the four of us knew that it would be our end time, too. If we were returned to Kerberos, or taken by the Hel'ss, then we would either be trapped within a dying entity above a dying world or within an entity adrift in the cosmos, possibly for the remainder of time. We were faced with a situation where the kattra might never return. Before either could take us, therefore, we assigned our souls to a different place…"

Kali let out an involuntary laugh of disbelief. "You said 'no' to the gods?"

"In essence. In practice, we found a way to bind part of our souls to the threads – to *particular* threads – that would one day release them where and when we wished. For thousands upon thousands of years they remained hidden and dormant, drifting within the weave, waiting for the faint tremors in the Circle of Power that would signal the return of the Hel'ss. And then, they would be born again. The souls themselves were not enough, however, for being part souls, they carried with them no memory of what they were or the threat they faced, which is why this message awaited you today. We had, of course to ensure that you all survived long enough for one of you to receive the message, and to that end we granted the abilities which each of you possess."

"My – our – powers came through the threads?"

"No. With the exception of Silus Morlader – whose apparent abilities are the result of a tragic encounter and whose true legacy is not what you think – that was not possible. Physical abilities needed to be transferred physically, and so we instilled them – dormant once more – into bloodlines that paralleled the threads."

"Pits of Kerberos," Kali said. "Those bloodlines began with the humans you experimented on at the Crucible, didn't they? The yassan, the others. The ones – the *other* four – who were being prepared for the ship?"

"Themselves the children of the Chadassa and the Calma, some of whose dying kin, following a great disaster that struck them, crawled onto the land where they were adopted – *adapted* – by the Old Races, who pitied them. This magnanimous act was the best thing they could have done, for in creating the humans, they gave Twilight a second chance."

"But is it a second chance? I mean the very fact we're having this chat only confirms what you've already said. That every attempt by the kattra to stop the Pantheon has ended in failure. Why should this time be any different?"

"Because of what is happening. For the first time in our endless struggle the Four that were and the Four that are can work together. With the knowledge I have given you – with what you have already discovered and found – the Four can become *eight*. With that, we have a fighting chance."

Kali frowned. Despite everything Zharn had said, she'd gone through too much and been surprised so many times to accept her words hands down. She needed more.

"Who were you?" she asked. "You and your Four?"

Zharn paused, but when she answered her response was accompanied by a faint smile. "I was no one of consequence, like the others. And yet bound by my legacy, as you are by yours. As for the other three, Rollin Dumarest was a dwarf, but unlike so many of his race a gentle, kind and loving man. Tremayin Fireflak, an elf like myself, prone, as befitted her name, to combustible temperament and absolute disregard for authority of any kind. And last, but far from least, Traynor Boom, a dwarf again, whose contribution to our cause were the blades of his two-handed battleaxe, Bloody Banshee. Its eloquent use bought the Drakengrat facility additional time, though regrettably not enough to save it."

"He died there?"

"Alongside Tremayin, fighting to protect the ship even as the darkness enveloped them."

Kali warmed to Zharn, despite the sadness she related. The fact that they were both talking of similar experiences made her feel a kinship with the elf, even though she and Zharn had never met. A kinship with her and the other three that was beginning to make her believe everything she'd been told.

"And Rollin Dumarest? What happened to him?"

"Rollin? Lost with Rodolfo Domdruggle, somewhere in the Expanse."

There it was again – that common experience – and Kali's mind whirled. Were it not for the fact that she, Lucius Kane and Silus Morlader were still alive, Zharn could have been speaking of them. And of Gabriella before she'd sacrificed herself. The similarities between the present and the past continued to be staggering.

"I'm sorry," Kali said.

"Don't be. Though their sacrifices are fresh in my mind, in a sense it all happened a long time ago," Zharn responded. "As I imagine is the case with yourself, I did not know my companions well, for that is the nature of our legacy. But they are sadly missed."

What did it for Kali was the question she asked next.

"If we each have one of your souls, which of you am I?"

"Can't you guess?"

"Combustible temperament?" Kali said. "Absolute disregard for authority of any kind?"

"Hello, Tremayin."

Kali put a hand to her mouth, holding back a sob. It took a moment for her to recover, and when she did she *believed* Zharn. But a couple of problems remained.

"When I came here you called me Kali," she said. "How did you know my name?"

"Because you told me."

"No, I didn't."

"If you say so," Zharn said slowly. "There are some questions that I can't answer."

"Okay, then, here's another one. You said that our abilities were sent by a bloodline, but as far as I know I don't have one. I wasn't born to any family. I was found, as a baby, in a dome."

"And," Zharn sighed, "there are some things that you can't yet know."

"*Why*?"

"Because they haven't yet happened."

"I haven't come this far to hear more riddles! Tell me, dammit!"

Zharn considered for a moment.

"Then first tell me – would it benefit you to know that you are dead?"

For the first time since her ordeal had began, Kali felt freezing cold. "What?"

The way Zharn couched her response could have sounded threatening, pitying, even sad. But it didn't. It actually sounded rather amused.

"Poor Kali Hooper. The girl who never was."

Kali's anger was diffused in a swirl of confusion. "Zharn, I don't understand."

"I know. But you have to trust me. Trust yourself. Now is not the time to speak of this."

Kali remained silent for more than a minute, torn by what she'd heard. She couldn't deny that in coming this far to learn about the Old Races, she'd wanted to learn about herself also – *expected* to – and Zharn's words hadn't just sent her back to square one, they'd knocked her completely off the game board. The fact was, though, she now accepted what she'd been told, and as a result felt the time would come when she *would* discover her origin. With whomever it was that would finally give her the answer.

In the meantime there was the small matter of saving the world. Again. She might as well get on with it.

"What," Kali said at last, "do I need to do?"

"Many things, and none will be easy. Your first task will be to unite the Four, and when you are together, unite what lies within you all."

"What lies within us – ?" Kali began, and then suddenly her mind flashed back to the final encounter with Redigor in the cavern below. What had exploded from within. Somehow now she knew why it had had such an effect on Redigor and on what had remained of the Hel'ss Spawn.

"That was dra'gohn magic? What's missing from the Circle?"

"Yes. A sliver of it was implanted within each of your bloodlines."

"But how? I thought it was all gone?"

"There are some things –"

"That I can't yet know?"

"I'm sorry. But you will come to understand."

"Yeah, right. So, okay, unite what lies within us all. How do we do that?"

"There is an artefact – an enchanted rod of my own manufacture known as the Guardian Starlight – that was hidden in the Anclas Territories and is currently sought by Lucius Kane. Find this rod and it will provide you with the means."

"Me? All this magical gubbins sounds more like a job for Lucius himself."

Zharn smiled. "It will not be necessary for you to use 'magical gubbins'. The Guardian Starlight itself knows what it must do. But it is Lucius Kane who will wield the rod when the Guardian Starlight is complete, for only he has that power."

"Fair enough. Unite Lucius, Silus and Gabriella. But isn't there one small flaw in your plan?"

"There is?"

"Gabriella DeZantez is dead."

"Need I repeat that so, child, are you."

"*Riiigghhtt*," Kali said hesitantly. "So we've united and powered up this rod – what next?"

"You must travel beyond the World's Ridge Mountains and there use the rod to restore the Circle of Power."

"Whoa, stop. *Beyond* the World's Ridge Mountains? But I thought there was nothing there?"

"It is true that your journey will end beyond the mountains. But also begin. Be patient, Kali, and you will see."

Kali's mind flashed back to her rescue of Merrit Moon. And to the journal she'd read.

"At least I think I know a way through. Or a start. A place called the Hall of Tales?"

"Indeed."

Kali frowned. "The old man finding it is a bit convenient, don't you think?"

"Convenient, or destined?"

"O-ho, no, don't you start that. Don't you dare start that."

The dome rumbled and parts of the energies that surrounded Kali and Zharn started to diffuse. The dome wall reappeared and Kali saw cracks appearing throughout its structure. As Brundle had warned, the cap was beginning to fall apart.

"I think," said Zharn, "that our moment in time is almost over."

"Problem our end," Kali replied. "We're taking a bit of flak at the moment."

"Kali," Zharn said, her image starting to flicker, "Listen to me. You have the means to finish this once and for all, but I cannot tell you how because I do not know. But you have time to ask me one more question that might help you, and I will answer it as best I can."

Kali could think of a hundred, but her brain was so busy that she couldn't pin down one. Finally, she asked something that, despite sticking in her mind, she immediately thought may not have been relevant at all.

"Have you ever heard of someone called Marryme Moo?"

"The name" said Zharn, "is Marryme Moon."

And then the dome exploded.

CHAPTER EIGHTEEN

IT WAS OVER.

Kali found herself standing suddenly in what remained of the Thunderflux cap, wind whistling through the shattered structure, less dome now than a ring of jagged projections. The Thunderflux was gone, diffused, and with it the link to the past that had existed for uncountable centuries. She was alone, and any more questions she might have, she'd have to answer herself. Including the most personal ones of all.

Poor Kali Hooper, the girl who never was. And *the name is Marryme Moon.*

Kali shivered, exposed in more ways than one. She was therefore grateful when behind her a crunch of boots on debris signalled the arrival of Slowhand. She didn't even need to turn to know it was him, merely sensed his comforting presence, and murmured her thanks when the archer slipped his shirt over her naked body, helping when her aching arms struggled with the sleeves.

Now she did turn, looking up at him. Slowhand's shirt draped her like a tent, hanging below her knees, but it still couldn't fully disguise the bruises and burns, the patches of crusted muck and weed, and here and there the spots of blood that were already seeping through the thick cloth.

"Fark, Hooper," Slowhand said. "What happened to you?"

"Long story," Kali replied, numbly. "Old story."

"Want to share it?"

"Not yet."

Kali cocked her head. It had only just occurred to her that, other than the whistling of the wind, the island was silent. No more tremors, no more screams.

"The Hel'ss Spawn is gone," Slowhand said. "Come see."

He took Kali by the hand and led her out of the ruin. They walked slowly up the slope to the clifftop that was Horizon Point. The bodies

– what had been left of the bodies – of the Faith and their own people were gone, the landscape normal once more, and the only signs of the struggles that had taken place were the half-melted remains of the Brogmas, standing there slumped and still on the bleak promontory. Maybe one day, Kali thought, someone like herself would come to the island and see these things, wonder at their meaning and the role they had played in its history.

If there *was* a one day.

She took a breath. At least, as Slowhand had said, one small part of the battle was done. Gazing out to sea, she saw that the waters around the island were smooth, that the dra'gohn magic that had burst from her in the cavern far below had indeed delivered the killing blow to the alien entity and the bastard who'd possessed it. In a way, it had been the Hel'ss and Kerberos who'd fought the battle – their essences clashing in a preliminary skirmish – and for now, at least, Kerberos had won.

Kali took no comfort in the fact. Though the sea looked quite beautiful, coloured by the remains of the amberglow engines, as if lit by the rays of a glowing sunset, she knew now what she was really looking at. And all she could see was a series of majestic, spectral forms swooping above a slowly diffusing bloodstain that, when it was gone, would once again make Twilight an emptier place.

"Do you know what they did, 'Liam?" she said quietly. "Do you know what they did to the dra'gohn?"

The archer stepped up beside her, surprised to see tears on Kali's cheeks. She seemed only half aware of his presence, staring out to sea, haunted somehow, and he noted her fingering her breastbone, as if contemplating something a long way, or a long time, away.

"Do you want to tell me?"

Kali did, and Slowhand pulled her to him as she related the tale, and when it was over he found all he could do was hold her, because there was nothing to say.

"We're all that's left now," Kali said eventually. "The Four."

"So what happens now?"

"We get the dra'gohn magic out of us and where it's meant to be. One way or another, we end the wars of the Pantheon once and for all."

Slowhand moved her to arms' length, lips forming a small smile. "You never do anything *small*, do you?"

Kali laughed. "Well, the first thing we have to do is get off this farking island."

"Being sorted as we speak. The others are below."

"Then what are we waiting for?"

The two of them wound their way down the steps through the ruins, back to the beach where Redigor and his forces had landed. The place was a hive of activity, Sonpear and Pim and his men tinkering under Brundle's supervision on the flutterbys, while Hetty, Pete Two-Ties and Martha DeZantez were helping the rest of their people, who had taken refuge underground, out from the access hatches, assembling them back on the surface. Kali bit her lip, looking in vain for the stretcher carrying Dolorosa, and fearing the worst when it didn't appear. But as it happened, she shouldn't have been looking for a stretcher at all.

"You arra the mess," a voice criticised at the same time a bony finger prodded her in the shoulder. "We cannot take-a you anywhere."

Kali span. "Dolorosa?"

The old woman loomed in her face, eyes narrowed, though there was a hint of humour in them. "Who elsa you theenk speaka thees way?"

"But how?" Kali said. Her gaze was drawn to Dolorosa's wound, now nothing more than a patch of dried blood on her torn clothing with a hint of strange, gold stitching on her skin.

"If there's one thing yer can say for me wife, it's that she knows her 'erbs," Brundle said from where he lay under a flutterby, bashing it with a spanner. He rose, wiping his hands with a rag. "That an' a bit o' the old knitting, eh?"

"Clack-clack," Dolorosa said.

Kali smiled, patted the old woman on the shoulder, and moved towards Brundle.

"I wanted to thank you."

"Me? It's Brogma yer shou –"

"That isn't what I meant," Kali interrupted. And punched the dwarf hard in the face.

Brundle crashed onto his backside, hand over nose. Three streams of blood ran between his fingers.

"Owww! Wod de fark wad dad for?"

"The Trials," Kali said. "You did design them, didn't you?"

"Aye, well," Brundle said, but was spared further defence when Kali offered him a hand up.

"Forget it," she said. "They kept me on my toes, and I've a feeling I'm going to need to be kept on my toes."

The dwarf, like Slowhand and Dolorosa before him, looked her battered and bloody body up and down. "Looks like yer made a bit of a worgle's arse of it, to me."

"Hey! There were complications, all right?"

The dwarf's expression turned to one of surprising concern, knowing full well what the complications must have been. "If ah had a badge yer could have one. Bu ah don't. Good to see yer made it, smoothskin."

"Me, too. So what's happening?"

Brundle pointed at the flutterbys.

"It's taken a bit o' tinkerin', but these beasties should get most o' yer people home."

"That's a long way. I thought they were short range flyers?"

"They are. Which is why I've had to cannibalise some ta handle the journey. It'll take a week or so an' ah can't guarantee they'll make it intact through the Stormwall, but they should come down within' range o' the peninsula's shipping."

Kali nodded. "Good enough. But if you've stripped them down, there won't be enough room for everybody, surely?"

"No," Brundle said, and hesitated. "But with those lost on both sides, fewer'll have ta remain behind than yer think. Ah reckon five or six volunteers."

"My hand's up."

"Ah don't think so, lass. Yer know by now where yer should be."

"And I know where these people should be," Kali said, looking at the freed prisoners. "I'll get there, Brundle, don't you worry. Meantime, like I said – my hand's up."

"Fair enough," the dwarf conceded. "An' ah don't think yer'll havta look far for the rest."

Kali jumped, suddenly aware of the forms of Slowhand, Dolorosa, Sonpear, Pim and Freel beside her. She studied the Allantian, glad to have him back with her, but aware also that his efforts to help since he'd been freed of Redigor had left him exhausted. His experience wasn't something recovered from easily. "Jakub," she said, calling him by his given name for the first time, "please, go with the others. We might need your strength when we get home."

The Allantian faltered, then nodded, tromping wearily towards those who had been assembled to leave. Slowhand slapped his back as he departed.

"So the rest of us swim?" he asked Brundle. "Or do you have another plan?"

"Me scuttlebarge, o' course," Brundle said. He made an obvious point of staring at Kali's behind and then added, "She'll be a little low in the water, but we'll make it."

"Hey!" Kali protested.

"Hey yerself," the dwarf replied. "Now let's get these people on the move."

Brundle moved among the flutterbys, starting up their engines, and the beach was filled with the sound of their insect-like drones. The choice of pilots was left to Kali, and she chose those whose determination she knew would get them home – Martha, Hetty, Abra and Freel himself among them. Civilians were led to the flutterbys in small groups, settled in, and then with a series of complex hand gestures that Kali was sure were more to do with showing off than actually necessary, Brundle walked from machine to machine, signalling each pilot that they were ready for take off.

"Good luck to all of you," Martha DeZantez said.

"You, too," Kali replied.

"See you at home, Kalee!"

"The gods be with you, girly, lady, madam, missus-woman."

One by one, their noses dipping slightly, the flutterbys rose from the beach and headed out to sea. They skimmed the waves at first but then began to rise until they were silhouetted against the coming sunset, which was already starting to paint the waters. A few minutes later they were dots, and then they were gone.

"They'll be fine," Slowhand said, sensing Kali's concern.

"I hope so."

Kali studied the archer. He hadn't turned as he'd spoken, but continued to stare out to sea. No, Kali thought, not out to sea but across it, doubtless seeing the distant shoreline of the peninsula in his mind's eye. A peninsula that had one less thing to offer him when he returned.

"What about you? Will you be fine?"

Slowhand straightened, drawing in a deep breath through his nose.

"I guess I've finally realised what my destiny is."

"Which is?"

"Today, to have been right there on that clifftop, where I could save your life," Slowhand said. "And tomorrow... tomorrow, well, somewhere else where the shit hits the fan."

Kali smiled. "I'll try not to keep you too busy."

The archer turned at last. "So then – it's business as usual."

"Not quite usual," Kali said, regarding Slowhand's altered appearance disapprovingly. If he intended to remain by her side, there'd have to be changes. "Poul, can you do something about this?"

The mage approached, circling Slowhand and inspecting his features with darting, close cocks of the head that made the archer scowl and pull warily away.

"I think so," Sonpear said. "Presuming Mister Slowhand doesn't want me to rebreak *all* of his bones, returning his physiognomy to what it was should require only a minor incantation."

"Then would you please do it?" Kali asked.

"Hey, hey!" Slowhand objected. "I'm here too, remember. Do I get a say in this?"

"Not really," Brundle interjected. "Unless, that is, you actually *want* to spend the rest of your life looking like an orc's knob found its way into yer mammy's panties."

"*Listen, shortarse...*"

"Slowhand, shut up!" Kali said. "I mean, what's the problem here?"

"The problem? The fact that it farking *hurts* is the problem."

"Don't be such a baby."

"You weren't *there*, Hooper. I'm telling you, those few minutes I spent on the Big Top floor felt like an eternity and... ow," Slowhand concluded. "OW. OWW!"

Sonpear smiled, his hands already weaving the threads, and as he did the coarser elements of Slowhand's features began to dwindle, reforming themselves into the more familiar lines he had once possessed. Kali nodded approvingly as she witnessed the return of the lantern jaw, the cute, concave nose, the mouth whose edges splayed laughter lines, though they had clearly been challenged of late. Even his hair returned to its natural colour and length, which the archer wasted no time tossing manfully in the wind.

"What about the scar?" Kali said, frowning at the 'x'. "The scar's still there."

"It is?" Slowhand responded, running his hand over his cheek.

"It shouldn't be," Sonpear said slowly. "But it won't seem to go away."

"Dammit!" Slowhand cursed.

Kali stroked and then playfully slapped Slowhand's cheek. "Never mind, pretty boy. I've had worse scars and it kind of suits you in a an ugly kind of way."

"Oh, it's all right for you," Slowhand protested. "Your scars recover because of that... regeneration thing you have going on..."

"Why," Sonpear mused, "won't it go away?"

"What?" Slowhand said.

Something flared in their midst, and the archer let out a cry far surpassing those when Sonpear had begun his work. Maybe even surpassing those when Fitch had begun his work. It was only after a few seconds that Kali realised the flare had come *from* him.

Slowhand dropped to his knees, groaning in pain, hand clutching his scar. Kali bent to help but faltered. She hesitated because between the cracks of Slowhand's fingers, light was leaking. A light that was starting to grow so bright it was shining through his flesh.

Rays of it began to punch between his fingers.

"What the hells?" Kali said. "Sonpear?"

"Mister Slowhand," he said cautiously. "I want you to remove your hand. And I want you to do it very, very slowly."

Slowhand nodded, but clearly had difficulty. His teeth clenched, the rumble of what would become a roar filtering through them, his hand seemed adhered to his flesh, pulling glue like strands of light with it. Then at last it broke away, revealing what lay beneath.

The 'x' shaped scar was pulsing a brilliant white.

"What... the... fark... is... happening?" Slowhand rumbled.

"Haven't a clue," Kali said honestly.

Dolorosa worked her way through the group about the kneeling archer, saw the scar and drew in a sharp intake of breath. Her eyes narrowed suspiciously.

"This looka familiar," she said. "A horribly familiar..."

"Familiar?"

"Yessa," Dolorosa insisted. "Do you notta see?"

Kali realised she had been paying far too much attention to the glow than to the detail of the scar, and as she studied it saw that around the weal of raised flesh, another tracery of light was slowly appearing. Having started beneath the scar it was working its way up left and right, like a burning fuse on Slowhand's flesh, enclosing the 'x' in a perfect circle. Then, as its two paths joined, it flared as brightly as the rest of the scar.

"Did I notta tell you, Kali Hooper? That's –"

"Oh gods," Kali finished. "The symbol of the Final Faith."

"The what?" Slowhand said. "The *what*?"

Kali stared at the crossed circle, burning now as brightly as a white-hot furnace. Then she felt Sonpear's hand on her shoulder, easing her away.

"There's nothing that can be done," he said. "Stand back. Everybody stand back."

"Stand back?" Slowhand repeated, panicked. "What – *am I going to explode?*"

"Not quite."

"Not quite?" The archer responded, having become quite high-pitched. "What the fark do you mean, *not quite?*"

He doubled over once more, wanting but resisting the need to slap his hand back over the pulsating scar. For the crossed circle of the Faith lifted *away* from his skin, becoming something quite independent of him, floating in the air. Gasping in both shock and relief, Slowhand scrambled back as the glowing emblem began to grow, its diameter widening.

It stopped then burst into flame. The four arms of the 'x' burned away into the surrounding circle. And in the space that was left, the face of Querilous Fitch appeared. He smiled like some visiting deity, but a smile did not sit easily on the psychic manipulator's emaciated features and the last thing anything felt was that their visitor was here to do good.

"Fitch," Slowhand said, "what the hells is going on?"

"Ah, the archer," Fitch said. "I should like to thank you for acting on my behalf. Through you, I have been able to witness the emergence of that I have waited so long to see."

"What the hells are you talking about?"

"Your scar was a spell called a Roving Eye," Sonpear determined. "Not to be confused with an Eye of the Lord, it is a magical thing. An observer – a conduit, if you like – between here and the mainland. Or wherever it is Fitch currently lurks."

"Poul Sonpear," Fitch said. "It has been a long time since last we met."

"You two know each other?" Kali asked.

"Once upon a time, Querilous was a student of mine. I'm sorry to say I taught him many things he should never have known. Including the Roving Eye."

"Teachings long since surpassed, Poul. But I thank you for the human perspective on the power of the threads."

"What do you mean, human perspective?" Kali asked, suspiciously.

Fitch smiled. "Of all the things you should have learned from Slowhand, Redigor and your own recent discoveries about yourself, it is that few things are what they seem," the psychic manipulator said. Then his features began to change, seemingly to melt, his flesh becoming waxier, greyer and moister as it did. This unexpected physiognomy took on a number of new features, including a lipless mouth, enlarged eyes, and a pair of glowing, bulbous nodules that hung from the side of his head, swaying slightly, as if caught in a gentle stream.

Kali's mind whirled. A flashback of a face from long ago, in the floodwaters of Martak. Of a shadowy shape in Gransk harbour. And of a fleetingly sighted rescuer on the other side of a sealed hatch on the Black Ship.

"You," she said. "All the time."

"Me," Querilous Fitch responded. "All the time."

"Er, you want to tell me what's going on?" Slowhand prompted Kali. Like most people on the peninsula, he had never seen such a creature before.

"Fitch is one of them. A fish."

Slowhand paused.

"The slippery bastard."

"Was it you at Scholten, too?" Kali asked Fitch. "My liberator from the Deep Cells?"

"Of course. I could hardly leave you at the mercy of the elf, now, could I?"

"Somehow I never pictured you as my knight in shining armour."

Fitch smiled, though in his new form it was less of a smile and more the slow, crescent shaped gaping of a freshly slashed throat.

"I had no interest in protecting you, girl. Only that which you carry."

"The dra'gohn magic?" Kali gasped.

"Do you realise how long I have waited for you to manifest its power? To even realise you possessed such power?"

"Sorry to keep you waiting. I suppose you want it?"

"Of course."

"Well, guess what – you're not having it."

"We'll see about that, won't we?"

Fitch's face began to move towards Kali, and in doing so the whole of his form physically followed it through the Roving Eye. Slowhand noticed that it was no longer in the strange wheelchair he had seen but walking independently – if walking was the word. The psychic manipulator still retained the semblance of human legs but seemed to glide rather than walk towards them, slime trailing behind him, making his approach all the more threatening. The archer and everyone else backed away. Only Sonpear made any kind of move, his hands weaving what may have been the beginnings of a spell, but none of them would find out which because a second later the mage from the Three Towers was dead. Very, very dead. Fitch simply raised his hand and Sonpear was struck all over his body by what seemed like a hundred invisible sledgehammers, each of them pummelling him so hard his robes billowed beneath the impact, disregarded the flesh beneath, and shrouded the mage in explosive puffs of dust from his own, obliterated bones. Sonpear jerked and spasmed and then the floppy remains of what he had been fell onto the beach on what remained of his face.

Kali refused to be weakened by what had happened. She wouldn't let Fitch see that.

"Why, you bastard? What do you want from the magic?"

"What do you think I want? Its power! With it, all can be made as it should be. A world of water. One vast ocean in which my kind can flourish undisturbed, can thrive."

Kali laughed out loud. "You want to play god? Use the power of the Pantheon to remake Twilight?"

"Why not? Without the interference of the Four, the last of the Pantheon will destroy each other, consume themselves, and in the process you landwalkers will be gone."

"I'm sorry to disappoint you but the Four might have something to say about that. Or at least one of them."

"Which," Fitch said, "is that?"

His hand moved again and, behind him, the still fiery circle of the Final Faith started to unravel until it became an open-ended strand of fire, like a glowing whip. It flexed and snapped in the air and then straightened, less whip than spear, one end pointed directly at Kali. She swallowed, knowing, somehow, that she had only a second left.

"What I don't understand," she said, "is why the Faith? Why involve yourself with them?"

Fitch smiled. "Where better to hide yourself than amongst the blind?"

The spear of fire shot forward, straight into Kali's chest and out through her back, and then twisted in the air to return to Fitch. It penetrated him in the same way it had her but, this time, did not re-emerge. The psychic manipulator – the fish – took a deep, satisfied breath.

"At last," he said.

Kali slumped to the beach as heavily as Sonpear had, landing in an almost foetal position. Unlike Sonpear, she still lived, though it hardly seemed so. What Fitch had done – stripped her of the dra'gohn magic – had hurt more than when Redigor had tried to take her soul in the Chapel of Screams, but there was a worse pain. An emptiness. Everything she had fought for – the true nature of which she had only just discovered – had been taken from her the moment it mattered most. And the worst of it was, it had left her too weak to do anything about it.

Kali's foetal position tightened, her knees rising, her fists clenching, her head dipping into her chest.

"What," Dolorosa shouted, "have you done to my girl?"

The piratess moved towards Fitch but Slowhand grabbed her and held her back.

"Don't," he warned. "He's too dangerous."

"Dangerous, but leaving." Fitch said. "It's been a long, long time since I have been able to delegate my more unsavoury tasks. I miss that."

Slowhand glared at him. "And what exactly are you delegating?"

"Your deaths, of course."

A sneer formed on Slowhand's lips, but faded as Querilous Fitch began to retreat from him. Because the psychic manipulator – the *fishman* – glided once more, this time backwards down the beach, towards and then into the sea.

Staring at them all the time, Querilous Fitch receded beneath the waves, the water lapping about his waist, his chest, his head, until he was gone. And as he disappeared, in his place, other figures waded by him from the depths, at least twenty of them, sloughing dark water and seaweed from their muscular forms as they came. Forms green of skin and scaled, and even without their talons, armed to their very sharp teeth.

"I think," Jengo Pim said, "that we should get the hells out of here."

"I'm open to suggestions," Slowhand responded.

"Back up the steps. We can make a stand on the cliff."

Slowhand nodded and pulled Kali's slumped form to its feet, supporting her as they began the climb. Pim, Brundle and Dolorosa brought up the rear. The old woman hissed at the fishmen as they crossed the beach in pursuit.

The climb seemed to take forever, and night closed in, but there seemed to be more than shadows in the rocks and ancient ruins around them. Hisses and sibilant rattles punctuated the darkness, and shapes flitted here and there, preternaturally fast, leaving a peculiar dampness in the air. Every member of the party cast uneasy glances as they rose higher and higher, but it was down to Brundle, as they at last reached Horizon Point, to voice what they all feared.

"They're everywhere, yer know," the dwarf said. "There must be hundreds of 'em."

It was true. As Slowhand, Pim and the others formed themselves into a defensive huddle on the highest point of the island, those that Querilous Fitch had sent from the sea to be their executioners emerged from all points of the compass, up the steps, from behind rocks, out of the shattered remains of the Thunderflux's cap, and over the lip of the cliff behind them.

All of them swarming onto Trass Kattra in search of their prey.

"It's over," Kali said, lying weak in his arms.

Slowhand started at her words.

"That doesn't sound like the Kali Hooper I know."

"That's because I'm not the Kali Hooper you know. Not any more."

"The dra'gohn magic," the archer said. "We'll get it back. Finish the job."

Kali stared over his shoulder to where the blood red orb that was the Hel'ss hung in the sky. It was almost touching Kerberos, now. She shook her head. "Too late. Just like last time, too late."

"Not if I have anything to do with it," Slowhand said.

"Make that *we*," Brundle rumbled.

"I'd go with that," agreed Jengo Pim.

Dolorosa nodded. "We will make sure these feesh havva their cheeps."

Slowhand lowered Kali's head to the ground. "I have to leave you now. Just for a while."

"What the hells are you doing? This is suicide."

Slowhand grinned. "Hey, I'm your sidekick, aren't I?"

He rose, pulling Suresight from his back and notching an arrow, the tension of it creaking in the night. Beside him, Brundle unslung his battleaxe from its scabbard with a *sching* and hefted it before him. Pim drew a short sword and Dolorosa twin daggers, slashing the air with their blades.

Slowhand stared at the surrounding circle of fishmen, jaw clenching as it began to close in.

"Bring it on," he said.

THE END

ABOUT THE AUTHOR

Mike Wild is much older than he has a right to be, considering the kebabs, the booze and the fags. Maybe it's because he still thinks he's 15. Apart from dabbling occasionally in publishing and editing, he's been a freelance writer for ever, clawing his way up to his current dizzy heights by way of work as diverse as *Doctor Who*, *Masters of the Universe*, *Starblazer*, *'Allo 'Allo!* and – erm – *My Little Pony*. Counting one *Teen Romance*, one *ABC Warriors* and two *Caballistics Inc*, Mike has written nine novels. However, only his beloved wife and tuna-scoffing cat give him the recognition he deserves.

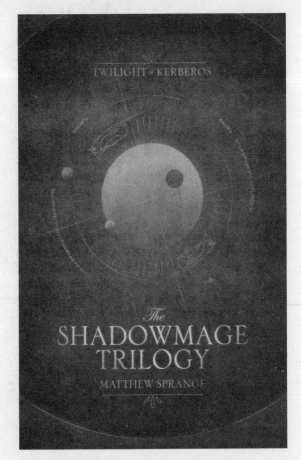

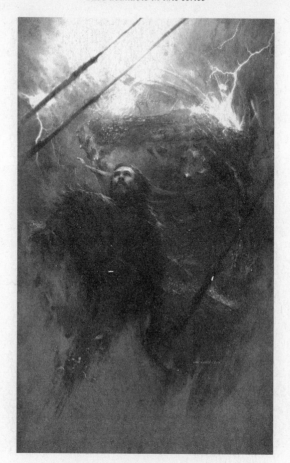

Also available in this series

THE WRATH OF KERBEROS
JONATHAN OLIVER

ISBN (EPUB): 978 1 84997 335 9 • ISBN (MOBI): 978 1 84997 336 6 • £4.99/$5.99

EBOOK EXCLUSIVE!

Silus and the crew of the *Llothriall* find themselves beached in the middle of a desert after a magical storm. Stranded, with supplies dwindling, Silus leads his companions across the landscape in search of civilisation. What they find will change their view of the world forever...

 # WWW.ABADDONBOOKS.COM
Follow us on Twitter! www.twitter.com/abaddonbooks